# STEPHEN KING

# FINDERS KEEPERS

### A NOVEL

SCRIBNER

New York   London   Toronto   Sydney   New Delhi

SCRIBNER
An Imprint of Simon & Schuster, Inc.
1230 Avenue of the Americas
New York, NY 10020

First Scribner hardcover edition June 2015

SCRIBNER and design are registered trademarks of The Gale Group, Inc., used under license by Simon & Schuster, Inc., the publisher of this work.

For information about special discounts for bulk purchases, please contact Simon & Schuster Special Sales at 1-866-506-1949 or business@simonandschuster.com.

The Simon & Schuster Speakers Bureau can bring authors to your live event. For more information or to book an event, contact the Simon & Schuster Speakers Bureau at 1-866-248-3049 or visit our website at www.simonspeakers.com.

Interior design by Erich Hobbing

Manufactured in the United States of America

1   3   5   7   9   10   8   6   4   2

Library of Congress Cataloging-in-Publication Data is available.

ISBN 978-1-5011-0007-9
ISBN 978-1-5011-0013-0 (ebook)

Thinking of John D. MacDonald

"It is by going down into the abyss that we recover
the treasures of life."

Joseph Campbell


"Shit don't mean shit."

Jimmy Gold

# FINDERS KEEPERS

# PART 1: BURIED TREASURE

# 1978

"Wake up, genius."

Rothstein didn't want to wake up. The dream was too good. It featured his first wife months before she became his first wife, seventeen and perfect from head to toe. Naked and shimmering. Both of them naked. He was nineteen, with grease under his fingernails, but she hadn't minded that, at least not then, because his head was full of dreams and that was what she cared about. She believed in the dreams even more than he did, and she was right to believe. In this dream she was laughing and reaching for the part of him that was easiest to grab. He tried to go deeper, but then a hand began shaking his shoulder, and the dream popped like a soap bubble.

He was no longer nineteen and living in a two-room New Jersey apartment, he was six months shy of his eightieth birthday and living on a farm in New Hampshire, where his will specified he should be buried. There were men in his bedroom. They were wearing ski masks, one red, one blue, and one canary-yellow. He saw this and tried to believe it was just another dream—the sweet one had slid into a nightmare, as they sometimes did—but then the hand let go of his arm, grabbed his shoulder, and tumbled him onto the floor. He struck his head and cried out.

"Quit that," said the one in the yellow mask. "You want to knock him unconscious?"

3

"Check it out." The one in the red mask pointed. "Old fella's got a woody. Must have been having one hell of a dream."

Blue Mask, the one who had done the shaking, said, "Just a piss hard-on. When they're that age, nothing else gets em up. My grandfather—"

"Be quiet," Yellow Mask said. "Nobody cares about your grandfather."

Although dazed and still wrapped in a fraying curtain of sleep, Rothstein knew he was in trouble here. Two words surfaced in his mind: *home invasion*. He looked up at the trio that had materialized in his bedroom, his old head aching (there was going to be a huge bruise on the right side, thanks to the blood thinners he took), his heart with its perilously thin walls banging against the left side of his ribcage. They loomed over him, three men with gloves on their hands, wearing plaid fall jackets below those terrifying balaclavas. Home invaders, and here he was, five miles from town.

Rothstein gathered his thoughts as best he could, banishing sleep and telling himself there was one good thing about this situation: if they didn't want him to see their faces, they intended to leave him alive.

Maybe.

"Gentlemen," he said.

Mr. Yellow laughed and gave him a thumbs-up. "Good start, genius."

Rothstein nodded, as if at a compliment. He glanced at the bedside clock, saw it was quarter past two in the morning, then looked back at Mr. Yellow, who might be the leader. "I have only a little money, but you're welcome to it. If you'll only leave without hurting me."

The wind gusted, rattling autumn leaves against the west side of the house. Rothstein was aware that the furnace was running for the first time this year. Hadn't it just been summer?

"According to our info, you got a lot more than a little." This was Mr. Red.

"Hush." Mr. Yellow extended a hand to Rothstein. "Get off the floor, genius."

Rothstein took the offered hand, got shakily to his feet, then sat on the bed. He was breathing hard, but all too aware (self-awareness had been both a curse and a blessing all his life) of the picture he must make: an old man in flappy blue pajamas, nothing left of his hair but white popcorn puffs above the ears. This was what had become of the writer who, in the year JFK became president, had been on the cover of *Time* magazine: JOHN ROTHSTEIN, AMERICA'S RECLUSIVE GENIUS.

*Wake up, genius.*

"Get your breath," Mr. Yellow said. He sounded solicitous, but Rothstein did not trust this. "Then we'll go into the living room, where normal people have their discussions. Take your time. Get serene."

Rothstein breathed slowly and deeply, and his heart quieted a little. He tried to think of Peggy, with her teacup-sized breasts (small but perfect) and her long, smooth legs, but the dream was as gone as Peggy herself, now an old crone living in Paris. On his money. At least Yolande, his second effort at marital bliss, was dead, thus putting an end to the alimony.

Red Mask left the room, and now Rothstein heard rummaging in his study. Something fell over. Drawers were opened and closed.

"Doing better?" Mr. Yellow asked, and when Rothstein nodded: "Come on, then."

Rothstein allowed himself to be led into the small living room, escorted by Mr. Blue on his left and Mr. Yellow on his right. In his study the rummaging went on. Soon Mr. Red would open the closet and push back his two jackets and three sweaters, exposing the safe. It was inevitable.

*All right. As long as they leave the notebooks, and why would they take them? Thugs like these are only interested in money. They probably can't even read anything more challenging than the letters in* Penthouse.

Only he wasn't sure about the man in the yellow mask. That one sounded educated.

All the lamps were on in the living room, and the shades weren't drawn. Wakeful neighbors might have wondered what was going on in the old writer's house . . . if he had neighbors. The closest ones were two miles away, on the main highway. He had no friends, no visitors. The occasional salesman was sent packing. Rothstein was just that peculiar old fella. The retired writer. The hermit. He paid his taxes and was left alone.

Blue and Yellow led him to the easy chair facing the seldom-watched TV, and when he didn't immediately sit, Mr. Blue pushed him into it.

"Easy!" Yellow said sharply, and Blue stepped back a bit, muttering. Mr. Yellow was the one in charge, all right. Mr. Yellow was the wheeldog.

He bent over Rothstein, hands on the knees of his corduroys. "Do you want a little splash of something to settle you?"

"If you mean alcohol, I quit twenty years ago. Doctor's orders."

"Good for you. Go to meetings?"

"I wasn't an *alcoholic*," Rothstein said, nettled. Crazy to be nettled in such a situation . . . or was it? Who knew how one was supposed to react after being yanked out of bed in the middle of the night by men in colorful ski masks? He wondered how he might write such a scene and had no idea; he did not write about situations like this. "People assume any twentieth-century white male writer must be an *alcoholic*."

"All right, all right," Mr. Yellow said. It was as if he were placating a grumpy child. "Water?"

"No, thank you. What I want is for you three to leave, so I'm going to be honest with you." He wondered if Mr. Yellow understood the most basic rule of human discourse: when someone says they're going to be honest with you, they are in most cases preparing to lie faster than a horse can trot. "My wallet is on the dresser in the bedroom. There's a little over eighty dollars in it. There's a ceramic teapot on the mantel . . ."

He pointed. Mr. Blue turned to look, but Mr. Yellow did not. Mr. Yellow continued to study Rothstein, the eyes behind the mask almost amused. *It's not working,* Rothstein thought, but he persevered. Now that he was awake, he was pissed off as well as scared, although he knew he'd do well not to show that.

"It's where I keep the housekeeping money. Fifty or sixty dollars. That's all there is in the house. Take it and go."

"Fucking liar," Mr. Blue said. "You got a lot more than that, guy. We know. Believe me."

As if this were a stage play and that line his cue, Mr. Red yelled from the study. "Bingo! Found a safe! Big one!"

Rothstein had known the man in the red mask would find it, but his heart sank anyway. Stupid to keep cash, there was no reason for it other than his dislike of credit cards and checks and stocks and instruments of transfer, all the tempting chains that tied people to America's overwhelming and ultimately destructive debt-and-spend machine. But the cash might be his salvation. Cash could be replaced. The notebooks, over a hundred and fifty of them, could not.

"Now the combo," said Mr. Blue. He snapped his gloved fingers. "Give it up."

Rothstein was almost angry enough to refuse, according to Yolande anger had been his lifelong default position ("Probably

7

even in your goddam cradle," she had said), but he was also tired and frightened. If he balked, they'd beat it out of him. He might even have another heart attack, and one more would almost certainly finish him.

"If I give you the combination to the safe, will you take the money inside and go?"

"Mr. Rothstein," Mr. Yellow said with a kindliness that seemed genuine (and thus grotesque), "you're in no position to bargain. Freddy, go get the bags."

Rothstein felt a huff of chilly air as Mr. Blue, also known as Freddy, went out through the kitchen door. Mr. Yellow, meanwhile, was smiling again. Rothstein already detested that smile. Those red lips.

"Come on, genius—give. Soonest begun, soonest done."

Rothstein sighed and recited the combination of the Gardall in his study closet. "Three left two turns, thirty-one right two turns, eighteen left one turn, ninety-nine right one turn, then back to zero."

Behind the mask, the red lips spread wider, now showing teeth. "I could have guessed that. It's your birth date."

As Yellow called the combination to the man in his closet, Rothstein made certain unpleasant deductions. Mr. Blue and Mr. Red had come for money, and Mr. Yellow might take his share, but he didn't believe money was the primary objective of the man who kept calling him *genius*. As if to underline this, Mr. Blue reappeared, accompanied by another puff of cool outside air. He had four empty duffel bags, two slung over each shoulder.

"Look," Rothstein said to Mr. Yellow, catching the man's eyes and holding them. "Don't. There's nothing in that safe worth taking except for the money. The rest is just a bunch of random scribbling, but it's important to me."

From the study Mr. Red cried: "Holy hopping Jesus, Morrie!

We hit the jackpot! Eee-doggies, there's a *ton* of cash! Still in the bank envelopes! Dozens of them!"

At least sixty, Rothstein could have said, maybe as many as eighty. With four hundred dollars in each one. From Arnold Abel, my accountant in New York. Jeannie cashes the expense checks and brings back the cash envelopes and I put them in the safe. Only I have few expenses, because Arnold also pays the major bills from New York. I tip Jeannie once in awhile, and the postman at Christmas, but otherwise, I rarely spend the cash. For years this has gone on, and why? Arnold never asks what I use the money for. Maybe he thinks I have an arrangement with a call girl or two. Maybe he thinks I play the ponies at Rockingham.

But here is the funny thing, he could have said to Mr. Yellow (also known as Morrie). I have never asked *myself*. Any more than I've asked myself why I keep filling notebook after notebook. Some things just *are*.

He *could* have said these things, but kept silent. Not because Mr. Yellow wouldn't understand, but because that knowing red-lipped smile said he just might.

And wouldn't care.

"What else is in there?" Mr. Yellow called. His eyes were still locked on Rothstein's. "Boxes? Manuscript boxes? The size I told you?"

"Not boxes, notebooks," Mr. Red reported back. "Fuckin safe's filled with em."

Mr. Yellow smiled, still looking into Rothstein's eyes. "Hand-written? That how you do it, genius?"

"Please," Rothstein said. "Just leave them. That material isn't meant to be seen. None of it's ready."

"And never will be, that's what I think. Why, you're just a great big hoarder." The twinkle in those eyes—what Rothstein thought of as an Irish twinkle—was gone now. "And hey, it isn't as if you *need* to publish anything else, right? Not like there's any *financial imperative*. You've got royalties from *The Runner*. And *The Runner Sees Action*. And *The Runner Slows Down*. The famous Jimmy Gold trilogy. Never out of print. Taught in college classes all over this great nation of ours. Thanks to a cabal of lit teachers who think you and Saul Bellow hung the moon, you've got a captive audience of book-buying undergrads. You're all set, right? Why take a chance on publishing something that might put a dent in your solid gold reputation? You can hide out here and pretend the rest of the world doesn't exist." Mr. Yellow shook his head. "My friend, you give a whole new meaning to anal retentive."

Mr. Blue was still lingering in the doorway. "What do you want me to do, Morrie?"

"Get in there with Curtis. Pack everything up. If there isn't room for all the notebooks in the duffels, look around. Even a cabin rat like him must have at least one suitcase. Don't waste time counting the money, either. I want to get out of here ASAP."

"Okay." Mr. Blue—Freddy—left.

"Don't do this," Rothstein said, and was appalled at the tremble in his voice. Sometimes he forgot how old he was, but not tonight.

The one whose name was Morrie leaned toward him, greenish-gray eyes peering through the holes in the yellow mask. "I want to know something. If you're honest, maybe we'll leave the notebooks. Will you be honest with me, genius?"

"I'll try," Rothstein said. "And I never called myself that, you know. It was *Time* magazine that called me a genius."

"But I bet you never wrote a letter of protest."

Rothstein said nothing. Sonofabitch, he was thinking. Smartass sonofabitch. You won't leave anything, will you? It doesn't matter what I say.

"Here's what I want to know—why in God's name couldn't you leave Jimmy Gold alone? Why did you have to push his face down in the dirt like you did?"

The question was so unexpected that at first Rothstein had no idea what Morrie was talking about, even though Jimmy Gold was his most famous character, the one he would be remembered for (assuming he was remembered for anything). The same *Time* cover story that had referred to Rothstein as a genius had called Jimmy Gold "an American icon of despair in a land of plenty." Pretty much horseshit, but it had sold books.

"If you mean I should have stopped with *The Runner*, you're not alone." But almost, he could have added. *The Runner Sees Action* had solidified his reputation as an important American writer, and *The Runner Slows Down* had been the capstone of his career: critical bouquets up the wazoo, on the *New York Times* bestseller list for sixty-two weeks. National Book Award, too—not that he had appeared in person to accept it. "The *Iliad* of postwar America," the citation had called it, meaning not just the last one but the trilogy as a whole.

"I'm not saying you should have stopped with *The Runner*," Morrie said. "*The Runner Sees Action* was just as good, maybe even better. They were *true*. It was the last one. Man, what a crap carnival. Advertising? I mean, *advertising*?"

Mr. Yellow then did something that tightened Rothstein's throat and turned his belly to lead. Slowly, almost reflectively, he stripped off his yellow balaclava, revealing a young man of classic Boston Irish countenance: red hair, greenish eyes, pasty-white skin that would always burn and never tan. Plus those weird red lips.

"House in the *suburbs*? Ford sedan in the *driveway*? Wife and two little *kiddies*? Everybody sells out, is that what you were trying to say? Everybody eats the poison?"

"In the notebooks . . ."

There were two more Jimmy Gold novels in the notebooks, that was what he wanted to say, ones that completed the circle. In the first of them, Jimmy comes to see the hollowness of his suburban life and leaves his family, his job, and his comfy Connecticut home. He leaves on foot, with nothing but a knapsack and the clothes on his back. He becomes an older version of the kid who dropped out of school, rejected his materialistic family, and decided to join the army after a booze-filled weekend spent wandering in New York City.

"In the notebooks what?" Morrie asked. "Come on, genius, speak. Tell me why you had to knock him down and step on the back of his head."

*In* The Runner Goes West *he becomes himself again,* Rothstein wanted to say. *His essential self.* Only now Mr. Yellow had shown his face, and he was removing a pistol from the right front pocket of his plaid jacket. He looked sorrowful.

"You created one of the greatest characters in American literature, then shit on him," Morrie said. "A man who could do that doesn't deserve to live."

The anger roared back like a sweet surprise. "If you think that," John Rothstein said, "you never understood a word I wrote."

Morrie pointed the pistol. The muzzle was a black eye.

Rothstein pointed an arthritis-gnarled finger back, as if it were his own gun, and felt satisfaction when he saw Morrie blink and flinch a little. "Don't give me your dumbass literary criticism. I got a bellyful of that long before you were born. What are you, anyway, twenty-two? Twenty-three? What do you know about life, let alone literature?"

"Enough to know not everyone sells out." Rothstein was astounded to see tears swimming in those Irish eyes. "Don't lecture me about life, not after spending the last twenty years hiding away from the world like a rat in a hole."

This old criticism—how *dare* you leave the Fame Table?—sparked Rothstein's anger into full-blown rage—the sort of glass-throwing, furniture-smashing rage both Peggy and Yolande would have recognized—and he was glad. Better to die raging than to do so cringing and begging.

"How will you turn my work into cash? Have you thought of that? I assume you have. I assume you know that you might as well try to sell a stolen Hemingway notebook, or a Picasso painting. But your friends aren't as educated as you are, are they? I can tell by the way they speak. Do they know what you know? I'm sure they don't. But you sold them a bill of goods. You showed them a large pie in the sky and told them they could each have a slice. I think you're capable of that. I think you have a lake of words at your disposal. But I believe it's a shallow lake."

"Shut up. You sound like my mother."

"You're a common thief, my friend. And how stupid to steal what you can never sell."

"Shut up, genius, I'm warning you."

Rothstein thought, And if he pulls the trigger? No more pills. No more regrets about the past, and the litter of broken relationships along the way like so many cracked-up cars. No more obsessive writing, either, accumulating notebook after notebook like little piles of rabbit turds scattered along a woodland trail. A bullet in the head would not be so bad, maybe. Better than cancer or Alzheimer's, that prime horror of anyone who has spent his life making a living by his wits. Of course there would be headlines, and I'd gotten plenty of those even before that damned *Time* story . . . but if he pulls the trigger, I won't have to read them.

"You're *stupid*," Rothstein said. All at once he was in a kind of ecstasy. "You think you're smarter than those other two, but you're not. At least they understand that cash can be spent." He leaned forward, staring at that pale, freckle-spattered face. "You know what, kid? It's guys like you who give reading a bad name."

"Last warning," Morrie said.

"Fuck your warning. And fuck your mother. Either shoot me or get out of my house."

Morris Bellamy shot him.

# 2009

The first argument about money in the Saubers household—the first one the kids overheard, at least—happened on an evening in April. It wasn't a big argument, but even the greatest storms begin as gentle breezes. Peter and Tina Saubers were in the living room, Pete doing homework and Tina watching a *SpongeBob* DVD. It was one she'd seen before, many times, but she never seemed to tire of it. This was fortunate, because these days there was no access to the Cartoon Network in the Saubers household. Tom Saubers had canceled the cable service two months ago.

Tom and Linda Saubers were in the kitchen, where Tom was cinching his old pack shut after loading it up with PowerBars, a Tupperware filled with cut veggies, two bottles of water, and a can of Coke.

"You're nuts," Linda said. "I mean, I've always known you were a Type A personality, but this takes it to a whole new level. If you want to set the alarm for five, fine. You can pick up Todd, be at City Center by six, and you'll still be first in line."

"I wish," Tom said. "Todd says there was one of these job fairs in Brook Park last month, and people started lining up the day before. *The day before,* Lin!"

"Todd says a lot of things. And you listen. Remember when Todd said Pete and Tina would just *love* that Monster Truck Jam thingie—"

15

"This isn't a Monster Truck Jam, or a concert in the park, or a fireworks show. This is our *lives*."

Pete looked up from his homework and briefly met his little sister's eyes. Tina's shrug was eloquent: *Just the parents.* He went back to his algebra. Four more problems and he could go down to Howie's house. See if Howie had any new comic books. Pete certainly had none to trade; his allowance had gone the way of the cable TV.

In the kitchen, Tom had begun to pace. Linda caught up with him and took his arm gently. "I know it's our lives," she said.

Speaking low, partly so the kids wouldn't hear and be nervous (she knew Pete already was), mostly to lower the temperature. She knew how Tom felt, and her heart went out to him. Being afraid was bad; being humiliated because he could no longer fulfill what he saw as his primary responsibility to support his family was worse. And humiliation really wasn't the right word. What he felt was shame. For the ten years he'd been at Lakefront Realty, he'd consistently been one of their top salesmen, often with his smiling photo at the front of the shop. The money she brought in teaching third grade was just icing on the cake. Then, in the fall of 2008, the bottom fell out of the economy, and the Sauberses became a single-income family.

It wasn't as if Tom had been let go and might be called back when things improved; Lakefront Realty was now an empty building with graffiti on the walls and a FOR SALE OR LEASE sign out front. The Reardon brothers, who had inherited the business from their father (and their father from his), had been deeply invested in stocks, and lost nearly everything when the market tanked. It was little comfort to Linda that Tom's best friend, Todd Paine, was in the same boat. She thought Todd was a dingbat.

"Have you seen the weather forecast? I have. It's going to be cold. Fog off the lake by morning, maybe even freezing drizzle. *Freezing drizzle,* Tom."

"Good. I hope it happens. It'll keep the numbers down and improve the odds." He took her by the forearms, but gently. There was no shaking, no shouting. That came later. "I've *got* to get something, Lin, and the job fair is my best shot this spring. I've been pounding the pavement—"

"I know—"

"And there's *nothing*. I mean *zilch*. Oh, a few jobs down at the docks, and a little construction at the shopping center out by the airport, but can you see me doing that kind of work? I'm thirty pounds overweight and twenty years out of shape. I might find something downtown this summer—clerking, maybe—*if* things ease up a little . . . but that kind of job would be low-paying and probably temporary. So Todd and me're going at midnight, and we're going to stand in line until the doors open tomorrow morning, and I promise you I'm going to come back with a job that pays actual money."

"And probably with some bug we can all catch. Then we can scrimp on groceries to pay the doctor's bills."

That was when he grew really angry with her. "I would like a little support here."

"Tom, for God's sake, I'm *try*—"

"Maybe even an attaboy. 'Way to show some initiative, Tom. We're glad you're going the extra mile for the family, Tom.' That sort of thing. If it's not too much to ask."

"All I'm saying—"

But the kitchen door opened and closed before she could finish. He'd gone out back to smoke a cigarette. When Pete looked up this time, he saw distress and worry on Tina's face. She was only eight, after all. Pete smiled and dropped her a wink. Tina gave him a doubtful smile in return, then went back to the doings in the deepwater kingdom called Bikini Bottom, where dads did not lose their jobs or raise their voices, and kids did not lose their allowances. Unless they were bad, that was.

Before leaving that night, Tom carried his daughter up to bed and kissed her goodnight. He added one for Mrs. Beasley, Tina's favorite doll—for good luck, he said.

"Daddy? Is everything going to be okay?"

"You bet, sugar," he said. She remembered that. The confidence in his voice. "Everything's going to be just fine. Now go to sleep." He left, walking normally. She remembered that, too, because she never saw him walk that way again.

At the top of the steep drive leading from Marlborough Street to the City Center parking lot, Tom said, "Whoa, hold it, stop!"

"Man, there's cars behind me," Todd said.

"This'll just take a second." Tom raised his phone and snapped a picture of the people standing in line. There had to be a hundred already. At least that many. Running above the auditorium doors was a banner reading **1000 JOBS GUARANTEED!** And *"We Stand With the People of Our City!"*—**MAYOR RALPH KINSLER**.

Behind Todd Paine's rusty '04 Subaru, someone laid on his horn.

"Tommy, I hate to be a party pooper while you're memorializing this wonderful occasion, but—"

"Go, go. I got it." And, as Todd drove into the parking lot, where the spaces nearest the building had already been filled: "I can't wait to show that picture to Linda. You know what she said? That if we got here by six, we'd be first in line."

"Told you, my man. The Toddster does not lie." The Toddster parked. The Subaru died with a fart and a wheeze. "By daybreak, there's gonna be, like, a couple-thousand people here. TV, too. All the stations. *City at Six, Morning Report, MetroScan.* We might get interviewed."

"I'll settle for a job."

Linda had been right about one thing, it was damp. You could smell the lake in the air: that faintly sewery aroma. And it was almost cold enough for him to see his breath. Posts with yellow DO NOT CROSS tape had been set up, folding the job-seekers back and forth like pleats in a human accordion. Tom and Todd took their places between the final posts. Others fell in behind them at once, mostly men, some in heavy fleece workmen's jackets, some in Mr. Businessman topcoats and Mr. Businessman haircuts that were beginning to lose their finely barbered edge. Tom guessed that the line would stretch all the way to the end of the parking lot by dawn, and that would still be at least four hours before the doors opened.

His eye was caught by a woman with a baby hanging off the front of her. They were a couple of zigzags over. Tom wondered how desperate you had to be to come out in the middle of a cold, damp night like this one with an infant. The kiddo was in one of those papoose carriers. The woman was talking to a burly man with a sleeping bag slung over his shoulder, and the baby was peering from one to the other, like the world's smallest tennis fan. Sort of comical.

"Want a little warm-up, Tommy?" Todd had taken a pint of Bell's from his pack and was holding it out.

Tom almost said no, remembering Linda's parting shot—*Don't you come home with booze on your breath, mister*—and then took the bottle. It was cold out here, and a short one wouldn't hurt. He felt the whiskey go down, heating his throat and belly.

Rinse your mouth before you hit any of the job booths, he

reminded himself. Guys who smell of whiskey don't get hired for anything.

When Todd offered him another nip—this was around two o'clock—Tom refused. But when he offered again at three, Tom took the bottle. Checking the level, he guessed the Toddster had been fortifying himself against the cold quite liberally.

Well, what the hell, Tom thought, and bit off quite a bit more than a nip; this one was a solid mouthful.

"Atta-baby," Todd said, sounding the teensiest bit slurry. "Go with your bad self."

Job hunters continued to arrive, their cars nosing up from Marlborough Street through the thickening fog. The line was well past the posts now, and no longer zigzagging. Tom had believed he understood the economic difficulties currently besetting the country—hadn't he lost a job himself, a very good job?—but as the cars kept coming and the line kept growing (he could no longer see where it ended), he began to get a new and frightening perspective. Maybe *difficulties* wasn't the right word. Maybe the right word was *calamity*.

To his right, in the maze of posts and tape leading to the doors of the darkened auditorium, the baby began to cry. Tom looked around and saw the man with the sleeping bag holding the sides of the papoose carrier so the woman (God, Tom thought, she doesn't look like she's out of her teens yet) could pull the kid out.

"What the fuck's zat?" Todd asked, sounding slurrier than ever.

"A kid," Tom said. "Woman with a kid. *Girl* with a kid."

Todd peered. "Christ on a pony," he said. "I call that pretty irra . . . irry . . . you know, not responsible."

"Are you drunk?" Linda disliked Todd, she didn't see his good side, and right now Tom wasn't sure he saw it, either.

"L'il bit. I'll be fine by the time the doors open. Got some breath mints, too."

Tom thought of asking the Toddster if he'd also brought some Visine—his eyes were looking mighty red—and decided he didn't want to have that discussion just now. He turned his attention back to where the woman with the crying baby had been. At first he thought they were gone. Then he looked lower and saw her sliding into the burly man's sleeping bag with the baby on her chest. The burly man was holding the mouth of the bag open for her. The infant was still bawling his or her head off.

"Can't you shut that kid up?" a man called.

"Someone ought to call Social Services," a woman added.

Tom thought of Tina at that age, imagined her out on this cold and foggy predawn morning, and restrained an urge to tell the man and woman to shut up . . . or better yet, lend a hand somehow. After all, they were in this together, weren't they? The whole screwed-up, bad-luck bunch of them.

The crying softened, stopped.

"She's probably feeding im," Todd said. He squeezed his chest to demonstrate.

"Yeah."

"Tommy?"

"What?"

"You know Ellen lost her job, right?"

"Jesus, no. I *didn't* know that." Pretending he didn't see the fear in Todd's face. Or the glimmering of moisture in his eyes. Possibly from the booze or the cold. Possibly not.

"They said they'd call her back when things get better, but they said the same thing to me, and I've been out of work going on half a year now. I cashed my insurance. That's gone. And you know what we got left in the bank? Five hundred dollars. You know how long five hundred dollars lasts when a loaf of bread at Kroger's costs a buck?"

"Not long."

"You're fucking A it doesn't. I *have* to get something here. *Have* to."

"You will. We both will."

Todd lifted his chin at the burly man, who now appeared to be standing guard over the sleeping bag, so no one would accidentally step on the woman and baby inside. "Think they're married?"

Tom hadn't considered it. Now he did. "Probably."

"Then they both must be out of work. Otherwise, one of em would have stayed home with the kid."

"Maybe," Tom said, "they think showing up with the baby will improve their chances."

Todd brightened. "The pity card! Not a bad idea!" He held out the pint. "Want a nip?"

He took a small one, thinking, If I don't drink it, Todd will.


Tom was awakened from a whiskey-assisted doze by an exuberant shout: "Life is discovered on other planets!" This sally was followed by laughter and applause.

He looked around and saw daylight. Thin and fog-draped, but daylight, just the same. Beyond the bank of auditorium doors, a fellow in gray fatigues—a man with a job, lucky fellow—was pushing a mop-bucket across the lobby.

"Whuddup?" Todd asked.

"Nothing," Tom said. "Just a janitor."

Todd peered in the direction of Marlborough Street. "Jesus, and still they come."

"Yeah," Tom said. Thinking, And if I'd listened to Linda, we'd be at the end of a line that stretches halfway to Cleveland. That was a good thought, a little vindication was always good, but he wished he'd said no to Todd's pint. His mouth tasted like kitty litter. Not that he'd ever actually *eaten* any, but—

Someone a couple of zigzags over—not far from the sleeping bag—asked, "Is that a Benz? It looks like a Benz."

Tom saw a long shape at the head of the entrance drive leading up from Marlborough, its yellow fog-lamps blazing. It wasn't moving; it just sat there.

"What's he think he's doing?" Todd asked.

The driver of the car immediately behind must have wondered the same thing, because he laid on his horn—a long, pissed-off blat that made people stir and snort and look around. For a moment the car with the yellow fog-lamps stayed where it was. Then it shot forward. Not to the left, toward the now full-to-overflowing parking lot, but directly at the people penned within the maze of tapes and posts.

"Hey!" someone shouted.

The crowd swayed backward in a tidal motion. Tom was shoved against Todd, who went down on his ass. Tom fought for balance, almost found it, and then the man in front of him—yelling, no, *screaming*—drove his butt into Tom's crotch and one flailing elbow into his chest. Tom fell on top of his buddy, heard the bottle of Bell's shatter somewhere between them, and smelled the sharp reek of the remaining whiskey as it ran across the pavement.

*Great, now I'll smell like a barroom on Saturday night.*

He struggled to his feet in time to see the car—it was a Mercedes, all right, a big sedan as gray as this foggy morning—plowing into the crowd, spinning bodies out of its way as it came, describing a drunken arc. Blood dripped from the grille. A woman went skidding and rolling across the hood with her hands out and her shoes gone. She slapped at the glass, grabbed at one of the windshield wipers, missed, and tumbled off to one side. Yellow DO NOT CROSS tapes snapped. A post clanged against the side of the big sedan, which did not slow its roll in the slightest. Tom saw the front wheels pass over the sleeping bag and the burly man, who had been crouched protectively over it with one hand raised.

Now it was coming right at him.

"Todd!" he shouted. "Todd, *get up!*"

He grabbed at Todd's hands, got one of them, and pulled. Someone slammed into him and he was driven back to his knees. He could hear the rogue car's motor, revving full-out. Very close now. He tried to crawl, and a foot clobbered him in the temple. He saw stars.

"Tom?" Todd was behind him now. How had that happened? "Tom, what the *fuck?*"

A body landed on top of him, and then something else was on top of him, a huge weight that pressed down, threatening to turn him to jelly. His hips snapped. They sounded like dry turkey bones. Then the weight was gone. Pain with its own kind of weight rushed in to replace it.

Tom tried to raise his head and managed to get it off the pavement just long enough to see taillights dwindling into the fog. He saw glittering shards of glass from the busted pint. He saw Todd sprawled on his back with blood coming out of his head and pooling on the pavement. Crimson tire-tracks ran away into the foggy half-light.

He thought, Linda was right. I should have stayed home.

He thought, I'm going to die, and maybe that's for the best. Because, unlike Todd Paine, I never got around to cashing in my insurance.

He thought, Although I probably would have, in time.

Then, blackness.


When Tom Saubers woke up in the hospital forty-eight hours later, Linda was sitting beside him. She was holding his hand. He asked her if he was going to live. She smiled, squeezed his hand, and said you bet your patootie.

"Am I paralyzed? Tell me the truth."

"No, honey, but you've got a lot of broken bones."

"What about Todd?"

She looked away, biting her lips. "He's in a coma, but they think he's going to come out of it eventually. They can tell by his brainwaves, or something."

"There was a car. I couldn't get out of the way."

"I know. You weren't the only one. It was some madman. He got away with it, at least so far."

Tom could have cared less about the man driving the Mercedes-Benz. Not paralyzed was good, but—

"How bad did I get it? No bullshit—be honest."

She met his eyes but couldn't hold them. Once more looking at the get-well cards on his bureau, she said, "You . . . well. It's going to be awhile before you can walk again."

"How long?"

She raised his hand, which was badly scraped, and kissed it. "They don't know."

Tom Saubers closed his eyes and began to cry. Linda listened to that awhile, and when she couldn't stand it anymore, she leaned forward and began to punch the button on the morphine pump. She kept doing it until the machine stopped giving. By then he was asleep.

# 1978

Morris grabbed a blanket from the top shelf of the bedroom closet and used it to cover Rothstein, who now sprawled askew in the easy chair with the top of his head gone. The brains that had conceived Jimmy Gold, Jimmy's sister Emma, and Jimmy's self-involved, semi-alcoholic parents—so much like Morris's own—were now drying on the wallpaper. Morris wasn't shocked, exactly, but he was certainly amazed. He had expected some blood, and a hole between the eyes, but not this gaudy expectoration of gristle and bone. It was a failure of imagination, he supposed, the reason why he could *read* the giants of modern American literature—read them and appreciate them—but never *be* one.

Freddy Dow came out of the study with a loaded duffel bag over each shoulder. Curtis followed, head down and carrying nothing at all. All at once he sped up, hooked around Freddy, and bolted into the kitchen. The door to the backyard banged against the side of the house as the wind took it. Then came the sound of retching.

"He's feelin kinda sick," Freddy said. He had a talent for stating the obvious.

"You all right?" Morris asked.

"Yuh." Freddy went out through the front door without looking back, pausing to pick up the crowbar leaning against the porch glider. They had come prepared to break in, but the front door had been unlocked. The kitchen door, as well. Rothstein had put all his confidence in the Gardall safe, it seemed. Talk about failures of the imagination.

Morris went into the study, looked at Rothstein's neat desk and covered typewriter. Looked at the pictures on the wall. Both ex-wives hung there, laughing and young and beautiful in their fifties clothes and hairdos. It was sort of interesting that Rothstein would keep those discarded women where they could look at him while he was writing, but Morris had no time to consider this, or to investigate the contents of the writer's desk, which he would dearly have loved to do. But was such investigation even necessary? He had the notebooks, after all. He had the contents of the writer's *mind*. Everything he'd written since he stopped publishing eighteen years ago.

Freddy had taken the stacks of cash envelopes in the first load (of course; cash was what Freddy and Curtis understood), but there were still plenty of notebooks on the shelves of the safe. They were Moleskines, the kind Hemingway had used, the kind Morris had dreamed of while in the reformatory, where he had also dreamed of becoming a writer himself. But in Riverview Youth Detention he had been rationed to five sheets of pulpy Blue Horse paper each week, hardly enough to begin writing the Great American Novel. Begging for more did no good. The one time he'd offered Elkins, the commissary trustee, a blowjob for a dozen extra sheets, Elkins had punched him in the face. Sort of funny, when you considered all the non-consensual sex he had been forced to participate in during his nine-month stretch, usually on his knees and on more than one occasion with his own dirty undershorts stuffed in his mouth.

He didn't hold his mother *entirely* responsible for those rapes, but she deserved her share of the blame. Anita Bellamy, the famous history professor whose book on Henry Clay Frick had been nominated for a Pulitzer. So famous that she presumed to know all about modern American literature, as well. It was an argument about the Gold trilogy that had sent him out one night, furious and determined to get drunk. Which he did, although he was underage and looked it.

Drinking did not agree with Morris. He did things when he was drinking that he couldn't remember later, and they were never good things. That night it had been breaking and entering, vandalism, and fighting with a neighborhood rent-a-cop who tried to hold him until the regular cops got there.

That was almost six years ago, but the memory was still fresh. It had all been so stupid. Stealing a car, joyriding across town, then abandoning it (perhaps after pissing all over the dashboard) was one thing. Not smart, but with a little luck, you could walk away from that sort of deal. But breaking into a place in Sugar Heights? Double stupid. He had wanted *nothing* in that house (at least nothing he could remember later). And when he *did* want something? When he offered up his mouth for a few lousy sheets of Blue Horse paper? Punched in the face. So he'd laughed, because that was what Jimmy Gold would have done (at least before Jimmy grew up and sold out for what he called the Golden Buck), and what happened next? Punched in the face again, even harder. It was the muffled crack of his nose breaking that had started him crying.

Jimmy never would have cried.

He was still looking greedily at the Moleskines when Freddy Dow returned with the other two duffel bags. He also had a scuffed leather carryall. "This was in the pantry. Along with like a billion cans of beans and tuna fish. Go figure, huh? Weird guy. Maybe he was waiting for the Acropolipse. Come on, Morrie, put it in gear. Someone might have heard that shot."

29

"There aren't any neighbors. Nearest farm is two miles away. Relax."

"Jails're full of guys who were relaxed. We need to get out of here."

Morris began gathering up handfuls of notebooks, but couldn't resist looking in one, just to make sure. Rothstein *had* been a weird guy, and it wasn't out of the realm of possibility that he had stacked his safe with blank books, thinking he might write something in them eventually.

But no.

This one, at least, was loaded with Rothstein's small, neat handwriting, every page filled, top to bottom and side to side, the margins as thin as threads.

*—wasn't sure why it mattered to him and why he couldn't sleep as the empty boxcar of this late freight bore him on through rural oblivion toward Kansas City and the sleeping country beyond, the full belly of America resting beneath its customary comforter of night, yet Jimmy's thoughts persisted in turning back to—*

Freddy thumped him on the shoulder, and not gently. "Get your nose out of that thing and pack up. We already got one puking his guts out and pretty much useless."

Morris dropped the notebook into one of the duffels and grabbed another double handful without a word, his thoughts brilliant with possibility. He forgot about the mess under the blanket in the living room, forgot about Curtis Rogers puking his guts in the roses or zinnias or petunias or whatever was growing out back. Jimmy Gold! Headed west, in a boxcar! Rothstein hadn't been done with him, after all!

"These're full," he told Freddy. "Take them out. I'll put the rest in the valise."

"That what you call that kind of bag?"

"I think so, yeah." He knew so. "Go on. Almost done here."

Freddy shouldered the duffels by their straps, but lingered a moment longer. "Are you sure about these things? Because Rothstein said—"

"He was a hoarder trying to save his hoard. He would have said anything. Go on."

Freddy went. Morris loaded the last batch of Moleskines into the valise and backed out of the closet. Curtis was standing by Rothstein's desk. He had taken off his balaclava; they all had. His face was paper-pale and there were dark shock circles around his eyes.

"You didn't have to kill him. You weren't *supposed* to. It wasn't in the plan. Why'd you do that?"

Because he made me feel stupid. Because he cursed my mother and that's my job. Because he called me a kid. Because he needed to be punished for turning Jimmy Gold into one of *them*. Mostly because nobody with his kind of talent has a right to hide it from the world. Only Curtis wouldn't understand that.

"Because it'll make the notebooks worth more when we sell them." Which wouldn't be until he'd read every word in them, but Curtis wouldn't understand the need to do that, and didn't need to know. Nor did Freddy. He tried to sound patient and reasonable. "We now have all the John Rothstein output there's ever going to be. That makes the unpublished stuff even more valuable. You see that, don't you?"

Curtis scratched one pale cheek. "Well . . . I guess . . . yeah."

"Also, he can never claim they're forgeries when they turn up. Which he would have done, just out of spite. I've read a lot about him, Curtis, just about everything, and he was one spiteful motherfucker."

"Well . . ."

Morrie restrained himself from saying *That's an extremely deep subject for a mind as shallow as yours.* He held out the valise instead. "Take it. And keep your gloves on until we're in the car."

"You should have talked it over with us, Morrie. We're your *partners.*"

Curtis started out, then turned back. "I got a question."

"What is it?"

"Do you know if New Hampshire has the death penalty?"

They took secondary roads across the narrow chimney of New Hampshire and into Vermont. Freddy drove the Chevy Biscayne, which was old and unremarkable. Morris rode shotgun with a Rand McNally open on his lap, thumbing on the dome light from time to time to make sure they didn't wander off their pre-planned route. He didn't need to remind Freddy to keep to the speed limit. This wasn't Freddy Dow's first rodeo.

Curtis lay in the backseat, and soon they heard the sound of his snores. Morris considered him lucky; he seemed to have puked out his horror. Morris thought it might be awhile before he himself got another good night's sleep. He kept seeing the brains dribbling down the wallpaper. It wasn't the killing that stayed on his mind, it was the spilled talent. A lifetime of honing and shaping torn apart in less than a second. All those stories, all those images, and what came out looked like so much oatmeal. What was the point?

"So you really think we'll be able to sell those little books of his?" Freddy asked. He was back to that. "For real money, I mean?"

"Yes."

"And get away with it?"

"Yes, Freddy, I'm sure."

Freddy Dow was quiet for so long that Morris thought the issue was settled. Then he spoke to the subject again. Two words. Dry and toneless. "I'm doubtful."

Later on, once more incarcerated—not in Youth Detention this time, either—Morris would think, That's when I decided to kill them.

But sometimes at night, when he couldn't sleep, his asshole slick and burning from one of a dozen soap-assisted shower-room buggeries, he would admit that wasn't the truth. He'd known all along. They were dumb, and career criminals. Sooner or later (probably sooner) one of them would be caught for something else, and there would be the temptation to trade what they knew about this night for a lighter sentence or no sentence at all.

I just knew they had to go, he would think on those cellblock nights when the full belly of America rested beneath its customary comforter of night. It was inevitable.


In upstate New York, with dawn not yet come but beginning to show the horizon's dark outline behind them, they turned west on Route 92, a highway that roughly paralleled I-90 as far as Illinois, where it turned south and petered out in the industrial city of Rockford. The road was still mostly deserted at this hour, although they could hear (and sometimes see) heavy truck traffic on the interstate to their left.

They passed a sign reading REST AREA 2 MI., and Morris thought of *Macbeth*. If it were to be done, then 'twere well it were done quickly. Not an exact quote, maybe, but close enough for government work.

"Pull in there," he told Freddy. "I need to drain the dragon."

"They probably got vending machines, too," said the puker in the backseat. Curtis was sitting up now, his hair crazy around his head. "I could get behind some of those peanut butter crackers."

Morris knew he'd have to let it go if there were other cars in the rest area. I-90 had sucked away most of the through traffic that used to travel on this road, but once daybreak arrived, there would be lots of local traffic, pooting along from one Hicksville to the next.

For now the rest area was deserted, at least in part because of the sign reading OVERNIGHT RVS PROHIBITED. They parked and got out. Birds chirruped in the trees, discussing the night just past and plans for the day. A few leaves—in this part of the world they were just beginning to turn—drifted down and scuttered across the lot.

Curtis went to inspect the vending machines while Morris and Freddy walked side by side to the men's half of the restroom facility. Morris didn't feel particularly nervous. Maybe what they said was true, after the first one it got easier.

He held the door for Freddy with one hand and took the pistol from his jacket pocket with the other. Freddy said thanks without looking around. Morris let the door swing shut before raising the gun. He placed the muzzle less than an inch from the back of Freddy Dow's head and pulled the trigger. The gunshot was a flat loud bang in the tiled room, but anyone who heard it from a distance would think it was a motorcycle backfiring on I-90. What he worried about was Curtis.

He needn't have. Curtis was still standing in the snack alcove, beneath a wooden eave and a rustic sign reading ROADSIDE OASIS. In one hand he had a package of peanut butter crackers.

"Did you hear that?" he asked Morris. Then, seeing the gun, sounding honestly puzzled: "What's that for?"

"You," Morris said, and shot him in the chest.

Curtis went down, but—this was a shock—did not die. He didn't seem even *close* to dying. He squirmed on the pavement. A fallen leaf cartwheeled in front of his nose. Blood began to seep out from beneath him. He was still clutching his crackers. He looked up, his oily black hair hanging in his eyes. Beyond the screening trees, a truck went past on Route 92, droning east.

Morris didn't want to shoot Curtis again, out here a gunshot didn't have that hollow backfire sound, and besides, someone might pull in at any second. "If it were to be done, then 'twere well it were done quickly," he said, and dropped to one knee.

"You shot me," Curtis said, sounding breathless and amazed. "You fucking *shot* me, Morrie!"

Thinking how much he hated that nickname—he'd hated it all his life, and even teachers, who should have known better, used it—he reversed the gun and began to hammer Curtis's skull with the butt. Three hard blows accomplished very little. It was only a .38, after all, and not heavy enough to do more than minor damage. Blood began to seep through Curtis's hair and run down his stubbly cheeks. He was groaning, staring up at Morris with desperate blue eyes. He waved one hand weakly.

"Stop it, Morrie! Stop it, that *hurts!*"

Shit. Shit, shit, *shit*.

Morris slid the gun back into his pocket. The butt was now slimy with blood and hair. He went to the Biscayne, wiping his hand on his jacket. He opened the driver's door, saw the empty ignition, and said *fuck* under his breath. Whispering it like a prayer.

On 92, a couple of cars went by, then a brown UPS truck.

He trotted back to the men's room, opened the door, knelt down, and began to go through Freddy's pockets. He found the car keys in the left front. He got to his feet and hurried back to the snack alcoves, sure a car or truck would have pulled in by now, the traffic was getting heavier all the time, *somebody* would have to piss out his or her morning coffee, and he would have to kill *that* one, too, and possibly the one after that. An image of linked paper dolls came to mind.

No one yet, though.

He got into the Biscayne, legally purchased but now bearing stolen Maine license plates. Curtis Rogers was slithering a slow course down the cement walkway toward the toilets, pulling with his hands and pushing feebly with his feet and leaving a snail-trail of blood behind. It was impossible to know for sure, but Morris thought he might be trying to reach the pay telephone on the wall between the mens' and the ladies'.

This wasn't the way it was supposed to go, he thought, starting the car. It was spur-of-the-moment stupid, and he was probably going to be caught. It made him think of what Rothstein had said at the end. *What are you, anyway, twenty-two? Twenty-three? What do you know about life, let alone literature?*

"I know I'm no sellout," he said. "I know that much."

He put the Biscayne in drive and rolled slowly forward toward the man eeling his way up the cement walkway. He wanted to get out of here, his brain was *yammering* at him to get out of here, but this had to be done carefully and with no more mess than was absolutely necessary.

Curtis looked around, his eyes wide and horrified behind the jungle foliage of his dirty hair. He raised one hand in a feeble *stop* gesture, then Morris couldn't see him anymore because the hood was in the way. He steered carefully and continued creeping forward. The front of the car bumped up over the curbing. The pine tree air freshener on the rearview mirror swung and bobbed.

There was nothing . . . and nothing . . . and then the car bumped

36

up again. There was a muffled *pop*, the sound of a small pumpkin exploding in a microwave oven.

Morris cut the wheel to the left and there was another bump as the Biscayne went back into the parking area. He looked in the mirror and saw that Curtis's head was gone.

Well, no. Not exactly. It was there, but all spread out. Mooshed. No loss of talent in *that* mess, Morrie thought.

He drove toward the exit, and when he was sure the road was empty, he sped up. He would need to stop and examine the front of the car, especially the tire that had run over Curtis's head, but he wanted to get twenty miles farther down the road first. Twenty at least.

"I see a car wash in my future," he said. This struck him funny (*inordinately* funny, and there was a word neither Freddy nor Curtis would have understood), and he laughed long and loud. He kept exactly to the speed limit. He watched the odometer turn the miles, and even at fifty-five, each revolution seemed to take five minutes. He was sure the tire had left a blood-trail going out of the exit, but that would be gone now. Long gone. Still, it was time to turn off onto the secondary roads again, maybe even the tertiary ones. The smart thing would be to stop and throw all the notebooks—the cash, too—into the woods. But he would not do that. Never would he do that.

Fifty-fifty odds, he told himself. Maybe better. After all, no one saw the car. Not in New Hampshire and not at that rest area.

He came to an abandoned restaurant, pulled into the side lot, and examined the Biscayne's front end and right front tire. He thought things looked pretty good, all in all, but there was some blood on the front bumper. He pulled a handful of weeds and wiped it off. He got back in and drove on west. He was prepared for roadblocks, but there were none.

Over the Pennsylvania state line, in Gowanda, he found a coin-op car wash. The brushes brushed, the jets rinsed, and the car came out spanking clean—underside as well as topside.

Morris drove west, headed for the filthy little city residents called the Gem of the Great Lakes. He had to sit tight for awhile, and he had to see an old friend. Also, home was the place where, when you go there, they have to take you in—the gospel according to Robert Frost—and that was especially true when there was no one to bitch about the return of the prodigal son. With dear old Dad in the wind for years now and dear old Mom spending the fall semester at Princeton guest-lecturing on the robber barons, the house on Sycamore Street would be empty. Not much of a house for a fancy-schmancy teacher—not to mention a writer once nominated for the Pulitzer—but blame dear old Dad for that. Besides, Morris had never minded living there; that had been Mother's resentment, not his.

Morris listened to the news, but there was nothing about the murder of the novelist who, according to that *Time* cover story, had been "a voice shouting at the children of the silent fifties to wake up and raise their own voices." This radio silence was good news, but not unexpected; according to Morris's source in the reformatory, Rothstein's housekeeper only came in once a week. There was also a handyman, but he only came when called. Morris and his late partners had picked their time accordingly, which meant he could reasonably hope the body might not be discovered for another six days.

That afternoon, in rural Ohio, he passed an antiques barn and made a U-turn. After a bit of browsing, he bought a used trunk for twenty dollars. It was old, but looked sturdy. Morris considered it a steal.

# 2010

Pete Saubers's parents had lots of arguments now. Tina called them the arkie-barkies. Pete thought she had something there, because that was what they sounded like when they got going: ark-ark-ark, bark-bark-bark. Sometimes Pete wanted to go to the head of the stairs and scream down at them to quit it, just quit it. *You're scaring the kids,* he wanted to yell. *There are kids in this house,* kids, *did you two stupes forget that?*

Pete was home because Honor Roll students with nothing but afternoon study hall and activity period after lunch were allowed to cut out early. His door was open and he heard his father go thumping rapidly across the kitchen on his crutches as soon as his mother's car pulled into the driveway. Pete was pretty sure today's festivities would start with his dad saying Gosh, she was home early. Mom would say he could never seem to remember that Wednesdays were now her early days. Dad would reply that he still wasn't used to living in this part of the city, saying it like they'd been forced to relocate into deepest darkest Lowtown instead of just the Tree Streets section of Northfield. Once the preliminaries were taken care of, they could get down to the real arking and barking.

Pete wasn't crazy about the North Side himself, but it wasn't *terrible,* and even at thirteen he seemed to understand the economic realities of their situation better than his father. Maybe because he wasn't swallowing OxyContin pills four times a day like his father.

They were here because Grace Johnson Middle School, where her mother used to teach, had been closed as part of the city council's cost-cutting initiative. Many of the GJ teachers were now unemployed. Linda, at least, had been hired as a combination librarian and study hall monitor at Northfield Elementary. She got out early on Wednesdays because the library closed at noon that day. All the school libraries did. It was another cost-cutting initiative. Pete's dad railed at this, pointing out that the council members hadn't cut their *salaries*, and calling them a bunch of goddam Tea Party hypocrites.

Pete didn't know about that. What he knew was that these days Tom Saubers railed at everything.

The Ford Focus, their only car now, pulled up in the driveway and Mom slid out, dragging her old scuffed briefcase. She skirted the patch of ice that always formed in the shady spot under the front porch downspout. It had been Tina's turn to salt that down, but she had forgotten, as usual. Mom climbed the steps slowly, her shoulders low. Pete hated to see her walk that way, as if she had a sack of bricks on her back. Dad's crutches, meanwhile, thumped a double-time rhythm into the living room.

The front door opened. Pete waited. Hoped for something nice like *Hiya, honey, how was your morning?*

As if.

He didn't exactly *want* to eavesdrop on the arkie-barkies, but the house was small and it was practically impossible not to over-hear . . . unless he left, that is, a strategic retreat he made more and more frequently this winter. And he sometimes felt that, as the older kid, he had a *responsibility* to listen. Mr. Jacoby liked to say in history class that knowledge was power, and Pete supposed that was why he felt compelled to monitor his parents' escalating war of words. Because each arkie-barkie stretched the fabric of the marriage thinner, and one of these days it would tear wide open. Best to be prepared.

Only prepared for what? Divorce? That seemed the most likely outcome. In some ways things might be better if they did split up—Pete felt this more and more strongly, although he had not yet articulated it as a conscious thought—but what exactly would a divorce mean in (another of Mr. Jacoby's faves) *real world terms*? Who would stay and who would go? If his dad went, how would he get along without a car when he could hardly walk? For that matter, how could either of them *afford* to go? They were broke already.

At least Tina wasn't here for today's spirited exchange of parental views; she was still in school, and probably wouldn't be home directly after. Maybe not until dinner. She had finally made a friend, a bucktoothed girl named Ellen Briggs, who lived on the corner of Sycamore and Elm. Pete thought Ellen had the brains of a hamster, but at least Tina wasn't always moping around the house, missing her friends in the old neighborhood, and sometimes crying. Pete hated it when Tina cried.

Meanwhile, silence your cell phones and turn off your pagers, folks. The lights are going down and this afternoon's installment of *We're in Deep Shit* is about to begin.

TOM: "Hey, you're home early."

LINDA (wearily): "Tom, it's—"

TOM: "Wednesday, right. Early day at the library."

LINDA: "You've been smoking in the house again. I can smell it."

TOM (getting his sulk on): "Just one. In the kitchen. With the window open. There's ice on the back steps, and I didn't want to risk a tumble. Pete forgot to salt them again."

PETE (aside to the audience): "As he should know, since he

made the schedule of chores, it's actually Tina's week to salt. Those OxyContins he takes aren't just pain pills, they're stupid pills."

LINDA: "I can still smell it, and you know the lease specifically prohibits—"

TOM: "All right, okay, I get it. Next time I'll go outside and risk falling off my crutches."

LINDA: "It's not *just* the lease, Tommy. The secondary smoke is bad for the kids. We've discussed that."

TOM: "And discussed it, and discussed it . . ."

LINDA (now wading into even deeper water): "Also, how much does a pack of cigarettes cost these days? Four-fifty? Five dollars?"

TOM: "I smoke a pack a *week*, for Christ's sake!"

LINDA (overrunning his defenses with an arithmetic Panzer assault): "At five a pack, that's over twenty dollars a month. And it all comes out of my salary, because it's the only one—"

TOM: "Oh, here we go—"

LINDA: "—we've got now."

TOM: "You never get tired of rubbing that in, do you? Probably think I got run over on purpose. So I could laze around the house."

LINDA (after a long pause): "Is there any wine left? Because I could use half a glass."

PETE (aside): "Say there is, Dad. Say there is."

TOM: "It's gone. Maybe you'd like me to crutch my way down to the Zoney's and get another bottle. Of course you'd have to give me an advance on my *allowance*."

LINDA (not crying, but sounding on the verge): "You act as though what happened to you is my fault."

TOM (shouting): "It's *nobody's* fault, and that's what drives me crazy! Don't you get that? They never even caught the guy who did it!"

At this point Pete decided he'd had enough. It was a stupid play. Maybe they didn't see that, but he did. He closed his lit book. He would read the assigned story—something by a guy named John Rothstein—that night. Right now he had to get out and breathe some uncontentious air.

LINDA (quiet): "At least you didn't die."

TOM (going totally soap opera now): "Sometimes I think it would be better if I had. Look at me—hooked through the bag on Oxy, and still in pain because it doesn't work for shit anymore unless I take enough to half-kill me. Living on my wife's salary—which is a thousand less than it used to be, thanks to the fucking Tea-Partiers—"

LINDA: "Watch your lang—"

TOM: "House? Gone. Motorized wheelchair? Gone. Savings? Almost used up. And now I can't even have a fucking cigarette!"

LINDA: "If you think whining will solve anything, be my guest, but—"

TOM (roaring): "Is whining what you call it? I call it reality. You want me to drop my pants so you can get a good look at what's left of my legs?"

Pete floated downstairs in his stocking feet. The living room was right there at the bottom, but they didn't see him; they were face-to-face and busy acting in a dipshit play no one would ever pay to see. His father hulking on his crutches, his eyes red and his cheeks scruffy with beard, his mother holding her purse in front of her breasts like a shield and biting her lips. It was awful, and the worst part? He loved them.

His father had neglected to mention the Emergency Fund, started a month after the City Center Massacre by the town's one remaining newspaper, in cooperation with the three local TV stations. Brian Williams had even done a story about it on *NBC*

*Nightly News*—how this tough little city took care of its own when disaster struck, all those caring hearts, all those helping hands, all that blah-blah-blah, and now a word from our sponsor. The Emergency Fund made everybody feel good for like six days. What the media didn't talk about was how little the fund had actually raised, even with the charity walks, and the charity bike rides, and a concert by an *American Idol* runner-up. The Emergency Fund was thin because times were hard for everyone. And, of course, what *was* raised had to be divided among so many. The Saubers family got a check for twelve hundred dollars, then one for five hundred, then one for two. Last month's check, marked FINAL INSTALL-MENT, came to fifty dollars.

Big whoop.


Pete slipped into the kitchen, grabbed his boots and jacket, and went out. The first thing he noticed was that there wasn't any ice on the back stoop; his father had been totally lying about that. The day was too warm for ice, at least in the sun. Spring was still six weeks away, but the current thaw had gone on for almost a week, and the only snow left in the backyard was a few crusty patches under the trees. Pete crossed to the fence and let himself out through the gate.

One advantage to living in the Tree Streets of the North Side was the undeveloped land behind Sycamore. It was easily as big as a city block, five tangled acres of undergrowth and scrubby trees running downhill to a frozen stream. Pete's dad said the land had been that way for a long time and was apt to stay that way even longer, due to some endless legal wrangle over who owned it and what could be built on it. "In the end, no one wins these things but the lawyers," he told Pete. "Remember that."

FINDERS KEEPERS

In Pete's opinion, kids who wanted a little mental health vacation from their parents also won.

A path ran through the winter-barren trees on a meandering diagonal, eventually coming out at the Birch Street Rec, a long-time Northfield youth center whose days were now numbered. Big kids hung out on and around the path in warm weather—smoking cigarettes, smoking dope, drinking beer, probably laying their girlfriends—but not at this time of year. No big kids equaled no hassle.

Sometimes Pete took his sister along the path if his mother and father were seriously into it, as was more and more often the case. When they arrived at the Rec, they'd shoot baskets or watch videos or play checkers. He didn't know where he could take her once the Rec closed. There was no place else except for Zoney's, the convenience store. On his own, he mostly just went as far as the creek, splooshing stones into it if it was flowing, bouncing them off the ice when it was frozen. Seeing if he could make a hole and enjoying the quiet.

The arkie-barkies were bad enough, but his worst fear was that his dad—now always a little high on the Oxy pills—might someday actually take a swing at his mother. That would almost certainly tear the thin-stretched cloth of the marriage. And if it didn't? If she put up with being hit? That would be even worse.

Never happen, Pete told himself. Dad never would.

But if he did?

Ice still covered the stream this afternoon, but it looked rotten, and there were big yellow patches in it, as if some giant had stopped to take a leak. Pete wouldn't dare walk on it. He wouldn't drown or anything if the ice gave way, the water was only ankle deep, but he had no wish to get home and have to explain why his pants and socks were wet. He sat on a fallen log, tossed a few stones (the small ones bounced and rolled, the big ones went through the yellow patches), then just looked at the sky for awhile. Big fluffy clouds floated along up there, the kind that looked more like spring than winter, moving from west to east. There was one that looked like an old woman with a hump on her back (or maybe it was a packsack); there was a rabbit; there was a dragon; there was one that looked like a—

A soft, crumbling thump on his left distracted him. He turned and saw an overhanging piece of the embankment, loosened by a week's worth of melting snow, had given way, exposing the roots of a tree that was already leaning precariously. The space created by the fall looked like a cave, and unless he was mistaken—he supposed it might be just a shadow—there was something in there.

Pete walked to the tree, grabbed one of its leafless branches, and bent for a better look. There was something there, all right, and it looked pretty big. The end of a box, maybe?

He worked his way down the bank, creating makeshift steps by digging the heels of his boots into the muddy earth. Once he was below the site of the little landspill, he squatted. He saw cracked black leather and metal strips with rivets in them. There was a handle the size of a saddle-stirrup on the end. It was a trunk. Someone had buried a trunk here.

Excited now as well as curious, Pete grabbed the handle and yanked. The trunk didn't budge. It was socked in good and tight. Pete gave another tug, but just for form's sake. He wasn't going to get it out. Not without tools.

He hunkered with his hands dangling between his thighs, as his father often used to do before his hunkering days came to an end. Just staring at the trunk jutting out of the black, root-snarled earth. It was probably crazy to be thinking of *Treasure Island* (also "The Gold Bug," a story they'd read in English the year before), but he *was* thinking of it. And was it crazy? Was it really? As well as telling them that knowledge was power, Mr. Jacoby stressed the importance of logical thinking. Wasn't it logical to think that someone wouldn't bury a trunk in the woods unless there was something valuable inside?

It had been there for awhile, too. You could tell just looking at it. The leather was cracked, and gray in places instead of black. Pete had an idea that if he pulled on the handle with all his might and kept pulling, it might break. The metal binding-strips were dull and lacy with rust.

He came to a decision and pelted back up the path to the house. He let himself in through the gate, went to the kitchen door, listened. There were no voices and the TV was off. His father had probably gone into the bedroom (the one on the first floor, Mom and Dad had to sleep there even though it was small, because Dad couldn't climb stairs very well now) to take a nap. Mom might have gone in with him, they sometimes made up that way, but more likely she was in the laundry room that doubled as her study, working on her résumé and applying for jobs online. His dad might have given up (and Pete had to admit he had his reasons), but his mom hadn't. She wanted to go back to teaching full-time, and not just for the money.

There was a little detached garage, but his mom never put the Focus in it unless there was going to be a snowstorm. It was full of stuff from the old house that they had no room for in this smaller rented place. His dad's toolbox was in there (Tom had listed the tools on craigslist or something, but hadn't been able to get what he considered a fair price for them), and some of Tina's and his old toys, and the tub of salt with its scoop, and a few lawn-and-garden implements leaning against the back wall. Pete selected a spade and ran back down the path, holding it in front of him like a soldier with his rifle at high port.

He eased his way almost all the way down to the stream, using the steps he'd made, and went to work on the little landslide that had revealed the trunk. He shoveled as much of the fallen earth as he could back into the hole under the tree. He wasn't able to fill it all the way to the gnarled roots, but he was able to cover the end of the trunk, which was all he wanted.

For now.

There was some arking and barking at dinner, not too much, and Tina didn't seem to mind, but she came into Pete's room just as he was finishing his homework. She was wearing her footy pajamas and dragging Mrs. Beasley, her last and most important comfort-doll. It was as if she had returned to the age of five.

"Can I get in your bed for awhile, Petie? I had a bad dream."

He considered making her go back, then decided (thoughts of the buried trunk flickering in his mind) that to do so might be bad luck. It would also be mean, considering the dark hollows under her pretty eyes.

"Yeah, okay, for awhile. But we're not going to make a practice of it." One of their mom's favorite phrases.

Tina scooted across the bed until she was against the wall—her sleeping position of choice, as if she planned to spend the night. Pete closed his Earth Science book, sat down beside her, and winced.

"Doll warning, Teens. Mrs. Beasley's head is halfway up my butt."

"I'll scrunch her down by my feet. There. Is that better?"

"What if she smothers?"

"She doesn't breathe, stupid. She's just a doll and Ellen says pretty soon I'll get tired of her."

"Ellen's a doofus."

"She's my friend." Pete realized with some amusement that this wasn't exactly disagreeing. "But she's probably right. People grow up."

"Not you. You'll always be my little sister. And don't go to sleep. You're going back to your room in like five minutes."

"Ten."

"Six."

She considered. "Okay."

From downstairs came a muffled groan, followed by the thump of crutches. Pete tracked the sound into the kitchen, where Dad would sit down, light a cigarette, and blow the smoke out the back door. This would cause the furnace to run, and what the furnace burned, according to their mother, was not oil but dollar bills.

"Are they gonna get divorced, do you think?"

Pete was doubly shocked: first by the question, then by the adult matter-of-factness of it. He started to say No, course not, then thought how much he disliked movies where adults lied to children, which was like *all* movies.

"I don't know. Not tonight, anyway. The courts are closed."

She giggled. That was probably good. He waited for her to say something else. She didn't. Pete's thoughts turned to the trunk buried in the embankment, beneath that tree. He had managed to keep those thoughts at arm's length while he did his homework, but . . .

*No, I didn't. Those thoughts were there all the time.*

"Teens? You better not go to sleep."

"I'm not . . ." But damn close, from the sound.

"What would you do if you found a treasure? A buried treasure chest full of jewels and gold doubloons?"

"What are doubloons?"

"Coins from olden days."

"I'd give it to Daddy and Mommy. So they wouldn't fight anymore. Wouldn't you?"

"Yes," Pete said. "Now go back to your own bed, before I have to carry you."

Under his insurance plan, Tom Saubers only qualified for therapy twice a week now. A special van came for him every Monday and Friday at nine o'clock and brought him back at four in the afternoon, after hydrotherapy and a meeting where people with long-term injuries and chronic pain sat around in a circle and talked about their problems. All of which meant that the house was empty for seven hours on those days.

On Thursday night, Pete went to bed complaining of a sore throat. The next morning he woke up saying it was still sore, and now he thought he had a fever, too.

"You're hot, all right," Linda said after putting the inside of her wrist to his brow. Pete certainly hoped so, after holding his face two inches from his bedside lamp before going downstairs. "If you're not better tomorrow, you probably should see the doctor."

"Good idea!" Tom exclaimed from his side of the table, where he was pushing around some scrambled eggs. He looked like he hadn't slept at all. "A specialist, maybe! Just let me call Shorty the Chauffeur. Tina's got dibs on the Rolls for her tennis lesson at the country club, but I think the Town Car is available."

Tina giggled. Linda gave Tom a hard look, but before she could respond, Pete said he didn't feel all *that* bad, a day at home would probably fix him up. If that didn't, the weekend would.

"I suppose." She sighed. "Do you want something to eat?"

Pete did, but thought it unwise to say so, since he was supposed to have a sore throat. He cupped his hand in front of his mouth and created a cough. "Maybe just some juice. Then I guess I'll go upstairs and try to get some more sleep."

Tina left the house first, bopping down to the corner where she and Ellen would discuss whatever weirdo stuff nine-year-olds discussed while waiting for the schoolbus. Then Mom for her school, in the Focus. Last of all Dad, who made his way down the walk on his crutches to the waiting van. Pete watched him go from his bedroom window, thinking that his father seemed smaller now. The hair sticking out around his Groundhogs cap had started to turn gray.

When the van was gone, Pete threw on some clothes, grabbed one of the reusable grocery shopping bags Mom kept in the pantry, and went out to the garage. From his father's toolbox he selected a hammer and chisel, which he dumped into the bag. He grabbed the spade, started out, then came back and took the crowbar as well. He had never been a Boy Scout, but believed in being prepared.

The morning was cold enough for him to see his breath, but by the time Pete dug enough of the trunk free to feel he had a chance of pulling it out, the air had warmed up to well above freezing and he was sweating under his coat. He draped it over a low branch and peered around to make sure he was still alone here by the stream (he had done this several times). Reassured, he got some dirt and rubbed his palms with it, like a batter getting ready to hit. He grasped the handle at the end of the trunk, reminding himself to be ready if it broke. The last thing he wanted to do was tumble down the embankment ass over teapot. If he fell into the stream, he really might get sick.

Probably nothing in there but a bunch of moldy old clothes, anyway . . . except why would anyone bury a trunk filled with old clothes? Why not just burn them, or take them to the Goodwill?

Only one way to find out.

Pete took a deep breath, locked it down in his chest, and pulled. The trunk stayed put, and the old handle creaked warningly, but Pete was encouraged. He found he could now shift the trunk from side to side a little. This made him think of Dad tying a thread around one of Tina's baby teeth and giving a brisk yank when it wouldn't come out on its own.

He dropped to his knees (reminding himself he would do well to either wash these jeans later on or bury them deep in his closet) and peered into the hole. He saw a root had closed around the rear of the trunk like a grasping arm. He grabbed the spade, choked up on the handle, and chopped at it. The root was thick and he had to rest several times, but finally he cut all the way through. He laid the spade aside and grabbed the handle again. The trunk was looser now, almost ready to come out. He glanced at his watch. Quarter past ten. He thought of Mom calling home on her break to see how he was doing. Not a big problem, when he didn't answer she'd just think he was sleeping, but he reminded himself to check the answering machine when he got back. He grabbed the spade and began to dig around the trunk, loosening the dirt and cutting a few smaller roots. Then he took hold of the handle again.

"This time, you mother," he told it. "This time for sure."

He pulled. The trunk slid forward so suddenly and easily that he would have fallen over if his feet hadn't been braced far apart. Now it was leaning out of the hole, its top covered with sprays and clods of dirt. He could see the latches on the front, old-fashioned ones, like the latches on a workman's lunchbox. Also a big lock. He grabbed the handle again and this time it snapped. "Fuck a duck," Pete said, looking at his hands. They were red and throbbing.

Well, in for a penny, in for a pound (another of Mom's favorite sayings). He gripped the sides of the trunk in a clumsy bearhug and rocked back on his heels. This time it came all the way out of its hidey-hole and into the sunlight for the first time in what had to be years, a damp and dirty relic with rusty fittings. It looked to be two and a half feet long and at least a foot and a half deep. Maybe more. Pete hefted the end and guessed it might weigh as much as sixty pounds, half his own weight, but it was impossible to tell how much of that was the contents and how much the trunk itself. In any case, it wasn't doubloons; if the trunk had been filled with gold, he wouldn't have been able to pull it out at all, let alone lift it.

He snapped the latches up, creating little showers of dirt, and then bent close to the lock, prepared to bust it off with the hammer and chisel. Then, if it still wouldn't open—and it probably wouldn't—he'd use the crowbar. But first . . . you never knew until you tried . . .

He grasped the lid and it came up in a squall of dirty hinges. Later he would surmise that someone had bought this trunk secondhand, probably getting a good deal because the key was lost, but for now he only stared. He was unaware of the blister on one palm, or the ache in his back and thighs, or the sweat trickling down his dirt-streaked face. He wasn't thinking of his mother, his father, or his sister. He wasn't thinking of the arkie-barkies, either, at least not then.

The trunk had been lined with clear plastic to protect against moisture. Beneath it he could see piles of what looked like notebooks. He used the side of his palm as a windshield wiper and cleared a crescent of fine droplets from the plastic. They were notebooks, all right, nice ones with what almost had to be real leather covers. It looked like a hundred at least. But that wasn't all. There were also envelopes like the ones his mom brought home when she cashed a check. Pete pulled away the plastic and stared into the half-filled trunk. The envelopes had GRANITE STATE BANK and *"Your Hometown Friend!"* printed on them. Later he would notice certain differences between these envelopes and the ones his mom got at Corn Bank and Trust—no email address, and nothing about using your ATM card for withdrawals—but for now he only stared. His heart was beating so hard he saw black dots pulsing in front of his eyes, and he wondered if he was going to faint.

Bullshit you are, only girls do that.

Maybe, but he felt decidedly woozy, and realized part of the problem was that since opening the trunk he had forgotten to breathe. He inhaled deeply, whooshed it out, and inhaled again. All the way down to his toes, it felt like. His head cleared, but his heart was whamming harder than ever and his hands were shaking.

Those bank envelopes will be empty. You know that, don't you? People find buried money in books and movies, but not in real life.

Only they didn't *look* empty. They looked *stuffed*.

Pete started to reach for one, then gasped when he heard rustling on the other side of the stream. He whirled around and saw two squirrels there, probably thinking the weeklong thaw meant spring had arrived, making merry in the dead leaves. They raced up a tree, tails twitching.

Pete turned back to the trunk and grabbed one of the bank envelopes. The flap wasn't sealed. He flipped it up with a finger that felt numb, even though the temperature now had to be riding right around forty. He squeezed the envelope open and looked inside.

Money.

Twenties and fifties.

"Holy Jesus God Christ in heaven," Pete Saubers whispered.

He pulled out the sheaf of bills and tried to count, but at first his hands were shaking too badly and he dropped some. They fluttered in the grass, and before he scrambled them up, his overheated brain assured him that Ulysses Grant had actually winked at him from one of the bills.

He counted. Four hundred dollars. Four hundred in this one envelope, and there were *dozens* of them.

He stuffed the bills back into the envelope—not an easy job, because now his hands were shaking worse than Grampa Fred's in the last year or two of his life. He flipped the envelope into the trunk and looked around, eyes wide and bulging. Traffic sounds that had always seemed faint and far and unimportant in this overgrown stretch of ground now sounded close and threatening. This was not Treasure Island; this was a city of over a million people, many now out of work, and they would love to have what was in this trunk.

Think, Pete Saubers told himself. *Think,* for God's sake. This is the most important thing that's ever happened to you, maybe the most important thing that ever *will* happen to you, so think hard and think right.

What came to mind first was Tina, snuggled up next to the wall in his bed. *What would you do if you found a treasure?* he had asked.

*Give it to Daddy and Mommy,* she had replied.

But suppose Mom wanted to give it back?

It was an important question. Dad never would—Pete knew

that—but Mom was different. She had strong ideas about what was right and what wasn't. If he showed them this trunk and what was inside it, it might lead to the worst arkie-barkie about money ever.

"Besides, give it back to *who*?" Pete whispered. "The bank?"

That was ridiculous.

Or was it? Suppose the money really was pirate treasure, only from bank robbers instead of buccaneers? But then why was it in envelopes, like for withdrawals? And what about all those black notebooks?

He could consider such things later, but not now; what he had to do now was *act*. He looked at his watch and saw it was already quarter to eleven. He still had time, but he had to use it.

"Use it or lose it," he whispered, and began tossing the Granite State Bank cash envelopes into the cloth grocery bag that held the hammer and chisel. He placed the bag on top of the embankment and covered it with his jacket. He crammed the plastic wrap back into the trunk, closed the lid, and muscled the trunk back into the hole. He paused to wipe his forehead, which was greasy with dirt and sweat, then seized the spade and began to shovel like a maniac. He got the trunk covered—mostly—then seized the bag and his jacket and ran back along the path toward home. He would hide the bag in the back of his closet, that would do to start with, and see if there was a message from his mother on the answering machine. If everything was okay on the Mom front (and if Dad hadn't come home early from therapy—that would be horrible), he could whip back to the stream and do a better job of concealing the trunk. Later he might check out the notebooks, but as he made his way home on that sunny February morning, his only thought about them was that there might be more money envelopes mixed in with them. Or lying beneath them.

He thought, I'll have to take a shower. And clean the dirt out of the bathtub after, so she doesn't ask what I was doing outside when I was supposed to be sick. I have to be really careful, and I can't tell anyone. No one at all.

In the shower, he had an idea.

# 1978

Home is the place that when you go there, they have to take you in, but when Morris arrived at the house on Sycamore Street, there were no lights to brighten the evening gloom and no one to welcome him at the door. Why would there be? His mother was in New Jersey, lecturing about how a bunch of nineteenth-century businessmen had tried to steal America. Lecturing grad students who would probably go on to steal everything they could lay their hands on as they chased the Golden Buck. Some people would undoubtedly say that Morris had chased a few Golden Bucks of his own in New Hampshire, but that wasn't so. He hadn't gone there for money.

He wanted the Biscayne in the garage and out of sight. Hell, he wanted the Biscayne *gone*, but that would have to wait. His first priority was Pauline Muller. Most of the people on Sycamore Street were so wedded to their televisions once prime time started that they wouldn't have noticed a UFO if one landed on their lawn, but that wasn't true of Mrs. Muller; the Bellamys' next-door neighbor had raised snooping to a fine art. So he went there first.

"Why, look who it is!" she cried when she opened the door . . . just as if she hadn't been peering out her kitchen window when Morris pulled into the driveway. "Morrie Bellamy! Big as life and twice as handsome!"

Morris produced his best aw-shucks smile. "How you doin, Mrs. Muller?"

She gave him a hug which Morris could have done without but dutifully returned. Then she turned her head, setting her wattles in motion, and yelled, "Bert! *Bertie!* It's Morrie Bellamy!"

From the living room came a triple grunt that might have been *how ya doin.*

"Come in, Morrie! Come in! I'll put on coffee! And guess what?" She gave her unnaturally black eyebrows a horrifyingly flirtatious wiggle. "There's Sara Lee poundcake!"

"Sounds delicious, but I just got back from Boston. Drove straight through. I'm pretty beat. Just didn't want you to see lights next door and call the police."

She gave a monkey-shriek of laughter. "You're so *thoughtful*! But you always were. How's your mom, Morrie?"

"Fine."

He had no idea. Since his stint in reform school at seventeen and his failure to make a go of City College at twenty-one, relations between Morris and Anita Bellamy amounted to the occasional telephone call. These were frosty but civil. After one final argument the night of his arrest for breaking and entering and assorted other goodies, they had basically given up on each other.

"You've really put on some muscle," Mrs. Muller said. "The girls must love *that*. You used to be such a *scrawny* thing."

"Been building houses—"

"Building *houses*! *You!* Holy gosh! Bertie! *Morris has been building houses!*"

This produced a few more grunts from the living room.

"But then the work dried up, so I came back here. Mom said I was welcome to use the place unless she managed to rent it, but I probably won't stay long."

How right *that* turned out to be.

"Come in the living room, Morrie, and say hello to Bert."

"I better take a rain check." To forestall further importuning, he called, "*Yo, Bert!*"

Another grunt, unintelligible over the laugh track accompanying *Welcome Back, Kotter*.

"Tomorrow, then," Mrs. Muller said, her eyebrows once more waggling. She looked like she was doing a Groucho imitation. "I'll save the poundcake. I might even *whip* some *cream*."

"Great," Morris said. It wasn't likely Mrs. Muller would die of a heart attack before tomorrow, but it was possible; as another great poet said, hope springs eternal in the human breast.


The keys to house and garage were where they'd always been, hanging under the eave to the right of the stoop. Morris garaged the Biscayne and set the trunk from the antiques barn on the concrete. He itched to get at that fourth Jimmy Gold novel right away, but the notebooks were all jumbled up, and besides, his eyes would cross before he read a single page of Rothstein's tiny handwriting; he really was bushed.

Tomorrow, he promised himself. After I talk to Andy, get some idea of how he wants to handle this, I'll put them in order and start reading.

He pushed the trunk under his father's old worktable and covered it with a swatch of plastic he found in the corner. Then he went inside and toured the old homestead. It looked pretty much the same, which was lousy. There was nothing in the fridge except a jar of pickles and a box of baking soda, but there were a few Hungry Man dinners in the freezer. He stuck one in the oven, turned the dial to 350, then climbed the stairs to his old bedroom.

I did it, he thought. I made it. I'm sitting on eighteen years' worth of unpublished John Rothstein manuscripts.

He was too tired to feel exultation, or even much pleasure. He almost fell asleep in the shower, and again over some really crappy meatloaf and instant potatoes. He shoveled it in, though, then trudged back up the stairs. He was asleep forty seconds after his head hit the pillow, and didn't wake up until nine twenty the following morning.

Well rested and with a bar of sunlight pouring across his childhood bed, Morris *did* feel exultation, and he couldn't wait to share it. Which meant Andy Halliday.

He found khakis and a nice madras shirt in his closet, slicked back his hair, and peeked briefly into the garage to make sure all was well there. He gave Mrs. Muller (once more looking out through the curtains) what he hoped was a jaunty wave as he headed down the street to the bus stop. He arrived downtown just before ten, walked a block, and peered down Ellis Avenue to the Happy Cup, where the outside tables sat under pink umbrellas. Sure enough, Andy was on his coffee break. Better yet, his back was turned, so Morris could approach undetected.

*"Booga-booga!"* he cried, grabbing the shoulder of Andy's old corduroy sportcoat.

His old friend—really his only friend in this benighted joke of a city—jumped and wheeled around. His coffee overturned and spilled. Morris stepped back. He had meant to startle Andy, but not *that* much.

"Hey, sor—"

"What did you *do?*" Andy asked in a low, grinding whisper. His eyes were blazing behind his glasses—hornrims Morris had always thought of as sort of an affectation. "What the fuck did you *do?*"

This was not the welcome Morris had anticipated. He sat down. "What we talked about." He studied Andy's face and saw none of the amused intellectual superiority his friend usually affected. Andy looked scared. Of Morris? Maybe. For himself? Almost certainly.

"I shouldn't be seen with y—"

Morris was carrying a brown paper bag he'd grabbed from the kitchen. From it he took one of Rothstein's notebooks and put it on the table, being careful to avoid the puddle of spilled coffee. "A sample. One of a great many. At least a hundred and fifty. I haven't had a chance to do a count yet, but it's the total jackpot."

"Put that away!" Andy was still whispering like a character in a bad spy movie. His eyes shifted from side to side, always returning to the notebook. "Rothstein's murder is on the front page of the *New York Times* and all over the TV, you idiot!"

This news came as a shock. It was supposed to be at least three days before anyone found the writer's body, maybe as long as six. Andy's reaction was even more of a shock. He looked like a cornered rat.

Morris flashed what he hoped was a fair approximation of Andy's I'm-so-smart-I-bore-myself smile. "Calm down. In this part of town there are kids carrying notebooks everywhere." He pointed across the street toward Government Square. "There goes one now."

"Not Moleskines, though! Jesus! The housekeeper knew the kind Rothstein used to write in, and the paper says the safe in his bedroom was open and empty! Put . . . it . . . *away!*"

Morrie pushed it toward Andy instead, still being careful to avoid the coffee stain. He was growing increasingly irritated with Andy—PO'd, as Jimmy Gold would have said—but he also felt a perverse sort of pleasure at watching the man cringe in his seat, as if the notebook were a vial filled with plague germs.

"Go on, have a look. This one's mostly poetry. I was paging through it on the bus—"

"On the *bus*? Are you *insane*?"

"—and it's not very good," Morris went on as if he hadn't heard, "but it's his, all right. A holograph manuscript. Extremely valuable. We talked about that. Several times. We talked about how—"

"Put it *away*!"

Morris didn't like to admit that Andy's paranoia was catching, but it sort of was. He returned the notebook to the bag and looked at his old friend (his *one* friend) sulkily. "It's not like I was suggesting we have a sidewalk sale, or anything."

"Where are the rest?" And before Morris could answer: "Never mind. I don't want to know. Don't you understand how hot those things are? How hot *you* are?"

"I'm not hot," Morris said, but he was, at least in the physical sense; all at once his cheeks and the nape of his neck were burning. Andy was acting as if he'd shit his pants instead of pulling off the crime of the century. "No one can connect me to Rothstein, and I *know* it'll be awhile before we can sell them to a private collector. I'm not stupid."

"Sell them to a col— Morrie, do you *hear* yourself?"

Morris crossed his arms and stared at his friend. The man who used to be his friend, at least. "You act as if we never talked about this. As if we never planned it."

"We didn't plan *anything*! It was a story we were telling ourselves, I thought you understood that!"

What Morris understood was Andy Halliday would tell the police exactly that if he, Morris, were caught. And Andy *expected* him to be caught. For the first time Morris realized consciously that Andy was no intellectual giant eager to join him in an existential act of outlawry but just another nebbish. A bookstore clerk only a few years older than Morris himself.

*Don't give me your dumbass literary criticism,* Rothstein had said to Morris in the last two minutes of his life. *You're a common thief, my friend.*

His temples began to throb.

"I should have known better. All your big talk about private collectors, movie stars and Saudi princes and I don't know who-all. Just a lot of big talk. You're nothing but a blowhard."

That was a hit, a palpable hit. Morris saw it and was glad, just as he had been when he had managed to stick it to his mother once or twice in their final argument.

Andy leaned forward, cheeks flushed, but before he could speak, a waitress appeared with a wad of napkins. "Let me get that spill," she said, and wiped it up. She was young, a natural ash-blonde, pretty in a pale way, maybe even beautiful. She smiled at Andy. He returned a pained grimace, at the same time drawing away from her as he had from the Moleskine notebook.

He's a homo, Morris thought wonderingly. He's a goddam homo. How come I didn't know that? How come I never saw? He might as well be wearing a sign.

Well, there were a lot of things about Andy he'd never seen, weren't there? Morris thought of something one of the guys on the housing job liked to say: *All pistol and no bullets.*

With the waitress gone, taking her toxic atmosphere of girl with her, Andy leaned forward again. "Those collectors are out there," he said. "They pile up paintings, sculpture, first editions . . . there's an oilman in Texas who's got a collection of early wax-cylinder recordings worth a million dollars, and another one who's got a complete run of every western, science fiction, and shudder-pulp magazine published between 1910 and 1955. Do you think all of that stuff was legitimately bought and sold? The fuck it was. Collectors are insane, the worst of them don't care if the things they covet were stolen or not, and they most assuredly do not want to share with the rest of the world."

Morris had heard this screed before, and his face must have shown it, because Andy leaned even farther forward. Now their noses were almost touching. Morris could smell English Leather, and wondered if that was the preferred aftershave of homos. Like a secret sign, or something.

"But do you think any of those guys would listen to *me?*"

Morris Bellamy, who was now seeing Andy Halliday with new eyes, said he guessed not.

Andy pooched out his lower lip. "They will someday, though. Yeah. Once I get my own shop and build up a clientele. But that'll take *years.*"

"We talked about waiting five."

"*Five?*" Andy barked a laugh and drew back to his side of the table again. "I might be able to open my *shop* in five years—I've got my eye on a little place in Lacemaker Lane, there's a fabric store there now but it doesn't do much business—but it takes longer than that to find big-money clients and establish trust."

Lots of buts, Morris thought, but there were no buts before.

"How long?"

"Why don't you try me on those notebooks around the turn of the twenty-first century, if you still have them? Even if I *did* have a call list of private collectors right now, today, not even the nuttiest of them would touch anything so hot."

Morris stared at him, at first unable to speak. At last he said, "You never said anything like *that* when we were planning—"

Andy clapped his hands to the sides of his head and clutched it. "We planned *nothing*! And don't you try to lay this off on me! Don't you ever! I know you, Morrie. You didn't steal them to sell them, at least not until you've read them. Then I suppose you might be willing to give some of them to the world, if the price was right. Basically, though, you're just batshit-crazy on the subject of John Rothstein."

"Don't call me that." His temples were throbbing worse than ever.

"I will if it's the truth, and it is. You're batshit-crazy on the subject of Jimmy Gold, too. He's why you went to jail."

"I went to jail because of my mother. She might as well have locked me up herself."

"Whatever. It's water under the bridge. This is now. Unless you're lucky, the police are going to be paying you a visit very soon, and they'll probably arrive with a search warrant. If you have those notebooks when they knock on your door, your goose will be cooked."

"Why would they come to me? Nobody saw us, and my partners . . ." He winked. "Let's just say that dead men tell no tales."

"You . . . what? *Killed* them? Killed them, *too*?" Andy's face was a picture of dawning horror.

Morris knew he shouldn't have said that, but—funny how that *but* kept coming around—Andy was just being such an asshole.

"What's the name of the town that Rothstein lived in?" Andy's eyes were shifting around again, as if he expected the cops to be closing in even now, guns drawn. "Talbot Corners, right?"

"Yes, but it's mostly farms. What they call the Corners is nothing but a diner, a grocery store, and a gas station where two state roads cross."

"How many times were you there?"

"Maybe five." It had actually been closer to a dozen, between

1976 and 1978. Alone at first, then with either Freddy or Curtis or both.

"Ever ask questions about the town's most famous resident while you were there?"

"Sure, once or twice. So what? Probably everybody who ever stops at that diner asks about—"

"No, that's where you're wrong. Most out-of-towners don't give a shit about John Rothstein. If they've got questions, it's about when deer season starts or what kind of fish they could catch in the local lake. You don't think the locals will remember you when the police ask if there have been any strangers curious about the guy who wrote *The Runner*? Curious strangers who made repeat visits? Plus you have a *record*, Morrie!"

"Juvenile. It's sealed."

"Something as big as this, the seal might not hold. And what about your partners? Did either of *them* have records?"

Morris said nothing.

"You don't know who saw you, and you don't know who your partners might have bragged to about the big robbery they were going to pull off. The police could nail you *today*, you idiot. If they do and you bring my name up, I'll deny we ever talked about this. But I'll give you some advice. Get rid of *that*." He was pointing to the brown paper bag. "That and all the rest of the notebooks. Hide them somewhere. Bury them! If you do that, maybe you can talk your way out of it, if push comes to shove. Always supposing you didn't leave fingerprints, or something."

We didn't, Morris thought. I wasn't stupid. And I'm not a cowardly big-talking homo, either.

"Maybe we can revisit this," Andy said, "but it will be much later on, and only if they don't grab you." He got up. "In the meantime, stay clear of me, or I'll call the police myself."

He walked away fast with his head down, not looking back.

Morris sat there. The pretty waitress returned to ask if she could get him anything. Morris shook his head. When she left, he picked up the bag with the notebook inside it and walked away himself. In the opposite direction.


He knew what the pathetic fallacy was, of course—nature echoing the feelings of human beings—and understood it to be the cheap, mood-creating trick of second-rate writers, but that day it seemed to be true. The morning's bright sunlight had both mirrored and amplified his feeling of exultation, but by noon the sun was only a dim circle behind a blear of clouds, and by three o'clock that afternoon, as his worries multiplied, the day grew dark and it began to drizzle.

He drove the Biscayne out to the mall near the airport, constantly watching for police cars. When one came roaring up behind him on Airline Boulevard with its blues flashing, his stomach froze and his heart seemed to climb all the way into his mouth. When it sped by without slowing, he felt no relief.

He found a news broadcast on BAM-100. The lead story was about a peace conference between Sadat and Begin at Camp David (Yeah, like *that'll* ever happen, Morris thought distractedly), but the second one concerned the murder of noted American writer John Rothstein. Police were saying it was the work of "a gang of thieves," and that a number of leads were being followed. That was probably just PR bullshit.

Or maybe not.

Morris didn't think he could be tracked down as a result of interviews with the half-deaf old codgers who hung out at the Yummy Diner in Talbot Corners, no matter what Andy thought, but there was something else that troubled him far more. He, Freddy, and Curtis had all worked for Donahue Construction, which was building homes in both Danvers and North Beverly. There were two different work crews, and for most of Morris's sixteen months, spent carrying boards and nailing studs, he had been in Danvers while Curtis and Freddy toiled at the other site, five miles away. Yet for awhile they *had* worked on the same crew, and even after they were split up, they usually managed to eat lunch together.

Plenty of people knew this.

He parked the Biscayne with about a thousand others at the JC Penney end of the mall, wiped down every surface he had touched, and left the keys in the ignition. He walked away fast, turning up his collar and yanking down his Indians cap. At the mall's main entrance, he waited on a bench until a Northfield bus came, and dropped his fifty cents into the box. The rain grew heavier and the ride back was slow, but he didn't mind. It gave him time to think.

Andy was cowardly and full of himself, but he had been right about one thing. Morris had to hide the notebooks, and he had to do so immediately, no matter how much he wanted to read them, starting with that undiscovered Jimmy Gold novel. If the cops *did* come and he didn't have the notebooks, they could do nothing . . . right? All they'd have would be suspicion.

Right?

There was no one peeking through the curtains next door, which saved him another conversation with Mrs. Muller, and perhaps having to explain that he had sold his car. The rain had become a downpour, and that was good. There would be no one rambling around in the undeveloped land between Sycamore and Birch. Especially after dark.

He pulled everything out of the secondhand trunk, resisting an almost overpowering urge to look into the notebooks. He couldn't do that, no matter how much he wanted to, because once he started, he wouldn't be able to stop. Later, he thought. Must postpone your gratifications, Morrie. Good advice, but spoken in his mother's voice, and that started his head throbbing again. At least he wouldn't have to postpone his gratifications for long; if three weeks went by with no visits from the police—a month at most—he would be able to relax and begin his researches.

He lined the trunk with plastic to make sure the contents would stay dry, and put the notebooks, including the one he'd taken to show Andy, back inside. He dumped the money envelopes on top. He closed the trunk, considered, and opened it again. He pawed the plastic aside and took a couple of hundred dollars from one of the bank envelopes. Surely no cop would think that an excessive amount, even if he were searched. He could tell them it was his severance pay, or something.

The sound of the rain on the garage roof was not soothing. To Morris it sounded like skeletal tapping fingers, and made his headache worse. He froze every time a car went by, waiting for headlights and pulsing blue strobes to splash up the driveway. Fuck Andy Halliday for putting all these pointless worries in my head, he thought. Fuck him and the homo horse he rode in on.

Only the worries might not be pointless. As afternoon wound down toward twilight, the idea that the cops could put Curtis and Freddy together with Morris Bellamy seemed more and more likely. That fucking rest area! Why hadn't he dragged the bodies into the woods, at least? Not that it would have slowed the cops down much once someone pulled in, saw all the blood, and called 911. The cops would have dogs . . .

"Besides," he told the trunk, "I was in a hurry. Wasn't I?"

His father's hand dolly was still standing in the corner, along with a rusty pick and two rusty shovels. Morris tipped the trunk endwise onto the dolly, secured the straps, and peered out of the garage window. Still too much light. Now that he was so close to getting rid of the notebooks and the money—Temporarily, he soothed himself, this is just a temporary measure—he became more and more sure that the cops would be here soon. Suppose Mrs. Muller had reported him as acting suspicious? It didn't seem likely, she was thicker than an oak plank, but who really knew?

He forced himself to stuff down another frozen dinner, thinking it might soothe his head. It made the headache worse, instead. He looked in his mother's medicine cabinet for aspirin or Advil, and found . . . nothing. Fuck you, Mom, he thought. Really. Sincerely. Fuck . . . *you.*

He saw her smile. Thin as a hook, that smile.

It was still light at seven o'clock—goddam daylight saving time, what genius thought *that* up?—but the windows next door were still dark. That was good, but Morris knew the Mullers might be back at any time. Besides, he was too nervous to wait any longer. He rooted around in the front hall closet until he found a poncho.

He used the garage's rear door and yanked the dolly across the back lawn. The grass was wet, the ground underneath spongy, and it was hard going. The path he had used so many times as a kid—usually going to the Birch Street Rec—was sheltered by overhanging trees, and he was able to make better progress. By the time he got to the little stream that flowed diagonally across this block-sized square of waste ground, full dark had arrived.

He had brought a flashlight and used it in brief winks to pick out a likely location on the embankment of the stream, a safe distance from the path. The dirt was soft, and it was easy digging until he got to the tangle of roots from an overhanging tree. He thought about trying a different spot, but the hole was almost big enough for the trunk already, and he was damned if he was going to start all over again, especially when this was just a temporary precaution. He laid the flashlight in the hole, propping it on a rock so the beam shone on the roots, and chopped through them with the pick.

He slid the trunk into the hole and shoveled the dirt back around it and over it quickly. He finished by tamping it down with the flat of the shovel. He thought it would be okay. The bank wasn't particularly grassy, so the bald spot wouldn't stand out. The important thing was that it was out of the house, right?

Right?

He felt no relief as he dragged the dolly back along the path. Nothing was working out the way it was supposed to, nothing. It was as if malignant fate had come between him and the notebooks, just as fate had come between Romeo and Juliet. That comparison seemed both ludicrous and perfectly apt. He *was* a lover. Goddam Rothstein had jilted him with *The Runner Slows Down*, but that didn't change the fact.

His love was true.


When he got back to the house, he went immediately to the shower, as a boy named Pete Saubers would do many years later in this very same bathroom, after visiting that very same embankment and overhanging tree. Morris stayed in until his fingers were pruney and the hot water was gone, then dried off and dressed in fresh clothes from his bedroom closet. They looked childish and out of fashion to him, but they still fit (more or less). He put his dirt-smeared jeans and sweatshirt in the washer, an act that would also be replicated by Pete Saubers years later.

Morris turned on the TV, sat in his father's old easy chair—his mother said she kept it as a reminder, should she ever be tempted into stupidity again—and saw the usual helping of ad-driven inanity. He thought that any of those ads (jumping laxative bottles, primping moms, singing hamburgers) could have been written by Jimmy Gold, and that made his headache worse than ever. He decided to go down to Zoney's and get some Anacin. Maybe even a beer or two. Beer wouldn't hurt. It was the hard stuff that caused trouble, and he'd learned his lesson on that score.

He did get the Anacin, but the idea of drinking beer in a house full of books he didn't want to read and TV he didn't want to watch made him feel worse than ever. Especially when the stuff he *did* want to read was so maddeningly close. Morris rarely drank in bars, but all at once he felt that if he didn't get out and find some company and hear some fast music, he would go completely insane. Somewhere out in this rainy night, he was sure there was a young lady who wanted to dance.

He paid for his aspirin and asked the young guy at the register, almost idly, if there was a bar with live music that he could get to on the bus.

The young guy said there was.

# 2010

When Linda Saubers got home that Friday afternoon at three thirty, Pete was sitting at the kitchen table drinking a cup of cocoa. His hair was still damp from the shower. She hung her coat on one of the hooks by the back door, and placed the inside of her wrist against his forehead again. "Cool as a cucumber," she pronounced. "Do you feel better?"

"Yeah," he said. "When Tina came home, I made her peanut butter crackers."

"You're a good brother. Where is she now?"

"Ellen's, where else?"

Linda rolled her eyes and Pete laughed.

"Mother of Mercy, is that the dryer I hear?"

"Yeah. There were a bunch of clothes in the basket, so I washed em. Don't worry, I followed the directions on the door, and they came out okay."

She bent down and kissed his temple. "Aren't you the little do-bee?"

"I try," Pete said. He closed his right hand to hide the blister on his palm.

The first envelope came on a snow-showery Thursday not quite a week later. The address—Mr. Thomas Saubers, 23 Sycamore

75

Street—was typed. Stuck on the upper-right-hand corner was a
forty-four-cent stamp featuring the Year of The Tiger. There was
no return address on the upper left. Tom—the only member of
Clan Saubers home at midday—tore it open in the hall, expecting
either some sort of come-on or another past due notice. God knew
there had been plenty of those lately. But it wasn't a come-on, and
it wasn't a past due.

It was money.

The rest of the mail—catalogues for expensive stuff they
couldn't afford and advertising circulars addressed to OCCU-
PANT—fell from his hand and fluttered around his feet, unno-
ticed. In a low voice, almost a growl, Tom Saubers said, "What
the *fuck* is *this*?"

When Linda came home, the money was sitting in the middle of
the kitchen table. Tom was seated before the neat little pile with
his chin resting on his folded hands. He looked like a general considering a battle plan.

"What's that?" Linda asked.

"Five hundred dollars." He continued to look at the bills—
eight fifties and five twenties. "It came in the mail."

"From who?"

"I don't know."

She dropped her briefcase, came to the table, and picked up the
stack of currency. She counted it, then looked at him with wide
eyes. "My God, Tommy! What did the letter say?"

"There was no letter. Just the money."

"But who would—"

"I don't know, Lin. But I know one thing."

"What?"

"We can sure use it."

• • •

"Holy shit," Pete said when they told him. He had stayed late at school for intramural volleyball, and didn't come in until almost dinnertime.

"Don't be vulgar," Linda said, sounding distracted. The money was still on the kitchen table.

"How much?" And when his father told him: "Who sent it?"

"That's a good question," Tom said. "Now for Double Jeopardy, where the scores can really change." It was the first joke Pete had heard him make in a very long time.

Tina came in. "Daddy's got a fairy godmother, that's what I think. Hey, Dad, Mom! Look at my fingernails! Ellen got sparkle polish, and she shared."

"Excellent look for you, my little punkin," Tom said.

First a joke, then a compliment. Those things were all it took to convince Pete that he had done the right thing. *Totally* the right thing. They couldn't exactly send it back, could they? Not without a return address, they couldn't. And by the way, when was the last time Dad had called Teens his little punkin?

Linda gave her son a piercing look. "*You* don't know anything about this, do you?"

"Uh-uh, but can I have some?"

"Dream on," she said, and turned to her husband, hands on hips. "Tom, someone's obviously made a mistake."

Tom considered this, and when he spoke, there was no arking and barking. His voice was calm. "That doesn't seem likely." He pushed the envelope toward her, tapping his name and address.

"Yes, but—"

"But me no buts, Lin. We owe the oil company, and before we pay them, we have to pay down your MasterCard. Or you're going to lose it."

"Yes, but—"

"Lose the credit card, lose your credit rating." Still not arking and barking. Calm and reasonable. Persuasive. To Pete it was as if his father had been suffering from a high fever that had just broken. He even smiled. Smiled and touched her hand. "It so happens that for now, your credit rating is the only one we've got, so we have to protect it. Besides, Tina could be right. Maybe I've got a fairy godmother."

No, Pete thought. A fairy god*son* is what you've got.

Tina said, "Oh, wait! I know where it *really* came from."

They turned to her. Pete felt suddenly warm all over. She couldn't know, could she? *How* could she? Only he'd said that stupid thing about buried treasure, and—

"Where, hon?" Linda asked.

"The Emergency Fund thingy. It must have got some more money, and now they're spreading it out."

Pete let out a soundless breath of air, only realizing as it passed his lips that he had been holding it.

Tom ruffled her hair. "They wouldn't send cash, punkin. They'd send a check. Also a bunch of forms to sign."

Pete went to the stove. "I'm making more cocoa. Does anyone want some?"

Turned out they all did.


The envelopes kept coming.

The price of postage went up, but the amount never changed. An extra six thousand dollars per annum, give or take. Not a huge sum, but tax-free and just enough to keep the Saubers family from drowning in debt.

The children were forbidden to tell anyone.

"Tina will never be able to keep it to herself," Linda told Tom one night. "You know that, don't you? She'll tell her idiot friend, and Ellen Briggs will broadcast it to everyone she knows."

But Tina kept the secret, partly because her brother, whom she idolized, told her she would never be allowed in his room again if she spilled the beans, and mostly because she remembered the arkie-barkies.

Pete stowed the cash envelopes in the cobweb-festooned hollow behind a loose baseboard in his closet. Once every four weeks or so, he took out five hundred dollars and put it in his backpack along with an addressed envelope, one of several dozen he had prepared at school on a computer in the school's Business Ed room. He did the envelopes after intramurals one late afternoon when the room was empty.

He used a variety of city mailboxes to send them on their way to Mr. Thomas Saubers of 23 Sycamore Street, going about this family-sustaining charity with the craft of a master criminal. He was always afraid that his mom would discover what he was up to, object (probably strenuously), and things would go back to the way they had been. Things weren't perfect now, there was still the occasional arkie-barkie, but he supposed things weren't perfect in any family outside those old TV sitcoms on Nick at Nite.

They could watch Nick at Nite, and Cartoon Network, and MTV, and everything else, because, ladies and gentlemen, the cable was *back*.

In May, another good thing happened: Dad got a part-time job with a new real estate company, as something called a "pre-sell investigator." Pete didn't know what that was, and didn't give Shit One. Dad could do it on his phone and the home computer, it brought in a little money, and those were the things that mattered.

Two other things mattered in the months after the money

started coming in. Dad's legs were getting better, that was one thing. In June of 2010 (when the perpetrator of the so-called City Center Massacre was finally caught), Tom began walking without his crutches some of the time, and he also began stepping down on the pink pills. The other thing was more difficult to explain, but Pete knew it was there. So did Tina. Dad and Mom felt . . . well . . . *blessed*, and now when they argued they looked guilty as well as mad, as if they were shitting on the mysterious good fortune that had befallen them. Often they would stop and talk about other things before the shit got deep. Often it was the money they talked about, and who could be sending it. These discussions came to nothing, and that was good.

I will not be caught, Pete told himself. I must not, and I will not.

One day in August of that year, Dad and Mom took Tina and Ellen to a petting zoo called Happydale Farm. This was the opportunity Pete had been patiently waiting for, and as soon as they were gone, he went back to the stream with two suitcases.

After making sure the coast was clear, he dug the trunk out of the embankment again and loaded the notebooks into the suitcases. He reburied the trunk and then went back to the house with his booty. In the upstairs hall, he pulled down the ladder and carried the suitcases up to the attic. This was a small, low space, chilly in winter and stifling in summer. The family rarely used it; their extra stuff was still stored in the garage. The few relics up here were probably left over from one of the previous families that had owned 23 Sycamore. There was a dirty baby carriage listing on one wheel, a standing lamp with tropical birds on the shade, old issues of *Redbook* and *Good Housekeeping* tied up with twine, a pile of moldy blankets that smelled like yuck.

Pete piled the notebooks in the farthest corner and covered them with the blankets, but first he grabbed one at random, sat under one of the attic's two hanging lightbulbs, and opened it. The writing was cursive and quite small, but carefully made and easy to read. There were no cross-outs, which Pete thought remarkable. Although he was looking at the first page of the notebook, the small circled number at the top was 482, making him think that this was continued not just from one of the other notebooks, but from half a dozen. Half a dozen, at least.

*Chapter 27*

*The back room of the Drover was the same as it had been five years before; the same smell of ancient beer mingled with the stink of the stockyards and the tang of diesel from the trucking depots that fronted this half of Nebraska's great emptiness. Stew Logan looked the same, too. Here was the same white apron, the same suspiciously black hair, even the same parrots-and-macaws necktie strangling his rosy neck.*

*"Why, it's Jimmy Gold, as I live and breathe," he said, and smiled in his old dislikeable way that said we don't care for each other, but let's pretend. "Have you come to pay me what you owe, then?"*

*"I have," Jimmy said, and touched his back pocket where the pistol rested. It felt small and final, a thing capable—if used correctly, and with courage—of paying all debts.*

*"Then step in," Logan said. "Have a drink. You look dusty."*

*"I am," Jimmy said, "and along with a drink I could use*

A horn honked on the street. Pete jumped and looked around guiltily, as if he had been whacking off instead of reading. What if they'd come home early because that doofus Ellen had gotten carsick, or something? What if they found him up here with the notebooks? Everything could fall apart.

He shoved the one he had been reading under the old blankets (phew, they stank) and crawled back to the trapdoor, sparing a glance for the suitcases. No time for them. Going down the ladder, the change in temperature from boiling hot to August-normal made him shiver. Pete folded the ladder and shoved it up, wincing at the screek and bang the trapdoor made when it snapped shut on its rusty spring.

He went into his bedroom and peered out at the driveway.

Nobody there. False alarm.

Thank God.

He returned to the attic and retrieved the suitcases. He put them back in the downstairs closet, took a shower (once more remembering to clean up the tub afterwards), then dressed in clean clothes and lay down on his bed.

He thought, It's a novel. With that many pages, it's pretty much got to be. And there might be more than one, because no single novel's long enough to fill all those books. Not even the Bible would fill all those books.

Also . . . it was interesting. He wouldn't mind hunting through the notebooks and finding the one where it started. Seeing if it really was good. Because you couldn't tell if a novel was good from just a single page, could you?

Pete closed his eyes and began to drift napward. Ordinarily he wasn't much of a day-sleeper, but it had been a busy morning, the house was empty and quiet, and he decided to let himself go. Why not? Everything was right, at least right now, and that was his doing. He deserved a nap.

That name, though—Jimmy Gold.

Pete could swear he'd heard it before. In class, maybe? Mrs. Swidrowski giving them background on one of the authors they were reading? Maybe. She liked to do that.

Maybe I'll google it later on, Pete thought. I could do that. I could . . .

He slept.

# 1978

Morris sat on a steel bunk with his throbbing head lowered and his hands dangling between his orange-clad thighs, breathing in a poison atmosphere of piss, puke, and disinfectant. His stomach was a lead ball that seemed to have expanded until it filled him from crotch to Adam's apple. His eyes pulsed in their sockets. His mouth tasted like a dumpster. His gut ached and his face hurt. His sinuses were stuffed. Somewhere a hoarse and despairing voice was chanting, "I need a lover that won't drive me *cray-zee*, I need a lover that won't drive me *cray-zee*, I need a lover that won't drive me *cray-zee* . . ."

"Shut up!" someone shouted. "You're drivin *me* crazy, asshole!"

A pause. Then:

"I need a lover that won't drive me *cray-zee!*"

The lead in Morris's belly liquefied and gurgled. He slid off the bunk, landed on his knees (provoking a fresh bolt of agony in his head), and hung his gaping mouth over the functional steel toilet. For a moment there was nothing. Then everything clenched and he ejected what looked like two gallons of yellow toothpaste. For a moment the pain in his head was so huge that he thought it would simply explode, and in that moment Morris hoped it would. Anything to end the pain.

Instead of dying, he threw up again. A pint instead of a gallon this time, but it *burned*. The next one was a dry heave. Wait, not completely dry; thick strings of mucus hung from his lips like cobwebs, swinging back and forth. He had to brush them away.

"Somebody's *feelin* it!" a voice shouted.

Shouts and cackles of laughter greeted this sally. To Morris it sounded as if he were locked up in a zoo, and he supposed he was, only this was the kind where the cages held humans. The orange jumpsuit he was wearing proved it.

How had he gotten here?

He couldn't remember, any more than he could remember how he'd gotten into the house he'd trashed in Sugar Heights. What he *could* remember was his own house, on Sycamore Street. And the trunk, of course. Burying the trunk. There had been money in his pocket, two hundred dollars of John Rothstein's money, and he had gone down to Zoney's to get a couple of beers because his head ached and he was feeling lonely. He had talked to the clerk, he was pretty sure of that, but he couldn't remember what they had discussed. Baseball? Probably not. He had a Groundhogs cap, but that was as far as his interest went. After that, almost nothing. All he could be sure of was that something had gone horribly wrong. When you woke up wearing an orange jumpsuit, that was an easy deduction to make.

He crawled back to the bunk, pulled himself up, drew his knees to his chest, and clasped his hands around them. It was cold in the cell. He began to shiver.

*I might have asked that clerk what his favorite bar was. One I could get to on the bus. And I went there, didn't I? Went there and got drunk. In spite of all I know about what it does to me. Not just a little loaded, either—standing-up, falling-down shitfaced drunk.*

Oh yes, undoubtedly, in spite of all he knew. Which was bad, but he couldn't remember the crazy things afterwards, and that was worse. After the third drink (sometimes only second), he fell down a dark hole and didn't climb back out until he woke up hungover but sober. Blackout drinking was what they called it. And in those blackouts, he almost always got up to . . . well, call it hijinks. Hijinks was how he'd ended up in Riverview Youth Detention, and doubtless how he'd ended up here. Wherever *here* was.

Hijinks.

Fucking hijinks.

Morris hoped it had been a good old-fashioned bar fight and not more breaking and entering. Not a repeat of his Sugar Heights adventure, in other words. Because he was well past his teenage years now and it wouldn't be the reformatory this time, no sir. Still, he would do the time if he had done the crime. Just as long as the crime had nothing to do with the murder of a certain genius American writer, please God. If it did, he would not be breathing free air again for a long time. Maybe never. Because it wasn't just Rothstein, was it? And now a memory *did* arise: Curtis Rogers asking if New Hampshire had the death penalty.

Morris lay on the bunk, shivering, thinking, That can't be why I'm here. It *can't*.

Can it?

He had to admit that it was possible, and not just because the police might have put him together with the dead men in the rest area. He could see himself in a bar or a stripjoint somewhere, Morris Bellamy, the college dropout and self-proclaimed American lit scholar, tossing back bourbon and having an out-of-body experience. Someone starts talking about the murder of John Rothstein, the great writer, the reclusive American *genius*, and Morris Bellamy—drunk off his tits and full of that huge anger he usually kept locked in a cage, that black beast with the yellow eyes—turning to the speaker and saying, He didn't look much like a genius when I blew his head off.

"I would *never*," he whispered. His head was aching worse than ever, and there was something wrong on the left side of his face, too. It *burned*. "I would *never*."

Only how did he know that? When he drank, any day was Anything Can Happen Day. The black beast came out. As a teenager the beast had rampaged through that house in Sugar Heights, tearing the motherfucker pretty much to shreds, and when the cops responded to the silent alarm he had fought them until one belted him unconscious with his nightstick, and when they searched him they found a shitload of jewelry in his pockets, much of it of the costume variety but some, carelessly left out of madame's safe, extraordinarily valuable, and howdy-do, off we go to Riverview, where we will get our tender young buttsky reamed and make exciting new friends.

He thought, The person who put on a shit-show like that is perfectly capable of boasting while drunk about murdering Jimmy Gold's creator, and you know it.

Although it could have been the cops, too. If they had ID'd him and put out an APB. That was just as likely.

"I need a lover who won't drive me *cray-zee*!"

"Shut up!" This time it was Morris himself, and he tried to yell it, but what came out was nothing but a puke-clotted croak. Oh, his head hurt. And his *face*, yow. He ran a hand up his left cheek and stared stupidly at the flakes of dried blood in his palm. He explored again and felt scratches there, at least three of them. Fingernail scratches, and deep. What does that tell us, class? Well, ordinarily—although there are exceptions to every rule—men punch and women scratch. The ladies do it with their nails because more often than not they have nice long ones to scratch with.

Did I try to slap the make on some twist, and she refused me with her nails?

88

Morris tried to remember and couldn't. He remembered the rain, the poncho, and the flashlight shining on the roots. He remembered the pick. He *sort* of remembered wanting to hear fast loud music and talking to the clerk at Zoney's Go-Mart. After that? Just darkness.

He thought, Maybe it was the car. That damn Biscayne. Maybe somebody saw it coming out of the rest area on Route 92 with the front end all bloody on the right, and maybe I left something in the glove compartment. Something with my name on it.

But that didn't seem likely. Freddy had purchased the Chevy from a half-drunk bar-bitch in a Lynn taproom, paying with money the three of them had pooled. She had signed over the pink to Harold Fineman, which happened to be the name of Jimmy Gold's best friend in *The Runner*. She had never seen Morris Bellamy, who knew enough to stay out of sight while that particular deal went down. Besides, Morris had done everything but soap PLEASE STEAL ME on the windshield when he left it at the mall. No, the Biscayne was now sitting in a vacant lot somewhere, either in Lowtown or down by the lake, stripped to the axles.

So how did I wind up here? Back to that, like a rat running on a wheel. If some woman marked my face with her nails, did I haul off on her? Maybe break her jaw?

That rang a faint bell behind the blackout curtains. If it were so, then he was probably going to be charged with assault, and he might go up to Waynesville for it; a ride in the big green bus with the wire mesh on the windows. Waynesville would be bad, but he could do a few years for assault if he had to. Assault was not murder.

*Please* don't let it be Rothstein, he thought. I've got a lot of reading to do, it's stashed away all safe and waiting. The beauty part is I've got money to support myself with while I do it, more than twenty thousand dollars in unmarked twenties and fifties. That will last quite awhile, if I live small. So please don't let it be murder.

"I need a lover who won't drive me *cray-zee!*"

"One more time, motherfucker!" someone shouted. "One more time and I'll pull your asshole right out through your mouth!"

Morris closed his eyes.

Although he was feeling better by noon, he refused the slop that passed for lunch: noodles floating in what appeared to be blood sauce. Then, around two o'clock, a quartet of guards came down the aisle between the cells. One had a clipboard and was shouting names.

"Bellamy! Holloway! McGiver! Riley! Roosevelt! Titgarden! Step forward!"

"That's *Tea*garden, sir," said the large black man in the box next to Morris's.

"I don't give a shit if it's John Q. Motherfucker. If you want to talk to your court-appointed, step forward. If you don't, sit there and stack more time."

The half dozen named prisoners stepped forward. They were the last ones left, at least in this corridor. The others brought in the previous night (mercifully including the fellow who had been butchering John Mellencamp) had either been released or taken to court for the morning arraignment. They were the small fry. Afternoon arraignments, Morris knew, were for more serious shit. He had been arraigned in the afternoon after his little adventure in Sugar Heights. Judge Bukowski, that cunt.

Morris prayed to a God he did not believe in as the door of his holding cell snapped back. Assault, God, okay? Simple, not ag.

Just not murder. God, let them know nothing about what went down in New Hampshire, or at a certain rest area in upstate New York, okay? That okay with you?

"Step out, boys," the guard with the clipboard said. "Step out and face right. Arm's length from the upstanding American in front of you. No wedgies and no reach-arounds. Don't fuck with us and we will return the favor."


They went down in an elevator big enough to hold a small herd of cattle, then along another corridor, and then—God knew why, they were wearing sandals and the jumpsuits had no pockets— through a metal detector. Beyond that was a visitor's room with eight walled booths like library carrels. The guard with the clipboard directed Morris to number 3. Morris sat down and faced his court-appointed through Plexiglas that had been smeared often and wiped seldom. The guy on the freedom side was a nerd with a bad haircut and a dandruff problem. He had a coldsore below one nostril and a scuffed briefcase sitting on his lap. He looked like he might be all of nineteen.

This is what I get, Morris thought. Oh Jesus, this is what I get.

The lawyer pointed to the phone on the wall of Morris's booth, and opened his briefcase. From it he removed a single sheet of paper and the inevitable yellow legal pad. Once these were on the counter in front of him, he put his briefcase on the floor and picked up his own phone. He spoke not in the tentative tenor of your usual adolescent, but in a confident, husky baritone that seemed far too big for the chicken chest lurking behind the purple rag of his tie.

"You're in deep shit, Mr."—he looked at the sheet lying on top of his legal pad—"Bellamy. You must prepare for a very long stay in the state penitentiary, I think. Unless you have something to trade, that is."

Morris thought, He's talking about trading the notebooks.

Coldness went marching up his arms like the feet of evil fairies. If they had him for Rothstein, they had him for Curtis and Freddy. That meant life with no possibility of parole. He would never be able to retrieve the trunk, never find out Jimmy Gold's ultimate fate.

"Speak," the lawyer said, as if talking to a dog.

"Then tell me who I'm speaking to."

"Elmer Cafferty, temporarily at your service. You're going to be arraigned in . . ." He looked at his watch, a Timex even cheaper than his suit. "Thirty minutes. Judge Bukowski is very prompt."

A bolt of pain that had nothing to do with his hangover went through Morris's head. "No! Not her! It can't be! That bitch came over on the Ark!"

Cafferty smiled. "I deduce you've had doings with the Great Bukowski before."

"Check your file," Morris said dully. Although it probably wasn't there. The Sugar Heights thing would be under seal, as he had told Andy.

Fucking Andy Halliday. This is more his fault than mine.

"Homo."

Cafferty frowned. "*What* did you say?"

"Nothing. Go on."

"My *file* consists of last night's arrest report. The good news is that your fate will be in some other judge's hands when you come to trial. The better news, for me, at least, is that by that point, someone else will be representing you. My wife and I are moving to Denver and you, Mr. Bellamy, will be just a memory."

Denver or hell, it made no difference to Morris. "Tell me what I'm charged with."

"You don't remember?"

"I was in a blackout."

"Is that so."

"It actually is," Morris said.

Maybe he *could* trade the notebooks, although it hurt him to even consider it. But even if he made the offer—or if Cafferty made it—would a prosecutor grasp the importance of what was in them? It didn't seem likely. Lawyers weren't scholars. A prosecutor's idea of great literature would probably be Erle Stanley Gardner. Even if the notebooks—all those beautiful Moleskines—did matter to the state's legal rep, what would he, Morris, gain by turning them over? One life sentence instead of three? Whoopee-ding.

I can't, no matter what. I *won't*.

Andy Halliday might have been an English Leather–wearing homo, but he had been right about Morris's motivation. Curtis and Freddy had been in it for cash; when Morris assured them the old guy might have squirreled away as much as a hundred thousand, they had believed him. Rothstein's writings? To those two bumblefucks, the value of Rothstein's output since 1960 was just a misty maybe, like a lost goldmine. It was Morris who cared about the writing. If things had gone differently, he would have offered to trade Curtis and Freddy his share of the money for the written words, and he was sure they would have taken him up on it. If he gave that up now—especially when the notebooks contained the continuation of the Jimmy Gold saga—it would all have been for nothing.

Cafferty rapped his phone on the Plexi, then put it back to his ear. "Cafferty to Bellamy, Cafferty to Bellamy, come in, Bellamy."

"Sorry. I was thinking."

"A little late for that, wouldn't you say? Try to stick with me, if you please. You'll be arraigned on three counts. Your mission, should you choose to accept it, is to plead not guilty to each in turn. Later, when you go to trial, you can change to guilty, should it prove to your advantage to do so. Don't even think about bail, because Bukowski doesn't laugh; she cackles like Witch Hazel."

Morris thought, This is a case of worst fears realized. Rothstein, Dow, and Rogers. Three counts of Murder One.

"Mr. Bellamy? Our time is fleeting, and I'm losing patience."

The phone sagged away from his ear and Morris brought it back with an effort. Nothing mattered now, and still the lawyer with the guileless Richie Cunningham face and the weird middle-aged baritone voice kept pouring words into his ear, and at some point they began to make sense.

"They'll work up the ladder, Mr. Bellamy, from first to worst. Count one, resisting arrest. For arraignment purposes, you plead not guilty. Count two, aggravated assault—not just the woman, you also got one good one in on the first-responding cop before he cuffed you. You plead not guilty. Count three, aggravated rape. They may add attempted murder later, but right now it's just rape . . . if rape can be called just anything, I suppose. You plead—"

"Wait a minute," Morris said. He touched the scratches on his cheek, and what he felt was . . . hope. "I *raped* somebody?"

"Indeed you did," Cafferty said, sounding pleased. Probably because his client finally seemed to be following him. "After Miss Cora Ann Hooper . . ." He took a sheet of paper from his briefcase and consulted it. "This was shortly after she left the diner where she works as a waitress. She was heading for a bus stop on Lower Marlborough. Says you tackled her and pulled her into an alley next to Shooter's Tavern, where you had spent several hours imbibing Jack Daniel's before kicking the jukebox and being asked to leave. Miss Hooper had a battery-powered Police Alert in her purse and managed to trigger it. She also scratched your face. You broke her nose, held her down, choked her, and proceeded to insert your Johns Hopkins into her Sarah Lawrence. When Officer Philip Ellenton hauled you off, you were still matriculating."

"Rape. Why would I . . ."

Stupid question. Why had he spent three long hours tearing up that home in Sugar Heights, just taking a short break to piss on the Aubusson carpet?

"I have no idea," Cafferty said. "Rape is foreign to my way of life."

And mine, Morris thought. Ordinarily. But I was drinking Jack and got up to hijinks.

"How long will they give me?"

"The prosecution will ask for life. If you plead guilty at trial and throw yourself on the mercy of the court, you might only get twenty-five years."

Morris pleaded guilty at trial. He said he regretted what he'd done. He blamed the booze. He threw himself on the mercy of the court.

And got life.

# 2013–2014

By the time he was a high school sophomore, Pete Saubers had already figured out the next step: a good college in New England where literature instead of cleanliness was next to godliness. He began investigating online and collecting brochures. Emerson or BC seemed the most likely candidates, but Brown might not be out of reach. His mother and father told him not to get his hopes up, but Pete didn't buy that. He felt that if you didn't have hopes and ambitions when you were a teenager, you'd be pretty much fucked later on.

About majoring in English there was no question. Some of this surety had to do with John Rothstein and the Jimmy Gold novels; so far as Pete knew, he was the only person in the world who had read the final two, and they had changed his life.

Howard Ricker, his sophomore English teacher, had also been life-changing, even though many kids made fun of him, calling him Ricky the Hippie because of the flower-power shirts and bell-bottoms he favored. (Pete's girlfriend, Gloria Moore, called him Pastor Ricky, because he had a habit of waving his hands above his head when he got excited.) Hardly anyone cut Mr. Ricker's classes, though. He was entertaining, he was enthusiastic, and—unlike many of the teachers—he seemed to genuinely like the kids, whom he called "my young ladies and gentlemen." They rolled their eyes at his retro clothes and his screechy laugh . . . but the clothes had a certain funky cachet, and the screechy laugh was so amiably weird it made you want to laugh along.

On the first day of sophomore English, he blew in like a cool breeze, welcomed them, and then printed something on the board that Pete Saubers never forgot:

## This is stupid!

"What do you make of this, ladies and gentlemen?" he asked. "What on earth can it *mean*?"

The class was silent.

"I'll tell you, then. It happens to be the most common criticism made by young ladies and gentlemen such as yourselves, doomed to a course where we begin with excerpts from *Beowulf* and end with Raymond Carver. Among teachers, such survey courses are sometimes called GTTG: Gallop Through the Glories."

He screeched cheerfully, also waggling his hands at shoulder height in a yowza-yowza gesture. Most of the kids laughed along, Pete among them.

"Class verdict on Jonathan Swift's 'A Modest Proposal'? This is stupid! 'Young Goodman Brown,' by Nathaniel Hawthorne? This is stupid! 'Mending Wall,' by Robert Frost? This is moderately stupid! The required excerpt from *Moby-Dick*? This is *extremely* stupid!"

More laughter. None of them had read *Moby-Dick*, but they all knew it was hard and boring. Stupid, in other words.

"And sometimes!" Mr. Ricker exclaimed, raising one finger and pointing dramatically at the words on the blackboard. "Sometimes, my young ladies and gentlemen, *the criticism is spot-on*. I stand here with my bare face hanging out and admit it. I am required to teach certain antiquities I would rather not teach. I see the loss of enthusiasm in your eyes, and my soul groans. Yes! *Groans!* But I soldier on, because I know that much of what I teach is *not* stupid. Even some of the antiquities to which you feel you cannot relate now or ever will, have deep resonance that will eventually reveal itself. Shall I tell you how you judge the *not-stupid* from the *is-stupid*? Shall I impart this great secret? Since we have forty minutes left in this class and as yet no grist to grind in the mill of our combined intellects, I believe I will."

He leaned forward and propped his hands on the desk, his tie swinging like a pendulum. Pete felt that Mr. Ricker was looking directly at him, as if he knew—or at least intuited—the tremendous secret Pete was keeping under a pile of blankets in the attic of his house. Something far more important than money.

"At some point in this course, perhaps even tonight, you will read something difficult, something you only partially understand, and your verdict will be *this is stupid.* Will I argue when you advance that opinion in class the next day? Why would I do such a useless thing? My time with you is short, only thirty-four weeks of classes, and I will not waste it arguing about the merits of this short story or that poem. Why would I, when all such opinions are subjective, and no final resolution can ever be reached?"

Some of the kids—Gloria was one of them—now looked lost, but Pete understood exactly what Mr. Ricker, aka Ricky the Hippie, was talking about, because since starting the notebooks, he had read dozens of critical essays on John Rothstein. Many of them judged Rothstein to be one of the greatest American writers of the twentieth century, right up there with Fitzgerald, Hemingway, Faulkner, and Roth. There were others—a minority, but a vocal one—who asserted that his work was second-rate and hollow. Pete had read a piece in *Salon* where the writer had called Rothstein "king of the wisecrack and the patron saint of fools."

"Time is the answer," Mr. Ricker said on the first day of Pete's sophomore year. He strode back and forth, antique bellbottoms swishing, occasionally waving his arms. "Yes! Time mercilessly culls away the *is-stupid* from the *not-stupid*. It is a natural, Darwinian process. It is why the novels of Graham Greene are available in every good bookstore, and the novels of Somerset Maugham are not—those novels still exist, of course, but you must order them, and you would only do that if you knew about them. Most modern readers do not. Raise your hand if you have ever heard of Somerset Maugham. And I'll spell that for you."

No hands went up.

Mr. Ricker nodded. Rather grimly, it seemed to Pete. "Time has decreed that Mr. Greene is *not-stupid* while Mr. Maugham is . . . well, not exactly stupid but forgettable. He wrote some very fine novels, in my opinion—*The Moon and Sixpence* is remarkable, my young ladies and gentlemen, *remarkable*—and he also wrote a great deal of excellent short fiction, but none is included in your textbook.

"Shall I weep over this? Shall I rage, and shake my fists, and proclaim injustice? No. I will not. Such culling is a natural process. It will occur for you, young ladies and gentlemen, although I will be in your rearview mirror by the time it happens. Shall I tell you *how* it happens? You will read something—perhaps 'Dulce et Decorum Est,' by Wilfred Owen. Shall we use that as an example? Why not?"

Then, in a deeper voice that sent chills up Pete's back and tightened his throat, Mr. Ricker cried: " 'Bent double, like old beggars under sacks, Knock-kneed, coughing like hags, we cursed through sludge . . . ' And so on. Cetra-cetra. Some of you will say, *This is stupid.* Will I break my promise not to argue the point, even though I consider Mr. Owen's poems the greatest to come out of

World War I? No! It's just my opinion, you see, and opinions are like assholes: everybody has one."

They all roared at that, young ladies and gentlemen alike.

Mr. Ricker drew himself up. "I may give some of you detentions if you disrupt my class, I have no problem with imposing discipline, but *never* will I disrespect your opinion. And yet! And yet!"

Up went the finger.

"Time will pass! *Tempus* will *fugit*! Owen's poem may fall away from your mind, in which case your verdict of *is-stupid* will have turned out to be correct. For you, at least. But for some of you it will recur. And recur. And recur. Each time it does, the steady march of your maturity will deepen its resonance. Each time that poem steals back into your mind, it will seem a little less stupid and a little more vital. A little more important. Until it *shines*, young ladies and gentlemen. Until it *shines*. Thus endeth my opening day peroration, and I ask you to turn to page sixteen in that most excellent tome *Language and Literature*."

One of the stories Mr. Ricker assigned that year was "The Rocking-Horse Winner," by D. H. Lawrence, and sure enough, many of Mr. Ricker's young ladies and gentlemen (including Gloria Moore, of whom Pete was growing tired, in spite of her really excellent breasts) considered it stupid. Pete did not, in large part because events in his life had already caused him to mature beyond his years. As 2013 gave way to 2014—the year of the famed Polar Vortex, when furnaces all over the upper Midwest went into maximum overdrive, burning money by the bale—that story recurred to him often, and its resonance continued to deepen. And recur.

The family in it seemed to have everything, but they didn't; there was never quite enough, and the hero of the story, a young boy named Paul, always heard the house whispering, "There must be more money! There must be more money!" Pete Saubers guessed that there were kids who considered that stupid. They were the lucky ones who had never been forced to listen to nightly arkie-barkies about which bills to pay. Or the price of cigarettes.

The young protagonist in the Lawrence story discovered a supernatural way to make money. By riding his toy rocking-horse to the make-believe land of luck, Paul could pick horse-race winners in the real world. He made thousands of dollars, and still the house whispered, "There must be more money!"

After one final epic ride on the rocking-horse—and one final big-money pick—Paul dropped dead of a brain hemorrhage or something. Pete didn't have so much as a headache after finding the buried trunk, but it was still his rocking-horse, wasn't it? Yes. His very own rocking-horse. But by 2013, the year he met Mr. Ricker, the rocking-horse was slowing down. The trunk-money had almost run out.

It had gotten his parents through a rough and scary patch when their marriage might otherwise have crashed and burned; this Pete knew, and he never once regretted playing guardian angel. In the words of that old song, the trunk-money had formed a bridge over troubled waters, and things were better—*much*—on the other side. The worst of the recession was over. Mom was teaching full-time again, her salary three thousand a year better than before. Dad now ran his own small business, not real estate, exactly, but something called real estate search. He had several agencies in the city as clients. Pete didn't completely understand how it worked, but he knew it was actually making some money, and might make more in the years ahead, if the housing market continued to trend upward. He was agenting a few properties of his own, too. Best of all, he was drug-free and walking well. The crutches had been in the closet for over a year, and he only used his cane on rainy or snowy days when his bones and joints ached. All good. Great, in fact.

And yet, as Mr. Ricker said at least once in every class. And yet!

There was Tina to think about, that was one very large *and yet*. Many of her friends from the old neighborhood on the West Side, including Barbara Robinson, whom Tina had idolized, were going to Chapel Ridge, a private school that had an excellent record when it came to sending kids on to good colleges. Mom had told Tina that she and Dad didn't see how they could afford to send her there directly from middle school. Maybe she could attend as a sophomore, if their finances continued to improve.

"But I won't know *anybody* by then," Tina had said, starting to cry.

"You'll know Barbara Robinson," Mom said, and Pete (listening from the next room) could tell from the sound of her voice that Mom was on the verge of tears herself. "Hilda and Betsy, too."

But Teens had been a little younger than those girls, and Pete knew only Barbs had been a real friend to his sister back in the West Side days. Hilda Carver and Betsy DeWitt probably didn't even remember her. Neither would Barbara, in another year or two. Their mother didn't seem to remember what a big deal high school was, and how quickly you forgot your little-kid friends once you got there.

Tina's response summed up these thoughts with admirable succinctness. "Yeah, but they won't know *me*."

"Tina—"

"You have that *money*!" Tina cried. "That mystery money that comes every month! Why can't I have some for Chapel Ridge?"

"Because we're still catching up from the bad time, honey."

To this Tina could say nothing, because it was true.

His own college plans were another *and yet*. Pete knew that to

103

some of his friends, maybe most of them, college seemed as far away as the outer planets of the solar system. But if he wanted a good one (*Brown*, his mind whispered, *English Lit at Brown*), that meant making early applications when he was a first-semester senior. The applications themselves cost money, as did the summer class he needed to pick up if he wanted to score at least a 670 on the math part of the SATs. He had a part-time job at the Garner Street Library, but thirty-five bucks a week didn't go far.

Dad's business had grown enough to make a downtown office desirable, that was *and yet* number three. Just a low-rent place on an upper floor, and being close to the action would pay dividends, but it would mean laying out more money, and Pete knew—even though no one said it out loud—that Dad was counting on the mystery cash to carry him through the critical period. They had all come to depend on the mystery cash, and only Pete knew it would be gone before the end of '14.

And yeah, okay, he had spent some on himself. Not a huge amount—that would have raised questions—but a hundred here and a hundred there. A blazer and a pair of loafers for the class trip to Washington. A few CDs. And books. He had become a fool for books since reading the notebooks and falling in love with John Rothstein. He began with Rothstein's Jewish contemporaries, like Philip Roth, Saul Bellow, and Irwin Shaw (he thought *The Young Lions* was fucking awesome, and couldn't understand why it wasn't a classic), and spread out from there. He always bought paperbacks, but even those were twelve or fifteen dollars apiece these days, unless you could find them used.

"The Rocking-Horse Winner" had resonance, all right, bigtime resonance, because Pete could hear his own house whispering *There must be more money . . .* and all too soon there would be less. But money wasn't *all* the trunk had contained, was it?

That was another *and yet*. One Pete Saubers thought about more and more as time passed.

For his end-of-year research paper in Mr. Ricker's Gallop Through the Glories, Pete did a sixteen-page analysis of the Jimmy Gold trilogy, quoting from various reviews and adding in stuff from the few interviews Rothstein had given before retreating to his farm in New Hampshire and going completely dark. He finished by talking about Rothstein's tour of the German death camps as a reporter for the *New York Herald*—this four years before publishing the first Jimmy Gold book.

"I believe that was the most important event of Mr. Rothstein's life," Pete wrote. "Surely the most important event of his life as a writer. Jimmy's search for meaning always goes back to what Mr. Rothstein saw in those camps, and it's why, when Jimmy tries to live the life of an ordinary American citizen, he always feels hollow. For me, this is best expressed when he throws an ashtray through the TV in *The Runner Slows Down*. He does it during a CBS news special about the Holocaust."

When Mr. Ricker returned their papers, a big A+ was scrawled on Pete's cover, which was a computer-scanned photo of Rothstein as a young man, sitting in Sardi's with Ernest Hemingway. Below the A+, Mr. Ricker had written *See me after class*.

When the other kids were gone, Mr. Ricker looked at Pete so fixedly that Pete was momentarily scared his favorite teacher was going to accuse him of plagiarism. Then Mr. Ricker smiled. "That is the best student paper I've read in my twenty-eight years of teaching. Because it was the most confident, and the most deeply felt."

Pete's face heated with pleasure. "Thanks. Really. Thanks a lot."

"I'd argue with your conclusion, though," Mr. Ricker said, leaning back in his chair and lacing his fingers together behind his neck. "The characterization of Jimmy as 'a noble American hero, like Huck Finn,' is not supported by the concluding book of the trilogy. Yes, he throws an ashtray at the television screen, but it's not an act of heroism. The CBS logo is an eye, you know, and Jimmy's act is a ritual blinding of his inner eye, the one that sees the truth. That's not my insight; it's an almost direct quote from an essay called 'The Runner Turns Away,' by John Crowe Ransom. Leslie Fiedler says much the same in *Love and Death in the American Novel*."

"But—"

"I'm not trying to debunk you, Pete; I'm just saying you need to follow the evidence of any book *wherever* it leads, and that means not omitting crucial developments that run counter to your thesis. What does Jimmy do *after* he throws the ashtray through the TV, and after his wife delivers her classic line, 'You bastard, how will the kids watch Mickey Mouse now?'"

"He goes out and buys another TV set, but—"

"Not just *any* TV set, but *the first color TV set on the block*. And then?"

"He creates the big successful ad campaign for Duzzy-Doo household cleaner. But—"

Mr. Ricker raised his eyebrows, waiting for the but. And how could Pete tell him that a year later, Jimmy steals into the agency late one night with matches and a can of kerosene? That Rothstein foreshadows all the protests about Vietnam and civil rights by having Jimmy start a fire that pretty much destroys the building known as the Temple of Advertising? That he hitchhikes out of New York City without a look back, leaving his family behind and striking out for the territory, just like Huck and Jim? He couldn't say any of that, because it was the story told in *The Runner Goes West*, a novel that existed only in seventeen closely written notebooks that had lain buried in an old trunk for over thirty years.

"Go ahead and but me your buts," Mr. Ricker said equably. "There's nothing I like better than a good book discussion with someone who can hold up his end of the argument. I imagine you've already missed your bus, but I'll be more than happy to give you a ride home." He tapped the cover sheet of Pete's paper, Johnny R. and Ernie H., those twin titans of American literature, with oversized martini glasses raised in a toast. "Unsupported conclusion aside—which I put down to a touching desire to see light at the end of an extremely dark final novel—this is extraordinary work. Just extraordinary. So go for it. But me your buts."

"But nothing, I guess," Pete said. "You could be right."

Only Mr. Ricker wasn't. Any doubt about Jimmy Gold's capacity to sell out that remained at the end of *The Runner Goes West* was swept away in the last and longest novel of the series, *The Runner Raises the Flag*. It was the best book Pete had ever read. Also the saddest.

"In your paper you don't go into how Rothstein died."

"No."

"May I ask why not?"

"Because it didn't fit the theme, I guess. And it would have made the paper too long. Also . . . well . . . it was such a bummer for him to die that way, getting killed in a stupid burglary."

"He shouldn't have kept cash in the house," Mr. Ricker said mildly, "but he did, and a lot of people knew it. Don't judge him too harshly for that. Many writers have been stupid and improvident about money. Charles Dickens found himself supporting a family of slackers, including his own father. Samuel Clemens was all but bankrupted by bad real estate transactions. Arthur Conan

Doyle lost thousands of dollars to fake mediums and spent thousands more on fake photos of fairies. At least Rothstein's major work was done. Unless you believe, as some people do—"

Pete looked at his watch. "Um, Mr. Ricker? I can still catch my bus if I hurry."

Mr. Ricker did that funny yowza-yowza thing with his hands. "Go, by all means go. I just wanted to thank you for such a wonderful piece of work . . . and to offer a friendly caution: when you approach this kind of thing next year—and in college—don't let your good nature cloud your critical eye. The critical eye should always be cold and clear."

"I won't," Pete said, and hurried out.

The last thing he wanted to discuss with Mr. Ricker was the possibility that the thieves who had taken John Rothstein's life had stolen a bunch of unpublished manuscripts as well as money, and maybe destroyed them after deciding they had no value. Once or twice Pete had played with the idea of turning the notebooks over to the police, even though that would almost surely mean his parents would find out where the mystery money had been coming from. The notebooks were, after all, evidence of a crime as well as a literary treasure. But it was an *old* crime, ancient history. Better to leave well enough alone.

Right?

The bus had already gone, of course, and that meant a two-mile walk home. Pete didn't mind. He was still glowing from Mr. Ricker's praise, and he had a lot to think about. Rothstein's unpublished works, mostly. The short stories were uneven, he thought, only a few of them really good, and the poems he'd tried to write were, in Pete's humble opinion, pretty lame. But those last two

Jimmy Gold novels were . . . well, gold. Judging by the evidence scattered through them, Pete guessed the last one, where Jimmy raises a burning flag at a Washington peace rally, had been finished around 1973, because Nixon was still president when the story ended. That Rothstein had never published the final Gold books (plus yet another novel, this one about the Civil War) blew Pete's mind. They were so good!

Pete took only one Moleskine at a time down from the attic, reading them with his door closed and an ear cocked for unexpected company when there were other members of his family in the house. He always kept another book handy, and if he heard approaching footsteps, he would slide the notebook under his mattress and pick up the spare. The only time he'd been caught was by Tina, who had the unfortunate habit of walking around in her sock feet.

"What's that?" she'd asked from the doorway.

"None of your beeswax," he had replied, slipping the notebook under his pillow. "And if you say anything to Mom or Dad, you're in trouble with me."

"Is it porno?"

"No!" Although Mr. Rothstein could write some pretty racy scenes, especially for an old guy. For instance the one where Jimmy and these two hippie chicks—

"Then why don't you want me to see it?"

"Because it's private."

Her eyes lit up. "Is it yours? Are you writing a *book*?"

"Maybe. So what if I am?"

"I think that's cool! What's it about?"

"Bugs having sex on the moon."

She giggled. "I thought you said it wasn't porno. Can I read it when you're done?"

"We'll see. Just keep your trap shut, okay?"

She had agreed, and one thing you could say for Teens, she rarely broke a promise. That had been two years ago, and Pete was sure she'd forgotten all about it.

Billy Webber came rolling up on a gleaming ten-speed. "Hey, Saubers!" Like almost everyone else (Mr. Ricker was an exception), Billy pronounced it *Sobbers* instead of *SOW-bers*, but what the hell. It was sort of a dipshit name however you said it. "What you doin this summer?"

"Working at the Garner Street libe."

"Still?"

"I talked em into twenty hours a week."

"Fuck, man, you're too young to be a wage-slave!"

"I don't mind," Pete said, which was the truth. The libe meant free computer-time, among the other perks, with no one looking over your shoulder. "What about you?"

"Goin to our summer place up in Maine. China Lake. Many cute girls in bikinis, man, and the ones from Massachusetts know what to do."

Then maybe they can show you, Pete thought snidely, but when Billy held out his palm, Pete slapped him five and watched him go with mild envy. Ten-speed bike under his ass; expensive Nike kicks on his feet; summer place in Maine. It seemed that some people had already caught up from the bad time. Or maybe the bad time had missed them completely. Not so with the Saubers family. They were doing okay, but—

There must be more money, the house had whispered in the Lawrence story. There must be more money. And honey, that was *resonance.*

Could the notebooks be turned into money? Was there a way? Pete didn't even like to think about giving them up, but at the same time he recognized how wrong it was to keep them hidden away in the attic. Rothstein's work, especially the last two Jimmy Gold books, deserved to be shared with the world. They would remake Rothstein's reputation, Pete was sure of that, but his rep still wasn't that bad, and besides, it wasn't the important part. People would like them, that was the important part. *Love* them, if they were like Pete.

Only, handwritten manuscripts weren't like untraceable twenties and fifties. Pete would be caught, and he might go to jail. He wasn't sure exactly what crime he could be charged with—not receiving stolen property, surely, because he hadn't received it, only found it—but he was positive that trying to sell what wasn't yours had to be *some* kind of crime. Donating the notebooks to Rothstein's alma mater seemed like a possible answer, only he'd have to do it anonymously, or it would all come out and his parents would discover that their son had been supporting them with a murdered man's stolen money. Besides, for an anonymous donation you got zilch.

Although he hadn't written about Rothstein's murder in his term paper, Pete had read all about it, mostly in the computer room at the library. He knew that Rothstein had been shot "execution-style." He knew that the cops had found enough different tracks in the dooryard to believe two, three, or even four people had been involved, and that, based on the size of those tracks, all were probably men. They also thought that two of the men had been killed at a New York rest area not long after.

Margaret Brennan, the author's first wife, had been interviewed in Paris not long after the killing. "Everyone talked about him in that provincial little town where he lived," she said. "What else did they have to talk about? Cows? Some farmer's new manure spreader? To the provincials, John was a big deal. They had the erroneous idea that writers make as much as corporate bankers, and believed he had hundreds of thousands of dollars stashed away on that rundown farm of his. Someone from out of town heard the loose talk, that's all. Closemouthed Yankees, my Irish fanny! I blame the locals as much as the thugs who did it."

When asked about the possibility that Rothstein had squirreled away manuscripts as well as cash, Peggy Brennan had given what the interview called "a cigarette-raspy chuckle."

"More rumors, darling. Johnny pulled back from the world for one reason and one reason only. He was burned out and too proud to admit it."

Lot you knew, Pete thought. He probably divorced you because he got tired of that cigarette-raspy chuckle.

There was plenty of speculation in the newspaper and magazine articles Pete had read, but he himself liked what Mr. Ricker called "the Occam's razor principle." According to that, the simplest and most obvious answer was usually the right one. Three men had broken in, and one of them had killed his partners so he could keep all the swag for himself. Pete had no idea why the guy had come to this city afterwards, or why he'd buried the trunk, but one thing he *was* sure of: the surviving robber was never going to come back and get it.

Pete's math skills weren't the strongest—it was why he needed that summer course to bone up—but you didn't have to be an Einstein to run simple numbers and assess certain possibilities. If the surviving robber had been thirty-five in 1978, which seemed like a fair estimate to Pete, he would have been sixty-seven in 2010, when Pete found the trunk, and around seventy now. Seventy was ancient. If he turned up looking for his loot, he'd probably do so on a walker.

Pete smiled as he turned onto Sycamore Street.

He thought there were three possibilities for why the surviving robber had never come back for his trunk, all equally likely. One, he was in prison somewhere for some other crime. Two, he was dead. Three was a combination of one and two: he had died in prison. Whichever it was, Pete didn't think he had to worry about the guy. The notebooks, though, were a different story. About them he had plenty of worries. Sitting on them was like sitting on a bunch of beautiful stolen paintings you could never sell.

Or a crate filled with dynamite.

In September of 2013—almost exactly thirty-five years from the date of John Rothstein's murder—Pete tucked the last of the trunk-money into an envelope addressed to his father. The final installment amounted to three hundred and forty dollars. And because he felt that hope which could never be realized was a cruel thing, he added a one-line note:

This is the last of it. I am sorry there's not more.

He took a city bus to Birch Hill Mall, where there was a mailbox between Discount Electronix and the yogurt place. He looked around, making sure he wasn't observed, and kissed the envelope. Then he slipped it through the slot and walked away. He did it Jimmy Gold–style: without looking back.

A week or two after New Year's, Pete was in the kitchen, making himself a peanut butter and jelly sandwich, when he overheard his parents talking to Tina in the living room. It was about Chapel Ridge.

"I thought maybe we *could* afford it," his dad was saying. "If I gave you false hope, I'm just as sorry as can be, Teens."

"It's because the mystery money stopped coming," Tina said. "Right?"

Mom said, "Partly but not entirely. Dad tried for a bank loan, but they wouldn't give it to him. They went over his business records and did something—"

"A two-year profit projection," Dad said. Some of the old post-accident bitterness crept into his voice. "Lots of compliments, because those are free. They said they might be able to make the loan in 2016, if the business grows by five percent. In the meantime, this goddam Polar Vortex thing . . . we're way over your mom's budget on heating expenses. Everyone is, from Maine to Minnesota. I know that's no consolation, but there it is."

"Honey, we're so, so sorry," Mom said.

Pete expected Tina to explode into a full-fledged tantrum—there were lots more of those as she approached the big thirteen—but it didn't happen. She said she understood, and that Chapel Ridge was probably a snooty school, anyway. Then she came out to the kitchen and asked Pete if he would make her a sandwich, because his looked good. He did, and they went into the living room, and all four of them watched TV together and had some laughs over *The Big Bang Theory*.

Later that night, though, he heard Tina crying behind the closed door of her room. It made him feel awful. He went into his own room, pulled one of the Moleskines out from under his mattress, and began rereading *The Runner Goes West*.


He was taking Mrs. Davis's creative writing course that semester, and although he got As on his stories, he knew by February that he was never going to be a fiction-writer. Although he was good with words, a thing he didn't need Mrs. Davis to tell him (although she often did), he just didn't possess that kind of creative spark. His chief interest was in *reading* fiction, then trying to analyze what he had read, fitting it into a larger pattern. He had gotten a taste for this kind of detective work while writing his paper on Rothstein. At the Garner Street Library he hunted out one of the books Mr. Ricker had mentioned, Fiedler's *Love and Death in the American Novel*, and liked it so much that he bought his own copy in order to highlight certain passages and write in the margins. He wanted to major in English more than ever, and teach like Mr. Ricker (except maybe at a university instead of in high school), and at some point write a book like Mr. Fiedler's, getting into the faces of more traditional critics and questioning the established way those traditional critics looked at things.

And yet!

There had to be more money. Mr. Feldman, the guidance counselor, told him that getting a full-boat scholarship to an Ivy League school was "rather unlikely," and Pete knew even that was an exaggeration. He was just another whitebread high school kid from a so-so Midwestern school, a kid with a part-time library job and a few unglamorous extracurriculars like newspaper and yearbook. Even if he did manage to catch a boat, there was Tina to think about. She was basically trudging through her days, getting mostly Bs and Cs, and seemed more interested in makeup and shoes and pop music than school these days. She needed a change, a clean break. He was wise enough, even at not quite seventeen, to know that Chapel Ridge might not fix his little sister . . . but then again, it might. Especially since she wasn't broken. At least not yet.

I need a plan, he thought, only that wasn't precisely what he needed. What he needed was a *story*, and although he was never going to be a great fiction-writer like Mr. Rothstein or Mr. Lawrence, he *was* able to plot. That was what he had to do now. Only every plot stood on an idea, and on that score he kept coming up empty.

He had begun to spend a lot of time at Water Street Books, where the coffee was cheap and even new paperbacks were thirty percent off. He went by one afternoon in March, on his way to his afterschool job at the library, thinking he might pick up something by Joseph Conrad. In one of his few interviews, Rothstein had called Conrad "the first great writer of the twentieth century, even though his best work was written before 1900."

Outside the bookstore, a long table had been set up beneath an awning. SPRING CLEANING, the sign said. EVERYTHING ON THIS TABLE 70% OFF! And below it: WHO KNOWS WHAT BURIED TREASURE YOU WILL FIND! This line was flanked by big yellow smiley-faces, to show it was a joke, but Pete didn't think it was funny.

He finally had an idea.

A week later, he stayed after school to talk to Mr. Ricker.

"Great to see you, Pete." Mr. Ricker was wearing a paisley shirt with billowy sleeves today, along with a psychedelic tie. Pete thought the combination said quite a lot about why the love-and-peace generation had collapsed. "Mrs. Davis says great things about you."

"She's cool," Pete said. "I'm learning a lot." Actually he wasn't, and he didn't think anyone else in her class was, either. She was nice enough, and quite often had interesting things to say, but Pete was coming to the conclusion that creative writing couldn't really be taught, only learned.

"What can I do for you?"

"Remember when you were talking about how valuable a hand-written Shakespeare manuscript would be?"

Mr. Ricker grinned. "I always talk about that during a midweek class, when things get dozy. There's nothing like a little avarice to perk kids up. Why? Have you found a folio, Malvolio?"

Pete smiled politely. "No, but when we were visiting my uncle Phil in Cleveland during February vacation, I went out to his garage and found a whole bunch of old books. Most of them were about Tom Swift. He was this kid inventor."

"I remember Tom and his friend Ned Newton well," Mr. Ricker said. "*Tom Swift and His Motor Cycle, Tom Swift and His Wizard Camera* . . . when I was a kid myself, we used to joke about *Tom Swift and His Electric Grandmother*."

Pete renewed his polite smile. "There were also a dozen or so about a girl detective named Trixie Belden, and another one named Nancy Drew."

"I believe I see where you're going with this, and I hate to disappoint you, but I must. Tom Swift, Nancy Drew, the Hardy Boys, Trixie Belden . . . all interesting relics of a bygone age, and a wonderful yardstick to judge how much what is called 'YA fiction' has changed in the last eighty years or so, but those books have little or no monetary value, even when found in excellent condition."

"I know," Pete said. "I checked it out later on *Fine Books*. That's a blog. But while I was looking those books over, Uncle Phil came out to the garage and said he had something else that might interest me even more. Because I'd told him I was into John Rothstein.

It was a signed hardback of *The Runner*. Not dedicated, just a flat signature. Uncle Phil said some guy named Al gave it to him because he owed my uncle ten dollars from a poker game. Uncle Phil said he'd had it for almost fifty years. I looked at the copyright page, and it's a first edition."

Mr. Ricker had been rocked back in his chair, but now he sat down with a bang. "Whoa! You probably know that Rothstein didn't sign many autographs, right?"

"Yeah," Pete said. "He called it 'defacing a perfectly good book.'"

"Uh-huh, he was like Raymond Chandler that way. And you know signed volumes are worth more when it's just the signature? *Sans* dedication?"

"Yes. It says so on *Fine Books*."

"A signed first of Rothstein's most famous book probably *would* be worth money." Mr. Ricker considered. "On second thought, strike the probably. What kind of condition is it in?"

"Good," Pete said promptly. "Some foxing on the inside cover and title page, is all."

"You *have* been reading up on this stuff."

"More since my uncle showed me the Rothstein."

"I don't suppose you're in possession of this fabulous book, are you?"

I've got something a lot better, Pete thought. If you only knew.

Sometimes he felt the weight of that knowledge, and never more than today, telling these lies.

*Necessary* lies, he reminded himself.

"I don't, but my uncle said he'd give it to me, if I wanted it. I said I needed to think about it, because he doesn't . . . you know . . ."

"He doesn't have any idea of how much it might really be worth?"

"Yeah. But then I started wondering . . ."

"What?"

Pete dug into his back pocket, took out a folded sheet of paper, and handed it to Mr. Ricker. "I went looking on the Internet for book dealers here in town that buy and sell first editions, and I found these three. I know you're sort of a book collector your-self—"

"Not much, I can't afford serious collecting on my salary, but I've got a signed Theodore Roethke that I intend to hand down to my children. *The Waking*. Very fine poems. Also a Vonnegut, but that's not worth so much; unlike Rothstein, Father Kurt signed everything."

"Anyway, I wondered if you knew any of these, and if you do, which one might be the best. If I decided to let him give me the book . . . and then, you know, sell it."

Mr. Ricker unfolded the sheet, glanced at it, then looked at Pete again. That gaze, both keen and sympathetic, made Pete feel uneasy. This might have been a bad idea, he really *wasn't* much good at fiction, but he was in it now and would have to plow through somehow.

"As it happens, I know all of them. But jeez, kiddo, I also know how much Rothstein means to you, and not just from your paper last year. Annie Davis says you bring him up often in Creative Writing. Claims the Gold trilogy is your Bible."

Pete supposed this was true, but he hadn't realized how blabby he'd been until now. He resolved to stop talking about Rothstein so much. It might be dangerous. People might think back and remember, if—

If.

"It's good to have literary heroes, Pete, especially if you plan to major in English when you get to college. Rothstein is yours—at least for now—and that book could be the beginning of your own library. Are you sure you want to sell it?"

Pete could answer this question with fair honesty, even though it wasn't really a signed book he was talking about. "Pretty sure, yeah. Things have been a little tough at home—"

"I know what happened to your father at City Center, and I'm sorry as hell. At least they caught the psycho before he could do any more damage."

"Dad's better now, and both he and my mom are working again, only I'm probably going to need money for college, see . . ."

"I understand."

"But that's not the biggest thing, at least not now. My sister wants to go to Chapel Ridge, and my parents told her she couldn't, at least not this coming year. They can't quite swing it. Close, but no cigar. And I think she needs a place like that. She's kind of, I don't know, *lagging*."

Mr. Ricker, who had undoubtedly known lots of students who were lagging, nodded gravely.

"But if Tina could get in with a bunch of strivers—especially this one girl, Barbara Robinson, she used to know from when we lived on the West Side—things might turn around."

"It's good of you to think of her future, Pete. Noble, even."

Pete had never thought of himself as noble. The idea made him blink.

Perhaps seeing his embarrassment, Mr. Ricker turned his attention to the list again. "Okay. Grissom Books would have been your best bet when Teddy Grissom was still alive, but his son runs the shop now, and he's a bit of a tightwad. Honest, but close with a buck. He'd say it's the times, but it's also his nature."

"Okay . . ."

"I assume you've checked on the Net to find out how much a signed first-edition *Runner* in good condition is valued at?"

"Yeah. Two or three thousand. Not enough for a year at Chapel Ridge, but a start. What my dad calls earnest money."

Mr. Ricker nodded. "That sounds about right. Teddy Junior would start you at eight hundred. You might get him up to a grand, but if you kept pushing, he'd get his back up and tell you to take a hike. This next one, Buy the Book, is Buddy Franklin's shop. He's also okay—by which I mean honest—but Buddy doesn't have much interest in twentieth-century fiction. His big deal is selling old maps and seventeenth-century atlases to rich guys in Branson Park and Sugar Heights. But if you could talk Buddy into valuing the book, then go to Teddy Junior at Grissom, you might get twelve hundred. I'm not saying you would, I'm just saying it's possible."

"What about Andrew Halliday Rare Editions?"

Mr. Ricker frowned. "I'd steer clear of Halliday. He's got a little shop on Lacemaker Lane, in that walking mall off Lower Main Street. Not much wider than an Amtrak car, but damn near a block long. Seems to do quite well, but there's an odor about him. I've heard it said he's not too picky about the provenance of certain items. Do you know what that is?"

"The line of ownership."

"Right. Ending with a piece of paper that says *you* legally own what you're trying to sell. The only thing I know for sure is that about fifteen years ago, Halliday sold a proof copy of James Agee's *Let Us Now Praise Famous Men*, and it turned out to have been stolen from the estate of Brooke Astor. She was a rich old biddy from New York with a larcenous business manager. Halliday showed a receipt, and his story of how he came by the book was credible, so the investigation was dropped. But receipts can be forged, you know. I'd steer clear of him."

"Thanks, Mr. Ricker," Pete said, thinking that if he went ahead with this, Andrew Halliday Rare Editions would be his first stop.

But he would have to be very, very careful, and if Mr. Halliday wouldn't do a cash deal, that would mean *no* deal. Plus, under no circumstances could he know Pete's name. A disguise might be in order, although it wouldn't do to go overboard on that.

"You're welcome, Pete, but if I said I felt good about this, I'd be lying."

Pete could relate. He didn't feel so good about it himself.

He was still mulling his options a month later, and had almost come to the conclusion that trying to sell even one of the notebooks would be too much risk for too little reward. If it went to a private collector—like the ones he had sometimes read about, who bought valuable paintings to hang in secret rooms where only they could look at them—it would be okay. But he couldn't be sure that would happen. He was leaning more and more to the idea of donating them anonymously, maybe mailing them to the New York University Library. The curator of a place like that would understand the value of them, no doubt. But doing that would be a little more public than Pete liked to think about, not at all like dropping the letters with the money inside them into anonymous streetcorner mailboxes. What if someone remembered him at the post office?

Then, on a rainy night in late April of 2014, Tina came to his room again. Mrs. Beasley was long gone, and the footy pajamas had been replaced by an oversized Cleveland Browns football jersey, but to Pete she looked very much like the worried girl who had asked, during the Era of Bad Feelings, if their mother and father were going to get divorced. Her hair was in pigtails, and with her face cleansed of the little makeup Mom let her wear (Pete had an idea she put on fresh layers when she got to school), she looked closer to ten than going on thirteen. He thought, Teens is almost a teen. It was hard to believe.

"Can I come in for a minute?"

"Sure."

He was lying on his bed, reading a novel by Philip Roth called *When She Was Good*. Tina sat on his desk chair, pulling her jersey nightshirt down over her shins and blowing a few errant hairs from her forehead, where a faint scattering of acne had appeared.

"Something on your mind?" Pete asked.

"Um . . . yeah." But she didn't go on.

He wrinkled his nose at her. "Go on, spill it. Some boy you've been crushing on told you to buzz off?"

"You sent that money," she said. "Didn't you?"

Pete stared at her, flabbergasted. He tried to speak and couldn't. He tried to persuade himself she hadn't said what she'd said, and couldn't do that, either.

She nodded as if he had admitted it. "Yeah, you did. It's all over your face."

"It didn't come from me, Teens, you just took me by surprise. Where would I get money like that?"

"I don't know, but I remember the night you asked me what I'd do if I found a buried treasure."

"I did?" Thinking, You were half-asleep. You *can't* remember that.

"Doubloons, you said. Coins from olden days. I said I'd give it to Dad and Mom so they wouldn't fight anymore, and that's just what you did. Only it wasn't pirate treasure, it was regular money."

Pete put his book aside. "Don't you go telling them that. They might actually believe you."

She looked at him solemnly. "I never would. But I need to ask you . . . is it really all gone?"

"The note in the last envelope said it was," Pete replied cautiously, "and there hasn't been any more since, so I guess so."

She sighed. "Yeah. What I figured. But I had to ask." She got up to go.

"Tina?"

"What?"

"I'm really sorry about Chapel Ridge and all. I wish the money *wasn't* gone."

She sat down again. "I'll keep your secret if you keep one Mom and I have. Okay?"

"Okay."

"Last November she took me to Chap—that's what the girls call it—for one of their tour days. She didn't want Dad to know, because she thought he'd be mad, but back then she thought they maybe *could* afford it, especially if I got a need scholarship. Do you know what that is?"

Pete nodded.

"Only the money hadn't stopped coming then, and it was before all the snow and weird cold weather in December and January. We saw some of the classrooms, and the science labs. There's like a jillion computers. We also saw the gym, which is humongous, and the showers. They have private changing booths, too, not just cattle stalls like at Northfield. At least they do for the girls. Guess who my tour group had for a guide?"

"Barbara Robinson?"

She smiled. "It was great to see her again." Then the smile faded. "She said hello and gave me a hug and asked how everyone was, but I could tell she hardly remembered me. Why would she, right? Did you know her and Hilda and Betsy and a couple of other girls from back then were at the 'Round Here concert? The one the guy who ran over Dad tried to blow up?"

"Yeah." Pete also knew that Barbara Robinson's big brother had played a part in saving Barbara and Barbara's friends and maybe thousands of others. He had gotten a medal or a key to the city, or something. That was real heroism, not sneaking around and mailing stolen money to your parents.

"Did you know I was invited to go with them that night?"

"What? No!"

Tina nodded. "I said I couldn't because I was sick, but I wasn't. It was because Mom said they couldn't afford to buy me a ticket. We moved a couple of months later."

"Jesus, how about that, huh?"

"Yeah, I missed all the excitement."

"So how was the school tour?"

"Good, but not great, or anything. I'll be fine at Northfield. Hey, once they find out I'm your sister, they'll probably give me a free ride, Honor Roll Boy."

Pete suddenly felt sad, almost like crying. It was the sweetness that had always been part of Tina's nature combined with that ugly scatter of pimples on her forehead. He wondered if she got teased about those. If she didn't yet, she would.

He held out his arms. "C'mere." She did, and he gave her a strong hug. Then he held her by the shoulders and looked at her sternly. "But that money . . . it wasn't me."

"Uh-huh, okay. So was that notebook you were reading stuck in with the money? I bet it was." She giggled. "You looked so guilty that night when I walked in on you."

He rolled his eyes. "Go to bed, short stuff."

"Okay." At the door she turned back. "I liked those private changing booths, though. And something else. Want to know? You'll think it's weird."

"Go ahead, lay it on me."

"The kids wear uniforms. For the girls it's gray skirts with white blouses and white kneesocks. There are also sweaters, if you want.

Some gray like the skirts and some this pretty dark red—hunter red they call it, Barbara said."

"Uniforms," Pete said, bemused. "You like the idea of *uniforms*."

"Knew you'd think it was weird. Because boys don't know how girls are. Girls can be mean if you're wearing the wrong clothes, or even if you wear the right ones too much. You can wear different blouses, or your sneakers on Tuesdays and Thursdays, you can do different things with your hair, but pretty soon they—the mean girls—figure out you've only got three jumpers and six good school skirts. Then they say stuff. But when everyone wears the same thing every day . . . except maybe the sweater's a different color . . ." She blew back those few errant strands again. "Boys don't have the same problem."

"I actually do get it," Pete said.

"Anyway, Mom's going to teach me how to make my own clothes, then I'll have more. Simplicity, Butterick. Also, I've got friends. Plenty of them."

"Ellen, for instance."

"Ellen's okay."

And headed for a rewarding job as a waitress or a drive-thru girl after high school, Pete thought but did not say. If she doesn't get pregnant at sixteen, that is.

"I just wanted to tell you not to worry. If you were."

"I wasn't," Pete said. "I know you'll be fine. And it wasn't me who sent the money. Honest."

She gave him a smile, both sad and complicit, that made her look like anything but a little girl. "Okay. Gotcha."

She left, closing the door gently behind her.

Pete lay awake for a long time that night. Not long after, he made the biggest mistake of his life.

# 1979–2014

Morris Randolph Bellamy was sentenced to life in prison on January 11th, 1979, and for a brief time things went fast before they went slow. And slow. And slow. His intake at Waynesville State Prison was completed by six PM the day of his sentencing. His cellmate, a convicted murderer named Roy Allgood, raped him for the first time forty-five minutes after lights-out.

"Hold still and don't you shit on my cock, young man," he whispered in Morris's ear. "If you do that, I'll cut your nose. You'll look like a pig been bit by a allygator."

Morris, who had been raped before, held still, biting his forearm to keep from screaming. He thought of Jimmy Gold, as Jimmy had been before he started chasing the Golden Buck. When he had still been an authentic hero. He thought of Harold Fineman, Jimmy's high school friend (Morris had never had a high school friend himself), saying that all good things must end, which implied the converse was also true: bad things must end, too.

This particular bad thing went on for a long time, and while it did, Morris repeated Jimmy's mantra from *The Runner* over and over in his mind: *Shit don't mean shit, shit don't mean shit, shit don't mean shit.* It helped.

A little.

In the weeks that followed, he was ass-raped by Allgood on

some nights and mouth-raped on others. On the whole, he preferred taking it up the ass, where there were no tastebuds. Either way, he thought that Cora Ann Hooper, the woman he had so foolishly attacked while in a blackout, was getting what she would probably have considered perfect justice. On the other hand, she'd only had to endure an unwanted invader once.

There was a clothing factory attached to Waynesville. The factory made jeans and the kind of shirts workmen wore. On his fifth day in the dyehouse, one of Allgood's friends took him by the wrist, led Morris around the number three blue-vat, and told him to unbuckle his pants. "You just hold still and let me do the rest," he said. When he was finished, he said, "I ain't a fag, or anything, but I got to get along, same as anyone. Tell anyone I'm a fag and I'll fuckin kill you."

"I won't," Morris said. Shit don't mean shit, he told himself. Shit don't mean shit.


One day in mid-March of 1979, a Hell's Angel type with tattooed slabs of muscle strolled up to Morris in the exercise yard. "Can you write?" this fellow said with an unmistakable Deep-South accent—*kin you raht*? "I hear you can write."

"Yes, I can write," Morris said. He saw Allgood approach, notice who was walking beside Morris, and sheer off toward the basketball court at the far end of the yard.

"I'm Warren Duckworth. Most folks call me Duck."

"I'm Morris Bel—"

"I know who you are. Write purty well, do you?"

"Yes." Morris spoke with no hesitation or false modesty. The way Roy Allgood had suddenly found another place to be wasn't lost on him.

"Could you write a letter to my wife, if I sort of tell you what to say? Only put it in, like, better words?"

"I could do that, and I will, but I've got a little problem."

"I know what your problem is," his new acquaintance said. "You write my wife a letter that'll make her happy, maybe stop her divorce talk, you ain't gonna have no more trouble with that skinny bitchboy in your house."

*I'm* the skinny bitchboy in my house, Morris thought, but he felt the tiniest glimmer of hope. "Sir, I'm going to write your wife the prettiest letter she ever got in her life."

Looking at Duckworth's huge arms, he thought of something he'd seen on a nature program. There was a kind of bird that lived in the mouths of crocodiles, granted survival on a day-to-day basis by pecking bits of food out of the reptiles' jaws. Morris thought that kind of bird probably had a pretty good deal.

"I'd need some paper." Thinking of the reformatory, where five lousy sheets of Blue Horse was all you ever got, paper with big spots of pulp floating in it like pre-cancerous moles.

"I'll get you paper. All you want. You just write that letter, and at the end say ever' word came from my mouth and you just wrote it down."

"Okay, tell me what would make her most happy to hear."

Duck considered, then brightened. "That she throws a fine fuck?"

"She'll know that already." It was Morris's turn to consider. "What part of her does she say she'd change, if she could?"

Duck's frown deepened. "I dunno, she always says her ass is too big. But you can't say that, it'll make things worse instead of better."

"No, what I'll write is how much you love to put your hands on it and squeeze it."

129

Duck was smiling now. "Better watch out or I'll be rapin you myself."

"What's her favorite dress? Does she have one?"

"Yeah, a green one. It's silk. Her ma gave it to her last year, just before I went up. She wears that one when we go out dancin." He looked down at the ground. "She better not be dancin now, but she might be. I know that. Maybe I can't write much more than my own fuckin name, but I ain't no stupe."

"I could write how much you like to squeeze her bottom when she's wearing that green dress, how's that? I could say thinking of that gets you hot."

Duck looked at Morris with an expression that was utterly foreign to Morris's Waynesville experience. It was respect. "Say, that's not bad."

Morris was still working on it. Sex wasn't all women thought about when they thought about men; sex wasn't romance. "What color is her hair?"

"Well, right now I don't know. She's what you call a brownette when there ain't no dye in it."

*Brown* didn't sing, at least not to Morris, but there were ways you could skate around stuff like that. It occurred to him that this was very much like selling a product in an ad agency, and pushed the idea away. Survival was survival. He said, "I'll write how much you like to see the sun shining in her hair, especially in the morning."

Duck didn't reply. He was staring at Morris with his bushy eyebrows furrowed together.

"What? No good?"

Duck seized Morris's arm, and for one terrible moment Morris was sure he was going to break it like a dead branch. HATE was tattooed on the fingers of the big man's knuckles. Duck breathed,

"It's like poitry. I'll get you the paper tomorrow. There's lots in the liberry."

That night, when Morris returned to the cellblock after a three-to-nine shift spent blue-dying, his house was empty. Rolf Venziano, in the next cell, told Morris that Roy Allgood had been taken to the infirmary. When Allgood returned the next day, both his eyes were black and his nose had been splinted. He looked at Morris from his bunk, then rolled over and faced the wall.

Warren Duckworth was Morris's first client. Over the next thirty-six years, he had many.

Sometimes when he couldn't sleep, lying on his back in his cell (by the early '90s he had a single, complete with a shelf of well-thumbed books), Morris would soothe himself by remembering his discovery of Jimmy Gold. That had been a shaft of bright sunlight in the confused and angry darkness of his adolescence.

By then his parents had been fighting all the time, and although he had grown to heartily dislike both of them, his mother had the better armor against the world, and so he adopted her sarcastic curl of a smile and the superior, debunking attitude that went with it. Except for English, where he got As (when he wanted to), he was a straight-C student. This drove Anita Bellamy into report-card-waving frenzies. He had no friends but plenty of enemies. Three times he suffered beatings. Two were administered by boys who just didn't like his general attitude, but one boy had a more specific issue. This was a hulking senior football player named Pete Womack, who didn't care for the way Morris was checking out his girlfriend one lunch period in the cafeteria.

"What are you looking at, rat-face?" Womack enquired, as the tables around Morris's solitary position grew silent.

"Her," Morris said. He was frightened, and when clearheaded, fright usually imposed at least a modicum of restraint on his behavior, but he had never been able to resist an audience.

"Well, you want to quit it," Womack said, rather lamely. Giving him a chance. Perhaps Pete Womack was aware that he was six-two and two-twenty, while the skinny, red-lipped piece of freshman shit sitting by himself was five-seven and maybe a hundred and forty soaking wet. He might also have been aware that those watching—including his clearly embarrassed girlfriend—would take note of this disparity.

"If she doesn't want to be looked at," Morris said, "why does she dress like that?"

Morris considered this a compliment (of the left-handed variety, granted), but Womack felt differently. He ran around the table, fists raised. Morris got in a single punch, but it was a good one, blacking Womack's eye. Of course after that he got his shit handed to him, and most righteously, but that one punch was a revelation. He *would* fight. It was good to know.

Both boys were suspended, and that night Morris got a twenty-minute lecture on passive resistance from his mother, along with the acid observation that *fighting in cafeteria* was generally not the sort of extracurricular activity the finer colleges looked for on the applications of prospective enrollees.

Behind her, his father raised his martini glass and dropped him a wink. It suggested that, even though George Bellamy mostly resided beneath his wife's thumb and thin smile, he would also fight under certain circumstances. But running was still dear old dad's default position, and during the second semester of Morris's freshman year at Northfield, Georgie-Porgie ran right out of the marriage, pausing only to clean out what was left in the Bellamy bank account. The investments of which he had boasted either didn't exist or had gone tits-up. Anita Bellamy was left with a stack of bills and a rebellious fourteen-year-old son.

Only two assets remained following her husband's departure to parts unknown. One was the framed Pulitzer nomination for that book of hers. The other was the house where Morris had grown up, situated in the nicer section of the North Side. It was mortgage-free because she had steadfastly refused to co-sign the bank papers her husband brought home, for once immune to his rhapsodizing about an investment opportunity that was absolutely not to be missed. She sold it after he was gone, and they moved to Sycamore Street.

"A comedown," she admitted to Morris during the summer between his freshman and sophomore years, "but the financial reservoir will refill. And at least the neighborhood is white." She paused, replaying that remark, and added, "Not that I'm prejudiced."

"No, Ma," Morris said. "Who'd ever believe that?"

Ordinarily she hated being called Ma, and said so, but on that day she kept still, which made it a good day. It was always a good day when he got in a poke at her. There were so few opportunities.

During the early seventies, book reports were still a requirement in sophomore English at Northfield. The students were given a mimeographed list of approved books to choose from. Most looked like dreck to Morris, and, as usual, he wasn't shy about saying so. "Look!" he cried from his spot in the back row. "Forty flavors of American oatmeal!"

Some of the kids laughed. He could make them laugh, and although he couldn't make them like him, that was absolutely okay. They were dead-enders headed for dead-end marriages and dead-end jobs. They would raise dead-end kids and dandle dead-end grandkids before coming to their own dead ends in dead-end

hospitals and nursing homes, rocketing off into darkness believing they had lived the American Dream and Jesus would meet
them at the gates of heaven with the Welcome Wagon. Morris was meant for better things. He just didn't know what they
were.

Miss Todd—then about the age Morris would be when he and
his cohorts broke into John Rothstein's house—asked him to stay
after class. Morris lounged splay-legged at his desk as the other
kids went out, expecting Todd to write him a detention slip. It
would not be his first for mouthing off in class, but it would be
his first in an English class, and he was sort of sorry about that. A
vague thought occurred to him in his father's voice—*You're burning
too many bridges, Morrie*—and was gone like a wisp of steam.

Instead of giving him a detention, Miss Todd (not exactly fair
of face but with a holy-shit body) reached into her bulging book-
bag and brought out a paperback with a red cover. Sketched on it
in yellow was a boy lounging against a brick wall and smoking a
cigarette. Above him was the title: *The Runner*.

"You never miss a chance to be a smartass, do you?" Miss Todd
asked. She sat on the desk next to him. Her skirt was short, her
thighs long, her hose shimmery.

Morris said nothing.

"In this case, I saw it coming. Which is why I brought this book
today. It's a good-news bad-news thing, my know-it-all friend. You
don't get detention, but you don't get to choose, either. You get to
read this and only this. It's not on the schoolboard's Approved List,
and I suppose I could get in trouble for giving it to you, but I'm
counting on your better nature, which I like to believe is in there
somewhere, minuscule though it may be."

Morris glanced at the book, then looked over it at Miss Todd's
legs, making no attempt to disguise his interest.

She saw the direction of his gaze and smiled. For a moment Morris glimpsed a whole future for them, most of it spent in bed. He had heard of such things actually happening. *Yummy teacher seeks teenage boy for extracurricular lessons in sex education.*

This fantasy balloon lasted perhaps two seconds. She popped it with her smile still in place. "You and Jimmy Gold will get along. He's a sarcastic, self-hating little shit. A lot like you." She stood up. Her skirt fell back into place two inches above her knees. "Good luck with your book report. And the next time you peek up a woman's skirt, you might remember something Mark Twain said: 'Any idler in need of a haircut can *look.*'"

Morris slunk from the classroom with his face burning, for once not just put in his place but rammed into it and hammered flat. He had an urge to chuck the paperback down a sewer drain as soon as he got off the bus on the corner of Sycamore and Elm, but held on to it. Not because he was afraid of detention or suspension, though. How could she do *anything* to him when the book wasn't on the Approved List? He held on to it because of the boy on the cover. The boy looking through a drift of cigarette smoke with a kind of weary insolence.

*He's a sarcastic, self-hating little shit. A lot like you.*

His mother wasn't home, and wouldn't be back until after ten. She was teaching adult education classes at City College to make extra money. Morris knew she loathed those classes, believing they were far beneath her skill set, and that was just fine with him. Sit on it, Ma, he thought. Sit on it and spin.

The freezer was stocked with TV dinners. He picked one at random and shoved it in the oven, thinking he'd read until it was done. After supper he might go upstairs, grab one of his father's *Playboys* from under the bed (*my inheritance from the old man,* he sometimes thought), and choke the chicken for awhile.

He neglected to set the stove timer, and it was the stench of burning beef stew that roused him from the book a full ninety minutes later. He had read the first hundred pages, no longer in this shitty little postwar tract home deep in the Tree Streets but wandering the streets of New York City with Jimmy Gold. Like a boy in a dream, Morris went to the kitchen, donned oven gloves, removed the congealed mass from the oven, tossed it in the trash, and went back to *The Runner*.

I'll have to read it again, he thought. He felt as if he might be running a mild fever. And with a marker. There's so much to underline and remember. So much.

For readers, one of life's most electrifying discoveries is that they *are* readers—not just capable of doing it (which Morris already knew), but in love with it. Hopelessly. Head over heels. The first book that does that is never forgotten, and each page seems to bring a fresh revelation, one that burns and exalts: *Yes! That's how it is! Yes! I saw that, too!* And, of course, *That's what I think! That's what I FEEL!*

Morris wrote a ten-page book report on *The Runner*. It came back from Miss Todd with an A+ and a single comment: *I knew you'd dig it.*

He wanted to tell her it wasn't digging; it was loving. *True* loving. And true love would never die.

*The Runner Sees Action* was every bit as good as *The Runner*, only instead of being a stranger in New York City, Jimmy was now a stranger in Europe, fighting his way across Germany, watching his friends die, and finally staring with a blankness beyond horror through the barbed wire at one of the concentration camps. *The wandering, skeletal survivors confirmed what Jimmy had suspected for years,* Rothstein wrote. *It was all a mistake.*

Using a stencil kit, Morris copied this line in Roman Gothic print and thumbtacked it to the door of his room, the one that would later be occupied by a boy named Peter Saubers.

His mother saw it hanging there, smiled her sarcastic curl of a smile, and said nothing. At least not then. Their argument over the Gold trilogy came two years later, after she had raced through the books herself. That argument resulted in Morris getting drunk; getting drunk resulted in breaking and entering and common assault; these crimes resulted in nine months at Riverview Youth Detention Center.

But before all that came *The Runner Slows Down*, which Morris read with increasing horror. Jimmy got married to a nice girl. Jimmy got a job in advertising. Jimmy began putting on weight. Jimmy's wife got pregnant with the first of three little Golds, and they moved to the suburbs. Jimmy made friends there. He and his wife threw backyard barbecue parties. Jimmy presided over the grill wearing an apron that said THE CHEF IS ALWAYS RIGHT. Jimmy cheated on his wife, and his wife cheated right back. Jimmy took Alka-Seltzer for his acid indigestion and something called Miltown for his hangovers. Most of all, Jimmy pursued the Golden Buck.

Morris read these terrible developments with ever increasing dismay and growing rage. He supposed he felt the way his mother had when she discovered that her husband, whom she had believed comfortably under her thumb, had been cleaning out all the accounts even as he ran hither and yon, eagerly doing her bidding and never once raising a hand to slap that sarcastic curl of a smile off her overeducated face.

Morris kept hoping that Jimmy would wake up. That he would remember who he was—who he had been, at least—and trash the stupid and empty life he was leading. Instead of that, *The Runner Slows Down* ended with Jimmy celebrating his most successful ad campaign ever—Duzzy-Doo, for God's sake—and crowing *Just wait until next year!*

In the detention center, Morris had been required to see a shrink once a week. The shrink's name was Curtis Larsen. The boys called him Curd the Turd. Curd the Turd always ended their sessions by asking Morris the same question: "Whose fault is it that you're in here, Morris?"

Most boys, even the cataclysmically stupid ones, knew the right answer to that question. Morris did, too, but refused to give it. "My mother's," he said each time the question was asked.

At their final session, shortly before the end of Morris's term, Curd the Turd folded his hands on his desk and looked at Morris for a long space of silent seconds. Morris knew Curd the Turd was waiting for him to drop his eyes. He refused to do it.

"In my game," Curd the Turd finally said, "there's a term for your response. It's called blame avoidance. Will you be back in here if you continue to practice blame avoidance? Almost certainly not. You'll be eighteen in a few months, so the next time you hit the jackpot—and there *will* be a next time—you'll be tried as an adult. Unless, that is, you make a change. So, for the last time: whose fault is it that you're in here?"

"My mother's," Morris said with no hesitation. Because it wasn't blame avoidance, it was the truth. The logic was inarguable.

Between fifteen and seventeen, Morris read the first two books of the Gold trilogy obsessively, underlining and annotating. He reread *The Runner Slows Down* only once, and had to force himself to finish. Every time he picked it up, a ball of lead formed in his gut, because he knew what was going to happen. His resentment of Jimmy Gold's creator grew. For Rothstein to destroy Jimmy like that! To not even allow him to go out in a blaze of glory, but to *live*! To compromise, and cut corners, and believe that sleeping with the Amway-selling slut down the street meant he was still a rebel!

138

Morris thought of writing Rothstein a letter, asking—no, *demanding*—that he explain himself, but he knew from the *Time* cover story that the sonofabitch didn't even read his fan mail, let alone answer it.

As Ricky the Hippie would suggest to Pete Saubers years later, most young men and women who fall in love with the works of a particular writer—the Vonneguts, the Hesses, the Brautigans and Tolkiens—eventually find new idols. Disenchanted as he was with *The Runner Slows Down*, this might have happened to Morris. Before it could, there came the argument with the bitch who was determined to spoil his life since she could no longer get her hooks into the man who had spoiled hers. Anita Bellamy, with her framed near-miss Pulitzer and her sprayed dome of dyed blond hair and her sarcastic curl of a smile.

During her February vacation in 1973, she raced through all three Jimmy Gold novels in a single day. And they were *his* copies, his *private* copies, filched from his bedroom shelf. They littered the coffee table when he came in, *The Runner Sees Action* soaking up a condensation ring from her wineglass. For one of the few times in his adolescent life, Morris was speechless.

Anita wasn't. "You've been talking about these for well over a year now, so I finally decided I had to see what all the excitement was about." She sipped her wine. "And since I had the week off, I read them. I thought it would take longer than a day, but there's really not much *content* here, is there?"

"You . . ." He choked for a moment. Then: "You went in my room!"

"You've never raised an objection when I go in to change your sheets, or when I return your clothes, all clean and folded. Perhaps you thought the Laundry Fairy did those little chores?"

"Those books are mine! They were on my special shelf! You had no right to take them!"

"I'll be happy to put them back. And don't worry, I didn't disturb the magazines under your bed. I know boys need . . . amusement."

He stepped forward on legs that felt like stilts and gathered up the paperbacks with hands that felt like hooks. The back cover of *The Runner Sees Action* was soaking from her goddam glass, and he thought, If one volume of the trilogy had to get wet, why couldn't it have been *The Runner Slows Down?*

"I'll admit they're interesting artifacts." She had begun speaking in her judicious lecture-hall voice. "If nothing else, they show the growth of a marginally talented writer. The first two are painfully jejune, of course, the way *Tom Sawyer* is jejune when compared to *Huckleberry Finn*, but the last one—although no *Huck Finn*—*does* show growth."

"The last one *sucks!*" Morris shouted.

"You needn't raise your voice, Morris. You needn't *roar.* You can defend your position without doing that." And here was that smile he hated, so thin and so sharp. "We're having a discussion."

"I don't *want* to have a fucking discussion!"

"But we *should* have one!" Anita cried, smiling. "Since I've spent my day—I won't say *wasted* my day—trying to understand my self-centered and rather pretentiously intellectual son, who is currently carrying a C average in his classes."

She waited for him to respond. He didn't. There were traps everywhere. She could run rings around him when she wanted to, and right now she wanted to.

"I notice that the first two volumes are tattered, almost falling out of their bindings, nearly read to death. There are copious underlinings and notes, some of which show the budding—I won't say *flowering*, it can't really be called that, can it, at least not yet—of an acute critical mind. But the third one looks almost new, and there are no underlinings at all. You don't like what happened to him, do you? You don't care for your Jimmy once he—and, by logical transference, the author—grew up."

"He sold out!" Morris's fists were clenched. His face was hot and throbbing, as it had been after Womack tuned up on him that day in the caff with everyone watching. But Morris had gotten in that one good punch, and he wanted to get one in now. He needed to. "Rothstein *let* him sell out! If you can't see that, you're *stupid*!"

"No," she said. The smile was gone now. She leaned forward, set her glass on the coffee table, looking at him steadily all the while. "That's the core of your misunderstanding. A good novelist does not lead his characters, he follows them. A good novelist does not create events, he watches them happen and then writes down what he sees. A good novelist realizes he is a secretary, not God."

"That wasn't Jimmy's character! Fucking Rothstein changed him! He made Jimmy into a joke! He made him into . . . into everyone!"

Morris hated how weak that sounded, and he hated that his mother had baited him into defending a position that didn't need defending, that was self-evident to anyone with half a brain and any feelings at all.

"Morris." Very softly. "Once I wanted to be the female version of Jimmy, just as you want to be Jimmy now. Jimmy Gold, or someone like him, is the island of exile where most teenagers go to wait until childhood becomes adulthood. What you need to see—what Rothstein finally saw, although it took him three books to do it—is that most of us become everyone. I certainly did." She looked around. "Why else would we be living here on Sycamore Street?"

"Because you were stupid and let my father rob us blind!"

She winced at that (*a hit, a palpable hit,* Morris exulted), but then the sarcastic curl resurfaced. Like a piece of paper charring in an ashtray. "I admit there's an element of truth in what you say, although you're unkind to task me with it. But have you asked yourself *why* he robbed us blind?"

Morris was silent.

"Because he refused to grow up. Your father is a potbellied Peter Pan who's found some girl half his age to play Tinker Bell in bed."

"Put my books back or throw them in the trash," Morris said in a voice he barely recognized. To his horror, it sounded like his father's voice. "I don't care which. I'm getting out of here, and I'm not coming back."

"Oh, I think you will," she said, and she was right about that, but it was almost a year before he did, and by then she no longer knew him. If she ever had. "And you should read this third one a few more times, I think."

She had to raise her voice to say the rest, because he was plunging down the hall, in the grip of emotions so strong he was almost blind. "Find some pity! Mr. Rothstein did, *and it's the last book's saving grace!*"

The slam of the front door cut her off.

Morris stalked to the sidewalk with his head down, and when he reached it, he began to run. There was a strip mall with a liquor store in it three blocks away. When he got there, he sat on the bike rack outside Hobby Terrific and waited. The first two guys he spoke to refused his request (the second with a smile Morris longed to punch off his face), but the third was wearing thrift-shop clothes and walking with a pronounced list to port. He agreed to buy Morris a pint for two dollars, or a quart for five. Morris opted for the quart, and began drinking it beside the stream running through the undeveloped land between Sycamore and Birch Streets. By then the sun was going down. He had no memory of making his way to

Sugar Heights in the boosted car, but there was no doubt that once he was there, he'd gotten into what Curd the Turd liked to call a mega jackpot.

*Whose fault is it that you're in here?*

He supposed a little of the blame could go to the wino who'd bought an underage kid a quart of whiskey, but mostly it was his mother's fault, and one good thing had come of it: when he was sentenced, there had been no sign of that sarcastic curl of a smile. He had finally wiped it off her face.

During prison lockdowns (there was at least one a month), Morris would lie on his bunk with his hands crossed behind his head and think about the fourth Jimmy Gold novel, wondering if it contained the redemption he had so longed for after closing *The Runner Slows Down*. Was it possible Jimmy had regained his old hopes and dreams? His old fire? If only he'd had two more days with it! Even one!

Although he doubted if even John Rothstein could have made a thing like that believable. Based on Morris's own observations (his parents being his prime exemplars), when the fire went out, it usually went out for good. Yet some people *did* change. He remembered once bringing up that possibility to Andy Halliday, while they were having one of their many lunch-hour discussions. This was at the Happy Cup, just down the street from Grissom Books, where Andy worked, and not long after Morris had left City College, deciding what passed for higher education there was fucking pointless.

"Nixon changed," Morris said. "The old Commie-hater opened trade relations with China. And Lyndon Johnson pushed the Civil Rights Bill through Congress. If an old racist hyena like him could change his spots, I suppose anything is possible."

"Politicians." Andy sniffed, as at a bad smell. He was a skinny, crewcut fellow only a few years older than Morris. "*They* change out of expediency, not idealism. Ordinary people don't even do that. They can't. If they refuse to behave, they're punished. Then, after punishment, they say okay, yes sir, and get with the program like the good little drones they are. Look at what happened to the Vietnam War protestors. Most of them are now living middle-class lives. Fat, happy, and voting Republican. Those who refused to knuckle under are in jail. Or on the run, like Katherine Ann Power."

"How can you call Jimmy Gold *ordinary?*" Morris cried.

Andy had given him a patronizing look. "Oh, please. His entire story is an epic journey out of exceptionalism. The purpose of American culture is to create a *norm*, Morris. That means that extraordinary people must be leveled, and it happens to Jimmy. He ends up working in *advertising*, for God's sake, and what greater agent of the norm is there in this fucked-up country? It's Rothstein's main point." He shook his head. "If you're looking for optimism, buy a Harlequin Romance."

Morris thought Andy was basically arguing for the sake of argument. A zealot's eyes burned behind his nerdy hornrims, but even then Morris was getting the man's measure. His zeal was for books as objects, not for the stories and ideas inside them.

They had lunch together two or three times a week, usually at the Cup, sometimes across the street from Grissom's on the benches in Government Square. It was during one of these lunches that Andrew Halliday first mentioned the persistent rumor that John Rothstein had continued to write, but that his will specified all the work be burned upon his death.

"No!" Morris had cried, genuinely wounded. "That could never happen. Could it?"

Andy shrugged. "If it's in the will, anything he's written since he dropped out of sight is as good as ashes."

"You're just making it up."

"The stuff about the will might just be a rumor, I grant you that, but it's well accepted in bookstore circles that Rothstein never stopped writing."

"Bookstore circles," Morris had said doubtfully.

"We have our own grapevine, Morris. Rothstein's housekeeper does his shopping, okay? Not just groceries, either. Once every month or six weeks, she goes into White River Books in Berlin, which is the closest town of any size, to pick up books he's ordered by phone. She's told the people who work there that he writes every day from six in the morning until two in the afternoon. The owner told some other dealers at the Boston Book Fair, and the word got around."

"Holy shit," Morris had breathed. This conversation had taken place in June of 1976. Rothstein's last published story, "The Perfect Banana Pie," had been published in 1960. If what Andy was saying was true, it meant that John Rothstein had been piling up fresh fiction for sixteen years. At even eight hundred words a day, that added up to . . . Morris couldn't begin to do the math in his head, but it was a lot.

"Holy shit is right," Andy said.

"If he really wants all that burned when he dies, he's *crazy!*"

"Most writers are." Andy had leaned forward, smiling, as if what he said next were a joke. Maybe it was. To him, at least. "Here's what I think—someone should mount a rescue mission. Maybe you, Morris. After all, you're his number one fan."

"Not me," Morris said, "not after what he did to Jimmy Gold."

"Cool it, guy. You can't blame a man for following his muse."

"Sure I can."

"Then steal em," Andy said, still smiling. "Call it theft as a pro-test on behalf of English literature. Bring em to me. I'll sit on em awhile, then sell em. If they're not senile gibberish, they might fetch as much as a million dollars. I'll split with you. Fifty-fifty, even-Steven."

"They'd catch us."

"Don't think so," Andy Halliday had replied. "There are ways."

"How long would you have to wait before you could sell them?"

"A few years," Andy had replied, waving his hand as if he were talking about a couple of hours. "Five, maybe."

A month later, heartily sick of living on Sycamore Street and haunted by the idea of all those manuscripts, Morris packed his beat-up Volvo and drove to Boston, where he got hired by a con-tractor building a couple of housing developments out in the burbs. The work had nearly killed him at first, but he had muscled up a little (not that he was ever going to look like Duck Duck-worth), and after that he'd done okay. He even made a couple of friends: Freddy Dow and Curtis Rogers.

Once he called Andy. "Could you *really* sell unpublished Roth-stein manuscripts?"

"No doubt," Andy Halliday said. "Not right away, as I believe I said, but so what? We're young. He's not. Time would be on our side."

Yes, and that would include time to read everything Rothstein had written since "The Perfect Banana Pie." Profit—even half a million dollars—was incidental. I am not a mercenary, Morris told himself. I am not interested in the Golden Buck. That shit don't mean shit. Give me enough to live on—sort of like a grant—and I'll be happy.

I am a *scholar*.

On the weekends, he began driving up to Talbot Corners, New

Hampshire. In 1977, he began taking Curtis and Freddy with him. Gradually, a plan began to take shape. A simple one, the best kind. Your basic smash-and-grab.

Philosophers have debated the meaning of life for centuries, rarely coming to the same conclusion. Morris studied the subject himself over the years of his incarceration, but his inquiries were practical rather than cosmic. He wanted to know the meaning of life in a legal sense. What he found was pretty schizo. In some states, life meant exactly that. You were supposedly in until you died, with no possibility of parole. In some states, parole was considered after as little as two years. In others, it was five, seven, ten, or fifteen. In Nevada, parole was granted (or not) based on a complicated point system.

By the year 2001, the average life sentence of a man in the American prison system was thirty years and four months.

In the state where Morris was stacking time, lawmakers had created their own arcane definition of life, one based on demographics. In 1979, when Morris was convicted, the average American male lived to the age of seventy. Morris was twenty-three at the time, therefore he could consider his debt to society paid in forty-seven years.

Unless, that is, he were granted parole.

He became eligible the first time in 1990. Cora Ann Hooper appeared at the hearing. She was wearing a neat blue suit. Her graying hair was pulled back in a bun so tight it screeched. She held a large black purse in her lap. She recounted how Morris Bellamy had grabbed her as she passed the alley beside Shooter's Tavern and told her of his intention to "rip off a piece." She told the five-member Parole Board how he had punched her and broken her nose when she managed to trigger the Police Alert device she kept in her purse. She told the board about the reek of alcohol on his breath and how he had gouged her stomach with his nails when he ripped off her underwear. She told them how Morris was "still choking me and hurting me with his organ" when Officer Ellenton arrived and pulled him off. She told the board that she had attempted suicide in 1980, and was still under the care of a psychiatrist. She told the board that she was better since accepting Jesus Christ as her personal savior, but she still had nightmares. No, she told the board, she had never married. The thought of sex gave her panic attacks.

Parole was not granted. Several reasons were given on the green sheet passed to him through the bars that evening, but the one at the top was clearly the PB's major consideration: *Victim states she is still suffering.*

Bitch.

Hooper appeared again in 1995, and again in 2000. In '95, she wore the same blue suit. In the millennium year—by then she had gained at least forty pounds—she wore a brown one. In 2005, the suit was gray, and a large white cross hung on the growing shelf of her bosom. She held what appeared to be the same large black purse in her lap at each appearance. Presumably her Police Alert was inside. Maybe a can of Mace, as well. She was not summoned to these hearings; she volunteered.

And told her story.

Parole was not granted. Major reason given on the green sheet: *Victim states she is still suffering.*

Shit don't mean shit, Morris told himself. Shit don't mean shit. Maybe not, but *God*, he wished he'd killed her.

• • •

By the time of his third turndown, Morris's work as a writer was much in demand—he was, in the small world of Waynesville, a bestselling author. He wrote love letters to wives and girlfriends. He wrote letters to the children of inmates, a few of which confirmed the reality of Santa Claus in touching prose. He wrote job applications for prisoners whose release dates were coming up. He wrote themes for prisoners taking online college courses or working to get their GEDs. He was no jailhouse lawyer, but he did write letters to real lawyers on behalf of inmates from time to time, cogently explaining each case at hand and laying out the basis for appeal. In some cases lawyers were impressed by these letters, and—mindful of the money to be made from wrongful imprisonment suits that were successful—came on board. As DNA became of overriding importance in the appeals process, he wrote often to Barry Scheck and Peter Neufeld, the founders of the Innocence Project. One of those letters ultimately led to the release of an auto mechanic and part-time thief named Charles Roberson, who had been in Waynesville for twenty-seven years. Roberson got his freedom; Morris got Roberson's eternal gratitude and nothing else . . . unless you counted his own growing reputation, and that was *far* from nothing. It had been a long time since he had been raped.

In 2004, Morris wrote his best letter ever, laboring over four drafts to get it exactly right. This letter was to Cora Ann Hooper. In it he told her that he lived with terrible remorse for what he had done, and promised that if he were granted parole, he would spend the rest of his life atoning for his one violent act, committed during an alcohol-induced blackout.

"I attend AA meetings four times a week here," he wrote, "and now sponsor half a dozen recovering alcoholics and drug addicts. I would continue this work on the outside, at the St. Patrick's Halfway House on the North Side. I had a spiritual awakening, Ms. Hooper, and have allowed Jesus into my life. You will understand how important this is, because I know you have also accepted Christ as your Savior. 'Forgive us our trespasses,' He said, 'as we forgive those who trespass against us.' Won't you please forgive my trespass against you? I am no longer the man who hurt you so badly that night. I have had a soul conversion. I pray that you respond to my letter."

Ten days later, his prayer for a response was answered. There was no return address on the envelope, but *C.A. Hooper* had been printed neatly on the back flap. Morris didn't need to tear it open; some screw in the front office, assigned the duty of checking inmate mail, had already taken care of that. Inside was a single sheet of deckle-edged stationery. In the upper right corner and the lower left, fluffy kittens played with gray balls of twine. There was no salutation. A single line had been printed halfway down the page:

I hope you rot in there.

The bitch appeared at his hearing the following year, legs now clad in support hose, ankles slopping over her sensible shoes. She was like some overweight, vengeful swallow returning to the prison version of Capistrano. She once more told her story, and parole was once more not granted. Morris had been a model prisoner, and now there was just a single reason given on the inmate green sheet: *Victim states she is still suffering.*

Morris assured himself that shit did not mean shit and went back to his cell. Not exactly a penthouse apartment, just six by eight, but at least there were books. Books were escape. Books were freedom. He lay on his cot, imagining how pleasant it would be to have fifteen minutes alone with Cora Ann Hooper, and a power nailer.

Morris was by then working in the library, which was a wonderful change for the better. The guards didn't much care how he spent his paltry budget, so it was no problem to subscribe to *The American Bibliographer's Newsletter*. He also got a number of catalogues from rare book dealers around the country, which were free. Books by John Rothstein came up for sale frequently, offered at ever steeper prices. Morris found himself rooting for this the way some prisoners rooted for sports teams. The value of most writers went down after they died, but a fortunate few trended upward. Rothstein had become one of those. Once in awhile a signed Rothstein showed up in one of the catalogues. In the 2007 edition of Bauman's Christmas catalogue, a copy of *The Runner* signed to Harper Lee—a so-called association copy—went for $17,000.

Morris also kept an eye on the city newspaper during his years of incarceration, and then, as the twenty-first century wrought its technological changes, various city websites. The land between Sycamore Street and Birch Street was still mired in that unending legal suit, which was just the way Morris liked it. He would get out eventually, and his trunk would be there, with the roots of that overhanging tree wrapped firmly around it. That the worth of those notebooks must by now be astronomical mattered less and less to him.

Once he had been young, and he supposed he would have enjoyed all the things young men chased after when their legs were strong and their balls were tight: travel and women, cars and women, big homes like the ones in Sugar Heights and women. Now he rarely even dreamed of such things, and the last woman with whom he'd had sex remained largely instrumental in keeping him locked up. The irony wasn't lost on him. But that was okay. The things of the world fell by the wayside, you lost your speed and your eyesight and your fucking Electric Boogaloo, but literature was eternal, and that was what was waiting for him: a lost geography as yet seen by no eye but its creator's. If he didn't get to see that geography himself until he was seventy, so be it. There was the money, too—all those cash envelopes. Not a fortune by any means, but a nice little nest egg.

I have something to live for, he told himself. How many men in here can say that, especially once their thighs go flabby and their cocks only stand up when they need to pee?

Morris wrote several times to Andy Halliday, who now *did* have his own shop—Morris knew that from *American Bibliographer's Newsletter*. He also knew that his old pal had gotten into trouble at least once, for trying to sell a stolen copy of James Agee's most famous book, but had skated. Too bad. Morris would have dearly loved to welcome that cologne-wearing homo to Waynesville. There were plenty of bad boys here who would have been all too willing to put a hurt on him for Morrie Bellamy. Just a daydream, though. Even if Andy had been convicted, it probably would have been just a fine. At worst, he would have gotten sent to the country club at the west end of the state, where the white-collar thieves went.

None of Morris's letters to Andy were answered.

In 2010, his personal swallow once more returned to Capistrano, wearing a black suit again, as if dressed for her own funeral. Which will be soon if she doesn't lose some weight, Morris thought nastily. Cora Ann Hooper's jowls now hung down at the sides of her neck in fleshy flapjacks, her eyes were all but buried in pouches of fat, her skin was sallow. She had replaced the black purse with a blue one, but everything else was the same. Bad dreams! Endless therapy! Life ruined thanks to the horrible beast who sprang out of the alley that night! So on and so forth, blah-blah-blah.

Aren't you over that lousy rape yet? Morris thought. Aren't you *ever* going to move on?

Morris went back to his cell thinking Shit don't mean shit. It don't mean fucking *shit*.

That was the year he turned fifty-five.

One day in March of 2014, a turnkey came to get Morris from the library, where he was sitting behind the main desk, reading *American Pastoral* for the third time. (It was by far Philip Roth's best book, in Morris's opinion.) The turnkey told him he was wanted in Admin.

"What for?" Morris asked, getting up. Trips to Admin were not ordinarily good news. Usually it was cops wanting you to roll on somebody, and threatening you with all kinds of dark shit if you refused to cooperate.

"PB hearing."

"No," Morris said. "It's a mistake. The board doesn't hear me again until next year."

"I only do what they tell me," the turnkey said. "If you don't want me to give you a mark, find somebody to take the desk and get the lead out of your ass."

The Parole Board—now three men and three women—was convened in the conference room. Philip Downs, the Board's legal counsel, made lucky seven. He read a letter from Cora Ann Hooper. It was an amazing letter. The bitch had cancer. That was good news, but what followed was even better. She was dropping all objections to Morris Bellamy's parole. She said she was sorry she had waited so long. Downs then read a letter from the Midwest Culture and Arts Center, locally known as the MAC. They had hired many Waynesville parolees over the years, and were willing to take Morris Bellamy on as a part-time file clerk and computer operator starting in May, should parole be granted.

"In light of your clean record over the past thirty-five years, and in light of Ms. Hooper's letter," Downs said, "I felt that putting the subject of your parole before the board a year early was the right thing to do. Ms. Hooper informs us that she doesn't have much time, and I'm sure she'd like to get closure on this matter." He turned to them. "How say you, ladies and gentlemen?"

Morris already knew how the ladies and gentlemen would say; otherwise he never would have been brought here. The vote was 6–0 in favor of granting him parole.

"How do you feel about that, Morris?" Downs asked.

Morris, ordinarily good with words, was too stunned to say anything, but he didn't have to. He burst into tears.

Two months later, after the obligatory pre-release counseling and shortly before his job at the MAC was scheduled to begin, he walked through Gate A and back into the free world. In his pocket were his earnings from thirty-five years in the dyehouse, the furniture workshop, and the library. It amounted to twenty-seven hundred dollars and change.

The Rothstein notebooks were finally within reach.

# PART 2: OLD PALS

# 1

Kermit William Hodges—plain old Bill, to his friends—drives along Airport Road with the windows rolled down and the radio turned up, singing along with Dylan's "It Takes a Lot to Laugh, It Takes a Train to Cry." He's sixty-six, no spring chicken, but he looks pretty good for a heart attack survivor. He's lost forty pounds since the vapor-lock, and has quit eating the junk food that was killing him a little with each mouthful.

Do you want to live to see seventy-five? the cardiologist asked him. This was at his first full checkup, a couple of weeks after the pacemaker went in. If you do, give up the pork rinds and dough-nuts. Make friends with salads.

As advice goes, it's not up there with love thy neighbor as thy-self, but Hodges has taken it to heart. There's a salad in a white paper bag on the seat beside him. He'll have plenty of time to eat it, with Dasani to wash it down, if Oliver Madden's plane is on time. And if Madden comes at all. Holly Gibney has assured him that Madden is already on the way—she got his flight plan from a computer site called AirTracker—but it's always possible that Madden will smell something downwind and head in another direction. He has been out there doing dirt for quite some time now, and guys like that have very educated sniffers.

Hodges passes the feeder road to the main terminals and short-term parking and continues on, following the signs that read AIR FREIGHT and SIGNATURE AIR and THOMAS ZANE AVIA-TION. He turns in at this last. It's an independent fixed-based operator, huddled—almost literally—in the shadow of the much bigger Signature Air FBO next door. There are weeds sprouting from the cracked asphalt of the little parking lot, which is empty except for the front row. That has been reserved for a dozen or so rental cars. In the middle of the economies and mid-sizes, and hulking above them, is a black Lincoln Navigator with smoked glass windows. Hodges takes this as a good sign. His man *does* like to go in style, a common trait among dirtbags. And although his man may wear thousand-dollar suits, he is still very much a dirt-bag.

Hodges bypasses the parking lot and pulls into the turnaround out front, stopping in front of a sign reading LOADING AND UNLOADING ONLY.

Hodges hopes to be loading.

He checks his watch. Quarter to eleven. He thinks of his mother saying You must always arrive early on important occasions, Billy, and the memory makes him smile. He takes his iPhone off his belt and calls the office. It rings just once.

"Finders Keepers," Holly says. She always says the name of the company, no matter who's calling; it's one of her little tics. She has many little tics. "Are you there, Bill? Are you at the airport? Are you?"

Little tics aside, this Holly Gibney is very different from the one he first met four years ago, when she came to town for her aunt's funeral, and the changes are all for the better. Although she's sneaking the occasional cigarette again; he has smelled them on her breath.

"I'm here," he says. "Tell me I'm gonna get lucky."

"Luck has nothing to do with it," she says. "AirTracker is a very good website. You might like to know that there are currently six thousand, four hundred and twelve flights in U.S. airspace. Isn't that interesting?"

"Totally fascinating. Is Madden's ETA still eleven thirty?"

"Eleven thirty-seven, to be exact. You left your skim milk on your desk. I put it back in the fridge. Skim milk goes over very rapidly on hot days, you know. Even in an air-conditioned environment, which this is. Now." She nagged Hodges into the air-conditioning. Holly is a very good nagger, when she puts her mind to it.

"Chug-a-lug, Holly," he says. "I have a Dasani."

"No, thank you, I'm drinking my Diet Coke. Barbara Robinson called. She wanted to talk to you. She was all serious. I told her she could call you later this afternoon. Or you'd call her." Uncertainty creeps into her voice. "Was that all right? I thought you'd want your phone available for the time being."

"That's fine, Holly. Did she say what she was all serious about?"

"No."

"Call her back and tell her I'll be in touch as soon as this is wrapped up."

"You'll be careful, won't you?"

"I always am." Although Holly knows that's not exactly true; he damned near got himself, Barbara's brother, Jerome, and Holly herself blown to kingdom come four years ago . . . and Holly's cousin *was* blown up, although that came earlier. Hodges, who had been more than halfway to in love with Janey Patterson, still mourns her. And still blames himself. These days he takes care of himself *for* himself, but he also does it because he believes it's what Janey would have wanted.

He tells Holly to hold the fort and returns his iPhone to the place on his belt where he used to carry his Glock before he became a Det-Ret. In retirement he always used to forget his cell, but those days are gone. What he's doing these days isn't quite the same as carrying a badge, but it's not bad. In fact, it's pretty good. Most of the fish Finders Keepers nets are minnows, but today's is a bluefin tuna, and Hodges is stoked. He's looking at a big payday, but that's not the main thing. He's *engaged*, that's the main thing. Nailing bad boys like Oliver Madden is what he was made to do, and he intends to keep on doing it until he no longer can. With luck, that might be eight or nine years, and he intends to treasure every day. He believes Janey would have wanted that for him, too.

*Yeah*, he can hear her say, wrinkling her nose at him in that funny way she had.

Barbara Robinson was also nearly killed four years ago; she was at the fateful concert with her mother and a bunch of friends. Barbs was a cheerful, happy kid then and is a cheerful, happy teenager now—he sees her when he takes the occasional meal at the Robinson home, but he does that less often now that Jerome is away at school. Or maybe Jerome's back for the summer. He'll ask Barbara when he talks to her. Hodges hopes she's not in some kind of jam. It seems unlikely. She's your basic good kid, the kind who helps old ladies across the street.

Hodges unwraps his salad, douses it with lo-cal French, and begins to snark it up. He's hungry. It's good to be hungry. Hunger is a sign of health.

2

Morris Bellamy isn't hungry at all. A bagel with cream cheese is the most he can manage for lunch, and not much of that. He ate like a pig when he first got out—Big Macs, funnel cakes, pizza by the slice, all the stuff he had longed for while in prison—but that was before a night of puking after an ill-advised visit to Senor Taco in Lowtown. He never had a problem with Mexican when he was young, and youth seems like just hours ago, but a night spent on his knees praying to the porcelain altar was all it took to drive home the truth: Morris Bellamy is fifty-nine, on the doorstep of old age. The best years of his life were spent dying bluejeans, varnishing tables and chairs to be sold in the Waynesville Outlet Shop, and writing letters for an unending stream of dead-end Charlies in prison overalls.

Now he's in a world he hardly recognizes, one where movies show on bloated screens called IMAX and everyone on the street is either wearing phones in their ears or staring at tiny screens. There are television cameras watching inside every shop, it seems, and the prices of the most ordinary items—bread, for instance, fifty cents a loaf when he went up—are so high they seem surreal. Everything has changed; he feels glare-blind. He is way behind the curve, and he knows his prison-oriented brain will never catch up. Nor his body. It's stiff when he gets out of bed in the morning, achy when he goes to bed at night; a touch of arthritis, he supposes. After that night of vomiting (and when he wasn't doing that, he was shitting brown water), his appetite just died.

For food, at least. He has thought of women—how could he not, when they're everywhere, the young ones barely dressed in the early summer heat?—but at his age, he'd have to buy one younger than thirty, and if he went to one of the places where such transactions are made, he would be violating his parole. If he were caught, he'd find himself back in Waynesville with the Rothstein notebooks still buried in that patch of waste ground, unread by anyone except the author himself.

He knows they're still there, and that makes it worse. The urge to dig them up and have them at last has been a maddening constant, like a snatch of music (*I need a lover that won't drive me cray-zee*) that gets into your head and simply won't leave, but so far he has done almost everything by the book, waiting for his PO to relax and let up a little. This was the gospel according to Warren "Duck" Duckworth, handed down when Morris first became eligible for parole.

"You gotta be super-careful to start with," Duck had said. This was before Morris's first board hearing and the first vengeful appearance of Cora Ann Hooper. "Like you're walking on eggs. 'Cause, see, the bastard will show up when you least expect it. You can take that to the bank. If you get the idea to do something that might get you marked up on Doubtful Behavior—that's a category they have—wait until *after* your PO makes a surprise visit. Then you prob'ly be all right. Get me?"

Morris did.

And Duck had been right.

## 3

After not even one hundred hours as a free man (well, *semi*-free), Morris came back to the old apartment building where he now lived to find his PO sitting on the stoop and smoking a cigarette. The graffiti-decorated cement-and-breezeblock pile, called Bugshit Manor by the people who lived there, was a state-subsidized fish tank stocked with recovering druggies, alcoholics, and parolees like himself. Morris had seen his PO just that noon, and been sent on his way after a few routine questions and a *Seeya next week*. This was not next week, this was not even the next *day*, but here he was.

Ellis McFarland was a large black gentleman with a vast sloping gut and a shining bald head. Tonight he was dressed in an acre of bluejeans and a Harley-Davidson tee-shirt, size XXL. Beside him was a battered old knapsack. "Yo, Morrie," he said, and patted the cement next to one humongous haunch. "Take a pew."

"Hello, Mr. McFarland."

Morris sat, heart beating so hard it was painful. Please just a Doubtful Behavior, he thought, even though he couldn't think what he'd done that was doubtful. Please don't send me back, not when I'm so close.

"Where you been, homie? You finish work at four. It's now after six."

"I . . . I stopped and had a sandwich. I got it at the Happy Cup. I couldn't believe the Cup was still there, but it is." Babbling. Not able to stop himself, even though he knew babbling was what people did when they were high on something.

"Took you two hours to eat a sandwich? Fucker must have been three feet long."

"No, it was just regular. Ham and cheese. I ate it on one of the benches in Government Square, and fed some of the crusts to the pigeons. I used to do that with a friend of mine, back in the day. And I just . . . you know, lost track of the time."

All perfectly true, but how lame it sounded!

"Enjoying the air," McFarland suggested. "Digging the freedom. That about the size of it?"

"Yes."

"Well, you know what? I think we ought to go upstairs and then I think you ought to drop a urine. Make sure you haven't been digging the wrong kind of freedom." He patted the knapsack. "Got my little kit right here. If the pee don't turn blue, I'll get out of your hair and let you get on with your evening. You don't have any objection to that plan, do you?"

"No." Morris was almost giddy with relief.

"And I'll watch while you make wee-wee in the little plastic cup. Any objection to that?"

"No." Morris had spent over thirty-five years pissing in front of other people. He was used to it. "No, that's fine, Mr. McFarland."

McFarland flipped his cigarette into the gutter, grabbed his knapsack, and stood up. "In that case, I believe we'll forgo the test."

Morris gaped.

McFarland smiled. "You're okay, Morrie. For now, at least. So what do you say?"

For a moment Morris couldn't think what he should say. Then it came to him. "Thank you, Mr. McFarland."

McFarland ruffled the hair of his charge, a man twenty years older than himself, and said, "Good boy. Seeya next week."

Later, in his room, Morris replayed that indulgent, patronizing *good boy* over and over, looking at the few cheap furnishings and the few books he was allowed to bring with him out of purgatory, listening to the animal-house yells and gawps and thumps of his fellow housemates. He wondered if McFarland had any idea how much Morris hated him, and supposed McFarland did.

Good boy. I'll be sixty soon, but I'm Ellis McFarland's good boy.

He lay on his bed for awhile, then got up and paced, thinking of the rest of the advice Duck had given him: *If you get the idea to do something that might get you marked up on Doubtful Behavior, wait until* after *your PO makes a surprise visit. Then you prob'ly be all right.*

Morris came to a decision and yanked his jeans jacket on. He rode down to the lobby in the piss-smelling elevator, walked two blocks to the nearest bus stop, and waited for one with NORTH-FIELD in the destination window. His heart was beating double-time again, and he couldn't help imagining Mr. McFarland somewhere near. McFarland thinking, *Ah, now that I've lulled him, I'll double back. See what that bad boy's* really *up to.* Unlikely, of course; McFarland was probably home by now, eating dinner with his wife and three kids as humongous as he was. Still, Morris couldn't help imagining it.

And if he *should* double back and ask where I went? I'd tell him I wanted to look at my old house, that's all. No taverns or titty bars in that neighborhood, just a couple of convenience stores, a few hundred houses built after the Korean War, and a bunch of streets named after trees. Nothing but over-the-hill suburbia in that part of Northfield. Plus one block-sized patch of overgrown land caught in an endless, Dickensian lawsuit.

He got off the bus on Garner Street, near the library where he had spent so many hours as a kid. The libe had been his safe haven, because big kids who might want to beat you up avoided it like Superman avoids kryptonite. He walked nine blocks to Sycamore, then actually did idle past his old house. It still looked pretty rundown, all the houses in this part of town did, but the lawn had been mowed and the paint looked fairly new. He looked at the garage where he had stowed the Biscayne thirty-six years ago, away from Mrs. Muller's prying eyes. He remembered lining the secondhand trunk with plastic so the notebooks wouldn't get damp. A very good idea, considering how long they'd had to stay in there.

Lights were on inside Number 23; the people who lived here—their name was Saubers, according to computer research he'd done in the prison library—were home. He looked at the upstairs window on the right, the one overlooking the driveway, and wondered who was in his old room. A kid, most likely, and in degenerate times like these, one probably a lot more interested in playing games on his phone than reading books.

Morris moved on, turning the corner onto Elm Street, then walking up to Birch. When he got to the Birch Street Rec (closed for two years now due to budget cuts, a thing he also knew from his computer research), he glanced around, saw the sidewalks were deserted on both sides, and hurried up the Rec's brick flank. Once behind it, he broke into a shambling jog, crossing the outside basketball courts—rundown but still used, by the look—and the weedy, overgrown baseball field.

The moon was out, almost full and bright enough to cast his shadow beside him. Ahead of him now was an untidy tangle of bushes and runty trees, their branches entwined and fighting for space. Where was the path? He thought he was in the right location, but he wasn't seeing it. He began to course back and forth where the baseball field's right field had been, like a dog trying to catch an elusive scent. His heart was up to full speed again, his mouth dry and coppery. Revisiting the old neighborhood was one thing, but being here, behind the abandoned Rec, was another. This was Doubtful Behavior for sure.

He was about to give up when he saw a potato chip bag fluttering from a bush. He swept the bush aside and bingo, there was the path, although it was just a ghost of its former self. Morris supposed that made sense. Some kids probably still used it, but the number would have dropped after the Rec closed. That was a good thing. Although, he reminded himself, for most of the years he'd been in Waynesville, the Rec would have been open. Plenty of foot traffic passing near his buried trunk.

He made his way up the path, moving slowly, stopping completely each time the moon dove behind a cloud and moving on again when it came back out. After five minutes, he heard the soft chuckle of the stream. So that was still there, too.

Morris stepped out on the bank. The stream was open to the

sky, and with the moon now directly overhead, the water shone like black silk. He had no problem picking out the tree on the other bank, the one he had buried the trunk under. The tree had both grown and tilted toward the stream. He could see a couple of gnarled roots poking out below it and then diving back into the earth, but otherwise it all looked the same.

Morris crossed the stream in the old way, going from stone to stone and hardly getting his shoes wet. He looked around once— he knew he was alone, if there had been anyone else in the area he would have heard them, but the old Prison Peek was second nature—and then knelt beneath the tree. He could hear his breath rasping harshly in his throat as he tore at weeds with one hand and held on to a root for balance with the other.

He cleared a small circular patch and then began digging, tossing aside pebbles and small stones. He was in almost halfway to the elbow when his fingertips touched something hard and smooth. He rested his burning forehead against a gnarled elbow of protruding root and closed his eyes.

Still here.

His trunk was still here.

Thank you, God.

It was enough, at least for the time being. The best he could manage, and ah God, such a relief. He scooped the dirt back into the hole and scattered it with last fall's dead leaves from the bank of the stream. Soon the weeds would be back—weeds grew fast, especially in warm weather—and that would complete the job.

Once upon a freer time, he would have continued up the path to Sycamore Street, because the bus stop was closer when you went that way, but not now, because the backyard where the path came out belonged to the Saubers family. If any of them saw him there and called 911, he'd likely be back in Waynesville tomorrow, probably with another five years tacked on to his original sentence, just for good luck.

He doubled back to Birch Street instead, confirmed the sidewalks were still empty, and walked to the bus stop on Garner Street. His legs were tired and the hand he'd been digging with was scraped and sore, but he felt a hundred pounds lighter. Still there! He had been sure it would be, but confirmation was *so* sweet.

Back at Bugshit Manor, he washed the dirt from his hands, undressed, and lay down. The place was noisier than ever, but not as noisy as D Wing at Waynesville, especially on nights like tonight, with the moon big in the sky. Morris drifted toward sleep almost at once.

Now that the trunk was confirmed, he had to be careful: that was his final thought.

More careful than ever.

4

For almost a month he *has* been careful; has turned up for his day job on the dot every morning and gotten in early at Bugshit Manor every night. The only person from Waynesville he'll see is Charlie Roberson, who got out on DNA with Morris's help, and Charlie doesn't rate as a known associate, because Charlie was innocent all along. At least of the crime he was sent up for.

Morris's boss at the MAC is a fat, self-important asshole, barely computer literate but probably making sixty grand a year. Sixty at least. And Morris? Eleven bucks an hour. He's on food stamps and living in a ninth-floor room not much bigger than the cell where he spent the so-called "best years of his life." Morris isn't positive his office carrel is bugged, but he wouldn't be surprised. It seems to him that *everything* in America is bugged these days.

It's a crappy life, and whose fault is that? He told the Parole Board time after time, and with no hesitation, that it was his; he had learned how to play the blame game from his sessions with Curd the Turd. Copping to bad choices was a necessity. If you didn't give them the old *mea culpa* you'd never get out, no matter what some cancer-ridden bitch hoping to curry favor with Jesus might put in a letter. Morris didn't need Duck to tell him that. He might have been born at night, as the saying went, but it wasn't last night.

But had it *really* been his fault?

Or the fault of that asshole right over yonder?

Across the street and about four doors down from the bench where Morris is sitting with the remains of his unwanted bagel, an obese baldy comes sailing out of Andrew Halliday Rare Editions, where he has just flipped the sign on the door from OPEN to CLOSED. It's the third time Morris has observed this lunchtime ritual, because Tuesdays are his afternoon days at the MAC. He'll go in at one and busy himself until four, working to bring the ancient filing system up-to-date. (Morris is sure the people who run the place know a lot about art and music and drama, but they know fuckall about Mac Office Manager.) At four, he'll take the crosstown bus back to his crappy ninth-floor room.

In the meantime, he's here.

Watching his old pal.

Assuming this is like the other two midday Tuesdays—Morris has no reason to think it won't be, his old pal always was a creature of habit—Andy Halliday will walk (well, *waddle*) down Lacemaker Lane to a café called Jamais Toujours. Stupid fucking name, means absolutely nothing, but sounds pretentious. Oh, but that was Andy all over, wasn't it?

Morris's old pal, the one with whom he had discussed Camus and Ginsberg and John Rothstein during many coffee breaks and pickup lunches, has put on at least a hundred pounds, the horn-rims have been replaced by pricey designer spectacles, his shoes look like they cost more than all the money Morris made in his thirty-five years of prison toil, but Morris feels quite sure his old pal hasn't changed inside. As the twig is bent the bough is shaped, that was another old saying, and once a pretentious asshole, always a pretentious asshole.

The owner of Andrew Halliday Rare Editions is walking away from Morris rather than toward him, but Morris wouldn't have been concerned if Andy had crossed the street and approached. After all, what would he see? An elderly gent with narrow shoulders and bags under his eyes and thinning gray hair, wearing an el cheapo sport jacket and even cheaper gray pants, both purchased at Chapter Eleven. His old pal would accompany his growing stomach past him without a first look, let alone a second.

I told the Parole Board what they wanted to hear, Morris thinks. I had to do that, but the loss of all those years is really your fault, you conceited homo cocksucker. If it had been Rothstein and my partners I'd been arrested for, that would be different. But it wasn't. I was never even questioned about Mssrs. Rothstein, Dow, and Rogers. I lost those years because of a forced and unpleasant act of sexual congress I can't even remember. And why did that happen? Well, it's sort of like the house that Jack built. I was in the alley instead of the tavern when the Hooper bitch came by. I got booted out of the tavern because I kicked the jukebox. I kicked the jukebox for the same reason I was in the tavern in the first place: because I was pissed at *you.*

*Why don't you try me on those notebooks around the turn of the twenty-first century, if you still have them?*

# FINDERS KEEPERS

Morris watches Andy waddle away from him and clenches his fists and thinks, You were like a girl that day. The hot little virgin you get in the backseat of your car and she's all *yes, honey, oh yes, oh yes, I love you so much*. Until you get her skirt up to her waist, that is. Then she clamps her knees together almost hard enough to break your wrist and it's all *no, oh no, unhand me, what kind of girl do you think I am?*

You could have been a little more diplomatic, at least, Morris thinks. A little diplomacy could have saved all those wasted years. But you couldn't spare me any, could you? Not so much as an attaboy, that must have taken guts. All I got was *don't try to lay this off on me.*

His old pal walks his expensive shoes into Jamais Toujours, where he will no doubt have his expanding ass kissed by the maître d'. Morris looks at his bagel and thinks he should finish it—or at least use his teeth to scrape the cream cheese into his mouth—but his stomach is too knotted up to accept it. He will go to the MAC instead, and spend the afternoon trying to impose some order on their tits-up, bass-ackwards digital filing system. He knows he shouldn't come back here to Lacemaker Lane—no longer even a street but a kind of pricey, open-air mall from which vehicles are banned—and knows he'll probably be on the same bench next Tuesday. And the Tuesday after that. Unless he's got the notebooks. That would break the spell. No need to bother with his old pal then.

He gets up and tosses the bagel into a nearby trash barrel. He looks down toward Jamais Toujours and whispers, "You suck, old pal. You really suck. And for two cents—"

But no.

No.

Only the notebooks matter, and if Charlie Roberson will help

171

him out, he's going after them tomorrow night. And Charlie *will* help him. He owes Morris a large favor, and Morris means to call it in. He knows he should wait longer, until Ellis McFarland is absolutely sure Morris is one of the good ones and turns his attention elsewhere, but the pull of the trunk and what's inside it is just too strong. He'd love to get some payback from the fat sonofabitch now feeding his face with fancy food, but revenge isn't as important as that fourth Jimmy Gold novel. There might even be a fifth! Morris knows that isn't likely, but it's possible. There was a lot of writing in those books, a mighty lot. He walks toward the bus stop, sparing one baleful glance back at Jamais Toujours and thinking, You'll never know how lucky you were.

Old pal.

5

Around the time Morris Bellamy is chucking his bagel and heading for the bus stop, Hodges is finishing his salad and thinking he could eat two more just like it. He puts the Styrofoam box and plastic spork back in the carryout bag and tosses it in the passenger footwell, reminding himself to dispose of his litter later. He likes his new car, a Prius that has yet to turn ten thousand miles, and does his best to keep it clean and neat. The car was Holly's pick. "You'll burn less gas and be kind to the environment," she told him. The woman who once hardly dared to step out of her house now runs many aspects of his life. She might let up on him a little if she had a boyfriend, but Hodges knows that's not likely. He's as close to a boyfriend as she's apt to get.

It's a good thing I love you, Holly, he thinks, or I'd have to kill you.

He hears the buzz of an approaching plane, checks his watch, and sees it's eleven thirty-four. It appears that Oliver Madden is going to be johnny-on-the-spot, and that's lovely. Hodges is an on-time man himself. He grabs his sportcoat from the backseat and gets out. It doesn't hang just right because there's heavy stuff in the front pockets.

A triangular overhang juts out above the entrance doors, and it's at least ten degrees cooler in its shade. Hodges takes his new glasses from the jacket's inner pocket and scans the sky to the west. The plane, now on its final approach, swells from a speck to a blotch to an identifiable shape that matches the pictures Holly has printed out: a 2008 Beechcraft KingAir 350, red with black piping. Only twelve hundred hours on the clock, and exactly eight hundred and five landings. The one he's about to observe will be number eight-oh-six. Rated selling price, four million and change.

A man in a coverall comes out through the main door. He looks at Hodges's car, then at Hodges. "You can't park there," he says.

"You don't look all that busy today," Hodges says mildly.

"Rules are rules, mister."

"I'll be gone very shortly."

"Shortly is not the same as now. The front is for pickups and deliveries. You need to use the parking lot."

The KingAir floats over the end of the runway, now only feet from Mother Earth. Hodges jerks a thumb at it. "Do you see that plane, sir? The man flying it is an extremely dirty dog. A number of people have been looking for him for a number of years, and now here he is."

The guy in the coverall considers this as the extremely dirty dog lands the plane with nothing more than a small blue-gray puff of rubber. They watch as it disappears behind the Zane Aviation building. Then the man—probably a mechanic—turns back to Hodges. "Are you a cop?"

"No," Hodges says, "but I'm in that neighborhood. Also, I know presidents." He holds out his loosely curled hand, palm down. A fifty-dollar bill peeps from between the knuckles.

The mechanic reaches for it, then reconsiders. "Is there going to be trouble?"

"No," Hodges says.

The man in the coverall takes the fifty. "I'm supposed to bring that Navigator around for him. Right where you're parked. That's the only reason I gave you grief about it."

Now that Hodges thinks of it, that's not a bad idea. "Why don't you go on and do that? Pull it up behind my car, nice and tight. Then you might have business somewhere else for fifteen minutes or so."

"Always stuff to do in Hangar A," the man in the coverall agrees. "Hey, you're not carrying a gun, are you?"

"No."

"What about the guy in the KingAir?"

"He won't have one, either." This is almost certainly true, but in the unlikely event Madden *does* have one, it will probably be in his carryall. Even if it's on his person, he won't have a chance to pull it, let alone use it. Hodges hopes he never gets too old for excitement, but he has absolutely no interest in OK Corral shit.

Now he can hear the steady, swelling beat of the KingAir's props as it taxies toward the building. "Better bring that Navigator around. Then . . ."

"Hangar A, right. Good luck."

Hodges nods his thanks. "You have a good day, sir."

6

Hodges stands to the left of the doors, right hand in his sport-coat pocket, enjoying both the shade and the balmy summer air. His heart is beating a little faster than normal, but that's okay. That's just as it should be. Oliver Madden is the kind of thief who robs with a computer rather than a gun (Holly has discovered the socially engaged motherfucker has eight different Facebook pages, each under a different name), but it doesn't do to take things for granted. That's a good way to get hurt. He listens as Madden shuts the KingAir down and imagines him walking into the terminal of this small, almost-off-the-radar FBO. No, not just walking, *striding*. With a bounce in his step. Going to the desk, where he will arrange for his expensive turboprop to be hangared. And fueled? Probably not today. He's got plans in the city. This week he's buying casino licenses. Or so he thinks.

The Navigator pulls up, chrome twinkling in the sun, smoked gangsta glass reflecting the front of the building . . . and Hodges himself. Whoops! He sidles farther to the left. The man in the coverall gets out, tips Hodges a wave, and heads for Hangar A.

Hodges waits, wondering what Barbara might want, what a pretty girl with lots of friends might consider important enough to make her reach out to a man old enough to be her grandpa. Whatever she needs, he'll do his best to supply it. Why wouldn't he? He loves her almost as much as he loves Jerome and Holly. The four of them were in the wars together.

That's for later, he tells himself. Right now Madden's the priority. Keep your eyes on the prize.

The doors open and Oliver Madden walks out. He's whistling, and yes, he's got that Mr. Successful bounce in his step. He's at least four inches taller than Hodges's not inconsiderable six-two. Broad shoulders in a summerweight suit, the shirt open at the collar, the tie hanging loose. Handsome, chiseled features that fall somewhere between George Clooney and Michael Douglas. He's got a briefcase in his right hand and an overnight bag slung over his left shoulder. His haircut's the kind you get in one of those places where you have to book a week ahead.

Hodges steps forward. He can't decide between morning and afternoon, so just wishes Madden a good day.

Madden turns, smiling. "The same back to you, sir. Do I know you?"

"Not at all, Mr. Madden," Hodges says, returning the smile. "I'm here for the plane."

The smile withers a bit at the corners. A frown line appears between Madden's manicured brows. "I beg your pardon?"

"The plane," Hodges says. "Three-fifty Beech KingAir? Seating for ten? Tail number November-one-one-four-Delta-Kilo? Actually belongs to Dwight Cramm, of El Paso, Texas?"

The smile stays on, but boy, it's struggling. "You've mistaken me, friend. My name's Mallon, not Madden. James Mallon. As for the plane, mine's a King, all right, but the tail is N426LL, and it belongs to no one but little old me. You probably want Signature Air, next door."

Hodges nods as if Madden might be right. Then he takes out his phone, reaching crossdraw so he can keep his right hand in his pocket. "Why don't I just put through a call to Mr. Cramm? Clear this up. I believe you were at his ranch just last week? Gave him a bank check for two hundred thousand dollars? Drawn on First of Reno?"

"I don't know what you're talking about." Smile all gone.

"Well, you know what? He knows you. As James Mallon rather

than Oliver Madden, but when I faxed him a photo six-pack, he had no trouble circling you."

Madden's face is entirely expressionless now, and Hodges sees he's not handsome at all. Or ugly, for that matter. He's nobody, extra tall or not, and that's how he's gotten by as long as he has, pulling one scam after another, taking in even a wily old coyote like Dwight Cramm. He's *nobody*, and that makes Hodges think of Brady Hartsfield, who almost blew up an auditorium filled with kids not so long ago. A chill goes up his back.

"Are you police?" Madden asks. He looks Hodges up and down. "I don't think so, you're too old. But if you are, let me see your ID."

Hodges repeats what he told the guy in the coverall: "Not exactly police, but in the neighborhood."

"Then good luck to you, Mr. In The Neighborhood. I've got appointments, and I'm running a bit late."

He starts toward the Navigator, not running but moving fast.

"You were actually right on time," Hodges says amiably, falling in step. Keeping up with him would have been hard after his retirement from the police. Back then he was living on Slim Jims and taco chips, and would have been wheezing after the first dozen steps. Now he does three miles a day, either walking or on the treadmill.

"Leave me alone," Madden says, "or I'll call the real police."

"Just a few words," Hodges says, thinking, Damn, I sound like a Jehovah's Witness. Madden is rounding the Navigator's rear end. His overnight bag swings back and forth like a pendulum.

"No words," Madden says. "You're a nut."

"You know what they say," Hodges replies as Madden reaches for the driver's-side door. "Sometimes you feel like a nut, sometimes you don't."

Madden opens the door. This is really working out well, Hodges thinks as he pulls his Happy Slapper from his coat pocket. The Slapper is a knotted sock. Below the knot, the sock's foot is loaded with ball bearings. Hodges swings it, connecting with Oliver Madden's left temple. It's a Goldilocks blow, not too hard, not too soft, just right.

Madden staggers and drops his briefcase. His knees bend but don't quite buckle. Hodges seizes him above the elbow in the strong come-along grip he perfected as a member of this city's MPD and helps Madden into the driver's seat of the Navigator. The man's eyes have the floaty look of a fighter who's been tagged hard and can only hope for the round to end before his opponent follows up and puts him down for good.

"Upsa-daisy," Hodges says, and when Madden's ass is on the leather upholstery of the bucket seat, he bends and lifts in the trailing left leg. He takes his handcuffs from the left pocket of his sportcoat and has Madden tethered to the steering wheel in a trice. The Navigator's keys, on a big yellow Hertz fob, are in one of the cupholders. Hodges takes them, slams the driver's door, grabs the fallen briefcase, and walks briskly around to the passenger side. Before getting in, he tosses the keys onto the grass verge near the sign reading LOADING AND UNLOADING ONLY. A good idea, because Madden has recovered enough to be punching the SUV's start button over and over again. Each time he does it, the dashboard flashes KEY NOT DETECTED.

Hodges slams the passenger door and regards Madden cheerfully. "Here we are, Oliver. Snug as two bugs in a rug."

"You can't do this," Madden says. He sounds pretty good for a man who should still have cartoon birdies flying in circles around his head. "You assaulted me. I can press charges. Where's my briefcase?"

Hodges holds it up. "Safe and sound. I picked it up for you."

Madden reaches with his uncuffed hand. "Give it to me."

Hodges puts it in the footwell and steps on it. "For the time being, it's in protective custody."

"What do you want, asshole?" The growl is in stark contrast to the expensive suit and haircut.

"Come on, Oliver, I didn't hit you that hard. The plane. Cramm's plane."

"He sold it to me. I have a bill of sale."

"As James Mallon."

"That's my name. I had it changed legally four years ago."

"Oliver, you and legal aren't even kissing cousins. But that's beside the point. Your check bounced higher than Iowa corn in August."

"That's impossible." He yanks his cuffed wrist. "Get this off me!"

"We can discuss the cuff after we discuss the check. Man, that was slick. First of Reno is a real bank, and when Cramm called to verify your check, the Caller ID said First of Reno was what he was calling. He got the usual automated answering service, welcome to First of Reno where the customer is king, blah-de-blah, and when he pushed the right number, he got somebody claiming to be an accounts manager. I'm thinking that was your brother-in-law, Peter Jamieson, who was arrested early this morning in Fields, Virginia."

Madden blinks and recoils, as if Hodges has suddenly thrust a hand at his face. Jamieson really is Madden's brother-in-law, but he hasn't been arrested. At least not to Hodges's knowledge.

"Calling himself Fred Dawlings, Jamieson assured Mr. Cramm that you had over twelve million dollars in First of Reno in several different accounts. I'm sure he was convincing, but the Caller ID thing was the clincher. It's a fiddle accomplished with a highly illegal computer program. My assistant is good with computers, and she figured that part out. The use of that alone could get you sixteen to twenty months in a Club Fed. But there's so much more. Five years ago, you and Jamieson hacked your way into the General Accounting Office and managed to steal almost four million dollars."

"You're insane."

"For most people, four million split two ways would be enough. But you're not one to rest on your laurels. You're just a big old thrill-seeker, aren't you, Oliver?"

"I'm not talking to you. You assaulted me and you're going to jail for it."

"Give me your wallet."

Madden stares at him, wide-eyed, genuinely shocked. As if he himself hasn't lifted the wallets and bank accounts of God knows how many people. Don't like it when the shoe's on the other foot, do you? Hodges thinks. Isn't that just tough titty.

He holds out his hand. "Give it."

"Fuck you."

Hodges shows Madden his Happy Slapper. The loaded toe hangs down, a sinister teardrop. "Give it, asshole, or I'll darken your world and take it. The choice is yours."

Madden looks into Hodges's eyes to see if he means it. Then he reaches into his suitcoat's inner pocket—slowly, reluctantly—and brings out a bulging wallet.

"Wow," Hodges says. "Is that ostrich?"

"As a matter of fact, it is."

Hodges understands that Madden wants him to reach for it. He thinks of telling Madden to lay it on the console between the seats, then doesn't. Madden, it seems, is a slow learner in need of a refresher course on who's in charge here. So he reaches for the wallet, and Madden grabs his hand in a powerful, knuckle-grinding grip, and Hodges whacks the back of Madden's hand with the Slapper. The knuckle-grinding stops at once.

"Ow! *Ow! Shit!*"

Madden's got his hand to his mouth. Above it, his incredulous eyes are welling tears of pain.

"One must not grasp what one cannot hold," Hodges says. He picks up the wallet, wondering briefly if the ostrich is an endangered species. Not that this moke would give a shit, one way or the other.

He turns to the moke in question.

"That was your second courtesy-tap, and two is all I ever give. This is not a police-and-suspect situation. You make another move on me and I'll beat you like a rented mule, chained to the wheel or not. Do you understand?"

"Yes." The word comes through lips still tightened with pain.

"You're wanted by the FBI for the GAO thing. Do you know that?"

A long pause while Madden eyes the Slapper. Then he says yes again.

"You're wanted in California for stealing a Rolls-Royce Silver Wraith, and in Arizona for stealing half a million dollars' worth of construction equipment which you then resold in Mexico. Do you also know those things?"

"Are you wearing a wire?"

"No."

Madden decides to take Hodges's word for it. "Okay, yes. Although I got pennies on the dollar for those front-end loaders and bulldozers. It was a damn swindle."

"If anyone would know a swindle when it walks up and says howdy, it would be you."

Hodges opens the wallet. There's hardly any cash inside, maybe eighty bucks total, but Madden doesn't need cash; he's got at least two dozen credit cards in at least six different names. Hodges looks at Madden with honest curiosity. "How do you keep them all straight?"

Madden doesn't reply.

With that same curiosity, Hodges says: "Are you never ashamed?"

Still looking straight ahead, Madden says: "That old bastard in El Paso is worth a hundred and fifty million dollars. He made most of it selling worthless oil leases. All right, I flew off with his plane. Left him nothing but his Cessna 172 and his Lear 35. Poor baby."

Hodges thinks, If this guy had a moral compass, it would always point due south. Talking is no use . . . but when was it ever?

He hunts through the wallet and finds a bill of particulars in the matter of the KingAir: two hundred thousand down, the rest held in escrow at First of Reno, to be paid after a satisfactory test flight. The paper is worthless in a practical sense—the plane was bought under a false name, with nonexistent money—but Hodges isn't always practical, and he's not too old to count coup and take scalps.

"Did you lock it up or leave the key at the desk so they could do it after they put it in the hangar?"

"At the desk."

"Okay, good." Hodges regards Madden earnestly. "Here comes the important part of our little talk, Oliver, so listen closely. I was hired to find the plane and take possession of it. That's all, end of story. I'm not FBI, MPD, or even a private dick. My sources are good, though, and I know you're on the verge of making a deal to buy a controlling interest in a couple of casinos out on the lake, one on Grande Belle Coeur Island and one on P'tit Grand Coeur." He taps the briefcase with his foot. "I'm sure the paperwork is in here, as I'm sure that if you want to remain a free man, it's never going to be signed."

"Oh now wait a minute!"

"Shut your hole. There's a ticket in the James Mallon name at the Delta terminal. It's one-way to Los Angeles. Leaves in—" he looked at his watch—"in about ninety minutes. Which gives you just time enough to go through all the security shit. Be on that plane or you'll be in jail tonight. Do you understand?"

"I can't—"

"*Do you understand?*"

Madden—who is also Mallon, Morton, Mason, Dillon, Callen, and God knows how many others—thinks over his options, decides he has none, and gives a sullen nod.

"Great! I'll unlock you now, take my cuffs, and exit your vehicle. If you try making a move on me while I do either, I'll knock you into next week. Are you clear on that?"

"Yes."

"Your car key's on the grass. Big yellow Hertz fob, can't miss it. For now, both hands on the wheel. Ten and two, just like Dad taught you."

Madden puts both hands on the wheel. Hodges unlocks the cuffs, slips them back in his left pocket, and exits the Navigator. Madden doesn't move.

"You have a good day, now," Hodges says, and shuts the door.

7

He gets into his Prius, drives to the end of the Zane Aviation turn-around, parks, and watches Madden grub the Navigator's key out of the grass. He waves as Madden drives past him. Madden doesn't wave back, which doesn't even come close to breaking Hodges's heart. He follows the Navigator along the airport feeder road, not quite tailgating but close. When Madden turns off toward the main terminals, Hodges flashes a so-long with his lights.

Half a mile farther up, he pulls into the lot of Midwest Airmotive and calls Pete Huntley, his old partner. He gets a civil enough "Hey, Billy, how you doin," but nothing you'd call effusive. Since Hodges went his own way in the matter of the so-called Mercedes Killer (and barely escaped serious legal trouble as a result), his relationship with Pete has frosted over. Maybe this will thaw it out a bit. Certainly he feels no remorse about lying to the moke now heading for the Delta terminal; if ever there was a guy who deserved a heaping spoonful of his own medicine, it's Oliver Madden.

"How would you like to bag an extremely tasty turkey, Pete?"

"How tasty?" Still cool, but on the interested side of cool now.

"FBI Ten Most Wanted, that tasty enough? He's currently checking in at Delta, scheduled to leave for LA on Flight Onenineteen at one forty-five PM. Going under James Mallon, but his real name is Oliver Madden. He stole a bunch of money from the Feds five years ago as Oliver Mason, and you know how Uncle Sam feels about getting his pocket picked." He adds a few of the more colorful details on Madden's resume.

"You know he's at Delta how?"

"Because I bought the ticket. I'm leaving the airport now. I just repo'd his plane. Which was not his plane, because he made the down payment with a rubber check. Holly will call Zane Aviation and give them all the details. She loves that part of the job."

A long moment of silence. Then: "Aren't you ever going to retire, Billy?"

That sort of hurts. "You could say thanks. It wouldn't kill you."

Pete sighs. "I'll call airport security, then get on out there myself." A pause. Then: "Thank you. *Kermit*."

Hodges grins. It's not much, but it might be a start in repairing what has been, if not broken, then badly sprained. "Thank Holly. She's the one who tracked him down. She's still jumpy with people she doesn't know, but when she's on the computer, she kills."

"I'll be sure to do that."

"And say hi to Izzy." Isabelle Jaynes has been Pete's partner since Hodges pulled the pin. She's one dynamite redhead, and plenty smart. It occurs to Hodges, almost as a shock, that soon enough she'll be working with a new partner; Pete himself will be retiring ere long.

"I'll pass that on, too. Want to give me this guy's description for the airport security guys?"

"He's hard to miss. Six and a half feet tall, light brown suit, probably looking a little woozy just about now."

"You clocked him?"

"I *soothed* him."

Pete laughs. It's good to hear him do that. Hodges ends the call and heads back to the city, well on the way to being twenty thousand dollars richer, courtesy of a crusty old Texan named Dwight Cramm. He'll call and give Cramm the good news after he finds out what the Barbster wants.

8

Drew Halliday (Drew is what he prefers to be called now, among his small circle of friends) eats eggs Benedict at his usual corner table in Jamais Toujours. He ingests slowly, pacing himself, although he could gobble everything in four large gulps, then pick up the plate and lick the tasty yellow sauce like a dog licking its bowl. He has no close relatives, his lovelife has been in the rearview mirror for over fifteen years now, and—face it—his small circle of friends are really no more than acquaintances. The only things he cares about these days are books and food.

Well, no.

These days there's a third thing.

John Rothstein's notebooks have made a reappearance in his life.

The waiter, a young fellow in a white shirt and tight black pants, glides over. Longish dark blond hair, clean and tied back at the nape so his elegant cheekbones show. Drew has been in a little theater group for thirty years now (funny how time glides away . . . only not really), and he thinks William would make a perfectly adequate Romeo, always assuming he could act. And good waiters always can, a little.

"Will there be anything else, Mr. Halliday?"

Yes! he thinks. Two more of these, followed by two crème brûlées and a strawberry shortcake!

"Another cup of coffee, I think."

William smiles, exposing teeth that have received nothing but the best of dental care. "I'll be back with it in two shakes of a lamb's tail."

Drew pushes his plate away regretfully, leaving the last smear of yolk and hollandaise behind. He takes out his appointment book. It's a Moleskine, of course, the pocket-sized one. He pages past four months' worth of jottings—addresses, reminders to self, prices of books he's ordered or will order for various clients. Near the end, on a blank page all its own, are two names. The first is James Hawkins. He wonders if it's a coincidence or if the boy picked it deliberately. Do boys still read Robert Louis Stevenson these days? Drew tends to think this one did; after all, he claims to be a lit major, and Jim Hawkins is the hero-narrator of *Treasure Island*.

The name written below James Hawkins is Peter Saubers.

9

Saubers—aka Hawkins—came into the shop for the first time two weeks ago, hiding behind a ridiculous adolescent moustache that hadn't had a chance to grow out much. He was wearing black hornrims like the ones Drew (then Andy) affected back in the days when Jimmy Carter was president. Teenagers did not as a rule come into the shop, and that was fine with Drew; he might still be attracted to the occasional young male—William the Waiter being a case in point—but teens tended to be careless with valuable books, handling them roughly, reshelving them upside down, even dropping them. Also, they had a regrettable tendency to shoplift.

This one looked as if he would turn and sprint for the door if Drew so much as said boo. He was wearing a City College jacket, although the day was too warm for it. Drew, who'd read his share of Sherlock Holmes, put it together with the moustache and studious hornrims and deduced that here was a lad attempting to look older, as if he were trying to get into one of the dance clubs downtown instead of a bookshop specializing in rare volumes.

You want me to take you for at least twenty-one, Drew thought, but if you're a day past seventeen, I'll eat my hat. You're not here to browse, either, are you? I believe you are a young man on a mission.

Under his arm, the boy carried a large book and a manila envelope. Drew's first thought was that the kid wanted an appraisal on some moldy old thing he'd found in the attic, but as Mr. Moustache drew hesitantly closer, Drew saw a purple sticker he recognized at once on the spine of the book.

Drew's first impulse was to say Hello, son, but he quashed it. Let the kid have his college-boy disguise. What harm?

"Good afternoon, sir. May I help you?"

For a moment young Mr. Moustache said nothing. The dark brown of his new facial hair was in stark contrast to the pallor of his cheeks. Drew realized he was deciding whether to stay or mutter *Guess not* and get the hell out. One word would probably be enough to turn him around, but Drew suffered the not unusual antiquarian disease of curiosity. So he favored the boy with his most pleasant wouldn't-hurt-a-fly smile, folded his hands, and kept silent.

"Well . . ." the boy said at length. "Maybe."

Drew raised his eyebrows.

"You buy rarities as well as sell them, right? That's what your website says."

"I do. If I feel I can sell them at a profit, that is. It's the nature of the business."

The boy gathered his courage—Drew could almost see him doing it—and stepped all the way up to the desk, where the circular glow of an old-fashioned Anglepoise lamp spotlighted a semi-organized clutter of paperwork. Drew held out his hand. "Andrew Halliday."

The boy shook it briefly and then withdrew, as if fearful of being grabbed. "I'm James Hawkins."

"Pleased to meet you."

"Uh-huh. I think . . . I have something you might be interested in. Something a collector might pay a lot for. If it was the right collector."

"Not the book you're carrying, is it?" Drew could see the title now: *Dispatches from Olympus*. The subtitle wasn't on the spine, but Drew had owned a copy for many years and knew it well: *Letters from 20 Great American Writers in Their Own Hand*.

"Gosh, no. Not this one." James Hawkins gave a small, nervous laugh. "This is just for comparison."

"Very well, say on."

For a moment "James Hawkins" seemed unsure how to do that. Then he tucked his manila envelope more firmly under his arm and began to hurry through the glossy pages of *Dispatches from Olympus*, passing a note from Faulkner scolding an Oxford, Missississippi, feed company about a misplaced order, a gushy letter from Eudora Welty to Ernest Hemingway, a scrawl about who knew what from Sherwood Anderson, and a grocery list Robert Penn Warren had decorated with a doodle of two dancing penguins, one of them smoking a cigarette.

At last he found what he wanted, set the book on the desk, and turned it to face Drew. "Here," he said. "Look at this."

Drew's heart jumped as he read the heading: *John Rothstein to Flannery O'Connor*. The carefully photographed note had been written on lined paper tattered down the lefthand side where it had been torn from a dimestore notebook. Rothstein's small, neat handwriting, very unlike the scrawl of so many writers, was unmistakable.

*February 19, 1953*

*My dear Flannery O'Connor,*

*I am in receipt of your wonderful novel,* Wise Blood, *which you have so kindly inscribed to me. I can say <u>wonderful</u> because I purchased a copy as soon as it came out, and read it immediately. I am delighted to have a signed copy, as I am sure you are delighted to have the royalty accruing from one more sold volume! I enjoyed the* *entire motley cast of characters, especially Hazel Motes and Enoch Emery, a zookeeper I'm sure my own Jimmy Gold would have enjoyed and befriended. You have been called a "connoisseur of grotesqueries," Miss O'Connor, yet what the critics miss—probably because they have none themselves—is your lunatic sense of humor, which takes no prisoners. I know you are physically unwell, but I hope you will persevere in your work in spite of that. It is <u>important</u> work! Thanking you again,*

*John Rothstein*

*PS: I still laugh about the Famous Chicken!!!*

Drew scanned the letter longer than necessary, to calm himself, then looked up at the boy calling himself James Hawkins. "Do you understand the reference to the Famous Chicken? I'll explain, if you like. It's a good example of what Rothstein called her lunatic sense of humor."

"I looked it up. When Miss O'Connor was six or seven, she had—or claimed she had—a chicken that walked backwards. Some newsreel people came and filmed it, and the chicken was in the movies. She said it was the high point of her life, and everything afterwards was an anticlimax."

"Exactly right. Now that we've covered the Famous Chicken, what can I do for you?"

The boy took a deep breath and opened the clasp on his manila envelope. From inside he took a photocopy and laid it beside Rothstein's letter in *Dispatches from Olympus*. Drew Halliday's face remained placidly interested as he looked from one to the other, but beneath the desk, his fingers interlaced so tightly that his closely clipped nails dug into the backs of his hands. He knew what he was looking at immediately. The squiggles on the tails of the *y*s, the *b*s that always stood by themselves, the *h*s that stood high and the *g*s that dipped low. The question now was how much "James Hawkins" knew. Maybe not a lot, but almost certainly more than a little. Otherwise he would not be hiding behind a new moustache and specs looking suspiciously like the clear-glass kind that could be purchased in a drugstore or costume shop.

At the top of the page, circled, was the number 44. Below it was a fragment of poetry.

> *Suicide is circular, or so I think;*
> *you may have your own opinion.*
> *In the meantime, meditate on this.*
>
> *A plaza just after sunrise,*
> *You could say in Mexico.*
> *Or Guatemala, if you like.*
> *Anyplace where the rooms still come*
> *with wooden ceiling fans.*
>
> *In any case it's blanco up to the blue sky*
> *except for the ragged mops of palms and*
> *rosa where the boy outside the café*
> *is washing cobbles, half asleep.*
> *On the corner, waiting for the first*

It ended there. Drew looked up at the boy.

"It goes on about the first bus of the day," James Hawkins said. "The kind that runs on wires. A *trolebus*, he calls it. It's Spanish for trolley. The wife of the man narrating the poem, or maybe it's his girlfriend, is sitting dead in the corner of the room. She shot herself. He's just found her."

"It doesn't strike me as deathless poesy," Drew said. In his current gobsmacked state, it was all he could *think* of to say. Regardless of its quality, the poem was the first new work by John Rothstein to appear in over half a century. No one had seen it but the author, this boy, and Drew himself. Unless Morris Bellamy had happened to glimpse it, which seemed unlikely given the great number of notebooks he claimed to have stolen.

The great number.

My God, the great number of notebooks.

"No, it's sure not Wilfred Owen or T. S. Eliot, but I don't think that's the point. Do you?"

Drew was suddenly aware that "James Hawkins" was watching him closely. And seeing what? Probably too much. Drew was used to playing them close to the vest—you had to in a business where lowballing the seller was as important as highballing potential buyers—but this was like the *Titanic* suddenly floating to the surface of the Atlantic Ocean, dinged-up and rusty, but *there*.

Okay, then, admit it.

"No, probably not." The photocopy and the letter to O'Connor were still side by side, and Drew couldn't help moving his pudgy finger back and forth between points of comparison. "If it's a forgery, it's a damned good one."

"It's not." No lack of confidence there.

"Where did you get it?"

The boy then launched into a bullshit story Drew barely listened to, something about how his uncle Phil in Cleveland had died and willed his book collection to young James, and there had been six Moleskine notebooks packed in with the paperbacks and Book of the Month Club volumes, and it turned out, hidey-ho, that these six notebooks, filled with all sorts of interesting stuff— mostly poetry, along with some essays and a few fragmentary short stories—were the work of John Rothstein.

"How did you know it was Rothstein?"

"I recognized his style, even in the poems," Hawkins said. It was a question he had prepared for, obviously. "I'm majoring in American Lit at CC, and I've read most of his stuff. But there's more. For instance, this one is about Mexico, and Rothstein spent six months wandering around there after he got out of the service."

"Along with a dozen other American writers of note, including Ernest Hemingway and the mysterious B. Traven."

"Yeah, but look at this." The boy drew a second photocopy from his envelope. Drew told himself not to reach for it greedily . . . and reached for it greedily. He was behaving as though he'd been in this business for three years instead of over thirty, but who could blame him? This was big. This was *huge*. The difficulty was that "James Hawkins" seemed to know it was.

*Ah, but he doesn't know what I know, which includes where they came from. Unless Morrie is using him as a cat's paw, and how likely is that with Morrie rotting in Waynesville State Prison?*

The writing on the second photocopy was clearly from the same hand, but not as neat. There had been no scratch-outs and marginal notes on the fragment of poetry, but there were plenty here.

"I think he might have written it while he was drunk," the boy said. "He drank a lot, you know, then quit. Cold turkey. Read it. You'll see what it's about."

The circled number at the top of this page was 77. The writing below it started in mid-sentence.

*never anticipated. While good reviews are always sweet desserts in the short term, one finds they lead to indigestion—insomnia, nightmares, even problems taking that ever-more-important afternoon shit—in the long term. And the stupiddity is even more remarkable in the good notices than in the bad ones. To see Jimmy Gold as some*

*sort of benchmark, a HERO, even, is like calling someone like Billy*
*the Kid (or Charles Starkweather, his closest 20th century avatar)*
*an American icon. Jimmy is as Jimmy is, even as I am or you are; he*
*is modeled not on Huck Finn but Etienne Lantier, the greatest char-*
*acter in 19th century fiction! If I have withdrawn from the public*
*eye, it is because that eye is infected and there is no reason to put more*
*materiel before it. As Jimmy himself would say, "Shit don't*

It ended there, but Drew knew what came next, and he was sure
Hawkins did, too. It was Jimmy's famous motto, still sometimes
seen on tee-shirts all these years later.

"He misspelled *stupidity*." It was all Drew could think of to say.

"Uh-huh, and *material*. Real mistakes, not cleaned up by some
copyeditor." The boy's eyes glowed. It was a glow Drew had seen
often, but never in one so young. "It's *alive*, that's what I think.
Alive and breathing. You see what he says about Étienne Lantier?
That's the main character of *Germinal*, by Émile Zola. And it's
new! Do you get it? It's a new insight into a character everybody
knows, and from the author himself! I bet some collectors would
pay big bucks for the original of this, and all the rest of the stuff
I have."

"You say there are six notebooks in your possession?"

"Uh-huh."

Six. Not a hundred or more. If six was all the kid had, then he
certainly wasn't acting on Bellamy's behalf, unless Morris had for
some reason split his haul up. Drew couldn't see his old pal doing
that.

"They're the medium-sized ones, eighty pages in each. That's
four hundred and eighty pages. A lot of white space—with poems
there always is—but they're not all poems. There are those short
stories, too. One is about Jimmy Gold as a kid."

But here was a question: did he, Drew, really *believe* there were only six? Was it possible the boy was holding back the good stuff? And if so, was he holding back because he wanted to sell the rest later, or because he didn't want to sell it at all? To Drew, the glow in his eyes suggested the latter, although the boy might not yet know it consciously.

"Sir? Mr. Halliday?"

"Sorry. Just getting used to the idea that this really might be new Rothstein material."

"It is," the boy said. There was no doubt in his voice. "So how much?"

"How much would *I* pay?" Drew thought *son* would be okay now, because they were about to get down to the dickering. "Son, I'm not exactly made of money. Nor am I completely convinced these aren't forgeries. A hoax. I'd have to see the real items."

Drew could see Hawkins biting his lip behind the nascent moustache. "I wasn't talking about how much *you'd* pay, I was talking about private collectors. You must know some who are willing to spend big money for special items."

"I know a couple, yes." He knew a dozen. "But I wouldn't even write to them on the basis of two photocopied pages. As for getting authentication from a handwriting expert . . . that might be dicey. Rothstein was murdered, you know, which makes these stolen property."

"Not if he gave them to someone before he was killed," the boy countered swiftly, and Drew had to remind himself again that the kid had prepared for this encounter. But I have experience on my side, he thought. Experience and craft.

"Son, there's no way to prove that's what happened."

"There's no way to prove it wasn't, either."

So: impasse.

195

Suddenly the boy grabbed the two photocopies and jammed them back into the manila envelope.

"Wait a minute," Drew said, alarmed. "Whoa. Hold on."

"No, I think it was a mistake coming here. There's a place in Kansas City, Jarrett's Fine Firsts and Rare Editions. They're one of the biggest in the country. I'll try there."

"If you can hold off a week, I'll make some calls," Drew said. "But you have to leave the photocopies."

The boy hovered, unsure. At last he said, "How much could you get, do you think?"

"For almost five hundred pages of unpublished—hell, *unseen*— Rothstein material? The buyer would probably want at least a computer handwriting analysis, there are a couple of good programs that do that, but assuming that proved out, perhaps . . ." He calculated the lowest possible figure he could throw out without sounding absurd. "Perhaps fifty thousand dollars."

James Hawkins either accepted this, or seemed to. "And what would your commission be?"

Drew laughed politely. "Son . . . James . . . no dealer would take a *commission* on a deal like this one. Not when the creator— known as the proprietor, in legalese—was murdered and the material might have been stolen. We'd split right down the middle."

"No." The boy said it at once. He might not yet be able to grow the biker moustache he saw in his dreams, but he had balls as well as smarts. "Seventy-thirty. My favor."

Drew could give in on this, get maybe a quarter of a million for the six notebooks and give the boy seventy percent of fifty K, but wouldn't "James Hawkins" expect him to dicker, at least a little? Wouldn't he be suspicious if he didn't?

"Sixty-forty. My last offer, and of course contingent on finding a buyer. That would be thirty thousand dollars for something you found crammed into a cardboard box along with old copies of *Jaws* and *The Bridges of Madison County*. Not a bad return, I'd say."

The boy shifted from foot to foot, saying nothing but clearly conflicted.

Drew reverted to the wouldn't-hurt-a-fly smile. "Leave the photocopies with me. Come back in a week and I'll tell you how we stand. And here's some advice—stay away from Jarrett's place. The man will pick your pockets."

"I'd want cash."

Drew thought, Don't we all.

"You're getting way ahead of yourself, son."

The boy came to a decision and put the manila envelope down on the cluttered desk. "Okay. I'll come back."

Drew thought, I'm sure you will. And I believe my bargaining position will be much stronger when you do.

He held out his hand. The boy shook it again, as briefly as he could while still being polite. As if he were afraid of leaving fingerprints. Which in a way he had already done.

Drew sat where he was until "Hawkins" went out, then dropped into his office chair (it gave out a resigned groan) and woke up his sleeping Macintosh. There were two security cameras mounted above the front door, one pointing each way along Lacemaker Lane. He watched the kid turn the corner onto Crossway Avenue and disappear from sight.

The purple sticker on the spine of *Dispatches from Olympus*, that was the key. It marked the volume as a library book, and Drew knew every branch in the city. Purple meant a reference volume from the Garner Street Library, and reference volumes weren't supposed to circulate. If the kid had tried to smuggle it out under his City College jacket, the security gate would have buzzed when he went through, because that purple sticker was also an anti-theft device. Which led to another Holmesian deduction, once you added in the kid's obvious book-smarts.

Drew went to the Garner Street Library's website, where all sorts of choices were displayed: SUMMER HOURS, KIDS & TEENS, UPCOMING EVENTS, CLASSIC FILM SERIES, and, last but far from least: MEET OUR STAFF.

Drew Halliday clicked on this and needed to click no farther, at least to begin with. Above the thumbnail bios was a photo of the staff, roughly two dozen in all, gathered on the library lawn. The statue of Horace Garner, open book in hand, loomed behind them. They were all smiles, including his boy, sans moustache and bogus spectacles. Second row, third from the left. According to the bio, young Mr. Peter Saubers was a student at Northfield High, currently working part-time. He hoped to major in English, with a minor in Library Science.

Drew continued his researches, aided by the fairly unusual surname. He was sweating lightly, and why not? Six notebooks already seemed like a pittance, a tease. *All* of them—some containing a fourth Jimmy Gold novel, if his psycho friend had been right all those years ago—might be worth as much as fifty million dollars, if they were broken up and sold to different collectors. The fourth Jimmy Gold alone might fetch twenty. And with Morrie Bellamy safely tucked away in prison, all that stood in his way was one teenage boy who couldn't even grow a proper moustache.

10

William the Waiter returns with Drew's check, and Drew tucks his American Express card into the leather folder. It will not be refused, he's confident of that. He's less sure about the other two cards, but he keeps the Amex relatively clean, because it's the one he uses in business transactions.

Business hasn't been so good over the last few years, although God knew it *should* have been. It should have been terrific, especially between 2008 and 2012, when the American economy fell into a sinkhole and couldn't seem to climb back out. In such times the value of precious commodities—real things, as opposed to computer boops and bytes on the New York Stock Exchange— always went up. Gold and diamonds, yes, but also art, antiques, and rare books. Fucking Michael Jarrett in KC is now driving a Porsche. Drew has seen it on his Facebook page.

His thoughts turn to his second meeting with Peter Saubers. He wishes the kid hadn't found out about the third mortgage; that had been a turning point. Maybe *the* turning point.

Drew's financial woes go back to that damned James Agee book, *Let Us Now Praise Famous Men*. Gorgeous copy, mint condition, signed by Agee *and* Walker Evans, the man who'd taken the photographs. How was Drew supposed to know it had been stolen?

All right, he probably *did* know, certainly all the red flags were there and flying briskly, and he should have steered clear, but the seller had had no idea of the volume's actual worth, and Drew had let down his guard a little. Not enough to get fined or thrown in jail, and thank Christ for that, but the results have been long-term. Ever since 1999 he's carried a certain *aroma* with him to every convention, symposium, and book auction. Reputable dealers and buyers tend to give him a miss, unless—here is the irony—they've got something just a teensy bit sketchy they'd like to turn over for a quick profit. Sometimes when he can't sleep, Drew thinks, They are pushing me to the dark side. It's not my fault. Really, I'm the victim here.

All of which makes Peter Saubers even more important.

William comes back with the leather folder, face solemn. Drew doesn't like that. Maybe the card has been refused after all. Then his favorite waiter smiles, and Drew releases the breath he's been holding in a soft sigh.

"Thanks, Mr. Halliday. Always great to see you."

"Likewise, William. Likewise, I'm sure." He signs with a flourish and slides his Amex—a bit bowed but not broken—back into his wallet.

On the street, walking toward his shop (the thought that he might be waddling never crosses his mind), his thoughts turn to the boy's second visit, which went *fairly* well, but not nearly as well as Drew had hoped and expected. At their first meeting, the boy had been so uneasy that Drew worried he might be tempted to destroy the priceless trove of manuscript he'd stumbled across. But the glow in his eyes had argued against that, especially when he talked about that second photocopy, with its drunken ramblings about the critics.

*It's alive,* Saubers had said. *That's what I think.*

And can the boy kill it? Drew asks himself as he enters his shop and turns the sign from CLOSED to OPEN. I don't think so. Any more than he could let the authorities take all that treasure away, despite his threats.

Tomorrow is Friday. The boy has promised to come in immediately after school so they can conclude their business. The boy thinks it will be a negotiating session. He thinks he's still holding some cards. Perhaps he is . . . but Drew's are higher.

The light on his answering machine is blinking. It's probably someone wanting to sell him insurance or an extended warranty on his little car (the idea of Jarrett driving a Porsche around Kansas City pinches momentarily at his ego), but you can never tell until you check. Millions are within his reach, but until they are actually in his grasp, it's business as usual.

Drew goes to see who called while he was having his lunch, and recognizes Saubers's voice from the first word.

His fists clench as he listens.

11

When the artist formerly known as Hawkins came in on the Friday following his first visit, the moustache was a trifle fuller but his step was just as tentative—a shy animal approaching a bit of tasty bait. By then Drew had learned a great deal about him and his family. And about the notebook pages, those too. Three different computer apps had confirmed that the letter to Flannery O'Connor and the writing on the photocopies were the work of the same man. Two of these apps compared handwriting. The third—not entirely reliable, given the small size of the scanned-in samples—pointed out certain stylistic similarities, most of which the boy had already seen. These results were tools laid by for the time when Drew would approach prospective buyers. He himself had no doubts, having seen one of the notebooks with his own eyes thirty-six years ago, on a table outside the Happy Cup.

"Hello," Drew said. This time he didn't offer to shake hands.

"Hi."

"You didn't bring the notebooks."

"I need a number from you first. You said you'd make some calls."

Drew had made none. It was still far too early for that. "If you recall, I gave *you* a number. I said your end would come to thirty thousand dollars."

The boy shook his head. "That's not enough. And sixty-forty isn't enough, either. It would have to be seventy-thirty. I'm not stupid. I know what I have."

"I know things, too. Your real name is Peter Saubers. You don't go to City College; you go to Northfield High and work part-time at the Garner Street Library."

The boy's eyes widened. His mouth fell open. He actually swayed on his feet, and for a moment Drew thought he might faint.

"How—"

"The book you brought. *Dispatches from Olympus.* I recognized the Reference Room security sticker. After that it was easy. I even know where you live—on Sycamore Street." Which made perfect, even divine sense. Morris Bellamy had lived on Sycamore Street, in the same house. Drew had never been there—because Morris didn't want him to meet his vampire of a mother, Drew suspected—but city records proved it. Had the notebooks been hidden behind a wall in the basement, or buried beneath the floor of the garage? Drew was betting it was one or the other.

He leaned forward as far forward as his paunch would allow and engaged the boy's dismayed eyes.

"Here's some more. Your father was seriously injured in the City Center Massacre back in '09. He was there because he became unemployed after the downturn in '08. There was a feature story in the Sunday paper a couple of years ago, about how some of the people who survived were doing. I looked it up, and it made for interesting reading. Your family moved to the North Side after your father got hurt, which must have been a considerable come-down, but you Sauberses landed on your feet. A nip here and a tuck there with just your mom working, but plenty of people did worse. American success story. Get knocked down? Arise, brush yourself off, and get back in the race! Except the story never really said how your family managed that. Did it?"

The boy wet his lips, tried to speak, couldn't, cleared his throat, tried again. "I'm leaving. Coming here was a big mistake."

He turned away from the desk.

"Peter, if you walk out that door, I can just about guarantee you'll be in jail by tonight. What a shame that would be, with your whole life ahead of you."

Saubers turned back, eyes wide, mouth open and trembling.

"I researched the Rothstein killing, too. The police believed that the thieves who murdered him only took the notebooks because they were in his safe along with his money. According to the theory, they broke in for what thieves usually break in for, which is cash. Plenty of people in the town where he lived knew the old guy kept cash in the house, maybe a lot of it. Those stories circulated in Talbot Corners for years. Finally the wrong some-ones decided to find out if the stories were true. And they were, weren't they?"

Saubers returned to the desk. Slowly. Step by step.

"You found his stolen notebooks, but you also found some sto-len money, that's what I think. Enough to keep your family solvent until your dad could get back on his feet again. Literally on his feet, because the story said he was busted up quite badly. Do your folks know, Peter? Are they in on it? Did Mom and Dad send you here to sell the notebooks now that the money's gone?"

Most of this was guesswork—if Morris had said anything about money that day outside the Happy Cup, Drew couldn't remember it—but he observed each of his guesses hit home like hard punches to the face and midsection. Drew felt any detective's delight in see-ing he had followed a true trail.

"I don't know what you're talking about." The boy sounded more like a phone answering machine than a human being.

"And as for there only being six notebooks, that really doesn't compute. Rothstein went dark in 1960, after publishing his last short story in *The New Yorker*. He was murdered in 1978. Hard to believe he only filled six eighty-page notebooks in eighteen years. I bet there were more. A *lot* more."

"You can't prove anything." Still in that same robotic monotone. Saubers was teetering; two or three more punches and he'd fall. It was rather thrilling.

"What would the police find if they came to your house with a search warrant, my young friend?"

Instead of falling, Saubers pulled himself together. If it hadn't been so annoying, it would have been admirable. "What about you, Mr. Halliday? You've already been in trouble once about selling what wasn't yours to sell."

Okay, that was a hit . . . but only a glancing blow. Drew nodded cheerfully.

"It's why you came to me, isn't it? You found out about the Agee business and thought I might help you do something illegal. Only my hands were clean then and they're clean now." He spread them to demonstrate. "I'd say I took some time to make sure that what you were trying to sell was the real deal, and once I was, I did my civic duty and called the police."

"But that's not true! It's not and you know it!"

Welcome to the real world, Peter, Drew thought. He said nothing, just let the kid explore the box he was in.

"I could burn them." Saubers seemed to be speaking to himself rather than Drew, trying the idea on for size. "I could go h . . . to where they are, and just burn them."

"How many are there? Eighty? A hundred and twenty? A hundred and *forty*? They'd find residue, son. The ashes. Even if they didn't, I have the photocopied pages. They'd start asking questions about just how your family *did* manage to get through the big recession as well as it did, especially with your father's injuries and all the medical bills. I think a competent accountant might find that your family's outlay extended its income by quite a bit."

Drew had no idea if this was true, but the kid didn't, either. He was close to panic now, and that was good. Panicked people never thought clearly.

"There's no proof." Saubers could hardly talk above a whisper. "The money is gone."

"I'm sure it is, or you wouldn't be here. But the financial trail remains. And who will follow it besides the police? The IRS! Who knows, Peter, maybe your mother and dad can also go to jail, for tax evasion. That would leave your sister—Tina, I believe?—all alone, but perhaps she has a kind old auntie she can live with until your folks get out."

"What do you want?"

"Don't be dense. I want the notebooks. *All* of them."

"If I give them to you, what do I get?"

"The knowledge that you're free and clear. Which, given your situation, is priceless."

"Are you *serious*?"

"Son—"

"Don't call me that!" The boy clenched his fists.

"Peter, think it through. If you refuse to turn the notebooks over to me, I'm going to turn *you* over to the police. But once you hand them over, my hold on you vanishes, because I have received stolen property. You'll be safe."

While he spoke, Drew's right index finger hovered near the silent alarm button beneath his desk. Pushing it was the last thing in the world he wanted to do, but he didn't like those clenched fists. In his panic, it might occur to Saubers that there was one other way to shut Drew Halliday's mouth. They were currently being recorded on security video, but the boy might not have realized that.

"And you walk away with hundreds and thousands of dollars," Saubers said bitterly. "Maybe even millions."

"You got your family through a tough time," Drew said. He thought of adding *why be greedy*, but under the circumstances, that might sound a little . . . off. "I think you should be content with that."

The boy's face offered a wordless reply: *Easy for you to say.*

"I need time to think."

Drew nodded, but not in agreement. "I understand how you feel, but no. If you walk out of here now, I can promise a police car waiting for you when you get home."

"And you lose your big payday."

Drew shrugged. "It wouldn't be the first." Although never one of this size, that was true.

"My dad's in real estate, did you know that?"

The sudden change in direction put Drew off his stride a bit. "Yes, I saw that when I was doing my research. Has his own little business now, and good for him. Although I have an idea that John Rothstein's money might have paid for some of the start-up costs."

"I asked him to research all the bookstores in town," Saubers said. "I told him I was doing a paper on how e-books are impacting traditional bookstores. This was before I even came to see you, while I was still making up my mind if I should take the chance. He found out you took a third mortgage on this place last year, and said you only got it because of the location. Lacemaker Lane being pretty upscale and all."

"I don't think that has anything to do with the subject under discus—"

"You're right, we went through a really bad time, and you know something? That gives a person a nose for people who are in trouble. Even if you're a kid. Maybe especially if you're a kid. I think you're pretty strapped yourself."

Drew raised the finger that had been poised near the silent alarm button and pointed it at Saubers. "Don't fuck with me, kid."

Saubers's color had come back in big hectic patches, and Drew saw something he didn't like and certainly hadn't intended: he had made the boy angry.

"I know you're trying to rush me into this, and it's not going to work. Yes, okay, I've got his notebooks. There's a hundred and sixty-five. Not all of them are full, but most of them are. And guess what? It was never the Gold trilogy, it was the Gold *cycle*. There are two more novels, both in the notebooks. First drafts, yeah, but pretty clean."

The boy was talking faster and faster, figuring out everything Drew had hoped he would be too frightened to see even as he was speaking.

"They're hidden away, but I guess you're right, if you call the police, they'll find them. Only my parents never knew, and I think the police will believe that. As for me . . . I'm still a minor." He even smiled a little, as if just realizing this. "They won't do much to me, since I never stole the notebooks or the money in the first place. I wasn't even born. You'll come out clean, but you also won't have anything to show for it. When the bank takes this place—my dad says they will, sooner or later—and there's an Au Bon Pain here instead, I'll come in and eat a croissant in your honor."

"That's quite a speech," Drew said.

"Well, it's over. I'm leaving."

"I warn you, you're being very foolish."

"I told you, I need time to think."

"How long?"

"A week. You need to think, too, Mr. Halliday. Maybe we can still work something out."

"I hope so, son." Drew used the word deliberately. "Because if we can't, I'll make that call. I am not bluffing."

The boy's bravado collapsed. His eyes filled with tears. Before they could fall, he turned and walked out.

12

Now comes this voicemail, which Drew listens to with fury but also with fear, because the boy sounds so cold and composed on top and so desperate underneath.

"I can't come tomorrow like I said I would. I completely forgot the junior-senior retreat for class officers, and I got elected vice president of the senior class next year. I know that sounds like an excuse, but it's not. I guess it entirely slipped my mind, what with you threatening to send me to jail and all."

Erase this right away, Drew thinks, his fingernails biting into his palms.

"It's at River Bend resort, up in Victor County. We leave on a bus at eight tomorrow morning—it's a teacher in-service day, so there's no school—and come back Sunday night. Twenty of us. I thought about begging off, but my parents are already worried about me. My sister, too. If I skip the retreat, they'll know something's wrong. I think my mom thinks I might have gotten some girl pregnant."

The boy voices a brief, semi-hysterical laugh. Drew thinks there's nothing more terrifying than boys of seventeen. You have absolutely no idea what they'll do.

"I'll come on Monday afternoon instead," Saubers resumes. "If you wait that long, maybe we can work something out. A compromise. I've got an idea. And if you think I'm just shining you on about the retreat, call the resort and check the reservation. Northfield High School Student Government. Maybe I'll see you on Monday. If not, not. Goodb—"

That's where the message-time—extra-long, for clients who call after-hours, usually from the West Coast—finally runs out. *Beep.*

Drew sits down in his chair (ignoring its despairing squeal, as always), and stares at the answering machine for nearly a full minute. He feels no need to call the River Bend Resort . . . which is, amusingly enough, only six or seven miles upriver from the penitentiary where the original notebook thief is now serving a life sentence. Drew is sure Saubers was telling the truth about the retreat, because it's so easy to check. About his reasons for not ditching it he's far less sure. Maybe Saubers has decided to call Drew's bluff about bringing the police into it. Except it's not a bluff. He has no intention of letting Saubers have what Drew can't have himself. One way or another, the little bastard is going to give those notebooks up.

I'll wait until Monday afternoon, Drew thinks. I can afford to wait that long, but then this situation is going to be resolved, one way or the other. I've already given him too much rope.

He reflects that the Saubers boy and his old friend Morris Bellamy, although at opposite ends of the age-spectrum, are very much alike when it comes to the Rothstein notebooks. They lust for what's *inside* them. It's why the boy only wanted to sell him six, and probably the six he judged least interesting. Drew, on the other hand, cares little about John Rothstein. He read *The Runner*, but only because Morrie was bonkers on the subject. He never bothered with the other two, or the book of short stories.

That's your Achilles' heel, son, Drew thinks. That collector's lust. While I, on the other hand, only care about money, and money simplifies everything. So go ahead. Enjoy your weekend of pretend politics. When you come back, we'll play some hardball."

Drew leans over his paunch and erases the message.

<br>

## 13

Hodges gets a good whiff of himself on his way back into the city and decides to divert to his house long enough for a veggie burger and a quick shower. Also a change of clothes. Harper Road isn't much out of his way, and he'll be more comfortable in a pair of jeans. Jeans are one of the major perks of self-employment, as far as he's concerned.

Pete Huntley calls as he's heading out the door, to inform his old partner that Oliver Madden is in custody. Hodges congratulates Pete on the collar and has just settled behind the wheel of his Prius when his phone rings again. This time it's Holly.

"Where *are* you, Bill?"

Hodges looks at his watch and sees it's somehow gotten all the way to three fifteen. How the time flies when you're having fun, he thinks.

"My house. Just leaving for the office."

"What are you doing *there*?"

"Stopped for a shower. Didn't want to offend your delicate olfactories. And I didn't forget about Barbara. I'll call as soon as I—"

"You won't have to. She's here. With a little chum named Tina. They came in a taxi."

"A taxi?" Ordinarily, kids don't even *think* of taxis. Maybe whatever Barbara wants to discuss is a little more serious than he believed.

"Yes. I put them in your office." Holly lowers her voice. "Barbara's just worried, but the other one acts scared to death. I think she's in some kind of jam. You should get here as soon as you can, Bill."

"Roger that."

"Please hurry. You know I'm not good with strong emotions. I'm working on that with my therapist, but right now I'm just *not*."

"On my way. There in twenty."

"Should I go across the street and get them Cokes?"

"I don't know." The light at the bottom of the hill turns yellow. Hodges puts on speed and scoots through it. "Use your judgment."

"But I have so little," Holly mourns, and before he can reply, she tells him again to hurry and hangs up.

14

While Bill Hodges was explaining the facts of life to the dazed Oliver Madden and Drew Halliday was settling in to his eggs Benedict, Pete Saubers was in the nurse's office at Northfield High, pleading a migraine headache and asking to be dismissed from afternoon classes. The nurse wrote the slip with no hesitation, because Pete is one of the good ones: Honor Roll, lots of school activities (although no sports), near-perfect attendance. Also, he *looked* like someone suffering a migraine. His face was far too pale, and there were dark circles under his eyes. She asked if he needed a ride home.

"No," Pete said, "I'll take the bus."

She offered him Advil—it's all she's allowed to dispense for headaches—but he shook his head, telling her he had special pills for migraines. He forgot to bring one that day, but said he'd take one as soon as he got home. He felt okay about this story, because he really did have a headache. Just not the physical kind. His headache was Andrew Halliday, and one of his mother's Zomig tablets (she's the migraine sufferer in the family) wouldn't cure it.

Pete knew he had to take care of that himself.

## 15

He has no intention of taking the bus. The next one won't be along for half an hour, and he can be on Sycamore Street in fifteen minutes if he runs, and he will, because this Thursday afternoon is all he has. His mother and father are at work and won't be home until at least four. Tina won't be home at all. She *says* she has been invited to spend a couple of nights with her old friend Barbara Robinson on Teaberry Lane, but Pete thinks she might actually have invited herself. If so, it probably means his sister hasn't given up her hopes of attending Chapel Ridge. Pete thinks he might still be able to help her with that, but only if this afternoon goes perfectly. That's a very big if, but he has to do *something*. If he doesn't, he'll go crazy.

He's lost weight since foolishly making the acquaintance of Andrew Halliday, the acne of his early teens is enjoying a return engagement, and of course there are those dark circles under his eyes. He's been sleeping badly, and what sleep he's managed has been haunted by bad dreams. After awakening from these—often curled in a fetal position, pajamas damp with sweat—Pete has lain awake, trying to think his way out of the trap he's in.

He genuinely forgot the class officers' retreat, and when Mrs.

Gibson, the chaperone, reminded him of it yesterday, it shocked his brain into a higher gear. That was after period five French, and before he got to his calculus class, only two doors down, he has the rough outline of a plan in his head. It partly depends on an old red wagon, and even more on a certain set of keys.

Once out of sight of the school, Pete calls Andrew Halliday Rare Editions, a number he wishes he did not have on speed dial. He gets the answering machine, which at least saves him another arkie-barkie. The message he leaves is a long one, and the machine cuts him off as he's finishing, but that's okay.

If he can get those notebooks out of the house, the police will find nothing, search warrant or no search warrant. He's confident his parents will keep quiet about the mystery money, as they have all along. As Pete slips his cell back into the pocket of his chinos, a phrase from freshman Latin pops into his head. It's a scary one in any language, but it fits this situation perfectly.

*Alea iacta est.*

The die is cast.

## 16

Before going into his house, Pete ducks into the garage to make sure Tina's old Kettler wagon is still there. A lot of their stuff went in the yard sale they had before moving from their old house, but Teens had made such a fuss about the Kettler, with its old-fashioned wooden sides, that their mother relented. At first Pete doesn't see it and gets worried. Then he spots it in the corner and lets out a sigh of relief. He remembers Teens trundling back and forth across the lawn with all her stuffed toys packed into it (Mrs. Beasley holding pride of place, of course), telling them that they were going on a nik-nik in the woods, with devil-ham samwitches and ginger-snap tooties for children who could behave. Those had been good days, before the lunatic driving the stolen Mercedes had changed everything.

No more nik-niks after that.

Pete lets himself into the house and goes directly to his father's tiny home office. His heart is pounding furiously, because this is the crux of the matter. Things might go wrong even if he finds the keys he needs, but if he doesn't, this will be over before it gets started. He has no Plan B.

Although Tom Saubers's business mostly centers on real estate search—finding likely properties that are for sale or might come up for sale, and passing these prospects on to small companies and independent operators—he has begun creeping back into primary sales again, albeit in a small way, and only here on the North Side. That didn't amount to much in 2012, but over the last couple of years, he's bagged several decent commissions, and has an exclusive on a dozen properties in the Tree Streets neighborhood. One of these—the irony wasn't lost on any of them—is 49 Elm Street, the house that had belonged to Deborah Hartsfield and her son, Brady, the so-called Mercedes Killer.

"I may be awhile selling that one," Dad said one night at dinner, then actually laughed.

A corkboard is mounted on the wall to the left of his father's computer. The keys to the various properties he's currently agenting are thumbtacked to it, each on its own ring. Pete scans the board anxiously, sees what he wants—what he *needs*—and punches the air with a fist. The label on this keyring reads BIRCH STREET REC.

"Unlikely I can move a brick elephant like that," Tom Saubers said at another family dinner, "but if I do, we can kiss this place goodbye and move back to the Land of the Hot Tub and BMW." Which is what he always calls the West Side.

Pete shoves the keys to the Rec into his pocket along with his cell phone, then pelts upstairs and gets the suitcases he used when he brought the notebooks to the house. This time he wants them for short-term transport only. He climbs the pull-down ladder to the attic and loads in the notebooks (treating them with care even in his haste). He lugs the suitcases down to the second floor one by one, unloads the notebooks onto his bed, returns the suitcases to his parents' closet, and then races *downstairs*, all the way to the cellar. He's sweating freely from his exertions and probably smells like the monkey house at the zoo, but there will be no time to shower until later. He ought to change his shirt, though. He has a Key Club polo that will be perfect for what comes next. Key Club is always doing community service shit.

His mother keeps a good supply of empty cartons in the cellar. Pete grabs two of the bigger ones and goes back upstairs, first detouring into his father's office again to grab a Sharpie.

Remember to put that back when you return the keys, he cautions himself. Remember to put *everything* back.

He packs the notebooks into the cartons—all but the six he still hopes to sell to Andrew Halliday—and folds down the lids. He uses the Sharpie to print **KITCHEN SUPPLIES** on each, in big capital letters. He looks at his watch. Doing okay for time . . . as long as Halliday doesn't listen to his message and blow the whistle on him, that is. Pete doesn't believe that's likely, but it isn't out of the question, either. This is unknown territory. Before leaving his bedroom, he hides the six remaining notebooks behind the loose baseboard in his closet. There's just enough room, and if all goes well, they won't be there long.

He carries the cartons out to the garage and puts them in Tina's old wagon. He starts down the driveway, remembers he forgot to change into the Key Club polo shirt, and pelts back up the stairs again. As he's pulling it over his head, a cold realization hits him: he left the notebooks sitting in the driveway. They are worth a huge amount of money, and there they are, out in broad daylight where anyone could come along and take them.

Idiot! he scolds himself. Idiot, idiot, fucking idiot!

Pete sprints back downstairs, the new shirt already sweat-stuck to his back. The wagon is there, of course it is, who would bother stealing boxes marked kitchen supplies? Duh! But it was still a stupid thing to do, some people will steal anything that's not nailed down, and it raises a valid question: how many other stupid things is he doing?

He thinks, I never should have gotten into this, I should have called the police and turned in the money and the notebooks as soon as I found them.

But because he has the uncomfortable habit of being honest with himself (most of the time, at least), he knows that if he had it all to do over again, he would probably do most of it the same way, because his parents had been on the verge of breaking up, and he loved them too much not to at least try to prevent that.

And it worked, he thinks. The bonehead move was not quitting while I was ahead.

But.

Too late now.


17


His first idea had been to put the notebooks back in the buried trunk, but Pete rejected that almost immediately. If the police came with the search warrant Halliday had threatened, where might they try next when they didn't find the notebooks in the house? All they'd have to do was go into the kitchen and see that undeveloped land beyond the backyard. The perfect spot. If they followed the path and saw a patch of freshly turned ground by the stream, it would be ballgame over. No, this way is better.

Scarier, though.

He pulls Tina's old wagon down the sidewalk and turns left onto Elm. John Tighe, who lives on the corner of Sycamore and Elm, is out mowing his lawn. His son Bill is tossing a Frisbee to the family dog. It sails over the dog's head and lands in the wagon, coming to rest between the two boxes.

"Hum it!" Billy Tighe shouts, cutting across the lawn. His brown hair bounces. "Hum it *hard*!"

Pete does so, but waves Billy off when he goes to throw him another. Someone honks at him when he turns onto Birch, and Pete almost jumps out of his skin, but it's only Andrea Kellogg, the woman who does Linda Saubers's hair once a month. Pete gives her a thumbs-up and what he hopes is a sunny grin. At least she doesn't want to play Frisbee, he thinks.

And here is the Rec, a three-story brick box with a sign out front reading FOR SALE and CALL THOMAS SAUBERS REAL ESTATE, followed by his dad's cell number. The first-floor windows have been blocked with plywood to keep kids from breaking them, but otherwise it still looks pretty good. A couple of tags on the bricks, sure, but the Rec was prime tagger territory even when it was open. The lawn in front is mowed. That's Dad's doing, Pete thinks with some pride. He probably hired some kid to do it. I would've done it for free, if he'd asked.

He parks the wagon at the foot of the steps, lugs the cartons up one at a time, and is pulling the keys out of his pocket when a beat-up Datsun pulls over. It's Mr. Evans, who used to coach Little League when there was still a league on this side of town. Pete played for him when Mr. Evans coached the Zoney's Go-Mart Zebras.

"Hey, Centerfield!" He's leaned over to roll down the passenger window.

Shit, Pete thinks. Shit-shit-shit.

"Hi, Coach Evans."

"What're you doing? They opening the Rec up again?"

"I don't think so." Pete has prepared a story for this eventuality, but hoped he wouldn't have to use it. "It's some kind of political thing next week. League of Women Voters? Maybe a debate? I don't know for sure."

It's at least plausible, because this is an election year with primaries just a couple of weeks away and municipal issues up the wazoo.

"Plenty to argue about, that's for sure." Mr. Evans—overweight, friendly, never much of a strategist but big on team spirit and always happy to pass out sodas after games and practices—is wearing his old Zoney Zebras cap, now faded and lapped with sweat-stains. "Need a little help?"

Oh please no. *Please.*

"Nah, I got it."

"Hey, I'm happy to lend a hand." Pete's old coach turns off the Datsun's engine and begins horsing his bulk across the seat, ready to jump out.

"Really, Coach, I'm okay. If you help me, I'll be done too soon and have to go back to class."

Mr. Evans laughs and slides back under the wheel. "I get that." He keys the engine and the Datsun farts blue smoke. "But you be sure and lock up tight once you're done, y'hear?"

"Right," Pete says. The keys to the Rec slip through his sweaty fingers and he bends to pick them up. When he straightens, Mr. Evans is pulling away.

Thank you, God. And please don't let him call up my dad to congratulate him on his civic-minded son.

The first key Pete tries won't fit the lock. The second one does, but won't turn. He wiggles it back and forth as sweat streams down his face and trickles, stinging, into his left eye. No joy. He's thinking he may have to unbury the trunk after all—which will mean going back to the garage for tools—when the balky old lock finally decides to cooperate. He pushes open the door, carries the cartons inside, then goes back for the wagon. He doesn't want anyone wondering what it's doing sitting there at the foot of the steps.

The Rec's big rooms have been almost completely cleaned out, which makes them seem even bigger. It's hot inside with no air-conditioning, and the air tastes stale and dusty. With the windows blocked up, it's also gloomy. Pete's footfalls echo as he carries the cartons through the big main room where kids used to play boardgames and watch TV, then into the kitchen. The door leading down to the basement is also locked, but the key he tried first out front opens it, and at least the power is still on. A good thing, because he never thought to bring a flashlight.

He carries the first carton downstairs and sees something delightful: the basement is loaded with crap. Dozens of card tables are stacked against one wall, at least a hundred folding chairs are leaning in rows against another, there are old stereo components and outdated video game consoles, and, best of all, dozens of cartons pretty much like his. He looks in a few and sees old sports trophies, framed photos of intramural teams from the eighties and nineties, a set of beat-to-shit catcher's gear, a jumble of LEGOs. Good God, there are even a few marked KITCHEN! Pete puts his cartons with these, where they look right at home.

219

Best I can do, he thinks. And if I can just get out of here without anyone coming in to ask me what the hell I'm up to, I think it will be good enough.

He locks the basement, then returns to the main door, listening to the echo of his footfalls and remembering all the times he brought Tina here so she wouldn't have to listen to their parents argue. So neither of them would.

He peeps out at Birch Street, sees it's empty, and lugs Tina's wagon back down the steps. He returns to the main door, locks it, then heads back home, making sure to wave again to Mr. Tighe. Waving is easier this time; he even gives Billy Tighe a couple of Frisbee throws. The dog steals the second one, making them all laugh. With the notebooks stored in the basement of the abandoned Rec, hidden among all those legitimate cartons, laughing is also easy. Pete feels fifty pounds lighter.

Maybe a hundred.

18

When Hodges lets himself into the outer office of the tiny suite on the seventh floor of the Turner Building on lower Marlborough Street, Holly is pacing worry-circles with a Bic jutting from her mouth. She stops when she sees him. "At last!"

"Holly, we spoke on the phone just fifteen minutes ago." He gently takes the pen from her mouth and observes the bite marks incised on the cap.

"It seems much longer. They're in there. I'm pretty sure Barbara's friend has been crying. Her eyes were all red when I brought them the Cokes. Go, Bill. Go go go."

He won't try to touch Holly, not when she's like this. She'd jump out of her skin. Still, she's so much better than when he first met her. Under the patient tutelage of Tanya Robinson, Jerome and Barbara's mother, she's even developed something approximating clothes sense.

"I will," he says, "but I wouldn't mind a head start. Do you have any idea what it's about?" There are many possibilities, because good kids aren't *always* good kids. It could be minor shoplifting or weed. Maybe school bullying, or an uncle with Roman hands and Russian fingers. At least he can be sure (*fairly* sure, nothing is impossible) that Barbara's friend hasn't murdered anyone.

"It's about Tina's brother. Tina, that's Barbara's friend's name, did I tell you that?" Holly misses his nod; she's looking longingly at the pen. Denied it, she goes to work on her lower lip. "Tina thinks her brother stole some money."

"How old is the brother?"

"In high school. That's all I know. May I have my pen back?"

"No. Go outside and smoke a cigarette."

"I don't do that anymore." Her eyes shift up and to the left, a tell Hodges saw many times in his life as a cop. Oliver Madden even did it once or twice, come to think of it, and when it came to lying, Madden was a pro. "I qui—"

"Just one. It'll calm you down. Did you get them anything to eat?"

"I didn't think of it. I'm sor—"

"No, that's okay. Go back across the street and get some snacks. NutraBars, or something."

"NutraBars are *dog treats*, Bill."

Patiently, he says, "Energy bars, then. Healthy stuff. No chocolate."

"Okay."

She leaves in a swirl of skirts and low heels. Hodges takes a deep breath and goes into his office.

## 19

The girls are on the couch. Barbara is black and her friend Tina is white. His first amused thought is salt and pepper in matching shakers. Only the shakers don't quite match. Yes, they are wearing their hair in almost identical ponytails. Yes, they are wearing similar sneakers, whatever happens to be the in thing for tweenage girls this year. And yes, each of them is holding a magazine from his coffee table: *Pursuit*, the skip-tracing trade, hardly the usual reading material for young girls, but that's okay, because it's pretty clear that neither of them is actually reading.

Barbara is wearing her school uniform and looks relatively composed. The other one is wearing black slacks and a blue tee with a butterfly appliquéd on the front. Her face is pale, and her red-rimmed eyes look at him with a mixture of hope and terror that's hard on the heart.

Barbara jumps up and gives him a hug, where once she would have dapped him, knuckles to knuckles, and called it good. "Hi, Bill. It's great to see you." How adult she sounds, and how tall she's grown. Can she be fourteen yet? Is it possible?

"Good to see you, too, Barbs. How's Jerome? Is he going to be home this summer?" Jerome is a Harvard man these days, and his alter ego—the jive-talking Tyrone Feelgood Delight—seems to have been retired. Back when Jerome was in high school and doing chores for Hodges, Tyrone used to be a regular visitor. Hodges doesn't miss him much, Tyrone was always sort of a juvenile persona, but he misses Jerome.

Barbara wrinkles her nose. "Came back for a week, and now he's gone again. He's taking his girlfriend, she's from Pennsylvania somewhere, to a *cotillion*. Does that sound racist to you? It does to me."

Hodges is not going there. "Introduce me to your friend, why don't you?"

"This is Tina. She used to live on Hanover Street, just around the block from us. She wants to go to Chapel Ridge with me next year. Tina, this is Bill Hodges. He can help you."

Hodges gives a little bow in order to hold out his hand to the white girl still sitting on the couch. She cringes back at first, then shakes it timidly. As she lets go, she begins to cry. "I shouldn't have come. Pete is going to be *so mad* at me."

Ah, shit, Hodges thinks. He grabs a handful of tissues from the box on the desk, but before he can give them to Tina, Barbara takes them and wipes the girl's eyes. Then she sits down on the couch again and hugs her.

"Tina," Barbara says, and rather sternly, "you came to me and said you wanted help. This is help." Hodges is amazed at how much she sounds like her mother. "All you have to do is tell him what you told me."

Barbara turns her attention on Hodges.

"And you can't tell my folks, Bill. Neither can Holly. If you tell my dad, he'll tell Tina's dad. Then her brother really will be in trouble."

"Let's put that aside for now." Hodges works his swivel chair out from behind the desk—it's a tight fit, but he manages. He doesn't want a desk between himself and Barbara's frightened friend; he'd look too much like a school principal. He sits down, clasps his hands between his knees, and gives Tina a smile. "Let's start with your full name."

"Tina Annette Saubers."

Saubers. That tinkles a faint bell. Some old case? Maybe.

"What's troubling you, Tina?"

"My brother stole some money." Whispering it. Eyes welling

again. "Maybe a lot of money. And he can't give it back, because it's gone. I told Barbara because I knew her brother helped stop the crazy guy who hurt our dad when the crazy guy tried to blow up a concert at the MAC. I thought maybe Jerome could help me, because he got a special medal for bravery and all. He was on TV."

"Yes," Hodges says. Holly should have been on TV, too—she was just as brave, and they sure wanted her—but during that phase of her life, Holly Gibney would have swallowed drain-cleaner rather than step in front of television cameras and answer questions.

"Only Barbs said Jerome was in Pennsylvania and I should talk to you instead, because you used to be a policeman." She looks at him with huge, welling eyes.

Saubers, Hodges muses. Yeah, okay. He can't remember the man's first name, but the last one is hard to forget, and he knows why that little bell tinkled. Saubers was one of those badly hurt at City Center, when Hartsfield plowed into the job fair hopefuls.

"At first I was going to talk to you on my own," Barbara adds. "That's what me and Tina agreed on. Kind of, you know, feel you out and see if you'd be willing to help. But then Teens came to my school today and she was all upset—"

"Because he's *worse* now!" Tina bursts out. "I don't know what happened, but since he grew that stupid moustache, he's *worse*! He talks in his sleep—I hear him—and he's losing weight and he's got pimples again, which in Health class the teacher says can be from stress, and . . . and . . . I think sometimes he *cries*." She looks amazed at this, as if she can't quite get her head around the idea of her big brother crying. "What if he kills himself? That's what I'm really scared of, because teen suicide is a *big problem*!"

More fun facts from Health class, Hodges thinks. Not that it isn't true.

"She's not making it up," Barbara says. "It's an amazing story."

"Then let's hear it," Hodges says. "From the beginning."

Tina takes a deep breath and begins.

20

If asked, Hodges would have said he doubted that a thirteen-year-old's tale of woe could surprise, let alone amaze him, but he's amazed, all right. Fucking astounded. And he believes every word; it's too crazy to be a fantasy.

By the time Tina has finished, she's calmed down considerably. Hodges has seen this before. Confession may or may not be good for the soul, but it's undoubtedly soothing to the nerves.

He opens the door to the outer office and sees Holly sitting at her desk, playing computer solitaire. Beside her is a bag filled with enough energy bars to feed the four of them during a zombie siege. "Come in here, Hols," he says. "I need you. And bring those."

Holly steps in tentatively, checks Tina Saubers out, and seems relieved by what she sees. Each of the girls takes an energy bar, which seems to relieve her even more. Hodges takes one himself. The salad he had for lunch seems to have gone down the hatch a month ago, and the veggie burger hasn't really stuck to his ribs, either. Sometimes he still dreams of going to Mickey D's and ordering everything on the menu.

"This is good," Barbara says, munching. "I got raspberry. What'd you get, Teens?"

"Lemon," she says. "It *is* good. Thank you, Mr. Hodges. Thank you, Ms. Holly."

"Barb," Holly says, "where does your mom think you are now?"

"Movies," Barbara says. "*Frozen* again, the sing-along version. It

225

plays every afternoon at Cinema Seven. It's been there like for-*ev-er*." She rolls her eyes at Tina, who rolls hers in complicity. "Mom said we could take the bus home, but we have to be back by six at the very latest. Tina's staying over."

That gives us a little time, Hodges thinks. "Tina, I want you to tell it all again, so Holly can hear. She's my assistant, and she's smart. Plus, she can keep a secret."

Tina goes through it again, and in more detail now that she's calmer. Holly listens closely, her Asperger's-like tics mostly disappearing as they always do when she's fully engaged. All that remains are her restlessly moving fingers, tapping her thighs as if she's working at an invisible keyboard.

When Tina has come to the end, Holly asks, "The money started coming in February of 2010?"

"February or March," Tina says. "I remember, because our folks were fighting a lot then. Daddy lost his job, see . . . and his legs were all hurt . . . and Mom used to yell at him about smoking, how much his cigarettes cost . . ."

"I hate yelling," Holly says matter-of-factly. "It makes me sick in my stomach."

Tina gives her a grateful look.

"The conversation about the doubloons," Hodges puts in. "Was that before or after the money-train started to roll?"

"Before. But not *long* before." She gives the answer with no hesitation.

"And it was five hundred every month," Holly says.

"Sometimes the time was a little shorter than that, like three weeks, and sometimes it was a little longer. When it was more than a month, my folks would think it was over. Once I think it was like six weeks, and I remember Daddy saying to Mom, 'Well, it was good while it lasted.'"

"When was that?" Holly's leaning forward, eyes bright, fingers no longer tapping. Hodges loves it when she's like this.

"Mmm . . ." Tina frowns. "Around my birthday, for sure. When I was twelve. Pete wasn't there for my party. It was spring vacation, and his friend Rory invited him to go to Disney World with their family. That was a bad birthday, because I was so jealous he got to go and I . . ."

She stops, looking first at Barbara, then at Hodges, finally at Holly, upon whom she seems to have imprinted as Mama Duck. "That's *why* it was late that time! Isn't it? *Because he was in Florida!*"

Holly glances at Hodges with just the slightest smile edging her lips, then returns her attention to Tina. "Probably. Always twenties and fifties?"

"Yes. I saw it lots of times."

"And it ran out when?"

"Last September. Around the time school started. There was a note that time. It said something like, 'This is the last of it, I'm sorry there isn't more.'"

"And how long after that was it when you told your brother you thought he was the one sending the money?"

"Not very long. And he never exactly admitted it, but I know it was him. And maybe this is all my fault because I kept talking to him about Chapel Ridge . . . and he said he wished the money wasn't all gone so I could go . . . and maybe he did something stupid and now he's sorry, and it's too l-l-late!"

She starts crying again. Barbara enfolds her and makes comforting sounds. Holly's finger-tapping resumes, but she shows no other signs of distress; she's lost in her thoughts. Hodges can almost see the wheels turning. He has his own questions, but for the time being, he's more than willing to let Holly take the lead.

When Tina's weeping is down to sniffles, Holly says, "You said you came in one night and he had a notebook he acted guilty about. He put it under his pillow."

"That's right."

"Was that near the end of the money?"

"I think so, yeah."

"Was it one of his school notebooks?"

"No. It was black, and looked expensive. Also, it had an elastic strap that went around the outside."

"Jerome has notebooks like that," Barbara said. "They're made of moleskin. May I have another energy bar?"

"Knock yourself out," Hodges tells her. He grabs a pad from his desk and jots *Moleskine*. Then, returning his attention to Tina: "Could it have been an accounts book?"

Tina frowns in the act of peeling the wrapper from her own energy bar. "I don't get you."

"It's possible he was keeping a record of how much he'd paid out and how much was left."

"Maybe, but it looked more like a fancy diary."

Holly is looking at Hodges. He tips her a nod: *Continue*.

"This is all good, Tina. You're a terrific witness. Don't you think so, Bill?"

He nods.

"So, okay. When did he grow his moustache?"

"Last month. Or maybe it was the end of April. Mom and Daddy both told him it was silly, Daddy said he looked like a drugstore cowboy, whatever that is, but he wouldn't shave it off. I thought it was just something he was going through." She turns to Barbara. "You know, like when we were little and you tried to cut your hair yourself to look like Hannah Montana's."

Barbara grimaces. "Please don't talk about that." And to Hodges: "My mother hit the *roof*."

"And since then, he's been upset," Holly says. "Since the moustache."

"Not so much at first, although I could tell he was nervous even then. It's really only been the last couple of weeks that he's been scared. And now *I'm* scared! *Really* scared!"

Hodges checks to see if Holly has more. She gives him a look that says *Over to you.*

"Tina, I'm willing to look into this, but it has to begin with talking to your brother. You know that, right?"

"Yes," she whispers. She carefully places her second energy bar, with only one bite gone, on the arm of the sofa. "Oh my God, he'll be so mad at me."

"You might be surprised," Holly says. "He might be relieved that someone finally forced the issue."

Holly, Hodges knows, is the voice of experience in this regard.

"Do you think so?" Tina asks. Her voice is small.

"Yes." Holly gives a brisk nod.

"Okay, but you can't this weekend. He's going up to River Bend Resort. It's a thing for class officers, and he got elected vice president next year. If he's still in school next year, that is." Tina puts the palm of her hand to her forehead in a gesture of distress so adult that it fills Hodges with pity. "If he isn't in *jail* next year. For *robbery*."

Holly looks as distressed as Hodges feels, but she's not a toucher and Barbara is too horrified by this idea to be motherly. It's up to him. He reaches over and takes Tina's small hands in his big ones.

"I don't think that's going to happen. But I *do* think Pete might need some help. When does he come back to the city?"

"S-Sunday night."

"Suppose I were to meet him after school on Monday. Would that work?"

"I guess so." Tina looks utterly drained. "He mostly rides the bus, but you could probably catch him when he leaves."

"Are *you* going to be all right this weekend, Tina?"

"I'll make sure she is," Barbara says, and plants a smack on her friend's cheek. Tina responds with a wan smile.

"What's next for you two?" Hodges asks. "It's probably too late for the movie."

"We'll go to my house," Barbara decides. "Tell my mom we decided to skip it. That's not exactly lying, is it?"

"No," Hodges agrees. "Do you have enough for another taxi?"

"I can drive you if you don't," Holly offers.

"We'll take the bus," Barbara says. "We both have passes. We only took a taxi here because we were in a hurry. Weren't we, Tina?"

"Yes." She looks at Hodges, then back to Holly. "I'm so worried about him, but you can't tell our folks, at least not yet. Do you promise?"

Hodges promises for both of them. He can't see the harm in it, if the boy is going to be out of the city over the weekend with a bunch of his classmates. He asks Holly if she'll go down with the girls and make sure they get on to the West Side bus okay.

She agrees. And makes them take the leftover energy bars. There are at least a dozen.

21

When Holly comes back, she's got her iPad. "Mission accomplished. They're off to Teaberry Lane on the Number Four."

"How did the Saubers girl seem?"

"Much better. She and Barbara were practicing some dance step they learned on TV while we waited for the bus. They tried to get me to do it with them."

"And did you?"

"No. Homegirl don't dance."

She doesn't smile when she says this, but she still might be joking. He knows she sometimes does these days, but it's always hard to tell. Much of Holly Gibney is still a mystery to Hodges, and he guesses that will always be the case.

"Will Barb's mom get the story out of them, do you think? She's pretty perceptive, and a weekend can be a long time when you're sitting on a big secret."

"Maybe, but I don't think so," Holly says. "Tina was a lot more relaxed once she got it off her chest."

Hodges smiles. "If she was dancing at the bus stop, I guess she was. So what do you think, Holly?"

"About which part?"

"Let's start with the money."

She taps at her iPad, brushing absently at her hair to keep it out of her eyes. "It started coming in February of 2010, and stopped in September of last year. That's forty-four months. If the brother—"

"Pete."

"If Pete sent his parents five hundred dollars a month over that period, that comes to twenty-two thousand dollars. Give or take. Not exactly a fortune, but—"

"But a mighty lot for a kid," Hodges finishes. "Especially if he started sending it when he was Tina's age."

They look at each other. That she will sometimes meet his gaze like this is, in a way, the most extraordinary part of her change from the terrified woman she was when he first met her. After a silence of perhaps five seconds, they speak at the same time.

"So—" "How did—"

"You first," Hodges says, laughing.

Without looking at him (it's a thing she can only do in short bursts, even when she's absorbed by some problem), Holly says, "That conversation he had with Tina about buried treasure—gold and jewels and doubloons. I think that's important. I don't think he stole that money. I think he *found* it."

"Must have. Very few thirteen-year-olds pull bank jobs, no matter how desperate they are. But where does a kid stumble across that kind of loot?"

"I don't know. I can craft a computer search with a timeline and get a dump of cash robberies, I suppose. We can be pretty sure it happened before 2010, if he found the money in February of that year. Twenty-two thousand dollars is a large enough haul to have been reported in the papers, but what's the search protocol? What are the parameters? How far back should I go? Five years? Ten? I bet an info dump going back to just oh-five would be pretty big, because I'd need to search the whole tristate area. Don't you think so?"

"You'd only get a partial catch even if you searched the whole Midwest." Hodges is thinking of Oliver Madden, who probably conned hundreds of people and dozens of organizations during the course of his career. He was an expert when it came to creating false bank accounts, but Hodges is betting that Ollie didn't put much trust in banks when it came to his own money. No, he would have wanted a cushy cash reserve.

"Why only partial?"

"You're thinking about banks, check-cashing joints, fast credit outfits. Maybe the dog track or the concession take from a Ground-hogs game. But it might not have been public money. The thief or thieves could have knocked over a high-stakes poker game or ripped off a meth dealer over on Edgemont Avenue in Hillbilly Heaven. For all we know, the cash could have come from a home invasion in Atlanta or San Diego or anyplace in between. Cash from that kind of theft might not even have been reported."

"Especially if it was never reported to Internal Revenue in the first place," Holly says. "Right right right. So where does that leave us?"

"Needing to talk to Peter Saubers, and frankly, I can't wait. I thought I'd seen it all, but I've never seen anything like this."

"You could talk to him tonight. He's not going on his class trip until tomorrow. I took Tina's phone number. I could call her and get her brother's."

"No, let's let him have his weekend. Hell, he's probably left already. Maybe it will calm him down, give him time to think. And let Tina have hers. Monday afternoon will be soon enough."

"What about the black notebook she saw? The Moleskine? Any ideas about that?"

"Probably has nothing at all to do with the money. Could be his *50 Shades of Fun* fantasy journal about the girl who sits behind him in homeroom."

Holly makes a *hmph* sound to show what she thinks of that and begins to pace. "You know what bugs me? The lag."

"The lag?"

"The money stopped coming last September, along with a note that said he's sorry there isn't more. But as far as we know, Peter didn't start getting weird until April or May of this year. For seven months he's fine, then he grows a moustache and starts exhibiting symptoms of anxiety. What happened? Any ideas on that?"

One possibility stands out. "He decided he wanted more money, maybe so his sister could go to Barbara's school. He thought he knew a way to get it, but something went wrong."

"Yes! That's what I think, too!" She crosses her arms over her breasts and cups her elbows, a self-comforting gesture Hodges has seen often. "I wish Tina had seen what was in that notebook, though. The Moleskine notebook."

"Is that a hunch, or are you following some chain of logic I don't see?"

"I'd like to know why he was so anxious for her not to see it, that's all." Having successfully evaded Hodges's question, she heads for the door. "I'm going to build a computer search on robberies between 2001 and 2009. I know it's a longshot, but it's a place to start. What are you going to do?"

"Go home. Think this over. Tomorrow I'm repo'ing cars and looking for a bail-jumper named Dejohn Frasier, who is almost certainly staying with his stepmom or ex-wife. Also, I'll watch the Indians and possibly go to a movie."

Holly lights up. "Can I go to the movies with you?"

"If you like."

"Can I pick?"

"Only if you promise not to drag me to some idiotic romantic comedy with Jennifer Aniston."

"Jennifer Aniston is a very fine actress and a badly underrated comedienne. Did you know she was in the original *Leprechaun* movie, back in 1993?"

"Holly, you're a font of information, but you're dodging the issue here. Promise me no rom-com, or I go on my own."

"I'm sure we can find something mutually agreeable," Holly says, not quite meeting his eyes. "Will Tina's brother be all right? You don't think he'd really try to kill himself, do you?"

"Not based on his actions. He put himself way out on a limb for his family. Guys like that, ones with empathy, usually aren't suicidal. Holly, does it seem strange to you that the little girl figured out Peter was behind the money, and their parents don't seem to have a clue?"

The light in Holly's eyes goes out, and for a moment she looks very much like the Holly of old, the one who spent most of her adolescence in her room, the kind of neurotic isolate the Japanese call *hikikomori*.

"Parents can be very stupid," she says, and goes out.

Well, Hodges thinks, yours certainly were, I think we can agree on that.

He goes to the window, clasps his hands behind his back, and stares out at lower Marlborough, where the afternoon rush hour traffic is building. He wonders if Holly has considered the second plausible source of the boy's anxiety: that the mokes who hid the money have come back and found it gone.

And have somehow found out who took it.

## 22

Statewide Motorcycle & Small Engine Repair isn't statewide or even citywide; it's a ramshackle zoning mistake made of rusty corrugated metal on the South Side, a stone's throw from the minor league stadium where the Groundhogs play. Out front there's a line of cycles for sale under plastic pennants fluttering lackadaisically from a sagging length of cable. Most of the bikes look pretty sketchy to Morris. A fat guy in a leather vest is sitting against the side of the building, swabbing road rash with a handful of Kleenex. He looks up at Morris and says nothing. Morris says nothing right back. He had to walk here from Edgemont Avenue, over a mile in the hot morning sun, because the buses only come out this far when the Hogs are playing.

He goes into the garage and there's Charlie Roberson, sitting on a grease-smeared car seat in front of a half-disassembled Harley. He doesn't see Morris at first; he's holding the Harley's battery up and studying it. Morris, meanwhile, studies him. Roberson is still a muscular fireplug of a man, although he has to be over seventy, bald on top with a graying fringe. He's wearing a cut-off tee, and Morris can read a fading prison tattoo on one of his biceps: WHITE POWER 4EVER.

One of my success stories, Morris thinks, and smiles.

Roberson was doing life in Waynesville for bludgeoning a rich old lady to death on Wieland Avenue in Branson Park. She supposedly woke up and caught him creeping her house. He also raped her, possibly before the bludgeoning, perhaps after, as she lay dying on the floor of her upstairs hall. The case was a slam-dunk. Roberson had been seen in the area on several occasions leading up to the robbery, he had been photographed by the security camera outside the rich old lady's gate a day prior to the break-in, he had discussed the possibility of creeping that particular crib and robbing that particular lady with several of his low-life friends (all given ample reason to testify by the prosecution, having legal woes of their own), and he had a long record of robbery and assault. Jury said guilty; judge said life without parole; Roberson swapped motorcycle repair for stitching bluejeans and varnishing furniture.

"I done plenty, but I didn't do that," he told Morris time and time again. "I *woulda*, I had the fuckin security code, but someone else beat me to the punch. I know who it was, too, because there was only one guy I told those numbers to. He was one of the ones who fuckin testified against me, and if I ever get out of here, that man is gonna die. Trust me."

Morris neither believed nor disbelieved him—his first two years in the Ville had shown him that it was filled with men claiming to be as innocent as morning dew—but when Charlie asked him to write Barry Scheck, Morris was willing. It was what he did, his real job.

Turned out the robber-bludgeoner-rapist had left semen in the old lady's underpants, the underpants were still in one of the city's cavernous evidence rooms, and the lawyer the Innocence Project sent out to investigate Charlie Roberson's case found them. DNA testing unavailable at the time of Charlie's conviction showed the jizz wasn't his. The lawyer hired an investigator to track down several of the prosecution's witnesses. One of them, dying of liver cancer, not only recanted his testimony but copped to the crime, perhaps in hopes that doing so would earn him a pass through the pearly gates.

"Hey, Charlie," Morris says. "Guess who."

Roberson turns, squints, gets to his feet. "Morrie? Is that Morrie Bellamy?"

"In the flesh."

"Well, I'll be fucked."

Probably not, Morris thinks, but when Roberson puts the battery down on the seat of the Harley and comes forward with his arms outstretched, Morris submits to the obligatory back-pounding bro-hug. Even gives it back to the best of his ability. The amount of muscle beneath Roberson's filthy tee-shirt is mildly alarming.

Roberson pulls back, showing his few remaining teeth in a grin. "Jesus Christ! Parole?"

"Parole."

"Old lady took her foot off your neck?"

"She did."

"God-*dam*, that's great! Come on in the office and have a drink! I got bourbon."

Morris shakes his head. "Thanks, but booze doesn't agree with my system. Also, the man might come around anytime and ask me to drop a urine. I called in sick at work this morning, that's risky enough."

"Who's your PO?"

"McFarland."

"Big buck nigger, isn't he?"

"He's black, yes."

"Ah, he ain't the worst, but they watch you close to begin with, no doubt. Come on in the office, anyway, I'll drink yours. Hey, did you hear Duck died?"

Morris has indeed heard this, got the news shortly before his parole came through. Duck Duckworth, his first protector, the one who stopped the rapes by Morris's cellie and his cellie's friends. Morris felt no special grief. People came; people went; shit didn't mean shit.

Roberson shakes his head as he takes a bottle from the top shelf of a metal cabinet filled with tools and spare parts. "It was some kind of brain thing. Well, you know what they say—in the midst of fuckin life we're in fuckin death." He pours bourbon into a cup with WORLD'S BEST HUGGER on the side, and lifts it. "Here's to ole Ducky." He drinks, smacks his lips, and raises the cup again. "And here's to you. Morrie Bellamy, out on the street again, rollin and trollin. What they got you doin? Some kind of paperwork'd be my guess."

Morris tells him about his job at the MAC, and makes chitchat while Roberson helps himself to another knock of bourbon. Morris doesn't envy Charlie his freedom to drink, he lost too many years of his life thanks to high-tension booze, but he feels Roberson will be more amenable to his request if he's a little high.

When he judges the time is right, he says, "You told me to come to you if I ever got out and needed a favor."

"True, true . . . but I never thought you'd get out. Not with that Jesus-jumper you nailed ridin you like a motherfuckin pony." Roberson chortles and pours himself a fresh shot.

"I need you to loan me a car, Charlie. Short-term. Not even twelve hours."

"When?"

"Tonight. Well . . . this evening. Tonight's when I need it. I can return it later on."

Roberson has stopped laughing. "That's a bigger risk than takin a drink, Morrie."

"Not for you; you're out, free and clear."

"No, not for me, I'd just get a slap on the wrist. But drivin without a license is a big parole violation. You might go back inside. Don't get me wrong, I'm willin to help you out, just want to be sure you understand the stakes."

"I understand them."

Roberson tops up his glass and sips it as he considers. Morris wouldn't want to be the owner of the bike Charlie is going to be putting back together once their little palaver is done.

At last Roberson says, "You be okay with a truck instead of a car? One I'm thinking of is a small panel job. And it's an auto-matic. Says 'Jones Flowers' on the side, but you can hardly read it anymore. It's out back. I'll show it to you, if you want."

Morris wants, and one look makes him decide the little black panel truck is a gift from God . . . assuming it runs all right. Rob-erson assures him that it does, even though it's on its second trip around the clock.

"I shut up shop early on Fridays. Around three. I could put in some gas and leave the keys under the right front tire."

"That's perfect," Morris says. He can go in to the MAC, tell his fat fuck of a boss that he had a stomach bug but it passed, work until four like a good little office drone, then come back out here. "Listen, the Groundhogs play tonight, don't they?"

"Yeah, they got the Dayton Dragons. Why? You hankerin to take in a game? Because I could be up for that."

"Another time, maybe. What I'm thinking is I could return the truck around ten, park it in the same place, then take a stadium bus back into town."

"Same old Morrie," Roberson says, and taps his temple. His eyes have become noticeably bloodshot. "You are one thinking cat."

"Remember to put the keys under the tire." The last thing Morris needs is for Roberson to get shitfaced on cheap bourbon and forget.

"I will. Owe you a lot, buddy. Owe you the motherfuckin *world*."

This sentiment necessitates another bro-hug, redolent of sweat, bourbon, and cheap aftershave. Roberson squeezes so tightly that Morris finds it hard to breathe, but at last he's released. He accompanies Charlie back into the garage, thinking that tonight—in twelve hours, maybe less—the Rothstein notebooks will once more be in his possession. With such an intoxicating prospect as that, who needs bourbon?

"You mind me asking why you're working here, Charlie? I thought you were going to get a boatload of cash from the state for false imprisonment."

"Aw, man, they threatened to bring up a bunch of old charges." Roberson resumes his seat in front of the Harley he's been working on. He picks up a wrench and taps it against the grease-smeared leg of his pants. "Including a bad one in Missouri, could have put me away down there for the rest of my life. Three-strikes rule or some shit. So we kinda worked out a trade."

He regards Morris with his bloodshot eyes, and in spite of his meaty biceps (it's clear he never lost the prison workout habit), Morris can see he's really old, and will soon be unhealthy, as well. If he isn't already.

"They fuck you in the end, buddy. Right up the ass. Rock the boat and they fuck you even harder. So you take what you can get. This is what I got, and it's enough for me."

"Shit don't mean shit," Morris says.

Roberson bellows laughter. "What you always said! And it's the fuckin truth!"

"Just don't forget to leave the keys."

"I'll leave em." Roberson levels a grease-blackened finger at Morris. "And don't get caught. Listen to your daddy."

I won't get caught, Morris thinks. I've waited too long.

"One other thing?"

Roberson waits for it.

"I don't suppose I could get a gun." Morris sees the look on Charlie's face and adds hastily, "Not to use, just as insurance."

Roberson shakes his head. "No gun. I'd get a lot more than a slap on the wrist for that."

"I'd never say it came from you."

The bloodshot eyes regard Morris shrewdly. "Can I be honest? You're too jail-bit for guns. Probably shoot yourself in the nut-sack. The truck, okay. I owe you that. But if you want a gun, find it somewhere else."

23

At three o'clock that Friday afternoon, Morris comes within a whisker of trashing twelve million dollars' worth of modern art.

Well, no, not really, but he *does* come close to erasing the records

241

of that art, which include the provenance and the background info on a dozen rich MAC donors. He's spent weeks creating a new search protocol that covers all of the Arts Center's acquisitions since the beginning of the twenty-first century. That protocol is a work of art in itself, and this afternoon, instead of sliding the biggest of the subfiles into the master file, he has moused it into the trash along with a lot of other dreck he needs to get rid of. The MAC's lumbering, outdated computer system is overloaded with useless shit, including a ton of stuff that's no longer even in the building. Said ton got moved to the Metropolitan Museum of Art in New York back in '05. Morris is on the verge of emptying the trash to make room for more dreck, his finger is actually on the trigger, when he realizes he's about to send a very valuable live file to data heaven.

For a moment he's back in Waynesville, trying to hide contraband before a rumored cell inspection, maybe nothing more dangerous than a snack-pack of Keebler cookies but enough to get him marked down if the screw is in a pissy mood. He looks at his finger, hovering less than an eighth of an inch over that damned delete button, and pulls his hand back to his chest, where he can feel his heart thumping fast and hard. What in God's name was he thinking?

His fat fuck of a boss chooses that moment to poke his head into Morris's closet-sized workspace. The cubicles where the other office drones spend their days are papered with pictures of boyfriends, girlfriends, families, even the fucking family dog, but Morris has put up nothing but a postcard of Paris, which he has always wanted to visit. Like *that's* ever going to happen.

"Everything all right, Morris?" the fat fuck asks.

"Fine," Morris says, praying that his boss won't come in and look at his screen. Although he probably wouldn't know what he was looking at. The obese bastard can send emails, he even seems to have a vague grasp of what Google is for, but beyond that he's lost. Yet he's living out in the suburbs with the wife and kiddies instead of in Bugshit Manor, where the crazies yell at invisible enemies in the middle of the night.

"Good to hear. Carry on."

Morris thinks, Carry your fat ass on out of here.

The fat fuck does, probably headed down to the canteen to feed his fat fuck face. When he's gone, Morris clicks on the trash icon, grabs what he almost deleted, and moves it back into the master file. This isn't much of an operation, but when it's finished he blows out his breath like a man who has just defused a bomb.

Where was your head? he scolds himself. What were you thinking?

Rhetorical questions. He was thinking about the Rothstein notebooks, now so close. Also about the little panel truck, and how scary it's going to feel, driving again after all those years inside. All he needs is one fender-bender . . . one cop who thinks he looks suspicious . . .

I have to keep it together a little longer, Morris thinks. I have to.

But his brain feels overloaded, running in the red zone. He thinks he'll be all right once the notebooks are actually in his possession (also the money, although that's far less important). Get those puppies hidden away at the back of the closet in his room on the ninth floor of Bugshit Manor and he can relax, but right now the stress is killing him. It's also being in a changed world and working an actual job and having a boss who doesn't wear a gray uniform but still has to be kowtowed to. On top of all that, there's the stress of having to drive an unregistered vehicle without a license tonight.

He thinks, By ten PM, things will be better. In the meantime, strap down and tighten up. Shit don't mean shit.

"Right," Morris whispers, and wipes a prickle of sweat from the skin between his mouth and nose.

## 24

At four o'clock he saves his work, closes out the apps he's been running, and shuts down. He walks into the MAC's plush lobby and standing there like a bad dream made real, feet apart and hands clasped behind his back, is Ellis McFarland. His PO is studying an Edward Hopper painting like the art aficionado he surely isn't.

Without turning (Morris realizes the man must have seen his reflection in the glass covering the painting, but it's still eerie), McFarland says, "Yo, Morrie. How you doin, homie?"

He knows, Morris thinks. Not just about the panel truck, either. About everything.

Not true, and he knows it isn't, but the part that's still in jail and always will be assures him it *is* true. To McFarland, Morris Bellamy's forehead is a pane of glass. Everything inside, every turning wheel and overheated whirling cog, is visible to him.

"I'm all right, Mr. McFarland."

Today McFarland is wearing a plaid sportcoat approximately the size of a living room rug. He looks Morris up and down, and when his eyes return to Morris's face, it's all Morris can do to hold them.

"You don't *look* all right. You're pale, and you got those dark whack-off circles under your eyes. Been using something you hadn't oughtta been using, Morrie?"

"No, sir."

"Doing something you hadn't oughtta be doing?"

"No." Thinking of the panel truck with JONES FLOWERS

still visible on the side, waiting for him on the South Side. The keys probably already under the tire.

"No what?"

"No, sir."

"Uh-huh. Maybe it's the flu. Because, frankly speaking, you look like ten pounds of shit in a five-pound bag."

"I almost made a mistake," Morris says. "It could have been rectified—probably—but it would have meant bringing in an outside I-T guy, maybe even shutting down the main server. I would have been in trouble."

"Welcome to the workaday world," McFarland says, with zero sympathy.

"Well, it's different for me!" Morris bursts out, and oh God, it's such a *relief* to burst out, and to do it about something safe. "If anyone should know that, it's you! Someone else who did that would just get a reprimand, but not me. And if they fired me—for a lapse in attention, not anything I did on purpose—I'd end up back inside."

"Maybe," McFarland says, turning back to the picture. It shows a man and a woman sitting in a room and apparently working hard not to look at each other. "Maybe not."

"My boss doesn't like me," Morris says. He knows he sounds like he's whining, probably he *is* whining. "I know four times as much as he does about how the computer system in this place works, and it pisses him off. He'd love to see me gone."

"You sound a weensy bit paranoid," McFarland says. His hands are again clasped above his truly awesome buttocks, and all at once Morris understands why McFarland is here. McFarland followed him to the motorcycle shop where Charlie Roberson works and has decided he's up to something. Morris knows this isn't so. He knows it is.

"What are they doing, anyway, letting a guy like me screw with their files? A parolee? If I do the wrong thing, and I almost did, I could cost them a lot of money."

"What did you think you'd be doing on the outside?" McFarland says, still examining the Hopper painting, which is called *Apartment 16-A*. He seems fascinated by it, but Morris isn't fooled. McFarland is watching his reflection again. Judging him. "You're too old and too soft to shift cartons in a warehouse or work on a gardening crew."

He turns around.

"It's called mainstreaming, Morris, and I didn't make the policy. If you want to wah-wah-wah about it, find somebody who gives a shit."

"Sorry," Morris says.

"Sorry *what?*"

"Sorry, Mr. McFarland."

"Thank you, Morris, that's better. Now let's step into the men's room, where you will pee in the little cup and prove to me that your paranoia isn't drug-induced."

The last stragglers of the office staff are leaving. Several glance at Morris and the big black man in the loud sportcoat, then quickly glance away. Morris feels an urge to shout *That's right, he's my parole officer, get a good look!*

He follows McFarland into the men's, which is empty, thank God. McFarland leans against the wall, arms crossed on his chest, watching as Morris unlimbers his elderly thingamajig and produces a urine sample. When it doesn't turn blue after thirty seconds, McFarland hands the little plastic cup back to Morris. "Congratulations. Dump that, homie."

Morris does. McFarland is washing his hands methodically, lathering all the way to his wrists.

"I don't have AIDS, you know. If that's what you're worried about. I had to take the test before they let me out."

McFarland carefully dries his big hands. He studies himself in the mirror for a moment (maybe wishing he had some hair to comb), then turns to Morris. "You may be substance-free, but I really don't like the way you look, Morrie."

Morris keeps silent.

"Let me tell you something eighteen years in this job has taught me. There are two types of parolees, and two only: wolves and lambs. You're too old to be a wolf, but I'm not entirely sure you're hip to that. You may not have *internalized* it, as the shrinks say. I don't know what wolfish shit you might have on your mind, maybe it's nothing more than stealing paper clips from the supply room, but whatever it is, you need to forget about it. You're too old to howl and *much* too old to run."

Having imparted this bit of wisdom, he leaves. Morris heads for the door himself, but his legs turn to rubber before he can get there. He wheels around, grasps a washbasin to keep from falling, and blunders into one of the stalls. There he sits down and lowers his head until it almost touches his knees. He closes his eyes and takes long deep breaths. When the roaring in his head subsides, he gets up and leaves.

He'll still be here, Morris thinks. Staring at that damned picture with his hands clasped behind his back.

But this time the lobby is empty save for the security guard, who gives Morris a suspicious look as he passes.

25

The Hogs-Dragons game doesn't start until seven, but the buses with BASEBALL GAME 2NITE in their destination windows start running at five. Morris takes one to the park, then walks back to Statewide Motorcycle, aware of each car that passes and cursing himself for losing his shit in the men's room after McFarland departed. If he'd gotten out sooner, maybe he could have seen what the sonofabitch was driving. But he didn't, and now any one of these cars might be McFarland's. The PO would be easy enough to spot, given the size of him, but Morris doesn't dare look at any of the passing cars too closely. There are two reasons for this. First, he'd look guilty, wouldn't he? Yes indeed, like a man who's got wolfish shit on his mind and has to keep checking his perimeter. Second, he might see McFarland even if McFarland isn't there, because he's edging ever closer to a nervous breakdown. It isn't surprising, either. A man could only stand so much stress.

*What are you, twenty-two?* Rothstein had asked him. *Twenty-three?*

That was a good guess by an observant man. Morris *had* been twenty-three. Now he's on the cusp of sixty, and the years between have disappeared like smoke in a breeze. He has heard people say sixty is the new forty, but that's bullshit. When you've spent most of your life in prison, sixty is the new seventy-five. Or eighty. Too old to be a wolf, according to McFarland.

Well, we'll see about that, won't we?

He turns into the yard of Statewide Motorcycle—the shades pulled, the bikes that were out front this morning locked away—and expects to hear a car door slam behind him the moment he transgresses private property. Expects to hear McFarland saying *Yo, homie, what you doing in there?*

But the only sound is the traffic passing on the way to the stadium, and when he gets around to the back lot, the invisible band that's been constricting his chest eases a little. There's a high wall of corrugated metal cutting off this patch of yard from the rest of the world, and walls comfort Morris. He doesn't like that, knows it isn't natural, but there it is. A man is the sum of his experiences.

He goes to the panel truck—small, dusty, blessedly nondescript—and feels beneath the right front tire. The keys are there. He gets in, and is gratified when the engine starts on the first crank. The radio comes on in a blare of rock. Morris snaps it off.

"I can do this," he says, first adjusting the seat and then gripping the wheel. "I can do this."

And, it turns out, he can. It's like riding a bike. The only hard part is turning against the stream of traffic headed for the stadium, and even that isn't too bad; after a minute's wait, one of the BASE-BALL GAME 2NITE buses stops, and the driver waves for Morris to go. The northbound lanes are nearly empty, and he's able to avoid downtown by using the new city bypass. He almost enjoys driving again. *Would* enjoy it, if not for the nagging suspicion that McFarland is tailing him. Not busting him yet, though; he won't do that until he sees what his old pal—his *homie*—is up to.

Morris stops at the Bellows Avenue Mall and goes into Home Depot. He strolls around beneath the glaring fluorescents, taking his time; he can't do his business until after dark, and in June the evening light lasts until eight thirty or nine. In the gardening section he buys a spade and also a hatchet, in case he has to chop some roots—that tree overhanging the bank looks like it might have his trunk in a pretty tight grip. In the aisle marked CLEARANCE, he grabs a pair of Tuff Tote duffels, on sale for twenty bucks each. He stows his purchases in the back of the truck and heads around to the driver's door.

"Hey!" From behind him.

Morris freezes, listening to the approaching footsteps and waiting for McFarland to grab his shoulder.

"Do you know if there's a supermarket in this mall?"

The voice is young. And white. Morris discovers he can breathe again. "Safeway," he says, without turning. He has no idea if there's a supermarket in the mall or not.

"Oh. Okay. Thanks."

Morris gets into the truck and starts the engine. *I can do this,* he thinks.

*I can and I will.*

## 26

Morris cruises slowly through the Northfield tree streets that were his old stomping grounds—not that he ever did much stomping; usually he had his nose in a book. It's still too early, so he parks on Elm for awhile. There's a dusty old map in the glove compartment, and he pretends to read it. After twenty minutes or so, he drives over to Maple and does the same thing. Then down to the local Zoney's Go-Mart, where he bought snacks as a kid. Also cigarettes for his father. That was back in the day when a pack cost forty cents and kids buying smokes for their parents was taken for granted. He gets a Slushie and makes it last. Then he moves onto Palm Street and goes back to pretend map reading. The shadows are lengthening, but oh so slowly.

*Should have brought a book,* he thinks, then thinks *No*—a man with a map looks okay, somehow, but a man reading a book in an old truck would probably look like a potential child molester.

*Is that paranoid or smart?* He can no longer tell. All he knows for sure is that the notebooks are close now. They're pinging like a sonar blip.

Little by little, the long light of this June evening mellows to dusk. The kids who've been playing on sidewalks and front lawns go inside to watch TV or play video games or spend an educational evening texting various misspelled messages and dumbass emoticons to their friends.

Confident that McFarland is nowhere near (although not *completely* confident), Morris keys the panel truck's engine and drives slowly to his final destination: the Birch Street Rec, where he used to go when the Garner Street branch of the library was closed. Skinny, bookish, with a regrettable tendency to run his mouth, he rarely got picked for the outdoor games, and almost always got yelled at on the few occasions when he did: hey butterfingers, hey dumbo, hey fumblebutt. Because of his red lips, he earned the nickname Revlon. When he went to the Rec, he mostly stayed indoors, reading or maybe putting together a jigsaw puzzle. Now the city has shut the old brick building down and put it up for sale in the wake of municipal budget cuts.

A few boys toss up a few final baskets on the weedy courts out back, but there are no longer outside lights and they beat feet when it's too dark to see, yelling and dribbling and shooting passes back and forth. When they're gone, Morris starts the truck and pulls into the driveway running alongside the building. He does it without turning on his headlights, and the little black truck is exactly the right color for this kind of work. He snuggles it up to the rear of the building, where a faded sign still reads RESERVED FOR REC DEPT. VEHICLES. He kills the engine, gets out, and smells the June air, redolent of grass and clover. He can hear crickets, and the drone of traffic on the city bypass, but otherwise the newly fallen night is his.

Fuck you, Mr. McFarland, he thinks. Fuck you very much.

He gets his tools and Tuff Totes from the back of the truck and starts toward the tangle of unimproved ground beyond the baseball field where he dropped so many easy pop flies. Then an idea strikes him and he turns back. He braces a palm on the old brick, still warm from the heat of the day, slides down to a crouch, and pulls some weeds so he can peer through one of the basement windows. These haven't been boarded up. The moon has just risen, orange and full. It lends enough light for him to see folding chairs, card tables, and heaps of boxes.

Morris has planned on bringing the notebooks back to his room in Bugshit Manor, but that's risky; Mr. McFarland can search his room anytime he pleases, it's part of the deal. The Rec is a lot closer to where the notebooks are buried, and the basement, where all sorts of useless bric-a-brac has already been stored, would be the perfect hiding place. It might be possible to rathole most of them here, only taking a few at a time back to his room, where he could read them. Morris is skinny enough to fit through this window, although he might have to wriggle a bit, and how hard could it be to bust the thumb-lock he sees on the inside of the window and pry it up? A screwdriver would probably do the trick. He doesn't have one, but there are plenty at Home Depot. He even saw a small display of tools when he was in Zoney's.

He leans closer to the dirty window, studying it. He knows to look for alarm tapes (the state penitentiary is a very educational place when it comes to breaking and entering), but he doesn't see any. Only suppose the alarm uses contact points, instead? He wouldn't see those, and he might not hear the alarm, either. Some of them are silent.

Morris looks a little longer, then reluctantly gets to his feet. It doesn't seem likely to him that an old building like this one is alarmed—the valuable stuff has no doubt been moved elsewhere long ago—but he doesn't dare take the chance.

Better to stick with the original plan.

He grabs his tools and his duffel bags and once more starts for the overgrown waste ground, careful to skirt the ballfield. He's not going there, uh-uh, no way. The moon will help him once he's in the undergrowth, but out in the open, the world looks like a brightly lighted stage.

The potato chip bag that helped him last time is gone, and it takes awhile to find the path again. Morris beats back and forth through the undergrowth beyond right field (the site of several childhood humiliations), finally rediscovers it, and sets off. When he hears the faint chuckle of the stream, he has to restrain himself from breaking into a run.

Times have been hard, he thinks. There could be people sleeping in here, homeless people. If one of them sees me—

If one of them sees him, he'll use the hatchet. No hesitation. Mr. McFarland may think he's too old to be a wolf, but what his parole officer doesn't know is that Morris has already killed three people, and driving a car isn't the only thing that's like riding a bike.

### 27

The trees are runty, choking each other in their struggle for space and sun, but they are tall enough to filter the moonlight. Two or three times Morris loses the path and blunders around, trying to find it again. This actually pleases him. He has the sound of the stream to guide him if he really does lose his way, and the path's faintness confirms that fewer kids use it now than back in his day. Morris just hopes he's not walking through poison ivy.

The sound of the stream is very close when he finds the path for the last time, and less than five minutes later, he's standing on the bank opposite the landmark tree. He stops there for a bit in the moon-dappled shade, looking for any sign of human habitation: blankets, a sleeping bag, a shopping cart, a piece of plastic draped over branches to create a makeshift tent. There's nothing. Just the water purling along in its stony bed, and the tree tilting over the far side of the stream. The tree that has faithfully guarded his treasure all these years.

"Good old tree," Morris whispers, and steps his way across the stream.

He kneels and puts aside the tools and the duffel bags for a moment of meditation. "Here I am," he whispers, and places his palms on the ground, as if feeling for a heartbeat.

And it seems that he *does* feel one. It's the heartbeat of John Rothstein's genius. The old man turned Jimmy Gold into a sellout joke, but who can say Rothstein didn't redeem Jimmy during his years of solitary composition? If he did that . . . *if* . . . then everything Morris has gone through has been worthwhile.

"Here I am, Jimmy. Here I finally am."

He grabs the spade and begins digging. It doesn't take long to get to the trunk again, but the roots have embraced it, all right, and it's almost an hour before Morris can chop through enough of them to pull it out. It's been years since he did hard manual labor, and he's exhausted. He thinks of all the cons he knew— Charlie Roberson, for example—who worked out constantly, and how he sneered at them for what he considered obsessive-compulsive behavior (in his mind, at least; never on his face). He's not sneering now. His thighs ache, his back aches, and worst of all, his head is throbbing like an infected tooth. A little breeze has sprung up, which cools the sweat sliming his skin, but it also causes the branches to sway, creating moving shadows that make him afraid. They make him think of McFarland again. McFarland making his way up the path, moving with the eerie quiet some big men, soldiers and ex-athletes, mostly, are able to manage.

When he's got his breath and his heartbeat has slowed a little, Morris reaches for the handle at the end of the trunk and finds it's no longer there. He leans forward on his splayed palms, peering into the hole, wishing he'd remembered to bring a flashlight.

The handle *is* still there, only it's hanging in two pieces.

That's not right, Morris thinks. Is it?

He casts his mind back across all those years, trying to remember if either trunk handle was broken. He doesn't think so. In fact, he's almost sure. But then he remembers tipping the trunk endwise in the garage, and exhales a sigh of relief strong enough to puff out his cheeks. It must have broken when he put the trunk on the dolly. Or maybe while he was bumping and thumping his way along the path to this very location. He had dug the hole in a hurry and muscled the trunk in as fast as he could. Wanting to get out of there and much too busy to notice a little thing like a broken handle. That was it. Had to be. After all, the trunk hadn't been new when he bought it.

He grasps the sides, and the trunk slides out of its hole so easily that Morris overbalances and flops on his back. He lies there, staring up at the bright bowl of the moon, and tries to tell himself nothing is wrong. Only he knows better. He might be able to talk himself out of the broken handle, but not out of this new thing.

The trunk is too light.

Morris scrambles back to a sitting position with smears of dirt now sticking to his damp skin. He brushes his hair off his forehead with a shaking hand, leaving a fresh streak.

The trunk is too light.

He reaches for it, then draws back.

I can't, he thinks. I can't. If I open it and the notebooks aren't there, I'll just . . . *snap*.

But why would anyone take a bunch of notebooks? The money, yes, but the notebooks? There wasn't even any space left to write in most of them; in most, Rothstein had used it all.

What if someone took the money and then *burned* the notebooks? Not understanding their incalculable value, just wanting to get rid of something a thief might see as evidence?

"No," Morris whispers. "No one would do that. They're still in there. They have to be."

But the trunk is too light.

He stares at it, a small exhumed coffin tilted on the bank in the moonlight. Behind it is the hole, gaping like a mouth that has just vomited something up. Morris reaches for the trunk again, hesitates, then lunges forward and snaps the latches up, praying to a God he knows cares nothing for the likes of him.

He looks in.

The trunk is not quite empty. The plastic he lined it with is still there. He pulls it out in a crackling cloud, hoping that a few of the notebooks are left underneath—two or three, or oh please God even just one—but there are just a few small trickles of dirt caught in the corners.

Morris puts his filthy hands to his face—once young, now deeply lined—and begins to cry in the moonlight.


28


He promised to return the truck by ten, but it's after midnight when he parks it behind Statewide Motorcycle and puts the keys back under the right front tire. He doesn't bother with the tools or the empty Tuff Totes that were supposed to be full; let Charlie Roberson have them if he wants them.

The lights of the minor league field four blocks over have been turned off an hour ago. The stadium buses have stopped running, but the bars—in this neighborhood there are a lot of them—are roaring away with live bands and jukebox music, their doors open, men and women in Groundhogs tee-shirts and caps standing out on the sidewalks, smoking cigarettes and drinking from plastic cups. Morris plods past them without looking, ignoring a couple of friendly yells from inebriated baseball fans, high on beer and a home team win, asking him if he wants a drink. Soon the bars are behind him.

He has stopped obsessing about McFarland, and the thought of the three mile walk back to Bugshit Manor never crosses his mind. He doesn't care about his aching legs, either. It's as if they belong to someone else. He feels as empty as that old trunk in the moonlight. Everything he's lived for during the last thirty-six years has been swept away like a shack in a flood.

He comes to Government Square, and that's where his legs finally give out. He doesn't so much sit on one of the benches as collapse there. He glances around dully at the empty expanse of concrete, realizing that he'd probably look mighty suspicious to any cops passing in a squad car. He's not supposed to be out this late anyway (like a teenager, he has a *curfew*), but what does that matter? Shit don't mean shit. Let them send him back to Waynesville. Why not? At least there he won't have to deal with his fat fuck boss anymore. Or pee while Ellis McFarland watches.

Across the street is the Happy Cup, where he had so many pleasant conversations about books with Andrew Halliday. Not to mention their *last* conversation, which was far from pleasant. *Stay clear of me,* Andy had said. That was how the last conversation had ended.

Morris's brains, which have been idling in neutral, suddenly engage again and the dazed look in his eyes begins to clear. *Stay clear of me or I'll call the police myself,* Andy had said . . . but that wasn't *all* he said that day. His old pal had also given him some advice.

*Hide them somewhere. Bury them.*

Had Andy Halliday really said that, or was it only his imagination?

"He said it," Morris whispers. He looks at his hands and sees they have rolled themselves into grimy fists. "He said it, all right. Hide them, he said. *Bury* them." Which leads to certain questions.

Like who was the only person who knew he had the Rothstein notebooks?

Like who was the only person who had actually *seen* one of the Rothstein notebooks?

Like who knew where he had lived in the old days?

And—here was a big one—who knew about that stretch of undeveloped land, an overgrown couple of acres caught in an endless lawsuit and used only by kids cutting across to the Birch Street Rec?

The answer to all these questions is the same.

*Maybe we can revisit this in ten years,* his old pal had said. *Maybe in twenty.*

Well, it had been a fuck of a lot longer than ten or twenty, hadn't it? Time had gone slip-sliding away. Enough for his old pal to meditate on those valuable notebooks, which had never turned up—not when Morris was arrested for rape and not later on, when the house was sold.

Had his old pal at some point decided to visit Morris's old neighborhood? Perhaps to stroll any number of times along the path between Sycamore Street and Birch? Had he perhaps made those strolls with a metal detector, hoping it would sense the trunk's metal fittings and start to beep?

Did Morris even *mention* the trunk that day?

Maybe not, but what else could it be? What else made sense? Even a large strongbox would be too small. Paper or canvas bags would have rotted. Morris wonders how many holes Andy had to dig before he finally hit paydirt. A dozen? Four dozen? Four dozen was a lot, but back in the seventies, Andy had been fairly trim, not a waddling fat fuck like he was now. And the motivation would have been there. Or maybe he didn't have to dig any holes at all. Maybe there had been a spring flood or something, and the bank had eroded enough to reveal the trunk in its cradle of roots. Wasn't that possible?

Morris gets up and walks on, now thinking about McFarland again and occasionally glancing around to make sure he isn't there. It matters again now, because now he has something to live for again. A goal. It's possible that his old pal has sold the notebooks, selling is his business as sure as it was Jimmy Gold's in *The Runner Slows Down*, but it's just as possible that he's still sitting on some or all of them. There's only one sure way to find out, and only one way to find out if the old wolf still has some teeth. He has to pay his *homie* a visit.

His old pal.

# PART 3: PETER AND THE WOLF

# 1

It's Saturday afternoon in the city, and Hodges is at the movies with Holly. They engage in a lively negotiation while looking at the showtimes in the lobby of the AMC City Center 7. His suggestion of *The Purge: Anarchy* is rejected as too scary. Holly enjoys scary movies, she says, but only on her computer, where she can pause the film and walk around for a few minutes to release the tension. Her counter-suggestion of *The Fault in Our Stars* is rejected by Hodges, who says it will be too sentimental. What he actually means is too emotional. A story about someone dying young will make him think of Janey Patterson, who left the world in an explosion meant to kill him. They settle on *22 Jump Street*, a comedy with Jonah Hill and Channing Tatum. It's pretty good. They laugh a lot and share a big tub of popcorn, but Hodges's mind keeps returning to Tina's story about the money that helped her parents through the bad years. Where in God's name could Peter Saubers have gotten his hands on over twenty thousand dollars?

As the credits are rolling, Holly puts her hand over Hodges's, and he is a little alarmed to see tears standing in her eyes. He asks her what's wrong.

"Nothing. It's just nice to have someone to go to the movies with. I'm glad you're my friend, Bill."

Hodges is more than touched. "And I'm glad you're mine. What are you going to do with the rest of your Saturday?"

"Tonight I'm going to order in Chinese and binge on *Orange Is the New Black*," she says. "But this afternoon I'm going online to look at more robberies. I've already got quite a list."

"Do any of them look likely to you?"

She shakes her head. "I'm going to keep looking, but I think it's something else, although I don't have any idea what it could be. Do you think Tina's brother will tell you?"

At first he doesn't answer. They're making their way up the aisle, and soon they'll be away from this oasis of make-believe and back in the real world.

"Bill? Earth to Bill?"

"I certainly hope so," he says at last. "For his own sake. Because money from nowhere almost always spells trouble."

2

Tina and Barbara and Barbara's mother spend that Saturday afternoon in the Robinson kitchen, making popcorn balls, an operation both messy and hilarious. They are having a blast, and for the first time since she came to visit, Tina doesn't seem troubled. Tanya Robinson thinks that's good. She doesn't know what the deal is with Tina, but a dozen little things—like the way the girl jumps when a draft slams an upstairs door shut, or the suspicious I've-been-crying redness of her eyes—tells Tanya that something is wrong. She doesn't know if that something is big or little, but one thing she's sure of: Tina Saubers can use a little hilarity in her life just about now.

They are finishing up—and threatening each other with syrup-sticky hands—when an amused voice says, "Look at all these womenfolk dashing around the kitchen. I do declare."

Barbara whirls, sees her brother leaning in the kitchen doorway, and screams "*Jerome!*" She runs to him and leaps. He catches her, whirls her around twice, and sets her down.

"I thought you were going to a *cotillion!*"

Jerome smiles. "Alas, my tux went back to the rental place unworn. After a full and fair exchange of views, Priscilla and I have agreed to break up. It's a long story, and not very interesting. Anyway, I decided to drive home and get some of my ma's cooking."

"Don't call me Ma," Tanya says. "It's vulgar." But she also looks mightily pleased to see Jerome.

He turns to Tina and gives a small bow. "Pleased to meet you, little ma'am. Any friend of Barbara's, and so forth."

"I'm Tina."

She manages to say this in a tone of voice that's almost normal, but doing so isn't easy. Jerome is tall, Jerome is broad-shouldered, Jerome is extremely handsome, and Tina Saubers falls in love with him immediately. Soon she will be calculating how old she'll need to be before he might look upon her as something more than a little ma'am in an oversized apron, her hands all sticky from making popcorn balls. For the time being, however, she's too stunned by his beauty to run the numbers. And later that evening, it doesn't take much urging from Barbara for Tina to tell him everything. Although it's not always easy for her to keep her place in the story, with his dark eyes on her.

3

Pete's Saturday afternoon isn't nearly as good. In fact, it's fairly shitty.

At two o'clock, class officers and officers-elect from three high schools crowd into the River Bend Resort's largest conference room to listen as one of the state's two U.S. senators gives a long and boring talk titled "High School Governance: Your Introduction to Politics and Service." This fellow, who's wearing a three-piece suit and sporting a luxuriant, swept-back head of white hair (what Pete thinks of as "soap opera villain hair"), seems ready to go on until dinnertime. Possibly longer. His thesis seems to be something about how they are the NEXT GENERATION, and being class officers will prepare them to deal with pollution, global warming, diminishing resources, and, perhaps, first contact with aliens from Proxima Centauri. Each minute of this endless Saturday afternoon dies a slow and miserable death as he drones on.

Pete couldn't care less about assuming the mantle of student vice president at Northfield High this coming September. As far as he's concerned, September might as well be out there on Proxima Centauri with the aliens. The only future that matters is this coming Monday afternoon, when he will confront Andrew Halliday, a man he now wishes most heartily that he had never met.

But I can work my way out of this, he thinks. If I can hold my nerve, that is. And keep in mind what Jimmy Gold's elderly aunt says in *The Runner Raises the Flag*.

Pete has decided he'll begin his conversation with Halliday by quoting that line: *They say half a loaf is better than none, Jimmy, but in a world of want, even a single slice is better than none.*

Pete knows what *Halliday* wants, and will offer more than a single slice, but not half a loaf, and certainly not the whole thing. That is simply not going to happen. With the notebooks safely hidden away in the basement of the Birch Street Rec, he can afford to negotiate, and if Halliday wants anything at all out of this, he'll have to negotiate, too.

No more ultimatums.

*I'll give you three dozen notebooks,* Pete imagines saying. *They contain poems, essays, and nine complete short stories. I'm even going to split fifty-fifty, just to be done with you.*

He *has* to insist on getting money, although with no way of verifying how much Halliday actually receives from his buyer or buyers, Pete supposes he'll be cheated out of his fair share, and cheated badly. But that's okay. The important thing is making sure Halliday knows he's serious. That he's not going to be, in Jimmy Gold's pungent phrase, anyone's birthday fuck. Even more important is not letting Halliday see how scared he is.

How terrified.

The senator winds up with a few ringing phrases about how the VITAL WORK of the NEXT GENERATION begins in AMERICA'S HIGH SCHOOLS, and how they, the chosen few, must carry forward THE TORCH OF DEMOCRACY. The applause is enthusiastic, possibly because the lecture is finally over and they get to leave. Pete wants desperately to get out of here, go for a long walk, and check his plan a few more times, looking for loopholes and stumbling blocks.

Only they don't get to leave. The high school principal who has arranged this afternoon's endless chat with greatness steps forward to announce that the senator has agreed to stay another hour and answer their questions. "I'm sure you have lots," she says, and the hands of the butt-lickers and grade-grubbers—there seem to be plenty of both in attendance—shoot up immediately.

Pete thinks, This shit don't mean shit.

He looks at the door, calculates his chances of slipping through it without being noticed, and settles back into his seat. A week from now, all this will be over, he tells himself.

The thought brings him some comfort.

4

A certain recent parolee wakes up as Hodges and Holly are leaving their movie and Tina is falling in love with Barbara's brother. Morris has slept all morning and part of the afternoon following a wakeful, fretful night, only dropping off as the first light of that Saturday morning began to creep into his room. His dreams have been worse than bad. In the one that woke him, he opened the trunk to find it full of black widow spiders, thousands of them, all entwined and gorged with poison and pulsing in the moonlight. They came streaming out, pouring over his hands and glittering up his arms.

Morris gasps and chokes his way back into the real world, hugging his chest so tightly he can barely breathe.

He swings his legs out of bed and sits there with his head down, the same way he sat on the toilet after McFarland exited the MAC men's room the previous afternoon. It's the not knowing that's killing him, and that uncertainty cannot be laid to rest too soon.

Andy *must* have taken them, he thinks. Nothing else makes sense. And you better still have them, pal. God help you if you don't.

He puts on a fresh pair of jeans and takes a crosstown bus over to the South Side, because he's decided he wants at least one of his tools, after all. He'll also take back the Tuff Totes. Because you had to think positive.

Charlie Roberson is once more seated in front of the Harley, now so torn down it hardly looks like a motorcycle at all. He doesn't seem terribly pleased at this reappearance of the man who helped get him out of jail. "How'd it go last night? Did you do what you needed to do?"

"Everything's fine," Morris says, and offers a smile that feels too wide and loose to be convincing. "Four-oh."

Roberson doesn't smile back. "As long as *five*-o isn't involved. You don't look so great, Morrie."

"Well, you know. Things rarely get taken care of all at once. I've got a few more details to iron out."

"If you need the truck again—"

"No, no. I left a couple of things in it, is all. Okay if I grab them?"

"It's nothing that's going to come back on me later, is it?"

"Absolutely not. Just a couple of bags."

And the hatchet, but he neglects to mention that. He could buy a knife, but there's something scary about a hatchet. Morris drops it into one of the Tuff Totes, tells Charlie so long, and heads back to the bus stop. The hatchet slides back and forth in the bag with each swing of his arms.

*Don't make me use it,* he will tell Andy. *I don't want to hurt you.*

But of course part of him *does* want to use it. Part of him *does* want to hurt his old pal. Because—notebooks aside—he's owed a payback, and payback's a bitch.

5

Lacemaker Lane and the walking mall of which it is a part is busy
on this Saturday afternoon. There are hundreds of shops with cutie-
poo names like Deb and Buckle and Forever 21. There's also one
called Lids, which sells nothing but hats. Morris stops in there and
buys a Groundhogs cap with an extra-long brim. A little closer to
Andrew Halliday Rare Editions, he stops again and purchases a
pair of shades at a Sunglass Hut kiosk.

Just as he spots the sign of his old pal's business establishment,
with its scrolled gold leaf lettering, a dismaying thought occurs
to him: what if Andy closes early on Saturday? All the other shops
seem to be open, but some rare bookstores keep lazy hours, and
wouldn't that be just his luck?

But when he walks past, swinging the totes (*clunk* and *bump*
goes the hatchet), secure behind his new shades, he sees the OPEN
sign hanging in the door. He sees something else, as well: cameras peeking left and right along the sidewalk. There are probably
more inside, too, but that's okay; Morris has done decades of post-
graduate work with thieves.

He idles up the street, looking in the window of a bakery and
scanning the wares of a souvenir vendor's cart (although Morris
can't imagine who'd want a souvenir of this dirty little lakefront
city). He even pauses to watch a mime who juggles colored balls
and then pretends to climb invisible stairs. Morris tosses a couple
of quarters into the mime's hat. For good luck, he tells himself.
Pop music pours down from streetcorner loudspeakers. There's a
smell of chocolate in the air.

He walks back. He sees a couple of young men come out of
Andy's bookshop and head off down the sidewalk. This time

Morris pauses to look in the display window, where three books are open on stands beneath pinspots: *To Kill a Mockingbird*, *The Catcher in the Rye*, and—surely it's an omen—*The Runner Sees Action*. The shop beyond the window is narrow and high-ceilinged. He sees no other customers, but he *does* see his old pal, the one and only Andy Halliday, sitting at the desk halfway down, reading a paperback.

Morris pretends to tie his shoe and unzips the Tuff Tote with the hatchet inside. Then he stands and, with no hesitation, opens the door of Andrew Halliday Rare Editions.

His old pal looks up from his book and scopes the sunglasses, the long-brimmed cap, the tote bags. He frowns, but only a little, because *everyone* in this area is carrying bags, and the day is warm and bright. Morris sees caution but no signs of real alarm, which is good.

"Would you mind putting your bags under the coatrack?" Andy asks. He smiles. "Store policy."

"Not at all," Morris says. He puts the Tuff Totes down, removes his sunglasses, folds the bows, and slides them into his shirt pocket. Then he takes off his new hat and runs a hand through the short scruff of his white hair. He thinks, *See? Just an elderly geezer who's come in to get out of the hot sun and do a little browsing. Nothing to worry about here.* "Whew! It's hot outside today." He puts his cap back on.

"Yes, and they say tomorrow's going to be even hotter. Can I help you with something special?"

"Just browsing. Although . . . I *have* been looking for a rather rare book called *The Executioners*. It's by a mystery novelist named John D. MacDonald." MacDonald's books were very popular in the prison library.

"Know him well!" Andy says jovially. "Wrote all those Travis

McGee stories. The ones with colors in the titles. Paperback writer for the most part, wasn't he? I don't deal in paperbacks, as a rule; very few of collectible quality."

What about notebooks? Morris thinks. Moleskines, to be specific. Do you deal in those, you fat, thieving fuck?

"*The Executioners* was published in hardcover," he says, examining a shelf of books near the door. He wants to stay close to the door for the time being. And the bag with the hatchet in it. "It was the basis of a movie called *Cape Fear*. I'd buy a copy of that, if you happened to have one in mint condition. What I believe you people call very fine as new. And if the price was right, of course."

Andy looks engaged now, and why not? He has a fish on the line. "I'm sure I don't have it in stock, but I could check Book-Finder for you. That's a database. If it's listed, and a MacDonald hardcover probably is, especially if it was made into a film . . . *and* if it's a first edition . . . I could probably have it for you by Tuesday. Wednesday at the latest. Would you like me to look?"

"I would," Morris says. "But the price has to be right."

"Naturally, naturally." Andy's chuckle is as fat as his gut. He lowers his eyes to the screen of his laptop. As soon as he does this, Morris flips the sign hanging in the door from OPEN to CLOSED. He bends down and takes the hatchet from the open duffel bag. He moves up the narrow central aisle with it held beside his leg. He doesn't hurry. He doesn't have to hurry. Andy is clicking away at his laptop and absorbed by whatever he's seeing on the screen.

"Found it!" his old pal exclaims. "James Graham has one, very fine as new, for just three hundred dol—"

He ceases speaking as the blade of the hatchet floats first into his peripheral vision, then front and center. He looks up, his face slack with shock.

"I want your hands where I can see them," Morris says. "There's probably an alarm button in the kneehole of your desk. If you want to keep all your fingers, don't reach for it."

"What do you want? Why are you—"

"Don't recognize me, do you?" Morris doesn't know whether to be amused by this or infuriated. "Not even right up close and personal."

"No, I . . . I . . ."

"Not surprising, I guess. It's been a long time since the Happy Cup, hasn't it?"

Halliday stares into Morris's lined and haggard face with dreadful fascination. Morris thinks, He's like a bird looking at a snake. This is a pleasant thought, and makes him smile.

"Oh my God," Andy says. His face has gone the color of old cheese. "It can't be you. You're in jail."

Morris shakes his head, still smiling. "There's probably a database for parolees as well as rare books, but I'm guessing you never checked it. Good for me, not so good for you."

One of Andy's hands is creeping away from the keyboard of his laptop. Morris wiggles the hatchet.

"Don't do that, Andy. I want to see your hands on either side of your computer, palms down. Don't try to hit the button with your knee, either. I'll know if you try, and the consequences for you will be unpleasant in the extreme."

"What do you want?"

The question makes him angry, but his smile widens. "As if you don't know."

"I don't, Morrie, my God!" Andy's mouth is lying but his eyes tell the truth, the whole truth, and nothing but the truth.

"Let's go in your office. I'm sure you have one back there."

"No!"

Morris wiggles the hatchet again. "You can come out of this

whole and intact, or with some of your fingers lying on the desk. Believe me on this, Andy. I'm not the man you knew."

Andy gets up, his eyes never leaving Morris's face, but Morris isn't sure his old pal is actually seeing him anymore. He sways as if to invisible music, on the verge of passing out. If he does that, he won't be able to answer questions until he comes around. Also, Morris would have to *drag* him to the office. He's not sure he can do that; if Andy doesn't tip the scales at three hundred, he's got to be pushing it.

"Take a deep breath," he says. "Calm down. All I want is a few answers. Then I'm gone."

"You promise?" Andy's lower lip is pushed out, shining with spit. He looks like a fat little boy who's in dutch with his father.

"Yes. Now breathe."

Andy breathes.

"Again."

Andy's massive chest rises, straining the buttons of his shirt, then lowers. A bit of his color comes back.

"Office. Now. Do it."

Andy turns and lumbers to the back of the store, weaving his way between boxes and stacks of books with the finicky grace some fat men possess. Morris follows. His anger is growing. It's something about the girlish flex and sway of Andy's buttocks, clad in gray gabardine trousers, that fuels it.

There's a keypad beside the door. Andy punches in four numbers—9118—and a green light flashes. As he enters, Morris reads his mind right through the back of his bald head.

"You're not quick enough to slam the door on me. If you try, you're going to lose something that can't be replaced. Count on it."

Andy's shoulders, which have risen as he tenses to make just this attempt, slump again. He steps in. Morris follows and closes the door.

The office is small, lined with stuffed bookshelves, lit by hanging globes. On the floor is a Turkish rug. The desk in here is much nicer—mahogany or teak or some other expensive wood. On it is a lamp with a shade that looks like real Tiffany glass. To the left of the door is a sideboard with four heavy crystal decanters on it. Morris doesn't know about the two containing clear liquid, but he bets the others hold scotch and bourbon. The good stuff, too, if he knows his old pal. For toasting big sales, no doubt.

Morris remembers the only kinds of booze available in the joint, prunejack and raisinjack, and even though he only imbibed on rare occasions like his birthday (and John Rothstein's, which he always marked with a single jolt), his anger grows. Good booze to drink and good food to gobble—that's what Andy Halliday had while Morris was dyeing bluejeans, inhaling varnish fumes, and living in a cell not much bigger than a coffin. He was in the joint for rape, true enough, but he never would have been in that alley, in a furious drunken blackout, if this man had not denied him and sent him packing. *Morris, I shouldn't even be seen with you.* That's what he said that day. And then called him batshit-crazy.

"Luxy accommodations, my friend."

Andy looks around as if noting the luxy accommodations for the first time. "It looks that way," he admits, "but appearances can be deceiving, Morrie. The truth is, I'm next door to broke. This place never came back from the recession, and from certain . . . allegations. You have to believe that."

Morris rarely thinks about the money envelopes Curtis Rogers found along with the notebooks in Rothstein's safe that night, but he thinks about them now. His old pal got the cash as well as the notebooks. For all Morris knows, that money paid for the desk, and the rug, and the fancy crystal decanters of booze.

At this, the balloon of rage finally bursts and Morris slings the hatchet in a low sideways arc, his cap tumbling from his head. The hatchet bites through gray gabardine and buries itself in the bloated buttock beneath with a *chump* sound. Andy screams and stumbles forward. He breaks his fall on the edge of his desk with his forearms, then goes to his knees. Blood pours through a six-inch slit in his pants. He claps a hand over it and more blood runs through his fingers. He falls on his side, then rolls over on the Turkish rug. With some satisfaction, Morris thinks, You'll never get *that* stain out, homie.

Andy squalls, "You said you wouldn't hurt me!"

Morris considers this and shakes his head. "I don't believe I ever said that in so many words, although I suppose I might have implied it." He stares into Andy's contorted face with serious sincerity. "Think of it as DIY liposuction. And you can still come out of this alive. All you have to do is give me the notebooks. Where are they?"

This time Andy doesn't pretend not to know what Morris is talking about, not with his ass on fire and blood seeping out from beneath one hip. "I don't have them!"

Morris drops to one knee, careful to avoid the growing pool of blood. "I don't believe you. They're gone, nothing left but the trunk they were in, and nobody knew I had them but you. So I'm going to ask you again, and if you don't want to get a close look at your own guts and whatever you ate for lunch, you should be careful how you answer. *Where are the notebooks?*"

"A kid found them! It wasn't me, it was a kid! He lives in your old house, Morrie! He must have found them buried in the basement, or something!"

Morris stares into his old pal's face. He's looking for a lie, but he's also trying to cope with this sudden rearrangement of what he thought he knew. It's like a hard left turn in a car doing sixty.

"Please, Morrie, please! His name is Peter Saubers!"

It's the convincer, because Morris knows the name of the family now living in the house where he grew up. Besides, a man with a deep gash in his ass could hardly make up such specifics on the spur of the moment.

"How do you know that?"

"*Because he's trying to sell them to me!* Morrie, I need a doctor! I'm bleeding like a stuck pig!"

You *are* a pig, Morris thinks. But don't worry, old pal, pretty soon you'll be out of your misery. I'm going to send you to that big bookstore in the sky. But not yet, because Morris sees a bright ray of hope.

*He's trying,* Andy said, not *He tried.*

"Tell me everything," Morris says. "Then I'll leave. You'll have to call for an ambulance yourself, but I'm sure you can manage that."

"How do I know you're telling the truth?"

"Because if the kid has the notebooks, I have no more interest in you. Of course, you have to promise not to tell them who hurt you. It was a masked man, wasn't it? Probably a drug addict. He wanted money, right?"

Andy nods eagerly.

"It had nothing to do with the notebooks, right?"

"No, nothing! You think I want my name involved with this?"

"I suppose not. But if you tried making up some story—and if my name was in that story—I'd have to come back."

"I won't, Morrie, I won't!" Next comes a declaration as childish as that pushed-out, spit-shiny lower lip: "Honest injun!"

"Then tell me everything."

Andy does. Saubers's first visit, with photocopies from the notebooks and *Dispatches from Olympus* for comparison. Andy's identification of the boy calling himself James Hawkins, using no more than the library sticker on the spine of *Dispatches*. The boy's second visit, when Andy turned the screws on him. The voicemail about the weekend class-officer trip to River Bend Resort, and the promise to come in Monday afternoon, just two days from now.

"What time on Monday?"

"He . . . he didn't say. After school, I'd assume. He goes to Northfield High. Morrie, I'm still bleeding."

"Yes," Morris says absently. "I guess you are." He's thinking furiously. The boy claims to have all the notebooks. He might be lying about that, but probably not. The number of them that he quoted to Andy sounds right. *And he's read them.* This ignites a spark of poison jealousy in Morris Bellamy's head and lights a fire that quickly spreads to his heart. The Saubers boy has read what was meant for Morris and Morris alone. This is a grave injustice, and must be addressed.

He leans closer to Andy and says, "Are you gay? You are, aren't you?"

Andy's eyes flutter. "Am I . . . what does that matter? Morrie, I need an *ambulance*!"

"Do you have a partner?"

His old pal is hurt, but not stupid. He can see what such a question portends. "Yes!"

No, Morris thinks, and swings the hatchet: *chump*.

Andy screams and begins to writhe on the bloody rug. Morris swings again and Andy screams again. Lucky the room's lined with books, Morris thinks. Books make good insulation.

"Hold still, damn you," he says, but Andy doesn't. It takes four blows in all. The last one comes down above the bridge of Andy's

nose, splitting both of his eyes like grapes, and at last the writh-
ing stops. Morris pulls the hatchet free with a low squall of steel
on bone and drops it on the rug beside one of Andy's outstretched
hands. "There," he says. "All finished."

The rug is sodden with blood. The front of the desk is beaded
with it. So is one of the walls, and Morris himself. The inner office
is your basic abbatoir. This doesn't upset Morris much; he's pretty
calm. It's probably shock, he thinks, but so what if it is? He *needs*
to be calm. Upset people forget things.

There are two doors behind the desk. One opens on his old pal's
private bathroom, the other on a closet. There are plenty of clothes
in the closet, including two suits that look expensive. They're of
no use to Morris, though. He'd float in them.

He wishes the bathroom had a shower, but if wishes were horses,
et cetera, et cetera. He'll make do with the basin. As he strips off his
bloody shirt and washes up, he tries to replay everything he touched
since entering the shop. He doesn't believe there's much. He will
have to remember to wipe down the sign hanging in the front door,
though. Also the doorknobs of the closet and this bathroom.

He dries off and goes back into the office, dropping the towel
and bloody shirt by the body. His jeans are also spattered, a problem that's easily solved by what he finds on a shelf in the closet:
at least two dozen tee-shirts, neatly folded with tissue paper
between them. He finds an XL that will cover his jeans halfway
down his thighs, where the worst of the spotting is, and unfolds
it. ANDREW HALLIDAY RARE EDITIONS is printed on the
front, along with the shop's telephone number, website address,
and an image of an open book. Morris thinks, He probably gives
these away to big-money customers. Who take them, say thank
you, and never wear them.

He starts to put the tee-shirt on, decides he really doesn't want to be walking around wearing the location of his latest murder on his chest, and turns it inside-out. The lettering shows through a little, but not enough for anyone to read it, and the book could be any rectangular object.

His Dockers are a problem, though. The tops are splattered with blood and the soles are smeared with it. Morris studies his old pal's feet, nods judiciously, and returns to the closet. Andy's waist size may be almost twice Morris's, but their shoe sizes look approximately the same. He selects a pair of loafers and tries them on. They pinch a little, and may leave a blister or two, but blisters are a small price to pay for what he has learned, and the long-delayed revenge he has exacted.

Also, they're damned fine-looking shoes.

He adds his own footwear to the pile of gooey stuff on the rug, then examines his cap. Not so much as a single spot. Good luck there. He puts it on and circles the office, wiping the surfaces he knows he touched and the ones he might have touched.

He kneels by the body one last time and searches the pockets, aware that he's getting blood on his hands again and will have to wash them again. Oh well, so it goes.

That's Vonnegut, not Rothstein, he thinks, and laughs. Literary allusions always please him.

Andy's keys are in a front pocket, his wallet tucked against the buttock Morris didn't split with the hatchet. More good luck. Not much in the way of cash, less than thirty dollars, but a penny saved is a penny et cetera. Morris tucks the bills away along with the keys. Then he re-washes his hands and re-wipes the faucet handles.

Before leaving Andy's sanctum sanctorum, he regards the hatchet. The blade is smeared with gore and hair. The rubber handle clearly bears his palmprint. He should probably take it along in one of the Tuff Totes with his shirt and shoes, but some intuition—too deep for words but very powerful—tells him to leave it, at least for the time being.

Morris picks it up, wipes the blade and the handle to get rid of the fingerprints, then sets it gently down on the fancy desk. Like a warning. Or a calling card.

"Who says I'm not a wolf, Mr. McFarland?" he asks the empty office. "Who says?"

Then he leaves, using the blood-streaked towel to turn the knob.

6

In the shop again, Morris deposits the bloody stuff in one of the bags and zips it closed. Then he sits down to investigate Andy's laptop.

It's a Mac, much nicer than the one in the prison library but basically the same. Since it's still wide awake, there's no need to waste time hunting for a password. There are lots of business files on the screen, plus an app marked SECURITY in the bar at the bottom. He'll want to investigate that, and closely, but first he opens a file marked JAMES HAWKINS, and yes, here is the information he wants: Peter Saubers's address (which he knows), and also Peter Saubers's cell phone number, presumably gleaned from the voicemail his old pal mentioned. His father is Thomas. His mother is Linda. His sister is Tina. There's even a picture of young Mr. Saubers, aka James Hawkins, standing with a bunch of librarians from the Garner Street branch, a branch Morris knows well. Below this information—which may come in handy, who knows, who knows—is a John Rothstein bibliography, which Morris only glances at; he knows Rothstein's work by heart.

Except for the stuff young Mr. Saubers is sitting on, of course. The stuff he stole from its rightful owner.

There's a notepad by the computer. Morris jots down the boy's cell number and sticks it in his pocket. Next he opens the security app and clicks on CAMERAS. Six views appear. Two show Lacemaker Lane in all its consumer glory. Two look down on the shop's narrow interior. The fifth shows this very desk, with Morris sitting behind it in his new tee-shirt. The sixth shows Andy's inner office, and the body sprawled on the Turkish rug. In black-and-white, the splashes and splatters of blood look like ink.

Morris clicks on this image, and it fills the screen. Arrow buttons appear on the bottom. He clicks the double arrow for rewind, waits, then hits play. He watches, engrossed, as he murders his old pal all over again. Fascinating. Not a home movie he wants anyone to see, however, which means the laptop is coming with him.

He unplugs the various cords, including the one leading from a shiny box stamped VIGILANT SECURITY SYSTEMS. The cameras feed directly to the laptop's hard drive, and so there are no automatically made DVDs. That makes sense. A system like that would be a little too pricey for a small business like Andrew Halliday Rare Editions. But one of the cords he unplugged went to a disc-burner add-on, so his old pal could have made DVDs from stored security footage if he had desired.

Morris hunts methodically through the desk, looking for them. There are five drawers in all. He finds nothing of interest in the first four, but the kneehole is locked. Morris finds this suggestive. He sorts through Andy's keys, selects the smallest, unlocks the drawer, and strikes paydirt. He has no interest in the six or eight graphic photos of his old pal fellating a squat young man with a lot of tattoos, but there's also a gun. It's a prissy, overdecorated P238 SIG Sauer, red and black, with gold-inlaid flowers scrolling down the barrel. Morris drops the clip and sees it's full. There's even one in the pipe. He puts the clip back in and lays the gun on the desk—something else to take along. He searches deep into the drawer and finds an unmarked white envelope at the very back, the flap tucked under rather than sealed. He opens it, expecting more dirty pix, and is delighted to find money instead—at least five hundred dollars. His luck is still running. He puts the envelope next to the SIG.

There's nothing else, and he's about decided that if there *are* DVDs, Andy's locked them in a safe somewhere. Yet Lady Luck is not quite done with Morris Bellamy. When he gets up, his shoulder bumps an overloaded shelf to the left of the desk. A bunch of old books go tumbling to the floor, and behind them is a slim stack of plastic DVD cases bound together with rubber bands.

"How *do* you do," Morris says softly. "How *do* you do."

He sits back down and goes through them rapidly, like a man shuffling cards. Andy has written a name on each in black Sharpie. Only the last one means anything to him, and it's the one he was looking for. "HAWKINS" is printed on the shiny surface.

He's had plenty of breaks this afternoon (possibly to make up for the horrible disappointment he suffered last night), but there's no point in pushing things. Morris takes the computer, the gun, the envelope with the money in it, and the HAWKINS disc to the front of the store. He tucks them into one of his totes, ignoring the people passing back and forth in front. If you look like you belong in a place, most people think you do. He exits with a confident step, and locks the door behind him. The CLOSED sign swings briefly, then settles. Morris pulls down the long visor of his Groundhogs cap and walks away.

He makes one more stop before returning to Bugshit Manor, at a computer café called Bytes 'N Bites. For twelve of Andy Halliday's dollars, he gets an overpriced cup of shitty coffee and twenty minutes in a carrel, at a computer equipped with a DVD player. It takes less than five minutes to be sure of what he has: his old pal talking to a boy who appears to be wearing fake glasses and his father's moustache. In the first clip, Saubers has a book that has to be *Dispatches from Olympus* and an envelope containing several sheets of paper that have to be the photocopies Andy mentioned. In the second clip, Saubers and Andy appear to be arguing. There's no sound in either of these black-and-white mini-movies, which is fine. The boy could be saying anything. In the second one, the argument one, he could even be saying The next time I come, I'll bring my hatchet, you fat fuck.

As he leaves Bytes 'N Bites, Morris is smiling. The man behind the counter smiles back and says, "I guess you had a good time."

"Yes," says the man who has spent well over two-thirds of his life in prison. "But your coffee sucks, nerdboy. I ought to pour it on your fucking head."

The smile dies on the counterman's face. A lot of the people who come in here are crackpots. With those folks, it's best to just keep quiet and hope they never come back.

7

Hodges told Holly he intended to spend at least part of his weekend crashed out in his La-Z-Boy watching baseball, and on Sunday afternoon he does watch the first three innings of the Indians game, but then a certain restlessness takes hold and he decides to pay a call. Not on an old pal, but certainly an old acquaintance. After each of these visits he tells himself Okay, that's the end, this is pointless. He means it, too. Then—four weeks later, or eight, maybe ten—he'll take the ride again. Something nags him into it.

Besides, the Indians are already down to the Rangers by five, and it's only the third inning.

He zaps off the television, pulls on an old Police Athletic League tee-shirt (in his heavyset days he used to steer clear of tees, but now he likes the way they fall straight, with hardly any belly-swell above the waist of his pants), and locks up the house. Traffic is light on Sunday, and twenty minutes later he's sliding his Prius into a slot on the third deck of the visitors' parking garage, adjacent to the vast and ever metastasizing concrete sprawl of John M. Kiner Hospital. As he walks to the parking garage elevator, he sends up a prayer as he almost always does, thanking God that he's here as a visitor rather than as a paying customer. All too aware, even as he says this very proper thank-you, that most people *become* customers sooner or later, here or at one of the city's four other fine and not-so-fine sickbays. No one rides for free, and in the end, even the most seaworthy ship goes down, blub-blub-blub. The only way to balance that off, in Hodges's opinion, is to make the most of every day afloat.

But if that's true, what is he doing here?

The thought recalls to mind a snatch of poetry, heard or read long ago and lodged in his brain by virtue of its simple rhyme: *Oh do not ask what is it, let us go and make our visit.*

8

It's easy to get lost in any big city hospital, but Hodges has made this trip plenty of times, and these days he's more apt to give directions than ask for them. The garage elevator takes him down to a covered walkway; the walkway takes him to a lobby the size of a train terminal; the Corridor A elevator takes him up to the third floor; a skyway takes him across Kiner Boulevard to his final destination, where the walls are painted a soothing pink and the atmosphere is hushed. The sign above the reception desk reads:

**WELCOME TO LAKES REGION**
**TRAUMATIC BRAIN INJURY CLINIC**
**NO CELL PHONES OR TELECOMMUNICATIONS**
**DEVICES ALLOWED**
**HELP US MAINTAIN A QUIET ENVIRONMENT**
**WE APPRECIATE YOUR COOPERATION**

Hodges goes to the desk, where his visitor's badge is already waiting. The head nurse knows him; after four years, they are almost old friends.

"How's your family, Becky?"

She says they are fine.

"Son's broken arm mending?"

She says it is. The cast is off and he'll be out of the sling in another week, two at most.

"That's fine. Is my boy in his room or physical therapy?"

She says he's in his room.

Hodges ambles down the hall toward Room 217, where a certain patient resides at state expense. Before Hodges gets there, he meets the orderly the nurses call Library Al. He's in his sixties, and—as usual—he's pushing a trolley cart packed with paperbacks and newspapers. These days there's a new addition to his little arsenal of diversions: a small plastic tub filled with handheld e-readers.

"Hey, Al," Hodges says. "How you doin?"

Although Al is ordinarily garrulous, this afternoon he seems half asleep, and there are purple circles under his eyes. Somebody had a hard night, Hodges thinks with amusement. He knows the symptoms, having had a few hard ones himself. He thinks of snapping his fingers in front of Al's eyes, sort of like a stage hypnotist, then decides that would be mean. Let the man suffer the tail end of his hangover in peace. If it's this bad in the afternoon, Hodges hates to think of what it must have been like this morning.

But Al comes to and smiles before Hodges can pass by. "Hey there, Detective! Haven't seen your face in the place for awhile."

"It's just plain old mister these days, Al. You feeling okay?"

"Sure. Just thinking about . . ." Al shrugs. "Jeez, I dunno what I was thinking about." He laughs. "Getting old is no job for sissies."

"You're not old," Hodges says. "Somebody forgot to give you the news—sixty's the new forty."

Al snorts. "Ain't *that* a crock of you-know-what."

Hodges couldn't agree more. He points to the cart. "Don't suppose my boy ever asks for a book, does he?"

Al gives another snort. "Hartsfield? He couldn't read a Berenstain Bears book these days." He taps his forehead gravely. "Nothing left but oatmeal up top. Although sometimes he does hold out his hand for one of these." He picks up a Zappit e-reader. It's a bright girly pink. "These jobbies have games on em."

"He plays games?" Hodges is astounded.

"Oh God no. His motor control is shot. But if I turn on one of the demos, like Barbie Fashion Walk or Fishin' Hole, he stares at it for hours. The demos do the same thing over and over, but does he know that?"

"I'm guessing not."

"Good guess. I think he likes the noises, too—the beeps and boops and goinks. I come back two hours later, the reader's layin on his bed or windowsill, screen dark, battery flat as a pancake. But what the hell, that don't hurt em, three hours on the charger and they're ready to go again. *He* don't recharge, though. Probably a good thing." Al wrinkles his nose, as at a bad smell.

Maybe, maybe not, Hodges thinks. As long as he's not better, he's here, in a nice hospital room. Not much of a view, but there's air-conditioning, color TV, and every now and then a bright pink Zappit to stare at. If he was compos mentis—able to assist in his own defense, as the law has it—he'd have to stand trial for a dozen offenses, including nine counts of murder. Ten, if the DA decided to add in the asshole's mother, who died of poisoning. Then it would be Waynesville State Prison for the rest of his life.

No air-conditioning there.

"Take it easy, Al. You look tired."

"Nah, I'm fine, Detective Hutchinson. Enjoy your visit."

Al rolls on, and Hodges looks after him, brow furrowed. Hutchinson? Where the hell did *that* come from? Hodges has been coming here for years now, and Al knows his name perfectly well. Or did. Jesus, he hopes the guy isn't suffering from early-onset dementia.

For the first four months or so, there were two guards on the door of 217. Then one. Now there are none, because guarding Brady is a waste of time and money. There's not much danger of escape when the perp can't even make it to the bathroom by himself. Each year there's talk of transferring him to a cheaper institution upstate, and each year the prosecutor reminds all and sundry that this gentleman, brain-damaged or not, is technically still awaiting trial. It's easy to keep him here because the clinic foots a large portion of the bills. The neurological team—especially Dr. Felix Babineau, the Head of Department—finds Brady Hartsfield an extremely interesting case.

This afternoon he sits by the window, dressed in jeans and a checked shirt. His hair is long and needs cutting, but it's been washed and shines golden in the sunlight. Hair some girl would love to run her fingers through, Hodges thinks. If she didn't know what a monster he was.

"Hello, Brady."

Hartsfield doesn't stir. He's looking out the window, yes, but is he seeing the brick wall of the parking garage, which is his only view? Does he know it's Hodges in the room with him? Does he know *anybody* is in the room with him? These are questions to which a whole team of neuro guys would like answers. So would Hodges, who sits on the end of the bed, thinking *Was* a monster? Or still is?

"Long time no see, as the landlocked sailor said to the chorus girl."

Hartsfield makes no reply.

"I know, that's an oldie. I got hundreds, ask my daughter. How are you feeling?"

Hartsfield makes no reply. His hands are in his lap, the long white fingers loosely clasped.

In April of 2009, Brady Hartsfield stole a Mercedes-Benz belonging to Holly's aunt, and deliberately drove at high speed into a crowd of job-seekers at City Center. He killed eight and seriously injured twelve, including Thomas Saubers, father of Peter and Tina. He got away with it, too. Hartsfield's mistake was to write Hodges, by then retired, a taunting letter.

The following year, Brady killed Holly's cousin, a woman with whom Hodges had been falling in love. Fittingly, it was Holly herself who stopped Brady Hartsfield's clock, almost literally bashing his brains out with Hodges's own Happy Slapper before Hartsfield could detonate a bomb that would have killed thousands of kids at a pop concert.

The first blow from the Slapper had fractured Hartsfield's skull, but it was the second one that did what was considered to be irreparable damage. He was admitted to the Traumatic Brain Injury Clinic in a deep coma from which he was unlikely to ever emerge. So said Dr. Babineau. But on a dark and stormy night in November of 2011, Hartsfield opened his eyes and spoke to the nurse changing his IV bag. (When considering that moment, Hodges always imagines Dr. Frankenstein screaming, "It's alive! It's alive!") Hartsfield said he had a headache, and asked for his mother. When Dr. Babineau was fetched, and asked his patient to follow his finger to check his extraocular movements, Hartsfield was able to do so.

Over the thirty months since then, Brady Hartsfield has spoken on many occasions (although never to Hodges). Mostly he asks for his mother. When he's told she is dead, he sometimes nods as if he understands . . . but then a day or a week later, he'll repeat the request. He is able to follow simple instructions in the PT center, and can sort of walk again, although it's actually more of an orderly-assisted shamble. On good days he's able to feed himself, but cannot dress himself. He is classed as a semicatatonic. Mostly he sits in his room, either looking out the window at the parking garage, or at a picture of flowers on the wall of his room.

But there have been certain peculiar occurrences around Brady Hartsfield over the last year or so, and as a result he has become something of a legend in the Brain Injury Clinic. There are rumors and speculations. Dr. Babineau scoffs at these, and refuses to talk about them . . . but some of the orderlies and other nurses will, and a certain retired police detective has proved to be an avid listener over the years.

Hodges leans forward, hands dangling between his knees, and smiles at Hartsfield.

"Are you faking, Brady?"

Brady makes no reply.

"Why bother? You're going to be locked up for the rest of your life, one way or the other."

Brady makes no reply, but one hand rises slowly from his lap. He almost pokes himself in the eye, then gets what he was aiming for and brushes a lock of hair from his forehead.

"Want to ask about your mother?"

Brady makes no reply.

"She's dead. Rotting in her coffin. You fed her a bunch of gopher poison. She must have died hard. Did she die hard? Were you there? Did you watch?"

No reply.

"Are you in there, Brady? Knock, knock. Hello?"

No reply.

"I think you are. I hope you are. Hey, tell you something. I used to be a big drinker. And do you know what I remember best about those days?"

Nothing.

"The hangovers. Struggling to get out of bed with my head pounding like a hammer on an anvil. Pissing the morning quart and wondering what I did the night before. Sometimes not even knowing how I got home. Checking my car for dents. It was like being lost inside my own fucking mind, looking for the door so I could get out of there and not finding it until maybe noon, when things would finally start going back to normal."

This makes him think briefly of Library Al.

"I hope that's where you are right now, Brady. Wandering around inside your half-busted brain and looking for a way out. Only for you there isn't one. For you the hangover just goes on and on. Is that how it is? Man, I hope so."

His hands hurt. He looks down at them and sees his fingernails digging into his palms. He lets up and watches the white crescents there fill in red. He refreshes his smile. "Just sayin, buddy. Just sayin. You want to say anything back?"

Hartsfield says nothing back.

Hodges stands up. "That's all right. You sit right there by the window and try to find that way out. The one that isn't there. While you do that, I'll go outside and breathe some fresh air. It's a beautiful day."

On the table between the chair and the bed is a photograph Hodges first saw in the house on Elm Street where Hartsfield lived with his mother. This is a smaller version, in a plain silver frame. It shows Brady and his mom on a beach somewhere, arms around each other, cheeks pressed together, looking more like boyfriend and girlfriend than mother and son. As Hodges turns to go, the picture falls over with a toneless *clack* sound.

He looks at it, looks at Hartsfield, then looks back at the face-down picture.

"Brady?"

No answer. There never is. Not to him, anyway.

"Brady, did you do that?"

Nothing. Brady is staring down at his lap, where his fingers are once more loosely entwined.

"Some of the nurses say . . ." Hodges doesn't finish the thought. He sets the picture back up on its little stand. "If you did it, do it again."

Nothing from Hartsfield, and nothing from the picture. Mother and son in happier days. Deborah Ann Hartsfield and her honey-boy.

"All right, Brady. Seeya later, alligator. Leaving the scene, jellybean."

He does so, closing the door behind him. As he does, Brady Hartsfield looks up briefly. And smiles.

On the table, the picture falls over again.

*Clack.*

9

Ellen Bran (known as Bran Stoker by students who have taken the Northfield High English Department's Fantasy and Horror class) is standing by the door of a schoolbus parked in the River Bend Resort reception area. Her cell phone is in her hand. It's four PM on Sunday afternoon, and she is about to call 911 to report a missing student. That's when Peter Saubers comes around the restaurant side of the building, running so fast that his hair flies back from his forehead.

Ellen is unfailingly correct with her students, always staying on the teacher side of the line and never trying to buddy up, but on this one occasion she casts propriety aside and enfolds Pete in a hug so strong and frantic that it nearly stops his breath. From the bus, where the other NHS class officers and officers-to-be are waiting, there comes a sarcastic smatter of applause.

Ellen lets up on the hug, grabs his shoulders, and does another thing she's never done to a student before: gives him a good shaking. "Where *were* you? You missed all three morning seminars, you missed lunch, I was on the verge of calling the *police!*"

"I'm sorry, Ms. Bran. I was sick to my stomach. I thought the fresh air would help me."

Ms. Bran—chaperone and adviser on this weekend trip because she teaches American Politics as well as American History—decides she believes him. Not just because Pete is one of her best

293

students and has never caused her trouble before, but because the boy *looks* sick.

"Well . . . you should have informed me," she says. "I thought you'd taken it into your head to hitchhike back to town, or something. If anything had happened to you, I'd be blamed. Don't you realize you kids are my responsibility when we're on a class trip?"

"I lost track of the time. I was vomiting, and I didn't want to do it inside. It must have been something I ate. Or one of those twenty-four-hour bugs."

It wasn't anything he ate and he doesn't have a bug, but the vomiting part is true enough. It's nerves. Unadulterated fright, to be more exact. He's terrified about facing Andrew Halliday tomorrow. It could go right, he knows there's a chance for it to go right, but it will be like threading a moving needle. If it goes wrong, he'll be in trouble with his parents and in trouble with the police. College scholarships, need-based or otherwise? Forget them. He might even go to jail. So he has spent the day wandering the paths that crisscross the thirty acres of resort property, going over the coming confrontation again and again. What he will say; what Halliday will say; what he will say in return. And yes, he lost track of time.

Pete wishes he had never seen that fucking trunk.

He thinks, But I was only trying to do the right thing. Goddammit, that's all I was trying to do!

Ellen sees the tears standing in the boy's eyes, and notices for the first time—perhaps because he's shaved off that silly singles-bar moustache—how thin his face has become. Really just half a step from gaunt. She drops her cell back into her purse and comes out with a packet of tissues. "Wipe your face," she says.

A voice from the bus calls out, "Hey Saubers! D'ja get any?"

"Shut up, Jeremy," Ellen says without turning. Then, to Pete:

"I should give you a week's detention for this little stunt, but I'm going to cut you some slack."

Indeed she is, because a week's detention would necessitate an oral report to NHS Assistant Principal Waters, who is also School Disciplinarian. Waters would inquire into her own actions, and want to know why she had not sounded the alarm earlier, especially if she were forced to admit that she hadn't actually seen Pete Saubers since dinner in the restaurant the night before. He had been out of her sight and supervision for nearly a full day, and that was far too long for a school-mandated trip.

"Thank you, Ms. Bran."

"Do you think you're done throwing up?"

"Yes. There's nothing left."

"Then get on the bus and let's go home."

There's more sarcastic applause as Pete comes up the steps and makes his way down the aisle. He tries to smile, as if everything is okay. All he wants is to get back to Sycamore Street and hide in his room, waiting for tomorrow so he can get this nightmare over with.

## 10

When Hodges gets home from the hospital, a good-looking young man in a Harvard tee-shirt is sitting on his stoop, reading a thick paperback with a bunch of fighting Greeks or Romans on the cover. Sitting beside him is an Irish setter wearing the sort of happy-go-lucky grin that seems to be the default expression of dogs raised in friendly homes. Both man and dog rise when Hodges pulls into the little lean-to that serves as his garage.

The young man meets him halfway across the lawn, one fisted hand held out. Hodges bumps knuckles with him, thus acknowledging Jerome's blackness, then shakes his hand, thereby acknowledging his own WASPiness.

Jerome stands back, holding Hodges's forearms and giving him a once-over. "Look at you!" he exclaims. "Skinny as ever was!"

"I walk," Hodges says. "And I bought a treadmill for rainy days."

"Excellent! You'll live forever!"

"I wish," Hodges says, and bends down. The dog extends a paw and Hodges shakes it. "How you doing, Odell?"

Odell woofs, which presumably means he's doing fine.

"Come on in," Hodges says. "I have Cokes. Unless you'd prefer a beer."

"Coke's fine. I bet Odell would appreciate some water. We walked over. Odell doesn't walk as fast as he used to."

"His bowl's still under the sink."

They go in and toast each other with icy glasses of Coca-Cola. Odell laps water, then stretches out in his accustomed place beside the TV. Hodges was an obsessive television watcher during the first months of his retirement, but now the box rarely goes on except for Scott Pelley on *The CBS Evening News*, or the occasional Indians game.

"How's the pacemaker, Bill?"

"I don't even know it's there. Which is just the way I like it. What happened to the big country club dance you were going to in Pittsburgh with what's-her-name?"

"That didn't work out. As far as my parents are concerned, what's-her-name and I discovered that we are not compatible in terms of our academic and personal interests."

Hodges raises his eyebrows. "Sounds a tad lawyerly for a philosophy major with a minor in ancient cultures."

Jerome sips his Coke, sprawls his long legs out, and grins.

"Truth? What's-her-name—aka Priscilla—was using me to tweak the jealous-bone of her high school boyfriend. And it worked. Told me how sorry she was to get me down there on false pretenses, hopes we can still be friends, so on and so forth. A little embarrassing, but probably all for the best." He pauses. "She still has all her Barbies and Bratz on a shelf in her room, and I must admit that gave me pause. I guess I wouldn't mind *too* much if my folks found out I was the stick she stirred her pot of love-soup with, but if you tell the Barbster, I'll never hear the end of it."

"Mum's the word," Hodges says. "So what now? Back to Massachusetts?"

"Nope, I'm here for the summer. Got a job down on the docks swinging containers."

"That is not work for a Harvard man, Jerome."

"It is for this one. I got my heavy equipment license last winter, the pay is excellent, and Harvard ain't cheap, even with a partial scholarship." Tyrone Feelgood Delight makes a mercifully brief guest appearance. "Dis here black boy goan tote dat barge an' lift dat bale, Massa Hodges!" Then back to Jerome, just like that. "Who's mowing your lawn? It looks pretty good. Not Jerome Robinson quality, but pretty good."

"Kid from the end of the block," Hodges says. "Is this just a courtesy call, or . . . ?"

"Barbara and her friend Tina told me one hell of a story," Jerome says. "Tina was reluctant to spill it at first, but Barbs talked her into it. She's good at stuff like that. Listen, you know Tina's father was hurt in the City Center thing, right?"

"Yes."

"If her big brother was really the one sending cash to keep the fam afloat, good for him . . . but where did it come from? I can't figure that one out no matter how hard I try."

"Nor can I."

"Tina says you're going to ask him."

"After school tomorrow, is the plan."

"Is Holly involved?"

"To an extent. She's doing background."

"Cool!" Jerome grins big. "How about I come with you tomorrow? Get the band back together, man! Play all the hits!"

Hodges considers. "I don't know, Jerome. One guy—a golden oldie like me—might not upset young Mr. Saubers too much. *Two* guys, though, especially when one of them's a badass black dude who stands six-four—"

"Fifteen rounds and I'm still pretty!" Jerome proclaims, waving clasped hands over his head. Odell lays back his ears. "Still pretty! That bad ole bear Sonny Liston never touched me! I float like a butterfly, I sting like a . . ." He assesses Hodges's patient expression. "Okay, sorry, sometimes I get carried away. Where are you going to wait for him?"

"Out front was the plan. You know, where the kids actually exit the building?"

"Not all of them come out that way, and he might not, especially if Tina lets on she talked to you." He sees Hodges about to speak and raises a hand. "She says she won't, but big brothers know little sisters, you can take that from a guy who's got one. If he knows somebody wants to ask him questions, he's apt to go out the back and cut across the football field to Westfield Street. I could park there, give you a call if I see him."

"Do you know what he looks like?"

"Uh-huh, Tina had a picture in her wallet. Let me be a part of this, Bill. Barbie likes that chick. I liked her too. And it took guts for her to come to you, even with my sister snapping the whip."

"I know."

"Also, I'm curious as hell. Tina says the money started coming when her bro was only thirteen. A kid that young with access to that much money . . ." Jerome shakes his head. "I'm not surprised he's in trouble."

"Me either. I guess if you want to be in, you're in."

"My man!"

This cry necessitates another fist-bump.

"You went to Northfield, Jerome. Is there any other way he could go out, besides the front and Westfield Street?"

Jerome thinks it over. "If he went down to the basement, there's a door that takes you out to one side, where the smoking area used to be, back in the day. I guess he could go across that, then cut through the auditorium and come out on Garner Street."

"I could put Holly there," Hodges says thoughtfully.

"Excellent idea!" Jerome cries. "Gettin the band back together! What I said!"

"But no approach if you see him," Hodges says. "Just call. *I* get to approach. I'll tell Holly the same thing. Not that she'd be likely to."

"As long as we get to hear the story."

"If I get it, you'll get it," Hodges says, hoping he has not just made a rash promise. "Come by my office in the Turner Building around two, and we'll move out around two fifteen. Be in position by two forty-five."

"You're sure Holly will be okay with this?"

"Yes. She's fine with watching. It's confrontation that gives her problems."

"Not always."

"No," Hodges says, "not always."

They are both thinking of one confrontation—at the MAC, with Brady Hartsfield—that Holly handled just fine.

299

Jerome glances at his watch. "I have to go. Promised I'd take the Barbster to the mall. She wants a Swatch." He rolls his eyes.

Hodges grins. "I love your sis, Jerome."

Jerome grins back. "Actually, so do I. Come on, Odell. Let's shuffle."

Odell rises and heads for the door. Jerome grasps the knob, then turns back. His grin is gone. "Have you been where I think you've been?"

"Probably."

"Does Holly know you visit him?"

"No. And you're not to tell her. She'd find it vastly upsetting."

"Yes. She would. How is he?"

"The same. Although . . ." Hodges is thinking of how the picture fell over. That *clack* sound.

"Although what?"

"Nothing. He's the same. Do me one favor, okay? Tell Barbara to get in touch if Tina calls and says her brother found out the girls talked to me on Friday."

"Will do. See you tomorrow."

Jerome leaves. Hodges turns on the TV, and is delighted to see the Indians are still on. They've tied it up. The game is going into extra innings.

11

Holly spends Sunday evening in her apartment, trying to watch *The Godfather Part II* on her computer. Usually this would be a very pleasant occupation, because she considers it one of the two or three best movies ever made, right up there with *Citizen Kane* and *Paths of Glory*, but tonight she keeps pausing it so she can pace worry-circles around the living room of her apartment. There's a lot of room to pace. This apartment isn't as glitzy as the lakeside condo she lived in for awhile when she first moved to the city, but it's in a good neighborhood and plenty big. She can afford the rent; under the terms of her cousin Janey's will, Holly inherited half a million dollars. Less after taxes, of course, but still a very nice nest egg. And, thanks to her job with Bill Hodges, she can afford to let the nest egg grow.

As she paces, she mutters some of her favorite lines from the movie.

"I don't have to wipe everyone out, just my enemies.

"How do you say banana daiquiri?

"Your country ain't your blood, remember that."

And, of course, the one everyone remembers: "I know it was you, Fredo. You broke my heart."

If she was watching another movie, she would be incanting a different set of quotes. It is a form of self-hypnosis that she has practiced ever since she saw *The Sound of Music* at the age of seven. (Favorite line from that one: "I wonder what grass tastes like.")

She's really thinking about the Moleskine notebook Tina's brother was so quick to hide under his pillow. Bill believes it has nothing to do with the money Pete was sending his parents, but Holly isn't so sure.

She has kept journals for most of her life, listing all the movies she's seen, all the books she's read, the people she's talked to, the times she gets up, the times she goes to bed. Also her bowel movements, which are coded (after all, someone may see her journals after she's dead) as WP, which stands for *Went Potty*. She knows this is OCD behavior—she and her therapist have discussed how obsessive listing is really just another form of magical thinking— but it doesn't hurt anyone, and if she prefers to keep her lists in

Moleskine notebooks, whose business is that besides her own? The point is, she *knows* from Moleskines, and therefore knows they're not cheap. Two-fifty will get you a spiral-bound notebook in Walgreens, but a Moleskine with the same number of pages goes for ten bucks. Why would a kid want such an expensive notebook, especially when he came from a cash-strapped family?

"Doesn't make sense," Holly says. Then, as if just following this train of thought: "Leave the gun. Take the cannoli." That's from the original *Godfather*, but it's still a good line. One of the best.

Send the money. Keep the notebook.

An *expensive* notebook that got shoved under the pillow when the little sister appeared unexpectedly in the room. The more Holly thinks about it, the more she thinks there might be something there.

She restarts the movie but can't follow its well-worn and well-loved path with this notebook stuff rolling around in her head, so Holly does something almost unheard of, at least before bedtime: she turns her computer off. Then she resumes pacing, hands locked together at the small of her back.

Send the money. Keep the notebook.

"And the lag!" she exclaims to the empty room. "Don't forget that!"

Yes. The seven months of quiet time between when the money ran out and when the Saubers boy started to get his underpants all in a twist. Because it took him seven months to think up a way to get *more* money? Holly thinks yes. Holly thinks he got an idea, but it wasn't a *good* idea. It was an idea that got him in trouble.

"What gets people in trouble when it's about money?" Holly asks the empty room, pacing faster than ever. "Stealing does. So does blackmail."

Was that it? Did Pete Saubers try to blackmail somebody about something in the Moleskine notebook? Something about the stolen money, maybe? Only how could Pete blackmail someone about that money when he must have stolen it himself?

Holly goes to the telephone, reaches for it, then pulls her hand back. For almost a minute she just stands there, gnawing her lips. She's not used to taking the initiative in things. Maybe she should call Bill first, and ask him if it's okay?

"Bill doesn't think the notebook's important, though," she tells her living room. "I think different. And I can think different if I want to."

She snatches her cell from the coffee table and calls Tina Saubers before she can lose her nerve.

"Hello?" Tina asks cautiously. Almost whispering. "Who's this?"

"Holly Gibney. You didn't see my number come up because it's unlisted. I'm very careful about my number, although I'll be happy to give it to you, if you want. We can talk anytime, because we're friends and that's what friends do. Is your brother back home from his weekend?"

"Yes. He came in around six, while we were finishing up dinner. Mom said there was still plenty of pot roast and potatoes, she'd heat them up if he wanted, but he said they stopped at Denny's on the way back. Then he went up to his room. He didn't even want any strawberry shortcake, and he loves that. I'm really worried about him, Ms. Holly."

"You can just call me Holly, Tina." She hates Ms., thinks it sounds like a mosquito buzzing around your head.

"Okay."

"Did he say anything to you?"

"Just hi," Tina says in a small voice.

"And you didn't tell him about coming to the office with Barbara on Friday?"

"God, no!"

"Where is he now?"

"Still in his room. Listening to the Black Keys. I hate the Black Keys."

"Yes, me too." Holly has no idea who the Black Keys are, although she could name the entire cast of *Fargo*. (Best line in that one, delivered by Steve Buscemi: "Smoke a fuckin peace pipe.")

"Tina, does Pete have a special friend he might have talked to about what's bothering him?"

Tina thinks it over. Holly takes the opportunity to snatch a Nicorette from the open pack beside her computer and pop it into her mouth.

"I don't think so," Tina says at last. "I guess he has friends at school, he's pretty popular, but his only close friend was Bob Pearson, from down the block? And they moved to Denver last year."

"What about a girlfriend?"

"He used to spend a lot of time with Gloria Moore, but they broke up after Christmas. Pete said she didn't like to read, and he could never get tight with a girl who didn't like books." Wistfully, Tina adds: "I liked Gloria. She showed me how to do my eyes."

"Girls don't need eye makeup until they're in their thirties," Holly says authoritatively, although she has never actually worn any herself. Her mother says only sluts wear eye makeup.

"*Really?*" Tina sounds astonished.

"What about teachers? Did he have a favorite teacher he might have talked to?" Holly doubts if an older brother would have talked to his kid sister about favorite teachers, or if the kid sister would have paid any attention even if he did. She asks because it's the only other thing she can think of.

But Holly doesn't even hesitate. "Ricky the Hippie," she says, and giggles.

Holly stops in mid-pace. "Who?"

"Mr. Ricker, that's his real name. Pete said some of the kids call him Ricky the Hippie because he wears these old-time flower-power shirts and ties. Pete had him when he was a freshman. Or maybe a sophomore. I can't remember. He said Mr. Ricker knew what good books were all about. Ms. . . . I mean Holly, is Mr. Hodges still going to talk to Pete tomorrow?"

"Yes. Don't worry about that."

But Tina is plenty worried. She sounds on the verge of tears, in fact, and this makes Holly's stomach contract into a tight little ball. "Oh boy. I hope he doesn't hate me."

"He won't," Holly says. She's chewing her Nicorette at warp speed. "Bill will find out what's wrong and fix it. Then your brother will love you more than ever."

"Do you promise?"

"Yes! *Ouch!*"

"What's wrong?"

"Nothing." She wipes her mouth and looks at a smear of blood on her fingers. "I bit my lip. I have to go, Tina. Will you call me if you think of anyone he might have talked to about the money?"

"There's no one," Tina says forlornly, and starts to cry.

"Well . . . okay." And because something else seems required: "Don't bother with eye makeup. Your eyes are very pretty as they are. Goodbye."

She ends the call without waiting for Tina to say anything else and resumes pacing. She spits the wad of Nicorette into the wastebasket by her desk and blots her lip with a tissue, but the bleeding has already stopped.

No close friends and no steady girl. No names except for that one teacher.

Holly sits down and powers up her computer again. She opens

Firefox, goes to the Northfield High website, clicks OUR FAC-
ULTY, and there is Howard Ricker, wearing a flower-patterned
shirt with billowy sleeves, just like Tina said. Also a very ridiculous tie. Is it really so impossible that Pete Saubers said something
to his favorite English teacher, especially if it had to do with whatever he was writing (or reading) in a Moleskine notebook?

A few clicks and she has Howard Ricker's telephone number on
her computer screen. It's still early, but she can't bring herself to
cold-call a complete stranger. Phoning Tina was hard enough, and
that call ended in tears.

I'll tell Bill tomorrow, she decides. He can call Ricky the Hippie if he thinks it's worth doing.

She goes back to her voluminous movie folder and is soon once
more lost in *The Godfather Part II*.

12

Morris visits another computer café that Sunday night, and does
his own quick bit of research. When he's found what he wants, he
fishes out the piece of notepaper with Peter Saubers's cell number
on it, and jots down Andrew Halliday's address. Coleridge Street
is on the West Side. In the seventies, that was a middle-class and
mostly white enclave where all the houses tried to look a little
more expensive than they actually were, and as a result all ended
up looking pretty much the same.

A quick visit to several local real estate sites shows Morris that
things over there haven't changed much, although an upscale
shopping center has been added: Valley Plaza. Andy's car may still
be parked at his house out there. Of course it might be in a space
behind his shop, Morris never checked (Christ, you can't check

*everything*, he thinks), but that seems unlikely. Why would you put up with the hassle of driving three miles into the city every morning and three miles back every night, in rush-hour traffic, when you could buy a thirty-day bus-pass for ten dollars, or a six-month's pass for fifty? Morris has the keys to his old pal's house, although he'd never try using them; the house is a lot more likely to be alarmed than the Birch Street Rec.

But he also has the keys to Andy's car, and a car might come in handy.

He walks back to Bugshit Manor, convinced that McFarland will be waiting for him there, and not content just to make Morris pee in the little cup. No, not this time. This time he'll also want to toss his room, and when he does he'll find the Tuff Tote with the stolen computer and the bloody shirt and shoes inside. Not to mention the envelope of money he took from his old pal's desk.

*I'd kill him,* thinks Morris—who is now (in his own mind, at least) Morris the Wolf.

Only he couldn't use the gun, plenty of people in Bugshit Manor know what a gunshot sounds like, even a polite *ka-pow* from a little faggot gun like his old pal's P238, and he left the hatchet in Andy's office. That might not do the job even if he did have it. McFarland is big like Andy, but not all puddly-fat like Andy. McFarland looks *strong*.

That's okay, Morris tells himself. That shit don't mean shit. Because an old wolf is a crafty wolf, and that's what I have to be now: crafty.

McFarland isn't waiting on the stoop, but before Morris can breathe a sigh of relief, he becomes convinced that his PO will be waiting for him upstairs. Not in the hall, either. He's probably got a passkey that lets him into every room in this fucked-up, piss-smelling place.

Try me, he thinks. You just try me, you sonofabitch.

But the door is locked, the room is empty, and it doesn't look like it's been searched, although he supposes if McFarland did it carefully . . . *craftily*—

But then Morris calls himself an idiot. If McFarland had searched his room, he would have been waiting with a couple of cops, and the cops would have handcuffs.

Nevertheless, he snatches open the closet door to make sure the Tuff Totes are where he left them. They are. He takes out the money and counts it. Six hundred and forty dollars. Not great, not even close to what was in Rothstein's safe, but not bad. He puts it back, zips the bag shut, then sits on his bed and holds up his hands. They are shaking.

I have to get that stuff out of here, he thinks, and I have to do it tomorrow morning. But get it out to where?

Morris lies down on his bed and looks up at the ceiling, thinking. At last he falls asleep.

13

Monday dawns clear and warm, the thermometer in front of City Center reading seventy before the sun is even fully over the horizon. School is still in session and will be for the next two weeks, but today is going to be the first real sizzler of the summer, the kind of day that makes people wipe the backs of their necks and squint at the sun and talk about global warming.

When Hodges gets to his office at eight thirty, Holly is already there. She tells him about her conversation with Tina last night, and asks if Hodges will talk to Howard Ricker, aka Ricky the Hippie, if he can't get the story of the money from Pete himself.

Hodges agrees to this, and tells Holly that was good thinking (she glows at this), but privately believes talking to Ricker won't be necessary. If he can't crack a seventeen-year-old kid—one who's probably dying to tell someone what's been weighing him down— he needs to quit working and move to Florida, home of so many retired cops.

He asks Holly if she'll watch for the Saubers boy on Garner Street when school lets out this afternoon. She agrees, as long as she doesn't have to talk to him herself.

"You won't," Hodges assures her. "If you see him, all you need to do is call me. I'll come around the block and cut him off. Have we got pix of him?"

"I've downloaded half a dozen to my computer. Five from the yearbook and one from the Garner Street Library, where he works as a student aide, or something. Come and look."

The best photo—a portrait shot in which Pete Saubers is wearing a tie and a dark sportcoat—identifies him as CLASS OF '15 STUDENT VICE PRESIDENT. He's dark-haired and good-looking. The resemblance to his kid sister isn't striking, but it's there, all right. Intelligent blue eyes look levelly out at Hodges. In them is the faintest glint of humor.

"Can you email these to Jerome?"

"Already done." Holly smiles, and Hodges thinks—as he always does—that she should do it more often. When she smiles, Holly is almost beautiful. With a little mascara around her eyes, she probably would be. "Gee, it'll be good to see Jerome again."

"What have I got this morning, Holly? Anything?"

"Court at ten o'clock. The assault thing."

"Oh, right. The guy who tuned up on his brother-in-law. Belson the Bald Beater."

"It's not nice to call people names," Holly says.

This is probably true, but court is always an annoyance, and having to go there today is particularly trying, even though it will probably take no more than an hour, unless Judge Wiggins has slowed down since Hodges was on the cops. Pete Huntley used to call Brenda Wiggins FedEx, because she always delivered on time.

The Bald Beater is James Belson, whose picture should probably be next to *white trash* in the dictionary. He's a resident of the city's Edgemont Avenue district, sometimes referred to as Hillbilly Heaven. As part of his contract with one of the city's car dealerships, Hodges was hired to repo Belson's Acura MDX, on which Belson had ceased making payments some months before. When Hodges arrived at Belson's ramshackle house, Belson wasn't there. Neither was the car. Mrs. Belson—a lady who looked rode hard and put away still damp—told him the Acura had been stolen by her brother Howie. She gave him the address, which was also in Hillbilly Heaven.

"I got no love for Howie," she told Hodges, "but you might ought to get over before Jimmy kills him. When Jimmy's mad, he don't believe in talk. He goes right to beatin."

When Hodges arrived, James Belson was indeed beating on Howie. He was doing this work with a rake-handle, his bald head gleaming with sweat in the sunlight. Belson's brother-in-law was lying in his weedy driveway by the rear bumper of the Acura, kicking ineffectually at Belson and trying to shield his bleeding face and broken nose with his hands. Hodges stepped up behind Belson and soothed him with the Happy Slapper. The Acura was back on the car dealership's lot by noon, and Belson the Bald Beater was now up on assault.

"His lawyer is going to try to make you look like the bad guy," Holly says. "He's going to ask how you subdued Mr. Belson. You need to be ready for that, Bill."

"Oh, for goodness sake," Hodges says. "I thumped him one to keep him from killing his brother-in-law, that's all. Applied acceptable force and practiced restraint."

"But you used a weapon to do it. A sock loaded with ball bearings, to be exact."

"True, but Belson doesn't know that. His back was turned. And the other guy was semiconscious at best."

"Okay . . ." But she looks worried and her teeth are working at the spot she nipped while talking to Tina. "I just don't want you to get in trouble. Promise me you'll keep your temper and not *shout*, or wave your *arms*, or—"

"Holly." He takes her by the shoulders. Gently. "Go outside. Smoke a cigarette. Chillax. All will be well in court this morning and with Pete Saubers this afternoon."

She looks up at him, wide-eyed. "Do you promise?"

"Yes."

"All right. I'll just smoke *half* a cigarette." She heads for the door, rummaging in her bag. "We're going to have *such* a busy day."

"I suppose we are. One other thing before you go."

She turns back, questioning.

"You should smile more often. You're beautiful when you smile."

Holly blushes all the way to her hairline and hurries out. But she's smiling again, and that makes Hodges happy.

14

Morris is also having a busy day, and busy is good. As long as he's in motion, the doubts and fears don't have a chance to creep in. It helps that he woke up absolutely sure of one thing: this is the day he becomes a wolf for real. He's all done patching up the Culture and Arts Center's outdated computer filing system so his fat fuck of a boss can look good to *his* boss, and he's done being Ellis McFarland's pet lamb, too. No more baa-ing *yes sir* and *no sir* and *three bags full sir* each time McFarland shows up. Parole is finished. As soon as he has the Rothstein notebooks, he's getting the hell out of this pisspot of a city. He has no interest in going north to Canada, but that leaves the whole lower forty-eight. He thinks maybe he'll opt for New England. Who knows, maybe even New Hampshire. Reading the notebooks there, near the same mountains Rothstein must have looked at while he was writing—that had a certain novelistic roundness, didn't it? Yes, and that was the great thing about novels: that roundness. The way things always balanced out in the end. He should have known Rothstein couldn't leave Jimmy working for that fucking ad agency, because there was no roundness in that, just a big old scoop of ugly. Maybe, deep down in his heart, Morris *had* known it. Maybe it was what kept him sane all those years.

He's never felt saner in his life.

When he doesn't show up for work this morning, his fat fuck boss will probably call McFarland. That, at least, is what he's supposed to do in the event of an unexplained absence. So Morris has to disappear. Duck under the radar. Go dark.

Fine.

Terrific, in fact.

At eight this morning, he takes the Main Street bus, rides all the way to its turnaround point where Lower Main ends, and then strolls down to Lacemaker Lane. Morris has put on his only sportcoat and his only tie, and they're good enough for him to not look out of place here, even though it's too early for any of the fancyschmancy stores to have opened. He turns down the alley between

Andrew Halliday Rare Editions and the shop next door, La Bella Flora Children's Boutique. There are three parking spaces in the small courtyard behind the buildings, two for the clothing shop and one for the bookshop. There's a Volvo in one of the La Bella Flora spots. The other one is empty. So is the space reserved for Andrew Halliday.

Also fine.

Morris leaves the courtyard as briskly as he came, pauses for a comforting look at the CLOSED sign hanging inside the bookshop door, and then strolls back to Lower Main, where he catches an uptown bus. Two changes later, he's stepping off in front of the Valley Plaza Shopping Center, just two blocks from the late Andrew Halliday's home.

He walks briskly again, no strolling now. As if he knows where he is, where he's going, and has every right to be here. Coleridge Street is nearly deserted, which doesn't surprise him. It's quarter past nine (his fat fuck of a boss will by now be looking at Morris's unoccupied desk and fuming). The kids are in school; the workadaddies and workamommies are off busting heavies to keep up with their credit card debt; most delivery and service people won't start cruising the neighborhood until ten. The only better time would be the dozy hours of mid-afternoon, and he can't afford to wait that long. Too many places to go, too many things to do. This is Morris Bellamy's big day. His life has taken a long, long detour, but he's almost back on the mainline.

15

Tina starts feeling sick around the time Morris is strolling up the late Drew Halliday's driveway and seeing his old pal's car parked inside his garage. Tina hardly slept at all last night because she's so worried about how Pete will take the news that she ratted him out. Her breakfast is sitting in her belly like a lump, and all at once, while Mrs. Sloan is performing "Annabel Lee" (Mrs. Sloan *never* just reads), that lump of undigested food starts to crawl up her throat and toward the exit.

She raises her hand. It seems to weigh at least ten pounds, but she holds it up until Mrs. Sloan raises her eyes. "Yes, Tina, what is it?"

She sounds annoyed, but Tina doesn't care. She's beyond caring. "I feel sick. I need to go to the girls'."

"Then go, by all means, but hurry back."

Tina scuttles from the room. Some of the girls are giggling—at thirteen, unscheduled bathroom visits are always amusing—but Tina is too concerned with that rising lump to feel embarrassed. Once in the hall she breaks into a run, heading for the bathroom halfway down the hall as fast as she can, but the lump is faster and she doubles over before she can get there and vomits her breakfast all over her sneakers.

Mr. Haggerty, the school's head janitor, is just coming up the stairs. He sees her stagger backward from the steaming puddle of whoopsie and trots toward her, his toolbelt jingling.

"Hey, girl, you okay?"

Tina gropes for the wall with an arm that feels made of plastic. The world is swimming. Part of that is because she has vomited hard enough to bring tears to her eyes, but not all. She wishes with all her heart that she hadn't let Barbara persuade her into talking to Mr. Hodges, that she had left Pete alone to work out whatever was wrong. What if he never speaks to her again?

"I'm fine," she says. "I'm sorry I made a m—"

But the swimming gets worse before she can finish. She doesn't exactly faint, but the world pulls away from her, becomes something she's looking at through a smudged window rather than something she's actually *in*. She slides down the wall, amazed by the sight of her own knees, clad in green tights, coming up to meet her. That is when Mr. Haggerty scoops her up and carries her downstairs to the school nurse's office.

16

Andy's little green Subaru is perfect, as far as Morris is concerned—not apt to attract a first glance, let alone a second. There are only thousands just like it. He backs down the driveway and sets off for the North Side, keeping an eye out for cops and obeying every speed limit.

At first it's almost a replay of Friday night. He stops once more at the Bellows Avenue Mall and once more visits Home Depot. He goes to the tools section, where he picks out a screwdriver with a long blade and a chisel. Then he drives on to the square brick hulk that used to be the Birch Street Recreation Center and once more parks in the space marked RESERVED FOR REC DEPT. VEHICLES.

It's a good spot in which to do dirty business. There's a loading dock on one side and a high hedge on the other. He's visible only from behind—the baseball field and crumbling basketball courts—but with school in session, those areas are deserted. Morris goes to the basement window he noticed before, squats, and rams the blade of his screwdriver into the crack at the top. It goes in easily, because the wood is rotten. He uses the chisel to widen the crack. The glass rattles in its frame but doesn't break, because the putty is old and there's plenty of give. The possibility that this hulk of a building has alarm protection is looking slimmer all the time.

Morris swaps the chisel for the screwdriver again. He chivvies it through the gap he's made, catches the thumb-lock, and pushes. He looks around to make sure he's still unobserved—it's a good spot, yes, but breaking and entering in broad daylight is still a scary proposition—and sees nothing but a crow perched on a telephone pole. He inserts the chisel at the bottom of the window, beating it in as deep as it will go with the heel of his hand, then bears down on it. For a moment there's nothing. Then the window slides up with a squall of wood and a shower of dirt. Bingo. He wipes sweat from his face as he peers in at the stored chairs, card tables, and boxes of junk, verifying that it will be easy to slide in and drop to the floor.

But not quite yet. Not while there's the slightest possibility that a silent alarm is lighting up somewhere.

Morris takes his tools back to the little green Subaru, and drives away.


17


Linda Saubers is monitoring the mid-morning activity period at Northfield Elementary School when Peggy Moran comes in and tells her that her daughter has been taken sick at Dorton Middle, some three miles away.

"She's in the nurse's office," Peggy says, keeping her voice low. "I understand she vomited and then sort of passed out for a few minutes."

"Oh my God," Linda says. "She looked pale at breakfast, but when I asked her if she was okay, she said she was."

"That's the way they are," Peggy says, rolling her eyes. "It's either melodrama or *I'm fine, Mom, get a life.* Go get her and take her home. I'll cover this, and Mr. Jablonski has already called a sub."

"You're a saint." Linda is gathering up her books and putting them into her briefcase.

"It's probably a stomach thing," Peggy says, sliding into the seat Linda has just vacated. "I guess you could take her to the nearest Doc in the Box, but why bother spending thirty bucks? That stuff's going around."

"I know," Linda says . . . but she wonders.

She and Tom have been slowly but surely digging themselves out of two pits: a money pit and a marriage pit. The year after Tom's accident, they came perilously close to breaking up. Then the mystery cash started coming, a kind of miracle, and things started to turn around. They aren't all the way out of either hole even yet, but Linda has come to believe they *will* get out.

With their parents focused on brute survival (and Tom, of course, had the additional challenge of recovering from his injuries), the kids have spent far too much time flying on autopilot. It's only now, when she feels she finally has room to breathe and time to look around her, that Linda clearly senses something not right with Pete and Tina. They're good kids, *smart* kids, and she doesn't think either of them has gotten caught in the usual teenage traps—drink, drugs, shoplifting, sex—but there's *something*, and she supposes she knows what it is. She has an idea Tom does, too.

God sent manna from heaven when the Israelites were starving, but cash drops from more prosaic sources: banks, friends, an inheritance, relatives who are in a position to help out. The mystery money didn't come from any of those sources. Certainly not from relatives. Back in 2010, all their kinfolk were just as strapped as Tom and Linda themselves. Only kids are relatives, too, aren't they?

It's easy to overlook that because they're so close, but they are. It's absurd to think the cash came from Tina, who'd only been nine years old when the envelopes started arriving, and who couldn't have kept a secret like that, anyway.

Pete, though . . . he's the closemouthed one. Linda remembers her mother saying when Pete was only five, "That one's got a lock on his lips."

Only where could a kid of thirteen have come by that kind of money?

As she drives to Dorton Middle to pick up her ailing daughter, Linda thinks, We never asked *any* questions, not really, because we were afraid to. No one who didn't go through those terrible months after Tommy's accident could get that, and I'm not going to apologize for it. We had reasons to be cowardly. Plenty of them. The two biggest were living right under our roof, and counting on us to support them. But it's time to ask who was supporting whom. If it was Pete, if Tina found out and that's what's troubling her, I need to stop being a coward. I need to open my eyes.

I need some answers.

18

Mid-morning.

Hodges is in court, and on best behavior. Holly would be proud. He answers the questions posed by the Bald Beater's attorney with crisp succinctness. The attorney gives him plenty of opportunity to be argumentative, and although this was a trap Hodges sometimes fell into during his detective days, he avoids it now.

Linda Saubers is driving her pale, silent daughter home from school, where she will give Tina a glass of ginger ale to settle her stomach and then put her to bed. She is finally ready to ask Tina what she knows about the mystery money, but not until the girl feels better. The afternoon will be time enough, and she should make Pete a part of that conversation when he gets home from school. It will be just the three of them, and probably that's best. Tom and a group of his real estate clients are touring an office complex, recently vacated by IBM, fifty miles north of the city, and won't be back until seven. Even later, if they stop for dinner on the return trip.

Pete is in period three Advanced Physics, and although his eyes are trained on Mr. Norton, who is rhapsodizing about the Higgs boson and the CERN Large Hadron Collider in Switzerland, the mind behind those eyes is much closer to home. He is going over his script for this afternoon's meeting yet again, and reminding himself that just because he *has* a script doesn't mean Halliday will follow it. Halliday has been in this business a long time, and he's probably been skirting the edges of the law for much of it. Pete is just a kid, and it absolutely will not do to forget that. He must be careful, and allow for his inexperience. He must think before he speaks, every time.

Above all, he must be brave.

He tells Halliday: Half a loaf is better than none, but in a world of want, even a single slice is better than none. I'm offering you three dozen slices. You need to think about that.

He tells Halliday: I'm not going to be anyone's birthday fuck, you better think about that, too.

He tells Halliday: If you think I'm bluffing, go on and try me. But if you do, we both wind up with nothing.

He thinks, If I can hold my nerve, I can get out of this. And I will hold it. I will. I have to.

Morris Bellamy parks the stolen Subaru two blocks from Bug-shit Manor and walks back. He lingers in the doorway of a second-hand store to make sure Ellis McFarland isn't in the vicinity, then scurries to the miserable building and plods up the nine flights of stairs. Both elevators are busted today, which is par for the course. He scrambles random clothes into one of the Tuff Totes and then leaves his crappy room for the last time. All the way down to the first corner his back feels hot, his neck as stiff as an ironing board. He carries one Tuff Tote in each hand, and they seem to weigh a hundred pounds apiece. He keeps waiting for McFarland to call his name. To step out from beneath a shadowed awning and ask him why he's not at work. To ask him where he thinks he's going. To ask him what he's got in those bags. And then to tell him he's going back to prison: Do not pass Go, do not collect two hundred dollars. Morris doesn't relax until Bugshit Manor is out of sight for good.

Tom Saubers is walking his little pack of real estate agents through the empty IBM facility, pointing out the various features and encouraging them to take pictures. They're all excited by the possibilities. Come the end of the day, his surgically repaired legs and hips will ache like all the devils of hell, but for the time being, he's feeling fine. This abandoned office and manufacturing com-plex could be a big deal for him. Life is finally turning around.

Jerome has popped into Hodges's office to surprise Holly, who squeals with joy when she sees him, then with apprehension when he seizes her by the waist and swings her around as he likes to do with his little sister. They talk for an hour or more, catching up, and she gives him her views on the Saubers affair. She's happy when Jerome takes her concerns about the Moleskine notebook seriously, and happier still to find out he has seen *22 Jump Street*. They drop the subject of Pete Saubers and discuss the movie at great length, comparing it to others in Jonah Hill's filmography. Then they move on to a discussion of various computer apps.

Andrew Halliday is the only one not occupied. First editions no longer matter to him, nor do young waiters in tight black pants. Oil and water are the same as wind and air to him now. He's sleeping the big sleep in a patch of congealed blood, drawing flies.

## 19

Eleven o'clock. It's eighty degrees in the city, and the radio says the mercury's apt to touch ninety before subsiding. *Got* to be global warming, people tell each other.

Morris cruises past the Birch Street Rec twice, and is happy (though not really surprised) to see it's as deserted as ever, just an empty brick box baking under the sun. No police; no security cars. Even the crow has departed for cooler environs. He circles the block, noting that there's now a trim little Ford Focus parked in the driveway of his old house. Mr. or Mrs. Saubers has knocked off early. Hell, maybe both of them. It's nothing to Morris. He heads back to the Rec and this time turns in, going around to the rear of the building and parking in what he's now begun to think of as his spot.

He's confident that he's unobserved, but it's still a good idea to do this quickly. He carries his bags to the window he's forced up and drops them to the basement floor, where they land with a flat clap and twin puffs of dust. He takes a quick look around, then slides feet first through the window on his stomach.

A wave of dizziness runs through his head as he takes his first deep breath of the cool, musty air. He staggers a little, and puts his arms out for balance. It's the heat, he thinks. You've been too busy to realize it, but you're dripping with sweat. Also, you ate no breakfast.

Both true, but the main thing is simpler and self-evident: he's not as young as he used to be, and it's been years since the physical exertions of the dyehouse. He's got to pace himself. Over by the furnace are a couple of good-sized cartons with **KITCHEN SUPPLIES** printed on the sides. Morris sits down on one of these until his heartbeat slows and the dizziness passes. Then he unzips the tote with Andy's little automatic inside, tucks the gun into the waistband of his pants at the small of his back, and blouses his shirt over it. He takes a hundred dollars of Andy's money, just in case he runs into any unforeseen expenses, and leaves the rest for later. He'll be back here this evening, may even spend the night. It sort of depends on the kid who stole his notebooks, and what measures Morris needs to employ in order to get them back.

Whatever it takes, cocksucker, he thinks. Whatever it takes.

Right now it's time to move on. As a younger man, he could have pulled himself out of that basement window easily, but not now. He drags over one of the **KITCHEN SUPPLIES** cartons—it's surprisingly heavy, probably some old busted appliance inside—and uses it as a step. Five minutes later, he's headed for Andrew Halliday Rare Editions, where he will park his old pal's car in his old pal's space and then spend the rest of the day soaking up the air-conditioning and waiting for the young notebook thief to arrive.

James Hawkins indeed, he thinks.

20

Quarter past two.

Hodges, Holly, and Jerome are on the move, headed for their positions around Northfield High: Hodges out front, Jerome on the corner of Westfield Street, Holly beyond the high school's auditorium, on Garner Street. When they are in position, they'll let Hodges know.

In the bookshop on Lacemaker Lane, Morris adjusts his tie, turns the hanging sign from CLOSED to OPEN, and unlocks the door. He goes back to the desk and sits down. If a customer should come in to browse—not terribly likely at such a slack time of the day, but possible—he will be happy to help. If there's a customer here when the kid arrives, he'll think of something. Improvise. His heart is beating hard, but his hands are steady. The shakes are gone. *I am a wolf,* he tells himself. *I'll bite if I have to.*

Pete is in his creative writing class. The text is Strunk and White's *The Elements of Style,* and today they are discussing the famous Rule 13: *Omit needless words.* They have been assigned Hemingway's short story "The Killers," and it has provoked a lively class discussion. Many words are spoken on the subject of how Hemingway omits needless words. Pete barely hears any of them. He keeps looking at the clock, where the hands march steadily toward his appointment with Andrew Halliday. And he keeps going over his script.

At twenty-five past two, his phone vibrates against his leg. He slips it out and looks at the screen.

Mom: Come right home after school, we need to talk.

His stomach cramps and his heart kicks into a higher gear. It might be no more than some chore that needs doing, but Pete doesn't believe it. *We need to talk* is Momspeak for *Houston, we have a problem.* It could be the money, and in fact that seems likely to him, because problems come in bunches. If it is, then Tina let the cat out of the bag.

All right. If that's how it is, all right. He will go home, and they will talk, but he needs to resolve the Halliday business first. His parents aren't responsible for the jam he's in, and he won't *make* them responsible. He won't blame himself, either. He did what he had to do. If Halliday refuses to cut a deal, if he calls the police in spite of the reasons Pete can give him not to, then the less his parents know, the better. He doesn't want them charged as accessories, or something.

He thinks about switching his phone off and decides not to. If she texts him again—or if Tina does—it's better to know. He looks up at the clock and sees it's twenty to three. Soon the bell will ring, and he'll leave school.

Pete wonders if he'll ever be back.


21


Hodges parks his Prius fifty feet or so down from the high school's main entrance. He's on a yellow curb, but he has an old POLICE CALL card in his glove compartment, which he saves for just such parking problems. He places it on the dashboard. When the bell rings, he gets out of the car and leans against the hood with his arms folded, watching the bank of doors. Engraved above the entrance is the school's motto: EDUCATION IS THE LAMP OF LIFE. Hodges has his phone in one hand, ready to either make or receive a call, depending on who comes out or doesn't.

The wait isn't long, because Pete Saubers is among the first group of students to burst into the June day and come hurrying down the wide granite steps. Most of the kids are with friends. The Saubers boy is alone. Not the only one flying solo, of course, but there's a set look to his face, as if he's living in the future instead of the here and now. Hodges's eyes are as good as they ever were, and he thinks that could be the face of a soldier going into battle.

Or maybe he's just worried about finals.

Instead of heading toward the yellow buses parked beside the school on the left, he turns right, toward where Hodges is parked. Hodges ambles to meet him, speed-dialing Holly as he goes. "I've got him. Tell Jerome." He cuts the call without waiting for her to answer.

The boy angles to go around Hodges on the street side. Hodges steps in front of him. "Hey, Pete, got a minute?"

The kid's eyes snap front and center. He's good-looking, but his face is too thin and his forehead is spotted with acne. His lips are pressed so tightly together that his mouth is almost gone. "Who are you?" he asks. Not *Yes sir* or *Can I help you.* Just *Who are you.* The voice as tight-wired as the face.

"My name is Bill Hodges. I'd like to talk to you."

Kids are passing them, chattering, elbowing, laughing, shooting the shit, adjusting backpacks. A few glance at Pete and the man with the thinning white hair, but none show any interest. They have places to go and things to do.

"About what?"

"In my car would be better. So we can have some privacy." He points at the Prius.

The boy repeats, "About what?" He doesn't move.

"Here's the deal, Pete. Your sister Tina is friends with Barbara Robinson. I've known the Robinson family for years, and Barb persuaded Tina to come and talk to me. She's very worried about you."

"Why?"

"If you're asking why Barb suggested me, it's because I used to be a police detective."

325

Alarm flashes in the boy's eyes.

"If you're asking why Tina's worried, that's something we'd really be better off not discussing on the street."

Just like that the look of alarm is gone and the boy's face is expressionless again. It's the face of a good poker player. Hodges has questioned suspects who are able to wipe their faces like that, and they are usually the ones who are toughest to crack. If they crack at all.

"I don't know what Tina said to you, but she's got nothing to worry about."

"If what she told me is true, she might." Hodges gives Pete his best smile. "Come on, Pete. I'm not going to kidnap you. Swear to God."

Pete nods reluctantly. When they reach the Prius, the kid stops dead. He's reading the yellow card on the dashboard. "*Used* to be a police detective, or still are?"

"Used to be," Hodges says. "That card . . . call it a souvenir. Comes in handy sometimes. I've been off the force and collecting my pension for five years. Please get in so we can talk. I'm here as a friend. If we stand out here much longer, I'm going to melt."

"And if I don't?"

Hodges shrugs. "Then you're off."

"Okay, but only for a minute," Pete says. "I have to walk home today so I can stop at the drugstore for my father. He takes this stuff, Vioxx. Because he got hurt a few years ago."

Hodges nods. "I know. City Center. That was my case."

"Yeah?"

"Yeah."

Pete opens the passenger door and gets into the Prius. He doesn't seem nervous about being in a strange man's car. Careful and cautious, but not nervous. Hodges, who has done roughly ten thousand suspect and witness interviews over the years, is pretty sure the boy has come to a decision, although he can't tell if it's to spill what's on his mind or keep it to himself. Either way, it won't take long to find out.

He goes around and gets in behind the wheel. Pete is okay with that, but when Hodges starts the engine, he tenses up and grabs the doorhandle.

"Relax. I only want the air-conditioning. It's damn hot, in case you didn't notice. Especially for so early in the year. Probably global warm—"

"Let's get this over with so I can pick up my dad's scrip and go home. What did my sister tell you? You know she's only thirteen, right? I love her to death, but Mom calls her Tina the Drama Queen-a." And then, as if this explains everything, "She and her friend Ellen never miss *Pretty Little Liars*."

Okay, so the initial decision is not to talk. Not all that surprising. The job now is to change his mind.

"Tell me about the cash that came in the mail, Pete."

No tensing up; no *uh-oh* look flashing across the kid's face. He knew that was it, Hodges thinks. He knew as soon as his sister's name came up. He might even have had advance warning. Tina could have had a change of heart and texted him.

"You mean the mystery money," Pete says. "That's what we call it."

"Yeah. That's what I mean."

"It started coming four years ago, give or take. I was about the age Tina is now. There'd be an envelope addressed to my dad every month or so. Never any letter with it, just the money."

"Five hundred dollars."

"Once or twice it might have been a little less or a little more, I guess. I wasn't always there when it came, and after the first couple of times, Mom and Dad didn't talk about it very much."

"Like talking about it might jinx it?"

"Yeah, like that. And at some point, Teens got the idea I was the one sending it. Like as if. Back then I didn't even get an allowance."

"If you didn't do it, who did?"

"I don't know."

It seems he will stop there, but then he goes on. Hodges listens peacefully, hoping Pete will say too much. The boy is obviously intelligent, but sometimes even the intelligent ones say too much. If you let them.

"You know how every Christmas they have stories on the news about some guy giving out hundred-dollar bills in Walmart or wherever?"

"Sure."

"I think it was that type of deal. Some rich guy decided to play Secret Santa with one of the people who got hurt that day at City Center, and he picked my dad's name out of a hat." He turns to face Hodges for the first time since they got in the car, eyes wide and earnest and totally untrustworthy. "For all I know, he's sending money to some of the others, too. Probably the ones who got hurt the worst, and couldn't work."

Hodges thinks, *That's good, kiddo. It actually makes a degree of sense.*

"Giving out a thousand dollars to ten or twenty random shoppers at Christmas is one thing. Giving well over twenty grand to one family over four years is something else. If you add in other families, you'd be talking about a small fortune."

"He could be a hedge fund dude," Pete says. "You know, one of those guys who got rich while everyone else was getting poor and felt guilty about it."

He's not looking at Hodges anymore, now he's looking straight out of the windshield. There's an aroma coming off him, or so it seems to Hodges; not sweat but fatalism. Again he thinks of soldiers preparing to go into battle, knowing the chances are at least fifty-fifty that they'll be killed or wounded.

"Listen to me, Pete. I don't care about the money."

"I didn't send it!"

Hodges pushes on. It's the thing he was always best at. "It was a windfall, and you used it to help your folks out of a tough spot. That's not a bad thing, it's an admirable thing."

"Lots of people might not think so," Pete says. "If it was true, that is."

"You're wrong about that. Most people *would* think so. And I'll tell you something you can take as a hundred percent dead-red certainty, because it's based on forty years of experience as a cop. No prosecutor in this city, no prosecutor in the whole *country*, would try bringing charges against a kid who found some money and used it to help his family after his dad first lost his job and then got his legs crushed by a lunatic. The press would crucify a man or woman who tried to prosecute *that* shit."

Pete is silent, but his throat is working, as if he's holding back a sob. He wants to tell, but something is holding him back. Not the money, but related to the money. Has to be. Hodges is curious about where the cash in those monthly envelopes came from— anyone would be—but he's far more curious about what's going on with this kid now.

"You sent them the money—"

"For the last time, I *didn't*!"

"—and that went smooth as silk, but then you got into some kind of jackpot. Tell me what it is, Pete. Let me help you fix it. Let me help you make it right."

For a moment the boy trembles on the brink of revelation. Then his eyes shift to his left. Hodges follows them and sees the card he put on the dashboard. It's yellow, the color of caution. The color of danger. POLICE CALL. He wishes to Christ he'd left it in the glove compartment and parked a hundred yards farther down the street. Jesus Christ, he walks every day. A hundred yards would have been easy.

"There's nothing wrong," Pete says. He now speaks as mechanically as the computer-generated voice that comes out of Hodges's dashboard GPS, but there's a pulse beating in his temples and his hands are clasped tightly in his lap and there's sweat on his face in spite of the air-conditioning. "I didn't send the money. I have to get my dad's pills."

"Pete, listen. Even if I was still a cop, this conversation would be inadmissible in court. You're a minor, and there's no responsible adult present to counsel you. In addition I never gave you the words—the Miranda warning—"

Hodges sees the boy's face slam shut like a bank vault door. All it took was two words: *Miranda warning.*

"I appreciate your concern," Pete says in that same polite robot voice. He opens the car door. "But there's nothing wrong. Really."

"There is, though," Hodges says. He takes one of his cards from his breast pocket and holds it out. "Take this. Call me if you change your mind. Whatever it is, I can hel—"

The door closes. Hodges watches Pete Saubers walk swiftly away, puts the card back in his pocket, and thinks, Fuck me, I blew it. Six years ago, maybe even two, I would have had him.

But blaming his age is too easy. A deeper part of him, more analytical and less emotional, knows he was never really close. Thinking he might have been was an illusion. Pete has geared himself up for battle so completely that he's psychologically incapable of standing down.

The kid reaches City Drug, takes his father's prescription out of his back pocket, and goes inside. Hodges speed-dials Jerome.

"Bill! How did it go?"

"Not so good. You know City Drug?"

"Sure."

"He's getting a scrip filled there. Haul ass around the block as fast as you can. He told me he's going home, and maybe he is, but if he's not, I want to know where he *does* go. Do you think you can tail him? He knows my car. He won't know yours."

"No prob. I'm on my way."

Less than three minutes later Jerome is coming around the corner. He nips into a space just vacated by a mom picking up a couple of kids that look way too shrimpy to be in high school. Hodges pulls out, gives Jerome a wave, and heads for Holly's position on Garner Street, punching in her number as he goes. They can wait for Jerome's report together.

### 22

Pete's father does take Vioxx, has ever since he finally kicked the OxyContin, but he currently has plenty. The folded sheet of paper Pete takes from his back pocket and glances at before going into City Drug is a stern note from the assistant principal reminding juniors that Junior Skip Day is a myth, and the office will examine all absences that day with particular care.

Pete doesn't brandish the note; Bill Hodges may be retired, but he sure didn't seem retarded. No, Pete just looks at it for a moment, as if making sure he has the right thing, and goes inside. He walks rapidly to the prescription counter at the back, where Mr. Pelkey throws him a friendly salute.

"Yo, Pete. What can I get you today?"

"Nothing, Mr. Pelkey, we're all fine, but there are a couple of kids after me because I wouldn't let them copy some answers from our take-home history test. I wondered if you could help me."

Mr. Pelkey frowns and starts for the swing-gate. He likes Pete, who is always cheerful even though his family has gone through incredibly tough times. "Point them out to me. I'll tell them to get lost."

"No, I can handle it, but tomorrow. After they have a chance to cool off. Just, you know, if I could slip out the back . . ."

Mr. Pelkey drops a conspiratorial wink that says he was a kid once, too. "Sure. Come through the gate."

He leads Pete between shelves filled with salves and pills, then into the little office at the back. Here is a door with a big red sign on it reading ALARM WILL SOUND. Mr. Pelkey shields the code box next to it with one hand and punches in some numbers with the other. There's a buzz.

"Out you go," he tells Pete.

Pete thanks him, nips out onto the loading dock behind the drugstore, and jumps down to the cracked cement. An alley takes him to Frederick Street. He looks both ways for the ex-detective's Prius, doesn't see it, and breaks into a run. It takes him twenty minutes to reach Lower Main Street, and although he never spots the blue Prius, he makes a couple of sudden diversions along the way, just to be safe. He's just turning onto Lacemaker Lane when his phone vibrates again. This time the text is from his sister.

Tina: Did u talk 2 Mr. Hodges? Hope u did. Mom knows. I didn't tell she KNEW. Please don't be mad at me. ☹

As if I could, Pete thinks. Were they two years closer in age, maybe they could have gotten that sibling rivalry thing going, but maybe not even then. Sometimes he gets irritated with her, but really mad has never happened, even when she's being a brat.

The truth about the money is out, but maybe he can say money was *all* he found, and hide the fact that he tried to sell a murdered man's most private property just so his sister could go to a school where she wouldn't have to shower in a pack. And where her dumb friend Ellen would be in the rearview mirror.

He knows his chances of getting out of this clean are slim approaching none, but at some point—maybe this very afternoon, watching the hands of the clock move steadily toward the hour of three—that has become of secondary importance. What he really wants is to send the notebooks, especially the ones containing the last two Jimmy Gold novels, to NYU. Or maybe *The New Yorker*, since they published almost all of Rothstein's short stories in the fifties. And stick it to Andrew Halliday. Yes, and hard. All the way up. No way can Halliday be allowed to sell *any* of Rothstein's later work to some rich crackpot collector who will keep it in a climate-controlled secret room along with his Renoirs or Picassos or his precious fifteenth-century Bible.

When he was a kid, Pete saw the notebooks only as buried treasure. *His* treasure. He knows better now, and not just because he's fallen in love with John Rothstein's nasty, funny, and sometimes wildly moving prose. The notebooks were never just his. They were never just Rothstein's, either, no matter what he might have thought, hidden away in his New Hampshire farmhouse. They deserve to be seen and read by everyone. Maybe the little landslide that exposed the trunk on that winter day had been nothing but happenstance, but Pete doesn't believe it. He believes that, like the blood of Abel, the notebooks cried out from the ground. If that makes him a dipshit romantic, so be it. Some shit *does* mean shit.

Halfway down Lacemaker Lane, he spots the bookshop's old-fashioned scrolled sign. It's like something you might see outside an English pub, although this one reads Andrew Halliday Rare Editions instead of The Plowman's Rest, or whatever. Looking at it, Pete's last doubts disappear like smoke.

He thinks, John Rothstein is not your birthday fuck, either, Mr. Halliday. Not now and never was. You get none of the notebooks. *Bupkes*, honey, as Jimmy Gold would say. If you go to the police, I'll tell them everything, and after that business you went through with the James Agee book, we'll see who they believe.

A weight—invisible but very heavy—slips from his shoulders. Something in his heart seems to have come back into true for the first time in a long time. Pete starts for Halliday's at a fast walk, unaware that his fists are clenched.

### 23

At a few minutes past three—around the time Pete is getting into Hodges's Prius—a customer *does* come into the bookshop. He's a pudgy fellow whose thick glasses and gray-flecked goatee do not disguise his resemblance to Elmer Fudd.

"Can I help you?" Morris asks, although what first occurs to him is *Ehhh, what's up, Doc?*

"I don't know," Elmer says dubiously. "Where is Drew?"

"There was sort of a family emergency in Michigan." Morris knows Andy came from Michigan, so that's okay, but he'll have to be cagey about the family angle; if Andy ever talked about relatives, Morris has forgotten. "I'm an old friend. He asked if I'd mind the store this afternoon."

Elmer considers this. Morris's left hand, meanwhile, creeps around to the small of his back and touches the reassuring shape of the little automatic. He doesn't want to shoot this guy, doesn't want to risk the noise, but he will if he has to. There's plenty of room for Elmer back there in Andy's private office.

"He was holding a book for me, on which I have made a deposit. A first edition of *They Shoot Horses, Don't They?* It's by—"

"Horace McCoy," Morris finishes for him. The books on the shelf to the left of the desk—the ones the security DVDs were hiding behind—had slips sticking out of them, and since entering the bookstore today, Morris has examined them all. They're customer orders, and the McCoy is among them. "Fine copy, signed. Flat signature, no dedication. Some foxing on the spine."

Elmer smiles. "That's the one."

Morris takes it down from the shelf, sneaking a glance at his watch as he does. 3:13. Northfield High classes end at three, which means the boy should be here by three-thirty at the latest.

He pulls the slip and sees *Irving Yankovic, $750.* He hands the book to Elmer with a smile. "I remember this one especially. Andy—I guess he prefers Drew these days—told me he's only going to charge you five hundred. He got a better deal on it than he expected, and wanted to pass the savings along."

Any suspicion Elmer might have felt at finding a stranger in Drew's customary spot evaporates at the prospect of saving two hundred and fifty dollars. He takes out his checkbook. "So . . . with the deposit, that comes to . . ."

Morris waves a magnanimous hand. "He neglected to tell me what the deposit was. Just deduct it. I'm sure he trusts you."

"After all these years, he certainly ought to." Elmer bends over the counter and begins writing the check. He does this with excruciating slowness. Morris checks the clock. 3:16. "Have you read *They Shoot Horses?*"

"No," Morris says. "I missed that one."

What will he do if the kid comes in while this pretentious goateed asshole is still dithering over his checkbook? He won't be able to tell Saubers that Andy's in back, not after he's told Elmer Fudd he's in Michigan. Sweat begins to trickle out of his hairline and down his cheeks. He can feel it. He used to sweat like that in prison, while he was waiting to be raped.

"Marvelous book," Elmer says, pausing with his pen poised over the half-written check. "Marvelous noir, and a piece of social commentary to rival *The Grapes of Wrath*." He pauses, thinking instead of writing, and now it's 3:18. "Well . . . perhaps not *Grapes*, that might be going too far, but it certainly rivals *In Dubious Battle*, which is more of a socialist tract than a novel, don't you agree?"

Morris says he does. His hands feel numb. If he has to pull out the gun, he's apt to drop it. Or shoot himself straight down the crack of his ass. This makes him yawp a sudden laugh, a startling sound in this narrow, book-lined space.

Elmer looks up, frowning. "Something funny? About Steinbeck, perhaps?"

"Absolutely not," Morris says. "It's . . . I have a medical condition." He runs a hand down one damp cheek. "It makes me sweat, and then I start laughing." The look on Elmer Fudd's face makes him laugh again. He wonders if Andy and Elmer ever had sex, and the thought of that bouncing, slapping flesh makes him laugh some more. "I'm sorry, Mr. Yankovic. It's not you. And by the way . . . are you related to the noted popular-music humorist Weird Al Yankovic?"

"No, not at all." Yankovic scribbles his signature in a hurry, rips the check loose from his checkbook, and passes it to Morris, who is grinning and thinking that this is a scene John Rothstein could have written. During the exchange, Yankovic takes care that their fingers should not touch.

"Sorry about the laughing," Morris says, laughing harder. He's remembering that they used to call the noted popular-musical humorist Weird Al Yank-My-Dick. "I really can't control it." The clock now reads 3:21, and even that is funny.

"I understand." Elmer is backing away with the book clutched to his chest. "Thank you."

He hurries toward the door. Morris calls after him, "Make sure you tell Andy I gave you the discount. When you see him."

This makes Morris laugh harder than ever, because that's a good one. When you see him! Get it?

When the fit finally passes, it's 3:25, and for the first time it occurs to Morris that maybe he hurried Mr. Irving "Elmer Fudd" Yankovic out for no reason at all. Maybe the boy has changed his mind. Maybe he's not coming, and there's nothing funny about that.

Well, Morris thinks, if he doesn't show up here, I'll just have to pay a house call. Then the joke will be on him. Won't it?

## 24

Twenty to four.

There's no need to park on a yellow curb now; the parents who clogged the area around the high school earlier, waiting to pick up their kids, have all departed. The buses are gone, too. Hodges, Holly, and Jerome are in a Mercedes sedan that once belonged to Holly's cousin Olivia. It was used as a murder weapon at City Center, but none of them is thinking about that now. They have other things in mind, chiefly Thomas Saubers's son.

"The kid may be in trouble, but you have to admit he's a quick thinker," Jerome says. After ten minutes parked down the street from City Drug, he went inside and ascertained that the boy he was tasked to follow had departed. "A pro couldn't have done much better."

"True," Hodges says. The boy has turned into a challenge, certainly more of a challenge than the airplane-stealing Mr. Madden. Hodges hasn't questioned the pharmacist himself and doesn't need to. Pete's been getting prescriptions filled there for years, he knows the pharmacist and the pharmacist knows him. The kid made up some bullshit story, the pharmacist let him use the back door, and pop goes the weasel. They never covered Frederick Street, because there seemed to be no need.

"Now what?" Jerome asks.

"I think we should go over to the Saubers house. We had a slim chance of keeping his parents out of this, per Tina's request, but I think that just went by the boards."

"They must already have some idea it was him," Jerome says. "I mean, they're his *folks*."

Hodges thinks of saying *There are none so blind as those who will not see*, and shrugs instead.

Holly has contributed nothing to the discussion so far, has just sat behind the wheel of her big boat of a car, arms crossed over her bosom, fingers tapping lightly at her shoulders. Now she turns to Hodges, who is sprawled in the backseat. "Did you ask Peter about the notebook?"

"I never got a chance," Hodges says. Holly's got a bee in her hat about that notebook, and he *should* have asked, just to satisfy her, but the truth is, it never even crossed his mind. "He decided to go, and boogied. Wouldn't even take my card."

Holly points to the school. "I think we should talk to Ricky the Hippie before we leave." And when neither of them replies: "Peter's *house* will still *be* there, you know. It's not going to *fly away*, or anything."

"Guess it wouldn't hurt," Jerome says.

Hodges sighs. "And tell him what, exactly? That one of his students found or stole a stack of money and doled it out to his parents like a monthly allowance? The parents should find that out before some teacher who probably doesn't know jack-shit about anything. And Pete should be the one to tell them. It'll let his sister off the hook, for one thing."

"But if he's in some kind of jam he doesn't want them to know about, and he still wanted to talk to someone . . . you know, an adult . . ." Jerome is four years older than he was when he helped Hodges with the Brady Hartsfield mess, old enough to vote and buy legal liquor, but still young enough to remember how it is to be seventeen and suddenly realize you've gotten in over your head with something. When that happens, you want to talk to somebody who's been around the block a few times.

"Jerome's right," Holly says. She turns back to Hodges. "Let's talk to the teacher and find out if Pete asked for advice about anything. If he asks why we want to know—"

"Of *course* he'll want to know why," Hodges says, "and I can't exactly claim confidentiality. I'm not a lawyer."

"Or a priest," Jerome adds, not helpfully.

"You can tell him we're friends of the family," Holly says firmly. "And that's true." She opens her door.

"You have a hunch about this," Hodges says. "Am I right?"

"Yes," she says. "It's a Holly-hunch. Now come on."


25


As they are walking up the wide front steps and beneath the motto EDUCATION IS THE LAMP OF LIFE, the door of Andrew Halliday Rare Editions opens again and Pete Saubers steps inside. He starts down the main aisle, then stops, frowning. The man behind the desk isn't Mr. Halliday. He is in most ways the exact *opposite* of Mr. Halliday, pale instead of florid (except for his lips, which are weirdly red), white-haired instead of bald, and thin instead of fat. Almost gaunt. Jesus. Pete expected his script to go out the window, but not this fast.

"Where's Mr. Halliday? I had an appointment to see him."

The stranger smiles. "Yes, of course, although he didn't give me your name. He just said a young man. He's waiting for you in his office at the back of the shop." This is actually true. In a way. "Just knock and go in."

Pete relaxes a little. It makes sense that Halliday wouldn't want to have such a crucial meeting out here, where anybody looking for a secondhand copy of *To Kill a Mockingbird* could walk in and interrupt them. He's being careful, thinking ahead. If Pete doesn't do the same, his slim chance of coming out of this okay will go out the window.

"Thanks," he says, and walks between tall bookcases toward the back of the shop.

As soon as he goes by the desk, Morris rises and goes quickly and quietly to the front of the shop. He flips the sign in the door from OPEN to CLOSED.

Then he turns the bolt.

## 26

The secretary in the main office of Northfield High looks curiously at the trio of after-school visitors, but asks no questions. Perhaps she assumes they are family members come to plead the case of some failing student. Whatever they are, it's Howie Ricker's problem, not hers.

She checks a magnetic board covered with multicolored tags and says, "He should still be in his homeroom. That's three-oh-nine, on the third floor, but please peek through the window and make sure he's not with a student. He has conferences today until four, and with school ending in a couple of weeks, plenty of kids stop by to ask for help on their final papers. Or plead for extra time."

Hodges thanks her and they go up the stairs, their heels echoing. From somewhere below, a quartet of musicians is playing "Greensleeves." From somewhere above, a hearty male voice cries jovially, "You *suck*, Malone!"

Room 309 is halfway down the third-floor corridor, and Mr. Ricker, dressed in an eye-burning paisley shirt with the collar unbuttoned and the tie pulled down, is talking to a girl who is gesturing dramatically with her hands. Ricker glances up, sees he has visitors, then returns his attention to the girl.

The visitors stand against the wall, where posters advertise summer classes, summer workshops, summer holiday destinations, an end-of-year dance. A couple of girls come bopping down the hall, both wearing softball jerseys and caps. One is tossing a catcher's mitt from hand to hand, playing hot potato with it.

Holly's phone goes off, playing an ominous handful of notes from the "Jaws" theme. Without slowing, one of the girls says, "You're gonna need a bigger boat," and they both laugh.

Holly looks at her phone, then puts it away. "A text from Tina," she says.

Hodges raises his eyebrows.

"Her mother knows about the money. Her father will too, as soon as he gets home from work." She nods toward the closed door of Mr. Ricker's room. "No reason to hold back now."

27

The first thing Pete becomes aware of when he opens the door to the darkened inner office is the billowing stench. It's both metal-lic and organic, like steel shavings mixed with spoiled cabbage. The next thing is the sound, a low buzzing. Flies, he thinks, and although he can't see what's in there, the smell and the sound come together in his mind with a thud like a heavy piece of furniture falling over. He turns to flee.

The clerk with the red lips is standing there beneath one of the hanging globes that light the back of the store, and in his hand is a strangely jolly gun, red and black with inlaid gold curlicues. Pete's first thought is Looks fake. They never look fake in the movies.

"Keep your head, Peter," the clerk says. "Don't do anything foolish and you won't get hurt. This is just a discussion."

Pete's second thought is You're lying. I can see it in your eyes.

"Turn around, take a step forward, and turn on the light. The switch is to the left of the door. Then go in, but don't try to slam the door, unless you want a bullet in the back."

Pete steps forward. Everything inside him from the chest on down feels loose and in motion. He hopes he won't piss his pants like a baby. Probably that wouldn't be such a big deal—surely he wouldn't be the first person to spray his Jockeys when a gun is pointed at him—but it *seems* like a big deal. He fumbles with his left hand, finds the switch, and flips it. When he sees the thing lying on the sodden carpet, he tries to scream, but the muscles in his diaphragm aren't working and all that comes out is a watery moan. Flies are buzzing and lighting on what remains of Mr. Hal-liday's face. Which is not much.

"I know," the clerk says sympathetically. "Not very pretty, is he?

Object lessons rarely are. He pissed me off, Pete. Do you want to piss me off?"

"No," Pete says in a high, wavering voice. It sounds more like Tina's than his own. "I don't."

"Then you have learned your lesson. Go on in. Move very slowly, but feel free to avoid the mess."

Pete steps in on legs he can barely feel, edging to his left along one of the bookcases, trying to keep his loafers on the part of the rug that hasn't been soaked. There isn't much. His initial panic has been replaced by a glassy sheet of terror. He keeps thinking of those red lips. Keeps imagining the big bad wolf telling Red Riding Hood, *The better to kiss you with, my dear.*

I have to think, he tells himself. I have to, or I'm going to die in this room. Probably I will anyway, but if I can't think, it's for sure.

He keeps skirting the blotch of blackish-purple until a cherrywood sideboard blocks his path, and there he stops. To go farther would mean stepping onto the bloody part of the rug, and it might still be wet enough to *squelch*. On the sideboard are crystal decanters of booze and a number of squat glasses. On the desk he sees a hatchet, its blade throwing back a reflection of the overhead light. That is surely the weapon the man with the red lips used to kill Mr. Halliday, and Pete supposes it should scare him even more, but instead the sight of it clears his mind like a hard slap.

The door clicks shut behind him. The clerk who probably isn't a clerk leans against it, pointing the jolly little gun at Pete. "All right," he says, and smiles. "Now we can talk."

"Wh-Wh—" He clears his throat, tries again, this time sounds a little more like himself. "What? Talk about what?"

"Don't be disingenuous. The notebooks. The ones you stole."

It all comes together in Pete's mind. His mouth falls open.

The clerk who isn't a clerk smiles. "Ah. The penny drops, I see. Tell me where they are, and you might get out of this alive."

Pete doesn't think so.

He thinks he already knows too much for that.

## 28

When the girl emerges from Mr. Ricker's homeroom, she's smiling, so her conference must have gone all right. She even twiddles her fingers in a little wave—perhaps to all three of them, more likely just to Jerome—as she hurries off down the hall.

Mr. Ricker, who has accompanied her to the door, looks at Hodges and his associates. "Can I help you, lady and gentlemen?"

"Not likely," Hodges says, "but worth a try. May we come in?"

"Of course."

They sit at desks in the first row like attentive students. Ricker plants himself on the edge of his desk, an informality he eschewed when talking to his young conferee. "I'm pretty sure you're not parents, so what's up?"

"It's about one of your students," Hodges says. "A boy named Peter Saubers. We think he may be in trouble."

Ricker frowns. "Pete? That doesn't seem likely. He's one of the best students I've ever had. Demonstrates a genuine love of literature, especially American literature. Honor Roll every quarter. What kind of trouble do you think he's in?"

"That's the thing—we don't know. I asked, but he stonewalled me."

Ricker's frown deepens. "That doesn't sound like the Pete Saubers I know."

"It has to do with some money he seems to have come into a

few years back. I'd like to fill you in on what we know. It won't take long."

"Please say it has nothing to do with drugs."

"It doesn't."

Ricker looks relieved. "Good. Seen too much of that, and the smart kids are just as much at risk as the dumb ones. More, in some cases. Tell me. I'll help if I can."

Hodges starts with the money that began arriving at the Saubers house in what was, almost literally, the family's darkest hour. He tells Ricker about how, seven months after the monthly deliveries of mystery cash ceased, Pete began to seem stressed and unhappy. He finishes with Tina's conviction that her brother tried to get some more money, maybe from the same source the mystery cash came from, and is in his current jam as a result.

"He grew a moustache," Ricker muses when Hodges has finished. "He's in Mrs. Davis's Creative Writing course now, but I saw him in the hall one day and joshed him about it."

"How did he take the joshing?" Jerome asks.

"Not sure he even heard me. He seemed to be on another planet. But that's not uncommon with teenagers, as I'm sure you know. Especially when summer vacation's right around the corner."

Holly asks, "Did he ever mention a notebook to you? A Moleskine?"

Ricker considers it while Holly looks at him hopefully.

"No," he says at last. "I don't think so."

She deflates.

"Did he come to you about *anything*?" Hodges asks. "Anything at all that was troubling him, no matter how minor? I raised a daughter, and I know they sometimes talk about their problems in code. Probably you know that, too."

Ricker smiles. "The famous friend-who."

"Beg pardon?"

"As in 'I have a friend who might have gotten his girlfriend pregnant.' Or 'I have a friend who knows who spray-painted anti-gay
slogans on the wall in the boys' locker room.' After a couple of years
on the job, every teacher knows about the famous friend-who."

Jerome asks, "Did Pete Saubers have a friend-who?"

"Not that I can recall. I'm very sorry. I'd help you if I could."

Holly asks, in a small and not very hopeful voice, "Never a
friend who kept a secret diary or maybe found some valuable information in a notebook?"

Ricker shakes his head. "No. I'm really sorry. Jesus, I hate to
think of Pete in trouble. He wrote one of the finest term papers
I've ever gotten from a student. It was about the Jimmy Gold trilogy."

"John Rothstein," Jerome says, smiling. "I used to have a tee-
shirt that said—"

"Don't tell me," Ricker says. "Shit don't mean shit."

"Actually, no. It was the one about not being anyone's birthday . . . uh, present."

"Ah," Ricker says, smiling. "*That* one."

Hodges gets up. "I'm more of a Michael Connelly man. Thanks
for your time." He holds out his hand. Ricker shakes it. Jerome is
also getting up, but Holly remains seated.

"John Rothstein," she says. "He wrote that book about the kid
who got fed up with his parents and ran away to New York City,
right?"

"That was the first novel in the Gold trilogy, yes. Pete was crazy
about Rothstein. Probably still is. He may discover new heroes
in college, but when he was in my class, he thought Rothstein
walked on water. Have you read him?"

"I never have," Holly says, also getting up. "But I'm a big movie fan, so I always go to a website called Deadline. To read the latest Hollywood news? They had an article about how all these producers wanted to make a movie out of *The Runner*. Only no matter how much money they offered, he told them to go to hell."

"That sounds like Rothstein, all right," Ricker says. "A famous curmudgeon. Hated the movies. Claimed they were art for idiots. Sneered at the word *cinema*. Wrote an essay about it, I think."

Holly has brightened. "Then he got *murdered* and there was no *will* and they still can't make a movie because of all the *legal* problems."

"Holly, we ought to go," Hodges says. He wants to get over to the Saubers home. Wherever Pete is now, he'll turn up there eventually.

"Okay . . . I guess . . ." She sighs. Although in her late forties, and even with the mood-levelers she takes, Holly still spends too much time on an emotional rollercoaster. Now the light in her eyes is going out and she looks terribly downcast. Hodges feels bad for her, wants to tell her that, even though not many hunches pan out, you shouldn't stop playing them. Because the few that do pan out are pure gold. Not exactly a pearl of wisdom, but later, when he has a private moment with her, he'll pass it on. Try to ease the sting a little.

"Thank you for your time, Mr. Ricker." Hodges opens the door. Faintly, like music heard in a dream, comes the sound of "Greensleeves."

"Oh my gosh," Ricker says. "Hold the phone."

They turn back to him.

"Pete *did* come to me about something, and not so long ago. But I see so many students . . ."

Hodges nods understandingly.

"And it wasn't a big deal, no adolescent Sturm und Drang, it was actually a very pleasant conversation. It only came to mind now because it was about that book you mentioned, Ms. Gibney. *The Runner*." He smiles a little. "Pete didn't have a friend-who, though. He had an uncle-who."

Hodges feels a spark of something bright and hot, like a lit fuse. "What was it about Pete's uncle that made him worth discussing?"

"Pete said the uncle had a signed first edition of *The Runner*. He offered it to Pete because Pete was a Rothstein fan—that was the story, anyway. Pete told me he was interested in selling it. I asked him if he was sure he wanted to part with a book signed by his literary idol, and he said he was considering it very seriously. He was hoping to help send his sister to one of the private schools, I can't remember which one—"

"Chapel Ridge," Holly says. The light in her eyes has returned.

"I think that's right."

Hodges walks slowly back to the desk. "Tell me . . . *us* . . . everything you remember about that conversation."

"That's really all, except for one thing that kind of nudged my bullshit meter. He said his uncle won the book in a poker game. I remember thinking that's the kind of thing that happens in novels or movies, but rarely in real life. But of course, sometimes life *does* imitate art."

Hodges frames the obvious question, but Jerome gets there first. "Did he ask you about booksellers?"

"Yes, that's really why he came to me. He had a short list of local dealers, probably gleaned from the Internet. I steered him away from one of them. Bit of a shady reputation there."

Jerome looks at Holly. Holly looks at Hodges. Hodges looks at Howard Ricker and asks the obvious follow-up question. He's locked in now, the fuse in his head burning brightly.

"What's this shady book dealer's name?"

29

Pete sees only one chance to go on living. As long as the man with the red lips and pasty complexion doesn't know where the Rothstein notebooks are, he won't pull the trigger of the gun, which is looking less jolly all the time.

"You're Mr. Halliday's partner, aren't you?" he says, not exactly looking at the corpse—it's too awful—but lifting his chin in that direction. "In cahoots with him."

Red Lips utters a brief chuckle, then does something that shocks Peter, who believed until that moment he was beyond shock. He spits on the body.

"He was *never* my partner. Although he had his chance, once upon a time. Long before you were even a twinkle in your father's eye, Peter. And while I find your attempt at a diversion admirable, I must insist that we keep to the subject at hand. Where are the notebooks? In your house? Which used to be *my* house, by the way. Isn't that an interesting co-inky-dink?"

Here is another shock. "*Your—*"

"More ancient history. Never mind. Is that where they are?"

"No. They were for awhile, but I moved them."

"And should I believe that? I think not."

"Because of him." Pete again lifts his chin toward the body. "I tried to sell him some of the notebooks, and he threatened to tell the police. I *had* to move them."

Red Lips considers this, then gives a nod. "All right, I can see that. It fits with what he told me. So where did you put them? Out with it, Peter. Fess up. We'll both feel better, especially you. If 'twere to be done, 'twere well it were done quickly. *Macbeth,* act one."

Pete does not fess up. To fess up is to die. This is the man who stole the notebooks in the first place, he knows that now. Stole the notebooks and murdered John Rothstein over thirty years ago. And now he's murdered Mr. Halliday. Will he scruple at adding Pete Saubers to his list?

Red Lips has no trouble reading his mind. "I don't have to kill you, you know. Not right away, at least. I can put a bullet in your leg. If that doesn't loosen your lips, I'll put one in your balls. With those gone, a young fellow like you wouldn't have much to live for, anyway. Would he?"

Pushed into a final corner, Pete has nothing left but the burning, helpless outrage only adolescents can feel. "You killed him! *You killed John Rothstein!*" Tears are welling in his eyes; they run down his cheeks in warm trickles. "The best writer of the twentieth century and you broke into his house and killed him! For money! Just for money!"

"*Not* for money!" Red Lips shouts back. "*He sold out!*"

He takes a step forward, the muzzle of the gun dipping slightly.

"He sent Jimmy Gold to hell and called it advertising! And by the way, who are you to be high and mighty? You tried to sell the notebooks yourself! *I* don't want to sell them. Maybe once, when I was young and stupid, but not anymore. I want to read them. They're mine. I want to run my hand over the ink and feel the words he set down in his own hand. Thinking about that was all that kept me sane for thirty-six years!"

He takes another step forward.

"Yes, and what about the money in the trunk? Did you take that, too? Of course you did! You're the thief, not me! *You!*"

In that moment Pete is too furious to think about escape, because this last accusation, unfair though it may be, is all too true. He simply grabs one of the liquor decanters and fires it at his tormentor as hard as he can. Red Lips isn't expecting it. He flinches, turning slightly to the right as he does so, and the bottle strikes him in the shoulder. The glass stopper comes out when it hits the carpet. The sharp and stinging odor of whiskey joins the smell of old blood. The flies buzz in an agitated cloud, their meal interrupted.

Pete grabs another decanter and lunges at Red Lips with it raised like a cudgel, the gun forgotten. He trips over Halliday's sprawled legs, goes to one knee, and when Red Lips shoots—the sound in the closed room is like a flat handclap—the bullet goes over his head almost close enough to part his hair. Pete hears it: zzzzz. He throws the second decanter and this one strikes Red Lips just below the mouth, drawing blood. He cries out, staggers backward, hits the wall.

The last two decanters are behind him now, and there is no time to turn and grab another. Pete pushes to his feet and snatches the hatchet from the desk, not by the rubberized handle but by the head. He feels the sting as the blade cuts into his palm, but it's distant, pain felt by somebody living in another country. Red Lips has held on to the gun, and is bringing it around for another shot. Pete can't exactly think, but a deeper part of his mind, perhaps never called upon until today, understands that if he were closer, he could grapple with Red Lips and get the gun away from him. Easily. He's younger, stronger. But the desk is between them, so he throws the hatchet, instead. It whirls at Red Lips end over end, like a tomahawk.

Red Lips screams and cringes away from it, raising the hand holding the gun to protect his face. The blunt side of the hatchet's head strikes his forearm. The gun flies up, strikes one of the bookcases, and clatters to the floor. There's another handclap as it discharges. Pete doesn't know where this second bullet goes, but it's not into him, and that's all he cares about.

Red Lips crawls for the gun with his fine white hair hanging in his eyes and blood dripping from his chin. He's eerily fast, somehow lizardlike. Pete calculates, still without thinking, and sees that if he races Red Lips to the gun, he'll lose. It will be close, but he will. There's a chance he might be able to grab the man's arm before he can turn the gun to fire, but not a good one.

He bolts for the door instead.

"Come back, you shit!" Red Lips shouts. "We're not done!"

Coherent thought makes a brief reappearance. Oh yes we are, Pete thinks.

He rakes the door open and goes through hunched over. He slams it shut behind him with a hard fling of his left hand and sprints for the front of the shop, toward Lacemaker Lane and the blessed lives of other people. There's another gunshot—muffled—and Pete hunches further, but there's no impact and no pain.

He pulls at the front door. It doesn't open. He casts a wild glance back over his shoulder and sees Red Lips shamble out of Halliday's office, his chin wreathed in a blood goatee. He's got the gun and he's trying to aim it. Pete paws at the thumb-lock with fingers that have no feeling, manages to grasp it, and twists. A moment later he's on the sunny sidewalk. No one looks at him; no one is even in the immediate vicinity. On this hot weekday afternoon, the Lacemaker Lane walking mall is as close to deserted as it ever gets.

Pete runs blindly, with no idea of where he's going.

30

It's Hodges behind the wheel of Holly's Mercedes. He obeys the traffic signals and doesn't weave wildly from lane to lane, but he makes the best time he can. He isn't a bit surprised that this run from the North Side to the Halliday bookshop on Lacemaker Lane brings back memories of a much wilder ride in this same car. It had been Jerome at the wheel that night.

"How sure are you that Tina's brother went to this Halliday guy?" Jerome asks. He's in the back this afternoon.

"He did," Holly says without looking up from her iPad, which she has taken from the Benz's capacious glove compartment. "I know he did, and I think I know why. It wasn't any signed book, either." She taps at the screen and mutters, "Come on come on come on. *Load*, you bugger!"

"What are you looking for, Hollyberry?" Jerome asks, leaning forward between the seats.

She turns to glare at him. "Don't call me that, you know I hate that."

"Sorry, sorry." Jerome rolls his eyes.

"Tell you in a minute," she says. "I've almost got it. I just wish I had some WiFi instead of this buggery cell connection. It's so *slow* and *poopy*."

Hodges laughs. He can't help it. This time Holly turns her glare on him, punching away at the screen even as she does so.

Hodges climbs a ramp and merges onto the Crosstown Connector. "It's starting to fit together," he tells Jerome. "Assuming the book Pete talked about to Ricker was actually a writer's notebook—the one Tina saw. The one Pete was so anxious to hide under his pillow."

"Oh, it was," Holly says without looking up from her iPad. "Holly Gibney says that's a big ten-four." She punches something else in, swipes the screen, and gives a cry of frustration that makes both of her companions jump. "Oooh, these goddam pop-up ads make me *so fracking crazy*!"

"Calm down," Hodges tells her.

She ignores him. "You wait. You wait and see."

"The money and the notebook were a package deal," Jerome says. "The Saubers kid found them together. That's what you think, right?"

"Yeah," Hodges says.

"And whatever was in the notebook was worth more money. Except a reputable rare book dealer wouldn't touch it with a ten-foot po—"

"*GOT IT!*" Holly screams, making them both jump. The Mercedes swerves. The guy in the next lane honks irritably and makes an unmistakable hand gesture.

"Got what?" Jerome asks.

"Not *what*, Jerome, *who*! *John Fracking Rothstein!* Murdered in 1978! At least three men broke into his farmhouse—in New Hampshire, this was—and killed him. They also broke into his safe. Listen to this. It's from the Manchester *Union Leader*, three days after he was killed."

As she reads, Hodges exits the Crosstown onto Lower Main.

"'There is growing certainty that the robbers were after more than money. "They may also have taken a number of notebooks containing various writings Mr. Rothstein did after retiring from public life," a source close to the investigation said. The source went on to speculate that the notebooks, whose existence was confirmed late yesterday by John Rothstein's housekeeper, might be worth a great deal on the black market.'"

Holly's eyes are blazing. She is having one of those divine passages where she has forgotten herself entirely.

"The robbers hid it," she says.

"Hid the money," Jerome says. "The twenty thousand."

"*And* the notebooks. Pete found at least some of them, maybe even all of them. He used the money to help his folks. He didn't

354

get in trouble until he tried selling the notebooks to help his sister. Halliday knows. By now he may even have them. Hurry up, Bill. Hurry up hurry up hurry *up!*"

## 31

Morris lurches to the front of the store, heart pounding, temples thudding. He drops Andy's gun into his sportcoat pocket, snatches up a book from one of the display tables, opens it, and slams it against his chin to stanch the blood. He could have wiped it with the sleeve of his coat, almost did, but he's thinking again now and knows better. He'll have to go out in public, and he doesn't want to do that smeared with blood. The boy had some on his pants, though, and that's good. That's fine, in fact.

I'm thinking again, and the boy better be thinking, too. If he is, I can still rescue this situation.

He opens the shop door and looks both ways. No sign of Saubers. He expected nothing else. Teenagers are fast. They're like cockroaches that way.

Morris scrabbles in his pocket for the scrap of paper with Pete's cell phone number on it, and suffers a moment of raw panic when he can't find it. At last his fingers touch something scrunched far down in one corner and he breathes a sigh of relief. His heart is pounding, pounding, and he slams one hand against his bony chest.

Don't you give up on me now, he thinks. Don't you dare.

He uses the shop's landline to call Saubers, because that also fits the story he's constructing in his mind. Morris thinks it's a good story. He doubts if John Rothstein could have told a better one.

32

When Pete comes fully back to himself, he's in a place Morris Bellamy knows well: Government Square, across from the Happy Cup Café. He sits on a bench to catch his breath, looking anxiously back the way he's come. He sees no sign of Red Lips, and this doesn't surprise him. Pete is also thinking again, and knows the man who tried to kill him would attract attention on the street. *I got him pretty good*, Pete thinks grimly. Red Lips is now Bloody Chin.

Good so far, but what now?

As if in answer, his cell phone vibrates. Pete pulls it out of his pocket and looks at the number displayed. He recognizes the last four digits, 8877, from when he called Halliday and left a message about the weekend trip to River Bend Resort. It has to be Red Lips; it sure can't be Mr. Halliday. This thought is so awful it makes him laugh, although the sound that comes out sounds more like a sob.

His first impulse is to not answer. What changes his mind is something Red Lips said: *Your house used to be my house. Isn't that an interesting co-inky-dink?*

His mother's text instructed him to come home right after school. Tina's text said their mother knew about the money. So they're together at the house, waiting for him. Pete doesn't want to alarm them unnecessarily—especially when *he's* the cause for alarm—but he needs to know what this incoming call is about, especially since Dad isn't around to protect the two of them if the crazy guy should turn up on Sycamore Street. Dad's in Victor County, doing one of his show-and-tells.

I'll call the police, Pete thinks. When I tell him that, he'll head for the hills. He'll have to. This thought brings some marginal comfort, and he pushes ACCEPT.

"Hello, Peter," Red Lips says.

"I don't need to talk to you," Peter says. "You better run, because I'm calling the cops."

"I'm glad I reached you before you did something so foolish. You won't believe this, but I'm telling you as a friend."

"You're right," Pete says. "I don't believe it. You tried to kill me."

"Here's something else you won't believe: I'm glad I didn't. Because then I'd never find out where you hid the Rothstein notebooks."

"You never will," Pete says, and adds, "I'm telling you as a friend." He's feeling a little steadier now. Red Lips isn't chasing him, and he isn't on his way to Sycamore Street, either. He's hiding in the bookshop and talking on the landline.

"That's what you think now, because you haven't considered the long view. I have. Here's the situation: You went to Andy to sell the notebooks. He tried to blackmail you instead, so you killed him."

Pete says nothing. He can't. He's flabbergasted.

"Peter? Are you there? If you don't want to spend a year in the Riverview Youth Detention Center followed by twenty or so in Waynesville, you better be. I've been in both, and I can tell you they're no place for young men with virgin bottoms. College would be much better, don't you think?"

"I wasn't even in the city last weekend," Pete says. "I was at a school retreat. I can prove it."

Red Lips doesn't hesitate. "Then you did it before you left. Or possibly on Sunday night, after you got back. The police are going to find your voicemail—I was sure to save it. There's also DVD security footage of you arguing with him. I took the discs, but I'll be sure the police get them if we can't come to an agreement. Then there's the fingerprints. They'll find yours on the doorknob of his inner office. Better still, they'll find them on the murder weapon. I think you're in a box, even if you can account for every minute of your time this past weekend."

Pete realizes with dismay that he can't even do that. He missed *everything* on Sunday. He remembers Ms. Bran—alias Bran Stoker—standing by the door of the bus just twenty-four hours ago, cell phone in hand, ready to call 911 and report a missing student.

*I'm sorry,* he told her. *I was sick to my stomach. I thought the fresh air would help me. I was vomiting.*

He can see her in court, all too clearly, saying that yes, Peter *did* look sick that afternoon. And he can hear the prosecuting attorney telling the jury that any teenage boy probably *would* look sick after chopping an elderly book dealer into kindling with a hatchet.

*Ladies and gentlemen of the jury, I submit to you that Pete Saubers hitchhiked back to the city that Sunday morning because he had an appointment with Mr. Halliday, who thought Mr. Saubers had finally decided to give in to his blackmail demands. Only Mr. Saubers had no intention of giving in.*

It's a nightmare, Pete thinks. Like dealing with Halliday all over again, only a thousand times worse.

"Peter? Are you there?"

"No one would believe it. Not for a second. Not once they find out about you."

"And who am I, exactly?"

The wolf, Pete thinks. You're the big bad wolf.

People must have seen him that Sunday, wandering around the resort acreage. *Plenty* of people, because he'd mostly stuck to the paths. Some would surely remember him and come forward. But, as Red Lips said, that left before the trip and after. Especially Sunday night, when he'd gone straight to his room and closed the door. On *CSI* and *Criminal Minds*, police scientists were always able to figure out the exact time of a murdered person's death, but in real life, who knew? Not Pete. And if the police had a good suspect, one whose prints were on the murder weapon, the time of death might become negotiable.

But I *had* to throw the hatchet at him! he thinks. It was all I had!

Believing that things can get no worse, Pete looks down and sees a bloodstain on his knee.

Mr. Halliday's blood.

"I can fix this," Red Lips says smoothly, "and if we come to terms, I will. I can wipe your fingerprints. I can erase the voice-mail. I can destroy the security DVDs. All you have to do is tell me where the notebooks are."

"Like I should trust you!"

"You should." Low. Coaxing and reasonable. "Think about it, Peter. With you out of the picture, Andy's murder looks like an attempted robbery gone wrong. The work of some random crackhead or meth freak. That's good for both of us. With you *in* the picture, the existence of the notebooks comes out. Why would I want that?"

You won't care, Pete thinks. You won't have to, because you won't be anywhere near here when Halliday is discovered dead in his office. You said you were in Waynesville, and that makes you an ex-con, and you knew Mr. Halliday. Put those together, and you'd be a suspect, too. Your fingerprints are in there as well as mine, and I don't think you can wipe them all up. What you can do—if I let you—is take the notebooks and go. And once you're gone, what's to keep you from sending the police those security DVDs, just for spite? To get back at me for hitting you with that liquor bottle and then getting away? If I agree to what you're saying . . .

He finishes the thought aloud. "I'll only look worse. No matter what you say."

"I assure you that's not true."

He sounds like a lawyer, one of the sleazy ones with fancy hair who advertise on the cable channels late at night. Pete's outrage returns and straightens him on the bench like an electric shock.

"Fuck you. You're *never* getting those notebooks."

He ends the call. The phone buzzes in his hand almost immediately, same number, Red Lips calling back. Pete hits DECLINE and turns the phone off. Right now he needs to think harder and smarter than ever in his life.

Mom and Tina, they're the most important thing. He has to talk to Mom, tell her that she and Teens have to get out of the house right away. Go to a motel, or something. They have to—

No, not Mom. It's his sister he has to talk to, at least to begin with.

He didn't take that Mr. Hodges's card, but Tina must know how to get in touch with him. If that doesn't work, he'll have to call the police and take his chances. He will not put his family at risk, no matter what.

Pete speed-dials his sister.

33

"Hello? Peter? Hello? *Hello?*"

Nothing. The thieving sonofabitch has hung up. Morris's first impulse is to rip the desk phone out of the wall and throw it at one of the bookcases, but he restrains himself at the last moment. This is no time to lose himself in a rage.

So what now? What next? Is Saubers going to call the police despite all the evidence stacked against him?

Morris can't allow himself to believe that, because if he does, the notebooks will be lost to him. And consider this: Would the boy take such an irrevocable step without talking to his parents first? Without asking their advice? Without warning them?

I have to move fast, Morris thinks, and aloud, as he wipes his fingerprints off the phone: "If 'twere to be done, best it be done quickly."

And 'twere best he wash his face and leave by the back door. He doesn't believe the gunshots were heard on the street—the inner office must be damned near soundproof, lined with books as it is—but he doesn't want to take the risk.

He scrubs away the blood goatee in Halliday's bathroom, careful to leave the red-stained washcloth in the sink where the police will find it when they eventually turn up. With that done, he follows a narrow aisle to a door with an EXIT sign above it and boxes of books stacked in front of it. He moves them, thinking how stupid to block the fire exit that way. Stupid and shortsighted.

That could be my old pal's epitaph, Morris thinks. Here lies Andrew Halliday, a fat, stupid, shortsighted homo. He will not be missed.

The heat of late afternoon whacks him like a hammer, and he staggers. His head is thumping from being hit with that goddam decanter, but the brains inside are in high gear. He gets in the Subaru, where it's even hotter, and turns the air-conditioning to max as soon as he starts the engine. He examines himself in the rearview mirror. There's an ugly purple bruise surrounding a crescent-shaped cut on his chin, but the bleeding has stopped, and on the whole he doesn't look too bad. He wishes he had some aspirin, but that can wait.

He backs out of Andy's space and threads his way down the alley leading to Grant Street. Grant is more downmarket than

Lacemaker Lane with its fancy shops, but at least cars are allowed there.

As Morris stops at the mouth of the alley, Hodges and his two partners arrive on the other side of the building and stand looking at the CLOSED sign hanging in the door of Andrew Halliday Rare Editions. A break in the Grant Street traffic comes just as Hodges is trying the bookshop door and finding it unlocked. Morris makes a quick left and heads toward the Crosstown Connector. With rush hour only getting started, he can be on the North Side in fifteen minutes. Maybe twelve. He needs to keep Saubers from going to the police, assuming he hasn't already, and there's one sure way to do that.

All he has to do is beat the notebook thief to his little sister.

34

Behind the Saubers house, near the fence that separates the family's backyard from the undeveloped land, there's a rusty old swing set that Tom Saubers keeps meaning to take down, now that both of his children are too old for it. This afternoon Tina is sitting on the glider, rocking slowly back and forth. *Divergent* is open in her lap, but she hasn't turned a page in the last five minutes. Mom has promised to watch the movie with her as soon as she's finished the book, but today Tina doesn't want to read about teenagers in the ruins of Chicago. Today that seems awful instead of romantic. Still moving slowly back and forth, she closes both the book and her eyes.

God, she prays, please don't let Pete be in really bad trouble. And don't let him hate me. I'll die if he hates me, so please let him understand why I told. *Please.*

God gets right back to her. God says Pete won't blame her because Mom figured it out on her own, but Tina's not sure she believes Him. She opens the book again but still can't read. The day seems to hang suspended, waiting for something awful to happen.

The cell phone she got for her eleventh birthday is upstairs in her bedroom. It's just a cheapie, not the iPhone with all the bells and whistles she desired, but it's her most prized possession and she's rarely without it. Only this afternoon she is. She left it in her room and went out to the backyard as soon as she texted Pete. She *had* to send that text, she couldn't just let him walk in unprepared, but she can't bear the thought of an angry, accusatory callback. She'll have to face him in a little while, that can't be avoided, but Mom will be with her then. Mom will tell him it wasn't Tina's fault, and he'll believe her.

Probably.

Now the cell begins to vibrate and jiggle on her desk. She's got a cool Snow Patrol ringtone, but—sick to her stomach and worried about Pete—Tina never thought to switch it from the mandated school setting when she and her mother got home, so Linda Saubers doesn't hear it downstairs. The screen lights up with her brother's picture. Eventually, the phone falls silent. After thirty seconds or so, it starts vibrating again. And a third time. Then it quits for good.

Pete's picture disappears from the screen.

35

In Government Square, Pete stares at his phone incredulously. For the first time in his memory, Teens has failed to answer her cell while school is not in session.

STEPHEN KING

Mom, then . . . or maybe not. Not quite yet. She'll want to ask a billion questions, and time is tight.

Also (although he won't quite admit this to himself), he doesn't want to talk to her until he absolutely has to.

He uses Google to troll for Mr. Hodges's number. He finds nine William Hodgeses here in the city, but the one he wants has got to be K. William, who has a company called Finders Keepers. Pete calls and gets an answering machine. At the end of the message—which seems to last at least an hour—Holly says, "If you need immediate assistance, you may dial 555-1890."

Pete once more debates calling his mother, then decides to go with the number the recording has given him first. What convinces him are two words: *immediate assistance.*

36

"Oough," Holly says as they approach the empty service desk in the middle of Andrew Halliday's narrow shop. "What's that smell?"

"Blood," Hodges replies. It's also decaying meat, but he doesn't want to say that. "You stay here, both of you."

"Are you carrying a weapon?" Jerome asks.

"I've got the Slapper."

"That's all?"

Hodges shrugs.

"Then I'm coming with you."

"Me too," Holly says, and grabs a substantial book called *Wild Plants and Flowering Herbs of North America.* She holds it as if she means to swat a stinging bug.

"No," Hodges says patiently, "you're going to stay right here. Both of you. And race to see which one can dial nine-one-one first, if I yell for you to do so."

364

"Bill—" Jerome begins.

"Don't argue with me, Jerome, and don't waste time. I've got an idea time might be rather short."

"A hunch?" Holly asks.

"Maybe a little more."

Hodges takes the Happy Slapper from his coat pocket (these days he's rarely without it, although he seldom carries his old service weapon), and grasps it above the knot. He advances quickly and quietly to the door of what he assumes is Andrew Halliday's private office. It's standing slightly ajar. The Slapper's loaded end swings from his right hand. He stands slightly to one side of the door and knocks with his left. Because this seems to be one of those moments when the strict truth is dispensable, he calls, "It's the police, Mr. Halliday."

There's no answer. He knocks again, louder, and when there's still no answer, he pushes the door open. The smell is instantly stronger: blood, decay, and spilled booze. Something else, too. Spent gunpowder, an aroma he knows well. Flies are buzzing somnolently. The lights are on, seeming to spotlight the body on the floor.

"Oh Christ, his head's half off!" Jerome cries. He's so close that Hodges jerks in surprise, bringing the Slapper up and then lowering it again. My pacemaker just went into overdrive, he thinks. He turns and both of them are crowding up right behind him. Jerome has a hand over his mouth. His eyes are bulging.

Holly, on the other hand, looks calm. She's got *Wild Plants and Flowering Herbs of North America* clasped against her chest and appears to be assessing the bleeding mess on the rug. To Jerome she says, "Don't hurl. This is a crime scene."

"I'm not going to hurl." The words are muffled, thanks to the hand clutching his lower face.

"Neither one of you minds worth a tinker's dam," Hodges says.

"If I were your teacher, I'd send you both to the office. I'm going in. You two stand right where you are."

He takes two steps in. Jerome and Holly immediately follow, side by side. The fucking Bobbsey Twins, Hodges thinks.

"Did Tina's brother do this?" Jerome asks. "Jesus Christ, Bill, did he?"

"If he did, it wasn't today. That blood's almost dry. And there's the flies. I don't see any maggots yet, but—"

Jerome makes a gagging noise.

"Jerome, *don't*," Holly says in a forbidding voice. Then, to Hodges: "I see a little ax. Hatchet. Whatever you call it. That's what did it."

Hodges doesn't reply. He's assessing the scene. He thinks that Halliday—if it *is* Halliday—has been dead at least twenty-four hours, maybe longer. *Probably* longer. But something has happened in here since, because the smell of spilled liquor and gunpowder is fresh and strong.

"Is that a bullet hole, Bill?" Jerome asks. He's pointing at a bookshelf to the left of the door, near a small cherrywood table. There's a small round hole in a copy of *Catch-22*. Hodges goes to it, looks more closely, and thinks, That's *got* to hurt the resale price. Then he looks at the table. There are two crystal decanters on it, probably Waterford. The table is slightly dusty, and he can see the shapes where two others stood. He looks across the room, beyond the desk, and yep, there they are, lying on the floor.

"Sure it's a bullet hole," Holly says. "I can smell the gunpowder."

"There was a fight," Jerome says, then points to the corpse without looking at it. "But *he* sure wasn't part of it."

"No," Hodges says, "not him. And the combatants have since departed."

"Was one of them Peter Saubers?"

Hodges sighs heavily. "Almost for sure. I think he came here after he ditched us at the drugstore."

"Somebody took Mr. Halliday's computer," Holly says. "His DVD hookup is still there beside the cash register, and the wireless mouse—also a little box with a few thumb drives in it—but the computer is gone. I saw a big empty space on the desk out there. It was probably a laptop."

"What now?" Jerome asks.

"We call the police." Hodges doesn't want to do it, senses that Pete Saubers is in bad trouble and calling the cops may only make it worse, at least to begin with, but he played the Lone Ranger in the Mercedes Killer case, and almost got a few thousand kids killed.

He takes out his cell, but before he can turn it on, it lights up and rings in his hand.

"Peter," Holly says. Her eyes are shining and she speaks with utter certainty. "Bet you six thousand dollars. *Now* he wants to talk. Don't just stand there, Bill, answer your fracking phone."

He does.

"I need help," Pete Saubers says rapidly. "Please, Mr. Hodges, I really need help."

"Just a sec. I'm going to put you on speaker so my associates can hear."

"Associates?" Pete sounds more alarmed than ever. "What associates?"

"Holly Gibney. Your sister knows her. And Jerome Robinson. He's Barbara Robinson's older brother."

"Oh. I guess . . . I guess that's okay." And, as if to himself: "How much worse can it get?"

"Peter, we're in Andrew Halliday's shop. There's a dead man in his office. I assume it's Halliday, and I assume you know about it. Would those assumptions be correct?"

There's a moment of silence. If not for the faint sound of traffic wherever Pete is, Hodges might have thought he'd broken the connection. Then the boy starts talking again, the words spilling out in a waterfall.

"He was there when I got there. The man with the red lips. He told me Mr. Halliday was in the back, so I went into his office, and he followed me and he had a gun and he tried to kill me when I wouldn't tell him where the notebooks were. I wouldn't because . . . because he doesn't deserve to have them and besides he was going to kill me *anyway*, I could tell just by looking in his eyes. He . . . I . . ."

"You threw the decanters at him, didn't you?"

"Yes! The bottles! And he shot at me! He missed, but it was so close I heard it go by. I ran and got away, but then he called me and said they'd blame me, the police would, because I threw a hatchet at him, too . . . did you see the hatchet?"

"Yes," Hodges says. "I'm looking at it right now."

"And . . . and my fingerprints, see . . . they're on it because I threw it at him . . . and he has some video discs of me and Mr. Halliday arguing . . . because he was trying to blackmail me! Halliday, I mean, not the man with the red lips, only now *he's* trying to blackmail me, too!"

"This red-lips man has the store security video?" Holly asks, bending toward the phone. "Is that what you mean?"

"*Yes!* He said the police will arrest me and they will because I didn't go to any of the Sunday meetings at River Bend, and he also has a voicemail *and I don't know what to do!*"

"Where are you, Peter?" Hodges asks. "Where are you right now?"

There's another pause, and Hodges knows exactly what Pete's doing: checking for landmarks. He may have lived in the city his whole life, but right now he's so freaked he doesn't know east from west.

"Government Square," he says at last. "Across from this restaurant, the Happy Cup?"

"Do you see the man who shot at you?"

"N-No. I ran, and I don't think he could chase me very far on foot. He's kind of old, and you can't drive a car on Lacemaker Lane."

"Stay there," Hodges says. "We'll come and get you."

"Please don't call the police," Peter says. "It'll kill my folks, after everything else that's happened to them. I'll give you the notebooks. I never should have kept them, and I never should have tried to sell any of them. I should have stopped with the money." His voice is blurring now as he breaks down. "My parents . . . they were in such trouble. About *everything*. I only wanted to help!"

"I'm sure that's true, but I *have* to call the police. If you didn't kill Halliday, the evidence will show that. You'll be fine. I'll pick you up and we'll go to your house. Will your parents be there?"

"Dad's on a business thing, but my mom and sister will be." Pete has to hitch in a breath before going on. "I'll go to jail, won't I? They'll never believe me about the man with the red lips. They'll think I made him up."

"All you have to do is tell the truth," Holly says. "Bill won't let anything bad happen to you." She grabs his hand and squeezes it fiercely. "Will you?"

Hodges repeats, "If you didn't kill him, you'll be fine."

"I didn't! Swear to God!"

"This other man did. The one with the red lips."

"Yes. He killed John Rothstein, too. He said Rothstein sold out."

Hodges has a million questions, but this isn't the time.

"Listen to me, Pete. Very carefully. Stay where you are. We'll be at Government Square in fifteen minutes."

"If you let me drive," Jerome says, "we can be there in ten."

Hodges ignores this. "The four of us will go to your house. You'll tell the whole story to me, my associates, and your mother. She may want to call your father and discuss getting you legal representation. *Then* we're going to call the police. It's the best I can do."

And better than I *should* do, he thinks, eyeing the mangled corpse and thinking about how close he came to going to jail himself four years ago. For the same kind of thing, too: Lone Ranger shit. But surely another half hour or forty-five minutes can't hurt. And what the boy said about his parents hit home. Hodges was at City Center that day. He saw the aftermath.

"A-All right. Come as fast as you can."

"Yes." He breaks the connection.

"What do we do about *our* fingerprints?" Holly asks.

"Leave them," Hodges says. "Let's go get that kid. I can't wait to hear his story." He tosses Jerome the Mercedes key.

"Thanks, Massa Hodges!" Tyrone Feelgood screeches. "Dis here black boy is one *safe drivuh*! I is goan get'chall safe to yo destin—"

"Shut up, Jerome."

Hodges and Holly say it together.

37

Pete takes a deep, trembling breath and closes his cell phone. Everything is going around in his head like some nightmare amusement park ride, and he's sure he sounded like an idiot. Or a murderer scared of getting caught and making up any wild tale. He forgot to tell Mr. Hodges that Red Lips once lived in Pete's own house, and he should have done that. He thinks about calling Hodges back, but why bother when he and those other two are coming to pick him up?

The guy won't go the house, anyway, Pete tells himself. He can't. He has to stay invisible.

But he might, just the same. If he thinks I was lying about moving the notebooks somewhere else, he really might. Because he's crazy. A total whack-job.

He tries Tina's phone again and gets nothing but her message: "Hey, it's Teens, sorry I missed you, do your thing." *Beeep.*

All right, then.

Mom.

But before he can call her, he sees a bus coming, and in the destination window, like a gift from heaven, are the words NORTH SIDE. Pete suddenly decides he's not going to sit here and wait for Mr. Hodges. The bus will get him there sooner, and he wants to go home *now*. He'll call Mr. Hodges once he's on board and tell him to meet him at the house, but first he'll call his mother and tell her to lock all the doors.

The bus is almost empty, but he makes his way to the back, just the same. And he doesn't have to call his mother, after all; his phone rings in his hand as he sits down. **MOM**, the screen says. He takes a deep breath and pushes ACCEPT. She's talking before he can even say hello.

"Where are you, Peter?" Peter instead of Pete. Not a good start. "I expected you home an hour ago."

"I'm coming," he says. "I'm on the bus."

"Let's stick to the truth, shall we? The bus has come and gone. I saw it."

"Not the schoolbus, the North Side bus. I had to . . ." What? Run an errand? That's so ludicrous he could laugh. Except this is no laughing matter. Far from it. "There was something I had to do. Is Tina there? She didn't go down to Ellen's, or something?"

"She's in the backyard, reading her book."

The bus is picking its way past some road construction, moving with agonizing slowness.

"Mom, listen to me. You—"

"No, you listen to *me*. Did you send that money?"

He closes his eyes.

"Did you? A simple yes or no will suffice. We can go into the details later."

Eyes still closed, he says: "Yes. It was me. But—"

"Where did it come from?"

"That's a long story, and right now it doesn't matter. The *money* doesn't matter. There's a guy—"

"What do you *mean*, it doesn't matter? That was over *twenty thousand dollars*!"

He stifles an urge to say *Did you just figure that out?*

The bus continues lumbering its laborious way through the construction. Sweat is rolling down Pete's face. He can see the smear of blood on his knee, dark brown instead of red, but still as loud as a shout. *Guilty!* it yells. *Guilty, guilty!*

"Mom, please shut up and listen to me."

Shocked silence on the other end of the line. Not since the days of his toddler tantrums has he told his mother to shut up.

"There's a guy, and he's dangerous." He could tell her just *how* dangerous, but he wants her on alert, not in hysterics. "I don't think he'll come to the house, but he might. You should get Tina inside and lock the doors. Just for a few minutes, then I'll be there. Some other people, too. People who can help."

At least I hope so, he thinks.

God, I hope so.

## 38

Morris Bellamy turns onto Sycamore Street. He's aware that his life is rapidly narrowing to a point. All he has is a few hundred stolen dollars, a stolen car, and the need to get his hands on Rothstein's notebooks. Oh, he has one other thing, too: a short-term hideout where he can go, and read, and find out what happened to Jimmy Gold after the Duzzy-Doo campaign put him at the top of the advertising dungheap with a double fistful of those Golden Bucks. Morris understands this is a crazy goal, so he must be a crazy person, but it's all he has, and it's enough.

There's his old house, which is now the notebook thief's house. With a little red car in the driveway.

"Crazy don't mean shit," Morris Bellamy says. "Crazy don't mean shit. *Nothing* means shit."

Words to live by.

## 39

"Bill," Jerome says. "I hate to say it, but I think our bird has flown."

Hodges looks up from his thoughts as Jerome guides the Mercedes through Government Square. There are quite a few people sitting on the benches—reading newspapers, chatting and drinking coffee, feeding the pigeons—but there are no teenagers of either sex.

"I don't see him at any of the tables on the café side, either," Holly reports. "Maybe he went inside for a cup of coffee?"

"Right now, coffee would be the last thing on his mind," Hodges says. He pounds a fist on his thigh.

"North Side and South Side buses run through here every fifteen minutes," Jerome says. "If I were in his shoes, sitting and waiting around for someone to come and pick me up would be torture. I'd want to be doing something."

That's when Hodges's phone rings.

"A bus came along and I decided not to wait," Pete says. He sounds calmer now. "I'll be home when you get there. I just got off the phone with my mother. She and Tina are okay."

Hodges doesn't like the sound of this. "Why wouldn't they be, Peter?"

"Because the guy with the red lips knows where we live. He said *he* used to live there. I forgot to tell you."

Hodges checks where they are. "How long to Sycamore Street, Jerome?"

"Be there in twenty. Maybe less. If I'd known the kid was going to grab a bus, I would've taken the Crosstown."

"Mr. Hodges?" Pete.

"I'm here."

"He'd be stupid to go to my house, anyway. If he does that, I won't be framed anymore."

He's got a point. "Did you tell them to lock up and stay inside?"
"Yes."

"And did you give your mom his description?"
"Yes."

Hodges knows that if he calls the cops, Mr. Red Lips will be gone with the wind, leaving Pete to depend on the forensic evidence to get him off the hook. And they can probably beat the cops, anyway.

"Tell him to call the guy," Holly says. She leans toward Hodges and bellows, *"Call and say you changed your mind and will give him the notebooks!"*

"Pete, did you hear that?"

"Yeah, but I can't. I don't even know if he has a phone. He called me from the one in the bookshop. We didn't, you know, exactly have time to exchange info."

"How poopy is that?" Holly asks no one in particular.

"All right. Call me the minute you get home and verify that everything's okay. If I don't hear from you, I'll have to call for the police."

"I'm sure they're f—"

But this is where they came in. Hodges closes his phone and leans forward. "Punch it, Jerome."

"As soon as I can." He gestures at the traffic, three lanes going each way, chrome twinkling in the sunshine. "Once we get past the rotary up there, we'll be gone like Enron."

Twenty minutes, Hodges thinks. Twenty minutes at most. What can happen in twenty minutes?

The answer, he knows from bitter experience, is quite a lot. Life and death. Right now all he can do is hope those twenty minutes don't come back to haunt him.

## 40

Linda Saubers came into her husband's little home office to wait for Pete, because her husband's laptop is on the desk and she can play computer solitaire. She is far too upset to read.

After talking to Pete, she's more upset than ever. Afraid, too, but not of some sinister villain lurking on Sycamore Street. She's afraid for her son, because it's clear *he* believes in the sinister villain. Things are finally starting to come together. His pallor and weight loss . . . the crazy moustache he tried to grow . . . the return of his acne and his long silences . . . they all make sense now. If he's not having a nervous breakdown, he's on the verge of one.

She gets up and looks out the window at her daughter. Tina's got her best blouse on, the billowy yellow one, and no way should she be wearing it on a dirty old glider that should have been taken down years ago. She has a book, and it's open, but she doesn't seem to be reading. She looks drawn and sad.

What a nightmare, Linda thinks. First Tom hurt so badly he'll walk with a limp for the rest of his life, and now our son seeing monsters in the shadows. That money wasn't manna from heaven, it was acid rain. Maybe he just has to come clean. Tell us the whole story about where the money came from. Once he does that, the healing process can begin.

In the meantime, she'll do as he asked: call Tina inside and lock the house. It can't hurt.

A board creaks behind her. She turns, expecting to see her son, but it's not Pete. It's a man with pale skin, thinning white hair, and red lips. It's the man her son described, the sinister villain, and her first feeling isn't terror but an absurdly powerful sense of relief. Her son isn't having a nervous breakdown, after all.

Then she sees the gun in the man's hand, and the terror comes, bright and hot.

"You must be Mom," the intruder says. "Strong family resemblance."

"Who are you?" Linda Saubers asks. "What are you doing here?"

The intruder—in the doorway of her husband's study instead of in her son's mind—glances out the window, and Linda has to suppress an urge to say *Don't look at her.*

"Is that your daughter?" Morris asks. "Hey, she's pretty. I always liked a girl in yellow."

"What do you want?" Linda asks.

"What's mine," Morris says, and shoots her in the head. Blood flies up and spatters red droplets against the glass. It sounds like rain.

41

Tina hears an alarming bang from the house and runs for the kitchen door. It's the pressure cooker, she thinks. Mom forgot the damn pressure cooker again. This has happened once before, while her mother was making preserves. It's an old cooker, the kind that sits on the stove, and Pete spent most of one Saturday afternoon on a stepladder, scraping dried strawberry goo off the ceiling. Mom was vacuuming the living room when it happened, which was lucky. Tina hopes to God she wasn't in the kitchen this time, either.

"Mom?" She runs inside. There's nothing on the stove. "Mo—"

An arm grabs her around the middle, hard. Tina loses her breath in an explosive whoosh. Her feet rise from the floor, kicking. She can feel whiskers against her cheek. She can smell sweat, sour and hot.

"Don't scream and I won't have to hurt you," the man says into her ear, making her skin prickle. "Do you understand?"

Tina manages to nod, but her heart is hammering and the world is going dark. "Let me—breathe," she gasps, and the hold loosens. Her feet go back to the floor. She turns and sees a man with a pale face and red lips. There's a cut on his chin, it looks like a bad one. The skin around it is swollen and blue-black.

"Don't scream," he repeats, and raises an admonitory finger. "Do *not* do that." He smiles, and if it's supposed to make her feel better, it doesn't work. His teeth are yellow. They look more like fangs than teeth.

"What did you do to my mother?"

"She's fine," the man with the red lips says. "Where's your cell phone? A pretty little girl like you must have a cell phone. Lots of friends to chatter and text with. Is it in your pocket?"

"N-N-No. Upstairs. In my room."

"Let's go get it," Morris says. "You're going to make a call."

## 42

Pete's stop is Elm Street, two blocks over from the house, and the bus is almost there. He's making his way to the front when his cell buzzes. His relief at seeing his sister's smiling face in the little window is so great that his knees loosen and he has to grab one of the straphandles.

"Tina! I'll be there in a—"

"There's a man here!" Tina is crying so hard he can barely understand her. "He was in the house! He—"

Then she's gone, and he knows the voice that replaces hers. He wishes to God he didn't.

"Hello, Peter," Red Lips says. "Are you on your way?"

He can't say anything. His tongue is stuck to the roof of his mouth. The bus pulls over at the corner of Elm and Breckenridge Terrace, his stop, but Pete only stands there.

"Don't bother answering that, and don't bother coming home, because no one will be here if you do."

"He's lying!" Tina yells. "Mom is—"

Then she howls.

"Don't you hurt her," Pete says. The few other riders don't look around from their papers or handhelds, because he can't speak above a whisper. "Don't you hurt my sister."

"I won't if she shuts up. She needs to be quiet. You need to be quiet, too, and listen to me. But first you need to answer two questions. Have you called the police?"

"No."

"Have you called *anyone?*"

"No." Pete lies without hesitation.

"Good. Excellent. Now comes the listening part. Are you listening?"

A large lady with a shopping bag is clambering onto the bus, wheezing. Pete gets off as soon as she's out of the way, walking like a boy in a dream, the phone plastered to his ear.

"I'm taking your sister with me to a safe place. A place where we can meet, once you have the notebooks."

Pete starts to tell him they don't have to do it that way, he'll just tell Red Lips where the notebooks are, then realizes doing that would be a huge mistake. Once Red Lips knows they're in the basement at the Rec, he'll have no reason to keep Tina alive.

"Are you there, Peter?"

"Y-Yes."

"You better be. You just better be. Get the notebooks. When you have them—and not before—call your sister's cell again. If you call for any other reason, I'll hurt her."

"Is my mother all right?"

"She's fine, just tied up. Don't worry about her, and don't bother going home. Just get the notebooks and call me."

With that, Red Lips is gone. Pete doesn't have time to tell him he *has* to go home, because he'll need Tina's wagon again to haul the cartons. He also needs to get his father's key to the Rec. He returned it to the board in his father's office, and he needs it to get in.

## 43

Morris slips Tina's pink phone into his pocket and yanks a cord from her desktop computer. "Turn around. Hands behind you."

"Did you shoot her?" Tears are running down Tina's cheeks. "Was that the sound I heard? Did you shoot my moth—"

Morris slaps her, and hard. Blood flies from Tina's nose and the corner of her mouth. Her eyes widen in shock.

"You need to shut your quack and turn around. Hands behind you."

Tina does it, sobbing. Morris ties her wrists together at the small of her back, cinching the knots viciously.

"Ow! *Ow*, mister! That's too tight!"

"Deal with it." He wonders vaguely how many shots might be left in his old pal's gun. Two will be enough; one for the thief and one for the thief's sister. "Walk. Downstairs. Out the kitchen door. Let's go. Hup-two-three-four."

She looks back at him, her eyes huge and bloodshot and swimming with tears. "Are you going to rape me?"

"No," Morris says, then adds something that is all the more terrifying because she doesn't understand it: "I won't make that mistake again."

## 44

Linda comes to staring at the ceiling. She knows where she is, Tom's office, but not what has happened to her. The right side of her head is on fire, and when she raises a hand to her face, it comes away wet with blood. The last thing she can remember is Peggy Moran telling her that Tina had gotten sick at school.

*Go get her and take her home,* Peggy had said. *I'll cover this.*

No, she remembers something else. Something about the mystery money.

I was going to talk to Pete about it, she thinks. Get some answers. I was playing solitaire on Tom's computer, just killing time while I waited for him to come home, and then—

Then, black.

Now, this terrible pain in her head, like a constantly slamming door. It's even worse than the migraines she sometimes gets. Worse even than childbirth. She tries to raise her head and manages to do it, but the world starts going in and out with her heartbeat, first *sucking*, then *blooming*, each oscillation accompanied by such godawful agony . . .

She looks down and sees the front of her gray dress has changed to a muddy purple. She thinks, Oh God, that's a lot of blood. Have I had a stroke? Some kind of brain hemorrhage?

Surely not, surely those only bleed on the inside, but whatever it is, she needs help. She needs an ambulance, but she can't make her hand go to the phone. It lifts, trembles, and drops back to the floor.

She hears a yelp of pain from somewhere close, then crying she'd recognize anywhere, even while dying (which, she suspects, she may be). It's Tina.

She manages to prop herself up on one bloody hand, enough to look out the window. She sees a man hustling Tina down the back steps into the yard. Tina's hands are tied behind her.

Linda forgets about her pain, forgets about needing an ambulance. A man has broken in, and he's now abducting her daughter. She needs to stop him. She needs the police. She tries to get into the swivel chair behind the desk, but at first she can only paw at the seat. She does a lunging sit-up and for a moment the pain is so intense the world turns white, but she holds on to consciousness and grabs the arms of the chair. When her vision clears, she sees the man opening the back gate and shoving Tina through. *Herding* her, like an animal on its way to the slaughterhouse.

*Bring her back!* Linda screams. *Don't you hurt my baby!*

But only in her head. When she tries to get up, the chair turns and she loses her grip on the arms. The world darkens. She hears a terrible gagging sound before she blacks out, and has time to think, Can that be me?

45

Things are *not* golden after the rotary. Instead of open street, they see backed-up traffic and two orange signs. One says FLAGGER AHEAD. The other says ROAD CONSTRUCTION. There's a line of cars waiting while the flagger lets downtown traffic go through. After three minutes of sitting, each one feeling an hour long, Hodges tells Jerome to use the side streets.

"I wish I could, but we're blocked in." He jerks a thumb over his shoulder, where the line of cars behind them is now backed up almost to the rotary.

Holly has been bent over her iPad, whacking away. Now she looks up. "Use the sidewalk," she says, then goes back to her magic tablet.

"There are mailboxes, Hollyberry," Jerome says. "Also a chain-link fence up ahead. I don't think there's room."

She takes another brief look. "Yeah there is. You may scrape a little, but it won't be the first time for this car. Go on."

"Who pays the fine if I get arrested on a charge of driving while black? You?"

Holly rolls her eyes. Jerome turns to Hodges, who sighs and nods. "She's right. There's room. I'll pay your fucking fine."

Jerome swings right. The Mercedes clips the fender of the car stopped ahead of them, then bumps up onto the sidewalk. Here comes the first mailbox. Jerome swings even farther to the right, now entirely off the street. There's a thud as the driver's side knocks the mailbox off its post, then a drawn-out squall as the passenger side caresses the chainlink fence. A woman in shorts and a halter top is mowing her lawn. She shouts at them as the passenger side of Holly's German U-boat peels away a sign reading NO TRESPASS-ING NO SOLICITING NO DOOR TO DOOR SALESMEN. She rushes for her driveway, still shouting. Then she just peers, shading her eyes and squinting. Hodges can see her lips moving.

"Oh, goody," Jerome says. "She's getting your plate number."

"Just drive," Holly says. "Drive drive drive." And with no pause: "Red Lips is Morris Bellamy. That's his name."

It's the flagger yelling at them now. The construction work-ers, who have been uncovering a sewer pipe running beneath the street, are staring. Some are laughing. One of them winks at Jerome and makes a bottle-tipping gesture. Then they are past. The Mercedes thumps back down to the street. With traffic bound for the North Side bottlenecked behind them, the street ahead is blessedly empty.

"I checked the city tax records," Holly says. "At the time John Rothstein was murdered in 1978, the taxes on 23 Sycamore Street were being paid by Anita Elaine Bellamy. I did a Google search for her name and came up with over fifty hits, she's sort of a famous academic, but only one hit that matters. Her son was tried and convicted of aggravated rape late that same year. Right here in the city. He got a life sentence. There's a picture of him in one of the news stories. Look." She hands the iPad to Hodges.

Morris Bellamy has been snapped coming down the steps of a courthouse Hodges remembers well, although it was replaced by the concrete monstrosity in Government Square fifteen years ago. Bellamy is flanked by a pair of detectives. Hodges recalls one of them, Paul Emerson. Good police, long retired. He's wearing a suit. So is the other detective, but that one has draped his coat over Bellamy's hands to hide the handcuffs he's wearing. Bellamy is also in a suit, which means the picture was taken either while the trial was ongoing, or just after the verdict was rendered. It's a black-and-white photo, which only makes the contrast between Bellamy's pale complexion and dark mouth more striking. He almost looks like he's wearing lipstick.

"That's got to be him," Holly says. "If you call the state prison, I'll bet you six thousand bucks that he's out."

"No bet," Hodges says. "How long to Sycamore Street, Jerome?"

"Ten minutes."

"Firm or optimistic?"

Reluctantly, Jerome replies, "Well . . . maybe a tad optimistic."

"Just do the best you can and try not to run anybody ov—"

Hodge's cell rings. It's Pete. He sounds out of breath.

"Have you called the police, Mr. Hodges?"

"No." Although they'll probably have the license plate of Holly's car by now, but he sees no reason to tell Pete that. The boy sounds more upset than ever. Almost crazed.

"You can't. No matter what. He's got my sister. He says if he doesn't get the notebooks, he'll kill her. I'm going to give them to him."

"Pete, don't—"

But he's talking to no one. Pete has broken the connection.

## 46

Morris hustles Tina along the path. At one point a jutting branch rips her filmy blouse and scratches her arm, bringing blood.

"Don't make me go so fast, mister! I'll fall down!"

Morris whacks the back of her head above her ponytail. "Save your breath, bitch. Just be grateful I'm not making you run."

He holds on to her shoulders as they cross the stream, balancing her so she won't fall in, and when they reach the point where the scrub brush and stunted trees give way to the Rec property, he tells her to stop.

The baseball field is deserted, but a few boys are on the cracked asphalt of the basketball court. They're stripped to the waist, their shoulders gleaming. The day is really too hot for outside games, which is why Morris supposes there are only a few of them.

He unties Tina's hands. She gives a little whimper of relief and starts rubbing her wrists, which are crisscrossed with deep red grooves.

"We're going to walk along the edge of the trees," he tells her. "The only time those boys will be able to get a good look at us is when we get near the building and come out of the shade. If they say hello, or if there's someone you know, just wave and smile and keep walking. Do you understand?"

"Y-Yes."

"If you scream or yell for help, I'll put a bullet in your head. Do you understand *that*?"

"*Yes.* Did you shoot my mother? You did, didn't you?"

"Of course not, just fired one into the ceiling to settle her down. She's fine and you will be, too, if you do as you're told. Get moving."

They walk in the shade, the uncut grass of right field whickering against Morris's trousers and Tina's jeans. The boys are totally absorbed in their game and don't even look around, although if they had, Tina's bright yellow blouse would have stood out against the green trees like a warning flag.

When they reach the back of the Rec, Morris guides her past his old pal's Subaru, keeping a close eye on the boys as he does so. Once the brick flank of the building hides the two of them from the basketball court, he ties Tina's hands behind her again. No sense taking chances with Birch Street so close. Lots of houses on Birch Street.

He sees Tina draw in a deep breath and grabs her shoulder. "Don't yell, girlfriend. Open your mouth and I'll beat it off you."

"Please don't hurt me," Tina whispers. "I'll do whatever you want."

Morris nods, satisfied. It's a wise-con response if he ever heard one.

"See that basement window? The one that's open? Lie down, turn over on your belly, and drop through."

Tina squats and peers into the shadows. Then she turns her bloody swollen face up to him. "It's too far! I'll fall!"

Exasperated, Morris kicks her in the shoulder. She cries out. He bends over and places the muzzle of the automatic against her temple.

"You said you'd do whatever I wanted, and that's what I want. Get through that window right now, or I'll put a bullet in your tiny brat brain."

Morris wonders if he means it. He decides he does. Little girls also don't mean shit.

Weeping, Tina squirms through the window. She hesitates, half in and half out, looking at Morris with pleading eyes. He draws his foot back to kick her in the face and help her along. She drops, then yells in spite of Morris's explicit instructions not to.

"My ankle! I think I broke my ankle!"

Morris doesn't give a fuck about her ankle. He takes a quick look around to make sure he's still unobserved, then slides through the window and into the basement of the Birch Street Rec, landing on the closed carton he used for a step last time. The thief's sister must have landed on it wrong and tumbled to the floor. Her foot is twisted sideways and already beginning to swell. To Morris Bellamy, that doesn't mean shit, either.

47

Mr. Hodges has a thousand questions, but Pete has no time to answer any of them. He ends the call and sprints down Sycamore Street to his house. He has decided getting Tina's old wagon will take too long; he'll figure out some other way to transport the notebooks when he gets to the Rec. All he really needs is the key to the building.

He runs into his father's office to grab it and stops cold. His mother is on the floor beside the desk, her blue eyes shining from a mask of blood. There's more blood on his dad's open laptop, on the front of her dress, spattered on the desk chair and the window behind her. Music is tinkling from the computer, and even in his distress, he recognizes the tune. She was playing solitaire. Just playing solitaire and waiting for her kid to come home and bothering no one.

"*Mom!*" He runs to her, crying.

"My head," she says. "Look at my head."

He bends over her, parts bloody clumps of hair, trying to be gentle, and sees a trench running from her temple to the back of her head. At one point, halfway along the trench, he can see bleary gray-white. It's her skull, he thinks. That's bad, but at least it's not her brains, please God no, brains are soft, brains would be leaking. It's just her skull.

"A man came," she says, speaking with great effort. "He . . . took . . . Tina. I heard her cry out. You have to . . . oh Jesus Christ, how my head *rings*."

Pete hesitates for one endless second, wavering between his need to help his mother and his need to protect his sister, to get her back. If only this *was* a nightmare, he thinks. If only I could wake up.

Mom first. Mom right now.

He grabs the phone off his father's desk. "Be quiet, Mom. Don't say anything else, and don't move."

She closes her eyes wearily. "Did he come for the money? Did that man come for the money you found?"

"No, for what was with it," Pete says, and punches in three numbers he learned in grade school.

"Nine-one-one," a woman says. "What is your emergency?"

"My mom's been shot," Pete says. "Twenty-three Sycamore Street. Send an ambulance, right now. She's bleeding like crazy."

"What is your name, si—"

Pete hangs up. "Mom, I have to go. I have to get Tina back."

"Don't . . . be hurt." She's slurring now. Her eyes are still shut and he sees with horror that there's even blood in her eyelashes. This is his fault, all his fault. "Don't let . . . Tina be . . . hur . . ."

She falls silent, but she's breathing. Oh God, please let her keep breathing.

Pete takes the key to the Birch Street Rec's front door from his father's real estate properties board.

"You'll be okay, Mom. The ambulance will come. Some friends will come, too."

He starts for the door, then an idea strikes him and he turns back. "Mom?"

"Whaa . . ."

"Does Dad still smoke?"

Without opening her eyes, she says, "He thinks . . . I don't . . . know."

Quickly—he has to be gone before Hodges gets here and tries to stop him from doing what he has to do—Pete begins to search the drawers of his father's desk.

Just in case, he thinks.

Just in case.


### 48


The back gate is ajar. Pete doesn't notice. He pelts down the path. As he nears the stream, he passes a scrap of filmy yellow cloth hanging from a branch jutting out into the path. He reaches the stream and turns to look, almost without realizing it, at the spot where the trunk is buried. The trunk that caused all this horror.

When he reaches the stepping-stones at the bottom of the bank, Pete suddenly stops. His eyes widen. His legs go rubbery and loose. He sits down hard, staring at the foaming, shallow water that he has crossed so many times, often with his little sister babbling away about whatever interested her at the time. Mrs. Beasley. SpongeBob. Her friend Ellen. Her favorite lunch-box.

Her favorite clothes.

The filmy yellow blouse with the billowing sleeves, for instance. Mom tells her she shouldn't wear it so often, because it has to be dry-cleaned. Was Teens wearing it this morning when she left for school? That seems like a century ago, but he thinks . . .

He thinks she was.

*I'm taking her to a safe place,* Red Lips had said. *A place where we can meet, once you have the notebooks.*

Can it be?

Of course it can. If Red Lips grew up in Pete's house, he would have spent time at the Rec. All the kids in the neighborhood spent time there, until it closed. And he must have known about the path, because the trunk was buried less than twenty paces from where it crossed the stream.

But he doesn't know about the notebooks, Pete thinks. Not yet.

Unless he found out since the last call, that is. If so, he will have taken them already. He'll be gone. That would be okay if he's left Tina alive. And why wouldn't he? What reason would he have to kill her once he has what he wants?

For revenge, Pete thinks coldly. To get back at me. I'm the thief who took the notebooks, I hit him with a bottle and got away at the bookstore, and I deserve to be punished.

He gets up and staggers as a wave of lightheadedness rushes through him. When it passes, he crosses the creek. On the other side, he begins to run again.


## 49


The front door of 23 Sycamore is standing open. Hodges is out of the Mercedes before Jerome has brought it fully to a stop. He runs inside, one hand in his pocket, gripping the Happy Slapper. He hears tinkly music he knows well from hours spent playing computer solitaire.

He follows the sound and finds a woman sitting—*sprawling*—beside a desk in an alcove that has been set up as an office. One side of her face is swollen and drenched in blood. She looks at him, trying to focus.

"Pete," she says, and then, "He took Tina."

Hodges kneels and carefully parts the woman's hair. What he sees is bad, but nowhere near as bad as it could be; this woman has won the only lottery that really matters. The bullet put a groove six inches long in her scalp, has actually exposed her skull in one place, but a scalp wound isn't going to kill her. She's lost a lot of blood, though, and is suffering from both shock and concussion. This is no time to question her, but he has to. Morris Bellamy is laying down a trail of violence, and Hodges is still at the wrong end of it.

"Holly. Call an ambulance."

"Pete . . . already did," Linda says, and as if her weak voice has conjured it, they hear a siren. It's still distant but approaching fast. "Before . . . he left."

"Mrs. Saubers, did Pete take Tina? Is that what you're saying?"

"No. *He.* The man."

"Did he have red lips, Mrs. Saubers?" Holly asks. "Did the man who took Tina have red lips?"

"Irish . . . lips," she says. "But not . . . a redhead. White. He was old. Am I going to die?"

"No," Hodges says. "Help is on the way. But you have to help us. Do you know where Peter went?"

"Out . . . back. Through the gate. Saw him."

Jerome looks out the window and sees the gate standing ajar. "What's back there?"

"A path," she says wearily. "The kids used it . . . to go to the Rec. Before it closed. He took . . . I think he took the key."

"Pete did?"

"Yes . . ." Her eyes move to a board with a great many keys hung on it. One hook is empty. The DymoTape beneath it reads BIRCH ST. REC.

Hodges comes to a decision. "Jerome, you're with me. Holly, stay with Mrs. Saubers. Get a cold cloth to put on the side of her head." He draws in breath. "But before you do that, call the police. Ask for my old partner. Huntley."

He expects an argument, but Holly just nods and picks up the phone.

"He took his father's lighter, too," Linda says. She seems a little more with it now. "I don't know why he would do that. And the can of Ronson's."

Jerome looks a question at Hodges, who says: "It's lighter fluid."

50

Pete keeps to the shade of the trees, just as Morris and Tina did, although the boys who were playing basketball have gone home to dinner and left the court deserted except for a few crows scavenging spilled potato chips. He sees a small car nestled in the loading dock. Hidden there, actually, and the vanity license plate is enough to cause any doubts Pete might have had to disappear. Red Lips is here, all right, and he can't have taken Tina in by the front. That door faces the street, which is apt to be fairly busy at this time of day, and besides, he has no key.

Pete passes the car, and at the corner of the building, he drops to his knees and peers around. One of the basement windows is open. The grass and weeds that were growing in front of it have been beaten down. He hears a man's voice. They're down there, all right. So are the notebooks. The only question is whether or not Red Lips has found them yet.

Pete withdraws and leans against the sunwarmed brick, wondering what to do next. Think, he tells himself. You got Tina into this and you need to get her out of it, so *think*, goddam you!

Only he can't. His mind is full of white noise.

In one of his few interviews, the ever-irritable John Rothstein expressed his disgust with the where-do-you-get-your-ideas question. Story ideas came from nowhere, he proclaimed. They arrived without the polluting influence of the author's intellect. The idea that comes to Pete now also seems to arrive from nowhere. It's both horrible and horribly attractive. It won't work if Red Lips has already discovered the notebooks, but if that is the case, *nothing* will work.

Pete gets up and circles the big brick cube the other way, once more passing the green car with its tattletale license plate. He stops at the front right corner of the abandoned brick box, looking at the going-home traffic on Birch Street. It's like peering through a window and into a different world, one where things are normal. He takes a quick inventory: cell phone, cigarette lighter, can of lighter fluid. The can was in the bottom desk drawer with his father's Zippo. The can is only half full, based on the slosh when he shakes it, but half full will be more than enough.

He goes around the corner, now in full view of Birch Street, trying to walk normally and hoping that no one—Mr. Evans, his old Little League coach, for instance—will hail him.

No one does. This time he knows which of the two keys to use, and this time it turns easily in the lock. He opens the door slowly, steps into the foyer, and eases the door closed. It's musty and brutally hot in here. For Tina's sake, he hopes it's cooler in the basement. How scared she must be, he thinks.

If she's still alive to feel anything, an evil voice whispers back. Red Lips could have been standing over her dead body and talking to himself. He's crazy, and that's what crazy people do.

On Pete's left, a flight of stairs leads up to the second floor, which consists of a single large space running the length of the building. The official name was The North Side Community Room, but the kids had a different name for it, one Red Lips probably remembers.

As Pete sits on the stairs to take off his shoes (he can't be heard clacking and echoing across the floor), he thinks again, *I got her into this, it's my job to get her out. Nobody else's.*

He calls his sister's cell. From below him, muffled but unmistakable, he hears Tina's Snow Patrol ringtone.

Red Lips answers immediately. "Hello, Peter." He sounds calmer now. In control. That could be good or bad for his plan. Pete can't tell which. "Have you got the notebooks?"

"Yes. Is my sister okay?"

"She's fine. Where are you?"

"That's pretty funny," Pete says . . . and when you think about it, it actually is. "Jimmy Gold would like it, I bet."

"I'm in no mood for cryptic humor. Let us do our business and be done with each other, shall we? Where are you?"

"Do you remember the Saturday Movie Palace?"

"What are you—"

Red Lips stops. Thinks.

"Are you talking about the Community Room, where they used to show all those corny . . ." He pauses again as the penny drops. "You're *here*?"

"Yes. And you're in the basement. I saw the car out back. You were maybe ninety feet from the notebooks all along." Even closer than that, Pete thinks. "Come and get them."

He ends the call before Red Lips can try to set the terms more to his liking. Pete runs for the kitchen on tiptoe, shoes in hand. He has to get out of sight before Red Lips can climb the stairs from the basement. If he does that, all may be well. If he doesn't, he and his sister will probably die together.

From downstairs, louder than her ringtone—*much* louder—he hears Tina cry out in pain.

Still alive, Pete thinks, and then, The bastard hurt her. Only that's not the truth.

I did it. This is all my fault. Mine, mine, mine.

51

Morris, sitting on a box marked **KITCHEN SUPPLIES**, closes Tina's phone and at first only looks at it. There's but one question on the floor, really; just one that needs to be answered. Is the boy telling the truth, or is he lying?

Morris thinks he's telling the truth. They both grew up on Sycamore Street, after all, and they both attended Saturday movie-shows upstairs, sitting on folding chairs and eating popcorn sold by the local Girl Scout troop. It's logical to think they would both choose this nearby abandoned building as a place to hide, one close to both the house they had shared and the buried trunk. The clincher is the sign Morris saw out front, on his first reconnaissance: CALL THOMAS SAUBERS REAL ESTATE. If Peter's father is the selling agent, the boy could easily have filched a key.

He seizes Tina by the arm and drags her across to the furnace, a huge and dusty relic crouched in the corner. She lets out another of those annoying cries as she tries to put weight on her swollen ankle and it buckles under her. He slaps her again.

"Shut up," he says. "Stop being such a whiny bitch."

There isn't enough computer cord to make sure she stays in one place, but there's a cage-light hanging on the wall with several yards of orange electrical cord looped around it. Morris doesn't need the light, but the cord is a gift from God. He didn't think he could be any angrier with the thief, but he was wrong. *Jimmy Gold would like it, I bet,* the thief had said, and what right did he have to reference John Rothstein's work? Rothstein's work was *his.*

"Turn around."

Tina doesn't move quickly enough to suit Morris, who is still furious with her brother. He grabs her shoulders and whirls her. Tina doesn't cry out this time, but a groan escapes her tightly compressed lips. Her beloved yellow blouse is now smeared with basement dirt.

He secures the orange electrical cord to the computer cord binding her wrists, then throws the cage-light over one of the furnace pipes. He pulls the cord taut, eliciting another groan from the girl as her bound hands are jerked up almost to her shoulder blades.

Morris ties off the new cord with a double knot, thinking, They were here all along, and he thinks that's *funny*? If he wants funny, I'll give him all the funny he can stand. He can die laughing.

He bends down, hands on knees, so he's eye to eye with the thief's sister. "I'm going upstairs to get my property, girlfriend. Also to kill your pain-in-the-ass brother. Then I'm going to come back down and kill you." He kisses the tip of her nose. "Your life is over. I want you to think about that while I'm gone."

He trots toward the stairs.

## 52

Pete is in the pantry. The door is only open a crack, but that's enough to see Red Lips as he goes hustling by, the little red and black gun in one hand, Tina's phone in the other. Pete listens to the echo of his footfalls as they cross the empty downstairs rooms, and as soon as they become the *thud-thud-thud* of feet climbing the stairs to what was once known as the Saturday Movie Palace, he pelts for the stairs to the basement. He drops his shoes on the way. He wants his hands free. He also wants Red Lips to know exactly where he went. Maybe it will slow him down.

Tina's eyes widen when she sees him. "Pete! *Get me out of here!*"

He goes to her and looks at the tangle of knots—white cord, orange cord—that binds her hands behind her and also to the furnace. The knots are tight, and he feels a wave of despair as he looks at them. He loosens one of the orange knots, allowing her hands to drop a little and taking some of the pressure off her shoulders. As he starts work on the second, his cell phone vibrates. The wolf has found nothing upstairs and is calling back. Instead of answering, Pete hurries to the box below the window. His printing is on the side: **KITCHEN SUPPLIES.** He can see footprints on top, and knows to whom they belong.

"What are you *doing?*" Tina says. "Untie me!"

But getting her free is only part of the problem. Getting her out is the rest of it, and Pete doesn't think there's enough time to do both before Red Lips comes back. He has seen his sister's ankle, now so swollen it hardly looks like an ankle at all.

Red Lips is no longer bothering with Tina's phone. He yells from upstairs. *Screams* from upstairs. "*Where are you, you fucking son of a whore?*"

Two little piggies in the basement and the big bad wolf upstairs, Pete thinks. And us without a house made of straw, let alone one made of bricks.

He carries the carton Red Lips used as a step to the middle of the room and pulls the folded flaps apart as footfalls race across the kitchen floor above them, pounding hard enough to make the old strips of insulation hanging between the beams sway a little. Tina's face is a mask of horror. Pete upends the carton, pouring out a flood of Moleskine notebooks.

"Pete! What are you doing? He's *coming*!"

Don't I know it, Pete thinks, and opens the second carton. As he adds the rest of the notebooks to the pile on the basement floor, the footfalls above stop. He's seen the shoes. Red Lips opens the door to the basement. Being cautious now. Trying to think it through.

"Peter? Are you visiting with your sister?"

"Yes," Peter calls back. "I'm visiting her with a gun in my hand."

"You know what?" the wolf says. "I don't believe that."

Pete unscrews the cap on the can of lighter fluid and upends it over the notebooks, dousing the jackstraw heap of stories, poems, and angry, half-drunk rants that often end in mid-thought. Also the two novels that complete the story of a fucked-up American named Jimmy Gold, stumbling through the sixties and looking for some kind of redemption. Looking for—in his own words—some kind of shit that means shit. Pete fumbles for the lighter, and at first it slips through his fingers. God, he can see the man's shadow up there now. Also the shadow of the gun.

Tina is saucer-eyed with terror, hogtied with her nose and lips slathered in blood. The bastard beat her, Pete thinks. Why did he do that? She's only a little kid.

But he knows. The sister was a semi-acceptable substitute for the one Red Lips *really* wants to beat.

"You *better* believe it," Pete says. "It's a forty-five, lots bigger than yours. It was in my father's desk. You better just go away. That would be the smart thing."

Please, God, *please*.

But Pete's voice wavers on the last words, rising to the uncertain treble of the thirteen-year-old boy who found these notebooks in the first place. Red Lips hears it, laughs, and starts down the stairs. Pete grabs the lighter again—tight, this time—and thumbs up the top as Red Lips comes fully into view. Pete flicks the spark wheel, realizing that he never checked to see if the lighter had fuel, an oversight that could end his life and that of his sister in the next ten seconds. But the spark produces a robust yellow flame.

Peter holds the lighter a foot above the pile of notebooks. "You're right," he says. "No gun. But I did find this in his desk."

## 53

Hodges and Jerome run across the baseball field. Jerome is pulling ahead, but Hodges isn't too far behind. Jerome stops at the edge of the sorry little basketball court and points to a green Subaru parked near the loading dock. Hodges reads the vanity license plate—BOOKS4U—and nods.

They have just started moving again when they hear a furious yell from inside: "*Where are you, you fucking son of a whore?*"

That's got to be Bellamy. The fucking son of a whore is undoubtedly Peter Saubers. The boy let himself in with his father's key, which means the front door is open. Hodges points to himself, then to the Rec. Jerome nods, but says in a low voice, "You have no gun."

"True enough, but my thoughts are pure and my strength is that of ten."

"Huh?"

"Stay here, Jerome. I mean it."

"You sure?"

"Yes. You don't happen to have a knife, do you? Even a pocketknife?"

"No. Sorry."

"All right, then look around. Find a bottle. There must be some, kids probably come back here to drink beer after dark. Break it and then slash you some tires. If this goes sideways, he's not using Halliday's car to get away."

Jerome's face says he doesn't much care for the possible implications of this order. He grips Hodges's arm. "No kamikaze runs, Bill, you hear me? Because you have nothing to make up for."

"I know."

The truth is he knows nothing of the kind. Four years ago, a woman he loved died in an explosion that was meant for him. There's not a day that goes by when he doesn't think of Janey, not a night when he doesn't lie in bed thinking, *If only I had been a little quicker. A little smarter.*

He hasn't been quick enough or smart enough this time, either, and telling himself that the situation developed too quickly isn't going to get those kids out of the potentially lethal jam they're in. All he knows for sure is that neither Tina nor her brother can die on his watch today. He'll do whatever he needs to in order to prevent that from happening.

He pats the side of Jerome's face. "Trust me, kiddo. I'll do my part. You just take care of those tires. You might yank some plug wires while you're at it."

Hodges starts away, looking back just once when he reaches the corner of the building. Jerome is watching him unhappily, but this time he's staying put. Which is good. The only thing worse than Bellamy killing Peter and Tina would be if he killed Jerome.

He goes around the corner and runs to the front of the building.

This door, like the one at 23 Sycamore Street, is standing open.

54

Red Lips is staring at the heap of Moleskine notebooks as if hypnotized. At last he raises his eyes to Pete. He also raises the gun.

"Go ahead," Pete says. "Do it and see what happens to the notebooks when I drop the lighter. I only got a chance to really douse the ones on top, but by now it'll be trickling down. And they're old. They'll go up fast. Then maybe the rest of the shit down here."

"So it's a Mexican standoff," Red Lips says. "The only problem with that, Peter—I'm speaking from your perspective now— is that my gun will last longer than your lighter. What are you going to do when it burns out?" He's trying to sound calm and in charge, but his eyes keep ping-ponging between the Zippo and the notebooks. The covers of the ones on top gleam wetly, like sealskin.

"I'll know when that's going to happen," Pete says. "The second the flame starts to go lower, and turns blue instead of yellow, I'll drop it. Then, *poof*."

"You won't." The wolf's upper lip rises, exposing those yellow teeth. Those fangs.

"Why not? They're just words. Compared to my sister, they don't mean shit."

"Really?" Red Lips turns the gun on Tina. "Then douse the lighter or I'll kill her right in front of you."

Painful hands squeeze Pete's heart at the sight of the gun pointing at his sister's midsection, but he doesn't close the Zippo's cap. He bends over, very slowly lowering it toward the pile of notebooks. "There are two more Jimmy Gold novels in here. Did you know that?"

"You're lying." Red Lips is still pointing the gun at Tina, but

401

his eyes have been drawn—helplessly, it seems—back toward the Moleskines again. "There's one. It's about him going west."

"Two," Pete says again. "*The Runner Goes West* is good, but *The Runner Raises the Flag* is the best thing he ever wrote. It's long, too. An epic. What a shame if you never get to read it."

A flush is climbing up the man's pale cheeks. "How dare you? How dare you *bait* me? I gave my *life* for those books! I *killed* for those books!"

"I know," Pete says. "And since you're such a fan, here's a little treat for you. In the last book, Jimmy meets Andrea Stone again. How about that?"

The wolf's eyes widen. "Andrea? He does? How? What happens?"

Under such circumstances the question is beyond bizarre, but it's also sincere. Honest. Pete realizes that the fictional Andrea, Jimmy's first love, is real to this man in a way Pete's sister is not. *No* human being is as real to Red Lips as Jimmy Gold, Andrea Stone, Mr. Meeker, Pierre Retonne (also known as The Car Salesman of Doom), and all the rest. This is surely a marker of true, deep insanity, but that must make Pete crazy, too, because he knows how this lunatic feels. Exactly how. He lit up with the same excitement, the same *amazement*, when Jimmy glimpsed Andrea in Grant Park, during the Chicago riots of 1968. Tears actually came to his eyes. Such tears, Pete realizes—yes, even now, *especially* now, because their lives hang upon it—mark the core power of make-believe. It's what caused thousands to weep when they learned that Charles Dickens had died of a stroke. It's why, for years, a stranger put a rose on Edgar Allan Poe's grave every January 19th, Poe's birthday. It's also what would make Pete hate this man even if he wasn't pointing a gun at his sister's trembling, vulnerable midsection. Red Lips took the life of a great writer, and why? Because Rothstein dared to follow a character who went in a direction Red Lips didn't like? Yes, that was it. He did it out of his own core belief: that the writing was somehow more important than the writer.

Slowly and deliberately, Pete shakes his head. "It's all in the notebooks. *The Runner Raises the Flag* fills sixteen of them. You could read it there, but you'll never hear any of it from me."

Pete actually smiles.

"No spoilers."

"The notebooks are mine, you bastard! *Mine!*"

"They're going to be ashes, if you don't let my sister go."

"Petie, I can't even *walk!*" Tina wails.

Pete can't afford to look at her, only at Red Lips. Only at the wolf. "What's your name? I think I deserve to know your name."

Red Lips shrugs, as if it no longer matters. "Morris Bellamy."

"Throw the gun away, Mr. Bellamy. Kick it along the floor and under the furnace. Once you do that, I'll close the lighter. I'll untie my sister and we'll go. I'll give you plenty of time to get away with the notebooks. All I want to do is take Tina home and get help for my mom."

"I'm supposed to trust you?" Red Lips sneers it.

Pete lowers the lighter farther. "Trust me or watch the notebooks burn. Make up your mind fast. I don't know the last time my dad filled this thing."

Something catches the corner of Pete's eye. Something moving on the stairs. He doesn't dare look. If he does, Red Lips will, too. *And I've almost got him,* Pete thinks.

This seems to be so. Red Lips starts to lower the gun. For a moment he looks every year of his age, and more. Then he raises the gun and points it at Tina again.

"I won't kill her." He speaks in the decisive tone of a general who has just made a crucial battlefield decision. "Not at first. I'll just shoot her in the leg. You can listen to her scream. If you light the notebooks on fire after that, I'll shoot her in the other leg. Then in the stomach. She'll die, but she'll have plenty of time to hate you first, if she doesn't alre—"

There's a flat double clap from Morris's left. It's Pete's shoes, landing at the foot of the stairs. Morris, on a hair trigger, wheels in that direction and fires. The gun is small, but in the enclosed space of the basement, the report is loud. Pete gives an involuntary jerk, and the lighter falls from his hand. There's an explosive *whump*, and notebooks on top of the pile suddenly grow a corona of fire.

"*No!*" Morris screams, wheeling away from Hodges even as Hodges comes pelting down the stairs so fast he can barely keep his balance. Morris has a clear shot at Pete. He raises the gun to take it, but before he can fire, Tina swings forward on her bonds and kicks him in the back of the leg with her good foot. The bullet goes between Pete's neck and shoulder.

The notebooks, meanwhile, are burning briskly.

Hodges closes with Morris before he can fire again, grabbing at Morris's gun hand. Hodges is the heavier of the two, and in better shape, but Morris Bellamy possesses the strength of insanity. They waltz drunkenly across the basement, Hodges holding Morris's right wrist so the little automatic points at the ceiling, Morris using his left hand to rip at Hodges's face, trying to claw out his eyes.

Peter races around the notebooks—they are blazing now, the lighter fluid that has trickled deep into the pile igniting—and grapples with Morris from behind. Morris turns his head, bares his teeth, and snaps at him. His eyes are rolling in their sockets.

"*His hand! Get his hand!*" Hodges shouts. They have stumbled under the stairs. Hodges's face is striped with blood, several pieces of his cheek hanging in strips. "Get it before he skins me alive!"

Pete grabs Bellamy's left hand. Behind them, Tina is screaming. Hodges pounds a fist into Bellamy's face twice: hard, pistoning blows. That seems to finish him; his face goes slack and his knees buckle. Tina is still screaming, and the basement is growing brighter.

*"The roof, Petie! The roof is catching!"*

Morris is on his knees, his head hanging, blood gushing from his chin, lips, and broken nose. Hodges grabs his right wrist and twists. There's a crack as Morris's wrist breaks, and the little automatic clatters to the floor. Hodges has a moment to think it's over before the bastard rams his free hand forward and upward, punching Hodges squarely in the balls and filling his belly with liquid pain. Morris scuttles between his spread legs. Hodges gasps, hands pressed to his throbbing crotch.

*"Petie, Petie, the ceiling!"*

Pete thinks Bellamy is going after the gun, but the man ignores it entirely. His goal is the notebooks. They are now a bonfire, the covers curling back, the pages browning and sending up sparks that have ignited several strips of hanging insulation. The fire begins spreading above them, dropping burning streamers. One of these lands on Tina's head, and there's a stench of frying hair to go with the smell of the burning paper and insulation. She shakes it away with a cry of pain.

Pete runs to her, punting the little automatic deep into the basement as he goes. He beats at her smoldering hair and then begins struggling with the knots.

*"No!"* Morris screams, but not at Pete. He goes to his knees in front of the notebooks like a religious zealot in front of a blazing altar. He reaches into the flames, trying to push the pile apart. This sends fresh clouds of sparks spiraling upward. *"No no no no!"*

Hodges wants to run to Peter and his sister, but the best he can manage is a drunken shamble. The pain in his groin is spreading down his legs, loosening the muscles he has worked so hard to build up. Nevertheless, he gets to work on one of the knots in the orange electrical cord. He again wishes for a knife, but it would take a cleaver to cut this stuff. The shit is *thick*.

More blazing strips of insulation fall around them. Hodges bats them away from the girl, terrified that her gauzy blouse will catch fire. The knot is letting go, finally letting go, but the girl is struggling—

"Stop, Teens," Pete says. Sweat is pouring down his face. The basement is getting hot. "They're slipknots, you're pulling them tight again, you have to stop."

Morris's screams are changing into howls of pain. Hodges has no time to look at him. The loop he's pulling on abruptly loosens. He pulls Tina away from the furnace, her hands still tied behind her.

There's going to be no exit by way of the stairs; the lower ones are burning and the upper ones are catching. The tables, the chairs, the boxes of stored paperwork: all on fire. Morris Bellamy is also on fire. Both his sportcoat and the shirt beneath are blazing. Yet he continues to root his way into the bonfire, trying to get at any unburned notebooks still left at the bottom. His fingers are turning black. Although the pain must be excruciating, he keeps going. Hodges has time to think of the fairy tale where the wolf came down the chimney and landed in a pot of boiling water. His daughter, Alison, didn't want to hear that one. She said it was too sca—

"Bill! Bill! Over here!"

Hodges sees Jerome at one of the basement windows. Hodges remembers saying *Neither one of you minds worth a tinker's dam*, and now he's delighted that they don't. Jerome is on his belly, sticking his arms through and down.

"Lift her! Lift her up! Quick, before you all cook!"

It's mostly Pete who carries Tina across to the basement window, through the falling sparks and burning scarves of insulation. One lands on the kid's back, and Hodges swipes it away. Pete lifts her. Jerome grabs her under the arms and hauls her out, the plug of the computer cord Morris used to tie her hands trailing and bumping behind.

"Now you," Hodges gasps.

Pete shakes his head. "You first." He looks up at Jerome. "You pull. I'll push."

"Okay," Jerome says. "Lift your arms, Bill."

There's no time to argue. Hodges lifts his arms and feels them grabbed. He has time to think, Feels like wearing handcuffs, and then he's being hoisted. It's slow at first—he's a lot heavier than the girl—but then two hands plant themselves firmly on his ass and shove. He rises into clear, clean air—hot, but cooler than the basement—and lands next to Tina Saubers. Jerome reaches through again. "Come on, kid! Move it!"

Pete lifts his arms, and Jerome seizes his wrists. The basement is filling with smoke and Pete begins coughing, almost retching, as he uses his feet to pedal his way up the wall. He slides through the window, turns over, and peers back into the basement.

A charred scarecrow kneels in there, digging into the burning notebooks with arms made of fire. Morris's face is melting. He shrieks and begins hugging the blazing, dissolving remnants of Rothstein's work to his burning chest.

"Don't look at that, kid," Hodges says, putting a hand on his shoulder. "Don't."

But Pete wants to look. Needs to look.

He thinks, That could have been me on fire.

He thinks, No. Because I know the difference. I know what matters.

He thinks, Please God, if you're there . . . let that be true.

## 55

Pete lets Jerome carry Tina as far as the baseball field, then says, "Give her to me, please."

Jerome surveys him—Pete's pale, shocked face, the one blistered ear, the holes charred in his shirt. "You sure?"

"Yeah."

Tina is already holding out her arms. She has been quiet since being hauled from the burning basement, but when Pete takes her, she puts her arms around his neck, her face against his shoulder, and begins to cry loudly.

Holly comes running down the path. "Thank God!" she says. "There you are! Where's Bellamy?"

"Back there, in the basement," Hodges says. "And if he isn't dead yet, he wishes he was. Have you got your cell phone? Call the fire department."

"Is our mother okay?" Pete asks.

"I think she's going to be fine," Holly says, pulling her phone off her belt. "The ambulance is taking her to Kiner Memorial. She was alert and talking. The paramedics said her vital signs are good."

"Thank God," Pete says. Now he also starts to cry, the tears cutting clean tracks through the smears of soot on his cheeks. "If she died, I'd kill myself. Because this is all my fault."

"No," Hodges says.

Pete looks at him. Tina is looking, too, her arms still linked around her brother's neck.

"You found the notebooks and the money, didn't you?"

"Yes. By accident. They were buried in a trunk by the stream."

"Anyone would have done what you did," Jerome says. "Isn't that right, Bill?"

"Yes," Bill says. "For your family, you do all that you can. The way you went after Bellamy when he took Tina."

"I wish I'd never found that trunk," Pete says. What he doesn't say, will never say, is how much it hurts to know that the notebooks are gone. Knowing that burns like fire. He does understand how Morris felt, and that burns like fire, too. "I wish it had stayed buried."

"Wish in one hand," Hodges says, "spit in the other. Let's go. I need to use an icepack before the swelling gets too bad."

"Swelling where?" Holly asks. "You look okay to me."

Hodges puts an arm around her shoulders. Sometimes Holly stiffens when he does this, but not today, so he kisses her cheek, too. It raises a doubtful smile.

"Did he get you where it hurts boys?"

"Yes. Now hush."

They walk slowly, partly for Hodges's benefit, partly for Pete's. His sister is getting heavy, but he doesn't want to put her down. He wants to carry her all the way home.

# AFTER

# PICNIC

On the Friday that kicks off the Labor Day weekend, a Jeep Wrangler—getting on in years but loved by its owner—pulls into the parking lot above the McGinnis Park Little League fields and stops next to a blue Mercedes that is also getting on in years. Jerome Robinson makes his way down the grassy slope toward a picnic table where food has already been set out. A paper bag swings from one of his hands.

"Yo, Hollyberry!"

She turns. "How many times have I told you not to call me that? A hundred? A thousand?" But she's smiling as she says it, and when he hugs her, she hugs back. Jerome doesn't press his luck; he gives one good squeeze, then asks what's for lunch.

"There's chicken salad, tuna salad, and coleslaw. I also brought a roast beef sandwich. That's for you, if you want it. I'm off red meat. It upsets my circadian rhythms."

"I'll make sure you're not tempted, then."

They sit down. Holly pours Snapple into Dixie cups. They toast the end of summer and then munch away, gabbing about movies and TV shows, temporarily avoiding the reason they're here—this is goodbye, at least for awhile.

"Too bad Bill couldn't come," Jerome says as Holly hands him a piece of chocolate cream pie. "Remember when we all got together here for a picnic after his hearing? To celebrate that judge deciding not to put him in jail?"

"I remember perfectly well," Holly says. "You wanted to ride the bus."

"Because de bus be fo' free!" Tyrone Feelgood exclaims. "I takes all the fo' free I kin git, Miss Holly!"

"You've worn that out, Jerome."

He sighs. "I sort of have, I guess."

"Bill got a call from Peter Saubers," Holly said. "That's why he didn't come. He said I was to give you his best, and that he'd see you before you went back to Cambridge. Wipe your nose. There's a dab of chocolate on it."

Jerome resists the urge to say *Chocolate be mah favorite cullah*! "Is Pete all right?"

"Yes. He had some good news that he wanted to share with Bill in person. I can't finish my pie. Do you want the rest? Unless you don't want to eat after me. I'm okay with that, but I don't have a cold, or anything."

"I'd even use your toothbrush," Jerome says, "but I'm full."

"Oough," Holly says. "I'd never use another person's toothbrush." She collects their paper cups and plates and takes them to a nearby litter barrel.

"What time are you leaving tomorrow?" Jerome asks.

"The sun rises at six fifty-five AM. I expect to be on the road by seven thirty, at the latest."

Holly is driving to Cincinnati to see her mother. By herself. Jerome can hardly believe it. He's glad for her, but he's also afraid for her. What if something goes wrong and she freaks out?

"Stop worrying," she says, coming back and sitting down. "I'll be fine. All turnpikes, no night driving, and the forecast is for clear weather. Also, I have my three favorite movie soundtracks on CD: *Road to Perdition*, *The Shawshank Redemption*, and *Godfather II*. Which is the best, in my opinion, although Thomas Newman is, on the whole, much better than Nino Rota. Thomas Newman's music is *mysterious*."

"John Williams, *Schindler's List*," Jerome says. "Nothing tops it."

"Jerome, I don't want to say you're full of shit, but . . . actually, you are."

He laughs, delighted.

"I have my cell phone and iPad, both fully charged. The Mercedes just had its full maintenance check. And really, it's only four hundred miles."

"Cool. But call me if you need to. Me or Bill."

"Of course. When are you leaving for Cambridge?"

"Next week."

"Done on the docks?"

"All done, and glad of it. Physical labor may be good for the body, but I don't feel that it ennobles the soul."

Holly still has trouble meeting the eyes of even her close friends, but she makes an effort and meets Jerome's. "Pete's all right, Tina's all right, and their mother is back on her feet. That's all good, but is *Bill* all right? Tell me the truth."

"I don't know what you mean." Now it's Jerome who finds it difficult to maintain eye contact.

"He's too thin, for one thing. He's taken the exercise-and-salads regimen too far. But that's not what I'm really worried about."

"What is?" But Jerome knows, and isn't surprised *she* knows, although Bill thinks he's kept it from her. Holly has her ways.

She lowers her voice as if afraid of being overheard, although there's no one within a hundred yards in any direction. "How often does he visit him?"

Jerome doesn't have to ask who she's talking about. "I don't really know."

"More than once a month?"

"I think so, yes."

"Once a week?"

"Probably not that often." Although who can say?

"*Why?* He's . . ." Holly's lips are trembling. "Brady Hartsfield is next door to a *vegetable!*"

"You can't blame yourself for that, Holly. You absolutely can't. You hit him because he was going to blow up a couple of thousand kids."

He tries to touch her hand, but she snatches it away.

"I *don't*! I'd do it again! Again again again! But I hate to think of Bill obsessing about him. I know from obsession, and it's *not nice!*"

She crosses her arms over her bosom, an old self-comforting gesture that she has largely given up.

"I don't think it's obsession, exactly." Jerome speaks cautiously, feeling his way. "I don't think it's about the past."

"What else can it be? Because that monster has no future!"

*Bill's not so sure,* Jerome thinks, but would never say. Holly is better, but she's still fragile. And, as she herself said, she knows from obsession. Besides, he has no idea what Bill's continuing interest in Brady means. All he has is a feeling. A hunch.

"Let it rest," he says. This time when he puts his hand over hers she allows it to stay, and they talk of other things for awhile. Then he looks at his watch. "I have to go. I promised to pick up Barbara and Tina at the roller rink."

"Tina's in love with you," Holly says matter-of-factly as they walk up the slope to their cars.

"If she is, it'll pass," he says. "I'm heading east, and pretty soon some cute boy will appear in her life. She'll write his name on her book covers."

"I suppose," Holly says. "That's usually how it works, isn't it? I just don't want you to make fun of her. She'd think you were being mean, and feel sad."

"I won't," Jerome says.

They have reached the cars, and once more Holly forces herself to look him full in the face. "*I'm* not in love with you, not the way she is, but I love you quite a lot, just the same. So take care of yourself, Jerome. Some college boys do foolish things. Don't be one of them."

This time it's she who embraces him.

"Oh, hey, I almost forgot," Jerome says. "I brought you a little present. It's a shirt, although I don't think you'll want to wear it when you visit your mom."

He hands her his bag. She takes out the bright red tee and unfolds it. Printed on the front, in black, it shouts:

# SHIT DON'T MEAN SHIT
## Jimmy Gold

"They sell them at the City College bookstore. I got it in an XL, in case you want to wear it as a nightshirt." He studies her face as she considers the words on the front of the tee. "Of course, you can also return it for something else, if you don't like it."

"I like it very much," she says, and breaks into a smile. It's the one Hodges loves, the one that makes her beautiful. "And I *will* wear it when I visit my mother. Just to piss her off."

Jerome looks so surprised that she laughs.

"Don't you ever want to piss your mother off?"

"From time to time. And Holly . . . I love you, too. You know that, right?"

"I do," she says, holding the shirt to her chest. "And I'm glad. That shit means a lot."

# TRUNK

Hodges walks the path through the undeveloped land from the Birch Street end, and finds Pete sitting on the bank of the stream with his knees hugged to his chest. Nearby, a scrubby tree juts over the water, which is down to a trickle after a long, hot summer. Below the tree, the hole where the trunk was buried has been reexcavated. The trunk itself is sitting aslant on the bank nearby. It looks old and tired and rather ominous, a time traveler from a year when disco was still in bloom. A photographer's tripod stands nearby. There are also a couple of bags that look like the kind pros carry when they travel.

"The famous trunk," Hodges says, sitting down next to Pete.

Pete nods. "Yeah. The famous trunk. The picture guy and his assistant have gone to lunch, but I think they'll be back pretty soon. Didn't seem crazy about any of the local restaurant choices. They're from New York." He shrugs, as if that explains every-thing. "At first the guy wanted me sitting on it, with my chin on my fist. You know, like that famous statue. I talked him out of it, but it wasn't easy."

"This is for the local paper?"

Pete shakes his head, starting to smile. "That's my good news, Mr. Hodges. It's for *The New Yorker*. They want an article about what happened. Not a little one, either. They want it for what they call 'the well,' which means the middle of the magazine. A really big piece, maybe the biggest they've ever done."

"That's great!"

"It will be if I don't fuck it up."

Hodges studies him for a moment. "Wait. *You're* going to write it?"

"Yeah. At first they wanted to send out one of their writers—George Packer, he's a really good one—to interview me and write the story. It's a big deal because John Rothstein was one of their fiction stars in the old days, right up there with John Updike, Shirley Jackson . . . you know the ones I mean."

Hodges doesn't, but he nods.

"Rothstein was sort of the go-to guy for teenage angst, and then middle-class angst. Sort of like John Cheever. I'm reading Cheever now. Do you know his story 'The Swimmer'?"

Hodges shakes his head.

"You should. It's awesome. Anyhow, they want the story of the notebooks. The whole thing, from beginning to end. This was after they had three or four handwriting analysts check out the photocopies I made, and the fragments."

Hodges *does* know about the fragments. There were enough charred scraps in the burned-out basement to validate Pete's claim that the lost notebooks really had been Rothstein's work. Police backtrailing Morris Bellamy had further buttressed Pete's story. Which Hodges never doubted in the first place.

"You said no to Packer, I take it."

"I said no to *anyone*. If the story's going to get written, I have to be the one to do it. Not just because I was there, but because reading John Rothstein changed my . . ."

He stops and shakes his head.

"No. I was going to say his work changed my life, but that's not right. I don't think a teenager has much of a life to change. I just turned eighteen last month. I guess what I mean is his work changed my *heart*."

Hodges smiles. "I get that."

"The editor in charge of the story said I was too young—better than saying I had no talent, right?—so I sent him writing samples. That helped. Also, I stood up to him. It wasn't all that hard. Negotiating with a magazine guy from New York didn't seem like such a big deal after facing Bellamy. *That* was a negotiation."

Pete shrugs.

"They'll edit it the way they want, of course, I've read enough to know the process, and I'm okay with that. But if they want to publish it, it'll be my name over my story."

"Tough stance, Pete."

He stares at the trunk, for a moment looking much older than eighteen. "It's a tough world. I found that out after my dad got run down at City Center."

No reply seems adequate, so Hodges keeps silent.

"You know what they want most at *The New Yorker*, right?"

Hodges didn't spend almost thirty years as a detective for nothing. "A summary of the last two books would be my guess. Jimmy Gold and his sister and all his friends. Who did what to who, and how, and when, and how it all came out in the wash."

"Yeah. And I'm the only one who knows those things. Which brings me to the apology part." He looks at Hodges solemnly.

"Pete, no apology's necessary. There are no legal charges against you, and I'm not bearing even a teensy grudge about anything. Holly and Jerome aren't, either. We're just glad your mom and sis are okay."

"They almost weren't. If I hadn't stonewalled you that day in the car, then ducked out through the drugstore, I bet Bellamy never would have come to the house. Tina still has nightmares."

"Does she blame you for them?"

"Actually . . . no."

"Well, there you are," Hodges says. "You were under the gun. Literally as well as figuratively. Halliday scared the hell out of you, and you had no way of knowing he was dead when you went to his shop that day. As for Bellamy, you didn't even know he was still alive, let alone out of prison."

"That's all true, but Halliday threatening me wasn't the only reason I wouldn't talk to you. I still thought I had a chance to keep the notebooks, see? *That's* why I wouldn't talk to you. And why I ran away. I wanted to keep them. It wasn't the top thing on my mind, but it was there underneath, all right. Those notebooks . . . well . . . and I have to say this in the piece I write for *The New Yorker* . . . they cast a spell over me. I need to apologize because I really wasn't so different from Morris Bellamy."

Hodges takes Pete by the shoulders and looks directly into his eyes. "If that were true, you never would have gone to the Rec prepared to burn them."

"I dropped the lighter by accident," Pete says quietly. "The gunshot startled me. I *think* I would have done it anyway—if he'd shot Tina—but I'll never know for sure."

"*I* know," Hodges says. "And I'm sure enough for both of us."
"Yeah?"
"Yeah. So how much are they paying you for this?"
"Fifteen thousand dollars."
Hodges whistles.

"It's on acceptance, but they'll accept it, all right. Mr. Ricker is helping me, and it's turning out pretty well. I've already got the first half done in rough draft. I'm not much at fiction, but I'm okay at stuff like this. I could make a career of it someday, maybe."

"What are you going to do with the money? Put it in a college fund?"

He shakes his head. "I'll get to college, one way or another. I'm not worried about that. The money is for Chapel Ridge. Tina's going this year. You can't believe how excited she is."

"That's good," Hodges says. "That's really good."

They sit in silence for a little while, looking at the trunk. There are footfalls on the path, and men's voices. The two guys who appear are wearing almost identical plaid shirts and jeans that still show the store creases. Hodges has an idea they think this is how everybody dresses in flyover country. One has a camera around his neck; the other is toting a second light.

"How was your lunch?" Pete calls as they teeter across the creek on the stepping-stones.

"Fine," the one with the camera says. "Denny's. Moons Over My Hammy. The hash browns alone were a culinary dream. Come on over, Pete. We'll start with a few of you kneeling by the trunk. I also want to get a few of you looking inside."

"It's empty," Pete objects.

The photographer taps himself between the eyes. "People will *imagine*. They'll think, 'What must it have been like when he opened that trunk for the first time and saw all those literary treasures?' You know?"

Pete stands up, brushing the seat of jeans that are much more faded and more natural-looking. "Want to stick around for the shoot, Mr. Hodges? Not every eighteen-year-old gets a full-page portrait in *The New Yorker* next to an article he wrote himself."

"I'd love to, Pete, but I have an errand to run."

"All right. Thanks for coming out and listening to me."

"Will you put one other thing in your story?"

"What?"

"That this didn't start with you finding the trunk." Hodges looks at it, black and scuffed, a relic with scratched fittings and a moldy top. "It started with the man who put it there. And when

423

you feel like blaming yourself for how it went down, you might want to remember that thing Jimmy Gold keeps saying. Shit don't mean shit."

Pete laughs and holds out his hand. "You're a good guy, Mr. Hodges."

Hodges shakes. "Make it Bill. Now go smile for the camera."

He pauses on the other side of the creek and looks back. At the photographer's direction, Pete is kneeling with one hand resting on the trunk's scuffed top. It is the classic pose of ownership, reminding Hodges of a photo he once saw of Ernest Hemingway kneeling next to a lion he bagged. But Pete's face holds none of Hemingway's complacent, smiling, stupid confidence. Pete's face says *I never owned this.*

Hold that thought, kiddo, Hodges thinks as he starts back to his car.

Hold that thought.

# CLACK

He told Pete he had an errand to run. That wasn't precisely true. He could have said he had a case to work, but that isn't precisely true, either. Although it would have been closer.

Shortly before leaving for his meeting with Pete, he received a call from Becky Helmington at the Traumatic Brain Injury Clinic. He pays her a small amount each month to keep him updated on Brady Hartsfield, the patient Hodges calls "my boy." She also updates him on any strange occurrences on the ward, and feeds him the latest rumors. Hodges's rational mind insists there's nothing to these rumors, and certain strange occurrences have rational explanations, but there's more to his mind than the rational part on top. Deep below that rational part is an underground ocean—there's one inside every head, he believes—where strange creatures swim.

"How's your son?" he asked Becky. "Hasn't fallen out of any trees lately, I hope."

"No, Robby's fine and dandy. Read today's paper yet, Mr. Hodges?"

"Haven't even taken it out of the bag yet." In this new era, where everything is at one's fingertips on the Internet, some days he never takes it out of the bag at all. It just sits there beside his La-Z-Boy like an abandoned child.

"Check the Metro section. Page two. Call me back."

425

Five minutes later he did. "Jesus, Becky."

"Exactly what I thought. She was a nice girl."

"Will you be on the floor today?"

"No. I'm upstate, at my sister's. We're spending the weekend."
Becky paused. "Actually, I've been thinking about transferring to
ICU in the main hospital when I get back. There's an opening, and
I'm tired of Dr. Babineau. It's true what they say—sometimes the
neuros are crazier than the patients." She paused, then added: "I'd
say I'm tired of Hartsfield, too, but that wouldn't be exactly right.
The truth is, I'm a little scared of him. The way I used to be scared
of the local haunted house when I was a girl."

"Yeah?"

"Uh-huh. I knew there were no ghosts in there, but on the other
hand, what if there were?"

Hodges arrives at the hospital shortly after two PM, and on this
pre-holiday afternoon, the Brain Injury Clinic is as close to deserted
as it ever gets. In the daytime, at least.

The nurse on duty—Norma Wilmer, according to her badge—
gives him a visitor's pass. As he clips it to his shirt, Hodges says,
just passing the time, "I understand you had a tragedy on the ward
yesterday."

"I can't talk about that," Nurse Wilmer says.

"Were you on duty?"

"No." She goes back to her paperwork and her monitors.

That's okay; he may learn more from Becky, once she gets back
and has time to tap her sources. If she goes through with her plan
to transfer (in Hodges's mind, that's the best sign yet that something real may be going on here), he will find someone else to help
him out a little. Some of the nurses are dedicated smokers, in spite

of all they know about the habit, and these are always happy to earn butt-money.

Hodges ambles down to Room 217, aware that his heart is beating harder and faster than normal. Another sign that he has begun to take this seriously. The news story in the morning paper shook him up more than a little.

He meets Library Al on the way, pushing his little trolley, and gives his usual greeting: "Hi, guy. How you doin?"

Al doesn't reply at first. Doesn't even seem to see him. The bruised-looking circles under his eyes are more prominent than ever, and his hair—usually neatly combed—is in disarray. Also, his damn badge is on upside-down. Hodges wonders again if Al is starting to lose the plot.

"Everything all right, Al?"

"Sure," Al says emptily. "Never so good as what you don't see, right?"

Hodges has no idea how to reply to this non sequitur, and Al has continued on his way before he can think of one. Hodges looks after him, puzzled, then moves on.

Brady is sitting in his usual place by the window, wearing his usual outfit: jeans and a checked shirt. Someone has given him a haircut. It's a bad one, a real butch job. Hodges doubts if his boy cares. It's not like he's going out boot scootin' anytime soon.

"Hello, Brady. Long time no see, as the ship's chaplain said to the Mother Superior."

Brady just looks out the window, and the same old questions join hands and play ring-a-rosie in Hodges's head. Is Brady seeing anything out there? Does he know he has company? If so, does he know it's Hodges? Is he thinking at all? *Sometimes* he thinks— enough to speak a few simple sentences, anyway—and in the physio center he's able to shamble along the seventy feet or so the patients call Torture Avenue, but what does that really mean? Fish swim in an aquarium, but that doesn't mean they think.

Hodges thinks, Never so good as what you don't see.

Whatever *that* means.

He picks up the silver-framed photo of Brady and his mother with their arms around each other, smiling to beat the band. If the bastard ever loved anyone, it was dear old mommy. Hodges looks to see if there's any reaction to his visitor having Deborah Ann's picture in his hands. There doesn't seem to be.

"She looks hot, Brady. Was she hot? Was she a real hoochie-mama?"

No response.

"I only ask because when we broke into your computer, we found some cheesecake pix of her. You know, negligees, nylons, bras and panties, that kind of thing. She looked hot to me, dressed like that. To the other cops, too, when I passed them around."

Although he tells this lie with his usual panache, there's still no reaction. Nada.

"Did you fuck her, Brady? I bet you wanted to."

Was that the barest twitch of an eyebrow? The slightest downward jerk of a lip?

Maybe, but Hodges knows it could just be his imagination, because he *wants* Brady to hear him. Nobody in America deserves to have more salt rubbed in more wounds than this murderous motherfucker.

"Maybe you killed her and *then* fucked her. No need to be polite then, right?"

Nothing.

Hodges sits in the visitor's chair and puts the picture back on the table next to one of the Zappit e-readers Al hands out to patients who want them. He folds his hands and looks at Brady, who should never have awakened from his coma but did.

Well.

Sort of.

"Are you faking, Brady?"

He always asks this question, and there has never been any reply. There's none today, either.

"A nurse killed herself on the floor last night. In one of the bathrooms. Did you know that? Her name has been withheld for the time being, but the paper says she died of excessive bleeding. I'm guessing that means she cut her wrists, but I'm not sure. If you knew, I bet it made you happy. You always enjoyed a good suicide, didn't you?"

He waits. Nothing.

Hodges leans forward, staring into Brady's blank face and speaking earnestly. "The thing is—what I don't understand—is how she did that. The mirrors in these bathrooms aren't glass, they're polished metal. I suppose she could have used the mirror in her compact, or something, but that seems like pretty small shit for a job like that. Kind of like bringing a knife to a gunfight." He sits back. "Hey, maybe she *had* a knife. One of those Swiss Army jobs, you know? In her purse. Did you ever have one of those?"

Nothing.

Or is there? He has a sense, very strong, that behind that blank stare, Brady is watching him.

"Brady, some of the nurses believe you can turn the water on and off in your bathroom from here. They think you do it just to scare them. Is that true?"

Nothing. But that sense of being watched is strong. Brady *did* enjoy suicide, that's the thing. You could even say suicide was his signature. Before Holly tuned him up with the Happy Slapper, Brady tried to get Hodges to kill himself. He didn't succeed . . . but he *did* succeed with Olivia Trelawney, the woman whose Mercedes Holly Gibney now owns and plans to drive to Cincinnati.

"If you can, do it now. Come on. Show off a little. Strut your stuff. What do you say?"

Nothing.

Some of the nurses believe that being whopped repeatedly in the head on the night he tried to blow up Mingo Auditorium has somehow rearranged Hartsfield's brains. That being whopped repeatedly gave him . . . powers. Dr. Babineau says that's ridiculous, the hospital equivalent of an urban legend. Hodges is sure he's right, but that sense of being watched is undeniable.

So is the feeling that, somewhere deep inside, Brady Hartsfield is laughing at him.

He picks up the e-reader, this one bright blue. On his last visit to the clinic, Library Al said Brady enjoyed the demos. *He stares at it for hours,* Al said.

"Like this thing, do you?"

Nothing.

"Not that you can do much with it, right?"

Zero. Zippo. Zilch.

Hodges puts it down beside the picture and stands. "Let me see what I can find out about the nurse, okay? What I can't dig up, my assistant can. We have our sources. Are you glad that nurse is dead? Was she mean to you? Did she pinch your nose or twist your tiny useless peepee, maybe because you ran down a friend or relative of hers at City Center?"

Nothing.

Nothing.

Noth—

Brady's eyes roll in their sockets. He looks at Hodges, and Hodges feels a moment of stark, unreasoning terror. Those eyes are dead on top, but he sees something beneath that looks not quite human. It makes him think of that movie about the little girl who was possessed by Pazuzu. Then the eyes return to the window and Hodges tells himself not to be an idiot. Babineau says Brady's come back as far as he's ever going to, and that's not very far. He's your basic blank slate, and nothing is written on it but Hodges's own feelings for this man, the most despicable creature he has encountered in all his years of law enforcement.

I want him to be in there so I can hurt him, Hodges thinks. That's all it is. It'll turn out the nurse's husband ran off on her, or she had a drug habit and was going to be fired, or both.

"All right, Brady," he says. "Gonna put an egg in my shoe and beat it. Make like a bee and buzz. But I have to say, as one friend to another, that's a really *shitty* haircut."

No response.

"Seeya later, alligator. After awhile, crocodile."

He leaves, closing the door gently behind him. If Brady *is* in there, slamming it might give him the pleasure of knowing he's gotten under Hodges's skin.

Which, of course, he has.


When Hodges is gone, Brady raises his head. Beside the picture of his mother, the blue e-reader abruptly comes to life. Animated fish rush hither and yon while cheery, bubbly music plays. The screen switches to the Angry Birds demo, then to Barbie Fashion Walk, then to Galactic Warrior. After that, the screen goes dark again.

In the bathroom, the water in the sink gushes, then stops.

Brady looks at the picture of him and his mother, smiling with their cheeks pressed together. Stares at it. Stares at it.

The picture falls over.

*Clack.*

July 26, 2014

# AUTHOR'S NOTE

You write a book in a room by yourself, that's just how it's done. I wrote the first draft of this one in Florida, looking out at palm trees. I rewrote it in Maine, looking out at pine trees sloping down to a beautiful lake where the loons converse at sunset. But I wasn't entirely alone in either place; few writers are. When I needed help, help was there.

NAN GRAHAM edited the book. SUSAN MOLDOW and ROZ LIPPEL also work for Scribner, and I couldn't get along without them. Those women are invaluable.

CHUCK VERRILL agented the book. He's been my go-to guy for thirty years, smart, funny, and fearless. No yes-man he; when my shit's not right, he never hesitates to tell me.

RUSS DORR does research, and he's gotten better and better at the job as the years pass. Like a good first assist PA in the OR, he's ready with the next instrument I need before I even call for it. His contributions to this book are on almost every page. Literally: Russ gave me the title when I was stumped for one.

OWEN KING and KELLY BRAFFET, both excellent novelists, read the first draft and sharpened it considerably. Their contributions are also on just about every page.

MARSHA DeFILIPPO and JULIE EUGLEY run my office in Maine, and keep me tethered to the real world. BARBARA MacINTYRE runs the office in Florida and does the same. SHIRLEY SONDEREGGER is emeritus.

TABITHA KING is my best critic and one true love.

And you, CONSTANT READER. Thank God you're still there after all these years. If you're having fun, I am, too.

# STEPHEN KING

# MR. MERCEDES

A NOVEL

SCRIBNER

New York    London    Toronto    Sydney    New Delhi

SCRIBNER
A Division of Simon & Schuster, Inc.
1230 Avenue of the Americas
New York, NY 10020

First Scribner hardcover edition June 2014

SCRIBNER and design are registered trademarks of The Gale Group, Inc.,
used under license by Simon & Schuster, Inc., the publisher of this work.

For information about special discounts for bulk purchases,
please contact Simon & Schuster Special Sales at 1-866-506-1949
or business@simonandschuster.com.

The Simon & Schuster Speakers Bureau can bring authors to your live event.
For more information or to book an event contact the Simon & Schuster Speakers Bureau
at 1-866-248-3049 or visit our website at www.simonspeakers.com.

Interior design by Erich Hobbing
Jacket design by Tal Goretsky
Jacket illustration by Sam Weber

Manufactured in the United States of America

1  3  5  7  9  10  8  6  4  2

Library of Congress Control Number: 2013046172

ISBN 978-1-4767-5445-1
ISBN 978-1-4767-5446-8 (ebook)

Thinking of James M. Cain

*They threw me off the hay truck about noon . . .*

# MR. MERCEDES

# GRAY MERCEDES

*April 9–10, 2009*

Augie Odenkirk had a 1997 Datsun that still ran well in spite of high mileage, but gas was expensive, especially for a man with no job, and City Center was on the far side of town, so he decided to take the last bus of the night. He got off at twenty past eleven with his pack on his back and his rolled-up sleeping bag under one arm. He thought he would be glad of the down-filled bag by three A.M. The night was misty and chill.

"Good luck, man," the driver said as he stepped down. "You ought to get something for just being the first one there."

Only he wasn't. When Augie reached the top of the wide, steep drive leading to the big auditorium, he saw a cluster of at least two dozen people already waiting outside the rank of doors, some standing, most sitting. Posts strung with yellow DO NOT CROSS tape had been set up, creating a complicated passage that doubled back on itself, mazelike. Augie was familiar with these from movie theaters and the bank where he was currently over-drawn, and understood the purpose: to cram as many people as possible into as small a space as possible.

As he approached the end of what would soon be a conga-line of job applicants, Augie was both amazed and dismayed to see that the woman at the end of the line had a sleeping baby in a Papoose carrier. The baby's cheeks were flushed with the cold; each exhale came with a faint rattle.

The woman heard Augie's slightly out-of-breath approach, and turned. She was young and pretty enough, even with the dark circles under her eyes. At her feet was a small quilted carry-case. Augie supposed it was a baby support system.

"Hi," she said. "Welcome to the Early Birds Club."

"Hopefully we'll catch a worm." He debated, thought what the hell, and stuck out his hand. "August Odenkirk. Augie. I was recently downsized. That's the twenty-first-century way of saying I got canned."

She shook with him. She had a good grip, firm and not a bit timid. "I'm Janice Cray, and my little bundle of joy is Patti. I guess I got downsized, too. I was a housekeeper for a nice family in Sugar Heights. He, um, owns a car dealership."

Augie winced.

Janice nodded. "I know. He said he was sorry to let me go, but they had to tighten their belts."

"A lot of that going around," Augie said, thinking: *You could find no one to babysit? No one at all?*

"I had to bring her." He supposed Janice Cray didn't have to be much of a mind reader to know what he was thinking. "There's no one else. Literally no one. The girl down the street couldn't stay all night even if I could pay her, and I just can't. If I don't get a job, I don't know what we'll do."

"Your parents couldn't take her?" Augie asked.

"They live in Vermont. If I had half a brain, I'd take Patti and go there. It's pretty. Only they've got their own problems. Dad says their house is underwater. Not literally, they're not in the river or anything, it's something financial."

Augie nodded. There was a lot of that going around, too.

A few cars were coming up the steep rise from Marlborough Street, where Augie had gotten off the bus. They turned left, into the vast empty plain of parking lot that would no doubt be full by daylight tomorrow . . . still hours before the First Annual City Job

4

Fair opened its doors. None of the cars looked new. Their drivers parked, and from most of them three or four job-seekers emerged, heading toward the doors of the auditorium. Augie was no longer at the end of the line. It had almost reached the first switchback.

"If I can get a job, I can get a sitter," she said. "But for tonight, me and Patti just gotta suck it up."

The baby gave a croupy cough Augie didn't care for, stirred in the Papoose, and then settled again. At least the kid was bundled up; there were even tiny mittens on her hands.

*Kids survive worse,* Augie told himself uneasily. He thought of the Dust Bowl, and the Great Depression. Well, this one was great enough for him. Two years ago, everything had been fine. He hadn't exactly been living large in the 'hood, but he *had* been making ends meet, with a little left over at the end of most months. Now everything had turned to shit. They had done something to the money. He didn't understand it; he'd been an office drone in the shipping department of Great Lakes Transport, and what he knew about was invoices and using a computer to route stuff by ship, train, and air.

"People will see me with a baby and think I'm irresponsible," Janice Cray fretted. "I know it, I see it on their faces already, I saw it on yours. But what else could I do? Even if the girl down the street could stay all night, it would have cost eighty-four dollars. *Eighty-four!* I've got next month's rent put aside, and after that, I'm skint." She smiled, and in the light of the parking lot's high arc-sodiums, Augie saw tears beading her eyelashes. "I'm babbling."

"No need to apologize, if that's what you're doing." The line had turned the first corner now, and had arrived back at where Augie was standing. And the girl was right. He saw lots of people staring at the sleeping kid in the Papoose.

"Oh, that's it, all right. I'm a single unmarried mother with no job. I want to apologize to everyone, for everything." She turned and looked at the banner posted above the rank of doors. 1000 **JOBS GUARENTEED!** it read. And below that: *"We Stand With the People of Our City!"* —**MAYOR RALPH KINSLER.**

"Sometimes I want to apologize for Columbine, and 9/11, and Barry Bonds taking steroids." She uttered a semi-hysterical giggle. "Sometimes I even want to apologize for the space shuttle exploding, and when that happened I was still learning to walk."

"Don't worry," Augie told her. "You'll be okay." It was just one of those things that you said.

"I wish it wasn't so damp, that's all. I've got her bundled up in case it was really cold, but this damp . . ." She shook her head. "We'll make it, though, won't we, Patti?" She gave Augie a hopeless little smile. "It just better not rain."

It didn't, but the dampness increased until they could see fine droplets suspended in the light thrown by the arc-sodiums. At some point Augie realized that Janice Cray was asleep on her feet. She was hipshot and slump-shouldered, with her hair hanging in dank wings around her face and her chin nearly on her breastbone. He looked at his watch and saw it was quarter to three.

Ten minutes later, Patti Cray awoke and started to cry. Her mother (her *baby mama*, Augie thought) gave a jerk, voiced a horselike snort, raised her head, and tried to pull the infant out of the Papoose. At first the kid wouldn't come; her legs were stuck. Augie pitched in, holding the sides of the sling. As Patti emerged, now wailing, he could see drops of water sparkling all over her tiny pink jacket and matching hat.

"She's hungry," Janice said. "I can give her the breast, but she's also wet. I can feel it right through her pants. God, I can't change her in this—look how foggy it's gotten!"

Augie wondered what comical deity had arranged for him to be the one in line behind her. He also wondered how in hell this woman was going to get through the rest of her life—*all* of it, not just the next eighteen years or so when she would be responsible for the kid. To come out on a night like this, with nothing but a bag of diapers! To be that goddam desperate!

He had put his sleeping bag down next to Patti's diaper bag. Now he squatted, pulled the ties, unrolled it, and unzipped it.

"Slide in there. Get warm and get *her* warm. Then I'll hand in whatever doodads you need."

She gazed at him, holding the squirming, crying baby. "Are you married, Augie?"

"Divorced."

"Children?"

He shook his head.

"Why are you being so kind to us?"

"Because we're here," he said, and shrugged.

She looked at him a moment longer, deciding, then handed him the baby. Augie held her out at arms' length, fascinated by the red, furious face, the bead of snot on the tiny upturned nose, the bicycling legs in the flannel onesie. Janice squirmed into the sleeping bag, then lifted her hands. "Give her to me, please."

Augie did, and the woman burrowed deeper into the bag. Beside them, where the line had doubled back on itself for the first time, two young men were staring.

"Mind your business, guys," Augie said, and they looked away.

"Would you give me a diaper?" Janice said. "I should change her before I feed her."

He dropped one knee to the wet pavement and unzipped the quilted bag. He was momentarily surprised to find cloth diapers instead of Pampers, then understood. The cloth ones could be used over and over. Maybe the woman wasn't entirely hopeless.

"I see a bottle of Baby Magic, too. Do you want that?"

From inside the sleeping bag, where now only a tuft of her brownish hair showed: "Yes, please."

He passed in the diaper and the lotion. The sleeping bag began to wiggle and bounce. At first the crying intensified. From one of the switchbacks farther down, lost in the thickening fog, someone said: "Can't you shut that kid up?" Another voice added: "Someone ought to call Social Services."

Augie waited, watching the sleeping bag. At last it stopped moving around and a hand emerged, holding a diaper. "Would you put it in the bag? There's a plastic sack for the dirty ones." She looked out at him like a mole from its hole. "Don't worry, it's not pooey, just wet."

Augie took the diaper, put it in the plastic bag (COSTCO printed on the side), then zipped the diaper bag closed. The crying from inside the sleeping bag (*so many bags*, he thought) continued for another minute or so, then abruptly cut out as Patti began to nurse in the City Center parking lot. From above the ranked doors that wouldn't open for another six hours, the banner gave a single lackadaisical flap. **1000 JOBS GUARENTEED!**

*Sure,* Augie thought. *Also, you can't catch AIDS if you load up on vitamin C.*

Twenty minutes passed. More cars came up the hill from Marlborough Street. More people joined the line. Augie estimated there already had to be four hundred people waiting. At that rate, there would be two thousand by the time the doors opened at nine, and that was a conservative estimate.

*If someone offers me fry-cook at McDonald's, will I take it?*

Probably.

*What about a greeter at Walmart?*

Oh, mos def. Big smile and *how're you today?* Augie thought he could wallop a greeter job right out of the park.

*I'm a people person,* he thought. And laughed.

From the bag: "What's funny?"

"Nothing," he said. "Cuddle that kid."

"I am." A smile in her voice.

At three-thirty he knelt, lifted the flap of the sleeping bag, and peered inside. Janice Cray was curled up, fast asleep, with the baby at her breast. This made him think of *The Grapes of Wrath*. What was the name of the girl who had been in it? The one who ended up nursing the man? A flower name, he thought. Lily? No. Pansy? Absolutely not. He thought of cupping his hands around his mouth, raising his voice, and asking the crowd, *WHO HERE HAS READ* THE GRAPES OF WRATH?

As he was standing up again (and smiling at this absurdity), the name came to him. Rose. That had been the name of the *Grapes of Wrath* girl. But not just Rose; Rose of *Sharon*. It sounded biblical, but he couldn't say so with any certainty; he had never been a Bible reader.

He looked down at the sleeping bag, in which he had expected to spend the small hours of the night, and thought of Janice Cray saying she wanted to apologize for Columbine, and 9/11, and Barry Bonds. Probably she would cop to global warming as well. Maybe when this was over and they had secured jobs—or not; not was probably just as likely—he would treat her to breakfast. Not a date, nothing like that, just some scrambled eggs and bacon. After that they would never see each other again.

More people came. They reached the end of the posted switchbacks with the self-important DO NOT CROSS tape. Once that was used up, the line began to stretch into the parking lot. What surprised Augie—and made him uneasy—was how *silent* they were. As if they all knew this mission was a failure, and they were only waiting to get the official word.

The banner gave another lackadaisical flap.

The fog continued to thicken.

Shortly before five A.M., Augie roused from his own half-doze, stamped his feet to wake them up, and realized an unpleasant iron light had crept into the air. It was the furthest thing in the world from the rosy-fingered dawn of poetry and old Technicolor movies; this was an anti-dawn, damp and as pale as the cheek of a day-old corpse.

He could see the City Center auditorium slowly revealing itself in all its nineteen-seventies tacky architectural glory. He could see the two dozen switchbacks of patiently waiting people and then the tailback of the line disappearing into the fog. Now there was a little conversation, and when a janitor clad in gray fatigues passed through the lobby on the other side of the doors, a small satiric cheer went up.

"Life is discovered on other planets!" shouted one of the young men who had been staring at Janice Cray—this was Keith Frias, whose left arm would shortly be torn from his body.

There was mild laughter at this sally, and people began to talk. The night was over. The seeping light wasn't particularly encouraging, but it was marginally better than the long small hours just past.

Augie knelt beside his sleeping bag again and cocked an ear. The small, regular snores he heard made him smile. Maybe his worry about her had been for nothing. He guessed there were people who went through life surviving—perhaps even thriving—on the kindness of strangers. The young woman currently snoozing in his sleeping bag with her baby might be one of them.

It came to him that he and Janice Cray could present themselves at the various application tables as a couple. If they did that, the baby's presence might not seem an indicator of irresponsibility but rather of joint dedication. He couldn't say for sure, much of human nature was a mystery to him, but he thought it was possible. He decided he'd try the idea out on Janice when she woke up. See what she thought. They couldn't claim marriage; she wasn't wearing a wedding ring and he'd taken his off for good three years before, but they could claim to be . . . what was it people said now? Partners.

Cars continued to come up the steep incline from Marlborough Street at steady tick-tock intervals. There would soon be pedestrians as well, fresh off the first bus of the morning. Augie was pretty sure they started running at six. Because of the thick fog, the arriving cars were just headlights with vague shadow-shapes lurking behind the windshields. A few of the drivers saw the huge crowd already waiting and turned around, discouraged, but most kept on, heading for the few remaining parking spaces, their taillights dwindling.

Then Augie noticed a car-shape that neither turned around nor continued on toward the far reaches of the parking lot. Its unusually bright headlights were flanked by yellow fog-lamps.

*HD headers,* Augie thought. *That's a Mercedes-Benz. What's a Benz doing at a job fair?*

He supposed it might be Mayor Kinsler, here to make a speech to the Early Birds Club. To congratulate them on their gumption, their good old American git-up-and-git. If so, Augie thought, arriving in his Mercedes—even if it was an old one—was in bad taste.

An elderly fellow in line ahead of Augie (Wayne Welland, now in the last moments of his earthly existence) said: "Is that a Benz? It looks like a Benz."

Augie started to say of course it was, you couldn't mistake a Mercedes's HD headlamps, and then the driver of the car directly behind the vague shape laid on his horn—a long, impatient blast. The HD lights flashed brighter than ever, cutting brilliant white cones through the suspended droplets of the fog, and the car leaped forward as if the impatient horn had goosed it.

"Hey!" Wayne Welland said, surprised. It was his final word.

The car accelerated directly at the place where the crowd of job-seekers was most tightly packed, and hemmed in by the DO NOT CROSS tapes. Some of them tried to run, but only the ones at the rear of the crowd were able to break free. Those closer to the doors—the true Early Birds—had no chance. They struck the posts and knocked them over, they got tangled in the tapes, they rebounded off each other. The crowd swayed back and forth in a series of agitated waves. Those who were older and smaller fell down and were trampled underfoot.

Augie was shoved hard to the left, stumbled, recovered, and was pushed forward. A flying elbow struck his cheekbone just below his right eye and that side of his vision filled with bright Fourth of July sparkles. From the other eye he could see the Mercedes not just emerging from the fog but seeming to *create* itself from it. A big gray sedan, maybe an SL500, the kind with twelve cylinders, and right now all twelve were screaming.

Augie was driven to his knees beside the sleeping bag, and kicked repeatedly as he struggled to get back up: in the arm, in the shoulder, in the neck. People were screaming. He heard a woman cry, *"Look out, look out, he's not stopping!"*

He saw Janice Cray pop her head out of the sleeping bag, eyes

11

blinking in bewilderment. Once more he was reminded of a shy mole peering from its hole. A lady mole with a bad case of bed head.

He scrambled forward on his hands and knees and lay down on the bag and the woman and baby inside, as if by doing this he could successfully shield them from a two-ton piece of German engineering. He heard people yelling, the sound of them almost lost beneath the approaching roar of the big sedan's motor. Someone fetched him a terrific wallop on the back of his head, but he barely felt it.

There was time to think: *I was going to buy Rose of Sharon breakfast.*

There was time to think: *Maybe he'll veer off.*

That seemed to be their best chance, probably their only chance. He started to raise his head to see if it was happening, and a huge black tire ate up his vision. He felt the woman's hand grip his forearm. He had time to hope the baby was still sleeping. Then time ran out.

# DET.-RET.

1

Hodges walks out of the kitchen with a can of beer in his hand, sits down in the La-Z-Boy, and puts the can down on the little table to his left, next to the gun. It's a .38 Smith & Wesson M&P revolver, M&P standing for Military and Police. He pats it absently, the way you'd pat an old dog, then picks up the remote control and turns on Channel Seven. He's a little late, and the studio audience is already applauding.

He's thinking of a fad, brief and baleful, that inhabited the city in the late eighties. Or maybe the word he really wants is *infected*, because it had been like a transient fever. The city's three papers had written editorials about it all one summer. Now two of those papers are gone and the third is on life support.

The host comes striding onstage in a sharp suit, waving to the audience. Hodges has watched this show almost every weekday since his retirement from the police force, and he thinks this man is too bright to be doing this job, one that's a little like scuba diving in a sewer without a wetsuit. He thinks the host is the sort of man who sometimes commits suicide and afterward all his friends and close relatives say they never had a clue anything was wrong; they talk about how cheerful he was the last time they saw him.

At this thought, Hodges gives the revolver another absent pat. It is the Victory model. An oldie but a goodie. His own gun, when

15

he was active, was a Glock .40. He bought it—officers in this city are expected to buy their service weapons—and now it's in the safe in his bedroom. Safe in the safe. He unloaded it and put it in there after the retirement ceremony and hasn't looked at it since. No interest. He likes the .38, though. He has a sentimental attachment to it, but there's something beyond that. A revolver never jams.

Here is the first guest, a young woman in a short blue dress. Her face is a trifle on the vacant side but she's got a knockout bod. Somewhere inside that dress, Hodges knows, there will be the sort of tattoo now referred to as a tramp-stamp. Maybe two or three. The men in the audience whistle and stomp their feet. The women in the audience applaud more gently. Some roll their eyes. This is the kind of woman you don't like to catch your husband staring at.

The woman is pissed right from go. She tells the host that her boyfriend has had a baby with another woman and he goes over to see them all the time. She still loves him, she says, but she hates that—

The next couple of words are bleeped out, but Hodges can lip-read *fucking whore*. The audience cheers. Hodges takes a sip of his beer. He knows what comes next. This show has all the predictability of a soap opera on Friday afternoon.

The host lets her run on for a bit and then introduces . . . THE OTHER WOMAN! She also has a knockout bod and several yards of big blond hair. There's a tramp-stamp on one ankle. She approaches the other woman and says, "I understand how you feel, but I love him, too."

She's got more on her mind, but that's as far as she gets before Knockout Bod One goes into action. Someone offstage rings a bell, as if this were the start of a prizefight. Hodges supposes it is, since all the guests on this show must be compensated; why else would they do it? The two women punch and claw for a few seconds, and then the two beefcakes with SECURITY printed on their tee-shirts, who have been watching from the background, separate them.

They shout at each other for awhile, a full and fair exchange of views (much of it bleeped out), as the host watches benignly, and this time it's Knockout Bod Two who initiates the fight, swinging a big roundhouse slap that rocks Knockout Bod One's head back. The bell rings again. They fall to the stage, their dresses rucking up, clawing and punching and slapping. The audience goes bugshit. The security beefcakes separate them and the host gets between them, talking in a voice that is soothing on top, inciteful beneath. The two women declare the depth of their love, spitting it into each other's faces. The host says they'll be right back and then a C-list actress is selling a diet pill.

Hodges takes another sip of his beer and knows he won't even finish half the can. It's funny, because when he was on the cops, he was damned near an alcoholic. When the drinking broke up his marriage, he assumed he *was* an alcoholic. He summoned all his willpower and reined it in, promising himself he would drink just as much as he goddam wanted once he had his forty in—a pretty amazing number, when fifty percent of city cops retired after twenty-five and seventy percent after thirty. Only now that he has his forty, alcohol no longer interests him much. He forced himself to get drunk a few times, just to see if he could still do it, and he could, but being drunk turned out to be no better than being sober. Actually it was a little worse.

The show returns. The host says he has another guest, and Hodges knows who that will be. The audience does, too. They yap their anticipation. Hodges picks up his father's gun, looks into the barrel, and puts it back down on the DirecTV guide.

The man over whom Knockout Bod One and Knockout Bod Two are in such strenuous conflict emerges from stage right. You knew what he was going to look like even before he comes strutting out and yup, he's the guy: a gas station attendant or a Target warehouse carton-shuffler or maybe the fella who detailed your car (badly) at the Mr. Speedy. He's skinny and pale, with black hair clumping over his forehead. He's wearing chinos and a crazy green and yellow tie that has a chokehold on his throat just below his

prominent Adam's apple. The pointy toes of suede boots poke out
beneath his pants. You knew that the women had tramp-stamps
and you know this man is hung like a horse and shoots sperm more
powerful than a locomotive and faster than a speeding bullet; a vir-
ginal maid who sits on a toilet seat after this guy jerked off will get
up pregnant. Probably with twins. On his face is the half-smart
grin of a cool dude in a loose mood. Dream job: lifetime disability.
Soon the bell will ring and the women will go at each other again.
Later, after they have heard enough of his smack, they will look at
each other, nod slightly, and attack him together. This time the
security personnel will wait a little longer, because this final battle
is what the audience, both in the studio and at home, really wants
to see: the hens going after the rooster.

That brief and baleful fad in the late eighties—the infection—
was called "bum fighting." Some gutter genius or other got the
idea, and when it turned a profit, three or four other entrepreneurs
leaped in to refine the deal. What you did was pay a couple of
bums thirty bucks each to go at each other at a set time and in a
set place. The place Hodges remembered best was the service area
behind a sleazy crab-farm of a strip club called Bam Ba Lam, over
on the East Side. Once the fight card was set, you advertised (by
word of mouth in those days, with widespread Internet use still
over the horizon), and charged spectators twenty bucks a head.
There had been better than two hundred at the one Hodges and
Pete Huntley had busted, most of them making odds and fading
each other like mad motherfuckers. There had been women, too,
some in evening dress and loaded with jewelry, watching as those
two wetbrain stewbums went at each other, flailing and kicking
and falling down and getting up and yelling incoherencies. The
crowd had been laughing and cheering and urging the combatants on.

This show is like that, only there are diet pills and insurance
companies to fade the action, so Hodges supposes the contestants
(that's what they are, although the host calls them "guests") walk
away with a little more than thirty bucks and a bottle of Night

Train. And there are no cops to break it up, because it's all as legal as lottery tickets.

When the show is over, the take-no-prisoners lady judge will show up, robed in her trademark brand of impatient righteousness, listening with barely suppressed rage to the small-shit petitioners who come before her. Next up is the fat family psychologist who makes his guests cry (he calls this "breaking through the wall of denial"), and invites them to leave if any of them dare question his methods. Hodges thinks the fat family psychologist might have learned those methods from old KGB training videos.

Hodges eats this diet of full-color shit every weekday afternoon, sitting in the La-Z-Boy with his father's gun—the one Dad carried as a beat cop—on the table beside him. He always picks it up a few times and looks into the barrel. Inspecting that round darkness. On a couple of occasions he has slid it between his lips, just to see what it feels like to have a loaded gun lying on your tongue and pointing at your palate. Getting used to it, he supposes.

If I could drink successfully, I could put this off, he thinks. I could put it off for at least a year. And if I could put it off for two, the urge might pass. I might get interested in gardening, or bird-watching, or even painting. Tim Quigley took up painting, down in Florida. In a retirement community that was loaded with old cops. By all accounts Quigley had really enjoyed it, and had even sold some of his work at the Venice Art Festival. Until his stroke, that was. After the stroke he'd spent eight or nine months in bed, paralyzed all down his right side. No more painting for Tim Quigley. Then off he went. Booya.

The fight bell is ringing, and sure enough, both women are going after the scrawny guy in the crazy tie, painted fingernails flashing, big hair flying. Hodges reaches for the gun again, but he has no more than touched it when he hears the clack of the front door slot and the flump of the mail hitting the hall floor.

Nothing of importance comes through the mail slot in these days of email and Facebook, but he gets up anyway. He'll look through it and leave his father's M&P .38 for another day.

2

When Hodges returns to his chair with his small bundle of mail, the fight-show host is saying goodbye and promising his TV Land audience that tomorrow there will be midgets. Whether of the physical or mental variety he does not specify.

Beside the La-Z-Boy there are two small plastic waste containers, one for returnable bottles and cans, the other for trash. Into the trash goes a circular from Walmart promising ROLLBACK PRICES; an offer for burial insurance addressed to OUR FAVOR-ITE NEIGHBOR; an announcement that all DVDs are going to be fifty percent off for one week only at Discount Electronix; a postcard-sized plea for "your important vote" from a fellow running for a vacancy on the city council. There's a photograph of the candidate, and to Hodges he looks like Dr. Oberlin, the dentist who terrified him as a child. There's also a circular from Albertsons supermarket. This Hodges puts aside (covering up his father's gun for the time being) because it's loaded with coupons.

The last thing appears to be an actual letter—a fairly thick one, by the feel—in a business-sized envelope. It is addressed to **Det. K. William Hodges (Ret.)** at **63 Harper Road**. There is no return address. In the upper lefthand corner, where one usually goes, is his second smile-face of the day's mail delivery. Only this one's not the winking Walmart Rollback Smiley but rather the email emoticon of Smiley wearing dark glasses and showing his teeth.

This stirs a memory, and not a good one.

No, he thinks. No.

But he rips the letter open so fast and hard the envelope tears and four typed pages spill out—not real typing, not *typewriter* typing, but a computer font that looks like it.

**Dear Detective Hodges,** the heading reads.

He reaches out without looking, knocks the Albertsons circular to the floor, finger-walks across the revolver without even noticing it, and seizes the TV remote. He hits the kill-switch, shutting up the take-no-prisoners lady judge in mid-scold, and turns his attention to the letter.

## 3

Dear Detective Hodges,

I hope you do not mind me using your title, even though you have been retired for 6 months. I feel that if incompetent judges, venal politicians, and stupid military commanders can keep their titles after retirement, the same should be true for one of the most decorated police officers in the city's history.

So Detective Hodges it shall be!

Sir (another title you deserve, for you are a true Knight of the Badge and Gun), I write for many reasons, but must begin by congratulating you on your years of service, 27 as a detective and 40 in all. I saw some of the Retirement Ceremony on TV (Public Access Channel 2, a resource overlooked by many), and happen to know there was a party at the Raintree Inn out by the airport the following night.

I bet that was the <u>real</u> Retirement Ceremony!

I have certainly never attended such a "bash," but I watch a lot of TV cop shows, and while I am sure many of them present a very fictional picture of "the policeman's lot," several have shown such retirement parties (<u>NYPD Blue, Homicide, The Wire,</u> etc., etc.), and I like to think they are ACCURATE portrayals of how the Knights of the Badge and Gun say "so-long" to one of their compatriots. I think they might be, because I have also read "retirement party scenes" in at least two Joseph Wambaugh books, and they are similar. He should know because he, like you, is a "Det. Ret."

I imagine balloons hanging from the ceiling, a lot of drinking, a lot of bawdy conversation, and plenty of reminiscing about the Old Days and the old cases. There is probably lots of loud and happy music, and possibly a stripper or two "shaking her tailfeathers." There are probably speeches that are a lot funnier and a lot truer than the ones at the "stuffed shirt ceremony."

How am I doing?

Not bad, Hodges thinks. Not bad at all.

According to my research, during your time as a detective, you broke literally hundreds of cases, many of them the kind the press (who Ted Williams called the Knights of the Keyboard) terms "high profile." You have caught Killers and Robbery Gangs and Arsonists and Rapists. In one article (published to coincide with your Retirement Ceremony), your longtime partner (Det. 1st Grade Peter Huntley) described you as "a combination of by-the-book and intuitively brilliant."

A nice compliment!

If it is true, and I think it is, you will have figured out by now that I am one of those few you did not catch. I am, in fact, the man the press chose to call

a.) The Joker

b.) The Clown

or

c.) The Mercedes Killer.

I prefer the last!

I am sure you gave it "your best shot," but sadly (for you, not me), you failed. I imagine if there was ever a "perk" you wanted to catch, Detective Hodges, it was the man who deliberately drove into the Job Fair crowd at City Center last year, killing eight and wounding so many more. (I must say I exceeded my own wildest expectations.) Was I on your mind when they gave you that plaque at the Official Retirement Ceremony? Was I on your mind when your fellow Knights of the Badge and Gun were telling stories about (just guessing here) criminals who were caught with their pants actually down or funny practical jokes that were played in the good old Squad Room?

I bet I was!

I have to tell you how much fun it was. (I'm being honest here.) When I "put the pedal to the metal" and drove poor Mrs. Olivia Trelawney's Mercedes at that crowd of people, I had the biggest "hard-on" of my life! And was my heart beating 200 a minute? "Hope to tell ya!"

Here was another Mr. Smiley in sunglasses.

I'll tell you something that's true "inside dope," and if you want to laugh, go ahead, because it is sort of funny (although I think it also shows just how careful I was). I was wearing a condom! A "rubber"! Because I was afraid of Spontaneous Ejaculation, and the DNA that might result! Well, that did not happen, but I have masturbated many times since while thinking of how they tried to run and couldn't (they were packed in like <u>sardines</u>), and how scared they all looked (that was so funny), and the way I jerked forward when the car "plowed" into them. So hard the seatbelt locked. Gosh it was exciting.

To tell the truth, I didn't know <u>what</u> might happen. I thought the chances were 50-50 that I would get caught. But I am "a cockeyed optimist," and I prepared for Success rather than Failure. The condom is "inside dope," but I bet your Forensics Department (I also watch <u>CSI</u>) was pretty darn disappointed when they didn't get any DNA from inside the clown mask. They must have said, "Damn! That crafty perk must have been wearing a hair net underneath!"

And so I was! I also washed it out with BLEACH!

I still relive the thuds that resulted from hitting them, and the crunching noises, and the way the car bounced on its springs when it went over the bodies. For power and control, give me a Mercedes 12-cylinder every time! When I saw in the paper that a <u>baby</u> was one of my victims, I was delighted!! To snuff out a life that young! Think of all she missed, eh? Patricia Cray, RIP! Got the mom, too! Strawberry jam in a sleeping bag! What a thrill, eh? I also enjoy thinking of the man who lost his arm and even more of the two who are paralyzed. The man only from the waist down, but Martine Stover is now your basic "head on a stick!" They didn't die but probably WISH they did! <u>How about that, Detective Hodges?</u>

Now you are probably thinking, "What kind of sick and twisted Pervo do we have here?" Can't really blame you, but we could argue about that! I think a great many people would enjoy doing what I did, and that is why they enjoy books and movies (and even TV shows these days) that feature Torture and Dismemberment, etc., etc., etc. The only difference is <u>I really did it.</u> Not because I'm mad, though (in either sense of the word). Just because I didn't know exactly what the experience would be like, only that it would be totally thrilling, with "memories to last a lifetime," as they say. Most people are fitted with Lead Boots when they are just little kids and have to wear them all their lives. These Lead Boots are called A CONSCIENCE. I have none, so I can soar high above the heads of the Normal Crowd. And if they had caught me? Well if it had been right there, if Mrs. Trelawney's Mercedes had stalled or something (small chance of that as it seemed very well maintained), I suppose the crowd might have torn me apart, I understood that possibility going in, and it added to the excitement. But I didn't think they really would, because most people are sheep and sheep don't eat meat. (I suppose I might have been beaten up a little, but I can take a beating.) Probably I would have been arrested and gone to trial, where I would have pleaded insanity. Maybe I even <u>am</u> insane (the idea has certainly crossed my mind), but it is a <u>peculiar</u> kind of insanity. Anyway, the coin came down heads and I got away.

The fog helped!

Now here is something else I saw, this time in a movie. (I don't remember the name.) There was a Serial Killer who was very clever and at first the cops (one was Bruce Willis, back when he still had some hair) couldn't catch him. So Bruce Willis said, "He'll do it again because he can't help himself and sooner or later he'll make a mistake and we will catch him."

Which they did!

That is not true in my case, Detective Hodges, because I have <u>absolutely no urge</u> to do it again. In my case, <u>once was enough</u>. I have my memories, and they are as clear as a bell. And of course, there was how frightened people were afterward, because they were sure I <u>would</u> do it again. Remember the public gatherings that were cancelled? That wasn't as much fun, but it <u>was</u> "tres amusant."

So you see, we are <u>both</u> "Ret."

Speaking of which, my one regret is that I couldn't attend your Retirement Party at the Raintree Inn and raise a toast to you, my good Sir Detective. You absolutely did give it your best shot. Detective Huntley too, of course, but if the papers and Internet reports of your respective careers are right, you were Major League and he was and always will be Triple A. I'm sure the case is still in the Active File, and that he takes those old reports out every now and then to study them, but he won't get anywhere. I think we both know that.

May I close on a Note of Concern?

In some of those TV shows (and also in one of the Wambaugh books, I think, but it might have been a James Patterson), the big party with the balloons and drinking and music is followed by a sad final scene. The Detective goes home and finds out that without his Gun and Badge, his life is pointless. Which I can understand. When you think of it, what is sadder than an Old Retired Knight? Anyway, the Detective finally shoots himself (with his Service Revolver). I looked it up on the Internet and discovered this type of thing isn't just fiction. It really happens!

Retired police have an <u>extremely high suicide rate</u>!!

In most cases, the cops who do this sad thing have no close family members who might see the Warning Signs. Many, like you, are divorced. Many have grown children living far away from home. I think of you all alone in your house on Harper Road, Detective Hodges, and <u>I grow concerned</u>. What kind of life do you have, now that the "thrill of the hunt" is behind you? Are you watching a lot of TV? Probably. Are you drinking more? Possibly. Do the hours go by more slowly because your life is now so empty? Are you suffering from insomnia? Gee, I hope not.

But I fear that might be the case!

You probably need a Hobby, so you'll have something to think about instead of "the one that got away" and how you will never catch me. It would be too bad if you started thinking your whole career had been a waste of time because the fellow who killed all those Innocent People "slipped through your fingers."

I wouldn't want you to start thinking about your gun.

But you <u>are</u> thinking of it, aren't you?

I would like to close with one final thought from "the one that got away." That thought is:

FUCK YOU, LOSER.

Just kidding!

Very truly yours,

THE MERCEDES KILLER

Below this was yet another smile-face. And below that:

PS! Sorry about Mrs. Trelawney, but when you turn this letter over to Det. Huntley, tell him not to bother looking at any photos I'm sure the police took at her funeral. I attended, but only in my imagination. (My imagination is very powerful.)

PPS: Want to get in touch with me? Give me your "feedback"? Try Under Debbie's Blue Umbrella. I even got you a username: "kermitfrog19." I might not reply, but "hey, you never know."

PPPS: Hope this letter has cheered you up!

4

Hodges sits where he is for two minutes, four minutes, six, eight. Completely still. He holds the letter in his hand, looking at the Andrew Wyeth print on the wall. At last he puts the pages on the table beside his chair and picks up the envelope. The postmark is right here in the city, which doesn't surprise him. His correspondent wants him to know he's close by. It's part of the taunt. As his correspondent would say, it's . . .

Part of the fun!

New chemicals and computer-assisted scanning processes can pick up excellent fingerprints from paper, but Hodges knows that if he turns this letter in to Forensics, they will find no prints on it but his. This guy is crazy, but his self-assessment—*one crafty perp*—is absolutely correct. Only he wrote *perk*, not *perp*, and he wrote it twice. Also . . .

Wait a minute, wait a minute.

What do you mean, *when you turn it in?*

Hodges gets up, goes to the window carrying the letter, and looks out on Harper Road. The Harrison girl putts by on her moped. She's really too young to have one of those things, no matter what the law allows, but at least she's wearing her helmet. The Mr. Tastey truck jangles by; in warm weather it works the city's

East Side between school's out and dusk. A little black smart car trundles by. The graying hair of the woman behind the wheel is up in rollers. Or is it a woman? It could be a man wearing a wig and a dress. The rollers would be the perfect final touch, wouldn't they?

That's what he wants you to think.

But no. Not exactly.

Not *what*. It's *how* the self-styled Mercedes Killer (except he was right, it was really the papers and the TV news that styled him that) wants him to think.

It's the ice cream man!

No, it's the man dressed as a woman in the smart car!

Uh-uh, it's the guy driving the liquid propane truck, or the meter-reader!

How did you spark paranoia like that? It helps to casually let drop that you know more than the ex-detective's address. You know he's divorced and at least imply that he has a kid or kids somewhere.

Looking out at the grass now, noticing that it needs cutting. If Jerome doesn't come around pretty soon, Hodges thinks, I'll have to call him.

Kid or kids? Don't kid *yourself*. He knows my ex is Corinne and we have one adult child, a daughter named Alison. He knows Allie's thirty and lives in San Francisco. He probably knows she's five-six and plays tennis. All that stuff is readily available on the Net. These days, *everything* is.

His next move should be to turn this letter over to Pete and Pete's new partner, Isabelle Jaynes. They inherited the Mercedes thing, along with a few other danglers, when Hodges pulled the pin. Some cases are like idle computers; they go to sleep. This letter will wake up the Mercedes case in a hurry.

He traces the progress of the letter in his mind.

From the mail slot to the hall floor. From the hall floor to the La-Z-Boy. From the La-Z-Boy to here by the window, where he can now observe the mail truck going back the way it came—Andy Fenster done for the day. From here to the kitchen, where the letter would go into a totally unnecessary Glad bag, the kind with the zip top, because old habits are strong habits. Next to Pete and Isabelle. From Pete to Forensics for a complete dilation and curettage, where the unnecessariness of the Glad bag would be conclusively proved by: no prints, no hairs, no DNA of any kind, paper available by the caseload at every Staples and Office Depot in the city, and—last but not least—standard laser printing. They may be able to tell what kind of computer was used to compose the letter (about this he can't be sure; he knows little about computers, and when he has trouble with his he turns to Jerome, who lives handily nearby), and if so, it would turn out to be a Mac or a PC. Big whoop.

From Forensics the letter would bounce back to Pete and Isabelle, who'd no doubt convene the sort of idiotic kop kolloquium you see on BBC crime shows like *Luther* and *Prime Suspect* (which his psychopathic correspondent probably loves). This kolloquium would be complete with whiteboard and photo enlargements of the letter, maybe even a laser pointer. Hodges watches some of those British crime shows, too, and believes Scotland Yard somehow missed the old saying about too many cooks spoiling the broth.

The kop kolloquium would accomplish only one thing, and Hodges believes it's what the psycho wants: with ten or a dozen detectives in attendance, the existence of the letter will inevitably leak to the press. The psycho is probably not telling the truth when he says he has no urge to repeat his crime, but of one thing Hodges is completely sure: he misses being in the news.

Dandelions are sprouting on the lawn. It is definitely time to call Jerome. Lawn aside, Hodges misses his face around the place. Cool kid.

Something else. Even if the psycho *is* telling the truth about feeling no urge to perpetrate another mass slaughter (unlikely, but not out of the question), he's still extremely interested in death. The letter's subtext could not be clearer. *Off yourself. You're thinking about it already, so take the next step. Which also happens to be the final step.*

Has he seen me playing with Dad's .38?

Seen me putting it in my mouth?

Hodges has to admit it's possible; he has never even thought of pulling the shades. Feeling stupidly safe in his living room when anybody could have a set of binocs. Or Jerome could have seen. Jerome bopping up the walk to ask about chores: what he is pleased to call *chos fo hos*.

Only if Jerome had seen him playing with that old revolver, he would have been scared to death. He would have said something.

Does Mr. Mercedes really masturbate when he thinks about running those people down?

In his years on the police force, Hodges has seen things he would never talk about with anyone who has not also seen them. Such toxic memories lead him to believe that his correspondent could be telling the truth about the masturbation, just as he is certainly telling the truth about having no conscience. Hodges has read there are wells in Iceland so deep you can drop a stone down them and never hear the splash. He thinks some human souls are like that. Things like bum fighting are only halfway down such wells.

He returns to his La-Z-Boy, opens the drawer in the table, and takes out his cell phone. He replaces it with the .38 and closes the drawer. He speed-dials the police department, but when the receptionist asks how she can direct his call, Hodges says: "Oh, damn. I just punched the wrong button on my phone. Sorry to have bothered you."

"No bother, sir," she says with a smile in her voice.

No calls, not yet. No action of any kind. He needs to think about this.

He really, really needs to think about this.

Hodges sits looking at his television, which is off on a weekday afternoon for the first time in months.

5

That evening he drives down to Newmarket Plaza and has a meal at the Thai restaurant. Mrs. Buramuk serves him personally. "Haven't seen you long time, Officer Hodges." It comes out *Offica Hutches*.

"Been cooking for myself since I retired."

"You let me cook. Much better."

When he tastes Mrs. Buramuk's Tom Yum Gang again, he realizes how sick he is of half-raw fried hamburgers and spaghetti with Newman's Own sauce. And the Sang Kaya Fug Tong makes him realize how tired he is of Pepperidge Farm coconut cake. If I never eat another slice of coconut cake, he thinks, I could live just as long and die just as happy. He drinks two cans of Singha with his meal, and it's the best beer he's had since the Raintree retirement party, which went almost exactly as Mr. Mercedes said; there was even a stripper "shaking her tailfeathers." Along with everything else.

Had Mr. Mercedes been lurking at the back of the room? As the cartoon possum was wont to say, "It's possible, Muskie, it's possible."

At home again, he sits in the La-Z-Boy and takes up the letter. He knows what the next step must be—if he's not going to turn it over to Pete Huntley, that is—but he also knows better than to try doing it after a couple of brewskis. So he puts the letter in the drawer on top of the .38 (he never did bother with the Glad bag) and gets another beer. The one from the fridge is just an Ivory Special, the local brand, but it tastes every bit as good as the Singha.

When it's gone, Hodges powers up his computer, opens Firefox, and types in *Under Debbie's Blue Umbrella*. The descriptor beneath isn't very descriptive: *A social site where interesting people exchange interesting views.* He thinks of going further, then shuts the computer down. Not that, either. Not tonight.

He has been going to bed late, because that means fewer hours spent tossing and turning, going over old cases and old mistakes, but tonight he turns in early and knows he'll sleep almost at once. It's a wonderful feeling.

His last thought before he goes under is of how Mr. Mercedes's poison-pen letter finished up. Mr. Mercedes wants him to commit suicide. Hodges wonders what he would think if he knew he had given this particular ex–Knight of the Badge and Gun a reason to live, instead. At least for awhile.

Then sleep takes him. He gets a full and restful six hours before his bladder wakes him. He gropes to the bathroom, pees himself empty, and goes back to bed, where he sleeps for another three hours. When he wakes, sunshine is slanting in the windows and the birds are twittering. He heads into the kitchen, where he cooks himself a full breakfast. As he's sliding a couple of hard-fried eggs onto a plate already loaded with bacon and toast, he stops, startled.

Someone is singing.

It's him.

6

Once his breakfast dishes are in the dishwasher, he goes into the study to tear the letter down. This is a thing he's done at least two dozen times before, but never on his own; as a detective he always had Pete Huntley to help him, and before Pete, two previous partners. Most of the letters were threatening communications from ex-husbands (and an ex-wife or two). Not much challenge in those. Some were extortion demands. Some were blackmail—really just another form of extortion. One was from a kidnapper demanding a paltry and unimaginative ransom. And three—four, counting the one from Mr. Mercedes—were from self-confessed murderers. Two of those were clearly fantasy. One might or might not have been from the serial killer they called Turnpike Joe.

What about this one? True or false? Real or fantasy?

Hodges opens his desk drawer, takes out a yellow legal pad,

tears off the week-old grocery list on the top. Then he plucks one of the Uni-Ball pens from the cup beside his computer. He considers the detail about the condom first. If the guy really was wearing one, he took it with him . . . but that makes sense, doesn't it? Condoms can hold fingerprints as well as jizz. Hodges considers other details: how the seatbelt locked when the guy plowed into the crowd, the way the Mercedes bounced when it went over the bodies. Stuff that wouldn't have been in any of the newspapers, but also stuff he could have made up. He even said . . .

Hodges scans the letter, and here it is: *My imagination is very powerful*.

But there were two details he could not have made up. Two details that had been withheld from the news media.

On his legal pad, below IS IT REAL?, Hodges writes: HAIR-NET. BLEACH.

Mr. Mercedes had taken the net with him just as he had taken the condom (probably still hanging off his dick, assuming it had been there at all), but Gibson in Forensics had been positive there was one, because Mr. Mercedes had left the clown mask and there had been no hairs stuck to the rubber. About the swimming-pool smell of DNA-killing bleach there had been no doubt. He must have used a lot.

But it isn't just those things; it's everything. The *assuredness*. There's nothing tentative here.

He hesitates, then prints: THIS IS THE GUY.

Hesitates again. Scribbles out GUY and prints BASTARD.

7

It's been awhile since he thought like a cop, and even longer since he did this kind of work—a special kind of forensics that doesn't require cameras, microscopes, or special chemicals—but once he buckles down to it, he warms up fast. He starts with a series of headings.

ONE-SENTENCE PARAGRAPHS.
CAPITALIZED PHRASES.
PHRASES IN QUOTATION MARKS.
FANCY PHRASES.
UNUSUAL WORDS.
EXCLAMATION POINTS.

Here he stops, tapping the pen against his lower lip and reading the letter through again from Dear Detective Hodges to Hope this letter has cheered you up! Then he adds two more headings on the sheet, which is now getting crowded.

USES BASEBALL METAPHOR, MAY BE A FAN.
COMPUTER SAVVY (UNDER 50?).

He is far from sure about these last two. Sports metaphors have become common, especially among political pundits, and these days there are octogenarians on Facebook and Twitter. Hodges himself may be tapping only twelve percent of his Mac's potential (that's what Jerome claims), but that doesn't make him part of the majority. You had to start somewhere, though, and besides, the letter has a young feel.

He has always been talented at this sort of work, and a lot more than twelve percent of it is intuition.

He's listed nearly a dozen examples under UNUSUAL WORDS, and now circles two: *compatriots* and *Spontaneous Ejaculation*. Beside them he adds a name: *Wambaugh*. Mr. Mercedes is a shitbag, but a bright, book-reading shitbag. He has a large vocabulary and doesn't make spelling errors. Hodges can imagine Jerome Robinson saying, "Spellchecker, my man. I mean, *duh?*"

Sure, sure, these days anyone with a word processing program can spell like a champ, but Mr. Mercedes has written *Wambaugh*, not *Wombough*, or even *Wombow*, which is how it sounds. Just the fact that he's remembered to put in that silent *gh* suggests a fairly high level of intelligence. Mr. Mercedes's missive may not be high-class literature, but his writing is a lot better than the dialogue in shows like *NCIS* or *Bones.*

Homeschooled, public-schooled, or self-taught? Does it matter? Maybe not, but maybe it does.

Hodges doesn't think self-taught, no. The writing is too . . . what?

"Expansive," he says to the empty room, but it's more than that. "*Outward.* This guy writes outward. He learned with others. And wrote *for* others."

A shaky deduction, but it's supported by certain flourishes—those FANCY PHRASES. *Must begin by congratulating you,* he writes. *Literally hundreds of cases,* he writes. And—twice—*Was I on your mind.* Hodges logged As in his high school English classes, Bs in college, and he remembers what that sort of thing is called: incremental repetition. Does Mr. Mercedes imagine his letter being published in the newspaper, circulated on the Internet, quoted (with a certain reluctant respect) on *Channel Four News at Six?*

"Sure you do," Hodges says. "Once upon a time you read your themes in class. You liked it, too. Liked being in the spotlight. Didn't you? When I find you—*if* I find you—I'll find that you did as well in your English classes as I did." Probably better. Hodges can't remember ever using incremental repetition, unless it was by accident.

Only there are four public high schools in the city and God knows how many private ones. Not to mention prep schools, junior colleges, City College, and St. Jude's Catholic University. Plenty of haystacks for a poisoned needle to hide in. If he even went to school here at all, and not in Miami or Phoenix.

Plus, he's a sly dog. The letter is full of false fingerprints—the capitalized phrases like *Lead Boots* and *Note of Concern,* the phrases in quotation marks, the extravagant use of exclamation points, the punchy one-sentence paragraphs. If asked to provide a writing sample, Mr. Mercedes would include none of those stylistic devices. Hodges knows that as well as he knows his own unfortunate first name: Kermit, as in *kermitfrog19.*

But.

This asshole isn't quite as smart as he thinks. The letter almost certainly contains two *real* fingerprints, one smudged and one crystal clear.

The smudged print is his persistent use of numbers instead of the words for numbers: 27, not twenty-seven; 40 instead of forty. Det. 1st Grade instead of Det. First Grade. There are a few exceptions (he has written *one regret* instead of *1 regret*), but Hodges thinks they are the ones that prove the general rule. The numbers *might* only be more camouflage, he knows that, but the chances are good Mr. Mercedes is genuinely unaware of it.

*If I could get him in IR4 and tell him to write Forty thieves stole eighty wedding rings . . . ?*

Only K. William Hodges is never going to be in an interview room again, including IR4, which had been his favorite—his lucky IR, he always thought it. Unless he gets caught fooling with this shit, that is, and then he's apt to be on the wrong side of the metal table.

*All right, then. Pete gets the guy in an IR. Pete or Isabelle or both of them. They get him to write 40 thieves stole 80 wedding rings. What then?*

*Then they ask him to write The cops caught the perp hiding in the alley. Only they'd want to slur the perp part. Because, for all his writing skill, Mr. Mercedes thinks the word for a criminal doer is perk. Maybe he also thinks the word for a special privilege is a perp, as in Traveling 1st class was one of the CEO's perps.*

Hodges wouldn't be surprised. Until college, he himself had thought that the fellow who threw the ball in a baseball game, the thing you poured water out of, and the framed objects you hung on the wall to decorate your apartment were all spelled the same. He had seen the word *picture* in all sorts of books, but his mind somehow refused to record it. His mother said *straighten that pitcher, Kerm, it's crooked*, his father sometimes gave him money for the *pitcher show*, and it had simply stuck in his head.

*I'll know you when I find you, honeybunch,* Hodges thinks.

He prints the word and circles it again and again, hemming it in. You'll be the asshole who calls a perp a perk.

8

He takes a walk around the block to clear his head, saying hello to people he hasn't said hello to in a long time. Weeks, in some cases. Mrs. Melbourne is working in her garden, and when she sees him, she invites him in for a piece of her coffee cake.

"I've been worried about you," she says when they're settled in the kitchen. She has the bright, inquisitive gaze of a crow with its eye on a freshly squashed chipmunk.

"Getting used to retirement has been hard." He takes a sip of her coffee. It's lousy, but plenty hot.

"Some people never get used to it at all," she says, measuring him with those bright eyes. She wouldn't be too shabby in IR4, Hodges thinks. "Especially ones who had high-pressure jobs."

"I was a little at loose ends to start with, but I'm doing better now."

"I'm glad to hear it. Does that nice Negro boy still work for you?"

"Jerome? Yes." Hodges smiles, wondering how Jerome would react if he knew someone in the neighborhood thinks of him as *that nice Negro boy*. Probably he would bare his teeth in a grin and exclaim, *I sho is!* Jerome and his chos fo hos. Already with his eye on Harvard. Princeton as a fallback.

"He's slacking off," she says. "Your lawn's gotten rather shaggy. More coffee?"

Hodges declines with a smile. Hot can only do so much for bad coffee.

9

Back home again. Legs tingling, head filled with fresh air, mouth tasting like newspaper in a birdcage, but brain buzzing with caffeine.

He logs on to the city newspaper site and calls up several stories about the slaughter at City Center. What he wants isn't in the first story, published under scare headlines on April eleventh of '09, or the much longer piece in the Sunday edition of April twelfth. It's in the Monday paper: a picture of the abandoned kill-car's steering wheel. The indignant caption: HE THOUGHT IT WAS FUNNY. In the center of the wheel, pasted over the Mercedes emblem, is a yellow smile-face. The kind that wears sunglasses and shows its teeth.

There was a lot of police anger about that photo, because the detectives in charge—Hodges and Huntley—had asked the news media to hold back the smile icon. The editor, Hodges remembers, had been fawningly apologetic. A missed communication, he said. Won't happen again. Promise. Scout's honor.

"Mistake, my ass," he remembers Pete fuming. "They had a picture that'd shoot a few steroids into their saggy-ass circulation, and they fucking used it."

Hodges enlarges the news photo until that grinning yellow face fills the computer screen. The mark of the beast, he thinks, twenty-first-century style.

This time the number he speed-dials isn't PD Reception but Pete's cell. His old partner picks up on the second ring. "Yo, you ole hossy-hoss. How's retirement treating you?" He sounds really pleased, and that makes Hodges smile. It also makes him feel guilty, yet the thought of backing off never crosses his mind.

"I'm good," he says, "but I miss your fat and hypertensive face."

"Sure you do. And we won in Iraq."

"Swear to God, Peter. How about we have lunch and catch up a little? You pick the place and I'll buy."

"Sounds good, but I already ate today. How about tomorrow?"

"My schedule is jammed, Obama was coming by for my advice on the budget, but I suppose I could rearrange a few things. Seeing's how it's you."

"Go fuck yourself, *Kermit*."

"When you do it so much better?" The banter is an old tune with simple lyrics.

"How about DeMasio's? You always liked that place."

"DeMasio's is fine. Noon?"

"That works."

"And you're sure you've got time for an old whore like me?"

"Billy, you don't even need to ask. Want me to bring Isabelle?"

He doesn't, but says: "If you want."

Some of the old telepathy must still be working, because after a brief pause Pete says, "Maybe we'll make it a stag party this time."

"Whatever," Hodges says, relieved. "Looking forward."

"Me too. Good to hear your voice, Billy."

Hodges hangs up and looks at the teeth-bared smile-face some more. It fills his computer screen.

10

He sits in his La-Z-Boy that night, watching the eleven o'clock news. In his white pajamas he looks like an overweight ghost. His scalp gleams mellowly through his thinning hair. The big story is the Deepwater Horizon spill in the Gulf of Mexico where the oil is still gushing. The newsreader says the bluefin tuna are endangered, and the Louisiana shellfish industry may be destroyed for a generation. In Iceland, a billowing volcano (with a name the newsreader mangles to something like *Eeja-fill-kull*) is still screwing up transatlantic air travel. In California, police are saying they may have finally gotten a break in the Grim Sleeper serial killer case. No names, but the suspect (the *perk*, Hodges thinks) is described as "a well-groomed and well-spoken African-American." Hodges thinks, Now if only someone would bag Turnpike Joe. Not to mention Osama bin Laden.

The weather comes on. Warm temperatures and sunny skies, the weather girl promises. Time to break out the bathing suits.

"I'd like to see you in a bathing suit, my dear," Hodges says, and uses the remote to turn off the TV.

He takes his father's .38 out of the drawer, unloads it as he walks into the bedroom, and puts it in the safe with his Glock. He has spent a lot of time during the last two or three months obsessing about the Victory .38, but tonight it hardly crosses his mind as he locks it away. He's thinking about Turnpike Joe, but not really; these days Joe is someone else's problem. Like the Grim Sleeper, that well-spoken African-American.

Is Mr. Mercedes also African-American? It's technically possible—no one saw anything but the pullover clown mask, a long-sleeved shirt, and yellow gloves on the steering wheel—but Hodges thinks not. God knows there are plenty of black people capable of murder in this city, but there's the weapon to consider. The neighborhood where Mrs. Trelawney's mother lived is pre-dominantly wealthy and predominantly white. A black man hanging around a parked Mercedes SL500 would have been noticed.

Well. Probably. People can be stunningly unobservant. But experience has led Hodges to believe rich people tend to be slightly more observant than the general run of Americans, espe-cially when it comes to their expensive toys. He doesn't want to say they're *paranoid*, but . . .

The fuck they're not. Rich people can be generous, even the ones with bloodcurdling political views can be generous, but most believe in generosity on their own terms, and underneath (not so deep, either), they're always afraid someone is going to steal their presents and eat their birthday cake.

How about neat and well spoken, then?

Yes, Hodges decides. No hard evidence, but the letter suggests he is. Mr. Mercedes may dress in suits and work in an office, or he may dress in jeans and Carhartt shirts and balance tires in a garage, but he's no slob. He may not talk a lot—such creatures are careful in all aspects of their lives, and that includes promiscuous blabbing—but when he does talk, he's probably direct and clear. If you were lost and needed directions, he'd give you good ones.

As he's brushing his teeth, Hodges thinks: DeMasio's. Pete wants to have lunch at DeMasio's.

That's okay for Pete, who still carries the badge and gun, and it seemed okay to Hodges when they were talking on the phone, because then Hodges had been *thinking* like a cop instead of a retiree who's thirty pounds overweight. It probably would be okay—broad daylight and all—but DeMasio's is on the edge of Lowtown, which is not a vacation community. A block west of the restaurant, beyond the turnpike spur overpass, the city turns into a wasteland of vacant lots and abandoned tenements. Drugs are sold openly on streetcorners, there's a burgeoning trade in illegal weaponry, and arson is the neighborhood sport. If you can call Lowtown a neighborhood, that is. The restaurant itself—a really terrific Italian joint—is safe, though. The owner is connected, and that makes it like Free Parking in Monopoly.

Hodges rinses his mouth, goes back into the bedroom, and—still thinking of DeMasio's—looks doubtfully at the closet where the safe is hidden behind the hanging pants, shirts, and the sportcoats he no longer wears (he's now too big for all but two of them).

Take the Glock? The Victory, maybe? The Victory's smaller.

No to both. His carry-concealed license is still in good standing, but he's not going strapped to a lunch with his old partner. It would make him self-conscious, and he's already self-conscious about the digging he plans to do. He goes to his dresser instead, lifts up a pile of underwear, and looks underneath. The Happy Slapper is still there, has been there since his retirement party.

The Slapper will do. Just a little insurance in a high-risk part of town.

Satisfied, he goes to bed and turns out the light. He puts his hands into the mystic cool pocket under the pillow and thinks of Turnpike Joe. Joe has been lucky so far, but eventually he'll be caught. Not

41

just because he keeps hitting those highway rest areas but because he can't stop killing. He thinks of Mr. Mercedes writing, *That is not true in my case, because I have <u>absolutely no urge</u> to do it again.*

Telling the truth, or lying the way he was lying with his CAP-ITALIZED PHRASES and MANY EXCLAMATION POINTS and ONE-SENTENCE PARAGRAPHS?

Hodges thinks he's lying—perhaps to himself as well as to K. William Hodges, Det. Ret.—but right now, as Hodges lies here with sleep coming on, he doesn't care. What matters is the guy thinks he's safe. He's positively smug about it. He doesn't seem to realize the vulnerability he has exposed by writing a letter to the man who was, until his retirement, the lead detective on the City Center case.

You need to talk about it, don't you? Yes you do, honeybunch, don't lie to your old uncle Billy. And unless that Debbie's Blue Umbrella site is another red herring, like all those quotation marks, you've even opened a conduit into your life. You want to talk. You need to talk. And if you could goad me into something, that would just be the cherry on top of a sundae, wouldn't it?

In the dark, Hodges says: "I'm willing to listen. I've got plenty of time. I'm retired, after all."

Smiling, he falls asleep.

## 11

The following morning, Freddi Linklatter is sitting on the edge of the loading dock and smoking a Marlboro. Her Discount Elec-tronix jacket is folded neatly beside her with her DE gimme cap placed on top of it. She's talking about some Jesus-jumper who gave her hassle. People are always giving her hassle, and she tells Brady all about it on break. She gives him chapter and verse, because Brady is a good listener.

"So he says to me, he goes, All homosexuals are going to hell, and this tract explains all about it. So I take it, right? There's

a picture on the front of these two narrow-ass gay guys—in lei-
sure suits, I swear to God—holding hands and staring into a cave
filled with flames. Plus the devil! With a pitchfork! I am *not* shitting you. Still, I try to discuss it with him. I'm under the impression that he wants to have a dialogue. So I say, I go, You ought to
get your face out of the Book of LaBitticus or whatever it is long
enough to read a few scientific studies. Gays are *born* gay, I mean,
hello? He goes, That is simply not true. Homosexuality is learned
behavior and can be unlearned. So I can't believe it, right? I mean,
you have *got* to be shitting me. But I don't say that. What I say is,
Look at me, dude, take a real good look. Don't be shy, go top to
bottom. What do you see? And before he can toss some more of
his bullshit, I go, You see a *guy*, is what you see. Only God got distracted before he could slap a dick on me and went on to the next
in line. So *then* he goes . . ."

Brady sticks with her—more or less—until Freddi gets to the
Book of LaBitticus (she means Leviticus, but Brady doesn't care
enough to correct her), and then mostly loses her, keeping track
just enough to throw in the occasional *uh-huh*. He doesn't really
mind the monologue. It's soothing, like the LCD Soundsystem
he sometimes listens to on his iPod when he goes to sleep. Freddi
Linklatter is way tall for a girl, at six-two or -three she towers over
Brady, and what she's saying is true: she looks like a girl about
as much as Brady Hartsfield looks like Vin Diesel. She's togged
out in straight-leg 501s, motorcycle skids, and a plain white tee
that hangs dead straight, without even a touch of tits. Her dark
blond hair is butched to a quarter inch. She wears no earrings and
no makeup. She probably thinks Max Factor is a statement about
what some guy did to some girl out behind old Dad's barn.

He says *yeah* and *uh-huh* and *right*, all the time wondering what
the old cop made of his letter, and if the old cop will try to get in
touch at the Blue Umbrella. He knows that sending the letter was
a risk, but not a very big one. He made up a prose style that's completely different from his own. The chances of the old cop picking
up anything useful from the letter are slim to nonexistent.

Debbie's Blue Umbrella is a slightly bigger risk, but if the old cop thinks he can trace him down that way, he's in for a big surprise. Debbie's servers are in Eastern Europe, and in Eastern Europe computer privacy is like cleanliness in America: next to godliness.

"So he goes, I swear this is true, he goes, There are plenty of young Christian women in our church who could show you how to fix yourself up, and if you grew your hair out, you'd look quite pretty. Do you believe it? So I tell him, With a little lipumstickum, you'd look darn pretty yourself. Put on a leather jacket and a dog collar and you might luck into a hot date at the Corral. Get your first squirt on the Tower of Power. So that buzzes him bigtime and he goes, If you're going to get personal about this . . ."

Anyway, if the old cop wants to follow the computer trail, he'll have to turn the letter over to the cops in the technical section, and Brady doesn't think he'll do that. Not right away, at least. He's got to be bored sitting there with nothing but the TV for company. And the revolver, of course, the one he keeps beside him with his beer and magazines. Can't forget the revolver. Brady has never seen him actually stick it in his mouth, but several times he's seen him holding it. Shiny happy people don't hold guns in their laps that way.

"So I tell him, I go, Don't get mad. Somebody pushes back against your precious ideas, you guys always get mad. Have you noticed that about the Christers?"

He hasn't but says he has.

"Only this one listened. He actually did. And we ended up going down to Hosseni's Bakery and having coffee. Where, I know this is hard to believe, we actually did have something approaching a dialogue. I don't hold out much hope for the human race, but every now and then . . ."

Brady is pretty sure his letter will pep the old cop up, at least to start with. He didn't get all those citations for being stupid, and he'll see right through the veiled suggestion that he commit suicide the way Mrs. Trelawney did. *Veiled?* Not very. It's pretty much right out front. Brady believes the old cop will go all gung ho, at least for awhile. But when he fails to get anywhere, it will make the fall even more jarring. Then, assuming the old cop takes the Blue Umbrella bait, Brady can really go to work.

The old cop is thinking, *If I can get you talking, I can goad you.*

Only Brady is betting the old cop never read Nietzsche; Brady's betting the old cop is more of a John Grisham man. If he reads at all. *When you gaze into the abyss,* Nietzsche wrote, *the abyss also gazes into you.*

I am the abyss, old boy. Me.

The old cop is certainly a bigger challenge than poor guilt-ridden Olivia Trelawney . . . but getting to her was such a hot hit to the nervous system that Brady can't help wanting to try it again. In some ways prodding Sweet Livvy into high-siding it was a bigger thrill than cutting a bloody swath through that pack of job-hunting assholes at City Center. Because it took brains. It took dedication. It took planning. And a little bit of help from the cops didn't hurt, either. Did they guess their faulty deductions were partly to blame for Sweet Livvy's suicide? Probably not Huntley, such a possibility would never cross his plodder's mind. Ah, but Hodges. *He* might have his doubts. A few little mice nibbling at the wires back there in his smart-cop brain. Brady hopes so. If not, he may get a chance to tell him. On the Blue Umbrella.

Mostly, though, it was him. Brady Hartsfield. Credit where credit is due. City Center was a sledgehammer. On Olivia Tre-lawney, he used a scalpel.

"Are you listening to me?" Freddi asks.

He smiles. "Guess I drifted away there for a minute."

Never tell a lie when you can tell the truth. The truth isn't always the safest course, but mostly it is. He wonders idly what she'd say if he told her, *Freddi, I am the Mercedes Killer.* Or if he said, *Freddi, there are nine pounds of homemade plastic explosive in my basement closet.*

She is looking at him as if she can read these thoughts, and Brady has a moment of unease. Then she says, "It's working two jobs, pal. That'll wear you down."

"Yes, but I'd like to get back to college, and nobody's going to pay for it but me. Also there's my mother."

"The wino."

He smiles. "My mother is actually more of a vodka-o."

"Invite me over," Freddi says grimly. "I'll drag her to a fucking AA meeting."

"Wouldn't work. You know what Dorothy Parker said, right? You can lead a whore to culture, but you can't make her think."

Freddi considers this for a moment, then throws back her head and voices a Marlboro-raspy laugh. "I don't know who Dorothy Parker is, but I'm gonna save that one." She sobers. "Seriously, why don't you just ask Frobisher for more hours? That other job of yours is strictly rinky-dink."

"I'll tell you why he doesn't ask Frobisher for more hours," Frobisher says, stepping out onto the loading platform. Anthony Frobisher is young and geekily bespectacled. In this he is like most of the Discount Electronix employees. Brady is also young, but better-looking than Tones Frobisher. Not that this makes him handsome. Which is okay. Brady is willing to settle for nondescript.

"Lay it on us," Freddi says, and mashes her cigarette out. Across the loading zone behind the big-box store, which anchors the south end of the Birch Hill Mall, are the employees' cars (mostly old beaters) and three VW Beetles painted bright green. These are always kept spotless, and late-spring sun twinkles on their windshields. On the sides, in blue, is COMPUTER PROBLEMS? CALL THE DISCOUNT ELECTRONIX CYBER PATROL!

"Circuit City is gone and Best Buy is tottering," Frobisher says in a schoolteacherly voice. "Discount Electronix is *also* tottering, along with several other businesses that are on life support thanks to the computer revolution: newspapers, book publishers, record stores, and the United States Postal Service. Just to mention a few."

"Record stores?" Freddi asks, lighting another cigarette. "What are record stores?"

"That's a real gut-buster," Frobisher says. "I have a friend who claims dykes lack a sense of humor, but—"

"You have friends?" Freddi asks. "Wow. Who knew?"

"—but you obviously prove him wrong. You guys don't have more hours because the company is now surviving on computers alone. Mostly cheap ones made in China and the Philippines. The great majority of our customers no longer want the other shit we sell." Brady thinks only Tones Frobisher would say *the great majority*. "This is partly because of the technological revolution, but it's also because—"

Together, Freddi and Brady chant, "—*Barack Obama is the worst mistake this country ever made!*"

Frobisher regards them sourly for a moment, then says, "At least you listen. Brady, you're off at two, is that correct?"

"Yes. My other gig starts at three."

Frobisher wrinkles the overlarge schnozzola in the middle of his face to show what he thinks of Brady's other job. "Did I hear you say something about returning to school?"

Brady doesn't reply to this, because anything he says might be the wrong thing. Anthony "Tones" Frobisher must not know that Brady hates him. Fucking *loathes* him. Brady hates everybody, including his drunk mother, but it's like that old country song says: no one has to know right now.

"You're twenty-eight, Brady. Old enough so you no longer have to rely on shitty pool coverage to insure your automobile—which is good—but a little *too* old to be training for a career in electrical engineering. Or computer programming, for that matter."

"Don't be a turd," Freddi says. "Don't be a Tones Turd."

"If telling the truth makes a man a turd, then a turd I shall be."

"Yeah," Freddi says. "You'll go down in history. Tones the Truth-Telling Turd. Kids will learn about you in school."

"I don't mind a little truth," Brady says quietly.

"Good. You can don't-mind all the time you're cataloguing and stickering DVDs. Starting now."

Brady nods good-naturedly, stands up, and dusts the seat of his pants. The Discount Electronix fifty-percent-off sale starts the following week; management in New Jersey has mandated that DE must be out of the digital-versatile-disc business by January of 2011. That once profitable line of merchandise has been strangled by Netflix and Redbox. Soon there will be nothing in the store but home computers (made in China and the Philippines) and flat-screen TVs, which in this deep recession few can afford to buy.

"You," Frobisher says, turning to Freddi, "have an out-call." He hands her a pink work invoice. "Old lady with a screen freeze. That's what she says it is, anyway."

"Yes, *mon capitan*. I live to serve." She stands up, salutes, and takes the call-sheet he holds out.

"Tuck your shirt in. Put on your cap so your customer doesn't have to be disgusted by that weird haircut. Don't drive too fast. Get another ticket and life as you know it on the Cyber Patrol is over. Also, pick up your fucking cigarette butts before you go."

He disappears inside before she can return his serve.

"DVD stickers for you, an old lady with a CPU probably full of graham cracker crumbs for me," Freddi says, jumping down and putting her hat on. She gives the bill a gangsta twist and starts across to the VWs without even glancing at her cigarette butts. She does pause long enough to look back at Brady, hands on her nonexistent boy hips. "This is *not* the life I pictured for myself when I was in the fifth grade."

"Me, either," Brady says quietly.

He watches her putt away, on a mission to rescue an old lady who's probably going crazy because she can't download her favorite mock-apple pie recipe. This time Brady wonders what Freddi would say if he told her what life was like for *him* when he was a kid. That was when he killed his brother. And his mother covered it up.

Why would she not?

After all, it had sort of been her idea.

12

As Brady is slapping yellow 50% OFF stickers on old Quentin Tarantino movies and Freddi is helping out elderly Mrs. Vera Willkins on the West Side (it's her keyboard that's full of crumbs, it turns out), Bill Hodges is turning off Lowbriar, the four-lane street that bisects the city and gives Lowtown its name, and in to the parking lot beside DeMasio's Italian Ristorante. He doesn't have to be Sherlock Holmes to know Pete got here first. Hodges parks next to a plain gray Chevrolet sedan with blackwall tires that just about scream city police and gets out of his old Toyota, a car that just about screams old retired fella. He touches the hood of the Chevrolet. Warm. Pete has not beaten him by much.

He pauses for a moment, enjoying this almost-noon morning with its bright sunshine and sharp shadows, looking at the overpass a block down. It's been gang-tagged up the old wazoo, and although it's empty now (noon is breakfast time for the younger denizens of Lowtown), he knows that if he walked under there, he would smell the sour reek of cheap wine and whiskey. His feet would grate on the shards of broken bottles. In the gutters, more bottles. The little brown kind.

No longer his problem. Besides, the darkness beneath the overpass is empty, and Pete is waiting for him. Hodges goes in and is pleased when Elaine at the hostess stand smiles and greets him by name, although he hasn't been here for months. Maybe even a year. Of course Pete is in one of the booths, already raising a hand to him, and Pete might have refreshed her memory, as the lawyers say.

He raises his own hand in return, and by the time he gets to the booth, Pete is standing beside it, arms raised to envelop him in a bearhug. They thump each other on the back the requisite number of times and Pete tells him he's looking good.

"You know the three Ages of Man, don't you?" Hodges asks.

Pete shakes his head, grinning.

49

"Youth, middle age, and you look fuckin terrific."

Pete roars with laughter and asks if Hodges knows what the blond said when she opened the box of Cheerios. Hodges says he does not. Pete makes big amazed eyes and says, "Oh! Look at the cute little doughnut seeds!"

Hodges gives his own obligatory roar of laughter (although he does not think this a particularly witty example of Genus Blond), and with the amenities thus disposed of, they sit down. A waiter comes over—no waitresses in DeMasio's, only elderly men who wear spotless aprons tied up high on their narrow chicken chests—and Pete orders a pitcher of beer. Bud Lite, not Ivory Special. When it comes, Pete raises his glass.

"Here's to you, Billy, and life after work."

"Thanks."

They click and drink. Pete asks about Allie and Hodges asks about Pete's son and daughter. Their wives, both of the ex variety, are touched upon (as if to prove to each other—and themselves—that they are not afraid to talk about them) and then banished from the conversation. Food is ordered. By the time it comes, they have finished with Hodges's two grandchildren and have analyzed the chances of the Cleveland Indians, which happens to be the closest major league team. Pete has ravioli, Hodges spaghetti with garlic and oil, what he has always ordered here.

Halfway through these calorie bombs, Pete takes a folded piece of paper from his breast pocket and places it, with some ceremony, beside his plate.

"What's that?" Hodges asks.

"Proof that my detective skills are as keenly honed as ever. I don't see you since that horror show at Raintree Inn—my hangover lasted three days, by the way—and I talk to you, what, twice? Three times? Then, bang, you ask me to lunch. Am I surprised? No. Do I smell an ulterior motive? Yes. So let's see if I'm right."

Hodges gives a shrug. "I'm like the curious cat. You know what they say—satisfaction brought him back."

Pete Huntley is grinning broadly, and when Hodges reaches for the folded slip of paper, Pete puts a hand over it. "No-no-no-no. You have to say it. Don't be coy, *Kermit*."

Hodges sighs and ticks four items off on his fingers. When he's done, Pete pushes the folded piece of paper across the table. Hodges opens it and reads:

1. *Davis*
2. *Park Rapist*
3. *Pawnshops*
4. *Mercedes Killer*

Hodges pretends to be discomfited. "You got me, Sheriff. Don't say a thing if you don't want to."

Pete grows serious. "Jesus, if you weren't interested in the cases that were hanging fire when you hung up your jock, I'd be disappointed. I've been . . . a little worried about you."

"I don't want to horn in or anything." Hodges is a trifle aghast at how smoothly this enormous whopper comes out.

"Your nose is growing, Pinocchio."

"No, seriously. All I want is an update."

"Happy to oblige. Let's start with Donald Davis. You know the script. He fucked up every business he tried his hand at, most recently Davis Classic Cars. Guy's so deep in debt he should change his name to Captain Nemo. Two or three pretty kitties on the side."

"It was three when I called it a day," Hodges says, going back to work on his pasta. It's not Donald Davis he's here about, or the City Park rapist, or the guy who's been knocking over pawnshops and liquor stores for the last four years; they are just camouflage. But he can't help being interested.

"Wife gets tired of the debt and the kitties. She's prepping the divorce papers when she disappears. Oldest story in the world. He reports her missing and declares bankruptcy on the same day. Does TV interviews and squirts a bucket of alligator tears. We know he killed her, but with no body . . ." He shrugs. "You were in on the meetings with Diana the Dope." He's talking about the city's district attorney.

"Still can't persuade her to charge him?"

"No corpus delicious, no charge. The cops in Modesto knew Scott Peterson was guilty as sin and still didn't charge him until they recovered the bodies of his wife and kid. You know that."

Hodges does. He and Pete discussed Scott and Laci Peterson a lot during their investigation of Sheila Davis's disappearance.

"But guess what? Blood's turned up in their summer cabin by the lake." Pete pauses for effect, then drops the other shoe. "It's hers."

Hodges leans forward, his food temporarily forgotten. "When was this?"

"Last month."

"And you didn't tell me?"

"I'm telling you now. Because you're asking now. The search out there is ongoing. The Victor County cops are in charge."

"Did anyone see him in the area prior to Sheila's disappearance?"

"Oh yeah. Two kids. Davis claimed he was mushroom hunting. Fucking Euell Gibbons, you know? When they find the body—if they find it—ole Donnie Davis can quit waiting for the seven years to be up so he can petition to have her declared dead and collect the insurance." Pete smiles widely. "Think of the time he'll save."

"What about the Park Rapist?"

"It's really just a matter of time. We know he's white, we know he's in his teens or twenties, and we know he just can't get enough of that well-maintained matronly pussy."

"You're putting out decoys, right? Because he likes the warm weather."

"We are, and we'll get him."

"It would be nice if you got him before he rapes another fifty-something on her way home from work."

"We're doing our best." Pete looks slightly annoyed, and when their waiter appears to ask if everything's all right, Pete waves the guy away.

"I know," Hodges says. Soothingly. "Pawnshop guy?"

Pete breaks into a broad grin. "Young Aaron Jefferson."

"Huh?"

"That's his actual name, although when he played football for City High, he called himself YA. You know, like YA Tittle. Although his girlfriend—also the mother of his three-year-old—tells us he calls the guy YA Titties. When I asked her if he was joking or serious, she said she didn't have any idea."

Here is another story Hodges knows, another so old it could have come from the Bible . . . and there's probably a version of it in there someplace. "Let me guess. He racks up a dozen jobs—"

"It's fourteen now. Waving that sawed-off around like Omar on *The Wire*."

"—and keeps getting away with it because he has the luck of the devil. Then he cheats on baby mama. She gets pissed and rats him out."

Pete points a finger-gun at his old partner. "Hole in one. And the next time Young Aaron walks into a pawnshop or a check-cashing emporium with his bellygun, we'll know ahead of time, and it's angel, angel, down we go."

"Why wait?"

"DA again," Pete says. "You bring Diana the Dope a steak, she says cook it for me, and if it isn't medium-rare, I'll send it back."

"But you've got him."

"I'll bet you a new set of whitewalls that YA Titties is in County by the Fourth of July and in State by Christmas. Davis and the Park Rapist may take a little longer, but we'll get them. You want dessert?"

"No. Yes." To the waiter he says, "You still have that rum cake? The dark chocolate one?"

The waiter looks insulted. "Yes, sir. Always."

"I'll have a piece of that. And coffee. Pete?"

"I'll settle for the last of the beer." So saying, he pours it out of the pitcher. "You sure about that cake, Billy? You look like you've put on a few pounds since I saw you last."

It's true. Hodges eats heartily in retirement, but only for the last couple of days has food tasted good to him. "I'm thinking about Weight Watchers."

Pete nods. "Yeah? I'm thinking about the priesthood."

"Fuck you. What about the Mercedes Killer?"

"We're still canvassing the Trelawney neighborhood—in fact, that's where Isabelle is right now—but I'd be shocked if she or anyone else comes up with a live lead. Izzy's not knocking on any doors that haven't been knocked on half a dozen times before. The guy stole Trelawney's luxury sled, drove out of the fog, did his thing, drove back into the fog, dumped it, and . . . nothing. Never mind Monsewer YA Titties, it's the Mercedes guy who *really* had the luck of the devil. If he'd tried that stunt even an hour later, there would have been cops there. For crowd control."

"I know."

"Do you think *he* knew, Billy?"

Hodges tilts a hand back and forth to indicate it's hard to say. Maybe, if he and Mr. Mercedes should strike up a conversation on that Blue Umbrella website, he'll ask.

"The murdering prick could have lost control when he started hitting people and crashed, but he didn't. German engineering, best in the world, that's what Isabelle says. Someone could have jumped on the hood and blocked his vision, but no one did. One of the posts holding up the DO NOT CROSS tape could have bounced under the car and gotten hung up there, but that didn't happen, either. And someone could have seen him when he parked behind that warehouse and got out with his mask off, but no one did."

"It was five-twenty in the morning," Hodges points out, "and even at noon that area would have been almost as deserted."

"Because of the recession," Pete Huntley says moodily. "Yeah, yeah. Probably half the people who used to work in those warehouses were at City Center, waiting for the frigging job fair to start. Have some irony, it's good for your blood."

"So you've got nothing."

"Dead in the water."

Hodges's cake comes. It smells good and tastes better.

When the waiter's gone, Pete leans across the table. "My night-mare is that he'll do it again. That another fog will come rolling in off the lake and he'll do it again."

*He says he won't,* Hodges thinks, conveying another forkload of the delicious cake into his mouth. *He says he has absolutely no urge. He says once was enough.*

"That or something else," Hodges says.

"I got into a big fight with my daughter back in March," Pete says. "*Monster* fight. I didn't see her once in April. She skipped all her weekends."

"Yeah?"

"Uh-huh. She wanted to go see a cheerleading competition. Bring the Funk, I think it was called. Practically every school in the state was in it. You remember how crazy Candy always was about cheerleaders?"

"Yeah," Hodges says. He doesn't.

"Had a little pleated skirt when she was four or six or some-thing, we couldn't get her out of it. Two of the moms said they'd take the girls. And I told Candy no. You know why?"

Sure he does.

"Because the competition was at City Center, that's why. In my mind's eye I could see about a thousand tweenyboppers and their moms milling around outside, waiting for the doors to open, dusk instead of dawn, but you know the fog comes in off the lake then, too. I could see that cocksucker running at them in another sto-len Mercedes—or maybe a fucking Hummer this time—and the kids and the mommies just standing there, staring like deer in the headlights. So I said no. You should have heard her scream at me, Billy, but I still said no. She wouldn't talk to me for a month, and she still wouldn't be talking to me if Maureen hadn't taken her. I told Mo absolutely no way, don't you dare, and she said, *That's why I divorced you, Pete, because I got tired of listening to no way and don't you dare.* And of course nothing happened."

He drinks the rest of the beer, then leans forward again.

"I hope there are plenty of people with me when we catch him. If I nail him alone, I'm apt to kill him just for putting me on the outs with my daughter."

"Then why hope for plenty of people?"

Pete considers this, then smiles a slow smile. "You have a point there."

"Do you ever wonder about Mrs. Trelawney?" Hodges asks the question casually, but he has been thinking about Olivia Trelawney a lot since the anonymous letter dropped through the mail slot. Even before then. On several occasions during the gray time since his retirement, he has actually dreamed about her. That long face—the face of a woeful horse. The kind of face that says *nobody understands* and *the whole world is against me*. All that money and still unable to count the blessings of her life, beginning with freedom from the paycheck. It had been years since Mrs. T. had had to balance her accounts or monitor her answering machine for calls from bill collectors, but she could only count the curses, totting up a long account of bad haircuts and rude service people. Mrs. Olivia Trelawney with her shapeless boatneck dresses, said boats always listed either to starboard or to port. The watery eyes that always seemed on the verge of tears. No one had liked her, and that included Detective First Grade Kermit William Hodges. No one had been surprised when she killed herself, including that selfsame Detective Hodges. The deaths of eight people—not to mention the injuries of many more—was a lot to carry on your conscience.

"Wonder about her how?" Pete asks.

"If she was telling the truth after all. About the key."

Pete raises his eyebrows. "She thought she *was* telling it. You know that as well as I do. She talked herself into it so completely she could have passed a lie-detector test."

It's true, and Olivia Trelawney hadn't been a surprise to either of them. God knows they had seen others like her. Career criminals acted guilty even when they hadn't committed the crime or crimes they had been hauled in to discuss, because they knew damned well they were guilty of *something*. Solid citizens just couldn't believe it, and when one of them wound up being questioned prior to charging, Hodges knows, it was hardly ever because a gun was involved. No, it was usually a car. *I thought it was a dog I ran over*, they'd say, and no matter what they might have seen in the rearview mirror after the awful double thump, they'd believe it.

Just a dog.

"I wonder, though," Hodges says. Hoping he seems thoughtful rather than pushy.

"Come on, Bill. You saw what I saw, and any time you need a refresher course, you can come down to the station and look at the photos."

"I suppose."

The opening bars of "Night on Bald Mountain" sound from the pocket of Pete's Men's Wearhouse sportcoat. He digs out his phone, looks at it, and says, "I gotta take this."

Hodges makes a be-my-guest gesture.

"Hello?" Pete listens. His eyes grow wide, and he stands up so fast his chair almost falls over. *"What?"*

Other diners stop eating and look around. Hodges watches with interest.

"Yeah . . . yeah! I'll be right there. What? Yeah, yeah, okay. Don't wait, just go."

He snaps the phone closed and sits down again. All his lights are suddenly on, and in that moment Hodges envies him bitterly.

"I should eat with you more often, Billy. You're my lucky charm, always were. We talk about it, and it happens."

"What?" Thinking, It's Mr. Mercedes. The thought that follows is both ridiculous and forlorn: He was supposed to be mine.

"That was Izzy. She just got a call from a State Police colonel out in Victory County. A game warden spotted some bones in an old gravel pit about an hour ago. The pit's less than two miles from Donnie Davis's summer place on the lake, and guess what? The bones appear to be wearing the remains of a dress."

He raises his hand over the table. Hodges high-fives it.

Pete returns the phone to its sagging pocket and brings out his wallet. Hodges shakes his head, not even kidding himself about what he feels: relief. *Enormous* relief. "No, this is my treat. You're meeting Isabelle out there, right?"

"Right."

"Then roll."

"Okay. Thanks for lunch."

"One other thing—hear anything about Turnpike Joe?"

"That's State," Pete says. "And the Feebles now. They're welcome to it. What I hear is they've got nothing. Just waiting for him to do it again and hoping to get lucky." He glances at his watch.

"Go, go."

Pete starts out, stops, returns to the table, and puts a big kiss on Hodges's forehead. "Great to see you, sweetheart."

"Get lost," Hodges tells him. "People will say we're in love."

Pete scrams with a big grin on his face, and Hodges thinks of what they sometimes used to call themselves: the Hounds of Heaven.

He wonders how sharp his own nose is these days.

13

The waiter returns to ask if there will be anything else. Hodges starts to say no, then orders another cup of coffee. He just wants to sit here awhile, savoring double happiness: it wasn't Mr. Mercedes and it *was* Donnie Davis, the sanctimonious cocksucker who killed his wife and then had his lawyer set up a reward fund for information leading to her whereabouts. Because, oh Jesus, he loved her so much and all he wanted was for her to come home so they could start over.

He also wants to think about Olivia Trelawney, and Olivia Trelawney's stolen Mercedes. That it *was* stolen no one doubts. But in spite of all her protests to the contrary, no one doubts that she enabled the thief.

58

Hodges remembers a case that Isabelle Jaynes, then freshly arrived from San Diego, told them about after they brought her up to speed on Mrs. Trelawney's inadvertent part in the City Center Massacre. In Isabelle's story it *was* a gun. She said she and her partner had been called to a home where a nine-year-old boy had shot and killed his four-year-old sister. They had been playing with an automatic pistol their father had left on his bureau.

"The father wasn't charged, but he'll carry that for the rest of his life," she said. "This will turn out to be the same kind of thing, wait and see."

That was a month before the Trelawney woman swallowed the pills, maybe less, and nobody on the Mercedes Killer case had given much of a shit. To them—and him—Mrs. T. had just been a self-pitying rich lady who refused to accept her part in what had happened.

The Mercedes SL was downtown when it was stolen, but Mrs. Trelawney, a widow who lost her wealthy husband to a heart attack, lived in Sugar Heights, a suburb as rich as its name where lots of gated drives led up to fourteen- and twenty-room McMansions. Hodges grew up in Atlanta, and whenever he drives through Sugar Heights he thinks of a ritzy Atlanta neighborhood called Buckhead.

Mrs. T.'s elderly mother, Elizabeth Wharton, lived in an apartment—a very nice one, with rooms as big as a political candidate's promises—in an upscale condo cluster on Lake Avenue. The crib had space enough for a live-in housekeeper, and a private nurse came three days a week. Mrs. Wharton had advanced scoliosis, and it was her Oxycontin that her daughter had filched from the apartment's medicine cabinet when she decided to step out.

Suicide proves guilt. He remembers Lieutenant Morrissey saying that, but Hodges himself has always had his doubts, and lately those doubts have been stronger than ever. What he knows now is that guilt isn't the only reason people commit suicide.

Sometimes you can just get bored with afternoon TV.

14

Two motor patrol cops found the Mercedes an hour after the killings. It was behind one of the warehouses that cluttered the lakeshore.

The huge paved yard was filled with rusty container boxes that stood around like Easter Island monoliths. The gray Mercedes was parked carelessly askew between two of them. By the time Hodges and Huntley arrived, five police cars were parked in the yard, two drawn up nose-to-nose behind the car's back bumper, as if the cops expected the big gray sedan to start up by itself, like that old Plymouth in the horror movie, and make a run for it. The fog had thickened into a light rain. The patrol car roofracks lit the droplets in conflicting pulses of blue light.

Hodges and Huntley approached the cluster of motor patrolmen. Pete Huntley spoke with the two who had discovered the car while Hodges did a walk-around. The front end of the SL500 was only slightly crumpled—that famous German engineering—but the hood and the windshield were spattered with gore. A shirtsleeve, now stiffening with blood, was snagged in the grille. This would later be traced to August Odenkirk, one of the victims. There was something else, too. Something that gleamed even in that morning's pale light. Hodges dropped to one knee for a closer look. He was still in that position when Huntley joined him.

"What the hell is that?" Pete asked.

"I think a wedding ring," Hodges said.

So it proved. The plain gold band belonged to Francine Reis, thirty-nine, of Squirrel Ridge Road, and was eventually returned to her family. She had to be buried with it on the third finger of her right hand, because the first three fingers of the left had been torn off. The ME guessed this was because she raised it in an instinctive warding-off gesture as the Mercedes came down on her. Two of those fingers were found at the scene of the crime shortly before noon on April tenth. The index finger was never found. Hodges thought that a seagull—one of the big boys that patrolled the lakeshore—might have seized it and carried it away. He preferred that idea to the grisly alternative: that an unhurt City Center survivor had taken it as a souvenir.

Hodges stood up and motioned one of the motor patrolmen over. "We've got to get a tarp over this before the rain washes away any—"

"Already on its way," the cop said, and cocked a thumb at Pete. "First thing he told us."

"Well aren't *you* special," Hodges said in a not-too-bad Church Lady voice, but his partner's answering smile was as pale as the day. Pete was looking at the blunt, blood-spattered snout of the Mercedes, and at the ring caught in the chrome.

Another cop came over, notebook in hand, open to a page already curling with moisture. His name-tag ID'd him as F. SHAMMING-TON. "Car's registered to a Mrs. Olivia Ann Trelawney, 729 Lilac Drive. That's Sugar Heights."

"Where most good Mercedeses go to sleep when their long day's work is done," Hodges said. "Find out if she's at home, Officer Shammington. If she's not, see if you can track her down. Can you do that?"

"Yes, sir, absolutely."

"Just routine, right? A stolen-car inquiry."

"You got it."

Hodges turned to Pete. "Front of the cabin. Notice anything?"

"No airbag deployment. He disabled them. Speaks to premeditation."

"Also speaks to him knowing how to do it. What do you make of the mask?"

Pete peered through the droplets of rain on the driver's side window, not touching the glass. Lying on the leather driver's seat was a rubber mask, the kind you pulled over your head. Tufts of orange Bozo-ish hair stuck up above the temples like horns. The nose was a red rubber bulb. Without a head to stretch it, the red-lipped smile had become a sneer.

"Creepy as hell. You ever see that TV movie about the clown in the sewer?"

Hodges shook his head. Later—only weeks before his retirement—he bought a DVD copy of the film, and Pete was right. The mask-face was very close to the face of Pennywise, the clown in the movie.

The two of them walked around the car again, this time noting blood on the tires and rocker panels. A lot of it was going to wash off before the tarp and the techs arrived; it was still forty minutes shy of seven A.M.

"Officers!" Hodges called, and when they gathered: "Who's got a cell phone with a camera?"

They all did. Hodges directed them into a circle around what he was already thinking of as the deathcar—one word, deathcar, just like that—and they began snapping pictures.

Officer Shammington was standing a little apart, talking on his cell phone. Pete beckoned him over. "Do you have an age on the Trelawney woman?"

Shammington consulted his notebook. "DOB on her driver's license is February third, 1957. Which makes her . . . uh . . ."

"Fifty-two," Hodges said. He and Pete Huntley had been working together for a dozen years, and by now a lot of things didn't have to be spoken aloud. Olivia Trelawney was the right sex and age for the Park Rapist, but totally wrong for the role of spree killer. They knew there had been cases of people losing control of their vehicles and accidentally driving into groups of people—only five years ago, in this very city, a man in his eighties, borderline senile, had plowed his Buick Electra into a sidewalk café, killing one and injuring half a dozen others—but Olivia Trelawney didn't fit that profile, either. Too young.

Plus, there was the mask.

But . . .

*But.*

## 15

The bill comes on a silver tray. Hodges lays his plastic on top of it and sips his coffee while he waits for it to come back. He's comfortably full, and in the middle of the day that condition usually leaves him ready for a two-hour nap. Not this afternoon. This afternoon he has never felt more awake.

The *but* had been so apparent that neither of them had to say it out loud—not to the motor patrolmen (more arriving all the time, although the goddam tarp never got there until quarter past seven) and not to each other. The doors of the SL500 were locked and the ignition slot was empty. There was no sign of tampering that either detective could see, and later that day the head mechanic from the city's Mercedes dealership confirmed that.

"How hard would it be for someone to slim-jim a window?" Hodges had asked the mechanic. "Pop the lock that way?"

"All but impossible," the mechanic had said. "These Mercs are *built*. If someone did manage to do it, it would leave signs." He had tilted his cap back on his head. "What happened is plain and simple, Officers. She left the key in the ignition and ignored the reminder chime when she got out. Her mind was probably on something else. The thief saw the key and took the car. I mean, he *must* have had the key. How else could he lock the car when he left it?"

"You keep saying *she*," Pete said. They hadn't mentioned the owner's name.

"Hey, come on." The mechanic smiling a little now. "This is Mrs. Trelawney's Mercedes. Olivia Trelawney. She bought it at our dealership and we service it every four months, like clockwork. We only service a few twelve-cylinders, and I know them all." And then, speaking nothing but the utter grisly truth: "This baby's a tank."

The killer drove the Benz in between the two container boxes, killed the engine, pulled off his mask, doused it with bleach, and exited the car (the gloves and hairnet probably tucked inside his jacket). Then a final fuck-you as he walked away into the fog: he locked the car with Olivia Ann Trelawney's smart key.

There was your *but*.

16

She warned us to be quiet because her mother was sleeping, Hodges remembers. Then she gave us coffee and cookies. Sitting in DeMasio's, he sips the last of his current cup while he waits for his credit card to be returned. He thinks about the living room in that whopper of a condo apartment, with its kick-ass view of the lake.

Along with coffee and cookies, she had given them the wide-eyed *of-course-I-didn't* look, the one that is the exclusive property of solid citizens who have never been in trouble with the police. Who can't imagine such a thing. She even said it out loud, when Pete asked if it was possible she had left her ignition key in her car when she parked it on Lake Avenue just a few doors down from her mother's building.

"Of course I didn't." The words had come through a cramped little smile that said *I find your idea silly and more than a bit insulting.*

The waiter returns at last. He puts down the little silver tray, and Hodges slips a ten and a five into his hand before he can straighten up. At DeMasio's the waiters split tips, a practice of which Hodges strongly disapproves. If that makes him old school, so be it.

"Thank you, sir, and *buon pomeriggio*."

"Back atcha," Hodges says. He tucks away his receipt and his Amex, but doesn't rise immediately. There are some crumbs left on his dessert plate, and he uses his fork to snare them, just as he used to do with his mother's cakes when he was a little boy. To him those last few crumbs, sucked slowly onto the tongue from between the tines of the fork, always seemed like the sweetest part of the slice.

## 17

That crucial first interview, only hours after the crime. Coffee and cookies while the mangled bodies of the dead were still being identified. Somewhere relatives were weeping and rending their garments.

Mrs. Trelawney walking into the condo's front hall, where her handbag sat on an occasional table. She brought the bag back, rummaging, starting to frown, still rummaging, starting to be a little worried. Then smiling. "Here it is," she said, and handed it over.

The detectives looked at the smart key, Hodges thinking how ordinary it was for something that went with such an expensive car. It was basically a black plastic stick with a lump on the end of it. The lump was stamped with the Mercedes logo on one side. On the other were three buttons. One showed a padlock with its shackle down. On the button beside it, the padlock's shackle was up. The third button was labeled PANIC. Presumably if a mugger attacked you as you were unlocking your car, you could push that one and the car would start screaming for help.

"I can see why you had a little trouble locating it in your purse," Pete remarked in his best just-passing-the-time-of-day voice. "Most people put a fob on their keys. My wife has hers on a big plastic daisy." He smiled fondly as if Maureen were still his wife, and as if that perfectly turned-out fashion plate would ever have been caught dead hauling a plastic daisy out of her purse.

"How nice for her," Mrs. Trelawney said. "When may I have my car back?"

"That's not up to us, ma'am," Hodges said.

She sighed and straightened the boatneck top of her dress. It was the first of dozens of times they saw her do it. "I'll have to sell it, of course. I'd never be able to drive it after this. It's so upsetting. To think *my* car . . ." Now that she had her purse in hand, she prospected again and brought out a wad of pastel Kleenex. She dabbed at her eyes with them. "It's *very* upsetting."

"I'd like you to take us through it one more time," Pete said.

She rolled her eyes, which were red-rimmed and bloodshot. "Is that really necessary? I'm exhausted. I was up most of the night with my mother. She couldn't go to sleep until four. She's in such pain. I'd like a nap before Mrs. Greene comes in. She's the nurse."

Hodges thought, Your car was just used to kill eight people, and only eight if all the others live, and you want a nap. Later he would not be sure if that was when he started to dislike Mrs. Trelawney, but it probably was. When some people were in distress, you wanted to enfold them and say *there-there* as you patted them on the back. With others you wanted to slap them a hard one across the chops and tell them to man up. Or, in Mrs. T.'s case, to woman up.

"We'll be as quick as we can," Pete promised. He didn't tell her that this would be the first of many interviews. By the time they were done with her, she would hear herself telling her story in her sleep.

"Oh, very well, then. I arrived here at my mother's shortly after seven o'clock on Thursday evening . . ."

She visited at least four times a week, she said, but Thursdays were her night to stay over. She always stopped at B'hai, a very nice vegetarian restaurant located in Birch Hill Mall, and got their dinners, which she warmed up in the oven. ("Although Mother eats very little now, of course. Because of the pain.") She told them she always scheduled her Thursday trips so she arrived after seven, because that was when the all-night parking began, and most of the streetside spaces were empty. "I won't parallel park. I simply can't do it."

"What about the garage down the block?" Hodges asked.

She looked at him as though he were crazy. "It costs sixteen dollars to park there overnight. The streetside spaces are *free*."

Pete was still holding the key, although he hadn't yet told Mrs. Trelawney they would be taking it with them. "You stopped at Birch Hill and ordered takeout for you and your mother at—" He consulted his notebook. "B'hai."

"No, I ordered ahead. From my house on Lilac Drive. They are always glad to hear from me. I am an old and valued customer.

Last night it was kookoo sabzi for Mother—that's an herbal omelet with spinach and cilantro—and gheymeh for me. Gheymeh is a lovely stew with peas, potatoes, and mushrooms. Very easy on the stomach." She straightened her boatneck. "I've had terrible acid reflux ever since I was in my teens. One learns to live with it."

"I assume your order was—" Hodges began.

"And sholeh zard for dessert," she added. "That's rice pudding with cinnamon. And saffron." She flashed her strangely troubled smile. Like the compulsive straightening of her boatneck tops, the smile was a Trelawneyism with which they would become very familiar. "It's the saffron that makes it special. Even Mother always eats the sholeh zard."

"Sounds tasty," Hodges said. "And your order, was it boxed and ready to go when you got there?"

"Yes."

"One box?"

"Oh no, three."

"In a bag?"

"No, just the boxes."

"Must have been quite a struggle, getting all that out of your car," Pete said. "Three boxes of takeout, your purse . . ."

"And the key," Hodges said. "Don't forget that, Pete."

"Also, you'd want to get it all upstairs as fast as possible," Pete said. "Cold food's no fun."

"I see where you're going with this," Mrs. Trelawney said, "and I assure you . . ." A slight pause. ". . . you *gentlemen* that you are barking up the wrong path. I put my key in my purse as soon as I turned off the engine, it's the first thing I always do. As for the boxes, they were tied together in a stack . . ." She held her hands about eighteen inches apart to demonstrate. ". . . and that made them very easy to handle. I had my purse over my arm. Look." She crooked her arm, hung her purse on it, and marched around the big living room, holding a stack of invisible boxes from B'hai. "See?"

"Yes, ma'am," Hodges said. He thought he saw something else as well.

67

"As for hurrying—no. There was no need, since the dinners need to be heated up, anyway." She paused. "Not the sholeh zard, of course. No need to heat up rice pudding." She uttered a small laugh. Not a giggle, Hodges thought, but a titter. Given that her husband was dead, he supposed you could even call it a widder-titter. His dislike added another layer—almost thin enough to be invisible, but not quite. No, not quite.

"So let me review your actions once you got here to Lake Avenue," Hodges said. "Where you arrived at a little past seven."

"Yes. Five past, perhaps a little more."

"Uh-huh. You parked . . . what? Three or four doors down?"

"Four at most. All I need are two empty spaces, so I can pull in without backing. I hate to back. I always turn the wrong way."

"Yes, ma'am, my wife has exactly the same problem. You turned off the engine. You removed the key from the ignition and put it in your purse. You put your purse over your arm and picked up the boxes with the food in them—"

"The *stack* of boxes. Tied together with good stout string."

"The stack, right. Then what?"

She looked at him as though he were, of all the idiots in a generally idiotic world, the greatest. "Then I went to my mother's building. Mrs. Harris—the housekeeper, you know—buzzed me in. On Thursdays, she leaves as soon as I arrive. I took the elevator up to the nineteenth floor. Where you are now asking me questions instead of telling me when I can deal with my car. My *stolen* car."

Hodges made a mental note to ask the housekeeper if she had noticed Mrs. T.'s Mercedes when she left.

Pete asked, "At what point did you take your key from your purse again, Mrs. Trelawney?"

"Again? Why would I—"

He held the key up—Exhibit A. "To lock your car before you entered the building. You *did* lock it, didn't you?"

A brief uncertainty flashed in her eyes. They both saw it. Then it was gone. "Of course I did."

Hodges pinned her gaze. It shifted away, toward the lake view out the big picture window, and he caught it again. "Think carefully, Mrs. Trelawney. People are dead, and this is important. Do you specifically remember juggling those boxes of food so you could get your key out of your purse and push the LOCK button? And seeing the headlights flash an acknowledgement? They do that, you know."

"Of *course* I know." She bit at her lower lip, realized she was doing it, stopped.

"Do you remember that specifically?"

For a moment all expression left her face. Then that superior smile burst forth in all its irritating glory. "Wait. Now I remember. I put the key in my purse *after* I gathered up my boxes and got out. And after I pushed the button that locks the car."

"You're sure," Pete said.

"Yes." She was, and would remain so. They both knew that. The way a solid citizen who hit and ran would say, when he was finally tracked down, that of *course* it was a dog he'd hit.

Pete flipped his notebook closed and stood up. Hodges did likewise. Mrs. Trelawney looked more than eager to escort them to the door.

"One more question," Hodges said as they reached it.

She raised carefully plucked eyebrows. "Yes?"

"Where's your spare key? We ought to take that one, too."

There was no blank look this time, no cutting away of the eyes, no hesitation. She said, "I have no spare key, and no need of one. I'm very careful of my things, Officer. I've owned my Gray Lady—that's what I call it—for five years, and the only key I've ever used is now in your partner's pocket."

## 18

The table where he and Pete ate their lunch has been cleared of everything but his half-finished glass of water, yet Hodges goes on sitting there, staring out the window at the parking lot and the overpass that marks the unofficial border of Lowtown, where Sugar Heights residents like the late Olivia Trelawney never venture. Why would they? To buy drugs? Hodges is sure there are druggies in the Heights, plenty of them, but when you live there, the dealers make housecalls.

Mrs. T. was lying. She *had* to lie. It was that or face the fact that a single moment of forgetfulness had led to horrific consequences.

Suppose, though—just for the sake of argument—that she was telling the truth.

Okay, let's suppose. But if we were wrong about her leaving her Mercedes unlocked with the key in the ignition, how were we wrong? And what *did* happen?

He sits looking out the window, remembering, unaware that some of the waiters have begun to look at him uneasily—the overweight retiree sitting slumped in his seat like a robot with dead batteries.

19

The *deathcar* had been transported to Police Impound on a carrier, still locked. Hodges and Huntley received this update when they got back to their own car. The head mechanic from Ross Mercedes had just arrived, and was pretty sure he could unlock the damn thing. Eventually.

"Tell him not to bother," Hodges said. "We've got her key."

There was a pause at the other end, and then Lieutenant Morrissey said, "You do? You're not saying *she*—"

"No, no, nothing like that. Is the mechanic standing by, Lieutenant?"

"He's in the yard, looking at the damage to the car. Damn near tears, is what I heard."

"He might want to save a drop or two for the dead people," Pete said. He was driving. The windshield wipers beat back and forth. The rain was coming harder. "Just sayin."

"Tell him to get in touch with the dealership and check something," Hodges said. "Then have him call me on my cell."

The traffic was snarled downtown, partly because of the rain, partly because Marlborough Street had been blocked off at City Center. They had made only four blocks when Hodges's cell rang. It was Howard McGrory, the mechanic.

"Did you have someone at the dealership check on what I was curious about?" Hodges asked him.

"No need," McGrory said. "I've worked at Ross since 1987. Must have seen a thousand Mercs go out the door since then, and I can tell you they all go out with two keys."

"Thanks," Hodges said. "We'll be there soon. Got some more questions for you."

"I'll be here. This is terrible. *Terrible.*"

Hodges ended the call and passed on what McGrory had said.

"Are you surprised?" Pete asked. Ahead was an orange DETOUR sign that would vector them around City Center . . . unless they wanted to light their blues, that was, and neither did. What they needed now was to talk.

"Nope," Hodges said. "It's standard operating procedure. Like the Brits say, an heir and a spare. They give you two keys when you buy your new car—"

"—and tell you to put one in a safe place, so you can lay hands on it if you lose the one you carry around. Some people, if they need the spare a year or two later, they've forgotten where they put it. Women who carry big purses—like that suitcase the Trelawney woman had—are apt to dump both keys into it and forget all about the extra one. If she's telling the truth about not putting it on a fob, she was probably using them interchangeably."

"Yeah," Hodges said. "She gets to her mother's, she's preoccupied with the thought of spending another night dealing with Mom's pain, she's juggling the boxes and her purse . . ."

"And left the key in the ignition. She doesn't want to admit it—not to us and not to herself—but that's what she did."

"Although the warning chime . . ." Hodges said doubtfully.

"Maybe a big noisy truck was going by as she was getting out and she didn't hear the chime. Or a police car, winding its siren. Or maybe she was just so deep in her own thoughts she ignored it."

It made sense then and even more later when McGrory told them the deathcar hadn't been jimmied to gain entry or hotwired to start. What troubled Hodges—the only thing that troubled him, really—was how much he *wanted* it to make sense. Neither of them had liked Mrs. Trelawney, she of the boatneck tops, perfectly plucked brows, and squeaky widder-titter. Mrs. Trelawney who hadn't asked for any news of the dead and injured, not so much as a single detail. She wasn't the doer—no way was she—but it would be good to stick her with some of the blame. Give her something to think about besides veggie dinners from B'hai.

"Don't complicate what's simple," his partner repeated. The traffic snarl had cleared and he put the pedal down. "She was given two keys. She claims she only had one. And now it's the truth. The bastard who killed those people probably threw the one she left in the ignition down a handy sewer when he walked away. The one she showed us was the spare."

That had to be the answer. When you heard hoofbeats, you didn't think zebras.

20

Someone is shaking him gently, the way you shake a heavy sleeper. And, Hodges realizes, he almost *has* been asleep. Or hypnotized by recollection.

It's Elaine, the DeMasio's hostess, and she's looking at him with concern. "Detective Hodges? Are you all right?"

"Fine. But it's just Mr. Hodges now, Elaine. I'm retired."

He sees concern in her eyes, and something more. Something worse. He's the only patron left in the restaurant. He observes the waiters clustered around the doorway to the kitchen, and suddenly sees himself as they and Elaine must be seeing him, an old fellow who's been sitting here long after his dining companion (and everyone else) has left. An old overweight fellow who sucked the last of his cake off his fork like a child sucking a lollipop and then just stared out the window.

They're wondering if I'm riding into the Kingdom of Dementia on the Alzheimer's Express, he thinks.

He smiles at Elaine—his number one, wide and charming. "Pete and I were talking about old cases. I was thinking about one. Kind of replaying it. Sorry. I'll clear out now."

But when he gets up he staggers and bumps the table, knocking over the half-empty water glass. Elaine grabs his shoulder to steady him, looking more concerned than ever.

"Detective . . . Mr. Hodges, are you okay to drive?"

"Sure," he says, too heartily. Pins and needles are doing windsprints from his ankles to his crotch and then back down to his ankles again. "Just had two glasses of beer. Pete drank the rest. My legs went to sleep, that's all."

"Oh. Are you better now?"

"Fine," he says, and his legs really are better. Thank God. He remembers reading somewhere that older men, especially older overweight men, should not sit too long. A blood clot can form behind the knee. You get up, the released clot does its own lethal windsprint up to the heart, and it's angel, angel, down we go.

She walks with him to the door. Hodges finds himself thinking of the private nurse whose job it was to watch over Mrs. T.'s mother. What was her name? Harris? No, Harris was the housekeeper. The nurse was Greene. When Mrs. Wharton wanted to go into the living room, or visit the jakes, did Mrs. Greene escort her the way Elaine is escorting him now? Of course she did.

"Elaine, I'm fine," he says. "Really. Sober mind. Body in balance." He holds his arms out to demonstrate.

"All right," she says. "Come see us again, and next time don't wait so long."

"It's a promise."

He looks at his watch as he pushes out into the bright sunshine.

Past two. He's missing his afternoon shows, and doesn't mind a bit. The lady judge and the Nazi psychologist can go fuck themselves. Or each other.

<br>

## 21

He walks slowly into the parking lot, where the only cars left, other than his, likely belong to the restaurant staff. He takes his keys out and jingles them on his palm. Unlike Mrs. T.'s, the key to his Toyota is on a ring. And yes, there's a fob—a rectangle of plastic with a picture of his daughter beneath. Allie at seventeen, smiling and wearing her City High lacrosse uni.

In the matter of the Mercedes key, Mrs. Trelawney never recanted. Through all the interviews, she continued to insist she'd only ever had the one. Even after Pete Huntley showed her the invoice, with PRIMARY KEYS (2) on the list of items that went with her new car when she took possession back in 2004, she continued to insist. She said the invoice was mistaken. Hodges remembers the iron certainty in her voice.

Pete would say that she copped to it in the end. There was no need of a note; suicide is a confession by its very nature. Her wall of denial finally crumbled. Like when the guy who hit and ran finally gets it off his chest. *Yes, okay, it was a kid, not a dog. It was a kid and I was looking at my cell phone to see whose call I missed and I killed him.*

Hodges remembers how their subsequent interviews with Mrs. T. had produced a weird kind of amplifying effect. The more she denied, the more they disliked. Not just Hodges and Huntley but the whole squad. And the more they disliked, the more stridently she denied. Because she knew how they felt. Oh yes. She was self-involved, but not stu—

Hodges stops, one hand on the sun-warmed doorhandle of his car, the other shading his eyes. He's looking into the shadows beneath the turnpike overpass. It's almost mid-afternoon, and the denizens of Lowtown have begun to rise from their crypts. Four of them are in those shadows. Three big 'uns and one little 'un. The big 'uns appear to be pushing the little 'un around. The little 'un is wearing a pack, and as Hodges watches, one of the big 'uns rips it from his back. This provokes a burst of troll-like laughter.

Hodges strolls down the broken sidewalk to the overpass. He doesn't think about it and he doesn't hurry. He stuffs his hands in his sportcoat pockets. Cars and trucks drone by on the turnpike extension, projecting their shapes on the street below in a series of shadow-shutters. He hears one of the trolls asking the little kid how much money he's got.

"Ain't got none," the little kid says. "Lea me lone."

"Turn out your pockets and we see," Troll Two says.

The kid tries to run instead. Troll Three wraps his arms around the kid's skinny chest from behind. Troll One grabs at the kid's pockets and squeezes. "Yo, yo, I hear foldin money," he says, and the little kid's face squinches up in an effort not to cry.

"My brother finds out who you are, he bust a cap on y'asses," he says.

"That's a terrifyin idea," Troll One says. "Just about make me want to pee my—"

Then he sees Hodges, ambling into the shadows to join them with his belly leading the way. His hands deep in the pockets of his old shapeless houndstooth check, the one with the patches on the elbows, the one he can't bear to give up even though he knows it's shot to shit.

"Whatchoo want?" Troll Three asks. He's still hugging the kid from behind.

Hodges considers trying a John Wayne drawl, and decides not to. The only Wayne these scuzzbags would know is L'il. "I want you to leave the little man alone," he says. "Get out of here. Right now."

Troll One lets go of the little 'un's pockets. He is wearing a hoodie and the obligatory Yankees cap. He puts his hands on his slim hips and cocks his head to one side, looking amused. "Fuck off, fatty."

Hodges doesn't waste time. There are three of them, after all.

75

He takes the Happy Slapper from his right coat pocket, liking its old comforting weight. The Slapper is an argyle sock. The foot part is filled with ball bearings. It's knotted at the ankle to make sure the steel balls stay in. He swings it at the side of Troll One's neck in a tight, flat arc, careful to steer clear of the Adam's apple; hit a guy there, you were apt to kill him, and then you were stuck in the bureaucracy.

There's a metallic *thwap*. Troll One lurches sideways, his look of amusement turning to pained surprise. He stumbles off the curb and falls into the street. He rolls onto his back, gagging, clutching his neck, staring up at the underside of the overpass.

Troll Three starts forward. "Fuckin—" he begins, and then Hodges lifts his leg (pins and needles all gone, thank God) and kicks him briskly in the crotch. He hears the seat of his trousers rip and thinks, Oh you fat fuck. Troll Three lets out a yowl of pain. Under here, with the cars and trucks passing overhead, the sound is strangely flat. He doubles over.

Hodges's left hand is still in his coat. He extends his index finger so it pokes out the pocket and points it at Troll Two. "Hey, fuckface, no need to wait for the little man's big brother. I'll bust a cap on your ass myself. Three-on-one pisses me off."

"No, man, no!" Troll Two is tall, well built, maybe fifteen, but his terror regresses him to no more than twelve. "Please, man, we 'us just playin'!"

"Then run, playboy," Hodges says. "Do it now."

Troll Two runs.

Troll One, meanwhile, has gotten on his knees. "You gonna regret this, fat ma—"

Hodges takes a step toward him, lifting the Slapper. Troll One sees it, gives a girly shriek, covers his neck.

"You better run, too," Hodges says, "or the fat man's going to tool up on your face. When your mama gets to the emergency room, she'll walk right past you." In that moment, with his adrenaline flowing and his blood pressure probably over two hundred, he absolutely means it.

Troll One gets up. Hodges makes a mock lunge at him, and Troll One jerks back most satisfyingly.

"Take your friend with you and pack some ice on his balls," Hodges says. "They're going to swell."

Troll One gets his arm around Troll Three, and they hobble toward the Lowtown side of the overpass. When Troll One considers himself safe, he turns back and says, "I see you again, fat man."

"Pray to God you don't, fuckwit," Hodges says.

He picks up the backpack and hands it to the kid, who's looking at him with wide mistrustful eyes. He might be ten. Hodges drops the Slapper back into his pocket. "Why aren't you in school, little man?"

"My mama sick. I goin to get her medicine."

This is a lie so audacious that Hodges has to grin. "No, you're not," he says. "You're skipping."

The kid says nothing. This is five-o, nobody else would step to it the way this guy did. Nobody else would have a loaded sock in his pocket, either. Safer to dummy up.

"You go skip someplace safer," Hodges says. "There's a playground on Eighth Avenue. Try there."

"They sellin the rock on that playground," the kid says.

"I know," Hodges says, almost kindly, "but you don't have to buy any." He could add *You don't have to run any, either*, but that would be naïve. Down in Lowtown, most of the shorties run it. You can bust a ten-year-old for possession, but try making it stick.

He starts back to the parking lot, on the safe side of the overpass. When he glances back, the kid is still standing there and looking at him. Pack dangling from one hand.

"Little man," Hodges says.

The kid looks at him, saying nothing.

Hodges lifts one hand and points at him. "I did something good for you just now. Before the sun goes down tonight, I want you to pass it on."

Now the kid's look is one of utter incomprehension, as if Hodges just lapsed into a foreign language, but that's all right. Sometimes it seeps through, especially with the young ones.

People would be surprised, Hodges thinks. They really would.


### 22


Brady Hartsfield changes into his other uniform—the white one—and checks his truck, quickly going through the inventory sheet the way Mr. Loeb likes. Everything is there. He pops his head in the office to say hi to Shirley Orton. Shirley is a fat pig, all too fond of the company product, but he wants to stay on her good side. Brady wants to stay on *everyone's* good side. Much safer that way. She has a crush on him, and that helps.

"Shirley, you pretty girly!" he cries, and she blushes all the way up to the hairline of her pimple-studded forehead. Little piggy, oink-oink-oink, Brady thinks. You're so fat your cunt probably turns inside out when you sit down.

"Hi, Brady. West Side again?"

"All week, darlin. You okay?"

"Fine." Blushing harder than ever.

"Good. Just wanted to say howdy."

Then he's off, obeying every speed limit even though it takes him forty fucking minutes to get into his territory driving that slow. But it has to be that way. Get caught speeding in a company truck after the schools let out for the day, you get canned. No recourse. But when he gets to the West Side—this is the good part—he's in Hodges's neighborhood, and with every reason to be there. Hide in plain sight, that's the old saying, and as far as Brady is concerned, it's a wise saying, indeed.

He turns off Spruce Street and cruises slowly down Harper Road, right past the old Det-Ret's house. Oh look here, he thinks. The niggerkid is out front, stripped to the waist (so all the stay-at-home mommies can get a good look at his sweat-oiled sixpack, no doubt) and pushing a Lawn-Boy.

About time you got after that, Brady thinks. It was looking mighty shaggy. Not that the old Det-Ret probably took much notice. The old Det-Ret was too busy watching TV, eating Pop-Tarts, and playing with that gun he kept on the table beside his chair.

The niggerkid hears him coming even over the roar of the mower and turns to look. I know your name, niggerkid, Brady thinks. It's Jerome Robinson. I know almost everything about the old Det-Ret. I don't know if he's queer for you, but I wouldn't be surprised. It could be why he keeps you around.

From behind the wheel of his little Mr. Tastey truck, which is covered with happy kid decals and jingles with happy recorded bells, Brady waves. The niggerkid waves back and smiles. Sure he does.

Everybody likes the ice cream man.

# UNDER DEBBIE'S BLUE UMBRELLA

1

Brady Hartsfield cruises the tangle of West Side streets until seven-thirty, when dusk starts to drain the blue from the late spring sky. His first wave of customers, between three and six P.M., consists of after-school kids wearing backpacks and waving crumpled dollar bills. Most don't even look at him. They're too busy blabbing to their buddies or talking into the cell phones they see not as accessories but as necessities every bit as vital as food and air. A few of them say thank you, but most don't bother. Brady doesn't mind. He doesn't want to be looked at and he doesn't want to be remembered. To these brats he's just the sugar-pusher in the white uniform, and that's the way he likes it.

From six to seven is dead time, while the little animals go in for their dinners. Maybe a few—the ones who say thank you—even talk to their parents. Most probably go right on poking the buttons of their phones while Mommy and Daddy yak to each other about their jobs or watch the evening news so they can find out all about the big world out there, where movers and shakers are actually doing shit.

During his last half hour, business picks up again. This time it's the parents as well as the kids who approach the jingling Mr. Tastey truck, buying ice cream treats they'll eat with their asses (mostly fat ones) snugged down in backyard lawnchairs. He almost pities them. They are people of little vision, as stupid as ants crawling around their hill. A mass killer is serving them ice cream, and they have no idea.

From time to time, Brady has wondered how hard it would be to poison a truckload of treats: the vanilla, the chocolate, the Berry Good, the Flavor of the Day, the Tastey Frosteys, the Brownie Delites, even the Freeze-Stix and Whistle Pops. He has gone so far as to research this on the Internet. He has done what Anthony "Tones" Frobisher, his boss at Discount Electronix, would probably call a "feasibility study," and concluded that, while it would be possible, it would also be stupid. It's not that he's averse to taking a risk; he got away with the Mercedes Massacre when the odds of being caught were better than those of getting away clean. But he doesn't want to be caught now. He's got work to do. His work this late spring and early summer is the fat ex-cop, K. William Hodges.

He might cruise his West Side route with a truckload of poisoned ice cream after the ex-cop gets tired of playing with the gun he keeps beside his living room chair and actually uses it. But not until. The fat ex-cop bugs Brady Hartsfield. Bugs him bad. Hodges retired with full honors, they even threw him a *party*, and how was that right when he had failed to catch the most notorious criminal this city had ever seen?

2

On his last circuit of the day, he cruises by the house on Teaberry Lane where Jerome Robinson, Hodges's hired boy, lives with his mother, father, and kid sister. Jerome Robinson also bugs Brady. Robinson is good-looking, he works for the ex-cop, and he goes out every weekend with different girls. All of the girls are pretty. Some are even white. That's wrong. It's against nature.

"Hey!" Robinson cries. "Mr. Ice Cream Man! Wait up!"

He sprints lightly across his lawn with his dog, a big Irish setter, running at his heels. Behind them comes the kid sister, who is about nine.

"Get me a chocolate, Jerry!" she cries. *"Pleeeease?"*

He even has a white kid's name. Jerome. *Jerry.* It's offensive. Why can't he be Traymore? Or Devon? Or Leroy? Why can't he be fucking Kunta Kinte?

Jerome's feet are sockless in his moccasins, his ankles still green from cutting the ex-cop's lawn. He's got a big smile on his undeniably handsome face, and when he flashes it at his weekend dates, Brady just bets those girls drop their pants and hold out their arms. Come on in, *Jerry.*

Brady himself has never been with a girl.

"How you doin, man?" Jerome asks.

Brady, who has left the wheel and now stands at the service window, grins. "I'm fine. It's almost quitting time, and that always makes me fine."

"You have any chocolate left? The Little Mermaid there wants some."

Brady gives him a thumbs-up, still grinning. It's pretty much the same grin he was wearing under the clown mask when he tore into the crowd of sad-sack job-seekers at City Center with the accelerator pedal pushed to the mat. "It's a big ten-four on the chocolate, my friend."

The little sister arrives, eyes sparkling, braids bouncing. "Don't you call me Little Mermaid, Jere, I hate that!"

She's nine or so, and also has a ridiculously white name: Barbara. Brady finds the idea of a black child named Barbara so surreal it's not even offensive. The only one in the family with a nigger name is the dog, standing on his hind legs with his paws planted on the side of the truck and his tail wagging.

"Down, Odell!" Jerome says, and the dog sits, panting and looking cheerful.

"What about you?" Brady asks Jerome. "Something for you?"

"A vanilla soft-serve, please."

Vanilla's what you'd like to be, Brady thinks, and gets them their orders.

He likes to keep an eye on Jerome, he likes to *know about* Jerome, because these days Jerome seems to be the only person who spends any time with the Det-Ret, and in the last two months Brady has observed them together enough to see that Hodges treats the kid as a friend as well as a part-time employee. Brady has never had friends himself, friends are dangerous, but he knows what they are: sops to the ego. Emotional safety nets. When you're feeling bad, who do you turn to? Your friends, of course, and your friends say stuff like *aw gee* and *cheer up* and *we're with you* and *let's go out for a drink.* Jerome is only seventeen, not yet old enough to go out with Hodges for a drink (unless it's soda), but he can always say *cheer up* and *I'm with you.* So he bears watching.

Mrs. Trelawney didn't have any friends. No husband, either. Just her old sick mommy. Which made her easy meat, especially after the cops started working her over. Why, they had done half of Brady's work for him. The rest he did for himself, pretty much right under the scrawny bitch's nose.

"Here you go," Brady says, handing Jerome ice cream treats he wishes were spiked with arsenic. Or maybe warfarin. Load them up with that and they'd bleed out from their eyes and ears and mouths. Not to mention their assholes. He imagines all the kids on the West Side dropping their packs and their precious cell phones while the blood poured from every orifice. What a disaster movie that would make!

Jerome gives him a ten, and along with his change, Brady hands back a dog biscuit. "For Odell," he says.

"Thanks, mister!" Barbara says, and licks her chocolate cone. "This is good!"

"Enjoy it, honey."

He drives the Mr. Tastey truck, and he frequently drives a Cyber Patrol VW on out-calls, but his real job this summer is Detective K. William Hodges (Ret.). And making sure Detective Hodges (Ret.) uses that gun.

Brady heads back toward Loeb's Ice Cream Factory to turn in his truck and change into his street clothes. He keeps to the speed limit the whole way.

Always safe, never sorry.

## 3

After leaving DeMasio's—with a side-trip to deal with the bullies hassling the little kid beneath the turnpike extension overpass—Hodges simply drives, piloting his Toyota through the city streets without any destination in mind. Or so he thinks until he realizes he is on Lilac Drive in the posh lakeside suburb of Sugar Heights. There he pulls over and parks across the street from a gated drive with a plaque reading 729 on one of the fieldstone posts.

The late Olivia Trelawney's house stands at the top of an asphalt drive almost as wide as the street it fronts. On the gate is a FOR SALE sign inviting Qualified Buyers to call MICHAEL ZAFRON REALTY & FINE HOMES. Hodges thinks that sign is apt to be there awhile, given the housing market in this Year of Our Lord, 2010. But somebody is keeping the grass cut, and given the size of the lawn, the somebody must be using a mower a lot bigger than Hodges's Lawn-Boy.

Who's paying for the upkeep? Got to be Mrs. T.'s estate. She had certainly been rolling in dough. He seems to recall that the probated figure was in the neighborhood of seven million dollars. For the first time since his retirement, when he turned the unsolved case of the City Center Massacre over to Pete Huntley and Isabelle Jaynes, Hodges wonders if Mrs. T.'s mother is still alive. He remembers the scoliosis that bent the poor old lady almost double, and left her in terrible pain . . . but scoliosis isn't necessarily fatal. Also, hadn't Olivia Trelawney had a sister living somewhere out west?

He fishes for the sister's name but can't come up with it. What he does remember is that Pete took to calling Mrs. Trelawney

Mrs. Twitchy, because she couldn't stop adjusting her clothes, and brushing at tightly bunned hair that needed no brushing, and fiddling with the gold band of her Patek Philippe watch, turning it around and around on her bony wrist. Hodges disliked her; Pete had almost come to loathe her. Which made saddling her with some of the blame for the City Center atrocity rather satisfying. She had enabled the guy, after all; how could there be any doubt? She had been given two keys when she bought the Mercedes, but had been able to produce only one.

Then, shortly before Thanksgiving, the suicide.

Hodges remembers clearly what Pete said when they got the news: "If she meets those dead people on the other side—especially the Cray girl and her baby—she's going to have some serious questions to answer." For Pete it had been the final confirmation: somewhere in her mind, Mrs. T. had known all along that she had left her key in the ignition of the car she called her Gray Lady.

Hodges had believed it, too. The question is, does he still? Or has the poison-pen letter he got yesterday from the self-confessed Mercedes Killer changed his mind?

Maybe not, but that letter raises questions. Suppose Mr. Mercedes had written a similar missive to Mrs. Trelawney? Mrs. Trelawney with all those tics and insecurities just below a thin crust of defiance? Wasn't it possible? Mr. Mercedes certainly would have known about the anger and contempt with which the public had showered her in the wake of the killings; all he had to do was read the Letters to the Editor page of the local paper.

Is it possible—

But here his thoughts break off, because a car has pulled up behind him, so close it's almost touching his Toyota's bumper. There are no jackpot lights on the roof, but it's a late-model Crown Vic, powder blue. The man getting out from behind the wheel is burly and crewcut, his sportcoat no doubt covering a gun in a shoulder holster. If this were a city detective, Hodges knows, the gun would be a Glock .40, just like the one in his safe at home. But he's not a city detective. Hodges still knows them all.

He rolls down his window.

"Afternoon, sir," Crewcut says. "May I ask what you're doing here? Because you've been parked quite awhile."

Hodges glances at his watch and sees this is true. It's almost four-thirty. Given the rush-hour traffic downtown, he'll be lucky to get home in time to watch Scott Pelley on *CBS Evening News*. He used to watch NBC until he decided Brian Williams was a good-natured goof who's too fond of YouTube videos. Not the sort of newscaster he wants when it seems like the whole world is falling apa—

"Sir? Sincerely hoping for an answer here." Crewcut bends down. The side of his sportcoat gapes open. Not a Glock but a Ruger. Sort of a cowboy gun, in Hodges's opinion.

"And I," Hodges says, "am sincerely hoping you have the authority to ask."

His interlocutor's brow creases. "Beg pardon?"

"I think you're private security," Hodges says patiently, "but I want to see some ID. Then, you know what? I want to see your carry-concealed permit for the cannon you've got inside your coat. And it better be in your wallet and not in the glove compartment of your car, or you're in violation of section nineteen of the city firearms code, which, briefly stated, is this: 'If you carry concealed, you must also carry your *permit* to carry concealed.' So let's see your paperwork."

Crewcut's frown deepens. "Are you a cop?"

"Retired," Hodges says, "but that doesn't mean I've forgotten either my rights or your responsibilities. Let me see your ID and your carry permit, please. You don't have to hand them over—"

"You're damn right I don't."

"—but I want to see them. Then we can discuss my presence here on Lilac Drive."

Crewcut thinks it over, but only for a few seconds. Then he takes out his wallet and flips it open. In this city—as in most, Hodges thinks—security personnel treat retired cops as they would those on active duty, because retired cops have plenty of friends who *are* on active duty, and who can make life difficult if given a reason to do so. The guy turns out to be Radney Peeples, and his company card identifies him as an employee of Vigilant Guard Service. He also shows Hodges a permit to carry concealed, which is good until June of 2012.

"Radney, not Rodney," Hodges says. "Like Radney Foster, the country singer."

Foster's face breaks into a grin. "That's right."

"Mr. Peeples, my name is Bill Hodges, I ended my tour as a Detective First Class, and my last big case was the Mercedes Killer. I'm guessing that'll give you a pretty good idea of what I'm doing here."

"Mrs. Trelawney," Foster says, and steps back respectfully as Hodges opens his car door, gets out, and stretches. "Little trip down Memory Lane, Detective?"

"I'm just a mister these days." Hodges offers his hand. Peeples shakes it. "Otherwise, you're correct. I retired from the cops at about the same time Mrs. Trelawney retired from life in general."

"That was sad," Peeples said. "Do you know that kids egged her gate? Not just at Halloween, either. Three or four times. We caught one bunch, the others . . ." He shook his head. "Plus toilet paper."

"Yeah, they love that," Hodges says.

"And one night someone tagged the lefthand gatepost. We got it taken care of before she saw it, and I'm glad. You know what it said?"

Hodges shakes his head.

Peeples lowers his voice. "KILLER CUNT is what it said, in big drippy capital letters. Which was absolutely not fair. She goofed up, that's all. Is there any of us who haven't at one time or another?"

"Not me, that's for sure," Hodges says.

"Right. Bible says let him who is without sin cast the first stone."

That'll be the day, Hodges thinks, and asks (with honest curiosity), "Did you like her?"

Peeples's eyes shift up and to the left, an involuntary movement Hodges has seen in a great many interrogation rooms over
the years. It means Peeples is either going to duck the question or
outright lie.

It turns out to be a duck.

"Well," he says, "she treated us right at Christmas. She sometimes mixed up the names, but she knew who we all were, and we
each got forty dollars and a bottle of whiskey. *Good* whiskey. Do
you think we got that from her husband?" He snorts. "Ten bucks
tucked inside a Hallmark card was what we got when that skin-
flint was still in the saddle."

"Who exactly does Vigilant work for?"

"It's called the Sugar Heights Association. You know, one of
those neighborhood things. They fight over the zoning regulations
when they don't like em and make sure everyone in the neighborhood keeps to a certain . . . uh, standard, I guess you'd say. There
are lots of rules. Like you can put up white lights at Christmas but
not colored ones. And they can't blink."

Hodges rolls his eyes. Peeples grins. They have gone from
potential antagonists to colleagues—almost, anyway—and why?
Because Hodges happened to recognize the guy's slightly off-center
first name. You could call that luck, but there's always something
that will get you on the same side as the person you want to question, *something*, and part of Hodges's success on the cops came from
being able to recognize it, at least in most cases. It's a talent Pete
Huntley never had, and Hodges is delighted to find his remains in
good working order.

"I think she had a sister," he says. "Mrs. Trelawney, I mean.
Never met her, though, and can't remember the name."

"Janelle Patterson," Peeples says promptly.

"You *have* met her, I take it."

"Yes indeed. She's good people. Bears a resemblance to Mrs. Trelawney, but younger and better-looking." His hands describe an
hourglass shape in the air. "More filled out. Do you happen to know
if there's been any progress on the Mercedes thing, Mr. Hodges?"

This isn't a question Hodges would ordinarily answer, but if you want to get information, you have to give information. And what he has is safe enough, because it isn't information at all. He uses the phrase Pete Huntley used at lunch a few hours ago. "Dead in the water."

Peeples nods as if this is no more than he expected. "Crime of impulse. No ties to any of the vics, no motive, just a goddam thrill-killing. Best chance of getting him is if he tries to do it again, don't you think?"

Mr. Mercedes says he won't, Hodges thinks, but this is information he absolutely *doesn't* want to give out, so he agrees. Collegial agreement is always good.

"Mrs. T. left a big estate," Hodges says, "and I'm not just talking about the house. I wonder if the sister inherited."

"Oh yeah," Peeples says. He pauses, then says something Hodges himself will say to someone else in the not too distant future. "Can I trust your discretion?"

"Yes." When asked such a question, the simple answer is best. No qualifiers.

"The Patterson woman was living in Los Angeles when her sister . . . you know. The pills."

Hodges nods.

"Married, but no children. Not a happy marriage. When she found out she had inherited megabucks and a Sugar Heights estate, she divorced the husband like a shot and came east." Peeples jerks a thumb at the gate, the wide drive, and the big house. "Lived there for a couple of months while the will was going through probate. Got close with Mrs. Wilcox, down at 640. Mrs. Wilcox likes to talk, and sees me as a friend."

This might mean anything from coffee-buddies to afternoon sex.

"Miz Patterson took over visiting the mother, who lived in a condo building downtown. You know about the mother?"

"Elizabeth Wharton," Hodges says. "Wonder if she's still alive."

"I'm pretty sure she is."

"Because she had terrible scoliosis." Hodges takes a little hunched-over walk to demonstrate. If you want to get, you have to give.

"Is that so? Too bad. Anyway, Helen—Mrs. Wilcox—says that Miz Patterson visited as regular as clockwork, just like Mrs. Trelawney did. Until a month ago, that is. Then things must have got worse, because I believe the old lady's now in a nursing home in Warsaw County. Miz Patterson moved into the condo herself. And that's where she is now. I still see her every now and then, though. Last time was a week ago, when the real estate guy showed the house."

Hodges decides he's gotten everything he can reasonably expect from Radney Peeples. "Thanks for the update. I'm going to roll. Sorry we kind of got off on the wrong foot."

"Not at all," Peeples says, giving Hodges's offered hand two brisk pumps. "You handled it like a pro. Just remember, I never said anything. Janelle Patterson may be living downtown, but she's still part of the Association, and that makes her a client."

"You never said a word," Hodges says, getting back into his car. He hopes that Helen Wilcox's husband won't catch his wife and this beefcake in the sack together, if that is indeed going on; it would probably be the end of Vigilant Guard Service's arrangement with the residents of Sugar Heights. Peeples himself would immediately be terminated for cause. About that there is no doubt at all.

Probably she just trots out to his car with fresh-baked cookies, Hodges thinks as he drives away. You've been watching too much Nazi couples therapy on afternoon TV.

Not that Radney Peeples's love-life matters to him. What matters to Hodges as he heads back to his much humbler home on the West Side is that Janelle Patterson inherited her sister's estate, Janelle Patterson is living right here in town (at least for the time being), and Janelle Patterson must have done something with the late Olivia Trelawney's possessions. That would include her personal papers, and her personal papers might contain a letter—

possibly more than one—from the freako who has reached out to Hodges. If such correspondence exists, he would like to see it.

Of course this is police business and K. William Hodges is no longer a policeman. By pursuing it he is skating well beyond the bounds of what is legal and he knows it—for one thing, he is with-holding evidence—but he has no intention of stopping just yet. The cocky arrogance of the freako's letter has pissed him off. But, he admits, it's pissed him off in a good way. It's given him a sense of purpose, and after the last few months, that seems like a pretty terrific thing.

*If I do happen to make a little progress, I'll turn the whole thing over to Pete.*

He's not looking in the rearview mirror as this thought crosses his mind, but if he had been, he would have seen his eyes flick momentarily up and to the left.

4

Hodges parks his Toyota in the sheltering overhang to the left of his house that serves as his garage, and pauses to admire his freshly cut lawn before going to the door. There he finds a note sticking out of the mail slot. His first thought is Mr. Mercedes, but such a thing would be bold even for that guy.

It's from Jerome. His neat printing contrasts wildly with the bullshit jive of the message.

*Dear Massa Hodges,*

*I has mowed yo grass and put de mower back in yo cah-pote. I hopes you didn't run over it, suh! If you has any mo chos for dis heah black boy, hit me on mah honker. I be happy to talk to you if I is not on de job wit one of my hos. As you know dey needs a lot of work and sometimes some tunin up on em, as dey can be uppity, especially dem high yallers! I is always heah fo you, suh!*

*Jerome*

Hodges shakes his head wearily but can't help smiling. His hired kid gets straight As in advanced math, he can replace fallen gutters, he fixes Hodges's email when it goes blooey (as it frequently does, mostly due to his own mismanagement), he can do basic plumbing, he can speak French pretty well, and if you ask what he's reading, he's apt to bore you for half an hour with the blood symbolism of D. H. Lawrence. He doesn't want to be white, but being a gifted black male in an upper-middle-class family has presented him with what he calls "identity challenges." He says this in a joking way, but Hodges does not believe he's joking. Not really.

Jerome's college professor dad and CPA mom—both humor-challenged, in Hodges's opinion—would no doubt be aghast at this communication. They might even feel their son in need of psychological counseling. But they won't find out from Hodges.

"Jerome, Jerome, Jerome," he says, letting himself in. Jerome and his chos fo hos. Jerome who can't decide, at least not yet, on which Ivy League college he wants to attend; that any of the big boys will accept him is a foregone conclusion. He's the only person in the neighborhood whom Hodges thinks of as a friend, and really, the only one he needs. Hodges believes friendship is over-rated, and in this way, if in no other, he is like Brady Hartsfield.

He has made it in time for most of the evening news, but decides against it. There is only so much Gulf oil-spill and Tea Party politics he can take. He turns on his computer instead, launches Firefox, and plugs **Under Debbie's Blue Umbrella** into the search field. There are only six results, a very small catch in the vast fishy sea of the Internet, and only one that matches the phrase exactly. Hodges clicks on it and a picture appears.

Under a sky filled with threatening clouds is a country hillside. Animated rain—a simple repeating loop, he judges—is pouring down in silvery streams. But the two people seated beneath a large blue umbrella, a young man and a young woman, are safe and dry. They are not kissing, but their heads are close together. They appear to be in deep conversation.

Below the picture, there's a brief description of the Blue Umbrella's raison d'être.

> *Unlike sites such as Facebook and LinkedIn, Under Debbie's Blue Umbrella is a chat site where old friends can meet and new friends can get to know one another in TOTAL GUARENTEED ANONYMITY. No pictures, no porn, no 140-character Tweets, just GOOD OLD-FASHIONED CONVERSATION.*

Below this is a button marked GET STARTED NOW! Hodges mouses his cursor onto it, then hesitates. About six months ago, Jerome had to delete his email address and give him a new one, because everyone in Hodges's address book had gotten a message saying he was stranded in New York, someone had stolen his wallet with all his credit cards inside, and he needed money to get home. Would the email recipient please send fifty dollars—more if he or she could afford it—to a Mail Boxes Etc. in Tribeca. "I'll pay you back as soon as I get this mess straightened out," the message concluded.

Hodges was deeply embarrassed because the begging request had gone out to his ex, his brother in Toledo, and better than four dozen cops he'd worked with over the years. Also his daughter. He had expected his phone—both landline and cell—to ring like crazy for the next forty-eight hours or so, but very few people called, and only Alison seemed actually concerned. This didn't surprise him. Allie, a Gloomy Gus by nature, has been expecting her father to lose his shit ever since he turned fifty-five.

Hodges had called on Jerome for help, and Jerome explained he had been a victim of phishing.

"Mostly the people who phish your address just want to sell Viagra or knockoff jewelry, but I've seen this kind before, too. It happened to my Environmental Studies teacher, and he ended up paying people back almost a thousand bucks. Of course, that was in the old days, before people wised up—"

"Old days meaning exactly when, Jerome?"

Jerome had shrugged. "Two, three years ago. It's a new world out there, Mr. Hodges. Just be grateful the phisherman didn't hit you with a virus that ate all your files and apps."

"I wouldn't lose much," Hodges had said. "Mostly I just surf the Web. Although I *would* miss the computer solitaire. It plays 'Happy Days Are Here Again' when I win."

Jerome had given him his patented I'm-too-polite-to-call-you-dumb look. "What about your tax returns? I helped you do em online last year. You want someone to see what you paid Uncle Sugar? Besides me, I mean?"

Hodges admitted he didn't.

In that strange (and somehow endearing) pedagogical voice the intelligent young always seem to employ when endeavoring to educate the clueless old, Jerome said, "Your computer isn't just a new kind of TV set. Get that out of your mind. Every time you turn it on, you're opening a window into your life. If someone wants to look, that is."

All this goes through his head as he looks at the blue umbrella and the endlessly falling rain. Other stuff goes through it, too, stuff from his cop-mind, which had been asleep but is now wide awake.

Maybe Mr. Mercedes wants to talk. On the other hand, maybe what he really wants is to look through that window Jerome was talking about.

Instead of clicking on GET STARTED NOW!, Hodges exits the site, grabs his phone, and punches one of the few numbers he has on speed-dial. Jerome's mother answers, and after some brief and pleasant chitchat, she hands off to young Mr. Chos Fo Hos himself.

Speaking in the most horrible Ebonics dialect he can manage, Hodges says: "Yo, my homie, you keepin dem bitches in line? Dey earnin? You representin?"

"Oh, hi, Mr. Hodges. Yes, everything's fine."

"You don't likes me talkin dis way on yo honkah, brah?"

"Uh . . ."

STEPHEN KING

Jerome is honestly flummoxed, and Hodges takes pity on him. "The lawn looks terrific."

"Oh. Good. Thanks. Can I do anything else for you?"

"Maybe so. I was wondering if you could come by after school tomorrow. It's a computer thing."

"Sure. What's the problem this time?"

"I'd rather not discuss it on the phone," Hodges says, "but you might find it interesting. Four o'clock okay?"

"That works."

"Good. Do me a favor and leave Tyrone Feelgood *Dee*lite at home."

"Okay, Mr. Hodges, will do."

"When are you going to lighten up and call me Bill? Mr. Hodges makes me feel like your American History teacher."

"Maybe when I'm out of high school," Jerome says, very seriously.

"Just as long as you know you can make the jump any time you want."

Jerome laughs. The kid has got a great, full laugh. Hearing it always cheers Hodges up.

He sits at the computer desk in his little cubbyhole of an office, drumming his fingers, thinking. It occurs to him that he hardly ever uses this room during the evening. If he wakes at two A.M. and can't get back to sleep, yes. He'll come in and play solitaire for an hour or so before returning to bed. But he's usually in his La-Z-Boy between seven and midnight, watching old movies on AMC or TCM and stuffing his face with fats and sugars.

He grabs his phone again, dials Directory Assistance, and asks the robot on the other end if it has a number for Janelle Patterson. He's not hopeful; now that she is the Seven Million Dollar Woman, and newly divorced in the bargain, Mrs. Trelawney's sister has probably got an unlisted number.

But the robot coughs it up. Hodges is so surprised he has to fumble for a pencil and then punch 2 for a repeat. He drums his fingers some more, thinking how he wants to approach her. It will probably come to nothing, but it would be his next step if he were still on the cops. Since he's not, it will take a little extra finesse.

He is amused to discover how eagerly he welcomes this challenge.

5

Brady calls ahead to Sammy's Pizza on his way home and picks up a small pepperoni and mushroom pie. If he thought his mother would eat a couple of slices, he would have gotten a bigger one, but he knows better.

Maybe if it was pepperoni and Popov, he thinks. If they sold that, I'd have to skip the medium and go straight to a large.

There are tract houses on the city's North Side. They were built between Korea and Vietnam, which means they all look the same and they're all turning to shit. Most still have plastic toys on the crabgrassy lawns, although it's now full dark. Chaz Hartsfield is at 49 Elm Street, where there are no elms and probably never were. It's just that all the streets in this area of the city—known, reasonably enough, as Northfield—are named for trees.

Brady parks behind Ma's rustbucket Honda, which needs a new exhaust system, new points, and new plugs. Not to mention an inspection sticker.

Let *her* take care of it, Brady thinks, but she won't. He will. He'll have to. The way he takes care of everything.

The way I took care of Frankie, he thinks. Back when the basement was just the basement instead of my control center.

Brady and Deborah Ann Hartsfield don't talk about Frankie.

The door is locked. At least he's taught her that much, although God knows it hasn't been easy. She's the kind of person who thinks *okay* solves all of life's problems. Tell her *Put the half-and-half back in the fridge after you use it,* she says okay. Then you come home and there it sits on the counter, going sour. You say *Please do a wash so I can have a clean uni for the ice cream truck tomorrow,* she says okay.

But when you poke your head into the laundry room, everything's still there in the basket.

The cackle of the TV greets him. Something about an immunity challenge, so it's *Survivor*. He has tried to tell her it's all fake, a set-up. She says yes, okay, she knows, but she still never misses it.

"I'm home, Ma!"

"Hi, honey!" Only a moderate slur, which is good for this hour of the evening. If I was her liver, Brady thinks, I'd jump out of her mouth some night while she's snoring and run the fuck away.

He nonetheless feels that little flicker of anticipation as he goes into the living room, the flicker he hates. She's sitting on the couch in the white silk robe he got her for Christmas, and he can see more white where it splits apart high up on her thighs. Her underwear. He refuses to think the word *panties* in connection with his mother, it's too sexy, but it's down there in his mind, just the same: a snake hiding in poison sumac. Also, he can see the small round shadows of her nipples. It's not right that such things should turn him on—she's pushing fifty, she's starting to flab out around the middle, she's his *mother*, for God's sake—but . . .

But.

"I brought pizza," he says, holding up the box and thinking, I already ate.

"I already ate," she says. Probably she did. A few lettuce leaves and a teensy tub of yogurt. It's how she keeps what's left of her figure.

"It's your favorite," he says, thinking, You enjoy it, honey.

"You enjoy it, sweetie," she says. She lifts her glass and takes a ladylike sip. Gulping comes later, after he's gone to bed and she thinks he's asleep. "Get yourself a Coke and come sit beside me." She pats the couch. Her robe opens a little more. White robe, white panties.

Underwear, he reminds himself. Underwear, that's all, she's my mother, she's Ma, and when it's your ma it's just underwear.

She sees him looking and smiles. She does not adjust the robe. "The survivors are on Fiji this year." She frowns. "I think it's Fiji. One of those islands, anyway. Come and watch with me."

"Nah, I guess I'll go downstairs and work for awhile."

"What project is this, honey?"

"A new kind of router." She wouldn't know a router from a grouter, so that's safe enough.

"One of these days you'll invent something that will make us rich," she says. "I know you will. Then, goodbye electronics store. And goodbye to that ice cream truck." She looks at him with wide eyes that are only a little watery from the vodka. He doesn't know how much she puts down in the course of an ordinary day, and counting empty bottles doesn't work because she ditches them somewhere, but he knows her capacity is staggering.

"Thanks," he says. Feeling flattered in spite of himself. Feeling other stuff, too. Very much in spite of himself.

"Come give your Ma a kiss, honeyboy."

He approaches the couch, careful not to look down the front of the gaping robe and trying to ignore that crawling sensation just below his belt buckle. She turns her face to one side, but when he bends to kiss her cheek, she turns back and presses her damp half-open mouth to his. He tastes booze and smells the perfume she always dabs behind her ears. She dabs it other places, as well.

She places a palm on the nape of his neck and ruffles his hair with the tips of her fingers, sending a shiver all the way down to the small of his back. She touches his upper lip with the tip of her tongue, just a flick, there and gone, then pulls back and gives him the wide-eyed starlet stare.

"My honeyboy," she breathes, like the heroine of some romantic chick-flick—the kind where the men wave swords and the women wear low-cut dresses with their cakes pushed up into shimmery globes.

He pulls away hastily. She smiles at him, then looks back at the TV, where good-looking young people in bathing suits are running along a beach. He opens the pizza box with hands that are shaking slightly, takes out a slice, and drops it in her salad bowl.

"Eat that," he says. "It'll sop up the booze. Some of it."

"Don't be mean to Mommy," she says, but with no rancor and

certainly no hurt. She pulls her robe closed, doing it absently, already lost in the world of the survivors again, intent on discovering who will be voted off the island this week. "And don't forget about my car, Brady. It needs a sticker."

"It needs a lot more than that," he says, and goes into the kitchen. He grabs a Coke from the fridge, then opens the door to the basement. He stands there in the dark for a moment, then speaks a single word: "Control." Below him, the fluorescents (he installed them himself, just as he remodeled the basement himself) flash on.

At the foot of the stairs, he thinks of Frankie. He almost always does when he stands in the place where Frankie died. The only time he didn't think of Frankie was when he was preparing to make his run at City Center. During those weeks everything else left his mind, and what a relief that was.

*Brady*, Frankie said. His last word on Planet Earth. Gurgles and gasps didn't count.

He puts his pizza and his soda on the worktable in the middle of the room, then goes into the closet-sized bathroom and drops trou. He won't be able to eat, won't be able to work on his new project (which is certainly not a router), he won't be able to *think*, until he takes care of some urgent business.

In his letter to the fat ex-cop, he stated he was so sexually excited when he crashed into the job-seekers at City Center that he was wearing a condom. He further stated that he masturbates while reliving the event. If that were true, it would give a whole new meaning to the term autoerotic, but it isn't. He lied a lot in that letter, each lie calculated to wind Hodges up a little more, and his bogus sex-fantasies weren't the greatest of them.

He actually doesn't have much interest in girls, and girls sense it. It's probably why he gets along so well with Freddi Linklatter, his cyber-dyke colleague at Discount Electronix. For all Brady knows, she might think *he's* gay. But he's not gay, either. He's largely a mystery to himself—an occluded front—but one thing he knows for sure: he's not *asexual*, or not completely. He and his mother share a gothic rainbow of a secret, a thing not to be thought of unless it is absolutely necessary. When it does become necessary, it must be dealt with and put away again.

Ma, I see your panties, he thinks, and takes care of his business as fast as he can. There's Vaseline in the medicine cabinet, but he doesn't use it. He wants it to burn.

6

Back in his roomy basement workspace, Brady speaks another word. This one is *chaos*.

On the far side of the control room is a long shelf about three feet above the floor. Ranged along it are seven laptop computers with their darkened screens flipped up. There's also a chair on casters, so he can roll rapidly from one to another. When Brady speaks the magic word, all seven come to life. The number 20 appears on each screen, then 19, then 18. If he allows this countdown to reach zero, a suicide program will kick in, scrubbing his hard discs clean and overwriting them with gibberish.

"Darkness," he says, and the big countdown numbers disappear, replaced by desktop images that show scenes from *The Wild Bunch*, his favorite movie.

He tried *apocalypse* and *Armageddon*, much better start-up words in his opinion, full of ringing finality, but the word-recognition program has problems with them, and the last thing he wants is having to replace all his files because of a stupid glitch. Two-syllable words are safer. Not that there's much on six of the seven computers. Number Three is the only one with what the fat ex-cop would call "incriminating information," but he likes to look at that awesome array of computing power, all lit up as it is now. It makes the basement room feel like a real command center.

Brady considers himself a creator as well as a destroyer, but knows that so far he hasn't managed to create anything that will exactly set the world on fire, and he's haunted by the possibil-

STEPHEN KING

ity that he never will. That he has, at best, a second-rate creative mind.

Take the Rolla, for instance. That had come to him in a flash of inspiration one night when he'd been vacuuming the living room (like using the washing machine, such a chore is usually beneath his mother). He had sketched a device that looked like a footstool on bearings, with a motor and a short hose attachment on the underside. With the addition of a simple computer program, Brady reckoned the device could be designed to move around a room, vacuuming as it went. If it hit an obstacle—a chair, say, or a wall—it would turn on its own and start off in a new direction.

He had actually begun building a prototype when he saw a version of his Rolla trundling busily around the window display of an upscale appliance store downtown. The name was even similar; it was called a Roomba. Someone had beaten him to it, and that someone was probably making millions. It wasn't fair, but what is? Life is a crap carnival with shit prizes.

He has blue-boxed the TVs in the house, which means Brady and his ma are getting not just basic cable but all the premium channels (including a few exotic add-ins like Al Jazeera) for free, and there's not a damn thing Time Warner, Comcast, or XFINITY can do about it. He has hacked the DVD player so it will run not just American discs but those from every region of the world. It's easy—three or four quick steps with the remote, plus a six-digit recognition code. Great in theory, but does it get used? Not at 49 Elm Street, it doesn't. Ma won't watch anything that isn't spoon-fed to her by the four major networks, and Brady himself is mostly working one of his two jobs or down here in the control room, where he does his *actual* work.

The blue boxes are great, but they're also illegal. For all he knows, the DVD hacks are illegal, too. Not to mention his Redbox and Netflix hacks. *All* his best ideas are illegal. Take Thing One and Thing Two.

Thing One had been on the passenger seat of Mrs. Trelawney's Mercedes when he left City Center on that foggy morning the

104

previous April, with blood dripping from the bent grille and stippling the windshield. The idea came to him during the murky period three years ago, after he had decided to kill a whole bunch of people—what he then thought of as his *terrorist run*—but before he had decided just how, when, or where to do it. He had been full of ideas then, jittery, not sleeping much. In those days he always felt as though he had just swallowed a whole Thermos of black coffee laced with amphetamines.

Thing One was a modified TV remote with a microchip for a brain and a battery pack to boost its range . . . although the range was still pretty short. If you pointed it at a traffic light twenty or thirty yards away, you could change red to yellow with one tap, red to blinking yellow with two taps, and red to green with three.

Brady was delighted with it, and had used it several times (always while sitting parked in his old Subaru; the ice cream truck was far too conspicuous) at busy intersections. After several near misses, he had finally caused an actual accident. Just a fender-bender, but it had been fun to watch the two men arguing about whose fault it had been. For awhile it had looked like they might actually come to blows.

Thing Two came shortly afterward, but it was Thing One that settled Brady on his target, because it radically upped the chances of a successful getaway. The distance between City Center and the abandoned warehouse he had picked as a dumping spot for Mrs. Trelawney's gray Mercedes was exactly 1.9 miles. There were eight traffic lights along the route he planned to take, and with his splendid gadget, he wouldn't have to worry about any of them. But on that morning—Jesus Christ, wouldn't you know it?—every one of those lights had been green. Brady understood the early hour had something to do with it, but it was still infuriating.

*If I hadn't had it,* he thinks as he goes to the closet at the far end of the basement, *at least four of those lights would have been red. That's the way my life works.*

Thing Two was the only one of his gadgets that turned out to be an actual moneymaker. Not big money, but as everyone knew, money isn't everything. Besides, without Thing Two there would have been no Mercedes. And with no Mercedes, no City Center Massacre.

Good old Thing Two.

A big Yale padlock hangs from the hasp of the closet door. Brady opens it with a key on his ring. The lights inside—more new fluorescents—are already on. The closet is small and made even smaller by the plain board shelves. On one of them are nine shoeboxes. Inside each box is a pound of homemade plastic explosive. Brady has tested some of this stuff at an abandoned gravel pit far out in the country, and it works just fine.

*If I was over there in Afghanistan,* he thinks, dressed in a head-rag and one of those funky bathrobes, *I could have quite a career blowing up troop carriers.*

On another shelf, in another shoebox, are five cell phones. They're the disposable kind the Lowtown drug dealers call burn-ers. The phones, available at fine drugstores and convenience stores everywhere, are Brady's project for tonight. They have to be modi-fied so that a single number will ring all of them, creating the proper spark needed to detonate the boom-clay in the shoeboxes at the same time. He hasn't actually decided to use the plastic, but part of him wants to. Yes indeed. He told the fat ex-cop he has no urge to replicate his masterpiece, but that was another lie. A lot depends on the fat ex-cop himself. If he does what Brady wants— as Mrs. Trelawney did what Brady wanted—he's sure the urge will go away, at least for awhile.

If not . . . well . . .

He grabs the box of phones, starts out of the closet, then pauses and looks back. On one of the other shelves is a quilted wood-man's vest from L.L.Bean. If Brady were really going out in the woods, a Medium would suit him fine—he's slim—but this one is an XL. On the breast is a smile decal, the one wearing dark glasses and showing its teeth. The vest holds four more one-pound blocks of plastic explosive, two in the outside pockets, two in the slash pockets on the inside. The body of the vest bulges, because it's filled with ball bearings (just like the ones in Hodges's Happy

Slapper). Brady slashed the lining to pour them in. It even crossed his mind to ask Ma to sew the slashes up, and that gave him a good laugh as he sealed them shut with duct tape.

*My very own suicide vest,* he thinks affectionately.

He won't use it . . . *probably* won't use it . . . but this idea also has a certain attraction. It would put an end to everything. No more Discount Electronix, no more Cyber Patrol calls to dig peanut butter or saltine crumbs out of some elderly idiot's CPU, no more ice cream truck. Also no more crawling snakes in the back of his mind. Or under his belt buckle.

He imagines doing it at a rock concert; he knows Springsteen is going to play Lakefront Arena this June. Or how about the Fourth of July parade down Lake Street, the city's main drag? Or maybe on opening day of the Summer Sidewalk Art Festival and Street Fair, which happens every year on the first Saturday in August. That would be good, except wouldn't he look funny, wearing a quilted vest on a hot August afternoon?

True, but such things can always be worked out by the creative mind, he thinks, spreading the disposable phones on his worktable and beginning to remove the SIM cards. Besides, the suicide vest is just a whatdoyoucallit, doomsday scenario. It will probably never be used. Nice to have it handy, though.

Before going upstairs, he sits down at his Number Three, goes online, and checks the Blue Umbrella. Nothing from the fat ex-cop.

Yet.

7

When Hodges uses the intercom outside Mrs. Wharton's Lake Avenue condo at ten the next morning, he's wearing a suit for only the second or third time since he retired. It feels good to be in a suit again, even though it's tight at the waist and under the arms. A man in a suit feels like a working man.

A woman's voice comes from the speaker. "Yes?"

"It's Bill Hodges, ma'am. We spoke last night?"

"So we did, and you're right on time. It's 19-C, Detective Hodges."

He starts to tell her that he's no longer a detective, but the door is buzzing and so he doesn't bother. Besides, he told her he was retired when they talked on the phone.

Janelle Patterson is waiting for him at the door, just as her sister was on the day of the City Center Massacre, when Hodges and Pete Huntley came to interview her the first time. The resemblance between the two women is enough to give Hodges a powerful sense of déjà vu. But as he makes his way down the short hall from the elevator to the apartment doorway (trying to walk rather than lumber), he sees that the differences outweigh the similarities. Patterson has the same light blue eyes and high cheekbones, but where Olivia Trelawney's mouth was tight and pinched, the lips often white with a combination of strain and irritation, Janelle Patterson's seem, even in repose, ready to smile. Or to bestow a kiss. Her lips are shiny with wet-look gloss; they look good enough to eat. And no boatneck tops for this lady. She's wearing a snug turtleneck that cradles a pair of perfectly round breasts. They are not big, those breasts, but as Hodges's dear old father used to say, more than a handful is wasted. Is he looking at the work of good foundation garments or a post-divorce enhancement? Enhancement seems more likely to Hodges. Thanks to her sister, she can afford all the bodywork she wants.

She extends her hand and gives him a good no-nonsense shake. "Thank you for coming." As if it had been at her request.

"Glad you could see me," he says, following her in.

That same kick-ass view of the lake smacks him in the face. He remembers it well, although they had only the one interview with Mrs. T. here; all the others were either at the big house in Sugar Heights or at the station. She had gone into hysterics during one of those station visits, he remembers. *Everybody is blaming me*, she said. The suicide had come not much later, only a matter of weeks.

"Would you like coffee, Detective? It's Jamaican. Very tasty, I think."

Hodges makes it a habit not to drink coffee in the middle of the morning, because doing so usually gives him savage acid reflux in spite of his Zantac. But he agrees.

He sits in one of the sling chairs by the wide living room window while he waits for her to come back from the kitchen. The day is warm and clear; on the lake, sailboats are zipping and curving like skaters. When she returns he stands up to take the silver tray she's carrying, but Janelle smiles, shakes her head no, and sets it on the low coffee table with a graceful dip of her knees. Almost a curtsey.

Hodges has considered every possible twist and turn their conversation might take, but his forethought turns out to be irrelevant. It is as if, after carefully planning a seduction, the object of his desire has met him at the door in a shortie nightgown and fuck-me shoes.

"I want to find out who drove my sister to suicide," she says as she pours their coffee into stout china mugs, "but I didn't know how I should proceed. Your call was like a message from God. After our conversation, I think you're the man for the job."

Hodges is too dumbfounded to speak.

She offers him a mug. "If you want cream, you'll have to pour it yourself. When it comes to additives, I take no responsibility."

"Black is fine."

She smiles. Her teeth are either perfect or perfectly capped. "A man after my own heart."

He sips, mostly to buy time, but the coffee is delicious. He clears his throat and says, "As I told you when we talked last night, Mrs. Patterson, I'm no longer a police detective. On November twentieth of last year, I became just another private citizen. We need to have that up front."

She regards him over the rim of her cup. Hodges wonders if the moist gloss on her lips leaves an imprint, or if lipstick technology has rendered that sort of thing obsolete. It's a crazy thing to be wondering, but she's a pretty lady. Also, he doesn't get out much these days.

"As far as I'm concerned," Janelle Patterson says, "there are only two words that matter in what you just said. One is *private* and the other is *detective*. I want to know who meddled with her, who *toyed* with her until she killed herself, and nobody in the police department cares. They'd like to catch the man who used her car to kill those people, oh yes, but about my sister—may I be vulgar?—they don't give a shit."

Hodges may be retired, but he still has his loyalties. "That isn't necessarily true."

"I understand why you'd say that, Detective—"

"Mister, please. Just Mr. Hodges. Or Bill, if you like."

"Bill, then. And it *is* true. There's a connection between those murders and my sister's suicide, because the man who used the car is also the man who wrote the letter. And those other things. Those Blue Umbrella things."

Easy, Hodges cautions himself. Don't blow it.

"What letter are we talking about, Mrs. Patterson?"

"Janey. If you're Bill, I'm Janey. Wait here. I'll show you."

She gets up and leaves the room. Hodges's heart is beating hard—much harder than when he took on the trolls beneath the underpass—but he still appreciates that the view of Janey Patterson going away is as good as the one from the front.

Easy, boy, he tells himself again, and sips more coffee. Philip Marlowe you ain't. His mug is already half empty, and no acid. Not a trace of it. Miracle coffee, he thinks.

She comes back holding two pieces of paper by the corners and with an expression of distaste. "I found it when I was going through the papers in Ollie's desk. Her lawyer, Mr. Schron, was with me— she named him the executor of her will, so he had to be—but he was in the kitchen, getting himself a glass of water. He never saw this. I hid it." She says it matter-of-factly, with no shame or defiance. "I knew what it was right away. Because of *that*. The guy left one on the steering wheel of her car. I guess you could call it his calling-card."

She taps the sunglasses-wearing smile-face partway down the first page of the letter. Hodges has already noted it. He has also noted the letter's font, which he has identified from his own word processing program as American Typewriter.

"When did you find it?"

She thinks back, calculating the passage of time. "I came for the funeral, which was near the end of November. I discovered that I was Ollie's sole beneficiary when the will was read. That would have been the first week of December. I asked Mr. Schron if we could put off the inventory of Ollie's assets and possessions until January, because I had some business to take care of back in L.A. He agreed." She looks at Hodges, a level stare from blue eyes with a bright sparkle in them. "The business I had to take care of was divorcing my husband, who was—may I be vulgar again?—a philandering, coke-snorting asshole."

Hodges has no desire to go down this sidetrack. "You returned to Sugar Heights in January?"

"Yes."

"And found the letter then?"

"Yes."

"Have the police seen it?" He knows the answer, January was over four months ago, but the question has to be asked.

"No."

"Why not?"

"I already told you! Because I don't trust them!" That bright sparkle in her eyes overspills as she begins to cry.

8

She asks if he will excuse her. Hodges tells her of course. She disappears, presumably to get control of herself and repair her face. Hodges picks up the letter and reads it, taking small sips of coffee as he does so. The coffee really is delicious. Now, if he just had a cookie or two to go with it . . .

Dear Olivia Trelawney,

I hope you will read this letter all the way to the end
before throwing it away or burning it up. I know I don't
deserve your consideration, but I am begging for it just the
same. You see, I am the man who stole your Mercedes and
drove it into those people. Now I am burning like you might
burn my letter, only with shame and remorse and sorrow.

Please, please, please give me a chance to explain! I can
never have your forgiveness, that's another thing I know,
and I don't expect it, but if I can only get you to <u>under-
stand</u>, that would be enough. Will you give me that chance?
Please? To the public I am a monster, to the TV news I am
just another bloody story to sell commercials, to the police I
am just another perk they want to catch and put in jail, but
<u>I am also a human being</u>, just as you are. Here is my story.

I grew up in a physically and sexually abusive household. My stepfather was the first, and do you know what
happened when my mother found out? <u>She joined the fun</u>!
Have you stopped reading yet? I wouldn't blame you, it's
disgusting, but I hope you have not, because I have to get
this off my chest. I may not be "in the land of the living"
much longer, you see, but I cannot end my life without
someone knowing WHY I did what I did. Not that I understand it completely myself, but perhaps you, as an "outsider," will.

Here was Mr. Smiley-Face.

The sexual abuse went on until my stepfather died of a
heart attack when I was 12. My mother said if I ever told,
I would be blamed. She said if I showed the healed cigarette
burns on my arms and legs and privates, she would tell
people I did it myself. I was just a kid and I thought she was
telling the truth. She also told me that if people did believe

112

me, she would have to go to jail and I would be put in an orphan home (which was probably true).

I kept my mouth shut. Sometimes "the devil you know is better than the devil you don't!"

I never grew very much and I was very thin because I was too nervous to eat and when I did I often threw up (bulimia). Hence and because of this, I was bullied at school. I also developed a bunch of nervous tics, such as picking at my clothes and pulling at my hair (sometimes pulling it out in bunches). This caused me to be laughed at, not just by the other kids but by teachers too.

Janey Patterson has returned and is once again sitting opposite him, drinking her coffee, but for the moment Hodges barely notices her. He's thinking back to the four or five interviews he and Pete conducted with Mrs. T. He's remembering how she was always straightening the boatneck tops. Or tugging down her skirt. Or touching the corners of her pinched mouth, as if to remove a crumb of lipstick. Or winding a curl of hair around her finger and tugging at it. That too.

He goes back to the letter.

I was never a mean kid, Mrs. Trelawney. I swear to you. I never tortured animals or beat up kids that were even smaller than I was. I was just a scurrying little mouse of a kid, trying to get through my childhood without being laughed at or humiliated, but at that I did not succeed.

I wanted to go to college, but I never did. You see, I ended up taking care of the woman who abused me! It's almost funny, isn't it? Ma had a stroke, possibly because of her drinking. Yes, she is also an alcoholic, or was when she could get to the store to buy her bottles. She can walk a little, but really not much. I have to help her to the toilet and clean her up after she "does her business." I work all day at a low-paying job (probably lucky to have a job at all in this economy, I know) and then come home and take care of her, because having a woman come in for a few hours on week-days is all I can afford. It is a bad and stupid life. I have no friends and no possibility of advancement where I work. If Society is a bee-hive, then I am just another drone.

Finally I began to get angry. I wanted to make someone pay. I wanted to strike back at the world and make the world know I was alive. Can you understand that? Have you ever felt like that? Most likely not as you are wealthy and prob-ably have the best friends money can buy.

Following this zinger, there's another of those sunglasses-wearing smile-faces, as if to say Just kidding.

One day it all got to be too much and I did what I did. I didn't plan ahead . . .

The fuck you didn't, Hodges thinks.

. . . and I thought the chances were at least 50-50 that I would get caught. I didn't care. And I SURE didn't know how it would haunt me afterward. I still relive the thuds that resulted from hitting them, and I still hear their screams. Then when I saw the news and found out I had even killed a baby, it really came home to me what a terrible thing I had done. I don't know how I live with myself.

Mrs. Trelawney, why oh why oh why did you leave your key in your ignition? If I had not seen that, walking one early morning because I could not sleep, none of this would have happened. If you hadn't left your key in your ignition, that little baby and her mother would still be alive. I am not blaming you, I'm sure your mind was full of your own prob-lems and anxieties, but I wish things had turned out differ-ent and if you had remembered to take your key they would have. I would not be burning in this hell of guilt and remorse.

You are probably feeling guilt and remorse too, and I am sorry, especially because very soon you will find out how mean people can be. The TV news and the papers will talk about how your carelessness made my terrible act possible. Your friends will stop talking to you. The police will hound you. When you go to the supermarket, people will look at you and then whisper to each other. Some won't be content with just whispering and will "get in your face." I would not be surprised if there was vandalism to your home, so tell your security people (I'm sure you have them) to "watch out."

I don't suppose you would want to talk to me, would you? Oh, I don't mean face to face, but there is a safe place, <u>safe for both of us</u>, where we could talk using our computers. It's called Under Debbie's Blue Umbrella. I even got you a username if you should want to do this. The username is "otrelaw19."

I know what an ordinary person would do. An ordinary person would take this letter straight to the police, but let me ask a question. <u>What have they done for you except hound you and cause you sleepless nights</u>? Although here's a thought, if you want me dead, giving this letter to the police is the way to do it, as surely as putting a gun to my head and pulling the trigger, because I will kill myself.

Crazy as it may seem, you are <u>the only person keeping me alive</u>. Because you are the only one I can talk to. The only one who understands what it is like to be in Hell.

Now I will wait.

Mrs. Trelawney, I am so so so SORRY.

Hodges puts the letter down on the coffee table and says, "Holy shit."

Janey Patterson nods. "That was pretty much my reaction."

"He invited her to get in touch with him—"

Janey gives him an incredulous look. "*Invited* her? Try *blackmailed* her. 'Do it or I'll kill myself.'"

"According to you, she took him up on it. Have you seen any of their communications? Were there maybe printouts along with this letter?"

She shakes her head. "Ollie told my mother that she'd been chatting with what she called 'a very disturbed man' and trying to get him to seek help because he'd done a terrible thing. My mother was alarmed. She assumed Ollie was talking with the very disturbed man face-to-face, like in the park or a coffee shop or something. You have to remember she's in her late eighties now. She knows about computers, but she's vague on their practical uses. Ollie explained about chat-rooms—or tried to—but I'm not sure how much Mom actually understood. What she remembers is that Ollie said she talked to the very disturbed man underneath a blue umbrella."

"Did your mother connect the man to the stolen Mercedes and the killings at City Center?"

"She never said anything that would make me believe so. Her short-term memory's gotten very foggy. If you ask her about the Japanese bombing Pearl Harbor, she can tell you exactly when she heard the news on the radio, and probably who the newscaster was. Ask her what she had for breakfast, or even where she is . . ." Janey shrugged. "She might be able to tell you, she might not."

"And where is she, exactly?"

"A place called Sunny Acres, about thirty miles from here." She laughs, a rueful sound with no joy in it. "Whenever I hear the name, I think of those old melodramas you see on Turner Classic Movies, where the heroine is declared insane and socked away in some awful drafty madhouse."

She turns to look out at the lake. Her face has taken on an expression Hodges finds interesting: a bit pensive and a bit defensive. The more he looks at her, the more he likes her looks. The fine lines around her eyes suggest that she's a woman who likes to laugh.

"I know who I'd be in one of those old movies," she says, still looking out at the boats playing on the water. "The conniving sister who inherits the care of an elderly parent along with a pile of money. The cruel sister who keeps the money but ships the Aged P off to a creepy mansion where the old people get Alpo for dinner and are left to lie in their own urine all night. But Sunny's not like that. It's actually very nice. Not cheap, either. And Mom asked to go."

"Yeah?"

"*Yeah,*" she says, mocking him with a little wrinkle of her nose. "Do you happen to remember her nurse? Mrs. Greene. Althea Greene."

Hodges catches himself reaching into his jacket to consult a case notebook that's no longer there. But after a moment's thought he recalls the nurse without it. A tall and stately woman in white who seemed to glide rather than walk. With a mass of marcelled gray hair that made her look a bit like Elsa Lanchester in *The Bride of Frankenstein*. He and Pete had asked if she'd noticed Mrs. Trelawney's Mercedes parked at the curb when she left on that Thursday night. She had replied she was quite sure she had, which to the team of Hodges and Huntley meant she wasn't sure at all.

"Yeah, I remember her."

"She announced her retirement almost as soon as I moved back from Los Angeles. She said that at sixty-four she no longer felt able to deal competently with a patient suffering from such serious disabilities, and she stuck to her guns even after I offered to bring in a nurse's aide—two, if she wanted. I think she was appalled by the publicity that resulted from the City Center Massacre, but if it had been only that, she might have stayed."

"Your sister's suicide was the final straw?"

"I'm pretty sure it was. I won't say Althea and Ollie were bosom buddies or anything, but they got on, and they saw eye to eye about Mom's care. Now Sunny's the best thing for her, and Mom's relieved to be there. On her good days, at least. So am I. For one thing, they manage her pain better."

"If I were to go out and talk to her . . ."

"She might remember a few things, or she might not." She turns from the lake to look at him directly. "Will you take the job?

I checked private detective rates online, and I'm prepared to do considerably better. Five thousand dollars a week, plus expenses. An eight-week minimum."

Forty thousand for eight weeks' work, Hodges marvels. Maybe he could be Philip Marlowe after all. He imagines himself in a ratty two-room office that gives on the third-floor hallway of a cheap office building. Hiring a va-voom receptionist with a name like Lola or Velma. A tough-talking blonde, of course. He'd wear a trenchcoat and a brown fedora on rainy days, the hat pulled down to one eyebrow.

Ridiculous. And not what attracts him. The attraction is not being in his La-Z-Boy, watching the lady judge and stuffing his face with snacks. He also likes being in his suit. But there's more. He left the PD with strings dangling. Pete has ID'd the pawnshop armed robber, and it looks like he and Isabelle Jaynes may soon be arresting Donald Davis, the mope who killed his wife and then went on TV, flashing his handsome smile. Good for Pete and Izzy, but neither Davis or the pawnshop shotgunner is the Big Casino.

Also, he thinks, Mr. Mercedes should have left me alone. And Mrs. T. He should have left her alone, too.

"Bill?" Janey's snapping her fingers like a stage hypnotist bringing a subject out of a trance. "Are you there, Bill?"

He returns his attention to her, a woman in her mid-forties who's not afraid to sit in bright sunlight. "If I say yes, you'll be hiring me as a security consultant."

She looks amused. "Like the men who work for Vigilant Guard Service out in the Heights?"

"No, not like them. They're bonded, for one thing. I'm not." I never had to be, he thinks. "I'd just be private security, like the kind of guys who work the downtown nightclubs. That's nothing you'd be able to claim as a deduction on your income tax, I'm afraid."

Amusement broadens into a smile, and she does the nose-wrinkling thing again. A fairly entrancing sight, in Hodges's opinion. "Don't care. In case you didn't know, I'm rolling in dough."

"What I'm trying for is full disclosure, Janey. I have no private detective's license, which won't stop me from asking questions, but how well I can operate without either a badge or a PI ticket remains to be seen. It's like asking a blind man to stroll around town without his guide dog."

"Surely there's a Police Department old boys' network?"

"There is, but if I tried to use it, I'd be putting both the old boys and myself in a bad position." That he has already done this by pumping Pete for information is a thing he won't share with her on such short acquaintance.

He lifts the letter Janey has showed him.

"For one thing, I'm guilty of withholding evidence if I agree to keep this between us." That he's already withholding a similar letter is another thing she doesn't need to know. "Technically, at least. And withholding is a felony offense."

She looks dismayed. "Oh my God, I never thought of that."

"On the other hand, I doubt if there's much Forensics could do with it. A letter dropped into a mailbox on Marlborough Street or Lowbriar Avenue is just about the most anonymous thing in the world. Once upon a time—I remember it well—you could match up the typing in a letter to the machine that wrote it. If you could find the machine, that is. It was as good as a fingerprint."

"But this wasn't typed."

"Nope. Laser printer. Which means no hanging *A*s or crooked *T*s. So I wouldn't be withholding much."

Of course withholding is still withholding.

"I'm going to take the job, Janey, but five thousand a week is ridiculous. I'll take a check for two, if you want to write one. And bill you for expenses."

"That doesn't seem like anywhere near enough."

"If I get someplace, we can talk about a bonus." But he doesn't think he'll take one, even if he does manage to run Mr. Mercedes to ground. Not when he came here already determined to investigate the bastard, and to sweet-talk her into helping him.

"All right. Agreed. And thank you."

"Welcome. Now tell me about your relationship with Olivia. All I know is it was good enough for you to call her Ollie, and I could use more."

"That will take some time. Would you like another cup of coffee? And a cookie or two to go with it? I have lemon snaps."

Hodges says yes to both.

9

"Ollie."

Janey says this, then falls silent long enough for Hodges to sip some of his new cup of coffee and eat a cookie. Then she turns to the window and the sailboats again, crosses her legs, and speaks without looking at him.

"Have you ever loved someone without liking them?"

Hodges thinks of Corinne, and the stormy eighteen months that preceded the final split. "Yes."

"Then you'll understand. Ollie was my big sister, eight years older than I was. I loved her, but when she went off to college, I was the happiest girl in America. And when she dropped out three months later and came running back home, I felt like a tired girl who has to pick up a big sack of bricks again after being allowed to put it down for awhile. She wasn't mean to me, never called me names or pulled my pigtails or teased when I walked home from junior high holding hands with Marky Sullivan, but when she was in the house, we were always at Condition Yellow. Do you know what I mean?"

Hodges isn't completely sure, but nods anyway.

"Food made her sick to her stomach. She got rashes when she was stressed out about anything—job interviews were the worst, although she finally did get a secretarial job. She had good skills and she was very pretty. Did you know that?"

Hodges makes a noncommittal noise. If he were to reply honestly, he might have said, I can believe it because I see it in you.

"One time she agreed to take me to a concert. It was U2, and I was mad to see them. Ollie liked them, too, but the night of the show she started vomiting. It was so bad that my parents ended up taking her to the ER and I had to stay home watching TV instead of pogoing and screaming for Bono. Ollie swore it was food poisoning, but we all ate the same meal, and no one else got sick. Stress is what it was. Pure stress. And you talk about hypochondria? With my sister, every headache was a brain tumor and every pimple was skin cancer. Once she got pinkeye and spent a week convinced she was going blind. Her periods were horroramas. She took to her bed until they were over."

"And still kept her job?"

Janey's reply is as dry as Death Valley. "Ollie's periods always used to last exactly forty-eight hours and they always came on the weekends. It was amazing."

"Oh." Hodges can think of nothing else to say.

Janey spins the letter around a few times on the coffee table with the tip of her finger, then raises those light blue eyes to Hodges. "He uses a phrase in here—something about having nervous tics. Did you notice that?"

"Yes." Hodges has noticed a great many things about this letter, mostly how it is in many ways a negative image of the one he received.

"My sister had her share, too. You may have noticed some of them."

Hodges pulls his tie first one way, then the other.

Janey grins. "Yes, that's one of them. There were many others. Patting light switches to make sure they were off. Unplugging the toaster after breakfast. She always said bread-and-butter before she went out somewhere, because supposedly if you did that, you'd remember anything you'd forgotten. I remember one day she had to drive me to school because I missed the bus. Mom and Dad had already gone to work. We got halfway there, then she became convinced the oven was on. We had to turn around and go back and check it. Nothing else would do. It was off, of course. I didn't make it to school until second period, and got hit with my first and only detention. I was furious. I was often furious with her, but I loved her, too. Mom, Dad, we all did. Like it was hardwired. But man, was she ever a sack of bricks."

"Too nervous to go out, but she not only married, she married money."

"Actually, she married a prematurely balding clerk in the investment company where she worked. Kent Trelawney. A nerd—I use the word affectionately, Kent was absolutely okay—with a love of video games. He started to invest in some of the companies that made them, and those investments paid off. My mother said he had the magic touch and my father said he was dumb lucky, but it was neither of those things. He knew the field, that's all, and what he didn't know he made it his business to learn. When they got married near the end of the seventies, they were only wealthy. Then Kent discovered Microsoft."

She throws her head back and belts out a hearty laugh, startling him.

"Sorry," she says. "Just thinking about the pure American irony of it. I was pretty, also well adjusted and gregarious. If I'd ever been in a beauty contest—which I call meat-shows for men, if you want to know, and probably you don't—I would have won Miss Congeniality in a walk. Lots of girlfriends, lots of boyfriends, lots of phone calls, and lots of dates. I was in charge of freshman orientation during my senior year at Catholic High School, and did a great job, if I do say so myself. Soothed a lot of nerves. My sister was just as pretty, but she was the neurotic one. The obsessive-compulsive one. If she'd ever been in a beauty contest, she would have thrown up all over her bathing suit."

Janey laughs some more. Another tear trickles down her cheek as she does. She wipes it away with the heel of her hand.

"So here's the irony. Miss Congeniality got stuck with the coke-snorting dingbat and Miss Nervy caught the good guy, the money-making, never-cheat husband. Do you get it?"

"Yeah," Hodges says. "I do."

"Olivia Wharton and Kent Trelawney. A courtship with about as much chance of success as a six-months preemie. Kent kept asking her out and she kept saying no. Finally she agreed to have dinner with him—just to make him stop bothering her, she said— and when they got to the restaurant, she froze. Couldn't get out of the car. Shaking like a leaf. Some guys would have given up right there, but not Kent. He took her to McDonald's and got Value Meals at the drive-through window. They ate in the parking lot. I guess they did that a lot. She'd go to the movies with him, but always had to sit on the aisle. She said sitting on the inside made her short of breath."

"A lady with all the bells and whistles."

"My mother and father tried for years to get her to see a shrink. Where they failed, Kent succeeded. The shrink put her on pills, and she got better. She had one of her patented anxiety attacks on her wedding day—I was the one who held her veil while she vomited in the church bathroom—but she got through it." Janey smiles wistfully and adds, "She was a beautiful bride."

Hodges sits silently, fascinated by this glimpse of Olivia Tre-lawney before she became Our Lady of Boatneck Tops.

"After she married, we drifted apart. As sisters sometimes do. We saw each other half a dozen times a year until our father died, even less after that."

"Thanksgiving, Christmas, and the Fourth of July?"

"Pretty much. I could see some of her old shit coming back, and after Kent died—it was a heart attack—*all* of it came back. She lost a ton of weight. She went back to the awful clothes she wore in high school and when she was working in the office. Some of this I saw when I came back to visit her and Mom, some when we talked on Skype."

He nods his understanding. "I've got a friend who keeps trying to hook me up with that."

She regards him with a smile. "You're old school, aren't you? I mean *really*." Her smile fades. "The last time I saw Ollie was May of last year, not long after the City Center thing." Janey hesitates, then gives it its proper name. "The massacre. She was in terrible shape. She said the cops were hounding her. Was that true?"

"No, but she thought we were. It's true we questioned her repeatedly, because she continued to insist she took her key and locked the Mercedes. That was a problem for us, because the car wasn't broken into and it wasn't hotwired. What we finally decided . . ." Hodges stops, thinking of the fat family psychologist who comes on every weekday at four. The one who specializes in breaking through the wall of denial.

"You finally decided what?"

"That she couldn't bear to face the truth. Does that sound like the sister you grew up with?"

"Yes." Janey points to the letter. "Do you suppose she finally told the truth to this guy? On Debbie's Blue Umbrella? Do you think that's why she took Mom's pills?"

"There's no way to be sure." But Hodges thinks it's likely.

"She quit her antidepressants." Janey is looking out at the lake again. "She denied it when I asked her, but I knew. She never liked them, said they made her feel woolly-headed. She took them for Kent, and once Kent was dead she took them for our mother, but after City Center . . ." She shakes her head, takes a deep breath. "Have I told you enough about her mental state, Bill? Because there's plenty more if you want it."

"I think I get the picture."

She shakes her head in dull wonder. "It's as if the guy knew her."

Hodges doesn't say what seems obvious to him, mostly because he has his own letter for comparison: he did. Somehow he did.

"You said she was obsessive-compulsive. To the point where she turned around and went back to check if the oven was on."

"Yes."

"Does it seem likely to you that a woman like that would have forgotten her key in the ignition?"

Janey doesn't answer for a long time. Then she says, "Actually, no."

It doesn't to Hodges, either. There's a first time for everything, of course, but . . . did he and Pete ever discuss that aspect of the matter? He's not sure, but thinks maybe they did. Only they hadn't known the depths of Mrs. T.'s mental problems, had they?

He asks, "Ever try going on this Blue Umbrella site yourself? Using the username he gave her?"

She stares at him, gobsmacked. "It never even crossed my mind, and if it had, I would have been too scared of what I might find. I guess that's why you're the detective and I'm the client. Will you try that?"

"I don't know what I'll try. I need to think about it, and I need to consult a guy who knows more about computers than I do."

"Make sure you note down his fee," she says.

Hodges says he will, thinking that at least Jerome Robinson will get some good out of this, no matter how the cards fall. And why shouldn't he? Eight people died at City Center and three more were permanently crippled, but Jerome still has to go to college. Hodges remembers an old saying: even on the darkest day, the sun shines on some dog's ass.

"What's next?"

Hodges takes the letter and stands up. "Next, I take this to the nearest UCopy. Then I return the original to you."

"No need of that. I'll scan it into the computer and print you one. Hand it over."

"Really? You can do that?"

Her eyes are still red from crying, but the glance she gives him is nonetheless merry. "It's a good thing you have a computer expert on call," she says. "I'll be right back. In the meantime, have another cookie."

Hodges has three.

10

When she returns with his copy of the letter, he folds it into his inner jacket pocket. "The original should go into a safe, if there's one here."

"There's one at the Sugar Heights house—will that do?"

It probably would, but Hodges doesn't care for the idea. Too many prospective buyers tromping in and out. Which is probably stupid, but there it is.

"Do you have a safe-deposit box?"

"No, but I could rent one. I use Bank of America, just two blocks over."

"I'd like that better," Hodges says, going to the door.

"Thank you for doing this," she says, and holds out both of her hands. As if he has asked her to dance. "You don't know what a relief it is."

He takes the offered hands, squeezes them lightly, then lets go, although he would have been happy to hold them longer.

"Two other things. First, your mother. How often do you visit her?"

"Every other day or so. Sometimes I take her food from the Iranian restaurant she and Ollie liked—the Sunny Acres kitchen staff is happy to warm it up—and sometimes I bring her a DVD or two. She likes the oldies, like with Fred Astaire and Ginger Rogers. I always bring her something, and she's always happy to see me. On her good days she *does* see me. On her bad ones, she's apt to call me Olivia. Or Charlotte. That's my aunt. I also have an uncle."

"The next time she has a good day, you ought to call me so I can go see her."

"All right. I'll go with you. What's the other thing?"

"This lawyer you mentioned. Schron. Did he strike you as competent?"

"Sharpest knife in the drawer, that was my impression."

"If I *do* find something out, maybe even put a name on the guy, we're going to need someone like that. We'll go see him, we'll turn over the letters—"

"Letters? I only found the one."

Hodges thinks Ah, shit, then regroups. "The letter and the copy, I mean."

"Oh, right."

"If I find the guy, it's the job of the police to arrest him and charge him. Schron's job is to make sure *we* don't get arrested for going off the reservation and investigating on our own."

"That would be criminal law, isn't it? I'm not sure he does that kind."

"Probably not, but if he's good, he'll know somebody who does. Someone who's just as good as he is. Are we agreed on that? We have to be. I'm willing to poke around, but if this turns into police business, we let the police take over."

"I'm fine with that," Janey says. Then she stands on tiptoe, puts her hands on the shoulders of his too-tight coat, and plants a kiss on his cheek. "I think you're a good guy, Bill. And the right guy for this."

He feels that kiss all the way down in the elevator. A lovely little warm spot. He's glad he took pains about shaving before leaving the house.

11

The silver rain falls without end, but the young couple—lovers? friends?—are safe and dry under the blue umbrella that belongs to someone, likely a fictional someone, named Debbie. This time Hodges notices that it's the boy who appears to be speaking, and the girl's eyes are slightly widened, as if in surprise. Maybe he's just proposed to her?

Jerome pops this romantic thought like a balloon. "Looks like a porn site, doesn't it?"

"Now what would a young pre–Ivy Leaguer like yourself know about porn sites?"

They are seated side by side in Hodges's study, looking at the Blue Umbrella start-up page. Odell, Jerome's Irish setter, is lying on his back behind them, rear legs splayed, tongue hanging from one side of his mouth, staring at the ceiling with a look of good-humored contemplation. Jerome brought him on a leash, but only because that's the law inside the city limits. Odell knows enough to stay out of the street and is about as harmless to passersby as a dog can be.

"I know what you know and what everybody with a computer knows," Jerome says. In his khaki slacks and button-down Ivy League shirt, his hair a close-cropped cap of curls, he looks to Hodges like a young Barack Obama, only taller. Jerome is six-five. And around him is the faint, pleasantly nostalgic aroma of Old Spice aftershave. "Porn sites are thicker than flies on roadkill. You surf the Net, you can't help bumping into them. And the ones with the innocent-sounding names are the ones most apt to be loaded."

"Loaded how?"

"With the kinds of images that can get you arrested."

"Kiddie porn, you mean."

"Or torture porn. Ninety-nine percent of the whips-and-chains stuff is faked. The other one percent . . ." Jerome shrugs.

"And you know this how?"

Jerome gives him a look—straight, frank, and open. Not an act, just the way he is, and what Hodges likes most about the kid. His mother and father are the same way. Even his little sis.

"Mr. Hodges, *everybody* knows. If they're under thirty, that is."

"Back in the day, people used to say don't trust anyone over thirty."

Jerome smiles. "I trust em, but when it comes to computers, an awful lot of em are clueless. They beat up their machines, then expect em to work. They open bareback email attachments. They go to websites like this, and all at once their computer goes HAL 9000 and starts downloading pictures of teenage escorts or terrorist videos that show people getting their heads chopped off."

It was on the tip of Hodge's tongue to ask who Hal 9000 is—it sounds like a gangbanger tag to him—but the thing about terrorist videos diverts him. "That actually happens?"

"It's been known to. And then . . ." Jerome makes a fist and raps his knuckles against the top of his head. "Knock-knock-knock, Homeland Security at your door." He unrolls his fist so he can point a finger at the couple under the blue umbrella. "On the other hand, this might be just what it claims to be, a chat site where shy people can be electronic pen-pals. You know, a lonelyhearts deal. Lots of people out there lookin for love, dude. Let's see."

He reaches for the mouse but Hodges grabs his wrist. Jerome looks at him inquiringly.

"Don't see on my computer," Hodges says. "See on yours."

"If you'd asked me to bring my laptop—"

"Do it tonight, that'll be fine. And if you happen to unleash a virus that swallows your cruncher whole, I'll stand you the price of a new one."

Jerome shoots him a look of condescending amusement. "Mr. Hodges, I've got the best virus detection and prevention program money can buy, and the second best backing it up. Any bug trying to creep into my machines gets swatted pronto."

"It might not be there to eat," Hodges says. He's thinking about Mrs. T.'s sister saying, *It's as if the guy knew her.* "It might be there to watch."

Jerome doesn't look worried; he looks excited. "How did you get onto this site, Mr. Hodges? Are you coming out of retirement? Are you, like, on the case?"

Hodges has never missed Pete Huntley so bitterly as he does at that moment: a tennis partner to volley with, only with theories and suppositions instead of fuzzy green balls. He has no doubt Jerome could fulfill that function, he has a good mind and a demonstrated talent for making all the right deductive leaps . . . but he's also a year from voting age, four from being able to buy a legal drink, and this could be dangerous.

"Just peek into the site for me," Hodges says. "But before you do, hunt around on the Net. See what you can find out about it. What I want to know most of all is—"

"If it has an actual history," Jerome cuts in, once more demonstrating that admirable deductive ability. "A whatdoyoucallit, backstory. You want to make sure it's not a straw man set up for you alone."

"You know," Hodges says, "you should quit doing chores for me and get a job with one of those computer-doctor companies. You could probably make a lot more dough. Which reminds me, you need to give me a price for this job."

Jerome is offended, but not by the offer of a fee. "Those companies are for geeks with bad social skills." He reaches behind him and scratches Odell's dark red fur. Odell thumps his tail appreciatively, although he would probably prefer a steak sandwich. "In fact there's one bunch that drives around in VW Beetles. You can't get much geekier than that. Discount Electronix . . . you know them?"

"Sure," Hodges says, thinking of the advertising circular he got along with his poison-pen letter.

"They must have liked the idea, because they have the same deal, only they call it the Cyber Patrol, and their VWs are green instead of black. Plus there are *mucho* independents. Look online, you can find two hundred right here in the city. I thinks I stick to chos, Massa Hodges."

Jerome clicks away from Under Debbie's Blue Umbrella and back to Hodges's screensaver, which happens to be a picture of Allie, back when she was five and still thought her old man was God.

"But since you're worried, I'll take precautions. I've got an old iMac in my closet with nothing on it but Atari Arcade and a few other moldy oldies. I'll use that one to check out the site."

"Good idea."

"Anything else I can do for you today?"

Hodges starts to say no, but Mrs. T.'s stolen Mercedes is still bugging him. There is something very wrong there. He felt it then and feels it more strongly now—so strongly he almost sees it. But *almost* never won a kewpie doll at the county fair. The wrongness is a ball he wants to hit, and have someone hit back to him.

"You could listen to a story," he says. In his mind he's already making up a piece of fiction that will touch on all the salient points. Who knows, maybe Jerome's fresh eye will spot something he himself has missed. Unlikely, but not impossible. "Would you be willing to do that?"

130

"Sure."

"Then clip Odell on his leash. We'll walk down to Big Licks. I've got my face fixed for a strawberry cone."

"Maybe we'll see the Mr. Tastey truck before we get there," Jerome says. "That guy's been in the neighborhood all week, and he's got some awesome goodies."

"So much the better," Hodges says, getting up. "Let's go."

### 12

They walk down the hill to the little shopping center at the intersection of Harper Road and Hanover Street with Odell padding between them on the slack leash. They can see the buildings of downtown two miles distant, City Center and the Midwest Culture and Arts Complex dominating the cluster of skyscrapers. The MAC is not one of I. M. Pei's finer creations, in Hodges's opinion. Not that his opinion has ever been solicited on the matter.

"So what's the story, morning glory?" Jerome asks.

"Well," Hodges says, "let's say there's this guy with a long-term lady friend who lives downtown. He himself lives in Parsonville." This is a municipality just beyond Sugar Heights, not as lux but far from shabby.

"Some of my friends call Parsonville Whiteyville," Jerome says. "I heard my father say it once, and my mother told him to shut up with the racist talk."

"Uh-huh." Jerome's friends, the black ones, probably call Sugar Heights Whiteyville, too, which makes Hodges think he's doing okay so far.

Odell has stopped to check out Mrs. Melbourne's flowers. Jerome pulls him away before he can leave a doggy memo there.

"So anyway," Hodges resumes, "the long-term lady friend has a condo apartment in the Branson Park area—Wieland Avenue, Branson Street, Lake Avenue, that part of town."

"Also nice."

"Yeah. He goes to see her three or four times a week. One or two nights a week he takes her to dinner or a movie and stays over. When he does that, he parks his car—a nice one, a Beemer—on the street, because it's a good area, well policed, plenty of those high-intensity arc-sodiums. Also, the parking's free from seven P.M. to eight A.M."

"I had a Beemer, I'd put it in one of the garages down there and never mind the free parking," Jerome says, and tugs the leash again. "Stop it, Odell, nice dogs don't eat out of the gutter."

Odell looks over his shoulder and rolls an eye as if to say You don't know what nice dogs do.

"Well, rich people have some funny ideas about economy," Hodges says, thinking of Mrs. T.'s explanation for doing the same thing.

"If you say so." They have almost reached the shopping center. On the way down the hill they've heard the jingling tune of the ice cream truck, once quite close, but it fades again as the Mr. Tastey guy heads for the housing developments north of Harper Road.

"So one Thursday night this guy goes to visit his lady as usual. He parks as usual—all kinds of empty spaces down there once the business day is over—and locks up his car as usual. He and his lady take a walk to a nearby restaurant, have a nice meal, then walk back. His car's right there, he sees it before they go in. He spends the night with his lady, and when he leaves the building in the morning—"

"His Beemer's gone bye-bye." They are now standing outside the ice cream shop. There's a bicycle rack nearby. Jerome fastens Odell's leash to it. The dog lies down and puts his muzzle on one paw.

"No," Hodges says, "it's there." He is thinking that this is a damned good variation on what actually happened. He almost believes it himself. "But it's facing the other way, because it's parked on the other side of the street."

Jerome raises his eyebrows.

"Yeah, I know. Weird, right? So the guy goes across to it. Car looks okay, it's locked up tight just the way he left it, it's just in a new place. So the first thing he does is check for his key, and yep, it's still in his pocket. So what the hell happened, Jerome?"

"I don't know, Mr. H. It's like a Sherlock Holmes story, isn't it? A real three-pipe problem." There's a little smile on Jerome's face that Hodges can't quite parse and isn't sure he likes. It's a *knowing* smile.

Hodges digs his wallet out of his Levi's (the suit was good, but it's a relief to be back in jeans and an Indians pullover again). He selects a five and hands it to Jerome. "Go get our ice cream cones. I'll dog-sit Odell."

"You don't need to do that, he's fine."

"I'm sure he is, but standing in line will give you time to consider my little problem. Think of yourself as Sherlock, maybe that'll help."

"Okay." Tyrone Feelgood Delight pops out. "Only *you* is Sherlock! I is Doctah Watson!"

## 13

There's a pocket park on the far side of Hanover. They cross at the WALK light, grab a bench, and watch a bunch of shaggy-haired middle-school boys dare life and limb in the sunken concrete skateboarding area. Odell divides his time between watching the boys and the ice cream cones.

"You ever try that?" Hodges asks, nodding at the daredevils.

"No, suh!" Jerome gives him a wide-eyed stare. "I is *black*. I spends mah spare time shootin hoops and runnin on de cinder track at de high school. Us black fellas is mighty fast, as de whole worl' knows."

"Thought I told you to leave Tyrone at home." Hodges uses his finger to swop some ice cream off his cone and extends the dripping finger to Odell, who cleans it with alacrity.

"Sometimes dat boy jus' show up!" Jerome declares. Then

Tyrone is gone, just like that. "There's no guy and no lady friend and no Beemer. You're talking about the Mercedes Killer."

So much for fiction. "Say I am."

"Are you investigating that on your own, Mr. Hodges?"

Hodges thinks this over, very carefully, then repeats himself. "Say I am."

"Does the Debbie's Blue Umbrella site have something to do with it?"

"Say it does."

A boy falls off his skateboard and stands up with road rash on both knees. One of his friends buzzes over, jeering. Road Rash Boy slides a hand across one oozing knee, flings a spray of red droplets at Jeering Boy, then rolls away, shouting "AIDS! AIDS!" Jeering Boy rolls after him, only now he's Laughing Boy.

"Barbarians," Jerome mutters. He bends to scratch Odell behind the ears, then straightens up. "If you want to talk about it—"

Embarrassed, Hodges says, "I don't think at this point—"

"I understand," Jerome says. "But I *did* think about your problem while I was in line, and I've got a question."

"Yes?"

"Your make-believe Beemer guy, where was his spare key?"

Hodges sits very still, thinking how very quick this kid is. Then he sees a line of pink ice cream trickling down the side of his waffle cone and licks it off.

"Let's say he claims he never had one."

"Like the woman who owned the Mercedes did."

"Yes. Exactly like that."

"Remember me telling you how my mom got pissed at my dad for calling Parsonville Whiteyville?"

"Yeah."

"Want to hear about a time when my dad got pissed at my mom? The only time I ever heard him say, That's just like a woman?"

"If it bears on my little problem, shoot."

"Mom's got a Chevy Malibu. Candy-apple red. You've seen it in the driveway."

"Sure."

"He bought it new three years ago and gave it to her for her birthday, provoking massive squeals of delight."

Yes, Hodges thinks, Tyrone Feelgood has definitely taken a hike.

"She drives it for a year. No problems. Then it's time to re-register. Dad said he'd do it for her on his way home from work. He goes out to get the paperwork, then comes back in from the driveway holding up a key. He's not mad, but he's irritated. He tells her that if she leaves her spare key in the car, someone could find it and drive her car away. She asks where it was. He says in a plastic Ziploc bag along with her registration, her insurance card, and the owner's manual, which she had never opened. Still had the paper band around it that says thanks for buying your new car at Lake Chevrolet."

Another drip is trickling down Hodges's ice cream. This time he doesn't notice it even when it reaches his hand and pools there. "In the . . ."

"Glove compartment, yes. My dad said it was careless, and my mom said . . ." Jerome leans forward, his brown eyes fixed on Hodges's gray ones. *"She said she didn't even know it was there.* That's when he said it was just like a woman. Which didn't make her happy."

"Bet it didn't." In Hodges's brain, all sorts of gears are engaging.

"Dad says, Honey, all you have to do is forget once and leave your car unlocked. Some crack addict comes along, sees the buttons up, and decides to toss it in case there's anything worth stealing. He checks the glove compartment for money, sees the key in the plastic bag, and away he goes to find out who wants to buy a low-mileage Malibu for cash."

"What did your mother say to that?"

Jerome grins. "First thing, she turned it around. No one does that any better than my moms. She says, *You* bought the car and *you* brought it home. *You* should have told me. I'm eating my breakfast while they're having this little discussion and thought of saying, If you'd ever checked the owner's manual, Mom, maybe just to see what all those cute little lights on the dashboard signify, but I kept my mouth shut. My mom and dad don't get into it often, but when they do, a wise person steers clear. Even the Barbster knows that, and she's only nine."

It occurs to Hodges that when he and Corinne were married, this is something Alison also knew.

"The other thing she said was that she *never* forgets to lock her car. Which, so far as I know, is true. Anyway, that key is now hanging on one of the hooks in our kitchen. Safe, sound, and ready to go if the primary ever gets lost."

Hodges sits looking at the skateboarders but not seeing them. He's thinking that Jerome's mom had a point when she said her husband should have either presented her with the spare key or at least told her about it. You don't just assume people will do an inventory and find things by themselves. But Olivia Trelawney's case was different. She bought her own car, and should have known.

Only the salesman had probably overloaded her with info about her expensive new purchase; they had a way of doing that. When to change the oil, how to use the cruise control, how to use the GPS, don't forget to put your spare key in a safe place, here's how you plug in your cell phone, here's the number to call roadside assistance if you need it, click the headlight switch all the way to the left to engage the twilight function.

Hodges could remember buying his first new car and letting the guy's post-sales tutorial wash over him—uh-huh, yep, right, gotcha—just anxious to get his new purchase out on the road, to dig the rattle-free ride and inhale that incomparable new-car smell, which to the buyer is the aroma of money well spent. But Mrs. T. was obsessive-compulsive. He could believe she'd overlooked the spare key and left it in the glove compartment, but if she had taken her primary key that Thursday night, wouldn't she also have locked the car doors? She said she did, had maintained that to the very end, and really, think about it—

"Mr. Hodges?"

"With the new smart keys, it's a simple three-step process, isn't

136

it?" he says. "Step one, turn off the engine. Step two, remove the key from the ignition. If your mind's on something else and you forget step two, there's a chime to remind you. Step three, close the door and push the button stamped with the padlock icon. Why would you forget that, with the key right there in your hand? Theft-Proofing for Dummies."

"True-dat, Mr. H., but some dummies forget, anyway."

Hodges is too lost in thought for reticence. "She was no dummy. Nervous and twitchy but not stupid. If she took her key, I almost have to believe she locked her car. And the car wasn't broken into. So even if she *did* leave the spare in her glove compartment, how did the guy get to it?"

"So it's a locked-car mystery instead of a locked room. Dis be a *fo'*-pipe problem!"

Hodges doesn't reply. He's going over it and over it. That the spare might have been in the glove compartment now seems obvious, but did either he or Pete ever raise the possibility? He's pretty sure they didn't. Because they thought like men? Or because they were pissed at Mrs. T.'s carelessness and wanted to blame her? And she *was* to blame, wasn't she?

Not if she really did lock her car, he thinks.

"Mr. Hodges, what does that Blue Umbrella website have to do with the Mercedes Killer?"

Hodges comes back out of his own head. He's been in deep, and it's a pretty long trudge. "I don't want to talk about that just now, Jerome."

"But maybe I can help!"

Has he ever seen Jerome this excited? Maybe once, when the debate team he captained his sophomore year won the citywide championship.

"Find out about that website and you will be helping," Hodges says.

"You don't want to tell me because I'm a kid. That's it, isn't it?"

It is part of the reason, but Hodges has no intention of saying so. And as it happens, there's something else.

"It's more complicated than that. I'm not a cop anymore, and investigating the City Center thing skates right up to the edge of what's legal. If I find anything out and don't tell my old partner, who's now the lead on the Mercedes Killer case, I'll be over the edge. You have a bright future ahead of you, including just about any college or university you decide to favor with your presence. What would I say to your mother and father if you got dragged into an investigation of my actions, maybe as an accomplice?"

Jerome sits quietly, digesting this. Then he gives the end of his cone to Odell, who accepts it eagerly. "I get it."

"Do you?"

"Yeah."

Jerome stands up and Hodges does the same. "Still friends?"

"Sure. But if you think I can help you, promise me that you'll ask. You know what they say, two heads are better than one."

"That's a deal."

They start back up the hill. At first Odell walks between them as before, then starts to pull ahead because Hodges is slowing down. He's also losing his breath. "I've got to drop some weight," he tells Jerome. "You know what? I tore the seat out of a perfectly good pair of pants the other day."

"You could probably stand to lose ten," Jerome says diplomatically.

"Double that and you'd be a lot closer."

"Want to stop and rest a minute?"

"No." Hodges sounds childish even to himself. He means it about the weight, though; when he gets back to the house, every damn snack in the cupboards and the fridge is going into the trash. Then he thinks, Make it the garbage disposal. Too easy to weaken and fish stuff out of the trash.

"Jerome, it would be best if you kept my little investigation to yourself. Can I trust your discretion?"

Jerome replies without hesitation. "Absolutely. Mum's the word."

"Good."

A block ahead, the Mr. Tastey truck jingles its way across Harper Road and heads down Vinson Lane. Jerome tips a wave. Hodges can't see if the ice cream man waves back.

"*Now* we see him," Hodges said.

Jerome turns, gives him a grin. "Ice cream man's like a cop."

"Huh?"

"Never around when you need him."

## 14

Brady rolls along, obeying the speed limit (twenty miles per here on Vinson Lane), hardly hearing the jingle and clang of "Buffalo Gals" from the speakers above him. He's wearing a sweater beneath his white Mr. Tastey jacket, because the load behind him is cold.

Like my mind, he thinks. Only ice cream is *just* cold. My mind is also analytical. It's a machine. A Mac loaded with gigs to the googolplex.

He turns it to what he has just seen, the fat ex-cop walking up Harper Road Hill with Jerome Robinson and the Irish setter with the nigger name. Jerome gave him a wave and Brady gave it right back, because that's the way you blend in. Like listening to Freddi Linklatter's endless rants about how tough it was to be a gay woman in a straight world.

Kermit William "I wish I was young" Hodges and Jerome "I wish I was white" Robinson. What was the Odd Couple talking about? That's something Brady Hartsfield would like to know. Maybe he'll find out if the cop takes the bait and strikes up a conversation on Debbie's Blue Umbrella. It certainly worked with the rich bitch; once she started talking, nothing could stop her.

The Det-Ret and his darkie houseboy.

Also Odell. Don't forget Odell. Jerome and his little sister love that dog. It would really break them up if something happened to it. Probably nothing will, but maybe he'll research some more poisons on the Net when he gets home tonight.

STEPHEN KING

Such thoughts are always flitting through Brady's mind; they are the bats in his belfry. This morning at DE, as he was inventorying another load of cheap-ass DVDs (why more are coming in at the same time they're trying to dump stock is a mystery that will never be solved), it occurred to him that he could use his suicide vest to assassinate the president, Mr. Barack "I wish I was white" Obama. Go out in a blaze of glory. Barack comes to this state often, because it's important to his re-election strategy. And when he comes to the state, he comes to this city. Has a rally. Talks about hope. Talks about change. Rah-rah-rah, blah-blah-blah. Brady was figuring out how to avoid metal detectors and random checks when Tones Frobisher buzzed him and told him he had a service call. By the time he was on the road in one of the green Cyber Patrol VWs, he was thinking about something else. Brad Pitt, to be exact. Fucking matinee idol.

Sometimes, though, his ideas stick.

A chubby little boy comes running down the sidewalk, waving money. Brady pulls over.

*"I want chawww-klit!"* the little boy brays. *"And I want it with springles!"*

You got it, you fatass little creep, Brady thinks, and smiles his widest, most charming smile. Fuck up your cholesterol all you want, I give you until forty, and who knows, maybe you'll survive the first heart attack. That won't stop you, though, nope. Not when the world is full of beer and Whoppers and chocolate ice cream.

"You got it, little buddy. One chocolate with sprinkles coming right up. How was school? Get any As?"


15


That night the TV never goes on at 63 Harper Road, not even for the *Evening News*. Nor does the computer. Hodges hauls out his trusty legal pad instead. Janelle Patterson called him old school.

So he is, and he doesn't apologize for it. This is the way he has always worked, the way he's most comfortable.

Sitting in beautiful no-TV silence, he reads over the letter Mr. Mercedes sent him. Then he reads the one Mrs. T. got. Back and forth he goes for an hour or more, examining the letters line by line. Because Mrs. T.'s letter is a copy, he feels free to jot in the margins and circle certain words.

He finishes this part of his procedure by reading the letters aloud. He uses different voices, because Mr. Mercedes has adopted two different personae. The letter Hodges received is gloating and arrogant. *Ha-ha, you broken-down old fool*, it says. *You have nothing to live for and you know it, so why don't you just kill yourself?* The tone of Olivia Trelawney's letter is cringing and melancholy, full of remorse and tales of childhood abuse, but here also is the idea of suicide, this time couched in terms of sympathy: *I understand. I totally get it, because I feel the same.*

At last he puts the letters in a folder with MERCEDES KILLER printed on the tab. There's nothing else in it, which means it's mighty thin, but if he's still any good at his job, it will thicken with page after page of his own notes.

He sits for fifteen minutes, hands folded on his too-large middle like a meditating Buddha. Then he draws the pad to him and begins writing.

*I think I was right about most of the stylistic red herrings. In Mrs. T.'s letter he doesn't use exclamation points, capitalized phrases, or many one-sentence paragraphs (the ones at the end are for dramatic effect). I was wrong about the quotation marks, he likes those. Also fond of underlining things. He may not be young after all, I could have been wrong about that . . .*

But he thinks of Jerome, who has already forgotten more about computers and the Internet than Hodges himself will ever learn. And of Janey Patterson, who knew how to make a copy of her sister's letter by scanning, and who uses Skype. Janey Patterson, who's got to be almost twenty years younger than he is.

He picks up his pen again.

*. . . but I don't think I am. Probably not a teenager (altho can't rule it out) but let's say in the range 20–35. He's smart. Good vocabulary, able to turn a phrase.*

He goes through the letters yet again and jots down some of those turned phrases: *scurrying little mouse of a kid, strawberry jam in a sleeping bag, most people are sheep and sheep don't eat meat.*

Nothing that would make people forget Philip Roth, but Hodges thinks such lines show a degree of talent. He finds one more and prints it below the others: *What have they done for you except hound you and cause you sleepless nights?*

He taps the tip of his pen above this, creating a constellation of tiny dark blue dots. He thinks most people would write *give you sleepless nights* or *bring you sleepless nights*, but those weren't good enough for Mr. Mercedes, because he is a gardener planting seeds of doubt and paranoia. *They* are out to get you, Mrs. T., and *they* have a point, don't they? Because you *did* leave your key. The cops say so; I say so too, and I was there. How can we both be wrong?

He writes these ideas down, boxes them, then turns to a fresh sheet.

*Best point of identification is still PERK for PERP, he uses it in both letters, but also note HYPHENS in the Trelawney letter.* Bee-hive *instead of beehive.* Week-days *instead of weekdays. If I am able to ID this guy and get a writing sample, I can nail him.*

Such stylistic fingerprints wouldn't be enough to convince a jury, but Hodges himself? Absolutely.

He sits back again, head tilted, eyes fixed on nothing. He isn't aware of time passing; for Hodges, time, which has hung so heavy since his retirement, has been canceled. Then he lurches forward, office chair squalling an unheard protest, and writes in large capital letters: *HAS MR. MERCEDES BEEN WATCHING?*

Hodges feels all but positive he has been. That it's his MO.

He followed Mrs. Trelawney's vilification in the newspapers, he watched her two or three appearances on the TV news (curt and unflattering, those appearances drove her already low approval ratings into the basement). He may have done drive-bys on her house as well. Hodges should talk to Radney Peeples again and find out if Peeples or any other Vigilant employees noted certain cars cruising Mrs. Trelawney's Sugar Heights neighborhood in the weeks before she caught the bus. And someone sprayed KILLER CUNT on one of her gateposts. How long before her suicide was that? Maybe Mr. Mercedes did it himself. And of course, he could have gotten to know her better, *lots* better, if she took him up on his invitation to meet under the Blue Umbrella.

Then there's me, he thinks, and looks at the way his own letter ends: *I wouldn't want you to start thinking about your gun* followed by *But you* are *thinking of it, aren't you?* Is Mr. Mercedes talking about his theoretical service weapon, or has he seen the .38 Hodges sometimes plays with? No way of telling, but . . .

But I think he has. He knows where I live, you can look right into my living room from the street, and I think he's seen it.

The idea that he's been watched fills Hodges with excitement rather than dread or embarrassment. If he could match some vehicle the Vigilant people have noticed with a vehicle spending an inordinate amount of time on Harper Road—

That's when the telephone rings.

16

"Hi, Mr. H."

"S'up, Jerome?"

"I'm under the Umbrella."

Hodges puts his legal pad aside. The first four pages are now full of disjointed notes, the next three with a close-written case summary, just like in the old days. He rocks back in his chair.

"It didn't eat your computer, I take it?"

"Nope. No worms, no viruses. And I've already got four offers to talk with new friends. One's from Abilene, Texas. She says her name is Bernice, but I can call her Berni. With an *i*. She sounds cute as hell, and I won't say I'm not tempted, but she's probably a cross-dressing shoe salesman from Boston who lives with his mother. The Internet, dude—it's a wonderbox."

Hodges grins.

"First the background, which I partly got from poking around that selfsame Internet and mostly from a couple of Computer Science geeks at the university. You ready?"

Hodges grabs his legal pad again and turns to a fresh page. "Hit me." Which is exactly what he used to say to Pete Huntley when Pete came in with fresh information on a case.

"Okay, but first . . . do you know what the most precious Internet commodity is?"

"Nope." And, thinking of Janey Patterson: "I'm old school."

Jerome laughs. "That you are, Mr. Hodges. It's part of your charm."

Dryly: "Thank you, Jerome."

"The most precious commodity is privacy, and that's what Debbie's Blue Umbrella and sites like it deliver. They make Facebook look like a partyline back in the nineteen-fifties. Hundreds of privacy sites have sprung up since 9/11. That's when the various first-world governments really started to get snoopy. The powers that be fear the Net, dude, and they're right to fear it. Anyway, most of these EP sites—stands for *extreme privacy*—operate out of Central Europe. They are to Internet chat what Switzerland is to bank accounts. You with me?"

"Yeah."

"The Blue Umbrella servers are in Olovo, a Bosnian ville that was mostly known for bullfights until 2005 or so. Encrypted servers. We're talking NASA quality, okay? Traceback's impossible, unless NSA or the Kang Sheng—that's the Chinese version of the NSA—have got some super-secret software nobody knows about."

And even if they do, Hodges thinks, they'd never put it to use in a case like the Mercedes Killer.

"Here's another feature, especially handy in the age of sexting scandals. Mr. H., have you ever found something on the Net—like a picture or an article in a newspaper—that you wanted to print, and you couldn't?"

"A few times, yeah. You hit print, and the Print Preview shows nothing but a blank page. It's annoying."

"Same thing on Debbie's Blue Umbrella." Jerome doesn't sound annoyed; he sounds admiring. "I had a little back-and-forth with my new friend Berni—you know, how's the weather there, what're your favorite groups, that kind of thing—and when I tried to print our conversation, I got a pair of lips with a finger across them and a message that says SHHH." Jerome spells this out, just to be sure Hodges gets it. "You *can* make a record of the conversation . . ."

You bet, Hodges thinks, looking fondly down at the jotted notes on his legal pad.

". . . but you'd have to take screen-shots or something, which is a pain in the ass. You see what I mean about the privacy, right? These guys are serious about it."

Hodges does see. He flips back to the first page of his legal pad and circles one of his earliest notes: COMPUTER SAVVY (UNDER 50?).

"When you click in, you get the usual choice—ENTER USER-NAME or REGISTER NOW. Since I didn't have a username, I clicked REGISTER NOW and got one. If you want to talk with me under the Blue Umbrella, I'm tyrone40. Next, there's a question-naire you fill out—age, sex, interests, things like that—and then you have to punch in your credit card number. It's thirty bucks a month. I did it because I have faith in your powers of reimbursement."

"Your faith will be rewarded, my son."

"The computer thinks it over for ninety seconds or so—the Blue Umbrella spins and the screen says SORTING. Then you get a list of people with interests similar to yours. You just bang on a few and pretty soon you're chatting up a storm."

"Could people use this to exchange porn? I know the descriptor says you can't, but—"

"You could use it to exchange *fantasies*, but no pix. Although I could see how weirdos—child abusers, crush freaks, that kind of thing—could use the Blue Umbrella to direct like-minded friends to sites where outlaw images *are* available."

Hodges starts to ask what crush freaks are, then decides he doesn't want to know.

"Mostly just innocent chat, then."

"Well . . ."

"Well what?"

"I can see how crazies might use it to exchange badass info. Like how to build bombs and stuff."

"Let's say I already have a username. What happens then?"

"Do you?" The excitement is back in Jerome's voice.

"Let's say I do."

"That would depend on whether you just made it up or if you got it from someone who wants to chat with you. Like he gave it to you on the phone or in an email."

Hodges grins. Jerome, a true child of his times, has never considered the possibility that information could be conveyed by such a nineteenth-century vehicle as a letter.

"Say you got it from someone else," Jerome goes on. "Like from the guy who stole that lady's car. Like maybe he wants to talk to you about what he did."

He waits. Hodges says nothing, but he is all admiration.

After a few seconds of silence, Jerome says, "Can't blame a guy for trying. Anyway, you go on and enter the username."

"When do I pay my thirty bucks?"

"You don't."

"Why not?"

"Because someone's already paid it for you." Jerome sounds sober now. Dead serious. "Probably don't need to tell you to be careful, but I will, anyway. Because if you already have a username, this guy's waiting for you."

17

Brady stops on his way home to get them supper (subs from Little Chef tonight), but his mother is gorked out on the couch. The TV is showing another of those reality things, a program that pimps a bunch of good-looking young women to a hunky bachelor who looks like he might have the IQ of a floor lamp. Brady sees Ma has already eaten—sort of. On the coffee table is a half-empty bottle of Smirnoff's and two cans of NutraSlim. High tea in hell, he thinks, but at least she's dressed: jeans and a City College sweatshirt.

On the off-chance, he unwraps her sandwich and wafts it back and forth beneath her nose, but she only snorts and turns her head away. He decides to eat that one himself and put the other one in his private fridge. When he comes back from the garage, the hunky bachelor is asking one of his potential fuck-toys (a blonde, of course) if she likes to cook breakfast. The blonde's simpering reply: "Do you like something hot in the morning?"

Holding the plate with his sandwich on it, he regards his mother. He knows it's possible he'll come home some evening and find her dead. He could even help her along, just pick up one of the throw pillows and settle it over her face. It wouldn't be the first time murder was committed in this house. If he did that, would his life be better or worse?

His fear—unarticulated by his conscious mind but swimming around beneath—is that *nothing* would change.

He goes downstairs, voice-commanding the lights and computers. He sits in front of Number Three and goes on Debbie's Blue Umbrella, sure that by now the fat ex-cop will have taken the bait.

There's nothing.

He smacks his fist into his palm, feeling a dull throb at his temples that is the sure harbinger of a headache, a migraine that's apt to keep him awake half the night. Aspirin doesn't touch those headaches when they come. He calls them the Little Witches, only sometimes the Little Witches are big. He knows there are pills that are supposed to relieve headaches like that—he's researched them on the Net—but you can't get them without a prescription, and Brady is terrified of doctors. What if one of them discovered he was suffering from a brain tumor? A glioblastoma, which Wikipedia says is the worst? What if that's why he killed the people at the job fair?

*Don't be stupid, a glio would have killed you months ago.*

Okay, but suppose the doctor said his migraines were a sign of mental illness? Paranoid schizophrenia, something like that? Brady accepts that he *is* mentally ill, of course he is, normal people don't drive into crowds of people or consider taking out the President of the United States in a suicide attack. Normal people don't kill their little brothers. Normal men don't pause outside their mothers' doors, wondering if they're naked.

But abnormal men don't like other people to *know* they're abnormal.

He shuts off his computer and wanders aimlessly around his control room. He picks up Thing Two, then puts it down again. Even this isn't original, he's discovered; car thieves have been using gadgets like this for years. He hasn't dared to use it since the last time he used it on Mrs. Trelawney's Mercedes, but maybe it's time to bring good old Thing Two out of retirement—it's amazing what people leave in their cars. Using Thing Two is a little dangerous, but not very. Not if he's careful, and Brady can be very careful.

*Fucking ex-cop, why hasn't he taken the bait?*

Brady rubs his temples.


18


Hodges hasn't taken the bait because he understands the stakes: pot limit. If he writes the wrong message, he'll never hear from Mr. Mercedes again. On the other hand, if he does what he's sure Mr. Mercedes expects—coy and clumsy efforts to discover who the guy is—the conniving sonofabitch will run rings around him.

The question to be answered before he starts is simple: who is going to be the fish in this relationship, and who is going to be the fisherman?

He has to write something, because the Blue Umbrella is all he has. He can call on none of his old police resources. The letters Mr. Mercedes wrote to Olivia Trelawney and Hodges himself are worthless without a suspect. Besides, a letter is just a letter, while computer chat is . . .

"A dialogue," he says.

Only he needs a lure. The tastiest lure imaginable. He can pretend he's suicidal, it wouldn't be hard, because until very recently he has been. He's sure that meditations on the attractiveness of death would keep Mr. Mercedes talking for awhile, but for how long before the guy realized he was being played? This is no hopped-up moke who believes the police really are going to give him a million dollars and a 747 that will fly him to El Salvador. Mr. Mercedes is a very intelligent person who happens to be crazy.

Hodges draws his legal pad onto his lap and turns to a fresh page. Halfway down he writes half a dozen words in large capitals:

I HAVE TO WIND HIM UP.

He puts a box around this, places the legal pad in the case file he has started, and closes the thickening folder. He sits a moment longer, looking at the screensaver photo of his daughter, who is no longer five and no longer thinks he's God.

"Good night, Allie."

He turns off his computer and goes to bed. He doesn't expect to sleep, but he does.

## 19

He wakes up at 2:19 A.M. by the bedside clock with the answer as bright in his mind as a neon bar sign. It's risky but right, the kind of thing you do without hesitation or you don't do at all. He goes into his office, a large pale ghost in boxer shorts. He powers up his computer. He goes to Debbie's Blue Umbrella and clicks GET STARTED NOW!

A new image appears. This time the young couple is on what looks like a magic carpet floating over an endless sea. The silver

STEPHEN KING

rain is falling, but they are safe and dry beneath the blue umbrella. There are two buttons below the carpet, REGISTER NOW on the left and ENTER PASSWORD on the right. Hodges clicks ENTER PASSWORD, and in the box that appears he types **kermitfrog19**. He hits return and a new screen appears. On it is this message:

**merckill wants to chat with you!**
**Do you want to chat with merckill?**
**Y N**

He puts the cursor on **Y** and clicks his mouse. A box for his message appears. Hodges types quickly, without hesitation.

20

Three miles away, at 49 Elm Street in Northfield, Brady Hartsfield can't sleep. His head thumps. He thinks: *Frankie.* My brother, who should have died when he choked on that apple slice. Life would have been so much simpler if things had happened that way.

He thinks of his mother, who sometimes forgets her nightgown and sleeps raw.

Most of all, he thinks of the fat ex-cop.

At last he gets up and leaves his bedroom, pausing for a moment outside his mother's door, listening to her snore. The most unerotic sound in the universe, he tells himself, but still he pauses. Then he goes downstairs, opens the basement door, and closes it behind him. He stands in the dark and says, "Control." But his voice is too hoarse and the dark remains. He clears his throat and tries again. "Control!"

The lights come on. *Chaos* lights up his computers and *darkness* stops the seven-screen countdown. He sits in front of his Number Three. Among the litter of icons is a small blue umbrella. He clicks on it, unaware that he's been holding his breath until he lets it out in a long harsh gasp.

150

**kermitfrog19 wants to chat with you!**
**Do you want to chat with kermitfrog19?**
**Y N**

Brady hits **Y** and leans forward. His eager expression remains for a moment before puzzlement seeps in. Then, as he reads the short message over and over, puzzlement becomes first anger and then naked fury.

**Seen a lot of false confessions in my time, but this one's a dilly.**
**I'm retired but not stupid.**
**Withheld evidence proves you are not the Mercedes Killer.**
**Fuck off, asshole.**

Brady feels an almost insurmountable urge to slam his fist through the screen but restrains it. He sits in his chair, trembling all over. His eyes are wide and unbelieving. A minute passes. Two. Three.

Pretty soon I'll get up, he thinks. Get up and go back to bed.

Only what good will that do? He won't be able to sleep.

"You fat fuck," he whispers, unaware that hot tears have begun to spill from his eyes. "You fat stupid useless fuck. It *was* me! It *was* me! *It was me!*"

**Withheld evidence proves.**

That is impossible.

He seizes on the necessity of hurting the fat ex-cop, and with the idea the ability to think returns. How should he do that? He considers the question for nearly half an hour, trying on and rejecting several scenarios. The answer, when it comes, is elegantly simple. The fat ex-cop's friend—his only friend, so far as Brady has been able to ascertain—is a nigger kid with a white name. And what does the nigger kid love? What does his whole family love? The Irish setter, of course. Odell.

Brady recalls his earlier fantasy about poisoning a few gallons of Mr. Tastey's finest, and starts laughing. He goes on the Internet and begins doing research.

My due diligence, he thinks, and smiles.

At some point he realizes his headache is gone.

# POISON BAIT

1

Brady Hartsfield doesn't need long to figure out how he's going to poison Jerome Robinson's canine pal, Odell. It helps that Brady is also Ralph Jones, a fictional fellow with just enough bona fides— plus a low-limit Visa card—to order things from places like Amazon and eBay. Most people don't realize how easy it is to whomp up an Internet-friendly false identity. You just have to pay the bills. If you don't, things can come unraveled in a hurry.

As Ralph Jones he orders a two-pound can of Gopher-Go and gives Ralphie's mail drop address, the Speedy Postal not far from Discount Electronix.

The active ingredient in Gopher-Go is strychnine. Brady looks up the symptoms of strychnine poisoning on the Net and is delighted to find that Odell will have a tough time of it. Twenty minutes or so after ingestion, muscle spasms start in the neck and head. They quickly spread to the rest of the body. The mouth stretches in a grin (at least in humans; Brady doesn't know about dogs). There may be vomiting, but by then too much of the poison has been absorbed and it's too late. Convulsions set in and get worse until the backbone turns into a hard and constant arch. Sometimes the spine actually snaps. When death comes—as a relief, Brady is sure—it's as a result of asphyxiation. The neural pathways tasked with running air to the lungs from the outside world just give up.

155

Brady can hardly wait.

At least it won't be a *long* wait, he tells himself as he shuts off his seven computers and climbs the stairs. The stuff should be waiting for him next week. The best way to get it into the dog, he thinks, would be in a ball of nice juicy hamburger. All dogs like hamburger, and Brady knows exactly how he's going to deliver Odell's treat.

Barbara Robinson, Jerome's little sister, has a friend named Hilda. The two girls like to visit Zoney's GoMart, the convenience store a couple of blocks from the Robinson house. They say it's because they like the grape Icees, but what they really like is hanging out with their other little friends. They sit on the low stone wall at the back of the store's four-car parking lot, half a dozen chickadees gossiping and giggling and trading treats. Brady has seen them often when he's driving the Mr. Tastey truck. He waves to them and they wave back.

Everybody likes the ice cream man.

Mrs. Robinson allows Barbara to make these trips once or twice a week (Zoney's isn't a drug hangout, a thing she has probably investigated for herself), but she has put conditions on her approval that Brady has had no trouble deducing. Barbara can never go alone; she always must be back in an hour; she and her friend must always take Odell. No dogs are allowed in the GoMart, so Barbara tethers him to the doorhandle of the outside restroom while she and Hilda go inside to get their grape-flavored ice.

That's when Brady—driving his personal car, a nondescript Subaru—will toss Odell the lethal burger-ball. The dog is big; he may last twenty-four hours. Brady hopes so. Grief has a transitive power which is nicely expressed by the axiom *shit rolls downhill*. The more pain Odell feels, the more pain the nigger girl and her big brother will feel. Jerome will pass his grief on to the fat ex-cop, aka Kermit William Hodges, and the fat ex-cop will understand the dog's death is *his* fault, payback for sending Brady that infuriating and disrespectful message. When Odell dies, the fat ex-cop will know—

Halfway up to the second floor, listening to his mother snoring, Brady stops, eyes wide with dawning realization.

The fat ex-cop will *know*.

And that's the trouble, isn't it? Because actions have consequences. It's the reason why Brady might *daydream* about poisoning a load of the ice cream he sells the kiddies, but wouldn't actually *do* such a thing. Not as long as he wants to keep flying under the radar, that is, and for now he does.

So far Hodges hasn't gone to his pals in the police department with the letter Brady sent. At first Brady believed it was because Hodges wanted to keep it between the two of them, maybe take a shot at tracking down the Mercedes Killer himself and getting a little post-retirement glory, but now he knows better. Why would the fucking Det-Ret want to track him down when he thinks Brady's nothing but a crank?

Brady can't understand how Hodges could come to that conclusion when he, Brady, knew about the bleach and the hairnet, details never released to the press, but somehow he has. If Brady poisons Odell, Hodges will call in his police pals. Starting with his old partner, Huntley.

Worse, it may give the man Brady hoped to goad into suicide a new reason to live, defeating the whole *purpose* of the artfully composed letter. That would be completely unfair. Pushing the Trelawney bitch over the edge had been the greatest thrill of his life, far greater (for reasons he doesn't understand, or care to) than killing all those people with her car, and he wanted to do it again. To get the chief investigator in the case to kill himself—what a triumph that would be!

Brady is standing halfway up the stairs, thinking hard.

The fat bastard still might do it, he tells himself. Killing the dog might be the final push he needs.

Only he doesn't really buy this, and his head gives a warning throb.

He feels a sudden urge to rush back down to the basement, go on the Blue Umbrella, and demand that the fat ex-cop tell him what bullshit "withheld evidence" he's talking about so he, Brady, can knock it down. But to do that would be a bad mistake. It would look needy, maybe even desperate.

Withheld evidence.

**Fuck off, asshole.**

*But I did it! I risked my freedom, I risked my life, and I did it! You can't take away the credit! It's not fair!*

His head throbs again.

You stupid cocksucker, he thinks. One way or the other, you're going to pay, but not until after the dog dies. Maybe your nigger friend will die, too. Maybe that whole nigger family will die. And after them, maybe a whole lot of other people. Enough to make what happened at City Center look like a picnic.

He goes up to his room and lies down on his bed in his underwear. His head is banging again, his arms are trembling (it's as if *he* has ingested strychnine). He'll lie here in agony until morning, unless—

He gets up and goes back down the hall. He stands outside his mother's open door for almost four minutes, then gives up and goes inside. He gets into bed with her and his headache begins to recede almost at once. Maybe it's the warmth. Maybe it's the smell of her—shampoo, body lotion, booze. Probably it's both.

She turns over. Her eyes are wide in the dark. "Oh, honeyboy. Are you having one of those nights?"

"Yes." He feels the warmth of tears in his eyes.

"Little Witch?"

"*Big* Witch this time."

"Want me to help you?" She already knows the answer; it's throbbing against her stomach. "You do so much for me," she says tenderly. "Let me do this for you."

He closes his eyes. The smell of the booze on her breath is very strong. He doesn't mind, although ordinarily he hates it. "Okay."

She takes care of him swiftly and expertly. It doesn't take long. It never does.

"There," she says. "Go to sleep now, honeyboy."

He does, almost at once.

When he wakes in the early morning light she's snoring again, a lock of hair spit-stuck to the corner of her mouth. He gets out of bed and goes back to his own room. His mind is clear. The strychnine-laced gopher poison is on its way. When it arrives, he'll poison the dog, and damn the consequences. *God* damn the consequences. As for those suburban niggers with the white-people names? They don't matter. The fat ex-cop goes next, after he's had a chance to fully experience Jerome Robinson's pain and Barbara Robinson's sorrow, and who cares if it's suicide? The important thing is that he *go*. And after that . . .

"Something big," he says as he pulls on a pair of jeans and a plain white tee. "A blaze of glory." Just what the blaze will be he doesn't know yet, but that's okay. He has time, and he needs to do something first. He needs to demolish Hodges's so-called "withheld evidence" and convince him that he, Brady, is indeed the Mercedes Killer, the monster Hodges failed to catch. He needs to rub it in until it hurts. He also needs it because if Hodges believes in this bogus "withheld evidence," the other cops—the *real* cops—must believe it, too. That is unacceptable. He needs . . .

"Credibility!" Brady exclaims to the empty kitchen. "I need credibility!"

He sets about making breakfast: bacon and eggs. The smell may waft upstairs to Ma and tempt her. If not, no big deal. He'll eat her share. He's pretty hungry.

2

This time it works, although when Deborah Ann appears, she's still belting her robe and barely awake. Her eyes are red-rimmed, her cheeks are pale, and her hair flies out every whichway. She no longer suffers hangovers, exactly, her brain and body have gotten too used to the booze for that, but she spends her mornings in a state of soft focus, watching game shows and popping Tums. Around two in the afternoon, when the world starts to sharpen up for her, she pours the day's first drink.

If she remembers what happened last night, she doesn't mention it. But then, she never does. Neither of them do.

*We never talk about Frankie, either,* Brady thinks. *And if we did, what would we say? Gosh, too bad about that fall he took?*

"Smells good," she says. "Some for me?"

"All you want. Coffee?"

"Please. Lots of sugar." She sits down at the table and stares at the television on the counter. It isn't on, but she stares at it anyway. For all Brady knows, maybe she thinks it *is* on.

"You're not wearing your uniform," she says—meaning the blue button-up shirt with DISCOUNT ELECTRONIX on the pocket. He has three hanging in his closet. He irons them himself. Like vacuuming the floors and washing their clothes, ironing isn't in Ma's repertoire.

"Don't need to go in until ten," he says, and as if the words are a magic incantation, his phone wakes up and starts buzzing across the kitchen counter. He catches it just before it can fall off onto the floor.

"Don't answer it, honeyboy. Pretend we went out for breakfast."

It's tempting, but Brady is as incapable of letting a phone ring as he is of giving up his muddled and ever-changing plans for some grand act of destruction. He looks at the caller ID and isn't surprised to see TONES in the window. Anthony "Tones" Frobisher, the grand high panjandrum of Discount Electronix (Birch Hill Mall branch).

He picks up the phone and says, "It's my late day, Tones."

"I know, but I need you to make a service call. I really, really do." Tones can't *make* Brady take a call on his late day, hence the wheedling tone. "Plus it's Mrs. Rollins, and you know she tips."

Of course she does, she lives in Sugar Heights. The Cyber Patrol makes lots of service calls in Sugar Heights, and one of their customers—one of *Brady's* customers—was the late Olivia Trelawney.

He was in her house twice on calls after he began conversing with her beneath Debbie's Blue Umbrella, and what a kick *that* was. Seeing how much weight she'd lost. Seeing how her hands had started to tremble. Also, having access to her computer had opened all sorts of possibilities.

"I don't know, Tones . . ." But of course he'll go, and not only because Mrs. Rollins tips. It's fun to go rolling past 729 Lilac Drive, thinking: *I'm* responsible for those closed gates. All I had to do to give her the final push was add one little program to her Mac.

Computers are wonderful.

"Listen, Brady, if you take this call, you don't have to work the store at all today, how's that? Just return the Beetle and then hang out wherever until it's time to fire up your stupid ice cream wagon."

"What about Freddi? Why don't you send her?" Flat-out teasing now. If Tones could have sent Freddi, she'd already be on her way.

"Called in sick. Says she got her period and it's killing her. Of course it's fucking bullshit. I know it, she knows it, and she knows I know it, but she'll put in a sexual harassment claim if I call her on it. She knows I know *that*, too."

Ma sees Brady smiling, and smiles back. She raises a hand, closes it, and turns it back and forth. *Twist his balls, honeyboy.* Brady's smile widens into a grin. Ma may be a drunk, she may only cook once or twice a week, she can be as annoying as shit, but sometimes she can read him like a book.

"All right," Brady says. "How about I take my own car?"

"You know I can't give you a mileage allowance for your personal vehicle," Tones says.

"Also, it's company policy," Brady says. "Right?"

"Well . . . yeah."

Schyn Ltd., DE's German parent company, believes the Cyber Patrol VWs are good advertising. Freddi Linklatter says that anyone who wants a guy driving a snot-green Beetle to fix his computer is insane, and on this point Brady agrees with her. Still, there must be a lot of insane people out there, because they never lack for service calls.

Although few tip as well as Paula Rollins.

"Okay," Brady says, "but you owe me one."

"Thanks, buddy."

Brady kills the connection without bothering to say You're not my buddy, and we both know it.

3

Paula Rollins is a full-figured blonde who lives in a sixteen-room faux Tudor mansion three blocks from the late Mrs. T.'s pile. She has all those rooms to herself. Brady doesn't know exactly what her deal is, but guesses she's some rich guy's second or third ex–trophy wife, and that she did very well for herself in the settlement. Maybe the guy was too entranced by her knockers to bother with the prenup. Brady doesn't care much, he only knows she has enough to tip well and she's never tried to slap the make on him. That's good. He has no interest in Mrs. Rollins's full figure.

She *does* grab his hand and just about pull him through the door, though.

"Oh . . . Brady! Thank God!"

She sounds like a woman being rescued from a desert island after three days without food or water, but he hears the little pause before she says his name and sees her eyes flick down to read it off his shirt, even though he's been here half a dozen times. (So has Freddi, for that matter; Paula Rollins is a serial computer abuser.) He doesn't mind that she doesn't remember him. Brady likes being forgettable.

"It just . . . I don't know what's *wrong*!"

As if the dimwitted twat ever does. Last time he was here, six weeks ago, it was a kernel panic, and she was convinced a computer virus had gobbled up all her files. Brady shooed her gently from the office and promised (not sounding too hopeful) to do what he could. Then he sat down, re-started the computer, and surfed for awhile before calling her in and telling her he had been able to fix the problem just in time. Another half hour, he said, and her files really *would* have been gone. She had tipped him eighty dollars. He and Ma had gone out to dinner that night, and split a not-bad bottle of champagne.

"Tell me what happened," Brady says, grave as a neurosurgeon.

"I didn't do *anything*," she wails. She always wails. Many of his service call customers do. Not just the women, either. Nothing can unman a top-shelf executive more rapidly than the possibility that everything on his MacBook just went to data heaven.

She pulls him through the parlor (it's as long as an Amtrak dining car) and into her office.

"I cleaned up myself, I never let the housekeeper in here—washed the windows, vacuumed the floor—and when I sat down to do my email, the damn computer wouldn't even *turn on*!"

"Huh. Weird." Brady knows Mrs. Rollins has a spic maid to do the household chores, but apparently the maid isn't allowed in the office. Which is a good thing for her, because Brady has already spotted the problem, and if the maid had been responsible for it, she probably would have been fired.

"Can you fix it, Brady?" Thanks to the tears swimming in them, Mrs. Rollins's big blue eyes are bigger than ever. Brady suddenly flashes on Betty Boop in those old cartoons you can look at on You-Tube, thinks *Poop-poop-pe-doop!*, and has to restrain a laugh.

"I'll sure try," he says gallantly.

"I have to run across the street to Helen Wilcox's," she says, "but I'll only be a few minutes. There's fresh coffee in the kitchen, if you want it."

So saying, she leaves him alone in her big expensive house, with fuck knows how many valuable pieces of jewelry scattered around upstairs. She's safe, though. Brady would never steal from a service client. He might be caught in the act. Even if he weren't, who would be the logical suspect? Duh. He didn't get away with mowing down those job-seeking idiots at City Center only to be arrested for stealing a pair of diamond earrings he wouldn't have any idea how to get rid of.

He waits until the back door shuts, then goes into the parlor to watch her accompany her world-class tits across the street. When she's out of sight, he goes back to the office, crawls under her desk, and plugs in her computer. She must have yanked the plug so she could vacuum, then forgot to jack it back in.

Her password screen comes on. Idly, just killing time, he types PAULA, and her desktop, loaded with all her files, appears. God, people are so dumb.

He goes on Debbie's Blue Umbrella to see if the fat ex-cop has posted anything new. He hasn't, but Brady decides on the spur of the moment to send the Det-Ret a message after all. Why not?

He learned in high school that thinking too long about writing doesn't work for him. Too many other ideas get into his head and start sliding all over each other. It's better to just fire away. That was how he wrote to Olivia Trelawney—white heat, baby—and it's also the way he wrote to Hodges, although he went over the message to the fat ex-cop a couple of times to make sure he was keeping his style consistent.

He writes in the same style now, only reminding himself to keep it short.

> **How did I know about the hairnet and bleach, Detective Hodges? THAT STUFF was withheld evidence because it was never in the paper or on TV. You say you are not stupid but IT SURE LOOKS THAT WAY TO ME. I think all that TV you watch has rotted your brain.**
> **WHAT withheld evidence?**
> **I DARE YOU TO ANSWER THIS.**

Brady looks this over and makes one change: a hyphen in the middle of *hairnet*. He can't believe he'll ever become a person of interest, but he knows that if he ever does, they'll ask him to provide a writing sample. He almost wishes he could give them one. He wore a mask when he drove into the crowd, and he wears another when he writes as the Mercedes Killer.

He hits SEND, then pulls down Mrs. Rollins's Internet history. For a moment he stops, bemused, when he sees several entries for White Tie and Tails. He knows what that is from something Freddi Linklatter told him: a male escort service. Paula Rollins has a secret life, it seems.

But then, doesn't everybody?

It's no business of his. He deletes his visit to Under Debbie's Blue Umbrella, then opens his boxy service crate and takes out a bunch of random crap: utility discs, a modem (broken, but she won't know that), various thumb-drives, and a voltage regulator that has nothing whatsoever to do with computer repair but looks technological. He also takes out a Lee Child paperback that he reads until he hears his client come in the back door twenty minutes later.

When Mrs. Rollins pokes her head into the study, the paperback is out of sight and Brady is packing up the random shit. She favors him with an anxious smile. "Any luck?"

"At first it looked bad," Brady says, "but I tracked down your problem. The trimmer switch was bad and that shut down your danus circuit. In a case like that, the computer's programmed not to start up, because if it did, you might lose all your data." He looks at her gravely. "The darn thing might even catch fire. It's been known to happen."

"Oh . . . my . . . dear . . . *Jesus*," she says, packing each word with drama and placing one hand high on her chest. "Are you sure it's okay?"

"Good as gold," he says. "Check it out."

He starts the computer and looks politely away while she types in her numbfuck password. She opens a couple of files, then turns to him, smiling. "Brady, you are a gift from God."

"My ma used to tell me the same thing until I got old enough to buy beer."

She laughs as if this were the funniest thing she has heard in her whole life. Brady laughs with her, because he has a sudden vision: kneeling on her shoulders and driving a butcher knife from her own kitchen deep into her screaming mouth.

He can almost feel the gristle giving way.

4

Hodges has been checking the Blue Umbrella site frequently, and he's reading the Mercedes Killer's follow-up message only minutes after Brady hit SEND.

Hodges is grinning, a big one that smooths his skin and makes him almost handsome. Their relationship has been officially established: Hodges the fisherman, Mr. Mercedes the fish. But a *wily* fish, he reminds himself, one capable of making a sudden lunge and snapping the line. He will have to be played carefully, reeled toward the boat slowly. If Hodges is able to do that, if he's patient, sooner or later Mr. Mercedes will agree to a meeting. Hodges is sure of it.

Because if he can't nudge me into offing myself, that leaves just one alternative, and that's murder.

The smart thing for Mr. Mercedes to do would be to just walk away; if he does that, the road ends. But he won't. He's pissed, but that's only part of it, and the small part, at that. Hodges wonders if Mr. Mercedes knows just how crazy he is. And if he knows there's one nugget of hard information here.

**I think all that TV you watch has rotted your brain.**

Up to this morning, Hodges has only suspected that Mr. Mercedes has been watching his house; now he knows. Motherfucker has been on the street, and more than once.

He grabs his legal pad and starts jotting possible follow-up messages. It has to be good, because his fish feels the hook. The pain of it makes him angry even though he doesn't yet know what it is. He needs to be a lot angrier before he figures it out, and that means taking a risk. Hodges must jerk the line to seat the hook deeper, despite the risk the line may break. What . . . ?

He remembers something Pete Huntley said at lunch, just a remark in passing, and the answer comes to him. Hodges writes on his pad, then rewrites, then polishes. He reads the finished message over and decides it will do. It's short and mean. There's something you forgot, sucka. Something a false confessor couldn't know. Or a real confessor, for that matter . . . unless Mr. Mercedes checked out his rolling murder weapon from stem to stern before climbing in, and Hodges is betting the guy didn't.

If he's wrong, the line snaps and the fish swims away. But there's an old saying: no risk, no reward.

He wants to send the message right away, but knows it's a bad idea. Let the fish swim around in circles a little longer with that bad old hook in his mouth. The question is what to do in the meantime. TV never had less appeal for him.

He gets an idea—they're coming in bunches this morning—and pulls out the bottom drawer of his desk. Here is a box filled with the small flip-up pads he used to carry with him when he and Pete were doing street interviews. He never expected to need one of these again, but he takes one now and stows it in the back pocket of his chinos.

It fits just right.

5

Hodges walks halfway down Harper Road, then starts knocking on doors, just like in the old days. Crossing and re-crossing the street, missing no one, working his way back. It's a weekday, but a surprising number of people answer his knock or ring. Some are stay-at-home moms, but many are retirees like himself, fortunate enough to have paid for their homes before the bottom fell out of the economy, but in less than great shape otherwise. Not living day-to-day or even week-to-week, maybe, but having to balance out the cost of food against the cost of all those old-folks medicines as the end of the month nears.

His story is simple, because simple is always best. He says there have been break-ins a few blocks over—kids, probably—and he's checking to see if anyone in his own neighborhood has noticed any vehicles that seem out of place, and have shown up more than once. They'd probably be cruising even slower than the twenty-five-mile-an-hour speed limit, he says. He doesn't have to say any more; they all watch the cop shows and know what "casing the joint" means.

He shows them his ID, which has RETIRED stamped in red across the name and vitals below his photo. He's careful to say that no, he hasn't been asked by the police to do this canvassing (the last thing in the world he wants is one of his neighbors calling the Murrow Building downtown to check up on him), it was his own idea. He lives in the neighborhood, too, after all, and has a personal stake in its security.

Mrs. Melbourne, the widow whose flowers so fascinated Odell, invites him in for coffee and cookies. Hodges takes her up on it because she seems lonely. It's his first real conversation with her, and he quickly realizes she's eccentric at best, downright bonkers at worst. Articulate, though. He has to give her that. She explains about the black SUVs she's observed ("With tinted windows you can't see through, just like on *24*"), and tells him about their special antennas. Whippers, she calls them, waving her hand back and forth to demonstrate.

"Uh-huh," Hodges says. "Let me make a note of that." He turns a page in his pad and jots *I have to get out of here* on the new one.

"That's a good idea," she says, bright-eyed. "I've just got to tell you how sorry I was when your wife left you, Detective Hodges. She did, didn't she?"

"We agreed to disagree," Hodges says with an amiability he doesn't feel.

"It's so nice to meet you in person and know you're keeping an eye out. Have another cookie."

Hodges glances at his watch, snaps his pad closed, and gets up. "I'd love to, but I'd better roll. Got a noon appointment."

She scans his bulk and says, "Doctor?"

"Chiropractor."

She frowns, transforming her face into a walnut shell with eyes. "Think that over, Detective Hodges. Back-crackers are dangerous. There are people who have lain down on those tables and never walked again."

She sees him to the door. As he steps onto the porch, she says, "I'd check on that ice cream man, too. This spring it seems like he's *always* around. Do you suppose Loeb's Ice Cream checks out the people they hire to drive those little trucks? I hope so, because that one looks suspicious. He might be a peedaroast."

"I'm sure their drivers have references, but I'll look into it."

"Another good idea!" she exclaims.

Hodges wonders what he'd do if she produced a long hook, like in the old-time vaudeville shows, and tried to yank him back inside. A childhood memory comes to him: the witch in *Hansel and Gretel*.

"Also—I just thought of this—I've seen several vans lately. They *look* like delivery vans—they have business names on them—but anyone can make up a business name, don't you think?"

"It's always possible," Hodges says, descending the steps.

"You should call in to number seventeen, too." She points down the hill. "It's almost all the way down to Hanover Street. They have people who come late, and play loud music." She sways forward in the doorway, almost bowing. "It could be a dope den. One of those crack houses."

Hodges thanks her for the tip and trudges across the street. Black SUVs and the Mr. Tastey guy, he thinks. Plus the delivery vans filled with Al Qaeda terrorists.

Across the street he finds a stay-at-home dad, Alan Bowfinger by name. "Just don't confuse me with Goldfinger," he says, and invites Hodges to sit in one of the lawn chairs on the left side of his house, where there's shade. Hodges is happy to take him up on this.

Bowfinger tells him that he makes a living writing greeting cards. "I specialize in the slightly snarky ones. Like on the outside it'll say, 'Happy Birthday! Who's the fairest of them all?' And when you open it up, there's a piece of shiny foil with a crack running down the middle of it."

"Yeah? And what's the message?"

Bowfinger holds up his hands, as if framing it. "'Not you, but we love you anyway.'"

"Kind of mean," Hodges ventures.

"True, but it ends with an expression of love. That's what sells the card. First the poke, then the hug. As to your purpose today, Mr. Hodges . . . or do I call you Detective?"

"Just Mister these days."

"I haven't seen anything but the usual traffic. No slow cruisers except people looking for addresses and the ice cream truck after school lets out." Bowfinger rolls his eyes. "Did you get an earful from Mrs. Melbourne?"

"Well . . ."

"She's a member of NICAP," Bowfinger says. "That stands for National Investigations Committee on Aerial Phenomena."

"Weather stuff? Tornadoes and cloud formations?"

"Flying saucers." Bowfinger raises his hands to the sky. "She thinks they walk among us."

Hodges says something that would never have passed his lips if he'd still been on active duty and conducting an official investigation. "She thinks Mr. Tastey might be a peedaroast."

Bowfinger laughs until tears squirt out of his eyes. "Oh God," he says. "That guy's been around for five or six years, driving his little truck and jingling his little bells. How many peeds do you think he's roasted in all that time?"

"Don't know," Hodges says, getting to his feet. "Dozens, probably." He holds out his hand and Bowfinger shakes it. Another thing Hodges is discovering about retirement: his neighbors have stories and personalities. Some of them are even interesting.

As he's putting his notepad away, a look of alarm comes over Bowfinger's face.

"What?" Hodges asks, at once on point.

Bowfinger points across the street and says, "You didn't eat any of her cookies, did you?"

"Yeah. Why?"

"I'd stay close to the toilet for a few hours, if I were you."

6

When he gets back to his house, his arches throbbing and his ankles singing high C, the light on his answering machine is blinking. It's Pete Huntley, and he sounds excited. "Call me," he says. "This is unbelievable. Un-fucking-real."

Hodges is suddenly, irrationally sure that Pete and his pretty new partner Isabelle have nailed Mr. Mercedes after all. He feels a deep stab of jealousy, and—crazy but true—anger. He hits Pete on speed-dial, his heart hammering, but his call goes right to voicemail.

"Got your message," Hodges says. "Call back when you can."

He kills the phone, then sits still, drumming his fingers on the edge of his desk. He tells himself it doesn't matter who catches the psycho sonofabitch, but it does. For one thing, it's certainly going to mean that his correspondence with the perk (funny how that word gets in your head) will come out, and that may put him in some fairly warm soup. But it's not the important thing. The important thing is that without Mr. Mercedes, things will go back to what they were: afternoon TV and playing with his father's gun.

He takes out his yellow legal pad and begins transcribing notes on his neighborhood walk-around. After a minute or two of this, he tosses the pad back into the case-folder and slams it closed. If Pete and Izzy Jaynes have popped the guy, Mrs. Melbourne's vans and sinister black SUVs don't mean shit.

He thinks about going on Debbie's Blue Umbrella and sending **merckill** a message: *Did they catch you?*

Ridiculous, but weirdly attractive.

His phone rings and he snatches it up, but it's not Pete. It's Olivia Trelawney's sister.

"Oh," he says. "Hi, Mrs. Patterson. How you doing?"

"I'm fine," she says, "and it's Janey, remember? Me Janey, you Bill."

"Janey, right."

"You don't sound exactly thrilled to hear from me, Bill." Is she being the tiniest bit flirty? Wouldn't that be nice.

"No, no, I'm happy you called, but I don't have anything to report."

"I didn't expect you would. I called about Mom. The nurse at Sunny Acres who's most familiar with her case works the day shift in the McDonald Building, where my mother has her little suite of rooms. I asked her to call if Mom brightened up. She still does that."

"Yes, you told me."

"Well, the nurse called just a few minutes ago to tell me Mom's back, at least for the time being. She might be clear for a day or two, then it's into the clouds again. Do you still want to go see her?"

"I think so," Hodges says cautiously, "but it would have to be this afternoon. I'm waiting on a call."

"Is it about the man who took her car?" Janey's excited. As I should be, Hodges tells himself.

"That's what I need to find out. Can I call you back?"

"Absolutely. You have my cell number?"

"Yeah."

"*Yeah,*" she says, gently mocking. It makes him smile, in spite of his nerves. "Call me as soon as you can."

"I will."

He breaks the connection, and the phone rings while it's still in his hand. This time it's Pete, and he's more excited than ever.

"Billy! I gotta go back, we've got him in an interview room—

IR4, as a matter of fact, remember how you always used to say that was your lucky one?—but I had to call you. We got him, partner, we fucking got him!"

"Got who?" Hodges asks, keeping his voice steady. His heartbeat is steady now, too, but the beats are hard enough to feel in his temples: *whomp* and *whomp* and *whomp*.

"Fucking Davis!" Pete shouts. "Who else?"

Davis. Not Mr. Mercedes but Donnie Davis, the camera-friendly wife murderer. Bill Hodges closes his eyes in relief. It's the wrong emotion to feel, but he feels it nevertheless.

He says, "So the body that game warden found near his cabin turned out to be Sheila Davis's? You're sure?"

"Positive."

"Who'd you blow to get the DNA results so fast?" When Hodges was on the force, they were lucky to get DNA results within a calendar month of sample submission, and six weeks was the average.

"We don't need DNA! For the trial, sure, but—"

"What do you mean, you don't—"

"Shut up and listen, okay? He just walked in off the street and copped to it. No lawyer, no bullshit justifications. Listened to the Miranda and said he didn't want a lawyer, only wanted to get it off his chest."

"Jesus. As smooth as he was in all the interviews we had with him? Are you sure he's not fucking with you? Playing some sort of long game?"

Thinking it's the kind of thing Mr. Mercedes would try to do if they nailed him. Not just a game but a *long* game. Isn't that why he tries to create alternate writing styles in his poison-pen letters?

"Billy, *it's not just his wife*. You remember those dollies he had on the side? Girls with big hair and inflated tits and names like Bobbi Sue?"

"Sure. What about them?"

"When this breaks, those young ladies are going to get on their knees and thank God they're still alive."

"I'm not following you."

"Turnpike Joe, Billy! Five women raped and killed at various Interstate rest stops between here and Pennsylvania, starting back in ninety-four and ending in oh-eight! Donnie Davis says it's him! *Davis is Turnpike Joe!* He's giving us times and places and descriptions. It all fits. This . . . it blows my mind!"

"Mine, too," Hodges says, and he absolutely means it. "Congratulations."

"Thanks, but I didn't do anything except show up this morning." Pete laughs wildly. "I feel like I won the Megabucks."

Hodges doesn't feel like that, but at least he hasn't *lost* the Megabucks. He still has a case to work.

"I gotta get back in there, Billy, before he changes his mind."

"Yeah, yeah, but Pete? Before you go?"

"What?"

"Get him a court-appointed."

"Ah, Billy—"

"I'm serious. Interrogate the shit out of him, but before you start, announce—for the record—that you're getting him lawyered up. You can wring him dry before anyone shows up at Murrow, but you have to get this right. Are you hearing me?"

"Yeah, okay. That's a good call. I'll have Izzy do it."

"Great. Now get back in there. Nail him down."

Pete actually crows. Hodges has read about people doing that, but hasn't ever heard it done—except by roosters—until now. "Turnpike Joe, Billy! *Fucking Turnpike Joe!* Do you believe it?"

He hangs up before his ex-partner can reply. Hodges sits where he is for almost five minutes, waiting until a belated case of the shakes subsides. Then he calls Janey Patterson.

"It wasn't about the man we're looking for?"

"Sorry, no. Another case."

"Oh. Too bad."

"Yeah. You'll still come with me to the nursing home?"

"You bet. I'll be waiting on the sidewalk."

Before leaving, he checks the Blue Umbrella site one last time.

Nothing there, and he has no intention of sending his own carefully crafted message today. Tonight will be soon enough. Let the fish feel the hook awhile longer.

He leaves his house with no premonition that he won't be back.

7

Sunny Acres is ritzy. Elizabeth Wharton is not.

She's in a wheelchair, hunched over in a posture that reminds Hodges of Rodin's *Thinker*. Afternoon sunlight slants in through the window, turning her hair into a silver cloud so fine it's a halo. Outside the window, on a rolling and perfectly manicured lawn, a few golden oldies are playing a slow-motion game of croquet. Mrs. Wharton's croquet days are over. As are her days of standing up. When Hodges last saw her—with Pete Huntley beside him and Olivia Trelawney sitting next to her—she was bent. Now she's broken.

Janey, vibrant in tapered white slacks and a blue-and-white-striped sailor's shirt, kneels beside her, stroking one of Mrs. Wharton's badly twisted hands.

"How are you today, dear one?" she asks. "You look better." If this is true, Hodges is horrified.

Mrs. Wharton peers at her daughter with faded blue eyes that express nothing, not even puzzlement. Hodges's heart sinks. He enjoyed the ride out here with Janey, enjoyed looking at her, enjoyed getting to know her even more, and that's good. It means the trip hasn't been entirely wasted.

Then a minor miracle occurs. The old lady's cataract-tinged eyes clear; the cracked lipstickless lips spread in a smile. "Hello, Janey." She can only raise her head a little, but her eyes flick to Hodges. Now they look cold. "Craig."

Thanks to their conversation on the ride out, Hodges knows who that is.

"This isn't Craig, lovey. This is a friend of mine. His name is Bill Hodges. You've met him before."

175

"No, I don't believe . . ." She trails off—frowning now—then says, "You're . . . one of the detectives?"

"Yes, ma'am." He doesn't even consider telling her he's retired. Best to keep things on a straight line while there are still a few circuits working in her head.

Her frown deepens, creating rivers of wrinkles. "You thought Livvy left her key in her car so that man could steal it. She told you and told you, but you never believed her."

Hodges copies Janey, taking a knee beside the wheelchair. "Mrs. Wharton, I now think we might have been wrong about that."

"Of course you were." She shifts her gaze back to her remaining daughter, looking up at her from beneath the bony shelf of her brow. It's the only way she *can* look. "Where's Craig?"

"I divorced him last year, Mom."

She considers, then says, "Good riddance to bad rubbish."

"I couldn't agree more. Can Bill ask you a few questions?"

"I don't see why not, but I want some orange juice. And my pain pills."

"I'll go down to the nurses' suite and see if it's time," she says. "Bill, are you okay if I—?"

He nods and flicks two fingers in a *go, go* gesture. As soon as she's out the door, Hodges gets to his feet, bypasses the visitor's chair, and sits on Elizabeth Wharton's bed with his hands clasped between his knees. He has his pad, but he's afraid taking notes might distract her. The two of them regard each other silently. Hodges is fascinated by the silver nimbus around the old lady's head. There are signs that one of the orderlies combed her hair that morning, but it's gone its own wild way in the hours since. Hodges is glad. The scoliosis has twisted her body into a thing of ugliness, but her hair is beautiful. Crazy and beautiful.

"I think," he says, "we treated your daughter badly, Mrs. Wharton."

Yes indeed. Even if Mrs. T. was an unwitting accomplice, and Hodges hasn't entirely dismissed the idea that she left her key in the ignition, he and Pete did a piss-poor job. It's easy—too easy—

to either disbelieve or disregard someone you dislike. "We were blinded by certain preconceptions, and for that I'm sorry."

"Are you talking about Janey? Janey and Craig? He hit her, you know. She tried to get him to stop using that dope stuff he liked, and he hit her. She says only once, but I believe it was more." She lifts one slow hand and taps her nose with a pale finger. "A mother can tell."

"This isn't about Janey. I'm talking about Olivia."

"He made Livvy stop taking her pills. She said it was because she didn't want to be a dope addict like Craig, but it wasn't the same. She *needed* those pills."

"Are you talking about her antidepressants?"

"They were pills that made her able to go out." She pauses, considering. "There were other ones, too, that kept her from touching things over and over. She had strange ideas, my Livvy, but she was a good person, just the same. Underneath, she was a very good person."

Mrs. Wharton begins to cry.

There's a box of Kleenex on the nightstand. Hodges takes a few and holds them out to her, but when he sees how difficult it is for her to close her hand, he wipes her eyes for her.

"Thank you, sir. Is your name Hedges?"

"Hodges, ma'am."

"You were the nice one. The other one was very mean to Livvy. She said he was laughing at her. Laughing all the time. She said she could see it in his eyes."

Was that true? If so, he's ashamed of Pete. And ashamed of himself for not realizing.

"Who suggested she stop taking her pills? Do you remember?"

Janey has come back with the orange juice and a small paper cup that probably holds her mother's pain medication. Hodges glimpses her from the corner of his eye and uses the same two fingers to motion her away again. He doesn't want Mrs. Wharton's attention divided, or taking any pills that will further muddle her already muddled recollection.

Mrs. Wharton is silent. Then, just when Hodges is afraid she won't answer: "It was her pen-pal."

"Did she meet him under the Blue Umbrella? Debbie's Blue Umbrella?"

"She never met him. Not in person."

"What I mean—"

"The Blue Umbrella was make-believe." From beneath the white brows, her eyes are calling him a perfect idiot. "It was a thing in her computer. Frankie was her *computer* pen-pal."

He always feels a kind of electric shock in his midsection when fresh info drops. Frankie. Surely not the guy's real name, but names have power and aliases often have meaning. *Frankie*.

"He told her to stop taking her medicine?"

"Yes, he said it was hooking her. Where's Janey? I want my pills."

"She'll be back any minute, I'm sure."

Mrs. Wharton broods into her lap for a moment. "Frankie said he took all the same medicines, and that's why he did . . . what he did. He said he felt better after he stopped taking them. He said that after he stopped, he knew what he did was wrong. But it made him sad because he couldn't take it back. That's what he *said*. And that life wasn't worth living. I told Livvy she should stop talking to him. I said he was bad. That he was poison. And she said . . ."

The tears are coming again.

"She said she had to save him."

This time when Janey comes into the doorway, Hodges nods to her. Janey puts a pair of blue pills into her mother's pursed and seeking mouth, then gives her a drink of juice.

"Thank you, Livvy."

Hodges sees Janey wince, then smile. "You're welcome, dear." She turns to Hodges. "I think we should go, Bill. She's very tired."

He can see that, but is still reluctant to leave. There's a feeling you get when the interview isn't done. When there's at least one more apple hanging on the tree. "Mrs. Wharton, did Olivia say anything else about Frankie? Because you're right. He *is* bad. I'd like to find him so he can't hurt anyone else."

"Livvy never would have left her key in her car. *Never.*" Elizabeth Wharton sits hunched in her bar of sun, a human parenthesis in a fuzzy blue robe, unaware that she's topped with a gauze of silver light. The finger comes up again—admonitory. She says, "That dog we had never threw up on the rug again. Just that once."

Janey takes Hodges's hand and mouths, *Let's go.*

Habits die hard, and Hodges speaks the old formula as Janey bends down and kisses first her mother's cheek and then the corner of her dry mouth. "Thank you for your time, Mrs. Wharton. You've been very helpful."

As they reach the door, Mrs. Wharton speaks clearly. "She *still* wouldn't have committed suicide if not for the ghosts."

Hodges turns back. Beside him, Janey Patterson is wide-eyed.

"What ghosts, Mrs. Wharton?"

"One was the baby," she says. "The poor thing who was killed with all those others. Livvy heard that baby in the night, crying and crying. She said the baby's name was Patricia."

"In her house? Olivia heard this in her house?"

Elizabeth Wharton manages the smallest of nods, a mere dip of the chin. "And sometimes the mother. She said the mother would accuse her."

She looks up at them from her wheelchair hunch.

"She would scream, 'Why did you let him murder my baby?' *That's* why Livvy killed herself."

8

It's Friday afternoon and the suburban streets are feverish with kids released from school. There aren't many on Harper Road, but there are still some, and this gives Brady a perfect reason to cruise slowly past number sixty-three and peek in the window. Except he can't, because the drapes are drawn. And the overhang to the left of the house is empty except for the lawnmower. Instead of sitting in his house and watching TV, where he belongs, the Det-Ret is sporting about in his crappy old Toyota.

Sporting about where? It probably doesn't matter, but Hodges's absence makes Brady vaguely uneasy.

Two little girls trot to the curb with money clutched in their hands. They have undoubtedly been taught, both at home and at school, to never approach strangers, especially strange *men*, but who could be less strange than good old Mr. Tastey?

He sells them a cone each, one chocolate and one vanilla. He joshes with them, asks how they got so pretty. They giggle. The truth is one's ugly and the other's worse. As he serves them and makes change, he thinks about the missing Corolla, wondering if this break in Hodges's afternoon routine has anything to do with him. Another message from Hodges on the Blue Umbrella might cast some light, give an idea of where the ex-cop's head is at.

Even if it doesn't, Brady wants to hear from him.

"You don't dare ignore me," he says as the bells tinkle and chime over his head.

He crosses Hanover Street, parks in the strip mall, kills the engine (the annoying chimes fall blessedly silent), and hauls his laptop out from under the seat. He keeps it in an insulated case because the truck is always so fucking cold. He boots it up and goes on Debbie's Blue Umbrella courtesy of the nearby coffee shop's Wi-Fi.

Nothing.

"You fucker," Brady whispers. "You don't *dare* ignore me, you fucker."

As he zips the laptop back into its case, he sees a couple of boys standing outside the comic book shop, talking and looking at him and grinning. Given his five years of experience, Brady estimates that they're sixth- or seventh-graders with a combined IQ of one-twenty and a long future of collecting unemployment checks. Or a short one in some desert country.

They approach, the goofier-looking of the pair in the lead. Smiling, Brady leans out his window. "Help you boys?"

"We want to know if you got Jerry Garcia in there," Goofy says.

"No," Brady says, smiling more widely than ever, "but if I did, I'd sure let him out."

They look so ridiculously disappointed, Brady almost laughs. Instead, he points down at Goofy's pants. "Your fly's unzipped," he says, and when Goofy looks down, Brady flicks a finger at the soft underside of his chin. A little harder than he intended—actually quite a lot—but what the hell.

"Gotcha," Brady says merrily.

Goofy smiles to show yes, he's been gotten, but there's a red weal just above his Adam's apple and surprised tears swim in his eyes.

Goofy and Not Quite So Goofy start away. Goofy looks back over his shoulder. His lower lip is pushed out and now he looks like a third-grader instead of just another preadolescent come-stain who'll be fucking up the halls of Beal Middle School come September.

"That really hurt," he says, with a kind of wonder.

Brady's mad at himself. A finger-flick hard enough to bring tears to the kid's eyes means he's telling the straight-up truth. It also means Goofy and Not Quite So Goofy will remember him. Brady can apologize, can even give them free cones to show his sincerity, but then they'll remember *that*. It's a small thing, but small things mount up and then maybe you have a big thing.

"Sorry," he says, and means it. "I was just kidding around, son."

Goofy gives him the finger, and Not Quite So Goofy adds his own middle digit to show solidarity. They go into the comics store, where—if Brady knows boys like these, and he does—they will be invited to either buy or leave after five minutes' browsing.

They'll remember him. Goofy might even tell his parents, and his parents might lodge a complaint with Loeb's. It's unlikely but not impossible, and whose fault was it that he'd given Goofy Boy's unprotected neck a snap hard enough to leave a mark, instead of just the gentle flick he'd intended? The ex-cop has knocked Brady off-balance. He's making him screw things up, and Brady doesn't like that.

He starts the ice cream truck's engine. The bells begin bonging a tune from the loudspeaker on the roof. Brady turns left on Hanover Street and resumes his daily round, selling cones and Happy Boys and Pola Bars, spreading sugar on the afternoon and obeying all speed limits.

9

Although there are plenty of parking spaces on Lake Avenue after seven P.M.—as Olivia Trelawney well knew—they are few and far between at five in the afternoon, when Hodges and Janey Patterson get back from Sunny Acres. Hodges spots one three or four buildings down, however, and although it's small (the car behind the empty spot has poached a little), he shoehorns the Toyota into it quickly and easily.

"I'm impressed," Janey says. "I could never have done that. I flunked my driver's test on parallel parking the first two times I went."

"You must have had a hardass."

She smiles. "The third time I wore a short skirt, and that did the trick."

Thinking about how much he'd like to see her in a short skirt—the shorter the better—Hodges says, "There's really no trick to it. If you back toward the curb at a forty-five-degree angle, you can't go wrong. Unless your car's too big, that is. A Toyota's perfect for city parking. Not like a—" He stops.

"Not like a Mercedes," she finishes. "Come up and have coffee, Bill. I'll even feed the meter."

"I'll feed it. In fact, I'll max it out. We've got a lot to talk about."

"You learned some stuff from my mom, didn't you? That's why you were so quiet all the way back."

"I did, and I'll fill you in, but that's not where the conversation starts." He's looking at her full in the face now, and it's an easy face to look into. Christ, he wishes he were fifteen years younger. Even ten. "I need to be straight with you. I think you're under the impression that I came looking for work, and that's not the case."

"No," she says. "I think you came because you feel guilty about what happened to my sister. I simply took advantage of you. I'm not sorry, either. You were good with my mother. Kind. Very . . . very gentle."

She's close, her eyes a darker blue in the afternoon light and very wide. Her lips open as if she has more to say, but he doesn't give her a chance. He kisses her before he can think about how stupid it is, how reckless, and is astounded when she kisses him back, even putting her right hand on the nape of his neck to make their contact a little firmer. It goes on for no more than five seconds, but it seems much longer to Hodges, who hasn't had a kiss like this one in quite awhile.

She pulls back, brushes a hand through his hair, and says, "I've wanted to do that all afternoon. Now let's go upstairs. I'll make coffee and you make your report."

But there's no report until much later, and no coffee at all.

10

He kisses her again in the elevator. This time her hands link behind his neck, and his travel down past the small of her back to the white pants, snug across her bottom. He is aware of his too-big stomach pressing against her trim one and thinks she must be revolted by it, but when the elevator opens, her cheeks are flushed, her eyes are bright, and she's showing small white teeth in a smile. She takes his hand and pulls him down the short hall between the elevator and the apartment door.

"Come on," she says. "Come on, we're going to do this, so come on, before one of us gets cold feet."

It won't be me, Hodges thinks. Every part of him is warm.

At first she can't open the door because the hand holding the key is shaking too badly. It makes her laugh. He closes his fingers over hers, and together they push the Schlage into the slot.

The apartment where he first met this woman's sister and mother is shadowy, because the sun has traveled around to the other side of the building. The lake has darkened to a cobalt so deep it's almost purple. There are no sailboats, but he can see a freighter—

"Come on," she says again. "Come on, Bill, don't quit on me now."

Then they're in one of the bedrooms. He doesn't know if it's Janey's or the one Olivia used on her Thursday-night stays, and he doesn't care. The life of the last few months—the afternoon TV, the microwave dinners, his father's Smith & Wesson revolver— seems so distant that it might have belonged to a fictional character in a boring foreign movie.

She tries to pull the striped sailor shirt over her head and it gets caught on the clip in her hair. She gives a frustrated, muffled laugh. "Help me with this damn thing, would you please—"

He runs his hands up her smooth sides—she gives a tiny jump at his initial touch—and beneath the inside-out shirt. He stretches the fabric and lifts. Her head pops free. She's laughing in little out-of-breath gasps. Her bra is plain white cotton. He holds her by the waist and kisses between her breasts as she unbuckles his belt and pops the button on his slacks. He thinks, If I'd known this could happen at this stage of my life, I would have gotten back to the gym.

"Why—" he begins.

"Oh, shut up." She slides a hand down the front of him, pushing the zipper with her palm. His pants fall around his shoes in a jingle of change. "Save the talk for later." She grabs the hardness of him through his underpants and wiggles it like a gearshift, making him gasp. "That's a good start. Don't go limp on me, Bill, don't you dare."

They fall onto the bed, Hodges still in his boxer shorts, Janey in cotton panties as plain as her bra. He tries to roll her onto her back, but she resists.

"You're not getting on top of me," she says. "If you have a heart attack while we're screwing, you'll crush me."

"If I have a heart attack while we're screwing, I'll be the most disappointed man to ever leave this world."

"Stay still. Just stay still."

She hooks her thumbs into the sides of his boxers. He cups her hanging breasts as she does it.

"Now lift your legs. And keep busy. Use your thumbs a little, I like that."

He's able to obey both of these commands with no trouble; he's always been a multitasker.

A moment later she's looking down at him, a lock of her hair tumbled over one of her eyes. She sticks out her lower lip and blows it back. "Keep still. Let me do the work. And stay with me. I don't mean to be bossy, but I haven't had sex in two years, and the last I did have sucked. I want to enjoy this. I deserve it."

The clinging, slippery warmth of her encloses him in a warm hug, and he can't help raising his hips.

"Stay still, I said. Next time you can move all you want, but this is mine."

It's difficult, but he does as she says.

Her hair tumbles into her eyes again, and this time she can't use her lower lip to blow it back because she's gnawing at it in little bites he thinks she'll feel later. She spreads both hands and rubs them roughly through the graying hair on his chest, then down to the embarrassing swell of his gut.

"I need . . . to lose some weight," he gasps.

"You need to shut up," she says, then moves—just a little—and closes her eyes. "Oh God, that's deep. And nice. You can worry about your diet program later, okay?" She begins to move again, pauses once to readjust the angle, then settles into a rhythm.

"I don't know how long I can . . ."

"You better." Her eyes are still closed. "You just better hold out, Detective Hodges. Count prime numbers. Think of the books you liked when you were a kid. Spell *xylophone* backwards. Just stay with me. I won't need long."

He stays with her just long enough.

## 11

Sometimes when he's feeling upset, Brady Hartsfield retraces the route of his greatest triumph. It soothes him. On this Friday night he doesn't go home after turning in the ice cream truck and making the obligatory joke or two with Shirley Orton in the front office. He drives his clunker downtown instead, not liking the front-end shimmy or the too-loud blat of the engine. Soon he will have to balance off the cost of a new car (a new *used* car) against the cost of repairs. And his mother's Honda needs work even more desperately than his Subaru does. Not that she drives the Honda very often these days, and that's good, considering how much of her time she spends in the bag.

His trip down Memory Lane begins on Lake Avenue, just past the bright lights of downtown, where Mrs. Trelawney always parked her Mercedes on Thursday nights, and wends up Marlborough Street to City Center. Only this evening he gets no farther than the condo. He brakes so suddenly that the car behind almost rear-ends him. The driver hits his horn in a long, outraged blast, but Brady pays no attention. It might as well have been a foghorn on the other side of the lake.

The driver pulls around him, buzzing down his passenger-side window to yell *Asshole* at the top of his lungs. Brady pays no attention to that, either.

There must be thousands of Toyota Corollas in the city, and hundreds of *blue* Toyota Corollas, but how many blue Toyota Corollas with bumper stickers reading SUPPORT YOUR LOCAL POLICE? Brady is betting there's just one, and what the hell is the fat ex-cop doing in the old lady's condominium apartment? Why is he visiting Mrs. Trelawney's sister, who now lives there?

The answer seems obvious: Detective Hodges (Ret.) is hunting.

Brady is no longer interested in reliving last year's triumph. He pulls an illegal (and completely out-of-character) U-turn, now heading for the North Side. Heading for home with a single thought in his head, blinking on and off like a neon sign.

You bastard. You bastard. You bastard.

Things are not going the way they are supposed to. Things are slipping out of his control. It's not right.

Something needs to be done.

12

As the stars come out over the lake, Hodges and Janey Patterson sit in the kitchen nook, gobbling takeout Chinese and drinking oolong tea. Janey is wearing a fluffy white bathrobe. Hodges is in his boxers and tee-shirt. When he used the bathroom after making love (she was curled in the middle of the bed, dozing), he got on her scale and was delighted to see he's four pounds lighter than the last time he weighed himself. It's a start.

"Why me?" Hodges says now. "Don't get me wrong, I feel incredibly lucky—even blessed—but I'm sixty-two and overweight."

She sips tea. "Well, let's think about that, shall we? In one of the old detective movies Ollie and I used to watch on TV when we were kids, I'd be the greedy vixen, maybe a nightclub cigarette girl, who tries to charm the crusty and cynical private detective with her fair white body. Only I'm not the greedy type—nor do I have to be, considering the fact that I recently inherited several million dollars—and my fair white body has started to sag in several vital places. As you may have noticed."

He hasn't. What he has noticed is that she hasn't answered his question. So he waits.

"Not good enough?"

"Nope."

Janey rolls her eyes. "I wish I could think of a way to answer you that's gentler than 'Men are very stupid' or more elegant than 'I was horny and wanted to brush away the cobwebs.' I'm not com-

ing up with much, so let's go with those. Plus, I was attracted to
you. It's been thirty years since I was a dewy debutante and much
too long since I got laid. I'm forty-four, and that allows me to reach
for what I want. I don't always get it, but I'm allowed to reach."

He stares at her, honestly amazed. Forty-*four*?

She bursts into laughter. "You know what? That look's the nicest compliment I've had in a long, long time. And the most honest
one. Just that stare. So I'm going to push it a little. How old did
you think I was?"

"Maybe forty. At the outside. Which would make me a cradle-
robber."

"Oh, bullshit. If you were the one with the money instead of
me, everyone would take the younger-woman thing for granted.
In that case, people would take it for granted if you were sleeping
with a twenty-five-year-old." She pauses. "Although that *would* be
cradle-robbing, in my humble opinion."

"Still—"

"You're old, but not *that* old, and you're on the heavyweight
side, but not *that* heavy. Although you will be if you keep on the
way you're going." She points her fork at him. "That's the kind of
honesty a woman can only afford after she's slept with a man and
still likes him well enough to eat dinner with him. I said I haven't
had sex in two years. That's true, but do you know when I last had
sex with a man I actually liked?"

He shakes his head.

"Try junior college. And he wasn't a man, he was a second-
string tackle with a big red pimple on the end of his nose. He was
very sweet, though. Clumsy and far too quick, but sweet. He actually cried on my shoulder afterward."

"So this wasn't just . . . I don't know . . ."

"A thank-you fuck? A mercy-fuck? Give me a little credit. And
here's a promise." She leans forward, the robe gaping to show the
shadowed valley between her breasts. "Lose twenty pounds and I'll
risk you on top."

He can't help laughing.

"It was great, Bill. I have no regrets, and I have a thing for big guys. The tackle with the pimple on his nose went about two-forty. My ex was a beanpole, and I should have known no good could come of it the first time I saw him. Can we leave it at that?"

"Yeah."

"*Yeah,*" she says, smiling, and stands up. "Come on in the living room. It's time for you to make your report."

## 13

He tells her everything except for his long afternoons watching bad TV and flirting with his father's old service revolver. She listens gravely, not interrupting, her eyes seldom leaving his face. When he's done, she gets a bottle of wine out of the fridge and pours them each a glass. They are big glasses, and he looks at his doubtfully.

"Don't know if I should, Janey. I'm driving."

"Not tonight you're not. You're staying here. Unless you've got a dog or a cat?"

Hodges shakes his head.

"Not even a parrot? In one of those old movies, you'd at least have a parrot in your office that would say rude things to prospective clients."

"Sure. And you'd be my receptionist. Lola instead of Janey."

"Or Velma."

He grins. There's a wavelength, and they're on it.

She leans forward, once again creating that enticing view. "Profile this guy for me."

"That was never my job. We had guys who specialized in that. One on the force and two on call from the psych department at the state university."

"Do it anyway. I Googled you, you know, and it looks to me like you were just about the best the police department had. Commendations up the wazoo."

"I got lucky a few times."

It comes out sounding falsely modest, but luck really is a big part of it. Luck, and being ready. Woody Allen was right: eighty percent of success is just showing up.

"Take a shot, okay? If you do a good job, maybe we'll revisit the bedroom." She wrinkles her nose at him. "Unless you're too old for twosies."

The way he feels right now, he might not be too old for three-sies. There have been a lot of celibate nights, which gives him an account to draw on. Or so he hopes. Part of him—a large part—still can't believe this isn't an incredibly detailed dream.

He sips his wine, rolling it around in his mouth, giving himself time to think. The top of her robe is closed again, which helps him concentrate.

"Okay. He's probably young, that's the first thing. I'm guessing between twenty and thirty-five. That's partly because of his computer savvy, but not entirely. When an older guy murders a bunch of people, the ones he mostly goes after are family, co-workers, or both. Then he finishes by putting the gun to his own head. You look, you find a reason. A motive. Wife kicked him out, then got a restraining order. Boss downsized him, then humiliated him by having a couple of security guys stand by while he cleaned out his office. Loans overdue. Credit cards maxed out. House underwater. Car repo'd."

"But what about serial killers? Wasn't that guy in Kansas a middle-aged man?"

"Dennis Rader, yeah. And he was middle-aged when they bagged him, but only thirty or so when he started. Also, those were sex killings. Mr. Mercedes isn't a sex-killer, and he's not a serial killer in the traditional sense. He started with a bunch, but since then he's settled on individuals—first your sister, now me. And he didn't come after either of us with a gun or a stolen car, did he?"

"Not yet, anyway," Janey says.

"Our guy is a hybrid, but he has certain things in common with younger men who kill. He's more like Lee Malvo—one of the Belt-way Snipers—than Rader. Malvo and his partner planned to kill six white people a day. Just random killings. Whoever had the bad luck to walk into their gunsights went down. Sex and age didn't matter. They ended up getting ten, not a bad score for a couple of homicidal maniacs. The stated motive was racial, and with John Allen Muhammad—he was Malvo's partner, much older, a kind of father figure—that might have been true, or partially true. I think Malvo's motivation was a lot more complex, a whole stew of things he didn't understand himself. Look closely and you'd probably find sexual confusion and upbringing were major players. I think the same is true with our guy. He's young. He's bright. He's good at fitting in, so good that a lot of his associates don't realize he's basically a loner. When he's caught, they'll all say, 'I can't believe it was so-and-so, he was always so nice.'"

"Like Dexter Morgan on that TV show."

Hodges knows the one she's talking about and shakes his head emphatically. Not just because the show is fantasyland bullshit, either.

"Dexter knows why he's doing what he's doing. Our guy doesn't. He's almost certainly unmarried. He doesn't date. He may be impotent. There's a good chance he's still living at home. If so, it's probably with a single parent. If it's Father, the relationship is cold and distant—ships passing in the night. If it's Mother, there's a good chance Mr. Mercedes is her surrogate husband." He sees her start to speak and raises his hand. "That doesn't mean they're having a sexual relationship."

"Maybe not, but I'll tell you something, Bill. You don't have to sleep with a guy to be having a sexual relationship with him. Sometimes it's in the eye contact, or the clothes you wear when you know he's going to be around, or what you do with your hands— touching, patting, caressing, hugging. Sex has got to be in this somewhere. I mean, that letter he sent you . . . the stuff about wearing a condom while he did it . . ." She shivers in her white robe.

"Ninety percent of that letter is white noise, but sure, sex is in it somewhere. Always is. Also anger, aggression, loneliness, feelings of inadequacy . . . but it doesn't do to get lost in stuff like that. It's not profiling, it's analysis. Which was way above my pay-grade even when I had a pay-grade."

"Okay . . ."

"He's broken," Hodges says simply. "And evil. Like an apple that looks okay on the outside, but when you cut it open, it's black and full of worms."

"Evil," she says, almost sighing the word. Then, to herself rather than him: "Of course he is. He battened on my sister like a vampire."

"He could have some kind of job where he meets the public, because he's got a fair amount of surface charm. If so, it's probably a low-paying job. He never advances because he's unable to combine his above-average intelligence with long-term concentration. His actions suggest he's a creature of impulse and opportunity. The City Center killings are a perfect example. I think he had his eye on your sister's Mercedes, but I don't think he knew what he was actually going to do with it until just a few days before the job fair. Maybe only a few hours. I just wish I could figure out how he stole it."

He pauses, thinking that thanks to Jerome, he has a good idea about half of it: the spare key was very likely in the glove compartment all along.

"I think ideas for murder flip through this guy's head as fast as cards in a good dealer's fast shuffle. He's probably thought of blowing up airliners, setting fires, shooting up schoolbuses, poisoning the water system, maybe assassinating the governor or the president."

"Jesus, Bill!"

"Right now he's fixated on me, and that's good. It will make him easier to catch. It's good for another reason, too."

"Which is?"

"I'd rather keep him thinking small. Keep him thinking one-on-

one. The longer he keeps doing that, the longer it will be before he decides to try putting on another horror show like the one at City Center, maybe on an even grander scale. You know what creeps me out? He's probably already got a list of potential targets."

"Didn't he say in his letter that he had no urge to do it again?"

He grins. It lights up his whole face. "Yeah, he did. And you know how you tell when guys like this are lying? Their lips are moving. Only in the case of Mr. Mercedes, he's writing letters."

"Or communicating with his targets on the Blue Umbrella site. Like he did with Ollie."

"Yeah."

"If we assume he succeeded with her because she was psychologically fragile . . . forgive me, Bill, but does he have reason to believe he can succeed with you for the same reason?"

He looks at his glass of wine and sees it's empty. He starts to pour himself another half a glass, thinks what that might do to his chances of a successful return engagement in the bedroom, and settles for a small puddle in the bottom instead.

"Bill?"

"Maybe," he says. "Since my retirement, I've been drifting. But I'm not as lost as your sister . . ." Not anymore, at least. ". . . and that's not the important thing. It's not the take-away from the letters, and from the Blue Umbrella communications."

"Then what is?"

"*He's been watching*. That's the take-away. It makes him vulnerable. Unfortunately, it also makes him dangerous to my known associates. I don't think he knows I've been talking to you—"

"Quite a bit more than talking," she says, giving her eyebrows a Groucho waggle.

"—but he knows Olivia had a sister, and we have to assume he knows you're in the city. You need to start being super-careful. Make sure your door is locked when you're here—"

"I always do."

"—and don't believe what you hear on the lobby intercom. Anyone can say he's from a package service and needs a signature.

Visually identify all comers before you open your door. Be aware of your surroundings when you go out." He leans forward, the splash of wine untouched. He doesn't want it anymore. "Big thing here, Janey. When you *are* out, keep an eye on traffic. Not just driving but when you're on foot. Do you know the term BOLO?"

"Cop-speak for *be on the lookout*."

"That's it. When you're out, you're going to BOLO any vehicles that seem to keep reappearing in your immediate vicinity."

"Like that lady's black SUVs," she says, smiling. "Mrs. Whoze-whatsit."

Mrs. Melbourne. Thinking of her tickles some obscure associational switch in the back of Hodges's mind, but it's gone before he can track it down, let alone scratch it.

Jerome's got to be on the lookout, too. If Mr. Mercedes is cruising Hodges's place, he'll have seen Jerome mowing the lawn, putting on the screens, cleaning out the gutters. Both Jerome and Janey are probably safe, but probably isn't good enough. Mr. Mercedes is a random bundle of homicide, and Hodges has set out on a course of deliberate provocation.

Janey reads his mind. "And yet you're . . . what did you call it? Winding him up."

"Yeah. And very shortly I'm going to steal some time on your computer and wind him up a little more. I had a message all worked out, but I'm thinking of adding something. My partner got a big solve today, and there's a way I can use that."

"What was it?"

There's no reason not to tell her; it will be in the papers tomorrow, Sunday at the latest. "Turnpike Joe."

"The one who kills women at rest stops?" And when he nods: "Does he fit your profile of Mr. Mercedes?"

"Not at all. But there's no reason for our guy to know that."

"What do you mean to do?"

Hodges tells her.

14

They don't have to wait for the morning paper; the news that Donald Davis, already under suspicion for the murder of his wife, has confessed to the Turnpike Joe killings leads the eleven P.M. news. Hodges and Janey watch it in bed. For Hodges, the return engagement has been strenuous but sublimely satisfactory. He's still out of breath, he's sweaty and in need of a shower, but it's been a long, long time since he felt this happy. This *complete*.

When the newscaster moves on to a puppy stuck in a drainpipe, Janey uses the remote to kill the TV. "Okay. It could work. But *God*, is it risky."

He shrugs. "With no police resources to call on, I see it as my best way forward." And it's fine with him, because it's the way he *wants* to go forward.

He thinks briefly of the makeshift but very effective weapon he keeps in his dresser drawer, the argyle sock filled with ball bearings. He imagines how satisfying it would be to use the Happy Slapper on the sonofabitch who ran one of the world's heaviest passenger sedans into a crowd of defenseless people. That probably won't happen, but it's possible. In this best (and worst) of all worlds, most things are.

"What did you make of what my mother said at the end? About Olivia hearing ghosts?"

"I need to think about that a little more," Hodges says, but he's already thought about it, and if he's right, he might have another path to Mr. Mercedes. Given his druthers, he wouldn't involve Jerome Robinson any more than he already has, but if he's going to follow up on old Mrs. Wharton's parting shot, he may have to. He knows half a dozen cops with Jerome's computer savvy and can't call on a single one of them.

Ghosts, he thinks. Ghosts in the machine.

He sits up and swings his feet out onto the floor. "If I'm still invited to stay over, what I need right now is a shower."

"You are." She leans over and sniffs at the side of his neck, her hand lightly clamped on his upper arm giving him a pleasurable shiver. "And you certainly do."

When he's showered and back in his boxers, he asks her to power up her computer. Then, with her sitting beside him and looking on attentively, he slips under Debbie's Blue Umbrella and leaves a message for **merckill**. Fifteen minutes later, and with Janey Patterson nestled next to him, he sleeps . . . and never so well since childhood.

## 15

When Brady gets home after several hours of aimless cruising, it's late and there's a note on the back door: *Where you been, honey-boy? There's homemade lasagna in the oven.* He only has to look at the unsteady, downslanting script to know she was seriously loaded when she wrote it. He untacks the note and lets himself in.

Usually he checks on her first thing, but he smells smoke and hustles to the kitchen, where a blue haze hangs in the air. Thank God the smoke detector in here is dead (he keeps meaning to replace it and keeps forgetting, too many other fish to fry). Thanks are also due for the powerful stove fan, which has sucked up just enough smoke to keep the rest of the detectors from going off, although they soon will if he can't air the place out. The oven is set at three-fifty. He turns it off. He opens the windows over the sink, then the back door. There's a floor fan in the utility closet where they keep the cleaning supplies. He sets it up facing the runaway stove, and turns it on at the highest setting.

With that done he finally goes into the living room and checks on his mother. She's crashed out on the couch, wearing a house-dress that's open up top and rucked to her thighs below, snoring so loudly and steadily she sounds like an idling chainsaw. He averts his eyes and goes back into the kitchen, muttering *fuck-fuck-fuck-fuck* under his breath.

He sits at the table with his head bent, his palms cupping his temples, and his fingers plunged deep into his hair. Why is it that when things go wrong, they have to *keep on* going wrong? He finds himself thinking of the Morton Salt motto: "When it rains it pours."

After five minutes of airing-out, he risks opening the oven. As he regards the black and smoking lump within, any faint hunger pangs he might have felt when he got home pass away. Washing will not clean that pan; an hour of scouring and a whole box of Brillo pads will not clean that pan; an industrial laser probably wouldn't clean that pan. That pan is a gone goose. It's only luck that he didn't get home to find the fucking fire department here and his mother offering them vodka collinses.

He shuts the oven—he doesn't want to look at that nuclear meltdown—and goes back to look at his mother instead. Even as his eyes are running up and down her bare legs, he's thinking, It would be better if she *did* die. Better for her and better for me.

He goes downstairs, using his voice commands to turn on the lights and his bank of computers. He goes to Number Three, centers the cursor on the Blue Umbrella icon . . . and hesitates. Not because he's afraid there won't be a message from the fat ex-cop but because he's afraid there will be. If so, it won't be anything he wants to read. Not the way things are going. His head is fucked up already, so why fuck it up more?

Except there might be an answer to what the cop was doing at the Lake Avenue condo. Has he been questioning Olivia Trelawney's sister? Probably. At sixty-two, he's surely not boffing her.

Brady clicks the mouse, and sure enough:

**kermitfrog19 wants to chat with you!**
**Do you want to chat with kermitfrog19?**
**Y N**

Brady settles the cursor on **N** and circles the curved back of his mouse with the pad of his index finger. Daring himself to push it and end this thing right here and right now. It's obvious he won't be able to nudge the fat ex-cop into suicide the way he did Mrs. Trelawney, so why not? Isn't that the smart thing?

But he has to know.

More importantly, the Det-Ret doesn't get to win.

He moves the cursor to **Y**, clicks, and the message—quite a long one this time—flashes onto the screen.

**If it isn't my false-confessing friend again. I shouldn't even respond, guys like you are a dime a dozen, but as you point out, I'm retired and even talking to a nut is better than Dr. Phil and all those late-night infomercials. One more 30-minute OxiClean ad and I'll be as crazy as you are, HAHAHA. Also, I owe you thanks for introducing me to this site, which I otherwise would not have found. I have already made 3 new (and non-crazy) friends. One is a lady with a delightfully dirty mouth!!! So OK, my "friend," let me clue you in.**

**First, anyone who watches CSI could figure out that the Mercedes Killer was wearing a hairnet and used bleach on the clown mask. I mean, DUH.**

**Second, if you were really the guy who stole Mrs. Trelawney's Mercedes, you would have mentioned the valet key. That's something you couldn't have figured out from watching CSI. So, at the risk of repeating myself, DUH.**

**Third (I hope you're taking notes), I got a call from my old partner today. He caught a bad guy, one who specializes in TRUE confessions. Check the news, my friend, and then guess what else this guy's going to confess to in the next week or so.**

**Have a nice night and BTW, why don't you go bother someone else with your fantasies?**

Brady vaguely remembers some cartoon character—maybe it was Foghorn Leghorn, the big rooster with the southern accent—

who would get so mad first his neck and then his head would turn into a thermometer with the temperature going up and up from BAKE to BROIL to NUKE. Brady can almost feel that happening to him as he reads this arrogant, insulting, infuriating post.

Valet key?

*Valet* key?

"What are you talking about?" he says, his voice somewhere between a whisper and a growl. "What the fuck are you *talking* about?"

He gets up and strides around in an unsteady circle on legs like stilts, yanking at his hair so hard his eyes water. His mother is forgotten. The blackened lasagna is forgotten. Everything is forgotten except for this hateful post.

He has even had the nerve to put in a smiley-face!

A *smiley-face*!

Brady kicks his chair, hurting his toes and sending it rolling all the way across the room, where it bangs the wall. Then he turns and runs back to his Number Three computer, hunching over it like a vulture. His first impulse is to reply immediately, to call the fucking cop a liar, an idiot with fat-induced early-onset Alzheimer's, an anal ranger who sucks his nigger yardboy's cock. Then some semblance of rationality—fragile and wavering—reasserts itself. He retrieves his chair and goes to the city paper's website. He doesn't even have to click on BREAKING NEWS in order to see what Hodges has been raving about; it's right there on the front page of tomorrow's paper.

Brady follows local crime news assiduously, and knows both Donald Davis's name and his handsomely chiseled features. He knows the cops have been chasing Davis for the murder of his wife, and Brady has no doubt the man did it. Now the idiot has confessed, but not just to *her* murder. According to the newspaper story, Davis has also confessed to the rape-murders of five *more* women. In short, he's claiming to be Turnpike Joe.

At first Brady is unable to connect this with the fat ex-cop's hectoring message. Then it comes to him in a baleful burst of inspiration: while he's in a breast-baring mood, Donnie Davis also means to confess to the City Center Massacre. May have done so already.

Brady whirls around like a dervish—once, twice, three times. His head is splitting. His pulse is thudding in his chest, his neck, his temples. He can even feel it in his gums and tongue.

Did Davis say something about a valet key? Is that what brought this on?

"There *was* no valet key," Brady says . . . only how can he be sure of that? What if there was? And *if* there was . . . if they hang this on Donald Davis and snatch away Brady Hartsfield's great triumph . . . after the *risks* he took . . .

He can no longer hold back. He sits down at his Number Three again and writes a message to **kermitfrog19**. Just a short one, but his hands are shaking so badly it takes him almost five minutes. He sends it as soon as he's done, without bothering to read it over.

**YOU ARE FULL OF SHIT YOU ASSHOLE. OK the key wasn't in the ignition but it was no VALET KEY. It was a spare in the glove complartment and how I uynlocked the car IS FOR YOU TO FIGURE OUT FUCKFACE. Donald Davis did not do this crime. I repeat, DONALD DAVIUS DID NOT DO THIS CRIME. If you tell people he did I will kill you altho it wouldn'tr be killing much as washed up as you are.**
**Signed,**
**The REAL Mercedes Killer**
**PS: Your mother was a whore, she took it up the ass & licked cum out of gutters.**

Brady shuts off his computer and goes upstairs, leaving his mother to snore on the couch instead of helping her to bed. He takes three aspirin, adds a fourth, and then lies in his own bed, wide-eyed and shaking, until the first streaks of dawn come up in the east. At last he drops off for two hours, sleep that is thin and dream-haunted and unrestful.

16

Hodges is making scrambled eggs when Janey comes into the kitchen on Saturday morning in her white robe, her hair wet from the shower. With it combed back from her face, she looks younger than ever. He thinks again, Forty-*four*?

"I looked for bacon, but didn't see any. Of course it might still be there. My ex claims that the great majority of American men suffer from the disease of Refrigerator Blindness. I don't know if there's a help line for that."

She points at his midsection.

"Okay," he says. And then, because she seems to like it: "Yeah."

"And by the way, how's your cholesterol?"

He smiles and says, "Toast? It's whole grain. As you probably know, since you bought it."

"One slice. No butter, just a little jam. What are you going to do today?"

"Not sure yet." Although he's thinking he'd like to check in with Radney Peeples out in Sugar Heights if Radney's on duty and being Vigilant. And he needs to talk to Jerome about computers. Endless vistas there.

"Have you checked the Blue Umbrella?"

"Wanted to make you breakfast first. And me." It's true. He woke up actually wanting to feed his body rather than trying to plug some empty hole in his head. "Also, I don't know your password."

"It's Janey."

"My advice? Change it. Actually it's the advice of the kid who works for me."

"Jerome, right?"

"That's the one."

He has scrambled half a dozen eggs and they eat them all, split right down the middle. It has crossed his mind to ask if she had any regrets about last night, but decides the way she's going through her breakfast answers the question.

With the dishes in the sink, they go on her computer and sit silently for nearly four minutes, reading and re-reading the latest message from **merckill**.

"Holy cow," she says at last. "You wanted to wind him up, and I'd say he's fully wound. Do you see all the mistakes?" She points out *complartment* and *uynlocked*. "Is that part of his—what did you call it?—stylistic masking?"

"I don't think so." Hodges is looking at *wouldn'tr* and smiling. He can't help smiling. The fish is feeling the hook, and it's sunk deep. It hurts. It *burns*. "I think that's the kind of typing you do when you're mad as hell. The last thing he expected was that he'd have a credibility problem. It's making him crazy."

"*Er,*" she says.

"Huh?"

"*Crazier.* Send him another message, Bill. Poke him harder. He deserves it."

"All right." He thinks, then types.

<br>

17

When he's dressed, she walks down the hall with him and treats him to a lingering kiss at the elevator.

"I still can't believe last night happened," he tells her.

"Oh, it did. And if you play your cards right, it might happen again." She searches his face with those blue eyes of hers. "But no promises or long-term commitments, okay? We take it as it comes. A day at a time."

"At my age, I take everything that way." The elevator doors open. He steps in.

"Stay in touch, cowboy."

"I will." The elevator doors start to close. He stops them with his hand. "And remember to BOLO, cowgirl."

She nods solemnly, but he doesn't miss the twinkle in her eye. "Janey will BOLO her ass off."

"Keep your cell phone handy, and it might be wise to program nine-one-one on your speed dial."

He drops his hand. She blows him a kiss. The doors roll shut before he can blow one back.

His car is where he left it, but the meter must have run out before the free parking kicked in, because there's a ticket stuck under the windshield wiper. He opens the glove compartment, stuffs the ticket inside, and fishes out his phone. He's good at giving Janey advice that he doesn't take himself—since he pulled the pin, he's always forgetting the damned Nokia, which is pretty prehistoric, as cell phones go. These days hardly anyone calls him anyway, but this morning he has three messages, all from Jerome. Numbers two and three—one at nine-forty last night, the other at ten-forty-five—are impatient inquiries about where he is and why he doesn't call. They are in Jerome's normal voice. The original message, left at six-thirty yesterday evening, begins in his exuberant Tyrone Feelgood Delight voice.

"Massah Hodges, where you at? Ah needs to *jaw* to y'all!" Then he becomes Jerome again. "I think I know how he did it. How he stole the car. Call me."

Hodges checks his watch and decides Jerome probably won't be up quite yet, not on Saturday morning. He decides to drive over there, with a stop at his house first to pick up his notes. He turns on the radio, gets Bob Seger singing "Old Time Rock and Roll," and bellows along: take those old records off the shelf.

## 18

Once upon a simpler time, before apps, iPads, Samsung Galaxies, and the world of blazing-fast 4G, weekends were the busiest days of the week at Discount Electronix. Now the kids who used to come in to buy CDs are downloading Vampire Weekend from iTunes, while their elders are surfing eBay or watching the TV shows they missed on Hulu.

This Saturday morning the Birch Hill Mall DE is a wasteland. Tones is down front, trying to sell an old lady an HDTV that's already an antique. Freddi Linklatter is out back, chain-smoking Marlboro Reds and probably rehearsing her latest gay rights rant. Brady is sitting at one of the computers in the back row, an ancient Vizio that he's rigged to leave no keystroke tracks, let alone a history. He's staring at Hodges's latest message. One eye, his left, has picked up a rapid, irregular tic.

> **Quit dumping on my mother, okay? ☺ Not her fault you got caught in a bunch of stupid lies. Got a key out of the glove compartment, did you? That's pretty good, since Olivia Trelawney had both of them. The one missing was the valet key. She kept it in a small magnetic box under the rear bumper. The REAL Mercedes Killer must have scoped it.**
>
> **I think I'm done writing to you, dickwad. Your Fun Quotient is currently hovering around zero, and I have it on good authority that Donald Davis is going to cop to the City Center killings. Which leaves you where? Just living your shitty little unexciting life, I guess. One other thing before I close this charming correspondence. You threatened to kill me. That's a felony offense, but guess what? I don't care. Buddy, you are just another chickenshit asshole. The Internet is full of them. Want to come to my house (I know you know where I live) and make that threat in person? No? I thought not. Let me close with two words so simple even a thud like you should be able to understand them.**
>
> **Go away.**

Brady's rage is so great he feels frozen in place. Yet he's also still burning. He thinks he will stay this way, hunched over the piece-of-shit Vizio ridiculously sale-priced at eighty-seven dollars and eighty-seven cents, until he either dies of frostbite or goes up in flames or somehow does both at the same time.

But when a shadow rises on the wall, Brady finds he can move after all. He clicks away from the fat ex-cop's message just before Freddi bends over to peer at the screen. "What you looking at, Brades? You moved awful fast to hide it, whatever it was."

"A *National Geographic* documentary. It's called *When Lesbians Attack*."

"Your humor," she says, "might be exceeded by your sperm count, but I tend to doubt it."

Tones Frobisher joins them. "Got a service call over on Edgemont," he says. "Which one of you wants it?"

Freddi says, "Given a choice between a service call in Hillbilly Heaven and having a wild weasel stuck up my ass, I'd have to pick the weasel."

"I'll take it," Brady says. He's decided he has an errand to run. One that can't wait.

## 19

Jerome's little sis and a couple of her friends are jumping rope in the Robinson driveway when Hodges arrives. All of them are wearing sparkly tees with silkscreens of some boy band on them. He cuts across the lawn, his case-folder in one hand. Barbara comes over long enough to give him a high-five and a dap, then hurries back to grab her end of the rope. Jerome, dressed in shorts and a City College tee-shirt with the sleeves torn off, is sitting on the porch steps and drinking orange juice. Odell is by his side. He tells Hodges his folks are off Krogering, and he's got babysitting duty until they get back.

"Not that she really needs a sitter anymore. She's a lot hipper than our parents think."

Hodges sits down beside him. "You don't want to take that for granted. Trust me on this, Jerome."

"Meaning what, exactly?"

"Tell me what you came up with first."

Instead of answering, Jerome points to Hodges's car, parked at the curb so as not to interfere with the girls' game. "What year is that?"

"Oh-four. No show-stopper, but it gets good mileage. Want to buy it?"

"I'll pass. Did you lock it?"

"Yeah." Even though this is a good neighborhood and he's sitting right here looking at it. Force of habit.

"Give me your keys."

Hodges digs in his pocket and hands them over. Jerome examines the fob and nods. "PKE," he says. "Started to come into use during the nineteen-nineties, first as an accessory but pretty much standard equipment since the turn of the century. Do you know what it stands for?"

As lead detective on the City Center Massacre (and frequent interviewer of Olivia Trelawney), Hodges certainly does. "Passive keyless entry."

"Right." Jerome pushes one of the two buttons on the fob. At the curb, the parking lights of Hodges's Toyota flash briefly. "Now it's open." He pushes the other button. The lights flash again. "Now it's locked. And you've got the key." He puts it in Hodges's palm. "All safe and sound, right?"

"Based on this discussion, maybe not."

"I know some guys from the college who have a computer club. I'm not going to tell you their names, so don't ask."

"Wouldn't think of it."

"They're not bad guys, but they know all the bad tricks—hacking, cloning, info-jacking, stuff like that. They tell me that PKE systems are pretty much a license to steal. When you push the button to lock or unlock your car, the fob emits a low-frequency radio signal. A code. If you could hear it, it would sound like the boops and beeps you get when you speed-dial a fax number. With me?"

"So far, yeah."

In the driveway the girls chant Sally-in-the-alley while Barbara Robinson darts deftly in and out of the loop, her sturdy brown legs flashing and her pigtails bouncing.

"My guys tell me that it's easy to capture that code, if you have the right gadget. You can modify a garage door opener or a TV remote to do it, only with something like that, you have to be really close. Say within twenty yards. But you can also build one that's more powerful. All the components are available at your friendly neighborhood electronics store. Total cost, about a hundred bucks. Range up to a hundred yards. You watch for the driver to exit the target vehicle. When she pushes the button to lock her car, you push *your* button. Your gadget captures the signal and stores it. She walks away, and when she's gone, you push your button again. The car unlocks, and you're in."

Hodges looks at his key, then at Jerome. "This works?"

"Yes indeed. My friends say it's tougher now—the manufacturers have modified the system so that the signal changes every time you push the button—but not impossible. Any system created by the mind of man can be hacked by the mind of man. You feel me?"

Hodges hardly hears him, let alone feels him. He's thinking about Mr. Mercedes before he *became* Mr. Mercedes. He might have purchased one of the gadgets Jerome has just told him about, but it's just as likely he built it himself. And was Mrs. Trelawney's Mercedes the first car he ever used it on? Unlikely.

I have to check on car robberies downtown, he thinks. Starting in . . . let's say 2007 and going right through until early spring of 2009.

He has a friend in records, Marlo Everett, who owes him one. Hodges is confident Marlo will run an unofficial check for him without a lot of questions. And if she comes up with a bunch of reports where the investigating officer concludes that "complainant may have forgotten to lock his vehicle," he'll know.

In his heart he knows already.

"Mr. Hodges?" Jerome is looking at him a little uncertainly.

"What is it, Jerome?"

"When you were working on the City Center case, didn't you check out this PKE thing with the cops who handle auto theft? I mean, they have to know about it. It's not new. My friends say it's even got a name: stealing the peek."

"We talked to the head mechanic from the Mercedes dealership, and he told us a key was used," Hodges says. To his own ears, the reply sounds weak and defensive. Worse: incompetent. What the head mechanic did—what they all did—was *assume* a key had been used. One left in the ignition by a ditzy lady none of them liked.

Jerome offers a cynical smile that looks odd and out of place on his young face. "There's stuff that people who work at car dealerships don't talk about, Mr. Hodges. They don't lie, exactly, they just banish it from their minds. Like how airbag deployment can save your life but also drive your glasses into your eyes and blind you. The high rollover rate of some SUVs. Or how easy it is to steal a PKE signal. But the auto theft guys must be hip, right? I mean, they *must*."

The dirty truth is Hodges doesn't know. He should, but he doesn't. He and Pete were in the field almost constantly, working double shifts and getting maybe five hours of sleep a night. The paperwork piled up. If there was a memo from auto theft, it will probably be in the case files somewhere. He doesn't dare ask his old partner about it, but realizes he may have to tell Pete everything soon. If he can't work it out for himself, that is.

In the meantime, Jerome needs to know everything. Because the guy Hodges is dicking with is crazy.

Barbara comes running up, sweaty and out of breath. "Jay, can me n Hilda n Tonya watch *Regular Show*?"

"Go for it," Jerome says.

She throws her arms around him and presses her cheek to his. "Will you make us pancakes, my darling brother?"

"No."

She quits hugging and stands back. "You're *bad*. Also lazy."

"Why don't you go down to Zoney's and get some Eggos?"

"No money is why."

Jerome digs into his pocket and hands her a five. This earns him another hug.

"Am I still bad?"

"No, you're *good*! Best brother ever!"

"You can't go without your homegirls," Jerome says.

"And take Odell," Hodges says.

Barbara giggles. "We *always* take Odell."

Hodges watches the girls bop down the sidewalk in their matching tees (talking a mile a minute and trading Odell's leash back and forth), with a feeling of deep disquiet. He can hardly put the Robinson family in lockdown, but those three girls look so *little*.

"Jerome? If somebody tried to mess with them, would Odell—?"

"Protect them?" Jerome is grave now. "With his life, Mr. H. With his life. What's on your mind?"

"Can I continue to count on your discretion?"

"*Yassuh!*"

"Okay, I'm going to put a lot on you. But in return, you have to promise to call me Bill from now on."

Jerome considers. "It'll take some getting used to, but okay."

Hodges tells him almost everything (he omits where he spent the night), occasionally referring to the notes on his legal pad. By the time he finishes, Barbara and her friends are returning from the GoMart, tossing a box of Eggos back and forth and laughing. They go inside to eat their mid-morning treat in front of the television.

Hodges and Jerome sit on the porch steps and talk about ghosts.

20

Edgemont Avenue looks like a war zone, but being south of Lowbriar, at least it's a mostly *white* war zone, populated by the descendants of the Kentucky and Tennessee hillfolk who migrated here to work in the factories after World War II. Now the factories are closed, and a large part of the population consists of drug addicts who switched to brown-tar heroin when Oxy got too expensive. Edgemont is lined with bars, pawnshops, and check-cashing joints, all of them shut up tight on this Saturday morning. The only two stores open for business are a Zoney's and the site of Brady's service call, Batool's Bakery.

Brady parks in front, where he can see anybody trying to break into his Cyber Patrol Beetle, and totes his case inside to the good smells. The greaseball behind the counter is arguing with a Visa-waving customer and pointing to a cardboard sign reading CASH ONLY TIL COMPUTER FIX.

Paki Boy's computer is suffering the dreaded screen freeze. While continuing to monitor his Beetle at thirty-second intervals, Brady plays the Screen Freeze Boogie, which consists of pushing *alt*, *ctrl*, and *del* at the same time. This brings up the machine's Task Manager, and Brady sees at once that the Explorer program is currently listed as non-responsive.

"Bad?" Paki Boy asks anxiously. "Please tell me not bad."

On another day, Brady would string this out, not because guys like Batool tip—they don't—but to see him sweat a few extra drops of Crisco. Not today. This is just his excuse to get off the floor and go to the mall, and he wants to finish as soon as possible.

"Nah, gotcha covered, Mr. Batool," he says. He highlights END TASK and reboots Paki Boy's PC. A moment later the cash register function is back up, complete with all four credit card icons.

"You genius!" Batool cries. For one awful moment, Brady is afraid the perfume-smelling sonofabitch is going to hug him.

21

Brady leaves Hillbilly Heaven and drives north toward the airport. There's a Home Depot in the Birch Hill Mall where he could almost certainly get what he wants, but he makes the Skyway Shopping Complex his destination instead. What he's doing is risky, reckless, and unnecessary. He won't make matters worse by doing it in a store only one corridor over from DE. You don't shit where you eat.

Brady does his business at Skyway's Garden World and sees at once that he's made the right choice. The store is huge, and on this midday late-spring Saturday, it's crammed with shoppers. In the pesticide aisle, Brady adds two cans of Gopher-Go to a shopping cart already loaded with camouflage items: fertilizer, mulch, seeds, and a short-handled gardening claw. He knows it's madness to be buying poison in person when he's already ordered some which will come to his safe mail-drop in another few days, but he can't wait. Absolutely cannot. He probably won't be able to actually poison the nigger family's dog until Monday—and it might even be Tuesday or Wednesday—but he has to be doing *something*. He needs to feel he's . . . how did Shakespeare put it? Taking arms against a sea of troubles.

He stands in line with his shopping cart, telling himself that if the checkout girl (another greaseball, the city is drowning in them) says anything about the Gopher-Go, even something completely innocuous like *This stuff really works*, he'll drop the whole thing. Too great a chance of being remembered and identified: *Oh yes, he was being the nervous young man with the garden claw and the gopher poison.*

He thinks, Maybe I should have worn sunglasses. It's not like I'd stand out, half the men in here are wearing them.

Too late now. He left his Ray-Bans back at Birch Hill, in his Subaru. All he can do is stand here in the checkout line and tell himself not to sweat. Which is like telling someone not to think of a blue polar bear.

*I was noticing him because he was having the sweat,* the greaseball checkout girl (a relative of Batool the Baker, for all Brady knows) will tell the police. Also because he was buying the gopher poison. The kind having the strychnine.

For a moment he almost flees, but now there are people behind him as well as ahead of him, and if he breaks from the line, won't people notice *that*? Won't they wonder—

A nudge from behind him. "You're up, buddy."

Out of options, Brady rolls his cart forward. The cans of Gopher-

Go are a screaming yellow in the bottom of his shopping cart; to Brady they seem the very color of insanity, and that's just as it should be. Being here *is* insane.

Then a comforting thought comes to him, one that's as soothing as a cool hand on a fevered brow: Driving into those people at City Center was even more insane . . . but I got away with it, didn't I?

Yes, and he gets away with this. The greaseball runs his purchases under the scanner without so much as a glance at him. Nor does she look up when she asks him if it will be cash or credit.

Brady pays cash.

He's not *that* insane.

Back in the VW (he's parked it between two trucks, where its fluorescent green hardly shows at all), he sits behind the wheel, taking deep breaths until his heartbeat is steady again. He thinks about the immediate road ahead, and that calms him even more.

First, Odell. The mutt will die a miserable death, and the fat ex-cop will know it's his own fault, even if the Robinsons do not. (From a purely scientific standpoint, Brady will be interested to see if the Det-Ret owns up. He thinks Hodges won't.) Second, the man himself. Brady will give him a few days to marinate in his guilt, and who knows? He may opt for suicide after all. Probably not, though. So Brady will kill him, method yet to be determined. And third . . .

A grand gesture. Something that will be remembered for a hundred years. The question is, what might that grand gesture be?

Brady keys the ignition and tunes the Beetle's shitty radio to BAM-100, where every weekend is a rock-block weekend. He catches the end of a ZZ Top block and is about to punch the button for KISS-92 when his hand freezes. Instead of switching the station, he turns the volume up. Fate is speaking to him.

The deejay informs Brady that the hottest boy band in the country is coming to town for one gig only—that's right, 'Round Here will be playing the MAC next Thursday. "The show's already almost sold out, children, but the BAM-100 Good Guys are holding on to a dozen tickets, and we'll be giving em out in pairs starting on Monday, so listen for the cue to call in and—"

Brady switches the radio off. His eyes are distant, hazy, contemplative. The MAC is what people in the city call the Midwest Culture and Arts Complex. It takes up a whole city block and has a gigantic auditorium.

He thinks, What a way to go out. Oh my God, what a way that would be.

He wonders what exactly the capacity of the MAC's Mingo Auditorium might be. Three thousand? Maybe four? He'll go online tonight and check it out.

## 22

Hodges grabs lunch at a nearby deli (a salad instead of the loaded burger his stomach is rooting for) and goes home. His pleasant exertions of the previous night have caught up with him, and although he owes Janey a call—they have business at the late Mrs. Trelawney's Sugar Heights home, it seems—he decides that his next move in the investigation will be a short nap. He checks the answering machine in the living room, but the MESSAGE WAITING window shows zero. He peeks beneath Debbie's Blue Umbrella and finds nothing new from Mr. Mercedes. He lies down and sets his internal alarm for an hour. His last thought before closing his eyes is that he left his cell phone in the glove compartment of his Toyota again.

Ought to go get that, he thinks. I gave her both numbers, but she's new school instead of old school, and that's the one she'd call first if she needed me.

Then he's asleep.

It's the old school phone that wakes him, and when he rolls over to grab it, he sees that his internal alarm, which never let him down during his years as a cop, has apparently decided it is also retired. He's slept for almost three hours.

"Hello?"

"Do you never check your messages, Bill?" Janey.

It crosses his mind to tell her the battery in his cell phone died, but lying is no way to start a relationship, even one of the day-at-a-time variety. And that's not the important thing. Her voice is blurry and hoarse, as if she's been shouting. Or crying.

He sits up. "What's wrong?"

"My mother had a stroke this morning. I'm at Warsaw County Memorial Hospital. That's the one closest to Sunny Acres."

He swings his feet out onto the floor. "Christ, Janey. How bad is it?"

"Bad. I've called my aunt Charlotte in Cincinnati and uncle Henry in Tampa. They're both coming. Aunt Charlotte will undoubtedly drag my cousin Holly along." She laughs, but the sound has no humor in it. "Of course they're coming—it's that old saying about following the money."

"Do you want *me* to come?"

"Of course, but I don't know how I'd explain you to them. I can't very well introduce you as the man I hopped into bed with almost as soon as I met him, and if I tell them I hired you to investigate Ollie's death, it's apt to show up on one of Uncle Henry's kids' Facebook pages before midnight. When it comes to gossip, Uncle Henry's worse than Aunt Charlotte, but neither one of them is exactly a model of discretion. At least Holly's just weird." She takes a deep, watery breath. "*God*, I could sure use a friendly face right now. I haven't seen Charlotte and Henry in years, neither of them showed up at Ollie's funeral, and they sure haven't made any effort to keep up with *my* life."

Hodges thinks it over and says, "I'm a friend, that's all. I used to work for the Vigilant security company in Sugar Heights. You met me when you came back to inventory your sister's things and take care of the will with the lawyer. Chum."

"Schron." She takes a deep, watery breath. "That could work."

It will. When it comes to spinning stories, no one can do it with a straighter face than a cop. "I'm on my way."

"But . . . don't you have things to take care of in the city? To investigate?"

"Nothing that won't wait. It'll take me an hour to get there. With Saturday traffic, maybe even less."

"Thank you, Bill. With all my heart. If I'm not in the lobby—"

"I'll find you, I'm a trained detective." He's slipping into his shoes.

"I think if you're coming, you better bring a change of clothes. I've rented three rooms in the Holiday Inn down the street. I'll rent one for you as well. The advantages of having money. Not to mention an Amex Platinum Card."

"Janey, it's an easy drive back to the city."

"Sure, but she might die. If it happens today or tonight, I'm *really* going to need a friend. For the . . . you know, the . . ."

Tears catch her and she can't finish. Hodges doesn't need her to, because he knows what she means. For the arrangements.

Ten minutes later he's on the road, headed east toward Sunny Acres and Warsaw County Memorial. He expects to find Janey in the ICU waiting room, but she's outside, sitting on the bumper of a parked ambulance. She gets into his Toyota when he pulls up beside her, and one look at her drawn face and socketed eyes tells him everything he needs to know.

She holds together until he parks in the visitors' lot, then breaks down. Hodges takes her in his arms. She tells him that Elizabeth Wharton passed from the world at quarter past three, central daylight time.

*About the same time I was putting on my shoes,* Hodges thinks, and hugs her tighter.

## 23

Little League season is in full swing, and Brady spends that sunny Saturday afternoon at McGinnis Park, where a full slate of games is being played on three fields. The afternoon is warm and business is brisk. Lots of tweenybop girls have come to watch their little brothers do battle, and as they stand in line waiting for their ice cream, the only thing they seem to be talking about (the only thing Brady hears them talking about, anyway) is the upcoming 'Round Here concert at the MAC. It seems they are all going. Brady has decided that he will go, too. He just needs to dope out a way to get in wearing his special vest—the one loaded with the ball bearings and blocks of plastic explosive.

My final bow, he thinks. A headline for the ages.

The thought improves his mood. So does selling out his entire truckload of goodies—even the JuCee Stix are gone by four o'clock. Back at the ice cream factory, he hands the keys over to Shirley Orton (who never seems to leave) and asks if he can switch with Rudy Stanhope, who's down for the Sunday afternoon shift. Sundays—always assuming the weather cooperates—are busy days, with Loeb's three trucks working not just McGinnis but the city's other four large parks. He accompanies his request with the boyishly winning smile Shirley is a sucker for.

"In other words," Shirley says, "you want two afternoons off in a row."

"You got it." He explains that his mother wants to visit her brother, which means at least one overnight and possibly two. There is no brother, of course, and when it comes to trips, the only one his mother is interested in making these days is the scenic tour that takes her from the couch to the liquor cabinet and back to the couch.

"I'm sure Rudy will say okay. Don't you want to call him yourself?"

"If the request comes from you, it's a done deal."

The bitch giggles, which puts acres of flesh in rather disturbing motion. She makes the call while Brady's changing into his street clothes. Rudy is happy to give up his Sunday shift and take Brady's on Tuesday. This gives Brady two free afternoons to stake out Zoney's GoMart, and two should be enough. If the girl doesn't show up with the dog on either day, he'll call in sick on Wednesday. If he has to, but he doesn't think it will take that long.

After leaving Loeb's, Brady does a little Krogering of his own.

He picks up half a dozen items they need—staples like eggs, milk, butter, and Cocoa Puffs—then swings by the meat counter and picks up a pound of hamburger. Ninety percent lean. Nothing but the best for Odell's last meal.

At home, he opens the garage and unloads everything he bought at Garden World, being careful to put the canisters of Gopher-Go on a high shelf. His mother rarely comes out here, but it doesn't do to take chances. There's a mini-fridge under the worktable; Brady got it at a yard sale for seven bucks, a total steal. It's where he keeps his soft drinks. He stows the package of hamburger behind the Cokes and Mountain Dews, then totes the rest of the groceries inside. What he finds in the kitchen is delightful: his mother shaking paprika over a tuna salad that actually looks tasty.

She catches his look and laughs. "I wanted to make up for the lasagna. I'm sorry about that, but I was just so *tired*."

So drunk is what you were, he thinks, but at least she hasn't given up entirely.

She pouts her lips, freshly dressed in lipstick. "Give Mommy a kiss, honeyboy."

Honeyboy puts his arms around her and gives her a lingering kiss. Her lipstick tastes of something sweet. Then she slaps him briskly on the ass and tells him to go down and play with his computers until dinner's ready.

Brady leaves the cop a brief one-sentence message—**I'm going to fuck you up, Grampa.** Then he plays *Resident Evil* until his mother calls him to dinner. The tuna salad is great, and he has two helpings. She actually *can* cook when she wants, and he says nothing as she pours the first drink of the evening, an extra-big one to make up for the two or three smaller ones she denied herself that afternoon. By nine o'clock, she's snoring on the couch again.

Brady uses the opportunity to go online and learn all about the upcoming 'Round Here concert. He watches a YouTube video where a giggle of girls discusses which of the five boys is the hottest. The consensus is Cam, who sings lead on "Look Me in My Eyes," a piece of audio vomit Brady vaguely recalls hearing on the

radio last year. He imagines those laughing faces torn apart by ball
bearings, those identical Guess jeans in burning tatters.

Later, after he's helped his mother up to bed and he's sure she's
totally conked, he gets the hamburger, puts it in a bowl, and mixes
in two cups of Gopher-Go. If that isn't enough to kill Odell, he'll
run the goddam mutt over with the ice cream truck.

This thought makes him snicker.

He puts the poisoned hamburger in a Baggie and stows it back
in the mini-fridge, taking care to hide it behind the cans of soda
again. He also takes care to wash both his hands and the mixing
bowl in plenty of hot, soapy water.

That night, Brady sleeps well. There are no headaches and no
dreams about his dead brother.

24

Hodges and Janey are loaned a phone-friendly room down the hall
from the hospital lobby, and there they split up the deathwork.

He's the one who gets in touch with the funeral home (Soames,
the same one that handled Olivia Trelawney's exit rites) and makes
sure the hospital is prepared to release the body when the hearse
arrives. Janey, using her iPad with a casual efficiency Hodges
envies, downloads an obituary form from the city paper. She fills
it out quickly, speaking occasionally under her breath as she does
so; once Hodges hears her murmur the phrase *in lieu of flowers*.
When the obit's emailed back, she produces her mother's address
book from her purse and begins making calls to the old lady's
few remaining friends. She's warm with them, and calm, but also
quick. Her voice wavers only once, while she's talking to Althea
Greene, her mother's nurse and closest companion for almost ten
years.

By six o'clock—roughly the same time Brady Hartsfield arrives
home to find his mother putting the finishing touches on her tuna
salad—most of the *t*'s have been crossed and the *i*'s dotted. At ten

to seven, a white Cadillac hearse pulls into the hospital drive and rolls around back. The guys inside know where to go; they've been here plenty of times.

Janey looks at Hodges, her face pale, her mouth trembling. "I'm not sure I can—"

"I'll take care of it."

The transaction is like any other, really; he gives the mortician and his assistant a signed death certificate, they give him a receipt. He thinks, I could be buying a car. When he comes back to the hospital lobby, he spies Janey outside, once more sitting on the bumper of the ambulance. He sits down next to her and takes her hand. She squeezes his fingers hard. They watch the white hearse until it's out of sight. Then he leads her back to his car and they drive the two blocks to the Holiday Inn.

Henry Sirois, a fat man with a moist handshake, shows up at eight. Charlotte Gibney appears an hour later, herding an overloaded bellman ahead of her and complaining about the terrible service on her flight. And the crying babies, she says—you don't want to know. They don't, but she tells them anyway. She's as skinny as her brother is fat, and regards Hodges with a watery, suspicious eye. Lurking by Aunt Charlotte's side is her daughter Holly, a spinster roughly Janey's age but with none of Janey's looks. Holly Gibney never speaks above a mutter and seems to have a problem making eye contact.

"I want to see Betty," Aunt Charlotte announces after a brief dry embrace with her niece. It's as if she thinks Mrs. Wharton might be laid out in the motel lobby, lilies at her head and carnations at her feet.

Janey explains that the body has already been transported to Soames Funeral Home in the city, where Elizabeth Wharton's earthly remains will be cremated on Wednesday afternoon, after a viewing on Tuesday and a brief nondenominational service on Wednesday morning.

"Cremation is *barbaric*," Uncle Henry announces. Everything these two say seems to be an announcement.

# STEPHEN KING

"It's what she wanted." Janey speaks quietly, politely, but Hodges observes the color rising in her cheeks.

He thinks there may be trouble, perhaps a demand to see a written document specifying cremation over burial, but they hold their peace. Perhaps they're remembering all those millions Janey inherited from her sister—money that is Janey's to share. Or not. Uncle Henry and Aunt Charlotte might even be considering all the visits they did not make to their elderly sister during her final suffering years. The visits Mrs. Wharton got during those years were made by Olivia, whom Aunt Charlotte does not mention by name, only calling her "the one with the problems." And of course it was Janey, still hurting from her abusive marriage and rancorous divorce, who was there at the end.

The five of them have a late dinner in the almost deserted Holiday Inn dining room. From the speakers overhead, Herb Alpert toots his horn. Aunt Charlotte has a salad and complains about the dressing, which she has specified should come on the side. "They can put it in a little pitcher, but bottled from the supermarket is still bottled from the supermarket," she announces.

Her muttering daughter orders something that sounds like *sneezebagel hellbun*. It turns out to be a cheeseburger, well done. Uncle Henry opts for fettuccini alfredo and sucks it down with the efficiency of a high-powered Rinse N Vac, fine droplets of perspiration appearing on his forehead as he approaches the finish line. He sops up the remains of the sauce with a chunk of buttered bread.

Hodges does most of the talking, recounting stories from his days with Vigilant Guard Service. The job is fictional, but the stories are mostly true, adapted from his years as a cop. He tells them about the burglar who got caught trying to squirm through a basement window and lost his pants in his efforts to wriggle free (this earns a small smile from Holly); the twelve-year-old boy who stood behind his bedroom door and cold-cocked a home invader with his baseball bat; the housekeeper who stole several pieces of her employer's jewelry only to have them drop out of her under-

220

wear while she served dinner. There are darker stories, many of them, that he keeps to himself.

Over dessert (which Hodges skips, Uncle Henry's unapologetic gluttony serving as a minatory power of example), Janey invites the new arrivals to stay at the house in Sugar Heights starting tomorrow, and the three of them toddle off to their prepaid rooms. Charlotte and Henry seem cheered by the prospect of inspecting at first hand just how the other half lives. As for Holly . . . who knows?

The newcomers' rooms are on the first floor. Janey and Hodges are on the third. As they reach the side-by-side doors, she asks if he will sleep with her.

"No sex," she says. "I never felt less sexy in my life. Basically, I just don't want to be alone."

That's okay with Hodges. He doubts if he would be capable of getting up to dickens, anyway. His stomach and leg muscles are still sore from last night . . . and, he reminds himself, last night she did almost all the work. Once they're beneath the coverlet, she snuggles up to him. He can hardly believe the warmth and firmness of her. The *thereness* of her. It's true he feels no desire at the moment, but he's glad the old lady had the courtesy to stroke out after he got his ashes hauled rather than before. Not very nice, but there it is. Corinne, his ex, used to say that men were born with a shitty-bone.

She pillows her head on his shoulder. "I'm so glad you came."

"Me too." It's the absolute truth.

"Do you think they know we're in bed together?"

Hodges considers. "Aunt Charlotte knows, but she'd know even if we weren't."

"And you can be sure of that because you're a trained—"

"Right. Go to sleep, Janey."

She does, but when he wakes up in the early hours of the morning, needing to use the toilet, she's sitting by the window, looking out at the parking lot and crying. He puts a hand on her shoulder.

She looks up. "I woke you. I'm sorry."

"Nah, this is my usual three A.M. pee-muster. Are you all right?"

"Yes. *Yeah*." She smiles, then wipes at her eyes with her fisted hands, like a child. "Just hating on myself for shipping Mom off to Sunny Acres."

"But she wanted to go, you said."

"Yes. She did. It doesn't seem to change how I feel." Janey looks at him, eyes bleak and shining with tears. "Also hating on myself for letting Olivia do all the heavy lifting while I stayed in California."

"As a trained detective, I deduce you were trying to save your marriage."

She gives him a wan smile. "You're a good guy, Bill. Go on and use the bathroom."

When he comes back, she's curled up in bed again. He puts his arms around her and they sleep spoons the rest of the night.

### 25

Early on Sunday morning, before taking her shower, Janey shows him how to use her iPad. Hodges ducks beneath Debbie's Blue Umbrella and finds a new message from Mr. Mercedes. It's short and to the point: **I'm going to fuck you up, Grampa.**

"Yeah, but tell me how you *really* feel," he says, and surprises himself by laughing.

Janey comes out of the bathroom wrapped in a towel, steam billowing around her like a Hollywood special effect. She asks him what he's laughing about. Hodges shows her the message. She doesn't find it so funny.

"I hope you know what you're doing."

Hodges hopes so, too. Of one thing he's sure: when he gets back home, he'll take the Glock .40 he carried on the job out of his bedroom safe and start carrying it again. The Happy Slapper is no longer enough.

The phone next to the double bed warbles. Janey answers, converses briefly, hangs up. "That was Aunt Charlotte. She suggests the Fun Crew meet for breakfast in twenty minutes. I think she's anxious to get to Sugar Heights and start checking the silverware."

"Okay."

"She also shared that the bed was *much* too hard and she had to take an allergy pill because of the foam pillows."

"Uh-huh. Janey, is Olivia's computer still at the Sugar Heights house?"

"Sure. In the room she used for her study."

"Can you lock that room so they can't get in there?"

She pauses in the act of hooking her bra, for a moment frozen in that pose, elbows back, a female archetype. "Hell with that, I'll just tell them to keep out. I am *not* going to be intimidated by that woman. And what about Holly? Can you understand anything she says?"

"I thought she ordered a sneezebagel for dinner," Hodges admits.

Janey collapses into the chair he awoke to find her crying in last night, only now she's laughing. "Sweetie, you're one bad detective. Which in this sense means good."

"Once the funeral stuff is over and they're gone—"

"Thursday at the latest," she says. "If they stay longer, I'll have to kill them."

"And no jury on earth would convict you. Once they're gone, I want to bring my friend Jerome in to look at that computer. I'd bring him in sooner, but—"

"They'd be all over him. And me."

Hodges, thinking of Aunt Charlotte's bright and inquisitive eyes, agrees.

"Won't the Blue Umbrella stuff be gone? I thought it disappeared every time you left the site."

"It's not Debbie's Blue Umbrella I'm interested in. It's the ghosts your sister heard in the night."

26

As they walk down to the elevator, he asks Janey something that's been troubling him ever since she called yesterday afternoon. "Do you think the questions about Olivia brought on your mother's stroke?"

She shrugs, looking unhappy. "There's no way to tell. She was very old—at least seven years older than Aunt Charlotte, I think—and the constant pain beat her up pretty badly." Then, reluctantly: "It could have played a part."

Hodges runs a hand through his hastily combed hair, mussing it again. "Ah, Jesus."

The elevator dings. They step in. She turns to him and grabs both of his hands. Her voice is swift and urgent. "I'll tell you something, though. If I had to do it over again, I still would. Mom had a long life. Ollie, on the other hand, deserved a few more years. She wasn't terribly happy, but she was doing okay until that bastard got to her. That . . . that *cuckoo* bird. Stealing her car and using it to kill eight people and hurt I don't know how many more wasn't enough for him, was it? Oh, no. He had to steal her *mind*."

"So we push forward."

"Goddam right we do." Her hands tighten on his. "This is *ours*, Bill. Do you get that? This is *ours*."

He wouldn't have stopped anyway, the bit is in his teeth, but the vehemence of her reply is good to hear.

The elevator doors open. Holly, Aunt Charlotte, and Uncle Henry are waiting in the lobby. Aunt Charlotte regards them with her inquisitive crow's eyes, probably prospecting for what Hodges's old partner used to call the freshly fucked look. She asks what took them so long, then, without waiting for an answer, tells them that the breakfast buffet looks very thin. If they were hoping for an omelet to order, they're out of luck.

Hodges thinks that Janey Patterson is in for several very long days.

27

Like the day before, Sunday is brilliant and summery. Like the day before, Brady sells out by four, at least two hours before dinnertime approaches and the parks begin emptying. He thinks about calling home and finding out what his mom wants for supper, then decides to grab takeout from Long John Silver's and surprise her. She loves the Langostino Lobster Bites.

As it turns out, Brady is the one surprised.

He comes into the house from the garage, and his greeting— *Hey, Mom, I'm home!*—dies on his lips. This time she's remembered to turn off the stove, but the smell of the meat she charred for her lunch hangs in the air. From the living room there comes a muffled drumming sound and a strange gurgling cry.

There's a skillet on one of the front burners. He peers into it and sees crumbles of burnt hamburger rising like small volcanic islands from a film of congealed grease. On the counter is a half-empty bottle of Stoli and a jar of mayonnaise, which is all she ever uses to dress her hamburgers.

The grease-spotted takeout bags drop from his hands. Brady doesn't even notice.

No, he thinks. It can't be.

It is, though. He throws open the kitchen refrigerator and there, on the top shelf, is the Baggie of poisoned meat. Only now half of it is gone.

He stares at it stupidly, thinking, She never checks the minifridge in the garage. *Never.* That's *mine.*

This is followed by another thought: How do you know what she checks when you're not here? For all you know she's been through all your drawers and looked under your mattress.

That gurgling cry comes again. Brady runs for the living room, kicking one of the Long John Silver's bags under the kitchen table and leaving the refrigerator door open. His mother is sitting bolt upright on the couch. She's in her blue silk lounging pajamas.

The shirt is covered with a bib of blood-streaked vomit. Her belly protrudes, straining the buttons; it's the belly of a woman who is seven months pregnant. Her hair stands out from her parchment-pale face in a mad spray. Her nostrils are clotted with blood. Her eyes bulge. She's not seeing him, or so he thinks at first, but then she holds out her hands.

"Mom! *Mom!*"

His initial idea is to thump her on the back, but he looks at the mostly eaten hamburger on the coffee table next to the remains of what must have been a perfectly enormous screwdriver, and knows back-thumps will do no good. The stuff's not lodged in her throat. If only it were.

The drumming sound he heard when he came in recommences as her feet begin to piston up and down. It's as if she's marching in place. Her back arches. Her arms fly straight up. Now she's simultaneously marching and signaling that the field goal is good. One foot shoots out and kicks the coffee table. Her screwdriver glass falls over.

"Mom!"

She throws herself back against the sofa cushions, then forward. Her agonized eyes stare at him. She gurgles a muffled something that might or might not be his name.

What do you do for poisoning victims? Was it raw eggs? Or Coca-Cola? No, Coke's for upset stomachs, and she's gone far beyond that.

Have to stick my fingers down her throat, he thinks. Make her gag it up.

But then her teeth begin doing their own march and he pulls his tentatively extended hand back, pressing the palm over his mouth instead. He sees that she has already bitten her lower lip almost to tatters; that's where the blood on her shirt has come from. Some of it, anyway.

"*Brayvie!*" She draws in a hitching breath. What follows is guttural but understandable. "Caw . . . nie . . . wha . . . whan!"

*Call 911.*

He goes to the phone and picks it up before realizing he really can't do that. Think of the unanswerable questions that would ensue. He puts it back down and whirls to her.

"Why did you go snooping out there, Mom? *Why?*"

"*Brayvie!* Nie-wha-*whan!*"

"When did you eat it? How long has it been?"

Instead of answering, she begins to march again. Her head snaps up and her bulging eyes regard the ceiling for a second or two before her head snaps forward again. Her back doesn't move at all; it's as if her head is mounted on bearings. The gurgling sounds return—the sound of water trying to go down a partially clogged drain. Her mouth yawns and she belches vomit. It lands in her lap with a wet splat, and oh God, it's half blood.

He thinks of all the times he's wished her dead. But I never wanted it to be like this, he thinks. Never like this.

An idea lights up his mind like a single bright flare over a stormy ocean. He can find out how to treat her online. *Everything's* online.

"I'm going to take care of it," he says, "but I have to go downstairs for a few minutes. You just . . . you hang in there, Mom. Try . . ."

He almost says *Try to relax.*

He runs into the kitchen, toward the door that leads to his control room. Down there he'll find out how to save her. And even if he can't, he won't have to watch her die.

28

The word to turn on the lights is *control*, but although he speaks it three times, the basement remains in darkness. Brady realizes the voice-recognition program isn't working because he doesn't sound like himself, and is it any wonder? Any fucking wonder at all?

He uses the switch instead and goes down, first shutting the door—and the beastly sounds coming from the living room—behind him.

He doesn't even try to voice-ac his bank of computers, just turns on his Number Three with the button behind the monitor. The countdown to Total Erasure appears and he stops it by typing in his password. But he doesn't seek out poison antidotes; it's far too late for that, and now that he's sitting here in his safe place, he allows himself to know it.

He also knows how this happened. She was good yesterday, staying sober long enough to make a nice supper for them, so she rewarded herself today. Got schnockered, then decided she'd better eat a little something to soak up the booze before her honeyboy got home. Didn't find anything in the pantry or the refrigerator that tickled her fancy. Oh but say, what about the mini-fridge in the garage? Soft drinks wouldn't interest her, but perhaps there were snacks. Only what she found was even better, a Baggie filled with nice fresh hamburger.

It makes Brady think of an old saying—whatever *can* go wrong, *will* go wrong. Is that the Peter Principle? He goes online to find out. After some investigation he discovers it's not the Peter Principle but Murphy's Law. Named after a man named Edward Murphy. The guy made aircraft parts. Who knew?

He surfs a few other sites—actually quite a few—and plays a few hands of solitaire. When there's a particularly loud thump from upstairs, he decides to listen to a few tunes on his iPod. Something cheery. The Staple Singers, maybe.

And as "Respect Yourself" plays in the middle of his head, he goes on Debbie's Blue Umbrella to see if there's a message from the fat ex-cop.

29

When he can put it off no longer, Brady creeps upstairs. Twilight has come. The smell of seared hamburger is almost gone, but the smell of puke is still strong. He goes into the living room. His mother is on the floor next to the coffee table, which is now overturned. Her eyes glare up at the ceiling. Her lips are pulled back in a great big grin. Her hands are claws. She's dead.

Brady thinks, Why did you have to go out in the garage when you got hungry? Oh Mom, Mommy, what in God's name possessed you?

Whatever *can* go wrong *will* go wrong, he thinks, and then, looking at the mess she's made, he wonders if they have any carpet cleaner.

This is Hodges's fault. It all leads back to him.

He'll deal with the old Det-Ret, and soon. Right now, though, he has a more pressing problem. He sits down to consider it, taking the chair he uses on the occasions when he watches TV with her. He realizes she'll never watch another reality show. It's sad . . . but it does have its funny side. He imagines Jeff Probst sending flowers with a card reading *From all your* Survivor *pals*, and he just has to chuckle.

What is he to do with her? The neighbors won't miss her because she never ever had anything to do with them, called them stuck-up. She has no friends, either, not even of the barfly type, because she did all her drinking at home. Once, in a rare moment of self-appraisal, she told him she didn't go out to the bars because they were full of drunks just like her.

"That's why you didn't taste that shit and stop, isn't it?" he asks the corpse. "You were too fucking loaded."

He wishes they had a freezer case. If they did, he'd cram her body into it. He saw that in a movie once. He doesn't dare put her in the garage; that seems a little too public, somehow. He supposes he could wrap her in a rug and take her down to the basement, she'd certainly fit under the stairs, but how would he get any work done, knowing she was there? Knowing that, even inside a roll of rug, her eyes were glaring?

Besides, the basement's *his* place. His control room.

In the end he realizes there's only one thing to do. He grabs her under the arms and drags her toward the stairs. By the time he gets her there, her pajama pants have slid down, revealing what she sometimes calls (*called*, he reminds himself) her winky. Once, when he was in bed with her and she was giving him relief for a particularly bad headache, he tried to touch her winky and she slapped his hand away. Hard. Don't you *ever*, she had said. That's where you *came* from.

Brady pulls her up the stairs, a riser at a time. The pajama pants work down to her ankles and puddle there. He remembers how she did a sit-down march on the couch in her last extremity. How awful. But, like the thing about Jeff Probst sending flowers, it had its funny side, although it wasn't the kind of joke you could explain to people. It was kind of Zen.

Down the hall. Into her bedroom. He straightens up, wincing at the pain in his lower back. God, she's so *heavy*. It's as if death has stuffed her with some dense mystery meat.

Never mind. Get it done.

He yanks up her pants, making her decent again—as decent as a corpse in vomit-soaked pj's can be—and lifts her onto her bed, groaning as fresh pain settles into his back. When he straightens up this time, he can feel his spine crackling. He thinks about taking off her nightclothes and replacing them with something clean— one of the XL tee-shirts she sometimes wears to bed, maybe—but that would mean more lifting and manipulation of what is now just pounds of silent flesh hanging from bone coathangers. What if he threw his back out?

He could at least take off her top, that caught most of the mess, but then he'd have to look at her boobs. Those she did let him touch, but only once in awhile. My handsome boy, she'd say on these occasions. Running her fingers through his hair or massaging his neck where the headaches settled, crouched and snarling. My handsome honeyboy.

In the end he just pulls the bedspread up, covering her entirely. Especially those staring, glaring eyes.

"Sorry, Mom," he says, looking down at the white shape. "Not your fault."

No. It's the fat ex-cop's fault. Brady bought the Gopher-Go to poison the dog, true, but only as a way of getting to Hodges and messing with his head. Now it's Brady's head that's a mess. Not to mention the living room. He's got a lot of work to do down there, but he has something else to do first.

### 30

He's got control of himself again and this time his voice commands work. He doesn't waste time, just sits down in front of his Number Three and logs on to Debbie's Blue Umbrella. His message to Hodges is brief and to the point.

**I'm going to kill you.**
**You won't see me coming.**

# CALL FOR THE DEAD

1

On Monday, two days after Elizabeth Wharton's death, Hodges is once more seated in DeMasio's Italian Ristorante. The last time he was here, it was for lunch with his old partner. This time it's dinner. His companions are Jerome Robinson and Janelle Patterson.

Janey compliments him on his suit, which already fits better even though he's only lost a few pounds (and the Glock he's wearing on his hip hardly shows at all). It's the new hat Jerome likes, a brown fedora Janey bought Hodges on impulse that very day, and presented to him with some ceremony. Because he's a private detective now, she said, and every private dick should have a fedora he can pull down to one eyebrow.

Jerome tries it on and gives it that exact tilt. "What do you think? Do I look like Bogie?"

"I hate to disappoint you," Hodges says, "but Bogie was Caucasian."

"So Caucasian he practically shimmered," Janey adds.

"Forgot that." Jerome tosses the hat back to Hodges, who places it under his chair, reminding himself not to forget it when he leaves. Or step on it.

He's pleased when his two dinner guests take to each other at once. Jerome—an old head on top of a young body, Hodges often thinks—does the right thing as soon as the ice-breaking foolishness of the hat is finished, taking one of Janey's hands in both of his and telling her he's sorry for her loss.

"Both of them," he says. "I know you lost your sister, too. If I lost mine, I'd be the saddest guy on earth. Barb's a pain, but I love her to death."

She thanks him with a smile. Because Jerome's still too young for a legal glass of wine, they all order iced tea. Janey asks him about his college plans, and when Jerome mentions the possibility of Harvard, she rolls her eyes and says, "A *Hah*-vad man. Oh my *Gawd*."

"Massa Hodges goan have to find hisself a new lawnboy!" Jerome exclaims, and Janey laughs so hard she has to spit a bite of shrimp into her napkin. It makes her blush, but Hodges is glad to hear that laugh. Her carefully applied makeup can't completely hide the pallor of her cheeks, or the dark circles under her eyes.

When he asks her how Aunt Charlotte, Uncle Henry, and Holly the Mumbler are enjoying the big house in Sugar Heights, Janey grabs the sides of her head as if afflicted with a monster headache.

"Aunt Charlotte called six times today. I'm not exaggerating. *Six*. The first time was to tell me that Holly woke up in the middle of the night, didn't know where she was, and had a panic attack. Auntie C said she was on the verge of calling an ambulance when Uncle Henry finally got her settled down by talking to her about NASCAR. She's crazy about stock car racing. Never misses it on TV, I understand. Jeff Gordon is her idol." Janey shrugs. "Go figure."

"How old is this Holly?" Jerome asks.

"About my age, but she suffers from a certain amount of . . . emotional retardation, I guess you'd say."

Jerome considers this silently, then says: "She probably needs to reconsider Kyle Busch."

"Who?"

"Never mind."

Janey says Aunt Charlotte has also called to marvel over the monthly electrical bill, which must be huge; to confide that the neighbors seem very standoffish; to announce there is an *awfully* large number of pictures and all that modern art is not to her taste; to point out (although it sounds like another announcement) that if Olivia thought all those lamps were carnival glass, she had almost certainly been taken to the cleaners. The last call, received just before Janey left for the restaurant, had been the most aggravating. Uncle Henry wanted Janey to know, her aunt said, that he had looked into the matter and it still wasn't too late to change her mind about the cremation. She said the idea made her brother very upset—he called it "a Viking funeral"—and Holly wouldn't even discuss it, because it gave her the horrors.

"Their Thursday departure is confirmed," Janey says, "and I'm already counting the minutes." She squeezes Hodges's hand, and says, "There's one bit of good news, though. Auntie C says that Holly was *very* taken with you."

Hodges smiles. "Must be my resemblance to Jeff Gordon."

Janey and Jerome order dessert. Hodges, feeling virtuous, does not. Then, over coffee, he gets down to business. He has brought two folders with him, and hands one to each of his dinner companions.

"All my notes. I've organized them as well as I can. I want you to have them in case anything happens to me."

Janey looks alarmed. "What else has he said to you on that site?"

"Nothing at all," Hodges says. The lie comes out smoothly and convincingly. "It's just a precaution."

"You sure of that?" Jerome asks.

"Absolutely. There's nothing definitive in the notes, but that doesn't mean we haven't made progress. I see a path of investigation that might—I repeat *might*—take us to this guy. In the meantime, it's important that you both remain very aware of what's going on around you at all times."

"BOLO our asses off," Janey says.

"Right." He turns to Jerome. "And what, specifically, are you going to be on the lookout for?"

The reply is quick and sure. "Repeat vehicles, especially those driven by males on the younger side, say between the ages of twenty-five and forty. Although I think forty's pretty old. Which makes you practically ancient, Bill."

"Nobody loves a smartass," Hodges says. "Experience will teach you that in time, young man."

Elaine, the hostess, drifts over to ask how everything was. They tell her everything was fine, and Hodges asks for more coffee all around.

"Right away," she says. "You're looking much better than the last time you were here, Mr. Hodges. If you don't mind me saying so."

Hodges doesn't mind. He *feels* better than the last time he was here. Lighter than the loss of seven or eight pounds can account for.

When Elaine's gone and the waiter has poured more coffee, Janey leans over the table with her eyes fixed on his. "What path? Tell us."

He finds himself thinking of Donald Davis, who has confessed to killing not only his wife but five other women at rest stops along the highways of the Midwest. Soon the handsome Mr. Davis will be in State, where he will no doubt spend the rest of his life.

Hodges has seen it all before.

He's not so naïve as to believe that every homicide is solved, but more often than not, murder *does* out. Something (a certain wifely body in a certain abandoned gravel pit, for instance) comes to light. It's as if there's a fumble-fingered but powerful universal force at work, always trying to put wrong things right. The detectives assigned to a murder case read reports, interview witnesses, work the phones, study forensic evidence . . . and wait for that force to do its job. When it does (*if* it does), a path appears. It often leads straight to the doer, the sort of person Mr. Mercedes refers to in his letters as a *perk*.

Hodges asks his dinner companions, "What if Olivia Trelawney actually *did* hear ghosts?"

2

In the parking lot, standing next to the used but serviceable Jeep Wrangler his parents gave him as a seventeenth birthday present, Jerome tells Janey how good it was to meet her, and kisses her cheek. She looks surprised but pleased.

Jerome turns to Hodges. "You all set, Bill? Need anything tomorrow?"

"Just for you to look into that stuff we talked about so you'll be ready when we check out Olivia's computer."

"I'm all over it."

"Good. And don't forget to give my best to your dad and mom."

Jerome grins. "Tell you what, I'll pass your best on to Dad. As for Mom . . ." Tyrone Feelgood Delight makes a brief cameo appearance. "I be steppin round *dat* lady fo' de nex' week or so."

Hodges raises his eyebrows. "Are you in dutch with your mother? That doesn't sound like you."

"Nah, she's just grouchy. And I can relate." Jerome snickers.

"What are you talking about?"

"Oh, man. There's a concert at the MAC Thursday night. This dopey boy band called 'Round Here. Barb and her friend Hilda and a couple of their other friends are insane to see them, although they're as vanilla pudding as can be."

"How old's your sister?" Janey asks.

"Nine. Going on ten."

"Vanilla pudding's what girls that age like. Take it from a former eleven-year-old who was crazy about the Bay City Rollers." Jerome looks puzzled, and she laughs. "If you knew who they were, I'd lose all respect for you."

"Anyway, none of them have ever been to a live show, right? I mean, other than *Barney* or *Sesame Street on Ice* or something. So they pestered and pestered—they even pestered *me*—and finally the moms got together and decided that since it was an early show, the girls could go even if it was a school night, as long as one of *them* did the chaperone thing. They literally drew straws, and my mom lost."

He shakes his head. His face is solemn but his eyes are sparkling. "My mom at the MAC with three or four thousand screaming girls between the ages of eight and fourteen. Do I have to explain any more about why I'm keeping out of her way?"

"I bet she has a great time," Janey says. "She probably screamed for Marvin Gaye or Al Green not so long ago."

Jerome hops into his Wrangler, gives them a final wave, and pulls out onto Lowbriar. That leaves Hodges and Janey standing beside Hodges's car, in an almost-summer night. A quarter moon has risen above the underpass that separates the more affluent part of the city from Lowtown.

"He's a good guy," Janey says. "You're lucky to have him."

"Yeah," Hodges says. "I am."

She takes the fedora off his head and puts it on her own, giving it a small but provocative tilt. "What's next, Detective? Your place?"

"Do you mean what I hope you mean?"

"I don't want to sleep alone." She stands on tiptoe to return his hat. "If I must surrender my body to make sure that doesn't happen, I suppose I must."

Hodges pushes the button that unlocks his car and says, "Never let it be said I failed to take advantage of a lady in distress."

"You are no gentleman, sir," she says, then adds, "Thank God. Let's go."

3

It's better this time because they know each other a little. Anxiety has been replaced by eagerness. When the lovemaking is done, she slips into one of his shirts (it's so big her breasts disappear completely and the tails hang down to the backs of her knees) and explores his small house. He trails her a bit anxiously.

She renders her verdict after they've returned to the bedroom. "Not bad for a bachelor pad. No dirty dishes in the sink, no hair in the bathtub, no porn videos on top of the TV. I even spied a green vegetable or two in the crisper, which earns you bonus points."

She's filched two cans of beer from the fridge and touches hers to his.

"I never expected to be here with another woman," Hodges says. "Except maybe for my daughter. We talk on the phone and email, but Allie hasn't actually visited in a couple of years."

"Did she take your ex's side in the divorce?"

"I suppose she did." Hodges has never thought about it in exactly those terms. "If so, she was probably right to."

"You might be too hard on yourself."

Hodges sips his beer. It tastes pretty good. As he sips again, a thought occurs to him.

"Does Aunt Charlotte have this number, Janey?"

"No way. That's not the reason I wanted to come here instead of going back to the condo, but I'd be a liar if I said it never crossed my mind." She looks at him gravely. "Will you come to the memorial service on Wednesday? Say you will. Please. I need a friend."

"Of course. I'll be at the viewing on Tuesday as well."

She looks surprised, but happily so. "That seems above and beyond."

Not to Hodges, it doesn't. He's in full investigative mode now, and attending the funeral of someone involved in a murder case— even peripherally—is standard police procedure. He doesn't really believe Mr. Mercedes will turn up at either the viewing or the service on Wednesday, but it's not out of the question. Hodges hasn't seen today's paper, but some alert reporter might well have linked Mrs. Wharton and Olivia Trelawney, the daughter who committed suicide after her car was used as a murder weapon. Such a connection is hardly news, but you could say the same about Lindsay Lohan's adventures with drugs and alcohol. Hodges thinks there might at least have been a sidebar.

"I want to be there," he says. "What's the deal with the ashes?"

"The mortician called them the *cremains*," she says, and wrinkles her nose the way she does when she mocks his *yeah*. "Is that gross or what? It sounds like something you'd pour in your coffee. On the upside, I'm pretty sure I won't have to fight Aunt Charlotte or Uncle Henry for them."

"No, you won't have to do that. Is there going to be a reception?"

Janey sighs. "Auntie C insists. So the service at ten, followed by a luncheon at the house in Sugar Heights. While we're eating catered sandwiches and telling our favorite Elizabeth Wharton stories, the funeral home people will take care of the cremation. I'll decide what to do with the ashes after the three of them leave on Thursday. They'll never even have to look at the urn."

"That's a good idea."

"Thanks, but I dread the luncheon. Not Mrs. Greene and the rest of Mom's few old friends, but *them*. If Aunt Charlotte freaks, Holly's apt to have a meltdown. You'll come to lunch, too, won't you?"

"If you let me reach inside that shirt you're wearing, I'll do anything you want."

"In that case, let me help you with the buttons."

4

Not many miles from where Kermit William Hodges and Janelle Patterson are lying together in the house on Harper Road, Brady Hartsfield is sitting in his control room. Tonight he's at his worktable instead of his bank of computers. And doing nothing.

Nearby, lying amid the litter of small tools, bits of wire, and computer components, is the Monday paper, still rolled up inside its thin plastic condom. He brought it in when he got back from Discount Electronix, but only from force of habit. He has no interest in the news. He has other things to think about. How he's going to get the cop. How he's going to get into the 'Round Here concert at the MAC wearing his carefully constructed suicide vest. If he really intends to do it, that is. Right now it all seems like an awful lot of work. A long row to hoe. A high mountain to climb. A . . . a . . .

But he can't think of any other similes. Or are those metaphors?

Maybe, he thinks drearily, I just ought to kill myself now and be done with it. Get rid of these awful thoughts. These snapshots from hell.

Snapshots like the one of his mother, for instance, convulsing on the sofa after eating the poisoned meat meant for the Robinson family's dog. Mom with her eyes bugging out and her pajama shirt covered with puke—how would that picture look in the old family album?

He needs to think, but there's a hurricane going on in his head, a big bad Category Five Katrina, and everything is flying.

His old Boy Scout sleeping bag is spread out on the basement floor, on top of an air mattress he scrounged from the garage. The air mattress has a slow leak. Brady supposes he ought to replace it if he means to continue sleeping down here for whatever short stretch of life remains to him. And where else *can* he sleep? He can't bring himself to use his bed on the second floor, not with his mother lying dead in her own bed just down the hall, maybe already rotting her way into the sheets. He's turned on her air conditioner and cranked it up to HI COOL, but he's under no illusions about how well that will work. Or for how long. Nor is sleeping on the living room couch an option. He cleaned it as well as he could, and turned the cushions, but it still smells of her vomit.

No, it has to be down here, in his special place. His control room. Of course the basement has its own unpleasant history; it's where his little brother died. Only *died* is a bit of a euphemism, and it's a bit late for those.

Brady thinks about how he used Frankie's name when he posted to Olivia Trelawney under Debbie's Blue Umbrella. It was as if Frankie was alive again for a little while. Only when the Trelawney bitch died, Frankie died with her.

Died again.

"I never liked you anyway," he says, looking toward the foot of the stairs. It is a strangely childish voice, high and treble, but Brady doesn't notice. "And I had to." He pauses. "*We* had to."

He thinks of his mother, and how beautiful she was in those days.

Those old days.

5

Deborah Ann Hartsfield was one of those rare ex-cheerleaders who, even after bearing children, managed to hang on to the body that had danced and pranced its way along the sidelines under the Friday-night lights: tall, full-figured, honey-haired. During the early years of her marriage, she took no more than a glass of wine with dinner. Why drink to excess when life was good sober? She had her husband, she had her house on the North Side of the city—not exactly a palace, but what starter-home was?—and she had her two boys.

At the time his mother became a widow, Brady was eight and Frankie was three. Frankie was a plain child, and a bit on the slow side. Brady, on the other hand, had good looks and quick wits. Also, what a charmer! She doted on him, and Brady felt the same about her. They spent long Saturday afternoons cuddled together on the couch under a blanket, watching old movies and drinking hot chocolate while Norm puttered in the garage and Frankie crawled around on the carpet, playing with blocks or a little fire truck that he liked so well he had given it a name: Sammy.

Norm Hartsfield was a lineman for Central States Power. He made a good salary pole-climbing, but had his sights trained on bigger things. Perhaps it was those things he was eyeing instead of watching what he was doing that day beside Route 51, or maybe he just lost his balance a little and reached the wrong way in an effort to steady himself. No matter what the reason, the result was lethal. His partner was just reporting that they'd found the out-age and repair was almost complete when he heard a crackling sound. That was twenty thousand volts of coal-fired CSP electric-ity pouring into Norm Hartsfield's body. The partner looked up just in time to see Norm tumble out of the cherry-picker basket and plunge forty feet to the ground with his left hand melted and the sleeve of his uniform shirt on fire.

Addicted to credit cards, like most middle Americans as the end of the century approached, the Hartsfields had savings of less than two thousand dollars. That was pretty thin, but there was a good insurance policy, and CSP kicked in an additional seventy thou-sand, trading it for Deborah Ann's signature on a paper absolving the company of all blame in the matter of Norman Hartsfield's death. To Deborah Ann, that seemed like a huge bucketful of cash. She paid off the mortgage on the house and bought a new car. Never did it occur to her that some buckets fill but once.

She had been working as a hairdresser when she met Norm, and went back to that trade after his death. Six months or so into her widowhood, she began seeing a man she had met one day at the bank—only a junior executive, she told Brady, but he had what she called *prospects*. She brought him home. He ruffled Brady's hair and called him *champ*. He ruffled Frankie's hair and called him *lit-tle champ*. Brady didn't like him (he had big teeth, like a vampire in a scary movie), but he didn't show his dislike. He had already learned to wear a happy face and keep his feelings to himself.

One night, before taking Deborah Ann out to dinner, the boy-friend told Brady, Your mother's a charmer and so are you. Brady smiled and said thank you and hoped the boyfriend would get in a car accident and die. As long as his mother wasn't with him, that was. The boyfriend with the scary teeth had no right to take his father's place.

That was Brady's job.

Frankie choked on the apple during *The Blues Brothers*. It was supposed to be a funny movie. Brady didn't see what was so funny about it, but his mother and Frankie laughed fit to split. His mother was happy and all dressed up because she was going out with her boyfriend. In a little while the sitter would come in. The sitter was a stupid greedyguts who always looked in the refrigerator to see what was good to eat as soon as Deborah Ann left, bending over so her fat ass stuck out.

There were two snack-bowls on the coffee table; one contained popcorn, the other apple slices dusted with cinnamon. In one part of the movie people sang in church and one of the Blues Brothers did flips all the way up the center aisle. Frankie was sitting on the floor and laughed hard when the fat Blues Brother did his flips. When he drew in breath to laugh some more, he sucked a piece of cinnamon-dusted apple slice down his throat. That made him stop laughing. He began to jerk around and claw at his neck instead.

Brady's mother screamed and grabbed him in her arms. She squeezed him, trying to make the piece of apple come out. It didn't. Frankie's face went red. She reached into his mouth and down his throat, trying to get at the piece of apple. She couldn't. Frankie started to lose the red color.

"Oh-my-dear-Jesus," Deborah Ann cried, and ran for the phone. As she picked it up she shouted at Brady, "Don't just sit there like an asshole! Pound him on the back!"

Brady didn't like to be shouted at, and his mother had never called him an asshole before, but he pounded Frankie on the back. He pounded *hard*. The piece of apple slice did not come out. Now Frankie's face was turning blue. Brady had an idea. He picked Frankie up by his ankles so Frankie's head hung down and his hair brushed the rug. The apple slice did not come out.

"Stop being a brat, Frankie," Brady said.

Frankie continued to breathe—sort of, he was making little breezy whistling noises, anyway—almost until the ambulance got there. Then he stopped. The ambulance men came in. They were wearing black clothes with yellow patches on the jackets. They made Brady go into the kitchen, so Brady didn't see what they did, but his mother screamed and later he saw drops of blood on the carpet.

No apple slice, though.

Then everyone except Brady went away in the ambulance. He sat on the couch and ate popcorn and watched TV. Not *The Blues Brothers*; *The Blues Brothers* was stupid, just a bunch of singing and running around. He found a movie about a crazy guy who kidnapped a bunch of kids who were on their schoolbus. That was pretty exciting.

When the fat sitter showed up, Brady said, "Frankie choked on an apple slice. There's ice cream in the refrigerator. Vanilla Crunch. Have as much as you want." Maybe, he thought, if she ate enough ice cream, she'd have a heart attack and he could call 911.

Or just let the stupid bitch lay there. That would probably be better. He could watch her.

Deborah Ann finally came home at eleven o'clock. The fat sitter had made Brady go to bed, but he wasn't asleep, and when he came downstairs in his pj's, his mother hugged him to her. The fat babysitter asked how Frankie was. The fat babysitter was full of fake concern. The reason Brady knew it was fake was because *he* wasn't concerned, so why would the fat babysitter care?

"He's going to be fine," Deborah Ann said, with a big smile. Then, when the fat babysitter was gone, she started crying like crazy. She got her wine out of the refrigerator, but instead of pouring it into a glass, she drank straight from the neck of the bottle.

"He might not be," she told Brady, wiping wine from her chin. "He's in a coma. Do you know what that is?"

"Sure. Like in a doctor show."

"That's right." She got down on one knee, so they were face-to-face. Having her so close—smelling the perfume she'd put on for the date that never happened—gave him a feeling in his stomach. It was funny but good. He kept looking at the blue stuff on her eyelids. It was weird but good.

"He stopped breathing for a long time before the EMTs could make some room for the air to go down. The doctor at the hospital said that even if he comes out of his coma, there might be brain damage."

Brady thought Frankie was already brain-damaged—he was awful stupid, carrying around that fire truck all the time—but said nothing. His mother was wearing a blouse that showed the tops of her titties. That gave him a funny feeling in his stomach, too.

"If I tell you something, do you promise never to tell anyone? Not another living soul?"

Brady promised. He was good at keeping secrets.

"It might be better if he *does* die. Because if he wakes up and he's brain-damaged, I don't know what we'll do."

Then she clasped him to her and her hair tickled the side of his face and the smell of her perfume was very strong. She said: "Thank God it wasn't you, honeyboy. Thank God for that."

Brady hugged her back, pressing his chest against her titties. He had a boner.

Frankie *did* wake up, and sure enough, he was brain-damaged. He had never been smart ("Takes after his father," Deborah Ann said once), but compared to the way he was now, he had been a genius in those pre–apple slice days. He had toilet-trained late, not until he was almost three and a half, and now he was back in diapers. His vocabulary had been reduced to no more than a dozen words. Instead of walking he made his way around the house in a limping shuffle. Sometimes he fell abruptly and profoundly asleep, but that was only in the daytime. At night, he had a tendency to wander, and before he started out on these nocturnal safaris, he usually stripped off his Pampers. Sometimes he got into bed with his mother. More often he got in with Brady, who would awake to find the bed soaked and Frankie staring at him with goofy, creepy love.

Frankie had to keep going to the doctor. His breathing was never right. At its best it was a wet wheeze, at its worst, when he had one of his frequent colds, a rattling bark. He could no longer eat solid food; his meals had to be pureed in the blender and he ate them in a highchair. Drinking from a glass was out of the question, so it was back to sippy cups.

The boyfriend from the bank was long gone, and the fat baby-sitter didn't last, either. She said she was sorry, but she just couldn't cope with Frankie the way he was now. For awhile Deborah Ann got a full-time home care lady to come in, but the home care lady ended up getting more money than Deborah Ann made at the beauty shop, so she let the home care lady go and quit her job. Now they were living off savings. She began to drink more, switching from wine to vodka, which she called *a more efficient delivery system.* Brady would sit with her on the couch, drinking Pepsi. They would watch Frankie crawl around on the carpet with his fire truck in one hand and his blue sippy cup, also filled with Pepsi, in the other.

"It's shrinking like the icecaps," Deborah Ann would say, and Brady no longer had to ask her what *it* was. "And when it's gone, we'll be out on the street."

She went to see a lawyer (in the same strip mall where Brady would years later flick an annoying goofy-boy in the throat) and paid a hundred dollars for a consultation. She took Brady with her. The lawyer's name was Greensmith. He wore a cheap suit and kept sneaking glances at Deborah Ann's titties.

"I can tell you what happened," he said. "Seen it before. That piece of apple left just enough space around his windpipe to let him keep breathing. It's too bad you reached down his throat, that's all."

"I was trying to get it out!" Deborah Ann said indignantly.

"I know, any good mother would do the same, but you pushed it deeper instead, and blocked his windpipe entirely. If one of the EMTs had done that, you'd have a case. Worth a few hundred thousand at least. Maybe a million-five. Seen it before. But it was you. And you told them what you did. Didn't you?"

Deborah Ann admitted she had.

"Did they intubate him?"

Deborah Ann said they did.

"Okay, *that's* your case. They got an airway into him, but in doing so, they pushed that bad apple in even deeper." He sat back, spread his fingers on his slightly yellowed white shirt, and peeped at Deborah Ann's titties again, maybe just to make sure they hadn't slipped out of her bra and run away. "Hence, brain damage."

"So you'll take the case?"

"Happy to, if you can pay for the five years it'll drag through the courts. Because the hospital and their insurance providers will fight you every step of the way. Seen it before."

"How much?"

Greensmith named a figure, and Deborah Ann left the office, holding Brady's hand. They sat in her Honda (then new) and she cried. When that part was over, she told him to play the radio while she ran another errand. Brady knew what the other errand entailed: a bottle of efficient delivery system.

She relived her meeting with Greensmith many times over the years, always ending with the same bitter pronouncement: "I paid a hundred dollars I couldn't afford to a lawyer in a suit from Men's Wearhouse, and all I found out was I couldn't afford to fight the big insurance companies and get what was coming to me."

The year that followed was five years long. There was a life-sucking monster in the house, and the monster's name was Frankie. Sometimes when he knocked something over or woke Deborah Ann up from a nap, she spanked him. Once she lost it completely and punched him in the side of the head, sending him to the floor in a twitching, eye-rolling daze. She picked him up and hugged him and cried and said she was sorry, but there was only so much a woman could take.

She went into Hair Today as a sub whenever she could. On these occasions she called Brady in sick at school so he could babysit his little brother. Sometimes Brady would catch Frankie reaching for stuff he wasn't supposed to have (or stuff that belonged to Brady, like his Atari Arcade handheld), and then he would slap Frankie's hands until Frankie cried. When the wails started, Brady would remind himself that it wasn't Frankie's fault, he had brain damage from that damn, no, that *fucking* apple slice, and he would be overcome by a mixture of guilt, rage, and sorrow. He would take

Frankie on his lap and rock him and tell him he was sorry, but there was only so much a man could take. And he *was* a man, Mom said so: the man of the house. He got good at changing Frankie's diapers, but when there was poo (no, it was *shit*, not poo but *shit*), he would sometimes pinch Frankie's legs and shout at him to lay still, damn you, lay still. Even if Frankie *was* laying still. Laying there with Sammy the Fire Truck clutched to his chest and looking up at the ceiling with his big stupid brain-damaged eyes.

That year was full of sometimes.

Sometimes he loved Frankie up and kissed him.

Sometimes he'd shake him and say This is your fault, we're going to have to live in the street and it's your fault.

Sometimes, putting Frankie to bed after a day at the beauty parlor, Deborah Ann would see bruises on the boy's arms and legs. Once on his throat, which was scarred from the tracheotomy the EMTs had performed. She never commented on these.

Sometimes Brady loved Frankie. Sometimes he hated him. Usually he felt both things at the same time, and it gave him headaches.

Sometimes (mostly when she was drunk), Deborah Ann would rail at the train-wreck of her life. "I can't get assistance from the city, the state, or the goddam federal government, and why? Because we still have too much from the insurance and the settlement, that's why. Does anyone care that everything's going out and nothing's coming in? No. When the money's gone and we're living in a homeless shelter on Lowbriar Avenue, *then* I'll be eligible for assistance, and isn't that just *ducky*."

Sometimes Brady would look at Frankie and think, You're in the *way*. You're in the *way*, Frankie, you're in the fucking goddam shitass *waaay*.

Sometimes—often—Brady hated the whole fucking goddam shitass world. If there was a God, like the Sunday guys said on TV, wouldn't He take Frankie up to heaven, so his mother could go back to work fulltime and they wouldn't have to be out on the street? Or living on Lowbriar Avenue, where his mother said there was nothing but nigger drug addicts with guns? If there was a

God, why had He let Frankie choke on that fucking apple slice in the first place? And then letting him wake up brain-damaged afterward, that was going from bad to fucking goddam shitass *worse*. There was no God. You only had to watch Frankie crawling around the floor with goddam Sammy in one hand, then getting up and limping for awhile before giving that up and crawling again, to know that the idea of God was fucking ridiculous.

Finally Frankie died. It happened fast. In a way it was like running down those people at City Center. There was no forethought, only the looming reality that something had to be done. You could almost call it an accident. Or fate. Brady didn't believe in God, but he did believe in fate, and sometimes the man of the house had to be fate's right hand.

His mother was making pancakes for supper. Frankie was playing with Sammy. The basement door was standing open because Deborah Ann had bought two cartons of cheap off-brand toilet paper at Chapter 11 and they kept it down there. The bathrooms needed re-stocking, so she sent Brady down to get some. His hands had been full when he came back up, so he left the basement door open. He thought Mom would shut it, but when he came down from putting the toilet paper in the two upstairs bathrooms, it was still open. Frankie was on the floor, pushing Sammy across the linoleum and making *rrr-rrr* sounds. He was wearing red pants that bulged with his triple-thick diapers. He was working ever closer to the open door and the steep stairs beyond, but Deborah Ann still made no move to close the door. Nor did she ask Brady, now setting the table, to do it.

"*Rrr-rrr,*" said Frankie. "*Rrr-rrr.*"

He pushed the fire truck. Sammy rolled to the edge of the basement doorway, bumped against the jamb, and there he stopped.

Deborah Ann left the stove. She walked over to the basement door. Brady thought she would bend down and hand Frankie's fire truck back to him, but she didn't. She kicked it instead. There was a small clacking sound as it tumbled down the steps, all the way to the bottom.

"Oops," she said. "Sammy faw down go boom." Her voice was very flat.

Brady walked over. This was interesting.

"Why'd you do that, Mom?"

Deborah Ann put her hands on her hips, the spatula jutting from one of them. She said, "Because I'm just so sick of listening to him make that sound."

Frankie opened his mouth and began to blat.

"Quit it, Frankie," Brady said, but Frankie didn't. What Frankie did was crawl onto the top step and peer down into the darkness.

In that same flat voice Deborah Ann said, "Turn on the light, Brady. So he can see Sammy."

Brady turned on the light and peered over his blatting brother.

"Yup," he said. "There he is. Right down at the bottom. See him, Frankie?"

Frankie crawled a little farther, still blatting. He looked down. Brady looked at his mother. Deborah Ann Hartsfield gave the smallest, most imperceptible nod. Brady didn't think. He simply kicked Frankie's triple-diapered butt and down Frankie went in a series of clumsy somersaults that made Brady think of the fat Blues Brother flipping his way along the church aisle. On the first somersault Frankie kept on blatting, but the second time around, his head connected with one of the stair risers and the blatting stopped all at once, as if Frankie were a radio and someone had turned him off. That was horrible, but had its funny side. He went over again, legs flying out limply to either side in a **Y** shape. Then he slammed headfirst into the basement floor.

"Oh my God, Frankie fell!" Deborah Ann cried. She dropped the spatula and ran down the stairs. Brady followed her.

Frankie's neck was broken, even Brady could tell that, because it was all croggled in the back, but he was still alive. He was breathing in little snorts. Blood was coming out of his nose. More was coming from the side of his head. His eyes moved back and forth, but nothing else did. Poor Frankie. Brady started to cry. His mother was crying, too.

"What should we do?" Brady asked. "What should we do, Mom?"

"Go upstairs and get me a pillow off the sofa."

He did as she said. When he came back down, Sammy the Fire Truck was lying on Frankie's chest. "I tried to get him to hold it, but he can't," Deborah Ann said.

"Yeah," Brady said. "He's prob'ly paralyzed. Poor Frankie."

Frankie looked up, first at his mother and then his brother. "Brady," he said.

"It'll be okay, Frankie," Brady said, and held out the pillow.

Deborah Ann took it and put it over Frankie's face. It didn't take long. Then she sent Brady upstairs again to put the sofa pillow back and get a wet washcloth. "Turn off the stove while you're up there," she said. "The pancakes are burning. I can smell them."

She washed Frankie's face to get rid of the blood. Brady thought that was very sweet and motherly. Years later he realized she'd also been making sure there would be no threads or fibers from the pillow on Frankie's face.

When Frankie was clean (although there was still blood in his hair), Brady and his mother sat on the basement steps, looking at him. Deborah Ann had her arm around Brady's shoulders. "I better call nine-one-one," she said.

"Okay."

"He pushed Sammy too hard and Sammy fell downstairs. Then he tried to go after him and lost his balance. I was making the pancakes and you were putting toilet paper in the bathrooms upstairs. You didn't see anything. When you got down to the basement, he was already dead."

"Okay."

"Say it back to me."

Brady did. He was an A student in school, and good at remembering things.

"No matter what anybody asks you, never say more than that. Don't add anything, and don't change anything."

"Okay, but can I say you were crying?"

She smiled. She kissed his forehead and cheek. Then she kissed him full on the lips. "Yes, honeyboy, you can say that."

"Will we be all right now?"

"Yes." There was no doubt in her voice. "We'll be fine."

She was right. There were only a few questions about the accident and no hard ones. They had a funeral. It was pretty nice. Frankie was in a Frankie-size coffin, wearing a suit. He didn't look brain-damaged, just fast asleep. Before they closed the coffin, Brady kissed his brother's cheek and tucked Sammy the Fire Truck in beside him. There was just enough room.

That night Brady had the first of his really bad headaches. He started thinking Frankie was under his bed, and that made the headache worse. He went down to his mom's room and got in with her. He didn't tell her he was scared of Frankie being under his bed, just that his head ached so bad he thought it was going to explode. She hugged him and kissed him and he wriggled against her tight-tight-tight. It felt good to wriggle. It made the headache less. They fell asleep together and the next day it was just the two of them and life was better. Deborah Ann got her old job back, but there were no more boyfriends. She said Brady was the only boyfriend she wanted now. They never talked about Frankie's accident, but sometimes Brady dreamed about it. He didn't know if his mother did or not, but she drank plenty of vodka, so much she eventually lost her job again. That was all right, though, because by then he was old enough to go to work. He didn't miss going to college, either.

College was for people who didn't know they were smart.

6

Brady comes out of these memories—a reverie so deep it's like hypnosis—to discover he's got a lapful of shredded plastic. At first he doesn't know where it came from. Then he looks at the newspaper lying on his worktable and understands he tore apart the bag it was in with his fingernails while he was thinking about Frankie.

He deposits the shreds in the wastebasket, then picks up the paper and stares vacantly at the headlines. Oil is still gushing into the Gulf of Mexico and British Petroleum executives are squalling that they're doing the best they can and people are being mean to them. Nidal Hasan, the asshole shrink who shot up the Fort Hood Army base in Texas, is going to be arraigned in the next day or two. (You should have had a Mercedes, Nidal-baby, Brady thinks.) Paul McCartney, the ex-Beatle Brady's mom used to call Old Spaniel Eyes, is getting a medal at the White House. Why is it, Brady sometimes wonders, that people with only a little talent get so much of everything? It's just another proof that the world is crazy.

Brady decides to take the paper up to the kitchen and read the political columns. Those and a melatonin capsule might be enough to send him off to sleep. Halfway up the stairs he turns the paper over to see what's below the fold, and freezes. There are photos of two women, side by side. One is Olivia Trelawney. The other one is much older, but the resemblance is unmistakable. Especially those thin bitch-lips.

MOTHER OF OLIVIA TRELAWNEY DIES, the headline reads. Below it: *Protested Daughter's "Unfair Treatment," Claimed Press Coverage "Destroyed Her Life."*

What follows is a two-paragraph squib, really just an excuse to get last year's tragedy (If you want to use that word, Brady thinks—rather snidely) back on the front page of a newspaper that's slowly being strangled to death by the Internet. Readers are referred to the obituary on page twenty-six, and Brady, now sitting at the kitchen table, turns there double-quick. The cloud of dazed gloom that has surrounded him ever since his mother's death has been swept away in an instant. His mind is ticking over rapidly, ideas coming together, flying apart, then coming together again like pieces in a jigsaw puzzle. He's familiar with this process and knows it will continue until they connect with a click of finality and a clear picture appears.

# MR. MERCEDES

ELIZABETH SIROIS WHARTON, 87, passed away peacefully on May 29, 2010, at Warsaw County Memorial Hospital. She was born on January 19, 1923, the son of Marcel and Catherine Sirois. She is survived by her brother, Henry Sirois, her sister, Charlotte Gibney, her niece, Holly Gibney, and her daughter, Janelle Patterson. Elizabeth was predeceased by her husband, Alvin Wharton, and her beloved daughter, Olivia. Private visitation will be held from 10 AM to 1 PM at Soames Funeral Home on Tuesday, June 1, followed by a 10 AM memorial service at Soames Funeral Home on Wednesday, June 2. After the service, a reception for close friends and family members will take place at 729 Lilac Drive, in Sugar Heights. The family requests no flowers, but suggests contributions to either the American Red Cross or the Salvation Army, Mrs. Wharton's favorite charities.

Brady reads all this carefully, with several related questions in mind. Will the fat ex-cop be at the visitation? At the Wednesday memorial service? At the reception? Brady's betting on all three. Looking for the perk. Looking for *him*. Because that's what cops do.

He remembers the last message he sent to Hodges, the good old Det-Ret. Now he smiles and says it out loud: "You won't see me coming."

"Make sure he doesn't," Deborah Ann Hartsfield says.

He knows she's not really there, but he can almost see her sitting across the table from him, wearing a black pencil-skirt and the blue blouse he especially likes, the one that's so filmy you can see the ghost of her underwear through it.

"Because he'll be looking for you."

"I know," Brady says. "Don't worry."

"Of course I'll worry," she says. "I have to. You're my honeyboy."

He goes back downstairs and gets into his sleeping bag. The leaky air mattress wheezes. The last thing he does before killing the lights via voice-command is to set his iPhone alarm for six-thirty. Tomorrow is going to be a busy day.

Except for the tiny red lights marking his sleeping computer equipment, the basement control room is completely dark. From beneath the stairs, his mother speaks.

"I'm waiting for you, honeyboy, but don't make me wait too long."

"I'll be there soon, Mom." Smiling, Brady closes his eyes. Two minutes later, he's snoring.

7

Janey doesn't come out of the bedroom until just after eight the following morning. She's wearing her pantsuit from the night before. Hodges, still in his boxers, is on the phone. He waves one finger to her, a gesture that says both *good morning* and *give me a minute.*

"It's not a big deal," he's saying, "just one of those things that nibble at you. If you could check, I'd really appreciate it." He listens. "Nah, I don't want to bother Pete with it, and don't you, either. He's got all he can handle with the Donald Davis case."

He listens some more. Janey perches on the arm of the sofa, points at her watch, and mouths, *The viewing!* Hodges nods.

"That's right," he says into the phone. "Let's say between the summer of 2007 and the spring of 2009. In the Lake Avenue area downtown, where all those new ritzy condos are." He winks at Janey. "Thanks, Marlo, you're a doll. And I promise I'm not going to turn into an uncle, okay?" Listens, nodding. "Okay. Yeah. I have to run, but give my best to Phil and the kids. We'll get together soon. Lunch. Of *course* on me. Right. Bye."

He hangs up.

"You need to get dressed in a hurry," she says, "then take me back to the apartment so I can put on my damn makeup before we go over to the funeral home. It might also be fun to change my underwear. How fast can you hop into your suit?"

"Fast. And you don't really need the makeup."

She rolls her eyes. "Tell that to Aunt Charlotte. She's totally on crow's-feet patrol. Now get going, and bring a razor. You can shave at my place." She re-checks her watch. "I haven't slept this late in five years."

He heads for the bedroom to get dressed. She catches him at the door, turns him toward her, puts her palms on his cheeks, and kisses his mouth. "Good sex is the best sleeping pill. I guess I forgot that."

He lifts her high off her feet in a hug. He doesn't know how long this will last, but while it does, he means to ride it like a pony.

"And wear your hat," she says, looking down into his face and smiling. "I did right when I bought it. That hat is *you*."

8

They're too happy with each other and too intent on getting to the funeral parlor ahead of the relatives from hell to BOLO, but even on red alert they almost certainly wouldn't have seen anything that rang warning bells. There are already more than two dozen cars parked in the little strip mall at the intersection of Harper Road and Hanover Street, and Brady Hartsfield's mud-colored Subaru is the most unobtrusive of the lot. He has picked his spot carefully so that the fat ex-cop's street is squarely in the middle of his rearview. If Hodges is going to the old lady's viewing, he'll come down the hill and make a left on Hanover.

And here he comes, at just past eight-thirty—quite a bit earlier than Brady expected, since the viewing's not until ten and the funeral parlor's only twenty minutes or so away. As the car makes its left turn, Brady is further surprised to see the fat ex-cop is not alone. His passenger is a woman, and although Brady only gets a quick glimpse, it's enough for him to ID Olivia Trelawney's sister. She's got the visor down so she can look into the mirror as she brushes her hair. The obvious deduction is that she spent the night in the fat ex-cop's bachelor bungalow.

Brady is thunderstruck. Why in God's name would she do that? Hodges is *old*, he's *fat*, he's *ugly*. She can't really be having sex with him, can she? The idea is beyond belief. Then he thinks of how his mother relieved his worst headaches, and realizes—reluctantly— that when it comes to sex, no pairing is beyond belief. But the idea of Hodges doing it with Olivia Trelawney's sister is infuriating (not in the least because you could say it was Brady himself who brought them together). Hodges is supposed to be sitting in front of his television and contemplating suicide. He has no right to enjoy a jar of Vaseline and his own right hand, let alone a good-looking blonde.

Brady thinks, She probably took the bed while he slept on the sofa.

This idea at least approaches logic, and makes him feel better. He supposes Hodges could have sex with a good-looking blonde if he really wanted to . . . but he'd have to pay for it. The whore would probably want a weight surcharge, too, he thinks, and laughs as he starts his car.

Before pulling out, he opens the glove compartment, takes out Thing Two, and places it on the passenger seat. He hasn't used it since last year, but he's going to use it today. Probably not at the funeral parlor, though, because he doubts they will be going there right away. It's too early. Brady thinks they'll be stopping at the Lake Avenue condo first, and it's not necessary that he beat them there, only that he be there when they come back out. He knows just how he's going to do it.

It will be like old times.

At a stoplight downtown, he calls Tones Frobisher at Discount Electronix and tells him he won't be in today. Probably not all week. Pinching his nostrils shut with his knuckles to give his voice a nasal honk, he informs Tones that he has the flu. He thinks of the 'Round Here concert at the MAC on Thursday night, and the suicide vest, and imagines adding *Next week I won't have the flu, I'll just be dead*. He breaks the connection, drops his phone onto the seat next to Thing Two, and begins laughing. He sees a woman in the next lane, all gussied up for work, staring at him. Brady, now laughing so hard tears are streaming down his cheeks and snot is running out of his nose, gives her the finger.

9

"You were talking to your friend in the Records Department?" Janey asks.

"Marlo Everett, yeah. She's always in early. Pete Huntley, my old partner, used to swear that was because she never left."

"What fairy tale did you feed her, pray tell?"

"That some of my neighbors have mentioned a guy trying cars to see if they were unlocked. I said I seemed to recall a spate of car burglaries downtown a couple of years back, the doer never apprehended."

"Uh-huh, and that thing you said about not turning into an uncle, what was that about?"

"Uncles are retired cops who can't let go of the job. They call in wanting Marlo to run the plate numbers of cars that strike them as hinky for one reason or another. Or maybe they brace some guy who looks wrong, go all cop-faced on his ass and ask for ID. Then they call in and have Marlo run the name for wants and warrants."

"Does she mind?"

"Oh, she bitches about it for form's sake, but I don't really think so. An old geezer named Kenny Shays called in a six-five a few years ago—that's suspicious behavior, a new code since 9/11. The guy he pegged wasn't a terrorist, just a fugitive who killed his whole family in Kansas back in 1987."

"Wow. Did he get a medal?"

"Nothing but an attaboy, which was all he wanted. He died six months or so later." Ate his gun is what Kenny Shays did, pulling the trigger before the lung cancer could get traction.

Hodges's cell phone rings. It's muffled, because he's once more left it in the glove compartment. Janey fishes it out and hands it over with a slightly ironic smile.

"Hey, Marlo, that was quick. What did you find out? Anything?" He listens, nodding along with whatever he's hearing and saying uh-huh and never missing a beat in the heavy flow of morning traffic. He thanks her and hangs up, but when he attempts to hand the Nokia back to Janey, she shakes her head.

"Put it in your pocket. Someone else might call you. I know it's a strange concept, but try to get your head around it. What did you find out?"

"Starting in September of 2007, there were over a dozen car break-ins downtown. Marlo says there could have been even more, because people who don't lose anything of value have a tendency not to report car burglaries. Some don't even realize it happened. The last report was logged in March of 2009, less than three weeks before the City Center Massacre. It was our guy, Janey. I'm sure of it. We're crossing his backtrail now, and that means we're getting closer."

"Good."

"I think we're going to find him. If we do, your lawyer—Schron—goes downtown to fill in Pete Huntley. He does the rest. We still see eye to eye on that, don't we?"

"Yes. But until then, he's *ours*. We still see eye to eye on *that*, right?"

"Absolutely."

He's cruising down Lake Avenue now, and there's a spot right in front of the late Mrs. Wharton's building. When your luck is running, it's running. Hodges backs in, wondering how many times Olivia Trelawney used this same spot.

Janey looks anxiously at her watch as Hodges feeds the meter.

"Relax," he says. "We've got plenty of time."

As she heads for the door, Hodges pushes the LOCK button on his key-fob. He doesn't think about it, Mr. Mercedes is what he's thinking about, but habit is habit. He pockets his keys and hurries to catch up with Janey so he can hold the door for her.

He thinks, I'm turning into a sap.

Then he thinks, So what?

10

Five minutes later, a mud-colored Subaru cruises down Lake Avenue. It slows almost to a stop when it comes abreast of Hodges's Toyota, then Brady puts on his left-turn blinker and pulls into the parking garage across the street.

There are plenty of vacant spots on the first and second levels, but they're all on the inside and no use to him. He finds what he wants on the nearly deserted third level: a spot on the east side of the garage, directly overlooking Lake Avenue. He parks, walks to the concrete bumper, and peers across the street and down at Hodges's Toyota. He puts the distance at about sixty yards. With nothing in the way to block the signal, that's a piece of cake for Thing Two.

With time to kill, Brady gets back into his car, fires up his iPad, and investigates the Midwest Culture and Arts Complex website. Mingo Auditorium is the biggest part of the facility. That figures, Brady thinks, because it's probably the only part of the MAC that makes money. The city's symphony orchestra plays there in the winter, plus there are ballets and lectures and arty-farty shit like that, but from June to August the Mingo is almost exclusively dedicated to pop music. According to the website, 'Round Here will be followed by an all-star Summer Cavalcade of Song including the Eagles, Sting, John Mellencamp, Alan Jackson, Paul Simon, and Bruce Springsteen. Sounds good, but Brady thinks the people who bought All-Concert Passes are going to be disappointed. There's only going to be one show in the Mingo this summer, a short one ending with a punk ditty called "Die, You Useless Motherfuckers."

The website says the auditorium's capacity is forty-five hundred.

It also says that the 'Round Here concert is sold out.

Brady calls Shirley Orton at the ice cream factory. Once more pinching his nose shut, he tells her she better put Rudy Stanhope on alert for later in the week. He says he'll try to get in Thursday or Friday, but she better not count on it; he has the flu.

As he expected, the f-word alarms Shirley. "Don't you come near this place until you can show me a note from your doctor saying you're not contagious. You can't be selling ice cream to kids if you've got the flu."

"I dno," Brady says through his pinched nostrils. "I'be sorry, Shirley. I thing I got id fromb by mother. I had to put her to bed." That hits his funnybone and his lips begin to twitch.

"Well, you take care of yourse—"

"I hab to go," he says, and breaks the connection just before another gust of hysterical laughter sweeps through him. Yes, he had to put his mother to bed. And yes, it was the flu. Not the Swine Flu or the Bird Flu, but a new strain called Gopher Flu. Brady howls and pounds the dashboard of his Subaru. He pounds so hard he hurts his hand, and that makes him laugh harder still.

This fit goes on until his stomach aches and he feels a little like puking. It has just begun to ease off when he sees the lobby door of the condo across the street open.

Brady snatches up Thing Two and slides the on switch. The ready-lamp glows yellow. He raises the short stub of the antenna. He gets out of his car, not laughing now, and creeps to the concrete bumper again, being careful to stay in the shadow of the nearest support pillar. He puts his thumb on the toggle-switch and angles Thing Two down—but not at the Toyota. He's aiming at Hodges, who is rummaging in his pants pocket. The blonde is next to him, wearing the same pantsuit she had on earlier, but with different shoes and purse.

Hodges brings out his keys.

Brady pushes Thing Two's toggle-switch, and the yellow ready-lamp turns operational green. The lights of Hodges's car flash. At the same instant, the green light on Thing Two gives a single quick blink. It has caught the Toyota's PKE code and stored it, just as it caught the code of Mrs. Trelawney's Mercedes.

Brady used Thing Two for almost two years, stealing PKEs and unlocking cars so he could toss them for valuables and cash. The income from these ventures was uneven, but the thrill never faded. His first thought on finding the spare key in the glove compartment of Mrs. Trelawney's Mercedes (it was in a plastic bag along with her owner's manual and registration) was to steal the car and joyride it all the way across the city. Bang it up a little just for the hell of it. Maybe slice the upholstery. But some instinct had told him to leave everything just as it was. That the Mercedes might have a larger role to play. And so it had proved.

Brady hops into his car and puts Thing Two back in his own glove compartment. He's very satisfied with his morning's work, but the morning isn't over. Hodges and Olivia's sister will be going to a visitation. Brady has his own visitation to make. The MAC will be open by now, and he wants a look around. See what they have for security. Check out where the cameras are mounted.

Brady thinks, I'll find a way in. I'm on a roll.

Also, he'll need to go online and score a ticket to the concert Thursday night. Busy, busy, busy.

He begins to whistle.

11

Hodges and Janey Patterson step into the Eternal Rest parlor of the Soames Funeral Home at quarter to ten, and thanks to her insistence on hurrying, they're the first arrivals. The top half of the coffin is open. The bottom half is swaddled in a blue silk swag. Elizabeth Wharton is wearing a white dress sprigged with blue florets that match the swag. Her eyes are closed. Her cheeks are rosy.

Janey hurries down an aisle between two ranks of folding chairs, looks briefly at her mother, then hurries back. Her lips are trembling.

"Uncle Henry can call cremation pagan if he wants to, but this open-coffin shit is the real pagan rite. She doesn't look like my mother, she looks like a stuffed exhibit."

"Then why—"

"It was the trade-off I made to shut Uncle Henry up about the cremation. God help us if he looks under the swag and sees the coffin's pressed cardboard painted gray to look like metal. So it'll . . . you know . . ."

"I know," Hodges says, and gives her a one-armed hug.

The deceased woman's friends trickle in, led by Althea Greene, Wharton's nurse, and Mrs. Harris, who was her housekeeper. At twenty past ten or so (fashionably late, Hodges thinks), Aunt Charlotte arrives on her brother's arm. Uncle Henry leads her down the aisle, looks briefly at the corpse, then stands back. Aunt Charlotte stares fixedly into the upturned face, then bends and kisses the dead lips. In a barely audible voice she says, "Oh, sis, oh, sis." For the first time since he met her, Hodges feels something for her other than irritation.

There is some milling, some quiet talk, a few low outbursts of laughter. Janey makes the rounds, speaking to everyone (there aren't more than a dozen, all of the sort Hodges's daughter calls "goldie-oldies"), doing her due diligence. Uncle Henry joins her, and on the one occasion when Janey falters—she's trying to comfort Mrs. Greene—he puts an arm around her shoulders. Hodges is glad to see it. Blood tells, he thinks. At times like this, it almost always does.

He's the odd man out here, so he decides to get some air. He stands on the front step for a few moments, scanning the cars parked across the street, looking for a man sitting by himself in one of them. He sees no one, and realizes he hasn't seen Holly the Mumbler, either.

He ambles around to the visitors' parking lot and there she is, perched on the back step. She's dressed in a singularly unbecoming shin-length brown dress. Her hair is put up in unbecoming clumps at the sides of her head. To Hodges she looks like Princess Leia after a year on the Karen Carpenter diet.

She sees his shadow on the pavement, gives a jerk, and hides something behind her hand. He comes closer, and the hidden object turns out to be a half-smoked cigarette. She gives him a narrow, worried look. Hodges thinks it's the look of a dog that's been beaten too many times with a newspaper for piddling under the kitchen table.

"Don't tell my mother. She thinks I quit."

"Your secret's safe with me," Hodges says, thinking that Holly is surely too old to worry about Mommy's disapproval of what is probably her only bad habit. "Can I share your step?"

"Shouldn't you be inside with Janey?" But she moves over to make room.

"Just taking a breather. With the exception of Janey herself, I don't know any of those people."

She looks him over with the bald curiosity of a child. "Are you and my cousin lovers?"

He's embarrassed, not by the question but by the perverse fact that it makes him feel like laughing. He sort of wishes he'd just left her to smoke her illicit cigarette. "Well," he says, "we're good friends. Maybe we should leave it at that."

She shrugs and shoots smoke from her nostrils. "It's all right with me. I think a woman should have lovers if she wants them. I don't, myself. Men don't interest me. Not that I'm a lesbian. Don't get that idea. I write poetry."

"Yeah? Do you?"

"Yes." And with no pause, as if it's all the same thing: "My mother doesn't like Janey."

"Really?"

"She doesn't think Janey should have gotten all that money from Olivia. She says it isn't fair. It probably isn't, but I don't care, myself."

She's biting her lips in a way that gives Hodges an unsettling sense of déjà vu, and it takes only a second to realize why: Olivia Trelawney did the same thing during her police interviews. Blood tells. It almost always does.

"You haven't been inside," he says.

"No, and I'm not going, and *she* can't make me. I've never seen a dead person, and I'm not going to start now. It would give me nightmares."

She kills her cigarette on the side of the step, not rubbing it but *plunging* it out, stabbing it until the sparks fly and the filter splits. Her face is as pale as milk glass, she's started to quiver (her knees are almost literally knocking), and if she doesn't stop chewing her lower lip, it's going to split open.

"This is the worst part," she says, and she's not mumbling now. In fact, if her voice doesn't stop rising it will soon be a scream. "This is the worst part, this is the worst part, *this is the worst part*!"

He puts an arm around her vibrating shoulders. For a moment the vibration grows to a whole-body shake. He fully expects her to flee (perhaps lingering just long enough to call him a masher and slap his face). Then the shaking subsides and she actually puts her head on his shoulder. She's breathing rapidly.

"You're right," he says. "This is the worst part. Tomorrow will be better."

"Will the coffin be closed?"

"Yeah." He'll tell Janey it will have to be, unless she wants her cuz sitting out here with the hearses again.

Holly looks at him out of her naked face. She doesn't have a damn thing going for her, Hodges thinks, not a single scrap of wit, not a single wile. He will come to regret this misperception, but for now he finds himself once more musing on Olivia Trelawney. How the press treated her and how the cops treated her. Including him.

"Do you promise it'll be closed?"

"Yes."

"*Double* promise?"

"Pinky swear, if you want." Then, still thinking of Olivia and the computer-poison Mr. Mercedes fed her: "Are you taking your medication, Holly?"

Her eyes widen. "How do you know I take Lexapro? Did *she* tell you?"

"Nobody told me. Nobody had to. I used to be a detective." He tightens the arm around her shoulders a little and gives her a small, friendly shake. "Now answer my question."

"It's in my purse. I haven't taken it today, because . . ." She gives a small, shrill giggle. "Because it makes me have to *pee*."

"If I get a glass of water, will you take it now?"

"Yes. For you." Again that naked stare, the look of a small child sizing up an adult. "I like you. You're a good guy. Janey's lucky. I've never been lucky in my life. I've never even had a boyfriend."

"I'll get you some water," Hodges says, and stands up. At the corner of the building, he looks back. She's trying to light another cigarette, but it's hard going because the shakes are back. She's holding her disposable Bic in both hands, like a shooter on the police gun range.

Inside, Janey asks where he's been. He tells her, and asks if the coffin can be closed at the memorial service the following day. "I think it's the only way you'll get her inside," he says.

Janey looks at her aunt, now at the center of a group of elderly women, all of them talking animatedly. "That bitch hasn't even noticed Holly's not in here," she says. "You know what, I just decided the coffin's not even going to *be* here tomorrow. I'll have the funeral director stash it in the back, and if Auntie C doesn't like it, she can go spit. Tell Holly that, okay?"

The discreetly hovering funeral director shows Hodges into the next room, where drinks and snacks have been arranged. He gets a bottle of Dasani water and takes it out to the parking lot. He passes on Janey's message and sits with Holly until she takes one of her little white happy-caps. When it's down, she smiles at him. "I really do like you."

And, using that splendid, police-trained capacity for telling the convincing lie, Hodges replies warmly, "I like you too, Holly."

12

The Midwest Culture and Arts Complex, aka the MAC, is called "the Louvre of the Midwest" by the newspaper and the local Chamber of Commerce (the residents of this midwestern city call it "the Loovah"). The facility covers six acres of prime downtown real estate and is dominated by a circular building that looks to Brady like the giant UFO that shows up at the end of *Close Encounters of the Third Kind*. This is Mingo Auditorium.

He wanders around back to the loading area, which is as busy as an anthill on a summer day. Trucks bustle to and fro, and workers are unloading all sorts of stuff, including—weird but true—what looks like sections of a Ferris wheel. There are also flats (he thinks that's what they're called) showing a starry night sky and a white sand beach with couples walking hand-in-hand at the edge of the water. The workers, he notes, are all wearing ID badges around their necks or clipped to their shirts. Not good.

There's a security booth guarding the entrance to the loading area, and that's not good, either, but Brady wanders over anyway, thinking No risk, no reward. There are two guards. One is inside, noshing a bagel as he monitors half a dozen video screens. The other steps out to intercept Brady. He's wearing sunglasses. Brady can see himself reflected in the lenses, with a big old gosh-this-is-interesting smile on his face.

"Help you, sir?"

"I was just wondering what's going on," Brady says. He points. "That looks like a Ferris wheel!"

"Big concert here Thursday night," the guard says. "The band's flogging their new album. *Kisses on the Midway*, I think it's called."

"Boy, they really go all out, don't they?" Brady marvels.

The guard snorts. "The less they can sing, the bigger the set. You know what? When we had Tony Bennett here last September, it was just him. Didn't even have a band. The City Symphony backed him up. *That* was a show. No screaming kids. Actual music. What a concept, huh?"

"I don't suppose I could go over for a peek. Maybe snap a picture with my cell phone?"

"Nope." The guard is looking him over too closely. Brady doesn't like that. "In fact, you're not supposed to be here at all. So . . ."

"Gotcha, gotcha," Brady says, widening his smile. Time to go. There's nothing here for him, anyway; if they have two guys on duty now, there's apt to be half a dozen on Thursday night. "Thanks for taking the time to talk to me."

"No problem."

Brady gives him a thumbs-up. The security goon returns it, but stands in the doorway of the security booth, watching him walk away.

He strolls along the edge of a vast and nearly empty parking lot that will be filled to capacity on the night of the 'Round Here show. His smile is gone. He's musing on the numbfuck ragheads who ran a pair of jetliners into the World Trade Center nine years before. He thinks (without the slightest trace of irony), They spoiled it for the rest of us.

A five-minute trudge takes him to the bank of doors where concertgoers will enter on Thursday night. He has to pay a five-dollar "suggested donation fee" to get in. The lobby is an echoing vault currently filled with art-lovers and student groups. Straight ahead is the gift shop. To the left is the corridor leading to the Mingo Auditorium. It's as wide as a two-lane highway. In the middle of it is a chrome stand with a sign reading NO BAGS NO BOXES NO BACKPACKS.

Also no metal detectors. It's possible they haven't been set up yet, but Brady's pretty sure they won't be used at all. There are going to be over four thousand concertgoers pushing to get in, and metal detectors booping and beeping all over the place would create a nightmarish traffic jam. There will be *mucho* security guards, though, all of them just as suspicious and officious as the sunglasses-wearing ass-munch out back. A man in a quilted vest on a warm June evening would attract their attention at once. In fact, *any* man without a pigtailed teenybop daughter in tow would be apt to attract attention.

*Would you step over here for a minute, sir?*

Of course he could blow the vest right then and there and scrag a hundred or more, but that isn't what he wants. What he wants is to go home, search the Web, find out the name of 'Round Here's biggest song, and flick the switch halfway through it, when the little chickie-boos are screaming their very loudest and going out of their little chickie-boo minds.

But the obstacles are formidable.

Standing there in the lobby amid the guidebook-toting retirees and junior high school mouth-breathers, Brady thinks, I wish Frankie was alive. If he was, I'd take him to the show. He'd be just stupid enough to like it. I'd even let him bring Sammy the Fire Truck. The thought fills him with the deep and completely authentic sadness that often comes to him when he thinks about Frankie.

Maybe I ought to just kill the fat ex-cop, and myself, and then call it a career.

Rubbing at his temples, where one of his headaches has begun to gather (and now there's no Mom to ease it), Brady wanders across the lobby and into the Harlow Floyd Art Gallery, where a large hanging banner announces that JUNE IS MANET MONTH!

He doesn't know exactly who Manet was, probably another old frog painter like van Gogh, but some of the pictures are great. He doesn't care much for the still-lifes (why in God's name would you want to spend time painting a melon?), but some of the other ones are possessed of an almost feral violence. One shows a dead matador. Brady looks at it for nearly five minutes with his hands clasped behind him, ignoring the people who jostle by or peer over his shoulder for a look. The matador isn't mangled or anything, but the blood oozing from beneath his left shoulder looks more real than the blood in all the violent movies Brady has ever seen, and he's seen plenty. It calms him and clears him and when he finally walks on, he thinks: There has to be a way to do this.

On the spur of the moment he hooks into the gift shop and buys a bunch of 'Round Here shit. When he comes out ten minutes later, carrying a bag with I HAD A MAC ATTACK printed on the side, he again glances down the hallway leading to the Mingo. Just two nights from now, that hallway will become a cattle-chute filled with laughing, pushing, crazily excited girls, most accompanied by longsuffering parents. From this angle he can see that the far righthand side of the corridor has been sectioned off from the rest by velvet ropes. At the head of this sequestered mini-corridor is another sign on another chrome stand.

Brady reads it and thinks, Oh my God.

Oh . . . my . . . *God*!

## 13

In the apartment that used to belong to Elizabeth Wharton, Janey kicks off her heels and plunks down on the couch. "Thank God that's over. Did it last a thousand years, or two?"

"Two," Hodges says. "You look like a woman who could use a nap."

"I slept until eight," she protests, but to Hodges it sounds feeble.

"Still might be a good idea."

"Considering the fact that I'm having dinner with my relatives tonight in Sugar Heights, you could have something there, shamus. You're off the hook on dinner, by the way. I think they want to talk about everyone's favorite musical comedy, *Janey's Millions*."

"Wouldn't surprise me."

"I'm going to split Ollie's loot with them. Straight down the middle."

Hodges starts to laugh. He stops when he realizes she's serious.

Janey hoists her eyebrows. "Got a problem with that? Maybe think a paltry three and a half mil won't be enough to see me through to my old age?"

"I guess it would, but . . . it's *yours*. Olivia willed it to you."

"Yes, and the will's unbreakable, Lawyer Schron assures me of that, but that still doesn't mean Ollie was in her right mind when she made it. You know that. You saw her, talked to her." She's massaging her feet through her stockings. "Besides, if I give them half, I get to watch how they divvy it up. Think of the amusement value."

"Sure you don't want me to come with you tonight?"

"Not tonight but definitely tomorrow. That I can't do alone."

"I'll pick you up at quarter past nine. Unless you want to spend another night at my place, that is."

"Tempting, but no. Tonight is strictly earmarked for family fun. There's one other thing before you take off. Very important." She rummages in her purse for a notepad and a pen. She writes, then tears off a page and holds it out to him. Hodges sees two groups of numbers.

Janey says, "The first one opens the gates to the house in Sugar Hill. The second kills the burglar alarm. When you and your friend Jerome are working on Ollie's computer Thursday morning, I'll be taking Aunt Charlotte, Holly, and Uncle Henry to the airport. If the guy rigged her computer the way you think he did . . . and the program's still there . . . I don't think I could stand it." She's looking at him pleadingly. "Do you get that? Say you do."

"I get it," Hodges says. He kneels beside her like a man getting ready to propose in one of the romantic novels his ex-wife used to like. Part of him feels absurd. Mostly he doesn't.

"Janey," he says.

She looks at him, trying to smile, not quite making it.

"I'm sorry. For everything. So, so sorry." It isn't just her he's thinking of, or her late sister, who was so troubled and troublesome. He's thinking of the ones who were lost at City Center, especially the woman and her baby.

When he was promoted to detective, his mentor was a guy named Frank Sledge. Hodges thought of him as an old guy, but back then Sledge was fifteen years younger than Hodges is now.

*Don't you ever let me hear you call them the vics,* Sledge told him. *That shit's strictly for assholes and burnouts. Remember their names. Call them by their names.*

The Crays, he thinks. They were the Crays. Janice and Patricia.

Janey hugs him. Her breath tickles his ear when she speaks, giving him goosebumps and half a hardon. "I'm going back to California when this is finished. I can't stay here. I think the world of you, Bill, and if I stayed here I could probably fall in love with you, but I'm not going to do that. I need to make a fresh start."

"I know." Hodges pulls away and holds her by the shoulders so he can look her in the face again. It's a beautiful face, but today she's looking her age. "It's all right."

She dives into her purse again, this time for Kleenex. After she's dried her eyes, she says, "You made a conquest today."

"A . . . ?" Then he gets it. "Holly."

"She thinks you're wonderful. She told me so."

"She reminds me of Olivia. Talking to her feels like a second chance."

"To do the right thing?"

"Yeah."

Janey wrinkles her nose at him and grins. *"Yeah."*

14

Brady goes shopping that afternoon. He takes the late Deborah Ann Hartsfield's Honda, because it's a hatchback. Still, one of the items barely fits in the rear. He thinks of stopping at Speedy Postal on his way home and checking for the Gopher-Go he ordered under his Ralph Jones alias, but all that seems like a thousand years ago now, and really, what would be the point? That part of his life is over. Soon the rest will be, too, and what a relief.

He leans the largest of his purchases against the garage wall. Then he goes into the house, and after a brief pause in the kitchen to sniff at the air (no whiff of decay, at least not yet), he goes down to his control room. He speaks the magic word that powers up his row of computers, but only out of habit. He has no urge to slip beneath Debbie's Blue Umbrella, because he has nothing more to say to the fat ex-cop. That part of his life is also over. He looks at his watch, sees that it's three-thirty in the afternoon, and calculates that the fat ex-cop now has roughly twenty hours to live.

If you really are fucking her, Detective Hodges, Brady thinks, you better get your end wet while you've still *got* an end.

He unlocks the padlock on the closet door and steps into the dry and faintly oily odor of homemade plastique. He regards the shoe-boxes full of explosive and chooses the one that held the Mephisto walking shoes he's now wearing—a Christmas present from his mother just last year. From the next shelf up he grabs the shoebox filled with cell phones. He takes one of them and the box of boom-clay over to the table in the middle of the room and goes to work, putting the phone in the box and rigging it to a simple detonator powered by double-A batteries. He turns the phone on to make sure it works, then turns it off again. The chance of someone dial-ing this disposable's number by mistake and blowing his control room sky-high is small, but why risk it? The chances of his mother finding that poisoned meat and cooking it for her lunch were also small, and look how *that* turned out.

No, this baby is going to stay off until ten-twenty tomorrow morning. That's when Brady will stroll into the parking lot behind the Soames Funeral Home. If there's anyone back there, Brady will say he thought he could cut through the lot to the next street over, where there's a bus stop (which happens to be true; he checked it on MapQuest). But he doesn't expect anyone. They'll all be inside at the memorial service, bawling up a storm.

He'll use Thing Two to unlock the fat ex-cop's car and put the shoebox on the floor behind the driver's seat. He'll lock the Toyota again and return to his own car. To wait. To watch him go past. To let him reach the next intersection, where Brady can be sure that he, Brady, will be relatively safe from flying debris. Then . . .

"Ka-pow," Brady says. "They'll need another shoebox to bury him in."

That's pretty funny, and he's laughing as he goes back to the closet to get his suicide vest. He'll spend the rest of the afternoon disassembling it. Brady doesn't need the vest anymore.

He has a better idea.

## 15

Wednesday, June 2, 2010, is warm and cloudless. It may still be spring according to the calendar, and the local schools may still be in session, but those things don't change the fact that this is a perfect summer day in the heartland of America.

Bill Hodges, suited up but as yet blessedly tieless, is in his study, going over a list of car burglaries Marlo Everett sent him by fax. He has printed out a map of the city, and puts a red dot at each burglary location. He sees shoeleather in his future, maybe a lot of it if Olivia's computer doesn't pan out, but it's just possible that some of the burglary victims will mention seeing a similar vehicle. Because Mr. Mercedes *had* to watch the owners of his target vehicles. Hodges is sure of it. He had to make sure they were gone before he used his gadget to unlock their cars.

He watched them the way he was watching me, Hodges thinks.

This kicks something over in his mind—a brief spark of association that's bright but gone before he can see what it's illuminating. That's okay; if there's really something there, it will come back. In the meantime, he keeps on checking addresses and making red dots. He has twenty minutes before he has to noose on his tie and go after Janey.

Brady Hartsfield is in his control room. No headache today, and his thoughts, so often muddled, are as clear as the various *Wild Bunch* screensavers on his computers. He has removed the blocks of plastic explosive from his suicide vest, disconnecting them carefully from the detonator wires. Some of the blocks have gone into a bright red seat cushion printed with the saucy slogan ASS PARK-ING. He has slipped two more, re-molded into cylinders with det-onator wires attached, down the throat of a bright blue Urinesta peebag. With that accomplished, he carefully attaches a stick-on decal to the peebag. He bought it, along with a souvenir tee-shirt, in the MAC gift shop yesterday. The sticker says 'ROUND HERE FANBOY #1. He checks his watch. Almost nine. The fat ex-cop now has an hour and a half to live. Maybe a little less.

Hodges's old partner Pete Huntley is in one of the interroga-tion rooms, not because he has anyone to question but because it's away from the morning hustle and flow of the squadroom. He has notes to go over. He's holding a press conference at ten, to talk about the latest dark revelations Donald Davis has made, and he doesn't want to screw anything up. The City Center killer—Mr. Mercedes—is the furthest thing from his mind.

In Lowtown, behind a certain pawnshop, guns are being bought and sold by people who believe they are not being watched.

Jerome Robinson is at his computer, listening to audio clips available at a website called Sounds Good to Me. He listens to a woman laughing hysterically. He listens to a man whistling "Danny Boy." He listens to a man gargling and a woman appar-ently in the throes of an orgasm. Eventually he finds the clip he wants. The title is simple: CRYING BABY.

On the floor below, Jerome's sister Barbara comes bursting into the kitchen, closely followed by Odell. Barbara is wearing a span-gly skirt, clunky blue clogs, and a tee-shirt that shows a foxy teen-age boy. Below his brilliant smile and careful coif is the legend I LUV CAM 4EVER! She asks her mother if this outfit looks too babyish to wear to the concert. Her mother (perhaps remember-ing what she wore to her own first concert) smiles and says it's perfect. Barbara asks if she can wear her mother's dangly peace-sign earrings. Yes, of course. Lipstick? Well . . . okay. Eye shadow? No, sorry. Barbara gives a no-harm-in-trying laugh and hugs her mother extravagantly. "I can't wait until tomorrow night," she says.

Holly Gibney is in the bathroom of the house in Sugar Heights, wishing she could skip the memorial service, knowing her mother will never let her. If she protests that she doesn't feel well, her mother's return serve will be one that goes all the way back to Holly's childhood: *What will people think*. And if Holly should protest that it doesn't *matter* what people think, they are never going to see any of these people (with the exception of Janey) again in their lives? Her mother would look at her as if Holly were speaking a foreign language. She takes her Lexapro, but her insides knot while she's brushing her teeth and she vomits it back up. Charlotte calls to ask if she's almost ready. Holly calls back that she almost is. She flushes the toilet and thinks, At least Janey's boyfriend will be there. Bill. He's nice.

Janey Patterson is dressing carefully in her late mother's condominium apartment: dark hose, black skirt, black jacket over a blouse of deepest midnight blue. She's thinking of how she told Bill she'd probably fall in love with him if she stayed here. That was a bodacious shading of the truth, because she's already in love with him. She's sure a shrink would smile and say it was a daddy thing. If so, Janey would smile right back and tell him that was a load of Freudian bullshit. Her father was a bald accountant who was barely there even when he was there. And one thing you can say about Bill Hodges is that he's *there*. It's what she likes about him. She also likes the hat she bought him. That Philip Marlowe fedora. She checks her watch and sees it's quarter past nine. He'd better be here soon.

If he's late, she'll kill him.

16

He's not late, and he's wearing the hat. Janey tells him he looks nice. He tells her she looks better than that. She smiles and kisses him.

"Let's get this done," he says.

Janey wrinkles her nose and says, *"Yeah."*

They drive to the funeral parlor, where they are once more the first to arrive. Hodges escorts her into the Eternal Rest parlor. She looks around and nods her approval. Programs for the service have been laid out on the seats of the folding chairs. The coffin is gone, replaced by a vaguely altarish table with sprays of spring flowers on it. Brahms, turned down almost too low to hear, is playing through the parlor's sound system.

"Okay?" Hodges asks.

"It'll do." She takes a deep breath and repeats what he said twenty minutes before: "Let's get this done."

It's basically the same bunch as yesterday. Janey meets them at the door. While she shakes hands and gives hugs and says all the right things, Hodges stands nearby, scanning the passing traffic. He sees nothing that raises a red flag, including a certain mud-colored Subaru that trundles by without slowing.

A rental Chevy with a Hertz sticker on the side of the windshield swings around back to the parking lot. Soon Uncle Henry appears, preceded by his gently swinging executive belly. Aunt Charlotte and Holly follow him, Charlotte with one white-gloved hand clamped just above her daughter's elbow. To Hodges, Auntie C looks like a matron escorting a prisoner—probably a drug addict—into county lockup. Holly is even paler than she was yesterday, if that is possible. She's wearing the same shapeless brown gunnysack, and has already bitten off most of her lipstick.

She gives Hodges a tremulous smile. Hodges offers his hand, and she seizes it with panicky tightness until Charlotte pulls her into the Hall of the Dead.

A young clergyman, from the church Mrs. Wharton attended until she was too unwell to go out on Sundays, serves as master of ceremonies. He reads the predictable passage from Proverbs, the one about the virtuous woman. Hodges is willing to stipulate that the deceased may have been worth more than rubies, but has his doubts about whether she spent any time working with wool and flax. Still, it's poetical, and tears are flowing by the time the clergyman is finished. The guy may be young, but he's smart enough not to try eulogizing someone he hardly knew. Instead of that, he invites those with "precious memories" of the late Elizabeth to come forward. Several do, beginning with Althea Greene, the nurse, and ending with the surviving daughter. Janey is calm and brief and simple.

"I wish we'd had more time," she finishes.

17

Brady parks around the corner at five past ten and is careful to feed the meter until the green flag with MAX on it pops up. After all, it just took a parking ticket to catch Son of Sam in the end. From the back seat he takes a cloth carry-bag. Printed on the side is KROGER and REUSE ME! SAVE A TREE! Inside is Thing Two, resting on top of the Mephisto shoebox.

He turns the corner and strides briskly past the Soames Funeral Home, just some citizen on a morning errand. His face is calm, but his heart is hammering like a steam-drill. He sees no one outside the funeral parlor, and the doors are shut, but there's still a possibility the fat ex-cop isn't with the other mourners. He could be in a back room, watching for suspicious characters. Watching for *him*, in other words. Brady knows this.

No risk, no reward, honeyboy, his mother murmurs. It's true. Also, he judges that the risk is minimal. If Hodges is pronging the blond bitch (or hoping to), he won't leave her side.

Brady does an about-face at the far corner, strolls back, and turns in to the funeral home drive without hesitation. He can hear faint music, some kind of classical shit. He spots Hodges's Toyota parked against the rear fence, nose-out for a quick getaway once the festivities are over. The old Det-Ret's last ride, Brady thinks. It's going to be a short one, pal.

He walks behind the larger of the two hearses, and once it blocks him from the view of anyone looking out the rear windows of the funeral parlor, he takes Thing Two out of the shopping bag and pulls up the antenna. His heart is driving harder than ever. There were times—only a few—when his gadget didn't work. The green light would flash, but the car's locks wouldn't pop. Some random glitch in the program or the microchip.

If it doesn't work, just slide the shoebox under the car, his mother advises him.

Of course. That would work just as well, or *almost* as well, but it wouldn't be so elegant.

He pushes the toggle. The green light flashes. So do the Toyota's headlights. Success!

He goes to the fat ex-cop's car as if he has every right to be there. He opens the rear door, takes the shoebox out of the carry-bag, turns on the phone, and puts the box on the floor behind the driver's seat. He closes the door and starts for the street, forcing himself to walk slowly and steadily.

As he's rounding the corner of the building, Deborah Ann Hartsfield speaks again. Didn't you forget something, honeyboy?

He stops. Thinks it over. Then goes back to the corner of the building and points Thing Two's stub of an antenna at Hodges's car.

The lights flash as the locks re-engage.

## 18

After the remembrances and a moment of silent reflection ("to use as you wish"), the clergyman asks the Lord to bless them and keep them and give them peace. Clothes rustle; programs are stowed in purses and jacket pockets. Holly seems fine until she's halfway up the aisle, but then her knees buckle. Hodges darts forward with surprising speed for a big man and catches her beneath her arms before she can go down. Her eyes roll up and for a moment she's on the verge of a full-fledged swoon. Then they come back into place and into focus. She sees Hodges and smiles weakly.

"Holly, stop that!" her mother says sternly, as if her daughter has uttered some jocose and inappropriate profanity instead of almost fainting. Hodges thinks what a pleasure it would be to backhand Auntie C right across her thickly powdered chops. Might wake her up, he thinks.

"I'm okay, Mother," Holly says. Then, to Hodges: "Thank you."

He says, "Did you eat any breakfast, Holly?"

"She had oatmeal," Aunt Charlotte announces. "With butter and brown sugar. I made it myself. You're quite the attention-getter sometimes, aren't you, Holly?" She turns to Janey. "Please don't linger, dear. Henry's useless at things like this, and I can't hostess all these people on my own."

Janey takes Hodges's arm. "I'd never expect you to."

Aunt Charlotte gives her a pinched smile. Janey's smile in return is brilliant, and Hodges decides that her decision to turn over half of her inherited loot is equally brilliant. Once that happens, she will never have to see this unpleasant woman again. She won't even have to take her calls.

The mourners emerge into the sunshine. On the front walk there's chatter of the wasn't-it-a-lovely-service sort, and then people begin walking around to the parking lot in back. Uncle Henry and Aunt Charlotte do so with Holly between them. Hodges and Janey follow along. As they reach the back of the mortuary, Holly suddenly slips free of her minders and wheels around to Hodges and Janey.

"Let me ride with you. I want to ride with you."

Aunt Charlotte, lips thinned almost to nothing, looms up behind her daughter. "I've had just about enough of your gasps and vapors for one day, miss."

Holly ignores her. She seizes one of Hodges's hands in a grip that's icy. "Please. *Please.*"

"It's fine with me," Hodges says, "if Janey doesn't m—"

Aunt Charlotte begins to sob. The sound is unlovely, the hoarse cries of a crow in a cornfield. Hodges remembers her bending over Mrs. Wharton, kissing her cold lips, and a sudden unpleasant pos-

sibility comes to him. He misjudged Olivia; he may have misjudged Charlotte Gibney as well. There's more to people than their
surfaces, after all.

"Holly, you don't even *know* this man!"

Janey puts a much warmer hand on Hodges's wrist. "Why don't
you go with Charlotte and Henry, Bill? There's plenty of room.
You can ride in back with Holly." She shifts her attention to her
cousin. "Would that be all right?"

"Yes!" Holly is still gripping Hodges's hand. "That would be
good!"

Janey turns to her uncle. "Okay with you?"

"Sure." He gives Holly a jovial pat on the shoulder. "The more
the merrier."

"That's right, give her plenty of attention," Aunt Charlotte
says. "It's what she likes. Isn't it, Holly?" She starts for the parking lot without waiting for a reply, heels clacking a Morse code
message of outrage.

Hodges looks at Janey. "What about my car?"

"I'll drive it. Hand over the keys." And when he does: "There's
just one other thing I need."

"Yeah?"

She plucks the fedora from his head, puts it on her own, and
gives it the correct insouciant dip over her left eyebrow. She wrinkles her nose at him and says, *"Yeah."*

19

Brady has parked up the street from the funeral parlor, his heart
beating harder than ever. He's holding a cell phone. The number of
the burner attached to the bomb in the Toyota's back seat is inked
on his wrist.

He watches the mourners stand around on the walk. The fat
ex-cop is impossible to miss; in his black suit he looks as big as a
house. Or a hearse. On his head is a ridiculously old-fashioned hat,

the kind you saw cops wearing in black-and-white detective movies from the nineteen-fifties.

People are starting around to the back, and after awhile, Hodges and the blond bitch head that way. Brady supposes the blond bitch will be with him when the car blows. Which will make it a clean sweep—the mother and both daughters. It has the elegance of an equation where all the variables have been solved.

Cars start pulling out, all moving in his direction because that's the way you go if you're heading to Sugar Heights. The sun glares on the windshields, which isn't helpful, but there's no mistaking the fat ex-cop's Toyota when it appears at the head of the funeral home driveway, pauses briefly, then turns toward him.

Brady doesn't even glance at Uncle Henry's rental Chevy when it passes him. All his attention is focused on the fat ex-cop's ride. When it goes by, he feels a moment's disappointment. The blond bitch must have gone with her relatives, because there's no one in the Toyota but the driver. Brady only gets a glimpse, but even with the sunglare, the fat ex-cop's stupid hat is unmistakable.

Brady keys in a number. "I said you wouldn't see me coming. Didn't I say that, asshole?"

He pushes SEND.

20

As Janey reaches to turn on the radio, a cell phone begins to ring. The last sound she makes on earth—everyone should be so lucky—is a laugh. Idiot, she thinks affectionately, you went and left it again. She reaches for the glove compartment. There's a second ring.

That's not coming from the glove compartment, that's coming from behi—

There's no sound, at least not that she hears, only the momentary sensation of a strong hand pushing the driver's seat. Then the world turns white.

21

Holly Gibney, also known as Holly the Mumbler, may have mental problems, but neither the psychotropic drugs she takes nor the cigarettes she smokes on the sneak have slowed her down physically. Uncle Henry slams on the brakes and she bolts from the rental Chevy while the explosion is still reverberating.

Hodges is right behind her, running hard. There's a stab of pain in his chest and he thinks he might be having a heart attack. Part of him actually hopes for this, but the pain goes away. The pedestrians are behaving as they always do when an act of violence punches a hole in the world they have previously taken for granted. Some drop to the sidewalk and cover their heads. Others are frozen in place, like statues. A few cars stop; most speed up and exit the vicinity immediately. One of these is a mud-colored Subaru.

As Hodges pounds after Janey's mentally unstable cousin, the last message from Mr. Mercedes beats in his head like a ceremonial drum: *I'm going to kill you. You won't see me coming. I'm going to kill you. You won't see me coming. I'm going to kill you. You won't see me coming.*

He rounds the corner, skidding on the slick soles of his seldom-worn dress shoes, and almost runs into Holly, who has stopped dead with her shoulders slumped and her purse dangling from one hand. She's staring at what remains of Hodges's Toyota. Its body has been blown clean off the axles and is burning furiously in a litter of glass. The back seat lies on its side twenty feet away, its torn upholstery on fire. A man staggers drunkenly across the street, holding his bleeding head. A woman is sitting on the curb outside a card-and-gift shop with a smashed-in show window, and for one wild moment he thinks it's Janey, but this woman is wearing a green dress and she has gray hair and of course it isn't Janey, it can't be Janey.

He thinks, This is my fault. If I'd used my father's gun two weeks ago, she'd be alive.

There's still enough cop inside him to push the idea aside (although it doesn't go easily). A cold shocked clarity flows in to replace it. This is *not* his fault. It's the fault of the son of a bitch who planted the bomb. The same son of a bitch who drove a stolen car into a crowd of job-seekers at City Center.

Hodges sees a single black high-heeled shoe lying in a pool of blood, he sees a severed arm in a smoldering sleeve lying in the gutter like someone's cast-off garbage, and his mind clicks into gear. Uncle Henry and Aunt Charlotte will be here shortly, and that means there isn't much time.

He seizes Holly by the shoulders and turns her around. Her hair has come loose from its Princess Leia rolls and hangs against her cheeks. Her wide eyes look right through him. His mind—colder than ever—knows she's no good to him as she is now. He slaps first one cheek, then the other. Not hard slaps, but enough to make her eyelids flutter.

People are screaming. Horns are honking, and a couple of car alarms are blatting. He can smell gasoline, burning rubber, melting plastic.

"Holly. Holly. Listen to me."

She's looking, but is she listening? He doesn't know, and there's no time.

"I loved her, but you can't tell anyone. *You can't tell anyone I loved her.* Maybe later, but not now. Do you understand?"

She nods.

"I need your cell number. And I may need *you*." His cold mind hopes he won't, that the house in Sugar Heights will be empty this afternoon, but he doesn't think it will be. Holly's mother and uncle will have to leave, at least for awhile, but Charlotte won't want her daughter to go with them. Because Holly has mental problems. Holly is delicate. Hodges wonders just how many breakdowns she's had, and if there have been suicide attempts. These thoughts zip across his mind like shooting stars, there at one moment, gone the next. He has no time for Holly's delicate mental condition.

"When your mother and uncle go to the police station, tell them you don't need anyone to stay with you. Tell them you're okay by yourself. Can you do that?"

She nods, although she almost certainly has no idea what he's talking about.

"Someone will call you. It might be me, or it might be a young man named Jerome. *Jerome.* Can you remember that name?"

She nods, then opens her purse and takes out a glasses case.

This is not working, Hodges thinks. The lights are on but nobody's home. Still, he has to try. He grasps her shoulders.

"Holly, I want to catch the guy who did this. I want to make him pay. Will you help me?"

She nods. There's no expression on her face.

"Say it, then. Say you'll help me."

She doesn't. She slips a pair of sunglasses from the case instead, and pops them on as if there weren't a car burning in the street and Janey's arm in the gutter. As if there weren't people screaming and already the sound of an approaching siren. As if this were a day at the beach.

He shakes her lightly. *"I need your cell phone number."*

She nods agreeably but says nothing. She snaps her purse closed and turns back to the burning car. The greatest despair he has ever known sweeps through Hodges, sickening his belly and scattering the thoughts that were, for the space of thirty or forty seconds, perfectly clear.

Aunt Charlotte comes sidewheeling around the corner with her hair—mostly black but white at the roots—flying out behind her. Uncle Henry follows. His jowly face is pasty except for the clownish spots of red high on his cheeks.

"Sharlie, stop!" Uncle Henry cries. "I think I'm having a heart attack!"

His sister pays no attention. She grabs Holly's elbow, jerks her around, and hugs her fiercely, mashing Holly's not inconsiderable nose between her breasts. *"DON'T LOOK!"* Charlotte bellows, looking. *"DON'T LOOK, SWEETHEART, DON'T LOOK AT IT!"*

"I can hardly breathe," Uncle Henry announces. He sits on the curb and hangs his head down. "God, I hope I'm not dying."

More sirens have joined the first. People have begun to creep forward so they can get a closer look at the burning wreck in the street. A couple snap photos with their phones.

Hodges thinks, Enough explosive to blow up a car. How much more does he have?

Aunt Charlotte still has Holly in a deathgrip, bawling at her not to look. Holly isn't struggling to get away, but she's got one hand behind her. There's something in it. Although he knows it's probably just wishful thinking, Hodges hopes it might be for him. He takes what she's holding out. It's the case her sunglasses were in. Her name and address are embossed on it in gold.

There's also a phone number.

22

Hodges takes his Nokia from his inside suit coat pocket, aware as he flips it open that it would probably be so much melted plastic and fizzing wire in the glove compartment of his baked Toyota, if not for Janey's gentle chaffing.

He hits Jerome on speed-dial, praying the kid will pick up, and he does.

"Mr. Hodges? Bill? I think we just heard a big explo—"

"Shut up, Jerome. Just listen." He's walking down the glass-littered sidewalk. The sirens are closer now, soon they'll be here, and all he has to go on is pure intuition. Unless, that is, his subconscious mind is already making the connections. It's happened before; he didn't get all those department commendations on Craigslist.

"Listening," Jerome says.

"You know nothing about the City Center case. You know nothing about Olivia Trelawney or Janey Patterson." Of course the three of them had dinner together at DeMasio's, but he doesn't think the cops will get that far for awhile, if ever.

"I know squat," Jerome says. There's no distrust or hesitance in his voice. "Who'll be asking? The police?"

"Maybe later. First it'll be your parents. Because that explosion you heard was my car. Janey was driving. We swapped at the last minute. She's . . . gone."

"Christ, Bill, you have to tell five-oh! Your old partner!"

Hodges thinks of her saying He's *ours*. We still see eye to eye on *that*, right?

Right, he thinks. Still eye to eye on that, Janey.

"Not yet. Right now I'm going to roll on this, and I need you to help me. The scumbucket killed her, I want his ass, and I mean to have it. Will you help?"

"Yes." Not *How much trouble could I get in*. Not *This could totally screw me up for Harvard*. Not *Leave me out of it*. Just *Yes*. God bless Jerome Robinson.

"You have to go on Debbie's Blue Umbrella as me and send the guy who did this a message. Do you remember my username?"

"Yeah. Kermitfrog19. Let me get some pa—"

"No time. Just remember the gist of it. And don't post for at least an hour. He has to know I didn't send it *before* the explosion. He has to know I'm still alive."

Jerome says, "Give it."

Hodges gives it and breaks the connection without saying good-bye. He slips the phone into his pants pocket, along with Holly's sunglasses case.

A fire truck comes swaying around the corner, followed by two police cars. They speed past the Soames Funeral Home, where the mortician and the minister from Elizabeth Wharton's service are now standing on the sidewalk, shading their eyes against the glare of the sun and the burning car.

Hodges has a lot of talking to do, but there's something more important to do first. He strips off his suit coat, kneels down, and covers the arm in the gutter. He feels tears pricking at his eyes and forces them back. He can cry later. Right now tears don't fit the story he has to tell.

The cops, two young guys riding solo, are getting out of their cars. Hodges doesn't know them. "Officers," he says.

"Got to ask you to clear the area, sir," one of them says, "but if you witnessed that—" He points to the burning remains of the Toyota. "—I need you to stay close so someone can interview you."

"I not only saw it, I should have been in it." Hodges takes out his wallet and flips it open to show the police ID card with RETIRED stamped across it in red. "Until last fall, my partner was Pete Huntley. You should call him ASAP."

One of the other cops says, "It was your car, sir?"

"Yeah."

The first cop says, "Then who was driving it?"


## 23


Brady arrives home well before noon with all his problems solved. Old Mr. Beeson from across the street is standing on his lawn. "Didja hear it?"

"Hear what?"

"Big explosion somewheres downtown. There was a lot of smoke, but it's gone now."

"I was playing the radio pretty loud," Brady says.

"I think that old paint fact'ry exploded, that's what I think. I knocked on your mother's door, but I guess she must be sleepun." His eyes twinkle with what's unsaid: *Sleepun it off.*

"I guess she must be," Brady says. He doesn't like the idea that the nosy old cock-knocker did that. Brady Hartsfield's idea of great neighbors would be no neighbors. "Got to go, Mr. Beeson."

"Tell your mum I said hello."

He unlocks the door, steps in, and locks it behind him. Scents the air. Nothing. Or . . . maybe not *quite* nothing. Maybe the tiniest whiff of unpleasantness, like the smell of a chicken carcass that got left a few days too long in the trash under the sink.

Brady goes up to her room. He turns down the coverlet, exposing her pale face and glaring eyes. He doesn't mind them so much now, and so what if Mr. Beeson's a neb-nose? Brady only needs to keep things together for another few days, so *fuck* Mr. Beeson. Fuck her glaring eyes, too. He didn't kill her; she killed herself. The way the fat ex-cop was supposed to kill himself, and so what if he didn't? He's gone now, so *fuck* the fat ex-cop. The Det is definitely Ret. Ret in peace, Detective Hodges.

"I did it, Mom," he says. "I pulled it off. And you helped. Only in my head, but . . ." Only he's not completely sure of that. Maybe it really was Mom who reminded him to lock the fat ex-cop's car doors again. He wasn't thinking about that at all.

"Anyway, thanks," he finishes lamely. "Thanks for whatever. And I'm sorry you're dead."

The eyes glare up at him.

He reaches for her—tentatively—and uses the tips of his fingers to close her eyes the way people sometimes do in movies. It works for a few seconds, then they roll up like tired old windowshades and the glare resumes. The you-killed-me-honeyboy glare.

It's a major buzzkill and Brady pulls the coverlet back over her face. He goes downstairs and turns on the TV, thinking at least one of the local stations will be broadcasting from the scene, but none of them are. It's very annoying. Don't they know a car-bomb when one explodes in their faces? Apparently not. Apparently Rachael Ray making her favorite fucking meatloaf is more important.

He turns off the idiot box and hurries to the control room, saying *chaos* to light up his computers and *darkness* to kill the suicide program. He does a shuffling little dance, shaking his fists over his head and singing what he remembers of "Ding Dong the Witch Is Dead," only changing *witch* to *cop*. He thinks it will make him feel better, but it doesn't. Between Mr. Beeson's long nose and his mother's glaring eyes, his good feeling—the feeling he *worked for*, the feeling he *deserved*—is slipping away.

Never mind. There's a concert coming up, and he has to be ready for it. He sits at the long worktable. The ball bearings that used to be in his suicide vest are now in three mayonnaise jars. Next to them is a box of Glad food-storage bags, the gallon size. He begins filling them (but not overfilling them) with the steel bearings. The work soothes him, and his good feelings start to come back. Then, just as he's finishing up, a steamboat whistle toots.

Brady looks up, frowning. That's a special cue he programmed into his Number Three. It sounds when he's got a message on the Blue Umbrella site, but that's impossible. The only person he's been communicating with via the Blue Umbrella is Kermit William Hodges, aka the fat ex-cop, aka the permanently Ret Det.

He rolls over in his office chair, paddling his feet, and stares at Number Three. The Blue Umbrella icon is now sporting a **1** in a little red circle. He clicks on it. He stares, wide-eyed and open-mouthed, at the message on his screen.

**kermitfrog19 wants to chat with you!**
**Do you want to chat with kermitfrog19?**
**Y N**

Brady would like to believe this message was sent last night or this morning before Hodges and the blond bimbo left his house, but he can't. He just heard it come in.

Summoning his courage—because this is much scarier than looking into his dead mother's eyes—he clicks **Y** and reads.

**Missed me.**
☺
**And here's something to remember, asshole: I'm like your side mirror. You know, OBJECTS ARE CLOSER THAN THEY APPEAR.**

**I know how you got into her Mercedes, and it wasn't the valet key. But you believed me about that, didn't you? Sure you did. Because you're an asshole.**

**I've got a list of all the other cars you burglarized between 2007 and 2009.**

**I've got other info I don't want to share right now, but here's something I WILL share: it's PERP, not PERK.**

**Why am I telling you this? Because I'm no longer going to catch you and turn you in to the cops. Why should I? I'm not a cop anymore.**

**I'm going to kill you.**

**See you soon, mama's boy.**

Even in his shock and disbelief, it's that last line that Brady's eyes keep returning to.

He walks to his closet on legs that feel like stilts. Once inside with the door closed, he screams and beats his fists on the shelves. Instead of the nigger family's dog, he managed to kill his own mother. That was bad. Now he's managed to kill someone else instead of the cop, and that's worse. Probably it was the blond bitch. The blond bitch wearing the Det-Ret's hat for some weirdo reason only another blonde could understand.

One thing he *is* sure of: this house is no longer safe. Hodges is probably gaming him about being close, but he might not be. He knows about Thing Two. He knows about the car burglaries. He says he knows other stuff, too. And—

*See you soon, mama's boy.*

He has to get out of here. Soon. Something to do first, though.

Brady goes back upstairs and into his mother's bedroom, barely glancing at the shape under the coverlet. He goes into her bathroom and rummages in the drawers of her vanity until he finds her Lady Schick. Then he goes to work.

24

Hodges is in Interrogation Room 4 again—IR4, his lucky room—but this time he's on the wrong side of the table, facing Pete Huntley and Pete's new partner, a stunner with long red hair and eyes of misty gray. The interrogation is collegial, but that doesn't change the basic facts: his car has been blown up and a woman has been killed. Another fact is that an interrogation is an interrogation.

"Did it have anything to do with the Mercedes Killer?" Pete asks. "What do you think, Billy? I mean, that's the most likely, wouldn't you say? Given the vic was Olivia Trelawney's sister?"

There it is: the vic. The woman he slept with after he'd come to a point in his life where he thought he'd never sleep with any woman again. The woman who made him laugh and gave him comfort, the woman who was his partner in this last investigation as much as Pete Huntley ever was. The woman who wrinkled her nose at him and mocked his *yeah.*

*Don't you ever let me hear you call them the vics,* Frank Sledge told him, back in the old days . . . but right now he has to take it.

"I don't see how it can," he says mildly. "I know how it looks, but sometimes a cigar is just a smoke and a coincidence is just a coincidence."

"How did you—" Isabelle Jaynes begins, then shakes her head. "That's the wrong question. *Why* did you meet her? Were you investigating the City Center thing on your own?" Playing the uncle on a grand scale is what she doesn't say, perhaps in deference to Pete. After all, it's Pete's old running buddy they're questioning, this chunky man in rumpled suit pants and a blood-spotted white shirt, the tie he put on this morning now pulled halfway down his big chest.

"Could I have a drink of water before we get started? I'm still shook up. She was a nice lady."

Janey was a hell of a lot more than that, but the cold part of his mind, which is—for the time being—keeping the hot part in a cage, tells him this is the right way to go, the route that will lead into the rest of his story the way a narrow entrance ramp leads to a four-lane highway. Pete gets up and goes out. Isabelle says nothing until he gets back, just regards Hodges with those misty gray eyes.

Hodges drinks half the paper cup in a swallow, then says, "Okay. It goes back to that lunch we had at DeMasio's, Pete. Remember?"

"Sure."

"I asked you about all the cases we were working—the big ones, I mean—when I retired, but the one I was really interested in was the City Center Massacre. I think you knew that."

Pete says nothing, but smiles slightly.

"Do you remember me asking if you ever wondered about Mrs. Trelawney? Specifically if she was telling the truth about not having an extra key?"

"Uh-huh."

"What I was really wondering was if we gave her a fair shake. If we were wearing blinders because of how she was."

"What do you mean, how she was?" Isabelle asks.

"A pain in the ass. Twitchy and haughty and quick to take offense. To get a little perspective, turn it around a minute and think of all the people who believed Donald Davis when he claimed he was innocent. Why? Because he *wasn't* twitchy and haughty and quick to take offense. He could really put that grief-stricken haunted-husband thing across, and he was good-looking. I saw him on Channel Six once, and that pretty blond anchor's thighs were practically squeezing together."

"That's disgusting," Isabelle says, but she says it with a smile.

"Yeah, but true. He was a charmer. Olivia Trelawney, on the other hand, was an *anti*-charmer. So I started to wonder if we ever gave her story a fair shot."

"We did." Pete says it flatly.

"*Maybe* we did. Anyway, there I am, retired, with time on my hands. Too much time. And one day—just before I asked you to lunch, Pete—I say to myself, Assume she *was* telling the truth. If so, where was that second key? And then—this was right *after* our lunch—I went on the Internet and started to do some research. And do you know what I came across? A techno-fiddle called 'stealing the peek.'"

"What's that?" Isabelle asks.

"Oh, man," Pete says. "You really think some computer genius stole her key-signal? Then just happened to find her spare key stowed in the glove compartment or under the seat? Her spare key that she *forgot*? That's pretty far-fetched, Bill. Especially when you add in that the woman's picture could have been next to Type A in the dictionary."

Calmly, as if he had not used his jacket to cover the severed arm of a woman he loved not three hours before, Hodges summarizes what Jerome found out about stealing the peek, representing it as his own research. He tells them that he went to the Lake Avenue condo to interview Olivia Trelawney's mother ("If she was still alive—I didn't know for sure") and found Olivia's sister, Janelle, living there. He leaves out his visit to the mansion in Sugar Heights and his conversation with Radney Peeples, the Vigilant security guard, because that might lead to questions he'd be hard-pressed to answer. They'll find out in time, but he's close to Mr. Mercedes now, he knows he is. A little time is all he needs.

He hopes.

"Ms. Patterson told me her mother was in a nursing home about thirty miles from here—Sunny Acres. She offered to go up there with me and make the introduction. So I could ask a few questions."

"Why would she do that?" Isabelle asks.

"Because she thought we might have jammed her sister up, and that caused her suicide."

"Bullshit," Pete says.

"I'm not going to argue with you about it, but you can understand the thinking, right? And the hope of clearing her sister of negligence?"

Pete gestures for him to go on. Hodges does, after finishing his water. He wants to get out of here. Mr. Mercedes could have read Jerome's message by now. If so, he may run. That would be fine with Hodges. A running man is easier to spot than a hiding man.

"I questioned the old lady and got nothing. All I managed to do was upset her. She had a stroke and died soon after." He sighs. "Ms. Patterson—Janelle—was heartbroken."

"Was she also pissed at you?" Isabelle asks.

"No. Because she was for the idea, too. Then, when her mother died, she didn't know anyone in the city except her mother's nurse, who's pretty long in the tooth herself. I'd given her my number, and she called me. She said she needed help, especially with a bunch of relatives flying in that she hardly knew, and I was willing to give it. Janelle wrote the obituary. I made the other arrangements."

"Why was she in your car when it blew?"

Hodges explains about Holly's meltdown. He doesn't mention Janey appropriating his new hat at the last moment, not because it will destabilize his story but because it hurts too much.

"Okay," Isabelle says. "You meet Olivia Trelawney's sister, who you like well enough to call by her first name. The sister facilitates a Q-and-A with the mom. Mom strokes out and dies, maybe because reliving it all again got her too excited. The sister is blown up after the funeral—in your car—and you still don't see a connection to the Mercedes Killer?"

Hodges spreads his hands. "How would this guy know I was asking questions? I didn't take out an ad in the paper." He turns to Pete. "I didn't talk to anyone about it, not even you."

Pete, clearly still brooding over the idea that their personal feelings about Olivia Trelawney might have colored the investigation, is looking dour. Hodges doesn't much care, because that's exactly what happened. "No, you just sounded me out about it at lunch."

Hodges gives him a big grin. It makes his stomach fold in on itself like origami. "Hey," he says, "it was my treat, wasn't it?"

"Who else could have wanted to bomb you to kingdom come?" Isabelle asks. "You on Santa's naughty list?"

"If I had to guess, I'd put my money on the Abbascia Family. How many of those shitbags did we put away on that gun thing back in '04, Pete?"

"A dozen or more, but—"

"Yeah, and RICO'd twice as many a year later. We smashed them to pieces, and Fabby the Nose said they'd get us both."

"Billy, the Abbascias can't get anyone. Fabrizio is dead, his brother is in a mental asylum where he thinks he's Napoleon or someone, and the rest are in jail."

Hodges just gives him the look.

"Okay," Pete says, "so you never catch all the cockroaches, but it's still crazy. All due respect, pal, but you're just a retired flatfoot. Out to pasture."

"Right. Which means they could go after me without creating a firestorm. You, on the other hand, still have a gold shield pinned to your wallet."

"The idea is ridiculous," Isabelle says, and folds her arms beneath her breasts as if to say *That ends the matter.*

Hodges shrugs. "*Somebody* tried to blow me up, and I can't believe the Mercedes Killer somehow got an ESP vibe that I was looking into the Case of the Missing Key. Even if he did, why would he come after me? How could that lead to him?"

"Well, he's crazy," Pete says. "How about that for a start?"

"Sure, but I repeat—*how would he know?*"

"No idea. Listen, Billy, are you holding anything back? Anything at all?"

"No."

"I think you are," Isabelle says. She cocks her head. "Hey, you weren't sleeping with her, were you?"

Hodges shifts his gaze to her. "What do you think, Izzy? Look at me."

She holds his eyes for a moment, then drops them. Hodges can't believe how close she just came. *Women's intuition,* he thinks, and then, *Probably a good thing I haven't lost any more weight, or put that Just For Men shit in my hair.*

"Look, Pete, I want to shake. Go home and have a beer and try to get my head around this."

"You swear you're not holding anything back? This is you and me, now."

Hodges passes up his last chance to come clean without a qualm. "Not a thing."

Pete tells him to stay in touch; they'll want him in tomorrow or Friday for a formal statement.

"Not a problem. And Pete? In the immediate future I'd give my car a once-over before driving it, if I were you."

At the door, Pete puts an arm over Hodges's shoulders and gives him a hug. "I'm sorry about this," he says. "Sorry about what happened and about all the questions."

"It's okay. You're doing the job."

Pete tightens his grip and whispers in Hodges's ear. "You *are* holding back. You think I've been taking stupid pills?"

For a moment Hodges rethinks his options. Then he remembers Janey saying He's *ours*.

He takes Pete by the arms, looks him full in the face, and says, "I'm just as mystified about this as you are. Trust me."

## 25

Hodges crosses the Detective Division bullpen, fielding the curious glances and leading questions with a stone face that only breaks once. Cassie Sheen, with whom he worked most often when Pete was on vacation, says, "Look at you. Still alive and uglier than ever."

He smiles. "If it isn't Cassie Sheen, the Botox Queen." He lifts an arm in mock defense when she picks a paperweight up off her desk and brandishes it. It all feels both fake and real at the same time. Like one of those girl-fights on afternoon TV.

In the hall, there's a line of chairs near the snack and soda machines. Sitting in two of the chairs are Aunt Charlotte and Uncle Henry. Holly isn't with them, and Hodges instinctively touches the glasses case in his pants pocket. He asks Uncle Henry if he's feeling better. Uncle Henry says he is, and thanks him. He turns to Aunt Charlotte and asks how she's doing.

"I'm fine. It's Holly I'm worried about. I think she blames herself, because she's the reason . . . you know."

Hodges knows. The reason Janey was driving his car. Of course Janey would have been in it anyway, but he doubts if that changes the way Holly feels.

"I wish you'd talk to her. You *bonded* with her, somehow." Her eyes take on an unpleasant gleam. "The way you bonded with Janelle. You must have a way about you."

"I'll do that," Hodges says, and he will, but Jerome is going to talk to her first. Assuming the number on the glasses case works, that is. For all he knows, that number rings a landline in . . . where was it? Cincinnati? Cleveland?

"I hope we're not supposed to identify her," Uncle Henry says. In one hand he holds a Styrofoam cup of coffee. He's hardly touched it, and Hodges isn't surprised. The police department coffee is notorious. "How can we? She was blown to bits."

"Don't be an idiot," Aunt Charlotte says. "They don't want us to do that. They *can't*."

Hodges says, "If she's ever been fingerprinted—most people have—they'll do it that way. They may show you photographs of her clothes, or personal pieces of jewelry."

"How would we know about her jewelry?" Aunt Charlotte cries. A cop getting a soda turns to look at her. "And I hardly noticed what she was wearing!"

Hodges guesses she priced out every stitch, but doesn't comment. "They may have other questions." Some about him. "It shouldn't take long."

There's an elevator, but Hodges chooses the stairs. On the landing one flight down, he leans against the wall, eyes closed, and takes half a dozen big, shuddering breaths. The tears come now. He swipes them away with his sleeve. Aunt Charlotte expressed concern about Holly—a concern Hodges shares—but no sorrow about her blown-to-bits niece. He guesses that Aunt Charlotte's biggest interest in Janey right now is what happens to all the lovely dosh Janey inherited from her sister.

*I hope she left it to a fucking dog hospital,* he thinks.

Hodges sits down with an out-of-breath grunt. Using one of the stairs as a makeshift desk, he lays out the sunglasses case and, from his wallet, a creased sheet of notepaper with two sets of numbers on it.

26

"Hello?" The voice is soft, tentative. "Hello, who is this?"

"My name's Jerome Robinson, ma'am. I believe Bill Hodges said I might call you."

Silence.

"Ma'am?" Jerome is sitting by his computer, holding his Android almost tightly enough to crack the casing. "Ms. Gibney?"

"I'm here." It's almost a sigh. "He said he wants to catch the person who killed my cousin. There was a terrible explosion."

"I know," Jerome says. Down the hall, Barb starts playing her new 'Round Here record for the thousandth time. *Kisses on the Midway*, it's called. It hasn't driven him crazy yet, but crazy gets closer with every play.

Meanwhile, the woman on the other end of the line has started to cry.

"Ma'am? Ms. Gibney? I'm very sorry for your loss."

"I hardly knew her, but she was my cousin, and she was nice to me. So was Mr. Hodges. Do you know what he asked me?"

"No, uh-uh."

"If I'd eaten breakfast. Wasn't that considerate?"

"It sure was," Jerome says. He still can't believe the lively, vital lady he had dinner with is dead. He remembers how her eyes sparkled when she laughed and how she mocked Bill's way of saying *yeah*. Now he's on the phone with a woman he's never met, a very odd woman, from the sound of her. Talking to her feels like defusing a bomb. "Ma'am, Bill asked me to come out there."

"Will he come with you?"

"He can't right now. He's got other things he has to do."

There's more silence, and then, in a voice so low and timid he can barely hear it, Holly asks, "Are you safe? Because I worry about people, you know. I worry very much."

"Yes, ma'am, I'm safe."

"I want to help Mr. Hodges. I want to help catch the man who did it. He must be crazy, don't you think?"

"Yes," Jerome says. Down the hall another song starts and two little girls—Barbara and her friend Hilda—emit joyous shrieks almost high enough to shatter glass. He thinks of three or four thousand Barbs and Hildas all shrieking in unison tomorrow night, and thanks God his mother is pulling *that* duty.

"You could come, but I don't know how to let you in," she says. "My uncle Henry set the burglar alarm when he went out, and I don't know the code. I think he shut the gate, too."

"I've got all that covered," Jerome says.

"When will you come?"

"I can be there in half an hour."

"If you talk to Mr. Hodges, will you tell him something for me?"

"Sure."

"Tell him I'm sad, too." She pauses. "And that I'm taking my Lexapro."

27

Late that Wednesday afternoon, Brady checks in to a gigantic Motel 6 near the airport, using one of his Ralph Jones credit cards. He has a suitcase and a knapsack. In the knapsack is a single change of clothes, which is all he'll need for the few dozen hours of life that still remain to him. In the suitcase is the ASS PARKING cushion, the Urinesta peebag, a framed picture, several homemade detonator switches (he only expects to need one, but you can never have enough backup), Thing Two, several Glad storage bags filled with ball bearings, and enough homemade explosive to blow both the motel and the adjacent parking lot sky-high. He goes back to his Subaru, pulls out a larger item (with some effort; it barely fits), carries it into his room, and leans it against the wall.

He lies down on his bed. His head feels strange against the pillow. Naked. And sort of sexy, somehow.

He thinks, I've had a run of bad luck, but I've ridden it out and I'm still standing.

He closes his eyes. Soon he's snoring.

## 28

Jerome parks his Wrangler with the nose almost touching the closed gate at 729 Lilac Drive, gets out, and pushes the call button. He has a reason to be here if someone from the Sugar Heights security patrol should stop and query him, but it will only work if the woman inside confirms him, and he's not sure he can count on that. His earlier conversation with the lady has suggested that she's got one wheel on the road at most. In any case, he's not challenged, and after a moment or two of standing there and trying to look as if he belongs—this is one of those occasions when he feels especially black—Holly answers.

"Yes? Who is it?"

"Jerome, Ms. Gibney. Bill Hodges's friend?"

A pause so long he's about to push the button again when she says, "You have the gate code?"

"Yes."

"All right. And if you're a friend of Mr. Hodges, I guess you can call me Holly."

He pushes the code and the gate opens. He drives through and watches it close behind him. So far, so good.

Holly is at the front door, peering at him through one of the side windows like a prisoner in a high-security visitation area. She's wearing a housecoat over pajamas, and her hair is a mess. A brief nightmare scenario crosses Jerome's mind: she pushes the panic button on the burglar alarm panel (almost certainly right next to where she's standing), and when the security guys arrive, she accuses him of being a burglar. Or a would-be rapist with a flannel-pajama fetish.

The door is locked. He points to it. For a moment Holly just stands there like a robot with a dead battery. Then she turns the deadbolt. A shrill peeping sound commences when Jerome opens the door and she takes several steps backward, covering her mouth with both hands.

"Don't let me get in trouble! I don't want to get in trouble!"

She's twice as nervous as he is, and this eases Jerome's mind. He punches the code into the burglar alarm and hits ALL SECURE. The peeping stops.

Holly collapses into an ornately carved chair that looks like it might have cost enough to pay for a year at a good college (although maybe not Harvard), her hair hanging around her face in dank wings. "Oh, this has been the worst day of my life," she says. "Poor Janey. Poor poor Janey."

"I'm sorry."

"But at least it's not *my* fault." She looks up at him with thin and pitiable defiance. "No one can say it was. *I* didn't do anything."

"Of course you didn't," Jerome says.

It comes out sounding stilted, but she smiles a little, so maybe it's okay. "Is Mr. Hodges all right? He's a very, very, *very* nice man. Even though my mother doesn't like him." She shrugs. "But who *does* she like?"

"He's fine," Jerome says, although he doubts if that's true.

"You're *black*," she says, looking at him, wide-eyed.

Jerome looks down at his hands. "I am, aren't I?"

She bursts into peals of shrill laughter. "I'm sorry. That was rude. It's *fine* that you're black."

"Black is whack," Jerome says.

"Of course it is. Totally whack." She stands up, gnaws at her lower lip, then pistons out her hand with an obvious effort of will. "Put it there, Jerome."

He shakes. Her hand is clammy. It's like shaking the paw of a small and timid animal.

"We have to hurry. If my mother and Uncle Henry come back and catch you in here, I'm in trouble."

You? Jerome thinks. What about the black kid?

"The woman who used to live here was also your cousin, right?"

"Yes. Olivia Trelawney. I haven't seen her since I was in college. She and my mother never got along." She looks at him solemnly. "I had to drop out of college. I had issues."

Jerome bets she did. And does. Still, there's something about her he likes. God knows what. It's surely not that fingernails-on-a-blackboard laugh.

"Do you know where her computer is?"

"Yes. I'll show you. Can you be quick?"

I better be, Jerome thinks.


## 29


The late Olivia Trelawney's computer is password-protected, which is silly, because when he turns over the keyboard, he finds OTRELAW written there with a Sharpie.

Holly, standing in the doorway and flipping the collar of her housecoat nervously up and down, mutters something he doesn't catch.

"Huh?"

"I asked what you're looking for."

"You'll know it if I find it." He opens the finder and types CRY-ING BABY into the search field. No result. He tries WEEPING INFANT. Nothing. He tries SCREAMING WOMAN. Nothing.

"It could be hidden." This time he hears her clearly because her voice is right next to his ear. He jumps a little, but Holly doesn't notice. She's bent over with her hands on her housecoated knees, staring at Olivia's monitor. "Try AUDIO FILE."

That's a pretty good idea, so he does. But there's nothing.

"Okay," she says, "go to SYSTEM PREFERENCES and look at SOUND."

"Holly, all that does is control the input and output. Stuff like that."

"Well *duh*. Try it anyway." She's stopped biting her lips.

Jerome does. Under output, the menu lists SOUND STICKS, HEADPHONES, and LOG ME IN SOUND DRIVER. Under input, there's INTERNAL MICROPHONE and LINE IN. Nothing he didn't expect.

"Any other ideas?" he asks her.

"Open SOUND EFFECTS. Over there on the left."

He turns to her. "Hey, you know this stuff, don't you?"

"I took a computer course. From home. On Skype. It was interesting. Go on, look at SOUND EFFECTS."

Jerome does, and blinks at what he sees. In addition to FROG, GLASS, PING, POP, and PURR—the usual suspects—there's an item listed as SPOOKS.

"Never seen that one before."

"Me, either." She still won't look directly at his face, but her affect has changed remarkably otherwise. She pulls up a chair and sits beside him, tucking her lank hair behind her ears. "And I know Mac programs inside and out."

"Go with your bad self," Jerome says, and holds up a hand.

Still looking at the screen, Holly slaps him five. "Play it, Sam."

He grins. *"Casablanca."*

"Yes. I've seen that movie seventy-three times. I have a Movie Book. I write down everything I see. My mother says that's OCD."

*"Life* is OCD," Jerome says.

Unsmiling, Holly replies, "Go with your bad self."

Jerome highlights SPOOKS and bangs the return key. From the stereo sound sticks on either side of Olivia's computer, a baby begins to wail. Holly is okay with that; she doesn't clutch Jerome's shoulder until the woman shrieks, *"Why did you let him murder my baby?"*

"Fuck!" Jerome cries, and grabs Holly's hand. He doesn't even think about it, and she doesn't draw away. They stare at the computer as if it has grown teeth and bitten them.

There's a moment of silence, then the baby starts crying again. The woman screams again. The program cycles a third time, then stops.

Holly finally looks directly at him, her eyes so wide they seem in danger of falling out of her head. "Did you know that was going to happen?"

"Jesus, *no*." Maybe something, or Bill wouldn't have sent him here, but *that*? "Can you find out anything about the program, Holly? Like when it was installed? If you can't, that's all ri—"

"Push over."

Jerome is good with computers, but Holly plays the keyboard like a Steinway. After a few minutes of hunting around, she says, "Looks like it was installed on July first of last year. A whole bunch of stuff was installed that day."

"It could have been programmed to play at certain times, right? Cycle three times and then quit?"

She gives him an impatient glance. "Of course."

"Then how come it's not *still* playing? I mean, you guys have been staying here. You would have heard it."

She clicks the mouse like crazy and shows him something else. "I saw this already. It's a slave program, hidden in her Mail Contacts. I bet Olivia didn't know it was here. It's called Looking Glass. You can't use it to turn on a computer—at least I don't think so—but if it *is* on, you can run everything from your own computer. Open files, read emails, look at search histories . . . or deactivate programs."

"Like after she was dead," Jerome says.

"Oough." Holly grimaces.

"Why would the guy who installed this leave it? Why not erase it completely?"

"I don't know. Maybe he just forgot. I forget stuff all the time. My mother says I'd forget my own head if it wasn't attached to my neck."

"Yeah, mine says that, too. But who's *he*? Who are we talking about?"

She thinks it over. They both do. And after perhaps five seconds, they speak at the same time.

"Her I-T guy," Jerome says, just as Holly says, "Her geek freak."

Jerome starts going through the drawers of Olivia's computer station, looking for a computer-service invoice, a bill stamped PAID, or a business card. There ought to be at least one of those, but there's nothing. He gets on his knees and crawls into the knee-hole under the desk. Nothing there, either.

"Look on the fridge," he says. "Sometimes people put shit there, under little magnets."

"There are plenty of magnets," Holly says, "but nothing on the fridge except for a real estate agent's card and one from the Vigilant security company. I think Janey must have taken down everything else. Probably threw it away."

"Is there a safe?"

"Probably, but why would my cousin put her I-T guy's business card in her safe? It's not like it's worth *money*, or anything."

"True-dat," Jerome says.

"If it was here, it would be by her computer. She wouldn't *hide* it. I mean, she wrote her password right under her goshdarn *keyboard*."

"Pretty dumb," Jerome says.

"Totally." Holly suddenly seems to realize how close they are. She gets up and goes back to the doorway. She starts flipping the collar of her housecoat again. "What are you going to do now?"

"I guess I better call Bill."

He takes out his cell phone, but before he can make the call, she says his name. Jerome looks at her, standing there in the doorway, looking lost in her flappy comfort-clothes.

"There must be, like, a zillion I-T guys in this city," she says.

Nowhere near that many, but a lot. He knows it and Hodges knows it, too, because it was Jerome who told him.

30

Hodges listens carefully to everything Jerome has to say. He's pleased by Jerome's praise of Holly (and hopes Holly will be pleased, too, if she's listening), but bitterly disappointed that there's no link to the Computer Jack who worked on Olivia's machine. Jerome thinks it must be because Janey threw Computer Jack's business card away. Hodges, who has a mind trained to be suspicious, thinks Mr. Mercedes might have made damned sure Olivia didn't *have* a card. Only that doesn't track. Wouldn't you *ask* for one, if the guy did good work? And keep it handy? Unless, that is . . .

He asks Jerome to put Holly on.

"Hello?" So faint he has to strain to hear her.

"Holly, is there an address book on Olivia's computer?"

"Just a minute." He hears faint clicking. When she comes back, her voice is puzzled. "No."

"Does that strike you as weird?"

"Kinda, yeah."

"Could the guy who planted the spook sounds have deleted her address book?"

"Oh, sure. Easy. I'm taking my Lexapro, Mr. Hodges."

"That's great, Holly. Can you tell how much Olivia used her computer?"

"Sure."

"Let me talk to Jerome while you look."

Jerome comes on and says he's sorry they haven't been able to find more.

"No, no, you've done great. When you tossed her desk, you didn't find a *physical* address book?"

"Uh-uh, but lots of people don't bother with them anymore— they keep all their contacts on their computers and phones. You know that, right?"

Hodges supposes he *should* know it, but the world is moving too fast for him these days. He doesn't even know how to program his DVR.

"Hang on, Holly wants to talk to you again."

"You and Holly are getting along pretty well, huh?"

"We're cool. Here she is."

"Olivia had all kinds of programs and website faves," Holly says. "She was big on Hulu and Huffpo. And her search history . . . it looks to me like she spent even more time browsing than I do, and I'm online a *lot*."

"Holly, why would a person who really depends on her computer not have a service card handy?"

"Because the guy snuck in and took it after she was dead," Holly says promptly.

"Maybe, but think of the risk—especially with the neighborhood security service keeping an eye on things. He'd have to know the gate code, the burglar alarm code . . . and even then he'd need a housekey . . ." He trails off.

"Mr. Hodges? Are you still there?"

"Yes. And go ahead and call me Bill."

But she won't. Maybe she can't. "Mr. Hodges, is he a master criminal? Like in James Bond?"

"I think just crazy." And *because* he's crazy, the risk might not matter to him. Look at the risk he took at City Center, plowing into that crowd of people.

It still doesn't ring right.

"Give me Jerome again, will you?"

She does, and Hodges tells him it's time to get out before Aunt Charlotte and Uncle Henry come back and catch him computer-canoodling with Holly.

"What are you going to do, Bill?"

He looks out at the street, where twilight has started to deepen the colors of the day. It's close to seven o'clock. "Sleep on it," he says.

31

Before going to bed, Hodges spends four hours in front of the TV, watching shows that go in his eyes just fine but disintegrate before reaching his brain. He tries to think about nothing, because that's how you open the door so the right idea can come in. The right idea always arrives as a result of the right connection, and there *is* a connection waiting to be made; he feels it. Maybe more than one. He will not let Janey into his thoughts. Later, yes, but for now all she can do is jam his gears.

Olivia Trelawney's computer is the crux of the matter. It was rigged with spook sounds, and the most likely suspect is her I-T guy. So why didn't she have his card? He could delete her computer address book at long distance—and Hodges is betting he did—but did he break into her house to steal a fucking *business card* after she was dead?

He gets a call from a newspaper reporter. Then from a Channel Six guy. After the third call from someone in the media, Hodges shuts his phone down. He doesn't know who spilled his cell number, but he hopes the person was well paid for the info.

Something else keeps coming into his mind, something that has nothing to do with anything: *She thinks they walk among us.*

A refresher glance through his notes allows him to put his finger on who said that to him: Mr. Bowfinger, the greeting-card writer. He and Bowfinger were sitting in lawn chairs, and Hodges remembers being grateful for the shade. This was while he was doing his canvass, looking for anyone who might have seen a suspicious vehicle cruising the street.

*She thinks they walk among us.*

Bowfinger was talking about Mrs. Melbourne across the street. Mrs. Melbourne who belongs to an organization of UFO nuts called NICAP, the National Investigations Committee on Aerial Phenomena.

Hodges decides it's just one of those echoes, like a snatch of pop music, that can start resounding in an overstressed brain. He gets undressed and goes to bed and Janey comes, Janey wrinkling her nose and saying *yeah*, and for the first time since childhood, he actually cries himself to sleep.

He wakes up in the small hours of Thursday morning, takes a

leak, starts back to bed, and stops, eyes widening. What he's been looking for—the connection—is suddenly there, big as life.

You didn't bother keeping a business card if you didn't *need* one.

Say the guy wasn't an independent, running a little business out of his house, but someone who worked for a *company*. If that was the case, you could call the company number any time you needed him, because it would be something easy to remember, like 555-9999, or whatever the numbers were that spelled out COMPUTE.

If he worked for a company, he'd make his repair calls in a company car.

Hodges goes back to bed, sure that sleep will elude him this time, but it doesn't.

He thinks, *If he had enough explosive to blow up my car, he must have more.*

Then he's under again.

He dreams about Janey.

# KISSES ON
# THE MIDWAY

# 1

Hodges is up at six A.M. on Thursday morning and makes himself a big breakfast: two eggs, four slices of bacon, four slices of toast. He doesn't want it, but he forces himself to eat every bite, telling himself it's body gasoline. He might get a chance to eat again today, but he might not. Both in the shower and as he chews his way resolutely through his big breakfast (no one to watch his weight for now), a thought keeps recurring to him, the same one he went to sleep with the night before. It's like a haunting.

Just how much explosive?

This leads to other unpleasant considerations. Like how the guy—the *perk*—means to use it. And when.

He comes to a decision: today is the last day. He wants to track Mr. Mercedes down himself, and confront him. Kill him? No, not that (*probably* not that), but beating the shit out of him would be *excellent*. For Olivia. For Janey. For Janice and Patricia Cray. For all the other people Mr. Mercedes killed and maimed at City Center the year before. People so desperate for jobs they got up in the middle of the night and stood waiting in a dank fog for the doors to open. Lost lives. Lost hopes. Lost *souls*.

So yes, he wants the sonofabitch. But if he can't nail him today, he'll turn the whole thing over to Pete Huntley and Izzy Jaynes and take the consequences . . . which, he knows, may well lead to some jail time. It doesn't matter. He's got plenty on his conscience already, but he guesses it can bear a little more weight. Not another mass killing, though. That would destroy what little of him there is left.

He decides to give himself until eight o'clock tonight; that's the line in the sand. He can do as much in those thirteen hours as Pete and Izzy. Probably more, because he's not constrained by routine or procedure. Today he will carry his father's M&P .38. And the Happy Slapper—that, too.

The Slapper goes in the right front pocket of his sportcoat, the revolver under his left arm. In his study, he grabs his Mr. Mercedes file—it's quite fat now—and takes it back to the kitchen. While he reads through it again, he uses the remote to fire up the TV on the counter and tunes in *Morning at Seven* on Channel Six. He's almost relieved to see that a crane has toppled over down by the lakeshore, half-sinking a barge filled with chemicals. He doesn't want the lake any more polluted than it already is (assuming that's possible), but the spill has pushed the car-bomb story back to second place. That's the good news. The bad is that he's identified as the detective, now retired, who was the lead investigator of the City Center Massacre task force, and the woman killed in the car-bombing is identified as Olivia Trelawney's sister. There's a still photo of him and Janey standing outside the Soames Funeral Home, taken by God knows who.

"Police are not saying if there's a connection to last year's mass killing at City Center," the newscaster says gravely, "but it's worth noting that the perpetrator of that crime has as yet not been caught. In other crime news, Donald Davis is expected to be arraigned . . ."

Hodges no longer gives Shit One about Donald Davis. He kills the TV and returns to the notes on his yellow legal pad. He's still going through them when his phone rings—not the cell (although today he's carrying it), but the one on the wall. It's Pete Huntley.

"You're up with the birdies," Pete says.

"Good detective work. How can I help you?"

"We had an interesting interview yesterday with Henry Sirois and Charlotte Gibney. You know, Janelle Patterson's aunt and uncle?"

Hodges waits for it.

"The aunt was especially fascinating. She thinks Izzy was right, and you and Patterson were a lot more than just acquaintances. She thinks you were very good friends."

"Say what you mean, Pete."

"Making the beast with two backs. Laying some pipe. Slicing the cake. Hiding the salami. Doing the horizontal b—"

"I think I get it. Let me tell you something about Aunt Charlotte, okay? If she saw a photo of Justin Bieber talking to Queen Elizabeth, she'd tell you the Beeb was tapping her. 'Just look at their eyes,' she'd say."

"So you weren't."

"No."

"I'll take that on a try-out basis—mostly for old times' sake—but I still want to know what you're hiding. Because this stinks."

"Read my lips: not . . . hiding . . . *anything.*"

Silence from the other end. Pete is waiting for Hodges to grow uncomfortable and break it, for the moment forgetting who taught him that trick.

At last he gives up. "I think you're digging yourself a hole, Billy. My advice is to drop the shovel before you're in too deep to climb out."

"Thanks, partner. Always good to get life-lessons at quarter past seven in the morning."

"I want to interview you again this afternoon. And this time I may have to read you the words."

The Miranda warning is what he means.

"Happy to make that work. Call me on my cell."

"Really? Since you retired, you never carry it."

"I'm carrying it today." Yes indeed. Because for the next twelve or fourteen hours, he's totally unretired.

He ends the call and goes back to his notes, wetting the tip of his index finger each time he turns a page. He circles a name: Radney Peeples. The Vigilant Guard Service guy he talked to out in Sugar Heights. If Peeples is even halfway doing his job, he may hold the key to Mr. Mercedes. But there's no chance he won't remember Hodges, not after Hodges first braced him for his company ID and then questioned him. And he'll know that today Hodges is big news. There's time to think about how to solve the problem; Hodges doesn't want to call Vigilant until regular business hours. Because the call has to look like ordinary routine.

The next call he receives—on his cell this time—is from Aunt Charlotte. Hodges isn't surprised to hear from her, but that doesn't mean he's pleased.

"I don't know what to do!" she cries. "You have to help me, Mr. Hodges!"

"Don't know what to do about what?"

"The *body*! Janelle's *body*! I don't even know where it *is*!"

Hodges gets a beep and checks the incoming number.

"Mrs. Gibney, I have another call and I have to take it."

"I don't see why you can't—"

"Janey's not going anywhere, so just stand by. I'll call you back."

He cuts her off in the middle of a protesting squawk and goes to Jerome.

"I thought you might need a chauffeur today," Jerome says. "Considering your current situation."

For a moment Hodges doesn't know what the kid is talking about, then remembers that his Toyota has been reduced to charred fragments. What remains of it is now in the custody of the PD's Forensics Department, where later today men in white coats will be going over it to determine what kind of explosive was used to blow it up. He got home last night in a taxi. He *will* need a ride. And, he realizes, Jerome may be useful in another way.

"That would be good," he says, "but what about school?"

"I'm carrying a 3.9 average," Jerome says patiently. "I'm also working for Citizens United and team-teaching a computer class for disadvantaged kids. I can afford to skip a day. And I already cleared it with my mom and dad. They just asked me to ask you if anyone else was going to try to blow you up."

"Actually, that's not out of the question."

"Hang on a second." Faintly, Hodges hears Jerome calling: "He says no one will."

In spite of everything, Hodges has to smile.

"I'll be there double-quick," Jerome says.

"Don't break any speed laws. Nine o'clock will be fine. Use the time to practice your thespian skills."

"Really? What role am I thesping?"

"Law office paralegal," Hodges says. "And thanks, Jerome."

He breaks the connection, goes into his study, boots up his computer, and searches for a local lawyer named Schron. It's an unusual name and he finds it with no trouble. He notes down the firm and Schron's first name, which happens to be George. Then he returns to the kitchen and calls Aunt Charlotte.

"Hodges," he says. "Back atcha."

"I don't appreciate being hung up on, Mr. Hodges."

"No more than I appreciate you telling my old partner that I was fucking your niece."

He hears a shocked gasp, followed by silence. He almost hopes she'll hang up. When she doesn't, he tells her what she needs to know.

"Janey's remains will be at the Huron County Morgue. You won't be able to take possession today. Probably not tomorrow, either. There'll have to be an autopsy, which is absurd given the cause of death, but it's protocol."

"You don't understand! I have *plane* reservations!"

Hodges looks out his kitchen window and counts slowly to five.

"Mr. Hodges? Are you still there?"

"As I see it, you have two choices, Mrs. Gibney. One is to stay here and do the right thing. The other is to use your reservation, fly home, and let the city do it."

Aunt Charlotte begins to snivel. "I saw the way you were looking at her, and the way she was looking at you. All I did was answer the woman cop's questions."

"And with great alacrity, I have no doubt."

"With *what?*"

He sighs. "Let's drop it. I suggest you and your brother visit the County Morgue in person. Don't call ahead, let them see your faces. Talk to Dr. Galworthy. If Galworthy's not there, talk to Dr. Patel. If you ask them in person to expedite matters—and if you can manage to be nice about it—they'll give you as much help as they can. Use my name. I go back to the early nineties with both of them."

"We'd have to leave Holly again," Aunt Charlotte says. "She's locked herself in her room. She's clicking away on her laptop and won't come out."

Hodges discovers he's pulling his hair and makes himself stop. "How old is your daughter?"

A long pause. "Forty-five."

"Then you can probably get away with not hiring a sitter." He tries to suppress what comes next, and can't quite manage it. "Think of the money you'll save."

"I can hardly expect you to understand Holly's situation, Mr. Hodges. As well as being mentally unstable, my daughter is very sensitive."

Hodges thinks: That must make you especially difficult for her. This time he manages not to say it.

"Mr. Hodges?"

"Still here."

"You don't happen to know if Janelle left a will, do you?"

He hangs up.

2

Brady spends a long time in the motel shower with the lights off. He likes the womblike warmth and the steady drumming sound. He also likes the darkness, and it's good that he does because soon he'll have all he ever wanted. He'd like to believe there's going to be a tender mother-and-child reunion—perhaps even one of the mother-and-lover type—but in his heart he doesn't. He can pretend, but . . . no.

Just darkness.

He's not worried about God, or about spending eternity being slow-roasted for his crimes. There's no heaven and no hell. Anyone with half a brain knows those things don't exist. How cruel would a supreme being have to be to make a world as fucked-up as this one? Even if the vengeful God of the televangelists and child-molesting blackrobes *did* exist, how could that thunderbolt-thrower possibly blame Brady for the things he's done? Did Brady Hartsfield grab his father's hand and wrap it around the live power line that electrocuted him? No. Did he shove that apple slice down Frankie's throat? No. Was he the one who talked on and on about how the money was going to run out and they'd end up living in a homeless shelter? No. Did he cook up a poisoned hamburger and say, *Eat this, Ma, it's delicious?*

Can he be blamed for striking out at the world that has made him what he is?

Brady thinks not.

He muses on the terrorists who brought down the World Trade Center (he muses on them often). Those clowns actually thought they were going to paradise, where they'd live in a kind of eternal luxury hotel being serviced by gorgeous young virgins. Pretty funny, and the best part? The joke was on them . . . not that they knew it. What they got was a momentary view of all those windows and a final flash of light. After that, they and their thousands of victims were just gone. Poof. Seeya later, alligator. Off you go, killers and killed alike, off you go into the universal null set that surrounds one lonely blue planet and all its mindlessly bustling denizens. Every religion lies. Every moral precept is a delusion. Even the stars are a mirage. The truth is darkness, and the only thing that matters is making a statement before one enters it. Cutting the skin of the world and leaving a scar. That's all history is, after all: scar tissue.

3

Brady dresses and drives to a twenty-four-hour drugstore near the airport. He's seen in the bathroom mirror that his mother's electric razor left a lot to be desired; his skull needs more maintenance. He gets disposable razors and shaving cream. He grabs more batteries, because you can never have enough. He also picks up a pair of clear glass spectacles from a spinner rack. He chooses hornrims because they give him a studently look. Or so it seems to him.

On his way to the checkout, he stops at a cardboard stand-up display featuring the four clean-cut boys in 'Round Here. The copy reads GET YOUR GEAR ON FOR THE BIG SHOW JUNE 3RD! Only someone has crossed out JUNE 3RD and written 2NITE below it.

Although Brady usually takes an M tee-shirt—he's always been slim—he picks out an XL and adds it to the rest of his swag. No need to stand in line; this early he's the only customer.

"Going to the show tonight?" the checkout girl asks.

Brady gives her a big grin. "I sure am."

On his way back to the motel, Brady starts to think about his car. To *worry* about his car. The Ralph Jones alias is all very fine, but the Subaru is registered to Brady Hartsfield. If the Det-Ret discovers his name and tells five-oh, that could be a problem. The motel is safe enough—they no longer ask for plate numbers, just a driver's license—but the car is not.

The Det-Ret's not close, Brady tells himself. He was just trying to freak you out.

Except maybe not. This particular Det solved a lot of cases before he was Ret, and some of those skills still seem to be there.

Instead of going directly back to the Motel 6, Brady swings into the airport, takes a ticket, and leaves the Subaru in long-term parking. He'll need it tonight, but for now it's fine where it is.

He glances at his watch. Ten to nine. Eleven hours until the showtime, he thinks. Maybe twelve hours until the darkness. Could be less; could be more. But not *much* more.

He puts on his new glasses and carries his purchases the half-mile back to the motel, whistling.

4

When Hodges opens his front door, the first thing Jerome keys on is the .38 in the shoulder rig. "You're not going to shoot anyone with that, are you?"

"I doubt it. Think of it as a good luck charm. It was my father's. And I have a permit to carry concealed, if that was on your mind."

"What's on my mind," Jerome says, "is whether or not it's loaded."

"Of course it is. What did you think I was going to do if I did have to use it? Throw it?"

Jerome sighs and ruffles his cap of dark hair. "This is getting heavy."

"Want out? If you do, you're taillights. Right this minute. I can still rent a car."

"No, I'm good. It's you I'm wondering about. Those aren't bags under your eyes, they're suitcases."

"I'll be okay. Today is it for me, anyway. If I can't track this guy down by nightfall, I'm going to see my old partner and tell him everything."

"How much trouble will you be in?"

"Don't know and don't much care."

"How much trouble will *I* be in?"

"None. If I couldn't guarantee that, you'd be in period one algebra right now."

Jerome gives him a pitying look. "Algebra was four years ago. Tell me what I can do."

Hodges does so. Jerome is willing but doubtful.

"Last month—you can't ever tell my folks this—a bunch of us tried to get into Punch and Judy, that new dance club downtown? The guy at the door didn't even look at my beautiful fake ID, just waved me out of the line and told me to go get a milkshake."

Hodges says, "I'm not surprised. Your face is seventeen, but fortunately for me, your voice is at least twenty-five." He slides Jerome a piece of paper with a phone number written on it. "Make the call."

Jerome tells the Vigilant Guard Service receptionist who answers that he is Martin Lounsbury, a paralegal at the firm of Canton, Silver, Makepeace, and Jackson. He says he's currently working with George Schron, a junior partner assigned to tie up a few loose ends concerning the estate of the late Olivia Trelawney. One of those loose ends has to do with Mrs. Trelawney's computer. His job for the day is to locate the I-T specialist who worked on the machine, and it seems possible that one of the Vigilant employees in the Sugar Heights area may be able to help him locate the gentleman.

Hodges makes a thumb-and-forefinger circle to indicate Jerome is doing well, and passes him a note.

Jerome reads it and says, "One of Mrs. Trelawney's neighbors, Mrs. Helen Wilcox, mentioned a Rodney Peeples?" He listens, then nods. "*Radney*, I see. What an interesting name. Perhaps he could call me, if it's not too much trouble? My boss is a bit of a tyrant, and I'm really under the gun here." He listens. "Yes? Oh, that's great. Thanks so much." He gives the receptionist the numbers of his cell and Hodges's landline, then hangs up and wipes make-believe sweat from his forehead. "I'm glad that's over. Whoo!"

"You did fine," Hodges assures him.

"What if she calls Canton, Silver, and Whoozis to check? And finds out they never heard of Martin Lounsbury?"

"Her job is to pass messages on, not investigate them."

"What if the Peeples guy checks?"

Hodges doesn't think he will. He thinks the name Helen Wilcox will stop him. When he talked to Peeples that day outside the Sugar Heights mansion, Hodges caught a strong vibe that Peeples's relationship with Helen Wilcox was more than just platonic. Maybe a little more, maybe a lot. He thinks Peeples will give Martin Lounsbury what he wants so he'll go away.

"What do we do now?" Jerome asks.

What they do is something Hodges spent at least half his career doing. "Wait."

"How long?"

"Until Peeples or some other security grunt calls." Because right now Vigilant Guard Service is looking like his best lead. If it doesn't pan out, they'll have to go out to Sugar Heights and start interviewing neighbors. Not a prospect he relishes, given his current news-cycle celebrity.

In the meantime, he finds himself thinking again of Mr. Bowfinger, and Mrs. Melbourne, the slightly crackers woman who lives across the street from him. With her talk about mysterious black SUVs and her interest in flying saucers, Mrs. Melbourne could have been a quirky supporting character in an old Alfred Hitchcock movie.

*She thinks they walk among us*, Bowfinger had said, giving his eyebrows a satirical wiggle, and why in God's name should that keep bouncing around in Hodges's head?

It's ten of ten when Jerome's cell rings. The little snatch of AC/DC's "Hells Bells" makes them both jump. Jerome grabs it.

"It says CALL BLOCKED. What should I do, Bill?"

"Take it. It's him. And remember who you are."

Jerome opens the line and says, "Hello, this is Martin Lounsbury." Listens. "Oh, hello, Mr. Peeples. Thanks so much for getting back to me."

Hodges scribbles a fresh note and pushes it across the table. Jerome scans it quickly.

"Uh-huh . . . yes . . . Mrs. Wilcox speaks very highly of you. Very highly, indeed. But my job has to do with the late Mrs. Trelawney. We can't finish clearing her estate until we can inventory her computer, and . . . yes, I know it's been over six months. Terrible how slowly these things move, isn't it? We had a client last year who actually had to apply for food stamps, even though he had a seventy-thousand-dollar bequest pending."

Don't over-butter the muffin, Jerome, Hodges thinks. His heart is hammering in his chest.

"No, it's nothing like that. I just need the name of the fellow who worked on it for her. The rest is up to my boss." Jerome listens, eyebrows pulling together. "You can't? Oh, that's a sha—"

But Peeples is talking again. The sweat on Jerome's brow is no longer imaginary. He reaches across the table, grabs Hodges's pen, and begins to scribble. While he writes, he keeps up a steady stream of *uh-huh*s and *okay*s and *I see*s. Finally:

"Hey, that's great. Totally great. I'm sure Mr. Schron can roll with this. You've been a big help, Mr. Peeples. So I'll just . . ." He listens some more. "Yes, it's a terrible thing. I believe Mr. Schron is dealing with some . . . uh . . . some aspects of that even as we speak, but I really don't know anythi . . . you did? Wow! Mr. Peeples, you've been great. Yes, I'll mention that. I certainly will. Thanks, Mr. Peeples."

He breaks the connection and puts the heels of his hands to his temples, as if to quell a headache.

"Man, that was *intense*. He wanted to talk about what happened yesterday. And to say that I should tell Janey's relatives that Vigilant stands ready to help in any way they can."

"That's great, I'm sure he'll get an attaboy in his file, but—"

"He also said he talked to the guy whose car got blown up. He saw your picture on the news this morning."

Hodges isn't surprised and at this minute doesn't care. "Did you get a name? Tell me you got a name."

"Not of the I-T guy, but I did get the name of the company he works for. It's called Cyber Patrol. Peeples says they drive around in green VW Beetles. He says they're in Sugar Heights all the time, and you can't miss them. He's seen a woman and a man driving them, both probably in their twenties. He called the woman 'kinda dykey.'"

Hodges has never even considered the idea that Mr. Mercedes might actually be Ms. Mercedes. He supposes it's technically possible, and it would make a neat solution for an Agatha Christie novel, but this is real life.

"Did he say what the guy looked like?"

Jerome shakes his head.

"Come on in my study. You can drive the computer while I co-pilot."

In less than a minute they are looking at a rank of three green VW Beetles with CYBER PATROL printed on the sides. It's not an independent company, but part of a chain called Discount Electronix with one big-box store in the city. It's located in the Birch Hill Mall.

"Man, I've shopped there," Jerome says. "I've shopped there *lots* of times. Bought video games, computer components, a bunch of chop-sockey DVDs on sale."

Below the photo of the Beetles is a line reading MEET THE EXPERTS. Hodges reaches over Jerome's shoulder and clicks on it. Three photos appear. One is of a narrow-faced girl with dirty-blond hair. Number two is a chubby guy wearing John Lennon specs and looking serious. Number three is a generically hand-some fellow with neatly combed brown hair and a bland say-cheese smile. The names beneath are FREDDI LINKLATTER, ANTHONY FROBISHER, and BRADY HARTSFIELD.

"What now?" Jerome asks.

"Now we take a ride. I just have to grab something first."

Hodges goes into his bedroom and punches the combo of the small safe in the closet. Inside, along with a couple of insurance policies and a few other financial papers, is a rubber-banded stack of laminated cards like the one he currently carries in his wallet. City cops are issued new IDs every two years, and each time he got a new one, he stored the old one in here. The crucial difference is that none of the old ones have RETIRED stamped across them in red. He takes out the one that expired in December of 2008, removes his final ID from his wallet, and replaces it with the one from his safe. Of course flashing it is another crime—State Law 190.25, impersonating a police officer, a Class E felony punishable by a $25,000 fine, five years in jail, or both—but he's far beyond worrying about such things.

He tucks his wallet away in his back pocket, starts to close the safe, then re-thinks. There's something else in there he might want: a small flat leather case that looks like the sort of thing a frequent flier might keep his passport in. This was also his father's.

Hodges slips it into his pocket with the Happy Slapper.

5

After cleansing the stubble on his skull and donning his new plain glass specs, Brady strolls down to the Motel 6 office and pays for another night. Then he returns to his room and unfolds the wheelchair he bought on Wednesday. It was pricey, but what the hell. Money is no longer an issue for him.

He puts the explosives-laden ASS PARKING cushion on the seat of the chair, then slits the lining of the pocket on the back and inserts several more blocks of his homemade plastic explosive. Each block has been fitted with a lead azide blasting plug. He gathers the connecting wires together with a metal clip. Their ends are stripped down to the bare copper, and this afternoon he'll braid them into a single master wire.

The actual detonator will be Thing Two.

One by one, he tapes Baggies filled with ball bearings beneath the wheelchair's seat, using crisscrossings of filament tape to hold them in place. When he's done, he sits on the end of the bed, looking solemnly at his handiwork. He really has no idea if he'll be able to get this rolling bomb into the Mingo Auditorium . . . but he had no idea if he'd be able to escape from City Center after the deed was done, either. That worked out; maybe this will, too. After all, this time he won't have to escape, and that's half the battle. Even if they get wise and try to grab him, the hallway will be crammed with concertgoers, and his score will be a lot higher than eight.

Out with a bang, Brady thinks. Out with a bang, and fuck you, Detective Hodges. Fuck you very much.

He lies down on the bed and thinks about masturbating. Probably he should while he's still got a prick to masturbate with. But before he can even unsnap his Levi's, he's fallen asleep.

On the night table beside him stands a framed picture. Frankie smiles from it, holding Sammy the Fire Truck in his lap.

6

It's nearly eleven A.M. when Hodges and Jerome arrive at Birch Hill Mall. There's plenty of parking, and Jerome pulls his Wrangler into a spot directly in front of Discount Electronix, where all the windows are sporting big SALE signs. A teenage girl is sitting on the curb in front of the store, knees together and feet apart, bent studiously over an iPad. A cigarette smolders between the fingers of her left hand. It's only as they approach that Hodges sees there's gray in the teenager's hair. His heart sinks.

"Holly?" Jerome says, at the same time Hodges says, "What in the hell are you doing here?"

"I was pretty sure you'd figure it out," she says, butting her butt and standing up, "but I was starting to worry. I was going to call you if you weren't here by eleven-thirty. I'm taking my Lexapro, Mr. Hodges."

"So you said, and I'm glad to hear it. Now answer my question and tell me what you're doing here."

Her lips tremble, and although she managed eye contact to begin with, her gaze now sinks to her loafers. Hodges isn't surprised he took her for a teenager at first, because in many ways she still is one, her growth stunted by insecurities and by the strain of keeping her balance on the emotional highwire she's been walking all her life.

"Are you mad at me? *Please* don't be mad at me."

"We're not mad," Jerome says. "Just surprised."

Shocked is more like it, Hodges thinks.

"I spent the morning in my room, browsing the local I-T community, but it's like we thought, there are hundreds of them. Mom and Uncle Henry went out to talk to people. About Janey, I think. I guess there'll have to be another funeral, but I hate to think about what will be in the coffin. It just makes me cry and cry."

And yes, big tears are rolling down her cheeks. Jerome puts an arm around her. She gives him a shy grateful glance.

"Sometimes it's hard for me to think when my mother is around. It's like she puts interference in my head. I guess that makes me sound crazy."

"Not to me," Jerome says. "I feel the same way about my sister. Especially when she plays her damn boy-band CDs."

"When they were gone and the house was quiet, I got an idea. I went back down to Olivia's computer and looked at her email."

Jerome slaps his forehead. "Shit! I never even thought of checking her mail."

"Don't worry, there wasn't any. She had three accounts—Mac Mail, Gmail, and AO-Hell—but all three folders were empty. Maybe she deleted them herself, but I don't think so because—"

"Because her desktop and hard drive were full of stuff," Jerome says.

"That's right. She has *The Bridge on the River Kwai* in her iTunes. I've never seen that. I might check it out if I get a chance."

Hodges glances toward Discount Electronix. With the sun glaring on the windows it's impossible to tell if anyone's watching them. He feels exposed out here, like a bug on a rock. "Let's take a little stroll," he says, and leads them toward Savoy Shoes, Barnes & Noble, and Whitey's Happy Frogurt Shoppe.

Jerome says, "Come on, Holly, give. You're drivin me crazy here."

That makes her smile, which makes her look older. More her age. And once they're away from the big Discount Electronix show windows, Hodges feels better. It's obvious to him that Jerome is delighted with her, and he feels the same (more or less in spite of himself), but it's humbling to find he's been scooped by a Lexapro-dependent neurotic.

"He forgot to take off his SPOOK program, so I thought maybe he forgot to empty her junk mail as well, and I was right. She had like four dozen emails from Discount Electronix. Some of them were sales notices—like the one they're having now, although I bet the only DVDs they have left aren't much good, they're probably Korean or something—and some of them were coupons for twenty percent off. She also had coupons for thirty percent off. The thirty percent coupons were for her next Cyber Patrol out-call." She shrugs. "And here I am."

Jerome stares at her. "That's all it took? Just a peek into her junk mail folder?"

"Don't be so surprised," Hodges says. "All it took to catch the Son of Sam was a parking ticket."

"I walked around back while I was waiting for you," Holly says. "Their Web page says there are only three I-Ts in the Cyber Patrol, and there are three of those green Beetles back there. So I guess the guy is working today. Are you going to arrest him, Mr. Hodges?" She's biting her lips again. "What if he fights? I don't want you to get hurt."

Hodges is thinking hard. Three computer techs in the Cyber Patrol: Frobisher, Hartsfield, and Linklatter, the skinny blond woman. He's almost positive it will turn out to be Frobisher or Hartsfield, and whichever one it is won't be prepared to see **kermitfrog19** walking through the door. Even if Mr. Mercedes doesn't run, he won't be able to hide the initial shock of recognition.

"I'm going in. You two are staying here."

"Going in with no backup?" Jerome asks. "Gee, Bill, I don't think that's very sma—"

"I'll be all right, I've got the element of surprise going for me, but if I'm not back out in ten minutes, call nine-one-one. Got it?"

"Yes."

Hodges points at Holly. "You stay close to Jerome. No more lone-wolf investigations." I should talk, he thinks.

She nods humbly, and Hodges walks away before they can engage him in further discussion. As he approaches the doors of Discount Electronix, he unbuttons his sportcoat. The weight of his father's gun against his ribcage is comforting.

7

As they watch Hodges enter the electronics store, a question occurs to Jerome. "Holly, how did you get here? Taxi?"

She shakes her head and points into the parking lot. There, parked three rows back from Jerome's Wrangler, is a gray Mercedes sedan. "It was in the garage." She notes Jerome's slack-jawed amazement and immediately becomes defensive. "I *can* drive, you know. I have a valid driver's license. I've never had an accident, and I have Safe Driver's Insurance. From Allstate. Do you know that the man who does the Allstate ads on TV used to be the president on *24*?"

"That's the car . . ."

She frowns, puzzled. "What's the big deal, Jerome? It was in the garage and the keys were in a basket in the front hall. So what's the big fat deal?"

The dents are gone, he notes. The headlights and windshield have been replaced. It looks as good as new. You'd never know it was used to kill people.

"Jerome? Do you think Olivia would mind?"

"No," he says. "Probably not." He is imagining that grille covered with blood. Pieces of shredded cloth dangling from it.

"It wouldn't start at first, the battery was dead, but she had one of those portable jump-stations, and I knew how to use it because my father had one. Jerome, if Mr. Hodges doesn't make an arrest, could we walk down to the frogurt place?"

He barely hears her. He's still staring at the Mercedes. They returned it to her, he thinks. Well, of course they did. It was her property, after all. She even got the damage repaired. But he'd be willing to bet she never drove it again. If there were spooks—real ones—they'd be in there. Probably screaming.

"Jerome? Earth to Jerome."

"Huh?"

"If everything turns out okay, let's get frogurt. I was sitting in the sun and waiting for you guys and I'm awfully hot. I'll treat. I'd really like ice cream, but . . ."

He doesn't hear the rest. He's thinking Ice cream.

The click in his head is so loud he actually winces, and all at once he knows why one of the Cyber Patrol faces on Hodges's computer looked familiar to him. The strength goes out of his legs and he leans against one of the walkway support posts to keep from falling.

"Oh my God," he says.

"What's wrong?" She shakes his arm, chewing her lips frantically. "What's *wrong*? Are you sick, Jerome?"

But at first he can only say it again: "Oh my God."

8

Hodges thinks that the Birch Hill Mall Discount Electronix looks like an enterprise with about three months to live. Many of the shelves are empty, and the stock that's left has a disconsolate, neglected look. Almost all of the browsers are in the Home Entertainment department, where fluorescent pink signs proclaim WOW! DVD BLOWOUT! ALL DISCS 50% OFF! EVEN BLU-RAY! Although there are ten checkout lines, only three are open, staffed by women in blue dusters with the yellow DE logo on them. Two of these women are looking out the window; the third is reading *Twilight*. A couple of other employees are wandering the aisles, doing a lot of nothing much.

Hodges doesn't want any of them, but he sees two of the three he *does* want. Anthony Frobisher, he of the John Lennon specs, is talking to a customer who has a shopping basket full of discounted DVDs in one hand and a clutch of coupons in the other. Frobisher's tie suggests that he might be the store manager as well as a Cyber Patrolman. The narrow-faced girl with the dirty-blond hair is at the back of the store, seated at a computer. There's a cigarette parked behind one ear.

Hodges strolls up the center aisle of the DVD BLOWOUT. Frobisher looks at him and raises a finger to say *Be with you soon.* Hodges smiles and gives him a little *I'm okay* wave. Frobisher returns to the customer with the coupons. No recognition there. Hodges walks on to the back of the store.

The dirty blond looks up at him, then back at the screen of the computer she's using. No recognition from her, either. She's not wearing a Discount Electronix shirt; hers says WHEN I WANT MY OPINION, I'LL GIVE IT TO YOU. He sees she's playing an updated version of Pitfall!, a cruder version of which fascinated his daughter Alison a quarter of a century before. Everything that goes around comes around, Hodges thinks. A Zen concept for sure.

"Unless you've got a computer question, talk to Tones," she says. "I only do crunchers."

"Tones would be Anthony Frobisher?"

"Yeah. Mr. Spiffy in the tie."

"You'd be Freddi Linklatter. Of the Cyber Patrol."

"Yeah." She pauses Pitfall Harry in mid-jump over a coiled snake in order to give him a closer inspection. What she sees is Hodges's police ID, with his thumb strategically placed to hide its year of expiration.

"Oooh," she says, and holds out her hands with the twig-thin wrists together. "I'm a bad, bad girl and handcuffs are what I deserve. Whip me, beat me, make me write bad checks."

Hodges gives a brief smile and tucks his ID away. "Isn't Brady Hartsfield the third member of your happy band? I don't see him."

"Out with the flu. *He* says. Want my best guess?"

"Hit me."

"I think maybe he finally had to put dear old Mom in rehab. He says she drinks and he has to take care of her most of the time. Which is probably why he's never had a gee-eff. You know what that is, right?"

"I'm pretty sure, yeah."

She examines him with bright and mordant interest. "Is Brady in trouble? I wouldn't be surprised. He's a little on the, you know, peekee-*yoolier* side."

"I just need to speak to him."

Anthony Frobisher—Tones—joins them. "May I help you, sir?"

"It's five-oh," Freddi says. She gives Frobisher a wide smile that exposes small teeth badly in need of cleaning. "He found out about the meth lab in the back."

"Can it, Freddi."

She makes an extravagant lip-zipping gesture, finishing with the twist of an invisible key, but doesn't go back to her game.

In Hodges's pocket, his cell phone rings. He silences it with his thumb.

"I'm Detective Bill Hodges, Mr. Frobisher. I have a few questions for Brady Hartsfield."

"He's out with the flu. What did he do?"

"Tones is a poet and don't know it," Freddi Linklatter observes. "Although his feet show it, because they're Longfel—"

"Shut up, Freddi. For the last time."

"Can I have his address, please?"

"Of course. I'll get it for you."

"Can I un-shut for a minute?" Freddi asks.

Hodges nods. She punches a key on her computer. Pitfall Harry is replaced by a spread-sheet headed STORE PERSONNEL.

"Presto," she says. "Forty-nine Elm Street. That's on the—"

"North Side, yeah," Hodges says. "Thank you both. You've been very helpful."

As he leaves, Freddi Linklatter calls after him, "It's something with his mom, betcha anything. He's freaky about her."

9

Hodges has no more than stepped out into the bright sunshine when Jerome almost tackles him. Holly lurks just behind. She's stopped biting her lips and gone to her fingernails, which look badly abused. "I called you," Jerome says. "Why didn't you pick up?"

"I was asking questions. What's got you all white-eyed?"

"Is Hartsfield in there?"

Hodges is too surprised to reply.

"Oh, it's him," Jerome says. "Got to be. You were right about him watching you, and I know how. It's like that Hawthorne story about the purloined letter. Hide in plain sight."

Holly stops munching her fingernails long enough to say, "Poe wrote that story. Don't they teach you kids anything?"

Hodges says, "Slow down, Jerome."

Jerome takes a deep breath. "He's got two jobs, Bill. *Two.* He must only work here until mid-afternoon or something. After that he works for Loeb's."

"Loeb's? Is that the—"

"Yeah, the ice cream company. He drives the Mr. Tastey truck. The one with the bells. I've bought stuff from him, my sister has, too. All the kids do. He's on our side of town a lot. *Brady Hartsfield is the ice cream man!*"

Hodges realizes he's heard those cheerful, tinkling bells more than a lot lately. In the spring of his depression, crashed out in his La-Z-Boy, watching afternoon TV (and sometimes playing with the gun now riding against his ribs), it seems he heard them every day. Heard them and ignored them, because only kids pay actual attention to the ice cream man. Except some deeper part of his mind didn't *completely* ignore them. It was the deep part that kept coming back to Bowfinger, and his satiric comment about Mrs. Melbourne.

*She thinks they walk among us,* Mr. Bowfinger said, but it hadn't been space aliens Mrs. Melbourne had been concerned about on the day Hodges had done his canvass; it had been black SUVs, and chiropractors, and the people on Hanover Street who played loud music late at night.

Also, the Mr. Tastey man.

*That one looks suspicious,* she had said.

*This spring it seems like he's* always *around,* she had said.

A terrible question surfaces in his mind, like one of the snakes always lying in wait for Pitfall Harry: if he had paid attention to Mrs. Melbourne instead of dismissing her as a harmless crank (the way he and Pete dismissed Olivia Trelawney), would Janey still be alive? He doesn't think so, but he's never going to know for sure, and he has an idea that the question will haunt a great many sleepless nights in the weeks and months to come.

Maybe the years.

He looks out at the parking lot . . . and there he sees a ghost. A *gray* one.

He turns back to Jerome and Holly, now standing side by side, and doesn't even have to ask.

"Yeah," Jerome says. "Holly drove it here."

"The registration and the sticker decal on the license plate are both a tiny bit expired," Holly says. "Please don't be mad at me, okay? I had to come. I wanted to help, but I knew if I just called you, you'd say no."

"I'm not mad," Hodges says. In fact, he doesn't know *what* he is. He feels like he's entered a dreamworld where all the clocks run backward.

"What do we do now?" Jerome asks. "Call the cops?"

But Hodges is still not ready to let go. The young man in the picture may have a cauldron of crazy boiling away behind his bland face, but Hodges has met his share of psychopaths and knows that when they're taken by surprise, most collapse like puffballs. They're only dangerous to the unarmed and unsuspecting, like the broke folks waiting to apply for jobs on that April morning in 2009.

"Let's you and I take a ride to Mr. Hartsfield's place of residence," Hodges says. "And let's go in that." He points to the gray Mercedes.

"But . . . if he sees us pull up, won't he recognize it?"

Hodges smiles a sharklike smile Jerome Robinson has never seen before. "I certainly hope so." He holds out his hand. "May I have the key, Holly?"

Her abused lips tighten. "Yes, but I'm going."

"No way," Hodges says. "Too dangerous."

"If it's too dangerous for me, it's too dangerous for you." She won't look directly at him and her eyes keep skipping past his face, but her voice is firm. "You can make me stay, but if you do, I'll call the police and give them Brady Hartsfield's address just as soon as you're gone."

"You don't have it," Hodges says. This sounds feeble even to him.

Holly doesn't reply, which is a form of courtesy. She won't even need to go inside Discount Electronix and ask the dirty blonde; now that they have the name, she can probably suss out the Harts-field address from her devilish iPad.

Fuck.

"All right, you can come. But I drive, and when we get there, you and Jerome are going to stay in the car. Do you have a problem with that?"

"No, Mr. Hodges."

This time her eyes go to his face and stay there for three whole seconds. It might be a step forward. With Holly, he thinks, who knows.

## 10

Because of drastic budget cuts that kicked in the previous year, most city patrol cars are solo rides. This isn't the case in Lowtown. In Lowtown every shop holds a deuce, the ideal deuce containing at least one person of color, because in Lowtown the minorities are the majority. At just past noon on June third, Officers Laverty and Rosario are cruising Lowbriar Avenue about half a mile beyond the overpass where Bill Hodges once stopped a couple of trolls from robbing a shorty. Laverty is white. Rosario is Latina. Because their shop is CPC 54, they are known in the department as Toody and Muldoon, after the cops in an ancient sitcom called

*Car 54, Where Are You?* Amarilis Rosario sometimes amuses her fellow blue knights at roll call by saying, "Ooh, ooh, Toody, I got an idea!" It sounds extremely cute in her Dominican accent, and always gets a laugh.

On patrol, however, she's Ms. Taking Care of Business. They both are. In Lowtown you have to be.

"The cornerboys remind me of the Blue Angels in this air show I saw once," she says now.

"Yeah?"

"They see us coming, they peel off like they're in formation. Look, there goes another one."

As they approach the intersection of Lowbriar and Strike, a kid in a Cleveland Cavaliers warmup jacket (oversized and totally superfluous on this day) suddenly decamps from the corner where he's been jiving around and heads down Strike at a trot. He looks about thirteen.

"Maybe he just remembered it's a schoolday," Laverty says.

Rosario laughs. "As if, esse."

Now they are approaching the corner of Lowbriar and Martin Luther King Avenue. MLK is the ghetto's other large thoroughfare, and this time half a dozen cornerboys decide they have business elsewhere.

"That's formation flying, all right," Laverty says. He laughs, although it's not really funny. "Listen, where do you want to eat?"

"Let's see if that wagon's on Randolph," she says. "I'm in a taco state of mind."

"Señor Taco it is," he says, "but lay off the beans, okay? We've got another four hours in this . . . huh. Check it, Rosie. That's weird."

Up ahead, a man is coming out of a storefront with a long flower box. It's weird because the storefront isn't a florist's; it's King Virtue Pawn & Loan. It's also weird because the man looks Caucasian and they are now in the blackest part of Lowtown. He's approaching a dirty white Econoline van that's standing on a yellow curb: a twenty-dollar fine. Laverty and Rosario are hungry, though, they've got their faces fixed for tacos with that nice hot picante sauce Señor Taco keeps on the counter, and they might have let it go. Probably would have.

But.

With David Berkowitz, it was a parking ticket. With Ted Bundy, it was a busted taillight. Today a florist's box with badly folded flaps is all it takes to change the world. As the guy fumbles for the keys to his old van (not even Emperor Ming of Mongo would leave his vehicle unlocked in Lowtown), the box tilts downward. The end comes open and something slides partway out.

The guy catches it and shoves it back in before it can fall into the street, but Jason Laverty spent two tours in Iraq and he knows an RPG launcher when he sees it. He flips on the blues and hooks in behind the guy, who looks around with a startled expression.

"Sidearm!" he snaps at his partner. "Get it out!"

They fly out the doors, double-fisted Glocks pointing at the sky.

"Drop the box, sir!" Laverty shouts. "Drop the box and put your hands on the van! Lean forward. Do it now!"

For a moment the guy—he's about forty, olive-skinned, round-shouldered—hugs the florist's box tighter against his chest, like a baby. But when Rosie Rosario lowers her gun and points it at his chest, he drops the box. It splits wide open and reveals what Laverty tentatively identifies as a Russian-made Hashim antitank grenade launcher.

"Holy shit!" Rosario says, and then: "Toody, Toody, I got an id—"

"Officers, lower your weapons."

Laverty keeps his focus on Grenade Launcher Guy, but Rosario turns and sees a gray-haired Cauc in a blue jacket. He's wearing an earpiece and has his own Glock. Before she can ask him anything, the street is full of men in blue jackets, all running for King Virtue Pawn & Loan. One is carrying a Stinger battering ram, the kind cops call a baby doorbuster. She sees ATF on the backs of the jackets, and all at once she has that unmistakable I-stepped-in-shit feeling.

*"Officers, lower your weapons.* Agent James Kosinsky, ATF."

Laverty says, "Maybe you'd like one of us to cuff him first? Just asking."

ATF agents are piling into the pawnshop like Christmas shoppers into Walmart on Black Friday. A crowd is gathering across the street, as yet too stunned by the size of the strike force to start casting aspersions. Or stones, for that matter.

Kosinsky sighs. "You may as well," he says. "The horse has left the barn."

"We didn't know you had anything going," Laverty says. Meanwhile, Grenade Launcher Guy already has his hands off the van and behind him with the wrists pressed together. It's pretty clear this isn't his first rodeo. "He was unlocking his van and I saw *that* poking out of the end of the box. What was I supposed to do?"

"What you did, of course." From inside the pawnshop there comes the sound of breaking glass, shouts, and then the boom of the doorbuster being put to work. "Tell you what, now that you're here, why don't you throw Mr. Cavelli there in the back of your car and come on inside. See what we've got."

While Laverty and Rosario are escorting their prisoner to the cruiser, Kosinsky notes the number.

"So," he says. "Which one of you is Toody and which one is Muldoon?"

11

As the ATF strike force, led by Agent Kosinsky, begins its inventory of the cavernous storage area behind King Virtue Pawn & Loan's humble façade, a gray Mercedes sedan is pulling to the curb in front of 49 Elm Street. Hodges is behind the wheel. Today Holly is riding shotgun—because, she claims (with at least some logic), the car is more hers than theirs.

"Someone is home," she points out. "There's a very badly maintained Honda Civic in the driveway."

Hodges notes the shuffling approach of an old man from the

house directly across the street. "I will now speak with Mr. Concerned Citizen. You two will keep your mouths shut."

He rolls down his window. "Help you, sir?"

"I thought maybe I could help *you*," the old guy says. His bright eyes are busy inventorying Hodges and his passengers. Also the car, which doesn't surprise Hodges. It's a mighty fine car. "If you're looking for Brady, you're out of luck. That in the driveway is Missus Hartsfield's car. Haven't seen it move in weeks. Not sure it even runs anymore. Maybe Missus Hartsfield went off with him, because I haven't seen her today. Usually I do, when she toddles out to get her post." He points to the mailbox beside the door of 49. "She likes the catalogs. Most women do." He extends a knuckly hand. "Hank Beeson."

Hodges shakes it briefly, then flashes his ID, careful to keep his thumb over the expiration date. "Good to meet you, Mr. Beeson. I'm Detective Bill Hodges. Can you tell me what kind of car Mr. Hartsfield drives? Make and model?"

"It's a brown Subaru. Can't help you with the model or the year. All those rice-burners look the same to me."

"Uh-huh. Have to ask you to go back to your house now, sir. We may come by to ask you a few questions later."

"Did Brady do something wrong?"

"Just a routine call," Hodges says. "Go on back to your house, please."

Instead of doing that, Beeson bends lower for a look at Jerome. "Aren't you kinda young to be on the cops?"

"I'm a trainee," Jerome says. "Better do as Detective Hodges says, sir."

"I'm goin, I'm goin." But he gives the trio another stem-to-stern onceover first. "Since when do city cops drive around in Mercedes-Benzes?"

Hodges has no answer for that, but Holly does. "It's a RICO car. RICO stands for Racketeer Influenced and Corrupt Organizations. We take their stuff. We can use it any way we want because we're the police."

"Well, yeah. Sure. Stands to reason." Beeson looks partly satisfied and partly mystified. But he goes back to his house, where he soon appears to them again, this time looking out a front window.

"RICO is the feds," Hodges says mildly.

Holly tips her head fractionally toward their observer, and there's a faint smile on her hard-used lips. "Do you think *he* knows that?" When neither of them answers, she becomes businesslike. "What do we do now?"

"If Hartsfield's in there, I'm going to make a citizen's arrest. If he's not but his mother is, I'm going to interview her. You two are going to stay in the car."

"I don't know if that's a good idea," Jerome says, but by the expression on his face—Hodges can see it in the rearview mirror—he knows this objection will be overruled.

"It's the only one I have," Hodges says.

He gets out of the car. Before he can close the door, Holly leans toward him and says: "There's no one home." He doesn't say anything, but she nods as if he had. "Can't you feel it?"

Actually, he can.

12

Hodges walks up the driveway, noting the drawn drapes in the big front window. He looks briefly in the Honda and sees nothing worth noting. He tries the passenger door. It opens. The air inside is hot and stale, with a faintly boozy smell. He shuts the door, climbs the porch steps, and rings the doorbell. He hears it *cling-clong* inside the house. Nobody comes. He tries it again, then knocks. Nobody comes. He hammers with the side of his fist, very aware that Mr. Beeson from across the street is taking all this in. Nobody comes.

He strolls to the garage and peers through one of the windows in the overhead door. A few tools, a mini-fridge, not much else.

He takes out his cell phone and calls Jerome. This block of Elm

Street is very still, and he can hear—faintly—the AC/DC ringtone as the call goes through. He sees Jerome answer.

"Have Holly jump on her iPad and check the city tax records for the owner's name at 49 Elm. Can she do that?"

He hears Jerome asking Holly.

"She says she'll see what she can do."

"Good. I'm going around back. Stay on the line. I'll check in with you at roughly thirty-second intervals. If more than a minute goes by without hearing from me, call nine-one-one."

"You positive you want to do this, Bill?"

"Yes. Be sure Holly knows that getting the name isn't a big deal. I don't want her getting squirrelly."

"She's chill," Jerome says. "Already tapping away. Just make sure you stay in touch."

"Count on it."

He walks between the garage and the house. The backyard is small but neatly kept. There's a circular bed of flowers in the middle. Hodges wonders who planted them, Mom or Sonny Boy. He mounts three wooden steps to the back stoop. There's an aluminum screen door with another door inside. The screen door is unlocked. The house door isn't.

"Jerome? Checking in. All quiet."

He peers through the glass and sees a kitchen. It's squared away. There are a few plates and glasses in the drainer by the sink. A neatly folded dishwiper hangs over the oven handle. There are two placemats on the table. No placemat for Poppa Bear, which fits the profile he has fleshed out on his yellow legal pad. He knocks, then hammers. Nobody comes.

"Jerome? Checking in. All quiet."

He puts his phone down on the back stoop and takes out the flat leather case, glad he thought of it. Inside are his father's lockpicks—three silver rods with hooks of varying sizes at the ends. He selects the medium pick. A good choice; it slides in easily. He fiddles around, turning the pick first one way, then the other, feeling for the mechanism. He's just about to pause and check in with

Jerome again when the pick catches. He twists, quick and hard, just as his father taught him, and there's a click as the locking button pops up on the kitchen side of the door. Meanwhile, his phone is squawking his name. He picks it up.

"Jerome? All quiet."

"You had me worried," Jerome says. "What are you doing?"

"Breaking and entering."

## 13

Hodges steps into the Hartsfield kitchen. The smell hits him at once. It's faint, but it's there. Holding his cell phone in his left hand and his father's .38 in the right, Hodges follows his nose first into the living room—empty, although the TV remote and scattering of catalogs on the coffee table makes him think that the couch is Mrs. Hartsfield's downstairs nest—and then up the stairs. The smell gets stronger as he goes. It's not a stench yet, but it's headed in that direction.

There's a short upstairs hall with one door on the right and two on the left. He clears the righthand room first. It's guest quarters where no guests have stayed for a long time. It's as sterile as an operating theater.

He checks in with Jerome again before opening the first door on the left. This is where the smell is coming from. He takes a deep breath and enters fast, crouching until he's assured himself there's no one behind the door. He opens the closet—this door is the kind that folds on a center hinge—and shoves back the clothes. No one.

"Jerome? Checking in."

"Is anyone there?"

Well . . . sort of. The coverlet of the double bed has been pulled up over an unmistakable shape.

"Wait one."

He looks under the bed and sees nothing but a pair of slippers, a pair of pink sneakers, a single white ankle sock, and a few dust kitties. He pulls the coverlet back and there's Brady Hartsfield's mother. Her skin is waxy-pale, with a faint green undertint. Her mouth hangs ajar. Her eyes, dusty and glazed, have settled in their sockets. He lifts an arm, flexes it slightly, lets it drop. Rigor has come and gone.

"Listen, Jerome. I've found Mrs. Hartsfield. She's dead."

"Oh my God." Jerome's usually adult voice cracks on the last word. "What are you—"

"Wait one."

"You already said that."

Hodges puts his phone on the night table and draws the coverlet down to Mrs. Hartsfield's feet. She's wearing blue silk pajamas. The shirt is stained with what appears to be vomit and some blood, but there's no visible bullet hole or stab wound. Her face is swollen, yet there are no ligature marks or bruises on her neck. The swelling is just the slow death-march of decomposition. He pulls up her pajama top enough so he can see her belly. Like her face, it's slightly swollen, but he's betting that's gas. He leans close to her mouth, looks inside, and sees what he expected: clotted goop on her tongue and in the gutters between her gums and her cheeks. He's guessing she got drunk, sicked up her last meal, and went out like a rock star. The blood could be from her throat. Or an aggravated stomach ulcer.

He picks up the phone and says, "He might have poisoned her, but it's more likely she did it to herself."

"Booze?"

"Probably. Without a postmortem, there's no way to tell."

"What do you want us to do?"

"Sit tight."

"We still don't call the police?"

"Not yet."

"Holly wants to talk to you."

There's a moment of dead air, then she's on the line, and clear as a bell. She sounds calm. Calmer than Jerome, actually.

"Her name is Deborah Hartsfield. The kind of Deborah that ends in an H."

"Good job. Give the phone back to Jerome."

A second later Jerome says, "I hope you know what you're doing."

I don't, he thinks as he checks the bathroom. I've lost my mind and the only way to get it back is to let go of this. You *know* that.

But he thinks of Janey giving him his new hat—his snappy private eye fedora—and knows he can't. Won't.

The bathroom is clean . . . or almost. There's some hair in the sink. Hodges sees it but doesn't take note of it. He's thinking of the crucial difference between accidental death and murder. Murder would be bad, because killing close family members is all too often how a serious nutcase starts his final run. If it was an accident or suicide, there might still be time. Brady could be hunkered down somewhere, trying to decide what to do next.

Which is too close to what I'm doing, Hodges thinks.

The last upstairs room is Brady's. The bed is unmade. The desk is piled helter-skelter with books, most of them science fiction. There's a *Terminator* poster on the wall, with Schwarzenegger wearing dark glasses and toting a futuristic elephant gun.

I'll be back, Hodges thinks, looking at it.

"Jerome? Checking in."

"The guy from across the street is still scoping us. Holly thinks we should come inside."

"Not yet."

"When?"

"When I'm sure this place is clear."

Brady has his own bathroom. It's as neat as a GI's footlocker on inspection day. Hodges gives it a cursory glance, then goes back downstairs. There's a small alcove off the living room, with just enough space for a small desk. On it is a laptop. A purse hangs by its strap from the back of the chair. On the wall is a large framed photograph of the woman upstairs and a teenage version of Brady Hartsfield. They're standing on a beach somewhere with their arms around each other and their cheeks pressed together. They're wearing identical million-dollar smiles. It's more girlfriend-boyfriend than mother-son.

Hodges looks with fascination upon Mr. Mercedes in his salad days. There's nothing in his face that suggests homicidal tendencies, but of course there almost never is. The resemblance between the two of them is faint, mostly in the shape of the noses and the color of the hair. She was a pretty woman, really just short of beautiful, but Hodges is willing to guess that Brady's father didn't have similar good looks. The boy in the photo seems . . . ordinary. A kid you'd pass on the street without a second glance.

That's probably the way he likes it, Hodges thinks. The Invisible Man.

He goes back into the kitchen and this time sees a door beside the stove. He opens it and looks at steep stairs descending into darkness. Aware that he makes a perfect silhouette for anyone who might be down there, Hodges moves to one side while he feels for the light switch. He finds it and steps into the doorway again with the gun leveled. He sees a worktable. Beyond it, a waist-high shelf runs the length of the room. On it is a line of computers. It makes him think of Mission Control at Cape Canaveral.

"Jerome? Checking in."

Without waiting for an answer, he goes down with the gun in one hand and his phone in the other, perfectly aware of what a grotesque perversion of all established police procedure this is. What if Brady is under the stairs with his own gun, ready to shoot Hodges's feet off at the ankles? Or suppose he's set up a boobytrap? He can do it; this Hodges now knows all too well.

He strikes no tripwire, and the basement is empty. There's a storage closet, the door standing open, but nothing is stored there. He sees only empty shelves. In one corner is a litter of shoeboxes. They also appear to be empty.

The message, Hodges thinks, is Brady either killed his mother or came home and found her dead. Either way, he then decamped. If he *did* have explosives, they were on those closet shelves (possibly in the shoeboxes) and he took them along.

Hodges goes upstairs. It's time to bring in his new partners. He doesn't want to drag them in deeper than they already are, but there are those computers downstairs. He knows jack shit about computers. "Come around to the back," he says. "The kitchen door is open."

14

Holly steps in, sniffs, and says, "Oough. Is that Deborah Hartsfield?"

"Yes. Try not to think about it. Come downstairs, you guys. I want you to look at something."

In the basement, Jerome runs a hand over the worktable. "Whatever else he is, he's Mr. Awesomely Neat."

"Are you going to call the police, Mr. Hodges?" Holly is biting her lips again. "You probably are and I can't stop you, but my mother is going to be *so* mad at me. Also, it doesn't seem fair, since we're the ones who found out who he is."

"I haven't decided *what* I'm going to do," Hodges says, although she's right; it doesn't seem fair at all. "But I'd sure like to know what's on those computers. That might help me make up my mind."

"He won't be like Olivia," Holly says. "He'll have a *good* password."

Jerome picks one of the computers at random (it happens to be Brady's Number Six; not much on that one) and pushes the recessed button on the back of the monitor. It's a Mac, but there's no chime. Brady hates that cheery chime, and has turned it off on all his computers.

Number Six flashes gray, and the boot-up worry-circle starts going round and round. After five seconds or so, gray turns to blue. This should be the password screen, even Hodges knows that, but instead a large 20 appears on the screen. Then 19, 18, and 17.

He and Jerome stare at it in perplexity.

"No, no!" Holly nearly screams it. "Turn it *off*!"

When neither of them moves immediately, she darts forward and pushes the power button behind the monitor again, holding it down until the screen goes dark. Then she lets out a breath and actually smiles.

"Jeepers! That was a close one!"

"What are you thinking?" Hodges asks. "That they're wired up to explode, or something?"

"Maybe they only lock up," Holly says, "but I bet it's a suicide program. If the countdown gets to zero, that kind of program scrubs the data. *All* the data. Maybe just in the one that's on, but in all of them if they're wired together. Which they probably are."

"So how do you stop it?" Jerome asks. "Keyboard command?"

"Maybe that. Maybe voice-ac."

"Voice-what?" Hodges asks.

"Voice-activated command," Jerome tells him. "Brady says *Milk Duds* or *underwear* and the countdown stops."

Holly giggles through her fingers, then gives Jerome a timid push on the shoulder. "You're silly," she says.

15

They sit at the kitchen table with the back door open to let in fresh air. Hodges has an elbow on one of the placemats and his brow cupped in his palm. Jerome and Holly keep quiet, letting him think it through. At last he raises his head.

"I'm going to call it in. I don't want to, and if it was just between Hartsfield and me, I probably wouldn't. But I've got you two to consider—"

"Don't do it on my account," Jerome says. "If you see a way to go on, I'll stick with you."

*Of course you will,* Hodges thinks. *You might think you know what you're risking, but you don't. When you're seventeen, the future is strictly theoretical.*

As for Holly . . . previously he would have said she was a kind of human movie screen, with every thought in her head projected large on her face, but at this moment she's inscrutable.

"Thanks, Jerome, only . . ." Only this is hard. Letting go is hard, and this will be the second time he has to relinquish Mr. Mercedes. But.

"It's not just us, see? He could have more explosive, and if he uses it on a crowd . . ." He looks directly at Holly. ". . . the way he used your cousin Olivia's Mercedes on a crowd, it would be on me. I won't take that chance."

Speaking carefully, enunciating each word as if to make up for what has probably been a lifetime of mumbling, Holly says, "No one can catch him but you."

"Thanks, but no," he says gently. "The police have resources. They'll start by putting a BOLO out on his car, complete with license plate number. I can't do that."

It sounds good but he doesn't believe it *is* good. When he's not taking insane risks like the one he took at City Center, Brady's one of the smart ones. He will have stashed the car somewhere—maybe in a downtown parking lot, maybe in one of the airport parking lots, maybe in one of those endless mall parking lots. His ride is no Mercedes-Benz; it's an unobtrusive shit-colored Subaru, and it won't be found today or tomorrow. They might still be looking for it next week. And if they *do* find it, Brady won't be anywhere near it.

"No one but you," she insists. "And only with us to help you."

"Holly—"

"How can you give up?" she cries at him. She balls one hand into a fist and strikes herself in the middle of the forehead with it, leaving a red mark. "How can you? Janey *liked* you! She was even sort of your girlfriend! Now she's *dead*! Like the woman upstairs! Both of them, *dead*!"

She goes to hit herself again and Jerome takes her hand. "Don't," he says. "Please don't hit yourself. It makes me feel terrible."

Holly starts to cry. Jerome hugs her clumsily. He's black and she's white, he's seventeen and she's in her forties, but to Hodges Jerome looks like a father comforting his daughter after she came home from school and said no one invited her to the Spring Dance.

Hodges looks out at the small but neatly kept Hartsfield backyard. He also feels terrible, and not just on Janey's account, although that is bad enough. He feels terrible for the people at City Center. He feels terrible for Janey's sister, whom they refused to believe, who was reviled in the press, and who was then driven to suicide by the man who lived in this house. He even feels terrible about his failure to pay heed to Mrs. Melbourne. He knows that Pete Huntley would let him off the hook on that one, and that makes it worse. Why? Because Pete isn't as good at this job as he, Hodges, still is. Pete never will be, not even on his best day. A good enough guy, and a hard worker, but . . .

But.

But but *but*.

All that changes nothing. He needs to call it in, even if it feels like dying. When you shove everything else aside, there's just one thing left: Kermit William Hodges is at a dead end. Brady Hartsfield is in the wind. There might be a lead in the computers— something to indicate where he is now, what his plans might be, or both—but Hodges can't access them. Nor can he justify continuing to withhold the name and description of the man who perpetrated the City Center Massacre. Maybe Holly's right, maybe Brady Hartsfield will elude capture and commit some new atrocity, but kermitfrog19 is out of options. The only thing left for him to do is to protect Jerome and Holly if he can. At this point, he may not even be able to manage that. The nosyparker across the street has seen them, after all.

He steps out on the stoop and opens his Nokia, which he has used more today than in all the time since he retired.

He thinks Doesn't this just suck, and speed-dials Pete Huntley.

## 16

Pete picks up on the second ring. *"Partner!"* he shouts exuberantly. There's a babble of voices in the background, and Hodges's first thought is that Pete's in a bar somewhere, half-shot and on his way to totally smashed.

"Pete, I need to talk to you about—"

"Yeah, yeah, I'll eat all the crow you want, just not right now. Who called you? Izzy?"

"Huntley!" someone shouts. "Chief's here in five! With press! Where's the goddam PIO?"

PIO, Public Information Officer. Pete's not in a bar and not drunk, Hodges thinks. He's just over-the-moon fucking happy.

"No one called me, Pete. What's going on?"

"You don't know?" Pete laughs. "Just the biggest armaments bust in this city's history. Maybe the biggest in the history of the USA. Hundreds of M2 and HK91 machine guns, rocket launchers, fucking *laser cannons*, crates of Lahti L-35s in mint condition, Russian AN-9s still in grease . . . there's enough stuff here to stock two dozen East European militias. And the ammo! Christ! It's stacked two stories high! If the fucking pawnshop had caught on fire, all of Lowtown would have gone up!"

Sirens. He hears sirens. More shouts. Someone is bawling for someone else to get those sawhorses up.

"What pawnshop?"

"King Virtue Pawn & Loan, south of MLK. You know the place?"

"Yeah . . ."

"And guess who owns it?" But Pete is far too excited to give him a chance to guess. "Alonzo Moretti! Get it?"

Hodges doesn't.

"Moretti is Fabrizio Abbascia's grandson, Bill! Fabby the Nose! Is it starting to come into focus now?"

At first it still doesn't, because when Pete and Isabelle questioned him, Hodges simply plucked Abbascia's name out of his mental file of old cases where someone might bear him animus . . . and there have been several hundred of those over the years.

"Pete, King Virtue's black-owned. All the businesses down there are."

"The fuck it is. Bertonne Lawrence's name is on the sign, but the shop's a lease, Lawrence is a front, and he's spilling his guts. You know the best part? We own part of the bust, because a couple of patrol cops kicked it off a week or so before the ATF was gonna roll these guys up. Every detective in the department is down here. The Chief's on his way, and he's got a press caravan bigger than the Macy's Thanksgiving Day Parade with him. No way are the feds gonna hog this one! No *way*!" This time his laugh is positively loonlike.

Every detective in the department, Hodges thinks. Which leaves what for Mr. Mercedes? Bupkes is what.

"Bill, I gotta go. This . . . man, this is *amazing*."

"Sure, but first tell me what it has to do with me."

"What you said. The car-bomb was revenge. Moretti trying to pay off his grandfather's blood debt. In addition to the rifles, machine guns, grenades, pistols, and other assorted hardware, there's at least four dozen crates of Hendricks Chemicals Deta-sheet. Do you know what that is?"

"Rubberized explosive." *Now* it's coming into focus.

"Yeah. You set it off with lead azide detonators, and we know already that was the kind that was used to blow the stuff in your car. We haven't got a chem analysis on the explosive itself, but when we do, it'll turn out to be Detasheet. You can count on it. You're one lucky old sonofabitch, Bill."

"That's right," Hodges says. "I am."

He can picture the scene outside King Virtue: cops and ATF agents everywhere (probably arguing over jurisdiction already), and more coming all the time. Lowbriar closed off, probably MLK Avenue, too. Crowds of lookie-loos gathering. The Chief of Police and other assorted big boys on their way. The mayor won't miss the chance to make a speech. Plus all those reporters, TV crews, and live broadcast vans. Pete is bullshit with excitement, and is Hodges going to launch into a long and complicated story about the City Center Massacre, and a computer chat-room called Debbie's Blue Umbrella, and a dead mommy who probably drank herself to death, and a fugitive computer repairman?

No, he decides, I am not.

What he does is wish Pete good luck and push END.


17


When he comes back into the kitchen, Holly is no longer there, but he can hear her. Holly the Mumbler has turned into Holly the Revival Preacher, it seems. Certainly her voice has that special good-God-a'mighty cadence, at least for the moment.

"I'm with Mr. *Hodges* and his friend *Jerome*," she's saying. "They're my *friends*, Momma. We had a nice *lunch* together. Now we're seeing some of the *sights*, and this *evening* we're going to have a nice *supper* together. We're talking about *Janey*. I can do that if I *want*."

Even in his confusion over their current situation and his continuing sadness about Janey, Hodges is cheered by the sound of Holly standing up to Aunt Charlotte. He can't be sure it's for the first time, but by the living God, it might be.

"Who called who?" he asks Jerome, nodding toward her voice.

"Holly made the call, but it was my idea. She had her phone turned off so her mother couldn't call her. She wouldn't do it until I said her mother might call the cops."

"So what if I *did*," Holly is saying now. "It was *Olivia's* car and it's not like I *stole* it. I'll be back tonight, Momma. Until then, *leave me alone!*"

She comes back into the room looking flushed, defiant, years younger, and actually pretty.

"You rock, Holly," Jerome says, and holds his hand up for a high-five.

She ignores this. Her eyes—still snapping—are fixed on Hodges. "If you call the police and I get in trouble, I don't care. But unless you already did, you *shouldn't*. *They* can't find him. *We* can. I *know* we can."

Hodges realizes that if catching Mr. Mercedes is more important to anyone on earth than it is to him, that person is Holly Gibney. Maybe for the first time in her life she's doing something that matters. And doing it with others who like and respect her.

"I'm going to hold on to it a little longer. Mostly because the cops are otherwise occupied this afternoon. The funny part—or maybe I mean the ironic part—is that they think it has to do with me."

"What are you talking about?" Jerome asks.

Hodges glances at his watch and sees it's twenty past two. They have been here long enough. "Let's go back to my place. I can tell you on the way, and then we can kick this around one more time. If we don't come up with anything, I'll have to call my partner back. I'm not risking another horror show."

Although the risk is already there, and he can see by their faces that Jerome and Holly know it as well as he does.

"I went in that little study beside the living room to call my mother," Holly says. "Mrs. Hartsfield's got a laptop. If we're going to your house, I want to bring it."

"Why?"

"I may be able to find out how to get into his computers. She might have written down the keyboard prompts or voice-ac password."

"Holly, that doesn't seem likely. Mentally ill guys like Brady go to great lengths to hide what they are from everyone."

"I know that," Holly says. "Of course I do. Because *I'm* mentally ill, and *I* try to hide it."

"Hey, Hol, come on." Jerome tries to take her hand. She won't let him. She takes her cigarettes from her pocket instead.

"I am and I know I am. My mother knows, too, and she keeps an *eye* on me. She *snoops* on me. Because she wants to *protect* me. Mrs. Hartsfield will have been the same. He was her *son*, after all."

"If the Linklatter woman at Discount Electronix was right," Hodges says, "Mrs. Hartsfield would have been drunk on her ass a good deal of the time."

Holly replies, "She could have been a *high-functioning* drunk. Have you got a better idea?"

Hodges gives up. "Okay, take the laptop. What the hell."

"Not yet," she says. "In five minutes. I want to smoke a cigarette. I'll go out on the stoop."

She goes out. She sits down. She lights up.

Through the screen door, Hodges calls: "When did you become so assertive, Holly?"

She doesn't turn around to answer. "I guess when I saw pieces of my cousin burning in the street."


18


At quarter to three that afternoon, Brady leaves his Motel 6 room for a breath of fresh air and spies a Chicken Coop on the other side of the highway. He crosses and orders his last meal: a Clucker Delight with extra gravy and coleslaw. The restaurant section is almost deserted, and he takes his tray to a table by the windows so he can sit in the sunshine. Soon there will be no more of that for him, so he might as well enjoy a little while he still can.

He eats slowly, thinking of all the times he brought home take-out from the Chicken Coop, and how his mother always asked for a Clucker with double slaw. He has ordered her meal without even thinking about it. This brings tears, and he wipes them away with a paper napkin. Poor Mom!

Sunshine is nice, but its benefits are ephemeral. Brady considers the more lasting benefits darkness will provide. No more listening to Freddi Linklatter's lesbo-feminist rants. No more listening to Tones Frobisher explain why he can't go out on service calls because of his RESPONSIBILITY TO THE STORE, when it's really because he wouldn't know a hard drive crash if it bit him on the dick. No more feeling his kidneys turning to ice as he drives around in the Mr. Tastey truck in August with the freezers on high. No more whapping the Subaru's dashboard when the radio cuts out. No more thinking about his mother's lacy panties and long, long thighs. No more fury at being ignored and taken for granted. No more headaches. And no more sleepless nights, because after today it will be all sleep, all the time.

With no dreams.

When he's finished his meal (he eats every bite), Brady buses his table, wipes up a splatter of gravy with another napkin, and dumps his trash. The girl at the counter asks him if everything was all right. Brady says it was, wondering how much of the chicken and gravy and biscuits and coleslaw will have a chance to digest before the explosion rips his stomach open and sprays what's left everywhere.

*They'll remember me,* he thinks as he stands at the edge of the highway, waiting for a break in traffic so he can go back to the motel. *Highest score ever. I'll go down in history.* He's glad now that he didn't kill the fat ex-cop. Hodges should be alive for what's coming tonight. He should have to remember. He should have to live with it.

Back in the room, he looks at the wheelchair and the explosives-stuffed urine bag lying on the explosives-stuffed ASS PARKING cushion. He wants to get to the MAC early (but not *too* early; the last thing he wants is to stand out more than he will just by being male and older than thirteen), but there's still a little time. He's brought his laptop, not for any particular reason but just out of habit, and now he's glad. He opens it, connects to the motel's WiFi, and goes to Debbie's Blue Umbrella. There he leaves one final message—a kind of insurance policy.

With that attended to, he walks back to the airport's long-term parking lot and retrieves his Subaru.

## 19

Hodges and his two apprentice detectives arrive on Harper Road shortly before three-thirty. Holly shoots a cursory glance around, then totes the late Mrs. Hartsfield's laptop into the kitchen and powers it up. Jerome and Hodges stand by, both hoping there will be no password screen . . . but there is.

"Try her name," Jerome says.

Holly does. The Mac shakes its screen: *no.*

"Okay, try Debbie," Jerome says. "Both the *–ie* one and the one that ends with an *i.*"

Holly brushes a clump of mouse-brown hair out of her eyes so he can see her annoyance clearly. "Find something to do, Jerome, okay? I don't want you looking over my shoulder. I hate that." She shifts her attention to Hodges. "Can I smoke in here? I hope I can. It helps me think. Cigarettes help me think."

Hodges gets her a saucer. "Smoking lamp's lit. Jerome and I will be in my study. Give a holler if you find something."

Small chance of that, he thinks. Small chance of *anything*, really.

Holly pays no attention. She's lighting up. She's left the revival-preacher voice behind and returned to mumbling. "Hope she left a hint. I have hint-hope. Hint-hope is what Holly has."

Oh boy, Hodges thinks.

In the study, he asks Jerome if he has any idea what kind of hint she's talking about.

"After three tries, some computers will give you a password hint. To jog your memory in case you forget. But only if one has been programmed."

From the kitchen there comes a hearty, non-mumbled cry: *"Shit! Double shit! Triple shit!"*

Hodges and Jerome look at each other.

"Guess not," Jerome says.

20

Hodges turns his own computer on and tells Jerome what he wants: a list of all public gatherings for the next seven days.

"I can do that," Jerome says, "but you might want to check this out first."

"What?"

"It's a message. Under the Blue Umbrella."

"Click it." Hodges's hands are clenched into fists, but as he reads merckill's latest communiqué, they slowly open. The message is short, and although it's of no immediate help, it contains a ray of hope.

**So long, SUCKER.**
**PS: Enjoy your Weekend, I know I will.**

Jerome says, "I think you just got a Dear John, Bill."

Hodges thinks so, too, but he doesn't care. He's focused on the PS. He knows it might be a red herring, but if it's not, they have some time.

From the kitchen comes a waft of cigarette smoke and another hearty cry of *shit.*

"Bill? I just had a bad thought."

"What's that?"

"The concert tonight. That boy band, 'Round Here. At the Mingo. My sister and my mother are going to be there."

Hodges considers this. Mingo Auditorium seats four thousand, but tonight's attendees will be eighty percent female—mommies and their preteen daughters. There will be men in attendance, but almost every one of them will be chaperoning their daughters and their daughters' friends. Brady Hartsfield is a good-looking guy of about thirty, and if he tries going to that concert by himself, he'll stick out like a sore thumb. In twenty-first-century America, any single man at an event primarily aimed at little girls attracts notice and suspicion.

Also: **Enjoy your Weekend, I know I will.**

"Do you think I should call Mom and tell her to keep the girls home?" Jerome looks dismayed at the prospect. "Barb'll probably never speak to me again. Plus there's her friend Hilda and a couple of others . . ."

From the kitchen: "Oh, you damn thing! *Give it up!*"

Before Hodges can reply, Jerome says, "On the other hand, it sure sounds like he has something planned for the weekend, and this is only Thursday. Or is that just what he wants us to think?"

Hodges tends to think the taunt is real. "Find that Cyber Patrol picture of Hartsfield again, would you? The one you get when you click on MEET THE EXPERTS."

While Jerome does that, Hodges calls Marlo Everett in Police Records.

"Hey, Marlo, Bill Hodges again. I . . . yeah, lot of excitement in Lowtown, I heard about it from Pete. Half the force is down there, right? . . . uh-huh . . . well, I won't keep you long. Do you know if Larry Windom is still head of security at the MAC? Yeah, that's right, Romper-Stomper. Sure, I'll hold."

While he does, he tells Jerome that Larry Windom took early retirement because the MAC offered him the job at twice the salary he was making as a detective. He doesn't say that wasn't the only reason Windom pulled the pin after twenty. Then Marlo is back. Yes, Larry's still at the MAC. She even has the number of the MAC's security office. Before he can say goodbye, she asks him if there's a problem. "Because there's a big concert there tonight. My niece is going. She's crazy about those twerps."

"It's fine, Marls. Just some old business."

"Tell Larry we could use him today," Marlo says. "The squad-room is dead empty. Nary a detective in sight."

"I'll do that."

Hodges calls MAC Security, identifies himself as Detective Bill Hodges, and asks for Windom. While he waits, he stares at Brady Hartsfield. Jerome has enlarged the photo so it fills the whole screen. Hodges is fascinated by the eyes. In the smaller version, and in a line with the two I-T colleagues, those eyes seemed pleasant enough. With the picture filling the screen, however, that changes. The mouth is smiling; the eyes aren't. The eyes are flat and distant. Almost dead.

Bullshit, Hodges tells himself (*scolds* himself). This is a classic case of seeing something that's not there based on recently acquired knowledge—like a bank-robbery witness saying *I thought he looked shifty even before he pulled out that gun.*

Sounds good, sounds *professional*, but Hodges doesn't believe it.

He thinks the eyes looking out of the screen are the eyes of a toad hiding under a rock. Or under a cast-off blue umbrella.

Then Windom's on the line. He has the kind of booming voice that makes you want to hold the phone two inches from your ear while you talk to him, and he's the same old yapper. He wants to know all about the big bust that afternoon. Hodges tells him it's a mega-bust, all right, but beyond that he knows from nothing. He reminds Larry that he's retired.

But.

"With all that going on," he says, "Pete Huntley kind of drafted me to call you. Hope you don't mind."

"Jesus, no. I'd like to have a drink with you, Billy. Talk over old times now that we're both out. You know, hash and trash."

"That would be good." Pure hell is what it would be.

"How can I help?"

"You've got a concert there tonight, Pete says. Some hot boy band. The kind all the little girls love."

"Iy-yi-yi, do they ever. They're already lining up. And *tuning* up. Someone'll shout out one of those kids' names, and they all scream. Even if they're still coming in from the parking lot they scream. It's like Beatlemania back in the day, only from what I hear, this crew ain't the Beatles. You got a bomb threat or something? Tell me you don't. The chicks'll tear me apart and the mommies will eat the leftovers."

"What I've got is a tip that you may have a child molester on your hands tonight. This is a bad, bad boy, Larry."

"Name and description?" Hard and fast, no bullshit. The guy who left the force because he was a bit too quick with his fists. Anger issues, in the language of the department shrink. Romper-Stomper, in the language of his colleagues.

"His name is Brady Hartsfield. I'll email you his picture." Hodges glances at Jerome, who nods and makes a circle with his thumb and forefinger. "He's approximately thirty years old. If you see him, call me first, then grab him. Use caution. If he tries to resist, subdue the motherfucker."

"With pleasure, Billy. I'll pass this along to my guys. Any chance he'll be with a . . . I don't know . . . a beard? A teenage girl or someone even younger?"

"Unlikely but not impossible. If you spot him in a crowd, Lar, you gotta take him by surprise. He could be armed."

"How good are the chances he's going to be at the show?" He actually sounds hopeful, which is typical Larry Windom.

"Not very." Hodges absolutely believes this, and it's not just the Blue Umbrella hint Hartsfield dropped about the weekend. He *has* to know that in a girls-night-out audience, he'd have no way of being unobtrusive. "In any case, you understand why the department can't send cops, right? With all that's going on in Lowtown?"

"Don't need them," Windom says. "I've got thirty-five guys tonight, most of the regulars retired po-po. We know what we're doing."

"I know you do," Hodges says. "Remember, call me first. Us retired guys don't get much action, and we have to protect what we do get."

Windom laughs. "I hear you on that. Email me the picture." He recites an e-address which Hodges jots down and hands to Jerome. "If we see him, we grab him. After that, it's your bust . . . *Uncle* Bill."

"Fuck you, *Uncle* Larry," Hodges says. He hangs up, turns to Jerome.

"The pic just went out to him," Jerome says.

"Good." Then Hodges says something that will haunt him for the rest of his life. "If Hartsfield's as clever as I think he is, he won't be anywhere near the Mingo tonight. I think your mom and sis are good to go. If he does try crashing the concert, Larry's guys will have him before he gets in the door."

Jerome smiles. "Great."

"See what else you can find. Concentrate on Saturday and Sunday, but don't neglect next week. Don't neglect tomorrow, either, because—"

"Because the weekend starts on Friday. Gotcha."

Jerome gets busy. Hodges walks out to the kitchen to check on how Holly's doing. What he sees stops him cold. Lying next to the borrowed laptop is a red wallet. Deborah Hartsfield's ID, credit cards, and receipts are scattered across the table. Holly, already on her third cigarette, is holding up a MasterCard and studying it through a haze of blue smoke. She gives him a look that's both frightened and defiant.

"I'm just trying to find her diddly-dang password! Her purse was hanging over the back of her office chair, and her billfold was right there on top, so I put it in my pocket. Because sometimes people keep their passwords in their billfolds. Women especially. I didn't want her *money*, Mr. Hodges. I have my own *money*. I get an *allowance*."

An allowance, Hodges thinks. Oh, Holly.

Her eyes are brimming with tears and she's biting her lips again. "I'd never *steal*."

"Okay," he says. He thinks of patting her hand and decides it might be a bad idea just now. "I understand."

And Jesus-God, what's the BFD? On top of all the shit he's pulled since that goddam letter dropped through his mail slot, lifting a dead woman's wallet is chump-change. When all this comes out—as it surely will—Hodges will say he took it himself.

Holly, meanwhile, is not finished.

"I have my own credit card, and I have money. I even have a checking account. I buy video games and apps for my iPad. I buy clothes. Also earrings, which I like. I have fifty-six pairs. And I buy my own cigarettes, although they're very expensive now. It might interest you to know that in New York City, a pack of cigarettes now costs *eleven dollars*. I try not to be a burden because I can't work and she says I'm not but I know I *am*—"

"Holly, stop. You need to save that stuff for your shrink, if you have one."

"Of *course* I have one." She flashes a grim grin at the stubborn password screen of Mrs. Hartsfield's laptop. "I'm fucked up, didn't you notice?"

Hodges chooses to ignore this.

"I was looking for a slip of paper with the password on it," she says, "but there wasn't one. So I tried her Social Security number, first forwards and then backwards. Same deal with her credit cards. I even tried the credit card security codes."

"Any other ideas?"

"A couple. Leave me alone." As he leaves the room, she calls: "I'm sorry about the smoke, but it really does help me think."


21


With Holly crunching in the kitchen and Jerome doing likewise in his study, Hodges settles into the living room La-Z-Boy, staring at the blank TV. It's a bad place to be, maybe the worst place. The logical part of his mind understands that everything which has happened is Brady Hartsfield's fault, but sitting in the La-Z-Boy where he spent so many vapid, TV-soaked afternoons, feeling useless and out of touch with the essential self he took for granted during his working life, logic loses its power. What creeps in to take its place is a terrifying idea: he, Kermit William Hodges, has committed the crime of shoddy police work, and has aided and abetted Mr. Mercedes by so doing. They are the stars of a reality TV show called *Bill and Brady Kill Some Ladies*. Because when Hodges looks back, so many of the victims seem to be women: Janey, Olivia Trelawney, Janice Cray and her daughter Patricia . . . plus Deborah Hartsfield, who might have been poisoned instead of poisoning herself. And, he thinks, I haven't even added Holly, who'll likely come out of this even more grandly fucked up than she was going in, if she can't find that password . . . or if she *does* find it and there's nothing on Mom's computer that can help us to find Sonny Boy. And really, how likely is that?

Sitting here in this chair—knowing he should get up but as yet unable to move—Hodges thinks his own destructive record with women stretches back even further. His ex-wife is his ex for a reason. Years of near-alcoholic drinking were part of it, but for Corinne (who liked a drink or three herself and probably still does), not the major part. It was the coldness that first stole through the cracks in the marriage and finally froze it solid. It was how he shut her out, telling himself it was for her own good, because so much of what he did was nasty and depressing. How he made it clear in a dozen ways—some large, some small—that in a race between her and the job, Corinne Hodges always came in second. As for his daughter . . . well. Jeez. Allie never misses sending him birthday and Christmas cards (although the Valentine's Day cards stopped about ten years ago), and she hardly ever misses the Saturday-evening duty-call, but she hasn't been to see him in a couple of years. Which really says all that needs saying about how he bitched up *that* relationship.

His mind drifts to how beautiful she was as a kid, with those freckles and that mop of red hair—his little carrot-top. She'd pelt down the hall to him when he came home and jump fearlessly, knowing he'd drop whatever he was holding and catch her. Janey mentioned being crazy about the Bay City Rollers, and Allie'd had her own faves, her own bubble-gum boy-toys. She bought their records with her own allowance, little ones with the big hole in the center. Who was on them? He can't remember, only that one of the songs went on and on about every move you make and every step you take. Was that Bananarama or the Thompson Twins? He doesn't know, but he does know he never took her to a concert, although Corrie might have taken her to see Cyndi Lauper.

Thinking about Allie and her love of pop music rings in a new thought, one that makes him sit up straight, eyes wide, hands clutching the La-Z-Boy's padded arms.

Would he have let *Allie* go to that concert tonight?

The answer is absolutely not. No way.

Hodges checks his watch and sees it's closing in on four o'clock. He gets up, meaning to go into the study and tell Jerome to call his moms and tell her to keep those girls away from the MAC no matter how much they piss and moan. He's called Larry Windom and taken precautions, but precautions be damned. He would never have put Allie's life in Romper-Stomper's hands. *Never.*

Before he can get two steps toward the study, Jerome calls out: "Bill! Holly! Come here! I think I found something!"

## 22

They stand behind Jerome, Hodges looking over his left shoulder and Holly over his right. On the screen of Hodges's computer is a press release.

### SYNERGY CORP., CITIBANK, 3 RESTAURANT CHAINS TO PUT ON MIDWEST'S BIGGEST SUMMER CAREERS DAY AT EMBASSY SUITES

**FOR IMMEDIATE RELEASE.** Career businesspeople and military veterans are encouraged to attend the biggest Careers Day of the year on Saturday, June 5th, 2010. This recession-busting event will be held at the downtown Embassy Suites, 1 Synergy Square. Prior registration is encouraged but not necessary. You will discover <u>hundreds of exciting and high-paying jobs</u> at the Citibank website, at your local McDonald's, Burger King, and Chicken Coop, or at www.synergy.com. Jobs available include customer service, retail, security, plumbing, electrical, accounting, financial analysts, telemarketing, cashiers. You will find trained and helpful Job Guides and useful seminars in all conference rooms. <u>There is no charge</u>. Doors open at 8 AM. Bring your resume and dress for success. Remember that prior registration will speed the process and improve your chances of finding that job you've been looking for.
**TOGETHER WE WILL BEAT THIS RECESSION!**

"What do you think?" Jerome asks.

"I think you nailed it." An enormous wave of relief sweeps through Hodges. Not the concert tonight, or a crowded downtown dance club, or the Groundhogs-Mudhens minor league baseball game tomorrow night. It's this thing at Embassy Suites. Got to be, it's too perfectly rounded to be anything else. There's method in Brady Hartsfield's madness; to him, alpha equals omega. Hartsfield means to finish his career as a mass murderer the same way he started it, by killing the city's jobless.

Hodges turns to see how Holly is taking this, but Holly has left the room. She's back in the kitchen, sitting in front of Deborah Hartsfield's laptop and staring at the password screen. Her shoulders are slumped. In the saucer beside her, a cigarette has smoldered down to the filter, leaving a neat roll of ash.

This time he risks touching her. "It's okay, Holly. The password doesn't matter because now we've got the location. I'm going to get with my old partner in a couple of hours, when this Lowtown thing's had a chance to settle a bit, and tell him everything. They'll put out a BOLO on Hartsfield and his car. If they don't get him before Saturday morning, they'll get him as he approaches the job fair."

"Isn't there anything we can do tonight?"

"I'm thinking about that." There *is* one thing, although it's such a long shot it's practically a no-shot.

Holly says, "What if you're wrong about it being the career-day? What if he plans to blow up a movie theater *tonight?*"

Jerome comes into the room. "It's Thursday, Hol, and still too early for the big summer pictures. Most screens won't be playing to even a dozen people."

"The concert, then," she says. "Maybe he doesn't *know* it'll be all girls."

"He'll know," Hodges says. "He's a creature of improvisation, but that doesn't make him stupid. He'll have done at least some advance planning."

"Can I have just a little more time to try and crack her password? Please?"

Hodges glances at his watch. Ten after four. "Sure. Until four-thirty, how's that?"

A bargaining glint comes into her eyes. "Quarter to five?"

Hodges shakes his head.

Holly sighs. "I'm out of cigarettes, too."

"Those things will kill you," Jerome says.

She gives him a flat look. "Yes! That's part of their charm."

## 23

Hodges and Jerome drive down to the little shopping center at the intersection of Harper and Hanover to buy Holly a pack of cigarettes and give her the privacy she clearly wants.

Back in the gray Mercedes, Jerome tosses the Winstons from hand to hand and says, "This car gives me the creeps."

"Me too," Hodges admits. "But it didn't seem to bother Holly, did it? Sensitive as she is."

"Do you think she'll be all right? After this is over, I mean."

A week ago, maybe even two days, Hodges would have said something vague and politically correct, but he and Jerome have been through a lot since then. "For awhile," he says. "Then . . . no."

Jerome sighs the way people do when their own dim view of things has been confirmed. "Fuck."

"Yeah."

"So what now?"

"Now we go back, give Holly her coffin nails, and let her smoke one. Then we pack up the stuff she filched from the Hartsfield house. I drive you two back to the Birch Hill Mall. You return Holly to Sugar Heights in your Wrangler, then go home yourself."

"And just let Mom and Barb and her friends go to that show."

Hodges blows out a breath. "If it'll make you feel easier, tell your mother to pull the plug."

"If I do that, it all comes out." Still tossing the cigarettes back and forth. "Everything we've been doing today."

Jerome is a bright boy and Hodges doesn't need to confirm this. Or remind him that eventually it's all going to come out anyway.

STEPHEN KING

"What will you do, Bill?"

"Go back to the North Side. Park the Mercedes a block or two away from the Hartsfield place, just to be safe. I'll return Mrs. Hartsfield's laptop and billfold, then stake out the house. In case he decides to come back."

Jerome looks doubtful. "That basement room looked like he made a pretty clean sweep. What are the chances?"

"Slim and none, but it's all I've got. Until I turn this thing over to Pete."

"You really wanted to make the collar, didn't you?"

"Yes," Hodges says, and sighs. "Yes I did."

24

When they come back, Holly's head is down on the table and hidden in her arms. The deconstructed contents of Deborah Hartsfield's wallet are an asteroid belt around her. The laptop is still on and still showing the stubborn password screen. According to the clock on the wall, it's twenty to five.

Hodges is afraid she'll protest his plan to return her home, but Holly only sits up, opens the fresh pack of cigarettes, and slowly removes one. She's not crying, but she looks tired and dispirited.

"You did your best," Jerome says.

"I always do my best, Jerome. And it's never good enough."

Hodges picks up the red wallet and starts returning the credit cards to the slots. They're probably not in the same order Mrs. Hartsfield had them in, but who's going to notice? Not her.

There are photos in an accordion of transparent envelopes, and he flips through them idly. Here's Mrs. Hartsfield standing arm-in-arm with a broad-shouldered, burly guy in a blue work coverall—the absent Mr. Hartsfield, perhaps. Here's Mrs. Hartsfield standing with a bunch of laughing ladies in what appears to be a beauty salon. Here's one of a chubby little boy holding a fire truck—Brady at age three or four, probably. And one more, a wallet-sized version of the picture in Mrs. Hartsfield's alcove office: Brady and his mom with their cheeks pressed together.

Jerome taps it and says, "You know what that reminds me of a little? Demi Moore and what's-his-name, Ashton Kutcher."

"Demi Moore has black hair," Holly says matter-of-factly. "Except in *G.I. Jane*, where she hardly had any at all, because she was learning to be a SEAL. I saw that movie three times, once in the theater, once on videotape, and once on my iTunes. Very enjoyable. Mrs. Hartsfield is blond-headed." She considers, then adds: "Was."

Hodges slides the photo out of the pocket for a better look, then turns it over. Carefully printed on the back is *Mom and Her Honeyboy, Sand Point Beach, Aug 2007*. He flicks the picture against the side of his palm a time or two, almost puts it back, then slides it across to Holly, photo-side down.

"Try that."

She frowns at him. "Try what?"

"Honeyboy."

Holly types it in, hits RETURN . . . and utters a very un-Hollylike scream of joy. Because they're in. Just like that.

There's nothing of note on the desktop—an address book, a folder marked FAVORITE RECIPES and another marked SAVED EMAILS; a folder of online receipts (she seemed to have paid most of her bills that way); and an album of photos (most of Brady at various ages). There are a lot of TV shows in her iTunes, but only one album of music: *Alvin and the Chipmunks Celebrate Christmas*.

"Christ," Jerome says. "I don't want to say she deserved to die, but . . ."

Holly gives him a forbidding look. "Not funny, Jerome. Do not go there."

He holds up his hands. "Sorry, sorry."

Hodges scrolls rapidly through the saved emails and sees nothing of interest. Most appear to be from Mrs. Hartsfield's old high school buddies, who refer to her as Debs.

"There's nothing here about Brady," he says, and glances at the clock. "We should go."

"Not so fast," Holly says, and opens the finder. She types BRADY. There are several results (many in the recipe file, some tagged as *Brady Favorites*), but nothing of note.

"Try HONEYBOY," Jerome suggests.

She does and gets one result—a document buried deep in the hard drive. Holly clicks it. Here are Brady's clothing sizes, also a list of all the Christmas and birthday presents she's bought him for the last ten years, presumably so she won't repeat herself. She's noted his Social Security number. There's a scanned copy of his car registration, his car insurance card, and his birth certificate. She's listed his co-workers at both Discount Electronix and Loeb's Ice Cream Factory. Next to the name Shirley Orton is a notation that would have made Brady laugh hysterically: *Wonder is she his gf?*

"What's up with this crap?" Jerome asks. "He's a grown *man*, for God's sake."

Holly smiles darkly. "What I said. She knew he wasn't right."

At the very bottom of the HONEYBOY file, there's a folder marked BASEMENT.

"That's it," Holly says. "Gotta be. Open it, open it, open it!"

Jerome clicks BASEMENT. The document inside is less than a dozen words long.

*Control = lights*
*Chaos?? Darkness??*
*Why don't they work for me????*

They stare at the screen for some time without speaking. At last Hodges says, "I don't get it. Jerome?"

Jerome shakes his head.

Holly, seemingly hypnotized by this message from the dead woman, speaks a single word, almost too low to hear: "Maybe . . ." She hesitates, chewing her lips, and says it again. "Maybe."

## 25

Brady arrives at the Midwest Culture and Arts Complex just before six P.M. Although the show isn't scheduled to start for over an hour, the vast parking lot is already three-quarters full. Long lines have formed outside the doors that open on to the lobby, and they're getting longer all the time. Little girls are screeching at the top of their lungs. Probably that means they're happy, but to Brady they sound like ghosts in a deserted mansion. It's impossible to look at the growing crowd and not recall that April morning at City Center. Brady thinks, *If I had a Humvee instead of this Jap shitbox, I could drive into them at forty miles an hour, kill fifty or more that way, then hit the switch and blow the rest into the stratosphere.*

But he doesn't have a Humvee, and for a moment he's not even sure what to do next—he can't be seen while he makes his final preparations. Then, at the far end of the lot, he sees a tractor-trailer box. The cab is gone and it's up on jacks. On the side is a Ferris wheel and a sign reading 'ROUND HERE SUPPORT TEAM. It's one of the trucks he saw in the loading area during his reconnaissance. Later, after the show, the cab would be reconnected and driven around back for the load-out, but now it looks deserted.

He pulls in on the far side of the box, which is at least fifty feet long and hides the Subaru completely from the bustling parking lot. He takes his fake glasses from the glove compartment and puts them on. He gets out and does a quick walk-around to assure himself the trailer box is as deserted as it looks. When he's satisfied on that score, he returns to the Subaru and works the wheelchair out of the back. It's not easy. The Honda would have been better, but he doesn't trust its unmaintained engine. He places the ASS PARKING cushion on the wheelchair's seat, and connects the wire protruding from the center of the A in PARKING to the wires hanging from the side pockets, where there are more blocks of plastic explosive. Another wire, connected to a block of plastic in the rear pocket, dangles from a hole he has punched in the seatback.

Sweating profusely, Brady begins the final unification, braiding copper cores and wrapping exposed connection-points with pre-cut strips of masking tape he has stuck to the front of the oversized 'Round Here tee-shirt he bought that morning in the drugstore. The shirt features the same Ferris wheel logo as the one on the truck. Above it are the words KISSES ON THE MIDWAY. Below, it says I LUV CAM, BOYD, STEVE, AND PETE!

After ten minutes of work (with occasional breaks to peek around the edge of the box and make sure he still has this far edge of the parking lot to himself), a spiderweb of connected wires lies on the seat of the wheelchair. There's no way to wire in the explosives-stuffed Urinesta peebag, at least not that he could figure out on short notice, but that's okay; Brady has no doubt the other stuff will set it off.

Not that he'll know for sure, one way or the other.

He returns to the Subaru one more time and takes out the eight-by-ten framed version of a picture Hodges has already seen: Frankie holding Sammy the Fire Truck and smiling his dopey where-the-fuck-am-I smile. Brady kisses the glass and says, "I love you, Frankie. Do you love me?"

He pretends Frankie says yes.

"Do you want to help me?"

He pretends Frankie says yes.

Brady goes back to the wheelchair and sits down on ASS PARK-ING. Now the only wire showing is the master wire, dangling over the front of the wheelchair seat between his spread thighs. He connects it to Thing Two and takes a deep breath before flicking the power switch. If the electricity from the double-A batteries leaks through . . . even a little . . .

But it doesn't. The yellow ready-lamp goes on, and that's all. Somewhere, not far away but in a different world, little girls are screaming happily. Soon many of them will be vaporized; many more will be missing arms and legs and screaming for real. Oh well, at least they'll get to listen to some music by their favorite band before the big bang.

Or maybe not. He's aware of what a crude and makeshift plan this is; the stupidest no-talent screenwriter in Hollywood could do better. Brady remembers the sign in the corridor leading to the auditorium: NO BAGS NO BOXES NO BACKPACKS. He has none of those things, but all it will take to blow the deal is one sharp-eyed security guard observing a single unconcealed wire. Even if that doesn't happen, a cursory glance into the wheelchair's storage pockets will reveal the fact that it's a rolling bomb. Brady has stuck a 'Round Here pennant in one of those pockets, but otherwise made no effort at concealment.

It doesn't faze him. He doesn't know if that makes him confident or just fatalistic, and doesn't think it matters. In the end, confidence and fatalism are pretty much the same, aren't they? He got away with running those people over at City Center, and there was almost no planning involved with that, either—just a mask, a hairnet, and some DNA-killing bleach. In his heart, he never really expected to escape, and in this case his expectations are zero. In a don't-give-a-fuck world, he is about to become the ultimate don't-give-a-fucker.

He slips Thing Two beneath the oversized tee-shirt. There's a slight bulge, and he can see a dim yellow glimmer from the ready-lamp through the thin cotton, but both the bulge and the glimmer disappear when he places Frankie's picture in his lap. He's pretty much ready to go.

His fake glasses slide down the bridge of his sweat-slippery nose. Brady pushes them back up. By craning his neck slightly, he can see himself in the Subaru's passenger-side rearview mirror. Bald and bespectacled, he looks nothing like his former self. He looks sick, for one thing—pale and sweaty with dark circles under his eyes.

Brady runs his hand over the top of his head, feeling smooth skin where no stubble will ever have the chance to grow out. Then he backs the wheelchair out of the slot where he has parked his car and begins to roll himself slowly across the expanse of parking lot toward the growing crowd.

26

Hodges gets snared in rush-hour traffic and doesn't arrive back on the North Side until shortly after six P.M. Jerome and Holly are still with him; they both want to see this through, regardless of the consequences, and since they seem to understand what those consequences may be, Hodges has decided he can't refuse them. Not that he has much of a choice; Holly won't divulge what she knows. Or thinks she knows.

Hank Beeson is out of his house and crossing the street before Hodges can bring Olivia Trelawney's Mercedes to a stop in the Hartsfield driveway. Hodges sighs and powers down the driver's-side window.

"I sure would like to know what's going on," Mr. Beeson says. "Does it have anything to do with all that mess down in Low-town?"

"Mr. Beeson," Hodges says, "I appreciate your concern, but you need to go back to your house and——"

"No, wait," Holly says. She's leaning across the center console of Olivia Trelawney's Mercedes so she can look up at Beeson's face. "Tell me how Mr. Hartsfield sounds. I need to know how his voice sounds."

Beeson looks perplexed. "Like anyone, I guess. Why?"

"Is it low? You know, baritone?"

"You mean like one of those fat opera singers?" Beeson laughs. "Hell, no. What kind of question is that?"

"Not high and squeaky, either?"

To Hodges, Beeson says, "Is your partner crazy?"

Only a little, Hodges thinks. "Just answer the question, sir."

"Not low, not high and squeaky. Regular! What's going on?"

"No accent?" Holly persists. "Like . . . um . . . Southern? Or New England? Or Brooklyn, maybe?"

"No, I said. He sounds like anybody."

Holly sits back, apparently satisfied.

Hodges says, "Go back inside, Mr. Beeson. Please."

Beeson snorts but backs off. He pauses at the foot of his steps to cast a glare over his shoulder. It's one Hodges has seen many times before, the *I pay your salary, asshole* glare. Then he goes inside, slamming the door behind him to make sure they get the point. Soon he appears once more at the window with his arms folded over his chest.

"What if he calls the cop shop to ask what we're doing here?" Jerome asks from the back seat.

Hodges smiles. It's wintry but genuine. "Good luck with that tonight. Come on."

As he leads them single-file along the narrow path between the house and the garage, he checks his watch. Quarter past six. He thinks, How the time flies when you're having fun.

They enter the kitchen. Hodges opens the basement door and reaches for the light switch.

"No," Holly says. "Leave it off."

He looks at her questioningly, but Holly has turned to Jerome. "You have to do it. Mr. Hodges is too old and I'm a woman."

For a moment Jerome doesn't get it, then he does. "Control equals lights?"

She nods. Her face is tense and drawn. "It should work if your voice is anywhere close to his."

Jerome steps into the doorway, clears his throat self-consciously, and says, "Control."

The basement remains dark.

Hodges says, "You've got a naturally low voice. Not baritone, but low. It's why you sound older than you really are when you're on the phone. See if you can raise it up a little."

Jerome repeats the word, and the lights in the basement come on. Holly Gibney, whose life has not exactly been a sitcom, laughs and claps her hands.

## 27

It's six-twenty when Tanya Robinson arrives at the MAC, and as she joins the line of incoming vehicles, she wishes she'd listened to the girls' importuning and left for the concert an hour earlier. The lot is already three-quarters full. Guys in orange vests are flagging traffic. One of them waves her to the left. She turns that way, driving with slow care because she's borrowed Ginny Carver's Tahoe for tonight's safari, and the last thing she wants is to get into a fender-bender. In the seats behind her, the girls—Hilda Carver, Betsy DeWitt, Dinah Scott, and her own Barbara—are literally bouncing with excitement. They have loaded the Tahoe's CD changer with their 'Round Here CDs (among them they have all six), and they squeal "Oh, I *love* this one!" every time a new tune comes on. It's noisy and it's stressful and Tanya is surprised to find she's enjoying herself quite a lot.

"Watch out for the crippled guy, Mrs. Robinson," Betsy says, pointing.

The crippled guy is skinny, pale, and bald, all but floating inside his baggy tee-shirt. He's holding what looks like a framed picture in his lap, and she can also see one of those urine bags. A sadly jaunty 'Round Here pennant juts from a pocket on the side of his wheelchair. Poor man, Tanya thinks.

"Maybe we should help him," Barbara says. "He's going awful slow."

"Bless your kind heart," Tanya says. "Let me get us parked, and if he hasn't made it to the building when we walk back, we'll do just that."

She slides the borrowed Tahoe into an empty space and turns it off with a sigh of relief.

"Boy, look at the *lines*," Dinah says. "There must be a zillion people here."

"Nowhere near that many," Tanya says, "but it *is* a lot. They'll open the doors soon, though. And we've got good seats, so don't worry about that."

"You've still got the tickets, right, Mom?"

Tanya ostentatiously checks her purse. "Got them right here, hon."

"And we can have souvenirs?"

"One each, and nothing that costs over ten dollars."

"I've got my own money, Mrs. Robinson," Betsy says as they climb out of the Tahoe. The girls are a little nervous at the sight of the crowd growing outside the MAC. They cluster together, their four shadows becoming a single dark puddle in the strong early-evening sunlight.

"I'm sure you do, Bets, but this is on me," Tanya says. "Now listen up, girls. I want you to give me your money and phones for safekeeping. Sometimes there are pickpockets at these big public gatherings. I'll give everything back when we're safe in our seats, but no texting or calling once the show starts—are we clear on that?"

"Can we each take a picture first, Mrs. Robinson?" Hilda asks.

"Yes. One each."

"Two!" Barbara begs.

"All right, two. But hurry up."

They each take two pictures, promising to email them later, so everyone has a complete set. Tanya takes a couple of her own, with the four girls grouped together and their arms around each other's shoulders. She thinks they look lovely.

"Okay, ladies, hand over the cash and the cackleboxes."

The girls give up thirty dollars or so among them and their candy-colored phones. Tanya puts everything in her purse and locks Ginny Carver's van with the button on the key-fob. She hears the satisfying thump of the locks engaging—a sound that means safety and security.

"Now listen, you crazy females. We're all going to hold hands until we're in our seats, okay? Let me hear your okay."

"*Okaay!*" the girls shout, and grab hands. They're tricked out in their best skinny jeans and their best sneakers. All are wearing 'Round Here tees, and Hilda's ponytail has been tied with a white silk ribbon that says I LUV CAM in red letters.

"And we're going to have fun, right? Best time ever, right? Let me hear your okay."

*"OKAAAYYYY!"*

Satisfied, Tanya leads them toward the MAC. It's a long walk across hot macadam, but none of them seems to mind. Tanya looks for the bald man in the wheelchair and spies him making his way toward the back of the handicapped line. That one is much shorter, but it still makes her sad to see all those broken folks. Then the wheelchairs start to move. They're letting the handicapped people in first, and she thinks that's a good idea. Let all or at least most of them get settled in their own section before the stampede begins.

As Tanya's party reaches the end of the shortest line of abled people (which is still very long), she watches the skinny bald guy propel himself up the handicap ramp and thinks how much easier it would be for him if he had one of those motorized chairs. She wonders about the picture in his lap. Some loved relative who's gone on? That seems the most likely.

Poor man, she thinks again, and sends up a brief prayer to God, thanking Him that her own two kids are all right.

"Mom?" Barbara says.

"Yes, honey?"

"Best time ever, right?"

Tanya Robinson squeezes her daughter's hand. "You bet."

A girl starts singing "Kisses on the Midway" in a clear, sweet voice. *"The sun, baby, the sun shines when you look at me . . . The moon, baby, the moon glows when you're next to me . . ."*

More girls join in. *"Your love, your touch, just a little is never enough . . . I want to love you my way . . ."*

Soon the song is floating up into the warm evening air a thousand voices strong. Tanya is happy to add her voice, and after the CD-a-thon coming from Barbara's room these last two weeks, she knows all the words.

Impulsively, she bends down and kisses the top of her daughter's head.

Best time ever, she thinks.

28

Hodges and his junior Watsons stand in Brady's basement control room, looking at the row of silent computers.

"Chaos first," Jerome says. "Then darkness. Right?"

Hodges thinks, It sounds like something out of the Book of Revelation.

"I think so," Holly says. "At least that's the order she had them in." To Hodges, she says, "She was listening, see? I bet she was listening a lot more than he knew she was listening." She turns back to Jerome. "One thing. Very important. Don't waste time if you get *chaos* to turn them on."

"Right. The suicide program. Only what if I get nervous and my voice goes all high and squeaky like Mickey Mouse?"

She starts to reply, then sees the look in his eye. "Hardy-har-har." But she smiles in spite of herself. "Go on, Jerome. Be Brady Hartsfield."

He only has to say *chaos* once. The computers flash on, and the numbers start descending.

"Darkness!"

The numbers continue to count down.

"Don't *shout*," Holly says. "Jeez."

16. 15. 14.

"Darkness."

"I think you're too low again," Hodges says, trying not to sound as nervous as he feels.

12. 11.

Jerome wipes his mouth. "D-darkness."

"Mushmouth," Holly observes. Perhaps not helpfully.

8. 7. 6.

"Darkness."

5.

The countdown disappears. Jerome lets out a gusty sigh of relief. What replaces the numbers is a series of color photographs of men in old-timey Western clothes, shooting and being shot. One has been frozen as he and his horse crash through a plate glass window.

"What kind of screensavers are those?" Jerome asks.

Hodges points at Brady's Number Five. "That's William Holden, so I guess they must be scenes from a movie."

*"The Wild Bunch,"* Holly says. "Directed by Sam Peckinpah. I only watched it once. It gave me nightmares."

Scenes from a movie, Hodges thinks, looking at the grimaces and gunfire. Also scenes from inside Brady Hartsfield's head. "Now what?"

Jerome says, "Holly, you start at the first one. I'll start at the last one. We'll meet in the middle."

"Sounds like a plan," Holly says. "Mr. Hodges, can I smoke in here?"

"Why the hell not?" he says, and goes over to the cellar stairs to sit and watch them work. As he does, he rubs absently at the hollow just below his left collarbone. That annoying pain is back. He must have pulled a muscle running down the street after his car exploded.

## 29

The air conditioning in the MAC's lobby strikes Brady like a slap, causing his sweaty neck and arms to break out in gooseflesh. The main part of the corridor is empty, because they haven't let in the regular concertgoers yet, but the right side, where there are velvet ropes and a sign reading HANDICAPPED ACCESS, is lined with wheelchairs that are moving slowly toward the checkpoint and the auditorium beyond.

Brady doesn't like how this is playing out.

He had assumed that everyone would smoosh in at the same time, as they had at the Cleveland Indians game he'd gone to when he was eighteen, and the security guys would be overwhelmed, just giving everyone a cursory look and then passing them on. The concert staff letting in the crips and gooniebirds first is something he should have forseen, but didn't.

There are at least a dozen men and women in blue uniforms with brown patches on their shoulders reading MAC SECURITY, and for the time being they have nothing to do but check out the handicapped folks rolling slowly past them. Brady notes with growing coldness that although they're not checking the storage pockets on *all* the wheelchairs, they are indeed checking the pockets on some of them—every third or fourth, and sometimes two in a row. When the crips clear security, ushers dressed in 'Round Here tee-shirts are directing them toward the auditorium's handicapped section.

He always knew he might be stopped at the security checkpoint, but had believed he could still take plenty of 'Round Here's young fans with him if that happened. Another bad assumption. Flying glass might kill a few of those closest to the doors, but their bodies would also serve as a blast-shield.

Shit, he thinks. Still—I only got eight at City Center. I'm bound to do better than that.

He rolls forward, the picture of Frankie in his lap. The edge of the frame rests against the toggle-switch. The minute one of those security goons bends to look into the pockets on the sides of the wheelchair, Brady will press a hand down on the picture, the yellow lamp will turn green, and electricity will flow to the lead azide detonators nestled in the homemade explosive.

There are only a dozen wheelchairs ahead of him. Chilled air blows down on his hot skin. He thinks of City Center, and how the Trelawney bitch's heavy car jounced and rocked as it ran over the people after he hit them and knocked them down. As if it were having an orgasm. He remembers the rubbery air inside the mask, and how he screamed with delight and triumph. Screamed until he was so hoarse he could hardly speak at all and had to tell his mother and Tones Frobisher at DE that he had come down with laryngitis.

Now there's just ten wheelchairs between him and the checkpoint. One of the guards—probably the head honcho, since he's the oldest and the only one wearing a hat—takes a backpack from a young girl who's as bald as Brady himself. He explains something to her, and gives her a claim-check.

They're going to catch me, Brady thinks coldly. They are, so get ready to die.

He *is* ready. Has been for some time now.

Eight wheelchairs between him and the checkpoint. Seven. Six. It's like the countdown on his computers.

Then the singing starts outside, muffled at first.

*"The sun, baby, the sun shines when you look at me . . . The moon, baby . . ."*

When they hit the chorus, the sound swells to that of a cathedral choir: girls singing at the top of their lungs.

*"I WANT TO LOVE YOU MY WAY . . . WE'LL DRIVE THE BEACHSIDE HIGHWAY . . ."*

At that moment, the main doors swing open. Some girls cheer; most continue singing, and louder than ever.

*"IT'S GONNA BE A NEW DAY . . . I'LL GIVE YOU KISSES ON THE MIDWAY!"*

Chicks wearing 'Round Here tops and their first makeup pour in, their parents (mostly mommies) struggling to keep up and stay connected to their brats. The velvet rope between the main part of the corridor and the handicapped zone is knocked over and trampled underfoot. A beefy twelve- or thirteen-year-old with an ass the size of Iowa is shoved into the wheelchair ahead of Brady's, and the girl inside it, who has a cheerfully pretty face and sticks for legs, is almost knocked over.

"Hey, watch it!" the wheelchair-girl's mother shouts, but the fat bitch in the double-wide jeans is already gone, waving a 'Round Here pennant in one hand and her ticket in the other. Someone thumps into Brady's chair, the picture shifts in his lap, and for one cold second he thinks they're all going to go up in a white flash and a hail of steel bearings. When they don't, he raises the picture enough to peer underneath, and sees the ready-lamp is still glowing yellow.

Close one, Brady thinks, and grins.

It's happy confusion in the hallway, and all but one of the security guards who were checking the handicapped concertgoers move to do what they can with this new influx of crazed singing teens and preteens. The one guard who remains on the handicapped side of the corridor is a young woman, and she's waving the wheelchairs through with barely a glance. As Brady approaches her he spots the guy in charge, Hat Honcho, standing on the far side of the corridor almost directly opposite. At six-three or so, he's easy to see, because he towers over the girls, and his eyes never stop moving. In one hand he holds a piece of paper, which he glances down at every now and again.

"Show me your tickets and go," the security woman says to the pretty wheelchair-girl and her mother. "Righthand door."

Brady sees something interesting. The tall security guy in the hat grabs a guy of twenty or so who looks to be on his own and pulls him out of the scrum.

"Next!" the security woman calls to him. "Don't hold up the line!"

Brady rolls forward, ready to push Frankie's picture against the toggle-switch on Thing Two if she shows even a passing interest in the pockets of his wheelchair. The corridor is now wall to wall with pushing, singing girls, and his score will be a lot higher than thirty. If the corridor has to do, that will be fine.

The security woman points at the picture. "Who's that, hon?"

"My little boy," Brady says with a game smile. "He was killed in an accident last year. The same one that left me . . ." He indicates the chair. "He loved 'Round Here, but he never got to hear their new album. Now he will."

She's harried, but not too harried for sympathy; her eyes soften. "I'm so sorry for your loss."

"Thank you, ma'am," Brady says, thinking: You stupid cunt.

"Go straight ahead, sir, then bear to the right. You'll find the two handicapped aisles halfway down the auditorium. Great views. If you need help getting down the ramp—it's pretty steep—look for one of the ushers wearing the yellow armbands."

"I'll be okay," Brady says, smiling at her. "Great brakes on this baby."

"Good for you. Enjoy the show."

"Thank you, ma'am, I sure will. Frankie will, too."

Brady rolls toward the main entrance. Back at the security checkpoint, Larry Windom—known to his police colleagues as Romper-Stomper—releases the young man who decided on the spur of the moment to use his kid sister's ticket when she came down with mono. He looks nothing like the creep in the photo Bill Hodges sent him.

The auditorium features stadium seating, which delights Brady. The bowl shape will concentrate the explosion. He can imagine the packets of ball bearings taped under his seat fanning out. If he's lucky, he thinks, he'll get the band as well as half the audience.

Pop music plays from the overhead speakers, but the girls who are filling the seats and choking the aisles drown it out with their own young and fervent voices. Spotlights swing back and forth over the crowd. Frisbees fly. A couple of oversized beachballs bounce around. The only thing that surprises Brady is that there's no sign of the Ferris wheel and all that midway shit onstage. Why did they haul it all in, if they weren't going to use it?

An usher with a yellow armband has just finished placing the pretty girl with the stick legs, and comes up to assist Brady, but Brady waves him off. The usher gives him a grin and a pat on the shoulder as he goes by to help someone else. Brady rolls down to the first of the two sections reserved for the handicapped. He parks next to the pretty girl with the stick legs.

She turns to him with a smile. "Isn't this exciting?"

Brady smiles back, thinking, You don't know the half of it, you crippled bitch.

30

Tanya Robinson is looking at the stage and thinking of the first concert she ever went to—it was the Temps—and how Bobby Wilson kissed her right in the middle of "My Girl." Very romantic.

She's roused from these thoughts by her daughter, who's shaking her arm. "Look, Mom, there's the crippled man. Over there with the other wheelchair-people." Barbara points to the left and down a couple of rows. Here the seats have been removed to make room for two ranks of wheelchairs.

"I see him, Barb, but it's not polite to stare."

"I hope he has a good time, don't you?"

Tanya smiles at her daughter. "I sure do, honey."

"Can we have our phones back? We need them for the start of the show."

To take pictures with is what Tanya Robinson assumes . . . because it's been a long time since she's been to a rock show. She opens her purse and doles out the candy-colored phones. For a wonder, the girls just hold them. For the time being, they're too busy goggling around to call or text. Tanya puts a quick kiss on top of Barb's head and then sits back, lost in the past, thinking of Bobby Wilson's kiss. Not quite the first, but the first good one.

She hopes that when the time comes, Barb will be as lucky.

## 31

"Oh my happy clapping Jesus," Holly says, and hits her forehead with the heel of her hand. She's finished with Brady's Number One—nothing much there—and has moved on to Number Two.

Jerome looks up from Number Five, which seems to have been exclusively dedicated to video games, most of the *Grand Theft Auto* and *Call of Duty* sort. "What?"

"It's just that every now and then I run across someone even more screwed in the head than me," she says. "It cheers me up. That's terrible, I know it is, but I can't help it."

Hodges gets up from the stairs with a grunt and comes over to look. The screen is filled with small photos. They appear to be harmless cheesecake, not much different from the kind he and his friends used to moon over in *Adam* and *Spicy Leg Art* back in the late fifties. Holly enlarges three of them and arranges them in a row. Here is Deborah Hartsfield wearing a filmy robe. And Deborah Hartsfield wearing babydoll pajamas. And Deborah Hartsfield in a frilly pink bra-and-panty set.

"My God, it's his *mother*," Jerome says. His face is a study in revulsion, amazement, and fascination. "And it looks like she *posed*."

It looks that way to Hodges, too.

"Yup," Holly says. "Paging Dr. Freud. Why do you keep rubbing your shoulder, Mr. Hodges?"

"Pulled a muscle," he says. But he's starting to wonder about that.

Jerome glances at the desktop screen of Number Three, starts to check out the photos of Brady Hartsfield's mother again, then does a double-take. "Whoa," he says. "Look at this, Bill."

Sitting in the lower lefthand corner of Number Three's desktop is a Blue Umbrella icon.

"Open it," Hodges says.

He does, but the file is empty. There's nothing unsent, and as they now know, all old correspondence on Debbie's Blue Umbrella goes straight to data heaven.

Jerome sits down at Number Three. "This must be his go-to glowbox, Hols. Almost got to be."

She joins him. "I think the other ones are mostly for show—so he can pretend he's on the bridge of the Starship *Enterprise* or something."

Hodges points to a file marked **2009**. "Let's look at that one."

A mouse-click discloses a subfile titled CITY CENTER. Jerome opens it and they stare at a long list of stories about what happened there in April of 2009.

"The asshole's press clippings," Hodges says.

"Go through everything on this one," Holly tells Jerome. "Start with the hard drive."

Jerome opens it. "Oh man, look at this shit." He points to a file titled EXPLOSIVES.

"Open it!" Holly says, shaking his shoulder. "Open it, open it, open it!"

Jerome does, and reveals another loaded subfile. Drawers within drawers, Hodges thinks. A computer's really nothing but a Victorian rolltop desk, complete with secret compartments.

Holly says, "Hey guys, look at this." She points. "He downloaded the whole *Anarchist Cookbook* from BitTorrent. That's illegal!"

"Duh," Jerome says, and she punches him in the arm.

The pain in Hodges's shoulder is worse. He walks back to the stairs and sits heavily. Jerome and Holly, huddled over Number Three, don't notice him go. He puts his hands on his thighs (My overweight thighs, he thinks, my *badly* overweight thighs) and begins taking long slow breaths. The only thing that can make this evening worse would be having a heart attack in a house he's illegally entered with a minor and a woman who is at least a mile from right in the head. A house where a bullshit-crazy killer's pinup girl is lying dead upstairs.

Please God, no heart attack. *Please.*

He takes more long breaths. He stifles a belch and the pain begins to ease.

With his head lowered, he finds himself looking between the stairs. Something glints there in the light of the overhead fluorescents. Hodges drops to his knees and crawls underneath to see what it is. It turns out to be a stainless steel ball bearing, bigger than the ones in the Happy Slapper, heavy in his palm. He looks at the distorted reflection of his face in its curved side, and an idea starts to grow. Only it doesn't exactly grow; it *surfaces*, like the bloated body of something drowned.

Farther beneath the stairs is a green garbage bag. Hodges crawls to it with the ball bearing clutched in one hand, feeling the cobwebs that dangle from the undersides of the steps caress his receding hair and growing forehead. Jerome and Holly are chattering excitedly, but he pays no attention.

He grabs the garbage bag with his free hand and begins to back out from beneath the stairs. A drop of sweat runs into his left eye, stinging, and he blinks it away. He sits down on the steps again.

"Open his email," Holly says.

"God, you're bossy," Jerome says.

"Open it, open it, open it!"

Right you are, Hodges thinks, and opens the garbage bag. There are snippets of wire inside, and what appears to be a busted circuit board. They are lying on top of a khaki-colored garment that looks like a shirt. He brushes the bits of wire aside, pulls the garment out, holds it up. Not a shirt but a hiker's vest, the kind with lots of pockets. The lining has been slashed in half a dozen places. He reaches into one of these cuts, feels around, and pulls out two more ball bearings. It's *not* a hiker's vest, at least not anymore. It's been customized.

Now it's a suicide vest.

Or was. Brady unloaded it for some reason. Because his plans changed to the Careers Day thing on Saturday? That has to be it. The explosives are probably in his car, unless he's stolen another one already. He—

"No!" Jerome cries. Then he screams it. *"No! No, no, OH GOD NO!"*

"Please don't let it be," Holly whimpers. "Don't let it be that."

Hodges drops the vest and hurries across to the bank of computers to see what they're looking at. It's an email from a site called FanTastic, thanking Mr. Brady Hartsfield for his order.

*You may download your printable ticket at once. No bags or backpacks will be allowed at this event. Thank you for ordering from FanTastic, where all the best seats to all the biggest shows are only a click away.*

Below this: **'ROUND HERE MINGO AUDITORIUM MIDWEST CULTURE AND ARTS COMPLEX JUNE 3, 2010 7 PM.**

Hodges closes his eyes. It's the fucking concert after all. We made an understandable mistake . . . but not a forgivable one. Please God, don't let him get inside. Please God, let Romper-Stomper's guys catch him at the door.

But even that could be a nightmare, because Larry Windom is

under the impression that he's looking for a child molester, not a mad bomber. If he spots Brady and tries to collar him with his usual heavy-handed lack of grace—

"It's quarter of seven," Holly says, pointing to the digital readout on Brady's Number Three. "He might still be waiting in line, but he's probably inside already."

Hodges knows she's right. With that many kids going, seating will have started no later than six-thirty.

"Jerome," he says.

The boy doesn't reply. He's staring at the ticket receipt on the computer screen, and when Hodges puts his hand on Jerome's shoulder, it's like touching a stone.

"Jerome."

Slowly, Jerome turns around. His eyes are huge. "We been so stupid," he whispers.

"Call your moms." Hodges's voice remains calm, and it's not even that much of an effort, because he's in deep shock. He keeps seeing the ball bearing. And the slashed vest. "Do it now. Tell her to grab Barbara and the other kids she brought and beat feet out of there."

Jerome pulls his phone from the clip on his belt and speed-dials his mother. Holly stares at him with her arms crossed tightly over her breasts and her chewed lips pulled down in a grimace.

Jerome waits, mutters a curse, then says: "You have to get out of there, Mom. Just take the girls and go. Don't call me back and ask questions, just *go*. Don't run. But get out!"

He ends the call and tells them what they already know. "Voicemail. It rang plenty of times, so she's not talking on it and it's not shut off. I don't get it."

"What about your sister?" Hodges says. "She must have a phone."

Jerome is hitting speed-dial again before he can finish. He listens for what seems to Hodges like an age, although he knows it can only be ten or fifteen seconds. Then he says, "Barb! Why in hell aren't you picking up? You and Mom and the other girls have to get out of there!" He ends the call. "I don't get this. She *always* carries it, that thing is practically grafted to her, and she should at least feel it vibra—"

Holly says, "Oh shit and piss." But that's not enough for her. "Oh, *fuck!*"

They turn to her.

"How big is the concert place? How many people can fit inside?"

Hodges tries to retrieve what he knows about the Mingo Auditorium. "Seats four thousand. I don't know if they allow standees or not, I can't remember that part of the fire code."

"And for this show, almost all of them are girls," she says. "Girls with cell phones practically grafted to them. Most of them gabbing away while they wait for the show to start. Or texting." Her eyes are huge with dismay. "It's the circuits. They're overloaded. You have to keep trying, Jerome. You have to keep trying until you get through."

He nods numbly, but he's looking at Hodges. "You should call your friend. The one in the security department."

"Yeah, but not from here. In the car." Hodges looks at his watch again. Ten of seven. "We're going to the MAC."

Holly clenches a fist on either side of her face. *"Yes,"* she says, and Hodges finds himself remembering what she said earlier: *They* can't find him. *We* can.

In spite of his desire to confront Hartsfield—to wrap his hands around Hartsfield's neck and see the bastard's eyes bulge as his breath stops—Hodges hopes she's wrong about that. Because if it's up to them, it may already be too late.

## 32

This time it's Jerome behind the wheel and Hodges in back. Olivia Trelawney's Mercedes gathers itself slowly, but once the twelve-cylinder engine gets cranking, it goes like a rocket . . . and with the lives of his mother and sister on the line, Jerome drives it like one, weaving from lane to lane and ignoring the protesting honks of the cars around him. Hodges estimates they can be at the MAC in twenty minutes. If the kid doesn't pile them up, that is.

"Call the security man!" Holly says from the passenger seat. "Call him, call him, call him!"

As Hodges takes his Nokia out of his jacket pocket, he instructs Jerome to take the City Bypass.

"Don't backseat-drive me," Jerome says. "Just make the call. And hurry."

But when he tries to access his phone's memory, the fucking Nokia gives a single weak tweet and then dies. When was the last time he charged it? Hodges can't remember. He can't remember the number of the security office, either. He should have written it down in his notebook instead of depending on the phone.

Goddam technology, he thinks . . . but whose fault is it, really?

"Holly. Dial 555-1900 and then give me your phone. Mine's dead." Nineteen hundred is the department. He can get Windom's number from Marlo again.

"Okay, what's the area code here? My phone's on—"

She breaks off as Jerome swerves around a panel truck and drives straight at an SUV in the other lane, flashing his lights and yelling, *"Get out of the way!"* The SUV swerves and Jerome skates the Mercedes past with a coat of paint to spare.

"—on Cincinnati," Holly finishes. She sounds as cool as a Popsicle.

Hodges, thinking he could use some of the drugs she's on, recites the area code. She dials and hands her phone to him over the seat.

"Police Department, how may I direct your call?"

"I need to talk to Marlo Everett in Records, and right away."

"I'm sorry, sir, but I saw Ms. Everett leave half an hour ago."

"Have you got her cell number?"

"Sir, I'm not allowed to give that information ou—"

He has no inclination to engage in a time-consuming argument that will surely prove fruitless, and clicks off just as Jerome swings onto the City Bypass, doing sixty. "What's the holdup, Bill? Why aren't you—"

"Shut up and drive, Jerome," Holly says. "Mr. Hodges is doing the best he can."

The truth is, she really doesn't want me to reach anyone, Hodges thinks. Because it's supposed to be us and only us. A crazy idea comes to him, that Holly is using some weird psychic vibe to make sure it *stays* them and only them. And it might. Based on the way Jerome's driving, they'll be at the MAC before Hodges is able to get hold of *anyone* in authority.

A cold part of his mind is thinking that might be best. Because no matter who Hodges reaches, Larry Windom is the man in charge at the Mingo, and Hodges doesn't trust him. Romper-Stomper was always a bludgeoner, a go-right-at-em kind of guy, and Hodges doubts he has changed.

Still, he has to try.

He hands Holly's phone back to her and says, "I can't figure this fucking thing out. Call Directory Assistance and—"

"Try my sister again first," Jerome says, and raps off the number.

Holly dials Barbara's phone, her thumb moving so fast it's a blur. Listens. "Voicemail."

Jerome curses and drives faster. Hodges can only hope there's an angel riding on his shoulder.

"*Barbara!*" Holly hollers. No mumbling now. "*You and whoever's with you get your asses out of there right away! ASAP! Pronto!*" She clicks off. "Now what? Directory Assistance, you said?"

"Yeah. Get the MAC Security Department number, dial it, and give the phone back to me. Jerome, take Exit 4A."

"3B's the MAC."

"It is if you're going in front. We're going to the back."

"Bill, if my mom and sis get hurt—"

"They won't. Take 4A." Holly's discussion with Directory Assistance has lasted too long. "Holly, what's the holdup?"

"No direct line into their Security Department." She dials a new number, listens, and hands him the phone. "You have to go through the main number."

He presses Holly's iPhone to his ear hard enough to hurt. It rings. And rings. And rings some more.

As they pass Exits 2A and 2B, Hodges can see the MAC. It's lit up like a jukebox, the parking lot a sea of cars. His call is finally answered, but before he can say a word, a fembot begins to lecture him. She does it slowly and carefully, as if addressing a person who speaks English as a second language, and not well.

"Hello, and thank you for calling the Midwest Culture and Arts Complex, where we make life better and all things are possible."

Hodges listens with Holly's phone mashed against his ear and sweat rolling down his cheeks and neck. It's six past seven. The bastard won't do it until the show starts, he tells himself (he's actually praying), and rock acts always start late.

"Remember," the fembot says sweetly, "we depend on *you* for support, and season's passes to the City Symphony and this fall's Playhouse Series are available now. Not only will you save fifty percent—"

"What's happening?" Jerome shouts as they pass 3A and 3B. The next sign reads EXIT 4A SPICER BOULEVARD ½ MILE. Jerome has tossed Holly his own phone and Holly is trying first Tanya, then Barbara again, with no result.

"I'm listening to a fucking recorded ad," Hodges says. He's rubbing the hollow of his shoulder again. That ache is like an infected tooth. "Go left at the bottom of the ramp. You'll want a right turn I think about a block up. Maybe two. By the McDonald's, anyway." Although the Mercedes is now doing eighty, the sound of the engine has yet to rise above a sleepy purr.

"If we hear an explosion, I'm going to lose my mind," Jerome says matter-of-factly.

"Just drive," Holly says. An unlit Winston jitters between her teeth. "If you don't wreck us, we'll be fine." She's gone back to Tanya's number. "We're going to get him. We're going to get him get him get him."

Jerome snatches a glance at her. "Holly, you're nuts."

"Just drive," she repeats.

"You can also use your MAC card to obtain a ten percent discount at selected fine restaurants and local retail businesses," the fembot informs Hodges.

Then, at long last, she gets down to business.

"There is no one in the main office to take your call now. If you know the number of the extension you wish to reach, you may dial it at any time. If not, please listen carefully, because our menu options have changed. To call the Avery Johns Drama Office, dial one-oh. To call the Belinda Dean Box Office, dial one-one. To reach City Symphony—"

Oh dear Jesus, Hodges thinks, it's the fucking Sears catalogue. And in alphabetical order.

The Mercedes dips and swerves as Jerome takes the 4A exit and shoots down the curved ramp. The light is red at the bottom. "Holly. How is it your way?"

She checks with the phone still at her ear. "You're okay if you hurry. If you want to get us all killed, take your time."

Jerome buries the accelerator. Olivia's Mercedes shoots across four lanes of traffic listing hard to port, the tires squalling. There's a thud as they bounce across the concrete divider. Horns blare a discordant flourish. From the corner of his eye, Hodges sees a panel truck climb the curb to avoid them.

"To reach Craft Service and Set Design, dial—"

Hodges punches the roof of the Mercedes. "What happened to *HUMAN FUCKING BEINGS?*"

Just as the Golden Arches of McDonald's appear ahead on the right, the fembot tells Hodges he can reach the MAC's Security Department by dialing three-two.

He does so. The phone rings four times, then is picked up. What he hears makes him wonder if he is losing his mind.

"Hello, and thank you for calling the Midwest Culture and Arts Complex," the fembot says cordially. "Where we make life better and all things are possible."

## 33

"Why isn't the show starting, Mrs. Robinson?" Dinah Scott asks. "It's already ten past seven."

Tanya thinks of telling them about the Stevie Wonder concert she went to when she was in high school, the one that was scheduled to start at eight and finally got underway at nine-thirty, but decides it might be counterproductive.

Hilda's frowning at her phone. "I still can't get Gail," she complains. "All the darn circuits are b—"

The lights begin to dim before she can finish. This provokes wild cheering and waves of applause.

"Oh God, Mommy, I'm so excited!" Barbara whispers, and Tanya is touched to see tears welling in her daughter's eyes. A guy in a BAM-100 Good Guys tee-shirt struts out. A spotlight tracks him to center stage.

"Hey, you guys!" he shouts. "Howya doin out there?"

A fresh wave of noise assures him that the sellout crowd is doing just fine. Tanya sees the two ranks of Wheelchair People are also applauding. Except for the bald man. He's just sitting there. Probably doesn't want to drop his picture, Tanya thinks.

"Are you ready for some Boyd, Steve, and Pete?" the DJ host inquires.

More cheers and screams.

*"And are you ready for some CAM KNOWLES?"*

The girls (most of whom would be struck utterly dumb in their idol's actual presence) shriek deliriously. They're ready, all right. *God*, are they ready. They could just die.

"In a few minutes you're going to see a set that'll knock your eyes out, but for now, ladies and gentlemen—and especially you girls—give it up for . . . 'ROUND . . . HEEERRRRE!!!"

The audience surges to its feet, and as the lights on the stage go completely dark, Tanya understands why the girls just had to have their phones. In her day, everyone held up matches or Bic lighters. These kids hold up their cell phones, the combined light of all those little screens casting a pallid moonglow across the bowl of the auditorium.

How do they know to do these things? she wonders. Who tells them? For that matter, who told *us*?

She cannot remember.

The stage lights come up to bright furnace red. At that moment, a call finally slips through the clogged network and Barbara Robinson's cell vibrates in her hand. She ignores it. Answering a phone call is the last thing in the world she wants to do right now (a first in her young life), and she couldn't hear the person on the other end—probably her brother—even if she did. The racket inside the Mingo is deafening . . . and Barb loves it. She waves her vibrating phone back and forth above her head in big slow swoops. Everyone is doing the same, even her mom.

The lead singer of 'Round Here, dressed in the tightest jeans Tanya Robinson has ever seen, strides onstage. Cam Knowles throws back a tidal wave of blond hair and launches into "You Don't Have to Be Lonely Again."

Most of the audience remains on its feet for the time being, holding up their phones. The concert has begun.

34

The Mercedes turns off Spicer Boulevard and onto a feeder road marked with signs reading MAC DELIVERIES and EMPLOYEES ONLY. A quarter of a mile up is a rolling gate. It's closed. Jerome pulls up next to a post with an intercom on it. The sign here reads CALL FOR ENTRY.

Hodges says, "Tell them you're the police."

Jerome rolls down his window and pushes the button. Nothing happens. He pushes it again and this time holds it. Hodges has a nightmarish thought: When Jerome's buzz is finally answered, it will be the fembot, offering several dozen new options.

But this time it's an actual human, albeit not a friendly one. "Back's closed."

"Police," Jerome says. "Open the gate."

"What do you want?"

"I just told you. Open the goddam gate. This is an emergency."

The gate begins to trundle open, but instead of rolling forward, Jerome pushes the button again. "Are you security?"

"Head custodian," the crackly voice returns. "If you want security, you gotta call the Security Department."

"Nobody there," Hodges tells Jerome. "They're in the auditorium, the whole bunch of them. Just *go*."

Jerome does, even though the gate isn't fully open. He scrapes the side of the Mercedes's refurbished body. "Maybe they caught him," he says. "They had his description, so maybe they already caught him."

"They didn't," Hodges says. "He's in."

"How do you know?"

"Listen."

They can't pick up actual music yet, but with the driver's window still down, they can hear a thudding bass progression.

"The concert's on. If Windom's men had collared a guy with explosives, they would have shut it down right away and they'd be evacuating the building."

"How could he get in?" Jerome asks, and thumps the steering wheel. *"How?"* Hodges can hear the terror in the boy's voice. All because of him. Everything because of him.

"I have no idea. They had his photo."

Ahead is a wide concrete ramp leading down to the loading area. Half a dozen roadies are sitting on amp crates and smoking, their work over for the time being. There's an open door leading to the rear of the auditorium, and through it Hodges can hear music coalescing around the bass progression. There's another sound, as well: thousands of happily screaming girls, all of them sitting on ground zero.

How Hartsfield got in no longer matters unless it helps to find him, and just how in God's name are they supposed to do that in a dark auditorium filled with thousands of people?

As Jerome parks at the bottom of the ramp, Holly says: "De Niro gave himself a Mohawk. That could be it."

"What are you talking about?" Hodges asks as he heaves himself out of the back seat. A man in khaki Carhartts has come into the open door to meet them.

"In *Taxi Driver*, Robert De Niro played a crazy guy named Travis Bickle," Holly explains as the three of them hurry toward the custodian. "When he decided to assassinate the politician, he shaved his head so he could get close without being recognized. Except for the middle, that is, which is called a Mohawk. Brady Hartsfield probably didn't do that, it'd make him look too weird."

Hodges remembers the leftover hair in the bathroom sink. It was not the bright (and probably tinted) color of the dead woman's hair. Holly may be nuts, but he thinks she's right about this; Hartsfield has gone skinhead. Yet Hodges doesn't see how even that could have been enough, because—

The head custodian steps to meet them. "What's it about?"

Hodges takes out his ID and flashes it briefly, his thumb once more strategically placed. "Detective Bill Hodges. What's your name, sir?"

"Jamie Gallison." His eyes flick to Jerome and Holly.

"I'm his partner," Holly says.

"I'm his trainee," Jerome says.

The roadies are watching. Some have hurriedly snuffed smokes that may contain something a bit stronger than tobacco. Through the open door, Hodges can see work-lights illuminating a storage area loaded with props and swatches of canvas scenery.

"Mr. Gallison, we've got a serious problem," Hodges says. "I need you to get Larry Windom down here, right away."

"Don't do that, Bill." Even in his growing distress, he realizes it's the first time Holly has called him by his first name.

He ignores her. "Sir, I need you to call him on your cell."

Gallison shakes his head. "The security guys don't carry cell phones when they're on duty, because every time we have one of these big shows—big *kid* shows, I mean, it's different with adults—the circuits jam up. The security guys carry—"

Holly is twitching Hodges's arm. "Don't do it. You'll spook him and he'll set it off. I know he will."

"She could be right," Jerome says, and then (perhaps recalling his trainee status) adds, "Sir."

Gallison is looking at them with alarm. "Spook who? Set off what?"

Hodges remains fixed on the custodian. "They carry what? Walkies? Radios?"

"Radios, yuh. They have . . ." He pulls his earlobe. "You know, things that look like hearie-aids. Like the FBI and Secret Service wear. What's going on here? Tell me it's not a bomb." And, not liking what he sees on Hodges's pale and sweating face: "Christ, is it?"

Hodges walks past him into the cavernous storage area. Beyond the attic-like profusion of props, flats, and music stands, there's a carpentry shop and a costume shop. The music is louder than ever, and he's started to have trouble breathing. The pain is creeping down his left arm, and his chest feels too heavy, but his head is clear.

Brady has either gone bald or mowed it short and dyed what's left. He may have added makeup to darken his skin, or colored contacts, or glasses. But even with all that, he'd still be a single man at a concert filled with young girls. After the heads-up he gave Windom, Hartsfield still would have attracted notice and suspicion. And there's the explosive. Holly and Jerome know about that, but Hodges knows more. There were also steel ball bearings, probably a shitload. Even if he wasn't collared at the door, how could Hartsfield have gotten all that inside? Is the security here really that bad?

Gallison grabs his left arm, and when he shakes it, Hodges feels the pain all the way up to his temples. "I'll go myself. Grab the first security guy I see and have him radio for Windom to come down here and talk to you."

"No," Hodges says. "You will not do that, sir."

STEPHEN KING

Holly Gibney is the only one of them seeing clearly. Mr. Mercedes is in. He's got a bomb, and it's only by the grace of God that he hasn't triggered it already. It's too late for the police and too late for MAC Security. It's also too late for him.

But.

Hodges sits down on an empty crate. "Jerome. Holly. Get with me."

They do. Jerome is white-eyed, barely holding back panic. Holly is pale but outwardly calm.

"Going bald wouldn't have been enough. He had to make himself look harmless. I might know how he did that, and if I'm right, I know his location."

"Where?" Jerome asks. "Tell us. We'll get him. *We* will."

"It won't be easy. He's going to be on red alert right now, always checking his personal perimeter. And he knows you, Jerome. You've bought ice cream from that damn Mr. Tastey truck. You told me so."

"Bill, he's sold ice cream to thousands of people."

"Sure, but how many *black* people on the West Side?"

Jerome is silent, and now he's the one biting his lips.

"How big a bomb?" Gallison asks. "Maybe I should pull the fire alarm?"

"Only if you want to get a whole shitload of people killed," Hodges says. It's becoming progressively difficult to talk. "The minute he senses danger, he'll blow whatever he's got. Do you want that?"

Gallison doesn't reply, and Hodges turns back to the two unlikely associates God—or some whimsical fate—has ordained should be with him tonight.

"We can't take a chance on you, Jerome, and we *certainly* can't take a chance on me. He was stalking me long before I even knew he was alive."

"I'll come up from behind," Jerome says. "Blindside him. In the dark, with nothing but the lights from the stage, he'll never see me."

404

"If he's where I think he is, your chances of doing that would be fifty-fifty at best. That's not good enough."

Hodges turns to the woman with the graying hair and the face of a neurotic teenager. "It's got to be you, Holly. By now he'll have his finger on the trigger, and you're the only one who can get close without being recognized."

She covers her abused mouth with one hand, but that isn't enough and she adds the other. Her eyes are huge and wet. God help us, Hodges thinks. It isn't the first time he has had this thought in relation to Holly Gibney.

"Only if you come with me," she says through her hands. "Maybe then—"

"I can't," Hodges says. "I'm having a heart attack."

"Oh *great*," Gallison moans.

"Mr. Gallison, is there a handicapped area? There must be, right?"

"Sure. Halfway down the auditorium."

Not only did he get in with his explosives, Hodges thinks, he's perfectly located to inflict maximum casualties.

He says: "Listen, you two. Don't make me say this twice."

## 35

Thanks to the emcee's introduction, Brady has relaxed a bit. The carnival crap he saw being offloaded during his reconnaissance trip is either offstage or suspended overhead. The band's first four or five songs are just warm-ups. Pretty soon the set will roll in either from the sides or drop down from overhead, because the band's main job, the reason they're here, is to sell their latest helping of audio shit. When the kids—many of them attending their first pop concert—see those bright blinking lights and the Ferris wheel and the beachy backdrop, they're going to go out of their teeny-bop minds. It's then, right *then*, that he'll push the toggle-switch on Thing Two, and ride into the darkness on a golden bubble of all that happiness.

The lead singer, the one with all the hair, is finishing a syrupy ballad on his knees. He holds the last note, head bowed, emoting his faggy ass off. He's a lousy singer and probably already overdue for a fatal drug overdose, but when he raises his head and blares, *"How ya feelin out there?"* the audience goes predictably batshit.

Brady looks around, as he has every few seconds—checking his perimeter, just as Hodges said he would—and his eyes fix on a little black girl sitting a couple of rows up to his right.

*Do I know her?*

"Who are you looking for?" the pretty girl with the stick legs shouts over the intro to the next song. He can barely hear her. She's grinning at him, and Brady thinks how ridiculous it is for a girl with stick legs to grin at anything. The world has fucked her royally, up the ying-yang and out the wazoo, and how does that deserve even a small smile, let alone such a cheek-stretching moony grin? He thinks, *She's probably stoned.*

"Friend of mine!" Brady shouts back.

Thinking, *As if I had any.*

*As if.*

36

Gallison leads Holly and Jerome away to . . . well, to somewhere. Hodges sits on the crate with his head lowered and his hands planted on his thighs. One of the roadies approaches hesitantly and offers to call an ambulance for him. Hodges thanks him but refuses. He doesn't believe Brady could hear the warble of an approaching ambulance (or anything else) over the din 'Round Here is producing, but he won't take the chance. Taking chances is what brought them to this pass, with everyone in the Mingo Auditorium, including Jerome's mother and sister, at risk. He'd rather die than take another chance, and rather hopes he will before he has to explain this shit-coated clusterfuck.

Only . . . Janey. When he thinks of Janey, laughing and tipping his borrowed fedora at just the right insouciant angle, he knows that if he had it to do over again, he'd likely do it the same way.

Well . . . most of it. Given a do-over, he might have listened a little more closely to Mrs. Melbourne.

*She thinks they walk among us,* Bowfinger had said, and the two of them had had a manly chuckle over that, but the joke was on them, wasn't it? Because Mrs. Melbourne was right. Brady Hartsfield really *is* an alien, and he was among them all the time, fixing computers and selling ice cream.

Holly and Jerome are gone, Jerome carrying the .38 that belonged to Hodges's father. Hodges has grave doubts about sending the boy into a crowded auditorium with a loaded gun. Under ordinary circumstances he's a beautifully levelheaded kid, but he's not apt to be so levelheaded with his mom and sis in danger. Holly needs to be protected, though. *Remember you're just the backup,* Hodges told the boy before Gallison led them away, but Jerome made no acknowledgement. He's not sure Jerome even heard him.

In any case, Hodges has done all he can do. The only thing left is to sit here, fighting the pain and trying to get his breath and waiting for an explosion he prays will not come.

37

Holly Gibney has been institutionalized twice in her life, once in her teens and once in her twenties. The shrink she saw later on (in her so-called *maturity*) labeled these enforced vacations *breaks with reality*, which were not good but still better than *psychotic breaks*, from which many people never returned. Holly herself had a simpler name for said breaks. They were her *total freakouts*, as opposed to the state of low to moderate freakout in which she lived her day-to-day life.

The total freakout in her twenties had been caused by her boss at a Cincinnati real estate firm called Frank Mitchell Fine Homes and Estates. Her boss was Frank Mitchell, Jr., a sharp dresser with the face of an intelligent trout. He insisted her work was substandard, that her co-workers loathed her, and the only way she could be assured of remaining with the company would be if he continued to cover for her. Which he would do if she slept with him. Holly didn't want to sleep with Frank Mitchell, Jr., and she didn't want to lose her job. If she lost her job, she would lose her apartment, and have to go back home to live with her milquetoast father and overbearing mother. She finally resolved the conflict by coming in early one day and trashing Frank Mitchell, Jr.'s, office. She was found in her own cubicle, curled up in a corner. The tips of her fingers were bloody. She had chewed at them like an animal trying to escape a trap.

The cause of her first total freakout was Mike Sturdevant. He was the one who coined the pestiferous nickname Jibba-Jibba.

In those days, as a high school freshman, Holly had wanted nothing except to scurry from place to place with her books clutched to her newly arrived breasts and her hair screening her acne-spotted face. But even then she had problems that went far beyond acne. Anxiety problems. Depression problems. Insomnia problems.

Worst of all, stimming.

Stimming was short for self-stimulation, which sounded like masturbation but wasn't. It was compulsive movement, often accompanied by fragments of self-directed dialogue. Biting one's fingernails and chewing one's lips were mild forms of stimming. More extravagant stimmers waved their hands, slapped at their chests and cheeks, or did curling movements with their arms, as if lifting invisible weights.

Starting at roughly age eight, Holly began wrapping her arms around her shoulders and shivering all over, muttering to herself and making facial grimaces. This would go on for five or ten seconds, and then she would simply continue with whatever she had been doing—reading, sewing, shooting baskets in the driveway with her father. She was hardly aware that she was doing it unless her mother saw her and told her to stop shaking and making faces, people would think she was having a fit.

Mike Sturdevant was one of those behaviorally stunted males who look back on high school as the great lost golden age of their lives. He was a senior, and—very much like Cam Knowles—a boy of godlike good looks: broad shoulders, narrow hips, long legs, and hair so blond it was a kind of halo. He was on the football team (of course) and dated the head cheerleader (of course). He lived on an entirely different level of the high school hierarchy from Holly Gibney, and under ordinary circumstances, she never would have attracted his notice. But notice her he did, because one day, on her way to the caff, she had one of her stimming episodes.

Mike Sturdevant and several of his football-playing buddies happened to be passing. They stopped to stare at her—this girl who was clutching herself, shivering, and making a face that pulled her mouth down and turned her eyes into slits. A series of small, inarticulate sounds—perhaps words, perhaps not—came squeezing through her clenched teeth.

"What are you gibbering about?" Mike asked her.

Holly relaxed her grip on her shoulders, staring at him in wild surprise. She didn't know what he was saying; she only knew he was staring at her. All his friends were staring at her. And grinning.

She gaped at him. "What?"

"Gibbering!" Mike shouted. "Jibba-jibba-gibbering!"

The others took it up as she ran toward the cafeteria with her head lowered, bumping into people as she went. From then on, Holly Gibney was known to the student body at Walnut Hills High School as Jibba-Jibba, and so she remained until just after the Christmas break. That was when her mother found her curled up naked in the bathtub, saying that she would never go to Walnut Hills again. If her mother tried to make her, she said, she would kill herself.

Voilà! Total freakout!

When she got better (a little), she went to a different school where things were less stressful (a little less). She never had to see Mike Sturdevant again, but she still has dreams in which she's running down an endless high school corridor—sometimes dressed only in her underwear—while people laugh at her, and point at her, and call her Jibba-Jibba.

She's thinking of those dear old high school days as she and Jerome follow the head custodian through the warren of rooms below the Mingo Auditorium. That's what Brady Hartsfield will look like, she decides, like Mike Sturdevant, only bald. Which she hopes Mike is, wherever he may now reside. Bald . . . fat . . . pre-diabetic . . . afflicted with a nagging wife and ungrateful children . . .

Jibba-Jibba, she thinks.

Pay you back, she thinks.

Gallison leads them through the carpentry shop and costume shop, past a cluster of dressing rooms, then down a corridor wide enough to transport flats and completed sets. The corridor ends at a freight elevator with the doors standing open. Happy pop music booms down the shaft. The current song is about love and dancing. Nothing Holly can relate to.

"You don't want the elevator," Gallison says, "it goes backstage and you can't get to the auditorium from there without walking right through the band. Listen, is that guy really having a heart attack? Are you guys really cops? You don't look like cops." He glances at Jerome. "You're too young." Then to Holly, his expression even more doubtful. "And you're . . ."

"Too freaky?" Holly supplies.

"I wasn't going to say that." Maybe not, but it's what he's thinking. Holly knows; a girl once nicknamed Jibba-Jibba always does.

"I'm calling the cops," Gallison says. "The *real* cops. And if this is some kind of joke—"

"Do what you need to do," Jerome says, thinking Why not? Let him call in the National Guard if he wants to. This is going to be over, one way or the other, in the next few minutes. Jerome knows it, and he can see that Holly does, too. The gun Hodges gave him is in his pocket. It feels heavy and weirdly warm. Other than the air rifle he had when he was nine or ten (a birthday present given to him despite his mother's reservations), he has never carried a gun in his life, and this one feels *alive*.

Holly points to the left of the elevator. "What about that door?" And when Gallison doesn't reply immediately: "Help us. Please. Maybe we're not real cops, maybe you're right about that, but there really is a man in the audience tonight who's very dangerous."

She takes a deep breath and says words she can hardly believe, even though she knows they are true. "Mister, we're all you've got."

Gallison thinks it over, then says, "The stairs'll take you to Auditorium Left. It's a long flight. At the top, there's two doors. The one on the left goes outside. The one on the right opens on the auditorium, way down by the stage. That close, the music's apt to bust your eardrums."

Touching the grip of the pistol in his pocket, Jerome asks, "And exactly where's the handicapped section?"

### 38

Brady *does* know her. He *does*.

At first he can't get it, it's like a word that's stuck on the tip of your tongue. Then, as the band starts some song about making love on the dancefloor, it comes to him. The house on Teaberry Lane, the one where Hodges's pet boy lives with his family, a nest of niggers with white names. Except for the dog, that is. He's named O'dell, a nigger name for sure, and Brady meant to kill him . . . only he ended up killing his mother instead.

Brady remembers the day the niggerboy came running to the Mr. Tastey truck, his ankles still green from cutting the fat ex-cop's lawn. And his sister shouting, *Get me a chocolate! Pleeeease?*

The sister's name is Barbara, and that's her, big as life and twice as ugly. She's sitting two rows up to the right with her friends and a woman who has to be her mother. Jerome isn't with them, and Brady is savagely glad. Let Jerome live, that's fine.

But without his sister.

Or his mother.

Let him see what *that* feels like.

Still looking at Barbara Robinson, his finger creeps beneath Frankie's picture and finds Thing Two's toggle-switch. He caresses it through the thin fabric of the tee-shirt the way he was allowed—on a few fortunate occasions only—to caress his mother's nipples. Onstage, the lead singer of 'Round Here does a split that must just about crush his balls (always supposing he has any) in those tight jeans he's wearing, then springs to his feet and approaches the edge of the stage. Chicks scream. Chicks reach out as if to touch him, their hands waving, their fingernails—painted in every girlish color of the rainbow—gleaming in the footlights.

*"Hey, do you guys like an amusement park?"* Cam hollers.

They scream that they do.

*"Do you guys like a carnival?"*

They scream that they *love* a carnival.

*"Have you ever been kissed on the midway?"*

The screams are utterly delirious now. The audience is on its feet again, the roving spotlights once more skimming over the crowd. Brady can no longer see the band, but it doesn't matter. He already knows what's coming, because he was there at the load-in.

Lowering his voice to an intimate, amplified murmur, Cam Knowles says, "Well, you're gonna get that kiss tonight."

Carnival music starts up—a Korg synthesizer set to play a calliope tune. The stage is suddenly bathed in a swirl of light: orange, blue, red, green, yellow. There's a gasp of amazement as the midway set starts to descend. Both the carousel and the Ferris wheel are already turning.

*"THIS IS THE TITLE TRACK OF OUR NEW ALBUM, AND WE REALLY HOPE YOU ENJOY IT!"* Cam bellows, and the other instruments fall in around the synth.

*"The desert cries in all directions,"* Cam Knowles intones. *"Like eternity, you're my infection."* To Brady he sounds like Jim Morrison after a prefrontal lobotomy. Then he yells jubilantly: *"What'll cure me, guys?"*

The audience knows, and roars out the words as the band kicks in full-force.

*"BABY, BABY, YOU'VE GOT THE LOVE THAT I NEED . . . YOU AND I, WE GOT IT BAD . . . LIKE NOTHIN' THAT I EVER HAD . . ."*

Brady smiles. It is the beatific smile of a troubled man who at long last finds himself at peace. He glances down at the yellow glow of the ready-lamp, wondering if he will live long enough to see it turn green. Then he looks back at the niggergirl, who is on her feet, clapping and shaking her tail.

Look at me, he thinks. Look at me, Barbara. I want to be the last thing you ever see.

## 39

Barbara takes her eyes from the wonders onstage long enough to see if the bald man in the wheelchair is having as much fun as she is. He has become, for reasons she doesn't understand, *her* man in the wheelchair. Is it because he reminds her of someone? Surely that can't be, can it? The only crippled person she knows is Dustin Stevens at school, and he's just a little second-grader. Still, there's *something* familiar about the crippled bald man.

This whole evening has been like a dream, and what she sees now also seems dreamlike. At first she thinks the man in the wheelchair is waving to her, but that's not it. He's smiling . . . and he's giving her the finger. At first she can't believe it, but that's it, all right.

There's a woman approaching him, climbing the aisle stairs two by two, going so fast she's almost running. And behind her, almost on her heels . . . maybe all this really *is* a dream, because it looks like . . .

"Jerome?" Barbara tugs Tanya's sleeve to draw her attention away from the stage. "Mom, is that . . ."

Then everything happens.

40

Holly's initial thought is that Jerome could have gone first after all, because the bald and bespectacled man in the wheelchair isn't—for the moment, at least—even looking at the stage. He's turned away and staring at someone in the center section, and it appears to her that the vile son of a bitch is actually flipping that someone the bird. But it's too late to change places with Jerome, even though he's the one with the revolver. The man's got his hand beneath the framed picture in his lap and she's terribly afraid that means he's ready to do it. If so, there are only seconds left.

At least he's on the aisle, she thinks.

She has no plan, the extent of Holly's planning usually goes no further than what snack she might prepare to go with her evening movie, but for once her troubled mind is clear, and when she reaches the man they're looking for, the words that come out of her mouth seem exactly right. *Divinely* right. She has to bend down and shout to be heard over the driving, amplified beat of the band and the delirious shrieks of the girls in the audience.

*"Mike? Mike Sturdevant, is that you?"*

Brady turns from his contemplation of Barbara Robinson, startled, and as he does, Holly swings the knotted sock Bill Hodges has given her—his Happy Slapper—with adrenaline-loaded strength. It flies a short hard arc and connects with Brady's bald head just above the temple. She can't hear the sound it makes over the combined cacophony of the band and the fans, but she sees a section of skull the size of a small teacup cave in. His hands fly up, the one that was hidden knocking Frankie's picture to the floor, where the glass shatters. His eyes are sort of looking at her, except now they're rolled up in their sockets so that only the bottom halves of the irises show.

Next to Brady, the girl with the stick-thin legs is staring at Holly, shocked. So is Barbara Robinson. No one else is paying any attention. They're on their feet, clapping and swaying and singing along.

*"I WANT TO LOVE YOU MY WAY . . . WE'LL DRIVE THE
BEACHSIDE HIGHWAY . . ."*

Brady's mouth is opening and closing like the mouth of a fish
that has just been pulled from a river.

*"IT'S GONNA BE A NEW DAY . . . I'LL GIVE YOU KISSES
ON THE MIDWAY!"*

Jerome lays a hand on Holly's shoulder and shouts to be heard.
*"Holly! What's he got under his shirt?"*

She hears him—he's so close she can feel his breath puff against
her cheek with each word—but it's like one of those radio trans-
missions that come wavering in late at night, some DJ or gospel-
shouter halfway across the country.

"Here's a little present from Jibba-Jibba, Mike," she says, and
hits him again in exactly the same place, only even harder, deep-
ening the divot in his skull. The thin skin splits and the blood
comes, first in beads and then in a freshet, pouring down his neck
to color the top of his blue 'Round Here tee-shirt a muddy purple.
This time Brady's head snaps all the way over onto his right shoulder and he begins to shiver and shuffle his feet. She thinks, Like a
dog dreaming about chasing rabbits.

Before Holly can hit him again—and she really really wants
to—Jerome grabs her and spins her around. "He's out, Holly! He's
out! What are you doing?"

"Therapy," she says, and then all the strength runs out of her
legs. She sits down in the aisle. Her fingers relax on the knotted
end of the Happy Slapper, and it drops beside one sneaker.

Onstage, the band plays on.

## 41

A hand is tugging at his arm.

"Jerome? *Jerome!*"

He turns from Holly and the slumped form of Brady Hartsfield
to see his little sister, her eyes wide with dismay. His mom is right

behind her. In his current hyper state, Jerome isn't a bit surprised, but at the same time he knows the danger isn't over.

"What did you *do?*" a girl is shouting. "What did you *do* to him?"

Jerome wheels back the other way and sees the girl sitting one wheelchair in from the aisle reaching for Hartsfield. Jerome shouts, *"Holly! Don't let her do that!"*

Holly lurches to her feet, stumbles, and almost falls on top of Brady. It surely would have been the last fall of her life, but she manages to keep her feet and grab the wheelchair girl's hands. There's hardly any strength in them, and she feels an instant of pity. She bends down close and shouts to be heard. *"Don't touch him! He's got a bomb, and I think it's hot!"*

The wheelchair girl shrinks away. Perhaps she understands; perhaps she's only afraid of Holly, who's looking even wilder than usual just now.

Brady's shivers and twitches are strengthening. Holly doesn't like that, because she can see something, a dim yellow light, under his shirt. Yellow is the color of trouble.

"Jerome?" Tanya says. "What are you doing here?"

An usher is approaching. "Clear the aisle!" the usher shouts over the music. "You have to clear the aisle, folks!"

Jerome grasps his mother's shoulders. He pulls her to him until their foreheads are touching. "You have to get out of here, Mom. Take the girls and go. Right now. Make the usher go with you. Tell her your daughter is sick. Please don't ask questions."

She looks in his eyes and doesn't ask questions.

"Mom?" Barbara begins. "What . . ." The rest is lost in the crash of the band and the choral accompaniment from the audience. Tanya takes Barbara by the arm and approaches the usher. At the same time she's motioning for Hilda, Dinah, and Betsy to join her.

Jerome turns back to Holly. She's bent over Brady, who continues to shudder as cerebral storms rage inside his head. His feet tapdance, as if even in unconsciousness he's really feeling that goodtime 'Round Here beat. His hands fly aimlessly around, and when one of them approaches the dim yellow light under his tee-shirt, Jerome bats it away like a basketball guard rejecting a shot in the paint.

"I want to get out of here," the wheelchair girl moans. "I'm scared."

Jerome can relate to that—he also wants to get out of here, and he's scared to death—but for now she has to stay where she is. Brady has her blocked in, and they don't dare move him. Not yet.

Holly is ahead of Jerome, as she so often is. "You have to stay still for now, honey," she tells the wheelchair girl. "Chill out and enjoy the concert." She's thinking how much simpler this would be if she'd managed to kill him instead of just bashing his sicko brains halfway to Peru. She wonders if Jerome would shoot Harts-field if she asked him to. Probably not. Too bad. With all this noise, he could probably get away with it.

"Are you *crazy?*" the wheelchair girl asks wonderingly.

"People keep asking me that," Holly says, and—very gingerly—she begins to pull up Brady's tee-shirt. "Hold his hands," she tells Jerome.

"What if I can't?"

"Then OJ the motherfucker."

The sell-out audience is on its feet, swaying and clapping. The beachballs are flying again. Jerome takes one quick glance behind him and sees his mother leading the girls up the aisle to the exit, the usher accompanying them. That's one for our side, at least, he thinks, then turns back to the business at hand. He grabs Brady's flying hands and pins them together. The wrists are slippery with sweat. It's like holding a couple of struggling fish.

"I don't know what you're doing, but do it fast!" he shouts at Holly.

The yellow light is coming from a plastic gadget that looks like a customized TV remote control. Instead of numbered channel buttons, there's a white toggle-switch, the kind you use to flip on a light in your living room. It's standing straight up. There's a wire leading from the gadget. It goes under the man's butt.

Brady makes a grunting sound and suddenly there's an acidic smell. His bladder has let go. Holly looks at the peebag on his lap, but it doesn't seem to be attached to anything. She grabs it and hands it to the wheelchair girl. "Hold this."

"Eeuw, it's *pee*," the wheelchair girl says, and then: "It's *not* pee. There's something inside. It looks like clay."

"Put it down." Jerome has to shout to be heard over the music. "Put it on the floor. *Gently.*" Then, to Holly: "Hurry the hell up!"

Holly is studying the yellow ready-lamp. And the little white nub of the toggle-switch. She could push it forward or back and doesn't dare do either one, because she doesn't know which way is *off* and which way is *boom*.

She plucks Thing Two from where it was resting on Brady's stomach. It's like picking up a snake that's bloated with poison, and takes all her courage. "Hold his hands, Jerome, you just hold his hands."

"He's *slippery*," Jerome grunts.

We already knew that, Holly thinks. One slippery son of a bitch. One slippery *motherfucker*.

She turns the gadget over, willing her hands not to shake and trying not to think of the four thousand people who don't even know their lives now depend on poor messed-up Holly Gibney. She looks at the battery cover. Then, holding her breath, she slides it down and lets it drop to the floor.

Inside are two double-A batteries. Holly hooks a fingernail onto the ridge of one and thinks, God, if You're there, please let this work. For a moment she can't make her finger move. Then one of Brady's hands slips free of Jerome's grip and slaps her upside the head.

Holly jerks and the battery she's been worrying pops out of the compartment. She waits for the world to explode, and when it doesn't, she turns the remote control over. The yellow light has gone out. Holly begins to cry. She grabs the master wire and yanks it free of Thing Two.

"You can let him go n—" she begins, but Jerome already has.

He's hugging her so tight she can hardly breathe. Holly doesn't care. She hugs him back.

The audience is cheering wildly.

"They think they're cheering for the song, but they're really cheering for us," she manages to whisper in Jerome's ear. "They just don't know it yet. Now let me go, Jerome. You're hugging me too tight. Let me go before I pass out."

## 42

Hodges is still sitting on the crate in the storage area, and not alone. There's an elephant sitting on his chest. Something's happening. Either the world is going away from him or he's going away from the world. He thinks it's the latter. It's like he's inside a camera and the camera is going backwards on one of those dolly-track things. The world is as bright as ever, but getting smaller, and there's a growing circle of darkness around it.

He holds on with all the force of his will, waiting for either an explosion or no explosion.

One of the roadies is bending over him and asking if he's all right. "Your lips are turning blue," the roadie informs him. Hodges waves him away. He must listen.

Music and cheers and happy screams. Nothing else. At least not yet.

Hold on, he tells himself. Hold on.

"What?" the roadie asks, bending down again. "What?"

"I have to hold on," Hodges whispers, but now he can hardly breathe at all. The world has shrunk to the size of a fiercely gleaming silver dollar. Then even that is blotted out, not because he's lost consciousness but because someone is walking toward him. It's Janey, striding slow and hipshot. She's wearing his fedora tipped sexily over one eye. Hodges remembers what she said when he asked her how he had been so lucky as to end up in her bed: I have no regrets . . . Can we leave it at that?

419

Yeah, he thinks. *Yeah*. He closes his eyes, and tumbles off the crate like Humpty off his wall.

The roadie grabs him but can only soften the fall, not stop it. The other roadies gather.

"Who knows CPR?" asks the one who grabbed Hodges.

A roadie with a long graying ponytail steps forward. He's wearing a faded Judas Coyne tee-shirt, and his eyes are bright red. "I do, but man, I'm so stoned."

"Try it anyway."

The roadie with the ponytail drops to his knees. "I think this guy is on the way out," he says, but goes to work.

Upstairs, 'Round Here starts a new song, to the squeals and cheers of their female admirers. These girls will remember this night for the rest of their lives. The music. The excitement. The beachballs flying above the swaying, dancing crowd. They will read about the explosion that didn't happen in the newspapers, but to the young, tragedies that don't happen are only dreams.

The memories: they're the reality.


## 43


Hodges awakens in a hospital room, surprised to find himself still alive but not at all surprised to see his old partner sitting at his bedside. His first thought is that Pete—hollow-eyed, needing a shave, the points of his collar turning up so they almost poke his throat—looks worse than Hodges feels. His second thought is for Jerome and Holly.

"Did they stop it?" he rasps. His throat is bone-dry. He tries to sit up. The machines surrounding him begin to beep and scold. He lies back down, but his eyes never leave Pete Huntley's face. *"Did they?"*

"They did," Pete says. "The woman says her name is Holly Gibney, but I think she's really Sheena, Queen of the Jungle. That guy, the perp—"

"The perk," Hodges says. "He thinks of himself as the perk."

"Right now he doesn't think of himself as anything, and the doctors say his thinking days are probably over for good. Gibney belted the living shit out of him. He's in a deep coma. Minimal brain function. When you get on your feet again, you can visit him, if you want. He's three doors down."

"Where am I? County?"

"Kiner. The ICU."

"Where are Jerome and Holly?"

"Downtown. Answering a shitload of questions. Meanwhile, Sheena's mother is running around and threatening her own murder-spree if we don't stop harassing her daughter."

A nurse comes in and tells Pete he'll have to leave. She says something about Mr. Hodges's vital signs and doctor's orders. Hodges holds up his hand to her, although it's an effort.

"Jerome's a minor and Holly's got . . . issues. This is all on me, Pete."

"Oh, we know that," Pete says. "Yes indeed. This gives a whole new meaning to going off the reservation. What in God's name did you think you were doing, Billy?"

"The best I could," he says, and closes his eyes.

He drifts. He thinks of all those young voices, singing along with the band. They got home. They're okay. He holds that thought until sleep takes him under.

# THE PROCLAMATION

# THE OFFICE OF THE MAYOR

WHEREAS, Holly Rachel Gibney and Jerome Peter Robinson uncovered a plot to commit an act of Terrorism at the Mingo Auditorium adjacent to the Midwest Culture and Arts Complex; and

WHEREAS, in realizing that to inform MAC Security Personnel might cause said Terrorist to set off an explosive device of great power, said explosive device accompanied by several pounds of metal shrapnel, they raced to the Mingo Auditorium; and

WHEREAS, they did confront said Terrorist themselves, at great personal risk; and

WHEREAS, they did subdue said Terrorist and prevent great loss of life and injury; and

WHEREAS, they have done this City a great and heroic service,

NOW THEREFORE, I, Richard M. Tewky, Mayor, do hereby award Holly Rachel Gibney and Jerome Peter Robinson the Medal of Service, this city's highest honor, and proclaim that all City Services shall be rendered to them without charge for a period of ten (10) years; and

NOW THEREFORE, recognizing that some Acts are beyond repayment, we thank them with all our hearts.

In testimony thereof,
I set my signature and
The City Seal.

Richard M. Tewky
Mayor

# BLUE MERCEDES

1

On a warm and sunny day in late October of 2010, a Mercedes sedan pulls into the nearly empty lot at McGinnis Park, where Brady Hartsfield not so long ago sold ice cream to Little Leaguers. It snuggles up to a tidy little Prius. The Mercedes, once gray, has now been painted baby blue, and a second round of bodywork has removed a long scrape from the driver's side, inflicted when Jerome drove into the loading area behind the Mingo Auditorium before the gate was fully opened.

Holly's behind the wheel today. She looks ten years younger. Her long hair—formerly graying and untidy—is now a glossy black cap, courtesy of a visit to a Class A beauty salon, recommended to her by Tanya Robinson. She waves to the owner of the Prius, who's sitting at a table in the picnic area not far from the Little League fields.

Jerome gets out of the Mercedes, opens the trunk, and hauls out a picnic basket. "Jesus Christ, Holly," he says. "What have you got in here? Thanksgiving dinner?"

"I wanted to make sure there was plenty for everybody."

"You know he's on a strict diet, right?"

"You're not," she says. "You're a growing boy. Also, there's a bottle of champagne, so don't drop it."

From her pocket, Holly takes a box of Nicorette and pops a piece into her mouth.

"How's that going?" Jerome asks as they walk down the slope.

"I'm getting there," she says. "The hypnosis helps more than the gum."

"What if the guy tells you you're a chicken and gets you to run around his office, clucking?"

"First of all, my therapist is a she. Second of all, she wouldn't do that."

"How would *you* know?" Jerome asks. "You'd be, like, hypnotized."

"You're an idiot, Jerome. Only an idiot would want to take the *bus* down here with all this *food*."

"Thanks to the proclamation, we ride free. I like free."

Hodges, still wearing the suit he put on that morning (although the tie is now in his pocket), comes to meet them, moving slowly. He can't feel the pacemaker ticking away in his chest—he's been told they're very small now—but he senses it in there, doing its work. Sometimes he imagines it, and in his mind's eye it always looks like a smaller version of Hartsfield's gadget. Only his is supposed to stop an explosion instead of causing one.

"Kids," he says. Holly is no kid, but she's almost two decades younger than he is, and to Hodges that almost makes her one. He reaches for the picnic basket, but Jerome holds it away from him.

"Nuh-uh," he says. "I'll carry it. Your heart."

"My heart's fine," Hodges says, and according to his last checkup this is true, but he still can't quite believe it. He has an idea that anyone who's suffered a coronary feels the same way.

"And you look good," Jerome says.

"Yes," Holly agrees. "Thank God you got some new clothes. You looked like a scarecrow the last time I saw you. How much weight have you lost?"

"Thirty-five pounds," Hodges says, and the thought that follows, I wish Janey could see me now, sends a pang through his electronically regulated heart.

"Enough with the Weight Watchers," Jerome says. "Hols

brought champagne. I want to know if we have a reason to drink it. How did it go this morning?"

"The DA isn't going to prosecute anything. All charges dropped. Billy Hodges is good to go."

Holly throws herself into his arms and gives him a hug. Hodges hugs her back and kisses her cheek. With her short hair and her face fully revealed—for the first time since her childhood, although he doesn't know this—he can see her resemblance to Janey. This hurts and feels fine at the same time.

Jerome feels moved to call on Tyrone Feelgood Delight. "Massa Hodges, you free at last! Free at last! Great God A'mighty, you is free at last!"

"Stop talking like that, Jerome," Holly says. "It's juvenile." She takes the bottle of champagne from the picnic basket, along with a trio of plastic glasses.

"The district attorney escorted me into the chambers of Judge Daniel Silver, a guy who heard my testimony a great many times in my cop days," Hodges says. "He gave me a ten-minute tongue-lashing and told me that my reckless behavior had put four thousand lives at risk."

Jerome is indignant. "That's outrageous! You're the reason those people are still alive."

"No," Hodges says quietly. "You and Holly are the reason for that."

"If Hartsfield hadn't gotten in touch with you in the first place, the cops still wouldn't know him from Adam. And those people would be *dead*."

This may or may not be true, but in his own mind, Hodges is okay with how things turned out at the Mingo. What he's not okay with—and will never be—is Janey. Silver accused him of playing "a pivotal role" in her death, and he thinks that might be so. But he has no doubt that Hartsfield would have gone on to kill more, if not at the concert or the Careers Day at Embassy Suites, then somewhere else. He'd gotten a taste for it. So there's a rough equation here: Janey's life in exchange for the lives of all those hypothetical others. And if it *had* been the concert in that alternate (but very possible) reality, two of the victims would have been Jerome's mother and sister.

"What did you say back?" Holly asks. "What did you say back to him?"

"Nothing. When you're taken to the woodshed, the best thing you can do is wait out the whipping and shut up."

"That's why you weren't with us to get a medal, isn't it?" she asks. "And why you weren't on the proclamation. Those poops were punishing you."

"I imagine," Hodges says, although if the powers that be thought that was a punishment, they were wrong. The last thing in the world he wanted was to have a medal hung over his neck and to be presented with a key to the city. He was a cop for forty years. *That's* his key to the city.

"A shame," Jerome says. "You'll never get to ride the bus free."

"How are things on Lake Avenue, Holly? Settling down?"

"Better," Holly says. She's easing the cork out of the champagne bottle with all the delicacy of a surgeon. "I'm sleeping through the night again. Also seeing Dr. Leibowitz twice a week. She's helping a lot."

"And how are things with your mother?" This, he knows, is a touchy subject, but he feels he has to touch, just this once. "She still calling you five times a day, begging you to come back to Cincinnati?"

"She's down to twice a day," Holly says. "First thing in the morning, last thing at night. She's lonely. And I think more afraid for herself than she is for me. It's hard to change your life when you're old."

Tell me about it, Hodges thinks. "That's a very important insight, Holly."

"Dr. Leibowitz says habits are hard to break. It's hard for me to give up smoking, and it's hard for Mom to get used to living alone. Also to realize I don't have to be that fourteen-year-old-girl curled up in the bathtub for the rest of my life."

They're silent for awhile. A crow takes possession of the pitcher's rubber on Little League Field 3 and caws triumphantly.

Holly's partition from her mother was made possible by Janelle Patterson's will. The bulk of her estate—which came to Janey courtesy of another of Brady Hartsfield's victims—went to Uncle Henry Sirois and Aunt Charlotte Gibney, but Janey also left half a million dollars to Holly. It was in a trust fund to be administered by Mr. George Schron, the lawyer Janey had inherited from Olivia. Hodges has no idea when Janey did it. Or why she did it. He doesn't believe in premonitions, but . . .

But.

Charlotte had been dead set against Holly moving, claiming her daughter was not ready to live on her own. Given that Holly was closing in on fifty, that was tantamount to saying she would never be ready. Holly believed she was, and with Hodges's help, she had convinced Schron that she would be fine.

Being a heroine who had been interviewed on all the major networks no doubt helped with Schron. It didn't with her mother; in some ways it was Holly's status as heroine that dismayed that lady the most. Charlotte would never be entirely able to accept the idea that her precariously balanced daughter had played a crucial role (maybe *the* crucial role) in preventing a mass slaughter of the innocents.

By the terms of Janey's will, the condo apartment with its fabulous lake view is now owned jointly by Aunt Charlotte and Uncle Henry. When Holly asked if she could live there, at least to start with, Charlotte had refused instantly and adamantly. Her brother could not convince her to change her mind. It was Holly herself who had done that, saying she intended to stay in the city, and if her mother would not give in on the apartment, she'd find one in Lowtown.

"In the very worst part of Lowtown," she said. "Where I'll buy everything with cash. Which I will flash around ostentatiously."

That did it.

Holly's time in the city—the first extended period she has ever spent away from her mother—hasn't been easy, but her shrink gives her plenty of support, and Hodges visits her frequently. Far more important, Jerome visits frequently, and Holly is an even more frequent guest at the Robinson home on Teaberry Lane. Hodges believes that's where the real healing is taking place, not on Dr. Leibowitz's couch. Barbara has taken to calling her Aunt Holly.

"What about you, Bill?" Jerome asks. "Any plans?"

"Well," he says, smiling, "I was offered a job with Vigilant Guard Service, how about that?"

Holly clasps her hands together and bounces up and down on the picnic bench like a child. "Are you going to take it?"

"Can't," Hodges says.

"Heart?" Jerome asks.

"Nope. You have to be bonded, and Judge Silver shared with me this morning that my chances of being bonded and the chances of the Jews and Palestinians uniting to build the first interfaith space station are roughly equal. My dreams of getting a private investigator's license are equally kaput. However, a bail bondsman I've known for years has offered me a part-time job as a skip-tracer, and for that I don't need to be bonded. I can do it mostly from home, on my computer."

"I could help you," Holly says. "With the computer part, that is. I don't want to actually chase anybody. Once was enough."

"What about Hartsfield?" Jerome asks. "Anything new, or just the same?"

"Just the same," Hodges says.

"I don't care," Holly says. She sounds defiant, but for the first time since arriving at McGinnis Park, she's biting her lips. "I'd do it again." She clenches her fists. "Again again again!"

Hodges takes one of those fists and soothes it open. Jerome does the same with the other.

"Of course you would," Hodges says. "That's why the mayor gave you a medal."

"Not to mention free bus rides and trips to the museum," Jerome adds.

She relaxes, a little at a time. "Why should I ride the bus, Jerome? I have lots of money in trust, and I have Cousin Olivia's Mercedes. It's a wonderful car. And such low mileage!"

"No ghosts?" Hodges asks. He's not joking about this; he's honestly curious.

For a long time she doesn't reply, just looks up at the big German sedan parked beside Hodges's tidy Japanese import. At least she's stopped biting her lips.

"There were at first," she says, "and I thought I might sell it. I had it painted instead. That was *my* idea, not Dr. Leibowitz's." She looks at them proudly. "I didn't even ask her."

"And now?" Jerome is still holding her hand. He has come to love Holly, difficult as she sometimes is. They have both come to love her.

"Blue is the color of forgetting," she says. "I read that in a poem once." She pauses. "Bill, why are you crying? Are you thinking about Janey?"

Yes. No. Both.

"I'm crying because we're here," he says. "On a beautiful fall day that feels like summer."

"Dr. Leibowitz says crying is good," Holly says matter-of-factly. "She says tears wash the emotions."

"She could be right about that." Hodges is thinking about how Janey wore his hat. How she gave it just the right tilt. "Now are we going to have some of that champagne or not?"

Jerome holds the bottle while Holly pours. They hold up their glasses.

"To us," Hodges says.

They echo it. And drink.

2

On a rain-soaked evening in November of 2011, a nurse hurries down the corridor of the Lakes Region Traumatic Brain Injury

Clinic, an adjunct to John M. Kiner Memorial, the city's premier hospital. There are half a dozen charity cases at the TBI, including one who is infamous . . . although his infamy has already begun to fade with the passage of time.

The nurse is afraid the clinic's chief neurologist will have left, but he's still in the doctor's lounge, going through case files.

"You may want to come, Dr. Babineau," she says. "It's Mr. Hartsfield. He's awake." This only makes him look up, but what the nurse says next gets him to his feet. "He spoke to me."

"After seventeen months? Extraordinary. Are you sure?"

The nurse is flushed with excitement. "Yes, Doctor, absolutely."

"What did he say?"

"He says he has a headache. And he's asking for his mother."

September 14, 2013

# AUTHOR'S NOTE

While there is indeed such a thing as "stealing the peek" (as in PKE), it would be impossible to do so with any of the cars identified in the book, including the Mercedes-Benz SL500s made during the passive keyless entry age. SL500s, like all Benzes, are high-performance cars with high-performance security features.

Thanks are due to Russ Dorr and Dave Higgins, who provided research assistance. Also to my wife, Tabitha, who knows more about cell phones than I do, and to my son, the novelist Joe Hill, who helped me solve the problems Tabby pointed out. If I got it right, thank my support crew. If I got it wrong, chalk it up to my failure to understand.

Nan Graham of Scribner did her usual sterling editorial job, and my son Owen followed up with a valuable second pass. My agent, Chuck Verrill, is a Yankees fan, but I love him anyway.

# STEPHEN KING

# END OF WATCH

### A NOVEL

**SCRIBNER**

New York   London   Toronto   Sydney   New Delhi

SCRIBNER
An Imprint of Simon & Schuster, Inc.
1230 Avenue of the Americas
New York, NY 10020

First Scribner hardcover edition June 2016

SCRIBNER and design are registered trademarks of The Gale Group, Inc.,
used under license by Simon & Schuster, Inc., the publisher of this work.

For information about special discounts for bulk purchases,
please contact Simon & Schuster Special Sales at 1-866-506-1949
or business@simonandschuster.com.

The Simon & Schuster Speakers Bureau can bring authors to your live event.
For more information or to book an event, contact the Simon & Schuster Speakers Bureau
at 1-866-248-3049 or visit our website at www.simonspeakers.com.

Interior design by Erich Hobbing

Manufactured in the United States of America

1   3   5   7   9   10   8   6   4   2

Library of Congress Control Number: 2015039639

ISBN 978-1-5011-2974-2
ISBN 978-1-5011-3415-9 (ebook)

For Thomas Harris

Get me a gun
Go back into my room
I'm gonna get me a gun
One with a barrel or two
You know I'm better off dead than
Singing these suicide blues.
                    —*Cross Canadian Ragweed*

# END OF WATCH

# APRIL 10, 2009
# MARTINE STOVER

It's always darkest before the dawn.

This elderly chestnut occurred to Rob Martin as the ambulance he drove rolled slowly along Upper Marlborough Street toward home base, which was Firehouse 3. It seemed to him that whoever thought that one up really got hold of something, because it was darker than a woodchuck's asshole this morning, and dawn wasn't far away.

Not that this daybreak would be up to much even when it finally got rolling; call it dawn with a hangover. The fog was heavy and smelled of the nearby not-so-great Great Lake. A fine cold drizzle had begun to fall through it, just to add to the fun. Rob clicked the wiper control from intermittent to slow. Not far up ahead, two unmistakable yellow arches rose from the murk.

"The Golden Tits of America!" Jason Rapsis cried from the shotgun seat. Rob had worked with any number of paramedics over his fifteen years as an EMT, and Jace Rapsis was the best: easygoing when nothing was happening, unflappable and sharply focused when everything was happening at once. "We shall be fed! God bless capitalism! Pull in, pull in!"

1

"Are you sure?" Rob asked. "After the object lesson we just had in what that shit can do?"

The run from which they were now returning had been to one of the McMansions in Sugar Heights, where a man named Harvey Galen had called 911 complaining of terrible chest pains. They had found him lying on the sofa in what rich folks no doubt called "the great room," a beached whale of a man in blue silk pajamas. His wife was hovering over him, convinced he was going to punch out at any second.

"Mickey D's, Mickey D's!" Jason chanted. He was bouncing up and down in his seat. The gravely competent professional who had taken Mr. Galen's vitals (Rob right beside him, holding the First In Bag with its airway management gear and cardiac meds) had disappeared. With his blond hair flopping in his eyes, Jason looked like an overgrown kid of fourteen. "Pull in, I say!"

Rob pulled in. He could get behind a sausage biscuit himself, and maybe one of those hash brown thingies that looked like a baked buffalo tongue.

There was a short line of cars at the drive-thru. Rob snuggled up at the end of it.

"Besides, it's not like the guy had a for-real heart attack," Jason said. "Just OD'd on Mexican. Refused a lift to the hospital, didn't he?"

He had. After a few hearty belches and one trombone blast from his nether regions that had his social X-ray of a wife booking for the kitchen, Mr. Galen sat up, said he was feeling much better, and told them that no, he didn't think he needed to be transported to Kiner Memorial. Rob and Jason didn't think so, either, after listening to a recitation of what Galen had put away at Tijuana Rose the night before. His pulse was strong, and although his blood pressure was on the iffy side, it probably had been for years, and was currently stable. The automatic external defibrillator never came out of its canvas sack.

"I want two Egg McMuffins and two hash browns," Jason announced. "Black coffee. On second thought, make that three hash browns."

Rob was still thinking about Galen. "It was indigestion this time, but it'll be the real thing soon enough. Thunderclap infarction. What do you think he went? Three hundred? Three fifty?"

"Three twenty-five at least," Jason said, "and stop trying to spoil my breakfast."

Rob waved his arm at the Golden Arches rising through the lake-effect fog. "This place and all the other greasepits like it are half of what's wrong with America. As a medical person, I'm sure you know that. What you just ordered? That's nine hundred calories on the hoof, bro. Add sausage to the Egg McMuffdivers and you're riding right around thirteen hundred."

"What are *you* having, Doctor Health?"

"Sausage biscuit. Maybe two."

Jason clapped him on the shoulder. "My man!"

The line moved forward. They were two cars from the window when the radio beneath the in-dash computer blared. Dispatchers were usually cool, calm, and collected, but this one sounded like a radio shock jock after too many Red Bulls. "All ambulances and fire apparatus, we have an MCI! I repeat, MCI! This is a high-priority call for all ambulances and fire apparatus!"

MCI, short for mass casualty incident. Rob and Jason stared at each other. Plane crash, train crash, explosion, or act of terrorism. It almost had to be one of the four.

"Location is City Center on Marlborough Street, repeat City Center on Marlborough. Once again, this is an MCI with multiple deaths likely. Use caution."

Rob Martin's stomach tightened. No one told you to use caution when heading to a crash site or gas explosion. That left an act of terrorism, and it might still be in progress.

Dispatch was going into her spiel again. Jason hit the lights and siren while Rob cranked the wheel and pulled the Freightliner ambo into the lane that skirted the restaurant, clipping the bumper of the car ahead of him. They were just nine blocks from City Center, but if Al-Qaeda was shooting the place up with Kalashnikovs, the only thing they had to fire back with was their trusty external defibrillator.

Jason grabbed the mike. "Copy, Dispatch, this is 23 out of Firehouse 3, ETA just about six minutes."

Other sirens were rising from other parts of the city, but judging from the sound, Rob guessed their ambo was closest to the scene. A cast iron light had begun creeping into the air, and as they wheeled out of McDonald's and onto Upper Marlborough, a gray car knitted itself out of the gray fog, a big sedan with a dented hood and badly rusted grille. For a moment the HD headlights, on high beam, were pointed straight at them. Rob hit the dual air-horns and swerved. The car—it looked like a Mercedes, although he couldn't be sure—slewed back into its own lane and was then nothing but taillights dwindling into the fog.

"Jesus Christ, that was close," Jason said. "Don't suppose you got the license plate?"

"No." Rob's heart was beating so hard he could feel it pulsing on both sides of his throat. "I was busy saving our lives. Listen, how can there be multiple casualties at City Center? God isn't even up yet. It's gotta be closed."

"Could've been a bus crash."

"Try again. They don't start running until six."

Sirens. Sirens everywhere, beginning to converge like blips on a radar screen. A police car went bolting past them, but so far as Rob could tell, they were still ahead of the other ambos and fire trucks.

Which gives us a chance to be the first to get shot or blown up by a mad Arab shouting Allahu akbar, he thought. How nice for us.

But the job was the job, so he swung onto the steep drive leading up to the main city administration buildings and the butt-ugly auditorium where he'd voted until moving out to the suburbs.

"*Brake!*" Jason screamed. "*Jesus-fuck, Robbie, BRAKE!*"

Scores of people were coming at them from the fog, a few sprinting nearly out of control because of the incline. Some were screaming. One guy fell down, rolled, picked himself up, and ran on with his torn shirttail flapping beneath his jacket. Rob saw a woman with shredded hose, bloody shins, and only one shoe. He came to a panic stop, the nose of the ambo dipping, unsecured shit flying. Meds, IV bottles, and needle packs from a cabinet left unsecured—a violation of protocol—became projectiles. The stretcher they hadn't had to use for Mr. Galen bounced off one wall. A stethoscope found the pass-through, smacked the windshield, and fell onto the center console.

"Creep along," Jason said. "Just creep, okay? Let's not make it worse."

Rob feathered the gas and continued up the slope, now at walking pace. Still they came, hundreds, it seemed, some bleeding, most not visibly hurt, all of them terrified. Jason unrolled the passenger window and leaned out.

"*What's going on? Somebody tell me what's going on!*"

A man pulled up, red-faced and gasping. "It was a car. Tore through the crowd like a mowing machine. Fucking maniac just missed me. I don't know how many he hit. We were penned in like hogs because of the posts they set up to keep people in line. He did it on purpose and they're laying around up there like . . . like . . . oh man, dolls filled with blood. I saw at least four dead. There's gotta be more."

The guy started to move on, plodding now instead of running as the adrenaline faded. Jason unhooked his seatbelt and leaned out to call after him. "Did you see what color it was? The car that did it?"

The man turned back, pale and haggard. "Gray. Great big gray car."

Jason sat back down and looked at Rob. Neither of them had to say it out loud: it was the one they had swerved to avoid as they came out of McDonald's. And that hadn't been rust on its snout, after all.

"Go, Robbie. We'll worry about the mess in back later. Just get us to the prom and don't hit anyone, yeah?"

"Okay."

By the time Rob arrived in the parking lot, the panic was abating. Some people were leaving at a walk; others were trying to help those who had been struck by the gray car; a few, the assholes present in every crowd, were snapping photos or making movies with their phones. Hoping to go viral on YouTube, Rob assumed. Chrome posts with yellow DO NOT CROSS tape trailing from them lay on the pavement.

The police car that had passed them was parked close to the building, near a sleeping bag with a slim white hand protruding. A man lay sprawled crossways on top of the bag, which was in the center of a spreading bloodpuddle. The cop motioned the ambo forward, his beckoning arm seeming to stutter in the swinging blue glare of the lightbar atop his cruiser.

Rob grabbed the mobile data terminal and got out while Jason ran around to the rear of the ambo. He emerged with his First In Bag and the external defibrillator. The day continued to brighten, and Rob could read the sign flapping over the main doors of the auditorium: **1000 JOBS GUARANTEED!** *We Stand With the People of Our City!* **MAYOR RALPH KINSLER.**

Okay, that explained why there had been such a crowd, and so early in the morning. A job fair. Times were tough everywhere, had been since the economy had its own thunderclap infarction the year before, but they had been especially tough in this little lakefront city, where the jobs had started bleeding away even before the turn of the century.

Rob and Jason started toward the sleeping bag, but the cop shook his head. His face was ashen. "This guy and the two in the bag are dead. His wife and baby, I guess. He must have been trying to protect them." He made a brief sound deep in his throat, something between a burp and a retch, clapped a hand over his mouth, then took it away and pointed. "That lady there might still be with us."

The lady in question was sprawled on her back, her legs twisted away from her upper body at an angle that suggested serious trauma. The crotch of her dressy beige slacks was dark with urine. Her face—what remained of it—was smeared with grease. Part of her nose and most of her upper lip had been torn away. Her beautifully capped teeth were bared in an unconscious snarl. Her coat and half of her roll-neck sweater had also been torn away. Great dark bruises were flowering on her neck and shoulder.

Fucking car ran right over her, Rob thought. Squashed her like a chipmunk. He and Jason knelt beside her, snapping on blue gloves. Her purse lay nearby, marked by a partial tire track. Rob picked it up and heaved it into the back of the ambo, thinking the tire print might turn out to be evidence, or something. And of course the woman would want it.

If she lived, that was.

"She's stopped breathing, but I got a pulse," Jason said. "Weak and thready. Tear down that sweater."

Rob did it, and half the bra, straps shredded, came with it. He pushed the rest down to get it out of the way, then began chest compressions while Jason started an airway.

"She going to make it?" the cop asked.

"I don't know," Rob said. "We got this. You've got other problems. If more rescue vehicles come steaming up the drive like we almost did, someone's gonna get killed."

"Ah, man, there are people lying hurt everywhere. It's like a battlefield."

"Help the ones you can."

"She's breathing again," Jason said. "Get with me, Robbie, let's save a life here. Hop on the MDT and tell Kiner we're bringing in a possible neck fracture, spinal trauma, internal injuries, facial injuries, God knows what else. Condition critical. I'll feed you her vitals."

Rob made the call from the mobile data terminal while Jason continued squeezing the Ambu bag. Kiner ER answered immediately, the voice on the other end crisp and calm. Kiner was a Level I trauma center, what was sometimes called Presidential Class, and ready for something like this. They trained for it five times a year.

With the call-in made, he got an $O_2$ level (predictably lousy) and then grabbed both the rigid cervical collar and the orange backboard from the ambo. Other rescue vehicles were arriving now, and the fog had begun to lift, making the magnitude of the disaster clear.

All with one car, Rob thought. Who would believe it?

"Okay," Jason said. "If she ain't stable, it's the best we can do. Let's get her onboard."

Careful to keep the backboard perfectly horizontal, they lifted her into the ambo, placed her on the stretcher, and secured her. With her pallid, disfigured face framed by the cervical collar, she looked like one of the ritual female victims in a horror movie . . . except those were always young and nubile, and this woman looked to be in her forties or early fifties. Too old to be job-hunting, you would have said, and Rob only had to look at her to know she would never go job-hunting again. Or walk, from the look of her. With fantastic luck, she might avoid quadriplegia—assuming she got through this—but Rob guessed that her life from the waist down was over.

Jason knelt, slipped a clear plastic mask over her mouth and nose, and started the oxygen from the tank at the head of the stretcher. The mask fogged up, a good sign.

"Next thing?" Rob asked, meaning What else can I do?

"Find some epi in that junk that flew around, or get it out of my bag. I had a good pulse for awhile there, but it's gone thready again. Then fire this monkey up. With the injuries she's sustained, it's a miracle she's alive at all."

Rob found an ampoule of epinephrine under a tumbled box of bandages and handed it over. Then he slammed the back doors, dropped into the driver's seat, and got cranking. First to the scene at an MCI meant first to the hospital. That would improve this lady's slim chances just a little bit. Still, it was a fifteen-minute run even in light morning traffic, and he expected her to be dead by the time they got to Ralph M. Kiner Memorial Hospital. Given the extent of her injuries, that might be the best outcome.

But she wasn't.

• • •

At three o'clock that afternoon, long after their shift was over but too wired to even think about going home, Rob and Jason sat in the ready-room of Firehouse 3, watching ESPN on mute. They had made eight runs in all, but the woman had been the worst.

"Martine Stover, that was her name," Jason said at last. "She's still in surgery. I called while you were in the can."

"Any idea what her chances are?"

"No, but they didn't just let her crater, and that means something. Pretty sure she was there looking for an executive secretary's position. I went in her purse for ID—got a blood type from her driver's license—and found a whole sheaf of references. Looks like she was good at her job. Last position was at the Bank of America. Got downsized."

"And if she lives? What do you think? Just the legs?"

Jason stared at the TV, where basketball players were running fleetly up the court, and said nothing for a long while. Then: "If she lives, she's gonna be a quad."

"For sure?"

"Ninety-five percent."

A beer ad came on. Young people dancing up a storm in a bar. Everyone having fun. For Martine Stover, the fun was over. Rob tried to imagine what she would be facing if she pulled through. Life in a motorized wheelchair that she moved by puffing into a tube. Being fed either pureed gluck or through IV tubes. Respirator-assisted breathing. Shitting into a bag. Life in a medical twilight zone.

"Christopher Reeve didn't do so bad," Jason said, as if reading his thoughts. "Good attitude. Good role model. Kept his chin up. Even directed a movie, I think."

"Sure he kept his chin up," Rob said. "Thanks to a cervical collar that never came off. And he's dead."

"She was wearing her best clothes," Jason said. "Good slacks, expensive sweater, nice coat. Trying to get back on her feet. And some *bastard* comes along and takes it all."

"Did they get him yet?"

"Not the last I heard. When they do, I hope they string him up by the nutsack."

The following night, while delivering a stroke victim to Kiner Memorial, the partners checked on Martine Stover. She was in the ICU, and showing those signs of increasing brain function that signal the imminent recovery of consciousness. When she did come back, someone would have to give her the bad news: she was paralyzed from the chest down.

Rob Martin was just glad it wouldn't have to be him.

And the man the press was calling the Mercedes Killer still hadn't been caught.

# Z
## January 2016

1

A pane of glass breaks in Bill Hodges's pants pocket. This is followed by a jubilant chorus of boys, shouting *"That's a HOME RUN!"*

Hodges winces and jumps in his seat. Dr. Stamos is part of a four-doctor cabal, and the waiting room is full this Monday morning. Everyone turns to look at him. Hodges feels his face grow warm. "Sorry," he says to the room at large. "Text message."

"And a very loud one," remarks an old lady with thinning white hair and beagle dewlaps. She makes Hodges feel like a kid, and he's pushing seventy. She's hip to cell phone etiquette, though. "You should lower the volume in public places like this, or mute your phone entirely."

"Absolutely, absolutely."

The old lady goes back to her paperback (it's *Fifty Shades of Grey*, and not her first trip through it, from the battered look of the thing). Hodges drags his iPhone out of his pocket. The text is from Pete Huntley, his old partner when Hodges was on the cops. Pete is now on the verge of pulling the pin himself, hard to believe but true. End of watch is what they call it, but Hodges himself has found it impossible to give up watching. He now

15

runs a little two-person firm called Finders Keepers. He calls himself an independent skip-tracer, because he got into a little trouble a few years back and can't qualify for a private investigator's license. In this city you have to be bonded. But a PI is what he is, at least some of the time.

**Call me, Kermit. ASAP. Important.**

Kermit is Hodges's actual first name, but he goes by the middle one with most people; it keeps the frog jokes to a minimum. Pete makes a practice of using it, though. Finds it hilarious.

Hodges considers just pocketing the phone again (after muting it, if he can find his way to the DO NOT DISTURB control). He'll be called into Dr. Stamos's office at any minute, and he wants to get their conference over with. Like most elderly guys he knows, he doesn't like doctors' offices. He's always afraid they're going to find not just something wrong but something *really* wrong. Besides, it's not like he doesn't know what his ex-partner wants to talk about: Pete's big retirement bash next month. It's going to be at the Raintree Inn, out by the airport. Same place where Hodges's party took place, but this time he intends to drink a lot less. Maybe not at all. He had trouble with booze when he was active police, it was part of the reason his marriage crashed, but these days he seems to have lost his taste for alcohol. That's a relief. He once read a science fiction novel called *The Moon Is a Harsh Mistress*. He doesn't know about the moon, but would testify in court that whiskey is a harsh mistress, and that's made right here on earth.

He thinks it over, considers texting, then rejects the idea and gets up. Old habits are too strong.

The woman behind the reception desk is Marlee, according to her nametag. She looks about seventeen, and gives him a brilliant cheerleader's smile. "He'll be with you soon, Mr. Hodges,

I promise. We're just running a teensy bit behind. That's Monday for you."

"Monday, Monday, can't trust that day," Hodges says.

She looks blank.

"I'm going to step out for a minute, okay? Have to make a call."

"That's fine," Marlee says. "Just stand in front of the door. I'll give you a big wave if you're still out there when he's ready."

"That works." Hodges stops by the old lady on his way to the door. "Good book?"

She looks up at him. "No, but it's very energetic."

"So I've been told. Have you seen the movie?"

She stares up at him, surprised and interested. "There's a *movie?*"

"Yes. You should check it out."

Not that Hodges has seen it himself, although Holly Gibney— once his assistant, now his partner, a rabid film fan since her troubled childhood—tried to drag him to it. Twice. It was Holly who put the breaking pane of glass/home run text alert on his phone. She found it amusing. Hodges did, too . . . at first. Now he finds it a pain in the ass. He'll look up how to change it on the Internet. You can find anything on the Internet, he has discovered. Some of it is helpful. Some of it is interesting. Some of it is funny.

And some of it is fucking awful.

2

Pete's cell rings twice, and then his old partner is in his ear. "Huntley."

Hodges says, "Listen to me carefully, because you may be

tested on this material later. Yes, I'll be at the party. Yes, I'll make a few remarks after the meal, amusing but not raunchy, and I'll propose the first toast. Yes, I understand both your ex and your current squeeze will be there, but to my knowledge no one has hired a stripper. If anyone has, it would be Hal Corley, who is an idiot, and you'd have to ask hi—"

"Bill, stop. It's not about the party."

Hodges stops at once. It's not just the intertwined babble of voices in the background—police voices, he knows that even though he can't tell what they're saying. What stops him dead is that Pete has called him Bill, and that means it's serious shit. Hodges's thoughts fly first to Corinne, his own ex-wife, next to his daughter Alison, who lives in San Francisco, and then to Holly. Christ, if something has happened to Holly . . .

"What is it about, Pete?"

"I'm at the scene of what appears to be a murder-suicide. I'd like you to come out and take a look. Bring your sidekick with you, if she's available and agreeable. I hate to say this, but I think she might actually be a little smarter than you are."

Not any of his people. Hodges's stomach muscles, tightened as if to absorb a blow, loosen. Although the steady ache that's brought him to Stamos is still there. "Of course she is. Because she's younger. You start to lose brain cells by the millions after you turn sixty, a phenomenon you'll be able to experience for yourself in another couple of years. Why would you want an old carthorse like me at a murder scene?"

"Because this is probably my last case, because it's going to blow up big in the papers, and because—don't swoon—I actually value your input. Gibney's, too. And in a weird way, you're both connected. That's probably a coincidence, but I'm not entirely sure."

"Connected how?"

"Does the name Martine Stover ring a bell?"

For a moment it doesn't, then it clicks in. On a foggy morning in 2009, a maniac named Brady Hartsfield drove a stolen Mercedes-Benz into a crowd of job-seekers at City Center, downtown. He killed eight and seriously injured fifteen. In the course of their investigation, Detectives K. William Hodges and Peter Huntley interviewed a great many of those who had been present on that foggy morning, including all the wounded survivors. Martine Stover had been the toughest to talk to, and not only because her disfigured mouth made her all but impossible to understand for anyone except her mother. Stover was paralyzed from the chest down. Later, Hartsfield had written Hodges an anonymous letter. In it he referred to her as "your basic head on a stick." What made that especially cruel was the radioactive nugget of truth inside the ugly joke.

"I can't see a quadriplegic as a murderer, Pete . . . outside an episode of *Criminal Minds*, that is. So I assume—?"

"Yeah, the mother was the doer. First she offed Stover, then herself. Coming?"

Hodges doesn't hesitate. "I am. I'll pick up Holly on the way. What's the address?"

"1601 Hilltop Court. In Ridgedale."

Ridgedale is a commuter suburb north of the city, not as pricey as Sugar Heights, but still pretty nice.

"I can be there in forty minutes, assuming Holly's at the office."

And she will be. She's almost always at her desk by eight, sometimes as early as seven, and apt to be there until Hodges yells at her to go home, fix herself some supper, and watch a movie on her computer. Holly Gibney is the main reason Finders Keepers is in the black. She's an organizational genius, she's a computer wizard, and the job is her life. Well, along with Hodges and the Robinson family, especially Jerome and Barbara. Once, when Jerome and Barbie's mom called Holly an honorary Robinson, she lit up like the sun on a summer afternoon. It's a thing Holly does more often than she used to, but still not enough to suit Hodges.

"That's great, Kerm. Thanks."

"Have the bodies been transported?"

"Off to the morgue as we speak, but Izzy's got all the pictures on her iPad." He's talking about Isabelle Jaynes, who has been Pete's partner since Hodges retired.

"Okay. I'll bring you an éclair."

"There's a whole bakery here already. Where are you, by the way?"

"Nowhere important. I'll get with you as soon as I can."

Hodges ends the call and hurries down the hall to the elevator.

3

Dr. Stamos's eight-forty-five patient finally reappears from the exam area at the back. Mr. Hodges's appointment was for nine, and it's now nine thirty. The poor guy is probably impatient to do his business here and get rolling with the rest of his day. She looks out in the hall and sees Hodges talking on his cell.

Marlee rises and peeks into Stamos's office. He's sitting behind his desk with a folder open in front of him. **KERMIT WILLIAM HODGES** is computer-printed on the tab. The doctor is studying something in the folder and rubbing his temple, as though he has a headache.

"Dr. Stamos? Shall I call Mr. Hodges in?"

He looks up at her, startled, then at his desk clock. "Oh God, yes. Mondays suck, huh?"

"Can't trust that day," she says, and turns to go.

"I love my job, but I hate this part of it," Stamos says.

It's Marlee's turn to be startled. She turns to look at him.

"Never mind. Talking to myself. Send him in. Let's get this over with."

Marlee looks out into the hall just in time to see the elevator door closing at the far end.

<br>

4

<br>

Hodges calls Holly from the parking garage next to the medical center, and when he gets to the Turner Building on Lower Marlborough, where their office is located, she's standing out front with her briefcase planted between her sensible shoes. Holly Gibney: late forties now, tallish and slim, brown hair usually scrooped back in a tight bun, this morning wearing a bulky North Face parka with the hood up and framing her small face. You'd call that face plain, Hodges thinks, until you saw the eyes, which are beautiful and full of intelligence. And you might not really see them for a long time, because as a rule, Holly Gibney doesn't do eye contact.

Hodges slides his Prius to the curb and she jumps in, taking off her gloves and holding her hands up to the passenger-side heating vent. "It took you a very long time to get here."

"Fifteen minutes. I was on the other side of town. I caught all the red lights."

"It was *eighteen* minutes," Holly informs him as Hodges pulls into traffic. "Because you were speeding, which is counterproductive. If you keep your speed to exactly twenty miles an hour, you can catch almost all the lights. They're timed. I've told you that several times. Now tell me what the doctor said. Did you get an A on your tests?"

Hodges considers his options, which are only two: tell the truth or prevaricate. Holly nagged him into going to the doctor because he's been having stomach issues. Just pressure at first, now some pain. Holly may have personality problems, but she's a very efficient nagger. Like a dog with a bone, Hodges sometimes thinks.

"The results weren't back yet." This is not quite a lie, he tells himself, because they weren't back to *me* yet.

She looks at him doubtfully as he merges onto the Crosstown Expressway. Hodges hates it when she looks at him that way.

"I'll keep after this," he says. "Trust me."

"I do," she says. "I do, Bill."

That makes him feel even worse.

She bends, opens her briefcase, and takes out her iPad. "I looked up some stuff while I was waiting for you. Want to hear it?"

"Hit me."

"Martine Stover was fifty at the time Brady Hartsfield crippled her, which would make her fifty-six as of today. I suppose she could be fifty-seven, but since this is only January, I think that's very unlikely, don't you?"

"Odds are against, all right."

"At the time of the City Center event, she was living with her mother in a house on Sycamore Street. Not far from Brady Hartsfield and *his* mother, which is sort of ironic when you think of it."

Also close to Tom Saubers and his family, Hodges muses. He and Holly had a case involving the Saubers family not long ago, and that one also had a connection to what the local newspaper had taken to calling the Mercedes Massacre. There were all sorts of connections, when you thought about it, perhaps the strangest being that the car Hartsfield had used as a murder weapon belonged to Holly Gibney's cousin.

"How does an elderly woman and her severely crippled daughter make the jump from the Tree Streets to Ridgedale?"

"Insurance. Martine Stover had not one or two whopping big policies, but three. She was sort of a freak about insurance." Hodges reflects that only Holly could say that approvingly. "There were several articles about her afterward, because she was the most badly hurt of those who survived. She said she knew that if she didn't get a job at City Center, she'd have to start cashing her policies in, one by one. After all, she was a single woman with a widowed, unemployed mother to support."

"Who ended up taking care of her."

Holly nods. "Very strange, very sad. But at least there was a financial safety net, which is the purpose of insurance. They even moved up in the world."

"Yes," Hodges says, "but now they're out of it."

To this Holly makes no reply. Up ahead is the Ridgedale exit. Hodges takes it.

5

Pete Huntley has put on weight, his belly hanging over his belt buckle, but Isabelle Jaynes is as smashing as ever in her tight faded jeans and blue blazer. Her misty gray eyes go from Hodges to Holly and then back to Hodges again.

"You've gotten thin," she says. This could be either a compliment or an accusation.

"He's having stomach problems, so he had some tests," Holly says. "The results were supposed to be in today, but—"

"Let's not go there, Hols," Hodges says. "This isn't a medical consultation."

"You two are more like an old married couple every day," Izzy says.

Holly replies in a matter-of-fact voice. "Marriage to Bill would spoil our working relationship."

Pete laughs and Holly shoots him a puzzled glance as they step inside the house.

It's a handsome Cape Cod, and although it's on top of a hill and the day is cold, the house is toasty-warm. In the foyer, all four of them put on thin rubber gloves and bootees. How it all comes back, Hodges thinks. As if I was never away.

In the living room there's a painting of big-eyed waifs hung on one wall, a big-screen TV hung on another. There's an easy chair in front of the tube with a coffee table beside it. On the table is a careful fan of celebrity mags like *OK!* and scandal rags like *Inside View*. In the middle of the room there are two deep grooves in the rug. Hodges thinks, This is where they sat in the evenings to watch TV. Or maybe all day long. Mom in her easy chair, Martine in her wheelchair. Which must have weighed a ton, judging by those marks.

"What was her mother's name?" he asks.

"Janice Ellerton. Husband James died twenty years ago, according to . . ." Old-school like Hodges, Pete carries a notebook instead of an iPad. Now he consults it. "According to Yvonne Carstairs. She and the other aide, Georgina Ross, found the bodies when they arrived this morning shortly before six. They got paid extra for turning up early. The Ross woman wasn't much help—"

"She was gibbering," Izzy says. "Carstairs was okay, though. Kept her head throughout. Called the police right away, and we were on-scene by six forty."

"How old was Mom?" Hodges asks.

"Don't know exactly yet," Pete says, "but no spring chicken."

"She was seventy-nine," Holly says. "One of the news stories I searched while I was waiting for Bill to pick me up said she was seventy-three when the City Center Massacre happened."

"Awfully long in the tooth to be taking care of a quadriplegic daughter," Hodges says.

"She was in good shape, though," Isabelle says. "At least according to Carstairs. Strong. And she had plenty of help. There was money for it because—"

"—of the insurance," Hodges finishes. "Holly filled me in on the ride over."

Izzy gives Holly a glance. Holly doesn't notice. She's measuring the room. Taking inventory. Sniffing the air. Running a palm across the back of Mom's easy chair. Holly has emotional problems, she's breathtakingly literal, but she's also open to stimuli in a way few people are.

Pete says, "There were two aides in the morning, two in the afternoon, two in the evening. Seven days a week. Private company called"—back to the notebook—"Home Helpers. They did all the heavy lifting. There's also a housekeeper, Nancy Alderson, but apparently she's off. Note on the kitchen calendar says *Nancy in Chagrin Falls*. There's a line drawn through today, Tuesday, and Wednesday."

Two men, also wearing gloves and bootees, come down the hall. From the late Martine Stover's part of the house, Hodges assumes. Both are carrying evidence cases.

"All done in the bedroom and bathroom," one of them says.

"Anything?" Izzy asks.

"About what you'd expect," the other says. "We got quite a few white hairs from the tub, not unusual considering that's where the old lady highsided it. There was also excrement in the tub, but just a trace. Also as you would expect." Off Hodges's questioning look, the tech adds, "She was wearing continence pants. The lady did her homework."

"Oough," Holly says.

The first tech says, "There's a shower chair, but it's in the corner with extra towels stacked on the seat. Looks like it's never been used."

"They would have given her sponge baths," Holly says.

She still looks grossed out, either by the thought of continence pants or shit in the bathtub, but her eyes continue to flick everywhere. She may ask a question or two, or drop a comment, but mostly she'll remain silent, because people intimidate her, especially in close quarters. But Hodges knows her well—as well as anyone can, at least—and he can tell she's on high alert.

Later she will talk, and Hodges will listen closely. During the Saubers case the year before, he learned that listening to Holly pays dividends. She thinks outside the box, sometimes way outside it, and her intuitions can be uncanny. And although fearful by nature—God knows she has her reasons—she can be brave. Holly is the reason Brady Hartsfield, aka Mr. Mercedes, is now in the Lakes Region Traumatic Brain Injury Clinic at Kiner Memorial. Holly used a sock loaded with ball bearings to crush in his skull before Hartsfield could touch off a disaster much greater than the one at City Center. Now he's in a twilight world the head neuro guy at the Brain Injury Clinic refers to as "a persistent vegetative state."

"Quadriplegics can shower," Holly amplifies, "but it's diffi-

26

cult for them because of all the life-support equipment they're hooked up to. So mostly it's sponge baths."

"Let's go in the kitchen, where it's sunny," Pete says, and to the kitchen they go.

The first thing Hodges notices is the dish drainer, where the single plate that held Mrs. Ellerton's last meal has been left to dry. The countertops are sparkling, and the floor looks clean enough to eat on. Hodges has an idea that her bed upstairs will have been neatly made. She may even have vacuumed the carpets. And then there's the continence pants. She took care of the things she could take care of. As a man who once seriously considered suicide himself, Hodges can relate.

6

Pete, Izzy, and Hodges sit at the kitchen table. Holly merely hovers, sometimes standing behind Isabelle to look at the collection of photos on Izzy's iPad labeled ELLERTON/STOVER, sometimes poking into the various cupboards, her gloved fingers as light as moths.

Izzy takes them through it, swiping at the screen as she talks.

The first photo shows two middle-aged women. Both are beefy and broad-shouldered in their red nylon Home Helpers uniforms, but one of them—Georgina Ross, Hodges presumes—is crying and gripping her shoulders so that her forearms press against her breasts. The other one, Yvonne Carstairs, is apparently made of sterner stuff.

"They got here at five forty-five," Izzy says. "They have a key to let themselves in, so they don't have to knock or ring. Sometimes Martine slept until six thirty, Carstairs says. Mrs. Ellerton is always up, gets up around five, she told them, had to have her coffee first thing, only this morning she's not up and there's no smell of coffee. So they think the old lady overslept for once, good for her. They tiptoe into Stover's bedroom, right down the hall, to see if *she's* awake yet. This is what they find."

Izzy swipes to the next picture. Hodges waits for another *oough* from Holly, but she is silent and studying the photo closely. Stover is in bed with the covers pulled down to her knees. The damage to her face was never repaired, but what remains looks peaceful enough. Her eyes are closed and her twisted hands are clasped together. A feeding tube juts from her scrawny abdomen. Her wheelchair—which to Hodges looks more like an astronaut's space capsule—stands nearby.

"In Stover's bedroom there *was* a smell. Not coffee, though. Booze."

Izzy swipes. Here is a close-up of Stover's bedside table. There are neat rows of pills. There's a grinder to turn them to powder, so that Stover could ingest them. Standing among them and looking wildly out of place is a fifth of Smirnoff Triple Distilled vodka and a plastic syringe. The vodka bottle is empty.

"The lady was taking zero chances," Pete says. "Smirnoff Triple Distilled is a hundred and fifty proof."

"I imagine she wanted it to be as quick for her daughter as possible," Holly says.

"Good call," Izzy says, but with a notable lack of warmth. She doesn't care for Holly, and Holly doesn't care for her. Hodges is aware of this but has no idea why. And since they rarely see Isabelle, he's never bothered to ask Holly about it.

"Have you got a close-up of the grinder?" Holly asks.

"Of course." Izzy swipes, and in the next photo, the pill grinder looks as big as a flying saucer. A dusting of white powder remains in the cup. "We won't be sure until later this week, but we think it's oxycodone. Her scrip was refilled just three weeks ago, according to the label, but that bottle is as empty as the vodka bottle."

She goes back to Martine Stover, eyes closed, scrawny hands clasped as if in prayer.

"Her mother ground up the pills, funneled them into the bottle, and poured the vodka down Martine's feeding tube. Probably more efficient than lethal injection."

Izzy swipes again. This time Holly *does* say "Oough," but she doesn't look away.

The first photo of Martine's handicap-equipped bathroom is a wide shot, showing the extra-low counter with its basin, the extra-low towel racks and cabinets, the jumbo shower-tub combination. The slider in front of the shower is closed, the tub in full view. Janice Ellerton reclines in water up to her shoulders, wearing a pink nightgown. Hodges guesses it would have ballooned around her as she lowered herself in, but in this crime scene photo it clings to her thin body. There is a plastic bag over her head, secured by the kind of terrycloth belt that goes with a bathrobe. A length of tubing snakes from beneath it, attached to a small canister lying on the tile floor. On the side of the canister is a decal that shows laughing children.

"Suicide kit," Pete says. "She probably learned how to make it on the Internet. There are plenty of sites that explain how to do it, complete with pix. The water in the tub was cool when we got here, but probably warm when she climbed in."

"Supposed to be soothing," Izzy puts in, and although she doesn't say *oough*, her face tightens in a momentary expression of distaste as she swipes to the next picture: a close-up of Janice Ellerton. The bag had fogged with the condensation of her final breaths, but Hodges can see that her eyes were closed. She also went out looking peaceful.

"The canister contained helium," Pete says. "You can buy it at any of the big discount stores. You're supposed to use it to blow up the balloons at little Buster's birthday party, but it works just as well to kill yourself with, once you have a bag over your head. Dizziness is followed by disorientation, at which point you probably couldn't get the bag off even if you changed your mind. Next comes unconsciousness, followed by death."

"Go back to the last one," Holly says. "The one that shows the whole bathroom."

"Ah," Pete says. "Dr. Watson may have seen something."

Izzy goes back. Hodges leans closer, squinting—his near vision isn't what it once was. Then he sees what Holly saw. Next to a thin gray power cord plugged into one of the outlets, there's a Magic Marker. Someone—Ellerton, he presumes, because her daughter's writing days were long over—drew a single large letter on the counter: **Z**.

"What do you make of it?" Pete asks.

Hodges considers. "It's her suicide note," he says at last. "Z is the final letter of the alphabet. If she'd known Greek, it might have been omega."

"That's what I think, too," Izzy says. "Kind of elegant, when you think of it."

"Z is also the mark of Zorro," Holly informs them. "He was a masked Mexican cavalier. There have been a great many Zorro movies, one starring Anthony Hopkins as Don Diego, but it wasn't very good."

"Do you find that relevant?" Izzy asks. Her face expresses polite interest, but there's a barb in her tone.

"There was also a television series," Holly goes on. She's looking at the photo as though hypnotized by it. "It was produced by Walt Disney, back in the black-and-white days. Mrs. Ellerton might have watched it when she was a girl."

"Are you saying she maybe took refuge in childhood memories while she was getting ready to off herself?" Pete sounds dubious, which is how Hodges feels. "I guess it's possible."

"Bullshit, more likely," Izzy says, rolling her eyes.

Holly takes no notice. "Can I look in the bathroom? I won't touch anything, even with these." She holds up her small gloved hands.

"Be our guest," Izzy says at once.

In other words, Hodges thinks, buzz off and let the adults talk. He doesn't care for Izzy's 'tude when it comes to Holly, but since it seems to bounce right off her, he sees no reason to make an issue of it. Besides, Holly really is a bit skitzy this morning, going off in all directions. Hodges supposes it was the pictures. Dead people never look more dead than in police photos.

She wanders off to check out the bathroom. Hodges sits back, hands laced at the nape of his neck, elbows winged out. His troublesome gut hasn't been quite so troublesome this morning, maybe because he switched from coffee to tea. If so, he'll have to stock up on PG Tips. Hell, *buy* stock. He's really tired of the constant stomachache.

"Want to tell me what we're doing here, Pete?"

Pete raises his eyebrows and tries to look innocent. "Whatever can you mean, Kermit?"

"You were right when you said this would make the paper. It's the kind of sad soap-opera shit people love, it makes their own lives look better to them—"

"Cynical but probably true," Izzy says with a sigh.

"—but any connection to the Mercedes Massacre is casual

rather than causal." Hodges isn't entirely sure that means what he thinks it means, but it sounds good. "What you've got here is your basic mercy killing committed by an old lady who just couldn't stand to see her daughter suffer anymore. Probably Ellerton's last thought when she turned on the helium was I'll be with you soon, honey, and when I walk the streets of heaven, you'll be walking right beside me."

Izzy snorts at that, but Pete looks pale and thoughtful. Hodges suddenly remembers that a long time ago, maybe thirty years, Pete and his wife lost their first child, a baby daughter, to SIDS.

"It's sad, and the papers lap it up for a day or two, but it happens somewhere in the world every day. Every hour, for all I know. So tell me what the deal is."

"Probably nothing. Izzy says it *is* nothing."

"Izzy does," she confirms.

"Izzy probably thinks I'm going soft in the head as I approach the finish line."

"Izzy doesn't. Izzy just thinks that it's time you stop letting the bee known as Brady Hartsfield buzz around in your bonnet."

She switches those misty gray eyes to Hodges.

"Ms. Gibney there may be a bundle of nervous tics and strange associations, but she stopped Hartsfield's clock most righteously, and I give her full credit for it. He's zonked out in that brain trauma clinic at Kiner, where he'll probably stay until he catches pneumonia and dies, thereby saving the state a whole potful of money. He's never going to stand trial for what he did, we all know that. You didn't catch him for the City Center thing, but Gibney stopped him from blowing up two thousand kids at Mingo Auditorium a year later. You guys need to accept that. Call it a win and move on."

"Whew," Pete says. "How long have you been holding that in?"

Izzy tries not to smile, but can't help it. Pete smiles in return, and Hodges thinks, They work as well together as Pete and I did. Shame to break up that combination. It really is.

"Quite awhile," Izzy says. "Now go on and tell him." She turns to Hodges. "At least it's not little gray men from *The X-Files*."

"So?" Hodges asks.

"Keith Frias and Krista Countryman," Pete says. "Both were also at City Center on the morning of April tenth, when Hartsfield did his thing. Frias, age nineteen, lost most of his arm, plus four broken ribs and internal injuries. He also lost seventy percent of the vision in his right eye. Countryman, age twenty-one, suffered broken ribs, a broken arm, and spinal injuries that resolved after all sorts of painful therapy I don't even want to think about."

Hodges doesn't, either, but he's brooded over Brady Hartsfield's victims many times. Mostly on how the work of seventy wicked seconds could change the lives of so many for years . . . or, in the case of Martine Stover, forever.

"They met in weekly therapy sessions at a place called Recovery Is You, and fell in love. They were getting better . . . slowly . . . and planned to get married. Then, in February of last year, they committed suicide together. In the words of some old punk song or other, they took a lot of pills and they died."

This makes Hodges think of the grinder on the table beside Stover's hospital bed. The grinder with its residue of oxycodone. Mom dissolved all of the oxy in the vodka, but there must have been plenty of other narcotic medications on that table. Why had she gone to all the trouble of the plastic bag and the helium when she could have swallowed a bunch of Vicodin, chased it with a bunch of Valium, and called it good?

"Frias and Countryman were the sort of youngster suicides that also happen every day," Izzy says. "The parents were doubtful about the marriage. Wanted them to wait. And they could hardly run off together, could they? Frias could barely walk, and neither of them had jobs. There was enough insurance to pay for the weekly therapy sessions and to kick in for groceries at their respective homes, but nothing like the kind of Cadillac coverage Martine Stover had. Bottom line, shit happens. You can't even call it a coincidence. Badly hurt people get depressed, and sometimes depressed people kill themselves."

"Where did they do it?"

"The Frias boy's bedroom," Pete says. "While his parents were on a day trip to Six Flags with his little brother. They took the pills, crawled into the sack, and died in each other's arms, just like Romeo and Juliet."

"Romeo and Juliet died in a tomb," Holly says, coming back into the kitchen. "In the Franco Zeffirelli film, which is really the best—"

"Yes, okay, point taken," Pete says. "Tomb, bedroom, at least they rhyme."

Holly is holding the *Inside View* that was on the coffee table, folded to show a picture of Johnny Depp that makes him look either drunk, stoned, or dead. Has she been in the living room, reading a scandal sheet all this time? If so, she really is having an off day.

Pete says, "Have you still got the Mercedes, Holly? The one Hartsfield stole from your cousin Olivia?"

"No." Holly sits down with the folded newspaper in her lap and her knees primly together. "I traded it last November for a Prius like Bill's. It used a great deal of gas and was not eco-friendly. Also, my therapist recommended it. She said that after a year and a half, I had surely exorcised its hold over me, and its therapeutic value was gone. Why are you interested in that?"

Pete sits forward in his chair and clasps his hands together between his spread knees. "Hartsfield got into that Mercedes by using an electronic gizmo to unlock the doors. Her spare key was in the glove compartment. Maybe he knew it was there, or maybe the slaughter at City Center was a crime of opportunity. We'll never know for sure."

And Olivia Trelawney, Hodges thinks, was a lot like her cousin Holly: nervy, defensive, most definitely not a social animal. Far from stupid, but hard to like. We were sure she left her Mercedes unlocked with the key in the ignition, because that was the simplest explanation. And because, on some primitive level where logical thinking has no power, we *wanted* that to be the explanation. She was a pain in the ass. We saw her repeated denials as a haughty refusal to take responsibility for her own carelessness. The key in her purse, the one she showed us? We assumed that was just her spare. We hounded her, and when the press got her name, *they* hounded her. Eventually, she started to believe she'd done what we believed she'd done: enabled a monster with mass murder on his mind. None of us considered the idea that a computer geek might have cobbled together that unlocking gizmo. Including Olivia Trelawney herself.

"But we weren't the only ones who hounded her."

Hodges is unaware that he's spoken aloud until they all turn to look at him. Holly gives him a small nod, as if they have been following the exact same train of thought. Which wouldn't be all that surprising.

Hodges goes on. "It's true that we never believed her, no matter how many times she told us she took her key and locked her car, so we bear part of the responsibility for what she did, but

Hartsfield went after her with malice aforethought. That's what you're driving at, isn't it?"

"Yes," Pete says. "He wasn't content with stealing her Mercedes and using it as a murder weapon. He got inside her head, even bugged her computer with an audio program full of screams and accusations. And then there's you, Kermit."

Yes. There was him.

Hodges had received an anonymous poison pen letter from Hartsfield when he was at an absolute low point, living in an empty house, sleeping badly, seeing almost no one except Jerome Robinson, the kid who cut his grass and did general repairs around the place. Suffering from a common malady in career cops: end-of-watch depression.

*Retired police have an extremely high suicide rate*, Brady Hartsfield had written. This was before they began communicating by the twenty-first century's preferred method, the Internet. *I wouldn't want you to start thinking about your gun. But you are thinking of it, aren't you?* It was as if Hartsfield had sniffed out Hodges's thoughts of suicide and tried to push him over the edge. It had worked with Olivia Trelawney, after all, and he'd gotten a taste for it.

"When I first started working with you," Pete says, "you told me repeat criminals were sort of like Turkish rugs. Do you remember that?"

"Yes." It was a theory Hodges had expounded to a great many cops. Few listened, and judging by her bored expression, he guessed Isabelle Jaynes would have been one of those who did not. Pete had.

"They create the same pattern, over and over. Ignore the slight variations, you said, and look for the underlying sameness. Because even the smartest doers—like Turnpike Joe, who killed all those women at rest stops—seem to have a switch inside their brains that's stuck on Repeat. Brady Hartsfield was a connoisseur of suicide—"

"He was an *architect* of suicide," Holly says. She's looking down at the newspaper, her brow furrowed, her face paler than ever. It's hard for Hodges to relive the Hartsfield business (at least he's finally managed to quit going to see the son of a bitch in his room in the Brain Injury Clinic), but it's even harder for Holly. He hopes she won't backslide and start smoking again, but it wouldn't surprise him if she did.

"Call it what you want, but the pattern was there. He goaded his own mother into suicide, for Christ's sake."

Hodges says nothing to this, although he has always doubted Pete's belief that Deborah Hartsfield killed herself when she discovered—perhaps by accident—that her son was the Mercedes Killer. For one thing, they have no proof that Mrs. Hartsfield ever did find out. For another, it was gopher poison the woman ingested, and that had to be a nasty way to go. It's possible that Brady murdered his mother, but Hodges has never really believed that, either. If he loved anyone, it was her. Hodges thinks the gopher poison might have been intended for someone else . . . and perhaps not for a person at all. According to the autopsy, it had been mixed in with hamburger, and if there was anything dogs liked, it was a ball of raw ground meat.

The Robinsons have a dog, a loveable floppy-eared mutt. Brady would have seen him many times, because he was watching Hodges's house and because Jerome usually brought the dog along when he cut Hodges's lawn. The gopher poison could have been meant for Odell. This is an idea Hodges has never mentioned to any of the Robinsons. Or to Holly, for that matter. And hey, it's probably bullshit, but in Hodges's opinion, it's as likely as Pete's idea that Brady's mom offed herself.

Izzy opens her mouth, then shuts it when Pete holds up a hand to forestall her—he is, after all, still the senior member of their partnership, and by quite a few years.

"Izzy's getting ready to say Martine Stover was murder, not suicide, but I think there's a very good chance that the idea came from Martine herself, or that she and her mother talked it over and came to a mutual agreement. Which makes them both suicides in my book, even though it won't get written up that way in the official report."

"I assume you've checked on the other City Center survivors?" Hodges asks.

"All alive except for Gerald Stansbury, who died just after Thanksgiving last year," Pete says. "Had a heart attack. His wife told me coronary disease runs in his family, and that he lived longer than both his father and brother. Izzy's right, this is probably nothing, but I thought you and Holly should know." He looks at each of them in turn. "*You* haven't had any bad thoughts about pulling the pin, have you?"

"No," Hodges says. "Not lately."

Holly merely shakes her head, still looking down at the newspaper.

Hodges asks, "I don't suppose anyone found a mysterious letter Z in young Mr. Frias's bedroom after he and Ms. Countryman committed suicide?"

"Of course not," Izzy says.

"That you know of," Hodges corrects. "Isn't that what you mean? Considering you just found this one today?"

"Jesus please us," Izzy says. "This is silly." She looks pointedly at her watch and stands.

Pete gets up, too. Holly remains seated, looking down at her filched copy of *Inside View*. Hodges also stays put, at least for the moment. "You'll go back to the Frias-Countryman photos, right, Pete? Check it out, just to be sure?"

"Yes," Pete says. "And Izzy's probably right, I was silly to get you two out here."

"I'm glad you did."

"And . . . I still feel bad about the way we handled Mrs. Trelawney, okay?" Pete is looking at Hodges, but Hodges has an idea he's really speaking to the thin, pale woman with the junk newspaper in her lap. "I never once doubted that she left her key in the ignition. I closed my mind to any other possibility. I promised myself I'd never do that again."

"I understand," Hodges says.

"One thing I believe we all can agree on," Izzy says, "is that Hartsfield's days of running people down, blowing people up, and architecting suicides are behind him. So unless we've all stumbled into a movie called *Son of Brady*, I suggest we exit the late Ms. Ellerton's house and get on with our lives. Any objections to that idea?"

There are none.

7

Hodges and Holly stand in the driveway for a moment before getting into the car, letting the cold January wind rush past them. It's out of the north, blowing straight down from Canada, so the usually present smell of the large, polluted lake to the east is refreshingly absent. There are only a few houses at this end of Hilltop Court, and the closest has a FOR SALE sign on it. Hodges notices that Tom Saubers is the agent, and he smiles. Tom was also badly hurt in the Massacre, but has come almost all the way back. Hodges is always amazed by the resilience of which some men and women are capable. It doesn't exactly give him hope for the human race, but . . .

Actually, it does.

In the car, Holly puts the folded *Inside View* on the floor long enough to fasten her seatbelt, then picks it up again. Neither Pete nor Isabelle objected to her taking it. Hodges isn't sure they even noticed. Why would they? To them, the Ellerton house isn't really a crime scene, although the letter of the law may call it that. Pete was uneasy, true, but Hodges thinks that had little to do with cop intuition and was a quasi-superstitious response instead.

*Hartsfield should have died when Holly hit him with my Happy Slapper,* Hodges thinks. *That would have been better for all of us.*

"Pete *will* go back and look at the pictures from the Frias-Countryman suicides," he tells Holly. "Due diligence, and all that. But if he finds a Z scratched somewhere—on a baseboard, on a mirror—I will be one surprised human being."

She doesn't reply. Her eyes are far away.

"Holly? Are you there?"

She starts a little. "Yes. Just planning how I'll locate Nancy Alderson in Chagrin Falls. It shouldn't take too long with all the search programs I've got, but you'll have to talk to her. I can do cold calls now if I absolutely have to, you know that—"

"Yes. You've gotten good at it." Which is true, although she always makes such calls with her trusty box of Nicorette close at hand. Not to mention a stash of Twinkies in her desk for backup.

"But I can't be the one to tell her that her employers—her *friends*, for all we know—are dead. You'll have to do it. You're good at things like that."

Hodges feels that nobody is very good at things like that, but doesn't bother saying so. "Why? The Alderson woman wouldn't have been there since last Friday."

"She deserves to know," Holly says. "The police will get in touch with any relatives, that's their job, but they're not going to call the housekeeper. At least I don't think so."

Hodges doesn't, either, and Holly's right—the Alderson woman deserves to know, if only so she doesn't turn up to find an **X** of police tape on the door. But somehow he doesn't think that's Holly's only interest in Nancy Alderson.

"Your friend Pete and Miss Pretty Gray Eyes hardly did *any-thing*," Holly says. "There was fingerprint powder in Martine Stover's bedroom, sure, and on her wheelchair, and in the bathroom where Mrs. Ellerton killed herself, but none upstairs where she slept. They probably went up long enough to make sure there wasn't a body stashed under the bed or in the closet, and called it good."

"Hold on a second. You went upstairs?"

"Of course. *Somebody* needed to investigate thoroughly, and those two sure weren't doing it. As far as they're concerned, they know exactly what happened. Pete only called you because he was spooked."

*Spooked.* Yes, that was it. Exactly the word he was looking for and hadn't been able to find.

"I was spooked, too," Holly says matter-of-factly, "but that doesn't mean I lost my wits. The whole thing was wrong. Wrong wrong wrong, and you need to talk to the housekeeper. I'll tell you what to ask her, if you can't figure it out for yourself."

"Is this about the Z on the bathroom counter? If you know something I don't, I wish you'd fill me in."

"It's not what I know, it's what I saw. Didn't you notice what was *beside* that Z?"

"A Magic Marker."

She gives him a look that says *you can do better*.

Hodges calls on an old cop technique that comes in especially handy when giving trial testimony: he looks at the picture again, this time in his mind. "There was a power cord plugged into the wall beside the basin."

"Yes! At first I thought it must be for an e-reader and Mrs. Ellerton left it plugged in there because she spent most of her time in that part of the house. It would be a convenient charging point, because all the plugs in Martine's bedroom were probably in use for her life-support gear. Don't you think so?"

"Yeah, that could be."

"Only I have both a Nook and a Kindle—"

Of course you do, he thinks.

"—and neither of them has cords like that. Those cords are black. This one was gray."

"Maybe she lost the original charging cord and bought a replacement at Tech Village." Pretty much the only game in town for electronic supplies, now that Discount Electronix, Brady Hartsfield's old employer, has declared bankruptcy.

"No. E-readers have prong-type plug-ins. This one was wider, like for an electronic tablet. Only my iPad also has that kind, and the one in the bathroom was much smaller. That cord was for some kind of handheld device. So I went upstairs to look for it."

"Where you found . . . ?"

"Just an old PC on a desk by the window in Mrs. Ellerton's bedroom. And I mean *old*. It was hooked up to a modem."

"Oh my God, no!" Hodges exclaims. "Not a modem!"

"This is *not* funny, Bill. Those women are *dead*."

Hodges takes a hand from the wheel and holds it up in a peace gesture. "Sorry. Go on. This is the part where you tell me you powered up her computer."

Holly looks slightly discomfited. "Well, yes. But only in the service of an investigation the police are clearly not going to make. I wasn't *snooping*."

Hodges could argue the point, but doesn't.

"It wasn't password protected, so I looked at Mrs. Ellerton's search history. She visited quite a few retail sites, and lots of medical sites having to do with paralysis. She seemed very interested in stem cells, which makes sense, considering her daughter's condi—"

"You did all this in ten minutes?"

"I'm a fast reader. But you know what I *didn't* find?"

"I'm guessing anything to do with suicide."

"Yes. So how did she know about the helium thing? For that matter, how did she know to dissolve those pills in vodka and put them in her daughter's feeding tube?"

"Well," Hodges says, "there's this ancient arcane ritual called reading books. You may have heard of it."

"Did you see any books in that living room?"

He replays the living room just as he did the photo of Martine Stover's bathroom, and Holly is right. There were shelves of knickknacks, and that picture of big-eyed waifs, and the flat-screen TV. There were magazines on the coffee table, but spread in a way that spoke more to decoration than to voracious reading. Plus, none of them was exactly *The Atlantic Monthly*.

"No," he says, "no books in the living room, although I saw a couple in the photo of Stover's bedroom. One of them looked like a Bible." He glances at the folded *Inside View* in her lap. "What have you got in there, Holly? What are you hiding?"

When Holly flushes, she goes totally Defcon 1, the blood

crashing to her face in a way that's alarming. It happens now. "It wasn't stealing," she says. "It was *borrowing*. I never steal, Bill. Never!"

"Cool your jets. What is it?"

"The thing that goes with the power cord in the bathroom." She unfolds the newspaper to reveal a bright pink gadget with a dark gray screen. It's bigger than an e-reader, smaller than an electronic tablet. "When I came downstairs, I sat in Mrs. Ellerton's chair to think a minute. I ran my hands between the arms and the cushion. I wasn't even hunting for something, I was just doing it."

One of Holly's many self-comforting techniques, Hodges assumes. He's seen many in the years since he first met her in the company of her overprotective mother and aggressively gregarious uncle. In their company? No, not exactly. That phrase suggested equality. Charlotte Gibney and Henry Sirois had treated her more like a mentally defective child out on a day pass. Holly is a different woman now, but traces of the old Holly still remain. And that's okay with Hodges. After all, everyone casts a shadow.

"That's where it was, down on the right side. It's a Zappit."

The name chimes a faint chord far back in his memory, although when it comes to computer chip–driven gadgetry, Hodges is far behind the curve. He's always screwing up with his own home computer, and now that Jerome Robinson is away, Holly is the one who usually comes over to his house on Harper Road to straighten him out. "A whatsit?"

"A Zappit Commander. I've seen advertisements online, although not lately. They come pre-loaded with over a hundred simple electronic games like Tetris, Simon, and SpellTower. Nothing complicated like Grand Theft Auto. So tell me what it was doing there, Bill. Tell me what it was doing in a house where one of the women was almost eighty and the other one couldn't turn on a light switch, let alone play video games."

"It seems odd, all right. Not downright bizarre, but on the odd side, for sure."

"And the cord was plugged in right next to that letter Z," she says. "Not Z for the end, like a suicide note, but Z for Zappit. At least that's what I think."

Hodges considers the idea.

"Maybe." He wonders again if he has encountered that name before, or if it's only what the French call *faux souvenir*—a false memory. He could swear it has some connection to Brady Hartsfield, but he can't trust that idea, because Brady is very much on his mind today.

*How long has it been since I've gone to visit him? Six months? Eight? No, longer than that. Quite a bit longer.*

The last time was not long after the business having to do with Pete Saubers and the cache of stolen money and notebooks Pete discovered, practically buried in his backyard. On that occasion, Hodges found Brady much the same as ever—a gorked-out young man dressed in a plaid shirt and jeans that never got dirty. He was sitting in the same chair he was always sitting in when Hodges visited Room 217 in the Brain Injury Clinic, just staring out at the parking garage across the way.

The only real difference that day had been outside Room 217. Becky Helmington, the head nurse, had moved on to the surgical wing of Kiner Memorial, thereby closing Hodges's conduit to rumors about Brady. The new head nurse was a woman with stony scruples and a face like a closed fist. Ruth Scapelli refused Hodges's offer of fifty dollars for any little tidbits about Brady and threatened to report him if he ever offered her money for patient information again. "You're not even on his visitors list," she said.

"I don't want information about him," Hodges had said. "I've got all the information about Brady Hartsfield I'm ever going to need. I just want to know what the staff is saying about him. Because there have been rumors, you know. Some of them pretty wild."

Scapelli favored him with a disdainful look. "There's loose talk in every hospital, Mr. Hodges, and always about patients who are famous. Or infamous, as is the case with Mr. Hartsfield. I held a staff meeting shortly after Nurse Helmington moved from Brain Injury to her current situation, and informed my people that the talk about Mr. Hartsfield was to stop immediately, and if I caught wind of more rumors, I would trace them to their source and see that the person or persons spreading them was dismissed. As for you . . ." Looking down her nose at him, the fist of her face tightening even more. "I can't believe that a former police officer, and a decorated one at that, would resort to bribery."

Not long after that rather humiliating encounter, Holly and Jerome Robinson cornered him and staged a mini-intervention, telling Hodges that his visits to Brady had to end. Jerome had been especially serious that day, his usual cheerful patter nowhere to be found.

"There's nothing you can do in that room but hurt yourself," Jerome had said. "We always know when you've been to see him, because you go around with a little gray cloud over your head for the next two days."

"More like a week," Holly added. She wouldn't look at him, and she was twisting her fingers in a way that made Hodges want to grab them and make her stop before she broke something. Her voice, however, was firm and sure. "There's nothing left inside him, Bill. You need to accept that. And if there was, he'd be happy every time you showed up. He'd see what he's doing to you and be happy."

That was the convincer, because Hodges knew it was the truth. So he stays away. It was kind of like quitting smoking: hard at first, easier as time went by. Now whole weeks sometimes pass without thoughts of Brady and Brady's terrible crimes.

*There's nothing left inside him.*

Hodges reminds himself of that as he drives back into the heart of the city, where Holly will kick her computer into high gear and start hunting down Nancy Alderson. Whatever happened in that house at the end of Hilltop Court—the chain of thoughts and conversations, of tears and promises, all ending in the dissolved pills injected into the feeding tube and the tank of helium with the laughing children decaled on the side—it can have nothing to do with Brady Hartsfield, because Holly literally bashed his brains out. If Hodges sometimes doubts, it's because he can't stand the idea that Brady has somehow escaped punishment. That in the end, the monster eluded him. Hodges didn't even get to swing the ball bearing–loaded sock he calls his Happy Slapper, because he was busy suffering a heart attack at the time.

Still, a ghost of memory: Zappit.

He *knows* he has heard that before.

His stomach gives a warning twinge, and he remembers the doctor's appointment he blew off. He'll have to take care of that, but tomorrow should be soon enough. He has an idea that Dr. Stamos is going to tell him he has an ulcer, and for that news he can wait.

8

Holly has a fresh box of Nicorette by her telephone, but doesn't need to use a single chew. The first Alderson she calls turns out to be the housekeeper's sister-in-law, who of course wants to know why someone from a company called Finders Keepers wants to get in touch with Nan.

"Is it a bequest, or something?" she asks hopefully.

"One moment," Holly says. "I have to put you on hold while I get my boss." Hodges is not her boss, he made her a full part-ner after the Pete Saubers business last year, but it's a fiction she often falls back on when she's stressed.

Hodges, who has been using his own computer to read up on Zappit Game Systems, picks up the phone while Holly lingers by his desk, gnawing at the neck of her sweater. Hodges hovers his finger over the hold button on his phone long enough to tell Holly that eating wool probably isn't good for her, and certainly not for the Fair Isle she's wearing. Then he connects with the sister-in-law.

"I'm afraid I have some bad news for Nancy," he says, and fills her in quickly.

"Oh my God," Linda Alderson says (Holly has jotted the name on his pad). "She's going to be devastated to hear that, and not just because it means the end of the job. She's been working for those ladies since 2012, and she really likes them. She had Thanksgiving dinner with them just last November. Are you with the police?"

"Retired," he says, "but working with the team assigned to the case. I was asked to get in touch with Ms. Alderson." He doesn't think this lie will come back to haunt him, since Pete opened the door by inviting him to the scene. "Can you tell me how to get in touch with her?"

"I'll give you her cell number. She went to Chagrin Falls for her brother's birthday party on Saturday. It was the big four-oh, so Harry's wife made a fuss about it. She's staying until Wednesday or Thursday, I think—at least that was the plan. I'm sure this news will bring her back. Nan lives alone since Bill died— Bill was my husband's brother—with only her cat for company. Mrs. Ellerton and Ms. Stover were sort of a surrogate family. This will just make her so sad."

Hodges takes the number down and calls immediately. Nancy Alderson picks up on the first ring. He identifies himself, then gives her the news.

After a moment of shocked silence, she says, "Oh, no, that can't be. You've made a mistake, Detective Hodges."

He doesn't bother to correct her, because this is interesting. "Why do you say that?"

"Because they're *happy*. They get along so well, watching TV together—they love movies on the DVD player, and those shows about cooking, or where women sit around talking about fun things and having celebrity guests. You wouldn't believe it, but there's a lot of laughter in that house." Nancy Alderson hesitates, then says, "Are you *sure* you're talking about the right people? About Jan Ellerton and Marty Stover?"

"Sorry to say I am."

"But . . . she had accepted her condition! Marty, I'm talking about. Martine. She used to say that getting used to being paralyzed was actually easier than getting used to being a spinster. She and I used to talk about that all the time—being on our own. Because I lost my husband, you know."

"So there was never a Mr. Stover."

"Yes there was, Janice had an earlier marriage. Very short, I believe, but she said she never regretted it because she got Martine. Marty did have a boyfriend not long before her accident, but he had a heart attack. Carried him right off. Marty said he was very fit, used to exercise three days a week at a health club downtown. She said it was being so fit that killed him. Because his heart was strong, and when it backfired, it just blew apart."

Hodges, a coronary survivor, thinks, Reminder to self: no fitness club.

"Marty used to say that being alone after someone you love passes on was the worst kind of paralysis. I didn't feel exactly the same way about my Bill, but I knew what she meant. Reverend Henreid came in to see her often—Marty calls him her spiritual adviser—and even when he didn't, she and Jan did daily devotions and prayers. Every day at noon. And Marty was thinking about taking an accounting course online—they have special courses for people with her kind of disability, did you know that?"

"I didn't," Hodges says. On his pad he prints STOVER PLANNING TO TAKE ACCOUNTING COURSE BY COMPUTER and turns it so Holly can read it. She raises her eyebrows.

"There were tears and sadness from time to time, of course there was, but for the most part they were *happy*. At least . . . I don't know . . ."

"What are you thinking about, Nancy?" He makes the switch to her first name—another old cop trick—without thinking about it.

"Oh, it's probably nothing. *Marty* seemed as happy as ever—she's a real love-bug, that one, you wouldn't believe how spiritual she is, always sees the good side of everything—but Jan did seem a little withdrawn lately, as if she had something weighing on her mind. I thought it might be money worries, or maybe just the after-Christmas blues. I never *dreamed* . . ." She sniffles. "Excuse me, I have to blow."

"Sure."

Holly grabs his pad. Her printing is small—constipated, he often thinks—and he has to hold the pad almost touching his nose to read Ask her about Zappit!

There's a honking sound in his ear as Alderson blows her nose. "Sorry."

"That's all right. Nancy, would you know if Mrs. Ellerton happened to have a small handheld game console? It would have been pink."

"Goodness sakes, how did you know that?"

"I really don't know anything," Hodges says truthfully. "I'm just a retired detective with a list of questions I'm supposed to ask."

"She said a man gave it to her. He told her the game gadget was free as long as she promised to fill out a questionnaire and send it back to the company. The thing was a little bit bigger than a paperback book. It just sat around the house awhile—"

"When was this?"

"I can't remember exactly, but before Christmas, for sure. The first time I saw it, it was on the coffee table in the living room. It just stayed there with the questionnaire folded up beside it until after Christmas—I know because their little tree was gone—and then I spied it one day on the kitchen table. Jan said she turned it on just to see what it would do, and found out there were solitaire games on it, maybe as many as a dozen different kinds, like Klondike and Picture and Pyramid. So, since she was using it, she filled out the questionnaire and sent it in."

"Did she charge it in Marty's bathroom?"

"Yes, because that was the most convenient place. She was in that part of the house so much, you know."

"Uh-huh. You said that Mrs. Ellerton became withdrawn—"

"A *little* withdrawn," Alderson corrects at once. "Mostly she was the same as always. A love-bug, just like Marty."

"But something was on her mind."

"Yes, I think so."

"*Weighing* on her mind."

"Well . . ."

"Was this around the same time she got the handheld game machine?"

"I guess it was, now that I think about it, but why in the world would playing solitaire on a little pink tablet depress her?"

"I don't know," Hodges says, and prints DEPRESSED on his pad. He thinks there's a significant jump between being withdrawn and being depressed.

"Have their relations been told?" Alderson asks. "There aren't any in the city, but there are cousins in Ohio, I know that, and I think some in Kansas, too. Or maybe it was Indiana. The names would be in her address book."

"The police will be doing that as we speak," Hodges says, although he will call Pete later on to make sure. It will probably annoy his old partner, but Hodges doesn't care. Nancy Alderson's distress is in every word she utters, and he wants to offer what comfort he can. "May I ask one more question?"

"Of course."

"Did you happen to notice anyone hanging around the house? Anyone without an obvious reason to be there?"

Holly is nodding vigorously.

"Why would you ask that?" Alderson sounds astonished. "Surely you don't think some *outsider*—"

"I don't think anything," Hodges says smoothly. "I'm just helping the police because there's been such a staff reduction in the last few years. Citywide budget cuts."

"I know, it's awful."

"So they gave me this list of questions, and that's the last one."

"Well, there was nobody. I'd have noticed, because of the breezeway between the house and the garage. The garage is heated, so that's where the pantry and the washer-dryer are. I'm back and forth in that breezeway all the time, and I can see the street from there. Hardly anyone comes all the way up Hilltop Court, because Jan and Marty's is the last house. It's just the turnaround after that. Of course there's the postman, and UPS, and sometimes FedEx, but otherwise, unless someone gets lost, we've got that end of the street to ourselves."

"So there was no one at all."

"No, sir, there sure wasn't."

"Not the man who gave Mrs. Ellerton the game console?"

"No, he approached her in Ridgeline Foods. That's the grocery store at the foot of the hill, down where City Avenue crosses Hilltop Court. There's a Kroger about a mile further on, in the City Avenue Plaza, but Janice won't go there even though things are a little cheaper, because she says you should always buy locally if you . . . you . . ." She gives a sudden loud sob. "But she's done shopping *anywhere*, isn't she? Oh, I can't believe this! Jan would never hurt Marty, not for the world."

"It's a sad thing," Hodges says.

"I'll have to come back today." Alderson now talking to herself rather than to Hodges. "It may take awhile for her relatives to come, and someone will have to make the proper arrangements."

A final housekeeping duty, Hodges thinks, and finds the thought both touching and obscurely horrible.

"I want to thank you for your time, Nancy. I'll let you go n—"

"Of course there was that elderly fellow," Alderson says.

"What elderly fellow was that?"

"I saw him several times outside 1588. He'd park at the curb and just stand on the sidewalk, looking at it. That's the house across the street and down the hill a little way. You might not have noticed it, but it was for sale."

Hodges did notice, but doesn't say so. He doesn't want to interrupt.

"Once he walked right up the lawn to look in the bay window—this was before the last big snowstorm. I think he was window shopping." She gives a watery laugh. "Although my mother would have called it window *wishing*, because he surely didn't look like the sort who could afford a house like that."

"No?"

"Uh-uh. He was dressed in workman's clothes—you know, green pants, like Dickies—and his parka was mended with a piece of masking tape. Also, his car looked very old and had spots of primer on it. My late husband used to call that poor man's polish."

"You don't happen to know what kind of car it was, do you?" He flips his pad to a fresh sheet and writes, FIND DATE OF LAST BIG SNOWSTORM. Holly reads it and nods.

"No, I'm sorry. I don't know cars. I don't even remember the color, just those spots of primer paint. Mr. Hodges, are you sure there hasn't been some mistake?" She's almost begging.

"I wish I could tell you that, Nancy, but I can't. You've been very helpful."

Doubtfully: "Have I?"

Hodges gives her his number, Holly's, and the office number. He tells her to call if anything occurs to her that they haven't

54

covered. He reminds her that there may be press interest because Martine was paralyzed at City Center in 2009, and tells her she isn't obliged to talk to reporters or TV news people if she doesn't want to.

Nancy Alderson is crying again when he breaks the connection.

9

He takes Holly to lunch at Panda Garden a block down the street. It's early and they have the dining room almost to themselves. Holly is off meat and orders vegetable chow mein. Hodges loves the spicy shredded beef, but his stomach won't put up with it these days, so he settles for Ma La Lamb. They both use chopsticks, Holly because she's good with them and Hodges because they slow him down and make a post-lunch bonfire in his guts less likely.

She says, "The last big storm was December nineteenth. The weather service reported eleven inches in Government Square, thirteen in Branson Park. Not exactly huge, but the only other one so far this winter dropped just four inches."

"Six days before Christmas. Around the same time Janice Ellerton was given the Zappit, according to Alderson's recollection."

"Do you think the man who gave it to her was the same one looking at that house?"

Hodges snares a piece of broccoli. It's supposed to be good for you, like all veggies that taste bad. "I don't think Ellerton would have accepted *anything* from a guy wearing a parka mended with masking tape. I'm not counting the possibility out, but it seems unlikely."

55

"Eat your lunch, Bill. If I get any further ahead of you, I'll look like a pig."

Hodges eats, although he has very little appetite these days even when his stomach isn't giving him the devil. When a bite sticks in his throat, he washes it down with tea. Maybe a good idea, since tea seems to help. He thinks about those test results he is yet to see. It occurs to him that his problem could be worse than an ulcer, that an ulcer might actually be the best-case scenario. There's medicine for ulcers. Other things, not so much.

When he can see the middle of his plate (but Jesus, so much food left around the edges), he sets his chopsticks aside and says, "I found something out while you were hunting down Nancy Alderson."

"Tell me."

"I was reading about those Zappits. Amazing how these computer-based companies pop up, then disappear. They're like dandelions in June. The Commander didn't exactly corner the market. Too simple, too expensive, too much sophisticated competition. Zappit Inc. stock went down and they got bought out by a company called Sunrise Solutions. Two years ago *that* company declared bankruptcy and went dark. Which means Zappit is long gone and the guy giving out Commander consoles had to be running some kind of scam."

Holly is quick to see where that leads. "So the questionnaire was bullpoop just to add a little whatdoyoucallit, verisimilitude. But the guy didn't try to get money out of her, did he?"

"No. At least not that we know of."

"Something weird is going on here, Bill. Are you going to tell Detective Huntley and Miss Pretty Gray Eyes?"

Hodges has picked up the smallest piece of lamb left on his plate, and here is an excuse to drop it. "Why don't you like her, Holly?"

"Well, she thinks I'm crazy," Holly says matter-of-factly. "There's that."

"I'm sure she doesn't—"

"Yes. She does. She probably thinks I'm dangerous, too, because of the way I whopped Brady Hartsfield at the 'Round Here concert. But I don't care. I'd do it again. A thousand times!"

He puts a hand over hers. The chopsticks she's holding in her fist vibrate like a tuning fork. "I know you would, and you'd be right every time. You saved a thousand lives, and that's a conservative estimate."

She slides her hand from beneath his and starts picking up grains of rice. "Oh, I can deal with her thinking I'm crazy. I've been dealing with people thinking that all my life, starting with my parents. But there's something else. Isabelle only sees what she sees, and she doesn't like people who see more, or at least look for more. She feels the same way about you, Bill. She's jealous of you. Over Pete."

Hodges says nothing. He's never considered such a possibility.

She puts down her chopsticks. "You didn't answer my question. Are you going to tell them what we've learned so far?"

"Not quite yet. There's something I want to do first, if you'll hold down the office this afternoon."

Holly smiles down at the remainder of her chow mein. "I always do."

10

Bill Hodges isn't the only one who took an instant dislike to Becky Helmington's replacement. The nurses and orderlies who work in the Traumatic Brain Injury Clinic call it the Bucket, as in Brain Bucket, and before long Ruth Scapelli has become known as Nurse Ratched. By the end of her third month, she has gotten three nurses transferred for various small infractions, and one orderly fired for smoking in a supply closet. She has banned certain colorful uniforms as "too distracting" or "too suggestive."

The doctors like her, though. They find her swift and competent. With the patients she is also swift and competent, but she's cold, and there's an undertone of contempt there, as well. She will not allow even the most cataclysmically injured of them to be called a gork or a burn or a wipeout, at least not in her hearing, but she has a certain *attitude*.

"She knows her stuff," one nurse said to another in the break room not long after Scapelli took up her duties. "No argument about that, but there's something missing."

The other nurse was a thirty-year veteran who had seen it all. She considered, then said one word . . . but it was *le mot juste*. "Mercy."

Scapelli never exhibits coldness or contempt when she accompanies Felix Babineau, the head of Neuro, on his rounds, and he probably wouldn't notice if she did. Some of the other doctors *have* noticed, but few pay any mind; the doings of such lesser beings as nurses—even head nurses—are far below their lordly gaze.

It is as if Scapelli feels that, no matter what is wrong with them, the patients of the Traumatic Brain Injury Clinic must bear part of the responsibility for their current condition, and if they only tried harder, they would surely regain at least *some* of their faculties. She does her job, though, and for the most part she does it well, perhaps better than Becky Helmington, who was far better liked. If told this, Scapelli would have said she was not here to be liked. She was here to care for her patients, end of story, full stop.

There is, however, one long-term patient in the Bucket whom she hates. That patient is Brady Hartsfield. It isn't because she had a friend or relative who was hurt or killed at City Center; it's because she thinks he's shamming. Avoiding the punishment he so richly deserves. Mostly she stays away and lets other staff members deal with him, because just seeing him often infuses her with a daylong rage that the system should be so easily gamed by this vile creature. She stays away for another reason, too: she doesn't entirely trust herself when she's in his room. On two occasions she has done something. The kind of thing that, were it discovered, might result in *her* being the one fired. But on this early January afternoon, just as Hodges and Holly are finishing their lunch, she is drawn down to Room 217 as if by an invisible cable. Only this morning she was forced to go in there, because Dr. Babineau insists she accompany him on rounds, and Brady is his star patient. He marvels at how far Brady has come.

"He should never have emerged from his coma at all," Babineau told her shortly after she came on staff at the Bucket. He's a cold fish, but when he speaks of Brady he becomes almost jolly. "And look at him now! He's able to walk short distances—with help, I grant you—he can feed himself, and he can respond either verbally or with signs to simple questions."

He's also prone to poking himself in the eye with his fork, Ruth Scapelli could have added (but doesn't), and his verbal responses all sound like *wah-wah* and *gub-gub* to her. Then there's the matter of waste. Put a Depends on him and he holds it. Take it off, and he urinates in his bed, regular as clockwork. Defecates in it, if he can. It's as if he knows. She believes he *does* know.

Something else he knows—of this there can be no doubt—is that Scapelli doesn't like him. This very morning, after the exam was finished and Dr. Babineau was washing his hands in the en suite bathroom, Brady raised his head to look at her and lifted one hand to his chest. He curled it into a loose, trembling fist. From it his middle finger slowly extended.

At first Scapelli could barely comprehend what she was seeing: Brady Hartsfield, giving her the finger. Then, as she heard the water go off in the bathroom, two buttons popped from the front of her uniform, exposing the center of her sturdy Playtex 18-Hour Comfort Strap Bra. She doesn't believe the rumors she's heard about this waste of humanity, *refuses* to believe them, but then . . .

He smiled at her. *Grinned* at her.

Now she walks down to Room 217 while soothing music wafts from the speakers overhead. She's wearing her spare uniform, the pink one she keeps in her locker and doesn't like much. She looks both ways to make sure no one is paying any attention to her, pretends to study Brady's chart just in case there's a set of prying eyes she's missed, and slips inside. Brady sits in his chair by the window, where he always sits. He's dressed in one of his four plaid shirts and a pair of jeans. His hair has been combed and his cheeks are baby-smooth. A button on his breast pocket proclaims I WAS SHAVED BY NURSE BARBARA!

He's living like Donald Trump, Ruth Scapelli thinks. He killed eight people and wounded God knows how many more, he tried to kill thousands of teenage girls at a rock-and-roll concert, and here he sits with his meals brought to him by his own personal staff, his clothes laundered, his face shaved. He gets a *massage* three times a week. He visits the *spa* four times a week, and spends time in the *hot tub*.

Living like Donald Trump? Huh. More like a desert chieftain in one of those oil-rich Mideast countries.

And if she told Babineau that he gave her the finger?

Oh no, he'd say. Oh no, Nurse Scapelli. What you saw was nothing but an involuntary muscle twitch. He's still incapable of the thought processes that would lead to such a gesture. Even if that were not the case, why would he make such a gesture to you?

"Because you don't like me," she says, bending forward with her hands on her pink-skirted knees. "Do you, Mr. Hartsfield? And that makes us even, because I don't like you."

He doesn't look at her, or give any sign that he's heard her. He only looks out the window at the parking garage across the way. But he *does* hear her, she's sure he does, and his failure to acknowledge her in any way infuriates her more. When she talks, people are supposed to *listen*.

"Am I to believe you popped the buttons on my uniform this morning by some kind of mind control?"

Nothing.

"I know better. I'd been meaning to replace that one. The bodice was a bit too tight. You may fool some of the more credulous staff members, but you don't fool me, Mr. Hartsfield. All you can do is sit there. And make a mess in your bed every time you get the chance."

Nothing.

She glances around at the door to make sure it's shut, then removes her left hand from her knee and reaches out with it. "All those people you hurt, some of them still suffering. Does that make you happy? It does, doesn't it? How would *you* like it? Shall we find out?"

She first touches the soft ridge of a nipple beneath his shirt, then grasps it between her thumb and index finger. Her nails are short, but she digs in with what she has. She twists first one way, then the other.

"That's pain, Mr. Hartsfield. Do you like it?"

His face remains as bland as ever, which makes her angrier still. She bends closer, until their noses are almost touching. Her face more like a fist than ever. Her blue eyes bulge behind her glasses. There are tiny spit-buds at the corners of her lips.

"I could do this to your testicles," she whispers. "Perhaps I will."

Yes. She just might. It's not as if he can tell Babineau, after all. He has four dozen words at most, and few people can understand what he does manage to say. *I want more corn* comes out *Uh-wan-mo-ko*, which sounds like fake Indian talk in an old Western movie. The only thing he says that's perfectly clear is *I want my mother*, and on several occasions Scapelli has taken great pleasure in re-informing him that his mother is dead.

She twists his nipple back and forth. Clockwise, then counterclockwise. Pinching as hard as she can, and her hands are nurse's hands, which means they are strong.

"You think Dr. Babineau is your pet, but you've got that backwards. You're *his* pet. His pet guinea pig. He thinks I don't know about the experimental drugs he's been giving you, but I do. Vitamins, he says. Vitamins, my fanny. I know *everything* that goes on around here. He thinks he's going to bring you all the way back, but that will never happen. You're too far gone. And what if it did? You'd stand trial and go to jail for the rest of your life. And they don't have hot tubs in Waynesville State Prison."

She's pinching his nipple so hard the tendons on her wrist stand out, and he still shows no sign that he feels anything—just looks out at the parking garage, his face a blank. If she keeps on, one of the nurses is apt to see bruising, swelling, and it will go on his chart.

She lets go and steps back, breathing hard, and the venetian blind at the top of his window gives an abrupt, bonelike rattle. The sound makes her jump and look around. When she turns back to him, Hartsfield is no longer looking at the parking garage. He's looking at *her*. His eyes are clear and aware. Scapelli feels a bright spark of fear and takes a step back.

"I could report Babineau," she says, "but doctors have a way of wiggling out of things, especially when it's their word against a nurse's, even a head nurse's. And why would I? Let him experiment on you all he wants. Even Waynesville is too good for you, Mr. Hartsfield. Maybe he'll give you something that will kill you. That's what you deserve."

A food trolley rumbles by in the corridor; someone is getting a late lunch. Ruth Scapelli jerks like a woman awaking from a dream and backs toward the door, looking from Hartsfield to the now silent venetian blind and then back to Hartsfield again.

"I'll leave you to your thoughts, but I want to tell you one more thing before I go. If you ever show me your middle finger again, it *will* be your testicles."

Brady's hand rises from his lap to his chest. It trembles, but that's a motor control issue; thanks to ten sessions a week downstairs in Physical Therapy, he's gotten at least some muscle tone back.

Scapelli stares, unbelieving, as the middle finger rises and tilts toward her.

With it comes that obscene grin.

"You're a freak," she says in a low voice. "An aberration."

But she doesn't approach him again. She's suddenly, irrationally afraid of what might happen if she did.

## 11

Tom Saubers is more than willing to do the favor Hodges has asked of him, even though it means rescheduling a couple of afternoon appointments. He owes Bill Hodges a lot more than a tour through an empty house up in Ridgedale; after all, the ex-cop—with the help of his friends Holly and Jerome—saved the lives of his son and daughter. Possibly his wife's, as well.

He punches off the alarm in the foyer, reading the numbers from a slip of paper clipped to the folder he carries. As he leads Hodges through the downstairs rooms, their footfalls echoing, Tom can't help going into his spiel. Yes, it's quite a long way out from the city center, can't argue the point, but what that means is you get all the city services—water, plowing, garbage removal, school buses, municipal buses—without all the city noise. "The place is cable-ready, and *way* above code," he says.

"Great, but I don't want to buy it."

Tom looks at him curiously. "What *do* you want?"

Hodges sees no reason not to tell him. "To know if anyone has been using it to keep an eye on that house across the street. There was a murder-suicide there this past weekend."

"In 1601? Jesus, Bill, that's *awful*."

It is, Hodges thinks, and I believe you're already wondering who you should talk to about becoming the selling agent on that one.

Not that he holds that against the man, who went through his own hell as a result of the City Center Massacre.

"See you've left the cane behind," Hodges comments as they climb to the second floor.

"I sometimes use it at night, especially if the weather is rainy,"

Tom says. "The scientists claim that stuff about your joints hurting more in wet weather is bullshit, but I'm here to tell you
that's one old wives' tale you can take to the bank. Now, this is
the master bedroom, and you can see how it's set up to catch the
morning light. The bathroom is nice and big—the shower has
pulsing jets—and just down the hall here . . ."

Yes, it's a fine house, Hodges would expect nothing else here
in Ridgedale, but there's no sign anyone has been in it lately.

"Seen enough?" Tom asks.

"I think so, yes. Did you notice anything out of place?"

"Not a thing. And the alarm is a good one. If someone *had*
broken in—"

"Yeah," Hodges says. "Sorry to get you out on such a cold
day."

"Nonsense. I had to be out and about anyway. And it's good
to see you." They step out the kitchen door, which Tom relocks.
"Although you're looking awfully thin."

"Well, you know what they say—you can't be too thin or too
rich."

Tom, who in the wake of his City Center injuries was too
thin and too poor, gives this oldie an obligatory smile and starts
around to the front of the house. Hodges follows a few steps,
then stops.

"Could we look in the garage?"

"Sure, but there's nothing in there."

"Just a peek."

"Cross every *t* and dot every *i*, huh? Roger that, just let me
get the right key."

Only he doesn't need the key, because the garage door is standing two inches ajar. The two men look at the splinters around
the lock silently. At last Tom says, "Well. How about that."

"The alarm system doesn't cover the garage, I take it."

"You take it right. There's nothing to protect."

Hodges steps into a rectangle with bare wood walls and a poured concrete floor. There are boot prints visible on the concrete. Hodges can see his breath, and he can see something else, as well. In front of the left overhead door is a chair. Someone sat here, looking out.

Hodges has been feeling a growing discomfort on the left side of his midsection, one that's putting out tentacles that curl around to his lower back, but this sort of pain is almost an old friend by now, and it's temporarily overshadowed by excitement.

Someone sat here looking out at 1601, he thinks. I'd bet the farm on it, if I had a farm.

He walks to the front of the garage and sits where the watcher sat. There are three windows running horizontally across the middle of the door, and the one on the far right has been wiped clean of dust. The view is a straight shot to the big living room window of 1601.

"Hey, Bill," Tom says. "Something under the chair."

Hodges bends to look, although doing so turns up the heat in his gut. What he sees is a black disc, maybe three inches across. He picks it up by the edges. Embossed on it in gold is a single word: STEINER.

"Is it from a camera?" Tom asks.

"From a pair of binoculars. Police departments with fat budgets use Steiner binocs."

With a good pair of Steiners—and as far as Hodges knows, there's no such thing as a bad pair—the watcher could have put himself right into the Ellerton-Stover living room, assuming the blinds were up . . . and they had been when he and Holly were in that room this morning. Hell, if the women had been watching

CNN, the watcher could have read the news crawl at the bottom of the screen.

Hodges doesn't have an evidence Baggie, but there's a travel-sized pack of Kleenex in his coat pocket. He takes out two, carefully wraps the lens cap, and slips it into the inside pocket of his coat. He rises from the chair (provoking another twinge; the pain is bad this afternoon), then spies something else. Someone has carved a single letter into the wood upright between the two overhead doors, perhaps using a pocketknife.

It's the letter Z.

12

They are almost back to the driveway when Hodges is visited by something new: a searing bolt of agony behind his left knee. It feels as if he's been stabbed. He cries out as much in surprise as from the pain and bends over, kneading at the throbbing knot, trying to make it let go. To loosen up a little, at least.

Tom bends down next to him, and thus neither of them sees the elderly Chevrolet cruising slowly along Hilltop Court. Its fading blue paint is dappled with spots of red primer. The old gent behind the wheel slows down even more, so he can stare at the two men. Then the Chevrolet speeds up, sending a puff of blue exhaust from its tailpipe, and passes the Ellerton-Stover house, headed for the buttonhook turnaround at the end of the street.

"What is it?" Tom asks. "What happened?"

"Cramp," Hodges says through gritted teeth.

"Rub it."

Hodges gives him a look of pained humor through his tumbled hair. "What do you think I'm doing?"

"Let me."

Tom Saubers, a physical therapy veteran thanks to his attendance at a certain job fair six years ago, pushes Hodges's hand aside. He removes one of his gloves and digs in with his fingers. Hard.

"Ow! Jesus! That fucking hurts!"

"I know," Tom says. "Can't be helped. Move as much of your weight to your good leg as you can."

Hodges does so. The Malibu with its patches of dull red primer paint cruises slowly by once more, this time headed back down the hill. The driver helps himself to another long look, then speeds up again.

"It's letting go," Hodges says. "Thank God for small favors." It is, but his stomach is on fire and his lower back feels like he wrenched it.

Tom is looking at him with concern. "You sure you're all right?"

"Yeah. Just a charley horse."

"Or maybe a deep vein thrombosis. You're no kid anymore, Bill. You ought to get that checked out. If anything happened to you while you were with me, Pete would never forgive me. His sister, either. We owe you a lot."

"All taken care of, got a doctor's appointment tomorrow," Hodges says. "Come on, let's get out of here. It's freezing."

He limps the first two or three steps, but then the pain behind his knee lets go entirely and he's able to walk normally. More normally than Tom. Thanks to his encounter with Brady Hartsfield in April of 2009, Tom Saubers will limp for the rest of his life.

13

When Hodges gets home, his stomach is better but he's dog tired. He tires easily these days and tells himself it's because his appetite has gotten so lousy, but he wonders if that's really it. He's heard the pane of breaking glass and the boys giving their home run cheer twice on his way back from Ridgedale, but he never looks at his phone while driving, partly because it's dangerous (not to mention illegal in this state), mostly because he refuses to become a slave to it.

Besides, he doesn't need to be a mind reader to know from whom at least one of those texts came. He waits until he's hung his coat in the front hall closet, briefly touching the inside pocket to make sure the lens cap is still safe and sound.

The first text is from Holly. **We should talk to Pete and Isabelle, but call me first. I have a Q.**

The other isn't hers. It reads: **Dr. Stamos needs to talk to you urgently. You are scheduled tomorrow at 9 AM. Please keep this appointment!**

Hodges checks his watch and sees that, although this day seems to have lasted at least a month already, it's only quarter past four. He calls Stamos's office and gets Marlee. He can tell it's her by the chirpy cheerleader's voice, which turns grave when he introduces himself. He doesn't know what those tests showed, but it can't be good. As Bob Dylan once said, you don't need a weatherman to know which way the wind blows.

He bargains for nine thirty instead of nine, because he wants a sit-down with Holly, Pete, and Isabelle first. He won't allow himself to believe that his visit to Dr. Stamos's office may be followed by a hospital admission, but he is a realist, and that sudden bolt of pain in his leg scared the shit out of him.

Marlee puts him on hold. Hodges listens to the Young Rascals for awhile (They must be mighty old Rascals by now, he thinks), and then she comes back. "We can get you in at nine thirty, Mr. Hodges, but Dr. Stamos wants me to emphasize that it's imperative that you keep this appointment."

"How bad is it?" He asks before he can stop himself.

"I don't have any information on your case," Marlee tells him, "but I'd say that you should get going on what's wrong as soon as possible. Don't you think so?"

"I do," Hodges says heavily. "I'll keep the appointment for sure. And thank you."

He breaks the connection and stares at his phone. On the screen is a picture of his daughter at seven, bright and smiling, riding high on the backyard swing he put up when they lived on Freeborn Avenue. When they were still a family. Now Allie's thirty-six, divorced, in therapy, and getting over a painful relationship with a man who told her a story as old as Genesis: *I'm going to leave her soon, but this is a bad time.*

Hodges puts the phone down and lifts his shirt. The pain on the left side of his abdomen has subsided to a low mutter again, and that's good, but he doesn't like the swelling he sees below his sternum. It's as if he just put away a huge meal, when in fact he could only eat half of his lunch and breakfast was a bagel.

"What's going on with you?" he asks his swollen stomach. "I wouldn't mind a clue before I keep that appointment tomorrow."

He supposes he could get all the clues he wants by firing up his computer and going to Web MD, but he's come to believe that Internet-assisted self-diagnosis is a game for idiots. He calls Holly, instead. She wants to know if he found anything interesting at 1588.

"*Very* interesting, as that guy on *Laugh-In* used to say, but before I go into that, ask your question."

"Do you think Pete can find out if Martine Stover was buying a computer? Check her credit cards, or something? Because her mother's was *ancient*. If so, it means she was serious about taking an online course. And if she was serious, then—"

"Then the chances she was working up to a suicide pact with her mother drop drastically."

"Yes."

"But it wouldn't rule out the mother deciding to do it on her own. She could have dumped the pills and vodka down Stover's feeding tube while she was asleep, then got into the tub to finish the job."

"But Nancy Alderson said—"

"They were happy, yeah, I know. I'm only pointing it out. I don't really believe it."

"You sound tired."

"Just my usual end-of-the-day slump. I'll perk up after I get some chow." Never in his life has he felt less like eating.

"Eat a lot. You're too thin. But first tell me what you found in that empty house."

"Not in the house. In the garage."

He tells her. She doesn't interrupt. Nor does she say anything when he's done. Holly sometimes forgets she's on the phone, so he gives her a prompt.

"What do you think?"

"I don't know. I mean, I really don't. It's just . . . weird all over. Don't you think so? Or not? Because I could be overreacting. Sometimes I do that."

Tell me about it, Hodges thinks, but this time he doesn't think she is, and says so.

Holly says, "You told me you didn't think Janice Ellerton would take anything from a man in a mended parka and workman's clothes."

"Indeed I did."

"So that means . . ."

Now he's the one who stays silent, letting her work it out.

"It means two men were up to something. *Two*. One gave Janice Ellerton the Zappit and the bogus questionnaire while she was shopping, and the other watched her house from across the street. And with binoculars! *Expensive* binoculars! I guess those two men might not have been working together, but . . ."

He waits. Smiling a little. When Holly turns her thinking processes up to ten, he can almost hear the cogs spinning behind her forehead.

"Bill, are you still there?"

"Yeah. Just waiting for you to spit it out."

"Well, it seems like they must have been. To me, anyway. And like they might have had something to do with those two women being dead. There, are you happy?"

"Yes, Holly. I am. I've got a doctor's appointment tomorrow at nine thirty—"

"Your test results came back?"

"Yeah. I want to set up a meeting beforehand with Pete and Isabelle. Does eight thirty work for you?"

"Of course."

"We'll lay out everything, tell them about Alderson and the game console you found and the house at 1588. See what they think. Sound okay?"

"Yes, but *she* won't think anything."

"You could be wrong."

"Yes. And the sky could turn green with red polka dots tomorrow. Now go make yourself something to eat."

Hodges assures her he will, and heats up a can of chicken noodle soup while watching the early news. He eats most of it, spacing out each spoonful, cheering himself on: You can do it, you can do it.

While he's rinsing the bowl, the pain on the left side of his abdomen returns, along with those tentacles curling around to his lower back. It seems to plunge up and down with every heartbeat. His stomach clenches. He thinks of running to the bathroom, but it's too late. He leans over the sink instead, vomiting with his eyes closed. He keeps them that way as he fumbles for the faucet and turns it on full to rinse away the mess. He doesn't want to see what just came out of him, because he can taste a slime of blood in his mouth and throat.

Oy, he thinks, I am in trouble here.

I am in such trouble.

14

Eight PM.

When her doorbell rings, Ruth Scapelli is watching some stupid reality program which is just an excuse to show young men and women running around in their small clothes. Instead of going directly to the door, she slipper-scuffs into the kitchen and turns on the monitor for the security cam mounted on the porch. She lives in a safe neighborhood, but it doesn't pay to take chances; one of her late mother's favorite sayings was *scum travels*.

She is surprised and uneasy when she recognizes the man at

her door. He's wearing a tweed overcoat, obviously expensive, and a trilby with a feather in the band. Beneath the hat, his perfectly barbered silver hair flows dramatically along his temples. In one hand is a slim briefcase. It's Dr. Felix Babineau, chief of the Neurology Department and head honcho at the Lakes Region Traumatic Brain Injury Clinic.

The doorbell chimes again and she hurries to let him in, thinking *He can't know about what I did this afternoon because the door was shut and no one saw me go in. Relax. It's something else. Perhaps a union matter.*

But he has never discussed union matters with her before, although she's been an officer of Nurses United for the last five years. Dr. Babineau might not even know her if he passed her on the street unless she was wearing her nurse's uniform. That makes her remember what she's wearing now, an old housecoat and even older slippers (with bunny faces on them!), but it's too late to do anything about that. At least her hair isn't up in rollers.

He should have called, she thinks, but the thought that follows is disquieting: *Maybe he wanted to catch me by surprise.*

"Good evening, Dr. Babineau. Come in out of the cold. I'm sorry to be greeting you in my housecoat, but I wasn't expecting company."

He comes in and just stands there in the hall. She has to step around him to close the door. Seen up close instead of on the monitor, she thinks that perhaps they're even in the department of sartorial disarray. She's in her housecoat and slippers, true, but his cheeks are speckled with gray stubble. Dr. Babineau (no one would dream of calling him Dr. Felix) may be quite the fashion plate—witness the cashmere scarf fluffed up around his throat—but tonight he needs a shave, and quite badly. Also, there are purple pouches under his eyes.

"Let me take your coat," she says.

He puts his briefcase between his shoes, unbuttons the over-coat, and hands it to her, along with the luxy scarf. He still hasn't said a single word. The lasagna she ate for supper, quite delicious at the time, seems to be sinking, and pulling the pit of her stomach down with it.

"Would you like—"

"Come into the living room," he says, and walks past her as if he owns the place. Ruth Scapelli scurries after.

Babineau takes the remote control from the arm of her easy chair, points it at the television, and hits mute. The young men and women continue to run around, but they do so unaccompa-nied by the mindless patter of the announcer. Scapelli is no lon-ger just uneasy; now she's afraid. For her job, yes, the position she has worked so hard to attain, but also for herself. There's a look in his eyes that is really no look at all, only a kind of vacancy.

"Could I get you something? A soft drink or a cup of—"

"Listen to me, Nurse Scapelli. And very closely, if you want to keep your position."

"I . . . I . . ."

"Nor would it end with losing your job." Babineau puts his briefcase on the seat of her easy chair and undoes the cunning gold clasps. They make little thudding sounds as they fly up. "You committed an act of assault on a mentally deficient patient today, what might be construed a *sexual* assault, and followed it with what the law calls criminal threatening."

"I . . . I never . . ."

She can barely hear herself. She thinks she might faint if she doesn't sit down, but his briefcase is in her favorite chair. She makes her way across the living room to the sofa, barking her shin on the coffee table en route, almost hard enough to tip it over. She feels a thin trickle of blood sliding down to her ankle, but doesn't look at it. If she does that, she *will* faint.

"You twisted Mr. Hartsfield's nipple. Then you threatened to do the same to his testes."

"He made an obscene gesture to me!" Scapelli bursts out. "Showed me his middle finger!"

"I will see that you never work in the nursing profession again," he says, looking into the depths of his briefcase as she half-swoons onto the sofa. His initials are monogrammed on the side of the case. In gold, of course. He drives a new BMW, and that haircut probably cost fifty dollars. Maybe more. He's an overbearing, domineering boss, and now he's threatening to ruin her life over one small mistake. One small error in judgment.

She wouldn't mind if the floor opened up and swallowed her, but her vision is perversely clear. She seems to see every filament on the feather poking out of his hatband, every scarlet thread in his bloodshot eyes, every ugly gray speck of stubble on his cheeks and chin. His hair would be that same rat fur color, she thinks, if he didn't dye it.

"I . . ." Tears begin to come—hot tears running down her cold cheeks. "I . . . please, Dr. Babineau." She doesn't know how he knows, and it doesn't matter. The fact is, he does. "I'll never do it again. Please. *Please.*"

Dr. Babineau doesn't bother to answer.

15

Selma Valdez, one of four nurses who work the three-to-eleven shift in the Bucket, gives a perfunctory rap on the door of 217—

perfunctory because the resident never answers—and steps in. Brady is sitting in his chair by the window, looking out into the dark. His bedside lamp is on, showing the golden highlights in his hair. He is still wearing his button reading I WAS SHAVED BY NURSE BARBARA!

She starts to ask if he's ready for a little help in getting ready for bed (he can't unbutton his shirt or pants, but he is capable of shuffling out of them once that's accomplished), but then rethinks the idea. Dr. Babineau has added a note to Hartsfield's chart, one written in imperative red ink: "Patient is not to be disturbed when in a semiconscious state. During these periods, his brain may actually be 'rebooting' itself in small but appreciable increments. Come back and check at half-hour intervals. Do not ignore this directive."

Selma doesn't think Hartsfield is rebooting jack shit, he's just off in gorkland, but like all the nurses who work in the Bucket, she's a bit afraid of Babineau, and knows he has a habit of showing up at any time, even in the small hours of the morning, and right now it's just gone eight PM.

At some point since she last checked him, Hartsfield has managed to get up and take the three steps to his bedside table where his game gadget is kept. He doesn't have the manual dexterity needed to play any of the pre-loaded games, but he can turn it on. He enjoys holding it in his lap and looking at the demo screens. Sometimes he'll do it for an hour or more, bent over like a man studying for an important exam. His favorite is the Fishin' Hole demo, and he's looking at it now. A little tune that she remembers from her childhood is playing: *By the sea, by the sea, by the beautiful sea . . .*

She approaches, thinks of saying You really like that one, don't you, but remembers *Do not ignore this directive*, underlined, and looks down at the small five inches-by-three screen instead. She gets why he likes it; there's something beautiful and fascinating in the way the exotic fish appear, pause, and then zip away with a single flip of their tails. Some are red . . . some are blue . . . some are yellow . . . oh, and there's a pretty pink one—

"Stop looking."

Brady's voice grates like the hinges on a seldom-opened door, and while there is an appreciable space between the words, they are perfectly clear. Nothing at all like his usual mushy mumble. Selma jumps as if he goosed her instead of just speaking to her. On the Zappit screen there's a momentary flash of blue light that obliterates the fish, but then they're back. Selma glances down at the watch pinned upside-down to her smock and sees it's now eight twenty. Jesus, has she really been standing here for almost twenty minutes?

"Go."

Brady is still looking down at the screen where the fish swim back and forth, back and forth. Selma drags her eyes away, but it's an effort.

"Come back later." Pause. "When I'm done." Pause. "Looking."

Selma does as she's told, and once she's back in the hall, she feels like herself again. He spoke to her, big whoop. And if he enjoys watching the Fishin' Hole demo the way some guys enjoy watching girls in bikinis play volleyball? Again, big whoop. The real question is why they let *kids* have those consoles. They can't be good for their immature brains, can they? On the other hand, kids play computer games all the time, so maybe they're immune. In the meantime, she has plenty to do. Let Hartsfield sit in his chair and look at his gizmo.

After all, he's not hurting anybody.

16

Felix Babineau bends stiffly forward from the waist, like an android in an old sci-fi movie. He reaches into his briefcase and brings out a flat pink gadget that looks like an e-reader. The screen is gray and blank.

"There's a number in here I want you to find," he says. "A nine-digit number. If you can find that number, Nurse Scapelli, today's incident will remain between us."

The first thing that comes to mind is You must be crazy, but she can't say that, not when he holds her whole life in his hands. "How can I? I don't know anything about those electronic gadgets! I can barely work my phone!"

"Nonsense. As a surgical nurse, you were in great demand. Because of your dexterity."

True enough, but it's been ten years since she worked in the Kiner surgical suites, handing out scissors and retractors and sponges. She was offered a six-week course in microsurgery— the hospital would have paid seventy percent—but she had no interest. Or so she claimed; in truth, she was afraid of failing the course. He's right, though, in her prime she had been fast.

Babineau pushes a button on top of the gadget. She cranes her neck to see. It lights up, and the words WELCOME TO ZAPPIT! appear. This is followed by a screen showing all sorts of icons. Games, she supposes. He swipes the screen once, twice, then tells her to stand next to him. When she hesitates, he smiles. Perhaps it's meant to be pleasant and inviting, but it terrifies her, instead. Because there's nothing in his eyes, no human expression at all.

"Come, Nurse. I won't *bite* you."

Of course not. Only what if he does?

Nevertheless, she steps closer so she can see the screen, where exotic fish are swimming back and forth. When they flick their tails, bubbles stream up. A vaguely familiar little tune plays.

"Do you see this one? It's called Fishin' Hole."

"Y-Yes." Thinking, *He really is crazy. He's had some sort of mental breakdown from overwork.*

"If you were to tap the bottom of the screen, the game would come up and the music would change, but I don't want you to do that. The demo is all you need. Look for the pink fish. They don't come often, and they're fast, so you have to watch carefully. You can't take your eyes off the screen."

"Dr. Babineau, are you all right?"

It's her voice, but it seems to be coming from far away. He makes no reply, just keeps looking at the screen. Scapelli is looking, too. Those fish are interesting. And the little tune, that's sort of hypnotic. There's a flash of blue light from the screen. She blinks, and then the fish are back. Swimming to and fro. Flicking their flippy tails and sending up burbles of bubbles.

"Each time you see a pink fish, tap it and a number will come up. Nine pink fish, nine numbers. Then you will be done and all this will be behind us. Do you understand?"

She thinks of asking him if she's supposed to write the numbers down or just remember them, but that seems too hard, so she just says yes.

"Good." He hands her the gadget. "Nine fish, nine numbers. But just the pink ones, mind."

Scapelli stares at the screen where the fish swim: red and green, green and blue, blue and yellow. They swim off the left side of the little rectangular screen, then back on at the right. They swim off the right side of the screen, then back on at the left.

Left, right.

Right, left.

Some high, some low.

But where are the pink ones? She needs to tap the pink ones and when she's tapped nine of them, all of this will be behind her.

From the corner of one eye she sees Babineau refastening the clasps on his briefcase. He picks it up and leaves the room. He's going. It doesn't matter. She has to tap the pink fish, and then all of this will be behind her. A flash of blue light from the screen, and then the fish are back. They swim left to right and right to left. The tune plays: *By the sea, by the sea, by the beautiful sea, you and me, you and me, oh how happy we'll be.*

A pink one! She taps it! The number 11 appears! Eight more to go!

She taps a second pink fish as the front door quietly closes, and a third as Dr. Babineau's car starts outside. She stands in the middle of her living room, lips parted as if for a kiss, staring down at the screen. Colors shift and move on her cheeks and forehead. Her eyes are wide and unblinking. A fourth pink fish swims into view, this one moving slowly, as if inviting the tap of her finger, but she only stands there.

"Hello, Nurse Scapelli."

She looks up to see Brady Hartsfield sitting in her easy chair. He's shimmering a bit at the edges, ghostly, but it's him, all right. He's wearing what he was wearing when she visited him in his room that afternoon: jeans and a checked shirt. On the shirt is that button reading I WAS SHAVED BY NURSE BAR-BARA! But the vacant gaze everyone in the Bucket has grown used to is gone. He's looking at her with lively interest. She remembers her brother looking at his ant farm that way when they were children back in Hershey, Pennsylvania.

He must be a ghost, because fish are swimming in his eyes.

"He'll tell," Hartsfield says. "And it won't just be his word against yours, don't get that idea. He had a nanny-cam planted in my room so he can watch me. Study me. It's got a wide-angle lens so he can see the whole room. That kind of lens is called a fish-eye."

He smiles to show he's made a pun. A red fish swims across his right eye, disappears, and then appears in his left one. Scapelli thinks, His brain is full of fish. I'm seeing his thoughts.

"The camera is hooked up to a recorder. He'll show the board of directors the footage of you torturing me. It didn't actually hurt that much, I don't feel pain the way I used to, but torture is what he'll call it. It won't end there, either. He'll put it on YouTube. And Facebook. And Bad Medicine dot-com. It will go viral. You'll be famous. The Torturing Nurse. And who will come to your defense? Who will stand up for you? No one. Because nobody likes you. They think you're awful. And what do *you* think? Do you think you're awful?"

Now that the idea has been brought fully to her attention, she supposes she is. Anyone who would threaten to twist the testicles of a brain-damaged man *must* be awful. What was she thinking?

"Say it." He leans forward, smiling.

The fish swim. The blue light flashes. The tune plays.

"Say it, you worthless bitch."

"I'm awful," Ruth Scapelli says in her living room, which is empty except for her. She stares down at the screen of the Zappit Commander.

"Now say it like you mean it."

"I'm awful. I'm an awful worthless bitch."

"And what is Dr. Babineau going to do?"

"Put it on YouTube. Put it on Facebook. Put it on Bad Medicine dot-com. Tell everyone."

"You'll be arrested."

"I'll be arrested."

"They'll put your picture in the paper."

"Of course they will."

"You'll go to jail."

"I'll go to jail."

"Who will stand up for you?"

"No one."

## 17

Sitting in Room 217 of the Bucket, Brady stares down at the Fishin' Hole demo. His face is fully awake and aware. It's the face he hides from everyone except Felix Babineau, and Dr. Babineau no longer matters. Dr. Babineau hardly exists. These days he's mostly Dr. Z.

"Nurse Scapelli," Brady says. "Let's go into the kitchen."

She resists, but not for long.

## 18

Hodges tries to swim below the pain and stay asleep, but it pulls him up steadily until he breaks the surface and opens his eyes. He fumbles for the bedside clock and sees it's two AM. A bad time to be awake, maybe the worst time. When he suffered insomnia after his retirement, he thought of two AM as the suicide hour and now he thinks, That's probably when Mrs. Ellerton did it. Two in the morning. The hour when it seems daylight will never come.

He gets out of bed, walks slowly to the bathroom, and takes the giant economy-sized bottle of Gelusil out of the medicine cabinet, careful not to look at himself in the mirror. He chugalugs four big swallows, then leans over, waiting to see if his stomach will accept it or hit the ejector button, as it did with the chicken soup.

It stays down and the pain actually begins to recede. Sometimes Gelusil does that. Not always.

He thinks about going back to bed, but he's afraid that dull throb will return as soon as he's horizontal. He shuffles into his office instead and turns on his computer. He knows this is the very worst time to start checking out the possible causes for his symptoms, but he can no longer resist. His desktop wallpaper comes up (another picture of Allie as a kid). He mouses down to the bottom of the screen, meaning to open Firefox, then freezes. There's something new in the dock. Between the balloon icon for text messaging and the camera icon for FaceTime, there's a blue umbrella with a red *1* sitting above it.

"A message on Debbie's Blue Umbrella," he says. "I'll be damned."

A much younger Jerome Robinson downloaded the Blue Umbrella app to his computer almost six years ago. Brady Hartsfield, aka Mr. Mercedes, wanted to converse with the cop who had failed to catch him, and, although retired, Hodges was very willing to talk. Because once you got dirtbags like Mr. Mercedes talking (there weren't very many like him, and thank God for that), they were only a step or two from being caught. This was especially true of the arrogant ones, and Hartsfield had been arrogance personified.

They both had their reasons for communicating on a secure,

supposedly untraceable chat site with servers located someplace in deepest, darkest Eastern Europe. Hodges wanted to goad the perpetrator of the City Center Massacre into making a mistake that would help identify him. Mr. Mercedes wanted to goad Hodges into killing himself. He had succeeded with Olivia Trelawney, after all.

*What kind of life do you have?* he had written in his first communication to Hodges—the one that had arrived by snail-mail. *What kind, now that the "thrill of the hunt" is behind you?* And then: *Want to get in touch with me? Try Under Debbie's Blue Umbrella. I even got you a username: "kermitfrog19."*

With plenty of help from Jerome Robinson and Holly Gibney, Hodges tracked Brady down, and Holly clobbered him. Jerome and Holly got free city services for ten years; Hodges got a pacemaker. There were sorrows and loss Hodges doesn't want to think about—not even now, all these years later—but you'd have to say that for the city, and especially for those who had been attending the concert at the Mingo that night, all ended well.

At some point between 2010 and now, the blue umbrella icon disappeared from the dock at the bottom of his screen. If Hodges ever wondered what happened to it (he can't remember that he ever did), he probably assumed either Jerome or Holly dumped it in the trash on one of their visits to fix whatever current outrage he had perpetrated on his defenseless Macintosh. Instead, one of them must have tucked it into the apps folder, where the blue umbrella has remained, just out of sight, all these years. Hell, maybe he even did the dragging himself and has forgotten. Memory has a way of slipping a few gears after sixty-five, when people round the third turn start down the home stretch.

He mouses to the blue umbrella, hesitates, then clicks. His desktop screen is replaced by a young couple on a magic carpet floating over an endless sea. Silver rain is falling, but the couple is safe and dry beneath a protective blue umbrella.

Ah, such memories this brings back.

He enters **kermitfrog19** as both his username and his password—isn't that how he did it before, as per Hartsfield's instructions? He can't remember for sure, but there's one way to find out. He bangs the return key.

The machine thinks for a second or two (it seems longer), and then, presto, he's in. He frowns at what he sees. Brady Hartsfield used **merckill** as his handle, short for Mercedes Killer—Hodges has no trouble remembering that—but this is someone else. Which shouldn't surprise him, since Holly turned Hartsfield's fucked-up brain to oatmeal, but somehow it still does.

**Z-Boy wants to chat with you!**
**Do you want to chat with Z-Boy?**
**Y N**

Hodges hits **Y**, and a moment later a message appears. Just a single sentence, half a dozen words, but Hodges reads them over and over again, feeling not fear but excitement. He is onto something here. He doesn't know what it is, but it feels big.

**Z-Boy: He's not done with you yet.**

Hodges stares at it, frowning. At last he sits forward in his chair and types:

**kermitfrog19: Who's not done with me? Who is this?**

There's no answer.

19

Hodges and Holly get together with Pete and Isabelle at Dave's Diner, a greasy spoon a block down from the morning madhouse known as Starbucks. With the early breakfast rush over, they have their pick of tables and settle at one in the back. In the kitchen a Badfinger song is playing on the radio and waitresses are laughing.

"All I've got is half an hour," Hodges says. "Then I have to run to the doctor's."

Pete leans forward, looking concerned. "Nothing serious, I hope."

"Nope. I feel fine." This morning he actually does—like forty-five again. That message on his computer, cryptic and sinister though it was, seems to have been better medicine than the Gelusil. "Let's get to what we've found. Holly, they'll want Exhibit A and Exhibit B. Hand em over."

Holly has brought her small tartan briefcase to the meeting. From it (and not without reluctance) she brings the Zappit Commander and the lens cap from the garage at 1588. Both are in plastic bags, although the lens cap is still wrapped in tissues.

"What have you two been up to?" Pete asks. He's striving for humorous, but Hodges can hear a touch of accusation there, as well.

"Investigating," Holly says, and although she isn't ordinarily one for eye contact, she shoots a brief look at Izzy Jaynes, as if to say Get the point?

"Explain," Izzy says.

Hodges does so while Holly sits beside him with her eyes cast down, her decaf—all she drinks—untouched. Her jaws are moving, though, and Hodges knows she's back on the Nicorette.

"Unbelievable," Izzy says when Hodges has finished. She pokes at the bag with the Zappit inside. "You just *took* this. Wrapped it up in newspaper like a piece of salmon from the fish market and carried it out of the house."

Holly appears to shrink in her chair. Her hands are so tightly clasped in her lap that the knuckles are white.

Hodges usually likes Isabelle well enough, even though she once nearly tripped him up in an interrogation room (this during the Mr. Mercedes thing, when he had been hip-deep in an unauthorized investigation), but he doesn't like her much now. He can't like anyone who makes Holly shrink like that.

"Be reasonable, Iz. Think it through. If Holly hadn't found that thing—and purely by accident—it would still be there. You guys weren't going to search the house."

"You probably weren't going to call the housekeeper, either," Holly says, and although she still won't look up, there's metal in her voice. Hodges is glad to hear it.

"We would have gotten to the Alderson woman in time," Izzy says, but those misty gray eyes of hers flick up and to the left as she says it. It's a classic liar's tell, and Hodges knows when he sees it that she and Pete haven't even discussed the housekeeper yet, although they probably *would* have gotten around to her eventually. Pete Huntley may be a bit of a plodder, but plodders are usually thorough, you had to give them that.

"If there were any fingerprints on that gadget," Izzy says, "they're gone now. Kiss them goodbye."

Holly mutters something under her breath, making Hodges remember that when he first met her (and completely underestimated her), he thought of her as Holly the Mumbler.

Izzy leans forward, her gray eyes suddenly not misty at all. "*What* did you say?"

"She said that's silly," Hodges says, knowing perfectly well that the word was actually *stupid*. "She's right. It was shoved down between the arm of Ellerton's chair and the cushion. Any fingerprints on it would be blurred, and you know it. Also, *were* you going to search the whole house?"

"We might have," Isabelle says, sounding sulky. "Depending on what we get back from forensics."

Other than in Martine Stover's bedroom and bathroom, there *were* no forensics. They all know this, Izzy included, and there's no need for Hodges to belabor the point.

"Take it easy," Pete says to Isabelle. "I invited Kermit and Holly out there, and you agreed."

"That was before I knew they were going to walk out with . . ."

She trails off. Hodges waits with interest to see how she will finish. Is she going to say *with a piece of the evidence?* Evidence of what? An addiction to computer solitaire, Angry Birds, and Frogger?

"With a piece of Mrs. Ellerton's property," she finishes lamely.

"Well, you've got it now," Hodges says. "Can we move on? Perhaps discuss the man who gave it to her in the supermarket, claiming the company was eager for user input on a gadget that's no longer made?"

"And the man who was watching them," Holly says, still without looking up. "The man who was watching them from across the street with binoculars."

Hodges's old partner pokes the bag with the wrapped lens cap inside. "I'll have this dusted for fingerprints, but I'm not real hopeful, Kerm. You know how people take these caps on and off."

"Yeah," Hodges says. "By the rim. And it was cold in that garage. Cold enough so I could see my breath. The guy was probably wearing gloves, anyway."

"The guy in the supermarket was most likely working some kind of short con," Izzy says. "It's got that smell. Maybe he called a week later, trying to convince her that by taking the obsolete games gadget, she was obligated to buy a more expensive current one, and she told him to go peddle his papers. Or he might have used the info from the questionnaire to hack into her computer."

"Not *that* computer," Holly says. "It was older than dirt."

"Had a good look around, didn't you?" Izzy says. "Did you check the medicine cabinets while you were investigating?"

This is too much for Hodges. "She was doing what you should have done, Isabelle. And you know it."

Color is rising in Izzy's cheeks. "We called you in as a courtesy, that's all, and I wish we'd never done it. You two are always trouble."

"Stop it," Pete says.

But Izzy is leaning forward, her eyes flicking between Hodges's face and the top of Holly's lowered head. "These two mystery men—if they existed at all—have nothing to do with what happened in that house. One was probably running a con, the other was a simple peeper."

Hodges knows he should stay friendly here—increase the peace, and all that—but he just can't do it. "Some pervo salivating at the thought of watching an eighty-year-old woman undress, or seeing a quadriplegic get a sponge bath? Yeah, that makes sense."

"Read my lips," Izzy says. "Mom killed daughter, then self. Even left a suicide note of sorts—Z, the end. Couldn't be any clearer."

Z-Boy, Hodges thinks. Whoever's under Debbie's Blue Umbrella this time signs himself Z-Boy.

Holly lifts her head. "There was also a Z in the garage. Carved into the wood between the doors. Bill saw it. Zappit also begins with Z, you know."

"Yes," Izzy says. "And Kennedy and Lincoln have the same number of letters, proving they were both killed by the same man."

Hodges sneaks a peek at his watch and sees he'll have to leave soon, and that's okay. Other than upsetting Holly and pissing off Izzy, this meeting has accomplished nothing. Nor can it, because he has no intention of telling Pete and Isabelle what he discovered on his own computer early this morning. That information might shift the investigation into a higher gear, but he's going to keep it on the down-low until he does a little more investigation himself. He doesn't want to think that Pete would fumble it, but—

But he might. Because being thorough is a poor substitute for being thoughtful. And Izzy? She doesn't want to open a can of worms filled with a lot of pulp-novel stuff about cryptic letters and mystery men. Not when the deaths at the Ellerton house are already on the front page of today's paper, along with a complete recap of how Martine Stover came to be paralyzed. Not when Izzy's expecting to take the next step up the police department ladder just as soon as her current partner retires.

"Bottom line," Pete says, "this is going down as a murder-suicide, and we're gonna move on. We *have* to move on, Kermit. I'm retiring. Iz will be left with a huge caseload and no new partner for awhile, thanks to the damn budget cuts. This stuff"—he indicates the two plastic bags—"is sort of interesting, but it doesn't change the clarity of what happened. Unless you think some master criminal set it up? One who drives an old car and mends his coat with masking tape?"

"No, I don't think that." Hodges is remembering something Holly said about Brady Hartsfield yesterday. She used the word *architect*. "I think you've got it right. Murder-suicide."

Holly gives him a brief look of wounded surprise before lowering her eyes again.

"But will you do something for me?"

"If I can," Pete says.

"I tried the game console, but the screen stayed blank. Probably a dead battery. I didn't want to open the battery compartment, because that little slide panel *would* be a place to check for fingerprints."

"I'll see that it's dusted, but I doubt—"

"Yeah, I do, too. What I really want is for one of your cyberwonks to boot it up and check the various game applications. See if there's anything out of the ordinary."

"Okay," Pete says, and shifts slightly in his seat when Izzy rolls her eyes. Hodges can't be sure, but he thinks Pete just kicked her ankle under the table.

"I have to go," Hodges says, and grabs for his wallet. "Missed my appointment yesterday. Can't miss another one."

"We'll pick up the check," Izzy says. "After you brought us all this valuable evidence, it's the least we can do."

Holly mutters something else under her breath. This time Hodges can't be sure, even with his trained Holly-ear, but he thinks it might have been *bitch*.


20


On the sidewalk, Holly jams an unfashionable but somehow charming plaid hunting cap down to her ears and then thrusts her hands into her coat pockets. She won't look at him, only starts walking toward the office a block away. Hodges's car is parked outside Dave's, but he hurries after her.

"Holly."

"You see how she is." Walking faster. Still not looking at him.

The pain in his gut is creeping back, and he's losing his breath. "Holly, wait. I can't keep up."

She turns to him, and he's alarmed to see her eyes are swimming with tears.

"There's more to it! More more more! But they're just going to sweep it under the rug and they didn't even say the real reason which is so Pete can have a nice retirement party without this hanging over his head the way you had to retire with the Mercedes Killer hanging over yours and so the papers don't make a big deal of it and you know there's more to it I know you do and I know you have to get your test results I *want* you to get them because I'm so *worried*, but those poor women . . . I just don't think . . . they don't deserve to . . . to just be *shoveled under*!"

She halts at last, trembling. The tears are already freezing on her cheeks. He tilts her face to look at him, knowing she would shrink away if anyone else tried to touch her that way—yes, even Jerome Robinson, and she loves Jerome, probably has since the day the two of them discovered the ghost-program Brady left in Olivia Trelawney's computer, the one that finally pushed her over the edge and caused her to take her own overdose.

"Holly, we're not done with this. In fact I think we might just be getting started."

She looks him squarely in the face, another thing she will do with no one else. "What do you mean?"

"Something new has come up, something I didn't want to tell

Pete and Izzy. I don't know what the hell to make of it. There's no time to tell you now, but when I get back from the doctor's, I'll tell you everything."

"All right, that's fine. Go on, now. And although I don't believe in God, I'll say a prayer for your test results. Because a little prayer can't hurt, can it?"

"No."

He gives her a quick hug—long hugs don't work with Holly—and starts back to his car, once more thinking of that thing she said yesterday, about Brady Hartsfield being an architect of suicide. A pretty turn of phrase from a woman who writes poetry in her spare time (not that Hodges has ever seen any, or is likely to), but Brady would probably sneer at it, consider it a mile short of the mark. Brady would consider himself a *prince* of suicide.

Hodges climbs into the Prius Holly nagged him into buying and heads for Dr. Stamos's office. He's doing a little praying himself: Let it be an ulcer. Even the bleeding kind that needs surgery to sew it up.

Just an ulcer.

Please nothing worse than that.


21


He doesn't have to spend time cooling his heels in the waiting room today. Although he's five minutes early and the room is as full as it was on Monday, Marlee the cheerleader receptionist sends him in before he even has a chance to sit down.

Belinda Jensen, Stamos's nurse, usually greets him at his yearly physicals with smiling good cheer, but she's not smiling this morning, and as Hodges steps on the scale, he remembers his yearly physical is a bit overdue. By four months. Actually closer to five.

The armature on the old-fashioned scale balances at 165. When he retired from the cops in '09, he weighed 230 at the mandatory exit physical. Belinda takes his blood pressure, pokes something in his ear to get his current temperature, then leads him past the exam rooms and directly to Dr. Stamos's office at the end of the corridor. She knocks a knuckle on the door, and when Stamos says "Please come in," she leaves Hodges at once. Usually voluble, full of tales about her fractious children and bumptious husband, she has today spoken hardly a word.

Can't be good, Hodges thinks, but maybe it's not too bad. Please God, not too bad. Another ten years wouldn't be a lot to ask for, would it? Or if You can't do that, how about five?

Wendell Stamos is a fiftysomething with a fast-receding hairline and the broad-shouldered, trim-waisted build of a pro jock who's stayed in shape after retirement. He looks at Hodges gravely and invites him to sit down. Hodges does so.

"How bad?"

"Bad," Dr. Stamos says, then hastens to add, "but not hopeless."

"Don't skate around it, just tell me."

"It's pancreatic cancer, and I'm afraid we caught it . . . well . . . rather late in the game. Your liver is involved."

Hodges finds himself fighting a strong and dismaying urge to laugh. No, more than laugh, to just throw back his head and yodel like Heidi's fucking grandfather. He thinks it was Stamos saying *bad but not hopeless*. It makes him remember an old joke. Doctor tells his patient there's good news and bad news; which does the patient want first? Hit me with the bad news, says the patient. Well, says the doctor, you have an inoperable brain tumor. The patient starts to blubber and asks what the good news can possibly be after learning a thing like that. The doctor leans forward, smiling confidentially, and says, I'm fucking my receptionist, and she's *gorgeous*.

"I'll want you to see a gastroenterologist immediately. I'm talking today. The best one in this part of the country is Henry Yip, at Kiner. He'll refer you to a good oncologist. I'm thinking that guy will want to start you on chemo and radiation. These can be difficult for the patient, debilitating, but are far less arduous than even five years ago—"

"Stop," Hodges says. The urge to laugh has thankfully passed.

Stamos stops, looking at him in a brilliant shaft of January sun. Hodges thinks, Barring a miracle, this is the last January I'm ever going to see. Wow.

"What are the chances? Don't sugarcoat it. There's something hanging fire in my life right now, might be something big, so I need to know."

Stamos sighs. "Very slim, I'm afraid. Pancreatic cancer is just so goddamned *stealthy*."

"How long?"

"With treatment? Possibly a year. Even two. And a remission is not entirely out of the ques—"

"I need to think about this," Hodges says.

"I've heard that many times after I've had the unpleasant task of giving this kind of diagnosis, and I always tell my patients what I'm now going to tell you, Bill. If you were standing on top of a burning building and a helicopter appeared and dropped a rope ladder, would you say you needed to think about it before climbing up?"

Hodges mulls that over, and the urge to laugh returns. He's able to restrain it, but not a smile. It's broad and charming. "I

might," he says, "if the helicopter in question only had two gallons of gas left in the tank."

22

When Ruth Scapelli was twenty-three, before she began to grow
the hard shell that encased her in later years, she had a short and
bumpy affair with a not-exactly-honest man who owned a bowl-
ing alley. She became pregnant and gave birth to a daughter she
named Cynthia. This was in Davenport, Iowa, her hometown,
where she was working toward her RN at Kaplan University.
She was amazed to find herself a mother, more amazed still to
realize that Cynthia's father was a slack-bellied forty-year-old
with a tattoo reading LOVE TO LIVE AND LIVE TO LOVE
on one hairy arm. If he had offered to marry her (he didn't), she
would have declined with an inward shudder. Her aunt Wanda
helped her raise the child.

Cynthia Scapelli Robinson now lives in San Francisco, where
she has a fine husband (no tattoos) and two children, the older
of whom is an honor roll student in high school. Her household is a warm one. Cynthia works hard to keep it that way,
because the atmosphere in her aunt's home, where she did most
of her growing up (and where her mother began to develop that
formidable shell) was always chilly, full of recriminations and
scoldings that usually began *You forgot to*. The emotional atmosphere was mostly above freezing, but rarely went higher than
forty-five degrees. By the time Cynthia was in high school, she
was calling her mother by her first name. Ruth Scapelli never
objected to this; in fact, she found it a bit of a relief. She missed
her daughter's nuptials due to work commitments, but sent a

wedding present. It was a clock-radio. These days Cynthia and her mother talk on the phone once or twice a month, and occasionally exchange emails. *Josh doing fine in school, made the soccer team* is followed by a terse reply: *Good for him*. Cynthia has never actually missed her mother, because there was never all that much to miss.

This morning she rises at seven, fixes breakfast for her husband and the two boys, sees Hank off to work, sees the boys off to school, then rinses the dishes and gets the dishwasher going. That is followed by a trip to the laundry room, where she loads the washer and gets *that* going. She does these morning chores without once thinking *You must not forget to*, except someplace down deep she *is* thinking it, and always will. The seeds sown in childhood put down deep roots.

At nine thirty she makes herself a second cup of coffee, turns on the TV (she rarely looks at it, but it's company), and powers up her laptop to see if she has any emails other than the usual come-ons from Amazon and Urban Outfitters. This morning there's one from her mother, sent last night at 10:44 PM, which translates to 8:44, West Coast time. She frowns at the subject line, which is a single word: **Sorry**.

She opens it. Her heartbeat speeds up as she reads.

**I'm awful. I'm an awful worthless bitch. No one will stand up for me. This is what I have to do. I love you.**

*I love you*. When is the last time her mother said that to her? Cynthia—who says it to her boys at least four times a day—honestly can't remember. She grabs her phone off the counter where it's been charging, and calls first her mother's cell, then the landline. She gets Ruth Scapelli's short, no-nonsense message on both: "Leave a message. I'll call you back if that seems appropriate." Cynthia tells her mother to call her right away, but she's terribly afraid her mother may not be able to do that. Not now, perhaps not later, perhaps not at all.

She paces the circumference of her sunny kitchen twice, chewing at her lips, then picks up her cell again and gets the number for Kiner Memorial Hospital. She resumes pacing as she waits to be transferred to the Brain Injury Clinic. She's finally connected to a nurse who identifies himself as Steve Halpern. No, Halpern tells her, Nurse Scapelli hasn't come in, which is surprising. Her shift starts at eight, and in the Midwest it's now twenty to one.

"Try her at home," he advises. "She's probably taking a sick day, although it's unlike her not to call in."

You don't know the half of it, Cynthia thinks. Unless, that is, Halpern grew up in a house where the mantra was *You forgot to*.

She thanks him (can't forget that, no matter how worried she may be) and gets the number of a police department two thousand miles away. She identifies herself and states the problem as calmly as possible.

"My mother lives at 298 Tannenbaum Street. Her name is Ruth Scapelli. She's the head nurse at the Kiner Hospital Brain Injury Clinic. I got an email from her this morning that makes me think . . ."

That she's badly depressed? No. It might not be enough to get the cops out there. Besides, it's not what she really thinks. She takes a deep breath.

"That makes me think she might be considering suicide."

23

CPC 54 pulls into the driveway at 298 Tannenbaum Street. Officers Amarilis Rosario and Jason Laverty—known as Toody and Muldoon because their car number was featured in an old cop sitcom—get out and approach the door. Rosario rings the doorbell. There's no answer, so Laverty knocks, good and hard. There's still no answer. He tries the door on the off chance, and it opens. They look at each other. This is a good neighborhood, but it's still the city, and in the city most people lock their doors.

Rosario pokes her head in. "Mrs. Scapelli? This is Police Officer Rosario. Want to give us a shout?"

There is no shout.

Her partner chimes in. "Officer Laverty, ma'am. Your daughter is worried about you. Are you okay?"

Nothing. Laverty shrugs and gestures to the open door. "Ladies first."

Rosario steps in, unsnapping the strap on her service weapon without even thinking about it. Laverty follows. The living room is empty but the TV is on, the sound muted.

"Toody, Toody, I don't like this," Rosario says. "Can you smell it?"

Laverty can. It's the smell of blood. They find the source in the kitchen, where Ruth Scapelli lies on the floor next to an overturned chair. Her arms are splayed out as if she tried to break her fall. They can see the deep cuts she's made, long ones up the forearms almost to the elbows, short ones across the wrists. Blood is splattered on the easy-clean tiles, and a great deal more is on the table, where she sat to do the deed. A butcher knife from the wooden block beside the toaster lies on the lazy Susan, placed with grotesque neatness between the salt and pepper shakers and the ceramic napkin holder. The blood is dark, coagulating. Laverty guesses she's been dead for twelve hours, at least.

"Maybe there was nothing good on TV," he says.

Rosario gives him a dark look and takes a knee close to the

body, but not close enough to get blood on her uni, which just came back from the cleaners the day before. "She drew something before she lost consciousness," she says. "See it there on the tile by her right hand? Drew it in her own blood. What do you make of it? Is it a 2?"

Laverty leans down for a close look, hands on his knees. "Hard to tell," he says. "Either a 2 or a Z."

# BRADY

"My boy is a genius," Deborah Hartsfield used to tell her friends. To which she would add, with a winning smile: "It's not bragging if it's the truth."

This was before she started drinking heavily, when she still had friends. Once she'd had another son, Frankie, but Frankie was no genius. Frankie was brain-damaged. One evening when he was four years old, he fell down the cellar stairs and died of a broken neck. That was the story Deborah and Brady told, anyway. The truth was a little different. A little more complex.

Brady loved to invent things, and one day he'd invent something that would make the two of them rich, would put them on that famous street called Easy. Deborah was sure of it, and told him so often. Brady believed it.

He managed just Bs and Cs in most of his courses, but in Computer Science I and II he was a straight-A star. By the time he graduated from North Side High, the Hartsfield house was equipped with all sorts of gadgets, some of them—like the blue boxes by which Brady stole cable TV from Midwest Vision— highly illegal. He had a workroom in the basement where Deborah rarely ventured, and it was there that he did his inventing.

Little by little, doubt crept in. And resentment, doubt's fraternal twin. No matter how inspired his creations were, none were moneymakers. There were guys in California—Steve Jobs, for instance—who made incredible fortunes and changed the world just tinkering in their garages, but the things Brady came up with never quite made the grade.

His design for the Rolla, for instance. It was to be a computer-powered vacuum cleaner that would run by itself, turning on gimbals and starting in a new direction each time it met an obstacle. That looked like a sure winner until Brady spotted a Roomba vacuum cleaner in a fancy-shmancy appliance store on Lacemaker Lane. Someone had beaten him to the punch. The phrase *a day late and a dollar short* occurred to him. He pushed it away, but sometimes at night when he couldn't sleep, or when he was coming down with one of his migraines, it recurred.

Yet two of his inventions—and minor ones at that—made the slaughter at City Center possible. They were modified TV remotes he called Thing One and Thing Two. Thing One could change traffic signals from red to green, or vice-versa. Thing Two was more sophisticated. It could capture and store signals sent from automobile key fobs, allowing Brady to unlock those vehicles after their clueless owners had departed. At first he used Thing Two as a burglary tool, opening cars and tossing them for cash or other valuables. Then, as the idea of driving a big car into a crowd of people took vague shape in his mind (along with fantasies of assassinating the President or maybe a hot shit movie star), he used Thing Two on Mrs. Olivia Trelawney's Mercedes, and discovered she kept a spare key in her glove compartment.

That car he left alone, filing the existence of the spare key away for later use. Not long after, like a message from the dark powers that ran the universe, he read in the newspaper that a job fair was to be held at City Center on the tenth of April.

Thousands were expected to show up.

• • •

After he started working the Cyber Patrol at Discount Electronix and could buy crunchers on the cheap, Brady wired together seven off-brand laptops in his basement workroom. He rarely used more than one of them, but he liked the way they made the room look: like something out of a science fiction movie or a *Star Trek* episode. He wired in a voice-activated system, too, and this was years before Apple made a voice-ac program named Siri a star.

Once again, a day late and a dollar short.

Or, in this case, a few billion.

Being in a situation like that, who wouldn't want to kill a bunch of people?

He only got eight at City Center (not counting the wounded, some of them maimed really good), but could have gotten *thousands* at that rock concert. He'd have been remembered forever. But before he could push the button that would have sent ball bearings flying in a jet-propelled, ever-widening deathfan, mutilating and decapitating hundreds of screaming prepubescent girls (not to mention their overweight and overindulgent mommies), someone had turned out all his lights.

That part of his memory was blacked out permanently, it seemed, but he didn't *have* to remember. There was only one person it could have been: Kermit William Hodges. Hodges was supposed to commit suicide like Mrs. Trelawney, that was the plan, but he'd somehow avoided both that and the explosives Brady had stashed in Hodges's car. The old retired detective showed up at the concert and thwarted him mere seconds before Brady could achieve his immortality.

Boom, boom, out go the lights.

Angel, angel, down we go.

• • •

Coincidence is a tricksy bitch, and it so happened that Brady was transported to Kiner Memorial by Unit 23 out of Firehouse 3. Rob Martin wasn't on the scene—he was at that time touring Afghanistan, all expenses paid by the United States government—but Jason Rapsis was the paramedic onboard, trying to keep Brady alive as 23 raced toward the hospital. If offered a bet on his chances, Rapsis would have bet against. The young man was seizing violently. His heart rate was 175, his blood pressure alternately spiking and falling. Yet he was still in the land of the living when 23 reached Kiner.

There he was examined by Dr. Emory Winston, an old hand in the patch-em-up, fix-em-up wing of the hospital some vets called the Saturday Night Knife and Gun Club. Winston collared a med student who happened to be hanging around the ER and chatting up nurses. Winston invited him to do a quick-and-dirty evaluation of the new patient. The student reported depressed reflexes, a dilated and fixed left pupil, and a positive right Babinski.

"Meaning?" Winston asked.

"Meaning this guy is suffering an irreparable brain injury," said the student. "He's a gork."

"Very good, we may make a doctor of you yet. Prognosis?"

"Dead by morning," said the student.

"You're probably right," Winston said. "I hope so, because he's never coming back from this. We'll give him a CAT scan, though."

"Why?"

"Because it's protocol, son. And because I'm curious to see how much damage there actually is while he's still alive."

He was still alive seven hours later, when Dr. Annu Singh, ably assisted by Dr. Felix Babineau, performed a craniotomy to evacuate the massive blood clot that was pressing on Brady's brain and increasing the damage minute by minute, strangling divinely specialized cells in their millions. When the operation was finished, Babineau turned to Singh and offered him a hand that was still encased in a blood-stippled glove.

"That," he said, "was amazing."

Singh shook Babineau's hand, but he did so with a deprecating smile. "That was *routine*," he said. "Done a thousand of them. Well . . . a couple of hundred. What's amazing is this patient's constitution. I can't believe he lived through the operation. The damage to his poor old chump . . ." Singh shook his head. "Iy-yi-yi."

"You know what he was trying to do, I take it?"

"Yes, I was informed. Terrorism on a grand scale. He may live for awhile, but he will never be tried for his crime, and he will be no great loss to the world when he goes."

It was with this thought in mind that Dr. Babineau began slipping Brady—not quite brain-dead, but almost—an experimental drug which he called Cerebellin (although only in his mind; technically, it was just a six-digit number), this in addition to the established protocols of increased oxygenation, diuretics, antiseizure drugs, and steroids. Experimental drug 649558 had shown promising results when tested on animals, but thanks to a tangle of regulatory bureaucracies, human trials were years away. It had been developed in a Bolivian neuro lab, which added to the hassle. By the time human testing commenced (if it ever did), Babineau would be living in a Florida gated community, if his wife had her way. And bored to tears.

This was an opportunity to see results while he was still actively involved in neurological research. If he got some, it was not impossible to imagine a Nobel Prize for Medicine somewhere down the line. And there was no downside as long as he kept the results to himself until human trials were okayed. The man was

a murderous degenerate who was never going to wake up, anyway. If by some miracle he did, his consciousness would at best
be of the shadowy sort experienced by patients with advanced
Alzheimer's disease. Yet even that would be an amazing result.

You may be helping someone farther down the line, Mr. Hartsfield, he told his comatose patient. Doing a spoonful of good
instead of a shovelful of evil. And if you should suffer an adverse
reaction? Perhaps go entirely flatline (not that you have far to go),
or even die, rather than showing a bit of increased brain function?

No great loss. Not to you, and certainly not to your family,
because you have none.

Nor to the world; the world would be delighted to see you go.

He opened a file on his computer titled HARTSFIELD CER-
EBELLIN TRIALS. There were nine of these trials in all, spread
over a fourteen-month period in 2010 and 2011. Babineau saw
no change. He might as well have been giving his human guinea
pig distilled water.

He gave up.

The human guinea pig in question spent fifteen months in the
dark, an inchoate spirit who at some point in the sixteenth
month remembered his name. He was Brady Wilson Hartsfield. There was nothing else at first. No past, no present, no *him*
beyond the six syllables of his name. Then, not long before he
would have given up and just floated away, another word came.
The word was *control*. It had once meant something important,
but he could not think what.

In his hospital room, lying in bed, his glycerin-moistened lips
moved and he spoke the word aloud. He was alone; this was still
three weeks before a nurse would observe Brady open his eyes
and ask for his mother.

"Con . . . trol."

And the lights came on. Just as they did in his *Star Trek*–style computer workroom when he voice-activated them from the top of the stairs leading down from the kitchen.

That's where he was: in his basement on Elm Street, looking just as it had on the day he'd left it for the last time. There was another word that woke up another function, and now that he was here, he remembered that, as well. Because it was a good word.

"Chaos!"

In his mind, he boomed it out like Moses on Mount Sinai. In his hospital bed, it was a whispered croak. But it did the job, because his row of laptop computers came to life. On each screen was the number 20 . . . then 19 . . . then 18 . . .

What is this? What, in the name of God?

For a panicky moment he couldn't remember. All he knew was that if the countdown he saw marching across the seven screens reached zero, the computers would freeze. He would lose them, this room, and the little sliver of consciousness he had somehow managed. He would be buried alive in the darkness of his own hea—

And that was the word! The very one!

"Darkness!"

He screamed it at the top of his lungs—at least inside. Outside it was that same whispered croak from long unused vocal cords. His pulse, respiration, and blood pressure had all begun to rise. Soon Head Nurse Becky Helmington would notice and come to check on him, hurrying but not quite running.

In Brady's basement workroom, the countdown on the computers stopped at 14, and on each screen a picture appeared. Once upon a time, those computers (now stored in a cavernous police evidence room and labeled exhibits A through G) had booted up showing stills from a movie called *The Wild Bunch*. Now, however, they showed photographs from Brady's life.

On screen 1 was his brother Frankie, who choked on an apple, suffered his own brain damage, and later fell down the cellar stairs (helped along by his big brother's foot).

On screen 2 was Deborah herself. She was dressed in a clingy white robe that Brady remembered instantly. She called mc her honeyboy, he thought, and when she kissed me her lips were always a little damp and I got a hard-on. When I was little, she called that a stiffy. Sometimes when I was in the tub she'd rub it with a warm wet washcloth and ask me if it felt good.

On screen 3 were Thing One and Thing Two, inventions that had actually worked.

On screen 4 was Mrs. Trelawney's gray Mercedes sedan, the hood dented and the grille dripping with blood.

On screen 5 was a wheelchair. For a moment the relevance wouldn't come, but then it clicked in. It was how he had gotten into the Mingo Auditorium on the night of the 'Round Here concert. Nobody worried about a poor old cripple in a wheelchair.

On screen 6 was a handsome, smiling young man. Brady couldn't recall his name, at least not yet, but he knew who the young man was: the old Det.-Ret.'s nigger lawnboy.

And on screen 7 was Hodges himself, wearing a fedora cocked rakishly over one eye and smiling. Gotcha, Brady, that smile said. Whapped you with my whapper and there you lie, in a hospital bed, and when will you rise from it and walk? I'm betting never.

Fucking Hodges, who spoiled everything.

Those seven images were the armature around which Brady began to rebuild his identity. As he did so, the walls of his basement room—always his hideaway, his redoubt against a stupid and uncaring world—began to thin. He heard other voices coming through the walls and realized that some were nurses, some were doctors, and some—perhaps—were law enforcement types, checking up on him to make sure he wasn't faking. He both was and wasn't. The truth, like that concerning Frankie's death, was complex.

At first he opened his eyes only when he was sure he was alone, and didn't open them often. There wasn't a lot in his room to look at. Sooner or later he would have to come awake all the way, but even when he did they must not know that he could think much, when in fact he was thinking more clearly every day. If they knew that, they would put him on trial.

Brady didn't want to be put on trial.

Not when he still might have things to do.

A week before Brady spoke to Nurse Norma Wilmer, he opened his eyes in the middle of the night and looked at the bottle of saline suspended from the IV stand beside his bed. Bored, he lifted his hand to push it, perhaps even knock it to the floor. He did not succeed in doing that, but it was swinging back and forth from its hook before he realized both of his hands were still lying on the counterpane, the fingers turned in slightly due to the muscle atrophy physical therapy could slow but not stop—not, at least, when the patient was sleeping the long sleep of low brainwaves.

Did I do that?

He reached out again, and his hands still did not move much (although the left, his dominant hand, trembled a bit), but he felt his palm touch the saline bottle and put it back in motion.

He thought, That's interesting, and fell asleep. It was the first honest sleep he'd had since Hodges (or perhaps it had been his nigger lawnboy) put him in this goddam hospital bed.

On the following nights—late nights, when he could be sure no one might come in and see—Brady experimented with his phantom hand. Often as he did so he thought of a high school classmate named Henry "Hook" Crosby, who had lost his right hand in a car accident. He had a prosthetic—obviously fake, so he wore it with a glove—but sometimes he wore a stainless steel hook to school, instead. Henry claimed it was easier to pick things up with the hook, and as a bonus, it grossed out girls when he snuck up behind them and caressed a calf or bare arm with it. He once told Brady that, although he'd lost the hand seven years ago, he sometimes felt it itching, or prickling, as if it had gone numb and was just waking up. He showed Brady his stump, smooth and pink. "When it gets prickly like that, I'd swear I could scratch my head with it," he said.

Brady now knew exactly how Hook Crosby felt . . . except he, Brady, *could* scratch his head with his phantom hand. He had tried it. He had also discovered that he could rattle the slats in the venetian blinds the nurses dropped over his window at night. That window was much too far away from his bed to reach, but with the phantom hand he could reach it, anyway. Someone had put a vase of fake flowers on the table next to his bed (he later discovered it was Head Nurse Becky Helmington, the only one on staff to treat him with a degree of kindness), and he could slide it back and forth, easy as pie.

After a struggle—his memory was full of holes—he recalled the name for this sort of phenomenon: telekinesis. The ability to move objects by concentrating on them. Only any real concentration made his head ache fiercely, and his mind didn't seem to have much to do with it. It was his *hand*, his dominant left hand, even though the one lying splay-fingered on the bedspread never moved.

Pretty amazing. He was sure that Babineau, the doctor who came to see him most frequently (or had; lately he seemed to be losing interest), would be over the moon with excitement, but this was one talent Brady intended to keep to himself.

It might come in handy at some point, but he doubted it. Wiggling one's ears was also a talent, but not one that had any useful value. Yes, he could move the bottles on the IV stand, and rattle the blinds, and knock over a picture; he could send ripples through his blankets, as though a big fish were swimming beneath. Sometimes he did one of those things when a nurse was in the room, because their startled reactions were amusing. That, however, seemed to be the extent of this new ability. He had tried and failed to turn on the television suspended over his bed, had tried and failed to close the door to the en suite bathroom. He could grasp the chrome handle—he felt its cold hardness as his fingers closed around it—but the door was too heavy and his phantom hand was too weak. At least, so far. He had an idea that if he continued to exercise it, the hand might grow stronger.

*I need to wake up,* he thought, *if only so I can get some aspirin for this endless fucking headache and actually eat some real food. Even a dish of hospital custard would be a treat. I'll do it soon. Maybe even tomorrow.*

But he didn't. Because on the following day, he discovered that telekinesis wasn't the only new ability he'd brought back from wherever he'd been.

The nurse who came in most afternoons to check his vitals and most evenings to get him ready for the night (you couldn't say ready for bed when he was always *in* bed) was a young woman named Sadie MacDonald. She was dark-haired and pretty in a washed-out, no-makeup sort of way. Brady had observed her through half-closed eyes, as he observed all visitors to his room in the days since he had come through the wall from his basement workroom where he had first regained consciousness.

She seemed frightened of him, but he came to realize that didn't exactly make him special, because Nurse MacDonald was frightened of everyone. She was the kind of woman who scuttles rather than walks. If someone came into 217 while she was about her duties—Head Nurse Becky Helmington, for instance—Sadie had a tendency to shrink into the background. And she was terrified of Dr. Babineau. When she had to be in the room with him, Brady could almost taste her fear.

He came to realize that might not have been an exaggeration.

On the day after Brady fell asleep thinking of custard, Sadie MacDonald came into Room 217 at quarter past three, checked the monitor above the head of his bed, and wrote some numbers on the clipboard that hung at the foot. Next she'd check the bottles on the IV stand and go to the closet for fresh pillows. She would lift him with one hand—she was small, but her arms were strong—and replace his old pillows with the new ones. That might actually have been an orderly's job, but Brady had an idea that MacDonald was at the bottom of the hospital pecking order. Low nurse on the totem pole, so to speak.

He had decided he would open his eyes and speak to her just as she finished changing the pillows, when their faces were closest. It would scare her, and Brady liked to scare people. Much in his life had changed, but not that. Maybe she would even scream, as one nurse had when he made his coverlet do its rippling thing.

Only MacDonald diverted to the window on her way to the closet. There was nothing out there to see but the parking garage, yet she stood there for a minute . . . then two . . . then three. Why? What was so fascinating about a brick fucking wall?

Only it wasn't *all* brick, Brady realized as he looked out with her. There were long open spaces on each level, and as the cars went up the ramp, the sun flashed briefly on their windshields.

Flash. And flash. And flash.

Jesus Christ, Brady thought. *I'm* the one who's supposed to be in a coma, aren't I? It's like she's having some kind of seiz—

But wait. Wait just a goddam minute.

Looking out *with* her? How can I be looking out with her when I'm lying here in bed?

There went a rusty pickup truck. Behind it came a Jaguar sedan, probably some rich doctor's car, and Brady realized he wasn't looking out *with* her, he was looking out *from* her. It was like watching the scenery from the passenger side while someone else drove the car.

And yes, Sadie MacDonald *was* having a seizure, one so mild she probably didn't even know it was happening. The lights had caused it. The lights on the windshields of the passing cars. As soon as there was a lull in the traffic on that ramp, or as soon as the angle of the sunlight changed a bit, she would come out of it and go about her duties. She would come out of it without even knowing she'd been in it.

Brady knew this.

He knew because he was inside her.

He went a little deeper and realized he could see her thoughts. It was amazing. He could actually watch them flashing back and forth, hither and thither, high and low, sometimes crossing paths in a dark green medium that was—perhaps, he'd have to think about this, and very carefully to be sure—her core consciousness. Her basic Sadie-ness. He tried to go deeper, to identify some of the thoughtfish, although Christ, they went by so fast! Still . . .

Something about the muffins she had at home in her apartment.

Something about a cat she had seen in a pet shop window: black with a cunning white bib.

Something about . . . rocks? Was it rocks?

Something about her father, and that fish was red, the color of anger. Or shame. Or both.

As she turned from the window and headed for the closet, Brady felt a moment of tumbling vertigo. It passed, and he was back inside himself, looking out through his own eyes. She had ejected him without even knowing he was there.

When she lifted him to put two foam pillows with freshly laundered cases behind his head, Brady let his eyes remain in their fixed and half-lidded stare. He did not speak, after all.

He really did need to think about this.

During the next four days, Brady tried several times to get inside the heads of those who visited his room. He had a degree of success only once, with a young orderly who came in to mop the floor. The kid wasn't a Mongolian idiot (his mother's term for those with Down syndrome), but he wasn't a Mensa candidate, either. He was looking down at the wet stripes his mop left on the linoleum, watching the brightness of each one fade, and that opened him up just enough. Brady's visit was brief and uninteresting. The kid was wondering if they would have tacos in the caff that evening—big deal.

Then the vertigo, the sense of tumbling. The kid had spit him out like a watermelon seed, never once slowing the pendulum swings of his mop.

With the others who poked into his room from time to time, he had no success at all, and this failure was a lot more frustrating than being unable to scratch his face when it itched. Brady had taken an inventory of himself, and what he had found was dismaying. His constantly aching head sat on top of a skeletal body. He could move, he wasn't paralyzed, but his muscles had atrophied and even sliding a leg two or three inches one way or another took a herculean effort. Being inside Nurse MacDonald, on the other hand, had been like riding on a magic carpet.

But he'd only gotten in because MacDonald had some form of epilepsy. Not much, just enough to briefly open a door. Others seemed to have natural defenses. He hadn't even managed to stay inside the orderly for more than a few seconds, and if *that* ass-munch had been a dwarf, he would have been named Dopey.

Which made him remember a joke. Stranger in New York City asks a beatnik, "How do you get to Carnegie Hall?" Beatnik replies, "Practice, man, practice."

That's what I need to do, Brady thought. Practice and get stronger. Because Kermit William Hodges is out there someplace, and the old Det.-Ret. thinks he won. I can't allow that. I *won't* allow that.

And so on that rain-soaked evening in mid-November of 2011, Brady opened his eyes, said his head hurt, and asked for his mother. There was no scream. It was Sadie MacDonald's night off, and Norma Wilmer, the nurse on duty, was made of tougher stuff. Nevertheless, she gave a little cry of surprise, and ran to see if Dr. Babineau was still in the doctors' lounge.

Brady thought, Now the rest of my life begins.

Brady thought, Practice, man, practice.

# BLACKISH

1

Although Hodges has officially made Holly a full partner in Finders Keepers, and there's a spare office (small, but with a street view), she has elected to remain based in the reception area. She's seated there, peering at the screen of her computer, when Hodges comes in at quarter to eleven. And although she's quick to sweep something into the wide drawer above the kneehole of her desk, Hodges's olfactories are still in good working order (unlike some of his malfunctioning equipment further south), and he catches an unmistakable whiff of half-eaten Twinkie.

"What's the story, Hollyberry?"

"You picked that up from Jerome, and you know I hate it. Call me Hollyberry again and I'll go see my mother for a week. She keeps asking me to visit."

As if, Hodges thinks. You can't stand her, and besides, you're on the scent, my dear. As hooked as a heroin addict.

"Sorry, sorry." He looks over her shoulder and sees an article from *Bloomberg Business* dated April of 2014. The headline reads ZAPPIT ZAPPED. "Yeah, the company screwed the pooch and stepped out the door. Thought I told you that yesterday."

"You did. What's interesting, to me at least, is the inventory."

"What do you mean?"

"Thousands of unsold Zappits, maybe tens of thousands. I wanted to know what happened to them."

"And did you find out?"

"Not yet."

"Maybe they got shipped to the poor children in China, along with all the vegetables I refused to eat as a child."

"Starving children are not funny," she says, looking severe.

"No, of course not."

Hodges straightens up. He filled a prescription for painkillers on his way back from Stamos's office—heavy-duty, but not as heavy as the stuff he may be taking soon—and he feels almost okay. There's even a faint stirring of hunger in his belly, which is a welcome change. "They were probably destroyed. That's what they do with unsold paperback books, I think."

"That's a lot of inventory to destroy," she says, "considering the gadgets are loaded with games and still work. The top of the line, the Commanders, even came equipped with WiFi. Now tell me about your tests."

Hodges manufactures a smile he hopes will look both modest and happy. "Good news, actually. It's an ulcer, but just a little one. I'll have to take a bunch of pills and be careful about my diet. Dr. Stamos says if I do that, it should heal on its own."

She gives him a radiant smile that makes Hodges feel good about this outrageous lie. Of course, it also makes him feel like dogshit on an old shoe.

"Thank God! You'll do what he says, won't you?"

"You bet." More dogshit; all the bland food in the world won't cure what ails him. Hodges is not a giver-upper, and under other circumstances he would be in the office of gastroenterologist Henry Yip right now, no matter how bad the odds of beating pancreatic cancer. The message he received on the Blue Umbrella site has changed things, however.

"Well, that's fine. Because I don't know what I'd do without you, Bill. I just don't."

"Holly—"

"Actually, I do. I'd go back home. And that would be bad for me."

No shit, Hodges thinks. The first time I met you, in town for your aunt Elizabeth's funeral, your mom was practically leading you around like a mutt on a leash. Do this, Holly, do that, Holly, and for Christ's sake don't do anything embarrassing.

"Now tell me," she says. "Tell me the something new. Tell me tell me tell me!"

"Give me fifteen minutes, then I'll spill everything. In the meantime, see if you can find out what happened to all those Commander consoles. It's probably not important, but it might be."

"Okay. Wonderful news about your tests, Bill."

"Yeah."

He goes into his office. Holly swivels her chair to look after him for a moment, because he rarely closes the door when he's in there. Still, it's not unheard of. She returns to her computer.

2

"He's not done with you yet."

Holly repeats it in a soft voice. She puts her half-eaten veggie burger down on its paper plate. Hodges has already demolished his, talking between bites. He doesn't mention waking with pain; in this version he discovered the message because he got up to net-surf when he couldn't sleep.

"That's what it said, all right."

"From Z-Boy."

"Yeah. Sounds like some superhero's sidekick, doesn't it? 'Follow the adventures of Z-Man and Z-Boy, as they keep the streets of Gotham City safe from crime!'"

"That's Batman and Robin. They're the ones who patrol Gotham City."

"I know that, I was reading Batman comics before you were born. I was just saying."

She picks up her veggie burger, extracts a shred of lettuce, puts it down again. "When is the last time you visited Brady Hartsfield?"

Right to the heart of the matter, Hodges thinks admiringly. That's my Holly.

"I went to see him just after the business with the Saubers family, and once more later on. Midsummer, that would have been. Then you and Jerome cornered me and said I had to stop. So I did."

"We did it for your own good."

"I know that, Holly. Now eat your sandwich."

She takes a bite, dabs mayo from the corner of her mouth, and asks him how Hartsfield seemed on his last visit.

"The same . . . mostly. Just sitting there, looking out at the parking garage. I talk, I ask him questions, he says nothing. He gives Academy Award brain damage, no doubt about that. But there have been stories about him. That he has some kind of mind-power. That he can turn the water on and off in his bathroom, and does it sometimes to scare the staff. I'd call it bullshit, but when Becky Helmington was the head nurse, she said she'd actually seen stuff on a couple of occasions—rattling blinds, the TV going on by itself, the bottles on his IV stand swinging back and forth. And she's what I'd call a credible witness. I know it's hard to believe—"

"Not so hard. Telekinesis, sometimes called psychokinesis, is a documented phenomenon. You never saw anything like that yourself during any of your visits?"

"Well . . ." He pauses, remembering. "Something did happen on my second-to-last visit. There was a picture on the table beside his bed—him and his mother with their arms around each other and their cheeks pressed together. On vacation somewhere. There was a bigger version in the house on Elm Street. You probably remember it."

"Of course I do. I remember everything we saw in that house, including some of the cheesecake photos of her he had on his computer." She crosses her arms over her small bosom and makes a moue of distaste. "That was a *very* unnatural relationship."

"Tell me about it. I don't know if he ever actually had sex with her—"

"Oough!"

"—but I think he probably wanted to, and at the very least she enabled his fantasies. Anyway, I grabbed the picture and talked some smack about her, trying to get a rise out of him, trying to get him to respond. Because he's *in* there, Holly, and I mean all present and accounted for. I was sure of it then and I'm sure of it now. He just sits there, but inside he's the same human wasp that killed those people at City Center and tried to kill a whole lot more at Mingo Auditorium."

"And he used Debbie's Blue Umbrella to talk with you, don't forget that."

"After last night I'm not likely to."

"Tell me the rest of what happened that time."

"For just a second he stopped looking out his window at the

parking garage across the way. His eyes . . . they rolled in their sockets, and he looked at me. Every hair on the nape of my neck stood up at attention, and the air felt . . . I don't know . . . *electric.*" He forces himself to say the rest. It's like pushing a big rock up a steep hill. "I arrested some bad doers when I was on the cops, some *very* bad doers—one was a mother who killed her three-year-old for insurance that didn't amount to a hill of beans—but I never felt the presence of evil in any of them once they were caught. It's like evil's some kind of vulture that flies away once these mokes are locked up. But I felt it that day, Holly. I really did. I felt it in Brady Hartsfield."

"I believe you," she says in a voice so small it's barely a whisper.

"And he had a Zappit. That's the connection I was trying to make. If it is a connection, and not just a coincidence. There was a guy, I don't know his last name, everyone just called him Library Al, who used to hand Zappits out along with Kindles and paperbacks when he made his rounds. I don't know if Al was an orderly or a volunteer. Hell, he might even have been one of the janitors, doing a little good deed on the side. I think the only reason I didn't pick up on that right away was the Zappit you found at the Ellerton house was pink. The one in Brady's room was blue."

"How could what happened to Janice Ellerton and her daughter have anything to do with Brady Hartsfield? Unless . . . has anyone reported any telekinetic activity outside of his room? Have there been rumors of that?"

"Nope, but right around the time the Saubers business finished up, a nurse committed suicide in the Brain Injury Clinic. Sliced her wrists in a bathroom right down the hall from Hartsfield's room. Her name was Sadie MacDonald."

"Are you thinking . . ."

She's picking at her sandwich again, shredding the lettuce and dropping it onto her plate. Waiting for him.

"Go on, Holly. I'm not going to say it for you."

"You're thinking Brady talked her into it somehow? I don't see how that could be possible."

"I don't, either, but we know Brady has a fascination with suicide."

"This Sadie MacDonald . . . did she happen to have one of those Zappit things?"

"God knows."

"How . . . how did . . ."

This time he does help. "With a scalpel she filched from one of the surgical suites. I got that from the ME's assistant. Slipped her a gift card to DeMasio's, the Italian joint."

Holly shreds more lettuce. Her plate is starting to look like confetti at a leprechaun birthday party. It's driving Hodges a little nuts, but he doesn't stop her. She's working her way up to saying it. And finally does. "You're going to see Hartsfield."

"Yeah, I am."

"Do you really think you'll get anything out of him? You never have before."

"I know a little more now." But what, really, *does* he know? He's not even sure what he suspects. But maybe Hartsfield isn't a human wasp, after all. Maybe he's a spider, and Room 217 at the Bucket is the center of his web, where he sits spinning.

Or maybe it's all coincidence. Maybe the cancer is already eating into my brain, sparking a lot of paranoid ideas.

That's what Pete would think, and his partner—hard to stop thinking of her as Miss Pretty Gray Eyes, now that it's in his head—would say it right out loud.

He stands up. "No time like the present."

She drops her sandwich onto the pile of mangled lettuce so she can grasp his arm. "Be careful."

"I will."

"Guard your thoughts. I know how crazy that sounds, but I *am* crazy, at least some of the time, so I can say it. If you should have any ideas about . . . well, harming yourself . . . call me. Call me *right away*."

"Okay."

She crosses her arms and grasps her shoulders—that old fretful gesture he sees less often now. "I wish Jerome was here." Jerome Robinson is in Arizona, taking a semester off from college, building houses as part of a Habitat for Humanity crew. Once, when Hodges used the phrase *garnishing his resume* in relation to this activity, Holly scolded him, telling him Jerome was doing it because he was a good person. With that, Hodges has to agree—Jerome really is a good person.

"I'm going to be fine. And this is probably nothing. We're like kids worrying that the empty house on the corner is haunted. If we said anything about it to Pete, he'd have us both committed."

Holly, who actually has been committed (twice), believes some empty houses really might be haunted. She removes one small and ringless hand from one shoulder long enough to grasp his arm again, this time by the sleeve of his overcoat. "Call me when you get there, and call me again when you leave. Don't forget, because I'll be worrying and I can't call you because—"

"No cell phones allowed in the Bucket, yeah, I know. I'll do it, Holly. In the meantime, I've got a couple of things for you." He sees her hand dart toward a notepad and shakes his head. "No, you don't need to write this down. It's simple. First, go on eBay or wherever you go to buy stuff that's no longer available retail and order one of those Zappit Commanders. Can you do that?"

"Easy. What's the other thing?"

"Sunrise Solutions bought out Zappit, then went bankrupt. Someone will be serving as the trustee in bankruptcy. The trustee hires lawyers, accountants, and liquidators to help squeeze every cent out of the company. Get a name and I'll make a call later today or tomorrow. I want to know what happened to all those unsold Zappit consoles, because somebody gave one to Janice Ellerton a long time after both companies were out of business."

She lights up. "That's fracking brilliant!"

Not brilliant, just police work, he thinks. I may have terminal cancer, but I still remember how the job is done, and that's something.

That's something good.

### 3

As he exits the Turner Building and heads for the bus stop (the Number 5 is a quicker and easier way to get across town than retrieving his Prius and driving himself), Hodges is a deeply preoccupied man. He is thinking about how he should approach Brady—how he can open him up. He was an ace in the interrogation room when he was on the job, so there has to be a way. Previously he has only gone to Brady to goad him and confirm his gut belief that Brady is faking his semi-catatonic state. Now he has some real questions, and there must be *some* way he can get Brady to answer them.

I have to poke the spider, he thinks.

Interfering with his efforts to plan the forthcoming confrontation are thoughts of the diagnosis he's just received, and the inevitable fears that go with it. For his life, yes. But there are also questions of how much he may suffer a bit farther down the line, and how he will inform those who need to know. Corinne and Allie will be shaken up by the news but basically okay. The same goes for the Robinson family, although he knows Jerome and Barbara, his kid sister (not such a kid now; she'll turn sixteen in a few months), will take it hard. Mostly, though, it's Holly he worries about. She isn't crazy, despite what she said in the office, but she's fragile. Very. She's had two breakdowns in her past, one in high school and one in her early twenties. She's stronger now, but her main sources of support over these last few years have been him and the little company they run together. If they go, she'll be at risk. He can't afford to kid himself about that.

I won't let her break, Hodges thinks. He walks with his head down and his hands stuffed in his pockets, blowing out white vapor. I can't let that happen.

Deep in these thoughts, he misses the primer-spotted Chevy Malibu for the third time in two days. It's parked up the street, opposite the building where Holly is now hunting down the Sunrise Solutions bankruptcy trustee. Standing on the sidewalk next to it is an elderly man in an old Army surplus parka that has been mended with masking tape. He watches Hodges get on the bus, then takes a cell phone from his coat pocket and makes a call.

4

Holly watches her boss—who happens to be the person she loves most in the world—walk to the bus stop on the corner. He looks so *slight* now, almost a shadow of the burly man she first met six years ago. And he has his hand pressed to his side as he walks. He does that a lot lately, and she doesn't think he's even aware of it.

Nothing but a small ulcer, he said. She'd like to believe that— would like to believe *him*—but she's not sure she does.

The bus comes and Bill gets on. Holly stands by the window watching it go, gnawing at her fingernails, wishing for a cigarette. She has Nicorette gum, plenty of it, but sometimes only a cigarette will do.

Quit wasting time, she tells herself. If you really mean to be a rotten dirty sneak, there's no time like the present.

So she goes into his office.

His computer is dark, but he never turns it off until he goes home at night; all she has to do is refresh the screen. Before she can, her eye is caught by the yellow legal pad beside the keyboard. He always has one handy, usually covered with notes and doodles. It's how he thinks.

Written at the top of this one is a line she knows well, one that has resonated with her ever since she first heard the song on the radio: *All the lonely people.* He has underlined it. Beneath are names she knows.

Olivia Trelawney (Widowed)
Martine Stover (Unmarried, housekeeper called her "spinster")
Janice Ellerton (Widowed)
Nancy Alderson (Widowed)

And others. Her own, of course; she is also a spinster. Pete Huntley, who's divorced. And Hodges himself, also divorced.

131

Single people are twice as likely to commit suicide. Divorced people, four times as likely.

"Brady Hartsfield enjoyed suicide," she murmurs. "It was his hobby."

Below the names, circled, is a jotted note she doesn't understand: *Visitors list? What visitors?*

She hits a random key and Bill's computer lights up, showing his desktop screen with all his files scattered helter-skelter across it. She has scolded him about this time and again, has told him it's like leaving the door of your house unlocked and your valuables all laid out on the dining room table with a sign on them saying PLEASE STEAL ME, and he always says he will do better, and he never does. Not that it would have changed things in Holly's case, because she also has his password. He gave it to her himself. In case something ever happened to him, he said. Now she's afraid something has.

One look at the screen is enough to tell her the something is no ulcer. There's a new file folder there, one with a scary title. Holly clicks on it. The terrible gothic letters at the top are enough to confirm that the document is indeed the last will and testament of one Kermit William Hodges. She closes it at once. She has absolutely no desire to paw through his bequests. Knowing that such a document exists and that he has been reviewing it this very day is enough. Too much, actually.

She stands there clutching at her shoulders and nibbling her lips. The next step would be worse than snooping. It would be prying. It would be burglary.

*You've come this far, so go ahead.*

"Yes, I have to," Holly whispers, and clicks on the postage stamp icon that opens his email, telling herself there will probably be nothing. Only there is. The most recent message likely

132

came in while they were talking about what he found early this morning under Debbie's Blue Umbrella. It's from the doctor he went to see. Stamos, his name is. She opens the email and reads: *Here is a copy of your most recent test results, for your files.*

Holly uses the password in the email to open the attachment, sits in Bill's chair, and leans forward, her hands clenched tightly in her lap. By the time she scrolls down to the second of the eight pages, she is crying.

5

Hodges has no more than settled in his seat at the back of the Number 5 when glass breaks in his coat pocket and the boys cheer the home run that just broke Mrs. O'Leary's living room window. A man in a business suit lowers his *Wall Street Journal* and looks disapprovingly at Hodges over the top of it.

"Sorry, sorry," Hodges says. "Keep meaning to change it."

"You should make it a priority," the businessman says, and raises his paper again.

The text is from his old partner. Again. Feeling a strong sense of *déjà vu*, Hodges calls him.

"Pete," he says, "what's with all the texts? It isn't as if you don't have my number on speed dial."

"Figured Holly probably programmed your phone for you and put on some crazy ringtone," Pete says. "That'd be her idea of a real knee-slapper. Also figured you'd have it turned up to max volume, you deaf sonofabitch."

"The text alert's the one on max," Hodges says. "When I get a call, the phone just has a mini-orgasm against my leg."

"Change the alert, then."

Hours ago he found out he has only months to live. Now he's discussing the volume of his cell phone.

"I'll absolutely do that. Now tell me why you called."

"Got a guy in computer forensics who landed on that game gadget like a fly on shit. He loved it, called it retro. Can you believe that? Gadget was probably manufactured all of five years ago and now it's retro."

"The world is speeding up."

"It's sure doing something. Anyway, the Zappit is zapped. When our guy plugged in fresh batteries, it popped half a dozen bright blue flashes, then died."

"What's wrong with it?"

"Some kind of virus is technically possible, the thing supposedly has WiFi and that's mostly how those bugs get downloaded, but he says it's more likely a bad chip or a fried circuit. The point is, it means nothing. Ellerton couldn't have used it."

"Then why did she keep the charger cord for it plugged in right there in her daughter's bathroom?"

That silences Pete for a moment. Then he says, "Okay, so maybe it worked for awhile and then the chip died. Or whatever they do."

It worked, all right, Hodges thinks. She played solitaire on it at the kitchen table. Lots of different kinds, like Klondike and Pyramid and Picture. Which you would know, Peter my dear, if you'd talked to Nancy Alderson. That must still be on your bucket list.

"All right," Hodges says. "Thanks for the update."

"It's your *final* update, Kermit. I have a partner I've worked with quite successfully since you pulled the pin, and I'd like her to be at my retirement party instead of sitting at her desk and sulking over how I preferred you to her right to the bitter end."

Hodges could pursue this, but the hospital is only two stops away now. Also, he discovers, he wants to separate himself from Pete and Izzy and go his own way on this thing. Pete plods, and Izzy actually drags her feet. Hodges wants to run with it, bad pancreas and all.

"I hear you," he says. "Again, thanks."

"Case closed?"

"Finito."

His eyes flick up and to the left.

6

Nineteen blocks from where Hodges is returning his iPhone to his overcoat pocket, there is another world. Not a very nice one. Jerome Robinson's sister is there, and she is in trouble.

Pretty and demure in her Chapel Ridge school uniform (gray wool coat, gray skirt, white kneesocks, red scarf wrapped around her neck), Barbara walks down Martin Luther King Avenue with a yellow Zappit Commander in her gloved hands. On it the Fishin' Hole fish dart and swim, although they are almost invisible in the cold bright light of midday.

MLK is one of two main thoroughfares in the part of the city known as Lowtown, and although the population is predominantly black and Barbara is herself black (make that café au lait), she has never been here before, and that single fact makes her feel stupid and worthless. These are her people, their collective ancestors might have toted barges and lifted bales on the same plantation back in the day, for all she knows, and yet she has never been here *one single time*. She has been warned away not only by her parents but by her brother.

"Lowtown's where they drink the beer and then eat the bottle it came in," he told her once. "No place for a girl like you."

A girl like me, she thinks. A nice upper-middle-class girl like me, who goes to a nice private school and has nice white girl-friends and plenty of nice preppy clothes and an allowance. Why, I even have a bank card! I can withdraw sixty dollars from an ATM anytime I want! Amazeballs!

She walks like a girl in a dream, and it's a little *like* a dream because it's all so strange and it's less than two miles from home, which happens to be a cozy Cape Cod with an attached two-car garage, mortgage all paid off. She walks past check cashing joints and pawnshops filled with guitars and radios and gleaming pearl-handled straight razors. She walks past bars that smell of beer even with the doors closed against the January cold. She walks past hole-in-the-wall restaurants that smell of grease. Some sell pizza by the slice, some sell Chinese. In the window of one is a propped sign reading HUSH PUPPYS AND COLLARD GREENS LIKE YOUR MOMMA USED TO MAKE.

Not *my* momma, Barbara thinks. I don't even know what a collard green is. Spinach? Cabbage?

On the corners—*every* corner, it seems—boys in long shorts and loose jeans are hanging out, sometimes standing close to rusty firebarrels to keep warm, sometimes playing hacky sack, sometimes just jiving in their gigantic sneakers, their jackets hung open in spite of the cold. They shout Yo to their homies and hail passing cars and when one stops they hand small glass-ine envelopes through the open window. She walks block after block of MLK (nine, ten, maybe a dozen, she's lost count) and each corner is like a drive-thru for drugs instead of for hamburgers or tacos.

She passes shivering women dressed in hotpants, short fake fur jackets, and shiny boots; on their heads they wear amazing wigs of many colors. She passes empty buildings with boarded-up windows. She passes a car that has been stripped to the axles and covered with gang tags. She passes a woman with a dirty bandage over one eye. The woman is dragging a screeching toddler by the arm. She passes a man sitting on a blanket who drinks from a bottle of wine and wiggles his gray tongue at her. It's poor and it's desperate and it's been *right here all along* and she never did anything about it. Never *did* anything? Never even *thought* about it. What she did was her homework. What she did was talk on the phone and text with her BFFs at night. What she did was update her Facebook status and worry about her complexion. She is your basic teen parasite, dining in nice restaurants with her mother and father while her brothers and sisters, *right here all along, less than two miles from her nice suburban home*, drink wine and take drugs to blot out their terrible lives. She is ashamed of her hair, hanging smoothly to her shoulders. She is ashamed of her clean white kneesocks. She is ashamed of her skin color because it's the same as theirs.

"Hey, blackish!" It's a yell from the other side of the street. "What you doin down here? You got no bi'ness down here!"

Blackish.

It's the name of a TV show, they watch it at home and laugh, but it's also what she is. Not black but blackish. Living a white life in a white neighborhood. She can do that because her parents make lots of money and own a home on a block where people are so screamingly non-prejudiced that they cringe if they hear one of their kids call another one dumbhead. She can live that wonderful white life because she is a threat to no one, she no rock-a da boat. She just goes her way, chattering with her friends about boys and music and boys and clothes and boys and the TV programs they all like and which girl they saw walking with which boy at the Birch Hill Mall.

She is blackish, a word that means the same as useless, and she doesn't deserve to live.

"Maybe you should just end it. Let that be your statement."

The idea is a voice, and it comes to her with a kind of revelatory logic. Emily Dickinson said her poem was her letter to the world that never wrote to her, they read that in school, but Barbara herself has never written a letter at all. Plenty of stupid essays and book reports and emails, but nothing that really matters.

"Maybe it's time that you did."

Not her voice, but the voice of a friend.

She stops outside a shop where fortunes are read and the Tarot is told. In its dirty window she thinks she sees the reflection of someone standing beside her, a white man with a smiling, boyish face and a tumble of blond hair on his forehead. She glances around, but there's no one there. It was just her imagination. She looks back down at the screen of the game console. In the shade of the fortune-telling shop's awning, the swimming fish are bright and clear again. Back and forth they go, every now and then obliterated by a bright blue flash. Barbara looks back the way she came and sees a gleaming black truck rolling toward her along the boulevard, moving fast and weaving from lane to lane. It's the kind with oversized tires, the kind the boys at school call a Bigfoot or a Gangsta Large.

"If you're going to do it, you better get to it."

It's as if someone really is standing beside her. Someone who understands. And the voice is right. Barbara has never considered suicide before, but at this moment the idea seems perfectly rational.

"You don't even need to leave a note," her friend says. She can see his reflection in the window again. Ghostly. "The fact that you did it down here will be your letter to the world."

True.

"You know too much about yourself now to go on living," her friend points out as she returns her gaze to the swimming fish. "You know too much, and all of it is bad." Then it hastens to add, "Which isn't to say you're a horrible person."

She thinks, No, not horrible, just useless.

*Blackish.*

The truck is coming. The Gangsta Large. As Jerome Robinson's sister steps toward the curb, ready to meet it, her face lights in an eager smile.

7

Dr. Felix Babineau is wearing a thousand-dollar suit beneath the white coat that goes flying out behind him as he strides down the hallway of the Bucket, but he now needs a shave worse than ever and his usually elegant white hair is in disarray. He ignores a cluster of nurses who are standing by the duty desk and talking in low, agitated tones.

Nurse Wilmer approaches him. "Dr. Babineau, have you heard—"

He doesn't even look at her, and Norma has to sidestep quickly to keep from being bowled over. She looks after him in surprise.

Babineau takes the red DO NOT DISTURB card he always keeps in the pocket of his exam coat, hangs it on the doorknob of Room 217, and goes in. Brady Hartsfield does not look up. All of his attention is fixed on the game console in his lap, where the fish swim back and forth. There is no music; he has muted the sound.

Often when he enters this room, Felix Babineau disappears and Dr. Z takes his place. Not today. Dr. Z is just another version of Brady, after all—a projection—and today Brady is too busy to project.

His memories of trying to blow up the Mingo Auditorium during the 'Round Here concert are still jumbled, but one thing has been clear since he woke up: the face of the last person he saw before the lights went out. It was Barbara Robinson, the sister of Hodges's nigger lawnboy. She was sitting almost directly across the aisle from Brady. Now she's here, swimming with the fish they share on their two screens. Brady got Scapelli, the sadistic cunt who twisted his nipple. Now he will take care of the Robinson bitch. Her death will hurt her big brother, but that's not the most important thing. It will put a dagger in the old detective's heart. That's the most important thing.

The most delicious thing.

He comforts her, tells her she's not a horrible person. It helps to get her moving. Something is coming down MLK, he can't be sure what it is because a down-deep part of her is still fighting him, but it's big. Big enough to do the job.

"Brady, listen to me. Z-Boy called." Z-Boy's actual name is Brooks, but Brady refuses to call him that anymore. "He's been watching, as you instructed. That cop . . . ex-cop, whatever he is—"

"Shut up." Not raising his head, his hair tumbled across his brow. In the strong sunlight he looks closer to twenty than thirty.

Babineau, who is used to being heard and who still has not entirely grasped his new subordinate status, pays no attention. "Hodges was on Hilltop Court yesterday, first at the Eller-

140

ton house and then snooping around the one across the street where—"

"*I said shut up!*"

"Brooks saw him get on a Number 5 bus, which means he's probably coming here! And if he's coming here, he *knows*!"

Brady looks at him for just a moment, his eyes blazing, then returns his attention to the screen. If he slips now, allows this educated idiot to divert his concentration—

But he won't allow it. He wants to hurt Hodges, he wants to hurt the nigger lawnboy, he owes them, and this is the way to do it. Nor is it just a matter of revenge. She's the first test subject who was at the concert, and she's not like the others, who were easier to control. But he *is* controlling her, all he needs is ten more seconds, and now he sees what's coming for her. It's a truck. A big black one.

Hey, honey, Brady Hartsfield thinks. Your ride is here.

8

Barbara stands on the curb, watching the truck approach, timing it, but just as she flexes her knees, hands grab her from behind.

"Hey, girl, what's up?"

She struggles, but the grip on her shoulders is strong and the truck passes by in a blare of Ghostface Killah. She whirls around, pulling free, and faces a skinny boy about her own age, wearing a Todhunter High letter jacket. He's tall, maybe six and a half feet, so she has to look up. He has a tight cap of brown curls and a goatee. Around his neck is a thin gold chain. He's smiling. His eyes are green and full of fun.

"You good-lookin, that's a fact as well as a compliment, but not from around here, correct? Not dressed like that, and hey, didn't your mom ever tell you not to jaywalk the block?"

"Leave me alone!" She's not scared; she's furious.

He laughs. "And tough! I like a tough girl. Want a slice and a Coke?"

"I don't want anything from you!"

Her friend has left, probably disgusted with her. It's not my fault, she thinks. It's this boy's fault. This *lout*.

Lout! A blackish word if ever there was one. She feels her face heat up and drops her gaze to the fish on the Zappit screen. They will comfort her, they always do. To think she almost threw the game console away after that man gave it to her! Before she found the fish! The fish always take her away, and sometimes they bring her friend. But she only gets a momentary look before the console vanishes. Poof! Gone! The lout has got it in his long-fingered hands and is staring down at the screen, fascinated.

"Whoa, this is old-school!"

"It's mine!" Barbara shouts. "Give it back!"

Across the street a woman laughs and yells in a whiskey voice, "Tell im, sister! Bring down that high neck!"

Barbara grabs for the Zappit. Tall Boy holds it over his head, smiling at her.

"Give it back, I said! Stop being a prick!"

More people are watching now, and Tall Boy plays to the audience. He jinks left, then stutter-steps to the right, probably a move he uses all the time on the basketball court, never losing that indulgent smile. His green eyes sparkle and dance. Every girl at Todhunter is probably in love with those eyes, and Barbara is no longer thinking about suicide, or being blackish, or what a socially unconscious bag of waste she is. Right now she's only mad, and him being cute makes her madder. She plays varsity soccer at Chapel Ridge and now she hoicks her best penalty kick into Tall Boy's shin.

He yells in pain (but it's somehow *amused* pain, which infuriates her even more, because that was a really hard kick), and bends over to grab his ouchy. It brings him down to her level, and Barbara snatches the precious rectangle of yellow plastic. She wheels, skirt flaring, and runs into the street.

*"Honey look out!"* the whiskey-voiced woman screams.

Barbara hears a shriek of brakes and smells hot rubber. She looks to her left and sees a panel truck bearing down on her, the front end heeling to the left as the driver stamps on the brake. Behind the dirty windshield, his face is all dismayed eyes and open mouth. She throws up her hands, dropping the Zappit. All at once the last thing in the world Barbara Robinson wants is to die, but here she is, in the street after all, and it's too late.

She thinks, My ride is here.

9

Brady shuts down the Zappit and looks up at Babineau with a wide smile. "Got her," he says. His words are clear, not the slightest bit mushy. "Let's see how Hodges and the Harvard jungle bunny like that."

Babineau has a good idea who *she* is, and he supposes he should care, but he doesn't. What he cares about is his own skin. How did he ever allow Brady to pull him into this? When did he stop having a choice?

"It's Hodges I'm here about. I'm quite sure he's on his way right now. To see you."

"Hodges has been here many times," Brady says, although it's true the old Det.-Ret. hasn't been around for awhile. "He never gets past the catatonic act."

"He's started putting things together. He's not stupid, you said as much yourself. Did he know Z-Boy when he was just Brooks? He must have seen him around here when he came to visit you."

"No idea." Brady is wrung out, sated. What he really wants now is to savor the death of the Robinson girl, then take a nap. There is a lot to be done, great things are afoot, but at the moment he needs rest.

"He can't see you like this," Babineau says. "Your skin is flushed and you're covered with sweat. You look like someone who just ran the City Marathon."

"Then keep him out. You can do that. You're the doctor and he's just another half-bald buzzard on Social Security. These days he doesn't even have the legal authority to ticket a car at an expired parking meter." Brady's wondering how the nigger lawnboy will take the news. *Jerome*. Will he cry? Will he sink to his knees? Will he rend his garments and beat his breast?

Will he blame Hodges? Unlikely, but that would be best. That would be wonderful.

"All right," Babineau says. "Yes, you're right, I can do that." He's talking to himself as much as to the man who was supposed to be his guinea pig. That turned out to be quite the joke, didn't it? "For now, at least. But he must still have friends on the police, you know. Probably lots of them."

"I'm not afraid of them, and I'm not afraid of him. I just don't want to see him. At least, not now." Brady smiles. "After he finds out about the girl. *Then* I'll want to see him. Now get out of here."

Babineau, who is at last beginning to understand who is the boss, leaves Brady's room. As always, it's a relief to do that as himself. Because every time he comes back to Babineau after being Dr. Z, there's a little less Babineau to come back to.

10

Tanya Robinson calls her daughter's cell for the fourth time in the last twenty minutes and for the fourth time gets nothing but Barbara's chirpy voicemail.

"Disregard my other messages," Tanya says after the beep. "I'm still mad, but mostly what I am right now is worried sick. Call me. I need to know you're okay."

She drops her phone on her desk and begins pacing the small confines of her office. She debates calling her husband and decides not to. Not yet. He's apt to go nuclear at the thought of Barbara skipping school, and he'll assume that's what she's doing. Tanya at first made that assumption herself when Mrs. Rossi, the Chapel Ridge attendance officer, called to ask if Barbara was home sick. Barbara has never played hooky before, but there's always a first time for bad behavior, especially with teenagers. Only she never would have skipped alone, and after further consultation with Mrs. Rossi, Tanya has confirmed that all of Barb's close friends are in school today.

Since then her mind has turned to darker thoughts, and one image keeps haunting her: the sign over the Crosstown Expressway the police use for Amber Alerts. She keeps seeing BAR-BARA ROBINSON on that sign, flashing on and off like some hellish movie marquee.

Her phone chimes the first few notes of "Ode to Joy" and she races to it, thinking Thank God, oh thank God, I'll ground her for the rest of the win—

Only it's not her daughter's smiling face in the window. It's an ID: CITY POLICE DEPT. MAIN BRANCH. Terror rolls through her stomach and her bowels loosen. For a moment she can't even take the call, because her thumb won't move. At last she manages to press the green ACCEPT button and silence the music. Everything in her office, especially the family photo on her desk, is too bright. The phone seems to float up to her ear.

"Hello?"

She listens.

"Yes, this is she."

She listens, her free hand rising to cover her mouth and stifle whatever sound wants to come out. She hears herself ask, "Are you sure it's my daughter? Barbara Rosellen Robinson?"

The policeman who has called to notify her says yes. He's sure. They found her ID in the street. What he doesn't tell her is that they had to wipe off the blood to see the name.


11


Hodges knows something's amiss as soon as he steps out of the skyway that connects Kiner Memorial proper to the Lakes Region Traumatic Brain Injury Clinic, where the walls are painted a soothing pink and soft music plays day and night. The usual patterns have been disrupted, and very little work seems to be getting done. Lunch carts stand marooned, filled with congealing plates of noodly stuff that might once have been the cafeteria's idea of Chinese. Nurses cluster, murmuring in low tones.

One appears to be crying. Two interns have their heads together by the water fountain. An orderly is talking on his cell phone, which is technically cause for suspension, but Hodges thinks he's safe enough; no one is paying him any mind.

At least Ruth Scapelli is nowhere in sight, which might improve his chances of getting in to see Hartsfield. It's Norma Wilmer at the duty desk, and along with Becky Helmington, Norma was his source for all things Brady before Hodges quit visiting Room 217. The bad news is that Hartsfield's doctor is also at the duty desk. Hodges has never been able to establish a rapport with him, although God knows he's tried.

He ambles down to the water fountain, hoping Babineau hasn't spotted him and will soon be off to look at PET scans or something, leaving Wilmer alone and approachable. He gets a drink (wincing and placing a hand to his side as he straightens up), then speaks to the interns. "Is something going on here? The place seems a little riled up."

They hesitate and glance at each other.

"Can't talk about it," says Intern One. He still has the remains of his adolescent acne, and looks about seventeen. Hodges shudders at the thought of him assisting in a surgery job more difficult than removing a thumb splinter.

"Something with a patient? Hartsfield, maybe? I only ask because I used to be a cop, and I'm sort of responsible for putting him here."

"Hodges," says Intern Two. "Is that your name?"

"Yeah, that's me."

"You caught him, right?"

Hodges agrees instantly, although if it had been left up to him, Brady would have bagged a lot more in Mingo Auditorium than he managed to get at City Center. No, it was Holly and

Jerome Robinson who stopped Brady before he could detonate his devil's load of homemade plastic explosive.

The interns exchange another glance and then One says, "Hartsfield's the same as ever, just gorking along. It's Nurse Ratched."

Intern Two gives him an elbow. "Speak no ill of the dead, asshole. Especially when the guy listening might have loose lips."

Hodges immediately runs a thumbnail across his mouth, as if sealing his dangerous lips shut.

Intern One looks flustered. "Head Nurse Scapelli, I mean. She committed suicide last night."

All the lights in Hodges's head come on, and for the first time since yesterday he forgets that he's probably going to die. "Are you sure?"

"Sliced her arms and wrists and bled out," says Two. "That's what I'm hearing, anyway."

"Did she leave a note?"

They have no idea.

Hodges heads for the duty desk. Babineau is still there, going over files with Wilmer (who looks flustered at her apparent battlefield promotion), but he can't wait. This is Hartsfield's dirt. He doesn't know how that can be, but it has Brady written all over it. The fucking suicide prince.

He almost calls Nurse Wilmer by her first name, but instinct makes him shy from that at the last moment. "Nurse Wilmer, I'm Bill Hodges." A thing she knows very well. "I worked both the City Center case and the Mingo Auditorium thing. I need to see Mr. Hartsfield."

She opens her mouth, but Babineau is there ahead of her. "Out of the question. Even if Mr. Hartsfield were allowed visitors, which he is not by order of the District Attorney's office, he wouldn't be allowed to see you. He needs peace and calm. Each of your previous unauthorized visits has shattered that."

"News to me," Hodges says mildly. "Every time I've been to see him, he just sits there. Bland as a bowl of oatmeal."

Norma Wilmer's head goes back and forth. She's like a woman watching a tennis match.

"You don't see what we see after you've left." Color is rising in Babineau's stubble-flecked cheeks. And there are dark circles under his eyes. Hodges remembers a cartoon from his Sunday school *Living with Jesus* workbook, back in the prehistoric era when cars had fins and girls wore bobby sox. Brady's doc has the same look as the guy in the cartoon, but Hodges doubts if he's a chronic masturbator. On the other hand, he remembers Becky telling him that the neuro doctors are often crazier than the patients.

"And what would that be?" Hodges asks. "Little psychic tantrums? Do things have a way of falling over after I'm gone? The toilet in his bathroom flushes by itself, maybe?"

"Ridiculous. What you leave is psychic *wreckage*, Mr. Hodges. He's not so brain damaged that he doesn't know you're obsessed with him. Malevolently so. I want you to leave. We've had a tragedy, and many of the patients are upset."

Hodges sees Wilmer's eyes widen slightly at this, and knows that the patients capable of cognition—many here in the Bucket are not—have no idea that the head nurse has offed herself.

"I only have a few questions for him, and then I'll be out of your hair."

Babineau leans forward. The eyes behind his gold-rimmed glasses are threaded with snaps of red. "Listen closely, Mr. Hodges. One, Mr. Hartsfield is not capable of answering your questions. If he could answer questions, he would have been brought to trial for his crimes by now. Two, you have no official standing. Three, if you don't leave now, I will call security and have you escorted from the premises."

Hodges says, "Pardon me for asking, but are you all right?"

Babineau draws back as if Hodges has brandished a fist in his face. "*Get out!*"

The little clusters of medical personnel stop talking and look around.

"Gotcha," Hodges says. "Going. All good."

There's a snack alcove near the entrance to the skyway. Intern Two is leaning there, hands in pockets. "Ooh, baby," he says. "You been schooled."

"So it would seem." Hodges studies the wares in the Nibble-A-Bit machine. He sees nothing in there that won't set his guts on fire, but that's okay; he's not hungry.

"Young man," he says, without turning around, "if you would like to make fifty dollars for doing a simple errand that will cause you no trouble, then get with me."

Intern Two, a fellow who looks like he might actually attain adulthood at some point in the not-too-distant future, joins him at the Nibble-A-Bit. "What's the errand?"

Hodges keeps his pad in his back pocket, just as he did when he was a Detective First Class. He scribbles two words—*Call me*—and adds his cell number. "Give this to Norma Wilmer once Smaug spreads his wings and flies away."

Intern Two takes the note and folds it into the breast pocket of his scrubs. Then he looks expectant. Hodges takes out his wallet. Fifty is a lot for delivering a note, but he has discovered at least one good thing about terminal cancer: you can toss your budget out the window.

## 12

Jerome Robinson is balancing boards on his shoulder under the hot Arizona sun when his cell phone rings. The houses they are building—the first two already framed—are in a low-income but respectable neighborhood on the southern outskirts of Phoenix. He puts the boards across the top of a handy wheelbarrow and plucks his phone from his belt, thinking it will be Hector Alonzo, the job foreman. This morning one of the workmen (a work*woman*, actually) tripped and fell into a stack of rebar. She broke her collarbone and suffered an ugly facial laceration. Alonzo took her to the St. Luke's ER, appointing Jerome temporary foreman in his absence.

It's not Alonzo's name he sees in the little window, but Holly Gibney's face. It's a photo he took himself, catching her in one of her rare smiles.

"Hey, Holly, how are you? I'll have to call you back in a few, it's been a crazy morning here, but—"

"I need you to come home," Holly says. She sounds calm, but Jerome knows her of old, and in just those six words he can sense strong emotions held in check. Fear chief among them. Holly is still a very fearful person. Jerome's mother, who loves her dearly, once called fear Holly's default setting.

"Home? Why? What's wrong?" His own fear suddenly grips him. "Is it my dad? Mom? Is it Barbie?"

"It's Bill," she says. "He has cancer. A very bad cancer. Pancreatic. If he doesn't get treatment he'll die, he'll probably die *anyway*, but he could have time and he told me it was just a little ulcer because . . . because . . ." She takes a great ragged breath that makes Jerome wince. "*Because of Brady Fracking Hartsfield!*"

Jerome has no idea what connection Brady Hartsfield can have to Bill's terrible diagnosis, but he knows what he's seeing right now: trouble. On the far side of the building site, two hard-hatted young men—Habitat for Humanity college volunteers like Jerome himself—are giving a beeping, backing cement truck conflicting directions. Disaster looms.

"Holly, give me five minutes and I'll call you back."

"But you'll come, won't you? Say you'll come. Because I don't think I can talk to him about this on my own and *he has to get into treatment right away*!"

"Five minutes," he says, and kills the call. His thoughts are spinning so fast that he's afraid the friction will catch his brains on fire, and the blaring sun isn't helping. Bill? With cancer? On one hand it doesn't seem possible, but on the other it seems *completely* possible. He was in top form during the Pete Saubers business, where Jerome and Holly partnered with him, but he'll be seventy soon, and the last time Jerome saw him, before leaving for Arizona in October, Bill didn't look all that well. Too thin. Too pale. But Jerome can't go anywhere until Hector gets back. It would be like leaving the inmates to run the asylum. And knowing the Phoenix hospitals, where the ERs are overrun twenty-four hours a day, he may be stuck here until quitting time.

He sprints for the cement truck, bawling *"Hold up! Hold UP, for Jesus' sake!"* at the top of his lungs.

He gets the clueless volunteers to halt the cement truck they've been misdirecting less than three feet from a freshly dug drainage ditch, and he's bending over to catch his breath when his phone rings again.

Holly, I love you, Jerome thinks, pulling it from his belt once more, but sometimes you drive me absolutely bugfuck.

Only this time it's not Holly's picture he sees. It's his mother's.

Tanya is crying. "You have to come home," she says, and Jerome has just long enough to think of something his grandfather used to say: *bad luck keeps bad company*.

It's Barbie after all.


## 13


Hodges is in the lobby and headed for the door when his phone vibrates. It's Norma Wilmer.

"Is he gone?" Hodges asks.

Norma doesn't have to ask who he's talking about. "Yes. Now that he's seen his prize patient, he can relax and do the rest of his rounds."

"I was sorry to hear about Nurse Scapelli." It's true. He didn't care for her, but it's still true.

"I was, too. She ran the nursing staff like Captain Bligh ran the *Bounty*, but I hate to think of anyone doing . . . that. You get the news and your first reaction is oh no, not her, never. It's the shock of it. Your second reaction is oh yes, that makes perfect sense. Never married, no close friends—not that I knew of, anyway—nothing but the job. Where everybody sort of loathed her."

"All the lonely people," Hodges says, stepping out into the cold and turning toward the bus stop. He buttons his coat one-handed and then begins to massage his side.

"Yes. There are a lot of them. What can I do for you, Mr. Hodges?"

"I have a few questions. Could you meet me for a drink?"

There's a long pause. Hodges thinks she's going to tell him

STEPHEN KING

no. Then she says, "I don't suppose your questions could lead to trouble for Dr. Babineau?"

"Anything is possible, Norma."

"That would be nice, but I guess I owe you one, regardless. For not letting on to him that we know each other from back in the Becky Helmington days. There's a watering hole on Revere Avenue. Got a clever name, Bar Bar Black Sheep, and most of the staff drinks closer to the hospital. Can you find it?"

"Yeah."

"I'm off at five. Meet me there at five thirty. I like a nice cold vodka martini."

"It'll be waiting."

"Just don't expect me to get you in to see Hartsfield. It would mean my job. Babineau was always intense, but these days he's downright weird. I tried to tell him about Ruth, and he blew right past me. Not that he's apt to care when he finds out."

"Got a lot of love for him, don't you?"

She laughs. "For that you owe me two drinks."

"Two it is."

He's slipping his phone back into his coat pocket when it buzzes again. He sees the call is from Tanya Robinson and his thoughts immediately flash to Jerome, building houses out there in Arizona. A lot of things can go wrong on building sites.

He takes the call. Tanya is crying, at first too hard for him to understand what she's saying, only that Jim is in Pittsburgh and she doesn't want to call him until she knows more. Hodges stands at the curb, one palm plastered against his non-phone ear to muffle the sound of traffic.

"Slow down. Tanya, slow down. Is it Jerome? Did something happen to Jerome?"

"No, Jerome's fine. Him I *did* call. It's *Barbara*. She was in Lowtown—"

"What in God's name was she doing in Lowtown, and on a school day?"

"I don't know! All I know is that some boy pushed her into the street and a truck hit her! They're taking her to Kiner Memorial. I'm on my way there now!"

"Are you driving?"

"Yes, what does that have to do with—"

"Get off the phone, Tanya. And slow down. I'm at Kiner now. I'll meet you in the ER."

He hangs up and heads back to the hospital, breaking into a clumsy trot. He thinks, This goddam place is like the Mafia. Every time I think I'm out, it pulls me back in.

## 14

An ambulance with its lights flashing is just backing into one of the ER bays. Hodges goes to meet it, pulling out the police ID he still keeps in his wallet. When the paramedic and the EMT pull the stretcher out of the back, he flashes the ID with his thumb placed over the red RETIRED stamp. Technically speaking this is a felony crime—impersonating an officer—and consequently it's a fiddle he uses sparingly, but this time it seems absolutely appropriate.

Barbara is medicated but conscious. When she sees Hodges, she grasps his hand tightly. "Bill? How did you get here so fast? Did Mom call you?"

"Yeah. How are you?"

"I'm okay. They gave me something for the pain. I have . . .

they say I have a broken leg. I'm going to miss the basketball season and I guess it doesn't matter because Mom will ground me until I'm, like, twenty-five." Tears begin to leak from her eyes.

He doesn't have long with her, so questions about what she was doing on MLK Ave, where there are sometimes as many as four drive-by shootings a week, will have to wait. There's something more important.

"Barb, do you know the name of the boy who pushed you in front of the truck?"

Her eyes widen.

"Or get a good look at him? Could you describe him?"

"Pushed . . . ? Oh, no, Bill! No, that's wrong!"

"Officer, we gotta go," the paramedic says. "You can question her later."

"Wait!" Barbara shouts, and tries to sit up. The EMT pushes her gently back down, and she's grimacing with pain, but Hodges is heartened by that shout. It was good and strong.

"What is it, Barb?"

"He only pushed me *after* I ran into the street! He pushed me out of the way! I think he might have saved my life, and I'm glad." She's crying hard now, but Hodges doesn't believe for a minute it's because of her broken leg. "I don't want to die, after all. I don't know what was *wrong* with me!"

"We really have to get her in an exam room, Chief," the paramedic says. "She needs an X-ray."

"Don't let them do anything to that boy!" Barbara calls as the ambo guys roll her through the double doors. "He's tall! He's got green eyes and a goatee! He goes to Todhunter—"

She's gone, the doors clapping back and forth behind her.

Hodges walks outside, where he can use his cell phone without being scolded, and calls Tanya back. "I don't know where you are, but slow down and don't run any red lights getting here. They just took her in, and she's wide awake. She has a broken leg."

"That's all? Thank God! What about internal injuries?"

"That's for the doctors to say, but she was pretty lively. I think maybe the truck just grazed her."

"I need to call Jerome. I'm sure I scared the hell out of him. And Jim needs to know."

"Call them when you get here. For now, get off your phone."

"*You* can call them, Bill."

"No, Tanya, I can't. I have to call someone else."

He stands there, breathing out plumes of white vapor, the tips of his ears going numb. He doesn't want the someone else to be Pete, because Pete is a tad pissed at him right now, and that goes double for Izzy Jaynes. He thinks about his other choices, but there's only one: Cassandra Sheen. He partnered up with her several times when Pete was on vacation, and on one occasion when Pete took six weeks of unexplained personal time. That was shortly after Pete's divorce, and Hodges surmised he was in a spin-dry center, but never asked and Pete never volunteered the information.

He doesn't have Cassie's cell number, so he calls Detective Division and asks to be connected, hoping she's not in the field. He's in luck. After less than ten seconds of McGruff the Crime Dog, she's in his ear.

"Is this Cassie Sheen, the Botox Queen?"

"Billy Hodges, you old whore! I thought you were dead!"

Soon enough, Cassie, he thinks.

"I'd love to bullshit with you, hon, but I need a favor. They haven't closed the Strike Avenue station yet, have they?"

"Nope. It's on the docket for next year, though. Which makes perfect sense. Crime in Lowtown? What crime, right?"

"Yeah, safest part of the city. They may have a kid in for booking, and if my information is right, he deserves a medal instead."

"Got a name?"

"No, but I know what he looks like. Tall, green eyes, goatee." He replays what Barbara said and adds, "He could be wearing a Todhunter High jacket. The arresting officers probably have him for pushing a girl in front of a truck. He actually pushed her out of the way, so she only got clipped instead of mashed."

"You know this for a fact?"

"Yeah." This isn't quite the truth, but he believes Barbara. "Find out his name and ask the cops to hold him, okay? I want to talk to him."

"I think I can do that."

"Thanks, Cassie. I owe you one."

He ends the call and looks at his watch. If he means to talk to the Todhunter kid and still keep his appointment with Norma, time is too tight to be messing around with the city bus service.

One thing Barbara said keeps replaying in his mind: *I don't want to die, after all. I don't know what was* wrong *with me!*

He calls Holly.

15

She's standing outside the 7-Eleven near the office, holding a pack of Winstons in one hand and plucking at the cellophane with the other. She hasn't had a cigarette in almost five months, a new record, and she doesn't want to start again now, but what she saw on Bill's computer has torn a hole in the middle of a life she has spent the last five years mending. Bill Hodges is her touchstone, the way she measures her ability to interact with the world. Which is only another way of saying that he is the way she measures her sanity. Trying to imagine her life with him gone is like standing on top of a skyscraper and looking at the sidewalk sixty stories below.

Just as she begins to pull the strip on the cellophane, her phone rings. She drops the Winstons into her purse and fishes it out. It's him.

Holly doesn't say hello. She told Jerome she didn't think she could talk to him on her own about what she's discovered, but now—standing on this windy city sidewalk and shivering inside her good winter coat—she has no choice. It just spills out. "I looked on your computer and I know that snooping's a lousy thing to do but I'm not sorry. I had to because I thought you were lying about it just being an ulcer and you can fire me if you want, I don't care, just as long as you let them fix what's wrong with you."

Silence at the other end. She wants to ask if he's still there, but her mouth feels frozen and her heart is beating so hard she can feel it all over her body.

At last he says, "Hols, I don't think it *can* be fixed."

"At least let them *try!*"

"I love you," he says. She hears the heaviness in his voice. The resignation. "You know that, right?"

"Don't be stupid, of course I know." She starts to cry.

"I'll try the treatments, sure. But I need a couple of days before I check into the hospital. And right now I need *you*. Can you come and pick me up?"

"Okay." Crying harder than ever, because she knows he's telling the truth about needing her. And being needed is a great thing. Maybe *the* great thing. "Where are you?"

He tells her, then says, "Something else."

"What?"

"I can't fire you, Holly. You're not an employee, you're my partner. Try to remember that."

"Bill?"

"Yeah?"

"I'm not smoking."

"That's good, Holly. Now come on over here. I'll be waiting in the lobby. It's freezing outside."

"I'll come as fast as I can while still obeying the speed limit."

She hurries to the corner lot where she parks her car. On the way, she drops the unopened pack of cigarettes into a litter basket.

## 16

Hodges sketches in his visit to the Bucket for Holly on the ride to the Strike Avenue police station, beginning with the news of Ruth Scapelli's suicide and ending with the odd thing Barbara said before they wheeled her away.

"I know what you're thinking," Holly says, "because I'm thinking it, too. That it all leads back to Brady Hartsfield."

"The suicide prince." Hodges has helped himself to another couple of painkillers while waiting for Holly, and he feels pretty much okay. "That's what I'm calling him. Got a ring to it, don't you think?"

"I guess so. But you told me something once." She's sitting bolt upright behind the wheel of her Prius, eyes darting everywhere as they drive deeper into Lowtown. She swerves to avoid a shopping cart someone has abandoned in the middle of the street. "You said coincidence doesn't equal conspiracy. Do you remember saying that?"

"Yeah." It's one of his faves. He has quite a few.

"You said you can investigate a conspiracy forever and come up with nothing if it's actually just a bunch of coincidences all strung together. If you can't find something concrete in the next two days—if *we* can't—you need to give up and start those treatments. Promise me you will."

"It might take a little longer to—"

She cuts him off. "Jerome will be back, and he'll help. It will be like the old days."

Hodges flashes on the title of an old mystery novel, *Trent's Last Case*, and smiles a little. She catches it from the corner of her eye, takes it for acquiescence, and smiles back, relieved.

"Four days," he says.

"Three. No more. Because every day you don't do something about what's going on inside you, the odds get longer. And they're long already. So don't start your poopy bargaining stuff, Bill. You're too good at it."

"Okay," he says. "Three days. If Jerome will help."

Holly says, "He will. And let's try to make it two."

17

The Strike Avenue cop shop looks like a medieval castle in a country where the king has fallen and anarchy rules. The windows are heavily barred; the motor pool is protected by chain-link fencing and concrete barriers. Cameras bristle in every direction, covering all angles of approach, and still the gray stone building has

161

been gang-tagged, and one of the globes hanging over the main doors has been shattered.

Hodges and Holly empty the contents of their pockets and Holly's purse into plastic baskets and go through a metal detector that beeps reproachfully at Hodges's metal watchband. Holly sits on a bench in the main lobby (which is also being scanned by multiple cameras) and opens her iPad. Hodges goes to the desk, states his business, and after a few moments is met by a slim, gray-haired detective who looks a little like Lester Freamon on *The Wire*—the only cop show Hodges can watch without wanting to throw up.

"Jack Higgins," the detective says, offering his hand. "Like the book-writer, only not white."

Hodges shakes with him and introduces Holly, who gives a little wave and her usual muttered hello before returning her attention to her iPad.

"I think I remember you," Hodges says. "You used to be at Marlborough Street station, didn't you? When you were in uniform?"

"A long time ago, when I was young and randy. I remember you, too. You caught the guy who killed those two women in McCarron Park."

"That was a group effort, Detective Higgins."

"Make it Jack. Cassie Sheen called. We've got your guy in an interview room. His name is Dereece Neville." Higgins spells the first name. "We were going to turn him loose, anyway. Several people who saw the incident corroborate his story—he was jiving around with the girl, she took offense and ran into the street. Neville saw the truck coming, ran after her, tried to push her out of the way, mostly succeeded. Plus, practically everyone down here knows this kid. He's a star on the Todhunter basketball team, probably going to get an athletic scholarship to a Division I school. Great grades, honor student."

"What was Mr. Great Grades doing on the street in the middle of a school day?"

"Ah, they were all out. Heating system at the high school shit the bed again. Third time this winter, and it's only January. The mayor says everything's cool down here in the Low, lots of jobs, lots of prosperity, shiny happy people. We'll see him when he runs for reelection. Riding in that armored SUV of his."

"Was the Neville kid hurt?"

"Scraped palms and nothing else. According to a lady across the street—she was closest to the scene—he pushed the girl and then, I quote, 'Went flyin over the top of her like a bigass bird.'"

"Does he understand he's free to go?"

"He does, and agreed to stay. Wants to know if the girl's okay. Come on. Have your little chat with him, and then we'll send him on his way. Unless you see some reason not to."

Hodges smiles. "I'm just following up for Miss Robinson. Let me ask him a couple of questions, and we're both out of your hair."

## 18

The interview room is small and stifling hot, the overhead heating pipes clanking away. Still, it's probably the nicest one they've got, because there's a little sofa and no perp table with a cuff-bolt sticking out of it like a steel knuckle. The sofa has been mended with tape in a couple of places, and that makes Hodges think of the man Nancy Alderson says she saw on Hilltop Court, the one with the mended coat.

Dereece Neville is sitting on the sofa. In his chino pants and white button-up shirt, he looks neat and squared away. His goatee and gold neck chain are the only real dashes of style. His school jacket is folded over one arm of the sofa. He stands when Hodges and Higgins come in, and offers a long-fingered hand that looks designed expressly for working with a basketball. The pad of the palm has been painted with orange antiseptic.

Hodges shakes with him carefully, mindful of the scrapes, and introduces himself. "You're in absolutely no trouble here, Mr. Neville. In fact, Barbara Robinson sent me to say thanks and make sure you were okay. She and her family are longtime friends of mine."

"Is *she* okay?"

"Broken leg," Hodges says, pulling over a chair. His hand creeps to his side and presses there. "It could have been a lot worse. I'm betting she'll be back on the soccer field next year. Sit down, sit down."

When the Neville boy sits, his knees seem to come almost up to his jawline. "It was my fault, in a way. I shouldn't have been goofing with her, but she was just so pretty and all. Still . . . I ain't blind." He pauses, corrects himself. "Not blind. What was she on? Do you know?"

Hodges frowns. The idea that Barbara might have been high hasn't crossed his mind, although it should have; she's a teenager, after all, and those years are the Age of Experimentation. But he has dinner with the Robinsons three or four times a month, and he's never seen anything in her that registered as drug use. Maybe he's just too close. Or too old.

"What makes you think she was on something?"

"Just her being down here, for one thing. Those were Chapel Ridge duds she was wearing. I know, because we play em twice every year. Blow em out, too. And she was like in a daze. Standing there on the curb near Mamma Stars, that fortune-telling place, looking like she was gonna walk right out into traffic." He shrugs. "So I chatted her up, teased her about jaywalking. She got mad, went all Kitty Pryde on my ass. I thought that was cute, so then . . ." He looks at Higgins, then back at Hodges. "This is the fault part, and I'm being straight with you about it, okay?"

"Okay," Hodges says.

"Well, look—I grabbed her game. Just for a joke, you know. Held it up over my head. I never meant to keep it. So then she kicked me—good hard kick for a girl—and grabbed it back. She sure didn't look stoned then."

"How *did* she look, Dereece?" The switch to the boy's first name is automatic.

"Oh, man, *mad*! But also scared. Like she just figured out where she was, on a street where girls like her—ones in private school uniforms—don't go, especially by themselves. MLK Ave? Come on, I mean bitch, please." He leans forward, long-fingered hands clasped between his knees, face earnest. "She didn't know I was just playing, you see what I mean? She was like in a panic, get me?"

"I do," Hodges says, and although he sounds engaged (at least he hopes so), he's on autopilot for the moment, stuck on what Neville has just said: *I grabbed her game.* Part of him thinks it can't be connected to Ellerton and Stover. Most of him thinks it must be, it's a perfect fit. "That must have made you feel bad."

Neville raises his scratched palms toward the ceiling in a philosophical gesture that says *What can you do?* "It's this place, man. It's the Low. She stopped being on cloud nine and realized where she was, is all. Me, I'm getting out as soon as I can. *While* I can. Gonna play Div I, keep my grades up so I can get a good job afterward if I ain't—aren't—good enough to go pro. Then I'm getting my family out. It's just me and my mom and my two brothers. My mom's the only reason I've got as far as I have. She ain't never let none of us play in the dirt." He replays what he just said and laughs. "She heard me say ain't never, she be in my face."

Hodges thinks, Kid's too good to be true. Except he is. Hodges is sure of it, and doesn't like to think what might have happened to Jerome's kid sister if Dereece Neville had been in school today.

Higgins says, "You were wrong to be teasing that girl, but I have to say you made it right. Will you think about what almost happened if you get an urge to do something like that again?"

"Yes, sir, I sure will."

Higgins holds a hand up. Rather than slap it, Neville taps it gently, with a slightly sarcastic smile. He's a good kid, but this is still Lowtown, and Higgins is still po-po.

Higgins stands. "Are we good to go, Detective Hodges?"

Hodges nods his appreciation at the use of his old title, but he isn't quite finished. "Almost. What kind of game was it, Dereece?"

"Old-school." No hesitation. "Like a Game Boy, but my little brother had one of those—Mom got it in a rumble sale, or whatever they call those things—and the one the girl had wasn't the same. It was bright yellow, I know that. Not the kind of color you'd expect a girl to like. Not the ones I know, at least."

"Did you happen to see the screen?"

"Just a glance. It was a bunch of fish swimming around."

"Thanks, Dereece. How sure are you that she was high? On a scale of one to ten, ten being absolutely positive."

"Well, say five. I would've said ten when I walked up to her, because she acted like she was going to walk right out into the street, and there was a bigass truck coming, a lot bigger than the panel job that come along behind and whumped her. I was thinking not coke or meth or molly, more something mellow, like ecstasy or pot."

"But when you started goofing with her? When you took her game?"

Dereece Neville rolls his eyes. "Man, she woke up *fast*."

"Okay," Hodges says. "All set. And thank you."

Higgins adds his thanks, then he and Hodges start toward the door.

"Detective Hodges?" Neville is on his feet again, and Hodges practically has to crane his neck to look at him. "You think if I wrote down my number, you could give it to her?"

Hodges thinks it over, then takes his pen from his breast pocket and hands it to the tall boy who probably saved Barbara Robinson's life.

## 19

Holly drives them back to Lower Marlborough Street. He tells her about his conversation with Dereece Neville on the way.

"In a movie, they'd fall in love," Holly says when he finishes. She sounds wistful.

"Life is not a movie, Hol . . . Holly." He stops himself from saying *Hollyberry* at the last second. This is not a day for levity.

"I know," she says. "That's why I go to them."

"I don't suppose you know if Zappit consoles came in yellow, do you?"

As is often the case, Holly has the facts at her fingertips. "They came in ten different colors, and yes, yellow was one of them."

"Are you thinking what I'm thinking? That there's a connection between what happened to Barbara and what happened to those women on Hilltop Court?"

"I don't know *what* I'm thinking. I wish we could sit down with Jerome the way we did when Pete Saubers got into trouble. Just sit down and talk it all out."

"If Jerome gets here tonight, and if Barbara's really okay, maybe we can do that tomorrow."

"Tomorrow's your second day," she says as she pulls to the curb outside the parking lot they use. "The second of three."

"Holly—"

"No!" she says fiercely. "Don't even start! You promised!" She shoves the gearshift into park and turns to face him. "You believe Hartsfield has been faking, isn't that right?"

"Yeah. Maybe not from the first time he opened his eyes and asked for his dear old mommy, but I think he's come a long way back since then. Maybe all the way. He's faking the semi-catatonic thing to keep from going to trial. Although you'd think Babineau would know. They must have tests, brain scans and things—"

"Never mind that. If he can think, and if he were to find out that you delayed treatment and died because of him, how do you think he'd feel?"

Hodges makes no answer, so Holly answers for him.

"He'd be happy happy happy! He'd be *fracking delighted*!"

"Okay," Hodges says. "I hear you. The rest of today and two

more. But forget about my situation for a minute. If he can somehow reach out beyond that hospital room . . . that's scary."

"I know. And nobody would believe us. That's scary, too. But nothing scares me as much as the thought of you dying."

He wants to hug her for that, but she's currently wearing one of her many hug-repelling expressions, so he looks at his watch instead. "I have an appointment, and I don't want to keep the lady waiting."

"I'm going to the hospital. Even if they won't let me see Barbara, Tanya will be there, and she'd probably like to see a friendly face."

"Good idea. But before you go, I'd like you to take a shot at tracking down the Sunrise Solutions bankruptcy trustee."

"His name is Todd Schneider. He's part of a law firm six names long. Their offices are in New York. I found him while you were talking to Mr. Neville."

"You did that on your iPad?"

"Yes."

"You're a genius, Holly."

"No, it's just computer research. You were the smart one, to think of it in the first place. I'll call him, if you want." Her face shows how much she dreads the prospect.

"You don't have to do that. Just call his office and see if you can make an appointment for me to talk to him. As early tomorrow as possible."

She smiles. "All right." Then her smile fades. She points to his midsection. "Does it hurt?"

"Only a little." For now that's true. "The heart attack was worse." That is true, too, but may not be for long. "If you get in to see Barbara, say hi for me."

"I will."

Holly watches him cross to his car, noting the way his left hand goes to his side after he turns up his collar. Seeing that makes her want to cry. Or maybe howl with outrage. Life can be very unfair. She's known that ever since high school, when she was the butt of everyone's joke, but it still surprises her. It shouldn't, but it does.

20

Hodges drives back across town, fiddling with the radio, looking for some good hard rock and roll. He finds The Knack on BAM-100, singing "My Sharona," and cranks the volume. When the song ends, the deejay comes on, talking about a big storm moving east out of the Rockies.

Hodges pays no attention. He's thinking about Brady, and about the first time he saw one of those Zappit game consoles. Library Al handed them out. What was Al's last name? He can't remember. If he ever knew it at all, that is.

When he arrives at the watering hole with the amusing name, he finds Norma Wilmer seated at a table in back, far from the madding crowd of businessmen at the bar, who are bellowing and backslapping as they jockey for drinks. Norma has ditched her nurse's uniform in favor of a dark green pantsuit and low heels. There's already a drink in front of her.

"I was supposed to buy that," Hodges says, sitting down across from her.

"Don't worry," she says. "I'm running a tab, which you will pay."

"Indeed I will."

"Babineau couldn't get me fired or even transferred if someone saw me talking to you here and reported back to him, but he could make my life difficult. Of course, I could make his a bit difficult, too."

"Really?"

"Really. I think he's been experimenting on your old friend Brady Hartsfield. Feeding him pills that contain God knows what. Giving him shots, as well. Vitamins, he says."

Hodges stares at her in surprise. "How long has this been going on?"

"Years. It's one of the reasons Becky Helmington transferred. She didn't want to be the whitecap on ground zero if Babineau gave him the wrong vitamin and killed him."

The waitress comes. Hodges orders a Coke with a cherry in it.

Norma snorts. "A Coke? Really? Put on your big boy pants, why don't you?"

"When it comes to booze, I spilled more than you'll ever drink, honeypie," Hodges says. "What the hell is Babineau up to?"

She shrugs. "No idea. But he wouldn't be the first doc to experiment on someone the world doesn't give shit one about. Ever hear of the Tuskegee Syphilis Experiment? The US government used four hundred black men like lab rats. It went on for forty years, and so far as I know, not a single one of *them* ran a car into a bunch of defenseless people." She gives Hodges a crooked smile. "Investigate Babineau. Get him in trouble. I dare you."

"It's Hartsfield I'm interested in, but based on what you're saying, I wouldn't be surprised if Babineau turned out to be collateral damage."

"Then hooray for collateral damage." It comes out *clatteral dammish*, and Hodges deduces she's not on her first drink. He is, after all, a trained investigator.

When the waitress brings his Coke, Norma drains her glass

and holds it up. "I'll have another, and since the gentleman's paying, you might as well make it a double." The waitress takes her glass and leaves. Norma turns her attention back to Hodges. "You said you have questions. Go ahead and ask while I can still answer. My mouth is a trifle numb, and will soon be number."

"Who is on Brady Hartsfield's visitors list?"

Norma frowns at him. "*Visitors* list? Are you kidding? Who told you he had a visitors list?"

"The late Ruth Scapelli. This was just after she replaced Becky as head nurse. I offered her fifty bucks for any rumors she heard about him—which was the going rate with Becky—and she acted like I'd just pissed on her shoes. Then she said, 'You're not even on his visitors list.'"

"Huh."

"Then, just today, Babineau said—"

"Some bullshit about the DA's office. I heard it, Bill, I was there."

The waitress sets Norma's new drink in front of her, and Hodges knows he'd better finish up fast, before Norma starts to bend his ear about everything from being underappreciated at work to her sad and loveless love life. When nurses drink, they have a tendency to go all in. They're like cops that way.

"You've been working the Bucket for as long as I've been coming there—"

"A lot longer. Twelve years." *Yearsh.* She raises her glass in a toast and swallows half of her drink. "And now I have been promoted to head nurse, at least temporarily. Twice the responsibility at the same old salary, no doubt."

"Seen anybody from the DA's office lately?"

"Nope. There was a whole briefcase brigade at first, along

with pet doctors just itching to declare the son of a bitch competent, but they went away discouraged once they saw him drooling and trying to pick up a spoon. Came back a few times just to double-check, fewer briefcase boys every time, but nothing lately. 'S'far's they're concerned, he's a total gork. Badda-boop, badda-bang, over and out."

"So they don't care." And why would they? Except for the occasional retrospective on slow news days, interest in Brady Hartsfield has died down. There's always fresh roadkill to pick over.

"You know they don't." A lock of hair has fallen in her eyes. She blows it back. "Did anyone try to stop you, all the times you were in to visit him?"

No, Hodges thinks, but it's been a year and a half since I dropped by. "If there *is* a visitors list—"

"It'd be Babineau's, not the DA's. When it comes to the Mercedes Killer, DA is like honeybadger, Bill. He don't give a shit."

"Huh?"

"Never mind."

"Could you check and see if there is such a list? Now that you've been promoted to head nurse?"

She considers, then says, "It wouldn't be on the computer, that would be too easy to check, but Scapelli kept a couple of file folders in a locked drawer at the duty desk. She was a great one for keeping track of who's naughty and who's nice. If I found something, would it be worth twenty to you?"

"Fifty, if you could call me tomorrow." Hodges isn't sure she'll even remember this conversation tomorrow. "Time is of the essence."

"If such a list exists, it's probably just power-tripping bullshit, you know. Babineau likes to keep Hartsfield to his little old self."

"But you'll check?"

"Yeah, why not? I know where she hides the key to her locked drawer. Shit, most of the nurses on the floor know. Hard to get used to the idea old Nurse Ratched's dead."

Hodges nods.

"He can move things, you know. Without touching them." Norma's not looking at him; she's making rings on the table with the bottom of her glass. It looks like she's trying to replicate the Olympic logo.

"Hartsfield?"

"Who are we talking about? Yeah. He does it to freak out the nurses." She raises her head. "I'm drunk, so I'll tell you something I'd never say sober. I wish Babineau *would* kill him. Just give him a hot shot of something really toxic and boot him out the door. Because he scares me." She pauses, then adds, "He scares all of us."

21

Holly reaches Todd Schneider's personal assistant just as he's getting ready to shut up shop and leave for the day. The PA says Mr. Schneider should be available between eight thirty and nine tomorrow. After that he has meetings all day.

Holly hangs up, washes her face in the tiny lavatory, reapplies deodorant, locks the office, and gets rolling toward Kiner Memorial just in time to catch the worst of the evening rush hour. It's six o'clock and full dark by the time she arrives. The woman at the information desk checks her computer and tells her that Barbara Robinson is in Room 528 of Wing B.

"Is that Intensive Care?" Holly asks.

"No, ma'am."

"Good," Holly says, and sets sail, sensible low heels clacking.

The elevator doors open on the fifth floor and there, waiting to get on, are Barbara's parents. Tanya has her cell phone in her hand, and looks at Holly as if at an apparition. Jim Robinson says he'll be damned.

Holly shrinks a little. "What? Why are you looking at me that way? What's wrong?"

"Nothing," Tanya says. "It's just that I was going to call you—"

The elevator doors start to close. Jim sticks out an arm and they bounce back. Holly gets out.

"—as soon as we got down to the lobby," Tanya resumes, and points to a sign on the wall. It shows a cell phone with a red line drawn through it.

"Me? Why? I thought it was just a broken leg. I mean, I know a broken leg is serious, of course it is, but—"

"She's awake and she's fine," Jim says, but he and Tanya exchange a glance which suggests that isn't precisely true. "It's a pretty clean break, actually, but they found a nasty bump on the back of her head and decided to keep her overnight just to be on the safe side. The doc who fixed her leg said he's ninety-nine percent sure she'll be good to go in the morning."

"They did a tox screen," Tanya said. "No drugs in her system. I wasn't surprised, but it was still a relief."

"Then what's wrong?"

"Everything," Tanya says simply. She looks ten years older than when Holly saw her last. "Hilda Carver's mom drove Barb and Hilda to school, it's her week, and she said Barbara was fine in the car—a little quieter than usual, but otherwise fine. Barbara told Hilda she had to go to the bathroom, and that was the last Hilda saw of her. She said Barb must have left by one of the side doors in the gym. The kids actually call those the skip doors."

"What does Barbara say?"

"She won't tell us *anything*." Her voice shakes, and Jim puts an arm around her. "But she says she'll tell you. That's why I was going to call you. She says you're the only one who might understand."

22

Holly walks slowly down the corridor to Room 528, which is all the way at the end. Her head is down, and she's thinking hard, so she almost bumps into the man wheeling the cart of well-thumbed paperback books and Kindles with PROPERTY OF KINER HOSP taped below the screens.

"Sorry," Holly tells him. "I wasn't looking where I was going."

"That's all right," Library Al says, and goes on his way. She doesn't see him pause and look back at her; she is summoning all her courage for the conversation to come. It's apt to be emotional, and emotional scenes have always terrified her. It helps that she loves Barbara.

Also, she's curious.

She taps on the door, which is ajar, and peeps around it when there's no answer. "Barbara? It's Holly. Can I come in?"

Barbara offers a wan smile and puts down the battered copy of *Mockingjay* she's been reading. Probably got it from the man with the cart, Holly thinks. She's cranked up in the bed, wearing pink pajamas instead of a hospital johnny. Holly guesses her mother must have packed the PJs, along with the ThinkPad she sees on Barb's night table. The pink top lends Barbara a bit of vivacity, but she still looks dazed. There's no bandage on her head, so the bump mustn't have been all *that* bad. Holly wonders if they are keeping Barbara overnight for some other reason. She can only think of one, and she'd like to believe it's ridiculous, but she can't quite get there.

"Holly! How did you get here so fast?"

"I was coming to see you." Holly enters and closes the door behind her. "When somebody's in the hospital, you go to see them if it's a friend, and we're friends. I met your parents at the elevator. They said you wanted to talk to me."

"Yes."

"How can I help, Barbara?"

"Well . . . can I ask you something? It's pretty personal."

"Okay." Holly sits down in the chair next to the bed. Gingerly, as if the seat might be wired for electricity.

"I know you had some bad times. You know, when you were younger. Before you worked for Bill."

"Yes," Holly says. The overhead light isn't on, just the lamp on the night table. Its glow encloses them and gives them their own little place to be. "Some very bad ones."

"Did you ever try to kill yourself?" Barbara gives a small, nervous laugh. "I told you it was personal."

"Twice." Holly says it without hesitation. She feels surprisingly calm. "The first time, I was just about your age. Because kids at school were mean to me, and called me mean names. I couldn't cope. But I didn't try very hard. I just took a handful of aspirin and decongestant tablets."

"Did you try harder the second time?"

It's a tough question, and Holly thinks it over carefully. "Yes and no. It was after I had some trouble with my boss, what they call sexual harassment now. Back then they didn't call it much of anything. I was in my twenties. I took stronger pills, but still not enough to do the job and part of me knew that. I was very unstable back then, but I wasn't stupid, and the part that wasn't stupid wanted to live. Partly because I knew Martin Scorsese would make some more movies, and I wanted to see them. Martin Scorsese is the best director alive. He makes long movies like novels. Most movies are only like short stories."

"Did your boss, like, *attack* you?"

"I don't want to talk about it, and it doesn't matter." Holly doesn't want to look up, either, but reminds herself that this is Barbara and forces herself to. Because Barbara has been her friend in spite of all of Holly's ticks and tocks, all of Holly's bells and whistles. And is now in trouble herself. "The reasons never matter, because suicide goes against every human instinct, and that makes it insane."

Except maybe in certain cases, she thinks. Certain *terminal* cases. But Bill isn't terminal.

I won't let him be terminal.

"I know what you mean," Barbara says. She turns her head from side to side on her pillow. In the lamplight, tear-tracks gleam on her cheeks. "I know."

"Is that why you were in Lowtown? To kill yourself?"

Barbara closes her eyes, but tears squeeze through the lashes. "I don't think so. At least not at first. I went there because the voice told me to. My friend." She pauses, thinks. "But he wasn't my friend, after all. A friend wouldn't want me to kill myself, would he?"

Holly takes Barbara's hand. Touching is ordinarily hard for her, but not tonight. Maybe it's because she feels they are enclosed in their own secret place. Maybe it's because this is Barbara. Maybe both. "What friend is this?"

Barbara says, "The one with the fish. The one inside the game."

23

It's Al Brooks who wheels the library cart through the hospital's main lobby (passing Mr. and Mrs. Robinson, who are waiting for Holly), and it's Al who takes another elevator up to the skyway that connects the main hospital to the Traumatic Brain Injury Clinic. It's Al who says hello to Nurse Rainier at the duty desk, a long-timer who hellos him back without looking up from her computer screen. It's still Al rolling his cart down the corridor, but when he leaves it in the hall and steps into Room 217, Al Brooks disappears and Z-Boy takes his place.

Brady is in his chair with his Zappit in his lap. He doesn't look up from the screen. Z-Boy takes his own Zappit from the left pocket of his loose gray tunic and turns it on. He taps the Fishin' Hole icon and on the starter screen the fish begin to swim: red ones, yellow ones, gold ones, every now and then a fast-moving pink one. The tune tinkles. And every now and then the console gives off a bright flash that paints his cheeks and turns his eyes into blue blanks.

They remain that way for almost five minutes, one sitting and one standing, both staring at the swimming fish and listening to the tinkling melody. The blinds over Brady's window rattle restlessly. The coverlet on his bed snaps down, then back up again. Once or twice Z-Boy nods his understanding. Then Brady's hands loosen and let go of the game console. It slides down his wasted legs, then between them, and clatters to the floor. His mouth falls open. His eyelids drop to half-mast. The rise and fall of his chest inside his checked shirt becomes imperceptible.

Z-Boy's shoulders straighten. He gives himself a little shake, clicks off his Zappit, and drops it back into the pocket from which it came. From his right pocket he takes an iPhone. A person with considerable computer skills has modified it with several state-of-the-art security devices, and the built-in GPS has been turned off. There are no names in the Contacts folder, only a few initials. Z-Boy taps *FL.*

The phone rings twice and FL answers in a fake Russian accent. "Ziss iss Agent Zippity-Doo-Dah, comrade. I avait your commands."

"You haven't been paid to make bad jokes."

Silence. Then: "All right. No jokes."

"We're moving ahead."

"We'll move ahead when I get the rest of my money."

"You'll have it tonight, and you'll go to work immediately."

"Roger-dodger," FL says. "Give me something hard next time."

There's not going to be a next time, Z-Boy thinks.

"Don't screw this up."

"I won't. But I don't work until I see the green."

"You'll see it."

Z-Boy breaks the connection, drops the phone into his pocket, and leaves Brady's room. He heads back past the duty desk and Nurse Rainier, who is still absorbed in her computer. He leaves the cart in the snack alcove and crosses the skyway. He walks with a spring in his step, like a much younger man.

In an hour or two, Rainier or one of the other nurses will find Brady Hartsfield either slumped in his chair or sprawled on the floor on top of his Zappit. There won't be much concern; he has slipped into total unconsciousness many times before, and always comes out of it.

Dr. Babineau says it's part of the re-booting process, that each time Hartsfield returns, he's slightly improved. Our boy is getting well, Babineau says. You might not believe it to look at him, but our boy is really getting well.

You don't know the half of it, thinks the mind now occupying Library Al's body. You don't know the fucking half of it. But you're starting to, Dr. B. Aren't you?

Better late than never.

24

"That man who yelled at me on the street was wrong," Barbara says. "I believed him because the voice told me to believe him, but he was wrong."

Holly wants to know about the voice from the game, but Barbara may not be ready to talk about that yet. So she asks who the man was, and what he yelled.

"He called me blackish, like on that TV show. The show is funny, but on the street it's a put-down. It's—"

"I know the show, and I know how some people use it."

"But I'm *not* blackish. Nobody with a dark skin is, not really. Not even if they live in a nice house on a nice street like Teaberry Lane. We're all black, all the time. Don't you think I know how I get looked at and talked about at school?"

"Of course you do," says Holly, who has been looked at and talked about plenty in her own time; her high school nickname was Jibba-Jibba.

"The teachers talk about gender equality, and racial equality.

They have a zero tolerance policy, and they mean it—at least most of them do, I guess—but anyone can walk through the halls when the classes are changing and pick out the black kids and the Chinese transfer students and the Muslim girl, because there's only two dozen of us and we're like a few grains of pepper that somehow got into the salt shaker."

She's picking up steam now, her voice outraged and indignant but also weary.

"I get invited to parties, but there are a lot of parties I don't get invited to, and I've only been asked out on dates twice. One of the boys who asked me was white, and everyone looked at us when we went into the movies, and someone threw popcorn at the back of our heads. I guess at the AMC 12, racial equality stops when the lights go down. And one time when I was playing soccer? Here I go, dribbling the ball up the sideline, got a clear shot, and this white dad in a golf shirt tells his daughter, 'Guard that jig!' I pretended I didn't hear it. The girl kind of smirked. I wanted to knock her over, right there where he could see it, but I didn't. I swallowed it. And once, when I was a freshman, I left my English book on the bleachers at lunch, and when I went back to get it, someone had put a note in it that said BUCKWHEAT'S GIRLFRIEND. I swallowed that, too. For days it can be good, weeks, even, and then there's something to swallow. It's the same with Mom and Dad, I know it is. Maybe it's different for Jerome at Harvard, but I bet sometimes even he has to swallow it."

Holly squeezes her hand, but says nothing.

"I'm not *blackish*, but the voice said I was, just because I didn't grow up in a tenement with an abusive dad and a drug addict mom. Because I never ate a collard green, or even knew exactly what it was. Because I say *pork chop* instead of *poke chop*. Because they're poor down there in the Low and we're doing just fine on Teaberry Lane. I have my cash card, and my nice school, and Jere goes to Harvard, but . . . but, don't you see . . . Holly, don't you *see* that I never—"

"You never had a choice about those things," Holly says. "You were born where you were and what you were, the same as me. The same as all of us, really. And at sixteen, you've never been asked to change anything but your clothes."

"*Yes!* And I know I shouldn't be ashamed, but the voice *made* me ashamed, it made me feel like a useless parasite, *and it's still not all gone.* It's like it left a trail of slime inside my head. Because I never *had* been in Lowtown before, and it's *horrible* down there, and compared to them I really *am* blackish, and I'm afraid that voice may never go away and my life will be *spoiled.*"

"You have to strangle it." Holly speaks with dry, detached certainty.

Barbara looks at her in surprise.

Holly nods. "Yes. You have to choke that voice until it's dead. It's the first job. If you don't take care of yourself, you can't get better. And if you can't get better, you can't make anything else better."

Barbara says, "I can't just go back to school and pretend Lowtown doesn't exist. If I'm going to live, I have to do something. Young or not, I have to do something."

"Are you thinking about some kind of volunteer work?"

"I don't know *what* I'm thinking about. I don't know what there is for a kid like me. But I'm going to find out. If it means going back down there, my parents won't like it. You have to help me with them, Holly. I know it's hard for you, but *please.* You have to tell them that I need to shut that voice up. Even if I can't choke it to death right away, maybe I can at least quiet it down."

"All right," Holly says, although she dreads it. "I will." An idea occurs to her and she brightens. "You should talk to the boy who pushed you out of the way of the truck."

"I don't know how to find him."

"Bill will help you," Holly says. "Now tell me about the game."

"It broke. The truck ran over it, I saw the pieces, and I'm glad. Every time I close my eyes I can see those fish, especially the pink number-fish, and hear the little song." She hums it, but it rings no bells with Holly.

A nurse comes in wheeling a meds cart. She asks Barbara what her pain level is. Holly is ashamed she didn't think to ask herself, and first thing. In some ways she is a very bad and thoughtless person.

"I don't know," Barbara says. "A five, maybe?"

The nurse opens a plastic pill tray and hands Barbara a little paper cup. There are two white pills in it. "These are custom-tailored Five pills. You'll sleep like a baby. At least until I come in to check your pupils."

Barbara swallows the pills with a sip of water. The nurse tells Holly she should leave soon and let "our girl" get some rest.

"Very soon," Holly says, and when the nurse is gone, she leans forward, face intent, eyes bright. "The game. How did you get it, Barb?"

"A man gave it to me. I was at the Birch Street Mall with Hilda Carver."

"When was this?"

"Before Christmas, but not much before. I remember, because I still hadn't found anything for Jerome, and I was starting to get worried. I saw a nice sport coat in Banana Republic, but it was *way* expensive, and besides, he's going to be building houses

184

until May. You don't have much reason to wear a sport coat when you're doing that, do you?"

"I guess not."

"Anyway, this man came up to us while Hilda and I were having lunch. We're not supposed to talk to strangers, but it's not like we're little kids anymore, and besides, it was in the food court with people all around. Also, he looked nice."

The worst ones usually do, Holly thinks.

"He was wearing a terrific suit that must have cost mucho megabucks and carrying a briefcase. He said his name was Myron Zakim and he worked for a company called Sunrise Solutions. He gave us his card. He showed us a couple of Zappits—his briefcase was full of them—and said we could each have one free if we'd fill out a questionnaire and send it back. The address was on the questionnaire. It was on the card, too."

"Do you happen to remember the address?"

"No, and I threw his card away. Besides, it was only a box number."

"In New York?"

Barbara thinks it over. "No. Here in the city."

"So you took the Zappits."

"Yes. I didn't tell Mom, because she would have given me a big lecture about talking to that guy. I filled out the questionnaire, too, and sent it in. Hilda didn't, because her Zappit didn't work. It just gave out a single blue flash and went dead. So she threw it away. I remember her saying that's all you could expect when someone said something was free." Barbara giggles. "She sounded just like her mother."

"But yours did work."

"Yes. It was old-fashioned but kind of . . . you know, kind of fun, in a silly way. At first. I wish mine had been broken,

185

then I wouldn't have the *voice*." Her eyes slip closed, then slowly reopen. She smiles. "Whoa! Feel like I might be floating away."

"Don't float away yet. Can you describe the man?"

"A white guy with white hair. He was old."

"Old-old, or just a little bit old?"

Barbara's eyes are growing glassy. "Older than Dad, not as old as Grampa."

"Sixtyish? Sixty-fiveish?"

"Yeah, I guess. Bill's age, more or less." Her eyes suddenly spring wide open. "Oh, guess what? I remember something. I thought it was a little weird, and so did Hilda."

"What was that?"

"He said his name was Myron Zakim, and his card said Myron Zakim, but there were initials on his briefcase that were different."

"Can you remember what they were?"

"No . . . sorry . . ." She's floating away, all right.

"Will you think about that first thing when you wake up, Barb? Your mind will be fresh then, and it might be important."

"Okay . . ."

"I wish Hilda hadn't thrown hers away," Holly says. She gets no reply, nor expects one; she often talks to herself. Barbara's breathing has grown deep and slow. Holly begins buttoning her coat.

"Dinah has one," Barbara says in a faraway dreaming voice. "*Hers* works. She plays Crossy Road on it . . . and Plants Vs. Zombies . . . also, she downloaded the whole *Divergent* trilogy, but she said it came in all jumbled up."

Holly stops buttoning. She knows Dinah Scott, has seen her at the Robinson house many times, playing board games or watching TV, often staying for supper. And drooling over Jerome, as all of Barbara's friends do.

"Did the same man give it to her?"

Barbara doesn't answer. Biting her lip, not wanting to press her but needing to, Holly shakes Barbara by the shoulder and asks again.

"No," Barbara says in the same faraway voice. "She got it from the website."

"What website was that, Barbara?"

Her only answer is a snore. Barbara is gone.

## 25

Holly knows that the Robinsons will be waiting for her in the lobby, so she hurries into the gift shop, lurks behind a display of teddy bears (Holly is an accomplished lurker), and calls Bill. She asks if he knows Barbara's friend Dinah Scott.

"Sure," he says. "I know most of her friends. The ones that come to the house, anyway. So do you."

"I think you should go to see her."

"You mean tonight?"

"I mean right away. She's got a Zappit." Holly takes a deep breath. "They're dangerous." She can't quite bring herself to say what she is coming to believe: that they are suicide machines.

## 26

In Room 217, orderlies Norm Richard and Kelly Pelham lift Brady back into bed while Mavis Rainier supervises. Norm picks up the Zappit console from the floor and stares at the swimming fish on the screen.

"Why doesn't he just catch pneumonia and die, like the rest of the gorks?" Kelly asks.

"This one's too ornery to die," Mavis says, then notices Norm staring down at the swimming fish. His eyes are wide and his mouth is hung ajar.

"Wake up, splendor in the grass," she says, and snatches the gadget away. She pushes the power button and tosses it into the top drawer of Brady's nightstand. "We've got miles to go before we sleep."

"Huh?" Norm looks down at his hands, as if expecting to see the Zappit still in them.

Kelly asks Nurse Rainier if maybe she wants to take Harts- field's blood pressure. "$O_2$ looks a little low," he says.

Mavis considers this, then says, "Fuck him."

They leave.

27

In Sugar Heights, the city's poshest neighborhood, an old Chevy Malibu spotted with primer paint creeps up to a closed gate on Lilac Drive. Artfully scrolled into the wrought iron are the initials Barbara Robinson failed to remember: *FB.* Z-Boy gets out from behind the wheel, his old parka (a rip in the back and another in the left sleeve thriftily mended with mask- ing tape) flapping around him. He taps the correct code into the keypad, and the gates begin to swing open. He gets back into the car, reaches under the seat, and brings out two items. One is a plastic soda bottle with the neck cut off. The inte- rior has been packed with steel wool. The other is a .32-caliber revolver. Z-Boy slips the muzzle of the .32 into this homemade silencer—another Brady Hartsfield invention—and holds it on his lap. With his free hand he pilots the Malibu up the smooth, curving driveway.

Ahead, the porch-mounted motion lights come on.

Behind, the wrought iron gates swing silently shut.

# LIBRARY AL

It didn't take Brady long to realize he was pretty much finished as a physical being. He was born stupid but didn't stay that way, as the saying goes.

Yes, there was physical therapy—Dr. Babineau decreed it, and Brady was hardly in a position to protest—but there was only so much therapy could accomplish. He was eventually able to shamble thirty feet or so along the corridor some patients called the Torture Highway, but only with the help of Rehab Care Coordinator Ursula Haber, the bull dyke Nazi who ran the place.

"One more step, Mr. Hartsfield," Haber would exhort, and when he managed one more step the bitch would ask for one more and one more after that. When Brady was finally allowed to collapse into his wheelchair, trembling and soaked with sweat, he liked to imagine stuffing oil-soaked rags up Haber's snatch and setting them on fire.

"Good job!" she'd cry. "*Good* job, Mr. Hartsfield!"

And if he managed to gargle something that bore a passing resemblance to *thank you*, she would look around at whoever happened to be near, smiling proudly. Look! My pet monkey can talk!

He *could* talk (more and better than they knew), and he could shamble ten yards up the Torture Highway. On his best days he could eat custard without spilling too much down his front. But he couldn't dress himself, couldn't tie his shoes, couldn't wipe himself after taking a shit, couldn't even use the remote control (so reminiscent of Thing One and Thing Two back in the good old days) to watch television. He could grasp it, but his motor control wasn't even close to good enough for him to manipulate the small buttons. If he did manage to hit the power button, he usually ended up staring at nothing but a blank screen and the SEARCHING FOR SIGNAL message. This infuriated him—in the early days of 2012, *everything* infuriated him—but he was careful not to show it. Angry people were angry for a reason, and gorks weren't supposed to have reasons for anything.

Sometimes lawyers from the District Attorney's office dropped by. Babineau protested these visits, telling the lawyers they were setting him back and therefore working against their own long-term interests, but it did no good.

Sometimes cops came with the lawyers from the DA's office, and once a cop came on his own. He was a fat cocksucker with a crewcut and a cheerful demeanor. Brady was in his chair, so the fat cocksucker sat on Brady's bed. The fat cocksucker told Brady that his niece had been at the 'Round Here concert. "Just thirteen years old and crazy about that band," he said, chuckling. Still chuckling, he leaned forward over his big stomach and punched Brady in the balls.

"A little something from my niece," the fat cocksucker said. "Did you feel it? Man, I hope so."

Brady did feel it, but not as much as the fat cocksucker probably hoped, because everything had gone kind of vague between his waist and knees. Some circuit in his brain that was supposed to be controlling that area had burned out, he supposed. That would ordinarily be bad news, but it was good news when you had to cope with a right hook to the family jewels. He sat there, his face blank. A little drool on his chin. But he filed away the fat cocksucker's name. Moretti. It went on his list.

Brady had a long list.

He retained a thin hold over Sadie MacDonald by virtue of that first, wholly accidental safari into her brain. (He retained an even greater hold over the idiot orderly's brain, but visiting there was like taking a vacation in Lowtown.) On several occasions Brady was able to nudge her toward the window, the site of her first seizure. Usually she only glanced out and then went about her work, which was frustrating, but one day in June of 2012, she had another of those mini-seizures. Brady found himself looking out through her eyes once more, but this time he was not content to stay on the passenger side, just watching the scenery. This time he wanted to drive.

Sadie reached up and caressed her breasts. Squeezed them. Brady felt a low tingle begin between Sadie's legs. He was getting her a little hot. Interesting, but hardly useful.

He thought of turning her around and walking her out of the room. Going down the corridor. Getting a drink of water from the fountain. His very own organic wheelchair. Only what if someone talked to him? What would he say? Or what if Sadie took over again once she was away from the sunflashes, and started screaming that Hartsfield was inside of her? They'd think she was crazy. They might put her on leave. If they did that, Brady would lose his access to her.

He burrowed deeper into her mind instead, watching the thoughtfish go flashing back and forth. They were clearer now, but mostly uninteresting.

One, though . . . the red one . . .

It came into view as soon as he thought about it, because he was making *her* think of it.

Big red fish.

A fatherfish.

Brady snatched at it and caught it. It was easy. His body was next to useless, but inside Sadie's mind he was as agile as a ballet dancer. The fatherfish had molested her regularly between the ages of six and eleven. Finally he had gone all the way and fucked her. Sadie told a teacher at school, and her father was arrested. He had killed himself while out on bail.

Mostly to amuse himself, Brady began to release his own fish into the aquarium of Sadie MacDonald's mind: tiny poisonous blowfish that were little more than exaggerations of thoughts she herself harbored in the twilight area that exists between the conscious mind and the subconscious.

That she had led him on.

That she had actually *enjoyed* his attentions.

That she was responsible for his death.

That when you looked at it that way, it hadn't been suicide at all. When you looked at it that way, she had murdered him.

Sadie jerked violently, hands flying up to the sides of her head, and turned away from the window. Brady felt that moment of nauseating, tumbling vertigo as he was ejected from her mind. She looked at him, her face pale and dismayed.

"I think I passed out for a second or two," she said, then laughed shakily. "But you won't tell, will you, Brady?"

Of course not, and after that he found it easier and easier to get into her head. She no longer had to look at the sunlight on the windshields across the way; all she had to do was come into the room. She was losing weight. Her vague prettiness was disappearing. Sometimes her uniform was dirty and sometimes her stockings were torn. Brady continued to plant his depth charges: you led him on, you enjoyed it, you were responsible, you don't deserve to live.

Hell, it was something to do.

Sometimes the hospital got freebies, and in September of 2012 it received a dozen Zappit game consoles, either from the company that made them or from some charity organization. Admin shipped them to the tiny library next to the hospital's nondenominational chapel. There an orderly unpacked them, looked them over, decided they were stupid and outdated, and stuck them on a back shelf. It was there that Library Al Brooks found them in November, and took one for himself.

Al enjoyed a few of the games, like the one where you had to get Pitfall Harry safely past the crevasses and poisonous snakes, but what he enjoyed most was Fishin' Hole. Not the game itself, which was stupid, but the demo screen. He supposed people would laugh, but it was no joke to Al. When he was upset about something (his brother yelling at him about not putting out the garbage for Thursday morning pickup, or a crabby call from his daughter in Oklahoma City), those slowly gliding fish and the little tune always mellowed him out. Sometimes he lost all track of time. It was amazing.

On an evening not long before 2012 became 2013, Al had an inspiration. Hartsfield in 217 was incapable of reading, and had shown no interest in books or music on CD. If someone put earphones on his head, he clawed at them until he got them off, as if he found them confining. He would also be incapable of manipulating the small buttons below the Zappit's screen, but he could look at the Fishin' Hole demo. Maybe he'd like it, or some of the other demo screens. If he did, maybe some of the other patients (to his credit, Al never thought of them as gorks) would, too, and that would be a good thing, because a few of the brain-damaged patients in the Bucket were occasionally violent. If the demo screens calmed them down, the docs, nurses, and orderlies—even the janitors—would have an easier time.

He might even get a bonus. It probably wouldn't happen, but a man could dream.

He entered Room 217 one afternoon in early December of 2012, shortly after Hartsfield's only regular visitor had left. This was an ex-detective named Hodges, who had been instrumental in Hartsfield's capture, although he hadn't been the one who had actually smacked his head and damaged his brain.

Hodges's visits upset Hartsfield. After he was gone, things fell over in 217, the water turned on and off in the shower, and sometimes the bathroom door flew open or slammed shut. The nurses had seen these things, and were sure Hartsfield was caus-ing them, but Dr. Babineau pooh-poohed that idea. He claimed it was exactly the kind of hysterical notion that got a hold on certain women (even though several of the Bucket nurses were men). Al knew the stories were true, because he had seen mani-festations himself on several occasions, and he did not think of himself as a hysterical person. Quite the opposite.

On one memorable occasion he had heard something in Hartsfield's room as he was passing, opened the door, and saw the window-blinds doing a kind of maniacal boogaloo. This was shortly after one of Hodges's visits. It had gone on for nearly thirty seconds before the blinds stilled again.

Although he tried to be friendly—he tried to be friendly with everyone—Al did not approve of Bill Hodges. The man seemed to be gloating over Hartsfield's condition. Reveling in it. Al knew Hartsfield was a bad guy who had murdered innocent people, but what the hell did that matter when the man who had done those things no longer existed? What remained was little more than a husk. So what if he could rattle the blinds, or turn the water on and off? Such things hurt no one.

"Hello, Mr. Hartsfield," Al said on that night in December. "I brought you something. Hope you'll take a look."

He turned the Zappit on and poked the screen to bring up the Fishin' Hole demo. The fish began to swim and the tune began to play. As always, Al was soothed, and took a moment to enjoy the sensation. Before he could turn the console so Hartsfield could see, he found himself pushing his library cart in Wing A, on the other side of the hospital.

The Zappit was gone.

This should have upset him, but it didn't. It seemed perfectly okay. He was a little tired, and seemed to be having trouble gathering his scattered thoughts, but otherwise he was fine. Happy. He looked down at his left hand and saw he had drawn a large **Z** on the back with the pen he always kept in the pocket of his tunic.

Z for Z-Boy, he thought, and laughed.

Brady did not make a decision to leap into Library Al; seconds after the old geezer looked down at the console in his hand, Brady was in. There was no sense of being an interloper in the library guy's head, either. For now it was Brady's body, as much as a Hertz sedan would have been his car for as long as he chose to drive it.

The library guy's core consciousness was still there—someplace—but it was just a soothing hum, like the sound of a furnace in the cellar on a cold day. Yet he had access to all of Alvin Brooks's memories and all of his stored knowledge. There was a fair amount of this latter, because before retiring from his full-time job at the age of fifty-eight, the man had been an electrician, then known as Sparky Brooks instead of Library Al. If Brady had wanted to rewire a circuit, he could have done so easily, although he understood he might no longer have this ability once he returned to his own body.

Thinking of his body alarmed him, and he bent over the man slumped in the chair. The eyes were half-closed, showing only the whites. The tongue lolled from one corner of the mouth. Brady put a gnarled hand on Brady's chest and felt a slow rise and fall. So *that* was all right, but God, he looked *horrible*. A skin-wrapped skeleton. This was what Hodges had done to him.

He left the room and toured the hospital, feeling a species of mad exhilaration. He smiled at everyone. He couldn't help it. With Sadie MacDonald he had been afraid of fucking up. He still was, but not so much. This was better. He was wearing Library Al like a tight glove. When he passed Anna Corey, the A Wing head housekeeper, he asked how her husband was bearing up with those radiation treatments. She told him Ellis was doing pretty well, all things considered, and thanked him for asking.

In the lobby, he parked his cart outside the men's bathroom, went in, sat on the toilet, and examined the Zappit. As soon as he saw the swimming fish, he understood what must have happened. The idiots who had created this particular game had also created, certainly by accident, a hypnotic effect. Not every-one would be susceptible, but Brady thought plenty of people would be, and not just those prone to mild seizures, like Sadie MacDonald.

He knew from reading he'd done in his basement control room that several electronic console and arcade games were capable of initiating seizures or light hypnotic states in perfectly normal people, causing the makers to print a warning (in extremely fine print) on many of the instruction sheets: do not play for prolonged periods, do not sit closer than three feet to the screen, do not play if you have a history of epilepsy.

The effect wasn't restricted to video games, either. At least one episode of the Pokémon cartoon series had been banned outright when thousands of kids complained of headaches, blurred vision, nausea, and seizures. The culprit was believed to be a sequence in the episode where a series of missiles were set off, causing a strobe effect. Some combination of the swimming fish and the little tune worked the same way. Brady was surprised the company that made the Zappit consoles hadn't been deluged with complaints. He found out later that there *had* been complaints, but not many. He came to believe that there were two reasons for that. First, the dumbshit Fishin' Hole game itself did not have the same effect. Second, hardly anybody bought the Zappit game consoles to begin with. In the jargon of computer commerce, it was a brick.

Still pushing his cart, the man wearing Library Al's body returned to Room 217 and placed the Zappit on the table by the bed—it merited further study and thought. Then (and not without regret) Brady left Library Al Brooks. There was that moment of vertigo, and then he was looking up instead of down. He was curious to see what would happen next.

At first Library Al just stood there, a piece of furniture that looked like a human being. Brady reached out to him with his invisible left hand and patted his cheek. Then he reached for Al's mind with his own, expecting to find it shut to him, as Nurse

MacDonald's had been once she came out of her fugue state.

But the door was wide open.

Al's core consciousness had returned, but there was a bit less now. Brady suspected that some of it had been smothered by his presence. So what? People killed off brain cells when they drank too much, but they had plenty of spares. The same was true of Al. At least for now.

Brady saw the Z he had drawn on the back of Al's hand—for no reason, just because he could—and spoke without opening his mouth.

"Hey there, Z-Boy. Go on now. Get out. Head over to A Wing. But you won't talk about this, will you?"

"Talk about what?" Al asked, looking puzzled.

Brady nodded as well as he could nod, and smiled as well as he could smile. He was already wishing to be in Al again. Al's body was old, but at least it *worked*.

"That's right," he told Z-Boy. "Talk about what."


2012 became 2013. Brady lost interest in trying to strengthen his telekinetic muscles. There was really no point, now that he had Al. Each time he got inside, his grip was stronger, his control better. Running Al was like running one of those drones the military used to keep an eye on the ragheads in Afghanistan . . . and then to bomb the living shit out of their bosses.

Lovely, really.

Once he had Z-Boy show the old Det.-Ret. one of the Zappits, hoping Hodges would become fascinated by the Fishin' Hole demo. Being inside Hodges would be wonderful. Brady would make it his first priority to pick up a pencil and poke out the old Det.-Ret.'s eyes. But Hodges only glanced at the screen and handed it back to Library Al.

Brady tried again a few days later, this time with Denise Woods, the PT associate who came into his room twice a week to exercise his arms and legs. She took the console when Z-Boy handed it to her, and looked at the swimming fish quite a bit longer than Hodges had. *Something* happened, but it wasn't quite enough. Trying to enter her was like pushing against a firm rubber diaphragm: it gave a little, enough for him to glimpse her feeding her young son scrambled eggs in his high chair, but then it pushed him back out.

She handed the Zappit back to Z-Boy and said, "You're right, they're pretty fish. Now why don't you go hand out some books, Al, and let Brady and me work on those pesky knees of his?"

So there it was. He didn't have the same instantaneous access to others that he'd had to Al, and a little thought was all it took for Brady to understand why. Al had been preconditioned to the Fishin' Hole demo, had watched it dozens of times before bringing his Zappit to Brady. That was a crucial difference, and a crushing disappointment. Brady had imagined having dozens of drones among whom he could pick and choose, but that wasn't going to happen unless there was a way to re-rig the Zappit and enhance the hypnotic effect. Might there be such a way?

As someone who had modified all sorts of gadgets in his time—Thing One and Thing Two, for instance—Brady believed there was. The Zappit was WiFi equipped, after all, and WiFi was the hacker's best friend. Suppose, for instance, he were to program in a flashing light? A kind of strobe, like the one that had buzzed the brains of those kids exposed to the missile-firing sequence in the Pokémon episode?

The strobe could serve another purpose, as well. While taking a community college course called Computing the Future (this was just before he dropped out of school for good), Brady's class had been assigned a long CIA report, published in 1995 and declassified shortly after 9/11. It was called "The Operational Potential of Subliminal Perception," and explained how computers could be programmed to transmit messages so rapidly that the brain recognized them not as messages per se, but as original thoughts. Suppose he were able to embed such a message inside the strobe flash? SLEEP NOW ALL OKAY, for instance, or maybe just RELAX. Brady thought those things, combined with the demo screen's existing hypnotics, would be pretty effective. Of course he might be wrong, but he would have given his mostly useless right hand to find out.

He doubted if he ever would, because there were two seemingly insurmountable problems. One was getting people to look at the demo screen long enough for the hypnotic effect to take hold. The other was even more basic: how in God's name was he supposed to modify *anything*? He had no computer access, and even if he had, what good would it be? He couldn't even tie his fucking shoes! He considered using Z-Boy, and rejected the idea almost immediately. Al Brooks lived with his brother and his brother's family, and if Al all of a sudden started demonstrating advanced computer knowledge and capability, there would be questions. Especially when they already had questions about Al, who had grown absentminded and rather peculiar. Brady supposed they thought he was suffering the onset of senility, which wasn't all that far from the truth.

It seemed that Z-Boy was running out of spare brain cells after all.

Brady grew depressed. He had reached the all too familiar point where his bright ideas collided head-on with gray reality. It had happened with the Rolla vacuum cleaner; it had happened with his computer-assisted vehicle backing device; it had happened with his motorized, programmable TV monitor, which was supposed to revolutionize home security. His wonderful inspirations always came to nothing.

Still, he had one human drone to hand, and after a particularly infuriating visit from Hodges, Brady decided he might cheer up if he put his drone to work. Accordingly, Z-Boy visited an Internet café a block or two down from the hospital, and after five minutes on a computer (Brady was exhilarated to be sitting in front of a screen again), he discovered where Anthony Moretti, aka the fat testicle-punching cocksucker, lived. After leaving the Internet café, Brady walked Z-Boy into an Army surplus store and bought a hunting knife.

The next day when he left the house, Moretti found a dead dog stretched out on the welcome mat. Its throat had been cut. Written in dogblood on the windshield of his car was YOUR WIFE & KIDS ARE NEXT.

Doing this—being *able* to do this—cheered Brady up. Payback is a bitch, he thought, and I am that bitch.

He sometimes fantasized about sending Z-Boy after Hodges and shooting him in the belly. How good it would be to stand over the Det.-Ret., watching him shudder and moan as his life ran through his fingers!

It would be great, but Brady would lose his drone, and once in custody, Al might point the police at *him*. There was something else, as well, something even bigger: *it wouldn't be enough.* He owed Hodges more than a bullet in the belly followed by ten or fifteen minutes of suffering. Much more. Hodges needed to live, breathing toxic air inside a bag of guilt from which there was no escape. Until he could no longer stand it, and killed himself.

Which had been the original plan, back in the good old days.

No way, though, Brady thought. No way to do any of it. I've got Z-Boy—who'll be in an assisted living home if he keeps on the way he's going—and I can rattle the blinds with my phantom hand. That's it. That's the whole deal.

But then, in the summer of 2013, the dark funk he'd been living in was pierced by a shaft of light. He had a visitor. A real one, not Hodges or a suit from the District Attorney's office, checking to see if he had magically improved enough to stand trial for a dozen different felony crimes, the list headed by eight counts of willful murder at City Center.

There was a perfunctory knock at the door, and Becky Helmington poked her head in. "Brady? There's a young woman here to see you. Says she used to work with you, and she's brought you something. Do you want to see her?"

Brady could think of only one young woman that might be. He considered saying no, but his curiosity had come back along with his malice (perhaps they were even the same thing). He gave one of his floppy nods, and made an effort to brush his hair out of his eyes.

His visitor entered timidly, as if there might be hidden mines under the floor. She was wearing a dress. Brady had never seen her in a dress, would have guessed she didn't even own one. But her hair was still cropped close to her skull in a half-assed crewcut, as it had been when they had worked together on the Discount Electronix Cyber Patrol, and she was still as flat as a board in front. He remembered some comedian's joke: If no tits count for shit, Cameron Diaz is gonna be around for a long time. But she had put on a little powder to cover her pitted skin (amazing)

204

and even a dash of lipstick (more amazing still). In one hand she held a wrapped package.

"Hey, man," Freddi Linklatter said with unaccustomed shyness. "How're you doing?"

This opened all sorts of possibilities.

Brady did his best to smile.

BADCONCERT.COM

1

Cora Babineau wipes the back of her neck with a monogrammed towel and frowns at the monitor in the basement exercise room. She has done only four of her six miles on the treadmill, she hates to be interrupted, and the weirdo is back.

*Cling-clong* goes the doorbell and she listens for her husband's footsteps above her, but there's nothing. On the monitor, the old man in the ratty parka—he looks like one of those bums you see standing at intersections, holding up signs that say things like HUNGRY, NO JOB, ARMY VETERAN, PLEASE HELP— just stands there.

"Dammit," she mutters, and pauses the treadmill. She climbs the stairs, opens the door to the back hallway, and shouts, "*Felix! It's your weirdo friend! That Al!*"

No response. He's in his study again, possibly looking at the game-thing he seems to have fallen in love with. The first few times she mentioned Felix's strange new obsession to her friends at the country club, it was a joke. It doesn't seem so funny now. He's sixty-three, too old for kids' computer games and too young to have gotten so forgetful, and she's begun to wonder if he might not be suffering early-onset Alzheimer's. It has also crossed her mind that Felix's weirdo friend is some kind of drug pusher, but isn't the guy awfully old for that? And if her husband wants drugs, he can certainly supply himself; according to him, half the doctors at Kiner are high at least half the time.

*Cling-clong* goes the doorbell.

"Jesus on a pony," she says, and goes to the door herself, growing more irritated with each long stride. She's a tall, gaunt woman whose female shape has been exercised nearly to oblivion. Her golf tan remains even in the depths of winter, only turning a pale shade of yellow that makes her look as if she's suffering chronic liver disease.

She opens the door. The January night rushes in, chilling her sweaty face and arms. "I think I would like to know who you are," she says, "and what you and my husband are up to together. Would that be too much to ask?"

"Not at all, Mrs. Babineau," he says. "Sometimes I'm Al. Sometimes I'm Z-Boy. Tonight I'm Brady, and boy oh boy, it's nice to be out, even on such a cold night."

She looks down at his hand. "What's in that jar?"

"The end of all your troubles," says the man in the mended parka, and there's a muffled bang. The bottom of the soda bottle blows out in shards, along with scorched threads from the steel wool. They float in the air like milkweed fluff.

Cora feels something hit her just below her shrunken left breast and thinks, This weirdo son of a bitch just punched me. She tries to take a breath and at first can't. Her chest feels strangely dead; warmth is pooling above the elastic top of her tracksuit pants. She looks down, still trying to take that all-important breath, and sees a stain spreading on the blue nylon.

She raises her eyes to stare at the geezer in the doorway. He's holding out the remains of the bottle as if it's a present, a little gift to make up for showing up unannounced at eight in the evening. What's left of the steel wool pokes out of the bottom like a charred boutonniere. She finally manages a breath, but it's mostly liquid. She coughs, and sprays blood.

The man in the parka steps into her house and sweeps the door shut behind him. He drops the bottle. Then he pushes her. She staggers back, knocking a decorative vase from the end table by the coathooks, and goes down. The vase shatters on the hardwood floor like a bomb. She drags in another of those liquid breaths—I'm drowning, she thinks, drowning right here in my front hall—and coughs out another spray of red.

"Cora?" Babineau calls from somewhere deep in the house. He sounds as if he's just woken up. "Cora, are you okay?"

Brady raises Library Al's foot and carefully brings Library Al's heavy black workshoe down on the straining tendons of Cora Babineau's scrawny throat. More blood bursts from her mouth; her sun-cured cheeks are now stippled with it. He steps down hard. There's a crackling sound as stuff breaks inside her. Her eyes bulge . . . bulge . . . and then they glaze over.

"You were a tough one," Brady remarks, almost affectionately.

A door opens. Slippered feet come running, and then Babineau is there. He's wearing a dressing gown over ridiculous Hugh Hefner–style silk pajamas. His silver hair, usually his pride, is in wild disarray. The stubble on his cheeks has become an incipient beard. In his hand is a green Zappit console from which the little Fishin' Hole tune tinkles: *By the sea, by the sea, by the beautiful sea.* He stares at his wife lying on the hall floor.

"No more workouts for her," Brady says in that same affectionate tone.

"*What did you DO?*" Babineau screams, as if it isn't obvious. He runs to Cora and tries to fall to his knees beside her, but Brady hooks him under the armpit and hauls him back up. Library Al is by no means Charles Atlas, but he is ever so much stronger than the wasted body in Room 217.

"No time for that," Brady says. "The Robinson girl is alive, which necessitates a change of plan."

Babineau stares at him, trying to gather his thoughts, but they elude him. His mind, once so sharp, has been blunted. And it's this man's fault.

"Look at the fish," Brady says. "You look at yours and I'll look at mine. We'll both feel better."

"No," Babineau says. He wants to look at the fish, he always wants to look at them now, but he's afraid to. Brady wants to pour his mind into Babineau's head like some strange water, and each time that happens, less of his essential self remains afterward.

"Yes," Brady says. "Tonight you need to be Dr. Z."

"I refuse!"

"You're in no position to refuse. This is coming unraveled. Soon the police will be at your door. Or Hodges, and that would be even worse. He won't read you your rights, he'll just hit you with that homemade sap of his. Because he's a mean mother-fucker. And because you were right. He *knows*."

"I won't . . . I can't . . ." Babineau looks down at his wife. Ah God, her eyes. Her bulging eyes. "The police would never believe . . . I'm a respected doctor! We've been married for thirty-five years!"

"Hodges will. And when Hodges gets the bit in his teeth, he turns into Wyatt fucking Earp. He'll show the Robinson girl your picture. She'll look at it and say oh wow, yes, that's the man who gave me the Zappit at the mall. And if you gave her a Zappit, you probably gave one to Janice Ellerton. Oops! And there's Scapelli."

Babineau stares, trying to comprehend this disaster.

"Then there's the drugs you fed me. Hodges may know about them already, because he's a fast man with a bribe and most of the nurses in the Bucket know. It's an open secret, because you never tried to hide it." Brady gives Library Al's head a sad shake. "Your arrogance."

"Vitamins!" It's all Babineau can manage.

"Even the cops won't believe that if they subpoena your files and search your computers." Brady glances down at Cora Babineau's sprawled body. "And there's your wife, of course. How are you going to explain her?"

"I wish you'd died before they brought you in," Babineau says. His voice is rising, becoming a whine. "Or on the operating table. You're a *Frankenstein*!"

"Don't confuse the monster with the creator," Brady says, although he doesn't actually give Babineau much credit in the creation department. Dr. B.'s experimental drug may have something to do with his new abilities, but it had little or nothing to do with his recovery. He's positive that was his own doing. An act of sheer willpower. "Meanwhile, we have a visit to make, and we don't want to be late."

"To the man-woman." There's a word for that, Babineau used to know it, but now it's gone. Like the name that goes with it. Or what he ate for dinner. Each time Brady comes into his head, he takes a little more when he leaves. Babineau's memory. His knowledge. His *self*.

"That's right, the man-woman. Or, to give her sexual preference its scientific name, *Ruggus munchus*."

"No." The whine has become a whisper. "I'm going to stay right here."

Brady raises the gun, the barrel now visible within the blown-out remains of the makeshift silencer. "If you think I really need you, you're making the worst mistake of your life. And the last one."

Babineau says nothing. This is a nightmare, and soon he will wake up.

"Do it, or tomorrow the housekeeper will find you lying dead next to your wife, unfortunate victims of a home invasion. I would rather finish my business as Dr. Z—your body is ten years younger than Brooks's, and not in bad shape—but I'll do what I have to. Besides, leaving you to face Kermit Hodges would be mean of me. He's a nasty man, Felix. You have no idea."

Babineau looks at the elderly fellow in the mended parka and sees Hartsfield looking out of Library Al's watery blue eyes. Babineau's lips are trembling and wet with spittle. His eyes are rimmed with tears. Brady thinks that with his white hair standing up around his head as it is now, the Babster looks like Albert Einstein in that photo where the famous physicist is sticking his tongue out.

"How did I get into this?" he moans.

"The way everybody gets into everything," Brady says gently. "One step at a time."

"Why did you have to go after the girl?" Babineau bursts out.

"It was a mistake," Brady says. Easier to admit that than the whole truth: he couldn't wait. He wanted the nigger lawnboy's sister to go before anyone else blotted out her importance. "Now stop fucking around and look at the fishies. You know you want to."

And he does. That's the worst part. In spite of everything Babineau now knows, he does.

He looks at the fish.

He listens to the tune.

After awhile he goes into the bedroom to dress and get money out of the safe. He makes one more stop before leaving. The bathroom medicine cabinet is well stocked, on both her side and his.

He takes Babineau's BMW, leaving the old Malibu where it is for the time being. He also leaves Library Al, who has gone to sleep on the sofa.

2

Around the time Cora Babineau is opening her front door for the last time, Hodges is sitting down in the living room of the Scott family's home on Allgood Place, just one block over from Teaberry Lane, where the Robinsons live. He swallowed a couple of painkillers before getting out of the car, and isn't feeling bad, all things considered.

Dinah Scott is on the sofa, flanked by her parents. She looks quite a bit older than fifteen tonight, because she's recently back from a rehearsal at North Side High School, where the Drama Club will soon be putting on *The Fantasticks*. She has the role of Luisa, Angie Scott has told Hodges, a real plum. (This causes Dinah to roll her eyes.) Hodges is across from them in a La-Z-Boy very much like the one in his own living room. From the deep divot in the seat, he deduces it is Carl Scott's normal evening roost.

On the coffee table in front of the sofa is a bright green Zappit. Dinah brought it down from her room right away, which allows Hodges to further deduce that it wasn't buried under sports gear in her closet, or left under the bed with the dust bunnies. It wasn't sitting forgotten in her locker at school. No, it was where she could lay her hands on it at once. Which means she's been using it, old-school or not.

"I'm here at the request of Barbara Robinson," he tells them. "She was struck by a truck today—"

"Omigod," Dinah says, a hand going to her mouth.

"She's okay," Hodges says. "Broken leg is all. They're keeping her overnight for observation, but she'll be home tomorrow and probably back in school next week. You can sign her cast, if kids still do that."

Angie puts an arm around her daughter's shoulders. "What does that have to do with Dinah's game?"

"Well, Barbara had one, and it gave her a shock." Based on what Holly told Hodges while he was driving over here, that's no lie. "She was crossing a street at the time, lost her bearings for a minute, and bammo. A boy pushed her clear, or it would have been much worse."

"Jesus," Carl says.

Hodges leans forward, looking at Dinah. "I don't know how many of these gadgets are defective, but it's clear from what happened to Barb, and a couple of other incidents we know of, that at least some of them are."

"Let this be a lesson to you," Carl says to his daughter. "The next time someone tells you a thing's free, be on your guard."

This prompts another eye-roll of the perfect teenage variety.

"The thing I'm curious about," Hodges says, "is how you came by yours in the first place. It's kind of a mystery, because the Zappit company didn't sell many. They were bought out by another company when it flopped, and that company went bankrupt in April two years ago. You'd think the Zappit consoles would have been held for resale, to help pay the bills—"

"Or destroyed," Carl says. "That's what they do with unsold paperbacks, you know."

"I'm actually aware of that," Hodges says. "So tell me, Dinah, how *did* you get it?"

216

"I went on the website," she says. "I'm not in trouble, am I? I mean, I didn't know, but Daddy always says ignorance of the law is no excuse."

"You're in zero trouble," Hodges assures her. "What website was this?"

"It was called badconcert.com. I looked for it on my phone when Mom called me at rehearsal and said you were coming over, but it's gone. I guess they gave away all the ones they had."

"Or found out the things were dangerous, and folded their tents without warning anyone," Angie Scott says, looking grim.

"How bad could the shock be, though?" Carl asks. "I opened up the back when Dee brought it down from her room. There's nothing in there but four rechargeable double As."

"I don't know about that stuff," Hodges says. His stomach is starting to hurt again in spite of the dope. Not that his stomach is actually the problem; it's an adjacent organ only six inches long. He took a moment after his meeting with Norma Wilmer to check the survival rate of patients with pancreatic cancer. Only six percent of them manage to live five years. Not what you'd call cheery news. "So far I haven't even managed to re-program my iPhone's text message alert so it doesn't scare innocent bystanders."

"I can do that for you," Dinah says. "Easy-peasy. I have Crazy Frog on mine."

"Tell me about the website first."

"There was a tweet, okay? Someone at school told me about it. It got picked up on lots of social media sites. Facebook . . . Pinterest . . . Google Plus . . . you know the ones I'm talking about."

Hodges doesn't, but nods.

"I can't remember the tweet exactly, but pretty close. Because they can only be a hundred and forty characters long. You know that, right?"

217

"Sure," Hodges says, although he barely grasps what a tweet is. His left hand is trying to sneak its way to the pain in his side. He makes it stay put.

"This one said something like . . ." Dinah closes her eyes. It's rather theatrical, but of course she just *did* come from a Drama Club rehearsal. "'Bad news, some nut got the 'Round Here concert canceled. Want some good news? Maybe even a free gift? Go to badconcert.com.'" She opens her eyes. "That's probably not exact, but you get the idea."

"I do, yeah." He jots the website name in his notebook. "So you went there . . ."

"Sure. Lots of kids went there. It was kind of funny, too. There was a Vine of 'Round Here singing their big song from a few years ago, 'Kisses on the Midway,' it was called, and after about twenty seconds there's an explosion sound and this quacky voice saying, 'Oh damn, show canceled.'"

"I don't think that's so funny," Angie says. "You all could have been killed."

"There must have been more to it than that," Hodges says.

"Sure. It said that there were like two thousand kids there, a lot of them at their first concert, and they got screwed out of the experience of a lifetime. Although, um, *screwed* wasn't the word they used."

"I think we can fill in that blank, dear one," Carl says.

"And then it said that 'Round Here's corporate sponsor had received a whole bunch of Zappit game consoles, and they wanted to give them away. To, you know, kind of make up for the concert."

"Even though that was almost six years ago?" Angie looks incredulous.

"Yeah. Kind of weird, when you think of it."

"But you didn't," Carl said. "Think of it."

Dinah shrugs, looking petulant. "I did, but it seemed okay."

"Famous last words," her father says.

"So you just . . . what?" Hodges asks. "Emailed in your name and address and got that"—he points to the Zappit—"in the mail?"

"There was a little more to it than that," Dinah says. "You had to, like, be able to prove you were actually there. So I went to see Barb's mom. You know, Tanya."

"Why?"

"For the pictures. I think I have mine somewhere, but I couldn't find them."

"Her room," Angie says, and this time she's the one with the eye-roll.

Hodges's side has picked up a slow, steady throb. "What pictures, Dinah?"

"Okay, it was Tanya—she doesn't mind if we call her that— who took us to the concert, see? There was Barb, me, Hilda Carver, and Betsy."

"Betsy would be . . . ?"

"Betsy DeWitt," Angie says. "The deal was, the moms drew straws to see who would take the girls. Tanya lost. She took Ginny Carver's van, because it was the biggest."

Hodges nods his understanding.

"So anyway, when we got there," Dinah says, "Tanya took pictures of us. We *had* to have pictures. Sounds stupid, I guess, but we were just little kids. I'm into Mendoza Line and Raveonettes now, but back then 'Round Here was a really big deal to us. Especially Cam, the lead singer. Tanya used our phones. Or maybe she used her own, I can't exactly remember. But she made sure we all had copies, only I couldn't find mine."

"You had to send a picture to the website as proof of attendance."

"Right, by email. I was afraid the pics would only show us standing in front of Mrs. Carver's van and that wouldn't be enough, but there were two that showed the Mingo Auditorium in the background, with all the people lined up. I thought even that might not be good enough, because it didn't show the sign with the band's name on it, but it was, and I got the Zappit in the mail just a week later. It came in a big padded envelope."

"Was there a return address?"

"Uh-huh. I can't remember the box number, but the name was Sunrise Solutions. I guess they were the tour sponsors."

It's possible that they were, Hodges thinks, the company wouldn't have been bankrupt back then, but he doubts it. "Was it mailed from here in the city?"

"I don't remember."

"I'm pretty sure it was," Angie says. "I picked the envelope up off the floor and tossed it in the trash. I'm the French maid around here, you know." She shoots her daughter a look.

"Soh-ree," Dinah says.

In his notebook, Hodges writes *Sunrise Solutions based NYC, but pkg mailed from here.*

"When did all this go down, Dinah?"

"I heard about the tweet and went to the website last year. I can't remember exactly, but I know it was before the Thanksgiving break. And like I said, it came lickety-split. I was really surprised."

"So you've had it for two months, give or take."

"Yes."

"And no shocks?"

"No, nothing like that."

"Have you ever had any experiences where you were playing with it—let's say with the Fishin' Hole game—and you kind of lost track of your surroundings?"

Mr. and Mrs. Scott look alarmed at this, but Dinah gives him an indulgent smile. "You mean like being hypnotized? Eenie-meenie, chili-beanie?"

"I don't know *what* I mean, exactly, but okay, say that."

"Nope," Dinah says cheerily. "Besides, Fishin' Hole is really dumb. It's for little kids. You use the joystick thingie beside the keypad to operate Fisherman Joe's net, see? And you get points for the fish you catch. But it's too easy. Only reason I check back on that one is to see if the pink fish are showing numbers yet."

"Numbers?"

"Yes. The letter that came with the game explained about them. I tacked it on my bulletin board, because I'd really like to win that moped. Want to see it?"

"I sure would."

When she bounces upstairs to get it, Hodges asks if he can use the bathroom. Once in there, he unbuttons his shirt and looks at his throbbing left side. It seems a little swollen and feels a little hot to the touch, but he supposes both of those things could be his imagination. He flushes the toilet and takes two more of the white pills. Okay? he asks his throbbing side. Can you just shut up awhile and let me finish here?

Dinah has scrubbed off most of her stage makeup, and now it's easy for Hodges to imagine her and the other three girls at nine or ten, going to their first concert and as excited as Mexican jumping beans in a microwave. She hands him the letter that came with the game.

At the top of the sheet is a rising sun, with the words SUN-RISE SOLUTIONS bent over it in an arc, pretty much what you'd expect, only it doesn't look like any corporate logo Hodges has ever seen. It's strangely amateurish, as if the original was drawn by hand. It's a form letter with the girl's name plugged in to give it a more personal feel. Not that anybody's apt to be fooled by that in this day and age, Hodges thinks, when even mass mailings from insurance companies and ambulance chasing lawyers come personalized.

Dear Dinah Scott!

Congratulations! We hope you will enjoy your Zappit game console, which comes pre-loaded with 65 fun and challenging games. It is also WiFi equipped so you can visit your favorite Internet sites and download books as a member of the Sunrise Readers Circle! You are receiving this FREE GIFT to make up for the concert you missed, but of course we hope you will tell all your friends about your wonderful Zappit experience. And there's more! Keep checking the Fishin' Hole demo screen, and keep tapping those pink fish, because someday—you won't know when until it happens!—you will tap them and they will turn into numbers! If the fish you tap add up to one of the numbers below, you will win a GREAT PRIZE! But the numbers will only be visible for a short time, so KEEP CHECKING! Add to the fun by staying in touch with others in "The Zappit Club" by going to zeetheend .com, where you can also claim your prize if you are one of the lucky ones! Thanks from all of us at Sunrise Solutions, and the whole Zappit team!

There was an unreadable signature, hardly more than a scribble. Below that:

Lucky numbers for Dinah Scott:

1034=$25 gift certificate at Deb
1781=$40 gift card at Atom Arcade
1946=$50 gift certificate at Carmike Cinemas
7459=Wave 50cc moped-scooter (Grand Prize)

"You actually believed this bullshit?" Carl Scott asks.

Although the question is delivered with a smile, Dinah tears up. "All right, I'm stupid, so shoot me."

Carl hugs her, kisses her temple. "Know what? I would have swallowed it at your age, too."

"Have you been checking the pink fish, Dinah?" Hodges asks.

"Yes, once or twice a day. That's actually harder than the game, because the pink ones are fast. You have to concentrate."

Of course you do, Hodges thinks. He likes this less and less. "But no numbers, huh?"

"Not so far."

"Can I take that?" he asks, pointing to the Zappit. He thinks about telling her he'll give it back later, but doesn't. He doubts if he will. "And the letter?"

"On one condition," she says.

Hodges, pain now subsiding, is able to smile. "Name it, kiddo."

"Keep checking the pink fish, and if one of my numbers comes up, *I* get the prize."

"It's a deal," Hodges says, thinking, Someone wants to give you a prize, Dinah, but I doubt very much if it's a moped or a cinema gift certificate. He takes the Zappit and the letter, and stands up. "I want to thank you all very much for your time."

"Welcome," Carl says. "And when you figure out just what the hell this is all about, will you tell us?"

"You got it," Hodges says. "One more question, Dinah, and if I sound stupid, remember that I'm pushing seventy."

She smiles. "At school, Mr. Morton says the only stupid question—"

"Is the one you don't ask, yeah. I've always felt that way myself, so here it comes. Everybody at North Side High knows about this, right? The free consoles, the number fish, and the prizes?"

"Not just our school, all the other ones, too. Twitter, Facebook, Pinterest, Yik Yak . . . that's how they *work*."

"And if you were at the concert and you could prove it, you were eligible to get one of these."

"Uh-huh."

"What about Betsy DeWitt? Did she get one?"

Dinah frowns. "No, and that's kind of funny, because she still had her pictures from that night, and she sent one to the website. But she didn't do it as soon as I did, she's an awful procrastinator, so maybe they were all out. If you snooze, you lose type of thing."

Hodges thanks the Scotts again for their time, wishes Dinah good luck with the play, and goes back down the walk to his car. When he slides behind the wheel, it's cold enough inside to see his breath. The pain surfaces again: four hard pulses. He waits them out, teeth clamped, trying to tell himself these new, sharper pains are psychosomatic, because he now knows what's wrong with him, but the idea won't quite wash. Two more days suddenly seems like a long time to wait for treatment, but he will wait. Has to, because an awful idea is rising in his mind. Pete Huntley wouldn't believe it, and Izzy Jaynes would probably think he needed a quick ambulance ride to the nearest funny farm. Hodges doesn't quite believe it himself, but the pieces are coming together, and although the picture that's being revealed is a crazy one, it also has a certain nasty logic.

He starts his Prius and points it toward home, where he will call Holly and ask her to try and find out if Sunrise Solutions ever sponsored a 'Round Here tour. After that he will watch TV. When he can no longer pretend that what's on interests him, he'll go to bed and lie awake and wait for morning.

Only he's curious about the green Zappit.

Too curious, it turns out, to wait. Halfway between Allgood Place and Harper Road, he pulls into a strip mall, parks in front of a dry cleaning shop that's closed for the night, and powers the gadget up. It flashes bright white, and then a red **Z** appears, growing closer and bigger until the slant of the Z colors the whole screen red. A moment later it flashes white again, and a message appears: WELCOME TO **ZAPPIT**! WE LOVE TO PLAY! HIT ANY KEY TO BEGIN, OR JUST SWIPE THE SCREEN!

Hodges swipes, and game icons appear in neat rows. Some are console versions of ones he watched Allie play at the mall when she was a little girl: Space Invaders, Donkey Kong, Pac-Man, and that little yellow devil's main squeeze, Ms. Pac-Man. There are also the various solitaire games Janice Ellerton had been hooked on, and plenty of other stuff Hodges has never heard of. He swipes again, and there it is, between SpellTower and Barbie's Fashion Walk: Fishin' Hole. He takes a deep breath and taps the icon.

THINKING ABOUT **FISHIN' HOLE**, the screen advises. A little worry-circle goes around for ten seconds or so (it seems longer), and then the demo screen appears. Fish swim back and forth, or do loop-the-loops, or shoot up and down on diagonals. Bubbles rise from their mouths and flipping tails. The water is greenish at the top, shading to blue farther down. A little tune plays, not one Hodges recognizes. He watches and waits to feel something—sleepy seems the most likely.

The fish are red, green, blue, gold, yellow. They're probably supposed to be tropical fish, but they have none of the hyper-reality Hodges has seen in Xbox and PlayStation commercials on TV. These fish are basically cartoons, and primitive ones, at that. No wonder the Zappit flopped, he thinks, but yeah, okay, there's something mildly hypnotic about the way the fish move, sometimes alone, sometimes in pairs, every now and then in a rainbow school of half a dozen.

And jackpot, here comes a pink one. He taps at it, but it's moving just a mite too fast, and he misses. Hodges mutters "Shit!" under his breath. He looks up at the darkened dry clean-ing store's window for a moment, because he really is feeling a trifle dozy. He lightly smacks first his left cheek and then his right with the hand not holding the game, and looks back down. There are more fish now, weaving back and forth in complicated patterns.

Here comes another pink one, and this time he succeeds in tapping it before it whisks off the left side of the screen. It blinks (almost as if to say Okay, Bill, you got me that time) but no number appears. He waits, watches, and when another pink one appears, he taps again. Still no number, just a pink fish that has no counterpart in the real world.

The tune seems louder now, and at the same time slower. Hodges thinks, It really is having some kind of effect. It's mild, and probably completely accidental, but it's there, all right.

He pushes the power button. The screen flashes THANKS FOR PLAYING SEE YOU SOON and goes dark. He looks at the dashboard clock and is astonished to see he has been sitting here looking at the Zappit for over ten minutes. It felt more like two or three. Five, at the very most. Dinah didn't talk about losing time while looking at the Fishin' Hole demo screen, but he hadn't asked about that, had he? On the other hand, he's on two fairly heavy-duty painkillers, and that probably played a part in what just happened. If anything actually did, that is.

No numbers, though.

The pink fish had just been pink fish.

Hodges slips the Zappit into his coat pocket along with his phone and drives home.

3

Freddi Linklatter—once a computer-repair colleague of Brady's before the world discovered Brady Hartsfield was a monster—sits at her kitchen table, spinning a silver flask with one finger as she waits for the man with the fancy briefcase.

Dr. Z is what he calls himself, but Freddi is no fool. She knows the name that goes with the briefcase initials: Felix Babineau, head of neurology at Kiner Memorial.

Does he know that *she* knows? She's guessing he does, and doesn't care. But it's weird. *Very*. He's in his sixties, an authentic golden oldie, but he reminds her of somebody much younger. Someone who is, in fact, this Dr. Babineau's most famous (infamous, really) patient.

Around and around goes the flask. Etched on the side is *GH & FL, 4Ever*. Well, 4Ever lasted just about two years, and Gloria Hollis has been gone for quite awhile now. Babineau—or Dr. Z, as he styles himself, like the villain in a comic book—was part of the reason why.

"He's creepy," Gloria said. "The older guy is, too. And the money's creepy. It's too much. I don't know what they got you into, Fred, but sooner or later it's going to blow up in your face, and I don't want to be part of the collateral damage."

Of course Gloria had also met someone else—someone quite a bit better-looking than Freddi, with her angular body and lantern jaw and pitted cheeks—but she didn't want to talk about that part of it, oh no.

Around and around goes the flask.

It all seemed so simple at first, and how could she refuse the money? She never saved much when she worked on the Discount Electronix Cyber Patrol, and the work she'd been able to find as an independent IT when the store closed had barely been enough to keep her off the street. It might have been different if she'd had what Anthony Frobisher, her old boss, liked to call "people skills," but those had never been her forte. When the old geezer who called himself Z-Boy made his offer (and dear God, that was *really* a comic book handle), it had been like a gift from God. She had been living in a shitty apartment on the South Side, in the part of town commonly referred to as Hillbilly Heaven, and a month behind on the rent in spite of the cash the guy had already given her. What was she supposed to do? Refuse five thousand dollars? Get real.

Around and around goes the flask.

The guy is late, maybe he's not coming at all, and that might be for the best.

She remembers the geezer casting his eyes around the two-room apartment, most of her possessions in paper bags with handles (all too easy to see those bags gathered around her as she tried to sleep beneath a Crosstown Expressway underpass). "You'll need a bigger place," he said.

"Yeah, and the farmers in California need rain." She remembers peering into the envelope he handed her. Remembers riffling the fifties, and what a comfy sound they made. "This is nice, but by the time I get square with all the people I owe, there won't be much left." She could stiff most of those people, but the geezer didn't need to know that.

"There'll be more, and my boss will take care of getting you an apartment where you may be asked to accept certain shipments."

That started alarm bells ringing. "If you're thinking about drugs, let's just forget the whole thing." She held out the cash-stuffed envelope to him, much as it hurt to do that.

He pushed it back with a little grimace of contempt. "No drugs. You'll not be asked to sign for anything even slightly illegal."

So here she is, in a condo close to the lakeshore. Not that there's much of a lake view from only six stories up, and not that the place is a palace. Far from it, especially in the winter. You can only catch a wink of the water between the newer, nicer highrises, but the wind finds its way through just fine, thanks, and in January, that wind is *cold*. She has the joke thermostat cranked to eighty, and is still wearing three shirts and longjohns under her carpenter jeans. Hillbilly Heaven is in the rearview mirror, though, that's something, but the question remains: is it enough?

Around and around goes the silver flask. *GH & FL, 4Ever.* Only nothing is 4Ever.

The lobby buzzer goes, making her jump. She picks up the flask—her one souvenir of the glorious Gloria days—and heads to the intercom. She quashes an urge to do her Russian spy accent again. Whether he calls himself Dr. Babineau or Dr. Z, the guy is a little scary. Not Hillbilly-Heaven, crystal-meth-dope-dealer scary, but in a different way. Better to play this straight, get it over with, and hope to Christ she doesn't find herself in too much trouble if the deal blows up in her face.

"Is this the famous Dr. Z?"

"Of course it is."

"You're late."

"Am I keeping you from something important, Freddi?"

No, nothing important. Nothing she does is particularly important these days.

"You brought the money?"

"Of course." Sounding impatient. The old geezer with whom she had commenced this nutty business had the same impatient way of speaking. He and Dr. Z looked nothing alike, but they *sounded* alike, enough to make her wonder if they weren't brothers. Only they also sounded like that someone else, the old colleague she used to work with. The one who turned out to be Mr. Mercedes.

Freddi doesn't want to think about that any more than she wants to think about the various hacks she's done on Dr. Z's behalf. She hits the buzzer beside the intercom.

She goes to her door to wait for him, taking a nip of Scotch to fortify herself. She tucks the flask into the breast pocket of her middle shirt, then reaches into the pocket of the one beneath, where she keeps her breath mints. She doesn't believe Dr. Z would give Shit One if he smelled booze on her breath, but she always used to pop a mint after a nip when she was working at Discount Electronix, and old habits are strong habits. She takes her Marlboros from the pocket of her top shirt and lights one. It will further mask the smell of the booze, and calm her a little more, and if he doesn't like her secondhand smoke, tough titty.

"This guy has set you up in a pretty nice apartment and paid you almost thirty thousand dollars over the last eighteen months or so," Gloria had said. "Tall tickets for something any hacker worth her salt could do in her sleep, at least according to you. So *why* you? And why so much?"

More stuff Freddi doesn't want to think about.

It all started with the picture of Brady and his mom. She found it in the junk room at Discount Electronix, shortly after the staff had been told the Birch Hill Mall store was closing. Their boss, Anthony "Tones" Frobisher, must have taken it out of Brady's work cubby and tossed it back there after the world found out that Brady was the infamous Mercedes Killer. Freddi had no great love for Brady (although they *did* have a few meaningful conversations about gender identity, back in the day). Wrapping the picture and taking it to the hospital was pure impulse. And the few times she'd visited him afterwards had been pure curiosity, plus a little pride at the way Brady had reacted to her. He *smiled*.

"He responds to you," the new head nurse—Scapelli—said after one of Freddi's visits. "That's very unusual."

By the time Scapelli replaced Becky Helmington, Freddi knew that the mysterious Dr. Z who took over supplying her with cash was in reality Dr. Felix Babineau. She didn't think about that, either. Or about the cartons that eventually began arriving from Terre Haute via UPS. Or the hacks. She became an expert in not thinking, because once you started doing that, certain connections became obvious. And all because of that damn picture. Freddi wishes now she'd resisted the impulse, but her mother had a saying: Too late always comes too early.

She hears his footsteps coming down the hall. She opens the door before he can ring the bell, and the question is out of her mouth before she knows she is going to ask it.

"Tell me the truth, Dr. Z—are you Brady?"

4

Hodges is barely inside his front door and still taking off his coat when his cell rings. "Hey, Holly."

"Are you all right?"

He can see a lot of calls from her starting with this exact same greeting. Well, it's better than Drop dead, motherfucker. "Yeah, I'm good."

"One more day, and then you start treatments. And once you start, you don't stop. Whatever the doctors say, you do."

"Stop worrying. A deal is a deal."

"I'll stop worrying when you're cancer free."

Don't, Holly, he thinks, and closes his eyes against the unexpected sting of tears. Don't, don't, don't.

"Jerome is coming tonight. He called from his plane to ask about Barbara, and I told him everything she told me. He'll be in at eleven o'clock. A good thing he left when he did, because a storm is coming. It's supposed to be a bad one. I offered to rent him a car the way I do for you when you go out of town, it's very easy now that we have the corporate account—"

"That you lobbied for until I gave in. Believe me, I know."

"But he doesn't need a car. His father is picking him up. They'll go in to see Barbara at eight tomorrow, and bring her home if the doctor says she can go. Jerome said he can be at our office by ten, if that's okay."

"Sounds fine," Hodges says, wiping his eyes. He doesn't know how much Jerome can help, but he knows it will be very good to see him. "Anything more he can find out from her about that damn gadget—"

"I asked him to do that. Did you get Dinah's?"

232

"Yeah. And tried it. There's something up with the Fishin' Hole demo screen, all right. It makes you sleepy if you look at it too long. Purely accidental, I think, and I don't see how most kids would be affected, because they'd want to go right to the game."

He fills her in on the rest of what he learned from Dinah.

Holly says, "So Dinah didn't get her Zappit the same way as Barbara and the Ellerton woman."

"No."

"And don't forget Hilda Carver. The man calling himself Myron Zakim gave her one, too. Only hers didn't work. Barb said it just gave a single blue flash and died. Did you see any blue flashes?"

"Nope." Hodges is peering at the scant contents of his refrigerator for something his stomach might accept, and settles on a carton of banana-flavored yogurt. "And there were pink fish, but when I succeeded in tapping a couple—which ain't easy—no numbers appeared."

"I bet they did on Mrs. Ellerton's."

Hodges thinks so, too. It's early to generalize, but he's starting to think the number-fish only show up on the Zappits that were handed out by the man with the briefcase, Myron Zakim. Hodges also thinks someone is playing games with the letter Z, and along with a morbid interest in suicide, games were part of Brady Hartsfield's modus operandi. Except Brady is stuck in his room at Kiner Memorial, goddammit. Hodges keeps coming up against that irrefutable fact. If Brady Hartsfield has stooges to do his dirt, and it's starting to seem that he does, how is he running them? And why would they run for him, anyway?

"Holly, I need you to heat up your computer and check something out. Not a biggie, just a *t* that needs to be crossed."

"Tell me."

"I want to know if Sunrise Solutions sponsored the 'Round

233

Here tour in 2010, when Hartsfield tried to blow up the Mingo Auditorium. Or *any* 'Round Here tour."

"I can do that. Did you have supper?"

"Taking care of that right now."

"Good. What are you having?"

"Steak, shoestring potatoes, and a salad," Hodges says, looking at the carton of yogurt with a mixture of distaste and resignation. "Got a leftover apple tart for dessert."

"Heat it up in the microwave and put a scoop of vanilla ice cream on top. Yummy!"

"I'll take that under consideration."

He shouldn't be amazed when she calls back five minutes later with the information he requested, it's just Holly being Holly, but he still is. "Jesus, Holly, already?"

With no idea that she is echoing Freddi Linklatter almost word for word, Holly says, "Ask for something hard next time. You might like to know that 'Round Here broke up in 2013. Those boy bands don't seem to last very long."

"No," Hodges says, "once they start having to shave, the little girls lose interest."

"I wouldn't know," Holly says. "I was always a Billy Joel fan. Also Michael Bolton."

Oh, Holly, Hodges mourns. And not for the first time.

"Between 2007 and 2012, the group did six nationwide tours. The first four were sponsored by Sharp Cereals, which gave out free samples at their concerts. The last two, including the one at the Mingo, were sponsored by PepsiCo."

"No Sunrise Solutions."

"No."

"Thanks, Holly. I'll see you tomorrow."

"Yes. Are you eating your dinner?"

234

"Sitting down to it now."

"All right. And try to see Barbara before you start your treatments. She needs friendly faces, because whatever was wrong with her hasn't worn off yet. She said it was like it left a trail of slime inside her head."

"I'll make sure of it," Hodges says, but that is a promise he's not able to keep.

5

*Are you Brady?*

Felix Babineau, who sometimes calls himself Myron Zakim and sometimes Dr. Z, smiles at the question. It wrinkles his unshaven cheeks in a decidedly creepy way. Tonight he's wearing a furry ushanka instead of his trilby, and his white hair kind of squishes out around the bottom. Freddi wishes she hadn't asked the question, wishes she didn't have to let him in, wishes she'd never heard of him. If he *is* Brady, he's a walking haunted house.

"Ask me no questions and I'll tell you no lies," he says.

She wants to let it go and can't. "Because you sound like him. And that hack the other one brought me after the boxes came . . . that was a Brady hack if I ever saw one. Good as a signature."

"Brady Hartsfield is a semi-catatonic who can barely walk, let alone write a hack to be used on a bunch of obsolete game consoles. Some of which have proved to be defective as well as obsolete. I did not get my money's worth from those Sunrise Solutions motherfuckers, which pisses me off to the max."

*Pisses me off to the max.* A phrase Brady used all the time back in their Cyber Patrol days, usually about their boss or some idiot customer who managed to spill a mocha latte into his CPU.

"You've been very well paid, Freddi, and you're almost done. Why don't we leave it at that?"

He brushes past her without waiting for a reply, puts his briefcase on the table, and snaps it open. He takes out an envelope with her initials, FL, printed on it. The letters slant backward. During her years on the Discount Electronix Cyber Patrol, she saw similar back-slanted printing on hundreds of work orders. Those were the ones Brady filled out.

"Ten thousand," Dr. Z says. "Final payment. Now go to work."

Freddi reaches for the envelope. "You don't need to hang around if you don't want to. The rest is basically automatic. It's like setting an alarm clock."

And if you're really Brady, she thinks, you could do it yourself. I'm good at this stuff, but you were better.

He lets her fingers touch the envelope, then pulls it back. "I'll stay. Not that I don't trust you."

Right, Freddi thinks. As if.

His cheeks once more wrinkle in that unsettling smile. "And who knows? We might get lucky and see the first hit."

"I'll bet most of the people who got those Zappits have already thrown them away. It's a fucking *toy*, and some of them don't even work. Like you said."

"Let me worry about that," says Dr. Z. Once again his cheeks wrinkle and pull back. His eyes are red, as if he's been smoking the rock. She thinks of asking him what, exactly, they are doing, and what he hopes to accomplish . . . but she already has an idea, and does she want to be sure? Besides, if this *is* Brady, what harm can it do? He had hundreds of ideas, all of them crackpot.

Well.

Most of them.

She leads the way into what was meant to be a spare bedroom

and has now become her workstation, the sort of electronic refuge she always dreamed of and could never afford—a hidey-hole that Gloria, with her good looks, infectious laugh, and "people skills," could never understand. In here the baseboard heaters hardly work at all, and it's five degrees colder than the rest of the apartment. The computers don't mind. They like it.

"Go on," he says. "Do it."

She sits down at the top-of-the-line desktop Mac with its twenty-seven-inch screen, refreshes it, and types in her password—a random collection of numbers. There's a file simply marked **Z**, which she opens with another password. The subfiles are marked Z-1 and Z-2. She uses a third password to open Z-2, then begins to rapidly click away at her keyboard. Dr. Z stands by her left shoulder. He's a disturbing negative presence at first, but then she gets lost in what she's doing, as she always does.

Not that it takes long; Dr. Z has given her the program, and executing it is child's play. To the right of her computer, sitting on a high shelf, is a Motorola signal repeater. When she finishes by simultaneously hitting COMMAND and the Z key, the repeater comes to life. A single word appears in yellow dots: SEARCHING. It blinks like a traffic light at a deserted intersection.

They wait, and Freddi becomes aware that she's holding her breath. She lets it go in a whoosh, momentarily puffing out her thin cheeks. She starts to get up, and Dr. Z puts a hand on her shoulder. "Let's give it a little longer."

They give it five minutes, the only sound the soft hum of her equipment and the keening of the wind off the frozen lake. SEARCHING blinks on and on.

"All right," he says at last. "I knew it was too much to hope for. All things in good time, Freddi. Let's go back into the other room. I'll give you your final payment and then be on my wa—"

SEARCHING in yellow suddenly turns to FOUND in green.

"*There!*" he shouts, making her jump. "*There, Freddi! There's the first one!*"

Her final doubts are swept away and she knows for sure. All it takes is that shout of triumph. It's Brady, all right. He's become a living Russian nesting doll, which goes perfectly with his furry Russian hat. Look inside Babineau and there's Dr. Z. Look inside Dr. Z, and there, pulling all the levers, is Brady Hartsfield. God knows how it can be, but it is.

FOUND in green is replaced with LOADING in red. After mere seconds, LOADING is replaced with TASK COMPLETE. After that, the repeater begins to search again.

"All right," he says, "I'm satisfied. Time for me to go. It's been a busy night, and I'm not done yet."

She follows him into the main room, shutting the door to her electronic hideaway behind her. She has come to a decision that's probably long overdue. As soon as he's gone, she's going to kill the repeater and delete the final program. Once that's done, she'll pack a suitcase and go to a motel. Tomorrow she's getting the fuck out of this city and heading south to Florida. She's had it with Dr. Z, and his Z-Boy sidekick, and winter in the Midwest.

Dr. Z puts on his coat, but drifts to the window instead of going to the door. "Not much of a view. Too many highrises in the way."

"Yeah, it sucks the big one."

"Still, it's better than mine," he says, not turning. "All I've had to look at for the last five and a half years is a parking garage."

Suddenly she's at her limit. If he's still in the same room with her sixty seconds from now, she'll go into hysterics. "Give me my money. Give it to me and then get the fuck out. We're done."

He turns. In his hand is the short-barreled pistol he used on Babineau's wife. "You're right, Freddi. We are."

She reacts instantly, knocking the pistol from his hand, kicking him in the groin, karate-chopping him like Lucy Liu when he doubles over, and running out the door while screaming her head off. This mental film-clip plays out in full color and Dolby sound as she stands rooted to the spot. The gun goes bang. She staggers back two steps, collides with the easy chair where she sits to watch TV, collapses across it, and rolls to the floor, coming down headfirst. The world begins to darken and draw away. Her last sensation is warmth above as she begins to bleed and below as her bladder lets loose.

"Final payment, as promised." The words come from a great distance.

Blackness swallows the world. Freddi falls into it and is gone.

## 6

Brady stands perfectly still, watching the blood seep from beneath her. He's listening for someone to pound on her door, wanting to know if everything is all right. He doesn't expect that will happen, but better safe than sorry.

After ninety seconds or so, he puts the gun back in his overcoat pocket, next to his Zappit. He can't resist one more look into the computer room before leaving. The signal repeater continues its endless, automated search. He has, against all odds, completed an amazing journey. What the final results will be is impossible to predict, but that there will be *some* result he is certain. And it will eat into the old Det.-Ret. like acid. Revenge really is best when eaten cold.

He has the elevator to himself going down. The lobby is similarly empty. He walks around the corner, turning up the collar of Babineau's expensive overcoat against the wind, and tweets the locks of Babineau's Beemer. He gets in and starts it up, but only for the heater. Something needs doing before he moves on to his next destination. He doesn't really *want* to do it, because, whatever his failings as a human being, Babineau has a gorgeously intelligent mind, and a great deal of it is still intact. Destroying that mind is too much like those dumb and superstitious ISIS fucks hammering irreplaceable treasures of art and culture to rubble. Yet it must be done. No risks can be allowed, because the body is also a treasure. Yes, Babineau has slightly high blood pressure and his hearing has gone downhill in the last few years, but tennis and twice-weekly trips to the hospital gym have kept his muscles in fairly good shape. His heart ticks along at seventy beats a minute, with no misses. He's not suffering from sciatica, gout, cataracts, or any of the other outrages that affect many men at his age.

Besides, the good doctor is what he's got, at least for now.

With that in mind, Brady turns inward and finds what remains of Felix Babineau's core consciousness—the brain within the brain. It has been scarred and ravaged and diminished by Brady's repeated occupancies, but it is still there, still Babineau, still capable (theoretically at least) of taking back control. It is, however, defenseless, like some armored creature stripped of its shell. It's not exactly flesh; Babineau's core self is more like densely packed wires made of light.

Not without regret, Brady seizes them with his phantom hand and tears them apart.

7

Hodges spends the evening slowly eating his yogurt and watching the Weather Channel. The winter storm, ridiculously dubbed Eugenie by the Weather Channel wonks, is still coming and is expected to hit the city sometime late tomorrow.

"Hard to be more exact as of now," the balding, bespectacled wonk says to the knockout blond wonk in the red dress. "This one gives new meaning to the term stop-and-go traffic."

The knockout wonk laughs as if her partner in meteorology has said something outrageously witty, and Hodges uses the remote to turn them off.

The zapper, he thinks, looking at it. That's what everyone calls these things. Quite the invention, when you stop to think of it. You can access hundreds of different channels by remote control. Never even have to get up. As if you're inside the television instead of in your chair. Or in both places at the same time. Sort of a miracle, really.

As he goes into the bathroom to brush his teeth, his cell phone buzzes. He looks at the screen and has to laugh, even though it hurts to do it. Now that he's in the privacy of his own home, with nobody to be bothered by the home run text alert, his old partner calls instead.

"Hey, Pete, nice to know you still remember my number."

Pete has no time for banter. "I'm going to tell you something, Kermit, and if you decide to run with it, I'm like Sergeant Schultz on *Hogan's Heroes*. Remember him?"

241

"Sure." What Hodges feels in his gut right now isn't a pain-cramp, but one of excitement. Weird how similar they are. "I know nothing."

"Right. It has to be that way, because as far as this department is concerned, the murder of Martine Stover and the suicide of her mother is officially a closed case. We are certainly not going to reopen it because of a coincidence, and that's right from the top. Are we clear on that?"

"As glass," Hodges says. "What's the coincidence?"

"The head nurse in the Kiner Brain Injury Clinic committed suicide last night. Ruth Scapelli."

"I heard," Hodges says.

"While on one of your pilgrimages to visit the delightful Mr. Hartsfield, I presume."

"Yeah." No need to tell Pete that he never got in to see the delightful Mr. Hartsfield.

"Scapelli had one of those game gadgets. A Zappit. She apparently threw it in the trash before she bled out. One of the forensics guys found it."

"Huh." Hodges goes back into the living room and sits down, wincing when his body folds in the middle. "And that's your idea of a coincidence?"

"Not necessarily mine," Pete says heavily.

"But?"

"But I just want to retire in peace, goddammit! If there's a ball to carry on this one, Izzy can carry it."

"But Izzy don't want to carry no steenkin ball."

"No. Neither does the captain, or the commish."

Hearing this, Hodges is forced to slightly revise his opinion of his old partner as a burnt-out case. "You actually spoke to them? Tried to keep this thing alive?"

"To the captain. Over Izzy Jaynes's objections, may I add. Her *strident* objections. The captain talked to the commish. Late this evening I got the word to drop it, and you know why."

"Yeah. Because it connects to Brady two ways. Martine Stover was one of his City Center victims. Ruth Scapelli was his nurse. It would take a moderately bright reporter about six minutes to put those things together and stir up a nice fat scare story. That's what you got from Captain Pedersen?"

"That's what I got. No one in police administration wants the spotlight back on Hartsfield, not when he's still judged incompetent to assist in his own defense and thus unable to stand trial. Hell, no one in city government wants it."

Hodges is silent, thinking hard—maybe as hard as ever in his life. He learned the phrase *to cross the Rubicon* way back in high school, and grasped its meaning without Mrs. Bradley's explanation: to make an irrevocable decision. What he learned later, sometimes to his sorrow, is that one comes upon most Rubicons unprepared. If he tells Pete that Barbara Robinson also had a Zappit and may also have had suicide on her mind when she left school and went to Lowtown, Pete will almost have to go back to Pedersen. Two Zappit-related suicides can be written off as coincidence, but three? And okay, Barbara didn't actually succeed, thank God, but she's another person with a connection to Brady. She was at the 'Round Here concert, after all. Along with Hilda Carver and Dinah Scott, who *also* received Zappits. But are the police capable of believing what he's starting to believe? It's an important question, because Hodges loves Barbara Robinson and does not want to see her privacy violated without some concrete result to show for it.

"Kermit? Are you there?"

"Yeah. Just thinking. Did the Scapelli woman have any visitors last night?"

"Can't tell you, because the neighbors haven't been interviewed. It was a suicide, not a murder."

"Olivia Trelawney also committed suicide," Hodges says. "Remember?"

It's Pete's turn to be silent. Of course he remembers, and he also remembers it was an *assisted* suicide. Hartsfield planted a nasty malware worm in her computer, made her think she was being haunted by the ghost of a young mother killed at City Center. It helped that most people in the city had come to believe Olivia Trelawney's carelessness with her ignition key was partially responsible for the massacre.

"Brady always enjoyed—"

"I know what he always enjoyed," Pete says. "No need to belabor the point. I've got one other scrap for you, if you want it."

"Hit me."

"I spoke to Nancy Alderson around five this afternoon."

Good for you, Pete, Hodges thinks. Doing a little more than punching the clock in your last few weeks.

"She said that Mrs. Ellerton already bought her daughter a new computer. For her online class. Said it's under the basement stairs, still in the carton. Ellerton was going to give it to Martine for her birthday next month."

"Planning for the future, in other words. Not the act of a suicidal woman, is it?"

"No, I wouldn't say so. I have to go, Kerm. The ball is in your court. Play it or let it lie. Up to you."

"Thanks, Pete. I appreciate the heads-up."

"I wish it was like the old days," Pete says. "We would have gone after this thing and let the chips fall."

"But it's not." Hodges is rubbing his side again.

"No. It's not. You take care of yourself. Put on some goddam weight."

"I'll give it my best shot," Hodges says, but he's talking to no one. Pete is gone.

He brushes his teeth, takes a painkiller, and climbs slowly into his pajamas. Then he goes to bed and stares up into the darkness, waiting for sleep or morning, whichever comes first.

8

Brady was careful to take Babineau's ID badge from the top of his bureau after donning Babineau's clothes, because the magnetic strip on the back turns it into an all-access pass. At 10:30 that night, around the time Hodges is finally getting a bellyful of the Weather Channel, he uses it for the first time, to enter the gated employees' parking lot behind the main hospital building. The lot is loaded in the daytime, but at this hour he has his pick of spaces. He chooses one as far from the pervasive glare of the arc-sodiums as he can get. He tilts back the seat of Dr. B.'s luxury ride and kills the engine.

He drifts into sleep and finds himself cruising through a light fog of disconnected memories, all that remains of Felix Babineau. He tastes the peppermint lipstick of the first girl he ever kissed, Marjorie Patterson at East Junior High, in Joplin, Missouri. He sees a basketball with the word VOIT printed on it in fading black letters. He feels warmth in his training pants as he pees himself while coloring behind his gammer's sofa, a huge dinosaur covered in faded green velour.

Childhood memories are apparently the last things to go.

Shortly after two AM he flinches from a brilliant recollection of his father slapping him for playing with matches in the attic of their house and starts awake with a gasp in the Beemer's bucket seat. For a moment the clearest detail of that memory

245

lingers: a vein pulsing in his father's flushed neck, just above the collar of his blue Izod golf shirt.

Then he's Brady again, wearing a Babineau skin-suit.

9

While mostly confined to Room 217, and to a body that no longer works, Brady has had months to plan, to revise those plans, and revise the revisions. He has made mistakes along the way (he wishes he'd never used Z-Boy to send Hodges a message using the Blue Umbrella site, for instance, and he should have waited before going after Barbara Robinson), yet he has persevered, and here he is, on the verge of success.

He has mentally rehearsed this part of the operation dozens of times, and now moves ahead confidently. A swipe of Babineau's card gets him in the door marked MAINTENANCE A. On the floors above, the machines that run the hospital are heard as a muted hum, if they are heard at all. Down here they're a steady thunder, and the tile hallway is stiflingly hot. But it's deserted, as he expected. A city hospital never falls into a deep sleep, but in the early hours of the morning it shuts its eyes and dozes.

The maintenance crew's break room is also deserted, as is the shower and changing area beyond it. Padlocks secure some of the lockers, but the majority of them are open. He tries one after the other, checking sizes, until he finds a gray shirt and a pair of workpants that are Babineau's approximate size. He takes off Babineau's clothes and puts on the maintenance worker's stuff, not neglecting to transfer the bottle of pills he took from Babineau's bathroom. It's a potent his 'n hers mixture. On one of the hooks by the showers he sees the final touch: a red-and-blue

Groundhogs baseball cap. He takes it, adjusts the plastic band in back, and pulls it low over his forehead, making sure to get all of Babineau's silver hair covered up.

He walks the length of Maintenance A and turns right into the hospital laundry, which is humid as well as hot. Two housekeepers are sitting in plastic contour chairs between two rows of gigantic Foshan dryers. Both are fast asleep, one with an overturned box of animal crackers spilling into the lap of her green nylon skirt. Farther down, past the washing machines, two laundry carts are parked against the cinderblock wall. One is filled with hospital johnnies, the other piled high with fresh bedlinens. Brady takes a handful of johnnies, puts them on top of the neatly folded sheets, and rolls the cart on down the hall.

It takes a change of elevators and a walk across the skyway to reach the Bucket, and he sees exactly four people on the journey. Two are nurses whispering together outside a med supply closet; two are interns in the doctors' lounge, laughing quietly over something on a laptop computer. None of them notice the graveyard-shift maintenance man, head down as he pushes an overloaded cart of laundry.

The point where he's most apt to be noticed—and perhaps recognized—is the nurses' station in the middle of the Bucket. But one of the nurses is playing solitaire on her computer, and the other is writing notes, propping her head up with her free hand. That one catches movement out of the corner of her eye and without raising her head asks how he's doing.

"Yeah, good," Brady says. "Cold night, though."

"Uh-huh, and I heard there's snow coming." She yawns and goes back to her notes.

Brady rolls his basket down the hall, stopping just short of 217. One of the Bucket's little secrets is that here the patient rooms have two doors, one marked and one unmarked. The unmarked ones open into the closets, making it possible to restock linens and other necessaries at night without disturbing the patients' rest . . . or their disturbed minds. Brady grabs a few of the johnnies, takes a quick look around to make sure he is still unobserved, and slips through this unmarked door. A moment later he's looking down at himself. For years he has fooled everyone into believing that Brady Hartsfield is what the staff calls (only among themselves) a gork, a ding, or a LOBNH: lights are on but nobody's home. Now he really is one.

He bends and strokes one lightly stubbled cheek. Runs the pad of his thumb over one closed lid, feeling the raised curve of eyeball beneath. Lifts one hand, turns it over, and lays it gently palm-up on the coverlet. From the pocket of the borrowed gray trousers he takes the bottle of pills and spills half a dozen in the upturned palm. Take, eat, he thinks. This is my body, broken for you.

He enters that broken body one final time. He doesn't need to use the Zappit to do this now, nor does he have to worry that Babineau will seize control and run away like the Gingerbread Man. With Brady's mind gone, Babineau is the gork. Nothing left in there but a memory of his father's golf shirt.

Brady looks around the inside of his head like a man giving a hotel room one last check after a long-term stay. Anything hanging forgotten in the closet? A tube of toothpaste left in the bathroom? Maybe a cufflink under the bed?

No. Everything is packed and the room is empty. He closes his hand, hating the draggy way the fingers move, as if the joints are filled with sludge. He opens his mouth, lifts the pills, and drops them in. He chews. The taste is bitter. Babineau, meanwhile, has collapsed bonelessly to the floor. Brady swallows once.

And again. There. It's done. He closes his eyes, and when he opens them again, he's staring beneath the bed at a pair of slippers Brady Hartsfield will never wear again.

He gets to Babineau's feet, brushes himself off, and takes one more look at the body that carried him around for almost thirty years. The one that stopped being of any use to him the second time he was smashed in the head at Mingo Auditorium, just before he could trigger the plastic explosive strapped to the underside of his wheelchair. Once he might have worried that this drastic step would backfire on him, that his consciousness and all his grand plans would die along with his body. No more. The umbilical cord has been severed. He has crossed the Rubicon.

So long, Brady, he thinks, it was good to know you.

This time when he pushes the laundry cart past the nurses' station, the one who was playing solitaire is gone, probably to the bathroom. The other is asleep on her notes.

10

But it's quarter to four now, and there's so much more to do.

After changing back into Babineau's clothes, Brady leaves the hospital the same way he entered and drives toward Sugar Heights. Because Z-Boy's homemade silencer is kaput and an unmuffled gunshot is likely to be reported in the town's ritziest neighborhood (where rent-a-cops from Vigilant Guard Service are never more than a block or two away), he stops at Valley Plaza, which is on the way. He checks the empty lot for cop cars, sees none, and drives around to the loading area of Discount Home Furnishings.

God, it's so good to be out! Fucking *wonderful*!

Walking to the front of the Beemer, he breathes deeply of the cold winter air wrapping the sleeve of Babineau's expensive top-coat around the .32's short barrel as he goes. It won't be as good as Z-Boy's silencer, and he knows it's a risk, but not a big one. Just the one shot. He looks up first, wanting to see the stars, but clouds have blanked out the sky. Oh, well, there will be other nights. Many of them. Possibly thousands. He is not limited to Babineau's body, after all.

He aims and fires. A small round hole appears in the Beemer's windshield. Now comes another risk, driving the last mile to Sugar Heights with a bullet hole in the glass just above the steering wheel, but this is the time of night when the suburban streets are at their emptiest and the cops also doze, especially in the better neighborhoods.

Twice headlights approach him and he holds his breath, but both times they pass by without slowing. January air comes in through the bullet hole, making a thin wheezing sound. He makes it back to Babineau's McMansion without incident. No need to tap the code this time; he just hits the gate opener clipped to the visor. When he reaches the top of the drive, he veers onto the snow-covered lawn, bounces over a hard crust of plowed snow, clips a bush, and stops.

Home again, home again, jiggety-jog.

Only problem is, he neglected to bring a knife. He could get one in the house, he has another piece of business in there, but he doesn't want to make two trips. He has miles to go before he sleeps, and he's anxious to start rolling them. He opens the center console and paws through it. Surely a dandy like Babineau will keep spare grooming implements, even a fingernail clipper will do . . . but there's nothing. He tries the glove compartment, and in the folder containing the Beemer's documents (leather, of course) he finds an Allstate insurance card laminated in plastic. It will serve. They are, after all, the Good Hands people.

Brady pushes back the sleeve of Babineau's cashmere overcoat and the shirt beneath, then drags a corner of the laminated card over his forearm. It produces nothing but a thin red line. He goes again, bearing down much harder, lips pulled back in a grimace. This time the skin splits and blood flows. He gets out of the car holding his arm up, then leans back in. He tips a spatter of droplets first onto the seat and then onto the bottom arc of the steering wheel. There's not much, but it won't take much. Not when combined with the bullet hole in the windshield.

He bounds up the porch steps, each springy leap a small orgasm. Cora is lying beneath the hall coathooks, just as dead as ever. Library Al is still asleep on the couch. Brady shakes him, and when he only gets a few muffled grunts, he grabs Al with both hands and rolls him onto the floor. Al's eyes creak open.

"Huh? Wha?"

The stare is dazed but not completely blank. There's probably no Al Brooks left inside that plundered head, but there's still a bit of the alter ego Brady has created. Enough.

"Hey there, Z-Boy," Brady says, squatting down.

"Hey," Z-Boy croaks, struggling to sit up. "Hey there, Dr. Z. I'm watching that house, just like you told me. The woman—the one who can still walk—she uses that Zappit all the time. I watch her from the g'rage across the street."

"You don't have to do that anymore."

"No? Say, where are we?"

"My house," Brady says. "You killed my wife."

Z-Boy stares at the white-haired man in the overcoat, his mouth hung open. His breath is awful, but Brady doesn't draw away. Slowly, Z-Boy's face begins to crumple. It's like watching a car crash in slow motion. "Kill? . . . did not!"

"Yes."

"No! Never would!"

"You did, though. But only because I told you to."

"Are you sure? I don't remember."

Brady takes him by the shoulder. "It wasn't your fault. You were hypnotized."

Z-Boy's face brightens. "By Fishin' Hole!"

"Yes, by Fishin' Hole. And while you were, I told you to kill Mrs. Babineau."

Z-Boy looks at him with doubt and woe. "If I did, it wasn't my fault. I was hypnotized and can't even remember."

"Take this."

Brady hands Z-Boy the gun. Z-Boy holds it up, frowning as if at some exotic artifact.

"Put it in your pocket, and give me your car keys."

Z-Boy stuffs the .32 absently into his pants pocket and Brady winces, expecting the gun to go off and put a bullet in the poor sap's leg. At last Z-Boy holds out his keyring. Brady pockets it, stands up, and crosses the living room.

"Where are you going, Dr. Z?"

"I won't be long. Why don't you sit on the couch until I get back?"

"I'll sit on the couch until you get back," Z-Boy says.

"Good idea."

Brady goes into Dr. Babineau's study. There's an ego wall crammed with framed photos, including one of a younger Felix Babineau shaking hands with the second President Bush, both of them grinning like idiots. Brady ignores the pictures; he's seen them many times before, during the months when he was learning how to be in another person's body, what he now thinks of as his student driver days. Nor is he interested in the desktop computer. What he wants is the MacBook Air sitting on the credenza. He opens it, powers it up, and types in Babineau's password, which happens to be CEREBELLIN.

"Your drug didn't do shit," Brady says as the main screen comes up. He's actually not sure of this, but it's what he chooses to believe.

His fingers rattle the keyboard with a practiced speed of which Babineau would have been incapable, and a hidden program, one Brady installed himself on a previous visit to the good doctor's head, pops up. It's labeled FISHIN' HOLE. He types again, and the program reaches out to the repeater in Freddi Linklatter's computer hideaway.

WORKING, the laptop's screen says, and below this: 3 FOUND.

Three found! Three already!

Brady is delighted but not really surprised, even though it's the graveyard of the morning. There are a few insomniacs in every crowd, and that includes the crowd that has received free Zappits from badconcert.com. What better way to while away the sleepless hours before dawn than with a handy game console? And before playing solitaire or Angry Birds, why not check those pink fish on the Fishin' Hole demo screen, and see if they've finally been programmed to turn into numbers when tapped? A combination of the right ones will win prizes, but at four in the morning, that may not be the prime motivator. Four in the morning is usually an unhappy time to be awake. It's when unpleasant thoughts and pessimistic ideas come to the fore, and the demo screen is soothing. It's also addictive. Al Brooks knew that before he became Z-Boy; Brady knew from the moment he saw it. Just a lucky coincidence, but what Brady has done since—what he has *prepared*—is no coincidence. It's the result of long and careful planning in the prison of his hospital room and his wasted body.

He shuts down the laptop, tucks it under his arm, and starts to leave the study. At the doorway he has an idea and goes back to Babineau's desk. He opens the center drawer and finds exactly what he wants—he doesn't even have to rummage. When your luck is running, it's running.

Brady returns to the living room. Z-Boy is sitting on the sofa, head lowered, shoulders slumped, hands dangling between his thighs. He looks unutterably weary.

"I have to go now," Brady says.

"Where?"

"Not your business."

"Not my business."

"Exactly right. You should go back to sleep."

"Here on the couch?"

"Or in one of the bedrooms upstairs. But you need to do something first." He hands Z-Boy the felt-tip pen he found in Babineau's desk. "Make your mark, Z-Boy, just like when you were in Mrs. Ellerton's house."

"They were alive when I was watching from the g'rage, I know that much, but they might be dead now."

"They probably are, yes."

"I didn't kill them, too, did I? Because it seems like I was in the bathroom, at least. And drawed a Z there."

"No, no, nothing like th—"

"I looked for the Zappit like you asked me to, I'm sure of that. I looked hard, but I didn't find it anywhere. I think maybe she throwed it away."

"That doesn't matter anymore. Just make your mark here, okay? Make it in at least ten places." A thought occurs. "Can you still count to ten?"

"One . . . two . . . three . . ."

Brady glances at Babineau's Rolex. Quarter past four. Morning rounds in the Bucket begin at five. Time is fleeting on wingèd feet. "That's great. Make your mark in at least ten places. Then you can go back to sleep."

"Okay. I'll make my mark in at least ten places, then I'll sleep, then I'll drive over to that house you want me to watch. Or should I stop doing that now that they're dead?"

"I think you can stop now. Let's review, okay? Who killed my wife?"

"I did, but it wasn't my fault. I was hypnotized, and I can't even remember." Z-Boy begins to cry. "Will you come back, Dr. Z?"

Brady smiles, exposing Babineau's expensive dental work. "Sure." His eyes move up and to the left as he says it.

He watches the old guy shuffle to the huge God-I'm-rich television mounted on the wall and draw a large **Z** on the screen. Zs all over the murder scene aren't absolutely necessary, but Brady thinks it will be a nice touch, especially when the police ask the former Library Al for his name and he tells them it's Z-Boy. Just a bit of extra filigree on a finely crafted piece of jewelry.

Brady goes to the front door, stepping over Cora again on the way. He bops down the porch steps and does a dance move at the bottom, snapping Babineau's fingers. That hurts a little, just a touch of incipient arthritis, but so what? Brady knows what real pain is, and a few twinges in the old phalanges ain't it.

He jogs to Al's Malibu. Not much of a ride compared to the late Dr. Babineau's BMW, but it will get him where he needs to go. He starts it and frowns when classical shit comes pouring out of the dashboard speaker. He switches to BAM-100 and finds some Black Sabbath from back when Ozzy was still cool. He takes a final look at the Beemer parked askew on the lawn, then gets rolling.

Miles to go before he sleeps, and then the final touch, the cherry on top of the sundae. He won't need Freddi Linklatter for that, only Dr. B.'s MacBook. He's running without a leash now.

He's free.

11

Around the time Z-Boy is proving that he can still count to ten, Freddi Linklatter's blood-caked lashes come unstuck from her blood-caked cheeks. She finds herself looking into a gaping brown eye. It takes her several long moments to decide it isn't really an eye, only a swirl of woodgrain that *looks* like an eye. She is lying on the floor and suffering the worst hangover of her life, even worse than after that cataclysmic party to celebrate her twenty-first, when she mixed crystal meth with Ronrico. She thought later that she was lucky to have survived that little experiment. Now she almost wishes she hadn't, because this is worse. It's not only her head; her chest feels like Marshawn Lynch has been using her for a tackling dummy.

She tells her hands to move and they reluctantly answer the call. She places them in push-up position and shoves. She comes up, but her top shirt stays down, stuck to the floor in a pool of what looks like blood and smells suspiciously like Scotch. So that's what she was drinking, and fell over her own stupid feet. Smacked her head. But dear God, how much did she put away?

It wasn't like that, she thinks. Someone came, and you know who it was.

It's a simple process of deduction. Lately she's only had two visitors here, the Z-Dudes, and the one who wears the ratty parka hasn't been around for awhile.

She tries to get to her feet, and can't make it at first. Nor can she take more than shallow breaths. Deeper ones hurt her above her left breast. It feels like something is sticking in there.

*My flask?*

*I was spinning it while I waited for him to show up. To give me the final payment and get out of my life.*

"Shot me," she croaks. "Fucking Dr. Z shot me."

She staggers into the bathroom and is hardly able to believe the train wreck she sees in the mirror. The left side of her face is covered with blood, and there's a purple knob rising from a gash above her left temple, but that's not the worst. Her blue chambray shirt is also matted with blood—mostly from the head wound, she hopes, head wounds bleed like crazy—and there's a round black hole in the left breast pocket. He shot her, all right. Now she remembers the bang and the smell of gunsmoke just before she passed out.

She tweezes her shaking fingers into the breast pocket, still taking those shallow breaths, and pulls out her pack of Marlboro Lights. There's the bullet hole right through the middle of the M. She drops the cigarettes into the basin, works at the buttons of the shirt, and lets it fall to the floor. The smell of Scotch is stronger now. The shirt beneath is khaki, with big flap pockets. When she tries to pull the flask from the one on the left, she utters a low mewl of agony—all she can manage without taking a deeper breath—but when she gets it free, the pain in her chest lessens a little. The bullet also went through the flask, and the prongs on the side closest to her skin are bright with blood. She drops the ruined flask on top of the Marlboros, and goes to work on the khaki shirt's buttons. This takes longer, but eventually it also falls to the floor. Beneath it is an American Giant tee, the kind that also has a pocket. She reaches into it and takes out a tin of Altoids. There's a hole in this, too. The tee has no buttons, so she works her pinky finger into the bullet hole in the pocket and pulls. The shirt tears, and at last she's looking at her own skin, freckled with blood.

There's a hole just where the scant swell of her breast begins, and in it she can see a black thing. It looks like a dead bug. She tears the rip in the shirt wider, using three fingers now, then reaches in and grasps the bug. She wiggles it like a loose tooth.

"*Oooo . . . ooooh . . . ooooh, FUCK . . .*"

It comes free, not a bug but a slug. She looks at it, then drops it into the sink with the other stuff. In spite of her aching head and the throbbing in her chest, Freddi realizes how absurdly fortunate she has been. It was just a little gun, but at such close range, even a little gun should have done the job. It would have, too, if not for a one-in-a-thousand lucky break. First through the cigarettes, then through the flask—which had been the real stopper—then through the Altoids tin, then into her. How close to her heart? An inch? Less?

Her stomach clenches, wanting to puke. She won't let it, can't let it. The hole in her chest will start bleeding again, but that's not the main thing. Her head will explode. *That's* the main thing.

Her breathing is a little easier now that she's removed the flask with its nasty (but lifesaving) prongs of metal. She plods back into her living room and stares at the puddle of blood and Scotch on the floor. If he had bent over and put the muzzle of the gun to the back of her neck . . . just to make sure . . .

Freddi closes her eyes and fights to retain consciousness as waves of faintness and nausea float through her. When it's a little better, she goes to her chair and sits down very slowly. Like an old lady with a bad back, she thinks. She stares at the ceiling. What now?

Her first thought is to call 911, get an ambulance over here and go to the hospital, but what will she tell them? That a man claiming to be a Mormon or a Jehovah's Witness knocked on her door, and when she opened it, he shot her? Shot her why? For what? And why would she, a woman living alone, open her door to a stranger at ten thirty in the evening?

That isn't all. The police will come. In her bedroom is an ounce of pot and an eightball of coke. She could get rid of that shit, but what about the shit in her computer room? She's got half a dozen illegal hacks going on, plus a ton of expensive equipment that she didn't exactly buy. The cops will want to know if just perchance, Ms. Linklatter, the man who shot you had something to do with said electronic gear. Maybe you owed him money for it? Maybe you were working with him, stealing credit card numbers and other personal info? And they can hardly miss the repeater, blinking away like a Las Vegas slot machine as it sends out its endless signal via WiFi, delivering a customized malware worm every time it finds a live Zappit.

What's *this*, Ms. Linklatter? What exactly does it do?

And what will she tell them?

She looks around, hoping to see the envelope of cash lying on the floor or the couch, but of course he took it with him. If there was ever cash in there at all, and not just cut-up strips of news-paper. She's here, she's shot, she's had a concussion (please God not a fracture) and she's low on dough. What to do?

Turn off the repeater, that's the first thing. Dr. Z has got

Brady Hartsfield inside him, and Brady is a bad motorcycle. Whatever the repeater's doing is nasty shit. She was going to turn it off anyway, wasn't she? It's all a little vague, but wasn't that the plan? To turn it off and exit stage left? She doesn't have that final payment to help finance her flight, but despite her loose habits with cash, there's still a few thousand in the bank, and Corn Trust opens at nine. Plus, there's her ATM card. So turn off the repeater, nip that creepy zeetheend site in the bud, wash the gore off her face, and get the fuck out of Dodge. Not by plane, these days airport security areas are like baited traps, but by any bus or train headed into the golden west. Isn't that the best idea?

She's up and shuffling toward the door of the computer room when the obvious reason why it is *not* the best idea hits her. Brady is gone, but he wouldn't leave if he couldn't monitor his projects from a distance, especially the repeater, and doing that is the easiest thing in the world. He's smart about computers—brilliant, actually, although it pisses her off to admit it—and he's almost certainly left himself a back door into her setup. If so, he can check in anytime he wants; all it will take is a laptop. If she shuts his shit down, he'll know, and he'll know she's still alive.

He'll come back.

"So what do I do?" Freddi whispers. She trudges to her window, shivering—it's so fucking cold in this apartment once winter comes—and looks out into the dark. "What do I do now?"

12

Hodges is dreaming of Bowser, the feisty little mongrel he had when he was a kid. His father hauled Bowser to the vet and had him put down, over Hodges's weeping protests, after ole Bowse bit the newspaper boy badly enough to require stitches. In this dream Bowser is biting *him*, biting him in the side. He won't let go even when young Billy Hodges offers him the best treat in the treat bag, and the pain is excruciating. The doorbell is ringing and he thinks, That's the paperboy, go bite *him*, you're supposed to bite *him*.

Only as he swims up from this dream and back into the real world, he realizes it isn't the doorbell, it's the phone by his bed. The landline. He gropes for it, drops it, picks it up off the duvet, and manages a furry approximation of hello.

"Figured you'd have your cell on do not disturb," Pete Huntley says. He sounds wide awake and weirdly jovial. Hodges squints at the bedside clock but can't read it. His bottle of painkillers, already half empty, is blocking the digital readout. Jesus, how many did he take yesterday?

"I don't know how to do that, either." Hodges struggles to a sitting position. He can't believe the pain has gotten so bad so fast. It's as if it was just waiting to be identified before pouncing with all its claws out.

"You need to get a life, Kerm."

A little late for that, he thinks, swinging his legs out of bed.

"Why are you calling at . . ." He moves the bottle of pills. "At twenty to seven in the morning?"

"Couldn't wait to give you the good news," Pete says. "Brady Hartsfield is dead. A nurse discovered him on morning rounds."

Hodges shoots to his feet, producing a stab of pain he hardly feels. "What? *How?*"

"There'll be an autopsy later today, but the doctor who examined him is leaning toward suicide. There's a residue of *something* on his tongue and gums. The doc on call took a sample, and a guy from the ME's office is taking another as we speak. They're going to rush the analysis, Hartsfield being such a rock star and all."

"Suicide," Hodges says, running a hand through his already crazed hair. The news is simple enough, but he still can't seem to take it in. *"Suicide?"*

"He was always a fan," Pete says. "I believe you might have said that yourself, and more than once."

"Yeah, but . . ."

But what? Pete's right, Brady *was* a fan of suicide, and not just the other guy's. He had been ready to die at the City Center Job Fair in 2009, if things worked out that way, and a year later he rolled a wheelchair into Mingo Auditorium with three pounds of plastic explosive strapped to the seat. Which put his ass at ground zero. Only that was then, and things have changed. Haven't they?

"But what?"

"I don't know," Hodges says.

"I do. He finally found a way to do it. Simple as that. In any case, if you thought Hartsfield was somehow involved in the deaths of Ellerton, Stover, and Scapelli—and I have to tell you I had my own thoughts along that line—you can stop worrying. He's a gone goose, a toasty turkey, a baked buzzard, and we all say hooray."

"Pete, I need to process this a little."

"No doubt," Pete says. "You had quite the history with him. Meanwhile, I have to call Izzy. Get her day started on the good foot."

"Will you call me when you get back the analysis of whatever he swallowed?"

"Indeed I will. Meanwhile, *sayonara* Mr. Mercedes, right?"

"Right, right."

Hodges hangs up the phone, walks into the kitchen, and puts on a pot of coffee. He should have tea, coffee will burn the shit out of his poor struggling innards, but right now he doesn't care. And he won't take any pills, not for awhile. He needs to be as clearheaded about this as he possibly can.

He snatches his mobile off the charger and calls Holly. She answers at once, and he wonders briefly what time she gets up. Five? Even earlier? Maybe some questions are best left unanswered. He tells her what Pete just told him, and for once in her life, Holly Gibney does not gild her profanity.

"You've got to be fucking kidding me!"

"Not unless Pete was kidding, and I don't think he was. He doesn't try joking until mid-afternoon, and he's not very good at it then."

Silence for a moment, and then Holly asks, "Do you believe it?"

"That he's dead, yes. It could hardly be a case of mistaken identity. That he committed suicide? To me that seems . . ." He fishes for the right phrase, can't find it, and repeats what he said to his old partner not five minutes before. "I don't know."

"Is it over?"

"Maybe not."

"That's what I think, too. We have to find out what happened to the Zappits that were left over after the company went broke. I don't understand how Brady Hartsfield could have had anything to do with them, but so many of the connections go back to him. And to the concert he tried to blow up."

"I know." Hodges is again picturing a web with a big old spider at the center of it, one full of poison. Only the spider is dead.

And we all say hooray, he thinks.

"Holly, can you be at the hospital when the Robinsons come to pick up Barbara?"

"I can do that." After a pause she adds, "I'd like to do that. I'll call Tanya to make sure it's okay, but I'm sure it is. Why?"

"I want you to show Barb a six-pack. Five elderly white guys in suits, plus Dr. Felix Babineau."

"You think Myron Zakim was Hartsfield's *doctor*? That he was the one who gave Barbara and Hilda those Zappits?"

"At this point it's just a hunch."

But that's modest. It's actually a bit more. Babineau gave Hodges a cock-and-bull story to keep him out of Brady's room, then nearly blew a gasket when Hodges asked if he was all right. And Norma Wilmer claims he's been conducting unauthorized experiments on Brady. *Investigate Babineau*, she said in Bar Bar Black Sheep. *Get him in trouble. I dare you.* As a man who probably has only months to live, that doesn't seem like much of a dare.

"Okay. I respect your hunches, Bill. And I'm sure I can find a society-page picture of Dr. Babineau from one of those charity events they're always having for the hospital."

"Good. Now refresh me on the name of the bankruptcy trustee guy."

"Todd Schneider. You should call him at eight thirty. If I'm with the Robinsons, I won't be in until later. I'll bring Jerome with me."

"Yeah, good. Have you got Schneider's number?"

"I emailed it to you. You remember how to access your email, don't you?"

"It's cancer, Holly, not Alzheimer's."

"Today is your last day. Remember that, too."

How can he forget? They'll put him in the hospital where Brady died, and that will be that, Hodges's last case left hanging fire. He hates the idea, but there's no way around it. This is going fast.

"Eat some breakfast."

"I will."

He ends the call, and looks longingly at the fresh pot of coffee. The smell is wonderful. He turns it down the sink and gets dressed. He does not eat breakfast.

## 13

Finders Keepers seems very empty without Holly at her desk in the reception area, but at least the seventh floor of the Turner Building is quiet; the noisy crew from the travel agency down the hall won't start to arrive for at least another hour.

Hodges thinks best with a yellow pad in front of him, jotting down ideas as they come, trying to tease out the connections and form a coherent picture. It's the way he worked when he was on the cops, and he was capable of making those connections more often than not. He won a lot of citations over the years, but they're piled helter-skelter on a shelf in his closet instead of hanging on a wall. The citations never mattered to him. The reward was the flash of light that came with the connections. He found himself unable to give it up. Hence Finders Keepers instead of retirement.

This morning there are no notes, only doodles of stick men climbing a hill, and cyclones, and flying saucers. He's pretty sure most of the pieces to this puzzle are now on the table and all he has to do is figure out how to put them together, but Brady Hartsfield's death is like a pileup on his personal information highway, blocking all traffic. Every time he glances at his watch, another five minutes have gone by. Soon enough he'll have to call Schneider. By the time he gets off the phone with him, the noisy travel agency crew will be arriving. After them, Barbara and Jerome. Any chance of quiet thought will be gone.

*Think of the connections*, Holly said. *They all go back to him. And the concert he tried to blow up.*

Yes; yes they do. Because the only ones eligible to receive free Zappits from that website were people—young girls then, for the most part, teenagers now—who could prove they were at the 'Round Here show, and the website is now defunct. Like Brady, badconcert.com is a gone goose, a toasty turkey, a baked buzzard, and we all say hooray.

At last he prints two words amid the doodles, and circles them. One is *Concert*. The other is *Residue*.

He calls Kiner Memorial, and is transferred to the Bucket. Yes, he's told, Norma Wilmer is in, but she's busy and can't come to the phone. Hodges guesses she's *very* busy this morning, and hopes her hangover isn't too bad. He leaves a message asking that she call him back as soon as she can, and emphasizes that it's urgent.

He continues doodling until eight twenty-five (now it's Zappits he's drawing, possibly because he's got Dinah Scott's in his coat pocket), then calls Todd Schneider, who answers the phone personally.

Hodges identifies himself as a volunteer consumer advocate working with the Better Business Bureau, and says he's been tasked with investigating some Zappit consoles that have shown up in the city. He keeps his tone easy, almost casual. "This is no big deal, especially since the Zappits were given away, but it seems that some of the recipients are downloading books from something called the Sunrise Readers Circle, and they're coming through garbled."

"Sunrise Readers Circle?" Schneider sounds bemused. No sign he's getting ready to put up a shield of legalese, and that's the way Hodges wants to keep it. "As in Sunrise Solutions?"

"Well, yes, that's what prompted the call. According to my information, Sunrise Solutions bought out Zappit, Inc., before going bankrupt."

"That's true, but I've got a ton of paperwork on Sunrise Solutions, and I don't recall anything about a Sunrise Readers Circle. And it would have stood out like a sore thumb. Sunrise was basically involved in gobbling up small electronics companies, looking for that one big hit. Which they never found, unfortunately."

"What about the Zappit Club? Ring any bells?"

"Never heard of it."

"Or a website called zeetheend.com?" As he asks this question, Hodges smacks himself in the forehead. He should have checked that site for himself instead of filling a page with dumb doodles.

"Nope, never heard of that, either." Now comes a tiny rattle of the legal shield. "Is this a consumer fraud issue? Because bankruptcy laws are very clear on the subject, and—"

"Nothing like that," Hodges soothes. "Only reason we're even involved is because of the jumbled downloads. And at least one of the Zappits was dead on arrival. The recipient wants to send it back, maybe get a new one."

"Not surprised someone got a dead console if it was from the last batch," Schneider says. "There were a lot of defectives, maybe thirty percent of the final run."

"As a matter of personal curiosity, how many were in that final run?"

"I'd have to look up the number to be sure, but I think around forty thousand units. Zappit sued the manufacturer, even though suing Chinese companies is pretty much a fool's game, but by then they were desperate to stay afloat. I'm only giving you this information because the whole business is done and dusted."

"Understood."

"Well, the manufacturing company—Yicheng Electronics—came back with all guns blazing. Probably not because of the money at stake, but because they were worried about their reputation. Can't blame them there, can you?"

"No." Hodges can't wait any longer for pain relief. He takes out his bottle of pills, shakes out two, then reluctantly puts one back. He puts it under his tongue to melt, hoping it will work faster that way. "I guess you can't."

"Yicheng claimed the defective units were damaged in shipping, probably by water. They said if it had been a software problem, *all* the games would have been defective. Makes a degree of sense to me, but I'm no electronics genius. Anyway, Zappit went under, and Sunrise Solutions elected not to proceed with the suit. They had bigger problems by then. Creditors snapping at their heels. Investors jumping ship."

"What happened to that final shipment?"

"Well, they were an asset, of course, but not a very valuable one, due to the defect issue. I held onto them for awhile, and we advertised in the trades to retail companies that specialize in discounted items. Chains like the Dollar Store and Economy Wizard. Are you familiar with those?"

"Yeah." Hodges had bought a pair of factory-second loafers at the local Dollar Store. They cost more than a buck, but they weren't bad. Wore well.

"Of course we had to make it clear that as many as three in every ten Zappit Commanders—that's what the last iteration was called—might be defective, which meant each one would have to be checked. That killed any chance for selling the whole shipment. Checking the units one by one would have been too labor intensive."

268

"Uh-huh."

"So, as bankruptcy trustee, I decided to have them destroyed and claim a tax credit, which would have amounted to . . . well, quite a lot. Not by General Motors standards, but mid-six figures. Clear the books, you understand."

"Right, makes sense."

"But before I could do that, I got a call from a fellow at a company called Gamez Unlimited, right there in your city. That's games with a Z on the end. Called himself the CEO. Probably CEO of a three-man operation working out of two rooms or a garage." Schneider chuckles a big business New York chuckle. "Since the computer revolution really got rolling, these outfits pop up like weeds, although I never heard of any of them actually *giving* product away. It smells a trifle scammy, don't you think?"

"Yeah," Hodges says. The dissolving pill is exceedingly bitter, but the relief is sweet. He thinks that's the case with a great many things in life. A *Reader's Digest* insight, but that doesn't make it invalid. "It does, actually."

The legal shield has gone bye-bye. Schneider is animated now, wrapped up in his own story. "The guy offered to buy eight hundred Zappits at eighty dollars apiece, which was roughly a hundred dollars cheaper than the suggested retail. We dickered a bit and settled on a hundred."

"Per unit."

"Yes."

"Comes to eighty thousand dollars," Hodges says. He's thinking of Brady, who had been hit with God only knew how many civil suits, for sums mounting into the tens of millions of dollars. Brady, who'd had—if Hodges's memory serves him right—about eleven hundred dollars in the bank. "And you got a check for that amount?"

He's not sure he'll get an answer to the question—many law-yers would close the discussion off at this point—but he does. Probably because the Sunrise Solutions bankruptcy is all tied up in a nice legal bow. For Schneider, this is like a postgame inter-view. "Correct. Drawn on the Gamez Unlimited account."

"Cleared okay?"

Todd Schneider chuckles his big business chuckle. "If it hadn't, those eight hundred Zappit consoles would have been recycled into new computer goodies along with the rest."

Hodges scribbles some quick math on his doodle-decorated pad. If thirty percent of the eight hundred units were defective, that leaves five hundred and sixty working consoles. Or maybe not that many. Hilda Carver got one that had presumably been vetted—why else give it to her?—but according to Barbara, it had given a single blue flash and then died.

"So off they went."

"Yes, via UPS from a warehouse in Terre Haute. A very small recoupment, but something. We do what we can for our clients, Mr. Hodges."

"I'm sure you do." And we all say hooray, Hodges thinks. "Do you recall the address those eight hundred Zappits went to?"

"No, but it will be in the files. Give me your email and I'll be happy to send it to you, on condition you call me back and tell me what sort of scam these Gamez people have been working."

"Happy to do that, Mr. Schneider." It'll be a box number, Hodges thinks, and the box holder will be long gone. Still, it will need to be checked out. Holly can do it while he's in the hospital, getting treatment for something that almost certainly can't be cured. "You've been very helpful, Mr. Schneider. One more question, and I'll let you go. Do you happen to remember the name of the Gamez Unlimited CEO?"

"Oh, yes," Schneider says. "I assumed that's why the company was Gamez with a Z instead of an S."

"I don't follow."

"The CEO's name was Myron Zakim."


# 14


Hodges hangs up and opens Firefox. He types in zeetheend and finds himself looking at a cartoon man swinging a cartoon pickaxe. Clouds of dirt fly up, forming the same message over and over.

> **SORRY, WE'RE STILL UNDER CONSTRUCTION**
> **BUT KEEP CHECKING BACK!**
> **"We are made to persist, that's how we find out who we are."**
> **Tobias Wolfe**

Another idea worthy of *Reader's Digest*, Hodges thinks, and goes to his window. Morning traffic on Lower Marlborough is moving briskly. He realizes, with wonder and gratitude, that the pain in his side has entirely disappeared for the first time in days. He could almost believe nothing is wrong with him, but the bitter taste in his mouth contradicts that.

The bitter taste, he thinks. The *residue*.

His cell rings. It's Norma Wilmer, her voice pitched so low he has to strain to hear. "If this is about the so-called visitors list, I haven't had a chance to look for it yet. This place is crawling with police and cheap suits from the district attorney's office. You'd think Hartsfield escaped instead of died."

"It's not about the list, although I still need that info, and if you can get it to me today, it's worth another fifty dollars. Get it to me before noon, and I'll make it a hundred."

"Jesus, what's the big deal with this? I asked Georgia Frederick—she's been bouncing back and forth between Ortho and the Bucket for the last ten years—and she says the only person she ever saw visiting Hartsfield besides you was some ratty chick with tattoos and a Marine haircut."

This rings no bells with Hodges, but there *is* a faint vibration. Which he doesn't trust. He wants to put this thing together too badly, and that means he must step with special care.

"What *do* you want, Bill? I'm in a fucking linen closet, it's hot, and I've got a headache."

"My old partner called and told me Brady swallowed some shit and killed himself. What that says to me is he must have stockpiled enough dope over time to do it. Is that possible?"

"It is. It's also possible I could land a 767 jumbo jet if the whole flight crew died of food poisoning, but both things are very fucking unlikely. I'll tell you what I told the cops and the two most annoying yappers from the DA's office. Brady got Anaprox-DS on PE days, one pill with food before, one late in the day if he asked, which he rarely did. Anaprox isn't really much more powerful when it comes to controlling pain than Advil, which you can buy OTC. He also had Extra Strength Tylenol on his chart, but only asked for it on a few occasions."

"How did the DA guys react to that?"

"Right now they're operating under the theory that he swallowed a shitload of Anaprox."

"But you don't buy it?"

"Of course I don't! Where would he hide that many pills, up his bony bedsored ass? I have to go. I'll get back to you on the visitors list. If there ever was one, that is."

"Thank you, Norma. Try some Anaprox for that headache of yours."

"Fuck you, Bill." But she says it with a laugh.

15

The first thought to cross Hodges's mind when Jerome walks in is Holy shit, kiddo, you grew up!

When Jerome Robinson came to work for him—first as the kid who cut his grass, then as an all-around handyman, finally as the tech angel who kept his computer up and running—he was a weedy teenager, going about five-eight and a hundred and forty pounds. The young giant in the doorway is six-two if he's an inch, and at least a hundred and ninety. He was always good-looking, but now he's movie star good-looking and all muscled out.

The subject in question breaks into a grin, strides quickly across the office, and embraces Hodges. He squeezes, but lets go in a hurry when he sees Hodges wince. "Jesus, sorry."

"You didn't hurt me, just happy to see you, my man." His vision is a little blurry and he wipes at his eyes with the heel of his hand. "You're a sight for sore eyes."

"You too. How you feeling?"

"Right now, good. I've got pills for pain, but you're better medicine."

Holly is standing in the doorway, sensible winter coat unzipped, small hands linked at her waist. She's watching them with an unhappy smile. Hodges wouldn't have believed there was such a thing, but apparently there is.

"Come on over, Holly," he says. "No group hug, I promise. Have you filled Jerome in on this business?"

"He knows about Barbara's part, but I thought I'd better let you tell the rest."

Jerome briefly cups the back of Hodges's neck with a big warm hand. "Holly says you're going into the hospital tomorrow for more tests and a treatment plan, and if you try to argue, I'm supposed to tell you to shut up."

"Not shut up," Holly says, looking at Jerome severely. "I never used that phrase."

Jerome grins. "You had be quiet on your lips, but shut up in your eyes."

"Fool," she says, but the smile returns. Happy we're together, Hodges thinks, sad because of the reason why. He breaks up this strangely pleasant sibling rivalry by asking how Barbara is.

"Okay. Fractures of the tibia and fibula, mid-shaft. Could have happened on the soccer field or skiing on a bunny slope. Supposed to heal with no problem. She's got a cast and is already complaining about how it itches underneath. Mom went out to get her a scratcher thing."

"Holly, did you show her the six-pack?"

"I did, and she picked out Dr. Babineau. Never even hesitated."

I have a few questions for you, Doc, Hodges thinks, and I intend to get some answers before my last day is over. If I have to squeeze you to get them, make your eyes pop out a little, that will be just fine.

Jerome settles on one corner of Hodges's desk, his usual perch. "Run through the whole thing for me, from the beginning. I might see something new."

Hodges does most of the talking. Holly goes to the window and looks out on Lower Marlborough, arms crossed, hands cupping her shoulders. She adds something from time to time, but mostly she just listens.

When Hodges is done, Jerome asks, "How sure are you about this mind-over-matter thing?"

Hodges considers. "Eighty percent. Maybe more. It's wild, but there are too many stories to discount it."

"If he could do it, it's my fault," Holly says without turning from the window. "When I hit him with your Happy Slapper, Bill, it could have rearranged his brains somehow. Given him access to the ninety percent of gray matter we never use."

"Maybe," Hodges says, "but if you hadn't clobbered him, you and Jerome would be dead."

"Along with a lot of other people," Jerome says. "And the hit might not have had anything to do with it. Whatever Babineau was feeding him could have done more than bring him out of his coma. Experimental drugs sometimes have unexpected effects, you know."

"Or it could have been a combination of the two," Hodges says. He can't believe they're having this conversation, but not to have it would fly in the face of rule one in the detective biz: you go where the facts lead you.

"He hated you, Bill," Jerome says. "Instead of killing yourself, which is what he wanted, you came after him."

"And turned his own weapon against him," Holly adds, still without turning and still hugging herself. "You used Debbie's Blue Umbrella to force him into the open. It was him who sent you that message two nights ago, I know it was. Brady Harts-field, calling himself Z-Boy." Now she turns. "It's as plain as the nose on your face. You stopped him at the Mingo—"

"No, I was downstairs having a heart attack. You were the one who stopped him, Holly."

She shakes her head fiercely. "He doesn't know that, *because he never saw me.* Do you think I could forget what happened that night? I'll never forget it. Barbara was sitting across the aisle a few rows up, and it was her he was looking at, not me. I shouted something at him, and hit him as soon as he started to turn his head. Then I hit him again. Oh God, I hit him so *hard*."

Jerome starts toward her, but she motions him back. Eye contact is hard for her, but now she's looking straight at Hodges, and her eyes are blazing.

"*You* goaded him out into the open, *you* were the one who figured out his password so we could crack his computer and find out what he was going to do. You were the one he always blamed. I *know* that. And then you kept going to his room, sitting there and talking to him."

"And you think that's why he did this, whatever *this* is?"

"*No!*" She nearly shrieks it. "*He did it because he was fracking crazy!*" There's a pause, and then in a meek voice she says she's sorry for raising her voice.

"Don't apologize, Hollyberry," Jerome says. "You thrill me when you're masterful."

She makes a face at him. Jerome snorts a laugh and asks Hodges about Dinah Scott's Zappit. "I'd like a look at it."

"My coat pocket," Hodges says, "but watch out for the Fishin' Hole demo."

Jerome rummages in Hodges's coat, rejects a roll of Tums and the ever-present detective's notebook, and brings out Dinah's green Zappit. "Holy joe. I thought these things went out with VCRs and dial-up modems."

"They pretty much did," Holly says, "and the price didn't help. I checked. A hundred and eighty-nine dollars, suggested retail, back in 2012. Ridiculous."

Jerome tosses the Zappit from hand to hand. His face is grim, and he looks tired. Well, sure, Hodges thinks. He was building houses in Arizona yesterday. Had to rush home because his normally cheerful sister tried to kill herself.

Maybe Jerome sees some of this on Hodges's face. "Barb's leg will be fine. It's her mind I'm a little worried about. She talks about blue flashes, and a voice she heard. Coming from the game."

"She says it's still in her head," Holly adds. "Like some piece of music that turns into an earworm. It will probably pass in time, now that her game is broken, but what about the others who got the consoles?"

"With the badconcert website down, is there any way of finding out how many others did?"

Holly and Jerome look at each other, then give identical head shakes.

"Shit," Hodges says. "I mean I'm not all that surprised, but still . . . shit."

"Does this one give out blue flashes?" Jerome still hasn't turned the Zappit on, just keeps playing hot potato with it.

"Nope, and the pink fish don't turn into numbers. Try it for yourself."

Instead of doing that, Jerome turns it over and opens the battery compartment. "Plain old double As," he says. "The rechargeable kind. No magic there. But the Fishin' Hole demo really makes you sleepy?"

"It did me," Hodges says. He does not add that he was medicated up the wazoo at the time. "Right now I'm more interested in Babineau. He's part of this. I don't understand how that partnership came about, but if he's still alive, he's going to tell us. And there's someone else involved, too."

"The man the housekeeper saw," Holly says. "The one who drives an old car with the primer spots. Do you want to know what I think?"

"Hit me."

"One of them, either Dr. Babineau or the man with the old car, paid a visit to the nurse, Ruth Scapelli. Hartsfield must have had something against her."

"How could he send anyone anywhere?" Jerome asks, sliding the battery cover back into place with a click. "Mind control? According to you, Bill, the most he could do with his teleki-whatzis was turn on the water in his bathroom, and it's hard for me to accept even that. It could be just so much talk. A hospital legend instead of an urban one."

"It has to be the games," Hodges muses. "He did something to the games. Amped them up, somehow."

"From his hospital room?" Jerome gives him a look that says be serious.

"I know, it doesn't make sense, not even if you add in the tele-kinesis. But it has to be the games. *Has* to be."

"Babineau will know," Holly says.

"She's a poet and don't know it," Jerome says moodily. He's still tossing the console back and forth. Hodges has a feeling that he's resisting an impulse to throw it on the floor and stomp on it, and that's sort of reasonable. After all, one just like it almost got his sister killed.

No, Hodges thinks. Not just like it. The Fishin' Hole demo on Dinah's Zappit generates a mild hypnotic effect, but nothing else. And it's probably . . .

He straightens suddenly, provoking a twinge of pain in his side. "Holly, have you searched for Fishin' Hole info on the Net?"

"No," she says. "I never thought of it."

"Would you do it now? What I want to know—"

"If there's chatter about the demo screen. I should have

thought of that myself. I'll do it now." She hurries into the outer office.

"What I don't understand," Hodges says, "is why Brady would kill himself before seeing how it all came out."

"You mean before seeing how many kids he could get to off themselves," Jerome says. "Kids who were at that fucking concert. Because that's what we're talking about, isn't it?"

"Yeah," Hodges says. "There are too many blank spots, Jerome. Far too many. I don't even know *how* he killed himself. If he actually did."

Jerome presses the heels of his hands to his temples as if to keep his brain from swelling. "Please don't tell me you think he's still alive."

"No, he's dead, all right. Pete wouldn't make a mistake about that. What I'm saying is maybe somebody murdered him. Based on what we know, Babineau would be the prime suspect."

"Holy poop!" Holly cries from the other room.

Hodges and Jerome happen to be looking at each other when she says it, and there is a moment of divine harmony as they both struggle against laughter.

"What?" Hodges calls. It's all he can manage without bursting into mad brays of hilarity, which would hurt his side as well as Holly's feelings.

"I found a site called Fishin' Hole Hypnosis! The start-page warns parents not to let their kids look at the demo screen too long! It was first noticed in the arcade game version back in 2005! The Game Boy fixed it, but the Zappit . . . wait a sec . . . they *said* they did, but they didn't! There's a whole big long thread!"

Hodges looks at Jerome.

"She means an online conversation," Jerome says.

"A kid in Des Moines passed out, hit his head on the edge of his desk, and fractured his skull!" She sounds almost gleeful as she gets up and rushes back to them. Her cheeks are flushed and rosy. "There would have been lawsuits! I bet that's one of the reasons the Zappit company went out of business! It might even have been one of the reasons why Sunrise Solutions—"

The phone on her desk begins to ring.

"Oh, frack," she says, turning toward it.

"Tell whoever it is that we're closed today."

But after saying Hello, you've reached Finders Keepers, Holly just listens. Then she turns, holding out the handset.

"It's Pete Huntley. He says he has to talk to you right away, and he sounds . . . funny. Like he's sad or mad or something."

Hodges goes into the outer office to find out what's got Pete sounding sad or mad or something.

Behind him, Jerome finally powers up Dinah Scott's Zappit.

In Freddi Linklatter's computer nest (Freddi herself has taken four Excedrin and gone to sleep in her bedroom), 44 FOUND changes to 45 FOUND. The repeater flashes LOADING.

Then it flashes TASK COMPLETE.

16

Pete doesn't say hello. What he says is, "Take it, Kerm. Take it and beat it until the truth falls out. Bitch is in the house with a couple of SKIDs, and I'm out back in a whatever-it-is. Potting shed, I think, and it's cold as hell."

Hodges is at first too surprised to answer, and not because a pair of SKIDs—the city cops' acronym for State Criminal Investigation Division detectives—is on some scene Pete is working.

He's surprised (in truth almost flabbergasted) because in all their long association he's only heard Pete use the b-word in connection with an actual woman a single time. That was when speaking of his mother-in-law, who urged Pete's wife to leave, and took her in, along with the children, when she finally did. The bitch he's talking about this time can only be his partner, aka Miss Pretty Gray Eyes.

"Kermit? Are you there?"

"I'm here," Hodges says. "Where are you?"

"Sugar Heights. Dr. Felix Babineau's house on scenic Lilac Drive. Hell, his fucking *estate*. You know who Babineau is, I know you do. No one kept closer tabs on Brady Hartsfield than you. For awhile there he was your fucking hobby."

"*Who* you're talking about, yes. *What* you're talking about, no."

"This whole thing is going to blow up, partner, and Izzy doesn't want to get hit with the shrapnel when it does. She's got ambitions, see? Chief of Detectives in ten years, maybe Chief of Police in fifteen. I get it, but that doesn't mean I like it. She called Chief Horgan behind my back, and Horgan called the SKIDs. If it's not officially their case now, it will be by noon. They've got their perp, but the shit's not right. I know it, and Izzy does, too. She just doesn't give a rat's ass."

"You need to slow down, Pete. Tell me what's going on."

Holly is hovering anxiously. Hodges shrugs his shoulders and raises a finger: wait.

"Housekeeper gets here at seven thirty, okay? Nora Everly by name. And at the top of the drive she sees Babineau's BMW on the lawn, with a bullet hole in the windshield. She looks inside, sees blood on the steering wheel and the seat, calls 911. There's a cop car five minutes away—in the Heights there's *always* one five minutes away—and when it arrives, Everly's sitting in her car with all the doors locked, shaking like a leaf. The unis tell her to stay put, and go to the door. The place is unlocked. Mrs. Babineau—Cora—is lying dead in the hall, and I'm sure the bullet the ME digs out of her will match the one forensics dug out of the Beemer. On her forehead—are you ready for this?—there's the letter Z in black ink. More all around the downstairs, including one on the TV screen. Just like the one at the Ellerton place, and I think it was right about then my partner decided she wanted no part of this particular tarbaby."

Hodges says, "Yeah, probably," just to keep Pete talking. He grabs the pad beside Holly's computer and prints BABINEAU'S WIFE MURDERED in big block letters, like a newspaper headline. Her hand flies to her mouth.

"While one of the cops is calling Division, the other one hears snores coming from upstairs. Like a chainsaw on idle, he said. So they go up, guns drawn, and in one of the three guest bedrooms, count em, *three*, the place is fucking huge, they find an old fart fast asleep. They wake him up and he gives his name as Alvin Brooks."

"Library Al!" Hodges shouts. "From the hospital! The first Zappit I ever saw was one he showed me!"

"Yeah, that's the guy. He had a Kiner ID badge in his shirt pocket. And without prompting, he says he killed Mrs. Babineau. Claims he did it while he was hypnotized. So they cuff him, take him downstairs, and sit him on the couch. That's where Izzy and me found him when we entered the scene half an hour or so later. I don't know what's wrong with the guy, whether he had a nervous breakdown or what, but he's on Planet Purple. He keeps going off on tangents, spouting all sorts of weird shit."

Hodges recollects something Al said to him on one of his last visits to Brady's room—right around Labor Day weekend of

2014, that would have been. "Never so good as what you don't see."

"Yeah." Pete sounds surprised. "Like that. And when Izzy asked who hypnotized him, he said it was the fish. The ones by the beautiful sea."

To Hodges, this now makes sense.

"On further questioning—I did it, by then Izzy must have been in the kitchen, busy ditching the whole thing without asking for my input—he said Dr. Z told him to, I quote, 'make his mark.' Ten times, he said, and sure enough, there are ten Zs, including the one on the deceased's forehead. I asked him if Dr. Z was Dr. Babineau, and he said no, Dr. Z was Brady Hartsfield. Crazy, see?"

"Yeah," Hodges says.

"I asked him if he shot Dr. Babineau, too. He just shook his head and said he wanted to go back to sleep. Right around then Izzy comes tripping back from the kitchen and says Chief Horgan called the SKIDs, on account of Dr. B. is a high-profile guy and this is going to be a high-profile case, and besides, a pair of them happened to be right here in the city, waiting to be called to testify in a case, isn't that convenient. She won't meet my eye, she's all flushed, and when I start pointing around at all the Zs, asking her if they don't look familiar, she won't talk about it."

Hodges has never heard such anger and frustration in his old partner's voice.

"So then my cell rings, and . . . you remember when I reached out to you this morning I said the doc on call took a sample of the residue in Hartsfield's mouth? Before the ME guy even got there?"

"Yeah."

"Well, the phone call was from that doc. Simonson, his name is. The ME's analysis won't be back for two days at the soonest, but Simonson did one right away. The stuff in Hartsfield's mouth was a combination of Vicodin and Ambien. Hartsfield wasn't prescribed either one, and he could hardly dance his way down to the nearest med locker and score some, could he?"

Hodges, who already knows what Brady was taking for pain, agrees that that would be unlikely.

"Right now Izzy's in the house, probably watching from the background and keeping her mouth shut while the SKIDs question this Brooks guy, who honest-to-God can't remember his own name unless he's prompted. Otherwise he calls himself Z-Boy. Like something out of a Marvel comic book."

Clutching the pen in his hand almost hard enough to snap it in two, Hodges prints more headline caps on the pad, with Holly bending over to read as he writes: LIBRARY AL LEFT THE MESSAGE ON DEBBIE'S BLUE UMBRELLA.

Holly stares at him with wide eyes.

"Just before the SKIDs arrived—man, they didn't take long— I asked Brooks if he also killed Brady Hartsfield. Izzy says to him, 'Don't answer that!'"

"She said *what*?" Hodges exclaims. He doesn't have much room in his head right now to worry about Pete's deteriorating relationship with his partner, but he's still amazed. Izzy's a police detective, after all, not Library Al's defense attorney.

"You heard me. Then she looks at me and says, 'You haven't given him the words.' So I turn to one of the uniforms and ask, 'Did you guys Mirandize this gentleman?' And of course they say yeah. I look at Izzy and she's redder in the face than ever, but she won't back down. She says, 'If we fuck this up, it won't come back on you, you're done in another couple of weeks, but it'll come back on me, and hard.'"

"So the state boys turn up . . ."

"Yeah, and now I'm out here in the late Mrs. Babineau's potting shed, or whatever the fuck it is, freezing my ass off. The richest part of the city, Kerm, and I'm in a shack colder than a welldigger's belt buckle. I bet Izzy knows I'm calling you, too. Tattling to my dear old uncle Kermit."

Pete is probably right about that. But if Miss Pretty Gray Eyes is as set on climbing the ladder as Pete believes, she's probably thinking of an uglier word: snitching.

"This Brooks guy is out of whatever little mind he's got left, which makes him the perfect donkey to pin the tail on when this hits the media. You know how they're going to lay it out?"

Hodges does, but lets Pete say it.

"Brooks got it in his head that he was some avenger of justice called Z-Boy. He came here, he killed Mrs. Babineau when she opened the door, then killed the doc himself when Babineau got in his Beemer and tried to flee. Brooks then drove to the hospital and fed Hartsfield a bunch of pills from the Babineaus' private stash. I don't doubt that part, because they had a fucking pharmacy in their medicine cabinet. And sure, he could have gotten up to the Brain Injury Clinic without any problem, he's got an ID card, and he's been a hospital fixture for the last six or seven years, but *why*? And what did he do with Babineau's body? Because it's not here."

"Good question."

Pete plunges on. "They'll say Brooks loaded it into his own car and ditched it somewhere, probably in a ravine or a culvert, and probably when he was coming back from feeding Hartsfield those pills, but why do that when he left the woman's body lying right there in the hall? And why come back here in the first place?"

"They'll say—"

"Yeah, that he's crazy! Sure they will! Perfect answer for anything that doesn't make sense! And if Ellerton and Stover come up at all—which they probably won't—they'll say he killed them, too!"

If they do, Hodges thinks, Nancy Alderson will backstop the story, at least to a degree. Because it was undoubtedly Library Al that she saw watching the house on Hilltop Court.

"They'll hang Brooks out to dry, wade through the press coverage, and call it good. But there's more to it, Kerm. Got to be. If you know anything, if you've got even a single thread to pull, pull it. Promise me you will."

I have more than one, Hodges thinks, but Babineau's the key, and Babineau has disappeared.

"How much blood was in the car, Pete?"

"Not a lot, but forensics has already confirmed it's Babineau's type. That's not conclusive, but . . . shit. I gotta go. Izzy and one of the SKID guys just came out the back door. They're looking for me."

"All right."

"Call me. And if you need anything I can access, let me know."

"I will."

Hodges ends the call and looks up, wanting to fill Holly in, but Holly is no longer beside him.

"Bill." Her voice is low. "Come in here."

Puzzled, he walks to the door of his office, where he stops dead. Jerome is behind the desk, sitting in Hodges's swivel chair. His long legs are splayed out and he's looking at Dinah Scott's Zappit. His eyes are wide open but empty. His mouth hangs ajar. There are fine drops of spittle on his lower lip. A tune is tinkling from the gadget's tiny speaker, but not the same tune as last night—Hodges is sure of it.

"Jerome?" He takes a step forward, but before he can take another, Holly grabs him by the belt. Her grip is surprisingly strong.

"No," she says in the same low voice. "You shouldn't startle him. Not when he's like that."

"What, then?"

"I had a year of hypnotherapy when I was in my thirties. I was having problems with . . . well, never mind what I was having problems with. Let me try."

"Are you sure?"

She looks at him, her face now pale, her eyes fearful. "No, but we can't leave him like that. Not after what happened to Barbara."

The Zappit in Jerome's limp hands gives off a bright blue flash. Jerome doesn't react, doesn't blink, only continues staring at the screen while the music tinkles.

Holly takes a step forward, then another. "Jerome?"

No answer.

"Jerome, can you hear me?"

"Yes," Jerome says, not looking up from the screen.

"Jerome, where are you?"

And Jerome says, "At my funeral. Everyone is there. It's beautiful."

17

Brady became fascinated with suicide at the age of twelve, while reading *Raven*, a true-crime book about the mass suicides in Jonestown, Guyana. There, more than nine hundred people—a third of them children—died after drinking fruit juice laced with cyanide. What interested Brady, aside from the thrillingly high body count, was the lead-up to the final orgy. Long before the day when whole families swallowed the poison together and nurses (*actual nurses!*) used hypodermics to squirt death down the throats of squalling infants, Jim Jones was preparing his followers for their apotheosis with fiery sermons and suicide rehearsals he called White Nights. He first filled them with paranoia, then hypnotized them with the glamour of death.

As a senior, Brady wrote his only A paper, for a half-assed sociology class called American Life. The paper was called "American Deathways: A Brief Study of Suicide in the U.S." In it he cited the statistics for 1999, then the most recent year for which they were available. More than forty thousand people had killed themselves during that year, usually with guns (the most reliable go-to method), but with pills running a close second. They also hung themselves, drowned themselves, bled out, stuck their heads in gas ovens, set themselves on fire, and rammed their cars into bridge abutments. One inventive fellow (this Brady did not put into his report; even then he was careful not to be branded an oddity) stuck a 220-volt line up his rectum and electrocuted himself. In 1999, suicide was the tenth leading cause of death in America, and if you added in the ones that were reported as accidents or "natural causes," it would undoubtedly be right up there with heart disease, cancer, and car crashes. Most likely still behind them, but not *far* behind.

Brady quoted Albert Camus, who said, "There is but one truly serious philosophical problem, and that is suicide."

He also quoted a famous psychiatrist named Raymond Katz, who stated flatly, "Every human being is born with the suicide gene." Brady did not bother to add the second part of Katz's statement, because he felt it took some of the drama out of it: "In most of us, it remains dormant."

In the ten years between his graduation from high school and that disabling moment in the Mingo Auditorium, Brady's fascination with suicide—including his own, always seen as part of some grand and historic gesture—continued.

This seed has now, against all the odds, fully blossomed.

He will be the Jim Jones of the twenty-first century.

## 18

Forty miles north of the city, he can wait no longer. Brady pulls into a rest area on I-47, kills the laboring engine of Z-Boy's Malibu, and powers up Babineau's laptop. There's no WiFi here, as there is at some rest areas, but thanks to Big Momma Verizon, there's a cell tower not four miles away, standing tall against the thickening clouds. Using Babineau's MacBook Air, he can go anywhere he wants and never have to leave this nearly deserted parking lot. He thinks (and not for the first time) that a touch of telekinesis is nothing compared to the power of the Internet. He's sure thousands of suicides have incubated in the potent soup of its social media sites, where the trolls run free and the bullying goes on endlessly. That's *real* mind over matter.

He's not able to type as fast as he'd like to—the damp air pushing in with the coming storm has worsened the arthritis in Babineau's fingers—but eventually the laptop is mated to the high-powered gear back in Freddi Linklatter's computer room. He won't have to stay mated to it for long. He clicks on a hidden file he placed on the laptop during one of his previous visits inside Babineau's head.

OPEN LINK TO ZEETHEEND? Y N

He centers the cursor on Y, hits the return key, then waits. The worry-circle goes around and around and around. Just as he's begun to wonder if something has gone wrong, the laptop flashes the message he's been waiting for:

ZEETHEEND IS NOW ACTIVE

Good. Zeetheend is just a little icing on the cake. He has been able to disseminate only a limited number of Zappits—and a significant portion of his shipment was defective, for Christ's sake—but teenagers are herd creatures, and herd creatures are in mental and emotional lockstep. It's why fish school and bees swarm. It's why the swallows come back each year to Capistrano. In human behavior, it's why "the wave" goes around at football and baseball stadiums, and why individuals will lose themselves in a crowd simply because the crowd is there.

Teenage boys have a tendency to wear the same baggy shorts and grow the same scruff on their faces, lest they be excluded from the herd. Teenage girls adopt the same styles of dress and go crazy for the same musical groups. It's We R Your Bruthas this year; not so long ago it was 'Round Here and One Direction. Back in the day it was New Kids on the Block. Fads sweep through teenagers like a measles epidemic, and from time to time, one of those fads is suicide. In southern Wales, dozens of teens hung themselves between 2007 and 2009, with messages on social networking sites stoking the craze. Even the goodbyes they left were couched in Netspeak: Me2 and CU L8er.

Wildfires vast enough to burn millions of acres can be started by a single match thrown into dry brush. The Zappits Brady has distributed through his human drones are hundreds of matches. Not all of them will light, and some of those that do won't stay lit. Brady knows this, but he has zeetheend.com to serve as both backstop and accelerant. Will it work? He's far from sure, but time is too short for extensive tests.

And if it does?

Teen suicides all over the state, maybe all over the Midwest. Hundreds, perhaps thousands. How would you like that, ex-Detective Hodges? Would that improve your retirement, you meddlesome old fuck?

He swaps Babineau's laptop for Z-Boy's game console. It's fitting to use this one. He thinks of it as Zappit Zero, because it's the first one he ever saw, on the day Al Brooks brought it into his room, thinking Brady might like it. Which he did. Oh yes, very much.

The extra program, with the number-fish and the subliminal messages, hasn't been added to this one, because Brady doesn't need it. Those things are strictly for the targets. He watches the fish swim back and forth, using them to settle and focus, then closes his eyes. At first there's only darkness, but after a few moments red lights begin to appear—more than fifty now. They are like dots on a computer map, except they don't remain stationary. They swim back and forth, left to right, up and down, crisscrossing. He settles on one at random, his eyes rolling beneath his closed lids as he follows its progress. It begins to slow, and slow, and slow. It stills, then starts growing bigger. It opens like a flower.

He's in a bedroom. There's a girl, staring fixedly down at the fish on her own Zappit, which she received free from badcon cert.com. She's in her bed because she didn't go to school today. Maybe she said she was sick.

"What's your name?" Brady asks.

Sometimes they just hear a voice coming from the game console, but the ones who are most susceptible actually see him, like some kind of avatar in a video game. This girl is one of the latter, an auspicious beginning. But they always respond better to their names, so he'll keep saying it. She looks without surprise at the young man sitting beside her on the bed. Her face is pale. Her eyes are dazed.

"I'm Ellen," she says. "I'm looking for the right numbers."

Of course you are, he thinks, and slips into her. She's forty miles south of him, but once the demo screen has opened them, distance doesn't matter. He could control her, turn her into one of his drones, but he doesn't want to do that any more than he wanted to slip into Mrs. Trelawney's house some dark night and cut her throat. Murder isn't control; murder is just murder.

*Suicide* is control.

"Are you happy, Ellen?"

"I used to be," she says. "I could be again, if I find the right numbers."

Brady gives her a smile that's both sad and charming. "Yes, but the numbers are like life," he says. "Nothing adds up, Ellen. Isn't that true?"

"Uh-huh."

"Tell me something, Ellen—what are you worried about?" He could find it himself, but it will be better if she tells him. He knows there's something, because everyone worries, and teenagers worry most of all.

"Right now? The SAT."

Ah-ha, he thinks, the infamous Scholastic Assessment Test, where the Department of Academic Husbandry separates the sheep from the goats.

"I'm so bad at math," she says. "I reek."

"Bad at the numbers," he says, nodding sympathetically.

"If I don't score at least six-fifty, I won't get into a good school."

"And you'll be lucky to score four hundred," he says. "Isn't that the truth, Ellen?"

"Yes." Tears well in her eyes and begin to roll down her cheeks.

"And then you'll do badly on the English, too," Brady says. He's opening her up, and this is the best part. It's like reaching into an animal that's stunned but still alive, and digging its guts out. "You'll freeze up."

"I'll probably freeze up," Ellen says. She's sobbing audibly now. Brady checks her short-term memory and finds that her parents have gone to work and her little brother is at school. So crying is all right. Let the bitch make all the noise she wants.

"Not probably. You *will* freeze up, Ellen. Because you can't handle the pressure."

She sobs.

"Say it, Ellen."

"I can't handle the pressure. I'll freeze, and if I don't get into a good school, my dad will be disappointed and my mother will be mad."

"What if you can't get into *any* school? What if the only job you can get is cleaning houses or folding clothes in a laundrymat?"

"My mother will hate me!"

"She hates you already, doesn't she, Ellen?"

"I don't . . . I don't think . . ."

"Yes she does, she hates you. Say it, Ellen. Say 'My mother hates me.'"

"My mother hates me. Oh God, I'm so scared and my life is so awful!"

This is the great gift bestowed by a combination of Zappit-induced hypnosis and Brady's own ability to invade minds once they are in that open and suggestible state. Ordinary fears, the ones kids like this live with as a kind of unpleasant background noise, can be turned into ravening monsters. Small balloons of paranoia can be inflated until they are as big as floats in the Macy's Thanksgiving Day Parade.

"You could stop being scared," Brady says. "And you could make your mother very, very sorry."

Ellen smiles through her tears.

"You could leave all this behind."

"I could. I could leave it behind."

"You could be at peace."

"Peace," she says, and sighs.

How wonderful this is. It took weeks with Martine Stover's mother, who was always leaving the demo screen to play her goddam solitaire, and days with Barbara Robinson. With Ruth Scapelli and this pimple-faced crybaby in her poofy-pink girl's bedroom? Mere minutes. But then, Brady thinks, I always had a steep learning curve.

"Do you have your phone, Ellen?"

"Here." She reaches under a decorative throw pillow. Her phone is also poofy-pink.

"You should post on Facebook and Twitter. So all your friends can read it."

"What should I post?"

"Say 'I am at peace now. You can be, too. Go to zeetheend.com.'"

She does it, but at an oozingly slow speed. When they're in this state, it's like they're underwater. Brady reminds himself of how well this is going and tries not to become impatient. When she's done and the messages are sent—more matches flicked into dry tinder—he suggests that she go to the window. "I think you could use some fresh air. It might clear your head."

294

"I could use some fresh air," she says, throwing back the duvet and swinging her bare feet out of bed.

"Don't forget your Zappit," he says.

She takes it and walks to the window.

"Before you open the window, go to the main screen, where the icons are. Can you do that, Ellen?"

"Yes . . ." A long pause. The bitch is slower than cold molasses. "Okay, I see the icons."

"Great. Now go to WipeWords. It's the blackboard-and-eraser icon."

"I see it."

"Tap it twice, Ellen."

She does so, and the Zappit gives an acknowledging blue flash. If anyone tries to use this particular game console again, it will give a final blue flash and drop dead.

"*Now* you can open the window."

Cold air rushes in, blowing her hair back. She wavers, seems on the edge of waking, and for a moment Brady feels her slipping away. Control is still hard to maintain at a distance, even when they're in a hypnotic state, but he's sure he'll hone his technique to a nice sharp point. Practice makes perfect.

"Jump," Brady whispers. "Jump, and you won't have to take the SAT. Your mother won't hate you. She'll be sorry. Jump and all the numbers will come right. You'll get the best prize. The prize is sleep."

"The prize is sleep," Ellen agrees.

"Do it now," Brady murmurs as he sits behind the wheel of Al Brooks's old car with his eyes closed.

Forty miles south, Ellen jumps from her bedroom window. It's not a long drop, and there's banked snow against the house. It's old and crusty, but it still cushions her fall to a degree, so instead of dying, she only breaks a collarbone and three ribs. She begins to scream in pain, and Brady is blown out of her head like a pilot strapped to an F-111 ejection seat.

"Shit!" he screams, and pounds the steering wheel. Babineau's arthritis flares all the way up his arm, and that makes him angrier still. "Shit, shit, *shit*!"


19


In the pleasantly upscale neighborhood of Branson Park, Ellen Murphy struggles to her feet. The last thing she remembers is telling her mother she was too sick to go to school—a lie so she could tap pink fish and hunt for prizes on the pleasantly addictive Fishin' Hole demo. Her Zappit is lying nearby, the screen cracked. It no longer interests her. She leaves it and begins staggering toward the front door on bare feet. Each breath she takes is a stab in the side.

But I'm alive, she thinks. At least I'm alive. What was I thinking? What in God's name was I thinking?

Brady's voice is still with her: the slimy taste of something awful that she swallowed while it was still alive.


20


"Jerome?" Holly asks. "Can you still hear me?"

"Yes."

"I want you to turn off the Zappit and put it on Bill's desk." And then, because she's always been a belt-and-suspenders kind of girl, she adds: "Facedown."

A frown creases his broad brow. "Do I have to?"

"Yes. Right now. And without looking at the damn thing."

Before Jerome can follow this order, Hodges catches one final glimpse of the fish swimming, and one more bright blue flash. A momentary dizziness—perhaps caused by his pain pills, perhaps not—sweeps through him. Then Jerome pushes the button on top of the console, and the fish disappear.

What Hodges feels isn't relief but disappointment. Maybe that's crazy, but given his current medical problem, maybe it's not. He's seen hypnosis used from time to time to help witnesses achieve better recall, but has never grasped its full power until now. He has an idea, probably blasphemous in this situation, that the Zappit fish might be better medicine for pain than the stuff Dr. Stamos prescribed.

Holly says, "I'm going to count down from ten to one, Jerome. Each time you hear a number, you'll be a little more awake. Okay?"

For several seconds Jerome says nothing. He sits calmly, peacefully, touring some other reality and perhaps trying to decide if he would like to live there permanently. Holly, on the other hand, is vibrating like a tuning fork, and Hodges can feel his fingernails biting into his palms as he clenches his fists.

At last Jerome says, "Okay, I guess. Since it's you, Hollyberry."

"Here we go. Ten . . . nine . . . eight . . . you're coming back . . . seven . . . six . . . five . . . waking up . . ."

Jerome raises his head. His eyes are aimed at Hodges, but Hodges isn't sure the boy is seeing him.

"Four . . . three . . . almost there . . . two . . . one . . . *wake up!*" She claps her hands together.

Jerome gives a hard jerk. One hand brushes Dinah's Zappit and knocks it to the floor. Jerome looks at Holly with an expression of surprise so exaggerated it would be funny under other circumstances.

"What just happened? Did I go to sleep?"

Holly collapses into the chair ordinarily reserved for clients. She takes a deep breath and wipes her cheeks, which are damp with sweat.

"In a way," Hodges says. "The game hypnotized you. Like it hypnotized your sister."

"Are you sure?" Jerome asks, then looks at his watch. "I guess you are. I just lost fifteen minutes."

"Closer to twenty. What do you remember?"

"Tapping the pink fish and turning them into numbers. It's surprisingly hard to do. You have to watch closely, really concentrate, and the blue flashes don't help."

Hodges picks the Zappit up off the floor.

"I wouldn't turn that on," Holly says sharply.

"Not going to. But I did last night, and I can tell you there were no blue flashes, and you could tap pink fish until your finger went numb without getting any numbers. Also, the tune is different now. Not much, but a little."

Holly sings, pitch perfect: "'By the sea, by the sea, by the beautiful sea, you and me, you and me, oh how happy we'll be.' My mother used to sing it to me when I was little."

Jerome is staring at her with more intensity than she can deal with, and she looks away, flustered. "What? What is it?"

"There were words," he says, "but not those."

Hodges heard no words, only the tune, but doesn't say so. Holly asks Jerome if he can remember them.

His pitch isn't as good as hers, but it's close enough for them to be sure that yes, it's the tune they heard. "'You can sleep, you can sleep, it's a beautiful sleep . . .'" He stops. "That's all I can remember. If I'm not just making it up, that is."

Holly says, "Now we know for sure. Someone amped the Fishin' Hole screen."

"Shot it full of 'roids," Jerome adds.

"What does that even mean?" Hodges asks.

Jerome nods to Holly and she says, "Someone loaded a stealth program into the demo, which is mildly hypnotic to begin with. The program was dormant when Dinah had the Zappit, and still dormant when you looked at it last night, Bill—which was lucky for you—but someone turned it on after that."

"Babineau?"

"Him or someone else, if the police are right and Babineau is dead."

"It could have been a preset," Jerome says to Holly. Then, to Hodges: "You know, like an alarm clock."

"Let me get this straight," Hodges says. "The program was in there all along, and only became active once Dinah's Zappit was turned on today?"

"Yes," Holly says. "There's probably a repeater at work, don't you think, Jerome?"

"Yeah. A computer program that pumps out the update constantly, waiting for some schlub—me, in this case—to turn on a Zappit and activate the WiFi."

"This could happen with *all* of them?"

"If the stealth program is in all of them, sure," Jerome says.

"Brady set this up." Hodges begins to pace, hand going to his side as if to contain the pain and hold it in. "Brady fucking Hartsfield."

"How?" Holly asks.

"I don't know, but it's the only thing that fits. He tries to blow up the Mingo during that concert. We stop him. The audience, most of them young girls, is saved."

"By you, Holly," Jerome says.

"Be quiet, Jerome. Let him tell it." Her eyes suggest she knows where Hodges is going.

"Six years pass. Those young girls, most of them in elementary or middle school in 2010, are in high school. Maybe in college. 'Round Here is long gone and the girls are young women now, they've moved on to other kinds of music, but then they get an offer they can't refuse. A free game console, and all they have to do is be able to prove they were at the 'Round Here show that night. The console probably looks as out-of-date to them as a black-and-white TV, but what the hell, it's free."

"Yes!" Holly says. "Brady was still after them. This is his revenge, but not just on them. It's his revenge on *you*, Bill."

Which makes me responsible, Hodges thinks bleakly. Except what else could I do? What else could any of us do? He was going to bomb the place.

"Babineau, going under the name of Myron Zakim, bought eight hundred of those consoles. It had to be him, because he's loaded. Brady was broke and I doubt Library Al could have fronted even twenty thousand dollars from his retirement savings. Those consoles are out there now. And if they all get this amped-up program once they're turned on . . ."

"Hold it, go back," Jerome says. "Are you really saying that a respected neurosurgeon got involved in this shit?"

"That's what I'm saying, yeah. Your sister ID'd him, and we already know the respected neurosurgeon was using Brady Hartsfield as a lab rat."

"But now Hartsfield's dead," Holly says. "Which leaves Babineau, who may also be dead."

"Or not," Hodges says. "There was blood in his car, but no body. Wouldn't be the first time some doer tried to fake his own death."

"I've got to check something on my computer," Holly says. "If those free Zappits are getting a new program as of today, then maybe . . ." She hurries out.

Jerome begins, "I don't understand how any of this can be, but—"

"Babineau will be able to tell us," Hodges says. "If he's still alive."

"Yes, but wait a minute. Barb talked about hearing a voice, telling her all sorts of awful things. I didn't hear any voice, and I sure don't feel like offing myself."

"Maybe you're immune."

"I'm not. That screen got me, Bill, I mean I was *gone*. I heard words in the little tune, and I think there were words in the blue flashes, too. Like subliminal messages. But . . . no voice."

There could be all sorts of reasons for that, Hodges thinks, and just because Jerome didn't hear the suicide voice, it doesn't mean that most of the kids who got those free games won't.

"Let's say this repeater gadget was only turned on during the last fourteen hours," Hodges says. "We know it can't have been earlier than when I tried out Dinah's game, or I would have seen the number-fish and the blue flashes. So here's a question: can those demo screens be amped up even if the gadgets are off?"

"No way," Jerome says. "They have to be turned on. But once they are . . ."

"*It's active!*" Holly shouts. "*That fracking zeetheend site is active!*"

Jerome rushes to her desk in the outer office. Hodges follows more slowly.

Holly turns up the volume on her computer, and music fills the offices of Finders Keepers. Not "By the Beautiful Sea" this time, but "Don't Fear the Reaper." As it spools out—*forty thousand men and women every day, another forty thousand coming every day*—Hodges sees a candlelit funeral parlor and a coffin buried in flowers. Above it, smiling young men and women come and go, moving side to side, crisscrossing, fading, reappearing. Some of them wave; some flash the peace sign. Below the coffin is a series of messages in letters that swell and contract like a slowly beating heart.

AN END TO PAIN
AN END TO FEAR
NO MORE ANGER
NO MORE DOUBT
NO MORE STRUGGLE
PEACE
PEACE
PEACE

Then a stuttering series of blue flashes. Embedded in them are words. Or call them what they really are, Hodges thinks. Drops of poison.

"Turn it off, Holly." Hodges doesn't like the way she's looking at the screen—that wide-eyed stare, so much like Jerome's a few minutes ago.

She moves too slowly to suit Jerome. He reaches over her shoulder and crashes her computer.

"You shouldn't have done that," she says reproachfully. "I could lose data."

"That's exactly what the fucking website is for," Jerome says. "To make you lose data. To make you lose your *shit*. I could read the last one, Bill. In the blue flash. It said *do it now*."

Holly nods. "There was another one that said *tell your friends*."

"Does the Zappit direct them to that . . . that thing?" Hodges asks.

"It doesn't have to," Jerome says. "Because the ones who find it—and plenty will, including kids who never got a free Zappit—will spread the word on Facebook and all the rest."

"He wanted a suicide epidemic," Holly says. "He set it in motion somehow, then killed himself."

"Probably to get there ahead of them," Jerome says. "So he can meet them at the door."

Hodges says, "Am I supposed to believe a rock song and a picture of a funeral is going to get kids to kill themselves? The Zappits, I can accept that. I've seen how they work. But this?"

Holly and Jerome exchange a glance, one that Hodges can read easily: How do we explain this to him? How do you explain a robin to someone who's never seen a bird? The glance alone is almost enough to convince him.

"Teenagers are vulnerable to stuff like this," Holly says. "Not all of them, no, but plenty. I would have been when I was seventeen."

"And it's catching," Jerome says. "Once it starts . . . *if* it starts . . ." He finishes with a shrug.

"We need to find that repeater gadget and turn it off," Hodges says. "Limit the damage."

"Maybe it's at Babineau's house," Holly says. "Call Pete. Find out if there's any computer stuff there. If there is, make him pull all the plugs."

"If he's with Izzy, he'll let it go to voicemail," Hodges says, but he makes the call and Pete picks up on the first ring. He tells Hodges that Izzy has gone back to the station with the SKIDs to await the first forensics reports. Library Al Brooks is already gone, taken into custody by the first responding cops, who will get partial credit for the bust.

Pete sounds tired.

"We had a blow-up. Me and Izzy. Big one. I tried to tell her what you told me when we started working together—how the case is the boss, and you go where it leads you. No ducking, no handing it off, just pick it up and follow the red thread all the way home. She stood there listening with her arms folded, nodding her head every now and then. I actually thought I was getting through to her. Then you know what she asked me? If I knew the last time there was a woman in the top echelon of the city police. I said I didn't, and she said that was because the answer was never. She said the first one was going to be her. Man, I thought I knew her." Pete utters what may be the most humorless laugh Hodges has ever heard. "I thought she was *police*."

Hodges will commiserate later, if he gets a chance. Right now there's no time. He asks about the computer gear.

"We found nothing except an iPad with a dead battery," Pete says. "Everly, the housekeeper, says he had a laptop in his study, almost brand new, but it's gone."

"Like Babineau," Hodges says. "Maybe it's with him."

"Maybe. Remember, if I can help, Kermit—"

"I'll call, believe me."

Right now he'll take all the help he can get.


21


The result with the girl named Ellen is infuriating—like the Robinson bitch all over again—but at last Brady calms down. It worked, that's what he needs to focus on. The shortness of the drop combined with the snowbank was just bad luck. There will be plenty of others. He has a lot of work ahead of him, a lot of matches to light, but once the fire is burning, he can sit back and watch.

It will burn until it burns itself out.

He starts Z-Boy's car and pulls out of the rest area. As he merges with the scant traffic headed north on I-47, the first flakes spin out of the white sky and hit the Malibu's windshield. Brady drives faster. Z-Boy's piece of crap isn't equipped for a snowstorm, and once he leaves the turnpike, the roads will grow progressively worse. He needs to beat the weather.

Oh, I'll beat it, all right, Brady thinks, and grins as a wonderful idea hits him. Maybe Ellen is paralyzed from the neck down, a head on a stick, like the Stover bitch. It's not likely, but it's possible, a pleasant daydream with which to while away the miles.

He turns on the radio, finds some Judas Priest, and lets it blast. Like Hodges, he enjoys the hard stuff.

# THE SUICIDE PRINCE

Brady won many victories in Room 217, but necessarily had to keep them to himself. Coming back from the living death of coma; discovering that he could—because of the drug Babineau had administered, or because of some fundamental alteration in his brainwaves, or perhaps due to a combination of the two— move small objects simply by thinking about them; inhabiting Library Al's brain and creating inside him a secondary personality, Z-Boy. And mustn't forget getting back at the fat cop who hit him in the balls when he couldn't defend himself. Yet the best, the absolute best, was nudging Sadie MacDonald into committing suicide. That was power.

He wanted to do it again.

The question that desire raised was a simple one: who next? It would be easy to make Al Brooks jump from a bridge overpass or swallow drain cleaner, but Z-Boy would go with him, and without Z-Boy, Brady would be stuck in Room 217, which was really nothing more than a prison cell with a parking garage view. No, he needed Brooks just where he was. And *as* he was.

More important was the question of what to do about the bastard responsible for putting him here. Ursula Haber, the Nazi who ran the PT department, said rehab patients needed GTG: goals to grow. Well, he was growing, all right, and revenge against Hodges was a worthy goal, but how to get it? Inducing Hodges to commit suicide wasn't the answer, even if there was a way to try it. He'd played the suicide game already with Hodges. And lost.

When Freddi Linklatter appeared with the picture of him and his mother, Brady was still over a year and a half from realizing how he could finish his business with Hodges, but seeing Freddi gave him a badly needed jump-start. He would need to be careful, though. Very careful.

A step at a time, he told himself as he lay awake in the small hours of the night. Just one step at a time. I have great obstacles, but I also have extraordinary weapons.

Step one was having Al Brooks remove the remaining Zappits from the hospital library. He took them to his brother's house, where he lived in an apartment over the garage. That was easy, because no one wanted them, anyway. Brady thought of them as ammo. Eventually he would find a gun that could use it.

Brooks took the Zappits on his own, although operating under commands—thoughtfish—that Brady implanted in the shallow but useful Z-Boy persona. He had become wary of entering Brooks completely and taking him over, because it burned through the old fellow's brains too fast. He had to ration those times of total immersion, and use them wisely. It was a shame, he enjoyed his vacations outside the hospital, but people were starting to notice that Library Al had become a trifle foggy upstairs. If he became *too* foggy, he would be forced out of his volunteer job. Worse, Hodges might notice. That would not be good. Let the old Det.-Ret. vacuum up all the rumors about telekinesis he wanted, Brady was fine with that, but he didn't want Hodges to catch even a whiff of what was really going on.

Despite the risk of mental depletion, Brady took complete

command of Brooks in the spring of 2013, because he needed the library computer. *Looking* at it could be done without total immersion, but *using* it was another thing. And it was a short visit. All he wanted to do was set up a Google alert, using the keywords *Zappit* and *Fishin' Hole*.

Every two or three days he sent Z-Boy to check the alert and report back. His instructions were to switch to the ESPN site if someone wandered over to see what he was surfing (they rarely did; the library was really not much more than a closet, and the few visitors were usually looking for the chapel next door).

The alerts were interesting and informative. It seemed a great many people had experienced either semi-hypnosis or actual seizure activity after looking at the Fishin' Hole demo screen for too long. That effect was more powerful than Brady would have believed. There was even an article about it in the *New York Times* business section, and the company was in trouble because of it.

Trouble it didn't need, because it was already tottering. You didn't have to be a genius (which Brady believed he was) to know that Zappit, Inc. would soon either go bankrupt or be swallowed up by a larger company. Brady was betting on bankruptcy. What company would be stupid enough to pick up an outfit making game consoles that were hopelessly out of date and ridiculously expensive, especially when one of the games was dangerously defective?

Meanwhile, there was the problem of how to jigger the ones he had (they were stored in the closet of Z-Boy's apartment, but Brady considered them his property) so that people would look at them longer. He was stuck on that when Freddi made her visit. When she was gone, her Christian duty done (not that Frederica Bimmel Linklatter was or ever had been a Christian), Brady thought long and hard.

Then, in late August of 2013, after a particularly aggravating visit from the Det.-Ret., he sent Z-Boy to her apartment.

Freddi counted the money, then studied the old fellow in the green Dickies standing slump-shouldered in the middle of what passed for her living room. The money had come from Al Brooks's account at Midwest Federal. The first withdrawal from his meager savings, but far from the last.

"Two hundred bucks for a few questions? Yeah, I can do that. But if what you really came for is a blowjob, you need to go somewhere else, old-timer. I'm a dyke."

"Just questions," Z-Boy said. He handed her a Zappit and told her to look at the Fishin' Hole demo screen. "But you shouldn't look longer than thirty seconds or so. It's, um, weird."

"Weird, huh?" She gave him an indulgent smile and turned her attention to the swimming fish. Thirty seconds became forty. That was allowable according to the directives Brady had given him before sending him on this mission (he always called them missions, having discovered that Brooks associated the word with heroism). But after forty-five, he grabbed it back.

Freddi looked up, blinking. "Whoo. It messes with your brain, doesn't it?"

"Yeah. It kinda does."

"I read in *Gamer Programming* that the Star Smash arcade game does something like that, but you have to play it for like, half an hour before the effect kicks in. This is a lot faster. Do people know about it?"

Z-Boy ignored the question. "My boss wants to know how you would fix this so people would look at the demo screen longer, and not go right to the game. Which doesn't have the same effect."

Freddi adopted her fake Russian accent for the first time. "Who is fearless leader, Z-Boy? You be good fellow and tell Comrade X, *da?*"

Z-Boy's brow wrinkled. "Huh?"

Freddi sighed. "Who's your boss, handsome?"

"Dr. Z." Brady had anticipated the question—he knew Freddi of old—and this was another directive. Brady had plans for Felix Babineau, but as yet they were vague. He was still feeling his way. Flying on instruments.

"Dr. Z and his sidekick Z-Boy," she said, lighting a cigarette. "On the path to world domination. My, my. Does that make me Z-Girl?"

This wasn't part of his directives, so he stayed silent.

"Never mind, I get it," she said, chuffing out smoke. "Your boss wants an eye-trap. The way to do it is to turn the demo screen itself into a game. Gotta be simple, though. Can't get bogged down in a lot of complex programming." She held up the Zappit, now turned off. "This thing is pretty brainless."

"What kind of game?"

"Don't ask me, bro. That's the creative side. Never was my forte. Tell your boss to figure it out. Anyway, once this thing is powered up and getting a good WiFi signal, you need to install a root kit. Want me to write this down?"

"No." Brady had allocated a bit of Al Brooks's rapidly diminishing memory storage space for this very task. Besides, when the job needed to be done, Freddi would be the one doing it.

"Once the kit's in, source code can be downloaded from another computer." She adopted the Russian accent again. "From secret Base Zero under polar ice-kep."

"Should I tell him that part?"

"No. Just tell him root kit plus source code. Got it?"

"Yes."

"Anything else?"

"Brady Hartsfield wants you to come visit him again."

Freddi's eyebrows shot up almost to her crewcut. "He *talks* to you?"

"Yes. It's hard to understand him at first, but after awhile you can."

Freddi looked around her living room—dim, cluttered, smelling of last night's take-out Chinese—as if it interested her. She was finding this conversation increasingly creepy.

"I don't know, man. I did my good deed, and I was never even a Girl Scout."

"He'll pay you," Z-Boy said. "Not very much, but . . ."

"How much?"

"Fifty dollars a visit?"

"Why?"

Z-Boy didn't know, but in 2013, there was still a fair amount of Al Brooks behind his forehead, and that was the part that understood. "I think . . . because you were a part of his life. You know, when you and him used to go out to fix people's computers. In the old days."


Brady didn't hate Dr. Babineau with the same intensity that he hated K. William Hodges, but that didn't mean Dr. B. wasn't on his shit list. Babineau had used him as a guinea pig, which was bad. He had lost interest in Brady when his experimental drug didn't seem to be working, which was worse. Worst of all, the shots had resumed once Brady had regained consciousness, and who knew what they were doing? They could kill him, but as a man who had assiduously courted his own death, that wasn't what kept him awake nights. What did was the possibility that the shots might interfere with his new abilities. Babineau pooh-poohed Brady's supposed mind-over-matter powers in public, but he actually believed they might exist, even though Brady had been careful never to exhibit his talent to the doctor, despite Babineau's repeated urgings. He believed any psychokinetic abilities were also a result of what he called Cerebellin.

The CAT scans and MRIs had also resumed. "You're the Eighth Wonder of the World," Babineau told him after one of these—in the fall of 2013, this was. He was walking beside Brady as an orderly wheeled him back to Room 217. Babineau was wearing what Brady thought of as his gloaty face. "The current protocols have done more than halt the destruction of your brain cells; they have stimulated the growth of new ones. More robust ones. Do you have any idea how remarkable that is?"

You bet, asshole, Brady thought. So keep those scans to yourself. If the DA's office found out, I'd be in trouble.

Babineau was patting Brady's shoulder in a proprietary way Brady hated. Like he was patting his pet dog. "The human brain is made up of approximately one hundred billion nerve cells. Those in the Broca's Area of yours were gravely injured, but they have recovered. In fact, they are creating neurons unlike any I've ever seen. One of these days you're going to be famous not as a person who took lives, but as one responsible for saving them."

If so, Brady thought, it's a day you won't be around to see.

Count on it, dickweed.

*The creative side never was my forte*, Freddi told Z-Boy. True enough, but it was *always* Brady's, and as 2013 became 2014, he had plenty of time to think of ways the Fishin' Hole demo screen might be juiced up and turned into what Freddi had called an eye-trap. Yet none of them seemed quite right.

They did not talk about the Zappit effect during her visits; mostly they reminisced (with Freddi necessarily doing most of the talking) about the old days on the Cyber Patrol. All the crazy people they'd met on their outcalls. And Anthony "Tones" Frobisher, their asshole boss. Freddi went on about him constantly, turning things she should have said into things she had, and *right to his face*! Freddi's visits were monotonous but comforting. They balanced his desperate nights, when he felt he might spend the rest of his life in Room 217, at the mercy of Dr. Babineau and his "vitamin shots."

*I have to stop him,* Brady thought. *I have to* control *him.*

To do that, the amped-up version of the demo screen had to be just right. If he flubbed his first chance to get into Babineau's mind, there might not be another.

The TV now played at least four hours a day in Room 217. This was per an edict from Babineau, who told Head Nurse Helmington that he was "exposing Mr. Hartsfield to external stimuli."

Mr. Hartsfield didn't mind the *News at Noon* (there was always an exciting explosion or a mass tragedy somewhere in the world), but the rest of the stuff—cooking shows, talk shows, soap operas, bogus medicine men—was drivel. Yet one day, while sitting in his chair by the window and watching *Prize Surprise* (staring in that direction, at least), he had a revelation. The contestant who had survived to the Bonus Round was given a chance to win a trip to Aruba on a private jet. She was shown an oversized computer screen where big colored dots were shuffling around. Her job was to touch five red ones, which would turn into numbers.

If the numbers she touched added up to a total within a five-digit range of 100, she'd win.

Brady watched her wide eyes moving from side to side as she studied the screen, and knew he'd found what he was looking for. The pink fish, he thought. They're the ones that move the fastest, and besides, red is an angry color. Pink is . . . what? What was the word? It came, and he smiled. It was the radiant one that made him look nineteen again.

Pink was *soothing*.

Sometimes when Freddi visited, Z-Boy left his library cart in the hall and joined them. On one of these occasions, during the summer of 2014, he handed Freddi an electronic recipe. It had been written on the library computer, and during one of the increasingly rare occasions when Brady did not just give instructions but slid into the driver's seat and took over completely. He had to, because this had to be just right. There was no room for error.

Freddi scanned it, got interested, and read it more closely. "Say," she said, "this is pretty clever. And adding subliminal messaging is cool. Nasty, but cool. Did the mysterious Dr. Z think this up?"

"Yeah," Z-Boy said.

Freddi switched her attention to Brady. "Do you know who this Dr. Z is?"

Brady shook his head slowly back and forth.

"Sure it's not you? Because this looks like your work."

Brady only stared at her vacantly until she looked away. He had let her see more of him than Hodges or anyone on the nursing or PT staff, but he had no intention of letting her see *into* him. Not at this point, at least. Too much chance she might talk.

Besides, he still didn't know exactly what he was doing. They said that the world would beat a path to your door if you built a better mousetrap, but since he did not as yet know if this one would catch mice, it was best to keep quiet. And Dr. Z didn't exist yet.

But he would.

On an afternoon not long after Freddi received the electronic recipe explaining just how to jigger the Fishin' Hole demo screen, Z-Boy visited Felix Babineau in his office. The doctor spent an hour there most days he was in the hospital, drinking coffee and reading the newspaper. There was an indoor putting green by the window (no parking garage view for Babineau), where he sometimes practiced his short game. That was where he was when Z-Boy came in without knocking.

Babineau looked at him coldly. "Can I help you? Are you lost?"

Z-Boy held out Zappit Zero, which Freddi had upgraded (after buying several new computer components paid for out of Al Brooks's rapidly shrinking savings account). "Look at this," he said. "I'll tell you what to do."

"You need to leave," Babineau said. "I don't know what kind of bee you have in your bonnet, but this is my private space and my private time. Or do you want me to call security?"

"Look at it, or you'll be seeing yourself on the evening news. 'Doctor performs experiments with untested South American drug on accused mass murderer Brady Hartsfield.'"

Babineau stared at him with his mouth open, at that moment looking very much as he would after Brady began to whittle away his core consciousness. "I have no idea what you're talking about."

"I'm talking about Cerebellin. Years away from FDA approval, if ever. I accessed your file and took two dozen photos with my phone. I also took photos of the brain scans you've been keeping to yourself. You broke lots of laws, Doc. Look at the game and it stays between us. Refuse, and your career is over. I'll give you five seconds to decide."

Babineau took the game and looked at the swimming fish. The little tune tinkled. Every now and then there was a flash of blue light.

"Start tapping the pink ones, doctor. They'll turn into numbers. Add them up in your head."

"How long do I have to do this for?"

"You'll know."

"Are you crazy?"

"You lock your office when you're not here, which is smart, but there are lots of all-access security cards floating around this place. And you left your computer on, which seems kind of crazy to me. Look at the fish. Tap the pink ones. Add up the numbers. That's all you have to do, and I'll leave you alone."

"This is blackmail."

"No, blackmail is for money. This is just a trade. Look at the fish. I won't ask you again."

Babineau looked at the fish. He tapped at a pink one and missed. He tapped again, missed again. Muttered "Fuck!" under his breath. It was quite a bit harder than it looked, and he began to get interested. The blue flashes should have been annoying, but they weren't. They actually seemed to help him focus. Alarm at what this geezer knew started to fade into the background of his thoughts.

He succeeded in tapping one of the pink fish before it could shoot off the left side of the screen and got a nine. That was good. A good start. He forgot why he was doing this. Catching the pink fish was the important thing.

The tune played.

One floor up, in Room 217, Brady stared at his own Zappit, and felt his breathing slow. He closed his eyes and looked at a single red dot. That was Z-Boy. He waited . . . waited . . . and then, just as he was beginning to think his target might be immune, a second dot appeared. It was faint at first, but gradually grew bright and clear.

Like watching a rose blossom, Brady thought.

The two dots began to swim playfully back and forth. He settled his concentration on the one that was Babineau. It slowed and became stationary.

Gotcha, Brady thought.

But he had to be careful. This was a stealth mission.

The eyes he opened were Babineau's. The doctor was still staring at the fish, but he had ceased to tap them. He had become . . . what was the word they used? A gork. He had become a gork.

Brady did not linger on that first occasion, but it didn't take long to understand the wonders to which he'd gained access. Al Brooks was a piggy bank. Felix Babineau was a vault. Brady had access to his memories, his stored knowledge, his abilities. While in Al, he could have rewired an electrical circuit. In Babineau, he could have performed a craniotomy and rewired a human brain. Further, he had proof of something he had only theorized about and hoped for: he could take possession of others at a distance. All it took was that state of Zappit-induced hypnosis to open them up. The Zappit Freddi had modified made for a very efficient eye-trap, and good God, it worked so *fast*.

He couldn't wait to use it on Hodges.

Before leaving, Brady released a few thoughtfish into Babineau's brain, but only a few. He intended to move very carefully with the doctor. Babineau needed to be thoroughly habituated to the screen—which was now what those specializing in hypnosis called an inducement device—before Brady announced himself. One of that day's thoughtfish was the idea that the CAT scans on Brady weren't producing anything of real interest, and ought to cease. The Cerebellin shots should also cease.

Because Brady's not making sufficient progress. Because I'm a dead end. Also, I might be caught.

"Getting caught would be bad," Babineau murmured.

"Yes," Z-Boy said. "Getting caught would be bad for both of us."

Babineau had dropped his putter. Z-Boy picked it up and put it in his hand.

As that hot summer morphed into a cold and rainy fall, Brady strengthened his hold on Babineau. He released thoughtfish carefully, like a game warden stocking a pond with trout. Babineau began to feel an urge to get touchy-feely with a few of the younger nurses, risking a sexual harassment complaint. Babineau occasionally stole pain medication from the Bucket's Pyxis Med Station, using the ID card of a fictional doctor—a fiddle Brady set up via Freddi Linklatter. Babineau did this even though he was bound to be caught if he kept on, and had other, safer ways of getting pills. He stole a Rolex watch from the Neuro lounge one day (although he had one of his own) and put it in the bottom drawer of his office desk, where he promptly forgot it. Little by little, Brady Hartsfield—who could barely walk—took possession of the doctor who had presumed to take possession of him, and put him in a guilt-trap that had many teeth. If he did something foolish, like trying to tell someone what was going on, the trap would snap shut.

At the same time he began sculpting the Dr. Z personality, doing it much more carefully than he had with Library Al. For one thing, he was better at it now. For another, he had finer materials to work with. In October of that year, with hundreds of thoughtfish now swimming in Babineau's brain, he began assuming control of the doctor's body as well as his mind, taking it on longer and longer trips. Once he drove all the way to the Ohio state line in Babineau's BMW, just to see if his hold would weaken with distance. It didn't. It seemed that once you were in, you were in. And it was a fine trip. He stopped at a roadside restaurant and pigged out on onion rings.

Tasty!

As the 2014 holiday season approached, Brady found himself in a state he hadn't known since earliest childhood. It was so foreign to him that the Christmas decorations had been taken down and Valentine's Day was approaching before he realized what it was.

He felt contented.

Part of him fought this feeling, labeling it a little death, but part of him wanted to accept it. Embrace it, even. And why not? It wasn't as though he were stuck in Room 217, or even in his own body. He could leave whenever he wanted, either as a passenger or as a driver. He had to be careful not to be in the driver's seat too much or stay too long, that was all. Core consciousness, it seemed, was a limited resource. When it was gone, it was gone.

Too bad.

If Hodges had continued to make his visits, Brady would have had another of those goals to grow—getting him to look at the Zappit in his drawer, entering him, and planting suicidal thoughtfish. It would have been like using Debbie's Blue Umbrella all over again, only this time with suggestions that were much more powerful. Not really suggestions at all, but commands.

The only problem with the plan was that Hodges had stopped coming. He had appeared just after Labor Day, spouting all his usual bullshit—*I know you're in there, Brady, I hope you're suffering, Brady, can you really move things around without touching them, Brady, if you can let me see you do it*—but not since. Brady surmised that Hodges's disappearance from his life was the real source of this unusual and not entirely welcome contentment. Hodges had been a burr under his saddle, infuriating him and making him gallop. Now the burr was gone, and he was free to graze, if he wanted to.

He sort of did.

With access to Dr. Babineau's bank account and investment portfolio as well as his mind, Brady went on a computer spending spree. The Babster withdrew the money and made the purchases; Z-Boy delivered the equipment to Freddi Linklatter's cheesedog of a crib.

She really deserves an apartment upgrade, Brady thought. I ought to do something about that.

Z-Boy also brought her the rest of the Zappits he'd pilfered from the library, and Freddi amped the Fishin' Hole demos in all of them . . . for a price, of course. And although the price was high, Brady paid it without a qualm. It was the doc's money, after all, the dough of Babineau. As to what he might do with the juiced-up consoles, Brady had no idea. Eventually he might want another drone or two, he supposed, but he saw no reason to trade up right away. He began to understand what contentment actually was: the emotional version of the horse latitudes, where all the winds died away and one simply drifted.

It ensued when one ran out of goals to grow.

This state of affairs continued until February 13th of 2015, when Brady's attention was caught by an item on *News at Noon*. The anchors, who had been laughing it up over the antics of a couple of baby pandas, put on their Oh Shit This Is So Awful faces when the chyron behind them changed from the pandas to a broken-heart logo.

"It's going to be a sad Valentine's Day in the suburb of Sewickley," said the female half of the duo.

"That's right, Betty," said the male half. "Two survivors of the City Center Massacre, twenty-six-year-old Krista Countryman and twenty-four-year-old Keith Frias, have committed suicide in the Countryman woman's home."

It was Betty's turn. "Ken, the shocked parents say the couple was hoping to be married in May of this year, but both were badly injured in the attack perpetrated by Brady Hartsfield, and the continuing physical and mental pain was apparently too much for them. Here's Frank Denton, with more."

Brady was on high alert now, sitting as close to bolt upright in his chair as he could manage, eyes shining. Could he legitimately claim those two? He believed he could, which meant his City Center score had just gone up from eight to ten. Still shy of a dozen, but hey! Not bad.

Correspondent Frank Denton, also wearing his best Oh Shit

expression, went blah-de-blah for awhile, and then the picture switched to the Countryman chick's pore ole daddy, who read the suicide note the couple had left. He blubbered through most of it, but Brady caught the gist. They'd had a beautiful vision of the afterlife, where their wounds would be healed, the burden of their pain would be lifted, and they could be married in perfect health by their Lord and Savior, Jesus Christ.

"Boy, that's sad," the male anchor opined at the end of the story. "So sad."

"It sure is, Ken," Betty said. Then the screen behind them flashed a picture showing a bunch of idiots in wedding clothes standing in a swimming pool, and her sad face clicked off and the happy one came back on. "But this should cheer you up— twenty couples decided to get married in a swimming pool in Cleveland, where it's only *twenty degrees!*"

"I hope they had a hunka-hunka burning love," Ken said, showing his perfectly capped teeth in a grin. "*Brrrr!* Here's Patty Newfield with the details."

How many more could I get? Brady wondered. He was on fire. *I've got nine augmented Zappits, plus the two my drones have and the one in my drawer. Who says I have to be done with those job-hunting assholes?*

*Who says I can't run up the score?*

Brady continued to keep track of Zappit, Inc. during his fallow period, sending Z-Boy to check the Google alert once or twice weekly. The chatter about the hypnotic effect of the Fishin' Hole screen (and the lesser effect of the Whistling Birds demo) died down and was replaced by speculation about just when the company would go under—it was no longer a matter of if. When Sunrise Solutions bought Zappit out, a blogger who called himself Electric Whirlwind wrote, "Wow! This is like a couple of cancer patients with six weeks to live deciding to elope."

Babineau's shadow personality was now well established, and it was Dr. Z who began to research the survivors of the City Center Massacre on Brady's behalf, making a list of the ones most badly injured, and thus most vulnerable to suicidal thoughts. A couple of them, like Daniel Starr and Judith Loma, were still wheelchair bound. Loma might get out of hers; Starr, never. Then there was Martine Stover, paralyzed from the neck down and living with her mother over in Ridgedale.

I'd be doing them a favor, Brady thought. Really I would.

He decided Stover's mommy would make a good start. His first idea was to have Z-Boy mail her a Zappit ("A Free Gift for You!"), but how could he be sure she wouldn't just throw it away? He only had nine, and didn't want to risk wasting one. Juicing them up had cost him (well, Babineau) quite a lot of money. It might be better to send Babineau on a personal mission. In one of his tailored suits, set off by a sober dark tie, he looked a lot more trustworthy than Z-Boy in his rumpled green Dickies, and he was the sort of older guy that chicks like Stover's mother had a tendency to dig. All Brady had to do was work up a believable story. Something about test marketing, maybe? Possibly a book club? A prize competition?

He was still sifting scenarios—there was no hurry—when his Google alert announced an expected death: Sunrise Solutions had gone bye-bye. This was in early April. A trustee had been appointed to sell off the assets, and a list of so-called "real goods" would soon appear in the usual sell-sites. For those who couldn't wait, a list of all Sunrise Solutions' unsaleable crapola could be found in the bankruptcy filing. Brady thought this was interesting, but not interesting enough to have Dr. Z look up the list of assets. There were probably crates of Zappits among them, but he had nine of his own, and surely that would be enough to play with.

A month later he changed his mind about that.

One of *News at Noon*'s most popular features was called "Just A Word From Jack." Jack O'Malley was a fat old dinosaur who had probably started in the biz when TV was still black-and-white, and he bumbled on for five minutes or so at the end of every newscast about whatever was on what remained of his mind. He wore huge black-rimmed glasses, and his jowls quivered like Jell-O when he talked. Ordinarily Brady found him quite entertaining, a bit of comic relief, but there was nothing amusing about that day's Word From Jack. It opened whole new vistas.

"The families of Krista Countryman and Keith Frias have been flooded with condolences as a result of a story this station ran not long ago," Jack said in his grouchy Andy Rooney voice. "Their decision to terminate their lives when they could no longer live with unending and unmitigated pain has reignited the debate on the ethics of suicide. It also reminded us—unfortunately—of the coward who caused that unending, unmitigated pain, a monster named Brady Wilson Hartsfield."

That's me, Brady thought happily. When they even give your middle name, you know you're an authentic boogeyman.

"If there is a life after this one," Jack said (out-of-control Andy Rooney brows drawing together, jowls flapping), "Brady Wilson Hartsfield will pay the full price for his crimes when he gets there. In the meantime, let us consider the silver lining in this dark cloud of woe, because there really is one.

"A year after his cowardly killing spree at City Center, Brady

Wilson Hartsfield attempted an even more heinous crime. He smuggled a large quantity of plastic explosive into a concert at Mingo Auditorium, with the intent to murder thousands of teens who were there to have a good time. In this he was thwarted by retired detective William Hodges and a brave woman named Holly Gibney, who smashed the homicidal loser's skull before he could detonate . . ."

Here Brady lost the thread. Some woman named Holly Gibney had been the one to smash him in the head and almost kill him? Who the fuck was Holly Gibney? And why had no one ever told him this in the five years since she'd turned his lights out and landed him in this room? How was that possible?

Very easily, he decided. When the coverage was fresh, he'd been in a coma. Later on, he thought, I just assumed it was either Hodges or his nigger lawnboy.

He would look Gibney up on the Web when he got a chance, but she wasn't the important thing. She was part of the past. The future was a splendid idea that had come to him as his best inventions always had: whole and complete, needing only a few modifications along the way to make it perfect.

He powered up his Zappit, found Z-Boy (currently handing out magazines to patients waiting in OB/GYN), and sent him to the library computer. Once he was seated in front of the screen, Brady shoved him out of the driver's seat and took control, hunched over and squinting at the monitor with Al Brooks's nearsighted eyes. On a website called Bankruptcy Assets 2015, he found the list of all the stuff Sunrise Solutions had left behind. There was junk from a dozen different companies, listed alphabetically. Zappit was the last, but as far as Brady was concerned, far from least. Heading the list of their assets was 45,872 Zappit Commanders, suggested retail price

$189.99. They were being sold in lots of four hundred, eight hundred, and one thousand. Below, in red, was the caveat that part of the shipment was defective, "but most are in perfect working condition."

Brady's excitement had Library Al's old heart laboring. His hands left the keyboard and curled into fists. Getting more of the City Center survivors to commit suicide paled in comparison to the grand idea that now possessed him: finishing what he had tried to do that night at the Mingo. He could see himself writing to Hodges from beneath the Blue Umbrella: *You think you stopped me? Think again.*

How wonderful that would be!

He was pretty sure Babineau had more than enough money to buy a Zappit console for everyone who had been there that night, but since Brady would have to handle his targets one at a time, it wouldn't do to go overboard.

He had Z-Boy bring Babineau to him. Babineau didn't want to come. He was afraid of Brady now, which Brady found delicious.

"You're going to be buying some goods," Brady said.

"Buying some goods." Docile. No longer afraid. Babineau had entered Room 217, but it was now Dr. Z standing slump-shouldered in front of Brady's chair.

"Yes. You'll want to put money in a new account. I think we'll call it Gamez Unlimited. That's Gamez with a Z."

"With a Z. Like me." The head of the Kiner Neurology Department managed a small, vacuous smile.

"Very good. Let's say a hundred and fifty thousand dollars. You'll also be setting Freddi Linklatter up in a new and bigger apartment. So she can receive the goods you buy, and then work on them. She's going to be a busy girl."

"I'll be setting her up in a new and bigger apartment so—"

"Just shut up and listen. She'll be needing some more equipment, too."

Brady leaned forward. He could see a bright future ahead, one
where Brady Wilson Hartsfield was crowned the winner years
after the Det.-Ret. thought the game had ended.

"The most important piece of equipment is called a repeater."

# HEADS AND SKINS

1

It's not pain that wakes Freddi, but her bladder. It feels like it's bursting. Getting out of bed is a major operation. Her head is banging, and it feels like she's wearing a plaster cast on her chest. It doesn't hurt too much, mostly it's just stiff and so heavy. Each breath is a clean-and-jerk.

The bathroom looks like something out of a slasher movie, and she closes her eyes as soon as she sits on the john so she won't have to look at all the blood. So lucky to be alive, she thinks as something that feels like ten gallons of pee rushes out of her. Just so goddam lucky. And why am I in the center of this clusterfuck? Because I took him that picture. My mother was right, no good deed goes unpunished.

But if there was ever a time for clear thinking it's now, and she has to admit to herself that taking Brady the picture wasn't what has led her to this place, sitting in her bloody bathroom with a knot on her head and a gunshot wound in her chest. It was going *back* that had done that, and she'd gone back because she was being paid to do so—fifty dollars a visit. Which made her sort of a call girl, she supposed.

You know what all this is about. You could tell yourself you only knew when you peeked at the thumb drive Dr. Z brought you, the one that activates the creepy website, but you knew when you were installing updates on all those Zappits, didn't you? A regular assembly line of them, forty or fifty a day, until all the ones that weren't defective were loaded landmines. Over five hundred. You knew it was Brady all along, and Brady Hartsfield is crazy.

She yanks up her pants, flushes, and leaves the bathroom. The light coming in the living room window is muted, but it still hurts her eyes. She squints, sees it's starting to snow, and shuffles to the kitchen, working for every breath. Her fridge is mostly stocked with cartons of leftover Chinese, but there's a couple of cans of Red Bull in the door shelf. She grabs one, chugs half, and feels a bit better. It's probably a psychological effect, but she'll take it.

What am I going to do? What in the name of God? Is there any way out of this mess?

She goes into her computer room, shuffling a little faster now, and refreshes her screen. She googles her way to zeetheend, hoping she'll get the cartoon man swinging his cartoon pickaxe, and her heart sinks when the picture filling the screen shows a candlelit funeral parlor, instead—exactly what she saw when she booted up the thumb drive and looked at the starter screen, instead of just importing the whole thing blind, as instructed. That dopey Blue Oyster Cult song is playing.

She scrolls past the messages below the coffin, each one swelling and fading like slow heartbeats (AN END TO PAIN, AN END TO FEAR) and clicks on POST A COMMENT. Freddi doesn't know how long this electronic poison pill has been active, but long enough for it to have generated hundreds of comments already.

**Bedarkened77: This dares to speak the truth!**

**AliceAlways401: I wish I had the guts, things are so bad at home now.**

**VerbanaThe Monkey: Bear the pain, people, suicide is gutless!!!**

**KittycatGreeneyes: No, suicide is PAINLESS, it brings on many changes.**

Verbana the Monkey isn't the only naysayer, but Freddi doesn't have to scroll through all the comments to see that he (or she) is very much in the minority. *This is going to spread like the flu,* Freddi thinks.

*No, more like ebola.*

She looks up at the repeater just in time to see 171 FOUND tick up to 172. Word about the number-fish is spreading fast, and by tonight almost all of the rigged Zappits will be active. The demo screen hypnotizes them, makes them receptive. To what? Well, to the idea that they should visit zeetheend, for one thing. Or maybe the Zappit People won't even have to go there. Maybe they'll just highside it. Will people obey a hypnotic command to off themselves? Surely not, right?

*Right?*

Freddi doesn't dare risk killing the repeater for fear of a return visit from Brady, but the website?

"You're going down, motherfucker," she says, and begins to rattle away at her keyboard.

Less than thirty seconds later, she's staring with disbelief at a message on her screen: THIS FUNCTION IS NOT ALLOWED. She reaches out to try again, then stops. For all she knows, another go at the website may nuke all her stuff—not just her computer equipment, but her credit cards, her bank account, her cell phone, even her fucking driver's license. If anyone knows how to program such evil shit, it's Brady.

Fuck. I have to get out of here.

She'll throw some clothes in a suitcase, call a cab, go to the bank, and draw out everything she's got. There might be as much as four thousand dollars. (In her heart, she knows it's more like three.) From the bank to the bus station. The snow swirling outside her window is supposed to be the beginning of a big storm, and that may preclude a quick getaway, but if she has to wait a few hours at the station, she will. Hell, if she has to *sleep* there, she will. This is all Brady. He's set up an elaborate Jonestown protocol of which the rigged Zappits are only a part, and she helped him do it. Freddi has no idea if it will work, and she doesn't intend to wait around to find out. She's sorry for the people who might be sucked in by the Zappits, or tipped into attempting suicide by that fucking zeetheend website instead of just thinking about it, but she has to take care of *numero uno.* There's no one else to do it.

Freddi makes her way back to the bedroom as rapidly as she can. She gets her old Samsonite from the closet, and then oxygen depletion caused by shallow breathing and too much excitement turns her legs to rubber. She makes it to the bed, sits on it, and lowers her head.

Easy does it, she thinks. Get your breath back. One thing at a time.

Only, thanks to her foolish effort to crash the website, she doesn't know how much time she has, and when "Boogie Woogie Bugle Boy" begins to play from the top of her dresser, she utters a little scream. Freddi doesn't want to answer her phone, but gets up, anyway. Sometimes it's better to know.

2

The snow remains light until Brady gets off the interstate at Exit 7, but on State Road 79—he's out in the boondocks now— it starts to come down a little harder. The tar is still bare and wet, but the snow will start to accumulate on it soon enough, and he's still forty miles from where he intends to hole up and get busy.

Lake Charles, he thinks. Where the real fun begins.

That's when Babineau's laptop awakens and chimes three times—an alert Brady programmed into it. Because safe is always better than sorry. He has no time to pull over, not when he's racing this goddam storm, but he can't afford not to. Ahead on the right is a boarded-up building with two metal girls in rusting bikinis on the roof, holding up a sign reading PORNO PALACE and XXX and WE DARE TO BARE. In the middle of the dirt parking lot—which the snow is now starting to sugar-coat—there's a For Sale sign.

Brady pulls in, shifts to park, and opens the laptop. The message on the screen puts a significant crack right down the middle of his good mood.

11:04 AM: UNAUTHORIZED ATTEMPT
TO MODIFY/CANCEL ZEETHEEND.COM
DENIED
SITE ACTIVE

He opens the Malibu's glove compartment and there is Al Brooks's battered cell phone, right where he always kept it. A good thing, too, because Brady forgot to bring Babineau's.

So sue me, he thinks. You can't remember everything, and I've been busy.

He doesn't bother going to Contacts, just dials Freddi's number from memory. She hasn't changed it since the old Discount Electronix days.

### 3

When Hodges excuses himself to use the bathroom, Jerome waits until he's out the door, then goes to Holly, who's standing at the window and watching the snow fall. It's still light here in the city, the flakes dancing in the air and seeming to defy gravity. Holly once more has her arms crossed over her chest so she can grip her shoulders.

"How bad is he?" Jerome asks in a low voice. "Because he doesn't look good."

"It's pancreatic cancer, Jerome. How good does anyone look with that?"

"Can he get through the day, do you think? Because he wants to, and I really think he could use some closure on this."

"Closure on Hartsfield, you mean. Brady fracking Hartsfield. Even though he's fracking *dead*."

"Yes, that's what I mean."

"I think it's bad." She turns to him and forces herself to meet his eyes, a thing that always makes her feel stripped bare. "Do you see the way he keeps putting his hand against his side?"

Jerome nods.

"He's been doing that for weeks now and calling it indigestion. He only went to the doctor because I nagged him into it. And when he found out what was wrong, he tried to lie."

"You didn't answer the question. Can he get through the day?"

"I think so. I hope so. Because you're right, he needs this. Only we have to stick with him. Both of us." She releases one shoulder so she can grip his wrist. "Promise me, Jerome. No sending the skinny girl home so the boys can play in the tree-house by themselves."

He pries her hand loose and gives it a squeeze. "Don't worry, Hollyberry. No one's breaking up the band."

4

"Hello? Is that you, Dr. Z?"

Brady has no time to play games with her. The snow is thickening every second, and Z-Boy's crappy old Malibu, with no snow tires and over a hundred thousand miles on the clock, will be no match for the storm once it really gets whooping. Under other circumstances, he'd want to know how she's even alive, but since he has no intention of turning back and rectifying that situation, it's a moot question.

"You know who it is, and I know what you tried to do. Try it again and I'll send in the men who are watching the building. You're lucky to be alive, Freddi. I wouldn't tempt fate a second time."

"I'm sorry." Almost whispering. This is not the fuck-you-and-fuck-your-mother riot grrrl Brady worked with on the Cyber Patrol. Yet she's not entirely broken, or she wouldn't have tried messing with the computer gear.

"Have you told anyone?"

"No!" She sounds horrified at the thought. Horrified is good. "Will you?"

"*No!*"

"That's the right answer, because if you do, I'll know. You're under surveillance, Freddi. Remember it."

He ends the call without waiting for a reply, more furious with her for being alive than for what she tried to do. Will she believe that fictitious men are watching the building, even though he left her for dead? He thinks so. She's had dealings with both Dr. Z and Z-Boy; who knows how many other drones he might have at his command?

In any case, there's nothing else he can do about it now. Brady has a long, long history of blaming others for his problems, and now he blames Freddi for not dying when she was supposed to.

He drops the Malibu's gearshift into drive and steps on the gas. The tires spin in the thin carpet of snow covering the defunct Porno Palace's parking lot, but catch once they get on the state road again, where the formerly brown soft shoulders are now turning white. Brady eases Z-Boy's car up to sixty. That will soon be too fast for conditions, but he'll hold the needle there as long as he can.

5

Finders Keepers shares the seventh-floor bathrooms with the travel agency, but right now Hodges has the men's to himself, for which he is grateful. He's bent over one of the sinks, right hand gripping the washbasin's rim, left pressed to his side. His belt is still unbuckled, and his pants are sinking past his hips under the weight of the stuff in his pockets: change, keys, wallet, phone.

He came in here to take a shit, an ordinary excretory function he's been performing all his life, but when he started to strain, the left half of his midsection went nuclear. It makes his previous pain seem like a bunch of warm-up notes before the full concert begins, and if it's this bad now, he dreads to think what may lie ahead.

No, he thinks, dread is the wrong word. Terror is the right one. For the first time in my life, I'm terrified of the future, where I see everything that I am or ever was first submerged, then erased. If the pain itself doesn't do it, the heavier drugs they give me to stifle it will.

Now he understands why pancreatic is called the stealth cancer, and why it's almost always deadly. It lurks, building up its troops and sending out secret emissaries to the lungs, the lymph nodes, the bones, and the brain. Then it blitzkriegs, not understanding, in its stupid rapacity, that victory can only bring its own death.

Hodges thinks, Except maybe that's what it wants. Maybe it's self-hating, born with a desire not to murder the host but to kill itself. Which makes cancer the *real* suicide prince.

He brings up a long, resounding burp, and that makes him feel a little better, who knows why. It won't last long, but he'll take any measure of relief he can get. He shakes out three of his painkillers (already they make him think of shooting a popgun at a charging elephant) and swallows them with water from the tap. Then he splashes more cold water on his face, trying to bring up a little color. When that doesn't work, he slaps himself briskly—two hard ones on each cheek. Holly and Jerome must not know how bad it's gotten. He was promised this day and he means to take every minute of it. All the way to midnight, if necessary.

He's leaving the bathroom, reminding himself to straighten

up and stop pressing his side, when his phone buzzes. Pete wanting to resume his bitch-a-thon, he thinks, but it's not. It's Norma Wilmer.

"I found that file," she says. "The one the late great Ruth Scapelli—"

"Yeah," he says. "The visitors list. Who's on it?"

"There *is* no list."

He leans against the wall and closes his eyes. "Ah, sh—"

"But there is a single memo with Babineau's letterhead on it. It says, and I quote, 'Frederica Linklatter to be admitted both during and after visiting hours. She is aiding in B. Hartsfield's recovery.' Does that help?"

Some girl with a Marine haircut, Hodges thinks. A ratty chick with a bunch of tats.

It rang no bells at the time, but there *was* that faint vibration, and now he knows why. He met a skinny girl with buzz-cut hair at Discount Electronix back in 2010, when he, Jerome, and Holly were closing in on Brady. Even six years later he can remember what she said about her co-worker on the Cyber Patrol: *It's something with his mom, betcha anything. He's freaky about her.*

"Are you still there?" Norma sounds irritated.

"Yeah, but I have to go."

"Didn't you say there'd be some extra money if—"

"Yeah. I'll take care of you, Norma." He ends the call.

The pills are doing their work, and he's able to manage a medium-fast walk back to the office. Holly and Jerome are at the window overlooking Lower Marlborough Street, and he can tell by their expressions when they turn to the sound of the opening door that they've been talking about him, but he has no time to think about that. Or brood on it. What he's thinking about are those rigged Zappits. The question ever since they started to put things together was how Brady could have had anything to do with modifying them when he was stuck in a hospital room and barely able to walk. But he knew somebody who almost certainly had the skills to do it for him, didn't he? Someone he used to work with. Somebody who came to visit him in the Bucket, with Babineau's written approval. A punky chick with a lot of tats and a yard of attitude.

"Brady's visitor—his *only* visitor—was a woman named Frederica Linklatter. She—"

"Cyber Patrol!" Holly nearly screams. "He worked with her!"

"Right. There was also a third guy—the boss, I think. Do either of you remember his name?"

Holly and Jerome look at each other, then shake their heads.

"That was a long time ago, Bill," Jerome says. "And we were concentrating on Hartsfield by then."

"Yeah. I only remember Linklatter because she was sort of unforgettable."

"Can I use your computer?" Jerome asks. "Maybe I can find the guy while Holly looks for the girl's addy."

"Sure, go for it."

Holly is at hers already, sitting bolt upright and clicking away. She's also talking out loud as she often does when she's deeply involved in something. "Frack. Whitepages doesn't have a number or address. Long shot, anyway, a lot of single women don't . . . wait, hold the fracking phone . . . here's her Facebook page . . ."

"I'm not really interested in her summer vacation snaps or how many friends she's got," Hodges says.

"Are you sure about that? Because she's only got six friends, and one of them is Anthony Frobisher. I'm pretty sure that was the name of the—"

"*Frobisher!*" Jerome yells from Hodges's office. "*Anthony Frobisher was the third Cyber Patrol guy!*"

"Beat you, Jerome," Holly says. She looks smug. "Again."

## 6

Unlike Frederica Linklatter, Anthony Frobisher is listed, both as himself and as Your Computer Guru. Both numbers are the same—his cell, Hodges assumes. He evicts Jerome from his office chair and settles there himself, doing it slowly and carefully. The explosion of pain he felt while sitting on the toilet is still fresh in his mind.

The phone is answered on the first ring. "Computer Guru, Tony Frobisher speaking. How can I help you?"

"Mr. Frobisher, this is Bill Hodges. You probably don't remember me, but—"

"Oh, I remember you, all right." Frobisher sounds wary. "What do you want? If it's about Hartsfield—"

"It's about Frederica Linklatter. Do you have a current address for her?"

"Freddi? Why would I have *any* address for her? I haven't seen her since DE closed."

"Really? According to her Facebook page, you and she are friends."

Frobisher laughs incredulously. "Who else has she got listed? Kim Jong-un? Charles Manson? Listen, Mr. Hodges, that smartmouth bitch *has* no friends. The closest thing to one was Hartsfield, and I just got a news push on my phone saying he's dead."

Hodges has no idea what a news push is, and no desire to

learn. He thanks Frobisher and hangs up. He's guessing that none of Freddi Linklatter's half dozen Facebook friends are real friends, that she just added them to keep from feeling like a total outcast. Holly might have done that same thing, once upon a time, but now she actually *has* friends. Lucky for her, and lucky for them. Which begs the question: how does he locate Freddi Linklatter?

The outfit he and Holly runs isn't called Finders Keepers for nothing, but most of their specialized search engines are constructed to locate bad people with bad friends, long police records, and colorful want sheets. He *can* find her, in this computerized age few people are able to drop entirely off the grid, but he needs it to happen fast. Every time some kid turns on one of those free Zappits, it's loading up pink fish, blue flashes, and—based on Jerome's experience—a subliminal message suggesting that a visit to zeetheend would be in order.

You're a detective. One with cancer, granted, but still a detective. So let go of the extraneous shit and detect.

It's hard, though. The thought of all those kids—the ones Brady tried and failed to kill at the 'Round Here concert—keeps getting in the way. Jerome's sister was one of them, and if not for Dereece Neville, Barbara might be dead now instead of just in a leg cast. Maybe hers was a test model. Maybe the Ellerton woman's was, too. That makes a degree of sense. But now there are all those other Zappits, a flood of them, and they must have gone *somewhere*, goddammit.

That finally turns on a lightbulb.

"Holly! I need a phone number!"

7

Todd Schneider is in, and affable. "I understand you folks are in for quite a storm, Mr. Hodges."

"So they say."

"Having any luck tracking down those defective consoles?"

"That's actually why I'm calling. Do you happen to have the address that consignment of Zappit Commanders was sent to?"

"Of course. Can I call you back with it?"

"How about if I hang on? It's rather urgent."

"An urgent consumer advocacy issue?" Schneider sounds bemused. "That sounds almost un-American. Let me see what I can do."

A click and Hodges is on hold, complete with soothing strings that fail to soothe. Holly and Jerome are both in the office now, crowding the desk. Hodges makes an effort not to put his hand to his side. The seconds stretch out and form a minute. Then two. Hodges thinks, Either he's on another call and forgotten me, or he can't find it.

The hold music disappears. "Mr. Hodges? Still there?"

"Still here."

"I have that address. It's Gamez Unlimited—Gamez with a Z, if you remember—at 442 Maritime Drive. Care of Ms. Frederica Linklatter. Does that help?"

"It sure does. Thank you, Mr. Schneider." He hangs up and looks at his two associates, one slender and winter-pale, the other bulked up from his house-building stint in Arizona. Along with his daughter Allie, now living on the other side of the country, they are the people he loves most at this end of his life.

He says, "Let's take a ride, kids."

8

Brady turns off SR-79 and onto Vale Road at Thurston's Garage, where a number of local plow-for-pay boys are gassing their trucks, loading up with salted sand, or just standing around, drinking coffee and jabbering. It crosses Brady's mind to pull in and see if he can get some studded snow tires on Library Al's Malibu, but given the crowd the storm has brought to the garage, it would probably take all afternoon. He's close to his destination now, and decides to go for it. If he gets snowed in once he's there, who gives a shit? Not him. He's been out to the camp twice already, mostly to scope the place out, but the second time he also laid in some supplies.

There's a good three inches of snow on Vale Road, and the going is greasy. The Malibu slides several times, once almost all the way to the ditch. He's sweating heavily, and Babineau's arthritic fingers are throbbing from Brady's deathgrip on the steering wheel.

At last he sees the tall red posts that are his final landmark. Brady pumps the brakes and makes the turn at walking pace. The last two miles are on an unnamed, one-lane camp road, but thanks to the overarching trees, the driving here is the easiest he's had in the last hour. In some places the road is still bare. That won't last once the main body of the storm arrives, which will happen around eight o'clock tonight, according to the radio.

He comes to a fork where wooden arrows nailed to a huge old-growth fir point in different directions. The one on the right reads BIG BOB'S BEAR CAMP. The one on the left reads HEADS AND SKINS. Ten feet or so above the arrows, already wearing a thin hood of snow, a security camera peers down.

Brady turns left and finally allows his hands to relax. He's almost there.

9

In the city, the snow is still light. The streets are clear and traffic is moving well, but the three of them pile into Jerome's Jeep Wrangler just to be on the safe side. 442 Maritime Drive turns out to be one of the condos that sprang up like mushrooms on the south side of the lake in the go-go eighties. Back then they were a big deal. Now most are half empty. In the foyer, Jerome finds F. LINKLATTER in 6-A. He reaches for the buzzer, but Hodges stops him before he can push it.

"What?" Jerome asks.

Holly says primly, "Watch and learn, Jerome. This is how we roll."

Hodges pushes other buttons at random, and gets a male voice in return on the fourth try. "Yeah?"

"FedEx," Hodges says.

"Who'd send me something by FedEx?" The voice sounds mystified.

"Couldn't tell you, buddy. I don't make the news, I just report it."

The door to the lobby gives out an ill-tempered rattle. Hodges pushes through and holds it for the others. There are two elevators, one with an out-of-order sign taped to it. On the one that works someone has posted a note that reads, **Whoever has the barking dog on 4, I will find you.**

"I find that rather ominous," Jerome says.

The elevator door opens and as they get in, Holly begins to rummage in her purse. She finds her box of Nicorette and pops one. When the elevator opens on the sixth floor, Hodges says, "If she's there, let me do the talking."

6-A is directly across from the elevator. Hodges knocks. When there's no answer, he raps. When there's still no answer, he hammers with the side of his fist.

"Go away." The voice on the other side of the door sounds weak and thin. The voice of a little girl with the flu, Hodges thinks.

He hammers again. "Open up, Ms. Linklatter."

"Are you the police?"

He could say yes, it wouldn't be the first time since retiring from the force that he impersonated a police officer, but instinct tells him not to do it this time.

"No. My name is Bill Hodges. We met before, briefly, back in 2010. It was when you worked at—"

"Yeah, I remember."

One lock turns, then another. A chain falls. The door opens, and the tangy smell of pot wafts into the corridor. The woman in the doorway has got a half-smoked fatty tweezed between the thumb and forefinger of her left hand. She's thin almost to the point of emaciation, and pale as milk. She's wearing a strappy tee-shirt with BAD BOY BAIL BONDS, BRADENTON FLA on the front. Below this is the motto IN JAIL? WE BAIL!, but that part is hard to read because of the bloodstain.

"I should have called you," Freddi says, and although she's looking at Hodges, he has an idea it's really herself she's speaking to. "I would have, if I'd thought of it. You stopped him before, right?"

"Jesus, lady, what happened?" Jerome asks.

"I probably packed too much." Freddi gestures at a pair of mismatched suitcases standing behind her in the living room.

"I should have listened to my mother. She said to always travel light."

"I don't think he's talking about the suitcases," Hodges says, cocking a thumb at the fresh blood on Freddi's shirt. He steps in, Jerome and Holly right behind him. Holly closes the door.

"I know what he's talking about," Freddi says. "Fucker shot me. Bleeding started again when I hauled the suitcases out of the bedroom."

"Let me see," Hodges says, but when he steps toward her, Freddi takes a compensatory step back and crosses her arms in front of her, a Holly-esque gesture that touches Hodges's heart.

"No. I'm not wearing a bra. Hurts too much."

Holly pushes past Hodges. "Show me where the bathroom is. Let me look." She sounds okay to Hodges—calm—but she's chewing the shit out of that nicotine gum.

Freddi takes Holly by the wrist and leads her past the suitcases, pausing a moment to hit the joint. She lets the smoke out in a series of smoke signals as she talks. "The equipment is in the spare room. On your right. Get a good look." And then, returning to her original scripture: "If I hadn't packed so much, I'd be gone now."

Hodges doubts it. He thinks she would have passed out in the elevator.

10

Heads and Skins isn't as big as the Babineau McMansion in Sugar Heights, but damned near. It's long, low, and rambling. Beyond it, the snow-covered ground slopes down to Lake Charles, which has frozen over since Brady's last visit.

He parks in front and walks carefully around to the west side, Babineau's expensive loafers sliding in the accumulating snow. The hunting camp is in a clearing, so there's a lot more snow to slip around in. His ankles are freezing. He wishes he'd thought to bring some boots, and once more reminds himself that you can't think of everything.

He takes the key to the generator shed from inside the electric meter box, and the keys to the house from inside the shed. The gennie is a top-of-the-line Generac Guardian. It's silent now, but will probably kick on later. Out here in the boonies, the electricity goes down in almost every storm.

Brady returns to the car for Babineau's laptop. The camp is WiFi equipped, and the laptop is all he needs to keep him connected to his current project, and abreast of developments. Plus the Zappit, of course.

Good old Zappit Zero.

The house is dark and chilly, and his first acts upon entering are the prosaic ones any returning homeowner might perform: he turns on the lights and boosts the thermostat. The main room is huge and pine-paneled, lit by a chandelier made of polished caribou bones, from back in the days when there were still caribou in these woods. The fieldstone fireplace is a maw, almost big enough to roast a rhino in. Overhead are thick, crisscrossing beams, darkened by years of woodsmoke from the fireplace. Next to one wall stands a cherrywood buffet as long as the room itself, lined with at least fifty liquor bottles, some nearly empty, some with the seals still intact. The furniture is old, mismatched, and plushy—deep easy chairs, and a gigantic sofa where innumerable bimbos have been banged over the years. Plenty of extramarital fucking has gone on out here in addition to the hunting and fishing. The skin in front of the fireplace belonged to a bear brought down by Dr. Elton Marchant, who has now gone to that great operating room in the sky. The mounted heads and stuffed fish are trophies belonging to nearly a dozen other docs, past and present. There's a particularly fine sixteen-point buck that Babineau himself brought down back when he was really Babineau. Out of season, but what the hell.

Brady puts the laptop on an antique rolltop desk at the far end of the room and fires it up before taking off his coat. First he checks in on the repeater, and is delighted to see it's now reading 243 FOUND.

He thought he understood the power of the eye-trap, and has seen how addictive that demo screen is even *before* it's juiced up, but this is success beyond his wildest expectations. Far beyond. There haven't been any new warning chimes from zeetheend, but he goes there next anyway, just to see how it's doing. Once again his expectations are exceeded. Over seven thousand visitors so far, seven *thousand*, and the number ticks up steadily even as he watches.

He drops his coat and does a nimble little dance on the bearskin rug. It tires him out fast—when he makes his next switch, he'll be sure to choose someone in their twenties or thirties—but it warms him up nicely.

He snags the TV remote from the buffet and clicks on the enormous flatscreen, one of the camp's few nods to life in the twenty-first century. The satellite dish pulls in God knows how many channels and the HD picture is to die for, but Brady is more interested in local programming today. He punches the source button on the remote until he's looking back down the camp road leading to the outside world. He doesn't expect company, but he has two or three busy days ahead of him, the most important and productive days of his life, and if someone tries to interrupt him, he wants to know about it beforehand.

The gun closet is a walk-in job, the knotty-pine walls lined with rifles and hung with pistols on pegs. The pick of the litter, as far as Brady's concerned, is the FN SCAR 17S with the pistol grip. Capable of firing six hundred fifty rounds a minute and illegally converted to full auto by a proctologist who is also a gun nut, it is the Rolls-Royce of grease guns. Brady takes it out, along with a few extra clips and several heavy boxes of Winchester .308s, and props it against the wall beside the fireplace. He thinks about starting a fire—seasoned wood is already stacked in the hearth—but he has one other thing to do first. He goes to the site for city breaking news and scrolls down rapidly, looking for suicides. None yet, but he can remedy that.

"Call it a Zappitizer," he says, grinning, and powers up the console. He makes himself comfortable in one of the easy chairs and begins following the pink fish. When he closes his eyes, they're still there. At first, anyway. Then they become red dots moving on a field of black.

Brady picks one at random and goes to work.

## 11

Hodges and Jerome are staring at a digital display reading 244 FOUND when Holly leads Freddi into her computer room.

"She's all right," Holly says quietly to Hodges. "She shouldn't be, but she is. She's got a hole in her chest that looks like—"

"Like what I said it is." Freddi sounds a little stronger now. Her eyes are red, but that's probably from the dope she's been smoking. "He shot me."

"She had some mini-pads and I taped one over the wound," Holly says. "It was too big for a Band-Aid." She wrinkles her nose. "Oough."

"Fucker shot me." It's as if Freddi's still trying to get it straight in her mind.

"Which fucker would that be?" Hodges asks. "Felix Babineau?"

"Yeah, him. Fucking Dr. Z. Only he's really Brady. So is the other one. Z-Boy."

"Z-Boy?" Jerome asks. "Who the hell is Z-Boy?"

"Older guy?" Hodges asks. "Older than Babineau? Frizzy white hair? Drives a beater with primer paint on it? Maybe wears a parka with tape over some of the rips?"

"I don't know about his car, but I know the parka," Freddi says. "That's my boy Z-Boy." She sits in front of her desktop Mac—currently spinning out a fractal screensaver—and takes a final drag on her joint before crushing it out in an ashtray full of Marlboro butts. She's still pale, but some of the fuck-you attitude Hodges remembers from their previous meeting is coming back. "Dr. Z and his faithful sidekick, Z-Boy. Except they're both Brady. Fucking matryoshka dolls is what they are."

"Ms. Linklatter?" Holly says.

"Oh, go ahead and call me Freddi. Any chick who sees the teacups I call tits gets to call me Freddi."

Holly blushes, but goes ahead. When she's on the scent, she always does. "Brady Hartsfield is dead. It was an overdose last night or early this morning."

"Elvis has left the building?" Freddi considers the idea, then shakes her head. "Wouldn't that be nice. If it was true."

And wouldn't it be nice I could totally believe she's crazy, Hodges thinks.

Jerome points at the readout above her jumbo monitor. It's now flashing 247 FOUND. "Is that thing searching or downloading?"

"Both." Freddi's hand is pressing at the makeshift bandage under her shirt in an automatic gesture that reminds Hodges of himself. "It's a repeater. I can turn it off—at least I think I can—but you have to promise to protect me from the men who are watching the building. The website, though . . . no good. I've got the IP address and the password, but I still couldn't crash the server."

Hodges has a thousand questions, but as 247 FOUND clicks up to 248, only two seem of paramount importance. "What's it searching for? And what's it downloading?"

"You have to promise me protection first. You have to take me somewhere safe. Witness Protection, or whatever."

"He doesn't have to promise you anything, because I already know," Holly says. There's nothing mean in her tone; if anything, it's comforting. "It's searching for Zappits, Bill. Each time somebody turns one on, the repeater finds it and upgrades the Fishin' Hole demo screen."

"Turns the pink fish into number-fish and adds the blue flashes," Jerome amplifies. He looks at Freddi. "That's what it's doing, right?"

Now it's the purple, blood-caked lump on her forehead that her hand goes to. When her fingers touch it, she winces and pulls back her hand. "Yeah. Of the eight hundred Zappits that were delivered here, two hundred and eighty were defective. They either froze while they were booting up or went ka-bloosh the first time you tried to open one of the games. The others were okay. I had to install a root kit into each and every one of them. It was a lot of work. *Boring* work. Like attaching widgets to wadgets on an assembly line."

"That means five hundred and twenty were okay," Hodges says.

"The man can subtract, give him a cigar." Freddi glances at the readout. "And almost half of them have updated already." She laughs, a sound with absolutely no humor in it. "Brady may be nuts, but he worked this out pretty good, don't you think?"

Hodges says, "Turn it off."

"Sure. When you promise to protect me."

Jerome, who has firsthand experience with how fast the Zappits work and what unpleasant ideas they implant in a person's mind, has no interest in standing by while Freddi tries to dicker with Bill. The Swiss Army Knife he carried on his belt while in Arizona has been retrieved from his luggage and is now back in his pocket. He unfolds the biggest blade, shoves the repeater off its shelf, and slices the cables mating it to Freddi's system. It falls to the floor with a moderate crash, and an alarm begins to bong from the CPU under the desk. Holly bends down, pushes something, and the alarm shuts up.

"There's a switch, moron!" Freddi shouts. "You didn't have to do that!"

"You know what, I did," Jerome says. "One of those fucking Zappits almost got my sister killed." He steps toward her, and Freddi cringes back. "Did you have any idea what you were doing? Any fucking idea at all? I think you must have. You look stoned but not stupid."

Freddi begins to cry. "I didn't. I swear I didn't. Because I didn't want to."

Hodges takes a deep breath, which reawakens the pain. "Start from the beginning, Freddi, and take us through it."

"And as quickly as you can," Holly adds.

12

Jamie Winters was nine when he attended the 'Round Here concert at the Mac with his mother. Only a few subteen boys were
there that night; the group was one of those dismissed by most
boys his age as girly stuff. Jamie, however, liked girly stuff. At
nine he hadn't yet been sure that he was gay (wasn't even sure he
knew what that meant). All he knew was that when he saw Cam
Knowles, 'Round Here's lead singer, he felt funny in the pit of
his stomach.

Now he's pushing sixteen and knows exactly what he is. With
certain boys at school, he prefers to leave off the last letter of
his first name because with those boys he likes to be Jami. His
father knows what he is, as well, and treats him like some kind
of freak. Lenny Winters—a man's man if ever there was one—
owns a successful building company, but today all four of Winters Construction's current jobs are shut down because of the
impending storm. Lenny is in his home office instead, up to his
ears in paperwork and stewing over the spreadsheets covering his
computer screen.

"Dad!"

"What do you want?" Lenny growls without looking up.
"And why aren't you in school? Was it canceled?"

"*Dad!*"

This time Lenny looks around at the boy he sometimes refers
to (when he thinks Jamie isn't in earshot) as "the family queer."
The first thing he's aware of is that his son is wearing lipstick,
rouge, and eye shadow. The second thing is the dress. Lenny recognizes it as one of his wife's. The kid is too tall for it, and it
stops halfway down his thighs.

"*What* the *fuck*!"

Jamie is smiling. Jubilant. "It's how I want to be buried!"

"What are you—" Lenny gets up so fast his chair tumbles over. That's when he sees the gun the boy is holding. He must have taken it from Lenny's side of the closet in the master bedroom.

"Watch this, Dad!" Still smiling. As if about to demonstrate a really cool magic trick. He raises the gun and places the muzzle against his right temple. His finger is curled around the trigger. The nail has been carefully coated with sparkle polish.

"Put that down, Son! *Put it*—"

Jamie—or Jami, which is how he has signed his brief suicide note—pulls the trigger. The gun is a .357, and the report is deafening. Blood and brains fly in a fan and decorate the door-frame with gaud. The boy in his mother's dress and makeup falls forward, the left side of his face pushed out like a balloon.

Lenny Winters gives voice to a series of high, wavering screams. He screams like a girl.

13

Brady disconnects from Jamie Winters just as the boy puts the gun to his head, afraid—terrified, actually—of what may happen if he's still in there when the bullet enters the head he's been messing with. Would he be spit out like a seed, as he was when he was inside the half-hypnotized dumbo mopping the floor in 217, or would he die along with the kid?

For a moment he thinks he's left it until too late, and the steady chiming he hears is what everyone hears when they exit this life. Then he's back in the main room of Heads and Skins with the Zappit console in his sagging hand and Babineau's laptop in front of him. That's where the chiming is coming from. He looks at the screen and sees two messages. The first reads 248 FOUND. That's the good news. The second is the bad news:

REPEATER NOW OFFLINE

Freddi, he thinks. I didn't believe you had the guts. I really didn't.

You bitch.

His left hand gropes along the desk and closes on a ceramic skull filled with pens and pencils. He brings it up, meaning to smash it into the screen and destroy that infuriating message. What stops him is an idea. A horribly *plausible* idea.

Maybe she *didn't* have the guts. Maybe somebody else killed the repeater. And who could that someone else be? Hodges, of course. The old Det.-Ret. His fucking *nemesis*.

Brady knows he isn't exactly right in the head, has known that for years now, and understands this could be nothing but paranoia. Yet it makes a degree of sense. Hodges stopped his gloating visits to Room 217 almost a year and a half ago, but he was sniffing around the hospital just yesterday, according to Babineau.

And he always knew I was faking, Brady thinks. He said so, time and time again: *I know you're in there, Brady.* Some of the suits from the DA's office had said the same thing, but with them it had only been wishful thinking; they wanted to put him on trial and have done with him. Hodges, though . . .

"He said it with conviction," Brady says.

And maybe this isn't such terrible news, after all. Half of the Zappits Freddi loaded up and Babineau sent out are now active, which means most of those people will be as open to invasion as the little fag he just dealt with. Plus, there's the website. Once the Zappit people start killing themselves—with a little help from Brady Wilson Hartsfield, granted—the website will push others over the edge: monkey see, monkey do. At first it will be just the ones who were closest to doing it anyway, but they will lead by example and there will be many more. They'll march off the edge of life like stampeding buffalo going over a cliff.

But still.

Hodges.

Brady remembers a poster he had in his room when he was a boy: *If life hands you lemons, make lemonade!* Words to live by, especially when you kept in mind that the only way to make them into lemonade was to squeeze the hell out of them.

He grabs Z-Boy's old but serviceable flip phone and once again dials Freddi's number from memory.

## 14

Freddi gives a small scream when "Boogie Woogie Bugle Boy" starts tootling away from somewhere in the apartment. Holly puts a gentling hand on her shoulder and looks a question at Hodges. He nods and follows the sound, with Jerome on his heels. Her phone is on top of her dresser, amid a clutter of hand cream, Zig-Zag rolling papers, roach clips, and not one but two good-sized bags of pot.

The screen says Z-BOY, but Z-Boy, once known as Library Al Brooks, is currently in police custody and not likely to be making any calls.

"Hello?" Hodges says. "Is that you, Dr. Babineau?"

Nothing . . . or almost. Hodges can hear breathing.

"Or should I call you Dr. Z?"

Nothing.

"How about Brady, will that work?" He still can't quite believe this in spite of everything Freddi has told them, but he *can* believe that Babineau has gone schizo, and actually thinks that's who he is. "Is it you, asshole?"

The sound of the breathing continues for another two or three seconds, then it's gone. The connection has been broken.


15


"It's possible, you know," Holly says. She has joined them in Freddi's cluttered bedroom. "That it really could be Brady, I mean. Personality projection is well documented. In fact, it's the second-most-common cause of so-called demonic possession. The most common being schizophrenia. I saw a documentary about it on—"

"No," Hodges says. "Not possible. Not."

"Don't blind yourself to the idea. Don't be like Miss Pretty Gray Eyes."

"What's that supposed to mean?" Oh God, now the tendrils of pain are reaching all the way down to his balls.

"That you shouldn't turn away from the evidence just because it points in a direction you don't want to go. You know Brady was different when he regained consciousness. He came back with certain abilities most people don't have. Telekinesis may only have been one of them."

"I never saw him actually moving shit around."

"But you believe the nurses who did. Don't you?"

Hodges is silent, head lowered, thinking.

"Answer her," Jerome says. His tone is mild, but Hodges can hear impatience underneath.

"Yeah. I believed at least some of them. The levelheaded ones like Becky Helmington. Their stories matched up too well to be fabrications."

"Look at me, Bill."

This request—no, this *command*—coming from Holly Gibney is so unusual that he raises his head.

"Do you really believe *Babineau* reconfigured the Zappits and set up that website?"

"I don't have to believe it. He got Freddi to do those things."

"Not the website," a tired voice says.

They look around. Freddi is standing in the doorway.

"If I'd set it up, I could shut it down. I just got a thumb drive with all the website goodies on it from Dr. Z. Plugged it in and uploaded it. But once he was gone, I did a little investigating."

"Started with a DNS lookup, right?" Holly says.

Freddi nods. "Girl's got some skills."

To Hodges, Holly says, "DNS stands for Domain Name Server. It hops from one server to the next, like using stepping-stones to cross a creek, asking 'Do you know this site?' It keeps going and keeps asking until it finds the right server." Then, to Freddi: "But once you found the IP address, you still couldn't get in?"

"Nope."

Holly says, "I'm sure Babineau knows a lot about human brains, but I doubt very much if he has the computer smarts to lock up a website like that."

"I was just hired help," Freddi says. "It was Z-Boy who brought me the program for retooling the Zappits, written down like a recipe for coffee cake, or something, and I'd bet you a thousand dollars that all he knows about computers is how to turn them on—assuming he can find the button in back—and navigate to his favorite porn sites."

Hodges believes her about that much. He's not sure the police will when they finally catch hold of this thing, but Hodges does. And . . . *Don't be like Miss Pretty Gray Eyes.*

That stung. It stung like hell.

"Also," Freddi says, "there was a double dot after each step in the program directions. Brady used to do that. I think he learned it when he was taking computer classes in high school."

Holly grabs Hodges's wrists. There's blood on one of her hands, from patching Freddi's wound. Along with her other bells and whistles, Holly is a clean-freak, and that she's neglected to wash the blood off says all that needs to be said about how fiercely she's working this.

"Babineau was giving Hartsfield experimental drugs, which was unethical, but that's *all* he was doing, because bringing Brady back was all he was interested in."

"You don't know that for sure," Hodges says.

She's still holding him, more with her eyes than her hands. Because she's ordinarily averse to eye contact, it's easy to forget how burning that gaze can be when she turns it up to eleven and pulls the knobs off.

"There's really just one question," Holly says. "Who's the suicide prince in this story? Felix Babineau or Brady Hartsfield?"

Freddi speaks in a dreamy, sing-songy voice. "Sometimes Dr. Z was just Dr. Z and sometimes Z-Boy was just Z-Boy, only then it was like both of them were on drugs. When they were wide awake, though, it *wasn't* them. When they were awake, it was

Brady inside. Believe what you want, but it was him. It's not just the double dots or the backslanted printing, it's everything. I worked with that skeevy motherfucker. I know."

She steps into the room.

"And now, if none of you amateur detectives object, I'm going to roll myself another joint."

16

On Babineau's legs, Brady paces the big living room of Heads and Skins, thinking furiously. He wants to go back into the world of the Zappit, wants to pick a new target and repeat the delicious experience of pushing someone over the edge, but he has to be calm and serene to do that, and he's far from either.

Hodges.

Hodges in Freddi's apartment.

And will Freddi spill her guts? Friends and neighbors, does the sun rise in the east?

There are two questions, as Brady sees it. The first is whether or not Hodges can take down the website. The second is whether or not Hodges can find him out here in the williwags.

Brady thinks the answer to both questions is yes, but the more suicides he causes in the meantime, the more Hodges will suffer. When he looks at it in that light, he thinks that Hodges finding his way out here could be a good thing. It could be making lemonade from lemons. In any case, he has time. He's many miles north of the city, and he's got winter storm Eugenie on his side.

Brady goes back to the laptop and confirms that zeetheend is still up and running. He checks the visitors' count. Over nine thousand now, and most of them (but by no means all) will be

362

teenagers interested in suicide. That interest peaks in January and February, when dark comes early and it seems spring will never arrive. Plus, he's got Zappit Zero, and with that he can work on plenty of kids personally. With Zappit Zero, getting to them is as easy as shooting fish in a barrel.

*Pink* fish, he thinks, and snickers.

Calmer now that he sees a way of dealing with the old Det.-Ret. should he try showing up like the cavalry in the last reel of a John Wayne western, Brady picks up the Zappit and turns it on. As he studies the fish, a fragment of some poem read in high school occurs to him, and he speaks it aloud.

"Oh do not ask what is it, let us go and make our visit."

He closes his eyes. The zipping pink fish become zipping red dots, each one a bygone concertgoer who is at this very moment studying his or her gift Zappit and hoping to win prizes.

Brady picks one, brings it to a halt, and watches it bloom.

Like a rose.

## 17

"Sure, there's a police computer forensics squad," Hodges says, in answer to Holly's question. "If you want to call three part-time crunchers a squad, that is. And no, they won't listen to me. I'm just a civilian these days." Nor is that the worst of it. He's a civilian who used to be a cop, and when retired cops try meddling in police business, they are called uncles. It is not a term of respect.

"Then call Pete and have him do it," Holly says. "Because that fracking suicide site has to come down."

The two of them are back in Freddi Linklatter's version of Mission Control. Jerome is in the living room with Freddi. Hodges doesn't think she's apt to flee—Freddi's terrified of the probably fictional men posted outside her building—but stoner behavior is difficult to predict. Other than how they usually want to get more stoned, that is.

"Call Pete and tell him to have one of the computer geeks call me. Any cruncher with half a brain will be able to doss the site and knock it down that way."

"Doss it?"

"Big D, little o, big S. Stands for Denial of Services. The guy needs to connect to a BOT network and . . ." She sees Hodges's mystified expression. "Never mind. The idea is to flood the suicide site with requests for services—thousands, millions. Choke the fracking thing and crash the server."

"You can do that?"

"I can't, and Freddi can't, but a police department geek freak will be able to tap enough computing power. If he can't do it from the police computers, he'll get Homeland Security to do it. Because this *is* a security issue, right? Lives are at stake."

They are, and Hodges makes the call, but Pete's cell goes directly to voicemail. Next he tries his old pal Cassie Sheen, but the desk officer who takes his call tells him Cassie's mother had some sort of diabetic crisis and Cassie took her to the doctor.

Out of other options, he calls Isabelle.

"Izzy, it's Bill Hodges. I tried to get Pete, but—"

"Pete's gone. Done. Kaput."

For one awful moment Hodges thinks she means he's dead.

"Left a memo on my desk. It said he was going to go home, turn off his cell, pull the plug on the landline, and sleep for the next twenty-four hours. He further shared that today was his last day as working police. He can do it, too, doesn't even have to touch his vacation time, of which he has piles. He's got enough personal days to see him through to retirement. And I think you better scratch that retirement party off your calendar. You and your weirdo partner can hit a movie that night, instead."

"You're blaming me?"

"You and your Brady Hartsfield fixation. You infected Pete with it."

"No. He wanted to chase the case. You were the one who wanted to hand it off, then duck down in the nearest foxhole. Gotta say I'm kind of on Pete's side when it comes to that one."

"See? See? That's exactly the attitude I'm talking about. Wake up, Hodges, this is the real world. I'm telling you for the last time to quit sticking your long beak into what isn't your busi—"

"And I'm telling *you* that if you want to have any fucking chance of promotion, you need to get your head out of your ass and listen to me."

The words are out before he can think better of them. He's afraid she'll hang up, and if she does, where will he go then? But there's only shocked silence.

"Suicides. Have any been reported since you got back from Sugar Heights?"

"I don't kn—"

"Well, look! Right now!"

He can hear the faint tapping of Izzy's keyboard for five seconds or so. Then: "One just came over the wire. Kid in Lakewood shot himself. Did it in front of his father, who called it in. Hysterical, as you might expect. What's that got to do with—"

"Tell the cops on the scene to look for a Zappit game console. Just like the one Holly found at the Ellerton house."

"That again? You're like a broken rec—"

"They'll find one. And you may have more Zappit suicides before the day's over. Possibly a lot more."

*Website!* Holly mouths. *Tell her about the website!*

"Also, there's a suicide website called zeetheend. Just went up today. It needs to come down."

She sighs and speaks as though to a child. "There are all *kinds* of suicide websites. We got a memo about it from Juvenile Services just last year. They pop up on the Net like mushrooms, usually created by kids who wear black tee-shirts and spend all their free time holed up in their bedrooms. There's a lot of bad poetry and stuff about how to do it painlessly. Along with the usual bitching about how their parents don't understand them, of course."

"This one is different. It could start an avalanche. It's loaded with subliminal messages. Have someone from computer forensics call Holly Gibney ASAP."

"That would be outside of protocol," she says coolly. "I'll have a look, then go through channels."

"Have one of your rent-a-geeks call Holly in the next five minutes, or when the suicides start cascading—and I'm pretty sure they will—I'll make it clear to anyone who'll listen that I went to you and you tied me up in red tape. My listeners will include the daily paper and *8 Alive.* The department does not have a lot of friends in either place, especially since those two unis shot an unarmed black kid to death on MLK last summer."

Silence. Then, in a softer voice—a hurt voice, maybe—she says, "You're supposed to be on *our* side, Billy. Why are you acting this way?"

Because Holly was right about you, he thinks.

Out loud he says, "Because there isn't much time."

18

In the living room, Freddi is rolling another joint. She looks at Jerome over the top of it as she licks the paper closed. "You're a big one, aren't you?"

Jerome makes no reply.

"What do you go? Two-ten? Two-twenty?"

Jerome has nothing to say to this, either.

Undeterred, she sparks the joint, inhales, and holds it out to him. Jerome shakes his head.

"Your loss, big boy. This is pretty good shit. Smells like dog pee, I know, but pretty good shit, just the same."

Jerome says nothing.

"Cat got your tongue?"

"No. I was thinking about a sociology class I took when I was a high school senior. We did a four-week mod on suicide, and there was one statistic I never forgot. Every teen suicide that makes it onto social media spawns seven attempts, five that are show and two that are go. Maybe you should think about that instead of running the tough-girl act into the ground."

Freddi's lower lip trembles. "I didn't know. Not really."

"Sure you did."

She drops her eyes to the joint. It's her turn to say nothing.

"My sister heard a voice."

At that, Freddi looks up. "What kind of voice?"

"One from the Zappit. It told her all sorts of mean things. About how she was trying to live white. About how she was denying her race. About how she was a bad and worthless person."

"And that reminds you of someone?"

"Yes." Jerome is thinking of the accusatory shrieks he and Holly heard coming from Olivia Trelawney's computer long after that unfortunate lady was dead. Shrieks programmed by Brady Hartsfield, and designed to drive Trelawney toward suicide like a cow down a slaughterhouse chute. "Actually, it does."

"Brady was fascinated by suicide," Freddi says. "He was always reading about it on the web. He meant to kill himself with the others at that concert, you know."

Jerome does know. He was there. "Do you really think he got in touch with my sister telepathically? Using the Zappit as . . . what? A kind of conduit?"

"If he could take over Babineau and the other guy—and he did, whether you believe it or not—then yeah, I think he could do that."

"And the others with updated Zappits? Those two hundred and forty-something others?"

Freddi only looks at him through her veil of smoke.

"Even if we take down the website . . . what about them? What about when that voice starts telling them they're dogshit on the world's shoe, and the only answer is to take a long walk off a short dock?"

Before she can reply, Hodges does it for her. "We have to stop the voice. Which means stopping *him*. Come on, Jerome. We're going back to the office."

"What about me?" Freddi asks plaintively.

"You're coming. And Freddi?"

"What?"

"Pot's good for pain, isn't it?"

"Opinions on that vary, as you might guess, the establishment in this fucked-up country being what it is, so all I can tell you is that for me, it makes that delicate time of the month a lot less delicate."

"Bring it along," Hodges says. "Also the rolling papers."

### 19

They go back to Finders Keepers in Jerome's Jeep. The back is full of Jerome's junk, meaning Freddi has to sit on someone's lap, and it's not going to be Hodges's. Not in his current condition. So he drives and Jerome gets Freddi.

"Hey, this is sort of like getting a date with John Shaft," Freddi says with a smirk. "The big private dick who's a sex machine to all the chicks."

"Don't get used to it," Jerome says.

Holly's cell rings. It's a guy named Trevor Jeppson, from the police department's Computer Forensics Squad. Holly is soon speaking in a jargon Hodges doesn't understand—something about BOTS and the darknet. Whatever she's getting back from the guy seems to please her, because when she breaks the connection, she's smiling.

"He's never dossed a website before. He's like a kid on Christmas morning."

"How long will it take?"

"With the password and the IP address already in hand? Not long."

Hodges parks in one of the thirty-minute spaces in front of the Turner Building. They won't be here long—if he gets lucky, that is—and given his recent run of bad luck, he considers the universe owes him a good turn.

He goes into his office, closes the door, then hunts through his ratty old address book for Becky Helmington's number. Holly has offered to program the address book into his phone, but Hodges has kept putting it off. He *likes* his old address book. Probably never get around to making the changeover now, he thinks. Trent's Last Case, and all that.

Becky reminds him she doesn't work in the Bucket any longer. "Maybe you forgot that?"

"I didn't forget. You know about Babineau?"

Her voice drops. "God, yes. I heard that Al Brooks—Library Al—killed Babineau's wife and might have killed him. I can hardly believe it."

I could tell you lots of stuff you'd hardly believe, Hodges thinks.

"Don't count Babineau out yet, Becky. I think he might be on the run. He was giving Brady Hartsfield experimental drugs of some kind, and they may have played a part in Hartsfield's death."

"Jesus, for real?"

"For real. But he can't be too far, not with this storm coming in. Can you think of anyplace he might have gone? Does Babineau own a summer cottage, anything like that?"

She doesn't even need to think about it. "Not a cottage, a hunting camp. It isn't just him, though. Four or maybe five docs co-own the place." Her voice drops to that confidential pitch again. "I hear they do more than hunt out there. If you know what I mean."

"Where is out there?"

"Lake Charles. The camp has some cutesy-horrible name. I can't remember it offhand, but I bet Violet Tranh would know. She spent a weekend there once. Said it was the drunkest forty-eight hours of her life, and she came back with chlamydia."

"Will you call her?"

"Sure. But if he's on the run, he might be on a plane, you know. Maybe to California or even overseas. The flights were still taking off and landing this morning."

"I don't think he would have dared to try the airport with the police looking for him. Thanks, Becky. Call me back."

He goes to the safe and punches in the combination. The sock filled with ball bearings—his Happy Slapper—is back home, but both of his handguns are here. One is the Glock .40 he carried on the job. The other is a .38, the Victory model. It was his father's. He takes a canvas sack from the top shelf of the safe, puts the guns and four boxes of ammunition into it, then gives the drawstring a hard yank.

No heart attack to stop me this time, Brady, he thinks. This time it's just cancer, and I can live with that.

The idea surprises him into laughter. It hurts.

From the other room comes the sound of three people applauding. Hodges is pretty sure he knows what it means, and he's not wrong. The message on Holly's computer reads ZEETHEEND IS EXPERIENCING TECHNICAL DIFFICULTIES. Below is this: CALL 1-800-273-TALK.

"It was that guy Jeppson's idea," Holly says, not looking up from what she's doing. "It's the National Suicide Prevention Hotline."

"Good one," Hodges says. "And those are good, too. You're a woman with hidden talents." In front of Holly is a line of joints. The one she adds makes an even dozen.

"She's fast," Freddi says admiringly. "And look how neat they are. Like they came out of a machine."

Holly gives Hodges a defiant look. "My therapist says an occasional marijuana cigarette is perfectly okay. As long as I don't go overboard, that is. The way some people do." Her eyes glide to Freddi, then back to Hodges. "Besides, these aren't for me. They're for you, Bill. If you need them."

Hodges thanks her, and has a moment to reflect on how far the two of them have come, and how pleasant, by and large, the trip has been. But too short. Far too short. Then his phone rings. It's Becky.

"The name of the place is Heads and Skins. I told you it was cutesy-horrible. Vi doesn't remember how to get there—I'm guessing she had more than a few shots on the ride, just to get her motor running—but she does remember they went north on the turnpike for quite a ways, and stopped for gas at a place called Thurston's Garage after they got off. Does that help?"

"Yeah, a ton. Thanks, Becky." He ends the call. "Holly, I need you to find Thurston's Garage, north of the city. Then I want you to call Hertz at the airport and rent the biggest four-wheel drive they've got left. We're going on a road trip."

"My Jeep—" Jerome begins.

"Is small, light, and old," Hodges says . . . although these are not the only reasons he wants a different vehicle built to go in the snow. "It'll be fine to get us out to the airport, though."

"What about me?" Freddi asks.

"WITSEC," Hodges says, "as promised. It'll be like a dream come true."


20


Jane Ellsbury was a perfectly normal baby—at six pounds, nine ounces, a little underweight, in fact—but by the time she was seven, she weighed ninety pounds and was familiar with the chant that sometimes haunts her dreams to this day: *Fatty fatty, two by four, can't get through the bathroom door, so she does it on the floor.* In June of 2010, when her mother took her to the 'Round Here concert as a fifteenth birthday present, she weighed two hundred and ten. She could still get through the bathroom door with no problem, but it had become difficult for her to tie her shoes. Now she's twenty, her weight has risen to three hundred and twenty, and when the voice begins to speak to her from the free Zappit she got in the mail, everything it says makes perfect sense to her. The voice is low, calm, and reasonable. It tells her that nobody likes her and everybody laughs at her. It points out that she can't stop eating—even now, with tears running down her face, she's snarfing her way through a bag of chocolate pinwheel cookies, the kind with lots of gooey marshmallow inside. Like a more kindly version of the ghost of Christmas Yet to Come, who pointed out certain home truths to Ebenezer Scrooge, it sketches in a future which boils down to fat, fatter, fattest. The laughter along Carbine Street in Hillbilly Heaven, where she and her parents live in a walk-up apartment. The looks of disgust. The jibes, like *Here comes the Goodyear Blimp* and *Look out, don't let her fall on you!* The voice explains, logically and reasonably, that she will never have a date, will never be hired for a good job now that political correctness has rendered the circus fat lady extinct, that by the age of forty she will have to sleep sitting up because her enormous breasts will make it impossible for her lungs to do their work, and before she dies of a heart attack at fifty, she'll be using a DustBuster to get the crumbs out of the deepest creases in her rolls of fat. When she tries to suggest to the voice that she could lose some weight—go to one of those clinics, maybe—it doesn't laugh. It only asks her, softly and sympathetically, where the money will come from, when the combined incomes of her mother and father are barely enough to satisfy an appetite that is basically insatiable. When the voice suggests they'd be better off without her, she can only agree.

Jane—known to the denizens of Carbine Street as Fat Jane—lumbers into the bathroom and takes the bottle of OxyContin pills her father has for his bad back. She counts them. There are thirty, which should be more than enough. She takes them five at a time, with milk, eating a chocolate marshmallow cookie after each swallow. She begins to float away. I'm going on a diet, she thinks. I'm going on a long, long diet.

That's right, the voice from the Zappit tells her. And you'll never cheat on this one, Jane—will you?

She takes the last five Oxys. She tries to pick up the Zappit, but her fingers will no longer close on the slim console. And what does it matter? She could never catch the speedy pink fish in this condition, anyway. Better to look out the window, where the snow is burying the world in clean linen.

No more fatty-fatty-two-by-four, she thinks, and when she slips into unconsciousness, she goes with relief.

21

Before going to Hertz, Hodges swings Jerome's Jeep into the turnaround in front of the Airport Hilton.

"This is supposed to be Witness Protection?" Freddi asks. "*This?*"

Hodges says, "Since I don't happen to have a safe house at my disposal, it will have to do. I'll register you under my name. You go in, you lock the door, you watch TV, you wait until this thing is over."

"And change the dressing on that wound," Holly says.

Freddi ignores her. She's focused on Hodges. "How much trouble am I going to be in? When it's over?"

"I don't know, and I don't have time to discuss it with you now."

"Can I at least order room service?" There's a faint gleam in Freddi's bloodshot eyes. "I'm not in so much pain now, and I've got a wicked case of the munchies."

"Knock yourself out," Hodges says.

Jerome adds, "Only check the peephole before you let in the waiter. Make sure it isn't one of Brady Hartsfield's Men in Black."

"You're kidding," Freddi says. "Right?"

The hotel lobby is dead empty on this snowy afternoon. Hodges, who feels as if he woke up to Pete's telephone call approximately three years ago, walks to the desk, does his business there, and comes back to where the others are sitting. Holly is tapping away at something on her iPad, and doesn't look up. Freddi holds out her hand for the key folder, but Hodges gives it to Jerome, instead.

"Room 522. Take her up, will you? I want to talk to Holly."

Jerome raises his eyebrows, and when Hodges doesn't elaborate, he shrugs and takes Freddi by the arm. "John Shaft will now escort you to your suite."

She pushes his hand away. "Be lucky if it even has a minibar." But she gets up and walks with him toward the elevators.

"I found Thurston's Garage," Holly says. "It's fifty-six miles north on I-47, the direction the storm's coming from, unfortunately. After that it's State Road 79. The weather really doesn't look g—"

"We'll be okay," Hodges says. "Hertz is holding a Ford Expedition for us. It's a nice heavy vehicle. And you can give me the

turn-by-turn later. I want to talk to you about something else."
Gently, he takes her iPad and turns it off.

Holly looks at him with her hands clasped in her lap, waiting.

22

Brady comes back from Carbine Street in Hillbilly Heaven
refreshed and exhilarated—the Ellsbury fatso was both easy and
fun. He wonders how many guys it will take to get her body
down from that third-floor apartment. He's guessing at least
four. And think of the coffin! Jumbo size!

When he checks the website and finds it offline, his good
mood collapses again. Yes, he expected Hodges would find a
way to kill it, but he didn't expect it to happen so fast. And the
phone number on the screen is as infuriating as the fuck-you
messages Hodges left on Debbie's Blue Umbrella during their
first go-round. It's a suicide prevention hotline. He doesn't even
have to check. He *knows*.

And yes, Hodges will come. Plenty of people at Kiner Memorial know about this place; it's sort of legendary. But will he
come straight in? Brady doesn't believe that for a minute. For
one thing, the Det.-Ret. will know that many hunters leave
their firearms out at camp (although few are as fully stocked
with them as Heads and Skins). For another—and this is more
important—the Det.-Ret. is one sly hyena. Six years older than
when Brady first encountered him, true, undoubtedly shorter of
wind and shakier of limb, but sly. The sort of slinking animal
that doesn't come at you directly but goes for the hamstrings
while you're looking elsewhere.

So I'm Hodges. What do I do?

After giving this due consideration, Brady goes to the closet, and a brief check of Babineau's memory (what's left of it) is all it takes for him to choose outerwear that belongs to the body he's inhabiting. Everything fits perfectly. He adds a pair of gloves to protect his arthritic fingers and goes outside. The snow is only a moderate fall and the branches of the trees are still. All that will change later, but for now it's pleasant enough to go for a tramp around the property.

He walks to a woodpile whose surface is covered with an old canvas tarp and a few inches of fresh powder. Beyond it are two or three acres of old-growth pines and spruces separating Heads and Skins from Big Bob's Bear Camp. It's perfect.

He needs to visit the gun closet. The Scar is fine, but there are other things in there he can use.

Oh, Detective Hodges, Brady thinks, hurrying back the way he came. I've got such a surprise. Such a surprise for you.

### 23

Jerome listens carefully to what Hodges tells him, then shakes his head. "No way, Bill. I need to come."

"What you need to do is go home and be with your family," Hodges says. "You especially need to be with your sister. She had a close call yesterday."

They are sitting in a corner of the Hilton's reception area, speaking in low voices although even the desk clerk has retired to the nether regions. Jerome is leaning forward, hands planted on his thighs, his face set in a stubborn frown.

"If Holly's going—"

"It's different for us," Holly says. "You must see that, Jerome.

I don't get along with my mother, never have. I see her once or twice a year, at most. I'm always glad to leave, and I'm sure she's glad to see me go. As for Bill . . . you know he'll fight what he's got, but both of us know what the chances are. Your case is not like ours."

"He's dangerous," Hodges says, "and we can't count on the element of surprise. If he doesn't know I'll come for him, he's stupid. That's one thing he never was."

"It was the three of us at the Mingo," Jerome says. "And after you went into vapor lock, it was just Holly and me. We did okay."

"Last time was different," Holly says. "Last time he wasn't capable of mind control juju."

"I still want to come."

Hodges nods. "I understand, but I'm still the wheeldog, and the wheeldog says no."

"But—"

"There's another reason," Holly says. "A bigger reason. The repeater's offline and the website's shut down, but that leaves almost two hundred and fifty active Zappits. There's been at least one suicide already, and we can't tell the police all of what's going on. Isabelle Jaynes thinks Bill's a meddler, and anyone else would think we're crazy. If anything happens to us, there's only you. Don't you understand that?"

"What I understand is that you're cutting me out," Jerome says. All at once he sounds like the weedy young kid Hodges hired to mow his lawn all those years ago.

"There's more," Hodges says. "I might have to kill him. In fact, I think that's the most likely outcome."

"Jesus, Bill, I know that."

"But to the cops and the world at large, the man I killed

would be a respected neurosurgeon named Felix Babineau. I've wiggled out of some tight legal corners since opening Finders Keepers, but this one could be different. Do you want to risk being charged as an accessory to aggravated manslaughter, defined in this state as the reckless killing of a human being through culpable negligence? Maybe even Murder One?"

Jerome squirms. "You're willing to let Holly risk that."

Holly says, "You're the one with most of your life still ahead of you."

Hodges leans forward, even though it hurts to do so, and cups the broad nape of Jerome's neck. "I know you don't like it. I didn't expect you would. But it's the right thing, for all the right reasons."

Jerome thinks it over, and sighs. "I see your point."

Hodges and Holly wait, both of them knowing this is not quite good enough.

"Okay," Jerome says at last. "I hate it, but okay."

Hodges gets up, hand to his side to hold in the pain. "Then let's snag that SUV. The storm's coming, and I'd like to get as far up I-47 as possible before we meet it."


24


Jerome is leaning against the hood of his Wrangler when they come out of the rental office with the keys to an all-wheel drive Expedition. He hugs Holly and whispers in her ear. "Last chance. Take me along."

She shakes her head against his chest.

He lets her go and turns to Hodges, who's wearing an old fedora, the brim already white with snow. Hodges puts out a hand. "Under other circumstances I'd go with the hug, but right now hugs hurt."

Jerome settles for a strong grip. There are tears in his eyes. "Be careful, man. Stay in touch. And bring back the Hollyberry."

"I intend to do that," Hodges says.

Jerome watches them get into the Expedition, Bill climbing behind the wheel with obvious discomfort. Jerome knows they're right—of the three of them, he's the least expendable. That doesn't mean he likes it, or feels less like a little kid being sent home to Mommy. He would go after them, he thinks, except for the thing Holly said in that deserted hotel lobby. *If anything happens to us, there's only you.*

Jerome gets into his Jeep and heads home. As he merges onto the Crosstown, a strong premonition comes to him: he's never going to see either one of his friends again. He tries to tell himself that's superstitious bullshit, but he can't quite make it work.

## 25

By the time Hodges and Holly leave the Crosstown for I-47 North, the snow is no longer just kidding around. Driving into it reminds Hodges of a science fiction movie he saw with Holly—the moment when the Starship *Enterprise* goes into hyperdrive, or whatever they call it. The speed limit signs are flashing SNOW ALERT and 40 MPH, but he pegs the speedometer at sixty and will hold it there as long as he can, which might be for thirty miles. Perhaps only twenty. A few cars in the travel lane honk at him to slow down, and passing the lumbering eighteen-wheelers, each one dragging a rooster-tail fog of snow behind it, is an exercise in controlled fear.

It's almost half an hour before Holly breaks the silence. "You brought the guns, didn't you? That's what's in the drawstring bag."

"Yeah."

She unbuckles her seatbelt (which makes him nervous) and fishes the bag out of the backseat. "Are they loaded?"

"The Glock is. The .38 you'll have to load it yourself. That one's yours."

"I don't know how."

Hodges offered to take her to the shooting range with him once, start the process of getting her qualified to carry concealed, and she refused vehemently. He never offered again, believing she would never need to carry a gun. Believing he would never put her in that position.

"You'll figure it out. It's not hard."

She examines the Victory, keeping her hands well away from the trigger and the muzzle well away from her face. After a few seconds she succeeds in rolling the barrel.

"Okay, now the bullets."

There are two boxes of Winchester .38s—130-grain, full metal jacket. She opens one, looks at the shells sticking up like mini-warheads, and grimaces. "Oough."

"Can you do it?" He's passing another truck, the Expedition enveloped in snowfog. There are still strips of bare pavement in the travel lane, but this passing lane is now snow-covered, and the truck on their right seems to go on forever. "If you can't, that's okay."

"You don't mean can I load it," she says, sounding angry. "I see how to do that, a kid could do it."

Sometimes they do, Hodges thinks.

"What you mean is can I shoot him."

"It probably won't come to that, but if it did, could you?"

"Yes," Holly says, and loads the Victory's six chambers. She pushes the cylinder back into place gingerly, lips turned down and eyes squinted into slits, as if afraid the gun will explode in her hand. "Now where's the safety switch?"

"There isn't any. Not on revolvers. The hammer's down, and that's all the safety that you need. Put it in your purse. The ammo, too."

She does as he says, then places the bag between her feet.

"And stop biting your lips, you're going to make them bleed."

"I'll try, but this is a very stressful situation, Bill."

"I know." They're back in the travel lane again. The mile markers seem to float past with excruciating slowness, and the pain in his side is a hot jellyfish with long tentacles that now seem to reach everywhere, even up into his throat. Once, twenty years ago, he was shot in the leg by a thief cornered in a vacant lot. That pain had been like this, but eventually it had gone away. He doesn't think this one ever will. The drugs may mute it for awhile, but probably not for long.

"What if we find this place and he's not there, Bill? Have you thought about that? Have you?"

He has, and has no idea what the next step would be in that case. "Let's not worry about it unless we have to."

His phone rings. It's in his coat pocket, and he hands it to Holly without looking away from the road ahead.

"Hello, this is Holly." She listens, then mouths *Miss Pretty Gray Eyes* to Hodges. "Uh-huh . . . yes . . . okay, I understand . . . no, he can't, his hands are full right now, but I'll tell him." She listens some more, then says, "I could tell you, Izzy, but you wouldn't believe me."

She closes his phone with a snap and slips it back into his pocket.

"Suicides?" Hodges asks.

"Three so far, counting the boy who shot himself in front of his father."

"Zappits?"

"At two of the three locations. Responders at the third one haven't had a chance to look. They were trying to save the kid, but it was too late. He hung himself. Izzy sounds half out of her mind. She wanted to know everything."

"If anything happens to us, Jerome will tell Pete, and Pete will tell her. I think she's almost ready to listen."

"We have to stop him before he kills more."

He's probably killing more right now, Hodges thinks. "We will."

The miles roll by. Hodges is forced to reduce his speed to fifty, and when he feels the Expedition do a loose little shimmy in the slipstream of a Walmart double box, he drops to forty-five. It's past three o'clock and the light is starting to drain from this snowy day when Holly speaks again.

"Thank you."

He turns his head briefly, looking a question at her.

"For not making me beg to come along."

"I'm only doing what your therapist would want," Hodges says. "Getting you a bunch of closure."

"Is that a joke? I can never tell when you're joking. You have an extremely dry sense of humor, Bill."

"No joke. This is our business, Holly. Nobody else's."

A green sign looms out of the white murk.

"SR-79," Holly says. "That's our exit."

"Thank God," Hodges says. "I hate turnpike driving even when the sun's out."

26

Thurston's Garage is fifteen miles east along the state highway, according to Holly's iPad, but it takes them half an hour to get there. The Expedition handles the snow-covered road easily, but now the wind is picking up—it will be blowing at gale force by eight o'clock, according to the radio—and when it gusts, throwing sheets of snow across the road, Hodges eases down to fifteen miles an hour until he can see again.

As he turns in at the big yellow Shell sign, Holly's phone rings. "Handle that," he says. "I'll be as quick as I can."

He gets out, yanking his fedora down hard to keep it from blowing away. The wind machine-guns his coat collar against his neck as he tramps through the snow to the garage office. His entire midsection is throbbing; it feels as if he's swallowed live coals. The gas pumps and the adjacent parking area are empty except for the idling Expedition. The plowboys have departed to spend a long night earning their money as the first big storm of the year rants and raves.

For one eerie moment, Hodges thinks it's Library Al behind the counter: same green Dickies, same popcorn-white hair exploding around the edges of his John Deere cap.

"What brings you out on a wild afternoon like this?" the old guy asks, then peers past Hodges. "Or is it night already?"

"A little of both," Hodges says. He has no time for conversation—back in the city kids may be jumping out of apartment-building windows and swallowing pills—but it's how the job is done. "Would you be Mr. Thurston?"

"In the flesh. Since you didn't pull up at the pumps, I'd almost wonder if you came to rob me, but you look a little too prosperous for that. City fella?"

"I am," Hodges says, "and in kind of a hurry."

"City fellas usually are." Thurston puts down the *Field & Stream* he's been reading. "What is it, then? Directions? Man, I hope it's somewhere close, the way this one's shaping up."

"I think it is. A hunting camp called Heads and Skins. Ring a bell?"

"Oh, sure," Thurston says. "The doctors' place, right near Big Bob's Bear Camp. Those fellas usually gas up their Jags and Porsches here, either on their way out or their way back." He pronounces *Porsches* as if he's talking about the things old folks sit on in the evening to watch the sun go down. "Wouldn't be nobody out there now, though. Hunting season ends December ninth, and I'm talking bow hunting. Gun hunting ends the last day of November, and all those docs use rifles. Big ones. I think they like to pretend they're in Africa."

"Nobody stopped earlier today? Would have been driving an old car with a lot of primer on it?"

"Nope."

A young man comes out of the garage bay, wiping his hands on a rag. "I saw that car, Granddad. A Chev'alay. I was out front, talking with Spider Willis, when it went by." He turns his attention to Hodges. "I only noticed because there's not much the way he was headed, and that car was no snowdog like the one you've got out there."

"Can you give me directions to the camp?"

"Easiest thing in the world," Thurston says. "Or would be on a fair day. You keep on going the way you were heading, about . . ." He turns his attention to the younger man. "What would you say, Duane? Three miles?"

"More like four," Duane says.

"Well, split the difference and call it three and a half," Thurston says. "You'll be looking for two red posts on your left.

385

They're tall, six feet or so, but the state plow's been by twice already, so you want to keep a sharp eye, because there won't be much of em to see. You'll have to bull your way through the snowbank, you know. Unless you brought a shovel."

"I think what I'm driving will do it," Hodges says.

"Yeah, most likely, and no harm to your SUV, since the snow hasn't had a chance to pack down. Anyway, you go in a mile, or maybe two, and the road splits. One fork goes to Big Bob's, the other to Heads and Skins. I can't remember which one is which, but there used to be arrow signs."

"Still are," Duane says. "Big Bob's is on the right, Heads and Skins on the left. I ought to know, I reshingled Big Bob Rowan's roof last October. This must be pretty important, mister. To get you out on a day like this."

"Will my SUV make it on that road, do you think?"

"Sure," Duane says. "Trees'll still be holding up most of the snow, and the road runs downhill to the lake. Making it out might be a little trickier."

Hodges takes his wallet from his back pocket—Christ, even that hurts—and fishes out his police ID with RETIRED stamped on it. To it he adds one of his Finders Keepers business cards, and lays them both on the counter. "Can you gentlemen keep a secret?"

They nod, faces bright with curiosity.

"I've got a subpoena to serve, right? It's a civil case, and the money at stake runs to seven figures. The man you saw go by, the one in the primered-up Chevy, is a doctor named Babineau."

"See him every November," the elder Thurston says. "Got an attitude about him, you know? Like he's always seein you from under the end of his nose. But he drives a Beemer."

"Today he's driving whatever he could get his hands on,"

386

Hodges says, "and if I don't serve these papers by midnight, the case goes bye-bye, and an old lady who doesn't have much won't get her payday."

"Malpractice?" Duane asks.

"Don't like to say, but I'm going in."

Which you will remember, Hodges thinks. That, and Babineau's name.

The old man says, "There are a couple of snowmobiles out back. I could let you have one, if you want, and the Arctic Cat has a high windshield. It'd still be a chilly ride, but you'd be guaranteed getting back."

Hodges is touched by the offer, coming as it does to a complete stranger, but shakes his head. Snowmobiles are noisy beasts. He has an idea that the man now in residence at Heads and Skins—be he Brady or Babineau or a weird mixture of the two—knows he's coming. What Hodges has on his side is that his quarry doesn't know when.

"My partner and I will get in," he says, "and worry about getting out later."

"Nice and quiet, huh?" Duane says, and puts a finger to his lips, which are curved in a smile.

"That's the ticket. Is there someone I could call for a ride if I do get stuck?"

"Call right here." Thurston hands him a card from the plastic tray by the cash register. "I'll send either Duane or Spider Willis. It might not be until late tonight, and it'll cost you forty dollars, but with a case worth millions, I guess you can afford that."

"Do cell phones work out here?"

"Five bars even in dirty weather," Duane says. "There's a tower on the south side of the lake."

"Good to know. Thank you. Thank you both."

He turns to go and the old man says, "That hat you're wearing is no good in this weather. Take this." He's holding out a knit hat with a big orange pompom on top. "Can't do nothing about those shoes, though."

Hodges thanks him, takes the hat, then removes his fedora and puts it on the counter. It feels like bad luck; it feels like exactly the right thing to do. "Collateral," he says.

Both of them grin, the younger one with quite a few more teeth.

"Good enough," the old man says, "but are you a hundred percent sure you want to be driving out to the lake, Mr.—" he glances down at the Finders Keepers business card—"Mr. Hodges? Because you look a trifle peaky."

"It's a chest cold," Hodges says. "I get one every damn winter. Thank you, both of you. And if Dr. Babineau should by any chance call here . . ."

"Wouldn't give him the time of day," Thurston says. "He's a snooty one."

Hodges starts for the door, and a pain like none he's ever felt before comes out of nowhere, lancing up from his belly all the way to his jawline. It's like being shot by a burning arrow, and he staggers.

"Are you sure you're okay?" the old man asks, starting around the counter.

"Yeah, I'm fine." He's far from that. "Leg cramp. From driving. I'll be back for my hat."

With luck, he thinks.

27

"You were in there a long time," Holly says. "I hope you gave them a very good story."

"Subpoena." Hodges doesn't need to say more; they've used the subpoena story more than once. Everyone likes to help, as long as they're not the ones being served. "Who called?" Thinking it must have been Jerome, to see how they're doing.

"Izzy Jaynes. They've had two more suicide calls, one attempted and one successful. The attempted was a girl who jumped out of a second-story window. She landed on a snowbank and just broke some bones. The other was a boy who hung himself in his closet. Left a note on his pillow. Just one word, *Beth*, and a broken heart."

The Expedition's wheels spin a little when Hodges drops it into gear and rolls back onto the state road. He has to drive with his low beams on. The brights turn the falling snow into a sparkling white wall.

"We have to do this ourselves," she says. "If it's Brady, no one will ever believe it. He'll pretend to be Babineau and spin some story about how he was scared and ran away."

"And never called the police himself after Library Al shot his wife?" Hodges says. "I'm not sure that would hold."

"Maybe not, but what if he can jump to someone else? If he could jump to Babineau, who else could he jump to? We have to do this ourselves, even if it means we end up getting arrested for murder. Do you think that could happen, Bill? Do you do you do you?"

"We'll worry about it later."

"I'm not sure I could shoot a person. Not even Brady Hartsfield, if he looks like someone else."

389

He repeats, "We'll worry about it later."

"Fine. Where did you get that hat?"

"Swapped it for my fedora."

"The puffball on top is silly, but it looks warm."

"Do you want it?"

"No. But Bill?"

"Jesus, Holly, what?"

"You look awful."

"Flattery will get you nowhere."

"Be sarcastic. Fine. How far is it to where we're going?"

"The general consensus back there was three and a half miles on this road. Then a camp road."

Silence for five minutes as they creep through the blowing snow. And the main body of the storm is still coming, Hodges reminds himself.

"Bill?"

"What now?"

"You have no boots, and I'm all out of Nicorette."

"Spark up one of those joints, why don't you? But keep an eye out for a couple of red posts on the left while you do it. They should be coming up soon."

Holly doesn't light a joint, just sits forward, looking to the left. When the Expedition skids again, the rear end flirting first left and then right, she doesn't appear to notice. A minute later she points. "Is that them?"

It is. The passing plows have buried all but the last eighteen inches or so, but that bright red is impossible to miss or mistake. Hodges feathers the brakes, brings the Expedition to a stop, then turns it so it's facing the snowbank. He tells Holly what he sometimes used to tell his daughter, when he took her on the Wild Cups at Lakewood Amusement Park: "Hold onto your false teeth."

Holly—always the literalist—says, "I don't have any," but she does put a bracing hand on the dashboard.

Hodges steps down gently on the gas and rolls at the snowbank. The thud he expected doesn't come; Thurston was right about the snow not yet having a chance to pack and harden. It explodes away to either side and up onto the windshield, momentarily blinding him. He shoves the wipers into overdrive, and when the glass clears, the Expedition is pointing down a one-lane camp road rapidly filling with snow. Every now and then more flumps down from the overhanging branches. He sees no tracks from a previous car, but that means nothing. By now they'd be gone.

He kills the headlights and advances at a creep. The band of white between the trees is just visible enough to serve as a guide track. The road seems endless—sloping, switching back, then sloping again—but eventually they come to the place where it splits left and right. Hodges doesn't have to get out and check the arrows. Ahead on the left, through the snow and the trees, he can see a faint glimmer of light. That's Heads and Skins, and someone is home. He crimps the wheel and begins rolling slowly down the righthand fork.

Neither of them looks up and sees the video camera, but it sees them.

28

By the time Hodges and Holly burst through the snowbank left by the plow, Brady is sitting in front of the TV, fully dressed in Babineau's winter coat and boots. He's left off the gloves, he wants his hands bare in case he has to use the Scar, but there's a black balaclava lying across one thigh. When the time comes, he'll don it to cover Babineau's face and silver hair. His eyes never leave the television as he nervously stirs the pens and pencils sticking out of the ceramic skull. A sharp lookout is absolutely necessary. When Hodges comes, he'll kill his headlights.

Will he have the nigger lawnboy with him? Brady wonders. Wouldn't that be sweet! Two for the price of—

And there he is.

He was afraid the Det.-Ret.'s vehicle might get by him in the thickening snow, but that was a needless worry. The snow is white; the SUV is a solid black rectangle sliding through it. Brady leans forward, squinting, but can't tell if there's only one person in the cabin, or two, or half a fucking dozen. He's got the Scar, and with it he could wipe out an entire squad if he had to, but that would spoil the fun. He'd like Hodges alive.

To start with, at least.

Only one more question needs to be answered—will he turn left, and bore straight in, or right? Brady is betting K. William Hodges will choose the fork that leads to Big Bob's, and he's right. As the SUV disappears into the snow (with a brief flash of the taillights as Hodges negotiates the first turn), Brady puts the skull penholder down next to the TV remote and picks up an item that has been waiting on the end table. A perfectly legal item when used the right way . . . which it never was by Babineau and his cohorts. They may have been good doctors, but out here in the woods, they were often bad boys. He pulls this valuable piece of equipment over his head, and lets it hang against the front of his coat by the elastic strap. Then he pulls on the balaclava, grabs the Scar, and heads out. His heart is beating fast and hard, and for the time being, at least, the arthritis in Babineau's fingers seems to be completely gone.

Payback is a bitch, and the bitch is back.

## 29

Holly doesn't ask Hodges why he took the right-hand fork. She's neurotic, but not stupid. He drives at a walking pace, looking to his left, measuring the lights to his left. When he's even with them, he stops the SUV and switches off the engine. It's full dark now, and when he turns to look at Holly, she has the fleeting impression that his head has been replaced by a skull.

"Stay here," he says in a low voice. "Text Jerome, tell him we're okay. I'm going to cut through those woods and take him."

"You don't mean alive, do you?"

"Not if I see him with one of those Zappits." And probably even if I don't, he thinks. "We can't take the risk."

"Then you believe it's him. Brady."

"Even if it's Babineau, he's part of this. Neck-deep in it." But yes, at some point he has become convinced that Brady Harts-field's mind is now running Babineau's body. The intuition is too strong to deny, and has gained the weight of fact.

God help me if I kill him and I'm wrong, he thinks. Only how would I know? How could I ever be sure?

He expects Holly to protest, to tell him she has to come along, but all she says is, "I don't think I can drive this thing out of here if something happens to you, Bill."

He hands her Thurston's card. "If I'm not back in ten minutes—no, make it fifteen—call this guy."

"What if I hear shots?"

"If it's me, and I'm okay, I'll honk the horn of Library Al's car. Two quick beeps. If you don't hear that, drive the rest of the way to the other camp, Big Bob's Whatsit. Break in, find somewhere to hide, call Thurston."

Hodges leans across the center console, and for the first time since he's known her, kisses her lips. She's too startled to kiss him back, but she doesn't pull away. When he does, she looks down in confusion and says the first thing that comes into her mind. "Bill, you're in *shoes*! You'll *freeze*!"

"There's not so much snow in the trees, only a couple of inches." And really, cold feet are the least of his worries at this point.

He finds the toggle switch that kills the interior lights. As he leaves the Expedition, grunting with suppressed pain, she can hear the rising whisper of the wind in the fir trees. If it were a voice, it would be mourning. Then the door shuts.

Holly sits where she is, watching his dark shape merge with the dark shapes of the trees, and when she can no longer tell which is which, she gets out and follows his tracks. The Victory .38 that Hodges's father once carried as a beat cop back in the fifties, when Sugar Heights was still woodland, is in her coat pocket.

30

Hodges makes his way toward the lights of Heads and Skins one plodding step at a time. Snow flicks his face and coats his eyelids. That burning arrow is back, lighting him up inside. Frying him. His face is running with sweat.

At least my feet aren't hot, he thinks, and that's when he stumbles over a snow-covered log and goes sprawling. He lands squarely on his left side and buries his face in the arm of his coat to keep from screaming. Hot liquid spills into his crotch.

Wet my pants, he thinks. Wet my pants just like a baby.

When the pain recedes a little, he gathers his legs under him and tries to stand. He can't do it. The wetness is turning cold. He can actually feel his dick shriveling to get away from it. He grabs a low-hanging branch and tries again to get up. It snaps off. He looks at it stupidly, feeling like a cartoon character— Wile E. Coyote, maybe—and tosses it aside. As he does, a hand hooks into his armpit.

His surprise is so great he almost screams. Then Holly is whispering in his ear. "Upsa-daisy, Bill. Come on."

With her help, he's finally able to make it to his feet. The lights are close now, no more than forty yards through the screening trees. He can see the snow frosting her hair and lighting on her cheeks. All at once he finds himself remembering the office of an antique bookdealer named Andrew Halliday, and how he, Holly, and Jerome had discovered Halliday lying dead on the floor. He told them to stay back, but—

"Holly. If I told you to go back, would you do it?"

"No." She's whispering. They both are. "You'll probably have to shoot him, and you can't get there without help."

"You're supposed to be my backup, Holly. My insurance policy." The sweat is pouring off him like oil. Thank God his coat is a long one. He doesn't want Holly to know he pissed himself.

"*Jerome* is your insurance policy," she says. "I'm your partner. That's why you brought me, whether you know it or not. And it's what I want. It's all I ever wanted. Now come on. Lean on me. Let's finish this."

They move slowly through the remaining trees. Hodges can't believe how much of his weight she's taking. They pause at the edge of the clearing that surrounds the house. There are two lighted rooms. Judging by the subdued glow coming from the one closest to them, Hodges thinks it must be the kitchen. A single light on in there, maybe the one over the stove. Coming from the other window he can make out an unsteady flicker that probably means a fireplace.

"That's where we're going," he says, pointing, "and from here on we're soldiers on night patrol. Which means we crawl."

"Can you?"

"Yeah." It might actually be easier than walking. "See the chandelier?"

"Yes. It looks all bony. Oough."

"That's the living room, and that's where he'll probably be. If he's not, we'll wait until he shows. If he's got one of those Zappits, I intend to shoot him. No hands up, no lie down and put your hands behind your back. Do you have a problem with that?"

"Absolutely not."

They drop to their hands and knees. Hodges leaves the Glock in his coat pocket, not wanting to dunk it in the snow.

"Bill." Her whisper so low he can barely hear it over the rising wind.

He turns to look at her. She's holding out one of her gloves.

"Too small," he says, and thinks of Johnnie Cochran saying, *If the glove doesn't fit, you must acquit.* Crazy what goes through a person's mind at times like this. Only has there ever in his life been a time like this?

"Force it," she whispers. "You need to keep your gun hand warm."

She's right, and he manages to get it most of the way on. It's too short to get over all of his hand, but his fingers are covered, and that's all that matters.

They crawl, Hodges slightly in the lead. The pain is still bad, but now that he's off his feet, the arrow in his guts is smoldering rather than burning.

Got to save some energy, though, he thinks. Just enough.

It's forty or fifty feet from the edge of the woods to the window with the chandelier hanging in it, and his uncovered hand has lost all feeling by the time they're halfway there. He can't believe he's brought his best friend to this place and this moment, crawling through the snow like children playing a war game, miles from any help. He had his reasons, and they made sense back in that Airport Hilton. Now, not so much.

He looks left, at the silent hulk of Library Al's Malibu. He looks right, and sees a snow-covered woodpile. He starts to look ahead again, at the living room window, then snaps his head back to the woodpile, alarm bells ringing just a little too late.

There are tracks in the snow. The angle was wrong to see them from the edge of the woods, but he can see them clearly now. They lead from the back of the house to that stack of fireplace fuel. He came outside through the kitchen door, Hodges thinks. That's why the light was on in there. I should have guessed. I would have, if I hadn't been so sick.

He scrabbles for the Glock, but the too-small glove slows his grip, and when he finally gets hold of it and tries to pull it out, the gun snags in the pocket. Meanwhile, a dark shape has risen from behind the woodpile. The shape covers the fifteen feet between it and them in four great looping strides. The face is that of an alien in a horror movie, featureless except for the round, projecting eyes.

*"Holly, look out!"*

She lifts her head just as the butt of the Scar comes down to meet it. There's a sickening crack and she drops face-first into the snow with her arms thrown out to either side: a puppet with its strings cut. Hodges frees the Glock from his coat pocket just as the butt comes down again. Hodges both feels and hears his wrist break; he sees the Glock land in the snow and almost disappear.

Still on his knees, Hodges looks up and sees a tall man—much taller than Brady Hartsfield—standing in front of Holly's motionless form. He's wearing a balaclava and night-vision goggles.

*He saw us as soon as we came out of the trees,* Hodges thinks dully. *For all I know, he saw us* in *the trees, while I was pulling on Holly's glove.*

"Hello, Detective Hodges."

Hodges doesn't reply. He wonders if Holly is still alive, and if she'll ever recover from the blow she's just been dealt, if she is. But of course, that's stupid. Brady isn't going to give her any chance to recover.

"You're coming inside with me," Brady says. "The question is whether or not we bring her, or leave her out here, to turn into a Popsicle." And, as if he's read Hodges's mind (for all Hodges knows, he can do that): "Oh, she's still alive, at least for now. I can see her back going up and down. Although after a hit that hard, and with her face in the snow, who knows for how long?"

"I'll carry her," Hodges says, and he will. No matter how much it hurts.

"Okay." No pause to think it over, and Hodges knows it's what Brady expected and what Brady wanted. *He's one step ahead. Has been all along. And whose fault is that?*

*Mine. Entirely mine. It's what I get for playing the Lone Ranger yet again . . . but what else could I do? Who would ever have believed it?*

"Pick her up," Brady says. "Let's see if you really can. Because, tell you what, you look mighty shaky to me."

Hodges gets his arms under Holly. In the woods, he couldn't make it to his feet after he fell, but now he gathers everything he has left and does a clean-and-jerk with her limp body. He staggers, almost goes down, and finds his balance again. The burning arrow is gone, incinerated in the forest fire it has touched off inside him. But he hugs her to his chest.

"That's good." Brady sounds genuinely admiring. "Now let's see if you can make it to the house."

Somehow, Hodges does.

31

The wood in the fireplace is burning well and throwing a stuporous heat. Gasping for breath, the snow on his borrowed hat melting and running down his face in slushy streams, Hodges gets to the middle of the room and then goes to his knees, having to cradle Holly's neck in the crook of his elbow because of his broken wrist, which is swelling up like a sausage. He manages to keep her head from banging on the hardwood floor, and that's good. Her head has taken enough abuse tonight.

Brady has removed his coat, the night-vision goggles, and the balaclava. It's Babineau's face and Babineau's silvery hair (now in unaccustomed disarray), but it's Brady Hartsfield, all right. Hodges's last doubts have departed.

"Has she got a gun?"

"No."

The man who looks like Felix Babineau smiles. "Well, here's what I'm going to do, Bill. I'll search her pockets, and if I do find a gun, I'll blow her narrow ass into the next state. How's that for a deal?"

"It's a .38," Hodges says. "She's right-handed, so if she brought it, it's probably in the right front pocket of her coat."

Brady bends, keeping the Scar trained on Hodges as he does so, finger on the trigger and the butt-plate braced against the right side of his chest. He finds the revolver, examines it briefly, then tucks it into his belt at the small of his back. In spite of his pain and despair, Hodges feels a certain sour amusement. Brady's probably seen badass dudes do that in a hundred TV shows and action movies, but it really only works with automatics, which are flat.

On the hooked rug, Holly makes a snoring sound deep in her throat. One foot gives a spastic jerk, then goes still.

"What about you?" Brady asks. "Any other weapons? The ever-popular throwdown gun strapped to your ankle, perhaps?"

Hodges shakes his head.

"Just to be on the safe side, why don't you hoist up your pants-legs for me?"

Hodges does it, revealing soaked shoes, wet socks, and nothing else.

"Excellent. Now take off your coat and throw it on the couch."

Hodges unzips it and manages to keep quiet while he shrugs out of it, but when he tosses it, a bull's horn gores him from crotch to heart and he groans.

Babineau's eyes widen. "Real pain or fake? Live or Memorex? Judging from a quite striking weight loss, I'm going to say it's real. What's up, Detective Hodges? What's going on with you?"

"Cancer. Pancreatic."

"Oh, goodness, that's bad. Not even Superman can beat that one. But cheer up, I may be able to shorten your suffering."

"Do what you want with me," Hodges says. "Just let her alone."

Brady looks at the woman on the floor with great interest. "This would not by any chance be the woman who smashed in what used to be my head, is it?" The locution strikes him funny and he laughs.

"No." The world has become a camera lens, zooming in and out with every beat of his laboring, pacemaker-assisted heart. "Holly Gibney was the one who thumped you. She's gone back to live with her parents in Ohio. That's Kara Winston, my assistant." The name comes to him from nowhere, and there's no hesitation as he speaks it.

"An assistant who just decided to come with you on a do-or-die mission? I find that a little hard to believe."

"I promised her a bonus. She needs the money."

"And where, pray tell, is your nigger lawnboy?"

Hodges briefly considers telling Brady the truth—that Jerome is back in the city, that he knows Brady has probably gone to the hunting camp, that he will pass this information on to the police soon, if he hasn't already. But will any of those things stop Brady? Of course not.

"Jerome is in Arizona, building houses. Habitat for Humanity."

"How socially conscious of him. I was hoping he'd be with you. How badly hurt is his sister?"

"Broken leg. She'll be up and walking in no time."

"That's a shame."

"She was one of your test cases, wasn't she?"

"She got one of the original Zappits, yes. There were twelve of them. Like the twelve Apostles, you might say, going forth to spread the word. Sit in the chair in front of the TV, Detective Hodges."

"I'd rather not. All my favorite shows are on Monday."

Brady smiles politely. "Sit."

Hodges sits, bracing his good hand on the table beside the chair. Going down is agony, but once he actually makes it, sitting is a little better. The TV is off, but he stares at it, anyway. "Where's the camera?"

"On the signpost where the road splits. Above the arrows. You don't have to feel bad about missing it. It was covered with snow, nothing sticking out but the lens, and your headlights were off by then."

"Is there any Babineau left inside you?"

He shrugs. "Bits and pieces. Every now and then there's a small scream from the part that thinks it's still alive. It will stop soon."

"Jesus," Hodges mutters.

Brady drops to one knee, the barrel of the Scar resting on his thigh and still pointing at Hodges. He pulls down the back of Holly's coat and examines the tag. "H. Gibney," he says. "Printed in indelible ink. Very tidy. Won't wash off in the laundry. I like a person who takes care of her things."

Hodges closes his eyes. The pain is very bad, and he would give everything he owns to get away from it, and from what is going to happen next. He would give anything to just sleep, and sleep, and sleep. But he opens them again and forces himself to look at Brady, because you play the game to the end. That's how it works; play to the end.

"I have a lot of stuff to do in the next forty-eight or seventy-two hours, Detective Hodges, but I'm going to put it on hold in order to deal with you. Does that make you feel special? It should. Because I owe you so much for fucking me over."

"You need to remember that *you* came to *me*," Hodges says. "You were the one who started the ball rolling, with that stupid, bragging letter. Not me. You."

Babineau's face—the craggy face of an older character actor—darkens. "I suppose you might have a point, but look who's on top now. Look who *wins*, Detective Hodges."

"If you call getting a bunch of stupid, confused kids to commit suicide winning, I guess you're the winner. Me, I think doing that is about as challenging as striking out the pitcher."

"It's *control*! I assert *control*! You tried to stop me and you couldn't! You absolutely couldn't! And neither could she!" He kicks Holly in the side. Her body rolls a boneless half a turn toward the fireplace, then rolls back again. Her face is ashen, her closed eyes sunk deep in their sockets. "She actually made me better! Better than I ever was!"

"Then for Christ's sake, *stop kicking her*!" Hodges shouts.

Brady's anger and excitement have caused Babineau's face to flush. His hands are tight on the assault rifle. He takes a deep, steadying breath, then another. And smiles.

"Got a soft spot for Ms. Gibney, do you?" He kicks her again, this time in the hip. "Are you fucking her? Is that it? She's not much in the looks department, but I guess a guy your age has to take what he can get. You know what we used to say? Put a flag over her face and fuck her for Old Glory."

He kicks Holly again, and bares his teeth at Hodges in what he may think is a smile.

"You used to ask me if I was fucking my mother, remember? All those visits you made to my room, asking if I was fucking the only person who ever cared a damn for me. Talking about how hot she looked, and was she a hoochie mama. Asking if I was faking. Telling me how much you hoped I was suffering. And I just had to sit there and take it."

He's getting ready to kick poor Holly again. To distract him, Hodges says, "There was a nurse. Sadie MacDonald. Did you

403

nudge her into killing herself? You did, didn't you? She was the first one."

Brady likes that, and shows even more of Babineau's expensive dental work. "It was easy. It always is, once you get inside and start pulling the levers."

"How do you do that, Brady? How do you get inside? How did you manage to get those Zappits from Sunrise Solutions, and rig them? Oh, and the website, how about that?"

Brady laughs. "You've read too many of those mystery stories where the clever private eye keeps the insane murderer talking until help arrives. Or until the murderer's attention wavers and the private eye can grapple with him and get his gun away. I don't think help is going to arrive, and you don't look capable of grappling with a goldfish. Besides, you know most of it already. You wouldn't be here if you didn't. Freddi spilled her guts, and—not to sound like Snidely Whiplash—she will pay for that. Eventually."

"She claims she didn't set up the website."

"I didn't need her for that. I did it all by myself, in Babineau's study, on Babineau's laptop. During one of my vacations from Room 217."

"What about—"

"Shut up. See that table beside you, Detective Hodges?"

It's cherrywood, like the buffet, and looks expensive, but there are faded rings all over it, from glasses that were put down without benefit of coasters. The doctors who own this place may be meticulous in operating rooms, but out here they're slobs. On top of it now is the TV remote and a ceramic skull penholder.

"Open the drawer."

Hodges does. Inside is a pink Zappit Commander sitting on top of an ancient *TV Guide* with Hugh Laurie on the cover.

"Take it out and turn it on."

"No."

"All right, fine. I'll just take care of Ms. Gibney, then." He lowers the barrel of the Scar and points it at the back of Holly's neck. "On full auto, this will rip her head right off. Will it fly into the fireplace? Let's find out."

"Okay," Hodges says. "Okay, okay, okay. Stop."

He takes the Zappit and finds the button at the top of the console. The welcome screen lights up; the diagonal downstroke of the red Z fills the screen. He is invited to swipe and access the games. He does so without being prompted by Brady. Sweat pours down his face. He has never been so hot. His broken wrist throbs and pulses.

"Do you see the Fishin' Hole icon?"

"Yes."

Opening Fishin' Hole is the last thing he wants to do, but when the alternative is just sitting here with his broken wrist and his swollen, pulsing gut and watching a stream of high-caliber bullets divide Holly's head from her slight body? Not an option. And besides, he has read a person can't be hypnotized against his will. It's true that Dinah Scott's console almost put him under, but then he didn't know what was happening. Now he does. And if Brady thinks he's tranced out and he's not, then maybe . . . just maybe . . .

"I'm sure you know the drill by now," Brady says. His eyes are bright and lively, the eyes of a boy who is about to set a spider-web on fire so he can see what the spider will do. Will it scurry around its flaming web, looking for a way to escape, or will it just burn? "Tap the icon. The fish will swim and the music will play. Tap the pink fish and add up the numbers. In order to win the game, you have to score one hundred and twenty points in

405

one hundred and twenty seconds. If you succeed, I'll let Ms. Gibney live. If you fail, we'll see what this fine automatic weapon can do. Babineau saw it demolish a stack of concrete blocks once, so just imagine what it will do to flesh."

"You're not going to let her live even if I score five thousand," Hodges says. "I don't believe that for a second."

Babineau's blue eyes widen in mock outrage. "But you should! All that I am, I owe to this bitch sprawled out in front of me! The least I can do is spare her life. Assuming she isn't suffering a brain bleed and dying already, that is. Now stop playing for time. Play the game instead. Your one hundred and twenty seconds start as soon as your finger taps the icon."

With no other recourse, Hodges taps it. The screen blanks. There's a blue flash so bright it makes him squint, and then the fish are there, swimming back and forth, up and down, crisscrossing, sending up silvery trails of bubbles. The music begins to tinkle: *By the sea, by the sea, by the beautiful sea* . . .

Only it isn't *just* music. There are words mixed in. And there are words in the blue flashes, too.

"Ten seconds gone," Brady says. "Tick-tock, tick-tock."

Hodges taps at one of the pink fish and misses. He's right hand–dominant, and each tap makes the throbbing in his wrist that much worse, but the pain there is nothing compared to the pain now roasting him from groin to throat. On his third try he gets a pinky—that's how he thinks of them, as pinkies—and the fish turns into a number 5. He says it out loud.

"Only five points in twenty seconds?" Brady says. "Better step it up, Detective."

Hodges taps faster, eyes moving left and right, up and down. He no longer has to squint when the blue flashes come, because he's used to them. And it's getting easier. The fish seem bigger now, also a little slower. The music seems less tinkly. Fuller, somehow. *You and me, you and me, oh how happy we'll be.* Is that Brady's voice, singing along with the music, or just his imagination? Live or Memorex? No time to think about it now. *Tempus* is *fugiting.*

He gets a seven-fish, then a four, and then—jackpot!—one turns into a twelve. He says, "I'm up to twenty-seven." But is that right? He's losing count.

Brady doesn't tell him, Brady only says, "Eighty seconds to go," and now his voice seems to have picked up a slight echo, as if it's coming to Hodges from the far end of a long hallway. Meanwhile, a marvelous thing is happening: the pain in his gut is starting to recede.

Whoa, he thinks. The AMA should know about this.

He gets another pinky. It turns into a 2. Not so good, but there are plenty more. Plenty, plenty more.

That's when he starts to feel something like fingers fluttering delicately inside his head, and it's not his imagination. He's being invaded. *It was easy,* Brady said of Nurse MacDonald. *It always is, once you get inside and start pulling the levers.*

And when Brady gets to *his* levers?

He'll jump inside me the way he jumped inside Babineau, Hodges thinks . . . although this realization is now like the voice and the music, coming from the far end of a long hallway. At the end of that hallway is the door to Room 217, and the door is standing open.

Why would he want to do that? Why would he want to inhabit a body that's turned into a cancer factory? Because he wants me to kill Holly. Not with the gun, though, he'd never trust me with that. He'll use my hands to choke her, broken wrist and all. Then he'll leave me to face what I've done.

"You're getting better, Detective Hodges, and you still have a minute to go. Just relax and keep tapping. It's easier when you relax."

The voice is no longer echoing down a hallway; even though Brady is now standing right in front of him, it's coming from a galaxy far, far away. Brady bends down and stares eagerly into Hodges's face. Only there are fish swimming between them. Pinkies and blueies and reddies. Because Hodges is in the Fishin' Hole now. Except it's really an aquarium, and he's the fish. Soon he will be eaten. Eaten alive. "Come on, Billy-boy, tap those pink fish!"

I can't let him inside me, Hodges thinks, but I can't keep him out.

He taps a pink fish, it turns into a 9, and it isn't just fingers he feels now but another consciousness spilling into his mind. It's spreading like ink in water. Hodges tries to fight and knows he will lose. The strength of that invading personality is incredible.

I'm going to drown. Drown in the Fishin' Hole. Drown in Brady Hartsfield.

*By the sea, by the sea, by the beautiful s—*

A pane of glass shatters close by. It's followed by a jubilant chorus of boys shouting, *"That's a HOME RUN!"*

The bond binding Hodges to Hartsfield is broken by the pure, unexpected surprise of the thing. Hodges jerks back in the chair and looks up as Brady wheels toward the couch, eyes wide and mouth open in startlement. The Victory .38, held against the small of his back only by its short barrel (the cylinder won't allow it to go deeper), falls out of his belt and thumps to the bearskin rug.

Hodges doesn't hesitate. He throws the Zappit into the fireplace.

*"Don't you do that!"* Brady bellows, turning back. He raises the Scar. *"Don't you fucking da—"*

Hodges grasps the nearest thing to hand, not the .38 but the ceramic penholder. There's nothing wrong with his left wrist, and the range is short. He throws it at the face Brady has stolen, he throws it hard, and connects dead center. The ceramic skull shatters. Brady screams—pain, yes, but mostly shock—and his nose begins to gush blood. When he tries to bring up the Scar, Hodges pistons out his feet, enduring another deep gore of that bull's horn, and smashes them into Brady's chest. Brady back-pedals, almost catches his balance, then trips over a hassock and sprawls on the bearskin rug.

Hodges tries to launch himself out of the chair and only succeeds in overturning the end table. He goes to his knees as Brady sits up, bringing the Scar around. There's a gunshot before he can level it on Hodges, and Brady screams again. This time it's all pain. He looks unbelievingly at his shoulder, where blood is pouring through a hole in his shirt.

Holly is sitting up. There's a grotesque bruise over her left eye, in almost the same place as the one on Freddi's forehead. That left eye is red, filled with blood, but the other is bright and aware. She's holding the Victory .38 in both hands.

*"Shoot him again!"* Hodges roars. *"Shoot him again, Holly!"*

As Brady lurches to his feet—one hand clapped to the wound in his shoulder, the other holding the Scar, face slack with disbelief—Holly fires again. This bullet goes way high, ricocheting off the fieldstone chimney above the roaring fire.

"Stop that!" Brady shouts, ducking. At the same time he's struggling to raise the Scar. "Stop doing that, you bi—"

Holly fires a third time. The sleeve of Brady's shirt twitches, and he yelps. Hodges isn't sure she's winged him again, but she at least grooved him.

Hodges gets to his feet and tries to run at Brady, who is making another effort to raise the automatic rifle. The best he can manage is a slow plod.

"You're in the way!" Holly cries. *"Bill, you're in the fracking way!"*

Hodges drops to his knees and tucks his head. Brady turns and runs. The .38 bangs. Wood splinters fly from the doorframe a foot to Brady's right. Then he's gone. The front door opens. Cold air rushes in, making the fire do an excited shimmy.

"I missed him!" Holly shouts, agonized. "Stupid and useless! Stupid and useless!" She drops the Victory and slaps herself across the face.

Hodges catches her hand before she can do it again, and kneels beside her. "No, you got him at least once, maybe twice. You're the reason we're still alive."

But for how long? Brady held onto that goddam grease gun, he may have an extra clip or two, and Hodges knows he wasn't lying about the SCAR 17S's ability to demolish concrete blocks. He has seen a similar assault rifle, the HK 416, do exactly that, at a private shooting facility in the wilds of Victory County. He went there with Pete, and on the way back they joked about how the HK should be standard police issue.

"What do we do?" Holly asks. "What do we do now?"

Hodges picks up the .38 and rolls the barrel. Two rounds left, and the .38 is only good at short range, anyway. Holly has a concussion at the very least, and he's almost incapacitated. The bitter truth is this: they had a chance, and Brady got away.

He hugs her and says, "I don't know."

"Maybe we should hide."

"I don't think that would work," he says, but doesn't say why and is relieved when she doesn't ask. It's because there's still a little of Brady left inside of him. It probably won't last long, but for the time being, at least, Hodges suspects it's as good as a homing beacon.

32

Brady staggers through shin-deep snow, eyes wide with disbelief, Babineau's sixty-three-year-old heart banging away in his chest. There's a metallic taste on his tongue, his shoulder is burning, and the thought running through his head on a constant loop is *That bitch, that bitch, that dirty sneaking bitch, why didn't I kill her while I had the chance?*

The Zappit is gone, too. Good old Zappit Zero, and it's the only one he brought. Without it, he has no way to reach the minds of those with active Zappits. He stands panting in front of Heads and Skins, coatless in the rising wind and driving snow. The keys to Z-Boy's car are in his pocket, along with another clip for the Scar, but what good are the keys? That shitbox wouldn't make it halfway up the first hill before it got stuck.

I have to take them, he thinks, and not just because they owe me. The SUV Hodges drove down here is the only way *out* of here, and either he or the bitch probably has the keys. It's possible they left them in the vehicle, but that's a chance I can't afford to take.

Besides, it would mean leaving them alive.

He knows what he has to do, and switches the fire control to FULL AUTO. He socks the butt of the Scar against his good shoulder, and starts shooting, raking the barrel from left to right but concentrating on the great room, where he left them.

Gunfire lights up the night, turning the fast-falling snow into a series of flash photographs. The sound of the overlapping

411

reports is deafening. Windows explode inward. Clapboards rise from the façade like bats. The front door, left half-open in his escape, flies all the way back, rebounds, and is driven back again. Babineau's face is twisted in an expression of joyful hate that is all Brady Hartsfield, and he doesn't hear the growl of an approaching engine or the clatter of steel treads from behind him.

33

"*Down!*" Hodges shouts. "*Holly, down!*"

He doesn't wait to see if she'll obey on her own, just lands on top of her and covers her body with his. Above them, the living room is a storm of flying splinters, broken glass, and chips of rock from the chimney. An elk's head falls off the wall and lands on the hearth. One glass eye has been shattered by a Winchester slug, and it looks like it's winking at them. Holly screams. Half a dozen bottles on the buffet explode, releasing the stench of bourbon and gin. A slug strikes a burning log in the fireplace, busting it in two and sending up a storm of sparks.

Please let him have just the one clip, Hodges thinks. And if he aims low, let him hit me instead of Holly. Only a .308 Winchester slug that hits him will go through them both, and he knows it.

The gunfire stops. Is he reloading, or is he out? Live or Memorex?

"Bill, get off me, I can't breathe."

"Better not," he says. "I—"

"What's that? What's that sound?" And then, answering her own question, "Someone's coming!"

Now that his ears are clearing a little, Hodges can hear it, too.

At first he thinks it must be Thurston's grandson, on one of the snowmobiles the old man mentioned, and about to be slaughtered for trying to play Good Samaritan. But maybe not. The approaching engine sounds too heavy for a snowmobile.

Bright yellow-white light floods in through the shattered windows like the spotlights from a police helicopter. Only this is no helicopter.

34

Brady is ramming his extra clip home when he finally registers the growl-and-clank of the approaching vehicle. He whirls, wounded shoulder throbbing like an infected tooth, just as a huge silhouette appears at the end of the camp road. The headlamps dazzle him. His shadow leaps out long on the sparkling snow as the whatever-it-is comes rolling toward the shot-up house, throwing gouts of snow behind its clanking treads. And it's not just coming at the house. It's coming at *him*.

He depresses the trigger and the Scar resumes its thunder. Now he can see it's some kind of snow machine with a bright orange cabin sitting high above the churning treads. The windshield explodes just as someone dives for safety from the open driver's side door.

The monstrosity keeps coming. Brady tries to run, and Babineau's expensive loafers slip. He flails, staring at those oncoming headlights, and goes down on his back. The orange invader rises above him. He sees a steel tread whirring toward him. He tries to push it away, as he sometimes pushed objects in his room— the blinds, the bedclothes, the door to the bathroom—but it's like trying to beat off a charging lion with a toothbrush. He raises a hand and draws in breath to scream. Before he can, the left tread of the Tucker Sno-Cat rolls over his midsection and chews it open.

35

Holly has zero doubt concerning the identity of their rescuer, and doesn't hesitate. She runs through the bullet-pocked foyer and out the front door, crying his name over and over. Jerome looks as if he's been dusted in powdered sugar when he picks himself up. She's sobbing and laughing as she throws herself into his arms.

"How did you know? How did you know to come?"

"I didn't," he says. "It was Barbara. When I called to say I was coming home, she told me I had to go after you or Brady would kill you . . . only she called him the Voice. She was half crazy."

Hodges is making his way toward the two of them at a slow stagger, but he's close enough to overhear this, and remembers that Barbara told Holly some of that suicide-voice was still inside her. Like a trail of slime, she said. Hodges knows what she was talking about, because he's got some of that disgusting thought-snot in his own head, at least for the time being. Maybe Barbara had just enough of a connection to know that Brady was lying in wait.

Or hell, maybe it was pure woman's intuition. Hodges actually believes in such a thing. He's old-school.

"Jerome," he says. The word comes out in a dusty croak. "My man." His knees unlock. He's going down.

Jerome frees himself from Holly's deathgrip and puts an arm around Hodges before he can. "Are you all right? I mean . . . I know you're not all right, but are you shot?"

"No." Hodges puts his own arm around Holly. "And I should have known you'd come. Neither one of you minds worth a tinker's damn."

"Couldn't break up the band before the final reunion concert, could we?" Jerome says. "Let's get you in the—"

There comes an animal sound from their left, a guttural groan that struggles to be words and can't make it.

Hodges is more exhausted than ever in his life, but he walks toward that groan anyway. Because . . .

Well, because.

What was the word he used with Holly, on their way out here? Closure, wasn't it?

Brady's hijacked body has been laid open to the backbone. His guts are spread out around him like the wings of a red dragon. Pools of steaming blood are sinking into the snow. But his eyes are open and aware, and all at once Hodges can feel those fingers again. This time they're not just probing lazily. This time they're frantic, scrabbling for purchase. Hodges ejects them as easily as that floor-mopping orderly once pushed this man's presence out of his mind.

He spits Brady out like a watermelon seed.

"Help me," Brady whispers. "You have to help me."

"I think you're way beyond help," Hodges says. "You were run down, Brady. Run down by an extremely heavy vehicle. Now you know what that feels like. Don't you?"

"Hurts," Brady whispers.

"Yes," Hodges says. "I imagine it does."

"If you can't help me, shoot me."

Hodges holds out his hand, and Holly puts the Victory .38 into it like a nurse handing a doctor a scalpel. He rolls the cylinder and dumps out one of the two remaining bullets. Then he closes the gun up again. Although he hurts everywhere now, hurts like hell, Hodges kneels down and puts his father's gun in Brady's hand.

"You do it," he says. "It's what you always wanted."

Jerome stands by, ready in case Brady should decide to use that final round on Hodges instead. But he doesn't. Brady tries to point the gun at his head. He can't. His arm twitches, but won't rise. He groans again. Blood pours over his lower lip and seeps out from between Felix Babineau's capped teeth. It would almost be possible to feel sorry for him, Hodges thinks, if you didn't know what he did at City Center, what he tried to do at the Mingo Auditorium, and the suicide machine he's set in motion today. That machine will slow down and stop now that its prime operative is finished, but it will swallow up a few more sad young people before it does. Hodges is pretty sure of that. Suicide may not be painless, but it *is* catching.

You could feel sorry for him if he wasn't a monster, Hodges thinks.

Holly kneels, lifts Brady's hand, and puts the muzzle of the gun against his temple. "Now, Mr. Hartsfield," she says. "You have to do the rest yourself. And may God have mercy on your soul."

"I hope not," Jerome says. In the glare of the Sno-Cat's headlights, his face is a stone.

For a long moment the only sounds are the rumble of the snow machine's big engine and the rising wind of winter storm Eugenie.

Holly says, "Oh God. His finger's not even on the trigger. One of you needs to help me, I don't think I can—"

Then, a gunshot.

"Brady's last trick," Jerome says. "Jesus."

36

There's no way Hodges can make it back to the Expedition, but
Jerome is able to muscle him into the cab of the Sno-Cat. Holly
sits beside him on the outside. Jerome climbs behind the wheel
and throws it into gear. Although he backs up and then circles
wide around the remains of Babineau's body, he tells Holly not
to look until they're at least up the first hill. "We're leaving
blood-tracks."

"Oough."

"Correct," Jerome says. "Oough is correct."

"Thurston told me he had snowmobiles," Hodges says. "He
didn't mention anything about a Sherman tank."

"It's a Tucker Sno-Cat, and you didn't offer him your Master-
Card as collateral. Not to mention an excellent Jeep Wrangler
that got me out here to the williwags just fine, thanks."

"Is he really dead?" Holly asks. Her wan face is turned up to
Hodges's, and the huge knot on her forehead actually seems to
be pulsing. "Really and for sure?"

"You saw him put a bullet in his brain."

"Yes, but is he? Really and for sure?"

The answer he won't give is no, not yet. Not until the trails
of slime he's left in the heads of God knows how many people
are washed away by the brain's remarkable ability to heal itself.
But in another week, another month at the outside, Brady will
be all gone.

"Yes," he says. "And Holly? Thanks for programming that
text alert. The home run boys."

She smiles. "What was it? The text, I mean?"

Hodges struggles his phone out of his coat pocket, checks it,

417

and says, "I will be goddamned." He begins to laugh. "I completely forgot."

"What? Show me show me show me!"

He tilts the phone so she can read the text his daughter Alison has sent him from California, where the sun is no doubt shining:

**HAPPY BIRTHDAY, DADDY! 70 YEARS OLD AND STILL GOING STRONG! AM RUSHING OUT TO THE MARKET, WILL CALL U LATER. XXX ALLIE**

For the first time since Jerome returned from Arizona, Tyrone Feelgood Delight makes an appearance. "You is sem'ny years old, Massa Hodges? Laws! You don't look a day ovah sixty-fi'!"

"Stop it, Jerome," Holly says. "I know it amuses you, but that sort of talk sounds very ignorant and silly."

Hodges laughs. It hurts to laugh, but he can't help it. He holds onto consciousness all the way back to Thurston's Garage; is even able to take a few shallow tokes on the joint Holly lights and passes to him. Then the dark begins to slip in.

This could be it, he thinks.

Happy birthday to me, he thinks.

Then he's gone.

# AFTER

*Four Days Later*

Pete Huntley is far less familiar with Kiner Memorial than his old partner, who made many pilgrimages here to visit a long-term resident who has now passed away. It takes Pete two stops—one at the main desk and one in Oncology—before he locates Hodges's room, and when he gets there, it's empty. A cluster of balloons with HAPPY BIRTHDAY DAD on them are tethered to one of the siderails and floating near the ceiling.

A nurse pokes her head in, sees him looking at the empty bed, and gives him a smile. "The solarium at the end of the hall. They've been having a little party. I think you're still in time."

Pete walks down. The solarium is skylighted and filled with plants, maybe to cheer up the patients, maybe to provide them with a little extra oxygen, maybe both. Near one wall, a party of four is playing cards. Two of them are bald, and one has an IV drip running into his arm. Hodges is seated directly under the skylight, doling out slices of cake to his posse: Holly, Jerome, and Barbara. Kermit seems to be growing a beard, it's coming in snow-white, and Pete has a brief memory of going to the mall with his own kids to see Santa Claus.

"Pete!" Hodges says, smiling. He starts to get up and Pete

419

waves him back into his seat. "Sit down, have some cake. Allie brought it from Batool's Bakery. It was always her favorite place to go when she was growing up."

"Where is she?" Pete asks, dragging a chair over and placing it next to Holly. She's sporting a bandage on the left side of her forehead, and Barbara has a cast on her leg. Only Jerome looks hale and hearty, and Pete knows the kid barely escaped getting turned into hamburger out at that hunting camp.

"She went back to the Coast this morning. Two days off was all she could manage. She's got three weeks' vacation coming in March, and says she'll be back. If I need her, that is."

"How are you feeling?"

"Not bad," Hodges says. His eyes flick up and to the left, but only for a second. "I've got three cancer docs on my case, and the first tests came back looking good."

"That's fantastic." Pete takes the piece of cake Hodges is holding out. "This is too big."

"Man up and chow down," Hodges says. "Listen, about you and Izzy—"

"We worked it out," Pete says. He takes a bite. "Hey, nice. There's nothing like carrot cake with cream cheese frosting to cheer up your blood sugar."

"So the retirement party is . . . ?"

"Back on. Officially, it was never off. I'm still counting on you to give the first toast. And remember—"

"Yeah, yeah, ex-wife and current squeeze both there, nothing too off-color. Got it, got it."

"Just as long as we're clear on that." The too-big slice of cake is getting smaller. Barbara watches the rapid intake with fascination.

"Are we in trouble?" Holly asks. "Are we, Pete, are we?"

"Nope," Pete says. "Completely in the clear. That's mostly what I came to tell you."

Holly sits back with a sigh of relief that blows the graying bangs off her forehead.

"Bet they've got Babineau carrying the can for everything," Jerome says.

Pete points his plastic fork at Jerome. "Truth you speak, young Jedi warrior."

"You might be interested to know that the famous puppeteer Frank Oz did Yoda's voice," Holly says. She looks around. "Well, *I* find it interesting."

"I find this cake interesting," Pete says. "Could I have a little more? Maybe just a sliver?"

Barbara does the honors, and it's far more than a sliver, but Pete doesn't object. He takes a bite and asks how she's doing.

"Good," Jerome says before she can answer. "She's got a boy-friend. Kid named Dereece Neville. Big basketball star."

"Shut up, Jerome, he is not my boyfriend."

"He sure visits like a boyfriend," Jerome says. "I'm talking every day since you broke your leg."

"We have a lot to talk about," Barbara says in a dignified tone of voice.

Pete says, "Going back to Babineau, hospital administration has some security footage of him coming in through a back entrance on the night his wife was murdered. He changed into maintenance-worker duds. Probably raided a locker. He leaves, comes back fifteen or twenty minutes later, changes back into the clothes he came in, leaves for good."

"No other footage?" Hodges asks. "Like in the Bucket?"

"Yeah, some, but you can't see his face in that stuff, because he's wearing a Groundhogs cap, and you don't see him go into

Hartsfield's room. A defense lawyer might be able to make something of that stuff, but since Babineau's never going to stand trial—"

"No one gives much of a shit," Hodges finishes.

"Correct. City and state cops are delighted to let him carry the weight. Izzy's happy, and so am I. I could ask you—just between us chickens—if it was actually Babineau who died out there in the woods, but I don't really want to know."

"So how does Library Al fit into this scenario?" Hodges asks.

"He doesn't." Pete puts his paper plate aside. "Alvin Brooks killed himself last night."

"Oh, Christ," Hodges says. "While he was in County?"

"Yes."

"They didn't have him on suicide watch? After all this?"

"They did, and none of the inmates are supposed to have anything capable of cutting or stabbing, but he got hold of a ballpoint pen somehow. Might have been a guard who gave it to him, but it was probably another inmate. He drew Zs all over the walls, all over his bunk, and all over himself. Then he took the pen's metal cartridge out of the barrel and used it to—"

"Stop," Barbara says. She looks very pale in the winterlight falling on them from above. "We get the idea."

Hodges says, "So the thinking is . . . what? He was Babineau's accomplice?"

"Fell under his influence," Pete says. "Or maybe both of them fell under someone else's influence, but let's not go there, okay? The thing to concentrate on now is that the three of you are in the clear. There won't be any citations this time, or city freebies—"

"It's okay," Jerome says. "Me 'n Holly have still got at least four years left on our bus passes, anyway."

"Not that you ever use yours now that you're hardly ever here," Barbara says. "You should give it to me."

"It's non-transferrable," Jerome says smugly. "I better hold onto it. Wouldn't want you to get in any trouble with the law. Besides, soon you'll be going places with Dereece. Just don't go too far, if you know what I mean."

"You're being childish." Barbara turns to Pete. "How many suicides were there in all?"

Pete sighs. "Fourteen over the last five days. Nine of them had Zappits, which are now as dead as their owners. The oldest was twenty-four, the youngest thirteen. One was a boy from a family that was, according to the neighbors, fairly weird about religion—the kind that makes fundamentalist Christians look liberal. He took his parents and kid brother with him. Shotgun."

The five of them fall silent for a moment. At the table on the left, the card players burst into howls of laughter over something.

Pete breaks the silence. "And there have been over forty attempts."

Jerome whistles.

"Yeah, I know. It's not in the papers, and the TV stations are sitting on it, even Murder and Mayhem." This is a police nickname for WKMM, an indie station that has taken *If it bleeds, it leads* as an article of faith. "But of course a lot of those attempts— maybe even most of them—end up getting blabbed about on the social media sites, and that breeds still more. I hate those sites. But this will settle. Suicide clusters always do."

"Eventually," Hodges says. "But with social media or without it, with Brady or without him, suicide is a fact of life."

He looks over at the card players as he says this, especially the two baldies. One looks good (as Hodges himself looks good), but the other is cadaverous and hollow-eyed. One foot in the grave and the other on a banana peel, Hodges's father would have said. And the thought that comes to him is too complicated—too fraught with a terrible mixture of anger and sorrow—to be articulated. It's about how some people carelessly squander what others would sell their souls to have: a healthy, pain-free body. And why? Because they're too blind, too emotionally scarred, or too self-involved to see past the earth's dark curve to the next sunrise. Which always comes, if one continues to draw breath.

"More cake?" Barbara asks.

"Nope. Gotta split. But I will sign your cast, if I may."

"Please," Barbara says. "And write something witty."

"That's far beyond Pete's pay grade," Hodges says.

"Watch your mouth, *Kermit*." Pete drops to one knee, like a swain about to propose, and begins writing carefully on Barbara's cast. When he's finished, he stands up and looks at Hodges. "Now tell me the truth about how you're feeling."

"Damn good. I've got a patch that controls the pain a lot better than the pills, and they're kicking me loose tomorrow. I can't wait to sleep in my own bed." He pauses, then says: "I'm going to beat this thing."

Pete's waiting for the elevator when Holly catches up to him. "It meant a lot to Bill," she says. "That you came, and that you still want him to give that toast."

"It's not so good, is it?" Pete says.

"No." He reaches out to hug her, but Holly steps back. She does allow him to take her hand and give it a brief squeeze. "Not so good."

"Crap."

"Yes, crap. Crap is right. He doesn't deserve this. But since he's stuck with it, he needs his friends to stand by him. You will, won't you?"

"Of course I will. And don't count him out yet, Holly. Where there's life, there's hope. I know it's a cliché, but . . ." He shrugs.

"I *do* have hope. I have Holly hope."

You can't say she's as weird as ever, Pete thinks, but she's still peculiar. He sort of likes it, actually. "Just make sure he keeps that toast relatively clean, okay?"

"I will."

"And hey—he outlived Hartsfield. No matter what else happens, he's got that."

"We'll always have Paris, kid," Holly says in a Bogart drawl.

Yes, she's still peculiar. One of a kind, actually.

"Listen, Gibney, you need to take care of yourself, too. No matter what happens. He'd hate it if you didn't."

"I know," Holly says, and goes back to the solarium, where she and Jerome will clean up the remains of the birthday party. She tells herself that it isn't necessarily the last one, and tries to convince herself of that. She doesn't entirely succeed, but she continues to have Holly hope.


*Eight Months Later*


When Jerome shows up at Fairlawn, two days after the funeral and at ten on the dot, as promised, Holly is already there, on her knees at the head of the grave. She's not praying; she's planting a chrysanthemum. She doesn't look up when his shadow falls over her. She knows who it is. This was the arrangement they made after she told him she didn't know if she could make it all the way through the funeral. "I'll try," she said, "but I'm not good with those fracking things. I may have to book."

"You plant these in the fall," she says now. "I don't know much about plants, so I got a how-to guide. The writing was only so-so, but the directions are easy to follow."

"That's good." Jerome sits down crosslegged at the end of the plot, where the grass begins.

Holly scoops dirt carefully with her hands, still not looking at him. "I told you I might have to book. They all stared at me when I left, but I just couldn't stay. If I had, they would have wanted me to stand up there in front of the coffin and talk about him and I couldn't. Not in front of all those people. I bet his daughter is mad."

"Probably not," Jerome says.

"I *hate* funerals. I came to this city for one, did you know that?"

Jerome does, but says nothing. Just lets her finish.

"My aunt died. She was Olivia Trelawney's mother. That's where I met Bill, at that funeral. I ran out of that one, too. I was sitting behind the funeral parlor, smoking a cigarette, feeling terrible, and that's where he found me. Do you understand?" At last she looks up at him. "He *found* me."

"I get it, Holly. I do."

"He opened a door for me. One into the world. He gave me something to do that made a difference."

"Same here."

She wipes her eyes almost angrily. "This is just so fracking poopy."

"Got that right, but he wouldn't want you to go backward. That's the last thing he'd want."

"I won't," she says. "You know he left me the company, right?

The insurance money and everything else went to Allie, but the company is mine. I can't run it by myself, so I asked Pete if he'd like to work for me. Just part-time."

"And he said . . . ?"

"He said yes, because retirement sucked already. It should be okay. I'll run down the skippers and deadbeats on my computer, and he'll go out and get them. Or serve the subpoenas, if that's the job. But it won't be like it was. Working for Bill . . . working *with* Bill . . . those were the happiest days of my life." She thinks that over. "I guess the only happy days of my life. I felt . . . I don't know . . ."

"Valued?" Jerome suggests.

"Yes! Valued."

"You should have felt that way," Jerome says, "because you were very valuable. And still are."

She gives the plant a final critical look, dusts dirt from her hands and the knees of her pants, and sits down next to him. "He was brave, wasn't he? At the end, I mean."

"Yes."

"Yeah." She smiles a little. "That's what Bill would have said—not yes, but yeah."

"Yeah," he agrees.

"Jerome? Would you put your arm around me?"

He does.

"The first time I met you—when we found the stealth program Brady loaded into my cousin Olivia's computer—I was afraid of you."

"I know," Jerome says.

"Not because you were black—"

"Black is whack," Jerome says, smiling. "I think we agreed on that much right from the jump."

"—but because you were a stranger. You were from *outside*. I was scared of outside people and outside things. I still am, but not as much as I was then."

"I know."

"I loved him," Holly says, looking at the chrysanthemum. It is a brilliant orange-red below the gray gravestone, which bears a simple message: KERMIT WILLIAM HODGES, and, below the dates, END OF WATCH. "I loved him so much."

"Yeah," Jerome says. "So did I."

She looks up at him, her face timid and hopeful—beneath the graying bangs, it is almost the face of a child. "You'll always be my friend, won't you?"

"Always." He squeezes her shoulders, which are heartbreakingly thin. During Hodges's final two months, she lost ten pounds she couldn't afford to lose. He knows his mother and Barbara are just waiting to feed her up. "Always, Holly."

"I know," she says.

"Then why did you ask?"

"Because it's so good to hear you say it."

End of Watch, Jerome thinks. He hates the sound of that, but it's right. It's right. And this is better than the funeral. Being here with Holly on this sunny late summer morning is much better.

"Jerome? I'm not smoking."

"That's good."

They sit quiet for a little while, looking at the chrysanthemum burning its colors at the base of the headstone.

"Jerome?"

"What, Holly?"

"Would you like to go to a movie with me?"

"Yes," he says, then corrects himself. "Yeah."

"We'll leave a seat empty between us. Just to put our popcorn in."

"Okay."

"Because I hate putting it on the floor where there are probably roaches and maybe even rats."

"I hate it, too. What do you want to see?"

"Something that will make us laugh and laugh."

"Works for me."

He smiles at her. Holly smiles back. They leave Fairlawn and walk back out into the world together.

August 30, 2015

# AUTHOR'S NOTE

Thanks to Nan Graham, who edited this book, and to all my other friends at Scribner, including—but not limited to—Carolyn Reidy, Susan Moldow, Roz Lippel, and Katie Monaghan. Thanks to Chuck Verrill, my longtime agent (important) and longtime friend (more important). Thanks to Chris Lotts, who sells the foreign rights to my books. Thanks to Mark Levenfus, who oversees such business affairs as I have, and keeps an eye on the Haven Foundation, which helps freelance artists down on their luck, and the King Foundation, which helps schools, libraries, and small-town fire departments. Thanks to Marsha DeFilippo, my able personal assistant, and to Julie Eugley, who does everything Marsha doesn't. I'd be lost without them. Thanks to my son Owen King, who read the manuscript and made valuable suggestions. Thanks to my wife, Tabitha, who also made valuable suggestions . . . including what turned out to be the right title.

Special thanks to Russ Dorr, who has traded in his career as a physician's assistant to become my research guru. He went the extra mile on this book, patiently tutoring me on how computer programs are written, how they can be rewritten, and how they can be disseminated. Without Russ, *End of Watch* would have been a lesser book. I should add that in some cases I deliberately changed various computer protocols to serve my fiction. Tech-savvy individuals will see that, which is fine. Just don't blame Russ.

One last thing. *End of Watch* is fiction, but the high rate of suicides—both in the United States and in many other countries where my books are read—is all too real. The National Suicide Prevention Hotline number given in this book is also real. It's 1-800-273-TALK. If you are feeling poopy (as Holly Gibney would say), give them a call. Because things can get better, and if you give them a chance, they usually do.

Stephen King